The Tome of Horrors Complete

For Swords & Wizardry

Credits

Authors
Scott Greene, Erica Balsley

Lair Encounter Authors
John Stater, Jeff Harkness, Gary Schotter

Additional Authors
Kevin Baase, Casey Christofferson, Jim Collura, Meghan Greene, Lance Hawvermale, Travis Hawvermale, Ian S. Johnston, Bill Kenower, Patrick Lawinger, Nathan Paul, Clark Peterson, Greg Ragland, Robert Schwalb, Greg A. Vaughan, Bill Webb

Lead Developer
Greg A. Vaughan

Developers
Matt Finch, Scott Greene, Clark Peterson, Bill Webb

Producers
Bill Webb, Charles A. Wright

Swords & Wizardry Conversion
Jeff Harkness, John Stater, Gary Schotter

Managing Editor
Greg A. Vaughan

Editors
Erica Balsley, Dawn Fischer, Jeff Harkness, Stefen Styrsky, Brent Vaughan, Greg A. Vaughan

Layout & Graphic Design
Charles A. Wright

1

Front Cover Art

Charles A. Wright and Mike Chaney

Interior Art

Rowena Aitken, Andrew Bates, Peter Bergting, Ed Bourelle, John Bridges, Mike Chaney, Chris Curtin, David Day, Jim DiBartolo, Talon Dunning, Steve Ellis, Tom Gianni, Jeff Holt, Llyne Hunter, Leif Jones, Veronica Jones, Brian LeBlanc, Eric Lofgren, Chet Masters, Jeremy McHugh, Gary McKee, Cara Mitten, Jim Nelson, Eric Pollack, Claudio Pozas, Nate Pride, Jeff Rebner, Erik Roman, Chad Sergesketter, James Stowe, Richard Thomas, Tim Truman, Tyler Walpole, & UDON Studios (with Attila Adorjany, Eric Kim, Ramon Perez, Noi Sackda, Eric Vedder, Jef Wayne, and Jim Zubkavich)

Special Thanks

To Matt Finch for bringing us Swords & Wizardry Complete and without whom this conversion would never have happened. Thanks to John Stater, Jeff Harkness and Gary Schotter for putting in the long hours to create the new material for the book.
Thanks to Mike Chaney for the look of the original books.
Thanks to Bill Webb for resurrecting all the great things that Necromancer Games stood for with the creation of Frog God Games. And thank you to all the Frog God Games fans who demand support of the Swords & Wizardry system. Old school lives on!

Table of Contents

Table of Contents

Table of Contents

Table of Contents

Table of Contents

INTRODUCTION

Many Swords & Wizardry players will not be familiar with the past history of the Tome of Horrors. After all, the Tomes were not written until 2002, a time when many of us were no longer paying attention to "mainstream" gaming publications any more. For those who were content to remain entirely with the Original Edition, or the First Edition, or even the Second Edition of our game, the significance of these books is probably a complete mystery. On the other hand, those of us who – like me – were still playing later editions before deciding to return to our gaming roots, will almost certainly have encountered these books, if only by their tremendous reputation. To explain briefly what they are: the first Tome of Horrors was essentially a collection of existing monsters from earlier editions, re-described for the new D&D rules that were published by Wizards of the Coast Inc. The next two volumes offered multitudes of newly-invented monsters for gamers playing those rules. It is clear why the second two volumes are of tremendous use to old-school players – these are monsters that most of us have never seen before, huge numbers of them, that can be used to populate entire dungeons, confound players, and spark the sort of new-found wonder that comes from cracking open a brand-new book of resources. Why, though, is that first volume, the one that merely "updated" earlier monsters, of any value to those of us who already own the first edition books in which these monsters originally appeared? After all, Swords & Wizardry is all about a return to the game's roots, as I mentioned earlier. What is the value of taking the 2002 re-description of those monsters, and then doing a second re-description to get them right back to the original form? The First Edition monster books are there on Ebay and in used bookstores, still easily available – first edition books are getting more expensive, but the supply has certainly not run out, and probably will not run out for years to come. First Edition monster books simply aren't in the same situation as the supply of the original-edition rulebooks, which has dwindled so much that the Swords & Wizardry rules are desperately needed in order to preserve the continued existence of a community playing the original version of the game. But First Edition monsters? The answer, I think, depends on the lens through which you perceive the game itself. For one thing, the Swords & Wizardry version of Tome of Horrors is *not* a First Edition re-description of First Edition monsters – it is an *Original Edition* description of First Edition monsters. In creating this book, the authorial team for the Swords & Wizardry version embarked on an unusual journey, the task of forgetting as well as remembering, creating as well as documenting, re-imagining instead of reproducing. In many ways, interpreting the First Edition monsters in terms of the Original Edition is to explore new territory – familiar territory, but territory that still contains surprises, opportunities, and unexpected inspirations. This aspect of the book is highlighted by John Stater's, Jeff Harkness', and Gary Schotter's tremendously creative short scenarios for each monster, offering a view of the monster that captures the vital and vibrant spirit of the Original Edition's terse, folkloric, and evocative style in an entirely new way.

My challenge, to those old-school players who might be approaching this book with any degree of skepticism, is that you approach it as it was envisioned, with new eyes raised toward an unfamiliar horizon, the undiscovered country, the unexplored reaches of the game that have called to us with siren-song since the days of our youth when we first stumbled across the world of fantasy roleplaying. Once you have read this introduction, close the book. And then, just as you did years or perhaps decades ago, open the book with the same sense of wonder, the same willingness to imagine a world from scratch, that you had when you played the game for the first time. It is in here, waiting to be found by those who seek it out.

— Matthew J. Finch

The Tome of Horrors Complete

Aberrant

Hit Dice: 8
Armor Class: 4 [15]
Attacks: 1 great club (2d8)
Saving Throw: 8
Special: Physical deformity
Move: 12
Alignment: Chaos
Challenge Level/XP: 9/1,100

Aberrants are hideous giants standing about 14 feet tall, with deformed bodies and limbs. Aberrants are covered in coarse, dark hair or blisters (for those without body hair). They make their homes in caves, abandoned mines, or deep underground away from civilization. Many have physical deformities, such as a misplaced or extra arm (an extra attack), eyes on the sides or back of their head (to see people sneaking up on them), flapping ears (to better hear) or a huge nose (to smell creatures).

Cyst Fist's Pass

A small troop of 16 aberrants from the Cyst Fist Tribe have set up a camp at the crest of the mountain pass. Their leader is the biggest of the tribe, a mountain of a creature named Furgristle. This group has journeyed down from their caves higher up in the mountains to raid and pillage, hoping to bring back items to help the tribe get through the coming winter. The entire group is wary and alert for danger after coming so close to civilization, and have laid out an ambush along the path leading to their encampment.

The path leading through the dense temperate forest is eerily quiet, with the sounds of the wind through the evergreens creating an occasional whistle. Hiding in the trees at the ambush point are 4 aberrants, each camouflaged with branches and leaves covering their deformed hides. Two aberrants swing large logs suspended by vines down at the PCs to knock them from their horses or to sweep them off their feet (1d6 points of damage). When the logs hit, the remaining 2 aberrants charge the PCs from the front.

The area around the campsite consists of discarded boulders, demolished wagons, crates, barrels and other refuse taken during their raids. This debris forms an extremely crude wall around the camp. Makeshift tents made from overlapping canvas and torn leathers surround a large fire pit sitting in the center of the camp. A partially eaten horse impaled on a spit sits above the sputtering fire. A crow's cage hanging from a high post contains a halfling dressed as a jester. Furgristle keeps the "little human" as a pet because the halfling's acrobatics makes the aberrant laugh. Eight aberrants remain in the camp at all times, while 4 others walk the perimeter.

Copyright Notice

Abomination

Abominations (often called hybrids) are fusions of two normal creatures that are just as often intelligent as they are rampaging beasts. No one knows how abominations came to be: perhaps the result of experimentation by a mad wizard or druid, a *wish* spell gone awry, or the wrath of a deity. The end result that fuses two creatures together often destroys the mind of the hapless beings, forcing them into madness and evil. The most well known examples of abominations are hippogriffs, griffons, gorilla-bears, and the terrible owlbear.

Owlephant

Hit Dice: 10
Armor Class: 4 [15]
Attack: Slam (2d6) and 2 claws (2d8) or gore (2d8)
Saving Throw: 5
Special: Trample
Move: 12
Alignment: Neutrality
Challenge Level/XP: 10/1400

This massive creature looks like an elephant with the head of a giant owl. Beneath its tusks, two clawed arms protrude from its body, one to each side of its elephantine trunk. Its feathered owl head is dark brown, fading to gray as it blends into its elephant-like body. An owlephant can trample opponent simply by moving over them. Those who fail a saving throw suffer 2d8 points of damage each. Those who pass a saving throw leap to the side to avoid the beast. Folk who choose not to avoid the trample attack can make a counter attack at a +1 bonus to hit.

Tigrilla

Hit Dice: 5
Armor Class: 5 [14]
Attack: 2 claws (1d8)
Saving Throw: 12
Special: Rake with claws
Move: 15/9 (climbing)
Alignment: Neutrality
Challenge Level/XP: 5/240

This creature looks like a gorilla with the head of a tiger. Its arms end in sharpened claws and its fur is orange-brown. Its head is striped like that of a normal tiger.

A tigrilla attacks by raking with its claws and biting with its fangs. If it hits the same opponent with both claws attacks it rakes with the claws, inflicting an additional 1d8 points of damage.

The Old Hermit's Castle

The adventurers wander into a creepy jungle valley, thick with vegetation but bearing wide paths that local guides claim were made by elephants. Rising above the jungle there are the ruins of an old castle, one owned, the guides say, by a weird old hermit. The hermit was a magician of some ability who specialized in unnatural crossbreeds.

The castle sits upon a rocky hill covered with green vines and shrubbery. A nest of 1d6 tigrilla lives on the slopes of the hill. A troupe of 1d4+4 owlephants and several owlbears dwell in the valley.

The castle looks as though it was destroyed in an explosion. Those exploring the place will feel a sinister presence (the phantom of the magician, see phantom entry in this book). Under the rubble, one might find a partially collapsed staircase to the castle's dungeons. The dungeons consist of a large common room connected to a laboratory on one side and storage rooms and cells on the other. One of the cells holds two human skeletons and a bloody bones (see entry in this book). The storage rooms hold copper vats, some in need of repair, bottles of reagents and phosphorescent liquids (poisonous to touch or taste) and other odds and ends of a magicians laboratory. The laboratory's steel door is blown off its hinges and the laboratory is completely destroyed.

Copyright Notice

Authors Erica Balsley and Scott Greene.

Abyssal Harvester (Fourth-Category Demon)

Hit Dice: 15
Armor Class: 1 [18]
Attacks: 6 tentacles (2d6)
Saving Throw: 3
Special: Constrict, harvest
Move: 6
Alignment: Chaos
Challenge Level/XP: 17/3,500

This gigantic beast stands nearly 40 feet tall. It is a squat, bloated mass of grayish, leathery flesh, somewhat in an oval shape with six long, serpentine tentacles. A massive gaping maw dominates its top surface. Hundreds of smaller tentacles allow the creature to move. The tentacles, if they hit, constrict for automatic damage after the initial hit. An abyssal harvester – which normally resides in the Abyss – can push up to four tentacles into the world. These tentacles appear out of thin air and can attack and grab victims to "harvest" by dragging them back through the rift to the Abyss.

The Root Run Vanishings

The Root Run Tunnel is a winding, six-mile underground trade route. The tunnel is 20 feet wide and its dirt ceiling varies from 12 to 20 feet. Thick redwood roots stick through the ceiling like giant twisted serpents. A flagstone entry goes for about a mile in from each tunnel entrance, before turning into a smooth dirt floor. Crossbeams engraved with the names of traders to use the tunnel are set every so often hold the ceiling in place. Lanterns hang every 100 yards to light the path.

A group of travelers entered the tunnel a week ago but never came out. Three people later found an abandoned cart at the tunnel's halfway point, but no people. Rumors are flying that the Root Run is haunted. Fear has halted the trade route, and the trade group that maintains the tunnel is offering a 500 gp reward for the safe return of the missing travelers.

The reward won't ever be collected. The missing traders met a gruesome fate when an abyssal harvester broke through a hole in reality as they passed. The grasping tentacles dragged the victims into the Abyss where they were devoured. The abyssal harvester currently has four of its thick tentacles stretched across the tunnel's passage to snare new victims. The tentacles appear to be tree roots in the semi-darkness until they rise to attack.

Copyright Notice
Author Scott Greene.

Abyssal Larva

Hit Dice: 3
Armor Class: 8 [11]
Attacks: acidic bite (2d4)
Saving Throw: 14
Special: maggot spray
Move: 6
Alignment: Chaos
Challenge Level/XP: 4/120

Abyssal larva look like puffy, bloated human-sized whitish-yellow maggots with purplish veins pulsating under their fleshy forms. A vaguely humanoid head sits atop its body and its facial features are twisted and distraught, as if the creature was in a constant state of pain. A pair of large, downward-curving horns juts from its head, just above its sunken eyes. Its mouth is lined with filthy, sharpened fangs. Once per day, an abyssal larva can regurgitate and spray a stream of maggots at a victim within 10 feet. If the creature fails a save, it is sickened.

The Maggot Pits

This 70-foot-diameter circular room is a charnel house of gore. Twenty decaying bodies hang from the 40-foot-high ceiling on rusted, barbed chains. Transparent tubes wind among the chain links and siphon fluids from the corpses. These tubes drape over 10-foot-tall wooden vats filled with congealing blood.

Beneath the hanging bodies, millions of squirming maggots fill a 30-foot-wide pit in the center of the room. More maggots drop from the hanging bodies into the pits below. The central pit is 10 feet deep, and filled to floor level with maggots. Stone steps descend to the maggot pit's floor, although using the steps nauseate those who try (save avoids).

In the maggot pit are 3 abyssal larva that spew a stream of maggots at intruders before rising to attack. A magic-user summoned the creatures to protect himself. He feeds the hanging bodies to the creatures after he has drained their blood for his gruesome experiments.

Copyright Notice

Adherer

Hit Dice: 4
Armor Class: 3 [16]
Attack: 2 slams (1d4)
Saving Throw: 13
Special: Adhesive, double damage from fire, resistance to blunt weapons (50%), surprise on 1-3 on 1d6
Move: 12
Alignment: Chaos
Challenge Level/XP: 5/240

The adherer is a subterranean humanoid whose folds of filthy, pale skin cause it to resemble a mummy. It exudes sticky, sour smelling glue from its skin that sticks to anything other than stone, including melee attacks. Each successful melee attack requires a saving throw to avoid it sticking fast to the weird creature. Once a creature is stuck, it suffers 1d4 damage per round from the grapple. The glue is dissolved by boiling water, and it breaks down 1 hour after the creature dies.

It Could Use a Little Salt

In a subterranean gallery draped with sticky fungal ropes and made unbearably warm and humid by a hot spring that spews polychromatic salts a gang of 1d3+1 adherers has made its home. They keep their treasure in a sealed urn of terracotta which they have lowered into the spring – it is now encrusted by the salts and difficult to discern from the uneven floor of the pool created by the spring. Moreover, retrieving it is tricky without a couple 10-ft poles. The adherers are rarely (2 in 6 chance) in their little hideout, spending most of their time wandering the underworld looking for treasure-laden victims to carry home, where they are dismembered and boiled in the spring for a grisly repast, their treasure added to the urn. In time, the adherers hope to collect a fitting tribute to some demon lord, that they can request a release from their tortured existence.

Credit
The Adherer originally appeared in the First Edition *Fiend Folio* (© TSR/Wizards of the Coast, 1981) and is used by permission.

Copyright Notice
Authors Scott Greene and Clark Peterson, based on original material by Guy Shearer.

Aerial Servant

Hit Dice: 16
Armor Class: 3 [16]
Attack: Slam (4d4)
Saving Throw: 3
Special: Throttle, invisibility, only harmed by magic weapons, wind blast
Move: 24/24 (flying)
Alignment: Neutrality
Challenge Level/XP: 20/4400

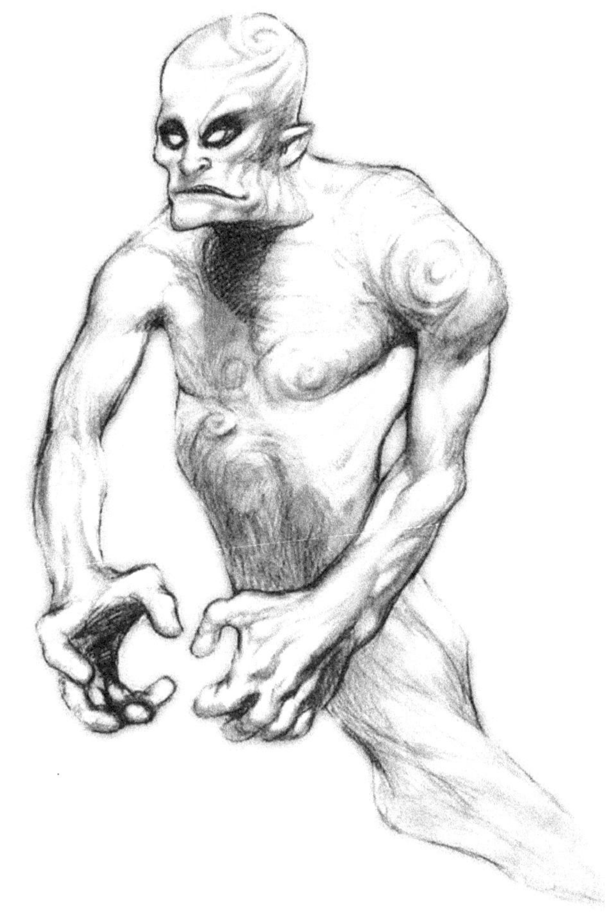

Aerial servants are semi-intelligent creatures from the Elemental Plane of Air that often roam the Astral and Ethereal planes. They normally are only found on the Material Plane as a result of being summoned by a cleric using the *aerial servant* spell and commanded to perform some task, often being required to use their immense strength to carry objects or aid the summoner. Though an aerial servant performs whatever task is asked of it, it resents being summoned and forced to do another's bidding; therefore, it attempts to pervert the conditions of the summoning and its mission. An aerial servant that fails or is thwarted in its mission becomes insane and immediately returns to the caster who summoned it, either killing the caster or carrying the caster back to the Elemental Plane of Air with it. Aerial servants are naturally invisible, and thus remain invisible even while attacking. Aerial servants can only be killed on their native plane. If slain elsewhere, they simply dissolve into wisps of vapor and return to their home plane.

Aerial servants attack by using a shearing blast of wind as a weapon or by grabbing an opponent and crushing it within their powerful grasp. An aerial servant can use its wind blast once every 1d4 rounds. The wind blast has a range of 80 feet and can be used against a single target, inflicting 4d8 points of damage and knocking them back 2d10 feet. The target can roll a saving throw to halve the damage and avoid being knocked back. An aerial servant grapple inflicts 4d4 points of damage each round and is notoriously difficult to break.

The Tomb of Zexus

When the archimage Zexus undertook the construction of his tomb, he plotted a petty revenge on the lords of elemental air who had most ungenerously done him wrong during his climb to the heights of wizardry. So it was that he summoned an aerial servant with all the ordinary perambulations and enticements and put it to the task of constructing a fitting tomb for one as grand as Zexus Yellow-Eyed. In due time, the tomb was constructed from massive slabs of precisely fitted marble. Zexus induced his servant to follow him into the tomb and place the last stone merely as a test. The slow-witted elemental saw no trickery, for surely the mage yet lived and would not seal himself into a tomb willingly. Alas, this was exactly the intention of Zexus, for a slow, persistent curse had been withering his body for ages. The tomb sealed, the aerial servant found itself standing in the middle of a cunningly designed magic circle, unable to do anything while the mage slumped down in a silver chair, died and over the course of a hundred years mouldered away. The servant remains in the tomb, invisible and waiting only for the great slab to be moved and a toe to step over the threshold, breaking the circle and releasing it to take its century of impotent rage out on the toe's hapless owner.

Credit
The Aerial Servant originally appeared in the First Edition *Monster Manual* (© TSR/Wizards of the Coast, 1977) and is used by permission.

Copyright Notice
Authors Scott Greene and Clark Peterson, based on original material by Gary Gygax.

Afanc

Hit Dice: 21
Armor Class: 2 [17]
Attacks: Bite (5d6), 2 claws (2d8)
Saving Throw: 3
Special: Swallow whole, sea swell
Move: 3/30 (swim)
Alignment: Chaos
Challenge Level/XP: 23/5,300

An afanc is a massive, gray-skinned whale with a bulbous head similar to a catfish. Its eyes are sullen and blue and its huge pectoral fins are serrated. These omnivorous hunters roam the deep sea. If an afanc rolls a 15 or above on its bite attack, it grasps a victim in its toothy maw and swallows the creature whole on the next round. When facing surface ships, an afanc can raise its entire body out of the water and crash down on the surface to generate a 30-foot-tall wave to swamp vessels.

The One That Got Away

The merchant ship Helene's Grace recently sailed into the port city of Borenstown, its keel splintered and its hull battered. The ship sits in port, listing badly against a redwood pier that juts into the Reaping Sea. Sailors swarm over the ship, patching holes and repairing a splintered mast. All look fearfully to the sea, watching for danger.

Helene's Grace has been on the run for three days after an afanc attacked it in the open sea. The ship accidentally rammed the surfacing afanc, and the angry fish turned on the vessel. It has trailed the ship ever since, battering the hull and nearly capsizing it twice as Grace made for shore. Captain Cor Balt fears the return of the giant sea creature, and is offering 100 gp to anyone who'll protect the ship while repairs are made. Around 20 townsfolk line the dock, scanning the waters. Most don't even know what they are watching for.

The afanc rams the pillars supporting the dock in anger before turning on the ship, throwing many of the unfortunate townsfolk into the harbor. Screams for help turn to terror as the giant afanc breaches among the anchored vessels.

Ahlinni (Cackle Bird)

Hit Dice: 4
Armor Class: 5 [14]
Attacks: 1 bite (1d8) or impale (2d8), 2 claws (1d4)
Saving Throw: 13
Special: Breath weapon, impale
Move: 15
Alignment: Neutrality
Challenge Level/XP: 5/240

The ahlinni, or cackle bird (so called because of its breath weapon) is a 5-foot-tall flightless bird that dwells in thick forests. It is covered in greenish feathers, and is nearly invisible when it lies motionless in its leafy surroundings. The bird's beak is half the length of its body, and as straight and strong as a long sword (2d8 damage). Wicked claws also sprout from its wings. Once every three rounds, an ahlinni can expel a pinkish gas that causes creatures that fail a save to fall to the ground laughing manically for 1d3 rounds.

A Bird in the Hand

A 30-foot-wide marble fountain sits in a clearing deep in the Kajaani Forest, its cool, clear waters gurgling in the foot-deep basin. Vine-covered ruins around the fountain are slowly being reclaimed by the forest. Standing at the cardinal points of the fountain are four statues of laughing nymphs holding vases of sculpted flowers. Diamond chips are worked into the marble surfaces, so the entire fountain glints and gleams in the sunlight.

A 20-foot-tall central statue of a massive crane-like man stands in the center of the fountain, its sculpted feathers also decorated with bits of sparkling glass and precious stones. Its bird head has a beak that is partly open. The giant figure has two outstretched arms with its palms cupped together. Water pours from between the statues intertwined fingers and drops into the basin below. A pink mist floats across the splashing waters, and birds cackle noisily in the treetops.

The clearing is the home of a flock of cackle birds. The flock leader has her nest in the statue's cupped hands, while the rest of the flock shelters in the treetops surrounding the clearing. The flock leader considers the fountain her "treasure" and frequently breathes her pinkish gas out over the water to mark her territory. The gas floats across the surface, infusing the water with the laughing properties. Anyone drinking the water must save or fall to the ground laughing uncontrollably.

There are 10 total birds in the clearing. The nine in the treetops hop to the ground to defend their leader should PCs threaten her nest.

Copyright Notice
Authors Scott Greene and Erica Balsley.

Algoid

Hit Dice: 5
Armor Class: 4 [15]
Attack: 2 slams (1d10)
Saving Throw: 12
Special: Immunity to electricity and fire, resistance to blunt weapons (50%), mind blast, surprise on 1-3 on 1d6
Move: 9
Alignment: Neutrality
Challenge Level/XP: 7/600

The algoid is a living colony of algae that has developed some semblance of intelligence and mobility. It roughly resembles a green humanoid. Algoids make their lairs in marshes and swamps. They are often encountered with other marsh-dwelling sentient plants; though never with shambling mounds (they hate them and usually attack them on sight). In its natural surroundings, it is nearly invisible until it attacks and uses this to its advantage when prey is nearby. Algoids can "wake" trees as do treants. Once per day, an algoid can use a mind blast in a 60-foot cone. Any creature caught in the cone must succeed on a saving throw or be stunned for 3d4 rounds. *Control water* spells deal 1d6 points of damage per caster level to algoids, with no saving throw allowed.

Someone Should Clean This Up

Water features are a wonderful addition to any dungeon complex, but over time they become something of a bother without an apprentice to keep them clean. In a misty corridor of one dungeon adventurers might come across a truly impressive spectacle – a chamber 30-ft wide and 60-ft long taken up by a stepped pool that gets as deep as 5-ft. Drains trickle water into the pool from a number of lead pipes capped by copper grotesques set into the walls, which are further ornamented by panels of speculum, a highly reflective alloy of copper and tin. A clogged drain in the bottom of the pool, covered by a copper grill, allows water to slowly escape the pool for lower levels of the underworld. Over time, the pool has acquired a thick layer of algae and a cluster of 1d4+2 algoids that lurk just beneath the surface. The floor of the pool is littered with their accumulated treasures, which they sometimes use as bait – leaving a few coins or a nice gem resting on the edge of the pool. The corpses of felled adventurers are layered with algae and, eventually, join the cluster.

Credit

The Algoid originally appeared in the First Edition *Fiend Folio* (© TSR/Wizards of the Coast, 1981) and is used by permission.

Copyright Notice

Authors Scott Greene and Clark Peterson, based on original material by Mike Ferguson.

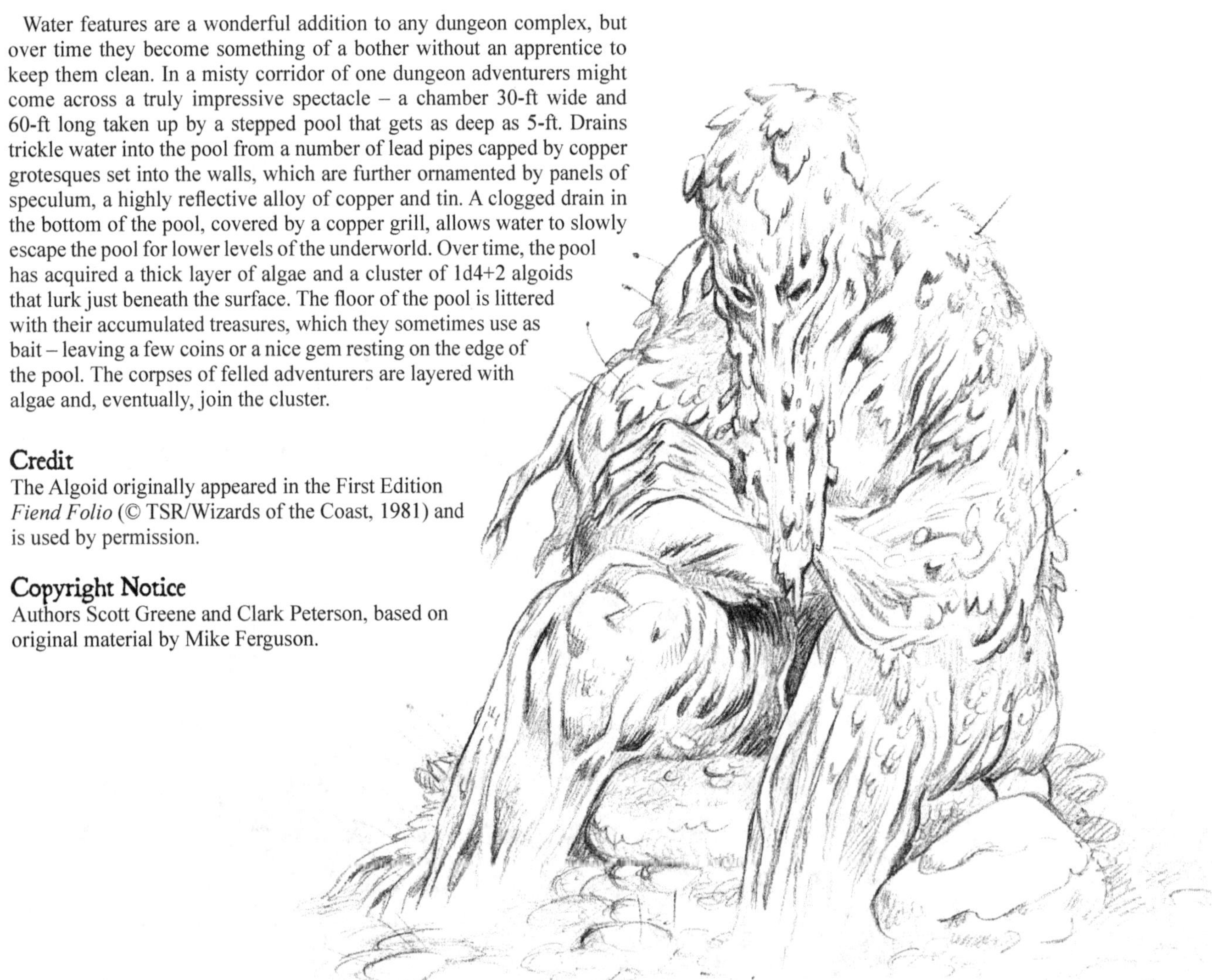

Al-mi'raj

Hit Dice: 1d6
Armor Class: 5 [14]
Attack: Horn (1d6)
Saving Throw: 18
Special: Blink, dimension door, immune to poison, magic resistance 30%
Move: 24
Alignment: Neutrality
Challenge Level/XP: 2/30

The al-mi'raj is a large rabbit with white, pink, yellow, or light green fur and a long golden or black horn. Al-mi'raj can *blink* (as the spell) and use a *dimension door* effect once per round. Rare al'mi'raj are more intelligent than their kin and have the following psionic powers: *Control winds, darkness 15-ft radius, levitate* and *telekinesis*. These psionic al-mi'raj have a challenge level of 3.

You've Been Warren-ed

On a green and pleasant pasture crossed by a lazy stream thick with lilypads and choked with reeds 1d10+10 al-mi'raj, including a psionic leader, have established a warren. During the daytime, one sees the creatures hopping around the meadow, grazing on the tender grasses and digging up roots, their golden horns shimmering in the sunlight. At the first sign of intruders, the creatures begin to hiss, and a swift wind sweeps across the meadow. Then the warm light of the sun is replaced by a thick, inky darkness. The intruders now discombobulated, the canny beasts quickly surround them and then charge into battle, blinking if the intruders find a way to defeat their darkness ability. The bones of an unfortunate mage lying in reeds bears silent witness to the effectiveness of the al-mi'raj's territorial defense.

Credit

The Al-mi'raj originally appeared in the First Edition *Fiend Folio* (© TSR/Wizards of the Coast, 1981) and is used by permission.

Copyright Notice

Authors Scott Greene and Clark Peterson, based on original material by Roger Musson.

Amphisbaena

Hit Dice: 6
Armor Class: 4 [15]
Attack: 2 bites (1d6 plus poison)
Saving Throw: 11
Special: Resistance to cold (50%), split, cannot be surprised
Move: 9/9 (climbing and swimming)
Alignment: Neutrality
Challenge Level/XP: 7/600

The amphisbaena is a giant poisonous snake about 10 feet long. It is often found lairing near a water source or in dark, damp locations. An amphisbaena moves on land by grasping one of its necks with its other head and rolling across the ground like a hoop. The amphisbaena's poison is deadly unless the victim passes a saving throw. Each of the amphisbaena's heads functions independently of the other. An amphisbaena that is cut in half continues to function normally (each with half its current hit points) and reattaches its body together in 1d2 days.

Twining the Fountain

This chamber is composed of massive granite blocks, each lovingly cut into a perfect cube and stacked. The chamber measures roughly 12-ft wide and 12-ft deep and has a conical ceiling 15-ft tall at its apex. A 4-ft diameter pool, raised about 2-ft above the beige-tiled floor has an amphisbaena wrapped around it. A stream of water falls from the apex of the ceiling into the pool. If the beast is killed and its blood drips into the pool, the water will turn murky red and then freeze solid for mere moments before it collapse into a pile of silver coins.

Credit

The Amphisbaena originally appeared in the First Edition *Monster Manual* (© TSR/Wizards of the Coast, 1977) as *Snake, Amphisbaena* and is used by permission.

Copyright Notice

Author Scott Greene, based on original material by Gary Gygax.

Amphisbaena Basilisk

Hit Dice: 6
Armor Class: 4 [15]
Attacks: 2 bites (2d6)
Saving Throw: 11
Special: Petrifying gaze
Move: 12
Alignment: Neutrality
Challenge Level/XP: 10/1,400

An amphisbaena basilisk is a single great lizard composed of two normal basilisks conjoined in the middle. Each head's gaze can turns to stone anyone meeting its eye. Fighting without trying to look at the creature incurs a -4 penalty to hit. If the amphisbaena basilisk's gaze is reflected back at it, it has a 10% chance to force the basilisk into a saving throw against being turned to stone itself.

Heads in the Clouds

Lazy coils of purple smoke roil from the 50-foot-by-30-foot room, filling the chamber waist high with thick clouds. The smoke smells of burnt lotus blossoms and is so thick it obscures the floor. The ceiling rises 15 feet over the thick mist. A 10-foot-tall statue of obsidian gilded with gold leaf stands in the center of the room. The statue is a massive satyr with two faces, one on each side of its head. It holds a cornucopia from which the purple wisps pour. One face is smiling, while the reverse side sneers. The purple smoke is harmless.

Curled around the base of the statue is an amphisbaena basilisk, with each of its heads on opposite sides of the statue facing toward the single entry into the room. The clouds obscure the creature's conjoined state, and it appears to be two creatures with its heads down in the mists.

Hidden in the base of the center statue is a compartment that contains 3 potions (levitate, healing and gaseous form), 3 rubies (100 gp each) and a silver *ring of mammal control* carved in the shape of a platypus.

Copyright Notice

Author Erica Balsley.

Anemone, Great (Giant) Sea

Hit Dice: 11
Armor Class: 8 [11]
Attacks: tendrils (paralysis)
Saving Throw: 4
Special: Acid cloud, swallow whole
Move: 0 (immobile)
Alignment: Neutrality
Challenge Level/XP: 13/2,300

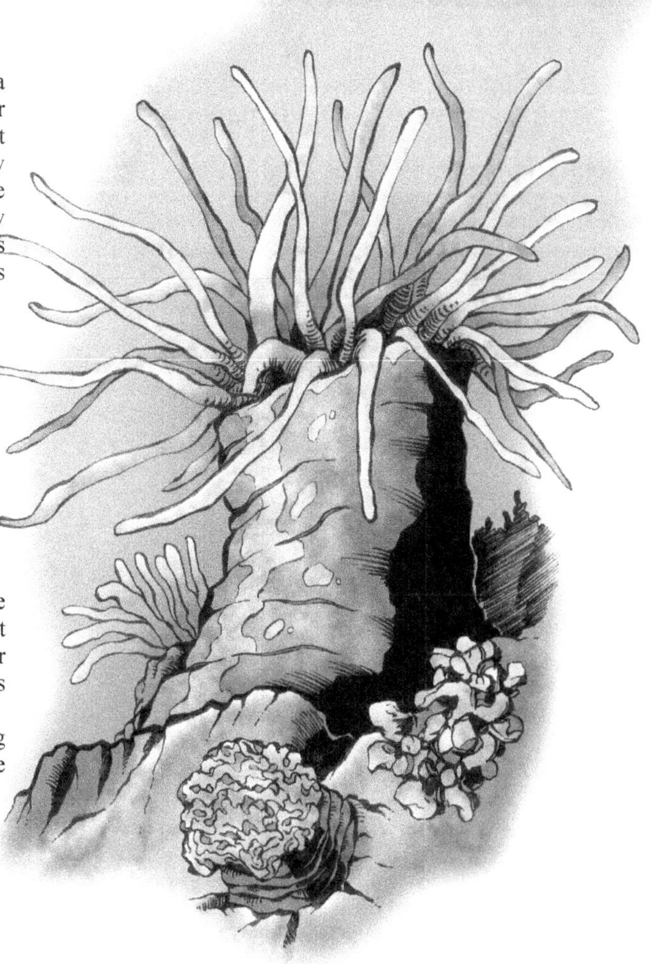

This gigantic flowerlike creature has a dark green to gray trunk and a brightly colored interior. At the center of the creature's front is a circular opening that leads into its interior. An anemone attacks any creature that swims into its many tendrils with a paralytic poison that immobilizes prey so it can be swallowed whole. A victim caught in the tendrils can save to resist the paralysis. If a creature fails, the anemone swallows the prey whole in the next round. If provoked, an anemone ejects the contents of its stomach in an acidic cloud that deals 1d8 damage to all creatures within 20 feet for 1d3 rounds.

Death Dive

A reef of jagged coral rises out of the surf, a deadly barrier shielding the rich seabed for the pearl divers of Markees. The hearty divers raft out into the deep water beyond the reef to swim deep beneath the azure waves. A bed of oysters containing rare fist-sized crimson pearls is located 40 feet beneath the waves.

A great sea anemone matured in the coral during the winter, however, and snatches divers who get too close to the aquatic vermin. The anemone appears to be a rock tube stuck near the base of the colorful coral, but it quickly lashes out with its tendrils. Crimson pearls litter the sea floor around the creature, as do the expelled bones of its victims. The pearls can be sold for 100 gp each.

The devious divers want to get rid of the anemone, and are spreading stories about a "mermaid stuck in the rocks" to get people to dive into the dangerous waters.

ANGELS

Angels are a race of celestials native to the lawfully-aligned outer planes.

Angel, Chalkydri

Hit Dice: 9
Armor Class: 0 [19]
Attacks: +2 flaming long sword (1d8+2 + 1d6 fire)
Save: 7
Special: Plane shift, spells
Move: 9/18 (flying)
Alignment: Lawful
Challenge Level/XP: 11/1,700

This angelic figure resembles a muscular humanoid with coppery skin and eyes. It has four large feathery, white wings and carries a longsword swathed in fire. Chalkydri take their role as protectors of good very seriously, and shift planes with ease, jumping from one reality to the next to do so. They are powerful spell casters (at will—*bless, detect evil, dispel magic, invisibility* (self only), *polymorph self, remove curse, cure disease, see invisible*; 3/day—*cure serious wounds, flame strike*; 1/day—*restoration, raise dead*)

Purgatory of the Nexus

A thick door made from an unearthly green stone blocks access to the area beyond. The looted remains of dozens of skeletons lie in heaps outside the door. A cryptic epitaph etched in the stone reads:

Away from the sight of mortals, cast deep beneath the sward.
A gate that seals the portal and a key forged from angel's sword.

The floor of the 60-foot-diameter cylindrical room beyond drops 30 feet down once past the door. The ceiling rises 30 feet above the entry. A round, 30-foot-tall pillar-like pedestal sits in the center of the room. The pedestal is 15 feet in diameter and the top is level with the entrance door. A plinth holding a small silver key sits in the exact center of the room atop the large pedestal.

Kneeling before the key is a solemn chalkydri angel who holds a sword in his hand. The blade has a small section carved from it that perfectly matches the silver key. The angel does not respond or acknowledge anyone standing outside the room. The angelic being attacks without reason those disturbing the room, regardless of their alignment. The chalkydri was tasked with protecting the key so that it does not fall into any mortal's possession. Despite the key's normal size, it weighs 400 pounds. It unlocks a gate to Hades in the city of Eminence.

Angel, Empyreal

Hit Dice: 12
Armor Class: -1 [20]
Attacks: 1 weapon (2d6)
Saving Throw: 3
Special: Radiant blast; immune to acid, cold and petrification; resists electricity and fire; spell-like abilities
Move: 15/25 (flying)
Alignment: Lawful
Challenge Level/XP: 15/2,900

Empyreals are powerful angelic warriors about 9 feet tall with silver hair, blue eyes and dressed in shining armor. They have large, feathery, silver wings and milk-white skin. Empyreals are fiery, quick-tempered, and forceful, but always fair. To non-Lawful beings and Lawful creatures with fewer HD, the empyreal appears as a column of white fire. Once per day, an empyreal can increase its radiance to deal 8d6 damage to creatures within 60 feet, and blind them for 3d6 minutes (save for half damage, avoid blindness). An empyreal also radiates an aura in a 30-foot-radius that forces Chaotic creatures to save before they can attack the angel. This aura grants Lawful creatures a -2[+2] armor bonus.

Empyreals have a number of spell-like abilities: at will—*continual light, detect evil, dispel magic, invisibility* (self only), *remove curse*; 2/day—*blade barrier, cure disease, cure serious wounds*; 1/day—*resurrection, raise dead*. Many can also cast spells as an 8th-level Cleric.

The Burning Angel

A column of white fire rises nearly 20 feet in the middle of 12 engraved brass plates set in the marble floor. Each pie-shaped plate is 20 feet long from the center flame to its outer edge, and the group forms a perfect circle around the knight. The white fire burns slowly with a blinding light, the overlapping flames flickering and receding in a slow-motion dance. Within the burning fire, obscured by the semi-solid flames, stands a warrior clad in shining plate armor decorated with swirling golden sigils. Two feathered wings curl up from the warrior's back, the tips nearly reaching the edge of the flames. The knight holds a crackling streak of lightning shaped into a long sword in his hands. Kneeling on the ground around the angelic knight are four brass figures, each holding a halberd pointing inward toward the knight. The tips of the halberds just touch the white fire sheathing the knight, and arcs of fire jump along their metal bodies.

The knight is an empyreal angel named Jemichar who was caught in a time trap during a battle more than 600 years ago. The angel landed among the brass plates and was caught in a temporal moment designed to repeat for 1,000 years. The brass plates originally burned at 1,000 degrees, but the spell loses a degree of heat for each year that passes. Right now, the plates burn at 400 degrees (4d6 points of damage to anyone touching them).

The brass figures are 4 brass men tasked with keeping the angel in the trap. The brass men attack anyone attempting to free the angelic warrior. The brass men heal 12 points of damage each round they are in contact with the brass floor plates. The angel can be freed by removing the runes engraved in the plates by destroying the copper plates or otherwise marring the sigils themselves. Each rune eliminated drops the temperature of the plates by 10 degrees. When the plates no longer burn, the angel's stasis lifts and Jemichar soars into the sky.

Copyright Notice

Angel, Monadic Deva

Hit Dice: 10
Armor Class: -2 [21]
Attack: 2 weapons (3d6)
Saving Throw: 5
Special: Immunities, +1 weapon to hit, magic resistance (60%), magical abilities
Move: 18/36 (flying)
Alignment: Law
Challenge Level/XP: 18/3500

Monadic devas are angels with silvery wings that patrol the Ethereal and Elemental planes. They serve as leaders and officers in celestial armies. Monadic devas wield two *maces +3/+5 vs. constructed creatures*. They are immune to acid and cold damage and death effects and suffer only half damage from electricity and fire. Monadic devas can use the following spells: *charm elemental* (per *charm monster*, but only affects elementals), *continual light*, *cure disease*, *cure light wounds* (7/day), *detect evil*, *dispel magic*, *hold monster* (1/day), *holy word*, *invisibility* (self only), *mirror image* (7/day), *polymorph self* and *remove curse*.

Eternal Vigilance

In a long forgotten temple to the gods of Law, a lone monadic deva sits in quiet contemplation of a shimmering, silvery pool set in the floor and surrounded by glossy tiles of sapphire blue set with fire opals. Ensconced on a throne of marble, he waits for the Intruder to once again attempt to enter the universe through that pool, for the deva is a gatekeeper, pledged for eternity to protect creation from something beyond and before and alien to creation. The chamber holds several idols of lawful deities, all hewn from marble and decorated with gold leaf. The deva is instantly hostile toward chaotics that enter the temple, but is friendly enough to lawful and neutral folk, provided they do not approach the silver pool.

Credit

The Monadic Deva originally appeared in *Dragon #63* (© TSR/Wizards of the Coast, 1982) and later in the First Edition *Monster Manual II* (© TSR/Wizards of the Coast, 1983) and is used by permission.

Copyright Notice

Author Scott Greene, based on original material by Gary Gygax.

Angel, Movanic Deva

Hit Dice: 8
Armor Class: -1 [20]
Attack: Weapon (3d6)
Saving Throw: 8
Special: Immunities, +1 weapon to hit, magic resistance (55%), magical abilities
Move: 18/36 (flying, swimming)
Alignment: Law
Challenge Level/XP: 15/2900

Movanic devas resemble broad-shouldered humans with silver hair, white eyes, and large feathery silver wings. Relatives of the monadic devas, they are usually found wandering the Positive or Negative Energy Planes or the Material Plane. Movanic devas directly aid powerful mortals when evil threatens the balance of the planes. In the celestial armies, movanic devas serve as soldiers.

Movanic devas wield *+1 flaming greatswords*. Animals do not willingly attack movanic devas, and plant creatures cannot and do not attack them unless attacked first. Movanic devas can shift between planes at will. They can also use the following spells: *Anti-magic shell* (3/day), *continual light*, *cure disease*, *cure light wounds* (7/day), *detect evil*, *dispel magic*, *invisibility* (self only), *plane shift*, *polymorph self*, *protection from normal missiles* (1/day) and *remove curse*.

Rooting Out a Thief

One night, a squad of exceptionally handsome men and women with sepia skin, glossy black hair pulled back and tied with saffron ribbons and opalescent eyes enters an otherwise quiet inn. They wear coats of gleaming mail and carry flamberges. After a quick survey of the room, they fan out and begin asking patrons if they have seen a ruddy-skinned merchant in these parts. While the men and women are charming in their manner and graceful in their speech, they are also quite insistent and rebuff all questions as to who they are or to the identity of their lord. They focus their most intense questioning on the chaotic, but make sure to question everyone in the place. The mysterious folk are actually movadic devas, polymorphed to resemble normal humans. They seek a demon or devil who has been plying the trade of soul stealer on the Material Plane in these parts, but are having difficulty locating him.

Credit

The Movanic Deva originally appeared in *Dragon #63* (© TSR/Wizards of the Coast, 1982) and later in the First Edition *Monster Manual II* (© TSR/Wizards of the Coast, 1983) and is used by permission.

Copyright Notice

Author Scott Greene, based on original material by Gary Gygax.

ANIMAL LORDS

For every animal species, there is a single ruler or lord, looked upon by those animals as a minor deity of sorts. The animal lord is the master of that species; for example, there is a fox lord, mouse lord, and a cat lord. Each animal can assume two forms: human and animal. Its animal form is always of a member of the species it represents. Animal lords are seen as protectors of nature and animals. They may step in and prevent hunters from destroying a race of animals or foresters from completely decimating a forest. They do not, however, interfere with nature itself (i.e., animals die, they are killed for food or clothing)—such is the way of the universe.

Animal lords are effectively immortal and nearly impossible to slay. When slain, an animal lord's soul reforms on the Astral Plane. Within one week, it inhabits another animal of its type on the Material Plane and reforms. No form of magic (such as magic that would contain or trap her soul) prevents this. To permanently kill an animal lord, one must destroy every animal it commands in existence (so her soul has no creature to inhabit).

Animal lords are immune to mind-affecting effects, including illusions. They can only be harmed by +1 or better weapons.

Animal Lord, Cat Lord

Hit Dice: 19
Armor Class: -5 [24]
Attack: 2 claws (2d6) and bite (1d6)
Saving Throw: 3
Special: Change shape, howl, lick wounds, magic resistance (95%), magical abilities, immune to mind-affecting effects, surprise on 1-4 on 1d6, +1 or better weapon to hit
Move: 24/12 (climbing)
Alignment: Neutrality
Challenge Level/XP: 26/6200

There is only one. The Cat Lord is the Lord of All Felines. His natural form is that of a black panther with dark, ruby eyes. He can assume a human form, and in this form, he appears as a dark-skinned human with black hair, chiseled features, and ruby eyes. In human form, he almost always dresses in black. The Cat Lord spends his days roaming the planes. The Cat Lord can speak the secret language of druids.

When the Cat Lord howls, all creatures except felines within a 20-foot spread must succeed on a saving throw or be stunned for 1d2 rounds. Once every 1d4 rounds the Cat Lord can spit a line of caustic saliva at a single target to a range of 30 feet. A creature hit must succeed on a saving throw or be blinded.

Twice per day, the Cat Lord can automatically summon 1d4+2 lions or tigers, 1d4+4 leopards or cheetahs, 1d2 smilodons, 1d2 weretigers, or 30 + 1d20 (normal) cats. No felines, including chimeras, caterwauls, sea cats, kamadans, tabaxis or feline lycanthropes willingly attack the Cat Lord. The Cat Lord can speak to all such creatures.

Nine times per day, the Cat Lord can lick his wounds, curing 2d4 points of damage. The Cat Lord can use the following spells: *Astral spell* (1/day), *detect evil, dimension door, ethereality* (2/day, as the potion), *haste* (2/day, self only), *invisibility* and *teleport* (1/day).

The Cat Lord sees five times as well as a human in shadowy illumination and normal light and can leap up to 30 feet forward, backward or laterally with minimal effort. The Cat Lord can communicate telepathically at a range of 100 feet.

Pomp and Circumstance

With baited breath do the people of this bustling market town await the coming of the Cat Lord, for his arrival has been presaged by the golden tiger that only last week entered the town and took its place in the market square. The yowling of a hundred cats announces his arrival, strutting in human form down the streets, empty of humans and demi-humans but swarming with cats of every shape and size, all come to pay homage to their master. For centuries, the Cat Lord has come to this town to receive tribute from the many feline tribes, each one sending their representative with a choice prize. But this year, he wears a look of concern on his face, for a new force has arrived in the town, something unknown but worrisome to him, something that will have to be uncovered and stamped out.

Credit

The Cat Lord originally appeared in *Monster Manual II* (© TSR/Wizards of the Coast, 1983) and is used by permission.

Copyright Notice

Author Scott Greene, based on original material by Gary Gygax.

Animal Lord, Mouse Lord

Hit Dice: 15
Armor Class: -5 [24]
Attack: Bite (2d6 + disease)
Saving Throw: 3
Special: Change shape, disease, magic resistance (95%), magical abilities, immune to mind-affecting effects (including illusions), surprise on 1-5 on 1d6, +1 or better weapon to hit
Move: 24/12 (climbing)
Alignment: Neutrality
Challenge Level/XP: 21/4700

Like the Cat Lord, there is only one Mouse Lord, and she is the Lord (or Lady) of all rodents. Her natural form is that of a large black-furred dire rat with copper eyes. She can assume a human form and this form is almost always of a female with darkened skin, raven-black hair, and copper eyes. She dresses in robes of flowing silver or gray. The Mouse Lord spends her days roaming the planes. She can speak the secret language of druids.

The Mouse Lord's bite causes black fever, which kills in 1d3 days unless cured.

Twice per day, the Mouse Lord can automatically summon 10-100 rats or mice, 2d8 brain rats* or shadow rats*, 2d6 dire rats or barics*, or 1d4 dire shadow rats*, ethereal rats*, or wererats, or 1d4+1 rat swarms. The Mouse Lord can speak to all of these creatures, and none of these creatures will willingly attack the Mouse Lord, although they can be compelled to do so using magic.

The Mouse Lord sees four times as well as a human in shadowy illumination and twice as well in normal light.

The Mouse Lord can use the following spells: *Astral spell* (1/day), *confusion, detect evil, ethereality* (2/day, as the potion), *teleport* (1/day).

** These creatures may be found in this book.*

The Circumstance

In a deep place, damp, pungent and unlit, the Mouse Lord reclines on a couch of stone before a platform that supports a large, silver idol in the shape of a rat, its carnelian eyes swallowed up by the darkness. She is marshalling her forces, in this hidden recess beneath the caravan town, unseen and unsuspected by the fools above. Tired of the persecution of her people, the Mouse Lord has come to establish a new order, where rat devours cat and humans bait no traps, instead leaving choice offerings on their tables at night for their four-footed masters. Here she rests, a swarm of rats around her ankles, awaiting news that the Cat Lord has arrived to receive his final tribute.

Copyright Notice

Authors Scott Greene and Erica Balsley.

Ant Lion

Hit Dice: 8
Armor Class: 2 [17]
Attack: Bite (2d8)
Saving Throw: 8
Special: Trap
Move: 12/6 (burrowing)
Alignment: Neutrality
Challenge Level/XP: 8/800

The ant lion is a vicious insect-like creature that resembles a giant gray or brown ant with leathery skin covered in coarse, black bristles. Its deep, inset eyes are black and its mouth is filled with rows of jagged teeth. Two large silver mandibles protrude just above its mouth. Each mandible has a barb on its inside midway between the creature's mouth and the end point of the mandible. The ant lion lurks in the bottom of pits and holes feeding on those unfortunates that fall in.

Ant lions dig deep, funnel-shaped pits in which to trap their prey. An ant lion pit is about 60 feet across and about 20 feet deep. A creature that steps on the pit must succeed at saving throw or slip and fall down into the center of the funnel. It is there the ant lion waits, buried just under the surface of the ground. When prey falls to the center of the funnel, the ant lion surfaces and attacks, using its mandibles to grab and tear its prey. An ant lion that gets a hold does not release its prey until either it or the prey is dead.

A Handy Trap

The sandstone monuments poke out of the desert sands, so weathered that they look to be part of the desert and inseperable from it. But a wise sage knows that these crooked pylons are much more than they seem, being as they are the fingers of a giant hand, a hand that awaits only a new crystalline matrix to re-awaken and deliver to its new master all the lands surrounding these butterscotch brown sands. What no sage could possibly know is that the great stone hand holds a terrible danger in the form of a large ant lion, its pit dug in the ruined courtyard just beyond those stone fingers. There, the ant lion preys on hapless caravaneers who pass through the fingers, anointing them with quinoa oil as the old stories say they must to avoid the depredations of the ghouls that lurk on the windswept expanses of the desert. Just a few feet beyond the old arch and into the ruined compound, and one loses their footing and plunges into the 20-ft deep pit and into the crushing mandibles of the ant lion. Mixed in with the bones of llamas and merchants there is a considerable treasure.

Credit

The Ant Lion originally appeared in the First Edition *Monster Manual II* (© TSR/Wizards of the Coast, 1983) and is used by permission.

Copyright Notice

Author Scott Greene, based on original material by Gary Gygax.

Apparition

Hit Dice: 8
Armor Class: 4 [15]
Attack: Spectral strangulation (see text)
Saving Throw: 8
Special: Strangulation, detect living, incorporeal, sunlight powerlessness
Move: 12/24 (flying)
Alignment: Chaos
Challenge Level/XP: 9/1100

Apparitions are undead spirits of creatures that died as the result of an accident. The twist of fate that ended their life prematurely has driven them totally and completely to the side of evil. An apparition is often mistaken for a ghost or spectre. Apparitions hate all living creatures and attack them on sight. Apparitions are ethereal creatures and they exist mainly on the Ethereal Plane.

An apparition has no physical attacks and attacks by fear alone. By implanting a *suggestion* in a victim's mind, it attempts to actually scare the life out of its opponent. Once the apparition selects a target, it shifts into the Material Plane and uses its *spectral strangulation* ability. If the target fails a saving throw made to disbelieve in the attack, it dies of fright. If the target succeeds at the saving throw, they are merely affected by the *fear* spell. Any humanoid slain by an apparition becomes an apparition in 1d4 hours. Apparitions are utterly powerless in natural sunlight and flee from it. An apparition caught in sunlight cannot attack.

The Mage's Fate

On that day twenty years ago, how could the old mage know he was sitting down to his last meal? It had been a common enough day, filled with researches into the recesses of the labyrinthine halls of the dungeon and little real success - always more questions than answers. He and his small retinue of apprentices had sat down around the old stone table in the room they called the "Grand Tomb". The table was made of marble, with a sculpture worked into the top depicting a gaunt man in full armor, hands clasped around a two-handed axe that extended all the way down to his pointed feet. An oddity to be sure, for the mage was quite sure it was not a repurposed sarcophagus lid - maybe a trophy memorializing a fallen foe? There they sat, the hired man bringing in a platter of boiled mushrooms they had discovered in a reeking cavern, a mismatched collection of found goblets and tankards holding souring wine, hard tack and salt pork spread out before them on the table. So involved were they with the feast and a good natured exploration into the meaning of the holes that dotted the floor of the Grand Tomb, they didn't notice the hiss of gas making its way through those holes, or the silent sliding of stone doors into place blocking their escape. And so, they died, coughing and hacking. And now, as soon as the party finds a way through that stone slab, the brave adventurer will discover the final fate of that mage and his apprentices, now 1d3+1 apparitions, still collected around the weird table wondering what it all means.

Credit

The Apparition originally appeared in the First Edition *Fiend Folio* (© TSR/Wizards of the Coast, 1981) and is used by permission.

Copyright Notice

Authors Scott Greene and Clark Peterson, based on original material by Underworld Oracle.

Arach

Hit Dice: 8
Armor Class: 5 [14]
Attacks: 6 slams (1d6) or 6 short swords (1d6), 1 bite (1d4 plus poison)
Save: 8
Special: Poison, summon spiders, spells
Move: 12/6 (climb)
Alignment: Chaos
Challenge Level: 9/1,100

This six-armed humanoid has a lithe build and stands just under seven feet tall. They have narrow aquiline faces and bony plates protruding from their thoraxes and limbs. Arach inject a poison with their bite, and may coat their weapons with the same substance. About 30% of arach are spell casters, able to cast spells as a 6th-level Magic-user.

Spider Colony

The underground tunnel opens into a cylindrical chamber filled with hanging vines and thick, twisted roots that drape down from the 50-foot-high ceiling. Three tunnels exit the chamber in various directions. Tiles inlaid in the jade floor depict a massive spider overrunning a city as black flames lick the night sky. The spider's eyes are red tiles that glow brightly in the darkened chamber. Spiders crawl in thick clusters through the roots and vines, and thick balls of webbing hang among the plants.

A nest of 6 arach lives in a series of chambers accessed by a hidden doorway 40 feet off the floor. The spider-like men and woman often lurk in the vines like giant hunting spiders, suspending themselves by gripping the roots and ivy in their six hands. The arach drop on unsuspecting explorers, and fight to subdue victims to sacrifice them in a grand ceremony to the spider god of destruction the tribe worships. The arach nest is decorated with spun webs, and thousands of spiders crawl inside the wide tunnels.

Copyright Notice
Author Scott Greene.

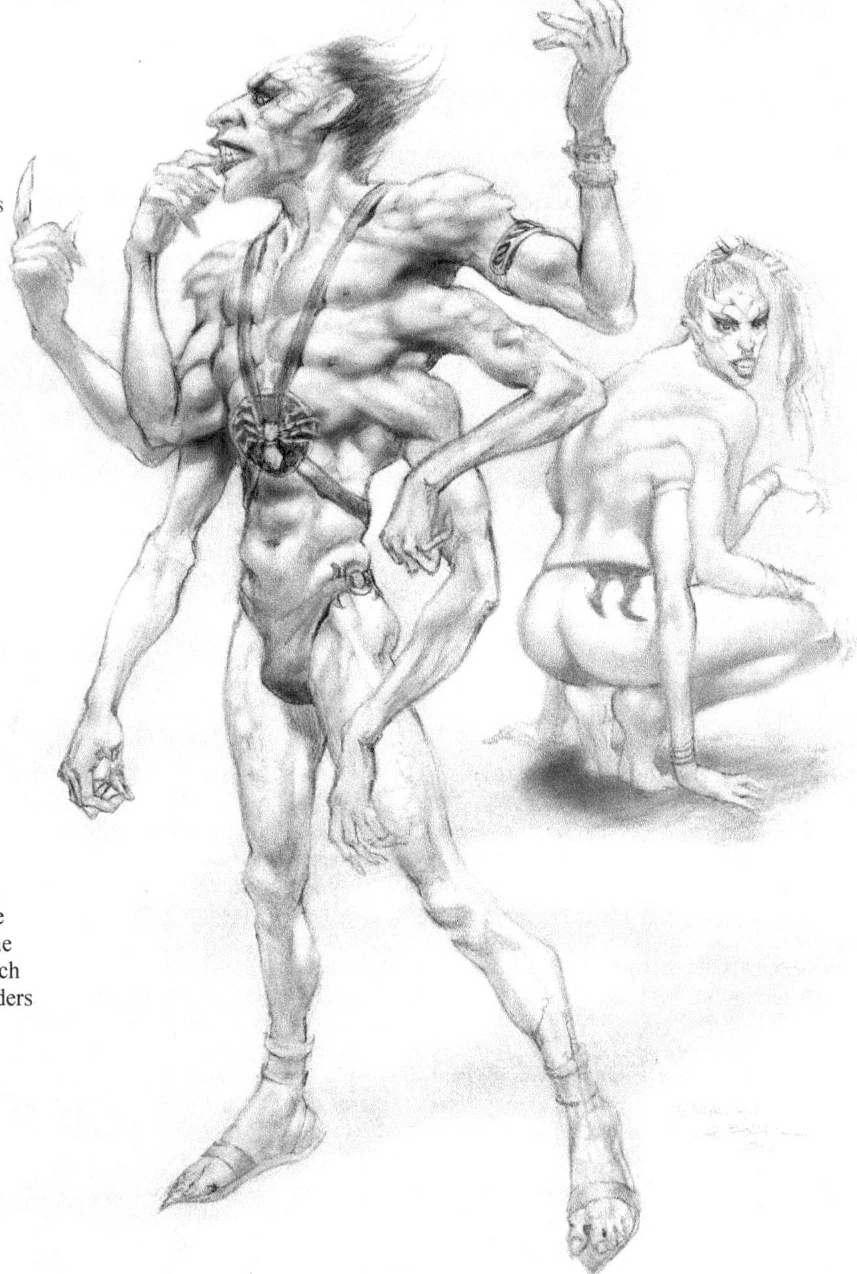

Arcanoplasm

Hit Dice: 5
Armor Class: 8 [11]
Attacks: 1 acid slam (2d4 plus 1d6 acid + grab)
Saving Throw: 12
Special: acid (1d6), absorb spells, spell mimicry, immunities
Move: 3
Alignment: Neutrality
Challenge Level/XP: 8/800

Arcanoplasms resemble giant pale yellow amoebas with "veins" of dark gray striping. Arcanoplasms are "tuned" to arcane magic and can detect magic-users within 100 feet. They can mimic any 5th-level or lower magic-user spell cast within 30 feet on their next action. Any arcane spell cast is automatically absorbed to heal 1 point for every 3 points of damage otherwise done (non-damaging spells heal 1 point per spell level of the spell). Spells that affect an area are not absorbed, but also don't affect the arcanoplasm. Cleric spells affect the ooze normally. Arcanoplasms are immune to poison, *sleep* effects, paralysis and polymorph.

The Glass Menagerie

The hallway opens into a 30-foot-by-30-foot room melted from within. The walls, floor and ceiling bow outward as if a pressure wave of heat slammed into them. Wall sconces droop like melted wax, the metal lanterns attached to them nothing more than molten puddles running in gray streaks down the stone walls.

Glass statues of cats, dogs and other wildlife sit on shelves or stand freely about the room. Some of the life-size sculptures are incredibly detailed, showing matted fur and antler scarring. The room gleams with reflected light from the hundreds of statues, which range from small glass tree frogs glued to the wall to a massive moose that dominates one corner of the chamber. All of the glass animals are incredibly detailed sculptures, but nothing more. A fine layer of dust collects on all of the animals.

Floating in the center of the room is a 5-foot-diameter glass sphere whose interior roils with yellows and grays. The sphere floats a foot off the floor, and can be pushed around the room with ease. There is a 1 in 6 chance that anyone pushing on the glass shatters it accidentally. The yellow mass inside the sphere twists and turns wildly whenever a magic-user comes within 5 feet. This wild thrashing has a 1 in 20 chance of shattering the glass. Anyone tapping the glass with a weapon shatters it instantly.

Trapped inside the sphere in an arcanoplasm that has been held captive for nearly a year. The creature melted the room, but was then trapped in the sphere by a magic-user named Chripat the Green. The effort cost the magic-user dearly; he fell sick and died of his injuries before he could get rid of the creature permanently. The arcanoplasm is folded tightly upon itself inside the glass sphere, and twists and turns unable to escape. It expands to fill a 10-foot square if released.

Copyright Notice

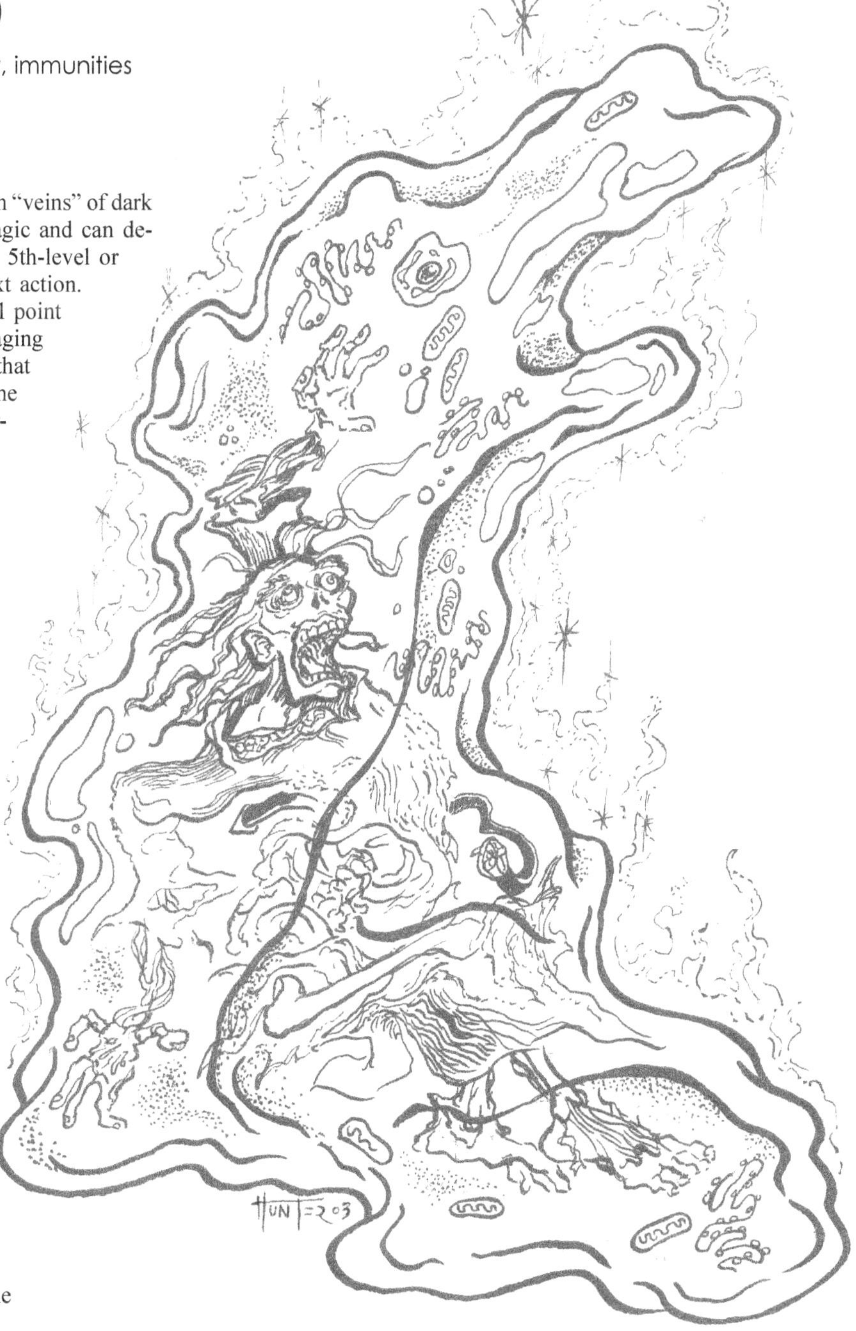

Archer Bush

A

Hit Dice: 2
Armor Class: 5 [14]
Attack: Thorns (1d8)
Saving Throw: 16
Special: Thorns
Move: 3
Alignment: Neutrality
Challenge Level/XP: 2/30

The archer bush is a subterranean, semi-mobile plant that looks like a small mound of brownish-green leaves with pale buds of gold and purple. It takes sustenance from the blood of living creatures. Hidden beneath its trunk is the archer bush's mouth, which appears to be nothing more than a dark recess or cavity. It attacks by firing a cluster of thorns at a single creature that comes within 20 feet of its location. These thorns inflict 1d8 points of damage and impose a -1 penalty to hit and to saving throws until removed.

A Way Out

A long, inclined passage leading toward the surface ends in a strange chamber measuring 30-ft wide and deep and 40-ft from floor to ceiling. The floor of the chamber is an inverted pyramid 15 feet deep with stepped sides. The upper portion of the chamber is similarly shaped with a 5-ft wide opening in the roof that appears to let in daylight. In floor of the chamber is inhabited by a patch of 1d4+4 archer bushes as well as a few pale vines bearing plutonic grapes (edible, but narcotic and with a deep, sharp taste). While the hole in the ceiling appears to provide a way out of the dungeon, it is actually a trick - just a few feet above the hole there is a large, silver plate enchanted with a permanent *light* spell - a fairly convincing illusion. The chamber is visited every few days by a gang of kobolds who use silver flutes to put the plant monsters into a trance, gathering any dropped treasure and picking a few grapes to turn into black wine.

Credit
The Archer Bush originally appeared in the module *B3 Palace of the Silver Princess* (© TSR/Wizards of the Coast, 1981) and is used by permission.

Copyright Notice
Author Scott Greene, based on original material by Jean Wells.

Ascomoid

Hit Dice: 6
Armor Class: 3 [16]
Attack: Run over or slam (1d8)
Saving Throw: 11
Special: Run over, spores, resistance to blunt weapons, fire and electricity (50%)
Move: 15
Alignment: Neutrality
Challenge Level/XP: 8/800

Ascomoids are subterranean fungus monsters that exist on a diet of living creatures. They appear as 10-ft diameter brownish-green puffballs pocked by small dots that function as sensory organs. Ascomoids feed by sitting atop a slain creature and absorbing its body fluids into its own form. Creatures slain in this manner appear as rotting husks. Ascomoids generally avoid light and the surface world, though they have no adverse reaction to sunlight or bright light. They attack by rolling over its opponents or slamming into them. Creatures that are run over or slammed must pass a saving throw or be knocked prone. Ascomoids can also fire spores at attackers. The spores have a range of 30-ft and billow into a cloud with a 20-ft radius and 20-ft height. Creatures caught in the cloud must pass a saving throw or suffer 2d6 points of damage. All creatures, whether they save or not, are blinded and nauseated for 1d4 rounds.

The King's Sauna

Damp and musty, the tunnel lead downward towards a large, natural cavern. As the tunnel approaches the cavern one notices whitish, downy fungus covering the walls and floor. The fungus is occaisionally interupted by small, tan puffballs that seem to quiver as people pass by. The cavern is monstrously large, with sulfur encrusted cracks in the walls and floor emitting a thin vapor that coats the cavern in moisture and allows fungus to thrive. A second tunnel, really a subterranean riverbed, exits the cavern. Dwellers of the underworld call this place The King's Sauna, referring to the warm, moist air and to the cavern's only inhabitant, a massive ascomoid. The ascomoid knows when people are approaching, and often lies in wait for them on an inclined shelf near the entrance, waiting for them to reach the center of the room, where the foot-wide cracks hinder their movement, before attacking. Any treasure found littering the floor is most likely tarnished or rusted unless made of gold, silver or stone.

Credit

The Ascomoid originally appeared in *Dragon #68* (© TSR/Wizards of the Coast, 1982) and later in the First Edition *Monster Manual II* (© TSR/Wizards of the Coast, 1983) and is used by permission.

Copyright Notice

Author Scott Greene, based on original material by Gary Gygax.

Asrai

Hit Dice: 1
Armor Class: 8 [11]
Attacks: 1 cold touch (1d6)
Saving Throw: 17
Special: Chill touch, spells, water dependent
Move: 12/24 (swim)
Alignment: Neutrality
Challenge Level/XP: 3/60

An asrai is a 1-foot tall female fey with long golden hair, slightly pointed elf-like ears and pale blue skin. Her eyes are emerald or gold and her features are delicate. Male asrai are thought to exist, though none have ever been encountered. Asrai can't leave their watery homes for more than an hour. An asrai's touch chills opponents for 1d6 points of damage. Asrai cast spells as 5th-level Magic-Users. Twice per day, they can also cast *create water* and *obscuring mist*.

The Lady in the Lake

A small pond sits amid the rolling hills under a peaceful blue sky. Elms sway in a gentle breeze. Frogs croak a natural melody and dragonflies flit across the still waters. Fallen logs sit in a jumble on the pond's edge.

An overturned rowboat floats in the lake about 15 feet offshore. Its wooden hull is scratched and battered, and small icicles of hoarfrost drape off the boat despite the dale's warm weather. The lake is shallow for about 5 feet along the edge, then drops to about 20 feet. The boat stays in one spot, resisting the slight wind pushing against it. A long sword with a gleaming golden hilt is thrust through the boat's wooden hull. The weapon has a small red jewel on the end that pulses like a beating heart. From the boat, a woman's voice pleads, "Help me."

An asrai named Nemedia became trapped in this small pond as she was traveling overland after drought forced the water creature from her river home. She had hoped to move on by now, heading eastward in small hops to a river about a day away. Her luck held until she reached this idyllic pond.

The pond was already the hunting ground of 7 stirges that live in the breakdown of fallen logs and in the trees on the edges of the pond. The stirges attacked Nemedia as the exhausted asrai dove into the lifesaving water. She was able to overturn a rowboat to shield herself from the flying pests, but has been unable to escape.

Nemedia hides in the pond's deep water, but occasionally surfaces beneath the rowboat to see if she might yet escape. She pleads with rescuers to help, promising them riches. The sword is a *phantasmal force* image she hopes will entice rescuers. The stirges refuse to let their meal get away so easily, however, and attack if PCs move toward the rowboat.

The asrai takes any help offered, including being carried in a container of water to the nearest river if PCs offer. If transported in such a manner, she repays her rescuers by drawing them a map to a small treasure hoard of 100 gp and 4 small rubies (50 gp each).

STIRGES (7): HD 1+1; AC 7[12]; Atk Sting (1d3 + blood drain); Move 3 (Fly 18); Save 17; Alignment: Neutrality; CL/XP 1/15; Special: Drain blood 1d4/round

Copyright Notice
Author Erica Balsley.

Assassin Bug, Giant

Hit Dice: 6
Armor Class: 5 [14]
Attacks: 2 claws (1d6) and 1 bite (1d8 + liquefy organ)
Saving Throw: 11
Special: Liquefy organs
Move: 9/6/12 (climb/flying)
Alignment: Neutrality
Challenge Level/XP: 8/800

A giant assassin bug has a narrow head ending in a segmented beak or proboscis. The 5-foot-tall creature's carapace is dull brownish-black and its front jackknife legs are covered in thousands of small hairs. Two long segmented antennae jut from its head. Assassin bugs are predatory insects that feed on the blood and tissue of living creatures. An assassin bug has two pairs of wings that it keeps folded against its back when not using them to fly. The bite of an assassin bug injects a corrosive poison that liquefies its prey's insides (save to resist).

Don't Mess With Mama

In the depths of the Primian Forest, the trees grow in thick clusters with conjoined canopies blocking the sunlight. Thick fronds catch the area's scant rainwater and hold it in the tops of the trunks. The ground is dusty and brown and dead. A giant assassin bug hunts in this seared wasteland, running through the upper branches before leaping down to pin prey. The creature has a clutch of young it protects in the hollow formed beneath a couple of fallen oak trees. The body of a half-digested fighter lies slumped over the log. His legs are still solid, but his torso a liquefied mess of soft flesh and gooey organs. The three young assassin bugs leap to attack if disturbed, but the real threat is their mother who viciously tears into any creature approaching her nest and young.

Copyright Notice

Author Scott Greene.

Astral Shark

Hit Dice: 8
Armor Class: 3 [16]
Attack: Bite (1d8)
Saving Throw: 8
Special: Astral scent, sever silver cord
Move: 24
Alignment: Neutrality
Challenge Level/XP: 9/1100

Astral sharks are sleek, piscean creatures with blotchy skin of sickly white and pink. They measure between 12 and 30 feet in length. Astral sharks have jagged, slightly curved dorsal fins and large, bulbous, lidless eyes that show no trace of pity. Astral sharks dwell on the Astral Plane, sitting atop that weird dimension's food chain. They seem to be drawn to the strange energies of visitors to the Astral Plane, relishing the silver cords that connect an astral traveler to its material body. Astral sharks can detect the presence of an astral traveler within 180 feet. When such a traveler is detected, it streaks toward them and begins to circle, darting in to bite with its powerful jaws. On a roll of a natural 20, the astral shark manages to sever the traveler's astral cord, destroying its material body and astral form.

Titanic Skeleton

Making their way across the great astral expanse, the adventurers might come across a giant skeleton drifting aimlessly, almost gracefully. Although it might be mistaken for the bones of a storm giant, the skeleton actually belonged to a young titan that fled battle with a great wyrm into the Astral Plane, only to die there. A passing school of 1d4+1 astral sharks stripped the titanic body of flesh, leaving only a few gibbets of amber-colored meat, shredded vestments and a smattering of treasure, much of it now floating in the vicinity of the corpse. The sharks remain nearby, and there is a 2 in 6 chance per minute spent examining the body that they detect the presence of visitors and attack.

Copyright Notice
Author Scott Greene.

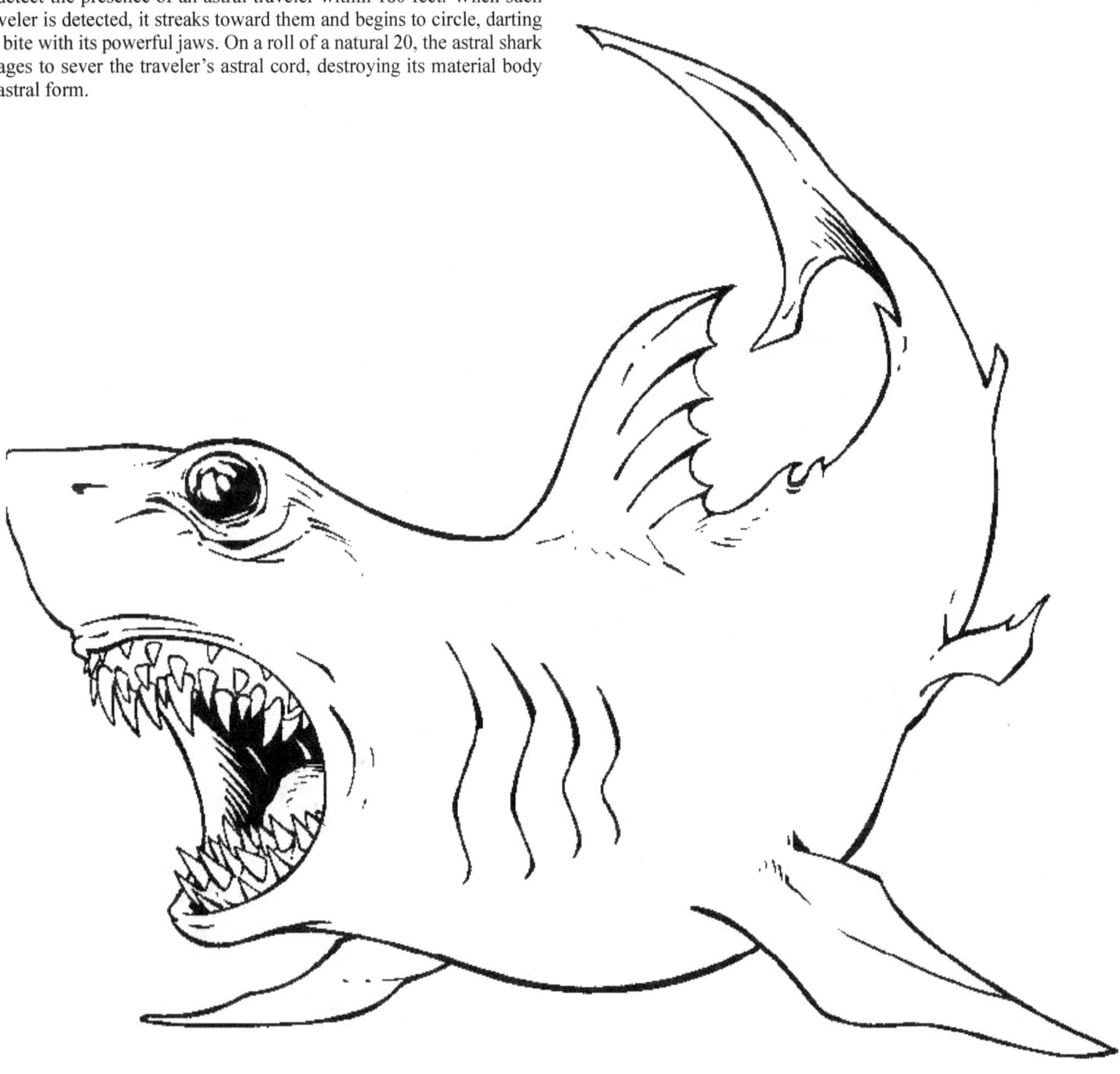

Atomie

Hit Dice: 1d3
Armor Class: 4 [15]
Attack: Weapon (1d3)
Saving Throw: 18
Special: Spells, magic resistance (20%), surprise on 1-2 on 1d6
Move: 15/24 (flying)
Alignment: Neutrality
Challenge Level/XP: 2/30

Atomies are among the smallest of the fey, looking like 1-foot tall elves with gangly limbs and greenish skin. They dwell in arboreal regions, with a single atomie family staking their claim to a single tree. Atomies are attractive, especially when compared to other sprites. Atomie clothing is almost always magical, made to change color with the seasons to help hide the wearer during all times of the year. Atomies can cast the following spells: *Blink, entangle, invisibility* (self), *pass without trace* and *speak with animals*.

There Goes the Neighborhood

When the archduke laid siege to the baroness' castle, he felled many trees and heaped one depredation after another on the woodlands that had housed a tribe of atomies since time immemorial. Fearing the iron weapons of the soldiers, the 2d4x10 atomies have moved on, taking up residence in a large forest of walnuts and wild apple trees. The people of a small village have gleaned much of their sustenance from this forest for years, grazing their swine in it and gathering walnuts and apples. The atomie, having just been driven from their own lands, are in no mood for sharing with humans and are thus doing their best to drive the humans away - tormenting hogs, tying fairy knots in hair, petty theft, scouring the woodlands of walnuts and apples, etc. The atomies have no leaders as such, with each female among believing herself to be a queen, so some of the creatures are against this campaign of terror and may be inclined to help the hapless villagers. The tree top hovels of the atomie are woven from fallen and living branches and very difficult to spot. The woods are now filled with simple traps - small holes to turn ankles, arrows coated with painful toxins and the like. At heart, the atomies do not wish to kill the humans, just drive them away.

Credit
The Atomie originally appeared in the First Edition *Monster Manual II* (© TSR/Wizards of the Coast, 1983) and is used by permission.

Copyright Notice
Author Scott Greene, based on original material by Gary Gygax.

Aurumvorax (Golden Gorger)

Hit Dice: 12
Armor Class: 0 [19]
Attack: Bite (1d8)
Saving Throw: 3
Special: Rake with claws, surprise on 1-2 on 1d6, resistance to fire (50%), immunity to poison
Move: 12/3 (burrowing)
Alignment: Neutrality
Challenge Level/XP: 13/2300

The aurumvorax (also called the golden gorger) is an extremely vicious creature that resembles an 8-legged badger with bright, golden fur. Only 3 feet long, aurumvoraces are extremely territorial, coming together only rarely to mate. The aurumvorax attacks by biting a foe and holding on with its powerful jaws. Victims of the creature's bite attack must pass a saving throw to avoid being held in jaws and raked with four claw attacks, each inflicting 1d4 points of damage. Aurumvorax feed on gold, devouring the coins and using the gold to strengthen their bones and stiffen their bristles. The pelt and bones of the animal are worth 2,000 gp.

Laying Claim

A grumpy old aurumvorax has made a lair for itself in a shallow, rocky cave overlooking a small gully that holds a trickling river that is quite rich in gold. More than a few prospectors have made the mistake of setting up camp along the stream, all of them quickly run off by the territorial and aggressive beast. This particular aurumvorax is now nursing a litter of 1d4+1 young. At the back of the beast's lair, one might find a tarnished metal wheel with five spokes sticking up out of the rock. With some effort (total strength score of 18) it can be turned to no immediate, obvious effect. One turn after turning the wheel, one might discern a low rumbling. 1d4 rounds after that, the rumbling becomes a roar and a wall of water sweeps down the gully, taking anything in its path with it and inflicting 6d6 points of damage on them. Folks in the cave will be drowned unless they can fight the current and swim free. The deluge continues for 1d4+1 rounds before settling down and leaving a small, swift river in place of the stream. The water comes from a dam constructed by the ancients about twelve miles up river.

Credit

The Aurumvorax originally appeared in the First Edition *Monster manual II* (© TSR/Wizards of the Coast, 1983) and is used by permission.

Copyright Notice

Author Scott Greene, based on original material by Gary Gygax.

Babbler

Hit Dice: 5
Armor Class: 4 [15]
Attack: 2 claws (1d6) and bite (1d8)
Saving Throw: 12
Special: Surprise on 1-4 on 1d6
Move: 15/9 (bipedal)
Alignment: Chaos
Challenge Level/XP: 5/240

Babblers are tall creatures that appear to a cross between a lizardman and a gorgosaurus. They heave yellow scales, grey underbellies, and large, strong tails that keep them balanced when they stand on their hind legs. Most of their time is spent slithering on their stomach in search of prey. The babbler is a carnivore and is quite fond of human, elven, and dwarven flesh. They speak their own weird, gutteral language and understand Common but cannot speak it. A babbler making a surprise attack enjoys a +2 bonus to hit and damage.

The Babbler Step

A stepped pyramid has long stood in the midst of the marshlands, rising from a shallow lake, the shores of which are choked with reeds that pipe weird tunes in the frequent winds that sweep over the area. The pyramid is constructed of large blocks of a chalky, ochre colored stone, and though now very weathered, once were decorated with angular glyphs of grimacing dragons and water lilies. At the top of the pyramid, which stands about 60-ft tall at the pinnacle, there is a small altar stained with wine and blood, for this pyramid was dedicated to an elder god who granted euphoria and madness in exchange for sacrifices. A hidden catch on the altar causes it to slide slightly, revealing a narrow flight of steps that winds its way into the heart of the pyramid.

The steps finally end in a large chamber lit by etheric orbs of light that bob gently on the surface of a dank, slimy pond. The pond is connected to the outer lake via submerged tunnels. Once a holy place to the lizard men who ruled these lands in ancient times, it is now occupied by the descendants of the priests who presided over that final sacrifice that helped tear down the wall between the Material Plane and the pocket dimension of Agothustlaat. A pack of 1d3+1 babblers lairs in this pond, relaxing in the cool waters and awaiting the day when the stars realign and Agothustlaat can return to our world.

A small hole drilled through the wall allows a small beam of light to enter the pond chamber. When the beam of light strikes the sapphire (300 gp) eye of a bas-relief of a reptilian priest in full regalia on the opposite wall, the babblers will know it is time. A copper urn, sealed with wax, holds the sacrificial robes and knives of the babbler priests. A secret door in the cavern leads to a narrow hallway lined with small cells wherein are chained a number of human and demi-human captives taken in raids on surrounding settlements. The prisoners are kept alive on a diet of swamp roots and raw fish, and two have already perished.

Credit

The Babbler originally appeared in the First Edition *Fiend Folio* (© TSR/Wizards of the Coast, 1981) and is used by permission.

Copyright Notice

Authors Scott Greene and Clark Peterson, based on original material by Jeremy Goodwin and Ian McDowell.

Baccae

Hit Dice: 3
Armor Class: 7 [12]
Attacks: 2 claws (1d6) and 1 bite (1d4) or 1 weapon (1d10) and 1 bite (1d6)
Saving Throw: 14
Special: beast form, charming gaze
Move: 6
Alignment: Neutrality
Challenge Level/XP: 4/120

Baccae are attractive women with long flowing, rich, red hair and emerald green eyes. They wear billowy white robes emblazoned with archaic symbols and runes and stand between 5 and 6 feet tall and weigh around 120 to 130 pounds. When enraged or intoxicated, baccae become beastlike and attack with weapons, fangs and claws. When in human form, any creature withon 30 feet meeting their gaze must save or be charmed (as per the spell).

Wild Things

The forest's thick plants and clinging thorns give way to a strange sight: Six women wearing little more than silk scarves tied strategically around their bodies dance in unison around a proud stag in the middle of the leaf-covered clearing. A bonfire of aromatic wood sends a thin stream of smoke across the dancers. Their flesh glistens with a fine sheen of sweat as they dance. The leader is a tall woman with rich red hair and emerald eyes who moves a half-second ahead of the dancers, directing the bacchanalia.

If interrupted, the dancers halt immediately, and the stag bounds away, vanishing into the forest with a chaotic stamp of hooves and thrashing of its pronged head. The 6 baccae invite PCs to join their dance. Red wine is freely offered, and the women consume as much as their guests. PCs notice the changes in the women almost immediately as they become more bestial and belligerent, and the dance becomes wilder and more passionate.

The baccae have one enemy in the woods, however, a black-furred gang of 4 ruthless werewolves who hide in the woods waiting to end the dancers' revelry. These ruffians burst out of the forest intent on slaying the women, and any guests they encounter.

Banderlog

Hit Dice: 4
Armor Class: 5 [14]
Attack: Bite (1d6) or club (1d6) or coconut (1d4)
Saving Throw: 13
Special: Coconut throwing
Move: 15/12 (climb)
Alignment: Neutrality
Challenge Level/XP: 4/120

The banderlog is a somewhat intelligent baboon-like primate with grayish-brown fur that makes its home in warm forests and jungles. Though it appears as a larger version of the common baboon, it does not keep company with or associate with normal baboons. Banderlogs' intelligence allows them to form small tribal communities for protection and companionship. The leader of such a community is usually the largest and strongest banderlog of the tribe. Banderlogs sustain themselves on a diet of fruits and nuts, with coconuts being their favorite food. Though omnivorous, they rarely eat meat of any sort. Unaggressive unless threatened, banderlogs prefer to attack from a distance using small rocks or coconuts. They can hurl these projectiles up to 50 feet.

Banderlog Barque

A grand barque, the property of a noblewoman from the coast, has run aground on a sandbank near the bank a great jungle river. The barque ventured up the river in search of a great treasure, a treasure guarded by sinister powers who did not wish it found. One terrible night, these guardians descended from a moonless sky and killed or carried away the barque's entire complement.

The abandoned boat has now been taken over by a a pack of 6d4 banderlogs and their 1d2 leaders (6 HD each). The banderlogs have occupied themselves by dismantling just about everything they could get their hands on, swinging about on the slack ropes, tearing up the sails and feasting on the provisions below decks. The captain's cabin, fairly doused in blood, still holds a treasure map stuck to a table with a dagger.

Credit

The Banderlog originally appeared in the First Edition module *S3 Expedition to the Barrier Peaks* (© TSR/Wizards of the Coast, 1980) (as the baboonoid) and later in the First Edition *Monster Manual II* (© TSR/Wizards of the Coast, 1983) and is used by permission.

Copyright Notice

Author Scott Greene, based on original material by Gary Gygax.

Baobhan Sith

Hit Dice: 3
Armor Class: 9 [11]
Attacks: 1 slam (1d4) and 1 bite (1d4)
Saving Throw: 14
Special: Blood drain, captivating dance, dying words, spell-like abilities
Move: 15
Alignment: Chaos
Challenge Level/XP: 6/400

A baobhan sith appears as female elf with pearl white skin, golden or brown hair, and eyes of emerald, blue or hazel. Her figure is sleek and curved and she moves with a cat-like grace. By entrancing creatures with their dance, they lure men to their deaths. Those who see her dance must make a save, or become enthralled for 2d4 rounds. Once a target is captivated, the baobhan sith moves in and drains its blood with a bite (1d4 points of damage). When slain, the baobhan sith curses her killers with her dying words. At will, baobhan sith can *detect thoughts* and cast *plant growth* and *suggestion*.

The Prism Prison

A 100-foot-diameter reflecting pool of clear water fills this forgotten temple. Plants grow wildly about the room from golden planters, creating a jungle of vegetation within the building. Ten mirrored columns surround the pool, each rising to the arching ceiling 40 feet overhead. A gurgling fountain of water jets upward in the center of the pool, splashing against the sides of a 15-foot-diameter clear crystal sphere hovering above the pool. Within the crystal is a pale elf with golden hair and delicate features. She is dressed in a sheer gown that flows over her slender body like a waterfall.

The woman is a baobhan sith imprisoned by her sisters for leading a female warrior into their valley. If PCs approach the pool, the trapped baobhan sith begins dancing. The crystal prison reflects the dance into the water and onto the pillars, forcing anyone looking at any of these reflective surfaces to save or be charmed by the woman's seductive movements. Any charmed PCs are attacked by 8 baobhan sith hiding in the thick vegetation.

If the crystal is shattered, the baobhan sith within is freed and flees.

Copyright Notice

Author Scott Greene.

Barbegazi (Ice Gnome)

Hit Dice: 2
Armor Class: 8 [11]
Attacks: 1 weapon (1d4)
Saving Throw: 16
Special: Spell-like abilities, snow move, immune to cold, fire vulnerability
Move: 9
Alignment: Neutrality
Challenge Level/XP: 3/60

Barbegazis – also known as ice gnomes – stand about 3-1/2 feet tall and have white hair and long flowing whitish-blue beards that appear to be made of icicles. Their skin is pale and glossy-white and their eyes are deep blue. They have large, flat feet and never wear shoes. They are perfectly adapted to live in the coldest regions, and can walk on deep snow without being slowed. Once per day, a barbegazi can cause metal to freeze using a variation of *heat metal*. They are also able to shoot shards of ice from their hands (cold variation of *burning hands*, 1/day) to stop attackers.

Making Tracks

Two run-down wagons sit in the middle of the frozen wasteland, their battered wooden sides covered by thick polar bear pelts to keep out the cold. A weak fire burns in the middle of deep snowdrifts, the logs barely flickering with tiny licks of flame. The camp is empty, although boot prints from about six human travelers lead off into the trees.

The camp is a trap laid by a group of 8 barbegazi thieves journeying far from their Wailing Glacier home. The small band is wanted by their village for stealing a diamond idol that supposed to keep the Wailing Glacier from melting. The small group fled their village and has been robbing travelers for supplies as they stay a step ahead of the bounty hunters hired to return the idol.

The barbegazi hide in hollowed-out snowdrifts with their **2 polar bear** pets. The polar bears pull the wagon when the barbegazi travel. The human tracks leading out of the camp were made using wooden boot shapes the barbegazi strap onto their smaller feet to mislead travelers.

One of the wagons contains a fist-sized diamond carved to look like a small white dragon wrapping itself around a frozen icicle. The idol is worth 500 gp, but the barbegazi of the Wailing Glacier have hired agents to seek out and return the relic. They look harshly on anyone trying to sell the stolen relic.

POLAR BEAR (2): HD 7; AC 6[13]; Atk 2 claws (1d6+1), 1 bite (1d10+1); Move 12; Save 9; CL/XP 7/600; Special: Hug.

Copyright Notice
Author Scott Greene.

Baric

Hit Dice: 2
Armor Class: 6 [13]
Attack: 2 claws (1d3) and bite (1d8)
Saving Throw: 16
Special: None
Move: 15
Alignment: Neutrality
Challenge Level/XP: 2/30

Barics look like giant 6-legged rats with black fur and yellow eyes. They have long, duck-like bills lined with rows of needle-like teeth. The average baric is 3 feet long and weighs 50 pounds, though they can grow to a length of 7 feet and weigh about 150 pounds. Some races keep barics as pets, though more often than not, these unpredictable monsters turn on their masters within a short time of entering captivity.

Rat Pack

A pack of 1d8 barics has been placed into suspended animation within a large, long, silvey cannister. The cannister's origin is unclear, though it bears many dents and scuffs, as though it has come a long way. It is now resting in the midst of a large, vaulted cavern, having been carried there by the warriors of a tribe of troglodytes, their shaman having declared it a god when a patrol discovered it in the surface swamps.

The cannister can be opened by the turning of dials found on one end of the cannister. The dials are encrusted with dried muck from the swamp and one of them is damage, requiring a thief to succeed at an open locks roll at a -15% penalty, or not penalty if assisted by a magic-user with a *read languages* spell. When opened, the end of the cannister simply falls off, as though severed, ending the suspended animation and setting the barics loose on an unsuspecting world. Inside the cannister there is a thick layer of red dust and a treasure of 1d4 x 100 oblong gold coins in a leather sack.

Credit

The Baric originally appeared in the module *B3 Palace of the Silver Princess* (© TSR/Wizards of the Coast, 1981) and is used by permission.

Copyright Notice

Author Scott Greene, based on original material by Jean Wells.

Basidirond

Hit Dice: 5
Armor Class: 3 [16]
Attack: Slam (1d8 + spores)
Saving Throw: 12
Special: Hallucination cloud, spores, immune to cold
Move: 9
Alignment: Neutral (chaotic tendencies)
Challenge Level/XP: 8/800

Basidirons are fungal creatures that resemble inverted umbrellas with stems of dark green or brown hanging beneath it. The inside of its cone-shaped top is inky black. The basidirond stands 7 feet tall, and is believed to be related to the ascomoid (q.v.). It makes it lair in very dry underground caverns. The basidirond attacks by striking with its cone-shaped cap or by releasing a cloud of spores . This cloud of spores measures 20 feet in radius. Creatures within the cloud must succeed on a saving throw or be affected as by a *confusion* spell for as long as they remain in the cloud plus 1d4 rounds after leaving the area. A new save must be made each round a creature remains within the affected area. (For more specific hallucinations see the sidebar text.)

Basidirond Hallucination Cloud

Rather than affecting an opponent as by a *confusion* spell, you can randomly determine hallucinations for each creature affected. The duration remains the same as detailed under the creature's special attack.

1d8	Hallucination
1	Individual believes he is in a swamp and strips off gear and armor to avoid sinking.
2	Individual believes he is being attacked by a swarm of spiders. He attacks the floor and surrounding area.
3	Individual believes item held has turned into a viper; drops item and retreats back from it.
4	Suffocation—Individual believes he is suffocating and gasps for air and clutches throat.
5	Individual believes he has shrunk to 1/10 normal size. He begins yelling for help.
6	Individual believes his associates have contracted a disease. He will not come closer than 10 feet.
7	Individual believes he is melting; grasps self in attempt to hold together.
8	Individual believes his back is covered with leeches. He tears armor, clothing, etc. from his back to get at them.

A basidirond's slam attack transfers smothering, poisonous spores to its opponent. A creature struck must succeed on a saving throw or smother in 1d4+1 rounds unless a *cure disease* spell is cast on them. A basidirond takes no damage from a cold effect, but is *slowed* (as the spell). During this time, a basidirond cannot use its poisonous spores or hallucination cloud special attacks.

Fungus Among Us

As you proceed down the tunnel, you notice the air becoming warmer and drier, working you into a lather and parching your throat. After a few more yards, you hear the screams of a madman echoing down the tunnel. They grow louder and louder, and no more than a minute later you catch sight of an adventurer in chainmail running towards you screaming about "the spiders". If one attempts to stop him, he flails wildly for a couple rounds before coming to his senses. Otherwise, he continues running past the adventurers into the dungeon.

If calmed down, the man describes 1d3 weird fungal creatures with long, brown tendrils and a cone shaped bodies dwelling in a large cavern about 100 yards ahead. The cavern is horseshoe-shaped and measures about 300 feet from entrance to exit. It is terribly warm, caused by a volcanic vent that passes through the inner cavern wall and filled with bones, dozens of pieces of armor and weapons and a thick layer of dried fungus - either husks of the creature's "young", or flakes from its own body.

Besides any other treasure that might litter the area, the dried husks are valuable for brewing a bitter, nauseating tea that is said to give one the ability to see through illusions for up to one hour after drinking it. Imbibers of the tea will find that these rumors are true, but they must also pass a saving throw at +4 or lose their minds (per a *symbol of insanity* spell).

Credit

The Basidirond originally appeared in *Dragon #68* (© TSR/Wizards of the Coast, 1982) and later in the First Edition *Monster Manual II* (© TSR/Wizards of the Coast, 1983) and is used by permission.

Copyright Notice

Author Scott Greene, based on original material by Gary Gygax.

Basilisk, Crimson

Hit Dice: 6
Armor Class: 4 [15]
Attacks: 1 bite (1d8 + acid)
Saving Throw: 11
Special: Acid bite, blood frenzy, wounding gaze, camouflage
Move: 6
Alignment: Neutrality
Challenge Level/XP: 7/600

A crimson basilisk is about 6 feet long and weighs over 400 pounds. Its skin is dull crimson though it can easily change its color to match that of its surroundings. Its eight legs are thick and stout and end in sharpened claws. The spines on its back are crimson as well, though they tend to be darker than its overall body (especially in males). Its eyes glow with a ghostly blue light. A crimson basilisk's saliva is corrosive, dealing 1d6 points of acid damage with each bite. Any creature within 30 feet that meet's the creature's gaze must save or lose 1d4 hit points as their blood weeps from their eyes, ears, nose and mouth. A crimson basilisk that detects fresh blood within 30 feet enters a frenzied state that gives it a +2 to-hit bonus.

Tears of the God

The 20-foot-tall head of a statue sits on the ground. There are no clues to the whereabouts of the rest of the statue. Blood continually drips over the surface of the unknown bearded god, weeping from its hairline where a stone crown sits and down its cheeks and chin. The entire area reeks of rotting gore, and years of draining blood saturate the ground around the stone head. Clouds of flies swarm the area, driven by bloodlust. The blood pours over the head and coalesces in cracks and crevasses, creating a dramatic chiaroscuro effect on the white marble head. The flowing blood gives the statue the appearance that it is crying.

The blood is actually from the prey of a crimson basilisk that nests atop the stature in a natural hollow inside the stone crown. The crimson basilisk normally stays atop the statue to sun and devour its meals; otherwise, it is off hunting for prey and mates. Down-on-their-luck locals sometimes journey to the statue to make offerings of meat and fruits to the god. Sometimes they do not return.

Basilisk, Greater

Hit Dice: 10
Armor Class: 2 [17]
Attack: 2 claws (1d8 + poison) and bite (1d8)
Saving Throw: 5
Special: Foul breath, petrifying gaze, poison
Move: 9
Alignment: Neutrality
Challenge Level/XP: 13/2300

Greater basilisks are larger, more vicious cousins of the normal basilisk. They are 12-foot long reptilian monsters with dull brown skin, yellow underbellies and eyes that glow with an eerie, pale green incandescence. Sages believe the greater basilisk hails from the Elemental Plane of Earth.

In combat they rear up on their hind legs and slash opponents with their poisonous claws while also using their deadly gaze attack. The beast's poisonous claws inflict an additional 1d4 points of damage with each hit unless a successful saving throw is made. The breath of a greater basilisk is so foul that all creatures within 5 feet must succeed on a saving throw or take 1d4 points of damage each round they remain in the area. A creature need only succeed on this saving throw once to avoid further damage from the poisonous breath.

The greater basilisk's petrifying gaze has a 50-foot range. Those it looks at must succeed at a saving throw or be turned into stone. The greater basilisk is near-sighted and must be within 10 ft. of its reflected gaze to suffer the same fate.

Life-Giving Water

A mated pair of greater basilisks has made its home in a series of howling caverns in a wasteland of red sandstone and stunted creosote bushes. The entrance to their maze-like lair is partially obscures by large boulders. Within the caverns, the wind causes a constant roaring and whistling that makes it impossible to hear the greater basilisks moving about. The greater basilisks usually lie motionless within their caverns, allowing them to surprise opponents on a roll of 1-2 on 1d6. There is about a 25% chance that one or the other is in their lair, and a 10% chance that both are in their lair.

The beasts are careless about where they devour their prey, so bits of armor, clothing, weapons, treasure and clothing as well as petrified adventurers can be found throughout the caverns. In the heart of the caverns there is an ancient druidic altar composed of a wind-shaped boulder surrounded by the burned remains of the creosote and painted with shamanic symbols.

A depression in the top of the altar holds crystal clear water that can reverse the petrifying gaze of the basilisks if applied to the victim within 10 rounds of being turned to stone. A small mirror lies in the bottom of the basin.

Credit

The Greater Basilisk originally appeared in the First Edition *Monster Manual II* (© TSR/Wizards of the Coast, 1983) and is used by permission.

Copyright Notice

Author Scott Greene, based on original material by Gary Gygax.

Bat, Doombat

Hit Dice: 6
Armor Class: 2 [17]
Attack: Bite (1d8) and tail (1d6)
Saving Throw: 11
Special: Shriek
Move: 3/18 (flying)
Alignment: Chaos
Challenge Level/XP: 8/800

The doombat is a giant black bat with glowing yellow eyes. It is a nocturnal hunter that desires living flesh to sustain it. The doombat has a 10-foot wingspan, though specimens with wingspans reaching 25 feet have been reported. The approach of a doombat can be heard long before the creature arrives on the scene, the yipping growing louder as the doombat draws closer. When a doombat yips, all creatures (except other doombats) within a 100-foot spread must succeed on a saving throw or suffer a -1 penalty on attacks rolls and saving throws for the duration of the battle. The yipping is constant, and spellcasters in the area must succeed on a saving throw anytime they attempt to cast a spell. The effect of several doombats yipping at once is not cumulative. Doombats use echolocation to pinpoint creatures within 120 feet, allowing them to attack invisible opponents at no penalty.

Doom, the Bell Tolls

When the errant knight in the scarlet tunic emblazoned with a golden sun killed the old sage in the belltower, things in the village began to improve. The rains stopped, the sun shone strong and the animals, drawn and lean, fattened up almost immediately. The people became hale and healthy as well, and the old belltower, home of the curious sage who turned out to be a necromancer, was bricked up. All the people remembered well the final curse on the necromancer's lips - when next the bell rings, doom will come from the skies.

The necromancer wasn't just whistling Dixie. In the grey peaks that loom over the lush meadow valley of the village, there are a number of caves both small and large. Nobody living has ever ventured into these caves, for they are exceptionally difficult to reach and the stories that have passed down from past generations report they they are barren and useless. The highest cavern is not completely barren, though, for it connects to much deeper tunnels and vaults wherein dwell many colonies of doombats.

Should the bell in the tower ever ring again, at nightfall the cavern will belch forth 1d4+4 of these terrible creatures to wreak the necromancer's final vengeance against the village. And in the vault from whence the doombats come, there is a weird idol of spongy, grey stone that is warm and pulsating to the touch. The idol depicts a petty and forgotten god, and it holds a large, perfect sapphire (worth 2,500 gp) that serves as a mystic key to release that forgotten god from its extradimensional prison. All that must happen is for sapphire be bathed in the blood of an innocent and then shattered by a doombat's shriek.

Credit

The Doombat originally appeared in the First Edition *Fiend Folio* (© TSR/Wizards of the Coast, 1981) and is used by permission.

Copyright Notice

Author Scott Greene, based on original material by Julian Lawrence.

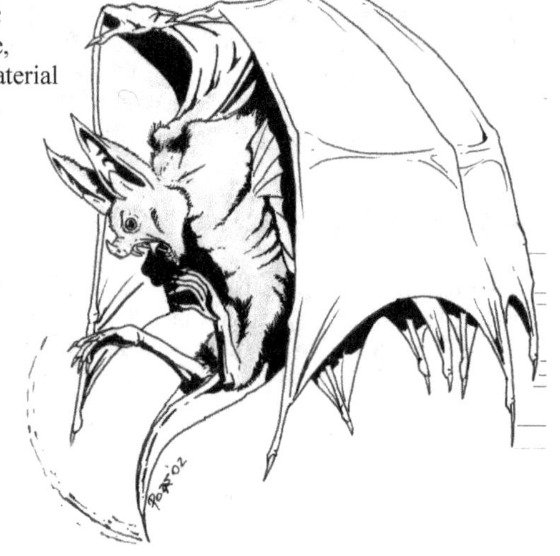

Bat, Mobat

Hit Dice: 4
Armor Class: 3 [16]
Attack: Bite (1d8)
Saving Throw: 13
Special: Sonic screech
Move: 9/15 (flying)
Alignment: Neutrality (chaotic tendencies)
Challenge Level/XP: 6/400

Mobats are large, brown bats with razor-sharp fangs and green, glowing eyes. The mobat has a wingspan of approximately 15 feet. It is a nocturnal creature, cruising silently through the night sky in its never ending quest for food. A mobat can blast an ear-splitting screech that affects all within a 20-foot spread. The screech stuns any creature in the area for 1d3 rounds if it fails a saving throw. Mobats use echolocation to pinpoint creatures within 120 feet, allowing them to attack invisible opponents at no penalty.

With This Ring

A colony of 2d4 mobats has been making a nuisance of itself to the people on the jungle's edge, ever since a mysterious, exotic woman was carried into the village by a hunting party. The woman has been locked in a deathless sleep since found, and the villager's now suspect that she is a witch calling the mobats to attack their livestock. The local priest finds this unlikely, but knows that the people's fear and anger cannot long be supressed.

The people are not entirely wrong. The mobats do search for the woman, who escaped from a reclusive wizard's tower with a magical ring, swallowing it to hide it from him. She is now in the grip of the wizard's curse, the ring attracting the mobats, the largest being the *polymorphed* wizard.

Credit

The Mobat originally appeared in the First Edition module *S4 Lost Caverns of Tsojcanth* (© TSR/Wizards of the Coast, 1982) and later in the First Edition *Monster Manual II* (© TSR/Wizards of the Coast, 1983) and is used by permission.

Copyright Notice

Author Scott Greene and Clark Peterson, based on original material by Gary Gygax.

Beast of Chaos

Hit Dice: 5
Armor Class: 0 [19]
Attack: 2 claws (1d4) and bite (1d8)
Saving Throw: 12
Special: Frightful presence, rage, immunities, magic resistance (25%)
Move: 15
Alignment: Chaos
Challenge Level/XP: 8/800

A chaos beast resembles a lion with dark, blackened fur, razor-sharp fangs, and oversized paws that wield sharpened claws.

When a beast of chaos growls, roars, hisses, or makes any other sound common to its animal type, all creatures within 30 feet that hear it and those with fewer HD than the beast of chaos must succeed on a saving throw or become shaken for 5d6 rounds.

In the presence of bright light, a beast of chaos flies into a berserk rage, attacking until either it or its opponent is dead. It gains a +1 bonus to hit and damage while enraged. If the source of light is removed, the creature's rage ends 1d4 rounds later.

Beasts of chaos are immune to *confusion*, *fear*, *hold animal*, *hold monster*, *slow,* and *haste*.

Chaos in the Savannah

When a party of adventurers toppled the blackened idol of the Ancient Traveler, the chaotic deity of the savannah, they unleashed a potent green mist that flowed across the landscape, tainting the grass and trees and twisting a pride of lions into beasts of chaos. The 1d6+5 lions now dwell in the shade of the fallen idol, collecting shamans from the savannah tribes and depositing their bodies into the hole from whence came the mists. The hole is the incarnate stomach of the Ancient Traveler, and the victims fuel his manifestation in the Material Plane.

The idol was 30 feet tall and up to 15 feet wide in places. The pieces of the idol (there are eight) now sprawl across the savannah. The grasses in the area have turned crimson and the trees are the color of jaundiced flesh, their leaves scarlet and oozing a weird sap (causes *confusion* to those who touch or taste them unless they pass a saving throw).

At the bottom of the hole of green mists, there is a pool of green acid. It is currently inhabited by seven wights, the risen remains of the shamans dropped into the hole by the beasts of chaos. The wights bear scars from the beasts and their legs and arms are twisted into weird angles.

Copyright Notice
Author Scott Greene.

Bedlam

Hit Dice: 8
Armor Class: 4 [15]
Attacks: 2 slams (2d4)
Saving Throw: 8
Special: Chaos burst, immune to polymorph, spell failure
Move: 30 (flying)
Alignment: Neutrality
Challenge Level/XP: 10/1,400

A bedlam is a semi-amorphous, nearly vaporous creature composed of pure chaos. The creature has no set shape or form. Every minute or so its form changes from that of a smoky gray and vaguely humanoid figure with arms, head, and torso to a swirling mass of grayish-black chaotic matter crackling with bluish-gray energy. A bedlam can unleash a burst of energy against nearby opponents for 4d8 damage (save for half). Spells fizzle around a bedlam, with magic-users needing to make a save to successfully cast a spell.

Rest in Peace and Quiet

Pilgrim House was a place of screams and insanity until about a week ago. The asylum sits on a hillside overlooking Dalerest, with wrought-iron gates keeping patients inside. Thick climbing streamers of ivy cover the fence, and azaleas planted by the insane surround the three interconnected buildings' granite foundations. The manor house is eerily silent, however, all of patients cowering in fear or whimpering silently in far corners by themselves. They run if approached. At night, the usual screams echoing through the hospital's halls are replaced by eerie silence.

An old man with wrinkled skin, a long white beard and scrawny legs walks half-naked through the yard around the hospital. He wears a gold "crown" made of folded paper on his head. Grubal Norton struts around the yard, having a grand old time. The patients either run from him or drop to the ground and grovel at his feet. He wears an assortment of rings on his toes and has a woman's silk scarf wrapped around his wrist. Norton was admitted to the hospital against his will more than a week ago when he was found dancing naked in the street with a bearskin rug. If PCs approach the old man, he puts his finger to his lips and shushes them.

Norton considers himself the emperor of Pilgrim House. As royalty, the screams of the other patients offend him. One of the worthless rings Norton wears on his toes is a dimensional prison that contains a bedlam in its opal depths. Norton's anger every sleepless night calls the bedlam forth, and the creature enforces the old man's wish for silence. The other patients know to keep quiet or face the bedlam's deadly torments. The creature floats freely through the manor halls at night looking for people making too much noise. Anyone angering Norton or touching the old man immediately draws the bedlam out of its dimensional lair.

Beetle, Giant Blister

Hit Dice: 2
Armor Class: 8 [11]
Attacks: 1 bite (1d6)
Saving Throw: 16
Special: Blister spray, immune to poison
Move: 15
Alignment: Neutrality
Challenge Level/XP: 3/60

Blister beetles are 3 feet long with slick, dark green carapaces. Their legs are dark green or black and their mandibles are serrated, and black or green in color. When they snap them together, their mandibles produce an audible clicking sound that can be heard up to 10 feet away. When attacked, the beetle releases a foul stream of oily liquid up to 20 feet that irritates an attacker's skin (1d3 damage, save avoids).

Blister Pack

The ground in a 20-foot-wide clearing is burned and blackened. A rotting, hollow tree trunk lies on the ground, its entire side bubbling with a green syrupy liquid. Other trees standing around the clearing are missing bark on the sides facing the clearing. Grass around the edges of the clearing is withered and brown. A giant sunflower lies across the clearing, its stem burned in half. A giant bee lies crushed beneath the fallen flower. The upper half of the bee has been burned away. The entire area smells of nail polish remover.

A giant blister beetle colony lives under the clearing. The opening into their colony is inside the fallen tree. Two beetles wait for creatures to enter their clearing, then spray the area with their oily blistering liquid through holes in the hollow trunk. They rush out opposite ends of the tree to attack, clicking their mandibles to bring other insects from the underground nest. The Game Referee should adjust the number of beetles to fit the Challenge Level of the PCs.

Copyright Notice

Author Scott Greene.

Beetle, Giant Boring

Hit Dice: 5
Armor Class: 2 [17]
Attack: Bite (2d8)
Saving Throw: 12
Special: Hive mind
Move: 9
Alignment: Neutrality
Challenge Level/XP: 5/240

Giant boring beetles are 9-foot long, with greenish-gray carapaces and wing-covers and black legs and mandibles. They feed primarily on wood, mold, fungus, and other organic matter and make their lairs inside ancient tunnels and caverns, where they harvest and grow molds and fungi. Shriekers are prized for both food and their use as alarms to warn the boring beetles of intrusion. Boring beetles are about 9 feet long. All boring beetles within 1 mile of each other are in constant communication. If one is aware of a particular danger, they all are. If one in the group is not surprised then none of them are.

Boring Temple

The temple that is supposed to hold the shinbone of Saint Alyssa of the Black Rose sank into the ground more than a century ago, sinkholes being common along the coast. The people merely filled it in with rubble and rebuilt, and for years never ventured into the dangerous corridors and crumbling rooms of the old temple, trusting that its inaccessibility would keep the relics safe.

But now, as a weird plague sweeps along the coast and strikes down man, woman and child indiscriminately, the priests have decided the holy reliquary must be recovered. To their dismay, they have discovered that the old temple has become something of a hub in the underworld. A tribe of venemous kobolds has moved into the old kitchen and turned the old fire pit into a place of sacrifice in honor of whatever minor demonic functionary they're worshipping this week.

The catacombs are now crawling with a hive of 1d8+10 giant boring beetles. The catacombs connect to the ancient crypt, the center of the beetles' hive. The vaulted crypt is now filled with all sorts of weird, pale fungi, including 2d4 shriekers. The sarcophagus of Saint Alyssa and the reliquary have not been harmed.

Credit

The Boring Beetle originally appeared in the First Edition *Monster Manual* (© TSR/Wizards of the Coast, 1977) and is used by permission.

Copyright Notice

Author Scott Greene, based on original material by Gary Gygax.

Beetle, Giant Death Watch

Hit Dice: 9
Armor Class: 2 [17]
Attack: Bite (1d8)
Saving Throw: 6
Special: Death rattle, immune to death spells, surprise on a 1-4 on 1d6
Move: 12
Alignment: Neutrality
Challenge Level/XP: 11/1700

This creature appears as a giant beetle with a dark green carapace and wing-covers. Its body is covered in leaves and sticks. Its mandibles are silver and its legs are black. The death watch beetle makes its lair in forests and uses a mixture of saliva and earth to stick rubbish (leaves and twigs, for instance) to itself in order to attack by surprise. Once every hour, a death watch beetle can vibrate its carapace to produce a clicking noise that sets up vibrations in all creatures within 30 feet. Affected creatures with 6 HD or less must succeed on a saving throw or die immediately. Creatures with more than 6 HD or those that succeed on their saving throw take 4d6 points of damage. Since the effect stems from the vibrations set up in a victim's body and not from the clicking noise itself, *silence* offers no protection against this attack. Likewise, a creature that cannot hear can still be affected.

Death Pyramid

The natives have always considered the valley hemmed in by the cliffs of white chalk to be a sacred, taboo place. To visitors, it appears to be little more than a gentle woodland of tall pines. The valley is abundant in game and the air here is always crisp and cool. In the midst of the valley there is a crude pyramid built of pale yellow chalk blocks, heavily weathered. What carvings still exist depict dancing skeletons and large scarabs.

A very narrow tunnel leads into the pyramid, which stands 30 feet tall and measures 20 feet on each side. The narrow tunnel leads downward, slightly, ending in a circular shaft open to the sky and also descending into a little cavern that holds a floating globe of wan light. When touched, this globe emits a sound inaudible to human beings that attracts a death watch beetle that lives nearby.

The death watch beetle will creep towards the pyramid and then lie low in a shallow, natural pit, its body covered with leaves and sticks. In this position, it will wait until the blasphemers come close enough to use its death rattle and then strike. The globe of light can be moved by touching it with a slim wand of knotty pine. It gives out light equal to a full moon and acts as a *protection from evil* spell.

Credit

The Death Watch Beetle originally appeared in the First Edition *Monster Manual II* (© TSR/Wizards of the Coast, 1983) and is used by permission.

Copyright Notice

Authors Scott Greene and Clark Peterson, based on original material by Gary Gygax.

Beetle, Giant Rhinoceros

Hit Dice: 12
Armor Class: 1 [18]
Attack: Bite (2d8) and gore (2d6)
Saving Throw: 3
Special: Trample (3d6)
Move: 9
Alignment: Neutrality
Challenge Level/XP: 12/2000

Giant rhinoceros beetles are 12-foot long beetles with grayish-brown carapaces and wing-covers and a large brownish-black "horns" between its mandibles. They are found in the warm jungles and forests of the world and spend their days searching for plants, fruits, and berries on which to sustain themselves. Giant rhinoceros beetles can trample smaller creatures by simply moving over them, inflicting 3d6 points of damage (save for half damage).

Fun With Explosions

For generations, the jungle people have kept the trading lanes clear with the use of a swarm of 1d6+5 semi-tamed giant rhinoceros beetles. The beetles are controlled by priestly maidens using long sticks scented with fragrant herbs. Slaves armed with sickles are connected to the beetle's carapace via long chains and neck collars, sweeping away the choking underbrush of the rain forest while the beetle topples trees and trods things underfoot.

The beetles are kept in a large enclosure - a pit surrounded by a wooden palisade, with their handlers living in long houses outside the enclosure and slaves living in subterranean chambers beneath the beetle enclosure.

All would be well with this situation were it not for the jungle goblins, mean-spirited little men with long green mustaches and broad, bald heads marred by scars and liver spots. The goblins like a good prank, and their acqisition of fire powder has given them the idea that a few well placed explosions in the beetle pen could make for a jolly afternoon.

Credit

The Rhinoceros Beetle originally appeared in the First Edition *Monster Manual* (© TSR/Wizards of the Coast, 1977) and is used by permission.

Copyright Notice

Author Scott Greene, based on original material by Gary Gygax.

Beetle, Giant Saw-Toothed

Hit Dice: 4
Armor Class: 7 [12]
Attacks: 1 bite (2d6)
Saving Throw: 13
Special: Grab
Move: 12
Alignment: Neutrality
Challenge Level/XP: 5/240

A giant saw-toothed beetle has oversized serrated mandibles to chew and crush its food. These creatures are about 6 feet long. Their wing covers and carapace are silvery-green in color and have a dull sheen. Their legs are long with spiraling bands of green and black. Its compound eyes aid it in detecting creatures moving close by, though it usually relies on motion and scent to pick up its prey. If a serrated beetle hits with a bite, it holds the prey in is massive mandibles, automatically inflicting 1d6 damage in the next round until the creature is freed.

Where the Trail Ends

A foot-deep carpet of colorful leaves covers the forest floor, the twisted trees standing bare above the multi-hued landscape. A wide path has been gouged recently through the leaves, the muddy trench dug a foot into the wet earth. The ragged trench wanders drunkenly from left to right along the path. The trench dead-ends in the middle of a clearing amid a stand of old oaks.

The center of the clearing where the trench stops is a 10-foot-wide pit that drops 15 feet straight down to a dirt floor in a 30-foot-wide chamber. Seven tunnels lead underground from this central room. The pit opening is covered by a lattice of small branches, leaves and chewed bark. At the bottom of the hole, a dead giant saw-toothed beetle lies in a crumpled heap. Part of its head is split by a sword stuck in the insect's serrated mandibles. Dirt cakes the large mandibles, and its carapace is covered with burns. The dead beetle returned to its nest, dragging its mandibles through the forest. Other saw-toothed beetles in the nest replaced the leaf and twig pit covering, but have yet to dismember the dead insect. The sword has a jewel-covered hilt and is worth 200 gp if sold.

Living in the tunnels are 6 giant saw-toothed beetles that pour out to attack anyone who falls into the pit. The insects climb out of the pit to attack creatures wandering around the clearing.

Beetle, Giant Slicer

Hit Dice: 6
Armor Class: 2 [17]
Attack: Bite (3d8)
Saving Throw: 11
Special: Vorpal bite
Move: 9
Alignment: Neutrality
Challenge Level/XP: 8/800

This creature appears as a giant beetle with a triangular head and two long, razor sharp mandibles. Its body is black in color. It closely resembles a large stag beetle and is often mistaken for such. However, the slicer beetle is more aggressive than the stag beetle. The creature dines on carrion, fresh meat, and leaves. Slicer beetles are about 10 feet long, but can grow to lengths of 20 feet or more. If a slicer beetle scores a natural 20 on its attack roll and its victim fails a saving throw, it severs one of the opponent's extremities (roll 1d6: 1-3 arm, 4-6 leg; 50% chance of either right or left).

Thistledown Justice

It isn't that the baron is not mad, but he certainly is not as bloodthirsty as his enemies would have people believe. Dwelling in his little, ancient stronghold on the craggy hill in the Thistledowns, he and his people herd sheep, and grow grains and bitter herbs, produce a fine, soft cheese from ewe milk and do their best to discourage visitors. The Thistledowners, as they are called, are an insular people who follow the old traditions, including trials by ordeal.

Within the baron's shell keep there is a deep pit that serves as the lair of a giant slicer beetle called "The Sword of Justice" by the locals. The slicer beetle is well fed on offal and straw, and therefore doesn't always attack when a criminal is dropped into the pit. They must stay in the pit for a few minutes based on the severity of the crime they allegedly committed and either come out intact (proving them innocent) or having lost a limb. The limb is then roasted on a fire as a sacrifice to the goddess of justice and the crime is duly forgotten.

The beetle is one of a mating pair, the "stallion" being kept in a similar pit located quite far from the stonghold to avoid potential burrowing.

Credit

The Slicer Beetle originally appeared in the First Edition *Monster Manual II* (© TSR/Wizards of the Coast, 1983) and is used by permission.

Copyright Notice

Author Scott Greene, based on original material by Gary Gygax.

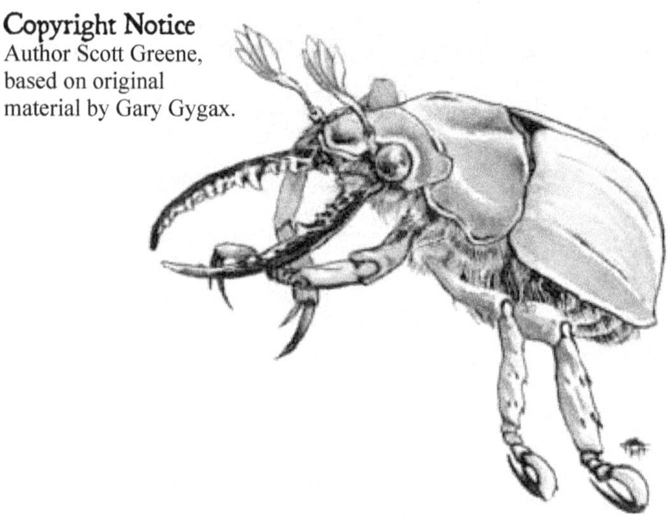

Beetle, Giant Water

Hit Dice: 3
Armor Class: 6 [13]
Attacks: 1 bite (1d8)
Saving Throw: 14
Special: Stench spray, aquatic
Move: 6/24 (swim)
Alignment: Neutrality
Challenge Level/XP: 3/60

The highly aggressive giant water beetles average about 6 feet long though they can grow to a length of about 10 feet. Their body is cylindrical and hydrodynamic, tapering into a pointed tail section. Their body shape allows them to move rapidly through the water and also aids them in hunting, allowing them to dive quickly through the water when a target is spotted. Typical coloration is black or dark brown with their wing covers following their body coloration. Some species of giant water beetle have yellow legs or a silver stripe on their dorsal side. Females are slightly larger than males and have a red band around their front legs. They rarely come on land, and never venture far from a water source. Once per minute, a water beetle can eject a foul-smelling liquid from its abdomen that sickens creatures nearby.

Cheese Log

A bridge built of 8-foot-diameter tree trunks roped together side-by-side floats low on the placid surface of Whisper Creek. The water is 30 feet deep and 300 feet wide. The bridge is shaky, but two ropes at waist height on either side of the 8-foot-long logs allow a person to stand upright while crossing. The logs are lashed together with a series of ropes and leather straps.

The 15-foot-center section of the bridge smells horrible, like moldy cheese left too long in the sun. The smell wafts over the water and seems to rise out of the logs. Three logs in the middle of the span are rotten, the wood eaten through from below. The upper surface of the bridge over this rotten section is extremely brittle. Anyone stepping on the center logs splinters the wood and steps right through the bridge deck into the water below.

A colony of giant water beetles lives underneath the bridge, protecting a queen that has chewed the logs open and frequently crawls inside the wet wood to deposit her eggs. The water beetles float in the water like logs, but submerge to attack anyone in the water.

The cheese smell is from the corpse of a halfling traveler who fell into the water a day ago and was killed by the giant beetles. The little man was carrying a sack full of cheeses to sell in a nearby market. His body is crammed into the hollow within the logs, and his leather pack reeks of cheese. The beetles put him into the crevice to feed the young water beetles when they hatch.

Copyright Notice

Author Scott Greene.

Beetle, Requiem

Hit Dice: 18
Armor Class: 2 [17]
Attacks: 2 claws (3d6+4) and bite (2d8+4)
Saving Throw: 3
Special: Constrict, earth-shaking
Move: 18
Alignment: Neutrality
Challenge Level/XP: 20/4,400

The gigantic requiem beetle has a dark red carapace, blackish-red wing covers, and black legs. Two large claw-like pincers protrude from its front to slash and rip the air around the creature. Its oversized mandibles are dark reddish-black. Requiem beetles measure about 40 feet long and weigh about 18 tons. A requiem beetle that hits a single opponent with both claws automatically constricts for 5d6 points of damage. Whenever a requiem beetle moves more than 10 feet in a round, all creatures within 10 feet must save or fall down as the earth shakes.

Potato Beetles

Buffalo Bur is a small mountain settlement situated in a quiet cove. Fields of wild potato plants surround the village. Countless beetles swarm over the land and congregate in and around the town. The beetles cover virtually everything in Buffalo Bur in inches-deep layers throughout the streets and inside dwellings. The beetles envelop the building like a thick living blanket, and the constant drone of clicking of legs and buzzing wings drowns out most noise. Although the beetles are slow to react, if agitated they fly en mass, obscuring vision until they settle down in about 1d3 hours.

This plague of beetles moved into Buffalo Bur overnight nearly two months ago. Although harmless, the number of beetles creates unsettling and unlivable conditions in Buffalo Bur. The villagers fled, unable to defend the town against the insurmountable beetle swarm. The beetles devastated the crops and contaminated the water, and the constant drone and large amount of pheromones in the air drew a much-larger relative to the devastated landscape. A requiem beetle now resides in a large potato barn on the far side of town. The beetle burrowed up from below the barn to feast on the stored potatoes. The barn sways and groans as the requiem beetle moves within the rickety wooden structure.

Copyright Notice

Author Scott Greene.

Belabra (Tangler)

Hit Dice: 4
Armor Class: 2 [17]
Attack: Slam (2d6) or 12 tentacles (1d2) and bite (1d6)
Saving Throw: 13
Special: Acidic blood, tentacle barbs
Move: 3/9 (flying)
Alignment: Neutrality
Challenge Level/XP: 6/400

Belabras resemble a man-sized flying jellyfish with a hard, chitinous shell and twelve long tentacles. Four thin, pupil-less eyestalks protrude from its cap. A small, bird-like beak is hidden among its array of tentacles. Its cap is blackish-gray and its eyestalks are dark gray. They dwell in deep forests and thick undergrowth and sustain themselves on a diet of plants, berries, and rodents. Particularly hungry belabras will attack larger creatures, such as humanoids. Each time a belabra is hit with a slashing or piercing weapon, all creatures within a 10-foot radius must succeed on a saving throw or be sprayed by the creature's acidic blood. A creature that fails its save is partially blinded and overcome with fits of sneezing. Both effects last 1d6+2 rounds. An affected creature takes a –4 penalty to hit, –1 penalty to AC, loses its Dexterity bonus to AC (if any) and moves at half speed. All checks relying on vision have a 50% chance of failing. A belabra's tentacles are lined with razor-sharp barbs. Anytime a grappled creature attempts to break free and fails, it takes 1d4 points of piercing damage from the barbs.

Air Jelly Baby

On a long, inaccessible ridge there lives an old belabra who fancies himself the "lord of the woods". Although solitary by nature, the old tangler has spent the past five years raising a lost human toddler he calls - well, belabra is almost impossible to write down in any meaningful way, but he calls the child something like "Zzzikikik". The child has become an expert at climbing and swinging and hunting, and he and his tutor dwell in a treetop nest of woven branches and twigs, protecting their domain from incursions by goblins, orcs and other humans.

Zzzikikik, who fights with a gnarly club studded with discarded belabra barbs, wears a teardrop shaped sapphire worth 500 gp, the only link to his parents, exiled nobles who were cast into the wild by an ambitious and wicked aunt. His adopted father is never far from him.

Credit

The Belabra originally appeared in the First Edition *Creature Catalog* (*Dragon #94*) (© TSR/Wizards of the Coast, 1985) and later in the Second Edition *Monstrous Compendium* (MC 3) (© TSR/Wizards of the Coast, 1991) and is used by permission.

Copyright Notice

Author Scott Greene, based on original material by Ed Greenwood.

Bhuta

Hit Dice: 7
Armor Class: 4 [15]
Attack: 2 claws (1d6)
Saving Throw: 9
Special: Death grip
Move: 12
Alignment: Chaos
Challenge Level/XP: 8/800

When a person is murdered, the spirit sometimes clings to the Material Plane, refusing to accept its mortal death. This spirit, called a bhuta, possesses its original body and seeks out those responsible for its murder. It will never rest until those responsible are sought out and slain. Since the transformation into unlife is almost instant (occurring within 1-2 hours after death), the bhuta appears as it did in life for about 2 weeks, taking on a more decayed appearance thereafter. Close inspection (spot on a roll of 1-2 on 1d6) reveals slight decay, and the body still shows signs of any trauma suffered prior to death (wounds, disease, burns, or the like), but outwardly, the bhuta for the most part appears as a normal creature of its race. In its undead state, the bhuta sustains itself on a diet of flesh, preferring that of humans and elves. A bhuta that scores two successful claw attacks on an opponent in the same round fastens its hands around its opponent's throat and deals 1d6+1 damage per round until the hold is broken with a successful attack by the victim. The bhuta's main objective is revenge on the person that killed it. So long as the bhuta and its killer are on the same plane of existence, it can find its target unerringly.

Wine (and Moan) Cellar

It was twelve years ago, twelve dark years, that the countess ended a night of debauchery by toppling into an open well. Her husband, a knightly rake known mostly for his womanizing and misfortune at the card table, immediately had the well sealed and a small memorial in her honor built nearby and then took the throne and coronet and began his rule as "the wastrel count".

It was a neat piece of work by the count, for his ex-wife's corpse, now risen as a bhuta, is physically incapable of getting through the seal. If she could, or if anyone was inclined to move the seal, they would discover a pallid, rotting corpse in an expensive gown with a deep slash across her throat (no doubt suffered in the fall) with vivid wine stains down her frock. Her jaw was shattered in the fall, and thus is capable of little more than a gibbering moan. The countess was wearing about 2d8 x 100 gp worth of jewelry when she fell into the well.

A secret door in the bottom of the dry well connects to secret tunnels to a wine cellar that was walled in a hundred years ago and is itself only accessible via a secret door in the friary, the friars being inclined to raid the wine cellar on special occaisions. The present count is unaware of these secret passages.

Copyright Notice
Author Scott Greene.

Biclops

Hit Dice: 12+2
Armor Class: 2[17]
Attacks: 2 weapons (4d6)
Saving Throw: 3
Special: Hurl boulders
Move: 12
Alignment: Chaos
Challenge Level/XP: 13/2,300

A biclops appears to be a filthy ettin, but has one eye in the center of each ugly head. They are feared by less intelligent monsters such as hill giants and trolls, whom they beat to death on sight. They throw two rocks for 3d6 points of damage.

Two Heads are Better than One Eye

Angry voices rise into shouts from behind a plank leaning against the cave opening. Two voices shout at one another and the sounds of meaty fists hitting flesh can be heard clearly behind the makeshift door.

Beyond the door is a truly odd sight: a biclops sits with its back against the rock wall, its two heads arguing loudly. The right head wears a pirate's eye patch over its lone eye, leaving it blind, while the left-side head shouts for a turn as the hand on that side of its body tries to grab the patch of black cloth. A giant club leans against the wall near the creature. A pirate's body lies battered and broken at the giant's feet, the corpse's head crushed into the floor. The feathery remains of a green parrot are punched into the rocks behind the biclops.

Lotney the biclops killed the pirate, but the two heads decided they wanted to wear the man's eye patch. They are quick to remove it if PCs enter the room, so the giants can see to attack. The eye patch can wait until the biclops sees what other interesting toys these new visitors carry – and what the two heads can argue over.

Copyright Notice
Author Scott Greene.

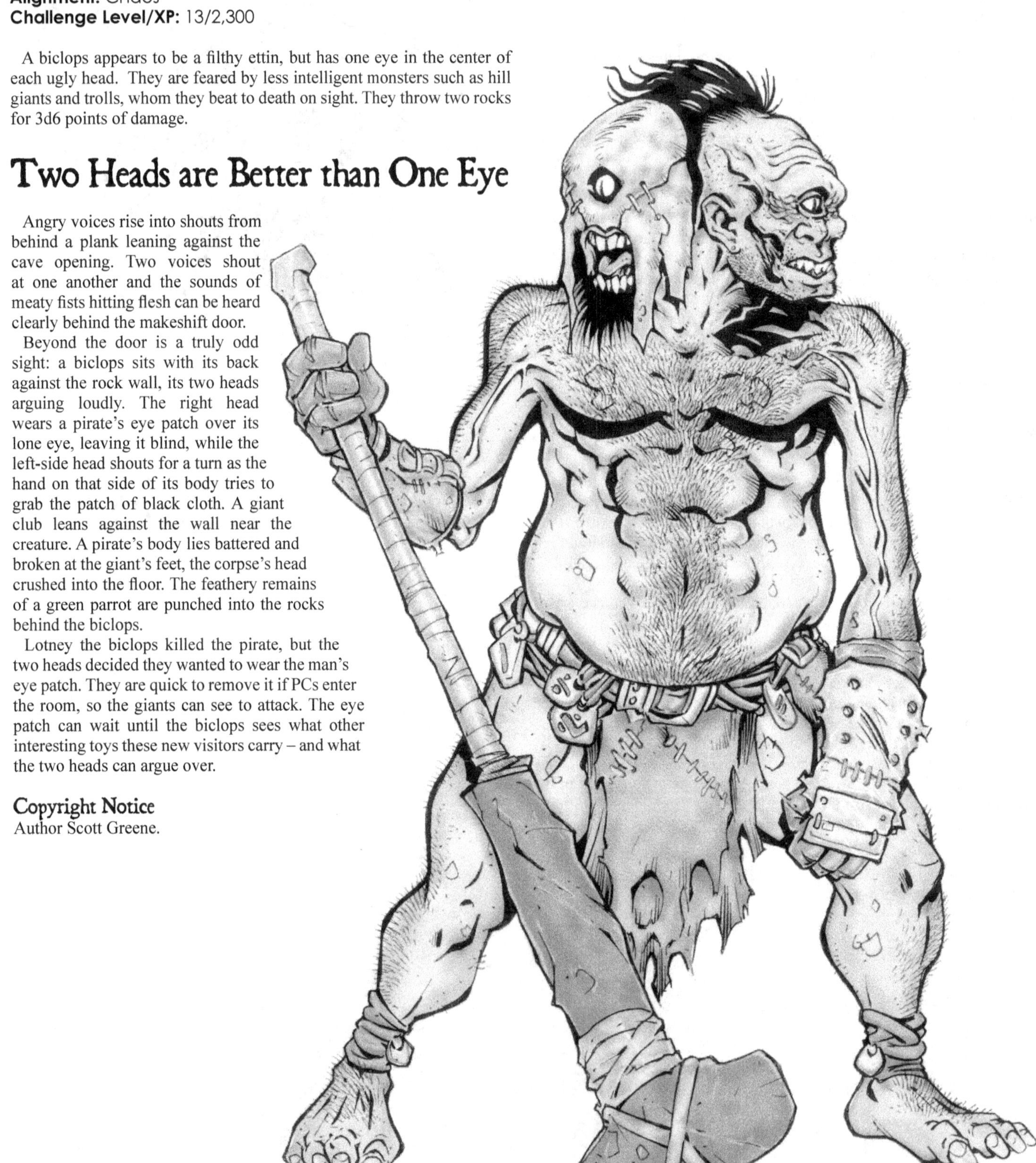

Bleeding Horror

Hit Dice: 6
Armor Class: -1 [20]
Attack: *Axe of Blood* (2d6) or 2 claws (1d8)
Saving Throw: 11
Special: Blood consumption, horrific appearance, +1 or better weapon to hit, magic resistance (10%)
Move: 12
Alignment: Chaos
Challenge Level/XP: 10/1400

Created by the *axe of blood*, these foul undead creatures drip with the blood they were so willing to sacrifice to the hungry blade. They are filled with the unquenchable desire for blood to feed the weapon that created them. Bleeding horrors appear as skeletons or sunken corpses covered in and continuously dripping thick red blood. Their eyes glow with a desire for blood. They may wear armor and wield weapons.

A living creature within 60 feet that views a bleeding horror must succeed on a saving throw or take 1d6 points of strength damage. This damage cannot reduce a victim's strength below 0, but anyone reduced to strength 0 is helpless.

When a bleeding horror successfully hits a living opponent with a claw attack, it heals a number of hit points equal to the damage dealt. However, it can't gain more than the subject's current hit points, which is enough to kill the subject. A bleeding horror can't gain more hit points than the maximum hit points allowed by its Hit Dice.

If a bleeding horror hits an opponent with both claw attacks in a single round, that opponent suffers catastrophic blood expulsion, taking 1d4 points of constitution damage. A successful saving throw reduces the damage by half. For each point of constitution damage dealt, a bleeding horror gains 4 temporary hit points. Any creature slain by the blood consumption attack of a bleeding horror becomes a bleeding horror in 1d4 minutes under the command of its creator.

If the *axe of blood* is taken from a bleeding horror before the creature is destroyed, it can find it unerringly.

Axe Murderer

When the dwarf warlord finally completed his quest and took possession of the *axe of blood*, he wasted no time in beginning the ritual to empower the axe with his own blood. Unfortunately, he fell to the axe's influence and is now a bleeding horror himself. His comrades soon fell to his axe, and were the first members of a rapidly expanding army of bleeding horrors. The warlord now commands thirty bleeding horrors drawn from kobold, orc, goblin and ogre tribes.

On the third level of a dungeon, the remnants of several humanoid tribes has managed to block the bleeding army behind several collapsed passages. They are trying to dig themselves out and threaten to engulf the civilized lands beyond the wilderness if they escape the dungeon. The humanoids, as chaotic as they are, will not refuse help from powerful adventurers. They know of a secret way into the sixth level of the dungeon (via an air shaft), so that they might come up behind the bleeding army and destroy it. The ogres will even send two or three of their number along to help.

Minor Artifact: The Axe of Blood

The *axe of blood* is rather nondescript, being made of dull iron. Only the large, strange rune carved into the side of its double-bladed head gives any immediate indication that the axe may be more than it seems. The rune is one of lesser life stealing, carved on it long ago by a sect of evil sorcerers. This is, in fact, the only remaining copy of that particular rune, thus making the axe a valuable item. Further inspection reveals another strange characteristic: the entire length of the axe's long haft of darkwood is wrapped in a thick leather thong stained black from years of being soaked in blood and sticky to the touch. When held, the axe feels strangely heavy but well balanced, and it possesses a keenly sharp blade.

Until activated, the axe is just a *+1 battleaxe*. The wielder must consult *legend lore* or some other similar source of information to learn the ritual required to feed the axe. Despite the gruesome ritual required to power the axe, the weapon is not chaotic but is instead neutral. Bound inside it is a rather savage earth spirit.

The axe draws power from its wielder in order to become a mighty magic weapon. Each day, the wielder of the axe can choose to "feed" the axe, sacrificing some of his blood in a strange ritual. This ritual takes 30 minutes and must be done at dawn.

Using the axe, the wielder opens a wound on his person (dealing 1d6 points of damage) and feeds the axe with his own blood. The wielder sacrifices blood in the form of hit points. For each 1d6 hit points sacrificed, the wielder gains a +1 bonus on attack rolls and weapon damage rolls with the axe (to a maximum of +3). Hit points sacrificed to the axe cannot be healed magically, but heal at the rate of 1 point per day. Similarly, the damage caused by the opening of the wound may not be healed by any means until the sacrificed hit points are regained.

There is a chance that the hit points sacrificed to the axe is lost permanently. If the wielder always skips a day in between powering the axe and always powers the axe with the morning ritual, there is no chance of permanent loss. If, however, the axe is fed on consecutive days, there is a 1% chance plus a 1% cumulative chance per consecutive day the axe is powered that hit points sacrificed to the axe on that day is permanently lost.

If reduced to 0 hit points as a result of feeding the axe, the wielder becomes a bleeding horror.

Blindheim

B

Hit Dice: 4
Armor Class: 3 [16]
Attack: Bite (1d6)
Saving Throw: 13
Special: Eye beams
Move: 12
Alignment: Chaos
Challenge Level/XP: 5/240

Blindheims are 4-foot tall frog-like humanoids with large, bulbous eyes that constantly emit bright yellow beams of light. A blindheim's skin is mottled yellow, growing darker across its back. Its feet are webbed as are its claws. Blindheims dwell in underground caverns and sustain themselves on a diet of fungi, molds, and small rodents. An extra eyelid allows the blindheim to "turn off" its eyes when it is sleeping or resting. A dead blindheim's eyes are dull gold in color. A blindheim can turn its eyes on and off as it wishes, but always leaves them on during combat. When open, the eyes emit a 30-foot cone of light. It can see normally in this light and functions normally in areas of magical darkness. A creature looking at a blindheim when its eye beams are "on" must succeed on a saving throw or be blinded for 1 hour.

Blind Intersection

A gang of 1d3+1 blindheims has taken up residence in a crystaline cavern. The interior of the cavern is highly irregular, with massive crystal columns jutting from the floor, some going from floor to ceiling, and thousands of smaller, multi-faceted crystals embedded in the walls and in between the larger crystals.

The blindheims dwell on a crystal shelf about 20 feet above the floor of the cavern, what treasures their victims have dropped being found either on the shelf or just below it. The cavern is usually pitch dark, and the mirrored crystals make navigating the cavern difficult with torch or lantern light. When the blindheim's turn on their lights, it becomes downright dazzling, requiring adventurers to make a saving throw to avoid suffering a -2 penalty on attack rolls due to the glare.

The cavern contains 1d6 x 1,000 sp, 1d4 x 100 gp, four lion skins (worth 25 gp each) a pink pearl worth 115 gp and magical *horseshoes of speed*.

Credit

The Blindheim originally appeared in the First Edition *Fiend Folio* (© TSR/Wizards of the Coast, 1981) and is used by permission.

Copyright Notice

Blood Bush

Hit Dice: 4
Armor Class: 7 [12]
Attacks: 4 tendrils (1d4), 6 flower darts (1d2)
Saving Throw: 13
Special: Paralysis
Move: 0
Alignment: Neutrality
Challenge Level/XP: 4/120

A blood bush is a 3-foot-tall flowering bush with a thick trunk and small whip-like branches. Each branch is topped with a blood-red flower and deep, rich green leaves. A victim hit by a dart must make a saving throw or be paralyzed for 1d6+1 rounds.

Unsafe Haven

A decaying mausoleum rises out of the forest. Crumbling columns surround the stone structure, and the faces of singing angels are worn away by the elements. Bushes blooming with red flowers grow abundantly around three stone steps leading up to the gravesite's sealed marble door. The word Haven is carved into the stone. A warm golden light filters out of cracks in the stone façade. The light is cast by a crystal globe held in a gold-colored statue's outstretched hands. The globe and statue are coated with yellow mold. The globe casts a radiant but heat-free light in a 20-foot radius. Three stone crypts are filled with brittle bones.

The bushes surrounding the crypt are 6 blood bushes. Bones from past victims poke out of the dirt around the mausoleum's foundation.

Copyright Notice

Blood Hawk

Hit Dice: 1
Armor Class: 4 [15]
Attack: 2 claws (1d4) and bite (1d6)
Saving Throw: 17
Special: None
Move: 6/36 (flying)
Alignment: Neutrality
Challenge Level/XP: 2/30

The blood hawk is nearly identical to a normal hawk and is often mistaken for one, but it is stronger and far more aggressive than a normal hawk and has red talons and a dull red beak. Blood hawks love the taste of human flesh and are relentless in their hunt of human prey. They often steal gems from the corpses of their humanoid prey, which they use to line their nests.

Predator or Prey?

A haggard and motley collection of hobgoblins is holed up in a shallow cave, a small fire pit having been dug just outside the cave entrance and several conies now roasting above in on a spit. The hobgoblins are on guard, but have no pickets posted, apparently being worried about leaving the cave.

Visitors soon discover the cause of the hobgoblin's worries if they remain in the open for more than a few moments. A flock of 1d6+5 blood hawks dwells on the ledges above the cave, nesting in natural alcoves dug into the stone. The lowest of the nests is 60 feet above the floor of the valley, the highest about 120 feet up and easily 80 feet below the cliffs above.

In one of those nests lies the golden crown (worth 250 gp) of the hobgoblin king, studded with jewels and stolen not three days ago from his head while he was hunting. The clans are gathering in a week's time, and the loss of the crown could mean the loss of his position. The 15 remaining hobgoblins sent to retreive the crown have failed on several attempts to reach the nests, and are considering fleeing into the wilderness. They might be open to some assistance.

Credit

The Blood Hawk originally appeared in the First Edition *Fiend Folio* (© TSR/Wizards of the Coast, 1981) and is used by permission.

Copyright Notice

Author Scott Greene, based on original material by Ian Livingstone.

Bloodsuckle

Hit Dice: 6
Armor Class: 7 [12]
Attacks: 2 tendrils (1d4), limb rake (1d6)
Saving Throw: 11
Special: Blood drain, create host, grab, summon host, seed
Move: 0
Alignment: Neutrality
Challenge Level/XP: 8/800

A bloodsuckle is a nightmarish bush consisting of a bulbous root from which sprout several vine-like tendrils. The tendrils end in hollow, needle-like points and can reach lengths of 60 feet. Woody limbs as thick as a human's leg sprout from the trunk of the bloodsuckle. The leaves of a bloodsuckle bush are a vile greenish color, and constantly ooze a sticky sap that reeks of decay, filth, and other unmentionable odors. Bloodsuckles are semi-intelligent. immobile plants that gain nourishment from the blood of living creatures. A bloodsuckle injects its sap into a host using its tendrils so it can control the creature to attack others or approach the plant to drain its blood. If a bloodsuckle hits a victim with both tendrils, it automatically begins draining the creature's blood (1d4 hit points per round). Once per month, a bloodsuckle can generate a walnut-sized seed that it implant's in a host's body. The host is then sent away, and a new bloodsuckle sprouts in the victim in 1d4 days. If threatened, the bloodsuckle can produce a high-pitched whine that draws nearby hosts to defend it.

Out to Pasture

Farmer Gertie knows that the cows are out to get her. She's seen them plotting to kill her. Every time she goes out to milk them in the morning, they look at her funny, like they were just talking about her and she interrupted them. They watch her every move, never mooing, and sometimes turn their heads as if listening to an unheard voice. A voice even she can't hear … and she hears lots of voices.

She's sure the cattle are plotting something. And don't you pay no mind to farmer Johnstone down the road, who says she's just been working the back forty in the sun too long. He's the one who samples the smelly grain alcohol he cranks out on his little backyard still.

Gertie's concerned now that 3 cows from her herd wandered off without a trace. She's not seen them for two days, and she's concerned they're out cavorting with Johnstone's bull. The cows stay in the barn at all times, when they leave, they do so in a single line all headed in the same direction. The bovines stare down anyone who enters the stalls, never making any sound. Bloody marks are visible along each cow's flank.

A little over a week ago, the cows stumbled into a bloodsuckle patch in Gertie's back field, and the plant is using the animals for food and protection. Two of the missing cows are protecting the patch, while the third was drained of blood and lies dead in the bloodsuckle patch.

And Gertie was right, the cows *are* cavorting with the bull in the next pasture, but only because it is also under the bloodsuckle plant's control. The bull comes running if the plant is threatened.

BULL: HD 4; AC 6[13]; Atk gore (2d4), trample 1d6; Move 12; Save 13; CL/ XP 4/120; Special: double damage from charge

Bloody Bones

Hit Dice: 5
Armor Class: 3 [16]
Attack: 4 tendrils (see below) and 2 claws (1d6)
Saving Throw: 12
Special: Tendrils, slippery, resistance to fire (50%)
Move: 12
Alignment: Chaos
Challenge Level/XP: 7/600

Bloody bones are evil undead spirits that haunts caverns, caves, and other desolate places. Their true origins are unknown, but they are believed to be the undead remains of those who desecrate evil temples and are punished by the gods for their wrongdoings. It appears as a skeletal humanoid with bits of muscle and sinew hanging from its body. Four long, sinewy tendrils writhe from its midsection. The entire creature constantly oozes a mixture of blood and mucus. Its eye sockets are hollow and show no pupils. A creature hit by the monster's tendril attack must pass a saving throw or be held fast and dragged toward the bloody bones. The bloody bones' tendrils have 10 hit points each and an AC of 3 [16]. Bloody bones are difficult to wrestle or snare due to the constant flow of blood and mucus across their bodies. Webs, magic or otherwise, do not affect bloody bones, and they usually wiggle free from most other forms of confinement.

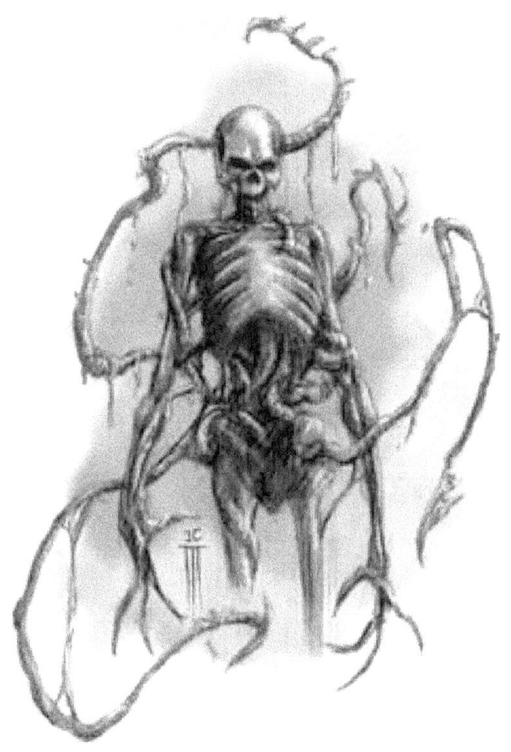

Bloody Pirates?

The people of the coast had long since become accustomed to the coming of the Black Galleass with the headless figurehead and its buff colored sails.. Framed by a blazing sunset, it would make its way to the coast and disembark a small launch carrying a basalt idol of the demon prince of evil sea creatures. Accompanied by men swathed in black and shuffling as though chained, the idol would be carried through a town preceeded by a tall man with golden eyes carrying a large urn. Coins would be placed into the urn by those wishing to avoid the attention of the demon prince and the village elders would make whatever gift they could of stores and supplies. The priests would carry their idol back to the launch and then their ship would disappear over the horizon for another happy year.

What a surprise, then, to find the galleass grounded on a windswept beach littered with the detritus of the sea. Listing slightly, its hull buffeted by the crashing surf, it lies there with not a sign of its rowers or priests. Closer inspection, of course, reveals a grisly scene - bodies strewn about the deck, their clothes and hides cleaved by axe blows. The carnage continues below decks, with the remains of a few skeletal rowers still in evidence, though most seem to have been blasted away by a divine fire.

The most terrible surprise, however, lies in the ship's shrine, located in the aftcastle. A shield, white and bearing a red cross, lies shattered outside the door and a thick spear holds the doors to the shrine open. Inside, in front of the toppled idol, are 1d4+1 bloody bones, still wearing the tattered surcoats that would identify them as crusaders. Although they succeeded in destroying the temple ship of a demon prince, they could not resist the ire of the dark gods with which that prince was allied.

Copyright Notice
Author Scott Greene.

Boalisk

Hit Dice: 5
Armor Class: 3 [16]
Attack: Bite (1d8)
Saving Throw: 12
Special: Constrict, gaze
Move: 9/9 (climbing, swimming)
Alignment: Neutrality
Challenge Level/XP: 6/400

A boalisk is a constrictor snake 12 to 30 feet long with dark scales interspersed with pale green and yellow daubs of color to help it blend in with its surroundings on the forest floor. The eyes of a boalisk are large and reddish in color. They dwell in misty jungles and along dark riverbanks. Boalisks have a powerful bite attack. Victims of a successful bite attack must succeed at a saving throw or be ensnared by the serpent's coils and constricted for 1d8 points of damage per round. The boalisk's more potent ability is its terrible gaze. Those within 30 feet that meet the boalisk's gaze must succeed on a saving throw or contract black rot. Black rot strikes at a victim almost immediately, causing the skin to become black and glossy and terrible swelling in the joints and face. Each day, a victim of the rot loses 1d6 points of constitution and charisma if they fail a saving throw. The disease persists until the victim succeeds at two consecutive daily saving throws. A victim of the disease dies when their constitution reaches 0. A recovering victim regains 1 point of charisma and 1 point of constitution per day of rest.

Quarantine

Tromping up the jungle trail that follows the lazy river into the highlands, you come across an old trading post of timber and stone. The trading post is two stories tall and looks abandoned at first blush. Dozens of barrels and crates lie outside the post, filled with basic trade goods and supplies. As one approaches, a voice will call out to them, weak and mournful.

"Come no closer," it says, "we have been invaded and the black rot is upon us. Take what you will and leave only your prayers."

Three days earlier, a boalisk crawled into the post, bringing with it the black rot and making a meal of a halfling trader. The others managed to escape to the second floor and bar the door. They do not know whether the serpent remains, but know that the disease will soon claim the last of them. The barrels and crates stores on the second story were thrown out in case folk came upon the post - better not to waste supplies in such a hostile country. The boalisk is now lodged between two water barrels on the ground floor, patiently waiting for new prey to enter the post.

Credit

The Boalisk originally appeared in the First Edition module *S4 Lost Caverns of Tsojcanth* (© TSR/Wizards of the Coast, 1982) and later in the First Edition *Monster Manual II* (© TSR/Wizards of the Coast, 1983) and is used by permission.

Copyright Notice

Author Scott Greene, based on original material by Gary Gygax.

Bog Beast

Hit Dice: 5
Armor Class: 5 [14]
Attack: 2 claws (1d6 + swamp fever)
Saving Throw: 12
Special: Swamp fever, rend with claws
Move: 12
Alignment: Neutrality
Challenge Level/XP: 6/400

Bog beasts make their homes in bogs and swamps and feed on creatures that dwell there. They are avid hunters and a bog beast's hunting area usually covers a large expanse of ground several miles around its lair. It makes its lair amid overgrown swamplands and attacks just about any creature that travels too close to its lair. They are large humanoids with shaggy fur and clawed hands and feet. Two, long, upright tusks protrude from its mouth. Its eyes are dull brown and its fur is brownish-yellow. A bog beast stands over 9 feet tall and weighs around 1,100 pounds. They seem to be able to communicate with one another through a series of guttural grunts and growls, but do not speak any known language. If a bog beast succeeds on both claw attacks against an opponent, they rend for an additional 2d6 damage. Characters who suffer damage from a bog beast's claws must pass a saving throw or come down with a case of swamp fever. The fever causes swelling of the joints and fills the lungs with fluid. The diseased character's movement rate is cut in half and they suffer a -2 penalty to AC and saving throws. Each day, they receive a saving throw at a -2 penalty to shake off the disease.

Cypress Swamp

A pack of 1d4+1 bog beasts has taken up residence beneath an ancient, black cypress in the heart of the swamp. The fish here are plentiful and the alligators are not terribly bothersome. The bog beasts serve the impetuous and often cruel dryad of the cypress, bringing her young fishermen that they kidnap from the nearby settlement of humans.

Most of these unfortunates are wracked with disease by the time they reach the cypress, and thus are not pleasing to the dryad and are quickly cast away into the mud of the swamp. The leader of the bog beasts is a barbaric individual with +2 HD who fights as a berserker. He carries a massive club constructed from the jawbone of a black dragon that he claims he killed with his bare hands (a lie - he found the body rotting in a small pool).

The bog beasts have 1d4 x 1,000 sp, 1d4 x 100 gp, a rhodochrosite worth 70 gp, a brass broach shaped like a salamander swallowing its own tail worth 95 gp and a limestone statuette of a knight worth 1 gp.

Copyright Notice

Author Scott Greene.

Bog Creeper

Hit Dice: 7
Armor Class: 6 [13]
Attacks: 1 slam (1d6), 4 tendrils (1d4) or bite (2d4)
Saving Throw: 9
Special: Constrict, spit acid, camouflage
Move: 4/9 (swim)
Alignment: Neutrality
Challenge Level/XP: 8/800

The bog creeper is a creature native to the thickest, darkest swamps. It superficially resembles a man-sized rotted tree trunk sprouting several thorny tendrils each about 10 feet long and a single 6-foot long limb. Bog creepers are carnivorous, lurking amid dead trees and stumps waiting to ambush unsuspecting prey. When prey comes within range, a bog creeper lashes out with its single limb and slashes with its tendrils. If two tendrils hit the same opponent, the creature grabs the victim and constricts it for 2d4 damage as it transfers the prey to its mouth. Three times per day, a bog creeper can vomit digestive sap on opponents (2d8 points of damage; save for half).

Stumped

Two loggers from Carson's Mill are missing. The men were last seen heading into the hills above the logging camp, making their way toward the deep woods. Their axes were found scattered amid the stumps of the cleared forest, along with a couple of goblin spears. The villagers fear the men have been abducted – or killed – by the ugly little humanoids. Worse still, two of the men searching for the missing loggers are now missing, and the villagers fear that the goblins are getting uppity and preparing to move against the isolated town.

The men are dead, but it wasn't goblins that got them. In fact, the goblins that stumbled upon the remains of the men and their scattered belongings were killed moments after the men by a bog creeper that makes its home among the hundreds of stumps in the cleared forest. The bog creeper grabbed the men and goblins and moved on once it had digested its meal. It now hides among the stumps, its tendrils spread out along the ground, waiting for more victims to stumble into its clutches.

Inside the creature's gullet are 60 gp, three small rubies (50 gp each) and a *+1 silver dagger*.

Copyright Notice

Author Erica Balsley.

Bog Mummy

Hit Dice: 8
Armor Class: 2 [17]
Attack: Slam (1d6 + bog rot)
Saving Throw: 8
Special: Bog rot, +1 or better weapon to hit, resistance to fire (50%)
Move: 9
Alignment: Chaos
Challenge Level/XP: 10/1400

Bog mummies resemble normal mummies, but are covered with a thin layer of swamp mud. Bog mummies rarely leave the swamp where they were formed. They hate life and attack any living creature that trespasses in their swamp. Bog mummies can only be harmed by magic weapons. Its touch infects victims who fail a saving throw with bog rot, a supernatural disease that does not allow wounds to heal naturally, and cuts magical healing in half until cured with the *cure disease* spell. Humanoids killed by a bog mummy rise as bog mummies themselves in 1d4 days unless their bodies are removed from the swamp or a *cure disease* spell is cast on the corpse. A bog mummy's movement is unaffected by mud, marshes and swamps.

Hanging Was Too Good for Him

On a peaty moor frequented only by ravens, scrawny ebon hares and the timid priests of the god of the scythe, one might have the misfortune to come across a low pool of water that is now home to a bog mummy. The mummy was a common thief that was strangled and thrown into the holy waters that are marked with a runic pillar.

The bog mummy has leathery, slate colored skin, dead eyes and stark white hair. It still wears the rope that hanged it, and has thin, atrophied arms and legs that, despite their appearance, are horribly strong. When it opens its mouth to groan, a thick, distended tongue lolls out. A terrible visage to be sure.

Bronze rings, bracelets, anklets and torques have been cast into the waters of the pond, and 1d10 x 100 gp worth of these goods can be found with an hour of uncomfortable searching. Such robberies will not go unnoticed by the god of the scythe.

Credit

The Bog Mummy originally appeared in the Second Edition *Return to White Plume Mountain* (© Wizards of the Coast, 1999) and is used by permission.

Copyright Notice

Author Scott Greene, based on original material by Bruce Cordell.

Bogeyman

Hit Dice: 6
Armor Class: 5 [12]
Attacks: claw (1d6)
Saving Throw: 11
Special: Frighten, create illusions, magical weapons to hit
Move: 12
Alignment: Chaos
Challenge Level/XP: 7/600

A bogeyman is a man-sized undead that lacks a corporeal body. A bogeyman can create realistic illusions and sounds to scare victims, and can only be hit by magical weapons. An opponent seeing a bogeyman must make a saving throw or run in fear (as per the spell).

Bump in the Night

This encounter takes place in a long hall (either a dungeon or inn or a similar setting) with many doors evenly spaced on either side. Some or all of the doors could be illusions. A bogeyman haunts this area. It uses its fear ability to scatter the party before running into one of the doors. Using illusions and its incorporeal form, it runs in and out of various doors. PCs chasing it will find an empty room – even as the creature exits from a different door across the hall.

Once the bogeyman has a victim alone, it attacks. The bogeyman is something of a coward and flees if cornered or outnumbered. One of the rooms has a shallow grave (possibly under floorboards) barely noticeable to casual observers. The grave is old and contains the remnants of the bogeyman (once a thief). His body still holds a short sword with a hollow pommel. Within the pommel are 4 rubies (50 gp each) and a treasure map (the reason he was slain).

Copyright Notice
Author Scott Greene.

Boggart

Hit Dice: 6
Armor Class: -1 [20]
Attack: Electrical discharge (2d6)
Saving Throw: 11
Special: Immune to magic, magical abilities
Move: 9
Alignment: Chaos
Challenge Level/XP: 8/800

Although a boggart's natural form is that of a small will-o'-wisp, boggarts usually take the form of a 2-foot tall humanoid with unkempt dark hair, an untrimmed shaggy beard, thick mustache, pale skin and green eyes. The boggart is a relative of the will-o-wisp. Sages believe it to be a sort of "larval" or immature form of said creature. Boggarts are immune to most spells or spell-like abilities that allow spell resistance, except *magic missile*, *protection from evil*, *protection from evil 10-ft radius* and *maze*. Boggarts can use *ESP* (as the spell) at will and can become *invisible* for 10 minutes each day. Once per day, a boggart can unleash a screech that causes *confusion* (per the spell) in all those within 30 feet who fail a saving throw. The confusion lasts for 6 rounds. Each additional boggart within 10 feet that joins the screeching imposes a -1 penalty to the saving throw. Boggarts not only deliver electrical shocks with their physical attacks, but also throw electrical current up to 10 feet, dealing 2d6 points of damage (save for half).

Acts of War

A pack of 1d4+1 boggarts haunts a lonely bridge on a rapid river that meanders through the lands between two baronies. The sole means of communication between these baronies, it was until recently stalked by a notorious highwayman. The boggarts electricuted the bandit (his life was a series of disasters that culminated in his fey encounter) and strung his body up in the branches of a gallows oak on the near side of the river.

The pitiless creatures entertain themselves by tossing the body down in front of travelers and making it dance. Folk who attempt to flee with their wagons are attacked on the bridge and tossed, alive or dead, into the rapids. More than a few unfortunates have washed up downshore, and one ambitious counsellor has asserted that their deaths are a clear act of war by the neighboring barony.

Credit

The Boggart originally appeared in the First Edition module *WG4 The Forgotten Temple of Tharizdun* (© TSR/Wizards of the Coast, 1982) and later in the First Edition *Monster Manual II* (© TSR/Wizards of the Coast, 1983) and is used by permission. This is not the same Boggart that appeared in *Dragon #54* (© TSR/Wizards of the Coast, 1981).

Copyright Notice

Author Scott Greene, based on original material by Gary Gygax.

Bone Cobbler

Hit Dice: 5
Armor Class: 5 [14]
Attack: 2 hammers (1d4) or 2 claws (1d3)
Saving Throw: 12
Special: Animate bones, breath weapon
Move: 12
Alignment: Chaos
Challenge Level/XP: 7/600

The bone cobbler is a tattered and desiccated humanoid often mistaken for a zombie in weak light. The bone cobbler is a malign and evil creature that delights in slaying its opponents and stripping the flesh from their bones. Bone cobblers take the skeletal remains of those they kill and combine them with other bones in their lair. From these bones they sculpt and form weird humanoid or half-humanoid skeletal statues. Once per day, a bone cobbler can animate up to 5 skeletal statues within 30 feet. These creatures fight as skeletons, though their forms and structures do not necessarily resemble anything remotely humanoid. A bone cobbler can rapidly strip all the flesh from a human-sized creature in 3 rounds using its claws and hammers. Once stripped, the bone cobbler devours the flesh and collects the victim's bones to use in its "sculptures". A creature slain in this manner can only be brought back to life by a *wish* spell. Finally, a bone cobbler can bellow forth a cloud of vapors every 1d4+1 rounds that covers a 10-foot-radius area. Creatures within the area must succeed on a saving throw or be slowed (as the *slow* spell) for 1d4 rounds.

Everybody Needs a Hobby

The sculptor of idols was never as reverent as his customers. His last object d'art was an idol of the love goddess for a shrine located out in the sticks. His progress on this particular sculpture had been hampered by the presence of his model, a peasant girl of very pleasing face and figure. Alas, a fortnight ago the maiden's paramour got wind of her new position and, with two boon companions struck, bashing the sculptor's head in and making a terrible mess of his workshop.

By the next night, one of the murderers had disappeared, his hovel turned into a bloody mess. The others followed, but the disappearances did not end with the trio of killers. In all, twenty villagers have gone missing. After the first five disappeared, the stripped bones of the others began to crop up, often jumbled and put together into bizarre shapes. The elders have sent for a priest from the imperial market town further down the river, but no help has yet arrived.

Copyright Notice
Author Scott Greene.

Boneneedle

Hit Dice: 2
Armor Class: 8 [11]
Attacks: 1 bite (1d3 + marrow poisoning)
Saving Throw: 16
Special: Marrow poisoning, aversion to daylight
Move: 18
Alignment: Neutrality
Challenge Level/XP: 3/60

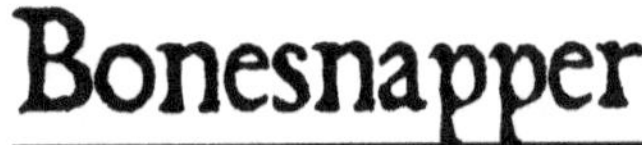

Boneneedles are bloated, yellowish-white blobs of rubbery flesh with spidery legs of black or gold. Two long, sharply-curved mandibles protrude from the monster. The mandibles are glossy-black and hollow, and aid the boneneedle in piercing its prey's flesh and bone and siphoning off its meal. After feeding, its form takes on a sickly yellow color. The boneneedle's bite secretes a thick, syrupy neurotoxin that breaks down bone (save resists). A creature with weakened bones suffers an extra +2 damage each time he is struck.

Bonesnapper

Hit Dice: 4
Armor Class: 3 [16]
Attack: Bite (1d8) and tail slap (1d3)
Saving Throw: 13
Special: Surprise on a roll of 1-2 on 1d6
Move: 9
Alignment: Neutrality
Challenge Level/XP: 4/120

The bonesnapper resembles a man-sized bipedal dinosaur with gray-green flesh mottled with gray spots. Its eyes are scarlet and its teeth are yellow. Though unintelligent, it is fond of collecting and decorating its lair with the jawbones of its victims.

Don't Feed the Animals

You wander into a vast cavern containing a number of cages composed of steel bars set in a circle 10-ft in diameter, the bars rising from floor to ceiling - the height ranges from 15 to 25 feet. There are fifteen cages in all, each containing a monster (you can choose them at random from this volume, if you like) save for one. One cage is empty, its only contents being a silvery skullcap and small patch of dried blood. The blood actually forms a trail from the cage to an exit some 30 yards away. It doesn't take a ranger to tell that some pour soul dragged itself from the cage to the door.

While the cage has no visible occupant, it does have an invisible occupant - a bonesnapper. The wizard who built this subterranean menagerie, made the mistake of quickly grasping through the bars for his hat and getting it stuck. The bonesnapper made quick work of the invading

Marrow Donor

Bones crunch underfoot in this narrow underground passage. A massive gray wolf lies collapsed amid the white heaps. It whimpers weakly but doesn't move. It has a red leather collar around its neck. Written on the collar is the word Jasper. Leg bones, spinal columns and arm bones surround the animal, each bone splintered and picked clean of flesh. The bones are mainly from animals, but a few humanoid remains can be found.

The wolf is the animal companion of Hollister, a ranger who entered the cave and died there. The wolf waited outside the cave for three days before venturing inside. He was attacked by the bone needles that live in the underground cavern among the bones. The animal is barely alive and in need of care.

A nest of 1d6+5 bone needles lives in the rocky passage. The bone needles burrow out of the broken bones to attack living creatures. One is wrapped around the underside of the wolf's throat. If rescued, the wolf follows PCs who rescued it.

Copyright Notice

appendage, which it so happened was equipped with a *ring of invisibility*, a ring which has, stewing in the beast's digestive juices, made it vanish from sight. The other members of the menagerie are particularly excited, having not been fed for several days.

Credit

The Bonesnapper originally appeared in the First Edition *Fiend Folio* (© TSR/Wizards of the Coast, 1981) and is used by permission.

Copyright Notice

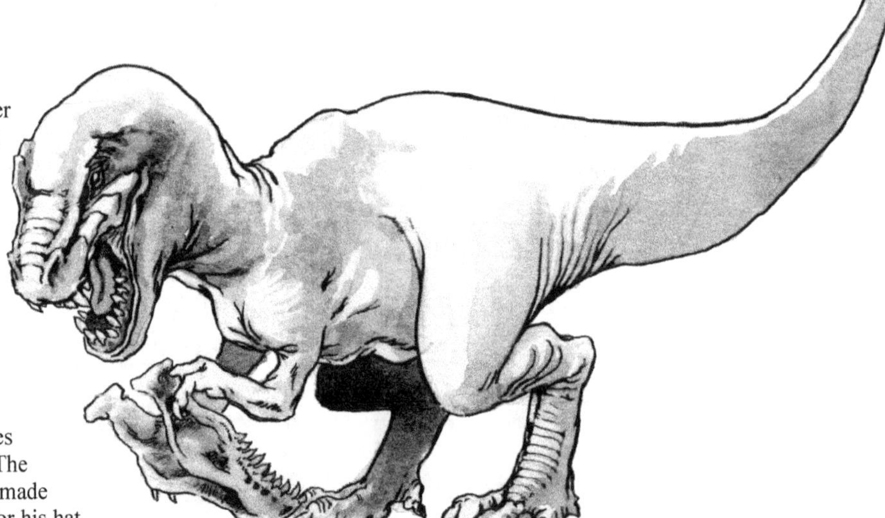

Bonesucker

Hit Dice: 8
Armor Class: 3 [16]
Attack: 4 tentacles (1d4+4 + liquefy bones)
Saving Throw: 8
Special: Liquefy bones, +1 or better weapon to hit
Move: 9
Alignment: Chaos
Challenge Level/XP: 10/1400

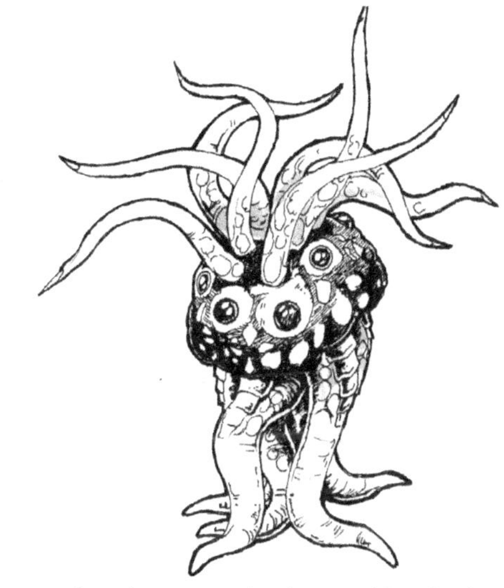

This bizarre creature resembles a fleshy tree trunk. Atop its main body protrudes a mass of writhing tentacles that constantly ooze and drip a brownish-yellow fluid. These tentacles appear to be only one or two feet long, but can be extended up to 10 feet. Near the top of its body is a ring of black, unblinking eyes that make it impossible for the monster to be surprised. Bonesuckers stand about 10 feet tall and move about through the use of 5 thick tentacles at their base. They stalk the darkness of wastelands and dank caves. Bonesuckers consume only the bones of an opponent by grabbing it and piercing its flesh with its hollow tentacles. Victims of a successful tentacle attack must pass a saving throw or be held fast and pierced by the hollow, bony protrusions that line the tentacle. These tubes inject digestive enzymes into the bones, inflicting 2d4 points of damage and causing 1d2 points of strength damage each round.

Fatal Error

The tunnel you are traveling down ends in an iron grate with a latch mechanism at the top. The grate is thick and studded with small spikes. Unhooking the latch causes the spring loaded grate to slam down on anyone standing in front of it, causing 2d6 points of damage to those who fail leap back (i.e. fail a saving throw).

Beyond the iron grate there is a large chamber, easily 100 feet wide and 200 feet long with a 30-foot high ceiling. The chamber is filled with bizarre, disturbing statues - most of them carved from basalt , but a few carved from greenish marble or limestone. The statues look to have been sculpted by a mad genius, suggesting humanoid and animal shapes that came out of a madman's nightmares.

In the center of the room there is a partial magic circle surrounded by a number of puddles of wax that used to be candles. A half-finished sculpture of what appears to be a twisted, evil tree stands next to the circle. On the margins of the circle lies the remains of a human body - just dried skin from which the bones and tissue have been removed.

The skin is swathed in robes of black velvet that were held on by a corded belt. A blank scroll, partially burned, lies next to the body. The body belongs to a wizard and artist whose model escaped from the magic circle. The model was a bonesucker, a bizarre entity brought from another dimension by means of the now useless scroll. The bonesucker is still lurking in the chamber, waiting for a new victim.

Copyright Notice

Bookworm

The bookworm is a tiny, 1-inch long, gray, seemingly normal worm. This miniscule creature is the bane of scholars, wizards, and sages, for its primary source of food is the paper, wood, and leather that make up books.

Bookworms cannot harm living creatures, but they burrow through wood, leather, rope, and paper very quickly. They ignore the hardness of such materials, and a burrowing bookworm deals 3 points of damage per round to dead wood, rope, paper, or leather. Bookworms are quick and agile (move 9) and seek to avoid being seen. To this end, they can alter their body color to match that of their surroundings. They surprise on a roll of 1-4 on 1d6.

Scrolls are destroyed in a single round and any spells contained on it are destroyed as well. A spellbook loses one spell level per round that a bookworm spends burrowing into it. For example, a spellbook has 100 pages and can hold a maximum of 100 total spell levels (a spell takes up one page per spell level). Multiple bookworms can destroy a spellbook much faster. Each bookworm burrowing through a book destroys one spell level per round.

A typical lair (or brood) contains 1d4 x 10 bookworms. They are easily killed by attacks that deal damage over an area (such as fire or cold). Consider one worm killed for each point of damage dealt.

Taking Out the Trash

You enter a cavern 60 feet long and between 15 feet and 20 feet wide. The cavern is piled up to waist height with trash and detritus, mostly in the form of worm-ridden books and tomes. The trash gives off a four odor (per the troglodyte stench ability) and a good amount of heat, making walking through the trash uncomfortable. The air in the cavern is very close and muggy. About a dozen holes in the ceiling spew more trash into the room (from an indeterminate source) as people walk through it. Those walking through the cavern are wading through both bookworms and rot grubs. Each round spent in the room brings a 1 in 6 chance of attack by one or the other.

Credit

The Bookworm originally appeared in the First Edition *Monster Manual II* (© TSR/Wizards of the Coast, 1983) and is used by permission.

Copyright Notice

Brass Man

Hit Dice: 10
Armor Class: 4 [15]
Attacks: 1 slam or 1 weapon (3d6)
Saving Throw: 5
Special: Spit molten brass (6d6), +1 or better magic weapon to hit, slowed by lightning, healed by fire, immune to spells
Move: 6
Alignment: Neutrality
Challenge Level/XP: 12/2,000

A brass man is an 8-foot tall humanoid composed of brass and weighing about 900 pounds. Its facial features are exquisitely and delicately worked. Some brass men have ancient runes and symbols carved into their bodies. Many are constructed with weapons, though the average brass golem relies on its fists. In combat, a brass man can spit a 30-foot stream of molten brass every 1d4 rounds (6d6 damage). Lightning slows a brass man, and fire heals it. They are immune to all other spells.

Head Games

An abandoned shrine sits deep in the Kriegh Forest, its flaking stucco columns entwined with clinging ivy. The stone portico rises above a marble entryway. Ornate double doors bordered in brass are closed but not locked.

The interior walls of the 20-foot-by-20-foot shrine are lined with 10 1-foot-deep niches that run the length of each side of the structure. These shelves start at floor level and rise to the ceiling 15 feet overhead. Each 20-foot-long niche houses a row of carved stone heads, about 20 in a row (around 200 stone heads per wall). Some are representations of influential leaders, while others are gods and goddesses. Nestled among the heads are bird nests and other debris carried in by forest creatures. A shattered skylight lets rain in, creating standing pools of stagnant water where mosquitos buzz in swirling clouds. A rope hangs down through the skylight to coil on the floor. Engravings on the walls of prancing satyrs and reveling druids are covered with green mold.

The heads are enchanted so that they all turn in unison to "watch" people who enter the shrine. The heads always turn to follow the person closest to them as they walk about the chamber. The effect is like being on a stage in the middle of a gallery of spectators. The heads are harmless, but disconcerting.

Against the wall opposite the brass entry sits a basalt altar, its sides decorated with idyllic pastoral scenes. A three-inch-thick glass top on the altar shields a depression in the stone that contains a shining gold ring carved with images of ivy and a scroll sealed with a wax signet. The burned body of a tomb robber lies in a heap of charred remains at the base of the altar. His armor is decayed and melted through, with obvious burn spots marring the leather. A crowbar in one of his skeletal hands is bent and twisted, the metal running like wax on the floor tiles. One corner of the glass atop the altar is scratched and chipped.

One of the heads behind the altar actually belongs to a brass man kneeling inside a space covered by a *phantasmal force*. The golem's entire body – except its head – is hidden by the spell so that it appears to be just one of the many moving heads lining the shelves. The brass man's features are coated with a thin patina of plaster to blend in with the stone heads beside it. It rotates to watch PCs, just like the rest of the heads in the gallery. The golem is tasked with protecting the altar and its contents.

The brass man kneels in its niche and doesn't bother PCs unless they touch the altar or harm the other carvings. If that happens, it spits a stream of molten brass at the closest PC then rises out of the phantasmal stone wall to attack. When it does so, a wall of fire ignites across the doorway, blocking the room's only entrance. The golem returns to its post after PCs are driven off.

The ring is a *ring of regeneration*, while the scroll contains three druid spells of the Game Referee's choosing.

*(See the **angel, empyreal** entry for another encounter with the brass man.)*

Copyright Notice
Authors Scott Greene and Casey Christofferson.

Brownie

Hit Dice: 1d3
Armor Class: 2 [17]
Attack: Tiny sword (1d3)
Saving Throw: 18
Special: Magic resistance (25%), spells
Move: 9
Alignment: Law
Challenge Level/XP: 1/15

A brownie is a timid, quiet fey creature that prefers to live only among its own kind. Most brownies dwell in pastoral areas untouched by civilization, such as deep forests and wild lands far from other creatures. They resemble 18-inch tall elves with greenish skin and brown, gray or tawny hair. Most brownies prefer green or otherwise brightly colored clothing. They may be distant relatives of pixies and halflings, but this has never been proven. In woodland areas, brownies surprise on a roll of 1-4 on 1d6, and is only surprised on a roll of 1 on 1d8. The can use the following spells once per day each: *Confusion*, *continual light*, *dimension door*, *protection from evil 10-ft radius* and *mirror image*.

Delectable Desserts

A band of 1d8+4 brownies lives together in a mossy cottage constructed next to an ancient oak. The brownies cultivate a small garden in and around the cottage, though it is so chaotic and overgrown one might never recognize it as such. The cottage has a two-level cellar, the upper level being used to store preserves and roots and the lower level for cultivating large, musty smelling mushrooms that are dried and turned into a delicious broth or powdered and turned into a cure for many diseases (+2 bonus to save vs. disease if applied to a wound).

The lower level has a secret door hidden behind shelves of mushrooms (the shelves swing out of the way if a secret lever is tripped). Behind the secret door there is a long tunnel winds its way beneath the woods, sometimes broken by a spiral stairway into a hollowed oak and finally ending in a hollowed hillock of greenish, marble boulders. In this hidden space there are a number of tree roots hanging from the ceiling and woven together into a single strand that drips moisture into a copper recepticle set in the floor.

A single draught from the copper basin acts as a *cure light wounds* spell. Two draughts acts as a *cure light wounds* and *cure disease* spell and three draughts acts simply as a very slow acting *polymorph*, turning a person into a wolfberry bush over the course of six hours. Not surprisingly, there are a number of well tended wolfberry bushes around the brownies' cottage, the fruit being used to make jelly tarts that act as half strength *cure light wounds* spells but take 2 rounds to consume.

Credit
The Brownie originally appeared in the First Edition *Monster Manual* (© TSR/Wizards of the Coast, 1977) and is used by permission.

Copyright Notice
Author Scott Greene, based on original material by Gary Gygax.

Brume

Hit Dice: 7
Armor Class: 2 [17]
Attacks: 2 claws (1d6)
Saving Throw: 9
Special: Magical weapons to hit, magical abilities
Move: 15
Alignment: Chaos
Challenge Level/XP: 8/800

A brume is an opaque spirit that takes human form. It can only be hit by magical weapons. A brume's claws cause an opponent to forget everything that has happened in the last 1d6 hours (save resists). A brume can create a billowing fog to appear three times a day.

Swept Away in the Moment

A maze made of narrow 5-foot-wide bridges stretches throughout a cavernous room. The bridge-path has many twists and turns that often end in dead ends. The floor of the room lies 60 feet down on each side of the bridge and appears to be covered in upward pointing sword blades. Oozing carefree through the blades are 3 black puddings. They make no attempt to climb the walls, contently dissolving refuse scattered along the bladed floor.

With careful study, a clear and safe path to the other side of the room can be navigated. The exact dimension of the bridge maze is left to the Game Referee, but the arching bridges should be expansive with many dead ends to force PCs to backtrack.

A brume hides beneath a bridge two-thirds of the way across the room. It creates a fog to cover the area while it attacks with its memory-robbing

claws. PCs robbed of their memory find themselves lost on a bridge maze without a clue as to where they are or why they are there.

Copyright Notice
Author Scott Greene.

Brykolakas

Hit Dice: 5
Armor Class: 5 [14]
Attacks: 2 claws (1d6 + infection)
Saving Throw: 12
Special: Create spawn, death throes, infection, change shape
Move: 6/24 (swim)
Alignment: Chaos
Challenge Level/XP: 7/600

Brykolakas are 6-foot-tall humanoid creatures with bluish-gray skin and unkempt black or gray hair. They can assume the shape of a dolphin or a manta ray at will. Their eyes burn with a hatred for living creatures, and their hands end in razor-sharp talons with black or broken nails. Brykolakas dress in flowing robes or gowns. When killed, a brykolakas' body changes into a pool of deadly poison (2d4 points of damage to all within 10 feet). The creature's claws also carry a deadly infection that deteriorates a victim's organs (save or die). Any humanoid slain by a byrkolakas rises as a kalanos in 1d4 days under the creature's control:

Kalanos: HD 3; AC 8[11]; Attack 1 slam (1d4 + 1 level drain); Save 14; Alignment Chaos; Move 6, Swim 24; CL/XP 4/120; Special: Level drain (1)

The Haunted Potty

Just offshore from the coastal town of Niborlyn dwells a brykolakas. The brykolakas lairs in an old place of worship dedicated to a sea goddess. The mostly intact ruins of a cathedral lie submerged in the bay, only the square top of the 60-foot-tall bell tower visible above the surface during low tide. Four stone sculptures of gargoyles (inanimate) stand watch on the corners of the tower. Although the stone church and bell tower remain, the tower's wooden access door rotted away long ago, leaving a square portal into the cathedral's black interior. The villagers call the tower "Hell's Well," not knowing of the submerged cathedral below. The fishermen stay clear of the top of the bell tower and believe it an ill omen to even view the gargoyles. The brykolakas occasionally raids the village of livestock or lone drunkards. The brykolakas has discovered that the village's sewer network empties into an undersea cave. Through this cave, the brykolakas can enter the village undetected by climbing the walls of the pit toilets.

Copyright Notice
Author Scott Greene.

Buckawn

Hit Dice: 1d6
Armor Class: 2 [17]
Attack: Dagger (1d3) or dart (1d3)
Saving Throw: 18
Special: Poison use, spells, magic resistance (10%)
Move: 12
Alignment: Neutrality
Challenge Level/XP: 2/30

Buckawns look like halfling-sized humanoids with swarthy skin, dark hair, greenish-brown eyes and brown clothes. Buckawns are somehow related to brownies, but they are nowhere near as kind-hearted and playful. Buckawns are extremely reclusive and rarely have dealings with outside races. Trade of any kind between a buckawn tribe and another race is virtually unheard of. Characters who journey into a buckawn's realm are usually left alone, providing they themselves leave the buckawn's realm alone. Buckawns readily use poisoned blades when confronted with a tough opponent, when outnumbered, or when battling opponents for whom they have great disdain. They favor moonseed berries as poison and usually have a plentiful supply readily available (see the sidebar).

Moonseed Berries

These small berries are bluish-purple and resemble wild grapes. They are highly poisonous and are often mixed with food or crushed and smeared on a weapon or object. The poison is deadly unless the victim succeeds at a saving throw. Even if the saving throw is successful, the poison inflicts 1d8 points of damage. A vial of the poison can be purchased from unsavory types for 1,500 gp.

Buckawns can use the following spells at will: *Phantasmal force*, *invisibility* and *insect plague* (1/day).

Children of the Berries

A band of 1d6+5 buckawn poachers has constructed a hunting blind on the outskirts of a bustling village. The buckawns prey on children who wander too far from home, bringing them back to their own hidden village in the dark forest to work as slaves. The children are put to the task of picking moonseed berries. The berries are quite acidic, raising boils on their fingers and staining them a deep crimson.

The slave children are kept in mildly comfortable cages in a tall, barn like structure disguised to look like a copse of trees. The buckawn village has a population of 1d10+10 living in teepee-like structures constructed from peeled tree bark. Most of the tribespeople work as quail hunters and bowyers. The buckawn are currently holding 15 children in their barn.

Credit

The Buckawn originally appeared in the First Edition *Monster Manual II* (© TSR/Wizards of the Coast, 1983) and is used by permission.

Copyright Notice

Author Scott Greene, based on original material by Gary Gygax.

Bumblebee, Giant

Worker

Hit Dice: 3
Armor Class: 3 [16]
Attacks: Sting (1d6 + poison)
Saving Throw: 14
Special: None
Move: 6/18 (flying)
Alignment: Neutrality
Challenge Level/XP: 5/240

Giant bees live in enormous hives in massive tress, along cliffs or even tunneled through soil. A hive can hold as many as 100 bees and always contains one queen. The poison of a bee does 2d6 points of damage if a saving throw is failed, 1d4 points of damage if the saving throw succeeds.

Queen

Hit Dice: 10
Armor Class: 3 [16]
Attacks: Sting (1d6 + poison)
Saving Throw: 5
Special: None
Move: 6/18 (flying)
Alignment: Neutrality
Challenge Level/XP: 12/2,000

The queen of a giant bee hive is larger and tougher, than the average giant bee. The poison of a bee does 2d6 points of damage if a saving throw is failed, 1d4 points of damage if the saving throw succeeds.

Mis-spelled Bee

The residents of the destitute and dwindling hamlet of Lessef scrape by farming on their barren lands. The people live with the very real fear of famine lingering above their heads. Only the locale tavern and church show any hint of prosperity.

Which is why the villagers were surprised to find a field on the outskirts overflowing with incredibly large clovers and sunflowers, some reaching heights of 15 to 20 feet. Recently, a good-hearted but inept druid named Hagglethorn Beefalo attempted to aid the impoverished citizens. By casting *plant growth* and administering a nutrient-rich potion in mass quantity, he secretly fed the clover and sunflower fields at night. His plan seemed flawless. The bountiful result would feed the remaining livestock and allow the town to sell the surplus of the plentiful crops. A humble man, Hagglethorn didn't hang around to take credit, desiring that the townsfolk credit the fertility goddess Freya for their good fortune. As fate would have it, though, the combination of spells and fertilizer had unfortunate results: The bees that collected the pollen and nectar also grew to gigantic sizes.

The territorial bees have now taken the village hostage. The citizens barricaded themselves into their homes a week ago, and their stored provisions are all but depleted. A few corpses of slain villagers lie around the village's well, some still grasping pitchforks and axes where they made a last stand. Their bodies are swollen and peppered with puncture wounds. Villagers plead for assistance, but do not open their doors or windows. The bees have taken over a large barn on the north side of town. A massive hive fills the interior of the barn. Only the destruction of the hive and the queen will keep the bees from returning. The nest contains 20-30 giant bees and one queen. The Game Referee should adjust the number of bees to challenge the players. While the people of Lessef are grateful, they can offer only small rewards to their saviors. They offer a jar of pickled eggs, a fox pelt (5 gp) and as much honey as the PCs can carry.

Copyright Notice
Author Scott Greene.

Bunyip

Hit Dice: 5
Armor Class: 4 [15]
Attack: Bite (1d6)
Saving Throw: 12
Special: Frenzy, roar, vorpal bite
Move: 21 (swimming)
Alignment: Neutrality (with lawful tendencies)
Challenge Level/XP: 7/600

Bunyips are aquatic creature with the front half of a black seal and the rear half of a grayish-black shark. The bunyip is about 6 feet long, though specimens of up to 10 feet long have been encountered. Bunyips do not attack creatures larger than themselves, except in self-defense or if they detect blood in the water. A bunyip that detects blood in the water goes into a killing frenzy, as do all other bunyips within a 90-foot radius. Frenzied bunyips attack twice per round until either they or their opponents are dead. A frenzied bunyip's swim speed increases to 24. This frenzy lasts for 10 rounds. When a bunyip roars, all creatures with 4 or less HD within a 100-foot spread must succeed on a saving throw or become panicked for 2d4 rounds, dropping their weapons and fleeing at top speed. If a bunyip scores a natural 20 on its attack roll, it severs one of the opponent's extremities (roll 1d6: 1-3 arm, 4-6 leg; 50% chance of either right or left).

Feeding Time

To label the lord of the coast a bastard would be accurate on two counts, namely parentage and personality. The veteran of many battles and intrigues maintains a stout tower on the limestone cliffs, as well as a narrow, rickety stair to the strand of beach below and a fairly large curtain wall encompassing his fields and meadows.

On the beach below his stronghold, the lord of the coast has a long, stone quay built into the crystal clear waters of the bay. A scaffolding has been constructed at the end of the quay, with a hook and winch device that allows a bound subject to be raised and lowered above the water. Swimming about the quay are is a large bunyip, well trained to circle the scaffolding when his "feeding gong" is struck at the top of the tower.

The lord keeps a fine collection of skulls on his scaffolding, and a few incomplete skeletons chained to the battlements of his tower.

Credit

The Bunyip originally appeared in the First Edition *Fiend Folio* (© TSR/Wizards of the Coast, 1981) and is used by permission.

Copyright Notice

Author Scott Greene, based on original material by Dermot Jackson.

Burning Dervish

Hit Dice: 8
Armor Class: 7 [12]
Attacks: 1 weapon (1d6 + 1d6 fire)
Saving Throw: 8
Special: Flame form, spell abilities, resist fire
Move: 9/6 (flying)
Alignment: Chaos
Challenge Level/XP: 9/1,100

Burning dervishes vary in appearance, but all resemble humans. Skin color, eye color, and hair color range across the same spectrum as that for normal humans. It is said that the burning dervishes were once a noble tribe of jann who sold their souls to the Sultan of Efreet in exchange for greater power over the Elemental Plane of Fire. Burning dervishes can shift into a flame form that resembles a column of fire to deal fire damage with each slam or weapon attack. Each day, a burning dervishes can become *invisible* 3 times, cast *pyrotechnics* 3 times, cast *enlarge* twice and cast *produce flame* twice. They can also transport themselves and up to eight creatures to any elemental plane, the Astral Plane or the Material Plane.

The Desert Toll

A burning sandstorm roars off the desert sands of the Veil, the leading edge of the blowing grit sparking a bluish flame that dances through the superheated air. Temperatures soar above 120 degrees, and the driving sand scours bare skin raw.

A shirtless man with tattoos inked in henna across his bare torso walks at the head of the storm, his arms wide in greeting even as he ignores the torrential winds whipping around him. A nimbus of blue flame hugs his body, but he pays it no mind, brushing the fire away as anyone else would an annoying gnat.

"Greetings, friends," he calls, his voice rising above the harsh winds. "I am Khalid al-Sin. Welcome to the grand desert! Do you have the gold needed to pass through my glorious desert?" Khalid steeples his hands before him and smiles.

Khalid is a burning dervish who delights in robbing travelers crossing "his" desert. He is an accomplished fighter and gladly takes his toll by beating travelers senseless, then taking their gold – and any other belongings he desires – while they are down.

Copyright Notice
Authors Scott Greene and Casey Christofferson.

Cadaver

Cadaver Lord

Bring Out Your Dead

A cloaked figure stands in the center of Arnelt, his wrinkled hand resting on a small cart pulled by a broken-down mare. Corpses lie heaped in the cart, stacked like cords of wood. The old man is as broken as his horse, but stands patiently by as two men load another body. A crying woman hands him a bag of coins and he nods silently. When the body is loaded, he takes the horse's reins and tugs it forward. His voice is loud as he calls out, "Bring out your dead!"

The old man never stays long in any town. He arrives at sunrise and leaves before the sun goes down. Rowling is a man with many secrets. First off, he's not actually an undertaker. And second, he's not and old man; he's actually a young thief named Rowling who concocted this scheme to make money. He's been traveling from town to town for a month now collecting the dead. He has no intention of burying the dead he collects, however. Instead, he takes the corpses outside town and dumps them in secluded spots where they won't be found.

His callousness has caused many of the unburied corpses left in his wake to rise as cadavers focused on finding the false undertaker. The undead charge into towns Rowling has visited, hoping to finally catch the liar before he moves on. They are mindless, but driven as a group to complete this single purpose. They spare no one in the towns they pass through as they follow the man who dumped their bodies.

Copyright Notice

Author Scott Greene.

Cadaver Lord

Hit Dice: 5
Armor Class: 3 [16]
Attacks: 2 claws (1d4 + disease) and bite (1d6 + disease)
Saving Throw: 12
Special: Disease, reanimation, create spawn, command undead, magical abilities, spell resistance (20%), +1 magic weapons to hit
Move: 9
Alignment: Chaos
Challenge Level/XP: 7/600

Cadavers lords are humanoids wearing tattered rags. Rotted flesh reveals corded muscles and sinew stretched tightly over its skeleton. Hollow eye sockets flicker with an unholy fire of orange or yellow light. The cadaver lord's mouth is lined with jagged and broken teeth, and its hands end in wicked claws. The creature's claws and bite transmit horrible diseases that waste victims' flesh (1d4 hit points damage; save resists). When killed, a cadaver lord regenerates 1 hit point per round. It stands up ready to fight again when it regains its full hit points. Damage caused by spells is not restored. A creature slain by a cadaver lord awakens in 1d4 rounds as a cadaver. The cadaver lord can command any undead to do its bidding. Once per day, a cadaver lord can cast *darkness (15-foot radius)* and *fear*.

The Wall of Thorns

A wall of darkness fills the corridor ahead. Just inside the perfect line of darkness is a spiked wall that fills the 10-foot-wide dungeon corridor. Ivory horns and metal spikes jut out at random angles across the boards forming the wall. Bodies of adventurers are spitted on the horns. Severed heads are mounted on spikes atop the 8-foot-tall wall. The wall leaves a three-foot gap between its top and the ceiling. The wall is mounted on steel wheels and can be pushed forward quite quickly. Anyone struck by the wall takes 3d6 points of damage and must save or become impaled on the racks of horns and spikes.

Chained to the back of the wall are two muscular minotaurs. The creatures' sole purpose is to push the wall forward against anyone approaching the darkness. The minotaurs wear blindfolds and are covered in thick scars. A line of six ghouls stand behind the minotaurs, whipping them mercilessly with cat-o-nine-tails.

A cadaver lord named Iniquitus Shaw sits on a bone throne pulled by another crouching minotaur. Shaw's eyes smolder a hellish flame as he watches his minions drive creature's before his wall of death. Rarely does he rise from the throne to attack, preferring to let his minions do the dirty work.

Copyright Notice

Carbuncle

Hit Dice: 1
Armor Class: 1 [18]
Attack: Bite (1d2)
Saving Throw: 17
Special: Discord, foresight, telepathy 100 ft.
Move: 9
Alignment: Neutrality
Challenge Level/XP: 2/30

Deep in the tangled underbrush of forests and in the remote regions of dismal swamps and bogs lives a strange creature called the carbuncle. The carbuncle resembles a cross between an anteater and armadillo with a large, red jewel embedded in its head. The carbuncle is a withdrawn creature and seeks to avoid encounters. Should it seek interaction, a carbuncle often begins by proudly announcing the value of the gem in its forehead just to watch the reaction such information arouses. Despite its overall shy nature, the carbuncle has a mischievous side as well, often seeking to join travelers in order to play pranks and gauge the reactions of the unfortunate victims of its curiosity. After joining with a party, a carbuncle will seek to cause discord by using selective telepathic images and prophesies to breed hostility and suspicion between party members. These images can be created once per round in the mind of a single creature within 30 feet of the carbuncle. Affected creatures must pass a saving throw or fall into loud bickering and arguing with those around them. If the affected creatures have different alignments, there is a 50% chance that they attack each other. Carbuncles might also telepathically contact nearby monsters and lead them to attack the party so that it can watch in fascination and read the thoughts of the party as they are attacked, slipping away at an opportune moment. A carbuncle can be coerced to surrender the gem in its forehead with some difficulty and much deception. When a carbuncle is slain, its forehead gem crumbles to dust. If the carbuncle relinquishes its gem, it grows another one within one month. Carbuncles enjoy watching others fight, but avoids engaging in combat itself.

Helpful Suggestions

You come across an abandoned caravan wagon. The wagon has been tipped over and several barrels of pale ale lie in a pile next to it. Sitting atop the pile, taking a long draught from one of the barrels, is a bizarre creature that looks like an armadillo with a long snout, low-slung ears and a large red jewel in its forehead. As the party looks upon the creature, they hear a voice in their heads, speaking their native language, asking them what they're waiting for and to come on over for a drink.

The creature is quite jovial, telling jokes and chattering on about the dangers of its forest home. It will explain that the caravan was struck by bandits who chased the merchants into the woods. It suggests moving on as soon as possible, and will offer to lead the party through the woods.

The carbuncle will take a winding, confusing path in an attempt to disorient the party, eventually leading them to an ancient tower in the woods. The tower is built of limestone caked with soil and heavily weathered and stands 100-ft in height.

The tower can be entered through a portcullis of rusty steel. Beyond the portcullis is a small, empty circular room. The carbuncle hangs back, explaining that it suffers from claustrophobia and explaining that the trapdoor in the ceiling leads to a magical chamber that holds an ancient relic (choose something important to your home campaign). When the party pulls on the rope tied to the trapdoor, the tower rapidly descends into the earth, the voice of the carbuncle in their heads laughing and wishing them a pleasant journey through the underworld.

When the tower hits bottom, inflicting 1d6 points of damage from the jarring stop, the exit now leads to a subterranean tunnel and whatever horrors the referee wishes to inflict on her players.

Credit

The Carbuncle originally appeared in the First Edition Fiend Folio (© TSR/Wizards of the Coast, 1981) and is used by permission.

Copyright Notice

Author Scott Greene, based on original material by Albie Fiore.

Carrion Moth

Hit Dice: 5
Armor Class: 3 [16]
Attack: 4 tentacles (paralysis) and bite (1d6)
Saving Throw: 12
Special: Drone, paralysis, stench
Move: 12/24 (flying)
Alignment: Neutrality
Challenge Level/XP: 8/800

Carrion moths resemble giant moths with long, beautiful wings covered in rippling patterns resembling skulls. Its head is centipede-like, with four long tentacles surrounding its mouth, which has a single pair of needle-like mandibles. Just as the caterpillar grows into a moth, sages believe the carrion crawler eventually sheds its form and transforms into the carrion moth. The carrion moth grows to a maximum length of 20 feet. Its wings are lined with tiny holes and veins that allow the carrion moth to emit a whining drone that affects all creatures that hear it. Affected creatures must pass a saving throw or be *confused* (as the spell) for 2d4 rounds. Creatures hit by the carrion moth's tentacles must pass a saving throw or be paralyzed for 2d6 rounds. Carrion moths are attracted to the stench of decaying flesh and the light of anything larger than a torch or lantern. When a carrion moth dies, its carcass splits open and releases a foul-smelling gas. All living creatures (except other carrion moths) within 5 feet of the carcass must succeed on a saving throw or be nauseated for 1d4+1 rounds.

Crystal Cone Cave

In a large, conical cavern (70 feet in diameter at the bottom, 80 feet high), 2d6 carrion moths swarm around a glowing crystal at the pinnacle of the cavern. The crystal is actually a gnomish construction of glass and filled with a glowing ooze that causes terrible burns and possible mutations to people who are exposed to it. The ooze can also be used to enchant weapons, imparting a +1 bonus to weapons dipped into it. Removing the crystal from the ceiling is not easy, and the carrion moths make the operation even more difficult. If the glowing ooze touches a moth, it swells to twice its size (double Hit Dice) and becomes especially aggressive.

Copyright Notice

Caryatid Column

Hit Dice: 5
Armor Class: 5 [14]
Attack: Longsword (1d8+1)
Saving Throw: 12
Special: Immune to magic, half damage from normal weapons, shatter weapons
Move: 9
Alignment: Neutrality
Challenge Level/XP: 7/600

A caryatid column is akin to the stone golem in that it is a magical construct created by a spellcaster. They look like exquisitely sculpted and chiseled statues of beautiful female warriors carrying longswords. The longsword is constructed of steel, but is melded with the column and made of stone until the column animates. Caryatid columns are programmed as guardians and activate when certain conditions or stipulations are met or broken (such as a living creature enters a chamber guarded by a caryatid column). It does not move more than 50 feet from the area it is guarding or protecting. They are immune to all spells except *transmute rock to mud*, which deals 1d6 points of damage per caster level to the caryatid column, *transmute mud to rock*, which heals the caryatid column of all damage and *stone to flesh*, which makes it subject to normal damage from weapons and suspends its immunity to magic for 1 round. Whenever a weapon strikes the caryatid column, the wielder must pass a saving throw or the weapon shatters into pieces. Magic weapons add their enchantment bonus to the saving throw.

Works of Art

You enter an opulent, though quite ancient and dusty, throne room clad in malachite. The ceiling is held aloft by a number of brass pillars. The room measures 20 feet in width and 40 feet in length, the ceiling being 15 feet overhead. At the end of the room there is a stately marble throne, ornately carved into images of cherubs, wood nymphs and panthers, flanked by two seven-foot-tall pillars of ghostly white marble.

The pillars are carved to represent twin maidens, naked, their waist-long hair adorned with stars and gleaming, curved longswords held above their heads, forming an arch. The pillars are caryatid columns and programmed to behead any who approaches the throne who is not crawling on all fours, nose pressed against the ground. The are likewise programmed to defend the rightful ruler of the kingdom.

Credit
The Caryatid Column originally appeared in the First Edition *Fiend Folio* (© TSR/Wizards of the Coast, 1981) and is used by permission.

Copyright Notice
Author Scott Greene, based on original material by Jean Wells.

Caterprism

Hit Dice: 6
Armor Class: 3 [16]
Attacks: 4 legs (1d8) and bite (1d6)
Saving Throw: 11
Special: Crystal silk, crystalline mandibles
Move: 9
Alignment: Neutrality
Challenge Level/XP: 8/800

A caterprism is a caterpillar made of crystal with hexagonal body segments and twelve sharply angled legs. Each body segment is about 2 feet long and contains a single pair of legs. The head of a caterprism is caterpillar-like, with large faceted eyes and huge mandibles. Three times per day, a caterprism can spew forth a crystalline silk up to 20 feet that instantly solidifies into a rock-like substance. Creatures caught in the silk are impaled for 3d6 points of damage (save for half) as it hardens. The crystalline mandibles of a caterprism are extremely sharp. If a caterprism rolls a natural 20 with its bite attack, it severs the head of its opponent.

The Crystal Cocoon

Gerdstall's Rock and Mineral Exchange is a small shop at the base of the Hollow Spire Mountains. Three days ago two well-liked former miners, the Gerdstall brothers, died in the shop they loved. Their bodies were impaled within a crystalline web of spikes. Sharp web filaments fill the tiny shack.

Behind the shop, a massive crystal cocoon hangs from a stout elm's branch. A dark hole beneath the split-open cocoon leads into the mountain, and several shallower holes are dug throughout the yard. The hole looks like a dog has been at work, frantically digging into the ground over and over.

A caterprism recently hatched from the crystalline cocoon (which the Gerdstalls thought was an elaborately carved chunk of crystal and not a real pod). The newly hatched caterprism chased the brothers into their shop, and lashed out when one of the men struck it with a broom. The creature's web of crystal spikes killed the brothers, and the giant earth creature bored its way into the mountains. It is now digging a series of tunnels for a lair, but returns each night to feast on exotic stones the brothers buried in their back yard to keep them safe.

Copyright Notice
Author Erica Balsley.

Caterwaul

Hit Dice: 5
Armor Class: 3 [16]
Attack: 2 claws (1d4) and bite (1d6)
Saving Throw: 12
Special: Screech
Move: 21/9 (climbing)
Alignment: Chaos
Challenge Level/XP: 6/400

Caterwauls are semi-intelligent bipedal felines with dark, blue fur and long tails. Caterwauls are terribly quick, and they use this speed to run down their prey. The caterwaul's lair is most often a cave littered with sticks, twigs, and leaves, with walls covered in scratch marks where the beast has honed its claws. Once every 10 rounds, a caterwaul can emit a piercing screech that deals 1d8 points of damage to all creatures within 60 feet that hear it. A creature that makes a successful saving throw takes half damage. About 1 in 6 caterwauls is so quick that it enjoys a +2 bonus to AC and can make an additional claw attack each round.

Catnip Tribute

Descending a rugged mountain trail - wide but precarious - you see an assemblage of thirty men in baggy trousers and long, heavy coats of blue-black velvet and brass buttons. The men in the front rank carry long poles topped by stylized brass panther heads holding lanterns in their mouths. Behind this front rank are two ranks of men holding wicked looking pole arms and wearing shirts of gleaming scales in place of velvet coats. Behind these soldiers stride eight men holding aloft a palanquin of teak and silver topped by a gauzy pavilion of red and yellow. The palanquin is followed by more soldiers, these men armed with long bows and curved swords.

At the head of the assemblage is a tall man with pink eyes and platinum hair. He rides a white charger, caparisoned in damask silks, and wears a coat of black mail and a velvet cape. Naturally, the assemblage expects travelers coming the opposite way to stand aside, and they will press this demand with a show of arms if necessary. The leader of the assemblage proclaims himself the grand vizier of a hidden country in the mountains, a country of teak forests and spice plantations and beautiful men and woman with honey-colored skin and hair as black as a starless night. On the palanquin is the kingdom's living goddess, she of the swift death who commands fear with her voice, which sounds like the scream of a thousand innocents.

The living goddess is a caterwaul. She is on her way into the lowlands to pay homage to the Cat Lord and bring a tribute of catnip in intricately carved pomanders of teak inlaid with silver images of hunting cats.

Credit

The Caterwaul originally appeared in the First Edition *Fiend Folio* (© TSR/Wizards of the Coast, 1981) and is used by permission.

Copyright Notice

Author Scott Greene, based on original material by Albie Fiore.

Cave Cricket

Hit Dice: 1
Armor Class: 3 [16]
Attack: 2 kicks (1d4)
Saving Throw: 17
Special: Chirp
Move: 12
Alignment: Neutrality
Challenge Level/XP: 1/15

Cave crickets are larger versions of normal crickets (3 feet long) and, much like the smaller crickets they resemble, are relatively harmless. The cave cricket's chirping can be heard to a range of 300 feet. Creatures within 20 feet of a chirping cave cricket cannot be heard unless they scream. Spellcasters in the area must succeed on a saving throw to successfully cast a spell. The chirping increases the chance of wandering monsters by 30%. Cave cricket usually avoid combat, making a couple kick attacks against an attacker and then fleeing.

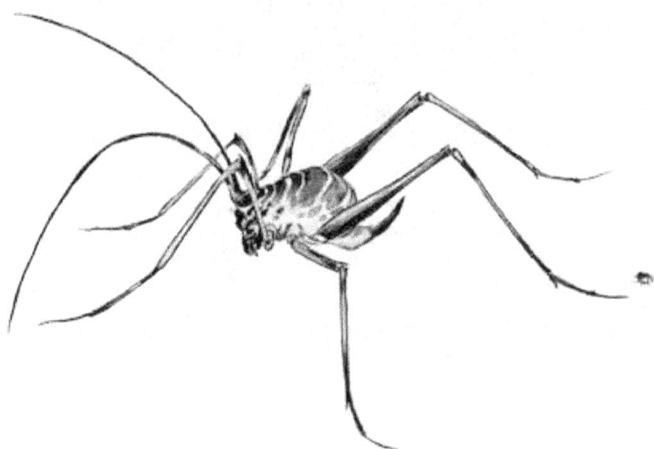

Kicking Cricket Style

You come to a very tricky portion of the underworld - a large cavernous tunnel of loose, toppled stones, many bearing signs of having been carved by some unknown subterranean race. At the bottom of this tunnel is a swiftly moving stream of icy cold water. The stream has cut a 10-foot deep channel through the tunnel. Narrow paths run alongside the stream, first one bank and then the other, with crossings either by leaping over a place where the stream narrows or via narrow, slippery bridges both natural and artificial.

Staring up from the shallower portions of the steam are the skulls of uncoordinated or unlucky adventurers, along with fragments of stone faces carved from the gold-colored rock of the tunnel.

The sound of the stream echoes through the tunnel, lulling one to sleep but for the incessant chirping of a cluster of 1d4+1 cave crickets. The echoe of the chirping is loud and unnerving, imposing a -1 penalty to all saving throws, including saving throws to avoid falling into the stream, which moves at a rate of 120 feet per round.

The tunnel has five such crossings, the banks near the middle crossing being occupied by the cave crickets in question. Though not terribly dangerous in and of themselves, a well-placed kick by a cave cricket can mean one's end if sent over the banks into freezing waters. Each round one is carried down the stream (which ultimately plunges into deeper portions of the underworld) inflicts 1d6 points of damage. During each round spent in the waters, one must pass a saving throw at a cumulative -1 penalty per round of exposure or be paralyzed by the chilling waters, meaning death by drowning in the next round.

Credit

The Cave Cricket originally appeared in the First Edition module *S4 The Lost Caverns of Tsojcanth* (© TSR/Wizards of the Coast, 1982) and later in the First Edition *Monster Manual II* (© TSR/Wizards of the Coast, 1983) and is used by permission.

Copyright Notice

Author Scott Greene, based on original material by Gary Gygax.

Cave Fisher

Hit Dice: 3
Armor Class: 3 [16]
Attack: Filament (see text) and 2 claws (1d6)
Saving Throw: 14
Special: Filaments
Move: 6
Alignment: Neutrality
Challenge Level/XP: 4/120

The cave fisher is a 7-foot long insect-like creature with a hard outer shell. It has eight legs, two of which end in serrated pincers. The cave fisher's snout fires a strong, web-like adhesive filament it uses to reel in its prey. The cave fisher lairs on ledges and cliffs underground, where it can quickly strike and reel in its prey. Its lair is always littered with bones and gear from its previous victims. Often, the ground and walls nearby are covered with this filament. The cave fisher's preferred method of attack is to anchor itself to its ledge and string its filament across the ground of its lair. When a living creature touches or passes near the filament (1 in 6 chance of spotting the filament, 2 in 6 for elves), the fisher attempts to trap it and reel it in. If the cave fisher fails this, it can fire its filament at an opponent up to 60 feet away. If a cave fisher hits with its filament attack, the filament latches onto the opponent's body. This deals no damage but drags the stuck opponent 10 feet closer each subsequent round unless that creature breaks free. An application of liquid with high alcohol content dissolves the adhesive and forces the cave fisher to release its hold. The filament has 10 hit points and is AC 2 [17]. If the filament is severed, it grows back within 1 hour.

Into the Cave Fisher's Mouth

If the subterranean river gorge inhabited by the cave crickets (q.v.) was not deadly enough, it becomes worse. The tunnel eventually narrows into a misty canyon. The stream here punges into the depths of the underworld, creating a terrible cacaphony that makes it impossible to hear somebody more than 5 feet away and imposes a 5% chance of spell failure on spell casters.

The canyon in question is really more of a vertical than horizontal reality, as it only extends another 200 feet ahead, but climbs more than 500 feet upwards, with many caves on precariously hung limestone ledges leading to other adventures. The canyon also drops 300 feet through a freezing shower caused by the stream, eventually ending in a cavern of ice.

The upper portions of the canyon are hunted by a gang of 1d4 cave fishers. The fishers mostly feed on cave crickets and the weird octopoid rats that lurk in this portion of the underworld.

Credit

The Cave Fisher originally appeared in the First Edition module *A4 In the Dungeons of the Slave Lords* (© TSR/Wizards of the Coast, 1981) and later in the First Edition *Monster Manual II* (© TSR/Wizards of the Coast, 1983) and is used by permission.

Copyright Notice

Author Scott Greene, based on original material by Lawrence Schick.

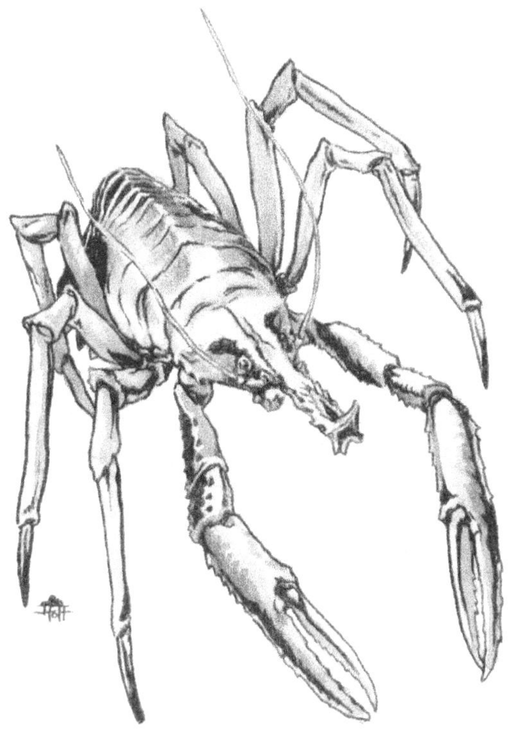

Cave Leech

Hit Dice: 5
Armor Class: 9 [10]
Attacks: 8 tentacles (1d4 blood drain) or bite (1d6)
Saving Throw: 12
Special: Blood drain
Move: 3
Alignment: Neutrality
Challenge Level/XP: 6/400

Cave leeches measure about 8 feet long and have a flattened semi-translucent body colored a sickly yellow or pale gray. Eight whip-like tentacles, each about 6 feet long protrude from the cave leech's body near its head. These tentacles contain rigid hairs that let the cave leech drain 1d4 hit points worth of blood with each strike. Hundreds of smaller tentacles line its body and aid in locomotion. The cave leech has a large, round mouth ringed with dozens of razor-like teeth.

The Opportunistic Leeches

A thin trickle of bloody water flows out of a rocky cave in the Malkan Peaks. The water courses over a jumble of recently fallen rocks that block much of the spillway. The streambed around the cave entrance is a muddy mess filled with blood-tinged puddles. Jutting lifelessly out of the rockfall dam is a hairy arm with a gold signet ring (20 gp) on one finger. Water seeps around the arm and flows down the rocks.

The ranger Hork Brambletread was looking for a lost bear cub when he discovered that a recent cave-in had nearly dammed up Flat Rock Creek. The intrepid outdoorsman clambered up a small waterfall to break loose the stone dam, but stumbled and fell into a narrow gap between two boulders. As water poured over him, the sputtering, frantic Hork flailed wildly, causing another rockfall that slowly suffocated the poor ranger. His body further blocks the flow of water. A four-foot-deep pool of water collects within the cave entry.

Feeding on Hork's pale, bloated corpse are three cave leeches. The cave leeches are aggressive, and fight to get at PCs investigating the dead ranger.

Copyright Notice
Author Scott Greene.

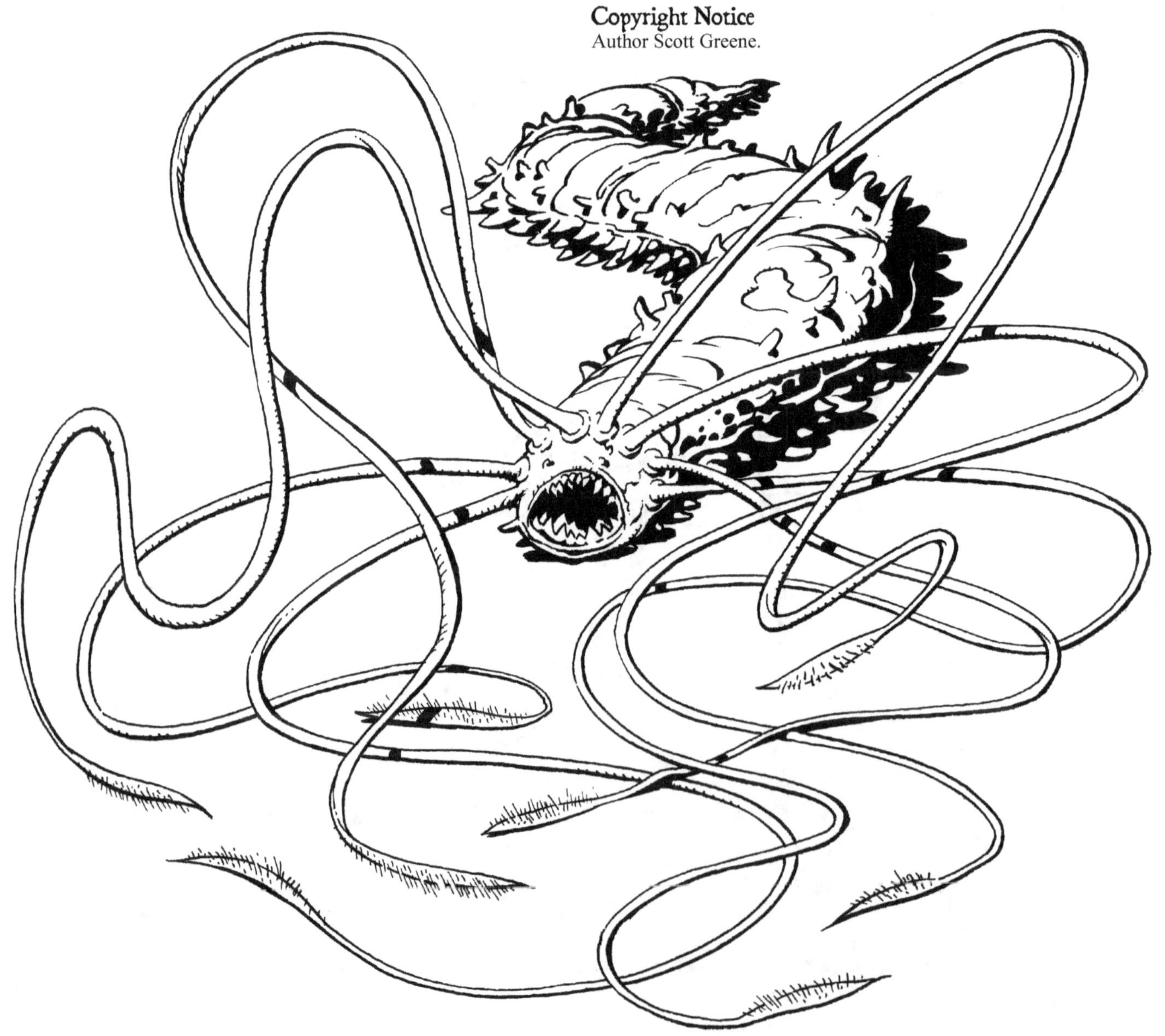

Cave Moray

Hit Dice: 4
Armor Class: 1 [18]
Attack: Bite (1d6)
Saving Throw: 13
Special: Recoil attack, surprise on 1-3 on 1d6
Move: 6
Alignment: Neutrality
Challenge Level/XP: 4/120

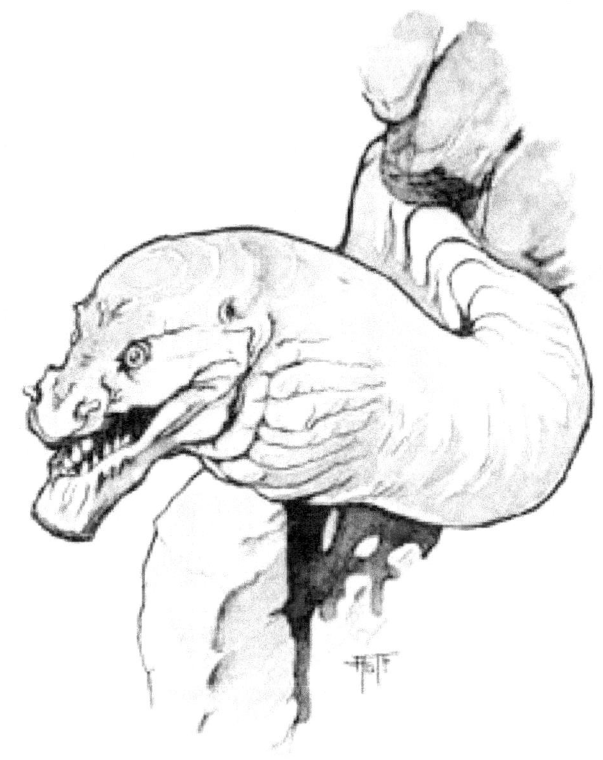

Cave morays are not related to moray eels, their name coming instead for a similarity in ferocity and habit between the two creatures. The cave moray is a slug-like creature, brownish-gray in color, about 5 feet long and 1 foot thick. Cave morays make their lairs underground in abandoned mines, dungeons, or natural occurring caves, usually near corridors, hallways or other areas of high traffic. Its lair is a burrow, just large enough for its body dug into the walls. Only one cave moray inhabits each burrow. Cave morays wait in their burrows, usually with a fellow on the opposite side of the passage, to ambush anyone walking down their passage. Cave morays enjoy a +1 bonus to hit when they attack a surprised opponent.

Curiosity Killed the Cat

The prospect of climbing into the circular shaft via the ice cold glass rungs is daunting. Add to that the brownish, bubbling liquid inside the rungs, greasy and smelling of cat fur and the blue vapors wafting gently out of the shaft and causing a tingling in the flesh and it is a bit too much. And that rheumatic cough that echoes from below. Egad! What could be down there?

Of course, no sane adventurer would have entered that shaft had they known it was inhabited by a colony of 1d6+10 cave morays, tucked neatly into their little burrows and perfectly aware of the weird lifting qualities of the vapor - that in fact living creatures cannot fall down the shaft after losing their grip on the rungs - just hanging in space, waiting for the pitiless beasts to recoil and attack.

Credit

The Cave Moray originally appeared in the First Edition module *S4 Lost Caverns of Tsojcanth* (© TSR/Wizards of the Coast, 1982) and later in the First Edition *Monster Manual II* (© TSR/Wizards of the Coast, 1983) and is used by permission. Cave morays made their first appearance in d20 in the Necromancer Games module *Tomb of Abysthor* by Clark Peterson (©2001, Clark Peterson, Necromancer Games, Inc.).

Copyright Notice

Authors Scott Greene and Clark Peterson, based on original material by Gary Gygax.

Cerberus

Hit Dice: 20 (120 hp)
Armor Class: 0 [19]
Attack: 3 bites (3d6)
Saving Throw: 3
Special: Breath weapon, howl, petrifying gaze, poisonous bite, +1 or better weapon to hit, regenerate 1d6 hit points per round, magic resistance (20%)
Move: 24
Alignment: Chaos
Challenge Level/XP: 29/6100

The triple-headed Cerberus (there is thankfully only one) is the guardian of Hades. He appears as a 10-foot long, three-headed black mastiff of the Molossian breed. Cerberus is tasked with the duty of keeping dead souls in Hades. If a dead soul attempts to pass beyond the Gates of Hades and back into the land of the living, Cerberus attacks relentlessly until that soul returns to Hades. If slain, the soul is immediately devoured by Cerberus and is lost forever. Cerberus is also tasked with keeping living creatures out of the land of the dead (adventurers being what they are, they love to journey to Hades). Living creatures that attempt to move past Cerberus into Hades (through the main gates) are immediately attacked.

Cerberus has a variety of potent attacks with which to carry out his duties. He usually begins a combat with a terrible, hair-raising howl that causes panic in those who hear it and fail a saving throw. This panic lasts for 2d4 rounds. Cerberus' saliva carries a deadly poison. The dog's center head can spit a stream of poison to a range of 30 feet. A creature meeting the gaze of all three heads must make a saving throw or be turned to stone (basalt, to be precise).

Cerberus is immune to any extraordinary, spell-like, or supernatural effect or spell that would teleport him or move him from his current location. Only deities can affect him with such magic. He is immune to death effects and disintegration and takes only half damage from acid, cold, electricity and fire.

Guard . . . Dogs?

On a gray plain, covered with a downy soft layer of lichens and interupted here and there with gnashing stalagmites hung with garlands of silvery blossoms, there stands a gate of black bronze. The gate bears no ornamentation and it is unlocked. No walls stand beside the gate, but it does pierce an ethereal barrier into the Land of the Dead, abode of Hades.

The gate swings open easily, though it gives an eerie groan. Beyond lies a heavy gloom and a light, sucking wind that chills the flesh and drowns the spirit. As one passes through the gate, they find themselves suddenly far beyond it, on a path of white pebbles edged by black poppies. Ahead there are pavilions of ghost-white marble, domed and unadorned and populated by spirits with downcast faces. The spirits do not speak or move, but one might glimpse one, now and then, bathed in an amber glow, their face upturned and for a mere moment smiling.

The path behind still leads to the gate, but between the trespasser and the gate stands a massive, black mastiff, three-headed and sitting on its haunches, its necks bent down vulture-style to allow its red eyes to leer and threaten. While one seeks the gate, they will alway find it at the center of the plain and Cerberus fronting it.

Copyright Notice
Author Scott Greene.

Cerebral Stalker

Hit Dice: 9
Armor Class: 7 [12]
Attacks: 2 claws (1d6+2) or bite (1d8+2)
Saving Throw: 6
Special: Consume brain, create zombie, fear gaze, web
Move: 6/3 (burrow)
Alignment: Chaos
Challenge Level/XP: 11/1,700

Cerebral stalkers are 6-foot tall bipedal creatures with blackish-gray scales covering their semi-reptilian form. A thick layer of mucus and slime drips from the creature's body. The cerebral stalker's bestial head sports vertical-slitted eyes of dull gray and a mouth filled with jagged teeth. Its hands are large and end in sharpened claws. A creature slain by a cerebral stalker's bite attack has its brain ripped out and consumed. The empty husk becomes a zombie in 1d4 rounds. A cerebral stalker's gaze instills fear (as per the spell of the same name) and three times per day, it can shoot sticky webbing from its body (as per a *web* spell).

Brrrrraaaiiiinnnsssss!

This large natural chamber overflows with zombies. At least 20 undead shuffle about the 50-foot-wide cavern, their eyes dull and lifeless. The sounds of their moaning bounces off the rocks. At the far end of the room, a 15-foot-tall hollow onyx skull hangs down from the ceiling, suspended about 10 feet over a flat brass altar. Blood drips down from a woman's torn body caught in the skull's carved teeth to spatter on the altar's engraved surface. Chunks of flesh and other unrecognizable bits of gore litter the brass plate. Behind the skull, a set of narrow stairs carved into the rock leads upward.

The stairs lead up to a cemetery crypt in the small village of Silhaven. Dismembered bodies lie in puddles of blood throughout the village, and the wails of people trapped inside the church can be heard. The church's doors and windows are boarded up from the inside, and 10 more zombies surround the structure, clawing at the building as they try to get at the tasty flesh trapped inside.

A cerebral stalker lairs in the underground temple. The zombies are Silhaven villagers it killed after finding this forgotten room beneath the town. The creature sleeps in the skull's lower jawbone and watches out the eye sockets if anyone enters the room. It uses its fear gaze on anyone meeting its stare, and leaps from the skull to attack while its zombies overrun intruders.

Copyright Notice
Author Scott Greene.

Chain Worm

Hit Dice: 12
Armor Class: 1 [18]
Attacks: 1 bite (2d6) and tail sting (2d6 + poison)
Saving Throw: 3
Special: Poison, trilling
Move: 9/6 (climb)
Alignment: Neutrality
Challenge Level/XP: 12/2,000

A chain worm is a massive centipede with a bright, reflective silver carapace. Its legs are dull silver and its oversized mandibles are black. A dull black stinger is located at the rear of its body. Chain worms stand nearly 6 feet tall and are about 10 feet long. By rapidly vibrating its carapace, a chain worm emits a high-pitched trilling sound that stuns and deafens all creatures within 30 feet (save resists).

As the Worm Turns

A thin, undulating portal of yellowish goo hangs suspended in the middle of this barren 80-foot square room, held upright by a gleaming silver frame carved with images of conquering worms consuming writhing humans. The goo wobbles if touched, but doesn't break, despite appearing to be paper thin. The chamber is nearly 60 feet tall.

The silver frame is a foot in diameter and stands nearly 15 feet tall. It is 10 feet wide from side to side and sits in the center of a 15-foot-diameter silver disk flush with the marble floor. A 20-foot-long chain worm skitters along the outer edge of the disk in a one-foot-wide groove, its movement causing the entire disk to rotate slowly. The worm ignores PCs unless they try to enter the frame or stop it from running in circles around the groove.

If the platform stops rotating, the shimmering goo pulses with an audible thrumming. Within 2d4 rounds of standing still, a purple worm is expelled through the goo curtain into the chamber. The portal could lead PCs anywhere the Game Referee wishes.

Purple Worm: HD 15; AC 6[13]; Atk 1 bite (2d12), 1 sting (1d8 + poison); Move 9; Save 3; CL/XP 17/3500; Special: Poison sting, swallow whole.

Copyright Notice
Author Scott Greene.

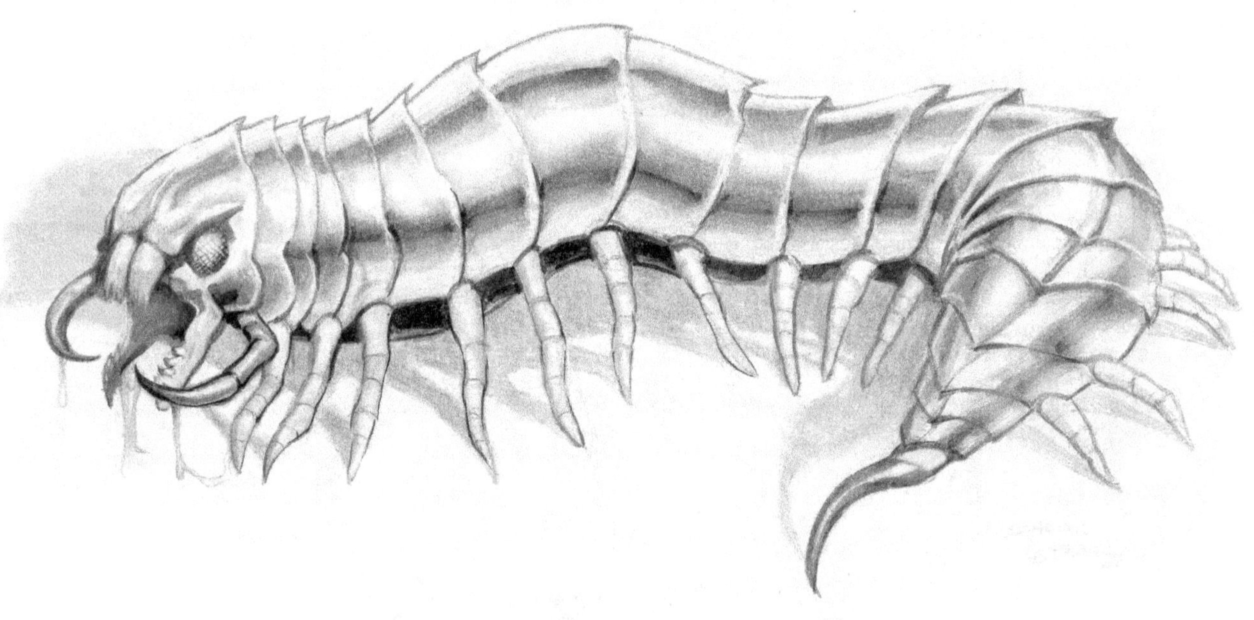

Cherum

Hit Dice: 24
Armor Class: -3 [22]
Attacks: 2 claws (2d8 + 1d6 fire) and bite (4d6 + 1d6 fire)
Saving Throw: 3
Special: Fiery aura, swallow whole, regenerate 5 hp/round, immune to fire and poison, vulnerable to cold, spell resistance (30%)
Move: 6
Alignment: Neutrality
Challenge Level/XP: 27/6,500

This hairless mountain of slick raw burning flesh constantly sizzles and oozes with the stench of burning fat. Two long meaty arms sprout from a hugely obese frame; its head appears to be little more than a bald sloping brow with black pits for eyes. Its maw splits open to reveal cavernous jaws, teeth glowing like huge red hot coals. A cherum stands about 70 feet tall and weighs well over 40,000 pounds. Anyone within 40 feet of a cherum takes 6d6 points of fire damage each round (save for half) from the blazing heat radiating off the creature's body. If a cherum rolls a natural 20 on its bite attack, it swallows an opponent whole and does an automatic 4d6 points of damage each round to the creature. Cherum's heal 5 hit points per round while touching flame or lava.

The Burning Crater of Ashgaba

Nearly a century ago a massive underground cavern collapsed near the sprawling city of Ashgaba on the outskirts of the Kanderi Desert. A cherum burrowing up from the depths caused the collapse. Natural gas swept into the city, killing most of the citizens overnight as the toxic fumes washed over dwellings. Flames ignited the gas, causing even more devastation. The gas in the city has since burnt off, and people have resettled the oasis city. The collapsed cavern left a massive crater just outside the walls of the city. The crater burns continuously as natural gas seeps through the rubble of the collapse. The result is a 100-foot-deep crater more than 600 feet across with a bowl-shaped floor filled with flaming rocks.

The citizens of Ashgaba blame the destruction of their city on the anger of the gods. Twice each year during a solar eclipse, Ashgaba holds a mass ritual sacrifice to appease the gods. They sacrifice eight virgins (two for each of the elements) by casting them into the flaming crater. The cherum remains in the bottom of the crater, content with the constant sacrifices. The cherum becomes quite angry if its needs are not met.

Elgra, an elderly woman, pleads on the streets for someone to save her teenage granddaughter, her only surviving relative. Darvaza was selected to be sacrificed during the next eclipse in 10 days. If Darvaza is rescued, Elgra offers Darvaza and her dowry as a reward for saving her grandchild.

Copyright Notice

Chrystone

Hit Dice: 5
Armor Class: 4 [15]
Attack: Longsword (1d8)
Saving Throw: 12
Special: Breath weapon, spells, immune to magic, resistance to non-magical weapons (50%), shatter weapons
Move: 9
Alignment: Neutrality
Challenge Level/XP: 8/800

Chrystones are humanoid creatures made of rock and crystal that normally stand just over 5 feet tall. Their coloration varies by the types of crystal and rock they absorb, giving each chrystone a unique pattern of striations and coloration that makes them easy to tell apart. Originally imbued with life by a spellcaster in a ritual involving the blood of several dragons and a demon, chrystones grow new offspring through budding. To form a new bud, a chrystone must consume several times its weight in crystals and consume at least 300 gp worth of gems. The bud continues to grow from the chrystone's back until it is large enough to separate. Each chrystone offspring retains the memories and knowledge of its entire parental line.

In battle, a chrystone can exhale a 20-foot cone of rainbow colors up to three times per day. Creatures with 2 HD or less are blinded and knocked unconscious for 2d4 rounds and remain blinded for an additional 1d4 rounds after regaining consciousness. Creatures with 3 or more HD are blinded for 1d4 rounds. Sightless creatures are not affected by the chrystone's breath weapon.

Chrystones can use the *stone shape* spell at will and the stone tell spell twice per day. They are immune to all spells save *transmute rock to mud*, which slows them for 2d6 rounds, *transmute mud to rock*, which restores all lost hit points to them, *stone shape*, which acts as a *cure light wounds* spell, and *stone to flesh*, which does not turn them into flesh, but does negate their immunity to magic for 1 round.

Whenever a character strikes a chrystone with a weapon (magical or nonmagical), the wielder must succeed on a saving throw or shatter into pieces. A magic weapon adds its own bonus to the saving throw. If the weapon breaks, the chrystone takes no damage from the attack.

When a chrystone is destroyed, it shatters, spraying razor-sharp fragments from its form. Creatures within 5 feet of the chrystone take 2d6 points of damage. A saving throw halves the damage.

Rock Band

The broad valley of the basalt pillars and the sheer bordering cliffs is a land of unceasing war. The largest of the pillars serve as fortresses with cunningly hidden entrances and arrow slits, each occupied by a squad of 1d6+14 chrystones. The prismatic crystalline creatures hide in their fortresses, hoarding gems and jewels they have stolen from travelers, one another, or retrieved from the ground. They drive their kobold slaves lower and lower, watching intently to make sure they do not undermine their own fortresses. Scouts sit atop each tower, watching the other scouts, hurling insults from time to time or rushing down into the fortress to announce the presence of outsiders.

When outsiders come to the valley, the pillars disgorge their warriors, who surround the hapless travelers demanding gems and fighting with the other chrystones for the right to the visitor's wealth. Perhaps someday one conglomerate of chrystones will destroy the others and found a kingdom in the valley, but given the requirements for budding and the enmity and cunning of the kobold slaves, this is unlikely.

Credit

The Chrystone first appeared in the **Necromancer Games** module *Hall of the Rainbow Mage* by Patrick Lawinger (©2002, Necromancer Games, Inc.).

Copyright Notice

Author Patrick Lawinger.

Chupacabra

Hit Dice: 3
Armor Class: 5 [14]
Attacks: 2 claws (1d3) and bite (1d4)
Saving Throw: 14
Special: Drain blood
Move: 9
Alignment: Neutrality
Challenge Level/XP: 4/120

The chupacabra is a fur-covered bipedal creature is 3 or 4 feet tall with a hunched back, red eyes, and a mouth filled with sharpened teeth. A flexible rows of spines run down its back. Chupacabras are small terrifying bloodsuckers that lurk on the fringes of society, emerging at night to drain the blood of warm-blooded creatures. If a chupacabra hits a single opponent with both claws, it latches on and begins sucking the creatures blood with an automatic bite attack that does 1d4 points of damage each round thereafter. There is a 10% chance that any chupacabra encountered has wings (Fly 15).

The Child in the Well

A crowd of people gathers around a stone well in the center of the small village of Reynwald. A few hold ropes and even a short ladder. People are pushing and jostling to get to the front of the group to see what's going on. Nearly 20 people are crowded around the scene, nearly the entire community. Jurgen Horstman, the village elder, tries to keep order. The villagers think a small child has fallen into the dry well, and are frantic to save the youth. They can just barely see him moving around in the dark at the bottom of the 60-foot-deep pit. A few are breaking out torches as the sun sets.

The "child" is actually a chupacabra lurking at the bottom of the well as bait. It is part of a colony of 10 that lives under the town in a large cavern containing a dry underground lake. The lake used to feed the well before it dried up. The chupacabras expanded the small opening to get into the well, and were going to invade the town that night. Instead, someone heard one of the diggers clawing at the tunnel and thought it was a child trying to get out. Anyone lowered into the well is dragged into the side tunnel where the chupacabra wait in the darkness.

Copyright Notice
Author Erica Balsley.

Church Grim

Hit Dice: 5
Armor Class: 7 [12]
Attacks: Bite (1d6)
Saving Throw: 12
Special: Howl, +1 or better weapons to hit, soul defender
Move: 15
Alignment: Lawful
Challenge Level/XP: 6/400

Church grims are good sprits that guard cemeteries from those who seek to steal from the dead, or those who wish to desecrate the sanctity of the graves there. They appear as large black dogs, roving protectively among the tombstones at night. The eyes of a church grim see all evil that crosses into its territory, and it spares no mercy for such trespassers. The howl of a church grim causes any Chaotic creature to save or flee in terror for 2d4 rounds (save resists). Church grims are partly incorporeal, requiring +1 or better weapons to hit. A church grim that is destroyed reforms in 24 hours. *Animate dead* or similar spells to create undead fizzle when a church grim is around as the creature defends the dead souls under its protection.

Watchers on the Water

The Bunford River winds through the Krieger hills at a leisurely pace, the 30-foot-deep channel funneling through narrow straits. The water runs green from floating algae, and glows at night under the full moon. Several low stone bridges rise barely 10 feet over the water. Several fishing poles are set in stone holders on the bridge, their long lines dragging in the water. Floating on the water are several funeral barges, each elaborately decorated and piled with weapons, shields and gold. Several appear to have been set ablaze, but haven't burned completely. The honored dead rest in silent repose in the center of the floating biers, their arms folded over their brawny chests. The dead are barbarians from a nearby tribe killed during a battle with the red dragon Horvoraxx the Crimson Death.

The barges are partially burned from fires set as they were pushed into the river. A rain squall extinguished the flames not long afterward. The barges drift until they sink. Five church grims walk alongside the funeral barges to protect the honored dead and their belongings. The dogs walk easily atop the slow-moving current, their heads down in a somber, silent processional. One occasionally raises its head in a mournful howl, the baying full of grief and pain. The church grims leave creatures on the banks alone, and only attack someone foolish enough to try to steal something off one of the barges. They don't react if PCs fire flaming arrows into the barges. The incorporeal grims vanish when the barges burn completely or sink into the deep river.

Churr

Hit Dice: 6
Armor Class: 4 [15]
Attacks: 2 claws (1d6) and bite (1d6)
Saving Throw: 11
Special: Constrict, howl
Move: 9/6 (climb)
Alignment: Neutrality
Challenge Level/XP: 6/400

Churrs are savage ape-like creatures found in heavily forested areas. They are fairly intelligent, standing 8 feet tall and weighing about 800 pounds. If a churr hits a single opponent with both claws, it grabs the foe and constricts for an additional 1d6 points of damage. A churr can unleash a frightening howl that causes all creatures within 60 feet to flee in fear (as per a *fear* spell) if they fail a save.

Knowledge for All and None

In the northern reaches of the Seething Jungle, hidden far from prying eyes, a fire-blasted landscape opens among the wild palm fronds and grasping vines. A village of churr lives on the edges of this forsaken desolation of blackened lava rock, their dwellings little more than mud huts dug into the jungle dirt. Sticks and wide-leaf palm fronds cover these bare huts.

Standing in the middle of the village is a 12-foot-tall smooth black monolith formed of igneous rock. This black featureless slab of stone has no markings, and absorbs the sunlight burning down on it. The churr carry bone clubs and protect the black stone with a fierce passion. The churr worship the stone as their "god" and claim it speaks to them in sibilant whispers to guide their lives. Anyone staring at the monolith starts seeing black sigils move across its depths, and points of unnoticed light sparking along the edges. Its true purpose is left to the Game Referee to decide.

Before the slab appeared on the volcanic field, the churr fought with their hands; they quickly learned to craft crude weapons after it appeared. Outsiders are not permitted to approach the deity and are viciously attacked if they try. The churr fear others will take their god and leave them clawing in the mud again.

Clam, Giant

Hit Dice: 4
Armor Class: 5 [14]
Attack: Bite (swallow)
Saving Throw: 13
Special: Acid, surprise on 1-3 on 1d6
Move: 3
Alignment: Neutrality
Challenge Level/XP: 4/120

Giant clams are generally found in coastal waters no deeper than 60 feet from the surface of the water. Many species of giant clams subsist strictly on a diet of sunlight, and as such are never found in deeper waters where sunlight cannot reach. Such giant clams are generally found in shallow seas or attached to coral reefs near the surface. Other species of giant clams feed not only on sunlight but also on what they can filter from the water, usually small plants and animals, and sometimes the occasional swimmer. A giant clam moves by pushing out a small "foot" and sliding itself along. Victims of the giant clam's bite attack must pass a saving throw or be swallowed. The giant clam uses a slow-acting acid to break down its meals, inflicting 1d2 points of damage each round. Victims lodged inside the creature can escape with a successful strength check. Otherwise, it opens on its own in 1d4 hours.

Seafood Cocktail

At the bottom of a sheer, chalk precipice the giant clams clutter the bottom of the shallow, silty sea. For lesser folk, the clam fields are best avoided. But for the stone giants of the coast, the clams are easy pickings. The stone giants are cliff divers, vaulting into the chilly waters and wrestling the giant clams from the bottom. From their shells they make ceremonial gowns and other tools. The meat is roasted or stewed and the juice is spiced with mint and imbibed as a cocktail (one few other living creatures will drink). The clams also serve as final justice for intruders condemned by the whispers of the sea goddess carried on the salty winds that sweep the coast.

Credit

The Giant Clam originally appeared in the First Edition module *EX2 Land Beyond the Magic Mirror* (© TSR/Wizards of the Coast, 1983) and is used by permission.

Copyright Notice

Author Scott Greene, based on original material by Gary Gygax.

Clamor

Hit Dice: 4
Armor Class: 3 [16]
Attacks: sonic ray (2d6)
Saving Throw: 13
Special: Sonic burst, mimic, +2 magic weapons to hit, invisibility
Move: 24 (flying)
Alignment: Neutrality
Challenge Level/XP: 7/600

A clamor is a strange, extraplanar creature composed entirely of sound waves. Normally invisible, a clamor looks like a field of shifting patterns of vibrations and oscillations approximately 5 feet across and about as tall. Clamors can perfectly mimic any sound they encounter. Clamors tend to avoid combat, instead staying back and "playing back" any sound they hear. If attacked, the clamor blasts opponents with a high frequency sonic beam. If overwhelmed, it uses its sonic burst to escape. This burst of sound can be heard for miles. Any creature within 100 feet of the clamor must save or be stunned for 1d3 rounds. Anyone within 50 feet must save or be permanently deafened. If attacked, the clamor focuses its sonic ray on the opponent.

Bar Fight

The Ruddy Rooster is alive with pretty maids dancing, men singing uproariously near the hearth, and celebrating patrons toasting the magic-user Zandon the Unpredictable. The magic-user recently (and quite by accident) drove off a horde of mimis infesting the city's grain silo. The miniature pranksters moved on, but decided to leave one last surprise for the townsfolk.

When the Rooster opened, the barkeep found 6 casks of wine lined up on the bar. A large red ribbon wrapped twice around the barrels. A bow sprinkled with glittering pollen sat on top. A note in flourishing handwriting read: "For Zandon, Raise a Glass – Loudly – For All He Does."

The tavern has tapped three of the kegs, and is pouring wine freely to anyone wanting a glass. Zandon sits in the middle of the revelry, downing glass after glass and getting quite drunk.

The fourth keg holds the mimis' surprise: They trapped a clamor in the cask as a farewell present to the town. Tapping the keg causes the barrel to explode and the clamor rises into the middle of the tavern.

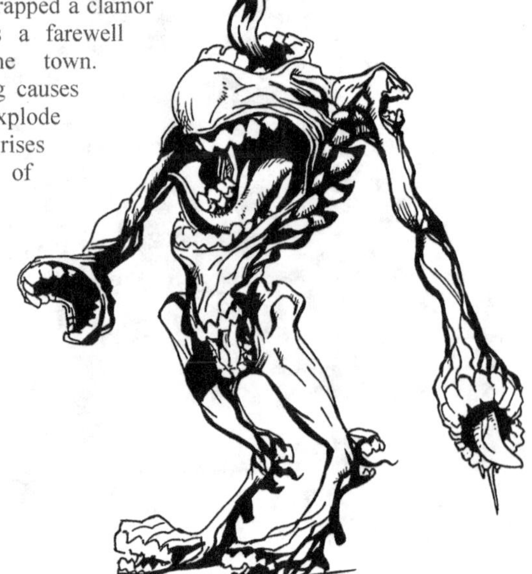

Copyright Notice

Author Erica Balsley.

CLOCKWORKS

Clockworks are the creations of powerful machines called brain gears.

Each clockwork creature varies from its brethren and each is assigned a task by the brain gear that created it. Clockworks are automatons and follow orders without question. It is through these various clockwork creations that brain gears seek to destroy all living creatures. They come in a wide variety of shapes and sizes.

The clockwork creations controlled by a brain gear share several characteristics. Most constructs are immediately destroyed when reduced to 0 hit points. Clockworks with the self-repair special quality, however, are not destroyed at 0 or less hit points. While they do cease to function, they continue to self-repair, only at a slower rate. Once it has self-repaired itself to at least 1 hit point, the clockwork begins functioning normally again.

Some clockworks (see below) can automatically repair themselves with spare parts and scrap, and a built-in mechanism allows them to self-repair even when seemingly destroyed. The clockwork automatically heals damage at a fixed rate per round, as given in the clockwork's entry. Certain attack forms, typically acid, cold, and fire cannot be self-repaired. The clockwork's descriptive text describes the details.

A clockwork with self-repair can repair lost limbs (including its head), but it takes 3d6 rounds to do so. A clockwork reduced to 0 or less hit points is not destroyed, but begins to self-repair damage at one-half its normal rate (minimum 1 hit point per round). It still cannot repair damage dealt by acid, cold, or fire effects. For example, a clockwork with self-repair 3 normally regains 3 hit points per round. If reduced to 0 or less hit points, it regains 1 hit point per round until it has at least 1 hit point (at which time it self-repairs at its normal rate).

Clockwork Brain Gear

Hit Dice: 5
Armor Class: 2 [17]
Attack: None
Saving Throw: 12
Special: Control clockworks, dream
Move: 0
Alignment: Neutrality
Challenge Level/XP: 3/60

The original brain gear began as little more than a collection of gears, chains, counterweights, and levers, but was enhanced and grown into a controlling intellect through a process very similar to flesh golem creation. A brain gear in its true form resembles nothing more than a copper or gold box or cube that shines with a pale blue light. It is immobile, cannot attack, or speak. The casing of a brain gear is so hard that it ignores up to 5 points of damage from physical attacks.

A brain gear is designed to control the actions of all other clockworks created by its own creator, relieving the creator of having to oversee simple operations of the clockworks. It is rumored that some brain gears occasionally develop an evil intellect and turn their charges against its creator. Any clockwork that comes within two miles of a brain gear immediately falls under that brain gear's control. If more than one brain gear attempts to control a clockwork (or if the clockwork is under the control of another brain gear or overseer), each gear must make a saving throw; the brain gear beating its saving throw by the most gains control of that clockwork.

When a clockwork moves more than 2 miles away from a brain gear, it continues to perform the last order given to it, but there is a 25% percent chance each hour that it ceases to function, collapsing into a pile of junk. If a brain gear later moves within two miles of the destroyed clockwork, the clockwork can reactivate if it has the self-repair ability. Otherwise, it remains destroyed.

A brain gear in control of at least one clockwork can use that clockwork to perceive the world through its senses. This ability has a range of 2 miles. A brain gear can switch control from one clockwork to another once per round. A brain gear uses this ability to give commands to its clockworks, allowing the usually mindless creatures to fight with highly coordinated tactics. Each clockwork is capable of receiving roughly 100 words worth of orders. Anything beyond that is too complicated for the clockwork to handle.

The brain gear has a limited ability to send psychic messages to multiple creatures of a particular type (human, ogre, etc) through their dreams.

The secrets of clockwork construction are known only to the brain gear and to those it employs.

Clockwork Drone

Hit Dice: 1d6
Armor Class: 2 [17]
Attack: Slam (1d3)
Saving Throw: 18
Special: None
Move: 9/24 (flying)
Alignment: Neutrality
Challenge Level/XP: B/10

Clockwork drones appear as human eyeballs encased within flat, metal disks. Imbued with magic that allows it to fly, a drone's approach is announced by a low buzzing sound caused by its tiny gears and pistons working furiously to maintain this magical field. These clockworks are designed to act as observers. When a drone finds an advantageous position from which to maintain its watch, it uses a small, metallic claw on its underside to attach itself to a surface. Drones usually avoid combat at all costs. When they are pressed into fighting, they prefer to aid their fellow clockworks by distracting their enemies.

Clockwork Overseer

Hit Dice: 2
Armor Class: 2 [17]
Attack: Slam (1d6)
Saving Throw: 16
Special: None
Move: 15
Alignment: Neutrality
Challenge Level/XP: 2/30

Overseers are a recent invention of the brain gears. They look like three-foot tall wooden dolls with long, slender limbs. An overseer can journey up to 10 miles away from a brain gear while maintaining contact with it. An overseer acts as a field commander for brain gears, controlling up to 20 HD worth of clockworks that are within 100 feet of its position so long as the overseer remains within 10 miles of the brain gear. An overseer avoids direct combat at all costs under direct orders of a brain gear. If cornered with no way of escaping, an overseer fights, and attempts to flee as soon as possible.

Clockwork Parasite

Hit Dice: 4
Armor Class: 4 [15]
Attack: Bite (1d4)
Saving Throw: 13
Special: Control host, self-repair
Move: 9
Alignment: Neutrality
Challenge Level/XP: 5/240

Clockwork parasites are fist-sized constructs that resemble mechanical beetles. They burrow into the skulls of the recently dead and reanimate the body using electrical impulses to control and direct the corpse. The animated corpses look and fight like zombies, though they cannot be turned or controlled. A host brought to 0 or less hit points is destroyed, but can be repaired by the clockwork parasite using its self-repair ability (though this only works if the host is brought to 0 or less hit points; a host does not gain the self-repair ability of the parasite while "alive"). A clockwork parasite regains 3 hit points per round. Damage dealt from acid, cold, or fire effects cannot be self-repaired. If reduced to 0 or less hit points, it regains 1 hit point per round (but still cannot repair damage caused by acid, cold, or fire effects) until it has at least 1 hit point (at which time it begins to self-repair at its normal rate of 3 hit points per round).

Clockwork Scout

Hit Dice: 1
Armor Class: 2 [17]
Attack: Slam (1d4)
Saving Throw: 17
Special: None
Move: 15
Alignment: Neutrality
Challenge Level/XP: 1/15

Scouts are constructed to resemble animals commonly found in the area that the brain gear operates within. Their inner wood and metal workings are covered by an animal's pelt. Characters have only a 1 in 6 chance to notice the deception (2 in 6 for demi-humans and 3 in 6 for druids and rangers). This camouflage helps them move about unnoticed and gives them the opportunity to strike from ambush. They are designed to serve as the mobile eyes and ears of a clockwork colony. While still restricted by the 2-mile radius they must remain within to keep contact with a brain gear, scouts serve an important role as reconnaissance, patrol, and pursuit troops. Only if the scouts have a chance to strike from a devastating ambush does the brain gear order them into battle.

Clockwork Swarm

Hit Dice: 4
Armor Class: 2 [17]
Attack: Swarm (1d6)
Saving Throw: 13
Special: Distraction, minimum damage from slashing and piercing weapons, self-repair
Move: 15
Alignment: Neutrality
Challenge Level/XP: 7/600

Clockwork swarms are a collection of tiny, insect-like clockworks that work together as a single creature. An individual member of the swarm poses little threat. Yet when acting in concert, a swarm poses a deadly threat to adventurers. Much like the clockwork warrior, the clockwork swarm forms a fighting frame from random pieces of trash, debris, and other cast-offs. The swarm, however, is much more capable of adapting to new situations and surviving combat. Unless the individual components of the swarm are destroyed, it simply reforms and continues its attack. Area of effect attacks, such as burning oil, *fireball*, or *lightning bolt* are the most effective means of destroying the swarm. A clockwork swarm typically appears as a ramshackle collection of spare parts and garbage draped in a thick, web-like substance and arranged in a vaguely humanoid form. Living creatures engulfed by the clockwork swarm must pass a saving throw or be unable to act during that round.

A clockwork swarm regains 3 hit points per round. Damage dealt from acid, cold, or fire effects cannot be self-repaired. If a clockwork swarm takes damage from an area attack, it is unable to repair itself for 1d6 rounds following the attack. If reduced to 0 or less hit points, it regains 1 hit point per round (but still cannot repair damage caused by acid, cold, or fire effects) until it has at least 1 hit point (at which time it begins to self-repair at its normal rate of 3 hit points per round).

Clockwork Titan

Hit Dice: 7
Armor Class: 0 [19]
Attack: Slam (2d8)
Saving Throw: 9
Special: None
Move: 12
Alignment: Neutrality
Challenge Level/XP: 8/800

Clockwork titans are huge, crab-like mechanical monstrosities. They have saucer-shaped hulls set atop four spindly legs that allow it to move with surprising speed and agility. Two iron-shod fists are mounted on the front of the hull. The clockwork titan has a long reach, and can attack from behind a line of clockwork warriors.

Clockwork Warrior

Hit Dice: 3
Armor Class: 2 [17]
Attack: Slam (1d8)
Saving Throw: 14
Special: Self-repair
Move: 9
Alignment: Neutrality
Challenge Level/XP: 4/120

Clockwork warriors are constructed from a wide range of materials but take the same general form of a 6-foot tall armored humanoid. They all feature a "nervous system" of thin steel wires that controls their individual pieces. Tiny clockworks that look much like metallic cockroaches infest the warrior, working to repair damage sustained by this construct. These tiny clockworks repair 1 hit point per round. Acid, fire, and cold effects destroy these maintenance clockworks, thus preventing the warrior from repairing damage from those sources. Unlike clockwork swarms (see below), the clockworks that repair the warrior lack the intelligence and sophistication to tackle any other task.

A.I. Spells Armageddon

The wizard's tomb (place it where you will) was a marvel to people near and far. On the exterior, a proper crypt of bronze decorated with automatons that, at different times of the day and year, performed complex pageants from the life and times of the wizard, from his apprenticeship to his mastery of the magical arts. What powered the giant clockwork device was unknown, but it was known that the crypt never wore down and assumed that some magical agent was responsible for the crypt's maintenance. At each winter solstice, an automaton of the wizard appears atop the crypt with a great cauldron, and shooting stars streak from his fingers as a sinuous marilith rises from the cauldron, flashes its blades and then returns to the cauldron.

Little do the onlookers know that the appearance of the cauldron offers them a chance, however slight, of preventing catastrophe. The old wizard had one final triumph before he expired - the creation of a brain gear. For decades he had slaved away in his workshop, making his clocks and his automatons and putting them to work excavating a large tomb, the top of which would be is marvelous clockwork crypt.

Beneath the surface, in cold, lightless halls, a terrible device was assembled. The halls now click and clack with the movement of gears and trip hammers, all centered around the mainspring and the brain gear. The appearance of the cauldron is the only time a small opening appears in the crypt - a way into the heart of the machine and the slim chance of stopping it before it completes the final phase of the wizard's revenge and unleashes an army of clockworks on the world bent on the final triumph of machine over man.

Credit

Clockworks and the Brain Gear first appeared in *G1 Siege of Durgam's Folly* by Mike Mearls (©2001, Necromancer Games, Inc.).

Copyright Notice

Authors Mike Mearls and Scott Greene.

Clockwork Bronze Giant

Hit Dice: 14
Armor Class: 0 [19]
Attacks: 1 Weapon (4d6 plus poison) or 1 fist (2d8)
Saving Throw: 3
Special: magic resistance (25%), +1 magic weapon needed to hit, throw rocks (2d8), lightning heals, immune to most spells
Move: 12
Alignment: Neutrality
Challenge Level/XP: 16/3,200

A clockwork bronze giant is a massive automaton standing 25 feet tall constructed entirely of bronze. Other clockwork giants are rumored to be crafted of iron, steel, bronze or other metals. Clockworks giants have no mind of their own and follow commands and orders given by their creator. Lightning heals a 3 hit points per level of the spell cast at a clockwork bronze giant. They are immune to all other spells.

Zenith of Time

On the plateau of a mountain peak stand seven clockwork bronze giants. Each one stands at the point of a mosaic eight-pointed star set into the rock. One of the clockwork giants is missing.

Coral and barnacles cover the first clockwork bronze giant, as if it has stood in the ocean for a long period of time. The second bronze clockwork giant stands tarnished and stained, and rotted vines and moss have left vein-like striations on the giant's bronze skin. The third giant is bright and shiny, its highly polished bronze shell glimmering in the sunlight. The fourth clockwork giant has muted features, as if it had stood in an extremely hot setting that softened its features almost to nonexistence. The next giant wears faded organic paint and necklaces of chains and crudely carved skulls. The sixth shows signs of battle, and its head is missing. Arrows of orcish origin remain wedged in its body. The seventh dirt-filled giant has plants and small trees growing from its cavities.

Each of these automated giants holds aloft a mace-like scepter toward the center of the star. An octahedron-shaped garnet the size of a human skull tops each scepter. The garnet tips atop the scepters touch in the air above the center of the star. Directly below the garnets in the center of the star pattern is a 12-inch-diameter brick hole that descends into the mountainside. The midday sun faintly sends a red beam of light from the garnets into the hole. The giants attack anyone disturbing the hole in the ground. Careful study of the star reveals that the eight-pointed star represents a solar calendar spanning 80-year intervals. Whatever the clockwork bronze giants were designed for will take place soon.

Clubnek

Hit Dice: 2
Armor Class: 6 [13]
Attack: 2 claws (1d4) and beak (1d6)
Saving Throw: 16
Special: Burst of speed
Move: 15
Alignment: Neutrality
Challenge Level/XP: 2/30

A clubnek is a large flightless bird resembling a green ostrich with an oversized beak that it uses to pound and bite. Found roaming meadowlands and forests, it is primarily a herbivore subsisting on a diet of plants and flowers, though it is given to flights of unpredictability when it takes the role of hunter and predator. A clubnek stands 7 feet tall and weighs about 350 pounds. Clubneks are generally nonaggressive unless threatened or frightened, though they are known to occasionally have fits of erratic behavior that cause them to become quite aggressive. In such a case, they attack until slain or driven off. If its prey attempts to flee, the clubnek often runs it down and continues combat. Once every 5 rounds, a clubnek can move five times its normal speed when it makes a charge.

Freedom

A flock of 2d4 clubnecks has managed to trap itself within the entrance to a dungeon. The birds have made a terrible mess of the place and are nearly starving when adventurers make the mistake of opening the door to their prison. All at once, the skiddish beasts will bolt for the opening (whether it is an exit or carries them deeper into the maze), trampling anyone in their path.

The room is now caked with feathers and dung. When disturbed, the powdery dung might enter the lungs, infecting them with a disease (save allowed) that causes shortness of breath and causes the skin around the mouth and eyes to become dry and brittle. The diseased suffer a -1 penalty to saving throws and temporarily lose 1 hit point per hit dice or level from exhaustion. A new saving throw can be made every three days, with back to back successful saves required to shake off the malady.

Credit

The Clubnek originally appeared in the First Edition *Fiend Folio* (© TSR/Wizards of the Coast, 1981) and is used by permission.

Copyright Notice

Author Scott Greene, based on original material by M. English.

Cobra Flower

Hit Dice: 6
Armor Class: 5 [14]
Attack: Bite (1d8 + 1d6 acid)
Saving Throw: 11
Special: Squeeze
Move: 3
Alignment: Neutrality
Challenge Level/XP: 7/600

Cobra flowers are tall, slender plants with large, flowering bulbs and brownish-green roots. Two large, green leaves flank its flowering top, giving the appearance of a cobra's hood. Its leaves are thin and have transparent blotches on them. Cobra flowers draw nutrients from sunlight, the soil, and water, but enjoy a diet of insects, rodents, animals, and even humans and demi-humans when available. The creatures can be found nesting in forests and often take up residence near small population areas where they can feed on humanoids who wander into their area. Many a child's or adult's disappearance can be attributed to a cobra flower. When a cobra flower detects a living creature, it remains motionless until its prey is within 5 feet. It then spreads its leafy hood, opens its flowery bulb, and bites its prey, secreting acidic enzymes to break down and digest the victim. Cobra flowers can also wrap their thick stems around an opponent with a successful attack, holding their prey still, squeezing them for 1d8 points of damage per round and increasing their chance to hit with their bite attack by +2.

Funeral Garland

In an octagonal room of swirled gray marble, measuring 30-ft across. The room contains 1d3+1 potted cobra flowers, basking under the light of several spheres hanging from the ceiling. In the center of the room, amidst the cobra flowers, there lies the dead body of a woman on a marble slab, her flesh eaten away and her white robes tattered.

The corpse is a wraith, and wears a large, bronze key around its neck. It waits to attack until one has battled through the cobra flowers and approached the slab. The bronze key only works if struck against the marble slab, releasing a tone that causes one of the stone walls of the octagonal room to vanish, revealing a chamber containing 3d6 x 1,000 sp and 1d6 x 1,000 gp.

Copyright Notice

Author Scott Greene.

Coffer Corpse

Hit Dice: 2
Armor Class: 5 [14]
Attack: Slam (1d6)
Saving Throw: 16
Special: Death grip, weapon resistance, deceiving death, cause fear
Move: 9
Alignment: Chaos
Challenge Level/XP: 5/240

The coffer corpse is an undead creature formed as the result of an incomplete death ritual. It looks like a desiccated corpse shrouded in rotting, tattered funerary clothes. It is often found haunting stranded funeral barges or in other situations where a corpse has not been delivered to its final resting place. The creature hates life and attacks living creatures on sight. In combat, coffer corpses attempt to grasp their opponents around the throat, strangling them for 1d6 damage per round. A creature in the coffer corpse's death grip cannot cast spells and can only break free by rolling an open doors check on a d8. Coffer corpses can only be harmed by magic weapons, and suffer minimal damage from edged and piercing weapons. Any time an attack is successful, regardless of the weapon used, damage dice should be rolled. If apparent (or real, in the case of magical bludgeoning damage) is 6 or higher, the coffer corpse appears to fall to the ground, destroyed. If the horror had a victim in its death grip, it will release its hold and then fall to the ground. On its next turn, however, it will rise again as if reanimated. A creature viewing this apparent reanimation must make a saving throw or become panicked for 2d4 rounds.

River of Corpses

Descending a set of narrow, stone stairs, you find yourself in a long tunnel, the ends of which disappear into darkness. The middle of the tunnel is taken up by a slowly flowing river of bilious green liquid. 1d6 corpses (coffer corpses, as it turns out) are either floating down the river or have run aground on the sloping banks, for the cross section of the tunnel would reveal it to be circular.

It's impossible to walk down the tunnel without getting one's feet wet, without the use of magic, of course. Spaced irregularly down the tunnel are openings covered with rusty grates. The entrances are placed at roughly chest height for an adult male. As soon as one enters the tunnel and wades a bit in the water (it is 2 feet deep at its deepest), the coffer corpses animate and attack.

Fleeing more than 120 feet in either direction brings adventurers into the grips of another 1d6 coffer corpses. The grates covering the exits can be removed with an open doors roll.

Credit

The Coffer Corpse originally appeared in the First Edition *Fiend Folio* (© TSR/Wizards of the Coast, 1981) and is used by permission.

Copyright Notice

Author Scott Greene, based on original material by Simon Eaton.

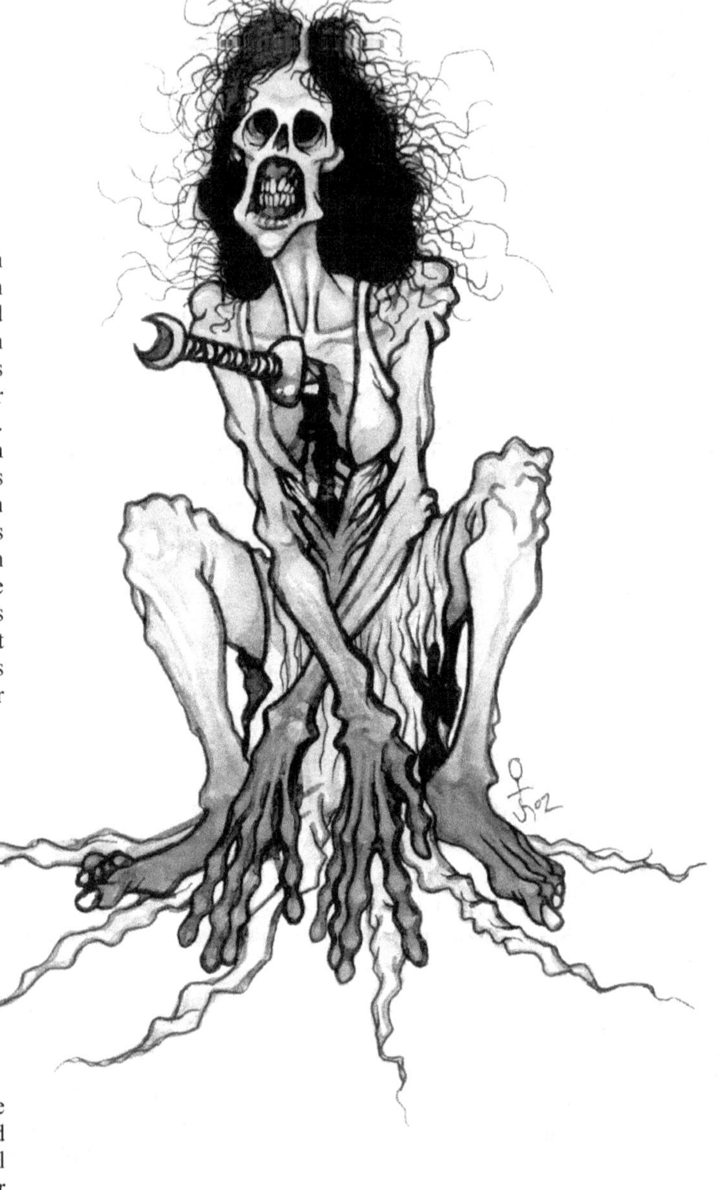

Colossus, Jade

Hit Dice: 30
Armor Class: -6 [25]
Attacks: 2 slams (4d8)
Saving Throw: 3
Special: Breath weapon, +3 weapons to hit, immune to fire, immune to magic
Move: 12
Alignment: Neutrality
Challenge Level/XP: 36/9,200

C

Jade colossi are massive constructs standing 35 feet tall and weighing about 60,000 pounds. It appears as a massive humanoid carved of smooth green stone. Its body is made up of perfect angles and contours. A jade colossus pummels a foe with its hardened fists. Once every 1d4 rounds, a jade colossus can spray a blast of green energy in a 60-foot cone or 120-foot line that does 15d6 points of damage (save for half). A creature slain by this blast is transformed into jade. Disintegrate slows a jade colossus for 1d6 rounds, while fire heals the construct. It is immune to all other magic.

When Stars Align

In the middle of the ruined bowl of a collapsed stone amphitheater, a gleaming marble pedestal rises 6 feet above the blistering desert sands claiming the ancient city. Low stone steps encircle the raised platform, and a railing carved with a fantastic depiction of a giant snake chasing its tail rings the dais. A slender golden pillar standing 3 feet tall sits in the middle of the platform. A mosaic star pattern inlaid with gleaming quartz covers the floor of the dais. A small platinum-and-gold lamp sits atop the pedestal. The lamp's curling handle sparkles with inset diamonds and emeralds.

A glowing green crystal dome encases the lamp, completely covering the top of the gold pedestal. This small dome is impervious to all efforts to remove it. The pedestal is similarly enchanted, and anyone striking it feels a heavy weight settle on their shoulders as if the weight of the world had settled over them. At the base of the pedestal are seven seven-pointed stars, each one representing a nation of the forsaken kingdoms of the Lands of Brass.

Engraved in the surface of the golden pedestal, beneath the dome, are words written in a flowing, mysterious script. The writing is the Covenant of Brass, and reads "Hail from the skies of molten metals, where the burning clouds of Ingol rain liquid fires over the lands of mortal fear. I plead for you, O Master of Fire and Brass, to now appear." After the greeting are written the seven forgotten kingdoms. The names are listed in alphabetical order. The seven-pointed stars at the base of the pillar each have the name of one of the kingdoms engraved on them. If pressed in the correct order by an efreeti as he recites the Covenant of Brass, the glass dome covering the lamp vanishes for 1 hour and grants everyone standing on the pedestal a single wish.

If pressed incorrectly (or by anyone other than an efreeti), the green glass clouds over, and a jade colossus materializes to destroy the would-be thieves.

Cooshee

Hit Dice: 3
Armor Class: 4 [15]
Attack: 2 claws (1d4) and bite (1d8)
Saving Throw: 14 (12 vs. charm)
Special: Sprint, trip, surprise on 1-3 on 1d6
Move: 15
Alignment: Neutrality (lawful tendencies)
Challenge Level/XP: 4/120

Cooshees are large, 200-pound, 4-foot tall hounds with green and brown spotted fur, a long, curling tail and ears that taper to points. They are known throughout the world as elven dogs, for their features resemble those of elves and they are often found in the employ of elves (who use them as guards). Though they only bark to warn their masters or other cooshees, the bark can be heard clearly up to one mile away. Cooshees enjoy a +2 bonus to save vs. charm effects. Once per hour, they can sprint at 10 times their normal speed. The victim of a cooshee's bite attack must pass a saving throw or be knocked prone.

Elven Safari

A pack of 1d6+3 cooshees has treed a kamadan (see that entry) in a large banyan, awakening 2d4 noisy banderlogs (see that entry) and, thus, most of the surrounding woodlands. The master of the pack, a 5th level elf fighter/magic-user, is about 1 turn behind the pack. The elf is mounted on a bay mare, extraordinarily intelligent, and is dressed in woodland green, a mail coat and carries a brass hunting horn (worth 40 gp), a longbow, 20 red-fletched arrows and a longsword. The hunter seeks the kamadan for its pituitary glands, required by a wise woman to effect a cure for his lady love.

Credit

The Cooshee originally appeared in *Dragon #67* (© TSR/Wizards of the Coast, 1983) and later in the First Edition module *S4 Lost Caverns of Tsojcanth* (© TSR/Wizards of the Coast, 1982) and still later in the First Edition *Monster Manual II* (© TSR/Wizards of the Coast, 1983) and is used by permission.

Copyright Notice

Author Scott Greene, based on original material by Gary Gygax.

Corpse Candle

Hit Dice: 6
Armor Class: 8 [11]
Attacks: Incorporeal touch (1d6)
Saving Throw: 11
Special: Hypnotic lights
Move: 6/18 (flying)
Alignment: Chaos
Challenge Level/XP: 8/800

A corpse candle appears as a translucent image of its living self. Its body shows little, if any, signs of death. Corpse candles can create dancing, twisting patterns of light that lure victims toward the colorful aura. A creature must save or be drawn onward – often into danger such as over cliffs, through fire or worse.

The Light at the End

A narrow channel of deep water runs down the center of a stone crypt. Bones are piled in niches along the route, spilling out onto the narrow ledges running alongside the water. The water is 10 feet deep. It is still and dark. Each niche is six feet wide and piled with miscellaneous bones from random corpses stuffed into the space. Ten-foot-tall statues of ancient kings stand in the spaces between the niches. Each holds a black candle in their outstretched hands. The candles sputter and flicker, thick tallow dripping down over the stone hands. Heavy shadows dance across the arched ceiling. A small boat sits on the edge of the water at the start of the crypt.

The watery channel runs throughout the entire crypt network. One dead-end passage opens into a 20-foot-diameter circular room filled with stain

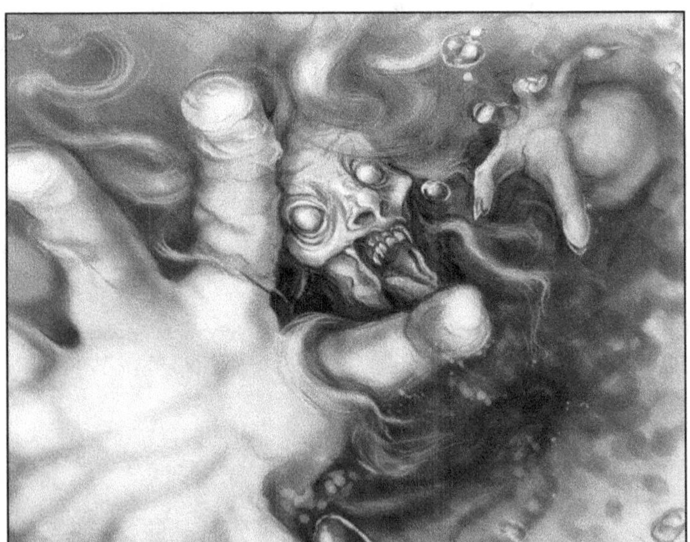

glass panels. The chamber glows with light reflected from candles set in the statues' hands and along the walls. The water here is 20 feet deep. An ancient hag was drowned in chamber 50 years ago when she tried to raise the dead to do her bidding. The crone rose as a corpse candle that haunts the crypts, although she prefers to remain in this chamber. Her bones lie at the bottom of the watery pit.

Copyright Notice

Author Scott Greene.

Corpse Orgy

Hit Dice: 14
Armor Class: 2 [17]
Attacks: 4 slams (2d6)
Saving Throw: 3
Special: Absorb body, pain shriek, half damage from blunt weapons
Move: 6
Alignment: Chaos
Challenge Level/XP: 16/3,200

A corpse orgy is a large, undulating mass of rotting corpses, sinew, bones, blood, muscle, mucus, and organs. It resembles an ooze and has no discernible features (other than the corpse parts that make up its form). A corpse orgy can absorb the physical body of any creature it has reduced to 0 hit points by moving over it and remaining in contact with it for at least one full round. When it absorbs a body, the corpse orgy gains 12 temporary hit points. A creature whose body is absorbed can only be raised or resurrected if the corpse orgy that absorbed its body is slain and the corpse in question is recovered. Twice per day, a corpse orgy can unleash a piercing shriek from the various heads captured in its form that deals 8d6 points of damage to all creatures within a 40-foot radius (save for half).

The jungle opens into a wide clearing that's been burned through the foliage. The dirt is churned and broken, and the impressions of hundreds of feet are pressed into the soft ground. A 10-foot-tall mound of freshly turned dirt rises in the center of the open area. Corpses are visible in the dirt hill, with decaying arms, legs and heads pushing out of the earthen mound. A fresh coat of lye is sprinkled over the raised earth.

Hundreds of human, goblin and other beings are piled in contorted heaps under the thin dirt layer. All were sacrificed at the temple of al-Sifon and the remains disposed of in this charnel pit. The dirt and lye only recently were applied.

A corpse orgy lives in the 10-foot-deep trench, and rises to the surface if the bodies are disturbed. The corpses above it begin pushing outward as the thing rises, the remains bursting out of the dirt as if alive. The corpse orgy attacks anyone bothering its "meal."

Copyright Notice

Author Scott Greene.

Dead Drop

Eric Lofgren

Corpse Rook

Hit Dice: 6
Armor Class: 6 [13]
Attacks: 2 claws (1d6) and 3 bites (1d8)
Saving Throw: 11
Special: Rend
Move: 6/24 (flying)
Alignment: Chaos
Challenge Level/XP: 7/600

Corpse rooks resemble large three-headed ravens or crows. Their feathers are oily black in color and have a pungent, almost sulfuric, odor. Their beak and talons are bright silver and their eyes are golden. The creature's wings are tipped with silver and the wingspan measures about 30 feet. From head to tail, the corpse rook is about 12 feet long. A corpse rook that hits with two or more bites on a single opponent latches on and tears at the victim's flesh for an additional 2d8 points of damage.

For the Birds

The scourge of the skies over Trivat, Mergond is really not much more than an amateurish thief at best. He can barely break into anything, his chances of pickpocketing a blind fool are slim to none, and he can't move without tripping over every noisy thing in his path. He's worthless as a thief, but excels in highway robbery.

What makes Mergond frightening is Moll, his corpse rook mount. He raised the bird from an egg and lovingly coddles her like a child. He feeds her dead squirrels from a pouch he carries. He rides on the bird's back in a special saddle.

A murder of crows fly in formation with Moll when she and Mergond set off to find gold. Mergond lets Moll sweep down on travelers before landy to demand tribute. He uses a *wand of metal detection* to make sure people don't hold out the good stuff. Moll has other ideas about what to take, and wouldn't mind a horse or a PCs.

Copyright Notice
Author Scott Greene.

Corpsespinner

Hit Dice: 12
Armor Class: 3 [16]
Attacks: 1 bite (2d8 + poison)
Saving Throw: 3
Special: Create corpsespun zombie, poison, web
Move: 9/6 (climb)
Alignment: Neutrality
Challenge Level/XP: 13/2,300

A corpsespinner is a huge tarantula-like creature, bone white in color with bands of gray, black, or silver ringing its abdomen and legs. The average corpsespinner is 15 feet long. Its body is covered in short, bristly hairs of white or silver. The corpsespinner has a skull-like marking on its thorax. Its eight eyes are silver, white, or gray. Creatures killed by a corpsespinner rise in 1 hour as corpsespun zombies. A corpsespinner's bite delivers a toxic poison, and they can fire sticky strands of webbing up to 80 feet up to 10 times per day (otherwise similar to a *web* spell)

Skeleton Key

A 150-foot stretch of hallway disappears into darkness and cobwebs. Dust covers everything in thick gray layers. Bone lanterns carved to resemble spiders give off a feeble bluish light. Halfway down the hall stands a skeleton wearing decaying finery and draped in thick layers of webbing. Alert PCs notice the skeleton doesn't touch the floor; sticky strands hold it aloft. The webs rise into a hollow nook where a corpsespinner waits, plucking at the webs to make the skeleton move. The spider toys with intruders by raising the skeleton's arms like a crude marionette. A gold key on a leather strap dangles enticingly from the skeleton's right arm.

A 25-foot-long stretch of floor beneath the skeleton is an open pit trap covered with webs. The thick webs bounce like a trampoline, but a roll of 1-3 on an 8-sided die causes the shroud to rip. PCs who fail a save land in the pit 10 feet below. Trapped in the pit are 10 corpsespun zombies. The corpsepinner attacks from above any PCs distracted by the zombies.

The gold key is worth 10 gp, and is enchanted to open any door (3 charges left).

Copyright Notice
Author Scott Greene.

Crab, Monstrous

Hit Dice: 3
Armor Class: 3 [16]
Attack: 2 claws (1d4)
Saving Throw: 14
Special: None
Move: 12/9 (swimming)
Alignment: Neutrality
Challenge Level/XP: 3/60

Monstrous crabs are omnivores and spend most of their time combing the ocean floors for food. Many act as vegetarians and sustain themselves on a diet of algae, fungus, and water-based plants, while others act as scavengers or predators. Some have been known to actively hunt giant clams and snails (the monstrous crab pries the shell open and devours the fleshy innards). Still others prefer to dwell in coastal waters and prey upon land-based creatures that wander too close to the shoreline. Monstrous crabs are often hunted as food by other races (particularly humans and sahuagin). They are about the size of a panther.

Guards of the Subterranean Sea

Could the fishermen of the coastal village have ever guessed at what lie beneath their feet? In the chalky hills, covered in scrawny blackberry bushes and tufts of yellow-green grass there was an old well, long since gone dry. Even if it had not gone dry, it was inconvenient to reach, sitting as it did atop a little mound of treacherous rocks, and there was such a nice little stream just a stone's throw from the village gate.

Should one ever decide to climb down the well – and why would a fisherman ever do such a daft thing – they would discover that the turquoise sea from which they drew their sustenance did not stop at the sandy beach where they parked their simple boats. Beneath the earth, that sea continued, strained through undersea tunnels and forming a vast, lightless sea that supported giant, albino crabs – 2d6 of them usually loitering at the bottom of that old well, waiting to greet anyone foolish enough to go exploring.

If one could get past those crabs, and the dozens of their fellows who would be drawn from the quiet waters to investigate any commotion, they might venture out onto that sea with its low ceiling and weird, lambent flames dancing above the glassy surface and beckoning the foolhardy into the Underworld.

Credit

The Monstrous Crab originally appeared in the First Edition *Monster Manual* (© TSR/Wizards of the Coast, 1977) and is used by permission.

Copyright Notice

Author Scott Greene, based on original material by Gary Gygax.

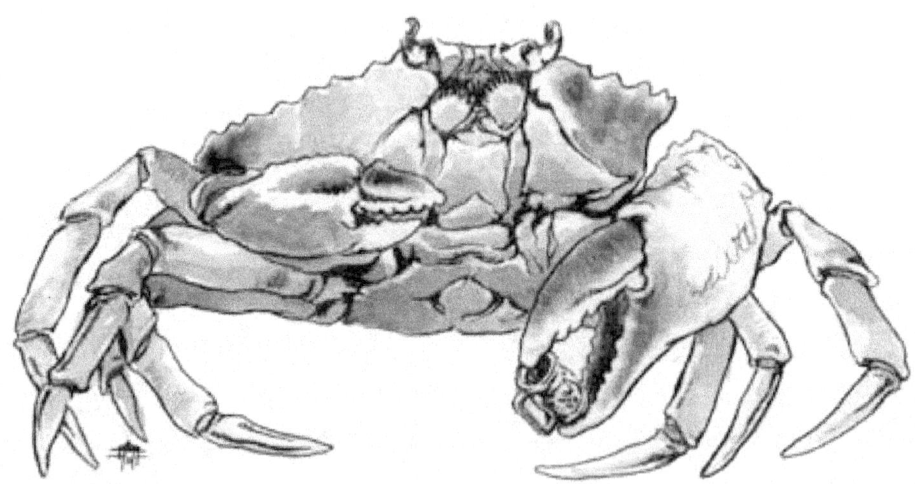

Crabman

Hit Dice: 3
Armor Class: 3 [16]
Attack: 2 claws (1d6)
Saving Throw: 14
Special: None
Move: 12/9 (swimming)
Alignment: Neutrality
Challenge Level/XP: 3/60

This giant-sized creature is a bipedal humanoid with a crab-like head, large hands that end in powerful pincers, feet that are splayed. It is covered with chitinous plates, reddish-brown in color. Two smaller humanoid arms protrude below its pincers. Crabmen inhabit coastal waters, hunting fish and gathering food. Crabmen communicate with others of their race through a series of hisses and clicks. A typical crabman stands about 9 feet tall. They speak their own language, and more intelligent examples of their species often speak Common. Crabmen are passive and peaceful creatures, rarely engaging in combat. Crabmen attack with their claws; their pincers prevent them from wielding weapons. Their humanoid arms end in human-like hands and are used for fine dexterity and manipulation; they are too weak to wield weapons effectively. Crabmen can survive indefinitely on land and under water. Crabmen make their homes in sea caves and coastal cliffs. Most tribes are led by male or female elders.

Crabmen as Characters

Crabmen are rather hulking brutes, despite their passive dispositions. They begin the game with an extra hit dice and are capable of swimming at a speed of 9. Their chitinous exoskeletons provide an AC of 3 [16], which is convenient since crabmen are incable of wearing armor or using shields. Their pincer attacks do 1d6 points of damage - again, this is convenient since they are incapable of using weapons, their second set of humanoid arms being too frail for such heavy work.

Crabmen may be fighters, advancing to the 4th level of ability (5th level with Strength of 17, 6th level with Strength of 18). Rare crabmen with prime requisites of 16 or higher can take up the profession of druid or magic-user, advancing to a maximum of 3rd level.

High Crustacean Society

A dozen miles across that shallow, subterranean sea, the ceiling rises high enough that the weird, upside-down towers built there by some unknown race can only be seen by following up the slowly swaying chains that descend from their battlements. The crabmen use these chains to climb into the towers from their own mazelike fortress in the shallows that they may access the upper world, but they do not relish entering those monuments to an extinct race, for they exude a peculiar malice for things born from the sea.

The crabmen of the subterranean sea have whitish-pink shells and bulbous eyes atop their crimson eye stalks. They have carved for themselves a fortress of mazelike passages from the living stone that lies no more than 20 feet below the surface of the sea. Into these corridors, which sink 50 feet into the sea floor, they herd their fish and raise their urchins, cultivating them for their toxins (which they turn into effective anti-ooze medicinal) and to decorate their burrow-like homes dug into the walls of the corridor.

A total of 2d6 x 20 crabmen dwell in the mazelike fortress, extracting copper from the sea floor and carrying it to the upper world to smelt and shape it into tools in forges hidden in the hills. They are ruled by a court of 3d4 sooks (females) with sorcerous powers. Each female dwells in a fortified burrow with its own egg chamber, the chamber being secured and trapped to discourage attacks from outsiders and other crabmen.

Credit

The Crabman originally appeared in the First Edition *Fiend Folio* (© TSR/Wizards of the Coast, 1981) and is used by permission.

Copyright Notice

Authors Scott Greene and Erica Balsley, based on original material by Ian Livingstone

Crag Man

Hit Dice: 6
Armor Class: 4 [15]
Attacks: 2 piercing slams (1d8+2)
Saving Throw: 11
Special: Pierce, piercer hellstorm, *passwall*
Move: 6
Alignment: Chaos
Challenge Level/XP: 7/600

Sometimes called living stalagmites, crag men appear as a normal stalagmite. In humanoid form, a crag man is a 6-foot tall human-shaped creature seemingly carved from stone. It is thick and squat and its features are jagged and broken. Small depressions on its head function as eyes, though no pupils are present. The crag man has no ears. A ridge on its "face" running between its eyes serves as a nose and its mouth is a wide, toothless crevice. Its arms end in powerful fists and its legs end in humanoid feet. A crag man's hands end in stony points that pierce an opponent's skin with each slam. Once a day, a crag man can summon 2d10 piercers with a 50% chance of success. A crag man can employ *passwall* (as per the spell) once per day.

Piercer: HD 3; AC 3[16]; Atk 1 drop and pierce (3d6); Move 1; Save 14; CL/XP 3/60; Special: None.

Dinner is Served

A dead gnoll sits upright on a round rock in the center of this large natural cavern. The corpse holds a silver knife and fork (1 gp total) in its lifeless paws. A wooden bowl sits on a flattened stalagmite, the dish filled with a dried-up rat and and heaps of crushed purple mushrooms. The gnoll has been dead less than a day.

The makeshift table is a crag man that killed the gnoll and propped the beast up to "entice" others to investigate. The stalactites hanging from the cavern's roof are piercers the crag man directs to drop on unsuspecting PCs.

The gnoll wears a leather belt containing 10 gp, a shiny rock good luck charm (it didn't work for him), and a wooden dog whistle that charms a creature blowing it into falling in love with the next gnoll he meets (save avoids).

Copyright Notice
Author Scott Greene.

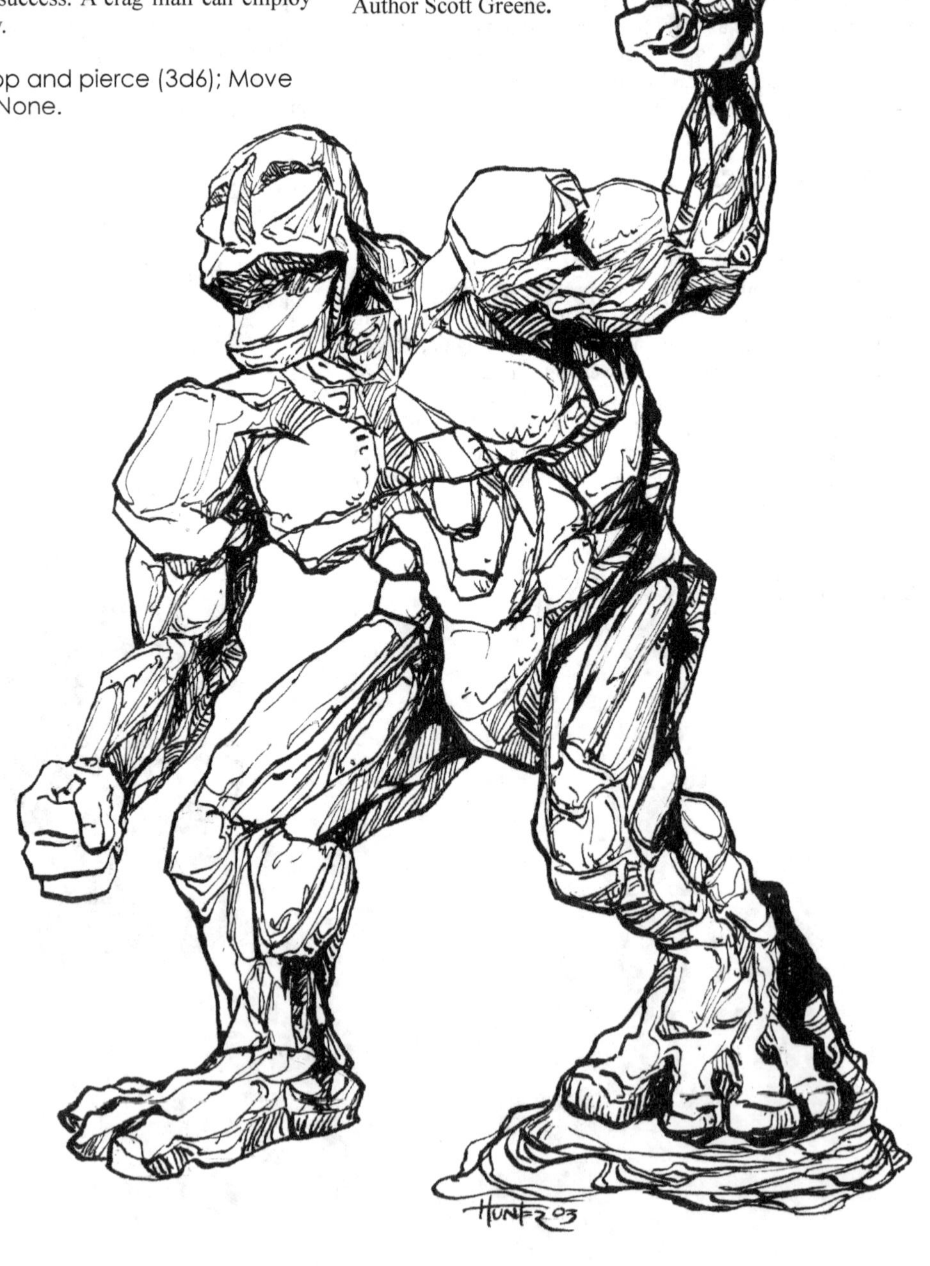

Crayfish, Monstrous

Hit Dice: 4
Armor Class: 4 [15]
Attack: 2 claws (1d6)
Saving Throw: 13
Special: Surprise on 1-2 on 1d6
Move: 9/15 (swimming)
Alignment: Neutrality
Challenge Level/XP: 4/120

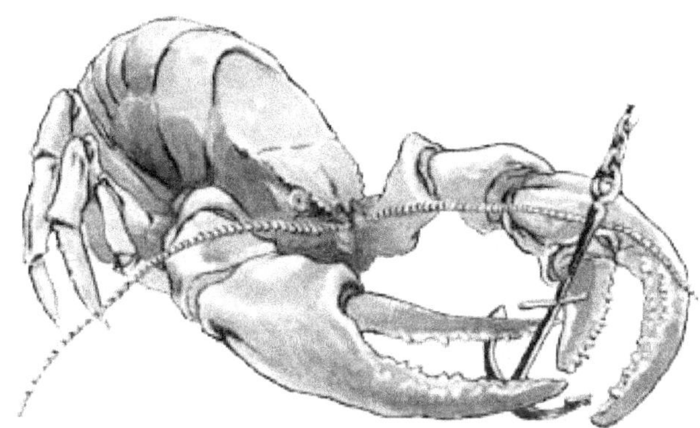

Giant crayfish are freshwater creatures that dwell on the bottom of seas, lakes, ponds, and other shallow waters. They are predators and scavengers and exist on a diet of decaying flesh (dead fish and other water-based animals), algae, snails, worms, and other animals (including swimmers who come to close to their lair). Giant crayfish make their homes under rocks or in underwater tunnels burrowed out by the crayfish. Most underwater tunnels extend over long distances and include a "chimney" found along the edge of the water or even as far as 100 feet away from the water which allows the giant crayfish to enter and exit its passageways onto dry ground. A giant crayfish can survive out of the water for up to 7 hours before suffocating.

Crayfish Fricassee

Trodding through the soggy bayou, you come across a brutish hill giant armed with a spiked club and a large sling. The hill giant is stalking giant crayfish for his chieftain's nuptial feast, and has just come across 1d4+1 of the pincered monstrosities. The hill giant will not refuse help, and if helped will invite his new friends to the feast.

The feast is being held on a barren cairn surrounded by fields of clover and daisies, many of the flowers having been woven into garlands to decorate the bride and groom. Visitors are welcome, but though the hill giant clans have sworn a promise of peace on this day, being around several dozen drunken hill giants is still very dangerous. Each wedding guest is required to bestow a valuable gift on the new couple - failure to do so being considered a grave insult.

Credit

The Monstrous Crayfish originally appeared in the First Edition *Monster Manual* (© TSR/Wizards of the Coast, 1977) and is used by permission.

Copyright Notice

Author Scott Greene, based on original material by Gary Gygax.

Crucifixion Spirit

Hit Dice: 12
Armor Class: 4 [15]
Attacks: Incorporeal touch (1d8 + paralysis) or crucify soul
Saving Throw: 3
Special: Crucify soul, paralysis
Move: 9/18 (flying)
Alignment: Chaos
Challenge Level/XP: 15/2,900

A crucifixion spirit is a translucent, gaunt humanoid with injuries to each wrist and to the arch of each foot. A crucifixion spirit makes no noise and its face is twisted in eternal pain. Its eyes flicker red. The incorporeal touch of a crucifixion spirit causes paralysis (save avoids). Five times per day, the spirit can point at a single target and crucify its soul if it hits its target. If the target fails a save, his body collapses as his soul is ripped out of his body and crucified to an X-shaped structure with translucent spikes. The victim is not dead, but loses 2 levels per round unless he is saved. A crucified victim can return to its body by making a save, but this leaves the victim stunned for one round.

Burning Revenge

Six boulders stand upright on the edge of the Corros Desert, the 10-foot-wide flat sides of each massive stone turned to face the harshest winds blowing off the burning sands. Heavy links of black chain wrap around each rock. Shackled to the rocks by red-hot metal manacles are six blackened bodies. Their faces and skin are sandblasted away, leaving them unidentifiable. Each was a thief sentenced to death and chained to the Rocks of Woe. The bodies are suspended against the superheated rocks. A man's head pokes out of the sand in front of the rocks, his wiry hair flapping in the harsh winds. His skin is streaked with blood. The howling winds drown his screams.

Four of the dead men hung on the rocks were killers and thugs who deserved their gruesome fate. Two were innocents wrongly convicted by Magistrate Chesle, the corrupt judge now buried up to his neck in the shifting sands. The innocent victims died horrible deaths on the rocks, and rose mere hours later as crucifixion spirits intent on revenge. Instead of killing Chesle outright, the pair dragged the elderly man to the desert hole to die slowly.

Chesle begs for his life and offers PCs gold and land if they free him. The crucifixion spirits rise out of the rocks supporting their blackened corpses if anyone helps the judge.

Copyright Notice

Author Scott Greene.

Crypt Thing

Hit Dice: 6
Armor Class: 2 [17]
Attack: 2 claws (1d6)
Saving Throw: 11
Special: Teleport other, +1 or better weapons to hit, turn as 10 HD monster
Move: 12
Alignment: Neutrality
Challenge Level/XP: 9/1100

Crypt things are hooded and robed skeletons found sitting in high-backed chairs, its eyes appearing as small pinpoints of reddish light. They are created by spellcasters as tomb guardians. They never leave their assigned area and never initiate combat. A crypt thing is content to sit (or stand) in its assigned area so long as intruders do not disturb it or anything in the assigned area. At the first sign of disturbance however, a crypt thing springs to life. Its first order of business is to attempt to remove the interlopers from its assigned area by teleporting them 1d10 x 100 feet in a random direction (roll 1d4: 1, north; 2, south; 3, east; 4, west). The recipient of this free, unplanned trip can resist it with a saving throw. A teleported creature arrives in the closest open space at the determined destination. A teleported creature can arrive in mid-air rather than on a solid surface, if the crypt thing wishes.

Crypt Guardian

There exists in some parts of the world (and perhaps only truly in legend; sages aren't sure) a variant of the crypt thing known as a crypt guardian. This variant has all the same abilities and powers as a normal crypt thing, with the following changes. The variant does not possess the ability to teleport others. Instead, it can simultaneously paralyze and turn invisible all creatures within 50 feet. An affected creature can make a saving throw to negate the effects. Affected creatures remain paralyzed and invisible for 2d4 days. A new save is allowed each day until the effects are broken, dispelled, or the duration ends.

Toga Party

Beyond the dusty antechamber there is a long passageway - 60 feet long - ending in a circular chamber lit by a single everburning brazier. On one wall there is a crypt, 20 feet long and 15 feet wide, with panes of amber-colored glass set into the walls - five panes on each wall. The glass apparently covers small alcoves, for a torch held up to the glass reveals a mouldering body partially covered in a funeral shroud behind it. A the end of the chamber there is a brass throne set with two large rubies (red glass, actually) set in the arms. Sitting in the throne there is a corpse, swathed in a woolen toga and wearing a brass helm surmounted by a horsehair crest.

The corpse is a crypt thing, and it will certainly teleport intruders far away. Now, it so happens that on the wall opposite the entrance to the crypt there is a large mirror - oval and measuring 5 feet tall and 3 feet wide. The mirror is set in a brass frame made to look like dozens of sinuous fire nymphs. The mirror is harder than steel and impossible to shatter, but one can walk through it by holding a burning ember from the brazier in their fist. Holding the ember in this way inflicts 1d4 points of (non-lethal) damage.

On the other side of the mirror, one finds an identical crypt, save for the fact that the throne is made of gold and set with actual rubies and worth easily 10,000 gp. The corpse on the throne is not a crypt thing, but rather the body of a long dead sorcerer. The bodies behind the amber glass are wights, and they will burst through the glass to attack intruders into the true tomb.

Create Crypt Thing

Spell Level: Cleric and Magic-User, 7th Level
Range: 60 feet
Duration: Instantaneous
This spell allows you to animate a single corpse into a crypt thing. This spell must be cast in the area the creature is to guard or it fails. The corpse must be mostly intact and must be humanoid-shaped and have a skeletal system or structure. Only one crypt thing is created with this spell, and it remains in the area where it was created until destroyed. A black pearl gem worth at least 300 gp must be placed inside the mouth of the corpse. When the corpse animates, the gem is destroyed.

Credit

The Crypt Thing originally appeared in the First Edition *Fiend Folio* (© TSR/Wizards of the Coast, 1981) and is used by permission. According to an article by Don Turnbull in *Dragon #55* (© TSR/Wizards of the Coast, 1981), the Crypt Thing was never intended to be an undead creature, though somehow it evolved into that over the years.

Copyright Notice
Author Scott Greene, based on original material by Roger Musson.

Crystalline Horror

Hit Dice: 7
Armor Class: 0 [19]
Attack: Shard spray (3d6) or claw (1d6)
Saving Throw: 9
Special: Shard spray, bend light, +1 or better weapons to hit, resistance to cold (50%)
Move: 12
Alignment: Chaos
Challenge Level/XP: 10/1400

A crystalline horror is a weird, unnatural humanoid made entirely of crystal and glass. It is man-sized and its head sports no eyes, nose, ears, or mouth. Its body appears razor-sharp and jagged. Its hands end in wicked claws. The origins of the crystalline horror are shrouded in mystery. A crystalline horror can loose a spray of razor-sharp shards of glass from its body in a 40-foot cone. A creature in the area takes 3d6 points of damage or half that amount if it succeeds on a saving throw. The crystalline horror can launch only five such sprays in a given day. Victims of any attack from the crystalline horror must pass an additional saving throw to avoid having an artery knicked. Unfortunates who fail such a saving throw suffer an additional 1d4 points of damage each round from bleeding until the wound is tended or magically healed. In place of attacking, a crystalline horror can refract natural light into a bright light that radiates out in a 10-foot spread. Creatures within this area must succeed on a saving throw or be blinded for 3 rounds.

Crystal Blue Confusion

In an icy cave in the high mountains, very near the blazing sun, a crystalline horror sits brooding. A skeleton is all that remains of the remorhaz that once called this cavern home. The crystalline horror puzzles over a blue metallic cube, a sort of puzzle box. Sadly, the creature's wickedly sharp claws are too clumsy to work the box.

Should one solve the puzzle (you can have players work on a real puzzle or allow their characters to attempt three 1d20 rolls, needing to roll under their intelligence scores on all three rolls) it opens into a strange metallic spider that roosts on one's shoulder for one hour. During this hour, the spider protects them from all evil mental effects. When the hour is up, the creature folds back into a cube and cannot be re-opened (a task which requires solving a new puzzle or re-rolling against intelligence) for 24 hours.

Fighting in the ice cave is treacherous, with each missed attack or move of more than 3 feet requiring a saving throw to avoid falling prone and suffering 1d4 damage.

Copyright Notice
Author Scott Greene.

Crystallis

Hit Dice: 14
Armor Class: 2 [17]
Attacks: 2 claws (2d6+3)
Saving Throw: 3
Special: Crystalline claws, wounding, petrification breath
Move: 6/6 (burrow)
Alignment: Neutrality
Challenge Level/XP: 17/3,500

A crystallis is formed of quartz, earth, and crystal and stands about 13 feet tall. Its powerful arms and legs end in razor-sharp claws that glint and shine like polished steel. Its large rounded head sports two sunken crystalline eyes and a gaping toothless maw. A crystallis attacks with razor-sharp crystalline claws that cause opponents to bleed each round for 2 hit points of damage until a healing spell is cast on the creature. Once every 1d4+1 rounds, the creature can breathe a cloud of orange smoke that fills a 10-foot cube in front of the crystallis. Anyone inside this smoke must save or be turned into a crystal, gem-encrusted statue.

Rock Garden

This humid cavern drips with condensation. Clear pools of warm water collect in low spots on the stone floor. Hundreds of fantastic cave formations are covered with quartz crystals of incredible beauty and color. Massive teardrop-shaped crystals hang delicately from the ceiling. Magical light brought into the room causes a dazzling display of brilliant light to reflect around the chamber. PCs must save or be blinded by the white glare of the reflected light (-2 to-hit penalty while in the room). Lanterns, torches and candlelights do not have this effect.

The hanging crystals are caterprisms in cocoons. They are at a delicate state and quickly die if the cocoon is harmed in anyway. A hermit-like crystallis tends to his rock garden beneath the hanging cocoons. Several caterprisms hide among the natural crystal formations. The protective crystallis dislikes intruders, and attacks anyone harming his garden or the crystal cocoons. The crystallis and the caterprisms are immune to the light effects and each other's special attacks. The crystals in this room have unusual qualities and exceptional clarity. They are highly prized and valuable.

Copyright Notice
Author Scott Greene.

Daemon, Cacodaemon

Hit Dice: 12
Armor Class: -3 [22]
Attack: Sword (2d6) or 2 claws (1d6)
Saving Throw: 3
Special: Spells, only harmed by silver weapons, immunity to acid and poison, magic resistance (60%), telepathy 100 ft.
Move: 12
Alignment: Chaos
Challenge Level/XP: 18/3800

Cacodaemons are tall, sleek, ebony humanoids with long, thick arms that end in powerful claws. The average cacodaemon stands about 7 feet tall and weighs about 800 pounds. They have sleek, hairless heads and bright, fiery red eyes. Their mouths are lined with sharpened teeth and fangs. They are employed as guards and soldiers in the Oinodaemon's palace. Cacodaemons are completely loyal to the Oinodaemon and never question their position or authority; they do not take orders from any other daemon. Cacodaemons are relentless combatants and never back down from a fight. They often begin combat by changing forms and appearing as a race friendly to their potential opponents. Once an opponent is lured close to the cacodaemon, it changes to its natural form and attacks. Cacodaemons can cast the following spells: *Darkness, ESP, fear* and *hold person* (3/day).

Slackers

Just beneath a large, oily rock covered in patches of pale, luminescent lichens that writhe under one's flesh, a squad of 1d5+5 cacodaemons is slacking off, smoking the ground leaves of the black lotus in stubby pipes carved from the thigh bones of sinners. The largest of the dull creatures is telling the others a story of some past battle against a horde of demons and devils that apparently culminated in his saving the life of the Oinodaemon. The others are rolling their eyes and glancing at one another sheepishly while blowing smoke rings. Two of the fiends is kicking a severed head back and forth between them, the head howling in pain as they do so. While the others hold the attention of the adventurers, one cacodaemon is creeping up behind them.

Copyright Notice
Author Scott Greene.

Daemon, Charon (Boatman of the Lower Planes)

Hit Dice: 32 (128 hp)
Armor Class: -5 (24)
Attack: Staff (2d6)
Saving Throw: 3
Special: Control Styx, fear gaze, paralysis, spells, +1 or better weapons to hit, immunity to acid and poison, magic resistance (90%), telepathy 100 ft.
Move: 18
Alignment: Chaos
Challenge Level/XP: 40/10800

Charon spends his time ferrying dead souls to their final resting place in the Lower Planes. He appears as a skeleton shrouded in a dark hooded robe with small pinpoints of crimson light burning in his empty eye sockets. He uses a large, flat skiff to ferry his passengers across the dangerous waters of the River Styx. On occasion, he ferries living souls to a desired location within the Lower Planes, though he charges a hefty price for such passage. A rare and costly (to one's sanity) spell can be used to summon the dread boatman. Passage for living souls across the River Styx costs a single magic item, 500 pp, or two gems of at least 1,000 gp total value. If his price is refused, Charon turns his skiff and moves away. If attacked, Charon attacks but seeks to escape as soon as possible. Those within 30 feet meeting Charon's gaze must succeed on a saving throw or be paralyzed with fear for a number of rounds equal to the value by which they failed their saving throw. A creature hit by Charon's staff must succeed on a saving throw or be paralyzed for 2d6 minutes. Charon can see through invisibility. Once per day he can trace a *symbol of fear* or *symbol of stunning*. Three times per day, Charon can summon 2d4 charonadaemons. Charon can control the waters of the River Styx as if using the *control water* spell. Additionally, he can form a 16 HD water elemental using this ability. A Styx elemental uses the standard 16 HD water elemental statistics with the addition that its touch causes *feeblemind* in those who fail a saving throw. Charon can roam the planes in its skiff at will.

Death in a Cup

Near the oily shore of the Styx, you discover a round table of stone. The table is set with a orichalcum ewer of dark, dry wine and two terracotta cups painted with black glaze and images of cavorting skeletons. Should one drop three pomegranate seeds and a copper coin in each cup and fill them with wine, they will, in the blink of an eye, be startled to see Charon accepting the cup and holding it to his mouth.

Charon does not drink until his "host" drinks. The wine is, of course, a deadly poison. Should the host survive his drink (saving throw at -2 penalty), he may initiate negotiations with Charon for passage on his skiff. If Charon's visitors prove troublesome, they will discover that they are surrounded by a band of summoned charonadaemons.

Credit
Charon originally appeared in the First Edition *Monster Manual II* (© TSR/Wizards of the Coast, 1983) and is used by permission.

Copyright Notice
Author Scott Greene, based on original material by Gary Gygax.

Daemon, Charonodaemon

Hit Dice: 10
Armor Class: -2 [21]
Attack: Staff (1d8)
Saving Throw: 5
Special: Fear gaze, spells, only harmed by silver weapons, immunity to acid and poison, magic resistance (45%), telepathy 100 ft.
Move: 15
Alignment: Chaos
Challenge Level/XP: 15/2900

Charonadaemons resemble their master, Charon, the Boatman of the Lower Planes, and are often mistaken for him. Unlike their master, they care nothing for ferrying souls across the River Styx and merely seek to murder or steal from those that request passage. Travel across the River Styx by a charonadaemon costs a single magic item, 50 pp, or 2 gems (total value of both gems must be at least 100 gp). Even if the price is paid, the charonadaemon usually betrays his passengers, attempting to dump them into the River Styx or kill them outright. If more money or fare is offered, the charonadaemon might be persuaded not to attack. A charonadaemon can be summoned to the banks of the River Styx by casting *symbol* (any). Those within 30 feet meeting the gaze of a charonadaemon must succeed on a saving throw or be paralyzed with fear for a number of rounds equal to the value by which they failed their saving throw. Charonadaemons can cast, at will, the spells *cause fear* and *darkness*, and they can discern invisible creatures. Charonadaemons can roam the planes in their skiffs at will.

A Boatman in the Lower Planes

On the shores of a subterranean sea, on a beach of gleaming, white sand, you come across a skeletal, robed figure standing on his skiff, looking absent-mindedly towards the mouth of a cave. The charonadaemon was summoned by an inhabitant of the Lower Planes to deliver them to the Material Plane and wait precisely 24 hours for its return with an important captive and message for the Oinodaemon. Every few minutes the charonadaemon holds aloft an hourglass and check the gray sands within.

There is a 3 in 6 chance that the passenger of the skiff, a cacodaemon, finally appears, a bound and gagged drow priestess slung over its shoulder. Should it appear, it ignores the adventurers unless they oppose it - either way, the charonadaemon gives it no aid other than to seize the priestess and deposit her on its skiff.

If the cacodaemon does not appear in time, the charonadaemon will launch its skiff and soon disappear from view. If the adventurers move quickly, they can hire the charonadaemon, who goes by the name of Blackjack and has a habit of referring to itself in the third person.

Credit

The Charonadaemon originally appeared in the First Edition *Monster Manual II* (© TSR/Wizards of the Coast, 1983) and is used by permission.

Copyright Notice

Author Scott Greene, based on original material by Gary Gygax.

Daemon, Derghodaemon

Hit Dice: 10
Armor Class: -2 [21]
Attack: 5 claws (1d4) or 2 claws (1d4) and 3 swords (2d6)
Saving Throw: 5
Special: Feeblemind, spells, only harmed by silver weapons, immunity to acid and poison, magic resistance (50%), telepathy 100 ft.
Move: 15
Alignment: Chaos
Challenge Level/XP: 16/3200

The derghodaemon is one of the strongest of the daemon races, but its low intelligence has relegated it to a position of brute warrior and little more. It is a tall, bloated, insect-like creature with five arms and three legs. Each of its arms ends in a sharpened, clawed hand. Its legs end in four-toed feet. Its flesh is mottled green and black and its eyes are large and black with no pupils. A derghodaemon stands 8 feet tall and weighs about 800 pounds. Twice per day, by clicking its mandibles, a derghodaemon can affect all creatures within 30 feet as if by a *feeblemind* spell. A derghodaemon's head can rotate 360 degrees, making it almost impossible to surprise the creatures or back stab them. In addition, they can see invisible creatures. Derghodaemons can cast, at will, the spells *cause fear, darkness* and *sleep*.

Fun and Games

A bloated, dim-witted dhergodaemon is rolling a massive, spherical stone up a barren, windswept hill. The stone is conmposed of a reddish black material that glows with an inner fire. The dhergodaemon will generally ignore adventurers unless they become bothersome, but it is not averse to chatting with them while it goes about its duties.

The strange stone is actually the egg of a fiendish roc, and the dhergodaemon is rolling it to the campsite of 1d3 other dhergodaemons, who intend to feast on it. Naturally, adventurers will be invited to share in this feast, though they will find the flesh of the roc bitter and nauseating. After devouring the embryonic roc, the dhergodaemons engage in a dizzying game of five-handed rock/paper/scissors.

Five adventurers can engage a single dhergodaemon in the game, each having a 3 in 6 chance of besting one of the daemon's arms. If they can best all five arms at once, the dhergodaemon will give out a chattering, wheezing laugh and offer them a bent golden coin that, it assures them, grants them entry and a single day's peace in any stronghold they should encounter in the Lower Planes.

Credit

The Derghodaemon originally appeared in the First Edition *Monster Manual II* (© TSR/Wizards of the Coast, 1983) and is used by permission.

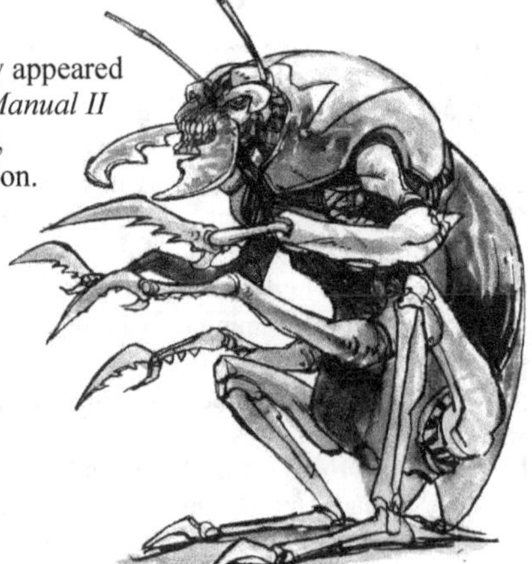

Copyright Notice

Author Scott Greene, based on original material by Gary Gygax.

Daemon, Guardian

Hit Dice: 8
Armor Class: -1 [20]
Attack: Bite (2d6), 2 claws (1d6)
Saving Throw: 8
Special: Breath weapon, +1 or better weapon to hit, immunity to acid and poison, limited domain, telepathy 100 ft.
Move: 12
Alignment: Chaos or Neutrality
Challenge Level/XP: 11/1700

A guardian daemon is summoned to the Material Plane by a spellcaster with the task of guarding an area or treasure. These daemons vary in size and appearance, though most resemble large bears, wild cats, or apes with added daemonic characteristics (horns, elongated fangs and nails, and so on). Despite its varying appearance and form, the guardian daemon is a dangerous adversary. Most guardian daemons are of neutral slant, though many, due to their daemonic heritage, are chaotic and usually only serve those of like alignment.

A guardian daemon only initiates combat if the area it is guarding is entered or the treasure it is watching over is disturbed. The realm of a guardian daemon encompasses only the area it is summoned to guard; a room, chamber, or treasure. The guardian daemon can wander freely in its area, but cannot move beyond the precincts of the designated area.

Three times per day a guardian daemon can breathe a cone of fire 30 feet long with a 15-foot wide base. This cone of fire deals 5d6 points of damage (save for half damage).

Guardian daemons are immune to mind-affecting effects (charms, compulsions, phantasms, patterns, and morale effects), *sleep*, hold, and polymorph. They cannot be harmed by acid and poison.

Lifeguard

A floating caravan of nine covered barges is making its way down a wide, golden river. Eight of the barges are carrying barrels of rice, plums, dried fish and other foodstuffs, along with 2 or 3 traders. One of the barges carries a lacquered altar case painted in gold dragons and sealed with a puzzle lock. Inside the case there are three peaches. One is a single peach of immortality (treat as a *potion of longevity*), while the other two contain deadly poison.

Lurking in the shadows of the barge is a guardian daemon that resembles a foo lion, with curved horns and skin that looks like golden marble. At first blush, one might easily mistake the daemon for a statue. The daemon can be placated by playing a bamboo flute. The men who steer the barge (3rd level assassins) carry such flutes in their sashes, along with poisoned daggers and lengths of chain. The caravan is on its way from a monastery high in the mountains to the palace of the emperor.

Credit

The Guardian Daemon originally appeared in the First Edition *Fiend Folio* (© TSR/Wizards of the Coast, 1981) and is used by permission.

Copyright Notice

Author Scott Greene, based on original material by Ian McDowall.

Daemon, Hydrodaemon

Hit Dice: 7
Armor Class: 0 [19]
Attack: 2 claws (1d6), bite (2d6) or spit (see below)
Saving Throw: Spittle, spells, only hamed by silver weapons, immunity to acid and poison, magic resistance (35%), telepathy 100 ft.
Special: 9
Move: 9/24/12 (swimming/flying)
Alignment: Chaos
Challenge Level/XP: 13/2300

Hydrodaemons are frog-like daemons that swim the River Styx. They are the only known creatures in existence that can touch the waters of the Styx without suffering any ill effects. Hydrodaemons are 10 feet tall and weight about 4,000 pounds. Large flaps of skin under their arms allow them to glide when leaping. The flesh of a hydrodaemon is warty and green. Its eyes are a sickly yellow in color. Up to five times per day a hydrodaemon can expel a 20-foot long line of sputum that causes those hit to save vs. sleep (as the spell) for 6 rounds. Hydrodaemons can, at will, cast *cause fear*, *darkness*, *detect magic* and *dimenson door*. Once per day, they can summon an 8 HD water elemental.

On Noisome Pond

On the banks of a noisesome pond, a hydrodaemon lurks. Summoned some ages before by a midling demonologist who got in way over his head (literally), the beast has since dwelled in this old mill pond that once served a large village, now abandoned. The mill is now crumbling, the interior coated in the dried spittle of the hydrodaemon, now a viscous ooze that acts as a contact poison (save at +3 or become drowsy for 1 hour, suffering a -1 penalty to all dice rolls).

The hydrodaemon lurks beneath the surface of the water, waiting for a single victim to stroll close. At this point, it strikes with its spittle and then leaps from the water to grab its dozing victim and drag them under the water.

In the shallows one may find numerous skeletons, mostly those of peasants in tattered and ruined woollens and leathers, but one skeleton belonged to a sorceress who still grips a *wand of enemy detection*, and another is the remains of a knight in *+1 gothic plate armor* that still gleams after spending several years in the muck.

Credit

The Hydrodaemon originally appeared in the First Edition *Monster Manual II* (© TSR/Wizards of the Coast, 1983) and is used by permission.

Copyright Notice

Author Scott Greene, based on original material by Gary Gygax.

Daemon, The Oinodaemon

Hit Dice: 25 (100 hp)
Armor Class: -3 [22]
Attack: 2 slams (2d6 plus disease)
Saving Throw: 3
Special: Disease, spells, *Staff of the Lower Planes*, transfixing gaze, +2 or better weapon to hit, magic resistance (90%), immune to disease and poison, telepathy 100 ft.
Move: 15
Alignment: Chaos
Challenge Level/XP: 34/8600

The Oinodaemon claims rulership over all other daemons. There is no other single figure in the lower planes that commands more respect (and fear) than the Oinodaemon (excepting a few powerful arch devils). His position is constantly threatened by those that would usurp the throne and take the position for themselves. There are believed to be at least seven other extremely powerful daemons vying for the throne and title. Through subtle machinations, sheer power, and fear, the Oinodaemon has staved them off thus far.

The Oinodaemon stands 9 feet tall. Its head resembles that of a diseased and rotting ram with downward, forward-curving horns. The wool and flesh of its humanoid body seem to pull away or drop away in sickly clumps. Its body is covered in boils, blisters, sores and scabs. Thick, white foam oozes from its mouth and a thin yellow ichor squeezes from its bloodshot eyes.

The touch of the Oinodaemon carries with its the daemon plague, a terrible disease that prevents magical and natural healing and rots the flesh while the victim yet lives. A person afflicted with the daemon plague is contagious until it dies, usually in one week.

Oinodaemon's gaze transfixes one target per round unless a saving throw is made. The transfixed target cannot move until permitted to do so.

Oinodaemon can cast spells as a 12th level cleric, as well as *detect magic*, *dispel magic* and *invisibility* at will and *feeblemind* once per day. Once per day, his touch can act as a *rod of cancellation*.

Staff of the Lower Planes: This 12-foot long, black wooden staff can only be wielded by the current Oinodaemon or any daemon he allows to wield it. In anyone else's hands, the staff functions as a normal quarterstaff. Upon the current Oinodaemon's death, the staff can be wielded (and it functions as detailed below) by the new Oinodaemon. The staff has the power of a staff of withering and can cast a charm monster spell that affects up to 20 targets, can lay a geas upon a person and can grant another's wish.

Servants of the Oinodaemon

Followers of the Oinodaemon are usually evil humanoids and often consist of clerics and necromancers. Clerics of the Oinodaemon are called Servants of Decay and must sign a pact of evil with the Oinodaemon. Servants of Decay can receive cleric spells up to 3rd level from the Oinodaemon.

Welcome to the Feast

As one tromps over the bleak wastes of the Lower Planes, they might discern on the horizon a looming shape - large and a dull, soul-sucking black. In mere moments it will be upon them, moving rapidly - a long corridor, hung in green, tapestry-like fungi, battered, rotting furniture, corroded copper candlesticks with dropping tapers, massive vases of terracotta filled with skulls - all moving rapidly past the adventurers before it finally and suddenly stops. The adventurers now find themselves facing a great door of rusted iron, the surface cast in the shape of terrible grotesques - beautiful lords and damsels, their joints twisted with palsey, their faces wracked with pox, starving dogs nipping at their hands, carrion crows pulling at their ears.

The doors are heavy, but swing open with some effort revealing a dank, damp chamber - a mockery of a feast hall furnished with a long, warped table covered in rotting victules picked over by giant, fiendish rats with the faces of dirty, runny-nosed urchins. At either end of the hall there is a great hearth filled with hellfire that gives out great gouts of oily, black smoke that fills the ceiling of the hall and provides no heat or comfort. Beyond the table, on a raised platform sits the lord of the feast, the Oinodaemon, and his court of seven rivals, all hidden beneath thick shrouds of dingy lace.

Each adventurer who has killed a daemon is commanded to come forward and take a place at the disgusting feast, a cacodaemon appearing behind them to guide them to their seat and place a goblet of thick, murky liquid before them. Those who have not killed a daemon are branded cowards and clapped in irons, their comrades finding it impossible to rise from the table until they have quaffed the rheumy mead that has been set before them.

The mead carries the daemon plague, of course. Those that die from the plague are reincarnated upon death as daemons. Those that survive are granted safe passage through the Lower Planes - at least in the presence of daemons.

Credit

Anthraxus (The Oinodaemon) originally appeared in the First Edition *Monster Manual II* (© TSR/Wizards of the Coast, 1983) and is used by permission.

Copyright Notice

Author Scott Greene, based on original material by Gary Gygax.

Daemon, Piscodaemon

Hit Dice: 10
Armor Class: -1 [20]
Attack: 2 claws (2d6), mouth tentacles (1d8 plus poison)
Saving Throw: 5
Special: Constrict, poison, spells, vorpal strike, only harmed by silver weapons, immunity to acid and poison, magic resistance (50%), telepathy 100 ft.
Move: 9/18 (swimming)
Alignment: Chaos
Challenge Level/XP: 20/4400

Piscodaemons look like 7-foot tall bipedal lobsters with long, gangly arms that end in powerful pincers. It has a short, fish-like tail on its posterior and a centipede-like head with several small tentacles located beneath its mouth and looking like a writhing beard. Piscodaemons are found throughout the Lower Planes bullying and killing weaker creatures. They are often themselves used as cannon fodder or slaves by the more powerful races of the Lower Planes. If a piscodaemon scores a natural 20 on its attack roll with a claw attack and its victim fails a saving throw, it severs one of the opponent's extremities (roll 1d6: 1-3 arm, 4-6 leg; 50% chance of either right or left). A piscodaemon's mouth tentacles are poisonous, affecting a victim as though with a *slow* spell for 1 minute if a saving throw is failed. Piscodaemons can cast the following spells: *Blink, cause fear, darkness, stinking cloud* and *mirror image* (2/day). The piscodaemon's faceted eyes can see in all directions, making it difficult to surprise. In addition, they can see invisible creatures and objects.

A Chip on the Shoulder

A solitary piscodaemon stalks across a landscape of twisted stone formations draped with brilliant reptilian skins that shimmer as though covered with jewels. The formations are separated by narrow gullies of freezing sand.

The piscodaemon and his fellows were set upon by a roaving band of mariliths, with this single specimen surviving the onslaught. It is now making its way back to its comrades with a king-sized chip on its chitinous shoulder. The piscodaemon would like nothing better than to unleash its fury on a band of outsiders, but it is wily enough to avoid a conflict it cannot hope to win, for it carries a stone tablet back to the greater daemon it serves.

The tablet contains the true name of a powerful bal-rukh in the language of demons. The tablet is composed of polished obsidian.

Credit

The Piscodaemon originally appeared in the First Edition *Monster Manual II* (© TSR/Wizards of the Coast, 1983) and is used by permission.

Copyright Notice

Author Scott Greene, based on original material by Gary Gygax.

Dakon

Hit Dice: 2
Armor Class: 4 [15]
Attack: 2 claws (1d6)
Saving Throw: 16
Special: None
Move: 12/12 (climbing)
Alignment: Neutrality
Challenge Level/XP: 2/30

Dakons are a race of intelligent apes that make their homes in the warmer regions of the world, though rarely, if ever, near a large expanse of water as they simply don't trust the stuff. They are generally friendly toward humans who share their alignment, and view all other races (even those races of the same alignment as the dakons) with caution and suspicion. Dakons stand 8 feet tall and weigh about 500 pounds. Dakons speak their own language and might speak Common if they dwell near humans. Dakons are very passive and docile creatures; they rarely attack except in self-defense. If forced into combat, a dakon attacks with its claws.

Skills: Dakons have a +8 racial bonus on Climb checks and can always choose to take 10 on a Climb check, even if rushed or threatened.

Dakons as Characters

Dakon characters enjoy a +1 bonus to Strength at character creation, though starting Strength cannot be higher than 18. Their large size and long arms allow them a +1 bonus to attacks involving grappling and they climb as well as a thief of equal level. A dakon's unarmed attacks inflict 1d4 damage instead of the normal 1d2. Dakon characters can see in the dark as well as elves. Dakons can take levels in fighter (advancing up to 7th level, or 8th level if their Strength score is 15 or higher) or magic-user (advancing up to 4th level, or 5th level if their Intelligence score is 15 or higher).

Gentle Masters

You come across a village sheltered by the overarching trees of the rain forest. The village is built near a small, swift stream and consists of several adobe buildings, some quite grand and a palisade of bamboo. The village is inhabited by 2d4 x 10 dakons. The dakons dwell in family bands, each in its own building. The buildings are domed structures, like large, mud brick igloos. The interiors are decorated with mosaics of stone and colorful glazes.

The village is ruled by several elder males with silvery fur. The elders are all druids of level 1d3+1. The dakon are friendly, though hesitant to allow travelers into their village without some gift of great value to prove their friendship. The villagers subsist on jungle vermin, fruits gathered in the forest and roots grown in their hidden gardens. The gardens are tended by bands of human servants, who trade their labor for the protection of the dakon. The dakon treat these servants gently, but consider them little more than beasts of burden or pets.

Credit

The Dakon originally appeared in the First Edition *Fiend Folio* (© TSR/Wizards of the Coast, 1981) and is used by permission.

Copyright Notice

Author Scott Greene, based on original material by Ian McDowall.

Dark Creeper

Hit Dice: 1
Armor Class: 3 [16]
Attack: Dagger (1d4)
Saving Throw: 17
Special: Darkness, death throes, light blindness, surprise on 1-2 on 1d6
Move: 12
Alignment: Neutrality (with chaotic inclinations)
Challenge Level/XP: 2/30

Dark creepers are dwellers that make their homes in the twisting passages and caverns of the subterranean world. They are small, thin humanoids with gray skin and eyes. Dark creepers dress in dark, filthy robes and smell of dung and rotted meat. When dark creepers' clothing begins to rot with age and fall from their bodies, they simply add another layer, rather than remove the tattered rags. Dark creepers speak their own babbling language (known as Darkling) understandable only by other dark creepers and dark stalkers (see that entry). Three times per day, a dark creeper can create an effect identical to the *darkness* spell. Dark creepers can see in all forms of darkness, including magical darkness. They also continuously *detect magic*. Abrupt exposure to bright light blinds dark creepers for 1d3 rounds. When killed, a dark creeper spontaneously explodes in a flash of white-hot light. All creatures within a 10-foot radius must succeed on a saving throw or be blinded for 1d6 x 10 minutes.

Sneak Thieves

In the dark of the tunnel you see a small, cloaked figure sitting alone,

hunched over some bauble in its hands and babbling like an idiot. From a distance, it looks as though it might be a dwarf or halfling, but as one approaches, it turns its head and you see the gray skin and the weird, gray eyes.

In the blink of an eye, the tunnel fills with a thick, impenetrable darkness and 1d6+1 additional dark creepers attack from forward and back, half of them having apparently trailing the adventurers for some time. The original dark creeper's bauble is a silver locket holding a strand of violet hair that once belonged to a high elven countess whose beauty was a legend. A portrait of the lady is painted inside the locket and the words "For Maximilian" are engraved on the back of the locket in the elven script.

Credit

The Dark Creeper originally appeared in the First Edition *Fiend Folio* (© TSR/Wizards of the Coast, 1981) and is used by permission.

Copyright Notice

Author Scott Greene, based on original material by Rik Shepard.

Dark Stalker

Hit Dice: 2
Armor Class: 1 [18]
Attack: Short sword (1d6)
Saving Throw: 16
Special: Darkness, fog cloud, death throes, light blindness, surprise on 1-2 on 1d6
Move: 12
Alignment: Neutrality (with a proclivity for chaos)
Challenge Level/XP: 4/120

If the dark creeper is rarely seen, the dark stalker is even rarer. They are the leaders and commanders of the dark creepers and rule the subterranean cities through might and fear. Dark stalkers are man-sized and have pallid skin. They wear the same type of filthy dark robes and clothes as the dark creepers. Dark stalkers speak their own babbling language understandable only to other dark stalkers and dark creepers. Some of the more intelligent dark stalkers speak Common. Dark stalkers generally try to avoid combat, using their powers to cover their escape. If forced into combat, they attack using their short swords, which they prefer to poison. If defeat is imminent, a dark stalker seeks the quickest means of escape possible. Three times per day, a dark stalker can create an effect identical to the *darkness* spell. Twice per day, a dark stalker can create a fog cloud (as *obscuring mist*). A dark stalker can continuously *detect magic* as the spell. Dark stalkers can see perfectly in darkness of any kind, including magical darkness. Abrupt exposure to bright light blinds dark stalkers for 1d3 rounds. When killed, a dark stalker spontaneously explodes in a flash of white-hot flame equal to a three dice *fireball* spell (save for half damage). Dark creepers within 60 feet that witness a dark stalker's death throes must succeed on a saving throw or flee in terror for 1d6 rounds.

Cult Leader

In a vast cavern, approximately 200 feet in diameter, with a high ceiling you discover numerous piles of junk. The piles contain all manner of refuse - rusted armor, broken weapons, candle stubs, bits of cord and rope - as well as a few good, even valuable items. The junkyard is the abode of 1d4 x 10 dark creepers and their leader, a dark stalker.

The darklings have been collecting bits and pieces for ages, and there is a 1% chance that any useful item resides in the yard, and a 1 in 1000 chance that a minor magic item is present. The items in question are buried in the piles of junk and thus take days to locate. The dark creepers have burrows in the piles of junk, and can find the item in question in mere moments if they have a mind to. The dark stalker dwells in a tent made of cast off cloaks over a wire frame atop the tallest pile in the yard.

Credit

The Dark Stalker originally appeared in the First Edition *Fiend Folio* (© TSR/Wizards of the Coast, 1981) and is used by permission.

Copyright Notice

Author Scott Greene, based on original material by Simon Muth.

Darnoc

Hit Dice: 8
Armor Class: 3 [16]
Attack: Slam (1d6)
Saving Throw: 8
Special: Curse of the grave, symbol of discord, ghostly
Move: 12
Alignment: Chaos
Challenge Level/XP: 10/1400

The darnoc is a corrupting evil presence whose very touch sucks the life from an opponent bit by painful bit. The darnoc are said to be the restless spirits of oppressive, cruel, and power hungry individuals cursed forever to a life of monotony and toil, forbidden by the gods to taste the spoils of the afterlife they so desperately craved in life. Often seen in the clothes and guise it wore in life, a darnoc often walks the same halls and repeats the same actions of its insipid existence over and over again.

Due to their great greed, a darnoc may be found within its treasury endlessly counting its coins, or within a graveyard noting the headstones of its vanquished foes with cruel mirth. When distracted from its reverie of its remembered past life, the creature flies into an inconsolable rage, often lashing out without warning or provocation at the first individual who attempts to speak to it. Creatures within a 30-foot radius and with less HD than the darnoc become flee in dear for 2d6 rounds when it flies into a rage if they fail a saving throw.

Once per day, a darnoc can scribe a symbol in the air. All creatures with an Intelligence score of 3 or higher within 60 feet who see the symbol must succeed on a saving throw or immediately fall into loud bickering and arguing. Meaningful communication is impossible. If the affected creatures have different alignments, there is a 50% chance that they attack each other. Bickering lasts 3d6 rounds. Fighting begins 1d6 rounds into the bickering and lasts 2d6 rounds. Once triggered, the symbol lasts 2 hours. Any damage dealt by a darnoc's slam attack does not heal naturally and resists all magical healing (potions, *cure* spells, and so on). Before the damage can be healed, the curse must first be broken with a *break enchantment* or *remove curse* spell (requiring a DC 20 caster level check for either spell).

A darnoc can become incorporeal for up to 10 minutes each day. While incorporeal, the darnoc can only be harmed by magic weapons and spells. Any humanoid slain by a darnoc becomes a darnoc in 1d4 rounds. Spawn are under the command of the darnoc that created them and remain enslaved until its destruction.

Insipid Greed

The ruler of the walled city-state was beside himself with worry. How was he to know that killing his exchequer would result in such calamity - after all, he had probably killed about one minister a month since he took the throne as a young man. Always the exchequer stood by, giving wise council and finding ways to fund the king's schemes.

But at the thought of giving the king his youngest daughter before her wedding day the minister balked, and for that he had to be killed. Death, however, did not part the exchequer from his post, for the next day his replacement fled in panic at the sight of the old man sitting in the treasury counting the coins.

Now, the wicked little king needs his money, and thus a team of adventurers capable of ridding the treasury of the minister's spirit. The king promises anything to get the deed done, but will certainly betray his saviors when they have completed their mission.

Copyright Notice
Author Scott Greene.

Death Dog

Hit Dice: 2
Armor Class: 4 [15]
Attack: 2 bites (1d6 plus rotting death)
Saving Throw: 16
Special: Rotting death
Move: 15
Alignment: Chaos
Challenge Level/XP: 3/60

Death dogs are two-headed, mastiff-like hounds; nocturnal killing machines that hunt their prey without hesitation across the desert sands and wastelands. Death dog packs have been known to share territory with little friction, although they do engage in dominance battles in leaner times when hunting is difficult. Victims of the death dog's bite must pass a saving throw or come down with the rotting death, losing 1d6 points of constitution each day until they succeed at a saving throw at a -5 penalty. Victims who lose all their points of constitution die. Constitution can be restored with powerful healing magic or be complete bed rest, with one point of constitution returning with each week of rest.

Killer Packs

While crossing the amber sands of the great desert you come across a lonely tower of sandstone that almost blends into the landscape. The tower shows some weathering, and appears to be quite ancient. The picked over bones of a horse lies half-buried in the sands near the tower. A sturdy iron door, scalding to the touch, blocks entry, and the tower has no windows, though a trap door allows access through the roof. The walls of the tower are five feet thick, and the circular rooms within measure 8 feet in diameter.

The ground floor is empty save for an old, dry straw mattress, some broken crockery and a longbow, the string snapped. The third floor is likewise empty, save for a dusty skull and a few empty wine bottles. The second floor, however, is inhabited by a maiden, beautiful but flushed and desperate, and her love, a young knight of the desert sands, his face haggard, his robes torn and a terrible wound on his right leg. The wound has been bound, but needs proper cleaning, for it looks septic. The knight is not long for the world, having perhaps two or three days before he dies unless given some powerful magical healing.

The maiden will explain that they were fleeing across the desert from her wicked uncle when they were attacked by a pack of 1d3+1 black, two-headed hounds. The knight was wounded by one of the dogs and they were fortunate to outrun them and find this tower. They've been trapped here for three days now, the dogs surrounding the tower each night and the knight too ill to walk, the horse having died from exhaution after their race across the desert.

Credit
The Death Dog originally appeared in the First Edition *Fiend Folio* (© TSR/Wizards of the Coast, 1981) and is used by permission.

Copyright Notice
Author Scott Greene, based on original material by Underworld Oracle.

Death Worm

Hit Dice: 7
Armor Class: 2 [17]
Attack: Bite (1d8 plus 1d6 acid)
Saving Throw: 9
Special: Spit lightning, surprise on 1-3 on 1d6
Move: 9/6 (burrowing)
Alignment: Neutrality
Challenge Level/XP: 8/800

Death worms are long, slender, reddish-brown monsters related to the purple worm. Its skin is mottled yellow across its back, tapering off as the colors near its head. Its mouth is huge and lined with rock hard teeth that allow it to break rocks and earth as it burrows underground. The death worm is a reclusive, desert-dwelling creature content to spend its life burrowing beneath the ground and sustaining itself on a diet of sand and earth. On occasion, it surfaces to devour more substantial prey (animals such as saiga, deer, yaks and humans). Death worms lay their eggs far beneath the surface of the earth. A death worm lurks under sand or loose earth, waiting for its prey to move close where it then ambushes its target, surprising on a 1-3 on 1d6. A death worm's mouth constantly drips highly corrosive saliva. Once every 1d4 rounds a death worm can spit a 3 dice lightning bolt (saving throw for half damage).

Opportunists

The guide you hired in the last village has been leading you over the rolling country of the steppe for several days when he finally stops cold and points to a distant outcropping of reddish-brown stones. The outcropping form a sort of natural gate to a lowland beyond. He will inform you that this is the entrance to the holy land of the great khan, the land of his birth and taboo for any to enter. He will go no further, but will explain that the place you seek (whatever goal is currently being sought by the players in your game) is beyond that land on the edge of a woodland of scrawny pines. The journey across the lowland should take approximately one week. At this he turns and heads away.

The lowland is sandy and barren, with strange stones, like monuments of chalk, breaking the endless sea of sand every few miles. The sands of the lowland are bronze colored, with strange streaks of darker, more reddish sand crisscrossing the landscape. The guide has, unfortunately, lied to you about this being holy land, for it is really the hunting ground of a death worm. The guide and his friends, who trailed about two days behind your band, plan to strike you when you flee the lowlands, bloodied and bruised by the worm, a few of your number maybe left to feed it. In all, the guide has 1d10+10 friends, bandits mounted on swift, light horses and wearing leather armor and carrying a short, jagged spear and a longbow with 25 arrows.

Copyright Notice

Authors Scott Greene and Erica Balsley.

Decapus

Hit Dice: 4
Armor Class: 4 [15]
Attack: 9 tentacles (1d4)
Saving Throw: 13
Special: Strangle, illusion
Move: 6/12 (climbing and swinging)
Alignment: Chaos
Challenge Level/XP: 7/600

A decapus is a large (4-foot in diameter), pale green spheroid with ten octopus-like tentacles protruding from its body. Hair grows in broken patches along its body. Its eyes are stark white and pupiless. Its large mouth sports long, yellow fangs. Decapuses are solitary creatures that dwell in dense forests or underground. Most prefer the forests as their ability to move among the trees allows them to either pursue their prey or flee in situations not to their advantage. On the ground, decapuses are slow-moving, thus they spend most of their time among the tree tops. Decapuses are nocturnal hunters and are quite fond of human, elf, and halfling flesh. In times when food is scarce, they exist on a diet of rats, snakes, and other small forest creatures (or dungeon denizens in the case of the subterranean decapus). Decapuses seem to be able to speak with others of their kind using a series of guttural noises.

Decapuses attack with their tentacles. A decapus that beats its opponent's Armor Class by 6 or more latches around their neck and scores automatic damage each round thereafter until it is killed (and 1d4 rounds even after it is killed) or its victim makes a successful open doors check. At will, a decapus can create an effect identical to the *phantasmal force* spell. The creature can also mimic any creature it has previously encountered with near total accuracy, though it cannot mimic humanoid speech longer than two or three words at a time.

Difficult Terrain

Regardless of the direction from which you enter this woodland of towering oaks, the ground slopes downward. The entire area is like a miles-wide funnel, eventually sinking into a series of flooded caverns featuring coursing rivers and waterfalls. Three swift streams run through the woodland and into the cave system. In many places in the woodland one will see the granite ledges that compose the landscape's foundation. One might also (1 in 10 chance, 1 in 6 for elves and rangers) notice broken limbs littering the ground, as though something heavy has moved through the trees, swinging from limb to limb. The funnel woods is home to a solitary decapus. The decapus keeps a lair of woven branches in a particularly tall tree that hangs over the open gulf that leads into the cavern system. A rushing waterfall runs past the tree. Any fight that occurs in the tree will be particularly dangerous, as a wrong move (missing an attack by more than 3 points or suffering maximum damage from a blow) might knock one into the vortex of water (saving throw to negate), a fall that will cause 10d6 points of damage and might very well end in drowning. The decapus keeps a modest treasure of 1d6 x 200 sp, 1d4 x 100gp in a terracotta coffer (worth 50 gp) in its lair.

Credit

The Decapus originally appeared in the First Edition module *B3 Palace of the Silver Princess* (© TSR/Wizards of the Coast, 1981) and is used by permission.

Copyright Notice

Author Scott Greene, based on original material by Jean Wells.

Demi-Lich

Hit Dice: 11
Armor Class: 0 [19]
Attacks: Steal soul
Saving Throw: 4
Special: Immune to most spells, +3 or better magic weapon to hit, immune to acid, electricity, fire, cold and polymorph, rejuvenation, steal souls
Move: 12 (flying)
Alignment: Chaos
Challenge Level/XP: 13/2,300

A demilich is a skull with gems in place of its eyes and teeth. Demiliches cannot be turned, and can cast cast *death spells* at will. Up to 8 times a day, a demilich can steal the soul of any creature within 30 feet unless the victim makes a save. After 24 hours, the demilich devours the soul, permanently slaying the creature. *Power word kill* and *dispel evil* spells deal 50 points of damage (no save) to a demilich. Demiliches are immune to all other spells. Unless its remains are consecrated, a demilich reforms in 1d10 days.

Tooth and Nail

This 75-foot-diameter room has but one entrance. The domed ceiling reaches 75 feet high at its peak, where a mural of an eclipsed sun looms. A crimson aura of light faintly glows from the mural and bathes the room in nightmarish light. The walls and half-sphere ceiling are covered in 6-inch-long rusted spikes set into the stone. A bier sits in the center of the room, draped with a sheer white burial shroud. A skull topped staff can be seen through the lattice shroud. The staff appears to be gem encrusted with platinum bands binding the shaft.

This is the burial vault of Akilha Harn, a little-known wizard from ancient times. In her day, she ruled a small kingdom with fear and cruelty. In her quest for immortality, she turned to lichdom. As an undead, she had her skull removed and replaced with one of copper (its location and terrible powers have yet to be discovered). She then created a staff of incredible power and topped it with her own skull. She ultimately evolved into the demilich that was placed in this vault. The skull is fastened to the magical staff, but can still attack normally anyone in the room.

The tomb is guarded by two aerial servants that are more of a distraction to the real danger that lurks within the room. A secret door on the side of the bier holds Akilha Harn's mostly disintegrated remains. Her moldering robes and funeral veil lie in tatters. Jewelry (both magical and regal) and other nonperishable items are entombed as well. The concealed treasure should be great to PCs matching wits with Akilha Harn's deadly legacy and utter iniquity. Destroying the demilich shatters the magical staff forever.

Credit

The Demi-Lich originally appeared in the First Edition module *S1 Tomb of Horrors* (© TSR/Wizards of the Coast, 1978) and is used by permission.

Copyright Notice

Author Scott Greene, based on original material by Gary Gygax.

Demiurge

Hit Dice: 8
Armor Class: 3 [16]
Attack: Incorporeal touch (1d4)
Saving Throw: 8
Special: Chill, soul touch, transfixing gaze, incorporeal, only harmed by cold-wrought iron or spells, magic resistance (50%)
Move: 12/15 (flying)
Alignment: Chaos
Challenge Level/XP: 14/2600

The demiurge is the undead spirit of an evil human returned from the grave with a wrathful vengeance against all living creatures that enter its domain. The demiurge is very territorial, usually haunting an area of up to three square miles from its place of death. It appears as a humanoid with sunken nose, hollow eye sockets, and sickly pale white, semi-transparent flesh. Its hair is unkempt and dirty, and its clothes are nothing more than rags that hang loosely from its translucent form. Any creature within 30 feet meeting the demiurge's gaze must succeed on a saving throw or be transfixed for one turn as if affected by a *hold person* spell. The touch of the demiurge brings the cold of the grave and deals 1d4 points of damage to a living creature touched. A creature that is moved through by a demiurge must pass a saving throw or die from shock. Animals can sense the unnatural presence of a demiurge at a distance of 30 feet. They will not willingly approach nearer than that and panic if forced to do so; they remain panicked as long as they are within that range.

Scorched Vengeance

While you were informed that the land beyond the mountain pass contained a fertile high meadow of dainty dun dairy cows and happy, though mildly xenophobic mountain herders, the land you see appears wild and uninhabited. You might come across a small herd of cattle, now half-wild and grazing, an alert bull challenging any who approach. About two miles into the meadowlands you discover a village surrounded by a low wall of field stone and consisting of a few dozen stone hovels and a ramshackle kirk with a blue door of oak and a large brass knocker in the shape of Jack o' the Green. Twenty or so bodies lie decomposing in the village, their faces twisted into masks of sheer horror, their flesh marbled and putrefaction setting in.

Most of the villagers have fled into the surrounding hills, most of them succumbing to the cold or packs of wolves. The source of their destruction was the burning of a foreign woman in front of the church - the charred post and bones and a pile of ashes still in evidence. The villagers believed her a witch, come to spread a pox among their cattle. Moments after the poor woman died, the grim villagers witnessed in horror her spectral image stepping out of the holocaust. Now a demiurge, she spread death and panic in her quest to revenge herself on the wicked peasants, blocking their attempts to flee into the mountain pass and sending most of them into the hills without food or adequate clothing. So enraged is this demiurge that she will attack any who enter the valley, provided they are within 3 miles of the charred post where she met her end.

The village's only treasure, besides two golden candlesticks in the kirk worth about 50 gp, are its cattle. About fifty of the creatures yet live and wander the valley.

Copyright Notice
Author Scott Greene.

Demodand, Shaggy

Hit Dice: 15
Armor Class: -3 [22]
Attack: 2 claws (1d8) and bite (2d6)
Saving Throw: 3
Special: Spells, +1 or better weapon to hit, magic resistance (75%), immunity to acid and poison, immune to mental effects
Move: 15/18 (flying)
Alignment: Chaos
Challenge Level/XP: 22/5000

The mighty shaggy demodands are the ruling class of the demodand race. No greater demodands are known to exist, though rumors lately hint at a single, powerful demodand of near-deity status. Shaggy demodands are by far the most malign, selfish, evil, and ruthless of the tripartite race of demodands. They are the nobility and upper class of demodand society and commanders of the demodand armies. A typical shaggy demodand stands 6 feet tall and weighs about 550 pounds. They resemble bipedal frog-like creatures with crimson skin. Shaggy demodands are bloated and their skin hangs in great folds about its body. Large, bat-like wings protrude from the creature's shoulders. Shaggy demodands can cast the following spells: *Charm monster (1/day), cloudkill (3/day), dispel magic (1/day), ESP, gaseous form, invisibility (self),* and *obscuring mist (3/day).*

Damn-sel in Distress

Atop the pinnacle of a citadel of cyclopean blocks of basalt on a basalt plain surrounded by plumes of acidic flame there sits the gloating conqueror, a massive shaggy demodand. The bloated fiend is surrounded by the spoils of its conquest - the bones of one thousand minor demons, licked clean of meat and sucked empty of marrow. Creeping about the citadel are 1d2 slime demodands and 1d4+1 tarry demodands, searching out the citadel for bits of treasure and hiding survivors of the assault.

Deep in the bowels (literally - the Netherworld is a frightening, confusing place) of the citadel, if one can dodge the slimes and otyughs, they might discover the princess of the citadel, an alu-demon, cradling her child and wearing the great treasure of the citadel, a crystalline gauntlet that can project hands of force and block magic missiles. She cannot escape the citadel without help, and might be willing to join forces with any adventurers treasure-hungry enough to have made it past the patrolling demodands.

Credit

The Shaggy Demodand originally appeared in the First Edition *Monster Manual II* (© TSR/Wizards of the Coast, 1983) and is used by permission.

Copyright Notice

Author Scott Greene, based on original material by Gary Gygax.

Demodand, Slime

Hit Dice: 13
Armor Class: -2 [21]
Attack: 2 claws (1d8 plus 1d6 acid) and bite (1d8)
Saving Throw: 3
Special: Enslime, spells, +1 or better weapon to hit, immunity to acid and poison, immune to mental effects, magic resistance (60%)
Move: 15/18 (flying)
Alignment: Chaos
Challenge Level/XP: 22/5000

Slime demodnads are 6 to 7-foot tall, bloated, slimy, black humanoids with large bat-like wings protruding from their shoulders. Its skin constantly drips and oozes a thick white-gray mucus. It has thick elephantine legs and long, powerful arms that end in razor-sharp talons. Slime demodands delight in torturing creatures of lesser skill and rank than themselves. The slimy secretions of the slime demodand are highly acidic, thus any contact with its skin causes 1d6 points of damage. Creatures hit by all three of the demodand's attacks in a round are covered in the acidic slime and suffer 1d6 points of damage per round until they are doused in either sand or alcohol. Wine cuts the damage in half and water has no effect. Slime demodands exude a stench to a range of 30 feet. Any living creature in the area must succeed on a saving throw or become sickened, suffering a -2 penalty to hit and save each round they are in the area and 2d6 rounds after leaving the area. Slime demodands can cast the following spells: *Cause fear*, *dispel magic* (1/day), *ESP*, *gaseous form*, *invisibility (self)* and *obscuring mist*.

The Lake of Slime

Amidst a shallow lake of gray slime there is a rocky island, and atop that island a twisted tower of barbed wrought iron. The tower has no entrance other than a circular stone portal in the base. A total strength of 50 is required to pivot the stone. Once inside the tower, one finds themselves at the bottom of a long, winding shaft studded with rusty spikes that can be used to climb. The shaft is 100 feet long and ends in a small observation chamber clad in cloudy crimson glass, warm to the touch.

Hanging from the ceiling by a brazen chain is a sword of damascus steel, black of blade and engraved with profane images. The longsword is a *+2 weapon* and, when swung, cries out in a terrible shriek that causes fear in creatures with 3 HD or less. Tendrils of malevolent force will burrow into the flesh of the wielder of the sword, clogging their minds with paranoia and hatred and turning them deeply and irrevocably evil if they do not pass a saving throw once a week to retain control of themselves. The slimy lake, 1 mile in diameter, is the hunting ground of 1d4+1 slime demodands, the lax guardians of the evil sword.

Credit

The Slime Demodand originally appeared in the First Edition *Monster Manual II* (© TSR/Wizards of the Coast, 1983) and is used by permission.

Copyright Notice

Author Scott Greene, based on original material by Gary Gygax.

Demodand, Tarry

Hit Dice: 11
Armor Class: -1 [20]
Attack: 2 claws (1d8), bite (1d8)
Saving Throw: 4
Special: Adhesive, spells, +1 or better weapon to hit, immune to acid and poison, immune to mental effects, magic resistance (50%)
Move: 15/21 (flying)
Alignment: Chaos
Challenge Level/XP: 18/3800

Tarry demodands are tall gray-skinned humanoids with green eyes and a long, oval heads. Two large, dull gray bat-like wings sprout from its shoulders. Its hands end in blackened claws. Cruel, malevolent creatures, they wander the planes of Tarterus as soldiers and warriors in the mighty demodand armies. Tarry demodands care little for anything and attack and kill just about anything weaker than themselves. When they take damage, they have a 50% chance of flying into a rage, gaining +2 bonus to hit and damage and suffering a -2 penalty to Armor Class. A tarry demodand exudes a thick tar-like substance that acts as a powerful adhesive, holding fast any creatures or items touching it. Removing a stuck item or body part requires an open door check. Because of their adhesive skin, tarry demodands enjoy a +2 bonus to grapple and pin opponents in combat. Strong alcohol dissolves the adhesive. A pint of wine or a similar liquid weakens it, but the tarry demodand can still grapple normally. A tarry demodand can dissolve its adhesive at will, and the substance breaks down 1 minute after the creature dies. Tarry demodands can cast the following spells: *cause fear*, *dispel magic (1/day)*, *ESP*, *gaseous form* and *invisibility (self)*.

Tar and Fungus

From beyond this small box canyon in a landscape of white bluffs shaped like supplicating demons and giant puffball fungi (ascomoids) that blow across the landscape like tumbleweeds one can hear the clash of arms, as two mighty armies of the Underworld go through one of the many pointless bloodlettings so common to these dimensions.

A troupe of 1d4+1 tarry demodands has fled from this battle and now hides in this canyon hoping to evade detection by the hell hounds of their master. The bizarre creatures now sit in the shade of one of the mighty bluffs (one can just make out a whimper coming from the stone), rolling the knuckle bones of a saintly man in some form of game and betting chips carved from the horns of devils. Although they had no desire to throw themselves into yet another battle for their master, the chaotic fiends are more than happy to attack a band of meddling adventures.

At the first sign of company, they vanish from view and make their way into a position of ambush.

Credit

The Tarry Demodand originally appeared in the First Edition *Monster Manual II* (© TSR/Wizards of the Coast, 1983) and is used by permission.

Copyright Notice

Author Scott Greene, based on original material by Gary Gygax.

Demon, Aeshma (Rage Demon)

Hit Dice: 12
Armor Class: -1 [20]
Attack: Weapon (2d6+1) or 2 claws (1d8)
Saving Throw: 3
Special: Rage, spells, wounding spear, +1 or better weapon to hit, immune to electricity, see invisibility, magic resistance (45%), telepathy 100 ft.
Move: 15/21 (flying)
Alignment: Chaos
Challenge Level/XP: 19/4100

Aeshma are demons of rage. They creature are 8-foot tall humanoids with basalt-colored skin. Dark hair covers its head and its hair is long and braided. Its arms are well-muscled and its hands end in powerful claws. Its head is human-like and its eyes are sapphire blue. Large leathery, bat-like wings protrude from its shoulders. Aeshma, sometimes called "fiends of the wounding spear", sometimes command battalions of lesser demons, usually vrocks or dretches. An aeshma that is reduced to half it normal hit points in combat flies into a berserk rage on its next turn, swinging madly with its longspear. A raging aeshma fights until either it or its opponent is dead and gains an additional attack each round. Aeshma continuously see invisibility. They can cast a *web* spell twice per day. Aeshma carry long *+1 spears* that cause terrible wounds when they hit. Creatures wounded by these spears suffer 1d2 points of damage each round after they are wounded from blood loss until the wounds are bound or magically healed.

A Whiter Shade of Rage

The strange palace of blue glass rising from the fetid swamplands of the Underworld seems an uncharacteristic island of calm in an otherwise abyssmal land of pain and torment. The palace measures 500 feet to a side and featured hundreds of slim towers, each ending in a perfect sphere. Weird, worm-like shapes can be seen wriggling inside the spheres to an unknown purpose. Four gates has the blue palace, each possessing a gate made of wrought iron, but each open to entry.

Inside the palace there are a myriad of passages, stairs up and down and domed chambers furnished with angular chairs and tables of white wood. As one approaches the center of the palace, they discern a strange droning coming from the walls, as though somebody is running a wet finger along the rim of a crystal goblet. The very center of the palace is a circular tower, the tallest of the palace.

The tower stands 300 feet tall and is open from floor to ceiling. In the center of the tower, floating three feet above the floor, there is a sphere of azure glass pulsing with brilliant white light. As a group studies the sphere, they might not notice the exits from the tower slowly closing, filling with glass until, when completely blocked, one would never know there were exits at all.

Once the exits are closed, the glass walls of the tower will begin to swirl, becoming blue-violet and then red-violet, and finally casting a light the color of freshly spilled blood. The droning becomes louder and more insistent, reaching into one's psyche and drawing out their ire and rage until all present must pass a saving throw each round to avoid attacking their allies.

The droning can be stopped by smashing the globe, releasing an aeshma, the genius loci of the palace. Once released, the aeshma attacks any present. The death of the demon is the only way to re-open the exits from the central tower. After the demon's death, the palace is filled with thousands of ghosts, the souls of those claimed by rage and violence. The ghosts ignore the adventurers unless attacked, though they might accidentally drift through them while wandering the halls.

Demon, Alu-

Hit Dice: 6
Armor Class: 1 [18]
Attack: Sword (1d8) or 2 claws (1d4)
Saving Throw: 11
Special: Spells, vampiric touch, immune to poison, magic resistance (15%), telepathy 100 ft.
Move: 12/18 (flying)
Alignment: Chaos
Challenge Level/XP: 10/1400

The alu-demon is the female demonic offspring of a succubus and human. Though part demon, not all alu-demons are inherently chaotic (although lawful alu-demons are extremely rare). The typical alu-demon has black or brown hair and dark green, brown, or black eyes. Alu-demons might be sent to the Material Plane to seduce mortals. When on such missions they typically arrange their flowing hair so it hides their horns and also fold their wings against their backs (and tuck them under their robe, shirt, or whatever garment of clothing one happens to be wearing at the time). Each time an alu-demon hits with its claw attack it gains temporary hit points equal to the damage she inflicts. These temporary hit points disappear in one hour. Alu-demons can cast the following spells: *Charm person* (3/day), *dimension door* (1/day), *ESP* (3/day) and *suggestion* (1/day).

Thar She Blows!

Across the storm-tossed seas of the Abyss there roams a sleek whaler, the *Broken Vow*, a stately ship of bone and laquered wood with three masts and a crew of 20 lost souls (zombies, but more mobile than usual and possessed of a malevolent intelligence).

The captain of the *Broken Vow* is a swaggering, foul-mouthed alu-demon who wears slops of black velvet, a vest of purple satin and veritable horde of ivory and gold jewelry (worth 500 gp). The alu-demon carries a curved sword and dagger, and can be seen pacing the decks, barking orders and periodically peering into the grey swirl that passes for an atmosphere above the ebony waves flecked with crimson foam.

The *Broken Vow* and its captain hunt abyssal whales with jagged harpoons fired from swivel guns. They are currently on the hunt for the whale that took the captain's last ship and crew.

Credit

The Alu-Demon originally appeared in the First Edition module *S4 Lost Caverns of Tsojcanth* (© TSR/Wizards of the Coast, 1982) and later in the First Edition *Monster Manual II* (© TSR/Wizards of the Coast, 1983) and is used by permission.

Copyright Notice

Author Scott Greene, based on original material by Gary Gygax.

Demon, Balban (Brute Demon)

Hit Dice: 9
Armor Class: 2 [17]
Attacks: 2 fists (1d6), 1 bite (1d8)
Saving Throw: 6
Special: Magic resistance (15%), pound, trample
Move: 14
Alignment: Chaos
Challenge Level/XP: 10/1,400

A balban demon resembles a 12-foot-tall bipedal elephant. Balbans attack with its two fists. If it hits a single opponent with both fists, it pounds the victim into the ground for an additional 2d6 points of damage. Balbans can charge and trample creatures for 2d8 points of damage (save avoids).

The Legless Wizard

The wizard Bidbleez suffered a horrific injury from an encounter with a wrath dragon that left him permanently scarred. His legs end at the knees and deep burn scars cover his flesh. Bidbleez, not one to let a mere flesh wound hamper him, arrived at a demented solution. Through his dark arts, he made a pact with a balban to allow the demon to serve as his legs. He rides the balban on a special chair attached to the balban's four horns and broad, flat head. The chair is bolted to the horns and Bidbleez is strapped securely into the chair. Together, these two roam and savage the lands in search of a treatment that will restore Bidbleez to health and fulfill the pact he made with the balban.

BIDBLEEZ: HD 9 (magic-user); HP 21; AC 9[10]; Atk 1 dagger (1d4); Move 12; Save 7; CL/XP 9/1,100; Special: Spells.

4/3/3/2/1; Spells: 1—*Charm Person, Magic Missile* **(x2)**, *Shield*; 2—*Invisibility, Levitate, Web*; 3—*Fireball, Invisibility (10-foot Radius)*, *Protection from Normal Missiles*; 4—*Confusion, Ice Strom*; 5—*Cloudkill*

Copyright Notice

Author Scott Greene.

Demon, Cambion

Hit Dice: 8
Armor Class: 1 [18]
Attack: Weapon or 2 claws (1d6)
Saving Throw: 8
Special: Spells, +1 or better weapon to hit, immune to electricity and poison, magic resistance (20%), telepathy 100 ft.
Move: 15
Alignment: Chaos
Challenge Level/XP: 12/2000

When an incubus mates with a human female, the offspring is a cambion. Cambions, unlike their "sisters" the alu-demons, are always chaotic and care little for anyone or anything but their own well-being. They are selfish, self-centered, and egotistical. Cambions hate humans and are often employed as assassins. Cambions are always male. The typical cambion stands 6 or 7 feet tall and weighs 200 pounds or more. It is stocky in build and has scaly skin of various colors, with blue being the most common, small fangs, tiny horns and crimson eyes. Cambions usually speak the common tongue of men, the secret language of demons and at least one other language. Cambions can cast *cause fear, ESP, levitate* and *polymorph self* at will.

Consorts of Demons

The old witch hill outside the village is best avoided - any attempt at gathering rumors in the village public house will garner that piece of advice. The ground on the hill is gray and spongy, with cruel, spiked stones forming a chaotic shrine (or so the locals say). The space inside those stones does show signs of fires burning there, and some digging will produce bones that might have come from animals or humanoids. The locals say that a coven of witches used to meet at that spot and conduct terrible revels under the dark of the new moon, conjuring spirits that would knock on doors at night and then flee or curdle the cow's milk.

The hill measures about 500 feet in diameter and rises about 35 feet at its highest point. Twelve runic stones have been erected around the base of the hill by local priests to hem in the malevolent influence of the site and, if not make it holy, at least make it useless to the unholy. On the far side of the hill there is a small cave that leads into the lair of an aged man with blue-gray hair. The old man is a hermit, a cambion demon born on the hill during one of the revels and now unable to leave it due to the presence of the holy stones.

Inside his humble lair he has a simple straw pallet, a gallery of skulls - adventurers who decided to investigate the odd rumors they had heard in the village - and wooden chest covered in the skin of those adventurers and branded with profane symbols. Inside this chest he keeps his treasure and a book of mystic investigations he has made in trying to break the influence of the holy stones. This book can be used by magic-users trying to develop spells to overcome magic or summon demons, giving them a bonus on rolls made to develop their spells.

Credit
The Cambion originally appeared in the First Edition *Monster Manual II* (© TSR/Wizards of the Coast, 1983) and is used by permission.

Copyright Notice
Author Scott Greene, based on original material by Gary Gygax.

Demon, Chaaor (Beast Demon)

Hit Dice: 11
Armor Class: 1 [19]
Attacks: 2 claws (1d8+3) and bite (2d6+3)
Saving Throw: 4
Special: Rend, roar, magical abilities, summon demons, +1 weapons to hit, immune to electricity and poison, resists cold, fire and acid
Move: 12
Alignment: Chaos
Challenge Level/XP: 15/2,900

A chaaor is a 12-foot-tall, hulking, ape-like brute with the head of a bear. Large downward curving, grayish-silver horns grow from its head and end in rounded points. A chaaor's body is covered in reddish-black fur and is almost always caked or matted in blood. The powerful arms of a chaaor end in razor-sharp and filthy black claws. Long rows of sharpened teeth fill the chaaor's mouth. When moving, the chaaor usually drops to all fours. When facing an aggressor it assumes a bipedal stance. If a chaaor hits with both claw attacks, it tears the flesh of its opponent for an automatic 2d8 points of damage. Three times per day, a chaaor can let loose a deadly roar that does 3d6 points of damage to all creatures within 60 feet (save for half). At will a chaaor can create *darkness* (15 foot radius) and *teleport*. Chaaor are immune to electricity and poison, and take half damage from cold, fire and acid.

Does a Bear Wreak Havoc In the Woods?

Dunslap Hollow's main commodity is swine. The entire town has developed into a massive swine farm where the overpopulated livestock run freely through the streets. Having only a population around hundred and fewer than 20 permanent structures, the few paths through town are quagmires of mud and feces. High councilman Hamish Talley runs the stockyard and the local tavern. The indentured townsfolk work for him and are paid in rent, sparse rations and cheap booze. Talley instantly dislikes anyone who questions how he runs his town, and his "boys" take care of people who raise too much of a fuss.

Hamish and his cronies recently ran a druid named Farlardo out of town. Farlardo arrived spouting off about the inhumane treatment of the swine in town and the damage to the environment from their waste. Hamish told his men the druid was right and ordered them to clean the streets … by pulling the haughty druid through the muck. They left the filth-covered druid on the outskirts of town and told him to never come back.

Since then, town workers and swine alike have disappeared nightly leaving only gore as a clue to their fate. The embarrassed Farlardo made a pact with a Chaaor demon to get even with the town, and the demonic bear is reveling in the torment it is causing. It allows people to enter Dunslap Hollow, but brutally attacks those who attempt to leave.

Demon, Choronzon (Chaos Demon)

Hit Dice: 16
Armor Class: 0 [19]
Attacks: 2 claws (1d8), 1 bite (2d6)
Saving Throw: 6
Special: Confusion, magic resistance (55%), +2 or better magic weapon required to hit, immune to electricity and fire, decomposing breath
Move: 14
Alignment: Chaos
Challenge Level/XP: 17/3,500

A choronzon is a 20-foot-tall behemoth weighing 9,000 pounds with a muscular demonic body. It has bluish-black scaly flesh and horns and claws. Choronzons radiate confusion (as per the spell of the same name) within 20 feet and its decomposing breath deals 8d6 points of damage in a 50-foot diameter (save for half damage). The massive demon can cause *darkness* in a 20-foot radius and resists magic.

When Looking Into the Abyss . . .

A large, ruined wall stands defiantly amid the spacious and partially collapsed room. A 15-foot-tall mirror remains imbedded into the far wall. It has miraculously survived unscathed. A nondescript wooden border encircles its oval shape. Its creators branded a prophecy into the frame in old and ornate script:

Envisage eras of arid seas and lands afire,
Whilst Legion devours souls impious and vain.
Look within the mirror, state your desire,
For the meek shall inherit and the faithful reign.

The mirror grants the first two wishes to those standing before it. Although the mirror is not inherently evil, the wishes appear to become reality. With time, however, the wishes distort and curse the individual. With a third wish, the reflective surface of the mirror becomes a *wall of fire* and a choronzon steps through the portal. The mirror's origin, purpose and powers lie with the Game Referee, as do the exact results and bane of the granted wishes.

Copyright Notice
Author Scott Greene.

CORRUPTOR DEMONS

Demons of corruption (also called corruptor demons) are used by the various greater demons (including the lords and princes) to destroy all that is good and just by seducing agents of good and law. Many spellcasters have fallen victim to the temptations and lies these demons spread. Those that fall from the side of good find themselves spiraling down into a sea of madness and despair from which they rarely return.

The demon lords and princes made it easy for even the weakest spellcaster (one not able to summon and control demons because of insufficient knowledge or understanding of the required spells) to summon a demon of corruption; if the demon can corrupt a lawful creature early in its career, the demon lord or prince can take that creature under its wing and mold it into a powerful tool of chaos.

When summoned, a demon of corruption automatically establishes a mental link between itself and the one who summoned it (the host). Distance is not a factor to maintain the link, and it can span across planes and dimensions. The demon need not concentrate to maintain the link. A corruptor demon can have in existence at one time a number of links equal to its Hit Dice. A corruptor demon can break a link it has established any time it likes.

The link allows the demon to speak (as if by *telepathy*) to the host and submit subconscious thoughts and messages to him or her. Once per task requested of the corruptor demon (or once per week if no task is requested), as long as the link is in existence, the host must succeed on a saving throw or have his alignment shift one increment toward Chaos.

When the host's alignment completely shifts to Chaos (or if the host is chaotic when the link is first established), he must immediately succeed on a saving throw or go permanently insane. A successful save negates the insanity for one month, after which time a new save must be made again. This cycle continues until the host fails a save and goes insane or until the link between host and corruptor demon is broken. The link is blocked by lead and magical circles and can be dispelled through magical means.

The alignment shift caused by these demons can only be removed after the link is broken. This requires the host to voluntarily subject himself to a ritual performed by a cleric (or druid) of at least 9th level of the alignment the subject originally possessed. The subject of the ritual might also have to atone through some specific act.

Call Lesser Demon

Conjuration (Calling)
Spell Level: Cleric and Magic-User, 3rd level
Range: 30 feet
Duration: Instantaneous

By casting this spell, you summon a lesser demon of 5 HD or less. You do not need to have the same alignment as the demon summoned. This spell was specifically created by a powerful demon prince (some say Orcus) and allowed to pass into the hands of mortal spellcasters to summon corruptor demons so they might corrupt the caster and turn him chaotic. Lawful creatures can freely employ this spell if desired.

The target creature receives a saving throw to avoid the calling. If the save fails, the creature is immediately drawn to your location. A demon subjected to this spell receives a penalty on its saving throw or magic resistance roll based on the alignment of the caster. Demons suffer a -2 or 10% penalty if summoned by a neutral spell caster and a -4 or 20% penalty if the spell caster is lawful.

You may ask the demon to perform one task for you, and the demon may ask for some service in return (note that corruptor demons never request anything in return, desiring only to use their whisper of madness against the caster). The more demanding the task, the greater the return favor asked for by the summoned demon. This bargaining takes at least 1 round, so any actions by the demon begin in the round after it arrives. If the character agrees to the service, the demon performs the task the character requested, reports back to the character afterward (if possible), and returns to its home plane. The character is honor bound to perform the return favor. If the return favor is not completed as promised, the summoner is visited by an appropriate number of demons that attempt to slay him and take his soul.

Demon, Corruptor - Azizou (Pain Demon)

Hit Dice: 4
Armor Class: 1 [18]
Attack: 2 claws (1d4), bite (1d6)
Saving Throw: 13
Special Attacks: Spells, whisper of madness, rending claws, +1 or better weapon to hit, immunity to electricity and poison, magic resistance (10%), telepathy 100 ft.
Movement: 12/18 (flying)
Alignment: Chaos
CL/XP: 7/600

The azizou is slightly larger than the barizou and is quite strong for its size. They are relentless combatants and love to inflict pain and suffering on their opponents in combat. Azizoiu have jackal heads, grayish skin covered in patches of course, black hair and large, round eyes with slit-pupils of gray. Membranous wings protrude from their backs and their hands and feet end in talons. A combatant who suffers damage from both of an azizou's claw attacks in the same round suffers an additional 1d6 damage as its flesh is rended. Azizous can cast *cause fear, ESP, invisibility (self)* and *stinking cloud.*

Demon, Corruptor - Barizou (Assassin Demon)

Hit Dice: 3
Armor Class: 2 [17]
Attack: 2 claws (1d4), bite (1d6)
Saving Throw: 14
Special Attacks: Spells, whisper of madness, chamelon, backstab, +1 or better weapon to hit, immunity to electricity and poison, magic resistance (5%), telepathy 100 ft.
Movement: 12/18 (flying)
Alignment: Chaos
CL/XP: 6/400

Called assassin demons or infiltrator demons, the barizou are employed as such because their small size allows them to move unseen in many places larger demons cannot go. They look like gray-skinned halflings with the heads of wolves, membranous wings and talons on their hands and feet. A barizou's mouth is filled with razor-sharp fangs and its back is mottled with sickly patches of bluish-gray. Barizou can cast *cause fear* and *invisibility (self)* at will. Barizou can alter their coloration to blend with their suroundings, allowing them to surprise on a roll of 1-4 on 1d6. When a barizou attacks a surprised opponent, they can backstab for double damage (as a thief).

Demon, Corruptor - Geruzou (Slime Demon)

Hit Dice: 5
Armor Class: 0 [19]
Attack: 2 claws (1d4), bite (1d6)
Saving Throw: 12
Special Attacks: Spells, whisper of madness, spit slime, +1 or better weapon to hit, immunity to electricity and poison, magic resistance (15%), telepathy 100 ft.
Movement: 12/18 (flying)
Alignment: Chaos
CL/XP: 8/800

Geruzou are sometimes called slime demons because their sickly-gray, leathery skin constantly drips and oozes thick, jelly-like mucus. Like their brethren, they are fierce combatants and are often employed as hunters and trackers by greater demons. The typical geruzou stands nearly 4 feet tall and has a horse-like head with downward-curving horns. It has long, sharp teeth exploding from its mouth, stretching its lips back in a perpetual snarl, and taloned hands and feet. A pair of large, membranous wings jut from its back. Three times per day, a geruzou can spit a stream of slimy goo in a 20-foot line. This spit attack requires a ranged attack against an AC of 10 plus its target's Dexterity bonus to AC (if any). A creature hit by the slime is coated and slowed (as the *slow* spell) for 6 rounds if it fails a saving throw. A geruzou can cast *cause fear, darkness, ESP, invisibility (self)* and *mirror image.*

Who's Tempting Whom?

Exploring the underworld, you come across a tall, octagonal chamber with a vaulted ceiling clad in prophyry. In the center of the room there is a large scrying pool surrounded by three demons, a barizou, azizou and geruzou. The demons are watching a sorcerous NPC known to the adventurers (but not an ally) as he thumbs through a book of demonology. The demons are not yet tempting the man, as he has not yet decided to call one of them. Although the adventurers may think they have arrived in time to stop the demons, they are in fact being lured into a trap of temptation themselves.

The NPC magic-user is of little interest to the demons, who are themselves intended to be sacrificed to the swords of the PCs. In fact, the PCs are being tempted into using their knowledge of the NPC against him. Whether the scrying pool is showing a true scene or not is up to the Referee, but it is a certainty that a different scrying pool in the Abyss is showing the activities of the PCs for the entertainment of a major demon.

Copyright Notice
Authors Scott Greene and Clark Peterson.

Demon, Daraka (Swarm Demon)

Hit Dice: 12
Armor Class: -3 [22]
Attack: 2 claws (1d10), bite (2d6) or scorpions (1d6 plus poison)
Saving Throw: 3
Special: Scorpions, spells, magic or silver weapons to hit, immunity to electricity and poison, magic resistance (50%), telepathy 100 ft.
Move: 15
Alignment: Chaos
Challenge Level/XP: 19/4100

Darakas are 9-foot tall, black-skinned humanoids with the heads of rams. A daraka's skin is leathery and oily and from a distance of 10 feet or more appears to be a mass of writhing flesh. Closer inspection reveals thousands of tiny scorpions swarming its flesh, skittering in and out of its mouth, ears and nose, seemingly unnoticed by the demon. They act as guards to the greater demons or as shock troops in demonic armies. Quite intelligent, they are often used as commanders or leaders, with each daraka having a battalion of minor demons at its command. Darakas can make themselves *invisible* at will and can cast the spell *feeblemind* once per day. They can sling scorpions at opponents as a range attacks. Those hit are covered in a swarm of the tiny vermin and stung repeatedly for 1d6 points of damage and, if a saving throw is failed, paralysis for 1d4 rounds.

Scorpions of the Swarm

A gang of 1d3+1 darakas guard the entrance to a massive subterranean temple. The entrance is in a subterranean canyon of gray stone that is warm to the touch. The walls of the canyon are covered in patches of white lichen in the shape of screaming faces. At the end of the canyon there is a facade of black onyx with large, brass portal into the depths of the temple.

The guardians stand in front of the portal, which is further blocked by a slab of basalt that requires a combined strength of 60 to shift. Several pits of rusty spikes are placed in front of the temple facade, the pits opening and closing randomly once battle is joined. Should the guardians be bested, the pits survived and the slab removed, the adventurers will discover that the "temple" consists of a 5-ft by 5-ft space occupied by a slimy shaft crawling with swarms of scorpions and descending 500 feet into the earth and ending in a giant vault of slime.

Copyright Notice

Author Scott Greene.

Demon, Gallu- (Faceless Demon)

Hit Dice: 7
Armor Class: 0 [19]
Attacks: 2 claws (1d3), 1 bite (2d6)
Saving Throw: 9
Special: Immune to poison and electricity, magical abilities
Move: 12
Alignment: Chaos
Challenge Level/XP: 9/1,100

A gallu-demon is a 9-foot-tall featureless black humanoid with a mouth filled with rows of sharpened teeth. A gallu-demon can *polymorph self* and *dimension door* at will. Gallu-demons are immune to poison and electricity.

Law and Orders

Mireeum Ubner and her two daughters, looking like vagrants, scrub soiled chamber pots with ragged sponges outside an untidy manor house. Deep bruises and lash marks cover their exposed flesh. Their ragged and soiled garments were once exquisite evening gowns. Blisters covering their hands, feet and knees tell of the hours of arduous work they endure every day.

Mireeum is the wife of chief constable Da' Ubner and until recently led an idyllic life few could even dream of. Da' Ubner was an influential and popular chief constable within the city and led his men justly and fairly.

What no one knows yet is that Da' Ubner was assassinated and replaced by a gallu-demon just weeks ago. His corpse still lies within the attic of the manor house. Since taking over as Da' Ubner, the malevolent gallu-demon has corrupted the city guard and destroyed their morale. Even worse, the new Da' Ubner has enslaved his wife and daughters. He routinely abuses them and intentionally prolongs their suffering, each day creating new and more-demeaning tasks for them to perform. Da' Ubner hosts lavish and decadent parties nightly, while his family sleeps chained in the kennel. The family has fallen far from their past nobility. The public scorns and ridicules them, but fears Da' Ubner's authority too much to not attend his gatherings when ordered to do so. With Da' Ubner's clout and a garrison of semi-loyal troops, few question his ethics publicly and live.

Demon, Gharros (Scorpion Demon)

Hit Dice: 16
Armor Class: -3 [22]
Attack: Axe (2d8) and 2 tail stings (1d8 plus poison)
Saving Throw: 3
Special: Poison, spells, +1 or better weapon to hit, immune to electricity and poison, magic resistance (50%), telepathy 100 ft.
Move: 12
Alignment: Chaos
Challenge Level/XP: 22/5000

This hideous creature appears to be half-scorpion and half-human. Its upper torso is that of a greenish-silver humanoid with long, flowing dark hair and stark white eyes while its lower torso is that of a reddish-brown scorpion. Its tail splits into two separate stingers and the creature's mouth is filled with razor-sharp teeth. Gharros serve as guards, soldiers, shock troops and assassins to some of the minor nobles and lesser demon lords of the Abyss. The poison from the gharros' scorpion sting is lethal if one fails a saving throw. Gharros can cast the spells *darkness* and *mirror image* at will.

Planar Gates

At the pinnacle of a tall mountain there is a gate of golden bars measuring 9 cubits wide by 12 cubits high. The gate sits in a tunnel that goes all the way through the mountain - about 1 mile. Travelers who enter the tunnel from the west will find the gate guarded by 1d3+1 monadic devas. From this direction the gate allows travel into the Ethereal Plane for chaotics, the Astral Plane for neutrals and the Upper Planes for lawfuls. Those who enter from the east will find the gate guarded by 1d3+1 gharros demons. From this direction, the gate allows access to the Elemental Plane of Fire for lawfuls, the Elemental Plane of Earth for neutrals and the Lower Planes for chaotics.

Copyright Notice
Author Scott Greene.

Demon, Greruor (Frog Demon)

Hit Dice: 10
Armor Class: -1 [20]
Attacks: gore (1d6) and bite (2d6) or polearm (2d6)
Saving Throw: 5
Special: Acid and fire spittle, magical abilities, summon demons, leap, immune to electricity and poison, resist cold, fire and acid
Move: 9
Alignment: Chaos
Challenge Level/XP: 14/2,600

A greruor is a squat, bloated, frog-like demon with arms in place of its forelegs. Its wide, frog-like head has two 3-foot-long horns protruding just above its deep, sunken eyes. It moves by hopping on its rear legs, leaping up to 20 feet. Its arms end in talons that are usually clutched around the greruor's deadly ranseur (2d6). Its huge mouth sports razor-sharp teeth of a dull gray color. The greruor's flesh is greenish-brown mottled with red or gray. Its skin constantly oozes and secretes a thick, mucus-like clear slime. Once every 1d4 rounds, a greruor can spit a line of acid up to 30 feet that deals 4d4 points of damage. On the greruor's next turn, the acid ignites and the opponent bursts into flame and takes 1d6 points of damage per round until extinguished. A save halves the acid damage and prevents the creature from bursting into flame. At will, a greruor can cause *confusion*, create *darkness* (15 foot radius), *hold person* and *detect good*. Greruor are immune to electricity and poison, and take half damage from cold, fire, and acid.

Village of the Damned

Kulkin's Vale is under siege, with the few villagers holed up in the town's small garrison. The town's soldiers were the first to die when Horrkurven, a greruor demon, leapt into town. In the chaos, the town was set ablaze and nearly burned to the ground. Horrkurven killed the guards with his acidic spittle, and drove the rest screaming from the town's gates.

The women and children retreated into the garrison and shut the doors, just in time to keep the demonic entity at bay. The walls are too high for it to leap, and its burning spit does little against the keep's fortified walls. The villagers are desperate. Horrkurven lurks in the burned-out homes.

PCs entering the village find skeletons lying in the street, the bones soft and brittle from acid and fire. Horrkurven lairs in the fire-ravaged temple. The demon has crafted a throne nest from the bones of his victims in the high rafters of the shrine, and leaps down on intruders. The demon was tasked with destroying the town by a magic-user who was run out of the village for consorting with demons. Inside the garrison are 15 women and 20 children (all under age 10). The rest of the villagers were killed or ran away during the chaos of the greruor's attack.

Copyright Notice
Author Scott Greene.

Demon, Mallor (Serpent Demon)

Hit Dice: 14
Armor Class: -4 [23]
Attacks: 2 claws (1d6 + poison) or *+1 longspear* (2d6+1)
Saving Throw: 3
Special: Fear gaze, foul liquid, poison, magical abilities, summon demons, summon serpents, +1 magic weapon to hit
Move: 12
Alignment: Chaos
Challenge Level/XP: 20/4,400

A mallor is a 10- to 12-foot-long, powerful humanoid with the lower torso of a giant coral snake. Its humanoid frame is crimson-colored while its snake body is black with bands of yellow and red. Its arms end in sharpened claws, slightly curved under, just enough to tear through flesh, sinew and muscle. Mallors have black, gold, or amber hair. Their eyes are white with red or green pupils. Anyone meeting a mallor's gaze must save or flee in fear for 1d6 rounds. All liquids, including potions, within 100 feet of a mallor automatically become foul and unsuitable to drink. Anyone drinking the water must save or become nauseated for 1 minute. A mallor injects a virulent poison when it hits an opponent with its claws. At will, a mallor can use *burning hands*, *dispel magic* and *teleport*. Once per day, a mallor can summon 1d6 giant vipers with a 50% chance of success. Mallors are immune to electricity and poison, and take half damage from cold, fire and acid.

Giant Viper: HD 4; AC 5[14]; Atk 1 bite (1d3 + poison); Move 12; Save 13; CL/XP 6/400; Special: Lethal poison

Snake Mass

A countless number of snakes (venomous and constrictors) entwine in a dance-like trance on the wide flagstone terrace. The snakes slide in and out of holes in the stones to an unknown subterranean lair. A shallow pit filled nearly to the rim with snakes sits in the center of the terrace. The mass of snakes sits just 5 feet below the pit's rim. Four braziers with glowing coals emit an intoxicating incense. A 15-foot-tall hooded cobra statue with its head hovering over the pit encircles the hole with its body. Subira the high priestess of Lachesiss (the Demon Lord of Snakes) often meditates and performs sensual ceremonies atop the hood. A ladder cleverly concealed in the statue's scales allows access to the top. Just below the surface of the snake mass lies Amaunet, the harbinger of Lashesiss. Amaunet lies in a state of euphoric mediation. He awakens in 1d4 rounds after any disturbance.

Subira: HD 12 (cleric); HP 64; AC 1[18]; Atk 1 staff (1d6+1); Move 12; Save 4; CL/XP 12/2,000; Special: Spells. 4/4/4/4/4/1; Spells: **1**—*cure light wounds, detect magic, light, protection from evil;* **2**—*bless, hold person, silence (15-foot radius), snake charm;* **3**—*cure disease, prayer, remove curse, speak with dead;* **4**—*cure serious wounds, neutralize poison, sticks to snakes (x2);* **5**—*commune, finger of death, insect plague, quest;* **6**—*blade barrier;* Equipment: +2 Snake Scale Plate Armor, Staff of the Snake

Copyright Notice
Author Scott Greene.

Demon, Mehrim (Goat Demon)

Hit Dice: 6
Armor Class: 3 [16]
Attacks: 2 hooves (1d4), 1 bite (2d6 + disease)
Saving Throw: 11
Special: Diseased bite, magic resistance (10%), magical abilities
Move: 14
Alignment: Chaos
Challenge Level/XP: 9/1,100

A mehrim is a man-sized black goat that exhales putrid black smoke when it breathes. It has three horns and jet black, glossy hooves. Its diseased bite inflicts 1 point of damage each day until cured. A mehrim can cast *darkness* at will, and *dispel magic* once per day. They are able to see invisible creatures at all times.

Got Your Goat

Wandering the rocky hillsides are Onslow, a hill giant goat herder, and his herd of large goats. For reasons unknown, scattered among the herd are 4 mehrims that command the goats with an uncanny intelligence. Onslow and his herd wander the rocky land tending his herd and trading with other giants. From a far distance, they appear as a normal-sized shepherd and herd. Once the herd is close enough, however, Onslow commands the mehrim and the goats to charge while he throws boulders. His tactics have worked exceeding well so far and he has amassed considerable treasure from caravans and travelers.

Onslow, Hill Giant: HD 8+2; hp 48, AC 4[15]; Atk 1 large barbed shepherd's hook (2d8); Move 12; Save 8; CL/XP 9/1100; Special: Throw boulders.
Giant Goats: HD 3; AC 7[12]; Atk 1 gore (2d6); Move 18; Save 14; CL/XP 3/60; Special: +4 damage on charge.

Copyright Notice
Author Scott Greene.

Demon, Mezzalorn (Wasp Demon)

Hit Dice: 12
Armor Class: -3 [22]
Attacks: 2 claws (1d6), 1 sting (2d6 + poison)
Saving Throw: 3
Special: Magic resistance (10%), immune to poison
Move: 6/14 (flying)
Alignment: Chaos
Challenge Level/XP: 13/2,300

A mezzalorn looks like a hellish giant wasp with the head and torso of a man. When reduced to half its hit points it releases a pheromone that gives it and all other mezzalorns a +1 to-hit bonus. The poison injected by a mezzalorn's stinger is lethal if the victim fails a saving throw.

The Droning Pipe Organ

The walls of this area reach about 20 feet high. An earthen mixture of mud and clay covers the stone walls. Long-dried clay cylinders start 5 feet from the floor and extend to the ceiling, the tubes resembling a crude pipe organ. The dirt is dry and brittle despite its four-inch thickness. The mud tubes are filled with paralyzed giant spiders that crash down out of the pipes in a huge pile if the clay tube is shattered. Once disturbed, 2 mezzalorn demons inside the top of the mud pipes begin droning in anticipation. The mezzalorns can be immature larvae or fully grown demons depending on the challenge needed for PCs. Alternatively, the parents could be lurking nearby guarding their offspring.

Copyright Notice
Author Scott Greene.

Demon, Nabasu (Death Stealer Demon)

	Demonling Nabasu	Mature Nabasu
Hit Dice:	7	13
Armor Class:	-1 [20]	-2 [21]
Attack:	2 claws (1d6), bite (1d6)	2 claws (1d8), bite (1d6)
Saving Throw:	9	3
Special:	Death gaze, feed, spells, magic or silver weapons to hit, immunity to electricity and poison, magic resistance (30%), telepathy 100 ft.	Death gaze, paralysis, spells, summon ghasts, magic or silver weapons to hit, immunity to electricity and poison, magic resistsance (40%), telepathy 100 ft.
Movement:	12/24 (flying)	12/24 (flying)
Alignment:	Chaos	Chaos
Challenge Level/XP:	15/2900	23/5300

Nabasu are tall and thin, with large, scaled wings and pale gray skin stretched tightly over their bones. Their hands end in long fingers tipped with razor-sharp talons and their mouths are filled with tusk-like teeth, including two overgrown tusks that jut upward from its bottom jaw. Their eyes glow with an eerie yellow light. Nabasu derive great pleasure from torturing and killing other creatures. Unlike other demons, a nabasu spends a portion of its life on the Material Plane. Those that reach the demonling stage in their growing process travel to the Material Plane where they feed on humanoids in order to continue their maturity. Once a nabasu reaches maturity, it returns to the Abyss to spend the rest of its immortal existence there.

A nabasu's gaze causes instant death in those who fail a saving throw. The death effect has a range of 20 feet. Humanoids who die from this attack are transformed into ghouls within 1d4 rounds and are under control of the nabasu that created them. A demonling nabasu can use its death gaze ability once per day. For every Hit Dice above 7 it has, it gains one more use per day of its death gaze.

When a demonling nabasu slays a humanoid opponent, it can feed on the corpse's heart, devouring both flesh and life force. Feeding destroys the victim's body and prevents any form of raising or resurrection that requires part of the corpse. There is a 50% chance that a *wish* spell can restore a devoured victim to life. Check once for each destroyed creature. If the check fails, the creature cannot be brought back to life by mortal magic.

A demonling nabasu advances in Hit Dice by consuming corpses in this fashion. For every three suitable corpses a nabasu devours, it gains 1 Hit Die and its AC improves by 1. The demonling nabasu only advances by consuming the corpses of creatures whose Hit Dice or levels are equal to or greater than its own current total. A nabasu that reaches 13 Hit Dice through feeding becomes a mature nabasu upon completion of the act. (A mature nabasu advances normally for its Hit Dice; see its statistics block above.)

Mature Nabasu

A demonling nabasu that reaches 13 Hit Dice through feeding becomes a mature nabasu. Mature nabasu do not have the feeding ability of demonlings. A mature nabasu can use its death gaze seven times per day. They can cast *darkness* at will and *silence* once per day and has the level drain ability of a vampire. They can also travel ethereally as though using a *potion of etherealness* two times per day.

Once per day, a mature nabasu can create an aura of paralysis in a 10-foot radius centered on its form. Creatures in the area must succeed on a saving throw or be paralyzed for 1d6+4 rounds. This ability functions as a *hold monster* spell. Demons are immune to this aura.

Once per day, a mature nabasu can automatically summon 2d4 ghasts while in the Abyss.

Heart of Black Oak

A tall, black oak a the crossroads between three mercantile towns has long been a source of superstitious fear among the townspeople. Travelers walking past the oak press their holy symbols to their lips and whisper prayers to ward its evil influence. Lately, however, it has become more than a source of imagined terror, as a nabasu demonling has taken residence in the oak, hiding in a hollow portion about 10 feet from the ground. The demonling now has 10 Hit Dice, and is selectively attacking more powerful individuals who pass by the tree. It has not fed on a heart in months, and will leap at the chance to take at least one of the adventurers, assuming they are experienced enough to be worth the while.

Credit
The Nabasu originally appeared in the First Edition *Monster Manual II* (© TSR/Wizards of the Coast, 1983) and is used by permission.

Copyright Notice
Author Scott Greene, based on original material by Gary Gygax.

Demon, Nerizo (Hound Demon)

Hit Dice: 10
Armor Class: -1 [20]
Attack: 2 claws (1d6), tail sting (1d6 plus poison)
Saving Throw: 5
Special: Poison, spit acid, spells, magic or silver weapons to hit, immune to electricity and poison, magic resistance (35%)
Move: 15
Alignment: Chaos
Challenge Level/XP: 17/3500

The bestial nerizo can be found on almost all planes of the Abyss. More animalistic than not, the nerizo are sometimes used as "hunting dogs" by the greater demons and lords. Neziro are man-sized demons with dark, blue-black skin. Their arms end in clawed hands and their legs in cloven hooves. They have long, barbed tails. These barbed tails deliver a poison that causes lethargy and weakness in the limbs; victims must pass a saving throw or suffer a -1 penalty to hit and damage and a 1 point penalty to AC. Once per hour, a nerizo can spit a glob of stomach bile in a 10-foot line. A creature hit takes 2d6 points of damage (saving throw allowed for half damage). Nerizos can cast *confusion* once per day.

Demonic Haunt

A pack of 1d4+1 disgruntled nerizo is chasing the adventurers through a demonic woodland of ashen, petrified trees inhabited by cackling, fiendish harpies who swoop down to harass the runners. The nerizo are relentless hunters, but they despise the task charged to them and so take their sweet time. If a person is caught, they are slowly tormented, all the while the demons complaining of their lot in life. They take their displeasure out on the victim, ultimately crippling them and spiking them to a petrified tree as they run down their friends.

Somewhere behind the nerizo is a nalfeshnee in the garb of a wealthy aristocrat, mounted on a fiendish water buffalo and surrounded by a hunting party consisting of his demonic court - succubi and alu-demons in gowns and stomachers of drider silk encrusted with bloodstones and onyx, cambions in the garb of huntsmen with barbed arrows and black bows, and other lesser demons on nightmares, all drinking a liquor distilled from the sorrows of tormented souls.

Copyright Notice
Author Scott Greene.

Demon, Nysrock (Cobra Demon)

Hit Dice: 10
Armor Class: 0 [19]
Attacks: 1 bite (1d8), 1 sting (2d4 + poison)
Saving Throw: 5
Special: Constrict, immune to poison, spit poison
Move: 12
Alignment: Chaos
Challenge Level/XP: 12/2,000

A nysrock is a 14-foot-long cobra-like demon with a humanoid head. After a nysrock hits with its bite, it automatically constricts for 1d8 points of damage per round thereafter. The poison of a nysrock deals 1d6 points of damage each round until healing is applied. A nysrock can spit poison up to 40 feet. The poison spit causes blindness unless a saving throw is made.

White Snake-Woman

This large room has 100 five-foot-diameter pits carved vertically into the floor. There is precisely five feet between each circular pit. Each pit is 10 feet deep. The ceiling rises 20 feet above the pocked floor. A white marble column hangs suspended from the ceiling directly above each pit, the lower half 10 feet off the floor. Each unique column is carved to resemble an upside-down woman whose lower half is morphing into the tail of a serpent as it joins with the ceiling. Each figure's face looks down toward the floor pits with expressions contorted in agony. Their arms are raised defensively. Entwined around the pillars along the ceiling is a nysrock demon that can move around the entire room without ever touching the floor.

Crossing between any of the floor pit openings and the hanging column above it causes the suspended pillar to swiftly slam down and crush beings into the pits for 4d6 points of damage. The columns remain in the downward position for 1 round before retracting back toward the ceiling. The nysrock has learned to trigger the pillars with its spit.

Copyright Notice
Author Scott Greene.

Demon, Ooze

Ooze demons are the forgotten children of Jubilex, The Faceless Lord, faithful servants that obey the will of their master without question. When the Faceless Lord went missing (see the module, *G5 Chaos Rising*, by **Necromancer Games** for details) the ooze demons formed search parties and scoured the planes for signs of his whereabouts.

Ooze demons, both lesser and greater, appear as a combination of ooze and demon. An ooze demon resembles a humanoid with a long, crocodilian snout, razor-sharp teeth, and long talons. From a distance, this monster looks like a typical demon (if such a thing exists). Up close, the horror is easily ascertainable; the creature is actually a single entity of swirling black and white or black and gray ooze in the shape of a humanoid.

Greater Ooze Demon

Hit Dice: 10
Armor Class: 0 [19]
Attacks: 1 slam (1d8) or bite (1d8 + 1d6 acid) and 2 claws (1d6 + 1d6 acid)
Saving Throw: 5
Special: Acid, summon demons, vomit
Move: 6
Alignment: Chaos
Challenge Level/XP: 13/2,300

A greater ooze demon takes the shape of a humanoid with a long, crocodilian snout, razor-sharp teeth, and long talons, but is composed entirely of ooze. Their claws drip with an acidic substance secreted by their bodies. The body of the demon is acidic and dissolves organic material and metal, but not stone. Greater ooze demons stand 12 feet tall but can reach heights of 20 feet or more. Ooze demons are immune to electricity, poison and paralysis, and take half damage from cold, fire and acid. Once every 1d4 rounds, a greater ooze demon can unleash a line of gastric juices up to 40 feet for 4d6 points of damage (save for half).

Lesser Ooze Demon

Hit Dice: 4
Armor Class: 4 [15]
Attacks: 1 slam (1d6) or bite (1d6 + 1d4 acid) and 2 claws (1d4 + 1d4 acid)
Saving Throw: 13
Special: Acid, summon demons
Move: 6
Alignment: Chaos
Challenge Level/XP: 6/400

An ooze demon takes the shape of a humanoid with a long, crocodilian snout, razor-sharp teeth, and long talons, but is composed entirely of ooze. Lesser ooze demons stand about 7 feet tall. Ooze demons are immune to electricity and poison, and take half damage from cold, fire and acid. Their claws drip with an acidic substance secreted by their bodies.

Crocodile Tears

The skulls of thousands of crocodiles cover the walls of this macabre chamber. The mortared skulls cover every inch of the domed ceiling except for a small hole in the center of the roof. A beam of light shines from the hole down onto an altar made of turtle shells and bones. A scepter made from the fused bones of a viper lies on the altar. The scepter has the power to cast *snake charm* once per day. Two ooze demons hide behind the crocodile skulls lining the ceiling. They pour out of the eyes sockets to attack anyone bothering the scepter.

Copyright Notice

Demon, Shadow

Hit Dice: 7
Armor Class: 4 [15]
Attack: 2 claws (1d6), bite (1d8)
Saving Throw: 9
Special: Incorporeal, spells, immunity to electricity and poison, shadow blend, sunlight powerlessness, telepathy 100 ft.
Move: 15 (flying)
Alignment: Chaos
Challenge Level/XP: 12/2000

This creature resembles a living shadow of inky darkness. Large bat-like wings protrude from its form. Shadow demons are the incorporeal form of a demon trapped in the form of a shadow as punishment for some wrongdoing. If anything can release a demon trapped in shadow form, only the dukes, princes, and lords of the Abyss know such secrets. As a result of their new form, shadow demons are especially malign and ill-tempered. In shadows and darkness, a shadow demon surprises foes on a roll of 1-5 on 1d6. Shadow demons are powerless in natural sunlight, and avoid it at all costs. Once per minute, a shadow demon can move at six times its normal speed. Shadow demons can cast *darkness*, *fear* and *magic jar* (1/week).

Of Shadowed Hearts and Betrayal

You discover a long tunnel shaped like a tube and formed of dark gray bricks. The tunnel is filled with mist and appears to have a bright light shining on the other end of the tunnel, though the light here is filtered through the mist and casts weird, constantly shifting shadows on the walls of the tunnel. The tunnel extends 300 feet, finally ending in a spherical chamber where four other tunnels of the same design meet. All five tunnels are studded with tripstones and spear traps, and they and the spherical center form the lair of a shadow demon.

The spherical chamber at the center of the shadow demon's lair extends about five feet below the floor of the tunnels and five feet above the ceiling of the tunnel. Both of these spaces are filled with an inky substance like liquid shadow, the demon often hiding in this substance, which doubles its natural rate of healing. Suspended in the middle of the sphere is a crown that shines with brilliant, dazzling light. Suspended in the middle of the crown is a large ruby shaped like a human heart.

The ruby is hot to the touch (1d4 damage) and holding it causes the possessor to believe he is Turaj of Tur, king of nomads, and inheritor to the vast empire of the steppes and destined to rule all the world. The crown is made of silver, and is heavy and angular. If placed upon the head, the cursed crown allows the wearer to believe he is reading minds. But in fact the crown weaves false thoughts, always of betrayal, into the thoughts the wearer perceives in the minds of his targets. The crown also grants the wearer a +2 bonus to Armor Class and the ability to fight as a berserker.

The shadow demon "guards" this cursed treasure, fighting any who come near it and then withdrawing down a tunnel when "defeated". Once the treasure has been claimed, the shadow demon will creep back and enter the liquid shadow to heal, emerging with a new crown and heart when fully restored to health.

Credit

The Shadow Demon originally appeared in the First Edition *Fiend Folio* (© TSR/Wizards of the Coast, 1981) and is used by permission.

Copyright Notice

Author Scott Greene, based on original material by Neville White.

Demon, Shrroth (Squid Demon)

Hit Dice: 12
Armor Class: 2 [17]
Attacks: 6 tentacles (2d6), 2 claws (1d6), 1 bite (1d8) and trident (3d6)
Saving Throw: 3
Special: Constrict, sickness cloud, magical abilities, summon demons, +1 weapons to hit
Move: 6/18 (swim)
Alignment: Chaos
Challenge Level/XP: 15/2,900

A shrroth is a 15-foot-tall copper-colored demon with the lower torso of an octopus and the upper torso of a powerful humanoid. Its arms end in 6-fingered talons. Its lower torso sports a mass of writing tentacles reaching lengths of 10 feet. Six larger tentacles stretching 20 feet surround the smaller tentacles. Its mouth is filled with serrated teeth. A mass of long black hair hangs from its head; from under which protrude two forward-curving, blackish horns. If a shrroth hits the same opponent with two tentacles, the victim is constricted for an automatic 2d6 points of damage each round thereafter. A shrroth can emit a cloud of grayish liquid in a 40-foot spread once per minute that conceals the creature (20% chance to miss) and forces any creature in the cloud to save or be sickened for 3 rounds. At will, a shrroth can *dispel magic*, create a *mirror image* or *teleport*. Twice a day it can use *feeblemind*, and once per day it can cast *power word blind*. A shrroth can jet backward in a straight line at a speed of 30 once per round. Shrroth are immune to electricity and poison, and take half damage from cold, fire and acid.

On the Beach and Under the Sea

The Sea of Pearls is violent in the face of a nor'easter, with 5-foot-high waves whipping the shore. A tangled fishing net lies on the beach. A bag containing pearls and gold coins lies scattered on the sand. Twisted in the net is a mermaid, her dark hair plastered to her beautiful features. Her eyes are dazed and glassy. Her mouth moves, but no understandable words come out. A dead flounder is caught in the net with her, its gills puffed out in misery. A crab walks sullenly over the beach.

The magic-user Carinea the Golden polymorphed herself into a mermaid to do some treasure hunting under the raging waters. Her efforts paid off when she discovered a sunken galleon 100 feet down containing a small amount of pearls and gold coins. As she was stuffing a bag with treasure, the "owner" of the shipwreck found her.

The shrroth demon Ursallah the Entwiner ripped the decking apart to get at the thieving magic-user. Carinea barely escaped by slipping through a metal porthole and fleeing for the surface. In her haste, she set off a *feeblemind* trap that shattered her mind. The magic-user blundered into a fisherman's net and barely dragged herself onto the beach mere moments ago. Carinea has no memory of what she was doing; she doesn't even remember she's really human. Ursallah rises out of the waves to retrieve her belongings, and assumes anyone near the trapped mermaid must be her partners in crime.

Demon, Skitterdark

Hit Dice: 2
Armor Class: 4 [15]
Attacks: 2 claws (1d2), 1 bite (1d2), or 1 weapon (1d3)
Saving Throw: 16
Special: Magic resistance (5%), immune to electricity, poison
Move: 8/12 (flying)
Alignment: Chaos
Challenge Level/XP: 3/60

Skitterdarks are small humanoid-shaped creature no more than 1 foot tall with crimson leathery bat wings. Its body is blood red and somewhat stocky for its size. Its hands end in sharp claws and its eyes and teeth are sickly yellow. Skitterdarks are commonly found in groups and sometimes use poison on their weapons.

Assassin's Parcel

The small manor house of Armandariz, a wealthy aristocrat, sits empty and abandoned. A hefty iron chest is the only item in the house's main room. The chest is neither locked nor trapped. The chest, a magical item, can open a gate to another plane within its interior.

This particular chest is attuned to hell and immediately gates a swarm of 2d4+4 skitterdark demons into existence. Once the last demon is slain, the lid slams shut with tremendous force and cannot be opened again for at least 24 hours. The demons grab anything and everyone and drag them back into the portal within the interior of the chest. Each time the chest is opened, another swarm of skitterdarks explode out of the iron chest. The chaotic and destructive skitterdarks relentlessly tear large matter into smaller pieces to fit into the chest. Items, bodies and living creatures taken into the chest are lost forever in the bowels of hell.

The corrupt Armandariz reneged on bad gambling debts with the local thieves' guild. A hired assassin named Thurid Hrolf sent the chest via a messenger to Armandariz's residence. Armandariz, his family, their servants and every possession he owned were dragged into the depths of hell.

Copyright Notice
Author Scott Greene.

Demon, Stirge

Hit Dice: 8
Armor Class: 0 [19]
Attack: 2 claws (2d6), bite (1d10)
Saving Throw: 8
Special: Blood drain, drone, spells, magic or silver weapons to hit, immunity to electricity and poison, magic resistance (40%), spider climb, telepathy 100 ft.
Move: 9/24 (flying)
Alignment: Chaos
Challenge Level/XP: 16/3200

One of the most foul and despicable of all demonkind, the stirge demon hates all other demonic races and usually attacks them on sight. It savors the blood of vrocks and hezrous, but generally avoids any more powerful demonic races. Stirge demons look like a cross between a human, stirge and demonic fly. They have four, stirge-like hind legs and human forearms that end in chitinous, claw-like fingers. Stirge demons have the wings of stirges and human heads topped with bristly manes. Stirge demons have long, sharp noses that are used to pierce the flesh and draw blood.

Stirge demons can drain blood by making a successful bite attack and rolling a natural '20'. The stirge deals 1d4 points of damage per round until the victim succeeds on an open doors check and breaks its hold.

Stirge demons constantly emit a droning sound from their winfs. All creatures within a 60-foot spread that hear it must succeed on a saving throw or fall into a comatose sleep for 1d4 hours.

Stirge demons can walk on walls, floors, ceilings, and other such surfaces at their normal movement rate. This is an inherent ability and cannot be dispelled or negated.

Blood Suckers

A stirge demon, summoned to the Material Plane by a now desiccated wizard, dwells in a cave atop a crooked mountain overlooking a land of massive blue cattle herded by hill giants. The hill giants produce wheels of strong, white cheese popular in the surrounding kingdoms. Trade between the humans and hill giants has proved profitable for all involved, and the hill giants only rarely cause trouble - usually young males drunk on fermented milk.

The stirge demon has been killing the cattle and the hill giants have no magical weapons with which to deal with it. The human merchants are likewise powerless, as is the prince who owes them a metric ton of gold to cover his monument building and gambling habit. As all are in fear of losing their livelihood, they are on the hunt for adventurers who can slay the demon or send it back to its own dimension.

Unfortunately, the would-be demonslayers will find they are opposed by a gang of assassins hired by the prince's rival, who wishes to see his reign collapse. It was on this rival's behalf that the wizard summoned the demon, and by the hands of the chief assassin that the magic circle was broken and the wizard destroyed.

Credit
The Stirge demon is loosely based on the Chasme Demon, which originally appeared in the First Edition module *S4 Lost Caverns of Tsojcanth* (© TSR/Wizards of the Coast, 1982) and later in the First Edition *Monster Manual II* (© TSR/Wizards of the Coast, 1983) and is used by permission. The stirge demon made its d20 debut in the Necromancer Games module *D1 Tomb of Abysthor* (©2001, Clark Peterson, Necromancer Games, Inc.).

Copyright Notice
Authors Scott Greene and Clark Peterson, based on original material by Gary Gygax.

Demon Lord, Baphomet (Demon Lord of Beasts)

Hit Dice: 25 (115 hp)
Armor Class: -5 [24]
Attack: Gore (2d6), bite (1d8), weapon (2d6+2)
Saving Throw: 3
Special: Roar, breath weapon, spells, +1 or better weapon to hit, immune to electricity, poison and charm, magic resistance (75%), teleapthy 100 ft.
Move: 18
Alignment: Chaos
Challenge Level/XP: 34/5600

Baphomet is the demon prince of brutes, most especially ogres and minotaurs, but also bull-headed humans and petty tyrants. His iron keep is located within a large stone cavern on a desolate plane of the Abyss. It is said his castle is a maze of twisting rooms and corridors, with his personal throne room located at the heart of his maze keep. Those that have ventured there remember little about the place other than the never-ending corridors and maze of rooms. Baphomet stands 12 feet tall and weighs about 4,500 pounds. He looks like a powerfully muscled minotaur, his body covered in shaggy, black fur and marred with battle scars. Baphomet wields a wicked-looking *+2 halberd*. When the halberd causes damage on an armored opponent, it reduces the armor value (i.e. the AC bonus afforded by the armor) by 2 points.

Baphomet is a dangerous combatant. Once every 1d4 rounds, he can belch forth a stream of unholy water in a 10-foot line at a single target. Lawful creatures take 10d6 points of damage (saving throw allowed for half damage). Neutral and chaotic creatures are unaffected. Three times per day, Baphomet can unleash a roar that instills fear in those within 30 feet that hear it and fail a saving throw.

Baphomet can cast spells as a 12th level magic-user. He can cast *darkness, dispel magic, maze, passwall* and *wall of iron* three times per day each as magical abilities. Baphomet can summon 2d10 minotaurs per day.

Servants of Baphomet

Followers of Baphomet are usually minotaurs or brutish humanoids like ogres, orcs or humans, and consist of clerics, necromancers, and sorcerers or adepts. Clerics of Baphomet are called Horned Ones and must sign a pact of evil with Baphomet. Horned ones are granted access to up to 3rd level cleric spells.

Why Wait?
Bring the Maze to Them

While exploring a fortified chapter house of a religious order of knights (perhaps it lies in ruins, perhaps it bustles with activity in the center of a frontier town) you might stumble upon a secret chamber in the wine cellar. The chamber lies behind a bricked up wall that is itself hidden by a pile of oak wine barrels. One of the barrels, beneath the others, it turned on its side and serves as the entrance to this secret chapel.

Once one has crawled through the barrel and a short tunnel through the brick wall, they will find themselves in a cramped room about 8 feet wide and deep with a 7-foot high ceiling. The room is dusty and musty and contains two objects - an idol carved from a glossy, reddish-black stone and a tome bound in blue scales (the hide of a blue dragon) and resting in the idol's lap. The tome is chained to the idol, which weighs 500 lb. The idol depicts a goat headed man with feathered wings, one hand raised, the other lowered. Both of the idol's hands have the pointer finger and middle finger upraised, the thumb extended and the other fingers curled under, as though giving a profane blessing. Its lower body is swathed in cloth. The book contains a number of profane spells usable by chaotic clerics, though they must be read from the book, as though on scrolls.

The idol is a touchstone. Should anyone make physical contact with the idol, the landscape around them will appear to change, the brick walls of the chapel turning into walls of iron that grow impossible tall - at least a mile high - until the ceiling disappears in a holocaust sky that occaisianly sends gouts of roiling flame that sears anyone in the room or the maze of iron passages that now connect with the room. The adventurers have been transported via the idol to the iron maze-fortress of Baphomet. Their only hope of returning home is to find a similar idol of white stone in the maze. While exploring, the adventurers are hunted by Baphomet and 2d4 minotaurs.

Credit

Baphomet originally appeared in the First Edition module *S4 Lost Caverns of Tsojcanth* (© TSR/Wizards of the Coast, 1982) and later in the First Edition *Monster Manual II* (© TSR/Wizards of the Coast, 1983) and is used by permission.

Copyright Notice

Author Scott Greene, based on original material by Gary Gygax.

Demon Lord, Beluiri (The Temptress)

Hit Dice: 16 (70 hp)
Armor Class: -2 [21]
Attack: 2 claws (1d8 plus poison)
Saving Throw: 3
Special: Dominating gaze, poison, seduction, spells, true sight, +1 or better weapon to hit, immune to electricity and poison, magic resistance (65%), telepathy 100 ft.
Move: 15
Alignment: Chaos
Challenge Level/XP: 25/5900

Beluiri is a bronze-skinned feminine demon standing about 6 feet tall. Her head is hairless and features four downward-curving horns jutting just above her forehead. The two lower horns are smaller than the topmost horns. A ridge of small spines runs from her brow down the center of her head and tapers off just below her shoulder blades. Her hands end in razor-sharp talons and her eyes are sapphire blue. Beluiri is one of the many concubines of Lord Baphomet (and one of his favorites). She is known throughout the Abyss as the Temptress, for in her many disguises she has seduced countless princes, lords, and generals of the demons. She sometimes journeys to the Material Plane (in one of her many guises) to tempt and seduce mortals, for she knows that all mortals, in their hearts, always give in to their true desires—be they power, greed, lust, or one of many countless other sins. Beluiri rarely wears clothing, but at times when she does, she enjoys gowns and robes of gold, white, and red.

Beluiri is a cunning combatant, preferring subterfuge to direct assaults, luring her victims by assuming a pleasing and non-threatening form. Three times per day she can turn her gaze upon a creature within 30 feet. The target of her gaze must pass a saving throw or become her slave, per a more powerful version of the *charm monster* spell. Her claws are coated with a debilitating poison that saps a person of their strength. Victims of the poison must pass a saving throw or temporarily lose 2d4 points of Strength (to a minimum of 1) for 1 hour.

Through body language and movement, Beluiri can fascinate all creatures of the opposite sex (which could be either sex, depending on her current form) within 30 feet that observe her dancing. Those viewing this dance must succeed on a saving throw or fall under her influence for 1d6+1 hours as if affected by a *charm monster* spell. In addition, Beluiri can cast the following spells: *Cause fear, darkness, dispel magic, polymorph self* and *wall of fire*. Beluiri is completely immune to illusions and can see invisible creatures.

She Gets Around

The daughter of the king, after reaching her 18th birthday, has become increasingly decadent and lacivious. Time and time again she has turned her father's wrath upon a former or potential ally when they were discovered in a compromising position with the beauteous maid. This increasing isolation and paranoia of the king even affected his relationship with the religious orders of the kingdom, several young monks having been found in unholy council with the princess. This is a particular problem given the presence of a known planar gate in the depths beneath the kingdom's ancient temple of Law.

The princess' chambers in the castle are now kept under lock and key, though no guards (or anyone other than the king) are permitted anywhere near her door. Her windows are barred, and though there is no secret door in the chamber, the princess still manages to get around. This is, of course, because the princess is actually the demon Beluiri, the real princess now a serving zombie in the catacombs beneath the estate of the king's rival. The rival, a duchess of malevolent mein, is a mere pawn in an attempt by Baphomet and his concubine to spark a war between the kingdom's ruler and its high priest, allowing followers of the duchess to infiltrate the temple and remove the mystic wards blocking the planar gate and a demonic invasion of the mortal realms.

Copyright Notice

Demon Lord, Caizel (Deposed Queen of Succubi)

Hit Dice: 18
Armor Class: -4 [23]
Attacks: +2 *dagger of returning* (Bonerazor) (2d4 + *hold person*) or 2 claws (1d6+3)
Saving Throw: 3
Special: Poison, magical abilities, summon demons, touch of ecstasy, +1 magic weapons to hit, immune to electricity and poison, resists cold, fire and acid
Move: 12
Alignment: Chaos
Challenge Level/XP: 22/5,000

Caizel is an astonishingly beautiful creature standing just under 6 feet tall. Her skin is delicate, soft, and copper in color. Her eyes are blue-green. Two tiny horns are hidden beneath her long, raven-black hair. Her hands, while clawed, are shapely and delicate. Small leather wings protrude from her back, but she usually keeps these hidden beneath her robes and gowns. Caizel's body courses with a virulent poison that she can intensify or suppress at will. It is not secreted through her skin (therefore her touch is not poisonous); rather it is delivered through the exchange of body fluids with another creature (kissing, consummating an encounter, etc.). At will she can cast *charm monster*, create *darkness* (15 foot radius), *detect good*, *teleport*, *read magic*, use *suggestion* and create a *wall of fire*. Once per day she can cast *mirror image*. Once per round, Caizel's touch can flood a creature's mind with pleasurable images if it fails a save. This stuns the creature for 1d4 rounds. Caizel is immune to electricity and poison, and takes half damage from cold, fire and acid. Any creature she hits with Bonerazor, her +2 dagger, must save or be held (as by a *hold person* spell).

Such a Lonely Place

Within the forest near the major city of Bargarsport resides Hotel Frenley, the most infamous house of ill repute in the lands. A bas-relief standard of a dove holding an olive branch hangs above the door and at the entrance gate to the low wall surrounding the complex. Those versed in plant knowledge may notice that the olive branch is actually the leaves of a toxic "bleeding heart flower." This luxurious four-story mansion has the infamous reputation of holding legendary parties that cater to the land's wealthiest and most powerful men and women.

It is from here that the matron of seduction, the demon princess Caizel enacts her will upon mortals. Hotel Frenley caters to a wide range of clientele; payments (not necessarily monetary) can be arranged for anyone willing to compensate in kind for services rendered. Hotel Frenley serves all classes of society, but payments are steep whether they are monetary or servitude. All transactions require a written and signed contract. Details and bartering are subjective. The majority of the soiled doves who work the delightful enterprise are harmless and legitimate, while a few have more sinister origins.

While Caizel is the undisputed matron, she only rarely makes appearances for notable patrons. Caizel and her succubi minions use this establishment to recruit the wicked and corrupt the righteous. Second Mother Iveene (10th-level magic-user) handles the daily responsibilities of running Hotel Frenley. A pair of rakshasas serves as guards with only their reversed hands belying their true nature. Only the finest furnishings adorn the building's interior and the sweet smell of jasmine permeates the air.

Demon Lord, Dagon (Demon Prince of the Sea)

Hit Dice: 20 (110 hp)
Armor Class: -5 [24]
Attack: +3 *trident* (2d6+3) or 2 meaty fists (1d10)
Saving Throw: 3
Special: Spells, master of the waters, summon sea creatures, only harmed by +2 or better weapons, immune to cold, electricity and poison, immune to water-based spells, magic resistance (80%), telepathy 100 ft.
Move: 9/24 (swimming)
Alignment: Chaos
Challenge Level/XP: 30/7400

Dagon is the demon prince of sea creatures. He is worshipped as a deity by legions of sahuagin, locathah, lizardfolk, tritons (those that have accepted the ways of chaos) and some merfolk. Dagon makes his home in a great underwater iron citadel called *Thos* located in the deepest recesses of his home plane. Dagon appears as a 10-foot tall merman and weighs about 2,000 pounds. He has blue-green skin and the lower torso of a black-scaled leviathan. A thin, translucent fin runs the length of his back, and a long mane of black hair falls from his head and down his finned back. His eyes are deep purple with glowing motes of crimson floating in them.

Dagon is a master of the seas. He is immune to all water-based spells and effects. When fighting in water, he gains a +2 bonus to hit and improves his AC by 2. As their prince, he can summon 20 HD worth of aquatic creatures per day and communicate with them telepathically.

Dagon casts spells as a 12th level magic-user. He has the following magical abilities: *Control water, create water, darkness, dispel magic, water breathing* and *feeblemind* (1/day).

Dagon wields a +3 trident that can telescope to up to 20 feet long on its master's command. The trident is forged of black bronze with adamantine barbs. Creatures struck by the trident and suffering more than 10 points of damage are caught on the barbs, suffering an addition 1d4 points of damage per round and unable to move until they make a successful open doors roll. Creatures that extract themselves from the trident suffer 1d8 points of damage from their rending of their flesh by the barbs.

Servants of Dagon

Followers of Dagon are mermen, locathah, sahuagin, lizardmen and evil humanoids that revere the seas and oceans. Clerics of Dagon are called Scaled Ones and must sign a pact of evil with Dagon. Scaled Ones can receive up to 3rd level spells from Dagon.

Black Pearl of Great Power

On the day of the new moon, the harbor of the mercantile city-state is thrown into confusion when small boats moving through the harbor are seized by thick tentacles belonging to 1d4 giant octopi and 1d6+2 giant squid, the occupants of those boats dragged to a watery grave and then, as soon as the attacks occur, the giant cephalopods disappear.

The next night of the new moon, chaos again erupts as those men and women who were lost on that fateful night a month ago emerge from the dark waters of the harbor, pale of skin, waterlogged and rotting, carrying on their shoulders a cassone of black bronze and studded with coral imbroglios of fiendish mermaids. Six wights, for wights they now are, carry the cassone on poles of black bronze, while another twelve wights serve as an honor guard, attacking anyone who comes near. This foul procession is making its way to the grand temple of the sea god.

While this is happening, the giant octopi and squid are back in the harbor, attacking ships and dragging sailors to their doom. Moments after a sailor drowns, its body climbs from the harbor as a draug. The draug run though the waterfront, killing indescriminately and spreading chaos in their wake.

When the procession of wights reaches the grand temple, they will force entry, set down their cassone before the idol of the sea god and open it. From the cassone will arise dozens of thick, black tentacles, which will grasp and throw down the idol of the sea god and replace it with a single, large black pearl, an idol of Dagon, the new master of the mercantile city-state.

Copyright Notice
Author Scott Greene.

Demon Lord, Fraz-Urb'luu (Demon Prince of Deception)

Hit Dice: 25 (130 hp)
Armor Class: -3 [22]
Attack: 2 clobbers (1d12), bite (1d10) or tail slash (2d6)
Saving Throw: 3
Special: Gnashing teeth, spells, summon demonic entity, +2 or better weapon to hit, immunity to electricity and poison, sealed mind, magic resistance (75%), telepathy 100 ft.
Move: 15/24 (flying)
Alignment: Chaos
Challenge Level/XP: 35/8900

Fraz-Urb'luu appears as a hulking, ape-like creature standing nearly three times as tall as a normal human. His head sports large, fan-like, pointed ears and a large, round mouth lined with sharpened teeth. His skin is gray and covered with fine, thin blue hair. A long, serpentine tail, gray and yielding to blue near the barbed end, trails behind him. Two large bat-like wings protrude from his back. Fraz-Urb'luu is one of the most physically powerful demon princes as well as one of the most cunning. His deceptions range far and wide, affecting and influencing not only those on the Material Plane but also other demon princes and demon lords. His malevolent nature lends itself well to his trickery and deception, and he bends others to do his will. Those that oppose him are quickly dispatched. Those he favors are often captured and taken back to his lair in the Abyss where they are forced into a life of servitude. When the day comes that Fraz-Urb'luu grows weary of them, he devours them or throws them to his other servants to do with as they wish. He makes his home deep within the Abyss on a smoldering and scarred layer devoid of most life. His keep is a large iron and stone castle situated near the very center of the layer. A constant stream of traffic emanates to and from his castle; demons and slaves tending to their daily tasks.

If Fraz-Urb'luu strikes the same creature with both of its clobber attacks in a single round it hugs them for an additional 1d12 points of damage and gains a +2 bonus to hit with his bite attack.

Fraz-Urb'luu is immune to all charms, compulsions and phantasms. He casts spells as a 12th level magic-user and can use the following magical abilities: *Charm monster*, *darkness*, *dispel magic*, *ESP*, *polymorph other* (1/day), *polymorph self* (3/day), *power word blind* (1/day), *prismatic sphere* (1/day) and *suggestion*. Once per day, Fraz-Urb'luu can attempt to summon a demon lord or demon prince with a 70% chance of success, and deceive the summoned demon into believing it was called by his opponents. The summoned lord or prince must succeed on a saving throw at -10 or fall for the deception.

Servants of Fraz-Urb'luu

Followers of Fraz-Urb'luu are usually evil humanoids and consist of charlatans, clerics, magic-users, politicians and aristocrats. Clerics of Fraz-Urb'luu are called Deceivers and must sign a pact of evil with Fraz-Urb'luu. Deceivers can receive spells up to 3rd level from Fraz-Urb'luu and are granted access to the magic-user spells *phantasmal force* and *suggestion* as though they were cleric spells of the same level.

Scary Funhouse

Nobody in the city remembered exactly when the funhouse appeared in a winding ally between the Modest Mermaid and Rampant Mallard taverns (though a few old timers would swear they remembered the day a hole was made in the wall the taverns shared after a drunken barbarian was bet he couldn't put his head through it), but most folks agreed that it had been there as long as they could remember.

The funhouse was an old brick building painted a myriad of colors with a door composed of a wooden frame and a stained glass window that looks like it came from a church - though the image is a bit unholy. Within the building are five floors of stuffed oddities, performing albinos, jugglers, exotic women, people with physical deformities and just about anything weird and disturbing. These exhibits line a maze of hallways one can easily become lost in - especially because some of these hallways, depending on the time of day, become portals into other dimensions. The funhouse is attended by 1d3+1 tall men in black velvet doublets and azure chausses that are actually nalfeshnee demons veiled in illusion.

In truth, everything in the building, itself just an old granary, is the product of illusion by its master, Fraz-Urb'luu. The demon lord uses the building as a nexus between dimensions and a place to weave his schemes. Fraz-Urb'luu can sometimes be found in the building, disguised as a shrunken man in gleaming brass armor sitting on an oversized throne of white oak. Powerful men and women who visit the funhouse are brought to visit Tiny Sir Knight, where they are brought into his service via his spells of enchantment. Those who resist are set adrift in the maze-like funhouse, eventually wandering into some other dimension and disappearing from the world until Fraz-Urb'luu sees fit to bring them back.

Credit

Fraz-Urb'luu originally appeared in the First Edition module *S4 Lost Caverns of Tsojcanth* (© TSR/Wizards of the Coast, 1982) and later in the First Edition *Monster Manual II* (© TSR/Wizards of the Coast, 1983) and is used by permission.

Copyright Notice

Author Scott Greene, based on original material by Gary Gygax.

Demon Lord, Jubilex (The Faceless Lord)

Hit Dice: 20 (120 hp)
Armor Class: -2 [21]
Attack: Slam (3d6)
Saving Throw: 3
Special: Acid slime, spells, summon oozes, +3 or better weapon to hit, immunity to electricity and poison, magic resistance (80%), telepathy 100 ft.
Move: 9/24 (flying)
Alignment: Chaos
Challenge Level/XP: 30/7400

Jubilex is a large, bubbling mass of greenish-black, foul-smelling liquid. Ooze, slime, and pus constantly squirt and seep from its form. Deep within the oozing form you notice several large red eyes. Jubilex is the ruler over all slimes, oozes, jellies, and other disgusting and foul ooze-like creatures – the cosmic ooze from which the forces of Law crafted reality and back to which reality always threatens to sink. Known by some as the Faceless Lord, his Abyssal home is a steaming, bubbling lair of putrid ooze and slime pits that are constantly shifting and changing at his whim. Even the other demonic rulers loathe to journey here. Jubilex makes his home in a huge slime pit somewhere on one of the many planes he controls. He is constantly attended by and surrounded with all sorts of slimes and oozes.

When confronted, he takes the form of a 12-foot tall column of bubbling and squirting ooze. Jubilex attacks with 10-foot long slimy appendages that emerge from its form. The demon prince secretes a digestive acid that dissolves organic material and metal quickly, but does not affect stone. Any melee hit deals 2d6 points of acid damage. Armor or clothing dissolves and becomes useless immediately unless the wearer succeeds on a saving throw. A metal or wooden weapon that strikes Jubilex also dissolves immediately unless the wielder succeeds on a saving throw. The save DCs are Constitution-based.

Once every six rounds, Jubilex can fire a stream of acidic slime in a 20-foot line. This requires a successful ranged attack that ignores armor. A creature hit takes 2d6 points of acid damage (save for half) and 1d6 points of acid damage on each round it remains on the target. On the first round after striking a target, the slime may be scraped off (most likely destroying the scraper in the process), but after that it must be burnt, frozen, or cut away (applying damage to the victim as well). Extreme cold or heat, sunlight, or a *cure disease* spell destroys the slime.

Jubilex can cast spells as a 15th level cleric. He can also use the following magical abilities: *Circle of cold* (emanate cold in a 10-ft. radius; 5d6 damage, save for half damage, lasts 1 minute per level), *cause disease* (reverse of *cure disease*), *darkness*, *dispel magic*, *ESP*, *hold monster*, *invisibility (self)*, *symbol of insanity* and *wall of acid* (as wall of fire, but deals acid damage). He is immune to illusions and can see invisible creatures without difficulty. Once per day, Jubilex can summon up to 2d4 ochre jellies, gray oozes, or gelatinous cubes, or 1d4 black puddings. Because of his ooze-like structure, Jubilex is immune to *sleep* effects, paralysis, polymorph, and stunning.

Servants of Jubilex

Followers of Jubilex are evil humanoids with an affinity for slimes, jellies, and all things that ooze. Clerics of Jubilex are called Masters of the Ooze and must sign a pact of evil with Jubilex. Masters of the Ooze can receive spells up to 3rd level from Jubilex and are granted access to the *circle of cold* and *wall of acid* spells described above. *Circle of cold* is a 5th level cleric spell and *wall of acid* is a 5th level cleric spell.

There Is No Third Choice

You enter a large, cylindrical chamber, 30 feet in diameter and 50 feet tall. The walls of the chamber are white marble and perfectly smooth. The floor is composed of hexagonal tiles of red and green, with a corroded silver fountain in the center of the room. The ceiling is carved to resemble a giant, moon-like face. Once several people have entered the chamber, the walls will begin to spin rapidly, making exit impossible (percentile chance to time one's leap correctly equal to their Dexterity score, otherwise suffer 2d6 points of damage and knocked prone). As the walls spin, the face on the ceiling will speak in a booming voice - "Supplicate yourself and petition the Faceless Lord".

At this prompt, the adventurers must crawl to the fountain on their knees and make offerings of their own blood using silver daggers (1d4 damage) into the fountain. If they do, an amethyst liquor will pour from the fountain's spout and mix with the blood. The petitioners may now drink from this liquor and petition Jubilex for some favor. Whether their favor is granted (or even if they make no such petition), they will suffer a geas from the Faceless Lord, forcing them to undertake some quest for his benefit.

If adventurers do not carry out the ritual described above, the face in the ceiling will proclaim them "Apostates!". From every opening on the face, oozes will begin to slowly drop to the floor - 2d4 ochre jellies, 1d4 gray oozes and 1d4 black puddings (you can change the numbers of the oozes depending on the level of your dungeon on which this chamber appears). If the oozes prove unable to destroy the adventurers, a column of slime, Jubilex itself, will arise from the fountain and attack with its slimy tendrils. It will attack each person a single time and, if it causes damage, will leave a purple mark in the shape of a triangle across their face. Adventurers who bear this mark are singled out for destruction by oozes, demons and evil cultists they might encounter. In addition, their presence will double the liklihood of random encounters in dungeons or the wilderness.

Credit
Jubilex originally appeared in the First Edition *Monster Manual* (© TSR/ Wizards of the Coast, 1977) and is used by permission. Jubilex is called J-u-i-b-l-e-x in the *Monster Manual* (notice the different spelling).

Copyright Notice
Author Scott Greene, based on original material by Gary Gygax.

Demon Lord, Kostchtchie (Demon Prince of Wrath)

Hit Dice: 15 (100 hp)
Armor Class: -4 [23]
Attack: *+3 warhammer* (3d6)
Saving Throw: 3
Special: Spells, +1 or better weapon to hit, immune to cold, electricity and poison, magic resistance (60%), telepathy 100 ft.
Move: 9
Alignment: Chaos
Challenge Level/XP: 23/5300

Kostchtchie is the demon lord of cold and is the epitome of hatred and evil. If there is a demon lord more ruthless and malevolent than he, that lord has never made his presence known. Kostchtchie is hated by all (including other demon lords and princes). He moves across his Abyssal landscape with a shuffling gait, and is rarely, if ever, encountered alone. He appears as a 10 foot tall, ogrish creature, with yellowish skin and hairless save for it bushy eyebrows. He has two twisted, stumpy legs and a thick torso. His head is flat and oval and sports two large, sunken, crystal-blue eyes of immeasurable beauty. Kostchtchie's Abyssal home is a frigid and mountainous realm of ice, rock, snow, and subfreezing temperatures. Unprotected travelers and those vulnerable to cold do not last long here.

Kostchtchie wields a cold-wrought *+3 warhammer* that must be wielded with two hands. It creates a cacophonous roar like thunder upon striking with a successful critical hit, deafening those who fail a saving throw. When Kostchtchie's attack roll is a natural '20', the hammer leaves a thick layer of frost and ice on whatever it strikes, causing an additional 1d6 points of freezing damage.

Kostchtchie can cast spells as a 12th level magic-user. He can cast *cause serious wounds* (reverse of cure serious wounds), *charm monster, darkness* and *dispel magic* at will. Three times per day he can summon 1d4 frost giants or 1 large, adult white dragon.

Servants of Kostchtchie

Followers of Kostchtchie are usually berserkers, frost giants and ogres. Clerics of Kostchtchie are called Ice Lords and must sign a pact of evil with Kostchtchie. Ice Lords cast receive spells up to 3rd level from Kostchtchie.

Devout to the End

Caught in a blizzard, you stumble across a stone roadhouse sending an inviting plume of smoke from its chimneys into the white sky. A knock on the door will elicit no response for one or two minutes, and then finally the door will swing open to reveal a rotund man with piggy eyes and a bald pate. He will silently invite the visitors into the roadhouse's common room, a large, low ceilinged chamber with a roaring hearth, several chairs and stools and a large cask of spiced amber ale served in pewter mugs. Besides the man at the door, the room contains a tall, harshly attractive woman with pale blue eyes and platinum hair pulled back in braids, twin maidens with raven hair and grey eyes and three well-dressed men who look like gentleman merchants. All sit quietly around the hearth, drinking from their mugs and trading glances with one another. Seats will be provided for the visitors and mugs of ale drawn.

A large trapdoor behind the bar grants access to a cellar, but the trapdoor is locked and the rotund man will never be far from it. At some point, the tall woman will emerge from the kitchen with a platter of steaming caribou steaks and boiled turnips, allowing the guests to take pieces of meat or turnips from the platter with their knife and enjoy the savory supper. During this repast, the sound of wolves - deep, sonorous howls - will first ring in the adventurer's ears from the outside. They are repeated once a turn, getting closer and closer, and each time eliciting a more excited/nervous response from the people in the room.

After an hour, you hear a crazed laugh from the rotund man and the others join in, rising and forming a circle in the middle of the room on their knees. At that moment, a heavy pounding is heard on the door. It finally flies open, hurled by a chill wind, the demon lord Kostchtchie standing in the entrance, come to claim the souls of his followers. The people in the circle do not move an inch as he approaches and, one by one, smashes them with his hammer, leaving naught but a pile of ash and a plume of sulfurous smoke where they once stood. He then turns his attention to the others in the room.

Credit

Kostchtchie originally appeared in the First Edition module *S4 Lost Caverns of Tsojcanth* (© TSR/Wizards of the Coast, 1982) and later in the First Edition *Monster Manual II* (© TSR/Wizards of the Coast, 1983) and is used by permission.

Copyright Notice

Author Scott Greene, based on original material by Gary Gygax.

Demon Lord, Maphistal (Second of Orcus)

Hit Dice: 20 (90 hp)
Armor Class: -3 [22]
Attack: +3 heavy mace (2d6) and bite (1d8 plus disease) or 2 claws (1d8) and bite (1d8 plus poison)
Saving Throw: 3
Special: Bone knit, disease, spells, summon undead, +1 or better weapon to hit, immunity to electricity and poison, magic resistance (70%), telepathy 100 ft.
Move: 15/30 (flying)
Alignment: Chaos
Challenge Level/XP: 30/7400

Maphistal is the second of Orcus, Demon Prince of the Undead. He makes his home on a stinking, smoldering layer of the Abyss and commands his troops from his great castle, *Maalstege* (The Keep of Bones, so called because it is believe to be constructed from the skeletal remains of those slain by Maphistal). He is loyal to no one but Orcus. He does not trust Sonechard, the General of Orcus's undead legions, and seeks to discredit him at any opportunity, though he does not do this openly for fear of rebellion by his troops or punishment by Orcus. His machinations against Sonechard are primarily through his agents and spies in Sonechard's camps.

Maphistal stands 9 feet tall and weighs 700 pounds. He is a feral-looking humanoid with two great horns protruding from his head and huge, bat wings sprouting from his shoulders. His legs end in sooty hooves and short, coarse, black hair covers his body save his face and clawed hands.

Maphistal's *+3 heavy mace* deals an extra 1d6 points of damage against lawful creatures and it drains one level from any lawful creature attempting to wield it. Each time a living creature is hit by Maphistal's mace, it must succeed on a saving throw or lose 1d4 points of Dexterity as its bones fuse together. Creatures reduced to 0 Dexterity can no longer move or attack. Only a *restoration* spell can repair this damage, restoring 1d4 points of Dexterity with each application.

Maphistal's bite infects victims with a demonic fever that incubates for 1 day and then begins inflicting 1d6 points of Constitution damage each day until the afflicted succeeds at a saving throw at a -3 penalty.

Maphistal can cast the following spells: *Animate dead, darkness, dispel magic, power word stun* and *suggestion*. Once per day, Maphistal can summon 3d10 zombies or skeletons, 2d6 ghouls, 2d4 ghasts, 1d6 wraiths or wights, or 1d4 spectres.

Within the Keep of Bones

Rising from the smoldering basalt plain is a truly awesome tower. Built in the style of a Scandinavian stave church, this tower is easily one mile tall and measures about half a mile on each side. The tower is constructed of bones, with flying demons flitting about the structure adding new bones at all times. The top of the tower, should one be able to see it, contains the throne of Maphistal, wings spread to catch the balmy, sulfurous winds of the plain, gazing out over the work crews extracting the spiritual bones of soldiers killed in suicidal battles on the Material Plane. The entrance to the tower is a door of bones that stands 20 feet high and can only be raised or lowered by heaping corpses upon a counterweight in a small weigh house located about 30 yards from the door. The weigh house is constructed of smoldering basalt and tiled with obsidian. It is overseen by a spectre, who liberally helps itself to the life force of visitors while they endeavor to pile 1 ton of corpses on the brazen scales to raise the door.

Inside the door there is a vast hall guarded by 1d4+4 wraiths that resemble knights in sooty armor atop crimson destriers. The walls of the hall are lined with raised alcoves in which bone sculptures (see Bone Cobbler) are displayed, alongside hundreds of pole arms, two-handed axes and swords and shields. Mulling about the hall are hundreds of zombies, tormented by skeletons in mail coats and wielding spiked maces. Should Maphistal enter the hall, the legions are quickly and painfully assembled in tight formations of ranks and columns.

From the hall four spiral staircases, each 20 feet wide, lead to upper levels of the tower. *Maalstege* holds hundreds of chambers and passages, and could take a lifetime to explore (though one's lifetime in *Maalstege* could be very short indeed).

Credit

Maphistal first appeared in the Necromancer Games module *R3 Rappan Athuk 3: The Lower Levels* (©2002, Necromancer Games, Inc.).

Copyright Notice

Author Scott Greene.

Demon Lord, Orcus (Demon Prince of the Undead)

Hit Dice: 30 (120 hp)
Armor Class: -5 [24]
Attack: *Wand of Orcus* (2d6 or death) or 2 fists (3d6) and tail sting (2d6 plus poison)
Saving Throw: 3
Special: Command undead, spells, summon undead, +3 or better weapon to hit, immunity to electricity and poison, speak with dead, magic resistance (75%), telepathy 100 ft.
Move: 18/24 (flying)
Alignment: Chaos
Challenge Level/XP: 40/10400

> Orcus is the Prince of the Undead, and it is said that he alone created the first undead that walked the worlds.

Orcus is one of the strongest (if not the strongest) and most powerful of all demon lords. He fights a never-ending war against rival demon princes that spans several Abyssal layers. From his great bone palace he commands his troops as they wage war across the smoldering and stinking planes of the Abyss. Orcus spends most of his days in his palace, rarely leaving its confines unless he decides to leads his troops into battle (which has happened on more than one occasion). Most of the time though, he is content to let his generals and commanders lead the battles.

Orcus is a squat, bloated humanoid standing 15 feet tall and weighing 3 tons. His goat-like head sports large, spiraling ram-like horns and his legs are covered in thick brown fur and end in hooves. Two large, black, bat-like wings protrude from its back and a long, snake-like tail, tipped with a sharpened barb, trails behind it.

When not warring against rival demon princes, Orcus likes to travel the planes, particularly the Material Plane. Should a foolish spellcaster open a *gate* and speak his name, he is more than likely going to hear the call and step through to the Material Plane. What happens to the spellcaster that called him usually depends on the reason for the summons and the power of the spellcaster. Extremely powerful spellcasters are usually slain after a while and turned into undead soldiers or generals in his armies.

Combat

Orcus prefers to fight using his *Wand*. His tail sting delivers a virulent poison (save or die).

Orcus can command or banish undead as a 15th-level cleric, controlling up to 150 HD worth of undead at one time. He casts spells as a 15th level cleric and 12th level magic-user, and can use the following magical abilities at will: *animate dead, charm monster, darkness, dispel magic, ESP, fear, feeblemind* (1/day), *lightning bolt, speak with dead, symbol (any)* and *wall of fire.*

Orcus radiates a 60-foot-radius aura of fear (as the spell). A creature in the area must succeed on a DC 44 Will save or be affected as though by a fear spell (caster level 35th). A creature that successfully saves cannot be affected again by Orcus's fear aura for one day. The save DC is Charisma-based.

Three times per day, Orcus can summon one balor, 1d3 nalfeshnees or 1d4 mariliths. As their prince, Orcus can summon up to 100 HD of any type of undead each day.

Wand of Orcus: Mighty Orcus wields a huge black skull-tipped rod that functions as a *+3 heavy mace*. It slays any living creature it touches if the target fails a saving throw. Orcus can shut this ability off so as to allow his wand to pass into the Material Plane, usually into the hands of one of his servants. Further, the *Wand* has the following magical powers: 3/day—*animate dead, darkness* and *fear*; 2/day—*unholy word.*

Servants of Orcus

The followers of the Prince of Undead are clerics that venerate death, magic-users fascinated with death, and cambions and alu-demons. His followers are most often clerics and necromancers. Clerics of Orcus are known as Disciples of Orcus and must sign a pact of evil. Disciples of Orcus can receive spells up to 3rd level from Orcus.

Seeds of Chaos

Amid an endless plain of writhing bodies on tall stakes and weeping women on torture wheels, the demon prince of the undead reclines on a chaise upholstered in the flayed skins of his enemies and feasting on eyes and tongues plucked from the field of victims. He directs the activity of 4d6 zombies equipped with scourges, conducting the cries of the damned as though they composed a symphony. Two mariliths guard the demon prince and see to his needs, while shadows flit through the field of sorrows, bringing messages of intriques and plots from the other lords of the damned.

Orcus is, on this day, in a generous mood, and will entertain his visitors so long as they can entertain him with tales of deception, sorrow, loss and regret. Should someone annoy him, a stake will erupt from the ground (saving throw to avoid) and impale them for 3d6 points of damage, lifting them five feet from the ground. After an hour or so, the demon prince will send his visitors (assuming they still live) on their way with a care package of delicacies wrapped in a flayed skin. As disgusting as these items are, they will provide invisibility to undead and demons for 1 hour if ingested, but also implant a seed of chaos in their eater.

Credit

Orcus originally appeared in the pre-First Edition *Eldritch Wizardry* (© TSR/Wizards of the Coast, 1976) and later in the First Edition *Monster Manual* (© TSR/Wizards of the Coast, 1977) and is used by permission. Orcus made his debut for the d20 system in the Necromancer Games module *R3 Rappan Athuk 3 — The Lower Levels* (©2002, Necromancer Games, Inc.).

Copyright Notice
Authors Scott Greene and Clark Peterson, based on original material by Gary Gygax.

Demon Lord, Pazuzu (Demon Prince of Air)

Hit Dice: 20 (110 hp)
Armor Class: -2 [21]
Attack: +2 sword (2d6+2), 2 claws (1d10)
Saving Throw: 3
Special: Breath weapon, dominate and summon aerial creatures, spells, aerial passivism, +2 or better weapon to hit, immunity to electricity and poison, magic resistance (70%), telepathy 100 ft.
Move: 15/30 (flying)
Alignment: Chaos
Challenge Level/XP: 32/8000

Pazuzu is the demon prince of aerial creatures, and is revered as such on both the Abyssal plane and the Material Plane. Unlike other demon princes, his lair is not confined to a single plane or multiple adjoining planes; Pazuzu rules the sky realms above all layers of the Abyss. (No demon prince has contested his rulership of the skies thus far.) Pazuzu appears as a muscular human being with the head of a hawk and four great, feathery wings spanning its shoulders. His feathers are red and gold, fading to black at the tip and his eyes are red. Pazuzu's heads and feet end in talons.

Pazuzu has three breath weapons. Regardless of which breath weapon he uses, he can't breathe more than once every 1d4 rounds. Each breath weapon is a 100-foot long cone. The first works like the *creeping doom* spell, the second like the *insect plague* spell and the last is a corrosive gas that deals 10d6 points of acid damage (saving throw for half damage) and ruins leather equipment, including armor.

Three times per day, Pazuzu can automatically summon 2d6 harpies, 2d8 gargoyles or 1d4 hieracosphinxes with a 50% chance of success. Pazuzu can automatically dominate any aerial creature of 6 HD or less that is within sight, no saving throw allowed. This functions as a *charm monster* spell. At any one time, Pazuzu can have a total of 20 HD of creatures dominated. Affected creatures must remain with sight or the effect ends. Aerial creatures are defined as avians, gargoyles, harpies, and elemental air creatures. No aerial creature of 10 HD or less willingly attacks Pazuzu, but they can be forced to magically.

Pazuzu can cast spells as a 12th level magic-user. He can use the following magical abilities: *Control weather*, *darkness*, *dispel magic*, *flesh to stone*, *lightning bolt*, *shape change*, *wind walk* and, once per day, *wish*.

Servants of Pazuzu

Followers of Pazuzu are chaotic humanoids that respect and revere the air and sky. Clerics of Pazuzu are called Aerial Lords and must sign a pact of evil with Pazuzu. Aerial Lords can receive up to 3rd level spells from Pazuzu.

Fly or Die

The tangled woodland of brambles and stinging wasps is blocked by a stone wall of cyclopean blocks that stretches as far as they eye can see in all directions. A multitude of perches jut out from this wall, as do black pipes dripping ichor that runs down the walls, forming streamlets and eventually oozing rivers of gore that form a wide moat at the base of the wall.

A host of the perches are now occupied by the demon prince Pazuzu and his court of 2d4 harpies and 1d6+5 gargoyles. The winged monstrosities stand on the perches, alternatively glaring out into the distance and then cleaning themselves. Some dive into the bramble, arising with the shriveled souls of the damned. These victims are torn apart in midair by other harpies and gargoyles, the pieced not consumed falling to the ground and slowing reforming into the shriveled, naked form and cowering again in the brambles.

If it pleases Pazuzu, he might raise a hot wind that will sweep over the woodland and carry intruders up to his presence, hanging them precariously over the moat of ichor. He is as likely to be cruel as kind, so one never knows what will come from an audience with the winged prince.

Credit

Pazuzu originally appeared in the First Edition *Monster Manual II* (© TSR/Wizards of the Coast, 1983) and is used by permission.

Copyright Notice

Author Scott Greene, based on original material by Gary Gygax.

Demon Lord, Sonechard (General of Orcus)

Hit Dice: 18
Armor Class: -2 [21]
Attack: *+2 military pick* (1d8+2) or 2 claws (1d10)
Saving Throw: 3
Special: Control undead, spells, stench, summon undead, +1 or better weapon to hit, immunity to electricity and poison, magic resistance (60%), telepathy 100 ft.
Move: 15/30 (flying)
Alignment: Chaos
Challenge Level/XP: 27/6500

Sonechard is a ram-headed demon standing 14 feet tall. He has gray, leathery skin, large, curved horns (half of the left horn broken off) and two large, bat-like wings. Sonechard's body is covered in thick, dark hair. Portions of the hair are torn away in areas revealing masses of battle-born scars and damage. Sonechard is a general in the infernal armies of Orcus and serves him—at least to all onlookers—with unswerving loyalty. He has countless numbers of demons and undead at his command. Though his true loyalty lies only to himself, he would never openly refuse a request by Orcus nor challenge his position as Prince of the Undead. Should the day come when Orcus weakens, Sonechard plans to be there to claim what he believes is rightfully his. Sonechard makes his home in a large castle that sits atop a plateau of scorched earth surrounded by a moat of blood. The walls are constructed of bone and sinew, and it is said that the souls of those who cross him are entombed within.

Sonechard's form secretes a nauseating odor that emanates from him to a range of 20 feet. All living creatures within this range must succeed on a saving throw or be nauseated, suffering a –1 penalty to hit for 1 hour. A *neutralize poison* spell removes the nausea.

Once per day, Sonechard can automatically summon 4d10 zombies or skeletons, 2d8 shadows, wights, or wraiths, 2d4 greater shadows or spectres, or 1d4 dread wraiths. He can create up to 50 HD of undead creatures with the *animate dead* spell and can control undead as a 20th level chaotic cleric.

Sonechard can cast the following spells: *Animate dead*, *fireball* (3/day), *power word stun*, *suggestion* and *wall of fire*.

Sonechard's *+2 military pick* deals an extra 1d3 points from blood loss when it hits a creature. This damage is inflicted every round thereafter until the wound is bound or magically healed.

Demonic Wars Never End

On a bone-white plain of bare granite bearing a thousand mile-high pillars of salt shaped in the form of dread Orcus there is assembled a mighty host of dretches, 200 strong. In their center is the bellowing form of Sonechard, surrounded by his personal guard of 1d4 wraiths in the form of friars in tattered black robes with sunken in faces that cough clouds of flies, 1d4+4 shadows in the form of long-legged hunting dogs and 1d10+10 skeletons in gleaming platemail and tabards emblazoned with a ram skull on a field striped black and green.

Treachery has forced this army, now depleted to one fiftieth its original strength, to retreat to the land of salt pillars, and Sonechard means to discover the culprit. In a 30-foot deep pit there are thirteen mortal magic-users and clerics, all potential leakers of information to the servants of Jubilex, whose army of slimes and jellies now wriggles in celebration, having driven off the army of Sonechard and taken residence in his massive castle, lapping at his bloody moat and releasing the souls of those who have crossed him that they might serve the Faceless Lord.

Copyright Notice
Author Scott Greene

Demon Lord, Tsathogga (The Frog God)

Hit Dice: 25 (130 hp)
Armor Class: -4 [23]
Attack: Bite (3d6) or tongue (see below)
Saving Throw: 3
Special: Blasphemous shriek, swallow whole, spells, +3 or better weapon to hit, immune to acid and poison, magic resistance (80%), telepathy 100 ft.
Move: 15
Alignment: Chaos
Challenge Level/XP: 34/8600

Tsathogga is a gigantic frog no less than 60 feet long with spindly, elongated limbs and fingers. His body is covered in warts and sores and all ooze a putrid, yellowish mucus. His eyes are red and glow with an inherent evil and his massive mouth sports rows of sharpened teeth, each at least as long as a sword. Tsathogga cares less about the machinations of men and power than he does about obliterating light and life with the slow oozing sickness and decay that he represents. He is the viscous dark evil bubbling up from beneath the surface, the foul corruption at the heart of the earth. Tsathogga makes his home on both Tarterus and the Abyss, spending equal amounts of time in both places. His lair is a vast swamp of filth deposited by the River Styx as it flows between the two planes. Tsathogga thoughtlessly commands a host of evil creatures, notably his own vile frog race, the tsathar (see that entry in this book).

Tsathogga's demonic form constantly oozes and drips acid, causing opponents to take an extra 1d8 points of acid damage every time he succeeds on a bite, claw, or tongue attack. Creatures attacking Tsathogga unarmed take this same acid damage each time one of their attacks hits. Any weapon striking Tsathogga's acidic body must succeed at a saving throw or suffer a cumulative -1 penalty to damage - a weapon that has its potential damage reduced to 0 is destroyed.

Creatures struck by Tsathogga's tongue suffer 1d8 points of acid damage and must succeed at a saving throw or be swallowed whole and consumed.

Three times per day, Tsathogga can unleash a piercing shriek that affects all non-chaotic creatures within a 100-foot radius as if by an *un-holy word* (reverse of holy word). Tsathogga can billow forth a cloud of thick, dark fog from his skin. This fog spreads to fill a 50-foot radius, 50 feet high. The darkness generated by the cloud nullifies normal lights (torches, candles, lanterns, and so forth) within the area. Light spells of 5th level or lower are incapable of brightening the area. This cloud remains for 10 minutes before dispersing. Tsathogga cannot use this ability underwater.

Tsathogga can cast spells as a 15th level magic-user. He can also use the following magical abilities: *Acid cone* (as *cone of cold*, but deals acid damage), *darkness, dispel magic, ESP, polymorph self* and *water breathing*. He can summon up to 30 HD of oozes, tsathar, giant frogs, or froghemoths each day.

Servants of Tsathogga

Followers of Tsathogga are the tsathar and some few evil and vile humans or giants. He has few other worshippers, though it is rumored that an evil cult of sahuagin worships him on the Material Plane. Clerics of Tsathogga are called Lords of the Gaping Maw and must sign a pact of evil with Tsathogga. Lords of the Gaping Maw receive up to 3rd level spells from Tsathogga.

The Court of His Frogginess

A large, natural amphitheatre looks out over the sea. The amphitheatre contains a natural lagoon, now filled with slime. Awful little creatures, like a combination of a green-skinned dwarf and maggot, emerge at random intervals from the slime, wading through it and attending their master, Tsathogga, who lives at the back of the amphitheatre. Some of the dwarf-maggots (they have the statistics of bugbears) are swallowed by the frog demon god, while others shuffle about collecting weird fish from the slime and offering them to Tsathogga and others climb the rocks to enter the wide world, bearing messages to Tsathogga's servants - tsathar, brutish lizard men, evil cultists and others.

Some of the dwarf-maggots carry stone jars containing weird slimes to the waiting boats of pirates who have been tempted into serving the frog god, their ships waiting further off shore, captains nervously reconsidering their oaths of blood and rum. The slime from the cavern has seeped into the sea, animating the seaweed and kelp (treat as assassin vines) and causing the native sharks to develop frog-like faces and a sinister intelligence. Beneath the fleshy form of Tsathogga there lies a stone casket occupied by the mummified remains of Blebb, Anti-Saint and servant of Tsathogga. Pieces of this anti-saint worn as pendants act as a *protection from good* (reverse of *protection from evil*) spell in a 30-foot radius.

Copyright Notice

Demon Lord, Vepar (Duke of Dagon)

Hit Dice: 22
Armor Class: -4 [23]
Attacks: +2 trident (Demonbrand) (2d6+4) or 2 claws (1d8+2 + hypothermic touch)
Saving Throw: 3
Special: Magical abilities, hypothermic touch, summon demons, +2 magic weapons to hit
Move: 6/24 (swim)
Alignment: Chaos
Challenge Level/XP: 26/6,200

Vepar is an Abyssal duke who resembles a 12-foot-tall merman. His upper torso is coppery-brown while his lower torso and fins are silver and scaled. Vepar's hair is long and black, and he usually wears it tied back or braided. His eyes, usually blue in color, burn with a silvery fire when he is angered or excited. Under his hair, two small copper horns can be seen just above his eyes. Vepar's hands end in wicked claws with silvery nails. At will, Vepar can *control winds*, *detect good*, cause *fear*, *dispel magic*, *teleport* and *polymorph self*. Once per day he can create an *ice storm*. Vepar wields his trident – named Demonbrand – which can fire up to seven *magic missiles* per day for 1d4+1 points of damage each. Anyone hit by Vepar's claws must save or be overcome by bone-numbing cold that does 1d8 points of damage (save for half). He is immune to electricity and poison, and takes half damage from cold, fire and acid.

Beggar in Irons

The lighthouse at Shipsgrave has shown for centuries without fail even though no living being has entered the structure in decades. The aptly named Shipsgrave Lighthouse stands amid a dead reef littered with the broken hulls of countless ships. During low tide, reef pillars and the masts of ships resemble a graveyard from a distance. High tide completely covers the remains of the ships and the jagged reef columns. The lighthouse never fails to light at night and extinguishes each morning. Mysteriously, the lighthouse's glow ceases during storms and heavy fog. Sailors know to avoid the entire coast during these times to avoid ending up as another victim of the deadly reefs.

The legendary ship the Beggar in Irons surfaces from the depths near the reef whenever the sea is at its worst. Sea-bound mummies and brykolakas man the ship and attempt to sink other ships at any cost. The demon lord Vepar commands the Beggar in Irons. The ship is an extension of Vepar's will as he fuses with the ship as its figurehead. While fused, Vepar can move the ship in any direction, albeit at a much slower speed than wind-powered craft. The Beggar in Irons under Vepar's command can submerge and move in any direction. It can even hover above the water. If Vepar is slain, the Beggar in Irons returns to a pristine and sailable state, although it must still be cleared of the demon's undead crew.

Demonic Knight

Hit Dice: 9
Armor Class: -1 [20]
Attack: +1 longsword (1d8+1) or 2 slams (1d6)
Saving Throw: 6
Special: Breath of unlife, fear, magic resistance (30%), +1 or better weapon to hit, spells, summon demons
Move: 12
Alignment: Chaos
Challenge Level/XP: 14/2600

The demonic knight—known by some as a death knight—is rumored to be the creation of the great demon prince Orcus, the Prince of the Undead. Some sages doubt the validity of such a claim, since the demonic knights are not undead. Though no link has been proven, however, it is known that three of the most powerful demonic knights (Baruliis, Caines, and Arrunes) make their home in the shadow of Orcus's great citadel. The demonic knights serve their master (whoever it may be) with unswerving loyalty. They never question their orders or station. They are often sent to the Material Plane to recruit new bodies for their master's next plot or deception, or to punish those that have offended their lord. On some occasions, they are simply sent to another plane to corrupt and slay those that are just and good (to the delight of their master). It is unknown exactly how many demonic knights exist, but they are believed to number no more than nine. Demonic knights appear as humanoids in black, gothic plate armor. They are armed with *+1 longswords*.

Those within sound of the demonic knight's voice must pass a saving throw or flee in terror for 2d4 rounds. Three times per day, a demonic knight can exhale a blast of negative energy in a 10-foot cone. Creatures in the area of the cone must pass a saving throw or suffer 2d4 points of Strength damage. Strength returns at the rate of 1 point per day. Creatures reduced to a strength score of 0 are killed, rising as shadow demons in 2d4 rounds. The shadow demons are slaves to the demonic knight until it is destroyed.

Demonic knights can cast the following spells: *dispel magic (2/day)*, *fireball (1/day)*, *symbol of fear (1/day)* and *wall of ice*. They are capable of seeing through invisibility and illusions.

Knight's Challenge

In a woodland of shadowy trees, tall and straight with overarching boughs that produce a canopy of blackness, you come across a pavilion of red damask silk. From afar, the embroidery appears to be of acanthus leaves, but on closer inspection it turns out to be lions devouring infants. Atop the pavilion there is a pennon or with a grisly lion's paw sable and claws sanquine. The pavilion rests in a clear area. By and by, a dretch garbed in black, rusty plate and mail and a yellow tabard charged with the same bloody paw as is on the pennon. The dretch is dragging a two-handed sword behind him and heading for nearby stump, next to which sit the tools necessary to clean and sharpen the blade. Upon seeing the adventurers, the dretch will hurry into the pavilion. His disappearance is followed swiftly by a deep growl and the ejection of the pitiable creature. The dretch will raise a golden ram's horn (worth 100 gp) to its blubbery lips and produce from it a low bellow. At this point, a demonic knight will emerge from the pavilion, swaggering and impressive. The knight will cuff the dretch, who will retrieve its sword. Pointing an armored, clawed finger at the adventurers, it will bellow out a challenge to the most impressive looking fighter or paladin. As a prize it will offer a carnelian pendant that, the knight claims, has the power to return the adventurers home with the command word "Zvid".

As the combatants take their positions in the middle of the dark clearing, the adventurers probably will not notice 1d3+1 shadows taking up positions within easy reach of the knight's opponent. These creatures, hidden effectively in the darkness, will aid the knight in any way they can, including attacking onlookers.

The pendant, should it be won, will prove to do just what the demonic knight claimed, in a manner of speaking. Anyone touching it while speaking the command word will be returned to their last permanent home polymorphed (if they fail a saving throw) into a dretch.

Copyright Notice
Author Scott Greene.

Devil, Amaimon

Hit Dice: 7
Armor Class: 2 [17]
Attacks: 2 claws (1d6), 1 bite (1d8)
Saving Throw: 9
Special: breath weapon, magic resistance (15%), immune to fire, fear aura, spell-like abilities
Move: 12
Alignment: Chaos
Challenge Level/XP: 3/60

Amaimons stand nearly 10 feet tall, weigh about 700 pounds and look like bloated, squat humanoids with scarlet flesh. They have a long, curved and forked tail, clawed hands and feet, and round, squashed heads with two small horns just above their sapphire colored eyes. Amiamons can breathe a cloud of poisonous fire that deals 3d8 points of damage. A saving throw halves the damage. Amaimons radiate fear in a 10-foot radius. At will, Amaimons can *teleport*, create a *phantasmal force* and cast *wall of fire*. Amaimons can use *ESP* at will.

Helly Tubby

The gray fleshy floor of this area has a 4-foot-high dome rising toward a center apex. The dome is 25 foot around and adheres to the floor with resin-like secretions. The spongy ground quivers with every step but is stable and does not impede movement.

Atop the flesh dome is an 8-foot-diameter closed, sinewy hole. The supple dome resists all damage and begins to swell 1 round after it is disturbed. After two rounds, the sphincter-like opening puckers and releases a rank plume of red vapor. The dome then discharges a slime-coated amaimon demon that was just birthed into this world. The bloated red demon is hungry for its first mortal meal. Only after the amaimon is slain does the flesh dome wither and rot away, leaving no trace of its existence. The dome may spew out more amaimons to incrrease the encounter's Challenge Level.

Copyright Notice
Author Scott Greene.

Devil, Blood Reaver (Garugin)

Hit Dice: 9
Armor Class: 1 [18]
Attacks: dual-headed barbed flail (1d10+3 + stun) or 2 claws (2d6+3)
Saving Throw: 6
Special: Siphoning aura, magical abilities, summon devils, +1 weapons to hit, regenerates 5 hp/round
Move: 12
Alignment: Chaos
Challenge Level/XP: 13/2,300

Blood reavers, also known as garugins, are 7-foot-tall bipedal humanoids with reddish-bronze leathery flesh and gleaming, gold eyes. Its hands end in blood-stained claws and the smell of fresh blood always hangs in the air around a blood reaver. Its fearsome visage sports a slightly curved mouth laced with sharp, flesh-rending fangs. The blood reaver has a long, forked tail the same color as its body. Blood reavers radiate an aura in a 20-foot radius that causes creatures to bleed from their mouths, noses, eyes and ears. Affected creatures must save or lose 1d6 hit points each round. When a blood reaver hits with its barbed flail, the opponent must save or be stunned for 1 round. At will a blood reaver can *teleport*, *turn invisible* and create a *wall of fire*. Once per day it can create a *lightning bolt*. Blood reavers are immune to fire and poison, and take half damage from cold and acid.

Stare into the Flames

A wall of flickering red fire rises 10 feet into the air in the center of the Enlightened Sanctuary of the Everlasting Conflagration. The wall of flame is 10 feet thick, and runs from wall to wall behind a 5-foot-wide square altar carved to resemble an open book. The wall of flame never goes out and changes colors with the seasons. It is currently red with flecks of orange and yellow to highlight the first days of autumn.

The bodies of nearly 30 worshippers lie slumped in the pews closest to the fire, their lifeless corpses staring at the dancing flames. Blood runs from their eyes and ears, and the floor is sticky with red puddles. Kazatul Chen, the temple's priest, lies across the altar, his skin ripped and torn into bloody strips. He is barely alive, but won't last long.

Chorcorat and Heekin, two blood reavers, dance within the flaming wall, their bodies barely visible. The pair teleported into the temple, using the fire for cover, to punish the headstrong Chen for his forays into the underworld. The reavers drained his congregation where they sat, then turned their flails on the priest. The demons lurk within the burning wall instead of leaving, waiting to have some fun with people coming to rescue the priest. The wall of flame burns fiercely, but does just 1d3 points of damage each round to Lawful PCs who enter it. Others, including the blood reavers, take 1d6 points each round.

Copyright Notice

Devil, Flayer (Marzach)

Hit Dice: 12
Armor Class: -1 [20]
Attacks: 2 claws (1d6+3) and bite (1d8+3)
Saving Throw: 3
Special: Flensing, magical abilities, summon devils, unholy burst, +1 magic weapons to hit, regenerate 5 hp/round, magic resistance (24%), immune to fire and poison, resists cold and acid
Move: 12
Alignment: Chaos
Challenge Level/XP: 18/3,800

A flayer demon is a 13-foot-tall hulking brute with leathery, crimson skin, a large mouth lined with razor-sharp teeth, and large, round horns protruding from the sides of its hairless head. Its hands and feet end in large, sharpened claws and its eyes are bronze-colored and slitted. A flayer devil that rolls a natural 20 with its claw attack rips the flesh from its opponent's body, dealing 2d6 points of damage. At will, a flayer can *detect good* and *teleport*. Once per day, it can cast *wall of fire*. Three times per day, the flayer devil can unleash a burst of hellish black vapor in a 30-foot radius that sickens anyone in the area for 1d6 rounds (save resists). Lawful creatures take 3d6 points of damage from this unholy aura if they fail their save. Flayers are immune to fire and poison, and take half damage from cold and acid.

Chamber of Bone

Once an enigmatic shrine to murder located below Bargarsport's streets, the Chamber of Bone has mostly fallen from common knowledge among the assassins of the land. To further their horrible goals, the mostly defunct murder cult enlisted the aid of a flayer demon. Within a short time, however, the flayer demon had devoured every last member of the Chamber of Bone. The flayer demon remains trapped on this plane, contentedly carrying out ritualistic murders in the city streets above.

The chambers that once housed the cult provide a safe haven for the flayer demon. The bones of his victims now decorate the compound's walls and ceiling. Bones sharpened to spear-like points protrude from the walls and ceiling. Furniture and eating utensils made from bone furnish the rooms, and the floors are caked with inches of powered bone dust. The flayer demon devours all flesh from its victims, leaving behind only heaps of gnawed bone.

Copyright Notice
Author Scott Greene.

Devil, Ghaddar

Hit Dice: 16
Armor Class: -2 [21]
Attack: 2 claws (2d8), bite (2d6)
Saving Throw: 3
Special: Feed, spells, vorpal bite, +1 or better weapon to hit, immunity to fire and poison, see in darkness, magic resistance (40%), telepathy 100 ft.
Move: 15
Alignment: Chaos
Challenge Level/XP: 23/5300

The terrible and mighty ghaddars roam the planes of Hell devouring the unfortunate souls of those they encounter. They also consume the essence and being of any outcast devils and dukes that cross their path. A typical ghaddar stands 15 feet tall and has the head of a donkey with large, downward-curving horns. A ghaddar's eyes are stark white, with hollow, black pupils. Its feet are splayed and it shuffles with a hunched gait.

If a ghaddar scores a natural "20" on its attack roll and its foe fails a saving throw, it severs the foe's head. When a ghaddar slays a humanoid, spending a minute to devour both flesh and life force. Feeding destroys the victim's body and prevents any form of raising and resurrection. For every three suitable corpses a ghaddar devours, it gains 1 Hit Die and its Armor Class increases by +1. The ghaddar only advances by consuming the corpses of creatures whose Hit Dice or levels are equal to or greater than its own current total.

Ghaddars can use the following spells: *Fireball* (3/day), *phantasmal force* and *wall of fire*.

Arena of the Lower Planes

Captured by devils, a band of adventurers might find themselves thrown into a great arena with walls a mile high banded with galleries crowded with bloodthirsty souls in ebon togas and clanging on bronze bells with great femur bones or disgorging their last nights repast into the sand of the arena. The largest galleries are occupied by Hell's aristocrats and their retinues. A prominent box seats Asmodeus and his concubines on crimson pillows, a great gong provided for him to quiet the cacaphonous crowd.

The sky above the arena boils and pops, with large chunks of magma falling into the sand and soon sinking out of sight. Combatants will discover that standing in the same place for more than one round results in the same effect. After one round of standing still, a combatant sinks to his ankles, losing his dexterity bonus to Armor Class and falling prone if more than 5 points of damage is suffered from a single hit. After two rounds if the combatant hasn't moved, he will be up to his knees and, in two more rounds, up to his neck. On the next round he'll be gone into the deep torture pits of Asmodeus.

As the new gladiators come to grips with this, the gong will sound and the crowd will quiet to a dull roar, followed by the rising shriek of one thousand fifes and the booming words "Release the ghaddar". Should the adventurers survive the first ghaddar, another will be loosed, until they have fought 1d3+1 of the beasts. If triumphant, they will be presented to Asmodeus who, after marking their foreheads with his glyph, will send them back to the Material Plane.

Copyright Notice

Devil, Hellstoker (Marnasoth)

Hit Dice: 5
Armor Class: 0 [19]
Attacks: 1 spear (1d8+3) or bellows (1d8 fire) or 2 claws (1d4+3)
Saving Throw: 12
Special: Bellows, fiery body, magical abilities, summon demons, +1 magic weapons to hit
Move: 9
Alignment: Chaos
Challenge Level/XP: 8/800

Hellstokers stand just less than 6 feet tall and weigh about 180 pounds. Their rubbery, grayish-black flesh hangs loosely on their bodies, and is always smeared with a fine layer of yellowish-brown oil. Hellstokers have ovoid heads, no hair, and small upward curving horns. A hardened ridge of bone runs from their brow across the top of their head and disappears into their spine. Hellstokers have long, serpentine, forked tails. Their eyes are round with red or black pupils. A hellstoker carries a set of bellows that can fire a line of flame up to 30 feet. The oil coating a hellstoker is highly flammable, and any fire-based spell causes them to burst into flame, which adds an extra 1d6 points of damage to their claw attacks. Hellstokers can *teleport* at will. Once per day, they can cast *burning hands*. Hellstokers are immune to fire and poison, and take half damage from cold and acid.

Sweet Shop

Chuzzlewit Pitt's pie-baking business is booming, with the ovens going day and night to fill orders from Dunstan's hungry townspeople. Chuzzlewit is the toast of the town, but he owes his success to an infernal pact made to keep his business alive. An old man promised Chuzzlewit fame beyond his wildest dreams. The poor baker jumped at the chance. That night, the ovens came alive with a hellish light, the fires burning hot and ready for Chuzzlewit's pies. Fanning the flames were 12 hellstoker demons that also help Chuzzlewit in the kitchen. Chuzzlewit doesn't even need to do anything anymore except wait on his happy customers. The entire shop is running quite efficiently by the demonic horde.

Unfortunately for the baker, he's winning fans but losing customers, as the vicious hellstokers kidnap a person every other day to rend into oil to power the stoves. A few missing people even make it into the delicious pies. Chuzzlewit desperately wants out of this horrible deal, but he's scared to say anything. He hints at "problems in the basement" to PCs, but is shifty and elusive about what's down there. He hopes someone can kill the demons destroying his businesss and his life. The demons boil out of the basement to protect their master's investment if the shop is attacked.

Copyright Notice
Author Scott Greene.

Devil, Lilin

Hit Dice: 7
Armor Class: 6 [13]
Attacks: 2 claws (1d3), 1 weapon (1d8)
Saving Throw: 9
Special: Magic resistance (15%), immune to fire, magical abilities, +1 magic weapons to hit
Move: 12/18 (flying)
Alignment: Chaos
Challenge Level/XP: 8/800

A lilin is a crimson-skinned woman about 5-1/2 feet tall with long dark hair. Her eyes are dark, almost black as is her hair. A pair of small bat-like wings protrudes from her shoulders. She wields a gleaming long sword. Lilins can use *ESP* and cast *charm person, charm monster* or *teleport* at will. Three times per day they can *animate dead*. They can see perfectly in darkness of any kind.

Innocence

Cobwebs and vines drape from the trees. The bones of many humanoids litter the earth; most appear to be dwarven in nature. An intricately carved wooden stake lies among the bones. A glass coffin sits on a latticework stone bier in the center of a small glade. The body of a young maiden of exquisite beauty lies within. She is adorned in black funerary shrouds and ornate silver plate armor. A wickedly curved sword lies across her breast. A scripted stone placard bearing a simple verse stands before the bier:

In the darkness of night, beauty in sight.
In the light of the moon, terror too soon.
In the shine of the sun, all will be undone.
Affection survive whilst thou alive.

Ezmersealla, a lilin, hides within the confines of the latticework bier. A *permanent darkness* spell envelops the hollow space within the bier. Ezmersealla delights in corrupting champions of good. With her immortal life span, she loves to devise intricate traps that tempt do-gooders with moral dilemmas. She incapacitated a farm girl with a debilitating poison and brought her to this location as bait. The girl's lips are coated with the same poison that immobilizes her. If not treated with an antidote, any victim of the poison will eventually die of starvation and dehydration as they continue to sleep. Ezmersealla uses her charm and ESP powers to dupe characters into slaying the innocent damsel.

Copyright Notice

Devil, Nupperibo

Hit Dice: 1
Armor Class: 7 [12]
Attack: Spear (1d6) or 2 claws (1d4)
Saving Throw: 17
Special: +1 or better weapon to hit, immunity to fire and poison, mindless, regeneration (1 hp/round), see in darkness
Move: 9
Alignment: Chaos
Challenge Level/XP: 4/120

Those evil souls that are taken to Hell and processed to become lemures but fail ultimately become nupperibo: a life-form even more disgusting and sad than the lowly lemure. Nupperibos are vaguely humanoid. They have clawed hands and dark, grayish-black flesh. They are gathered by the dukes and arch devils and used as fodder in their never-ending wars. A nupperibo killed in battle is 99% likely to be reformed (by a duke or arch devil) into another nupperibo; the remaining 1% are "promoted" to lemure status, having proved their worth in combat. Nupperibos are blind and deaf but can ascertain all foes within 60 feet using scent and vibration. Nupperibos are immune to all mind-influencing effects (charms, compulsions, phantasms, patterns, and morale effects).

The Ox King

In a depression of the landscape, you come across a horde of 1d4x20 nupperibo crawling over the mournfully bellowing carcass of some massive creature that must have once been an ox. The carcass is 30 feet long, its massive ribs rising 15 feet off the ground. Great chunks of flesh have been removed from the beast, which cannot die. Should one look into its eyes, they will see reflected back the image of a king, garbed in the Assyrian style with curled, blue-black beard and cylindrical crown, pleading for release.

The nupperibo are plenty busy feeding on the tortured king, but there is a 1 in 6 chance per round that 3d6 of the beasts will leave the giant oxen and attack the adventurers. Dead nupperibo will be replaced an hour later. In the meantime, if all the nupperibo are destroyed, the beast will open its mouth and, upon its tongue, you will find a cylinder seal made of faience (a man-made glass as valuable as a gemstone) measuring 1 foot in length and worth 600 gp. If rolled out onto a clay, the resulting image contains clues to the location of a princely treasure on the Material Plane.

Credit

The Nupperibo originally appeared in the First Edition *Monster Manual II* (© TSR/Wizards of the Coast, 1983) and is used by permission.

Copyright Notice

Author Scott Greene, based on original material by Gary Gygax.

Devil, Tormentor (Tormentor of Souls)

Hit Dice: 8
Armor Class: -1 [20]
Attack: *+1 battleaxe* (1d8+1) or *soulcatcher net* (1d4 plus entanglement) or 2 claws (1d8)
Saving Throw: 8
Special: Magic weapons, spells, +1 or better weapon to hit, immunity to fire and poison, regeneration (2 hp/round), magic resistance (45%), see in darkness, soul track, telepathy 100 ft.
Move: 12
Alignment: Chaos
Challenge Level/XP: 15/2900

These reddish-gray scaled humanoids stand taller than a human. Their hands are clawed and its feet cloven. Oversized fangs jut from their upper jaw and drip foul-smelling saliva. Small horns protrude from just above its eyes, curving backwards. Their bodies are hairless and they have small curving tails. Tormentors of Souls, known as tormentor devils, make their way across the uppermost plane of Hell searching for souls that have entered the realms of evil. They are in the employ of this devil lord or that devil lord and return captured souls to their current master, where they are justly rewarded. Tormentors often employ hell hounds when pursuing renegade or runaway souls.

Tormentor devils can cast the following spells: *ESP, scorching ray* (1/day, as fireball but a 30-ft long ray that requires a ranged attack). A tormentor devil can track the soul of any creature that enters the planes of Hell.

A tormentor devil's net looks like a normal net and acts like a normal net save that it can entrap incorporeal creatures. The net has many small razor-sharp barbs lining it. These barbs deal 1d4 points of damage each round to any creature caught in the net, including incorporeal creatures. A tormentor's *+1 battleaxe* can also deal damage against incorporeal creatures.

Devil Gets His Due

You come across a pitiful sight, a ghostly man (perhaps the soul of a vanquished villain) hiding in the cracks between two massive outcroppings of rock. The ghost is almost mad with worry, for it knows that a tormentor of souls and 1d4 hell hounds are on its trail. The hunters will arrive in 1d4+1 rounds, giving the ghost just enough time to bargain with the adventurers to save him. He will offer the location of a fabulous treasure he left behind on the Material Plane. Of course, this ghostly soul may be a mere illusion, meant to fool adventurers into finding the treasure and releasing some horror upon the world - devil's do that kind of thing all day long.

Copyright Notice

UNIQUE DEVILS

Certain unique devils serve as tyrants and enforcers among the ranks of Hell.

Devil, Alastor (Executioner of Hell)

Hit Dice: 25 (120)
Armor Class: -4 [23]
Attacks: 1 weapon (2d6+2), 1 claw (2d8), 1 bite (1d8), 1 tail (2d8)
Saving Throw: 3
Special: Magic resistance (75%), +3 magic weapon required to hit, immune to fire and charm, magical abilities
Move: 6/15 (flying)
Alignment: Chaos
Challenge Level/XP: 28/6,800

Alastor stands at least 16 feet tall, and his body is entirely cloaked in hellish red and yellow flames. Huge bat-like wings spread from his scaled body and his arms end in clawed hands that hold a tight grip on a wickedly curved iron battleaxe named Grimfang. Alastor's eyes are black with red pupils and its mouth is filled with rows of fangs. At will, Alastor can *dispel magic*, cast *fireball* or use *ESP*.

Red Erring

The medium-sized town of Red Erring is the site of recent warfare. Most of the thatch and sod residences lie in smoldering heaps. Barns, stables, fences and even outhouses are splintered ruins. The butchered remains townsfolk and livestock cover the ground in a nightmarish scene of bloated carcasses and fetid pools of blood. The fresh carnage and swarms of flies testify to the recent carnage. Despite the numerous corpses, it seems that most of the women and children fled or went into hiding. A small granite cathedral appears to have survived unscathed through the slaughter. A stone decorative parapet surrounds the church grounds and cemetery. Six men with swords and torches scream profanities and blasphemous curses toward the church from outside the wall. Their blades are heavy with gore and their eyes wild with fury. They lay siege upon those within the church. Weak and feeble hymns can be heard through the massive doors.

About 100 survivors cower within the church around the High Priest Galanfane (Cleric 15). The villagers are wounded, and weak from hunger and dehydration. Another score of villagers died from their wounds and their bodies are stacked along the walls. The remaining villagers feebly sing and chant prayers to ward off the evil that has ravaged their town. In fact only the consecrated grounds of the ancient church protect the survivors from the demon Alastor and his demonic allies surrounding the temple.

Only for the truly wicked does Alastor journey to the world of mortals to seek retribution. The High Priest Galanfane and his underlings committed grave sins against their fellow man and warranted such attention when his power and influence within the community put him above castigation. The cleric enjoyed his position of wealth and power for many years with impunity until one of Galafane's many victims pleaded to the dark lords for revenge. While Galanfane blessed Red Erring's cathedral with his presence (and brazenly stole from the townspeople), Alastor and his 5 nalfeshnee entered the world with a goal of returning to the nether depths with the immoral priest.

Helpless against the demonic horde invading the town, the villagers fell quickly to the demons' supremacy. Many fled into the wilds, while others turned to the high priest and his underlings (5th-level cleric) hiding in the church. High Priest Galanfane now uses his "flock" as human shields while he plans his escape. Alastor hides within a barn with the nalfeshnee assuming the form of the humans surrounding the church wall. The demons cannot cross into the hallowed grounds beyond the low stone partition. Galanfane promises his rescuers privileges and riches beyond their wildest dreams, although he will betray them at his earliest convenience.

Copyright Notice

Author Scott Greene.

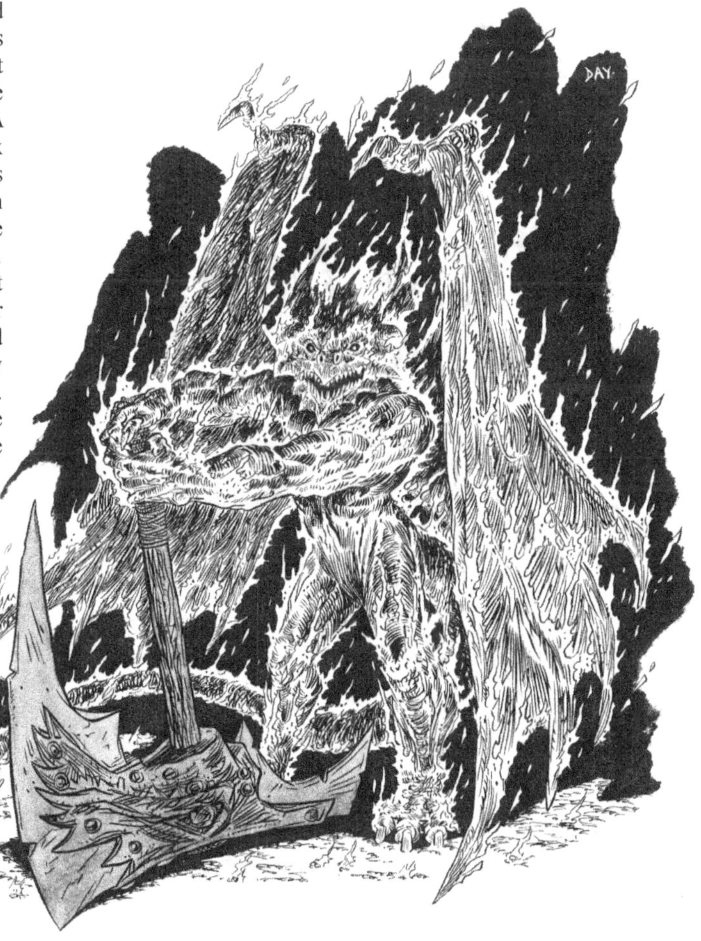

Devil, Amon (Duke of Hell)

Hit Dice: 20 (100 hp)
Armor Class: -3 [22]
Attack: +3 *heavy mace* (3d6), bite (2d6)
Saving Throw: 3
Special: Fear gaze, spells, control and summon wolves, summon demons, +2 or better weapon to hit, immunity to fire and poison, magic resistance (75%), regeneration (3 hp/round), teleapthy 100 ft.
Move: 24
Alignment: Chaos
Challenge Level/XP: 30/7400

Amon is a wolf-headed demon who stands 9 feet tall. His fur is brownish-black and his eyes and teeth are yellow. Amon is a vassal in service to Geryon, commanding no less than 3 legions of bone devils. He is completely loyal to the Great Serpent and never questions his post. On more than one occasion an arch devil has tried to seduce Amon into betraying his lord, but such attempts always fail Amon's iron citadel sits high on a flat-topped mountain within the domain of Hell's fifth plane. It is a great, dark place filled with devils, wolves, and creatures far worse.

Amon's gaze induces fear to a range of 30 feet. An affected creature must succeed on a saving throw or be affected as by a *fear* spell. Amon can cast the following spells: *Animate dead, charm monster, dispel magic, fly, produce flame, suggestion, symbol of discord* (1/day) and *wall of ice*. Once per day, Amon can summon a total of 40 HD of wolves and worgs. He can control up to 40 HD of wolves and worgs, whether summoned by him or not. Twice per day, Amon can summon 4d10 lemures or nupperibos, 2d4 bone devils, 1d4 barbed devils or 1 gaddar devil or pit fiend.

Hounds of Hell

In the ancient desert, in a shallow cave burrowed into the ground between two sandstone bluffs, there is a small shrine dedicated to Amon. The shrine contains a brass idol of the Hellish duke, a perfect sapphire worth 5,000 gp grasped in its fist. Piles of human bones surround the idol, and iron loops set into the floor and ceiling, along with copious patches of dried blood, speak to the terrible ceremonies that have taken place here. An alabaster cup rests before the idol containing a mixture of snake venom and the fermented pressings of one of the native agaves.

The sapphire is easily removed from the idol's hand. The possessor of the jewel must pass a saving throw or find themselves fascinated by the ripples of light across its surface, and fancy they can see an image deep in the stone. Each night they will stare into the stone and refuse to let others touch it, and each night the image will become more and more clear - a loved one, wandering in the wilderness, frightened and fleeing from the howls of wolves. The holder of the jewel must pass a new saving throw each night or find themselves unable to sleep. Those who do not sleep will not benefit from natural healing and after a week must save each morning or be struck with *confusion* (as the spell) for the next 24 hours. After falling into confusion three times, the unfortunate despoiler of shrines will find the condition is permanent.

The spell can be broken by smashing the gem, a task easily accomplished with a metal weapon. As the gem shatters, an azure cloud will envelop all assembled. When it clears, they will find themselves in the same desert landscape, but everything tinted a deep, midnight blue -everything except the starless sky, which is stained blood red. Almost instantly, the cry of wolves will be heard nearby - the hunting pack of Amon - 1d8+4 wolves and 2d4 bone devils. The devils are about 1 mile away from the adventurers, who now must hie back to the location of the shrine, where they must drink from the poisoned goblet and pray to the idol of Amon for forgiveness to return back to their own dimension. When (or if) they do, they will find themselves back in the shrine, the sapphire still in the idol's fist.

Bone Devil: HD 10; AC 0 [19]; Atk Bite (1d8) and 2 claws (1d4) and sting (3d4 plus poison); Move 15; Save 5; CL/XP 15/2900; Special: Spells, poison, +1 or better weapon to hit, immunity to fire and poison, resistance to acid and cold (50%), spell resistance (55%), telepathy 100 ft.

Credit

Amon originally appeared in *Dragon #75* (© TSR/Wizards of the Coast, 1983) and later in the First Edition *Monster Manual II* (© TSR/Wizards of the Coast, 1983) and is used by permission.

Copyright Notice

Author Scott Greene, based on original material by Gary Gygax.

Devil, Baal (Duke of Hell)

Hit Dice: 16 (80 hp)
Armor Class: -4 [23]
Attack: *+2 morning star* (3d6) or 2 claws (1d8)
Saving Throw: 3
Special: Fear aura, spells, summon devils, +1 or better weapon to hit, immunity to fire and poison, magic resistance (70%), regeneration (3 hp/round), telepathy 100 ft.
Move: 15
Alignment: Chaos
Challenge Level/XP: 26/6200

Baal is a tall, golden-skinned humanoid dressed in battered bronze chainmail. His bovine head features large, round eyes of black, a large nose, the ears of a wolf and a large mouth lined with razor sharp teeth. Tiny forward-curving horns protrude from his forehead. Baal is a duke in the employ of Great Mammon and leads 5 legions of barbed devils in his service. Baal follows Lord Mammon's orders without question but secretly plans one day to wrest the throne from his master (who has become complacent as of late). For now, though, he waits and schemes.

Baal attacks with a *+3 morningstar* that can telescope to up to 8 feet in length. He radiates a 20-foot-radius aura of fear (save or affected as *fear* spell). He can cast the following spells: *Animate dead, cause serious wounds, charm monster, dispel magic, invisibility* (self), *phantasmal force, produce fire, pyrotechnics, shape change* (2/day), *suggestion* and *symbol of stunning* (1/day). Twice per day Baal can summon 4d10 lemures or nupperibo, 2d4 barbed devils or bearded devils, 1d4 erinyes, or 1 ghaddar devil, horned devil, or 1 pit fiend.

The Bronze Pit of Baal

The brazen pit of Bael sits in a landscape of bronze hills (hills actually made of bronze) divided by rivers of molten copper spanned by searing bridges of iron chains. In the center of this landscape is a pit 300 feet deep and 100 feet in diameter. Bronze stairs lead into the pit, meandering over its surface up and down and leading here and there to doors - slabs of basalt framed in brass that only open when a bloodied palm is pressed against them and one speaks the words "Bael Indomitus Rex".

At the bottom of the pit is the magma sea upon which the bronze hills float. Behind the doors of Bael's pit are long, brazen halls stamped in bas reliefs of the lord of the palace and his servants engaged in all manner of horrors. Hidden in these bas reliefs are secret doors opened by sticking fingers into unsavory places (that sometimes biting those fingers off). Being the palace of a Duke of Hell, the place contains hundreds of chambers and passages, all steaming hot and occupied by all manner of fell beasts. The halls are patrolled by groups of 1d4+1 horned devils or 1d3+1 barbed devils. A cross section of the palace would reveal the halls and chambers situated in a conical shape, the point of the cone being the throne room of Baal, located in a spherical chamber underneath the magma pit.

The throne room is 50 feet in diameter, with a 10-foot diameter lodestone at its center. Baels throne is a red lacquered throne in the Asian style, and it rests on this lodestone sphere. The lodestone sphere is the soul source of gravity in the throne room, and this gravity only extends a mere 5 feet out from the lodestone. The rest of the room should be considered zero gravity. Bael keeps nine leaping lemures chained to the sphere. The lemure's chains are 15 feet long, and allow the beasts to leap into the zero gravity environment and attack and then be pulled back, or pull themselves back, to do it again.

Credit
Baal originally appeared as "Bael" in *Dragon #75* (© TSR/Wizards of the Coast, 1983) and later in the First Edition *Monster Manual II* (© TSR/Wizards of the Coast, 1983) and is used by permission.

Copyright Notice
Author Scott Greene, based on original material by Gary Gygax.

Devil, Baaphel (Duke of Hell)

Hit Dice: 18 (120 hp)
Armor Class: -2 [21]
Attack: +3 *scythe* (2d6) or 2 fists (1d8)
Saving Throw: 3
Special: Fear touch, spells, summon devils, +2 or better weapon to hit, immunity to fire and poison, magic resistance (65%), regeneration (3 hp/round), telepathy 100 ft.
Move: 12/18 (flying)
Alignment: Chaos
Challenge Level/XP: 28/6800

Baaphel is a grand duke in the service of Belial, leading 2 legions of bearded devils in battle for his lord. He is a dog-headed humanoid with grayish-brown skin, pale scarlet eyes, two crimson horns, two large bat wings, hooved feet and a forked crimson tail. Baaphel is constantly scheming against the other dukes in Belial's service and takes every opportunity to discredit them in the eyes of their lord, though he never does this openly; it is always through lesser dukes and other devils that his machinations come to fruition. Baaphel yearns to be ruler of an entire plane and is waiting anxiously until the time comes that he can overthrow his lord. Baaphel makes his home in a great castle of basalt and iron on Hell's fourth plane.

Baaphel can induce fear by touch, an affected creature affected by a *fear* spell if they fail a saving throw. Baaphel can cast the following spells: *Charm monster, dispel magic, invisibility, suggestion, symbol of sleep* (1/day) and *transmute flesh to stone* (1/day). Twice per day Baaphel can automatically summon 4d10 nupperibos, 2d6 bearded devils, 1d4 barbed devils, bone devils, or erinyes or 1 ghaddar devil.

Fortress of Basalt and Iron

The stronghold of Baaphel is a massive shell keep of basalt blocks and iron bindings that measures 500 feet in diameter, with 20-foot thick walls that rise 100 feet high and are topped by swallowtail merlons. The shell keep has three levels of battlements, with "X"-shaped arrow slits beneath the crenellations and beneath them machiolations backed by a walkway equipped with charcoal pits and vats of boiling oil. The keep has four gates, each composed of a iron pikes on which are skewered the heads of humans, demi-humans and demons, all animated and uttering screams of pain or sobbing and pleading for release. The tunnels that lead into the courtyard are covered in mosaics depicting the armies and battles of Baaphel. The figures in these mosaics seem to stare into one's eyes, and travelers must pass a saving throw or become hypnotized and believe them to be reaching out for them - the affected will cower on the ground until snapped out of the delusion.

The central courtyard of the keep consists of a perimeter walk of slightly gooey asphalt around a bubbling tar pit. Perched in the center of the pit, on a bronze pillar, is the seat of Baaphel, with two or three unfortunates chained to the seat in easy reach of Baaphels claws. Baaphel's stronghold is guarded by one hundred bearded devils and a staff of twenty lemures. Besides the aforementioned battlements, the stronghold contains long chains of chambers - some clad in pig iron, others in bare basalt, and still others decorated with mosaics (as above, only more profane and sometimes including people the adventurers know or the adventurers themselves and causing confusion for 1 hour in those who are hypnotized).

In each chamber there is an iron brazier, white hot, with the soul of a tormented soul suspended over it in ghostly chains, writhing in agony. These chains of rooms are connected by passages, stairs (up or down), trapdoors in the floors or ceilings and hidden doors in black wardrobes and coffers. A variety of devils and other monsters lurks in this pointless, never-ending labyrinth of rooms, along with all manner of weird treasures - coins stamped with the visage of Asmodeus or other archdevils that shriek when place in the same bag as coins bearing the image of a rival, dried monkey paws, chains of devil teeth that sup on any foolish enough to wear them around their necks, bronze masks that twist the face of the wearer into a replica of the mask, etc. Almost any magic item found in the stronghold will be cursed in the hands of a lawful person, but will function normally for chaotics and normally half the time for neutrals.

Devil, Caasimolar (Former President of Hell)

Hit Dice: 25
Armor Class: -8 [27]
Attacks: Caasimolar's rod (1d6 + *inflict serious wounds*)
Saving Throw: 3
Special: Fear, magical abilities, summon devils, +3 magic weapons to hit, regenerate 7 hp/round, magic resistance (40%), immune to fire and poison, resists acid and cold
Move: 32
Alignment: Chaos
Challenge Level/XP: 32/5,900

As President of Hell, Caasimolar was the second in command of the Abyss. Caasimolar appears as a wizened old man about 7 feet tall with a silver beard and balding head. His eyes are ruby red, as are the small rounded horns that jut from his head just above his eyes. His hands and feet are humanoid and his nails are ruby red. His long, snaky, thin forked tail is crimson. Caasimolar wears robes of purple, white, amber, or sapphire. Underneath his robes his body is crimson with small scales. By speaking, Caasimolar induces *fear* (as per the spell) in all creatures within 30 feet who fail a save. At will, Caasimolar can *animate dead*, cast a *cone of cold*, *detect magic*, *detect good*, use *ESP*, *dispel magic*, *teleport* and *polymorph self*. Three time a day he can cast *wall of ice*, and once a day he can cast *power word kill*. Caasimolar is immune to fire and poison, and takes half damage from cold and acid. Caasimolar's rod is a 6-foot long iron rod that functions as a *+3 quarterstaff*. In addition, once per day it can unleash a *lightning bolt* for 10d6 points of damage (save for half), and three times a day it can cast *finger of death*. Each strike by Caasimolar's rod does 1d6 points of damage and inflicts serious wounds (2d6+2).

Let's Make a Deal

A small hut sits among dead trees to the side of the dirt trail through the forest. Wind chimes carved from animal bones clatter in the weak wind. The air smells of coffee grounds. Thorny vines grow in abundance throughout this small clearing. Two gaunt goats graze among the brambles.

An elderly man sits on a swing suspended with barbed wire from two dead pine trees. His wrinkled scalp is sunburnt and cracked, and his eyes are sunken into deep pits beneath his heavy brow. A long silver beard flows down into his lap. A gnarled walking stick rests within easy reach. A smile creases his lips.

Caasimolar tempts PCs with riches, women and anything their hearts desire – all the while playing his offerings off as the whimsy of a forgetful old man. He is quite serious, however, and numerous visitors take him up on his offers – only to have things turn sour in the end. Caasimolar collects what's left of their broken souls in glass vials he stores on a rickety wooden shelf inside the hut. The Game Referee is free to offer PCs anything they desire, knowing that whatever wish is made will be twisted to benefit the demon.

If attacked, Caasimolar grabs his walking stick and defends himself. The two goats are polymorphed baalrochs that rise up to protect the old man.

Demon, Baalroch: HD 9; hp 68; AC 2 [17]; Atk Sword (1d12+2) and whip; Move 6/15 (flying); Save 6; CL/XP 10/1,400; Special: Magic resistance (75%), surrounded by fire

Copyright Notice
Author Scott Greene.

Devil, Demoriel (Twice-Exiled Seductress)

Hit Dice: 20
Armor Class: -2 [21]
Attacks: *+3 short sword (Reaver)* (1d6+6) or 2 claws (1d6+3)
Saving Throw: 3
Special: Enrapture, magical abilities, summon devils, +2 weapons to hit, regenerate 6 hp/round, magic resistance (30%), immune to fire and poison, resists cold and acid
Move: 15/24 (flying)
Alignment: Chaos
Challenge Level/XP: 26/6,200

Demoriel was once a powerful angel who made her home in the heavens among the other angels. Demoriel's journey into evil altered her appearance and left her with black hair, coal black eyes, amber skin, small horns protruding above her eyes, and a thin, snake-like forked tail. Small bat-like wings protrude from her shoulders, though she often keeps these folded against her back and hidden beneath her robes. Anyone seeing Demoriel must save or stand enthralled for 1 minute (as per a *hold person* spell). At will, Demoriel can *charm monster*, *detect good*, *detect magic*, *dispel magic*, cast a *fireball*, *teleport*, turn *invisible*, *polymorph self*, make a *suggestion*, and create a *wall of fire*. Once per day she can create a *meteor swarm* and use *power word stun*. Demorial is immune to fire and poison, and takes half damage from cold and acid. Demorial wields *Reaver*, a *+3 short sword*.

Mirror, Mirror

A floor-to-ceiling mirror fills a dead-end stone corridor within Bandar's Hold, the silver-backed glass filling the space from wall to wall and from floor to ceiling so completely that it appears the corridor simply continues on into infinity. The mirror glass is smoky, and reflections waver within it. The mirror's surface is unbreakable. PCs' reflections do not appear in the mirror. Hanging on a strand of silver wire from the ceiling before the mirror is a golden heart-shaped locket engraved with the words "What the Heart Wants." The locket also is not reflected. Written on the mirror in a foggy vaporous cloud as if someone had blown on the glass, is the word "Love."

Anyone who puts on the locket sees a beautiful woman wearing fuchsia robes standing in the center of the mirror. Her long black hair flows past her shapely waist. Her dark eyes burn seductively. Her lips are the color of roses. Merely touching the locket doesn't allow this vision; but anyone wearing the locket around their neck, even if taken off, still sees the woman's visage reflected back at them.

Demoriel's realm is a mirror image of the castle, except it sits on a level of hell amid clouds of volatile gases that burn in a fiery sky and where charmed demons roam the walkways guarding their mistress. Demoriel attempts to charm those who see her, and beckons them forward to be with her.

Charmed PCs pass easily through the mirror like stepping through a curtain of silver. The PC appears instantly beside the demon in the mirror's surface. The PC vanishes from the real world when he or she appears in the mirror universe. If they are wearing the golden locket, it vanishes and reappears on the silver string. Demoriel won't give up her conquests easily, and requires a favor from PCs first. It's left up to the Game Referee to determine the demon seductress's needs. Demoriel is not bound to this particular mirror, and can hound PCs through any reflective surface if they cross her.

Copyright Notice

Devil, Geryon (Arch-Devil)

Hit Dice: 20 (120 hp)
Armor Class: -4 [23]
Attack: 2 claws (2d10), tail sting (2d6 plus poison)
Saving Throw: 3
Special: Fear gaze, spells, *bull's horn*, summon devils, +2 or better weapon to hit, immunity to fire and poison, regeneration (3 hp/round), see in darkness, magic resistance (65%), telepathy 100 ft.
Move: 9/21 (flying)
Alignment: Chaos
Challenge Level/XP: 31/7700

Geryon is a towering creature with the upper torso of a humanoid with paw-like hands, blue-furred arms, dark hair, and piercing black eyes, and the lower torso of a massive black and gold banded snake. Called "the Great Serpent", he rules Hell's fifth plane. His fortress, a large iron citadel located in the heart of a great city, is situated at the center of his plane. Geryon often leaves his fortress to wander the city, but rarely ever journeys beyond the city's gates. The city is a large, dark place filled with all manner of filth. Geryon is one of the most powerful arch devils (by physical standards) and enjoys displaying his physical prowess to any who would watch, often destroying pit fiends or minor dukes for sheer pleasure and entertainment. While he is weaker than other arch devils (in station and overall power), he has allied himself with Mephistopheles and as such is feared by many. For all of Hell's inhabitants know, if any can wrest the throne of Hell from Asmodeus, it is Mephistopheles, and Geryon wants to make sure he is on the winning side when the time comes to challenge the current Overlord.

Geryon's gaze induces fear (as the spell) to a range of 30 feet. His tail sting delivers a deadly poison. Geryon casts spells as a 12th level magic-user. He can also use the following magical abilities: *Charm monster, dispel magic, geas, ice storm, invisibility, light, raise dead, symbol of stunning* (1/day) and *wall of ice*. Three times per day, Geryon can automatically summon 4d10 lemures or nupperibos, 2d8 bearded devils, 2d4 bone devils or barbed devils, or 2 ghaddar devils or pit fiends.

Geryon carries a great horn made of bone. He can blow this horn and summon 5d4 minotaurs who serve him until their death. This horn can be blown three times per week. Lawful creatures touching the horn take 5d6 points of electricity damage each round they touch it (no save).

Servants of Geryon

Followers of Geryon are evil humanoids that revere serpents, some clans and tribes of lizardfolk, and several inphidian communities. Devout followers of Geryon are called Serpent Masters and must sign a pact of evil with Geryon. Serpent Masters can receive up to 3rd level cleric spells from Geryon.

Phlegethon Falls

At a point where the flaming river Phlegethon topples from the cliffs of the fifth plane of Hell down to the sixth, a formation of basalt covered in hot ashes juts out, dividing the river into two falls. This basalt formation measures approximately 1 mile long and up to 1 mile wide, and has a vaguely diamond shape.

The outcropping is pocked with tunnels and caves, and serves as a retreat for Geryon, the three-bodied giant king turned into a reptilian horror by the weird energies of Hell. These halls are prowled by manticores, demonic snapping turtles and crocodiles, bone devils and barbed devils, and the ever present lemures. In the center of the outcropping is the great feast hall of Geryon, a smorgasbord of macabre delicacies surrouning the ravenous arch-devil, face and hands drenched in blood, great horn hung around his neck and splattered with the remnants of his feast. A host of imprisoned succubi dance for the king (or serve as between course snacks) and offer him large goblets of burgundy received in tribute from the vineyards of a mortal servant.

Credit

Geryon originally appeared in the First Edition *Monster Manual* (© TSR/Wizards of the Coast, 1977) and is used by permission.

Copyright Notice

Author Scott Greene, based on original material by Gary Gygax.

Devil, Gorson (The Blood Duke)

Hit Dice: 18 (90 hp)
Armor Class: -3 [22]
Attack: +2 battle axe (2d8), 2 forepaws (1d8)
Saving Throw: 3
Special: Spells, summon devils, +2 or better weapon to hit, immunity to fire and poison, magic resistance (80%), regeneration (3 hp/round), see in darkness, telepathy 100 ft.
Move: 18
Alignment: Chaos
Challenge Level/XP: 27/6500

The Blood Duke, Gorson, is a great lion-bodied centaur that serves Great Mammon as 2nd general of his infernal army. Gorson leads 5 legions of barbed devils in service to his lord. Gorson is called "The Lion" for his ferocity in battle and his general appearance. He often takes the entrails of those he has slain and makes a necklace, wrapping it around his neck or entwining them in his bloody mane-like hair. Wounds from his battleaxe do heal naturally, and until a *remove curse* is cast upon them, healing spells cure only 1 point of damage per casting.

Gorson can cast the following spells: *Animate dead, charm monster, dispel magic, produce flame, suggestion, symbol of stunning* (1/day) and *wall of fire*. Twice per day Gorson can automatically summon 2d10 lemures or nupperibos, 2d4 bearded devils, 1d4 bone devils, erinyes, or barbed devils, or 1 pit fiend.

Orcish Worship

You peer into a vaulted cavern veined with reddish stone. The floor has been ground flat, with broad steps leading into the cavern. On a long pedestal of the black and red stone there is a bronze idol of a lion centaur, its face raised in a terrible roar and two curved shamshir swords upraised in its hands. The ground around the idol is covered in prostrate orcs, easily four dozen of them. One orc, a high priest wearing a bulbous helm of silver and garbed in robes of scarlet embroidered with silver thread (worth 300 gp), stands in the sea of green-gray flesh, swords upraised in imitation of the idol. The orcs are calling "Gorson! Gorson!" in a sing-songy, baritone chant, getting louder and then softer in some rhythm only they seem to understand.

As they chant, the walls of the chamber begin to swirl, first in the black and red that are already present, but then with motes of golden brown and splashes of an indecent purple, swirling faster and faster that those looking at the walls eventually become nauseous. The orcs will ignore anything short of an attack, and the swirling of the walls takes four rounds to reach its height, more than enough time to flee to the exit on the other side of the cavern (which is, unfortunately, trapped with a spiked pit, 20 feet deep and filled an inch high with acid that deals 1d3 point sof damage per round). As the walls reach their peak, they will suddenly turn bright white, and 1d3 bone devils will emerge from the walls, walking on the backs of the orcs to the bronze idol. The devils receive tribute from the orcs in the form of dwarf hearts (each orc holds one heart).

An attack now, at the height of the ceremony, has a 1% chance per round, cumulative, of drawing the attention of Gorson and bringing him to the Material Plane to defend his temple, essentially swapping places with his idol. Even if the devils and orcs are destroyed without drawing Gorson's fiendish personage to the temple, the Blood Duke will take note of the adventurers and mark them for destruction.

Copyright Notice
Author Scott Greene.

Devil, Hutijin (Duke of Hell)

Hit Dice: 17 (85 hp)
Armor Class: -5 [24]
Attack: *+3 flaming trident* (2d8 plus 1d6 fire) or *net of snaring* or 2 claws (1d8)
Saving Throw: 3
Special: Fear, spells, summon devils, +2 or better weapon to hit, immunity to fire and poison, regeneration (3 hp/round), magic resistance (65%), see in darkness, telepathy 100 ft.
Move: 15/24 (flying)
Alignment: Chaos
Challenge Level/XP: 28/6800

Hutijin is a tall humanoid with bat-like wings, a whip-like tail and dark red, scaled skin. He has a mouth filled with sharpened teeth and two oversized canine teeth and upward curving horns project from his head. Hutijin is a loyal servant of Mephistopheles and commands 2 companies of pit fiends in the infernal armies of the eighth plane of Hell. Hutijin is a noble of Mephistopheles' court and commands much respect from the other dukes and nobles. His battle prowess and strong demeanor command respect from the other dukes of Hell.

Hutijin can cause fear by speaking. Creatures within 30 feet that hear his voice must succeed on a saving throw or be affected as though by a *fear* spell (caster level 20th). He can also cast the following spells: *Animate dead, cure serious wounds, dispel magic, fireball, hold monster, invisibility, polymorph self, produce flame, suggestion, symbol of stunning* (1/day) and *wall of fire*. Twice per day Hutijin can automatically summon 2d10 lemures, 2d4 ice devils or erinyes, 1d4 barbed devils, or 1d2 pit fiends.

Upon command, Hutijin's *trident* is sheathed in fire. The fire does not harm the wielder, but deals an extra 1d6 points of damage on a successful hit. His magical net holds fast any creature it hits.

8th Column Goes to War

A column of devils heads towards a conflict with a demonic army. The devils are mounted upon giant, fiendish elephants, their tusks encased in iron and houdahs of bronzewood and silver swaying atop their bony backs. In the center of the column, four of the beasts struggle beneath the weight of a giant palanquin of marble holding an onion-domed veranda of bronze and porphyry. The palaquin houses Hutijin, a duke of Hell, who lounges on ash gray pillows plucking on a sitar as six fire nymphs dance for him. The other elephants are mounted by 1d4+2 ice devils and 1d2 pit fiends lead the assemblage across the bleak steppe of ebon grasses and bleached white almond trees.

Credit

Hutijin originally appeared in *Dragon #75* (© TSR/Wizards of the Coast, 1983) and later in the First Edition *Monster Manual II* (© TSR/Wizards of the Coast, 1983) and is used by permission.

Copyright Notice

Devil, Lilith (Former Queen of Hell)

Hit Dice: 17 (71 hp)
Armor Class: -3 [22]
Attacks: 2 claws (1d4), 1 weapon (1d8)
Saving Throw: 3
Special: +2 magic weapons to hit, magic resistance (65%), immune to fire, magical abilities, summon minions
Move: 12/18 (flying)
Alignment: Chaos
Challenge Level/XP: 20/3,400

Lilith is an insanely comely female standing 5'7" tall and weighing roughly 130 pounds. Her skin is cinnamon colored and her hair is waist length and blood red. She has a small pair of leathery black bat-like wings. Lilith can use *ESP* and cast *fireball, hold person, charm person* or *charm monster, suggestion and teleport* at will. Three times a day she can cast *lightning bolt* and *wall of fire*. One a week she can grant a wish. She can see perfectly in darkness of any kind. Lilth can summon 1d4+4 lilins with a 100% chance. She carries a +2 longsword that can fire a *finger of death* spell 3 times each day.

Home Sweet Hell

The desposed queen of hell has no permanent home. Her castle of basalt destructively rises from the ground in seemingly random areas and planes. The roving castle remains only long enough for Lilith to subjugate the populace to her will and wicked ways before it sinks into the ground. Where it stood is a permanent barren scar burned upon the earth. The castle resembles a jagged stalagmite reaching nearly 500 feet at its peak. Concealed balconies and exposed stairs coil around the tower's exterior. Plumes of smoke billow from hollow spires and glowing red flames blast out of the windows each night. The tower has a single massive iron door that opens only at night. The spacious rooms of the castle are elegantly decorated and sparsely inhabited. Ghosts, demons (especially lilins and mariliths), cultist of Lilith and other servants populate the corridors and chambers. Depraved titans that have fallen from the heavens serve as guards and an ancient subdued gold dragon acts as a mount. Lilith managed to take her concubines and loyalists with her in her exodus from hell.

Occasionally, the castle appears without disrupting the area it settles in. More often, however, the arrival of the castle causes great battles to begin, children to be kidnapped, fires to spread unchecked across the land or entire villages to vanish. If Lilith has a master plan, it remains a secret. It is rumored that she has enslaved kingdoms and waged wars upon mankind only to disappear at her moment of triumph.

Copyright Notice

Devil, Lucifer (Prince of Darkness)

Hit Dice: 25 (150 hp)
Armor Class: -6 [25]
Attack: *Rod of Infernus* (3d6), bite (2d4 plus poison) or 2 claws (2d8), bite (2d4 plus poison), tail sting (1d8 plus poison)
Saving Throw: 3
Special: Gaze weapons, spells, summon devils, +3 or better weapon to hit, immunity to fire and poison, regeneration (4 hp/round), magic resistance (90%), see in darkness, telepathy 100 ft.
Move: 21/30 (flying)
Alignment: Chaos
Challenge Level/XP: 40/10400

Lucifer has many names: The Prince of Lies, The Prince of Darkness, The Adversary, The Prince of Light, and Satan. It is believed that Lucifer was the first devil in existence, having been cast down from the heavens when he challenged the rulings of the gods of law. After being cast down, Lucifer constructed a plane he called Hell. There he built his palace of iron and basalt on the lowest and darkest region of Hell. He divided this realm into nine distinct regions and appointed his closest allies to rule. Each lord was allowed to mold and shape his domain as he saw fit, but all paid homage to Lucifer.

A millennia passed and Lucifer reigned supreme in Hell. During this time, one of the lieutenants (each of which had now become known as arch-devils or rulers) decided he could do a much better job of running Hell than Lucifer could. Asmodeus coveted the Throne of Hell and wanted it for himself. Using his powers of persuasion, he promised each and every other arch-devil that stood with him and challenged Lucifer a larger role in the "new" Hells. Those that stood against him, he said, would be destroyed or cast out of Hell along with Lucifer when the end came. This time in Hell's history became known as the Great Uprising.

Asmodeus managed to sway every single arch-devil, save one. Belial refused to stand with Asmodeus and barely escaped capture at the hands of the other arch-devils. When the battle for Hell's Throne commenced, Belial, Lucifer, and their allies stood fast against the mighty armies of the other arch-devils. In the end however, the sheer numbers of devils that fought against Lucifer overwhelmed his armies and those that stood with him. Lucifer and his allies were forced to flee Hell or face destruction. The sole exception was Belial. Near the end of the war when he saw that Lucifer would likely lose the Throne, Belial turned and joined Asmodeus' ranks and helped oust Lucifer from Hell.

Cast out, Lucifer wanted vengeance. But vengeance required power, and he was tired, injured, and weakened from the time spent battling in Hell. He needed a place to rest, a place to grow in power, and a place to plan. Thus he created Infernus, a plane of eternal and everlasting fire and suffering: one plane, one ruler; created by his own hands, his own blood, and a portion of his very essence. From his great keep, *Malefacta*, Lucifer waits for the day he can challenge for the Throne of Hell again.

Lucifer is said to be one with the plane. As the gods of law are to the upper planes, so is Lucifer to Infernus. Nothing goes unnoticed by him on Infernus. All movements are seen, all whispers are heard. A plan is not hatched or contrived in this place without Lucifer's knowledge. When people speak of Infernus, they speak of Lucifer and vice versa. No creature, it is thought, stands a chance against

Lucifer on Infernus, not even the arch-devils that stood against him a millennia ago. But Lucifer knows that when the battle comes, he will have to fight the arch-devils on their own planes, not on Infernus, and he is preparing for just that. By sending his agents to the Material Plane to corrupt lawful beings and convert those currently paying homage to Hell's rulers, Lucifer grows in strength. And this strength gives him power, power that surpasses any he ever had—including his near deific powers he possessed in the planes of good. And when his power finally reaches its pinnacle, he will travel to Hell and destroy it and every single inhabitant.

Lucifer is an exquisitely handsome humanoid with jet black hair and a forked beard. His hands end in wicked claws and his feet are cloven. A long snake-like tail dances behind him and intertwines itself around the massive triple-pronged pitchfork he carries. Two oversized and

backward-curving blackened horns jut from his head. He is cloaked in a suit of banded armor that glistens with the color of the night sky.

Lucifer has two gaze weapons. Each gaze weapon has a range of 30 feet. His first forces victims to pass a saving throw or have their alignment shift one step toward chaotic. The second gaze weapon curses the victim with a -4 penalty to all attack rolls and saving throws.

Lucifer's tail ends in a deadly stinger that delivers lethal venom.

Lucifer casts spells as a 15th level cleric and a 12th level magic-user. He can also use the following magical abilities at will: *Animate dead, charm monster, darkness, dispel magic, ESP, fireball, geas, hold monster, ice storm, invisibility, locate object, meteor swarm* (2/day), *phantasmal force, polymorph self, produce flame, pyrotechnics, restoration* (2/day), *shapechange* (2/day), *symbol of death* (1/day), *symbol of fear* (2/day), *teleport, wall of fire, wall of ice* and *wish* (1/day).

Once per week, Lucifer can attempt to summon each arch devil to his palace on the nethermost plane of Hell. The arch devil can resist with its magic resistance, but gets no saving throw. Lucifer cannot currently use this ability while in Infernus. Three times per day, Lucifer can summon 4d10 lemures or nupperibos, 2d8 bearded devils or chain devils, 2d4 bone devils, ice devils, or erinyes, 1d6 barbed devils or ghaddar devils, or 1d3 pit fiends.

Rod of Infernus: Lucifer's black iron rod functions as a *+5 heavy mace*. Any lawful creature that touches the rod must pass a saving throw or suffer 10d6 points of electricity damage per round. Once per round, and no more than five times per day, the rod can fire a ray to a range of 60 feet. A creature struck by this ray must succeed on a saving throw at -2 or be annihilated instantly—not even a trace of dust is left behind. No form of mortal magic can restore life to a creature annihilated by this ray. Once per round, and no more than three times per day, the rod can fire a ray of hellish-red energy to a range of 60 feet that functions as a *magic jar* spell. A target can make a saving throw to resist the effects. If failed, the victim's soul vanishes into Lucifer's rod. Up to 10 such souls can be held in the rod at one time.

Servants of Lucifer

Followers of Lucifer are far and wide and consist of evil humanoids; usually clerics, magic-users, frustrated artists and ambitious politicans and nobles. Devout followers of Lucifer are called Dark Cardinals and must sign a pact of evil with Lucifer. Dark Cardinals can receive up to 5th level cleric spells from Lucifer.

Damned if You Do . . .

On a city street or country lane you come across a young boy, perhaps seven or eight years old, with a cherubic face and dressed in the garb of wealthy yeoman's son. He is kneeling on the ground looking over a ring he has drawn in the sand with a stick. Inside the ring, he has set two beetles against one another, tying them together with a length of yarn.

"It is terrible to see them fight, and father says I shouldn't, but I feel I must. What would you do?", he asks in a tone to old for his young face.

If the adventurers chide the boy, he will look up abruptly, a terrible grimace on his face and fire in his eyes and 1d3+1 pit fiends erupting from the ground around the adventurers.

If the adventurers side with the boy, he will pick up the beetles, slowly raise his ice blue eyes and give a smile devoid of mirth. Extending his hand as though to give the adventurers something, he will drop in his enabler's hand a scarab carved from lapis lazuli. Once per day, for one hour, this scarab can be set on the ground and annointed with a drop of blood. It will turn into a giant rhinoceros beetle and serve the enabler loyally, attacking his foes, trampling houses on his or her behest or serving as a mount.

Copyright Notice
Author Scott Greene.

Devil, Moloch (Arch-Devil)

Hit Dice: 20 (100 hp)
Armor Class: -4 [23]
Attack: +3 six-tailed whip (2d8 plus 1d6 electricity), bite (2d8) or 2 claws (2d6) and bite (2d8)
Saving Throw: 3
Special: Breath weapon, spells, summon devils, +2 or better weapon to hit, immunity to fire and poison, regeneration (3 hp/round), magic resistance (70%), see in darkness, telepathy 100 ft.
Move: 15
Alignment: Chaos
Challenge Level/XP: 31/7700

Moloch rules the sixth plane of Hell, a flat, stinking plane of acrid smoke and soot. He is currently plotting to wrest control of the plane completely from its true ruler, Baalzebul, for Moloch is nothing more than a lieutenant in Baalzebul's infernal army or seneschal to Baalzebul's court. Yet before he puts in motion steps to secure his plane, he must first deal with the machinations of the Great Serpent, Geryon. Geryon and Moloch hate each other; their infernal armies are constantly warring with each other either openly or through subterfuge.

Moloch is a massive, barrel-chested, hairless humanoid that stands 14 feet tall. His head is squat and large and its oversized mouth is filled with rows of wickedly-sharp teeth. His eyes are sapphire blue and his large, curving horns are black. His flesh is dark brown. He wields a long black metal rod with 6 long pliable metal tails.

Once per round, Moloch can breathe a cone of fear to a range of 30 feet. Affected creatures must succeed on a saving throw or be affected as by a *fear* spell.

Moloch casts spells as a 12th level cleric. He can use the following magical abilities at will: *Animate dead, charm monster, dispel magic, firestorm* (1/day), *fly, geas, phantasmal force, polymorph self, produce flame, raise dead, suggestion, symbol of stunning* (1/day), *wall of fire.* Twice per day, Moloch can summon 4d10 lemures or nupperibos, 2d6 bearded devils, 2d4 bone devils, 1d4 horned devils or barbed devils, or 1d2 pit fiends.

Unholy Shocking Six-Tailed Whip: Moloch's *+3 six-tailed whip* deals an extra 1d6 points of electricity damage on a successful hit.

Servants of Moloch

Followers of Moloch are evil humanoids and usually consist of assassins, clerics and magic-users. Devout followers of Moloch are called Knights of Moloch and must sign a pact of evil with Moloch. Knights can receive up to 3rd level cleric spells from Moloch.

Viva La Revolution!

The ground beneath the adventurers falls away and they find themselves falling through a twisted chimney of basalt and ash. The fall lasts a full minute and inflicts 4d6 points of damage (save for half). Finally depositing them in the hearth (not currently containing a fire, thankfully) of what appears to be a salon of revolutionary Paris. The room is 30 feet wide and 40 feet long and furnished with impeccable taste - cherrywood tables inlaid with ivory, bronze busts, tall vases of fragrant blooms, etc. Sitting on a crimson settee in the middle of the room is a tall man with bronzed skin in the garb of a French aristocrat. Four women, also dressed in finery and riches, huddle about him, all sipping on coffee from porcelain cups, a selection of sweets on the low table before them.

As the adventurers enter the chamber, the women leap up and draw their fans as the man slowly turns to regard them. A smile slowly comes to his face and he stands and bows and welcomes them with a sweep of his long arm. The women now hover around the newcomers and guide them to seats. Servants appear from nowhere holding trays of coffee and sandwiches. The women have alabaster skin, tall piles of scented and powdered hair in shades of aqua, puce and crimson and they are quite beautiful. They speak with the newcomers, discussing any subject one wishes and, though they chatter on and on, they never seem to reveal anything of any import.

Gradually, the room becomes warmer and warmer, and after a full turn, the women begin to melt like candles, grasping at the newcomers and burning their flesh and making it difficult to move. The paper on the walls begins to peel, revealing iron walls underneath that glow red. Each round, the room becomes hotter, causing 1d6 points of damage the first round, 1d8 the next, then 1d10, 2d6, 3d6 and so on until nothing remains in the room but ash and molten metal.

The bronze skinned man will regard all of this with amusement, for he is Moloch, the lord of fire. He makes no attempt to kill the adventurers or even stop them trying to escape up the chimney (200 feet high and filled by now with choking, suffocating smoke). Wise adventurers may notice a single cool spot in the center of the room, which turns out to be a circular trapdoor that requires great strength to lift, but which opens into a vertical shaft that leads to the caverns of the ice devils. One can also escape immolation by swearing themselves to Moloch, who gladly accepts their veneration.

Credit

Moloch originally appeared in *Dragon #75* (© TSR/Wizards of the Coast, 1983) and later in the First Edition *Monster Manual II* (© TSR/Wizards of the Coast, 1983) and is used by permission.

Copyright Notice

Author Scott Greene, based on original material by Gary Gygax.

Devil, Titivilus (Duke of Hell)

Hit Dice: 13 (65 hp)
Armor Class: -3 [22]
Attack: +2 silver rapier (1d8)
Saving Throw: 3
Special: Fear touch, spells, summon devils, +2 or better weapon to hit, immunity to fire and poison, magic resistance (70%), regeneration (3 hp/round), see in darkness, telepathy 100 ft.
Move: 18/24 (flying)
Alignment: Chaos
Challenge Level/XP: 24/5600

Titivilus the Confuser resembles a satyr with a round hairless head, the lower torso of a goat, cloven feet, and clawed hands. Small black leathery wings sprout from his back. His eyes are the color of coal. He serves Lord Dispater as messenger and chamberlain, and his ability to manipulate others is legendary throughout the Hells. Titivilus spends most of his days in his tower, a large structure composed of blackened iron. When encountered away from his tower he usually has a small retinue of bearded devils or erinyes with him.

Titivilus can induce fear by touch (requires a successful attack that ignores one's armor bonus to AC). An affected creature must succeed on a saving throw or be affected as by a *fear* spell. Titivilus can also cast *animate dead, charm person, confusion, dispel magic, feeblemind* (1/day), *invisibility, polymorph self, suggestion, symbol of stunning* (1/day), *ventriloquism*. Twice per day, Titivilus can automatically summon 4d10 lemures or nupperibos, 1d4 bone devils or erinyes, 1d2 horned devils, or 1 pit fiend.

Silver Rapier: Titivilus's *+2 rapier* is constructed of silver and causes burning wounds that cannot be healed naturally.

Dance With the Devil

In the throne room of a great prince and patron of the adventurers (or chambers of a senate or lord mayor or counting house of a wealthy merchant-prince) the doors will swing open to give entrance to Titivilus in all his glory. A lacy hankerchief at his nose and a sneer on his lips, he will slowly and gracefully approach the ruler of the place, tapping his black cane (his rapier in disguise) as he walks. At the foot of the throne, he will give a cursory bow with a grand flourish and speak thusly:

"You sit on your throne, throngs hanging on your every word, a beauteous lady by your side and a bonny child on your knee. Clearly, sir, the contract is fulfilled and your child now enters the house of Father Dis for tutelage in the dark arts. Stand and deliver, milord."

Should the king appear ungracious or hesitant, the Duke of Hell will doff his cap and, reaching into it, produce three black doves. Flinging them into the air, they will take the form of erinyes and swoop on the young princess, seizing her from her nurse. Titivilus will tap his cane upon the floor, opening up a sulfurous pit that bathes the throne room in a reddish glow and contorts the faces of the onlookers into masks of horror.

"Should you feel yourself misused, you may send representative to the iron city to petition for a renegotiation of terms."

At this, the erinyes will swoop over the crowd and into the pit. Titivilus will toss a black egg on the ground, remarking "This will guide you," and then step into the pit, which vanish from existance without a trace.

The egg holds an infant cockatrice which, if placed on a chain, will lead a band of petititioners into the hills to a deep and dark cavern that serves as a portal to the Nine Hells. It will further lead them to the city of Dis. Once there, they are on their own, but they'll probably want to bring along a few lawyers or a servant efreet to handle the negotiations.

Credit

Titivilus originally appeared in *Dragon #75* (© TSR/Wizards of the Coast, 1983) and later in the First Edition *Monster Manual II* (© TSR/Wizards of the Coast, 1983) and is used by permission.

Copyright Notice

Author Scott Greene, based on original material by Gary Gygax.

Devil, Xaphan (Duke of Infernus)

Hit Dice: 33
Armor Class: -7 [26]
Attacks: +4 *flaming falchion* (*Hellstorm*) (2d6 + 1d6 fire)
Saving Throw: 3
Special: Fiery aura, fiery gaze, spells, summon devils, magic resistance (75%), +3 magic weapons to hit, immune to fire and charm, magical abilities, spells, regenerate 10 hp/round,
Move: 9/24 (flying)
Alignment: Chaos
Challenge Level/XP: 38/9,800

Xaphan is 13 feet tall and resembles a satyr, with the lower torso of a goat and the upper body of a powerful humanoid. His skin is blackish-brown and the fur on his lower torso black. Two small horns jut from his forehead, just above his golden eyes. His hair is long and black, and he often wears it in a braided ponytail. Two large, leathery bat-like wings protrude from his back. Xaphan can cause his entire body to erupt in flame, doing 2d6 points of damage to all creatures within 5 feet (no save). In addition, any creature meeting his gaze must save or begin to burn from the inside out, dealing 1d6 points on the 1st round, 3d6 on the 2nd, and 6d6 on the 3rd. The victim gets a save each round to negate the continuing damage. Xaphan casts spells as a 20th-level Magic-User. At will he can cast *animate dead, create darkness (15 foot radius), cause fear, detect magic, dispel magic, fireball, pyrotechnics,* or *wall of fire.* Once per day he can cast *power word kill, symbol of fear* and *limited wish.*

Falling Angels

Roiling black thunderheads fill the sky, and harsh peals of thunder roll menacingly closer. Darkness covers the hills as the storm front arrives. PCs caught in the storm are pelted with driving winds and torrential rain. Jagged lightning tears at the night, the bolts of electricity sizzling in the air as they hit close by.

But the worst is yet to come.

As the heaviest rain passes, a burning body falls from the clouds, burning wings trailing its broken body. The angel slams hard into the muddy dirt, its wings broken and its head twisted nearly all the way around on its neck. The feathers of its wings are burnt and charred. Another body falls soon afterward, then another, and another, all burning angels that plummet like fiery meteors until they smash into the ground below.

Fighting in the clouds among the angry thunderheads are a host of angels and the demon Xaphan, who is intent on driving the angelic host out of the skies. PCs who jump into the fight find themselves facing off against the Burning Duke.

Copyright Notice
Author Scott Greene.

Devil Dog

Hit Dice: 6
Armor Class: 4 [15]
Attack: Bite (1d6)
Saving Throw: 11
Special: Frightening howl, immune to cold, throat attack
Move: 21
Alignment: Chaos
Challenge Level/XP: 8/800

The wolf-like devil dog is larger than a wolf — about 5 feet long and 3 feet high at the shoulder. It has frost white fur that blends in almost perfectly with its snowbound environment, becoming effectively invisible when more than 30 feet away. Devil dogs have glowing blue eyes. When a devil dog bays, all creatures within 30 feet with fewer HD than the devil dog that hear it must succeed on a saving throw or become frightened for 2d6 rounds, suffering a -1 penalty to all hit rolls and saving throws. When the devil dog's to hit roll beats its target's AC by 4 or more, the victim suffers a throat attack. A throat attack deals double damage and stuns the victim for 2d4 rounds if they fail a saving throw. Stunned creatures die unless healing magic is applied before the end of the duration of the stun.

Dogs on Ice

The icy stream you have been following in hopes of finding a friendly village eventually descends into a wide cavern. Carvings around the mouth of the cave, and just into it, suggest that it is or was inhabited. About 200 yeards into the cavern, you discover ice covering the floor of the cavern and made all the more slippery by the presence of the stream, still picking its way into the cavern. As you continue to explore, the cavern widens and the ice field grows. You eventually come across a tall pillar of stone jutting from the ice. Geometric symbols are carved into the post on all four sides.

As adventurers puzzle over the meaning of the symbols, they might not notice 1d10+6 pairs of sapphire eyes surrounding them just beyond the glow of the party's torches or lanterns. The eyes belong to a pack of devil dogs that have cut off a village of gnomes located deeper in the caverns. The large ice cavern with the pillar has three exits into the deeper caverns, the symbols on the pillar denoting what lies down each tunnel. The gnomes of the village speak in mathematical formulas, hence their geometric "alphabet".

Credit

The Devil Dog originally appeared in the First Edition *Fiend Folio* (© TSR/Wizards of the Coast, 1981) and is used by permission.

Copyright Notice

Author Scott Greene, based on original material by Louis Boschelli

Diger

Hit Dice: 2
Armor Class: 5 [14]
Attack: Slimy appendage (1d4 plus 1d4 acid), surprise in water on 1-5 on 1d6
Saving Throw: 16
Special: Acid, engulf, paralysis, limited flight
Move: 3/12 (flying, swimming)
Alignment: Neutrality
Challenge Level/XP: 4/60

Digers are semi-transparent oozes about 9 feet in diameter that live in abandoned ruins or underground areas where they spend most of their time hunting for food. A large, reddish-colored gem, actually an eye, floats near the center of the creature. A diger's gem-like eye offers it a means to lure its prey in so it can attack. A character has a 1 in 6 (2 in 6 for dwarves and elves) to realize the gem is not real. A diger attacks by hitting a foe with its slimy appendage, or by simply waiting, floating unnoticed until an opponent contacts it. A diger secretes a digestive acid that dissolves only flesh. Any melee hit deals acid damage. Digers also secrete an anaesthetizing slime. A creature making physical contact with a diger must succeed on a saving throw or be paralyzed for 1d6 rounds. Digers do not deliver this paralysis with an attack by one of their slimy appendages. A diger can automatically engulf a paralyzed foe. An opponent remains paralyzed for as long as it remains engulfed. A paralyzed foe is considered to be grappled and takes 1d4 points of acid damage every 10 minutes as the diger slowly digests it. By releasing naturally occurring helium from its body, a diger is able to fly for 2 rounds. After that, it must land and cannot fly again until it has rested for 2 rounds.

Medicinal Hot Springs

Proceeding from the large ice cavern (see Devil Dog lair) the tunnel that lies straight ahead takes a sharp turn downward, becoming a brutal ice slide for those without the proper equipment. Those attempting to make their way down the tunnel must pass a saving throw every 20 feet (or 5 saves in all), failure indicating they slip and fall and slide into the next cavern. For every 20 feet an adventurer slides, he or she suffers 1d4 points of damage.

The ice slide ends in a cavern filled with steam, the ice and water melting here due to the presence of an active hot spring. The steam is quite thick when one first enters the cavern due to the close confines, but as they proceed further, the cavern opens up, becoming 40 feet high and 60 feet wide. At this point, one can not only see the hot spring, surrounded by an outcropping of large crystals, and dozens of smaller, crystal clear pools where the steam has recondensed into water and filled hollows in the cavern floor.

One of these pools appears to hold a large, reddish-colored gem and is, of course, a diger. The crystals surrounding the spring are medicinal in nature, though quite poisonous if they haven't first been processed by a skilled alchemist. Once properly processed, the crystals can be used to make a bluish tincture that provides the imbiber a +2 bonus on saving throws vs. poison for 1 hour. A pound of crystals can produce six such tinctures.

Credit

The Diger originally appeared in the First Edition module *B3 Palace of the Silver Princess* (© TSR/Wizards of the Coast, 1981) and is used by permission.

Copyright Notice

Authors Scott Greene and Erica Balsley, based on original material by Jean Wells.

Dire Corby

Hit Dice: 2
Armor Class: 5 [14]
Attack: 2 claws (1d4)
Saving Throw: 16
Special: None
Move: 12
Alignment: Chaos
Challenge Level/XP: 2/30

Dire corbies are wingless bipedal crows with slick black feathers, powerful arms that end in razor-sharp claws and a gold beaks. They dwell deep beneath the surface world, making their homes in large, open caverns, hollowing out individual shelters in the walls themselves. These creatures do not possess wings now, but did in some remote part of their past. Dire corbies are omnivores but prefer a diet of fresh meat, enjoying the flesh of subterranean rodents, animals, and even other races. They are particularly fond of the flesh of bats, savoring the leathery grit of their flesh. Dire corbies speak their own language of clicks and tweets. More intelligent dire corbies have a 10% chance of speaking Common as well. Dire corbies hunt in flocks. They enjoy the thrill of the hunt and enjoy running their prey down, toying with it before swooping in and tearing it to shreds with their claws. Dire corbies always fight to the death and never flee, even when faced with overwhelming odds.

Dire corbies as Characters

Dire corby flocks are usually led by fighters. Dire corby characters are capable of seeing in the dark as elves. Their keen hearing assures that they never suffer penalties for fighting blind and succeed at listening through doors and thin walls on a roll of 1-3 on 1d6. A dire corby's feathers and thick skin give is a natural AC of 8 [11]. Their coloration allows them to surprise foes on a roll of 1-2 on 1d6 in areas of darkness. Dire corbies can advance to 8th level as fighters (or up to 9th level with a strength of 14 or higher) and 4th level as thieves (or up to 5th level with a dexterity of 16 or higher).

Flock to the Fire

The narrow tunnel the party has been following for the past 30 minutes finally ends in what appears to be a circular cage with copper bars. The cage contains a winch, and when turned the cage descends. The cage descends 20 feet through solid rock before emerging into a vast cavern shrouded in darkness. About 100 feet below the adventurers can see a small bonfire beneath the elevator, and then several more such bonfires, suggesting other elevators. They might also catch the dull roar of running water; and, if their ears are sensitive enough, the sound of cackling and movement over the sound of the water.

The cavern is inhabited by a flock of 1d6x10 dire corbies under the leadership of a cunning corby with the ability to cast spells as a 1d2+2 level druid. The corbies dwell here in the darkness, around the shores of a pond created by a waterfall that topples 40 feet into the cavern from a subterranean river. The cavern, should one manage to light it, is 100 feet tall and 500 feet in diameter and indeed contains 8 elevators and a large idol of black stone depicting something resembling a humanoid vulture with long arms that end in cruel hooks.

A small stone table stands before the idol, and from the bloodstains sees occaisional use as a sacrificial altar. The water from the waterfall runs into a completely submerged tunnel that descends much deeper into the earth.

Credit

The Dire Corby originally appeared in the First Edition *Fiend Folio* (© TSR/Wizards of the Coast, 1981) and is used by permission.

Copyright Notice

Author Scott Greene, based on original material by Jeff Wyndham.

DIRE CREATURES

Dire creatures are large, feral-looking animals. They are not just bigger versions of normal animals, however. On the whole, dire creatures are bigger, stronger, faster, and more aggressive than their normal counterparts. No one is certain what causes a dire creature to be born. Some druids maintain that Nature creates dire creatures as a direct response to some environmental threat, or as an adaptation to the magic and monsters that share the world with her creations. Others insist that, rather than an evolutionary step forward, dire creatures are a regression to more savage and prehistoric days. The majority of druids are not in the habit of questioning or explaining Nature's motives, however, and simply state that dire creatures exist and that is all that need be known.

Dire Bison

Hit Dice: 9
Armor Class: 3 [16]
Attack: Butt (2d6)
Saving Throw: 7
Special: Stampede
Move: 18
Alignment: Neutrality
Challenge Level/XP: 9/1100

Dire bison resemble their smaller normal-sized relatives. They can grow to a length of 20 feet and weigh up to 6,000 pounds. Humanoids often hunt dire bison for the value of their pelts as well as the copious amounts of meat they can provide. A single dire bison can feed a village for weeks.

A frightened herd of dire bison flees as a group in a random direction (but always away from the perceived source of danger). They literally run over anything smaller than they are that gets in their way, dealing 2d12 points of damage per each 5 dire bison in the herd (saving throw for half damage).

Stampede!

The curse and promise of the prairie are the dire buffalo. Massive beasts, their stampedes cause earth tremors and make settlement along the prairie's rivers highly dangerous, but a single beast can feed a village for weeks and their horns and pelts command a high price from the eastern men in their fancy cities.

It is the danger posed by the dire bison that currently interests a bitter exile from the single market town of the prairie. A horse thief and charlatan, he was driven into the wilderness stark naked and marked with welts on his back and the glyph of "chaos" branded into his forehead. Found by a band of goblin hunters, he was lucky to speak their language fluently. With his silver tongue, he convinced them he was a prophet of their crude gods, come to deliver them from the threat of humanity.

The charlatan's plan is simple - stampede a herd of 1d4+6 dire bison into the defensive walls of the market town and follow it up with a goblin invasion. To this end, he has equipped the goblin warriors with torches of hated fire and sent them to set the prairie ablaze. The goblin shaman has been set the task of controlling the winds, to send the dire bison toward the town. While the goblins carry out this horendous plot, the charlatan plans to be on his way south to more pleasant climes.

Copyright Notice

Author Scott Greene.

Dire Deer

Hit Dice: 5
Armor Class: 3 [16]
Attack: Gore (1d8) or 2 hooves (1d6)
Saving Throw: 12
Special: Surprise on roll of 1-3 on 1d6
Move: 18
Alignment: Neutrality
Challenge Level/XP: 5/240

A dire deer stands 6 feet at the shoulder and weighs 1,000 pounds. It has an impressive rack of antlers up to 8 feet wide. Dire deer are hunted for their meat as well as their tough hides. A reasonably intact dire deer hide is worth 50 gp. Dire deer usually flee combat, but rutting males are highly aggressive. A dire deer attacks by goring with its antlers or by rearing on its hind legs and smacking opponents with its hooves.

Check Out Those Racks

In a fantastic lake country of green grasses and ancient, gray woodlands there stands an old, fortified manor house, home of the Laird of the Lakes. The Laird is an old man, a warrior who proved himself in countless campaigns, now consigned to a cane and the ministrations of a flurry of servants. He employs twenty men-at-arms, harsh men in ring armor with longbows and longswords, and a court jester who spent time at the royal court plying the trade of a poisoner.

The old laird once enjoyed taking to the hills around his castle and hunting game, his preference being for the dire deer that stood as tall as a man at their shoulder and had racks of antlers up to 8 feet wide. The laird's home is decorated with many such racks. He now draws amusement from a very different activity.

Although the laird's castle is not on the main thoroughfares of the kingdom, he gets his share of visitors. Commoners are given a bowl of porridge and put in the barn, but adventures are brought into the manor to sit at the laird's table and enjoy a fine repast of venison, duck and other game meats. The next morning, they are awakened at dawn by the laird's servants and hustled into the main hall. There, the laird explains that they have all injested a very deadly poison, secreted in their food. As it stands, they have a mere 12 hours to live. The antidote is complicated, taking many days of effort to brew, but sufficient doses can be found in the hills in golden vials tied to the antlers of a herd of 1d6+5 dire deer. If they get started, they might even find the beasts before it is too late.

Copyright Notice

Dire Dog

Hit Dice: 3
Armor Class: 3 [16]
Attack: Bite (1d6)
Saving Throw: 18
Special: None
Move: 18
Alignment: Neutrality
Challenge Level/XP: 3/60

Dire dogs are the domestic equivalent of dire wolves. They are large, vicious canines highly prized for their ability to track and kill opponents much larger than themselves. Domesticated dire dogs are often trained and outfitted for war in spiked, studded leather armor. Orcs use trained dire dogs in warfare.

Baron Hunt

On the borders of a misty moor, one might find a tiny village and the manors of two rival lords. Both lords hail from the same ancient family, one from the baronial line, the other from a cadet line. Their grandfathers were cousins and much feared in the area for their daring cattle raids, piracy and smuggling along the nearby coast and wild behavior with women. The descendants have turned their backs on this behavior, the new baron being devout in his adherence to law and his cousin a well respected sage and magic-user.

The magician, however, holds a secret. The fires of his grandfather's generation still burn brightly in his breast, and despite his advanced age he has ambitions to usurp his cousin, the last of his line. To this end he has bargained with the orc tribes from beyond the moor in the land of white mountains and secured a single dire dog, a powerful creature resembling a mastiff. Securing articles of clothing from his cousin, he has released the "demon dog" onto the moor on successive nights to hunt for his cousin's scent. The baying of the beast has sent a chill through the villagers (and the baron, truth be told) and two peddlars have already been found dead and savaged by pheasant hunters.

Dire Elephant

Hit Dice: 24
Armor Class: 1 [18]
Attack: Slam (3d6) and 2 stomps (3d6) or gore (3d8)
Saving Throw: 3
Special: Trample
Move: 18
Alignment: Neutrality
Challenge Level/XP: 24/5600

A dire elephant is a truly tremendous animal, as large as some dinosaurs. It stands 20 feet high at the shoulder, and weighs many tons. Its trunk is thicker than a human's body and is 20 feet long.

A dire elephants is as intelligent as a normal elephant and can be trained to carry a howdah almost as big as a house. Trained and outfitted for war, a dire elephant is a nearly unstoppable dreadnaught from which warriors can launch swarms of arrows. Some dire elephants are trained as mobile siege engines, even to the point of having catapults and ballistae mounted on their backs. War engineers have for centuries pondered how to use dire elephants to pull down entire castles, but have been frustrated by the prospects of inventing ropes strong enough for the task.

The victim of a dire elephant's trunk attack must pass a saving throw or be grabbed and squeezed for 3d6 per round. The dire elephant can drop a creature it has snatched for 2d6 points of falling damage or fling it aside. A flung creature travels 1d6×10 feet, and takes 1d6 points of damage per 10 feet it traveled.

A dire elephant can inflict 3d8 points of trampling damage by moving over the top of smaller creatures.

A light load for a dire elephant is 33,200 pounds; a medium load, 33,201-66,402 pounds; and a heavy load, 66,402-99,600 pounds. A dire elephant can drag 498,000 pounds.

Bane of the Raj

A lone bull dire elephant has wandered into the territory of a powerful raj. The beast threatens to trample the raj's crops and the villages of his people if they cannot find a way to rid themselves of the beast. Alas, no champions dwell in the land of the raj, all of them driven away by the paranoid man's fear of a coup de'etat. The hapless peasants have tried to frighten the beast away with horns and clashing cymbols, by releasing giant rats in front of the beast (which resulted in the destruction of an ancient fortress and much of its garrison) and with fire (which resulted in the loss of jujube orchard). Still, the beast refuses to leave and the raj is beside himself with grief.

The young dire elephant was driven out of the deeper forests by a rival, and cannot return until it is properly healed and fed and ready to re-challenge the larger dire elephant. Speaking with the beast will elicit this information and the creature, which is fairly reasonable, will happily acquiesce to a plan to return him to his native country.

Copyright Notice

Dire Goat

Hit Dice: 3
Armor Class: 6 [13]
Attack: Head butt (1d6)
Saving Throw: 14
Special: Trample
Move: 18
Alignment: Neutrality
Challenge Level/XP: 3/60

Dire goats stand 3 feet tall at the shoulder and resemble their smaller cousins. Although they are normally wild, domesticated dire goats are not unheard of. They are domesticated their meat as well as the amounts of milk they can produce. Dire goats are non-aggressive unless threatened or provoked. A dire goat rams opponents with its head, or tries to run them over, inflicting 1d6 points of damage doing so.

Tall Tales

A hill giant maiden, attractive for her kind, tends a herd of 1d6+5 dire goats on a hill covered with wild thyme and bushes of sour, golden berries. The girl is a dreamer, given to spinning long, exciting stories of her ancestors and the other giant races in their heroic struggles against the petty gods and the hordes of avaricious humans that threaten their ancient homelands.

The maiden wears animal pelts and goes barefoot. She carries a bag of cheese pastries, a skin of sparkling, golden berry-wine and a large stick with a metal clapper on the end, the goats responding to the clapper. A dire dog sits with her on that hill, sometimes harassing the goats to keep them close and out of the berries, which have a tendency to send them into a frenzy of kicks and bleating that can attract predators.

Dire Hippopotamus (Behemoth)

Hit Dice: 13
Armor Class: 1 [18]
Attack: Bite (3d6)
Saving Throw: 3
Special: Capsize
Move: 15
Alignment: Neutrality
Challenge Level/XP: 13/2300

Dire hippos resemble their smaller cousins and grow up to 20 feet long and can weigh up to 10,000 pounds.

Dire hippos gave rise to the legends of the behemoth, a massive beast that can drink entire rivers, and make the earth tremble when it walks. Although they can't quite drink it all, dire hippos are the undisputed masters of the river in which they reside. All predators give them a wide berth.

A submerged dire hippo that surfaces under a boat or ship less than 20 feet long capsizes the vessel 95% of the time. It has a 50% chance to capsize a vessel from 20-60 feet long and a 20% chance to capsize a vessel over 60 feet long.

A dire hippo can hold its breath for 10 minutes before it risks drowning.

Trading Rights Rescinded

The queen of the nixies was tolerant when the humans came to her valley and established a trading post. There were not many humans, and they provided good sport and a few handsome strangers with whom she and her daughters and sons could pass their evenings and mingle their blood. But over time, the trading post became a village and then a river port, and the nixies have had enough.

Seeking the end of the river port, the queen has summoned a herd of five behemoths. Each is now ridden by one of her daughters, with two attacking river traffic from downriver, and three attacking river traffic from upriver. Effectively, they have choked all traffic to the river port. Although the lord mayor has a small fleet of galleys and almost 100 men-at-arms, the behemoths have proven more than he can handle. The beasts approach underwater and the capsize his boats, and acting in concert, they have destroyed two small galleys already.

The queen awaits the capitulation of the humans in her river palace, located on a tributary about eight miles away.

Dire Moose

Hit Dice: 9
Armor Class: 1 [18]
Attack: Head butt (2d6) and 2 hooves (1d8)
Saving Throw: 7
Special: Surprise on roll of 1-2 on 1d6
Move: 15
Alignment: Neutrality
Challenge Level/XP: 9/1100

A dire moose is over 20 feet long from nose to tail. Its rack of antlers is 18 feet across. Dire moose are hunted only by the brave, as their sheer size and strength makes them nearly unbeatable foes. A hunter that can mount a pair of dire moose antlers is sure to receive the praise and admiration of his fellows. A dire moose charges with its antlers, but it can rear onto its hind legs and batter opponents with its hooves.

Moose Tinkers

In a land of melting glaciers, rubble-stewn trenches and peat bogs, broad woodlands of maples and birch, a clan of gnomes uses a pack of 1d8+1 dire moose in much the same way tropical folk use elephants. The gnomes ride on the backs of these moose in wicker hoodahs, with a family of six fitting comfortably into each hoodah. One gnome rides on the moose's neck, directing it with vocal commands and rewarding it with maple candies delivered in a basket tied to a long stick. The gnomes arm themselves with short bows and long spears, and though they prefer not to put their mounts into dangerous situations, will make use of their devastating charges in dire situations.

The gnomes work as itinerant tinkers and traders, their caravan of dire moose traversing the primitive human villages that are following the retreating glaciers back into the north. The humans work as hunters and fishermen, and trade pelts, dried meat and bones for the metal and wicker goods of the gnomes. The gnomes also entertain them with stories and illusions and provide a means for one chief to communicate with another without the necessity of meeting face-to-face.

Dire Porcupine

Hit Dice: 1
Armor Class: 5 [14]
Attack: 1d6 quills (1d4) and bite (1d4)
Saving Throw: 17
Special: Quills
Move: 12
Alignment: Neutrality
Challenge Level/XP: 2/30

The dire porcupine ranges in size from 3 to 4 feet in height and can weigh up to 80 pounds. When the porcupine is relaxed, the hair and quills lie flat and point toward the rear of its body. When threatened, it draws up the skin of the back to expose quills facing all directions.

Dire porcupines are passive until threatened. When faced with possible combat, the dire porcupine raises the quills on its body and spins around, smashing an opponent with its quill-covered tail. If it bites an opponent, 1d4 quills break off from its body and lodge in the opponent.

When the dire porcupine strikes with its tail, it dislodges 1d6 quills that automatically break off and lodge in the opponent's flesh. A lodged quill imposes a -1 circumstance penalty to attacks and saving throws. Each 1 minute thereafter, the quill moves deeper into the opponent's flesh, dealing 1d3 additional points of damage. Removing the quill takes 1 round and deals 1d4 additional points of damage. If the quill has been embedded for more than 2 rounds, an open doors check is needed to remove the quill. An unarmed or melee touch attack against a dire porcupine causes 1d4 quills to break off and lodge in the attacker.

Saltpeter

In a comfortable tavern of craftsmen and a few men-at-arms, three men - thin, with the look of scholars about them - are speaking all at once in agitated voices, throwing their arms about and demanding quick action of a man in chainmail armor with a drooping mustache and tired eyes. The man is doing his best to quiet the men and get some sense out of them. The patrons are gathered about with their mugs of ale and enjoying the spectacle, some joining in the demonstrations of the scholars, others "helping" the armored man.

When some semblance of order is restored, the armored man will be revealed to be the local shire reeve and the scholars a trio of alchemists. They are complaining about the fact that 1d4+1 dire porcupines has invaded their operation in search of salt. In particular, they have surrounded great, 20-foot long heap of straw soaked with urine and covered with burlap taps. The heap is used to produce saltpeter, and it is ready to be harvested. This has thrown the excitable alchemists (too much mercury, don't you know) into a tizzy, and the shire reeve is taking the brunt of it since he's significantly less dangerous than the dire porcupine.

Copyright Notice

Dire Ram

Hit Dice: 5
Armor Class: 3 [16]
Attack: Butt (1d8)
Saving Throw: 12
Special: Ferocity
Move: 15
Alignment: Neutrality
Challenge Level/XP: 5/240

Dire rams are larger, meaner cousins of normal rams. They can grow to a length of 10 feet and weigh as much as 1,000 pounds. Dire rams are the majestic lords of their domain, and tolerate not incursion by predators.

A dire ram is such a tenacious combatant that it continues to fight without penalty for 1d4 rounds after its hit points are reduced to 0.

Between a Roc and a Ram's Place

Situated at the peak of a mountain is the nest of a black-feathered roc. The roc's nest currently holds the body of the princess royal, plucked from the deck of her pleasure barge and carried to the nest to feed its young. The feeding has already occurred, and the princess is far beyond saving, but her jewels remain in the nest ready to be plucked by a band of enterprising adventurers. The nest currently holds three fledglings and approximately 5,000 gp worth of jewels.

If the mother roc and her babies (they attack as clubnecks, see that entry in this book) weren't dangerous enough, the slopes of the mountain that holds their nest are inhabited by a dire ram and his harem of eight females. The ram controls the lower slopes of the mountain and does not take kindly to intruders.

Copyright Notice

Dire Skunk

Hit Dice: 1
Armor Class: 5 [14]
Attack: Bite (1d4)
Saving Throw: 17
Special: Musk
Move: 12
Alignment: Neutrality
Challenge Level/XP: 1/15

A dire skunk is 3 feet long, with a tail that rises 2 feet into the air. When aroused, it stamps it forefeet and hisses. A dire skunk gives its opponents every opportunity to back down and leave the area. If it is not left alone, a dire skunk rises onto its forelegs and sprays its musk. A dire skunk bites an opponent not driven away by the odor.

Once per round, and no more than 5 times per day, a dire skunk can release a cloud of stinking musk that quickly fills a 5-foot area in front of it. A creature within or entering the area must succeed on a saving throw or be sickened for 1d4 rounds. One round later a second save must be made (whether the first one succeeded or not) or the affected creature is blinded for 1d4 rounds. A *neutralize poison* spell removes the effect from the sickened creature, but does not remove the blindness.

The stench is highly potent, and short of magical means of cleaning, all cloth and such material continue to reek for 1d6 months. The odor is so strong that it doubles all chances for wandering monster encounters and imposes a -50% penalty on an assassin or thief's ability to hide in shadows while wearing clothing contaminated with a skunk's musk. Flesh, leather goods, and metal goods (weapons, armor, and so on) must be washed in a concentrated mixture of vinegar for a period of 1d3 days. Otherwise, the stench clings to them for at least 1 week.

Territorial Disputes

While traversing a river valley, one might come upon a camp of dwarves. The dwarves are in a foul humor for they have been driven from the gold mine in the surrounding hills by a family of 1d6+3 dire skunks. The skunks were driven from their old home in the woodlands by the action of the miners, who felled trees for use in constructing their mine and setting the fires that crack the rock, allowing them to extract ore.

The dwarves are twelve in number and they are hungry and miserable. They are miners, not hunters or warriors, and they're now cut off from their supplies in the mine. They are a shifty lot, and though they will promise the moon to be rid of the dire skunks, they may not deliver. Worse yet, they will leave out the problem of the kobolds that live deeper in the mine and the green slime that claimed Udolf.

Dire Sloth

Hit Dice: 3
Armor Class: 7 [12]
Attack: 2 claws (1d4) and bite (1d6)
Saving Throw: 14
Special: Move: 6/12 (climbing)
Alignment: Neutrality
Challenge Level/XP: 3/60

Dire sloths grow up to be 7 feet long and weigh up to 250 pounds. The fur of a dire sloth is stained green by algae. A dire sloth that hits with both claw attacks latches onto the opponent's body and tears the flesh for an additional 1d4 points of damage.

Sacrifices to the Green Gods

A copse of giant cecropias serves as the lair of a pair of dire sloths. The sloths are called the "Green Gods of the Tree Tops" by the natives of the area, who leave offerings of fruits to them regularly. The natives dwell about 4 miles away from the sacred copse in a large, riverside village of woven huts. Although not terribly aggressive, they fear outsiders. Armed with spears, blowguns and poisoned darts (sleep), the warriors of the tribe do their best to capture invaders, ambushing them from the trees. Captives are taken to the sacred copse. Vines are tied around their hands, legs and chest, and they are lifted into the tree tops as an offering to the "Green Gods". The natives return in three days. If the captives are still alive, they are lowered and welcomed into the village, being adopted by the chief and made his sons and daughters. Otherwise, their bodies are cut down and thrown into the river to feed its monstrous hunger.

Disenchanter

Hit Dice: 5
Armor Class: 4 [15]
Attack: Snout (disenchantment) or 2 hooves (1d6)
Saving Throw: 12
Special: Disenchant, +1 or better weapon to hit
Move: 12
Alignment: Neutrality
Challenge Level/XP: 7/600

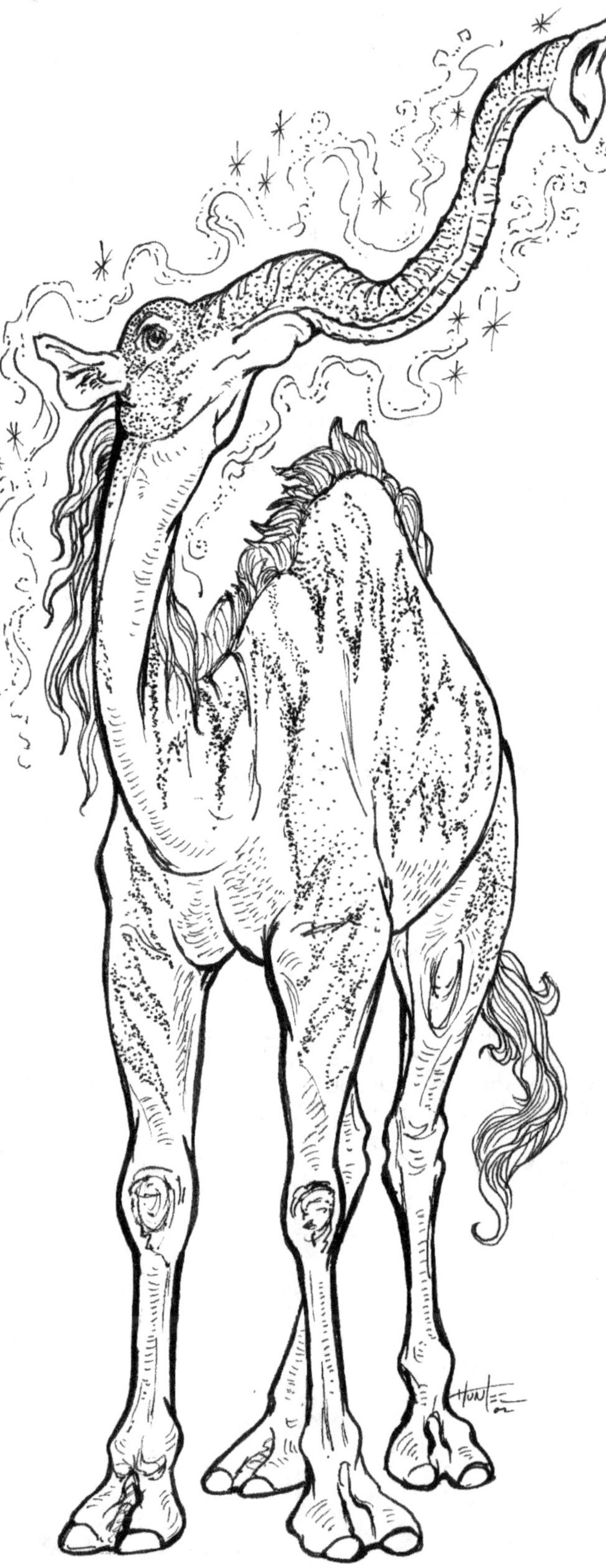

A disenchanter resembles a lightly-built, blue-furred dromedary with slightly translucent skin and a long snout ending in something akin to a suction cup. The disenchanter is greatly feared for the damage it can cause. Much like a rust monster, it feeds on objects most adventurers hold near and dear to their hearts—magic items. A typical disenchanter is about 8 feet long and weighs 600 pounds. A disenchanter targets magical items carried or worn by an opponent. A disenchanter is able to discern the most powerful magical items in a group and always attack those items first, unless those items are too difficult to reach (such as hidden in a backpack), in which case the disenchanter will choose to attack a more readily available item (such as a magical shield). It fastens its snout onto an item and drains the item's magical properties unless its owner passes a saving throw. The item hit is determined randomly by the Referee. If the disenchanter aims for a specific item, it suffers a -6 penalty to hit. Magical weapons are not drained of their magical properties if they merely strike a disenchanter - the weapon must be struck by the creature's snout to be drained.

An Adventurer's Worst Nightmare

Via an iron door you enter a corridor about 35 feet long with a door on each end, the door to the left being painted with the image of a magic-user, the door to the right bearing the image of an armored knight. Both images have their facial features twisted in looks of abject terror. You enter the corridor at its center, the iron door sealing tightly behind you. Walking more than 10 feet in either direction down the corridor causes the corridor to tilt (unless balanced by an equal weight down the other side of the corridor).

The doors bearing the magic-user and fighter spin on a horizontal access. If the corridor is not tilted, the doors will not move, having stone walls behind them. Otherwise, they grant access to level (i.e. not tilted) chambers 20 feet by 20 feet in size. The corridor does not "un-tilt" when a chamber is entered, latching tightly and not unlatching until people have climbed the slope to the middle of the corridor, at which point it rights itself.

The chamber of the fighter contains 1d4 rust monsters, while the chamber of the magic-user contains a pair of disenchanters. Both chambers contain a large wooden wheel which must be turned so that blue arrows align with one another to unlatch the iron door through which the adventurers entered the tilting corridor.

Credit

The Disenchanter originally appeared in the First Edition *Fiend Folio* (© TSR/Wizards of the Coast, 1981) and is used by permission.

Copyright Notice

Author Scott Greene, based on original material by Roger Musson.

Dracolisk

Hit Dice: 11
Armor Class: 2 [17]
Attack: 2 claws (1d6), bite (2d6)
Saving Throw: 4
Special: Breath weapon, petrifying gaze
Move: 12/24 (flying)
Alignment: Neutrality
Challenge Level/XP: 14/2600

This creature resembles a young six-legged dragon with glistening scales and gleaming eyes.

The vicious dracolisk is a rare crossbreed of dragon and basilisk. A dracolisk has a scaled body the same color as its dragon parent that fades to a lighter shade on its underside. A short, curved horn, similar to a rhino's, juts from its nose. Like the basilisk, it has six legs. Its dragon-like wings match its body color but fade to a slightly darker shade near the tips. A dracolisk's eyes are pale green with sparkles that match its dragon-parent color. Dracolisks speak a crude and broken form of the language of their dragon parent. Black dracolisks can be found in warm marshes, deserts, or underground; blue dracolisks favor warm hills and mountains, rarely being found underground; green dracolisks favor temperate or warm forests and underground settings; red dracolisks favor warm mountains and underground settings; and white dracolisks favor cold mountains, cold deserts, and underground. A dracolisk has the breath weapon of its parent. It can use its breath weapon three times per day, inflicting 4d8 points of damage with it.

Dracolisk Variety	Breath Weapon
Black	60-foot line of acid
Blue	60-foot line of electricity
Green	30-foot cone of acidic gas
Red	30-foot cone of fire
White	30-foot cone of cold

Like the basilisk, the dracolisk's gaze turns people to stone. The gaze has a range of 30 feet, and potential victims receive a saving throw to avoid the gaze.

The Hubris of Youth

A chill mountain pass that links the young kingdom with the old is rarely used these days due to the presence of a reptilian horror with alabaster scales and leering, green eyes as big as saucers. The beast is a white dracolisk, a young, rambunctious specimen who has recently fled his mother's lair deeper in the earth with a small portion of treasure. While the white dracolisk has held his new cave lair, he has managed to devour two peddlers, stealing their wares (a dozen copper pots worth about 5 gp and a large keg of fortified wine worth about 20 gp), which make up its entire treasure.

Credit

The Dracolisk originally appeared in the First Edition module *S4 Lost Caverns of Tsojcanth* (© TSR/Wizards of the Coast, 1982) and later in the First Edition *Monster Manual II* (© TSR/Wizards of the Coast, 1983) and is used by permission.

Copyright Notice

Author Scott Greene, based on original material by Gary Gygax

Draconid

Hit Dice: 15
Armor Class: 3 [16]
Attacks: 2 bites (2d6 + poison)
Saving Throw: 3
Special: Breath weapon, poison, web, resists fire
Move: 9/3 (climb)
Alignment: Neutrality
Challenge Level/XP: 17/3,500

A draconid appears as a giant spider with eight spindly legs. Where its head should be, two long serpentine necks sprout from its body. Atop each neck sits a dragon-like head. A draconid's spidery body is grayish-black and covered in short, coarse fur. Its heads and necks are scaled gray and fade to a grayish-black as they near the body. Each draconid head can breathe a jet of fire once every 1d4 rounds in a line 10 feet wide, 10 feet high and 30 feet long. Each jet deals 3d6 points of damage (save for half). A draconid's bite delivers a toxic poison. Draconids can throw a web up to six times per day up to 50 feet that is similar to a *web* spell.

Whack-a-Draconid

A 20-foot-wide limestone corridor is filled with odd calcite formations that appear to be crude statues and carvings worked out of the walls by an insane sculptor. Curling obstacles hinder movement, but don't completely block the corridor. These karst formations are natural creations formed by water droplets falling from the ceiling to erode the stone into fantastic shapes. The floor is pitted with hundreds of indentations from the dripping water. The corridor is 90 feet long, with the ceiling rising between 15 and 20 feet high.

About halfway down the natural corridor, the ceiling is pocked by eight wide circular openings. Looking through the holes, a second ceiling rises about eight feet above the lower ceiling, like an attic in a home. This second tunnel is dark and filled with more rock protrusions. This second corridor twists and turns and eventually rises to the surface.

A draconid roams this second tunnel, walking upside down on the ceiling to avoid the rock karsts. In the darkness, the draconid's strange shape and coloration make it appear to be another rock outcropping.

The draconid waits for creatures to pass beneath it, then sticks its two dragon heads through the limestone holes to attack PCs in lower corridor. The heads are long enough that they can reach PCs cowering on the floor. The draconid breathes fire at every opportunity. PCs fleeing through the sharp rock outcroppings take 1d6 points of damage (save avoids).

Copyright Notice
Author Scott Greene.

Dragon, Cloud (Draco Nimbus Caelo)

Hit Dice: 12-14
Armor Class: -1 [20]
Attack: 2 claws (1d8), bite (3d6)
Saving Throw: 3
Special: Cloud form, breath weapon, spells
Move: 9/24 (flying)
Alignment: Neutrality
Challenge Level/XP: 12 HD (14/2600), 13 HD (15/2900), 14 HD (16/3200)

Cloud dragons are the most reclusive of all dragons, rarely leaving the safety and sanctity of their cloudy lairs. They have fringed and frilled heads and wings that sweep back from shoulders to tail. Large, piercing rose colored eyes dominate their somewhat triangular heads. A cloud dragon wyrmling's scales are silvery-blue with a slight hint of red at the tip of each scale. As the dragon ages, its color slowly changes to a bright sunset orange. The oldest cloud dragons resemble gold dragons, save for the large bony plates on their heads and backs. Their tails trail off becoming misty and translucent near the tip. Cloud dragons have a great disdain for non-flying creatures and creatures that must use non-natural means to fly. Cloud dragons are not highly aggressive, but dislike interlopers and attack them on sight.

A cloud dragon has one type of breath weapon, a cone of icy cold air. Creatures smaller than the cloud dragon must succeed on a saving throw or be knocked down and blown back 2d12 feet plus 3 feet per age category of the cloud dragon. A creature takes 1d4 points of damage per 10 feet it is blown back. Flying creatures are buffeted and blown back twice the distance and sustain 2d6 points of damage per 10 feet.

The cloud dragon can assume a cloudy form and remain in this form indefinitely. While in cloud form, it can still use spells but cannot use its breath weapon or make physical attacks. This ability is otherwise identical to the *gaseous form* spell.

Twice per day, an adult or older cloud dragon can create a maximum of 81 cubic feet of water as per the *create water* spell, the water falling from the sky in the form of rain. In addition, it can cast the following spells: *Call lightning* (2/day), *control weather* (2/day), *obscuring mist* (3/day) and *stinking cloud* (2/day).

Head in the Clouds

A good millennia ago, an archimage spent many years ensorcelling dozens of glass spheres with permanent *levitation* spells. These orbs were used to fill the hold of a large treasure junk, its bow carved in the shape of a grimacing gold dragon and its timbers flecked with gold paint. Through the use of these orbs, a dozen large casks and a wand that allowed him to create water, the archimage had a (barely) functional flying ship. Taken with his own genius, he gathered his apprentices, friends and retainers and took the ship up for its maiden voyage. Having never been to so great a height, the poor archimage did not realize how powerful the wind can become in the upper atmosphere, and he and his crew were blown clean off the deck.

The ship still floats in the upper atmosphere, slightly beaten and battered, its lateen rigging in shreds. It serves as the lair of 1d3 cloud dragons, the kegs now holding their treasure and the ship slowly being dragged closer to the earth and, therefore, closer to the path of a range of jagged peaks. From these peaks, on certain days of the year, one can make out the ghostly ship emerging from the clouds, promising adventure to any who can find a way to reach it.

Credit

The Cloud Dragon originally appeared in the First Edition *Monster Manual II* (© TSR/Wizards of the Coast, 1983) and is used by permission.

Copyright Notice

Author Scott Greene, based on original material by Gary Gygax.

Dragon, Dungeon (Draco Carcer Dominus)

Hit Dice: 8-10
Armor Class: 2 [17]
Attacks: 2 claws (1d6) and bite (3d6)
Saving Throw: 8, 6 or 5
Special: Spits confusion mist
Move: 9/24 (flying)
Alignment: Neutrality
Challenge Level/XP: 8 HD (10/1,400), 9 HD (11/1,700), 10 HD (12/2,000)

The dungeon dragon is a rare dragon race that delights in building intricate underground dungeons and mazes in which to ensnare would-be-delvers. A dungeon dragon is approximately 15 feet long, with a long serpentine neck, small atrophied wings, and glistening scales. Two small horns dominate its triangular head. Its body is gray in color, with scales tipped in flecks of gold and green. Its eyes are rounded and gold or gray. A dungeon dragon spits a blast of warm mist in a 100-foot line or a 50-foot cone that causes confusion.

The Maze of Mystery

A boarded-up one-story building sits against the hillside. A once-colorful sign hanging from the roof proclaims it to be the Mind-Boggling Maze of Mystery. A board near the door has been pried open and a gold coin sits just inside the dilapidated structure on the wooden floor. The gold coin is glued to the floor, and trying to pick it up causes the floor to slant and drop PCs into a cavernous rock maze beneath the building.

The maze is built into the hillside behind and below the abandoned roadside attraction, and covers more than a square mile of twisting underground tunnels filled with pit traps, swinging scythe blades and dense spider webs. Heavy fake doors fall out of their hinges on PCs (1d6 damage to those who fail a save to get out of the way) and fountain nozzles shoot jets of acid out of holes hidden behind colorful murals of clowns.

The torture chamber maze is the creation of a dungeon dragon living in a stone cavern sealed off from the maze. Daedalintus the Twisted captures living creatures and dumps them into his maze for his personal delight. The demented little dragon uses a crystal ball to watch the fun as his playthings meet gruesome ends in his diabolical trap and while facing off against one another. Besides PCs, residents of the maze include six minotaurs with white skulls painted on the black fur of their faces, a pair of mated ahlinni with their clipped wings to keep them from flying away, four ghost-faced orcs with clown features added to their angry features and 2 leucrotta.

MINOTAUR (6): HD 6+4; hp 41; AC 6 [13]; Atk Head butt (2d4), bite (1d3) and weapon (1d8); Move 12; Save 11; CL/XP 6/400; Alignment: Chaos; Special: Never get lost in labyrinths

LEUCROTA (2): HD 6; AC 4[15]; Atk 1 bite (3d6); Move 18; Save 11; CL/XP 6/400; Special: None.

Copyright Notice

Dragon, Faerie (Draco Fraudatio Minimus)

Hit Dice: 2
Armor Class: 4 [15]
Attack: Bite (1d4)
Saving Throw: 16
Special: Breath weapon, spells, invisibility, magic resistance (10%), telepathy (2 miles)
Move: 9/36 (flying)
Alignment: Neutrality
Challenge Level/XP: 5/240

The faerie dragon is a tiny beast with delicate and brightly colored butterfly wings and a long, thin prehensile tail. Its scales are smooth and range in color from red to purple, with all colors of the spectrum falling in between. Its eyes are bluish-green, and its backward curving horns are silver with gold flecks. Faerie dragons are fey members of the dragon family and are believed to be distant cousins of the pseudodragon. Female faerie dragons have a golden sheen to their coloring while males have a silver sheen. Faerie dragons love to play pranks on passersby and employ their spells to this end. Some faerie dragons spend months on end preparing for the day they can unleash their single grand practical joke or prank. Faerie dragons avoid combat and only attack if cornered or if their lair or young are in immediate danger. A faerie dragon attacks with its breath weapon, spells, and bite.

The faerie dragon's breath weapon is a cone 5 feet long and 5 feet wide at the base. Those within the cone must pass a saving throw or or wander aimlessly in a state of euphoric bliss for 2d6 rounds (similar to a *confusion* effect). The faerie dragon can emit its breath weapon three times per day.

A faerie dragon can replicate magic-user (65% chance) or druid spells (35% chance) as a 4th level spell caster. A faerie dragon can become invisible at will and remain invisible even while attacking. This effect can be dispelled, but the faerie dragon can create it again on its next turn.

All Fun and Games Until Someone Gets Hurt

The House at the Edge of the Wood has been serving travelers on their way into and out of the sylvan valley for almost a century. The road house was once the fortified abbey of a chaotic and thoroughly repugnant order of clerics, long since put the sword by a band of tender adventurers. Much of the abbey was lost to a fire, the burnt out bits now reconstructed with timber taken from the nearby woodlands. The roadhouse provides stables, a large, comfortable great room (with tours of the old torture chamber in the cellar available for a silver piece, or for free for those who don't pay their check). The rooms are rather small, with clay pipes running through them from the hearth in the great room to provide a bit of heat and furnished with copper pots and feather mattresses atop straw pallettes.

The crowd at the House usually consists of a dozen or so travelers - merchants, pilgrims, adventurers, etc - in high spirits, their sore feet soaking in tubs of hot water, a mug of ale in their mitts. Of late, the place has fallen under a melancholy, for it is said that the restless spirits of the souls once tormented in the cellar have returned. Strange sights and sounds have been occuring in the place, and though none have died, none have waited about for the worst to happen. The roadhouse has fallen on hard times and the servants are especially eager to please their only guests. The trouble is being caused by a trio of faerie dragons who have taken up residence in the cellar. The beasts will stay as long as their are amusements to be had.

Credit

The Faerie Dragon originally appeared in *Dragon #62* (© TSR/Wizards of the Coast, 1982) and later in the First Edition *Monster Manual II* (© TSR/Wizards of the Coast, 1983) and is used by permission.

Copyright Notice

Author Scott Greene, based on original material by Brian Jaeger and Gary Gygax.

Dragon, Mist (Draco Nebulus Terra)

Hit Dice: 9/10/11
Armor Class: 0 [19]
Attack: 2 claws (1d6), bite (2d10)
Saving Throw: 6/5/4
Special: Gaseous form, breath weapon, spells
Move: 9/30 (flying)
Alignment: Neutrality
Challenge Level/XP: 9 HD (14/2600), 10 HD (15/2900), 11 HD (16/3200)

Mist dragons are relatively passive and reclusive, preferring to spend their time away from most other folk, including other mist dragons. Mist dragons make their lairs near large sources of water such as waterfalls, lakes, and seashores. A mist dragon resembles a gold dragon in shape and size. Its scales are shiny-blue white as a hatchling and gradually darken to a blue-gray color with metallic silver splotches. It possesses no visible wings.

A mist dragon can breathe a cloud of scalding vapor 20 feet in diameter up to three times per day. In still air, the vapor lingers for 1d4 rounds; on the second round, the vapor condenses into a heated smothering fog that deals 2d6 points of damage to creatures each round they remain in the area (saving throw for half damage) and additionally causes blindness (as the spell) as long as they remain within in the cloud and for 1d4+2 rounds after they leave the area.

A mist dragon can assume a mist form at will. This ability is as the *gaseous form* spell, but the mist dragon can remain in its mist form indefinitely and has a fly speed of 21 with perfect maneuverability. The mist dragon can use its spells in mist form, but not its physical attacks or breath weapon.

Twice per day, an adult or older mist dragon can create a maximum of 81 cubic feet of water as per the *create water* spell. It can also cast the following spells: *Control winds* (3/day), *lower water* (2/day), *obscuring mist* (2/day) and *part water* (2/day)

Mist dragons can breathe underwater indefinitely and can freely use their breath weapon, spells, and other abilities while submerged.

Overlooking the pounding surf, from the warmth of a deep, dark cave, a clan of 1d4+1 mist dragons awaits the approach of their students. The mist dragons have for generations served as the mentors of a clan of assassins. The cave lair contains dozens of censors in which burn cones of pleasant incense that fill the chamber with burgundy smoke. The entrance tunnel leads back about forty feet and contains three separate trip wires that trigger poisoned darts - the stock in trade of the assassins. The tunnel leads to a large cavern that contains a pool of sea water that connects to the sea. A ledge overlooking this pool leads to another cavern, wherein dwell the mist dragons, surrounded by the treasure they have collected from their students.

On any given day, there is a 1 in 10 chance that 1d4+2 of the assassins are present to sit at the feet of the dragons and benefit from their wisdom. They instruct their students in the art of stealth and the power of patience and perseverance, the latter lesson being taught through the use of a curious chatrang board consisting of three levels, one atop the other.

Credit
The Mist Dragon originally appeared in the First Edition *Monster Manual II* (© TSR/Wizards of the Coast, 1983) and is used by permission.

Copyright Notice
Author Scott Greene, based on original material by Gary Gygax.

Mist School

Dragon, Smoke (Draco Fumo Suffoco)

Hit Dice: 3-5
Armor Class: 3 [16]
Attacks: 2 claws (1d4) and bite (2d8)
Saving Throw: 14, 13 or 12
Special: Spits smoke
Move: 9/24 (flying)
Alignment: Neutrality
Challenge Level/XP: 3 HD (3/60), 4 HD (4/120), 5 HD (5/240)

Smoke dragons are small, 3-foot long, black dragons with grayish underbellies and are often mistaken for immature black dragons because of their dark colored scales. Smoke dragons have smoke-gray talons and red-tinged wings. Their eyes are gray or, in some rare instances, blue. Small under-curved horns protrude from their heads and their serpentine tails are about 5 feet long. Smoke dragons spit a cone of smoke up to 20 feet that causes opponents to choke and cough (save avoids). Once per day, a smoke dragon can assume a smoky form (similar to *gaseous form*).

Fire in the Sky

A waterfall's deep rumble in the underground network of caverns thrums across a shallow lake filling this 60-foot-diameter grotto. Ripples bounce across the surface of the water with each bass thump of falling water that echoes through the darkness. A 10-foot-wide underground river opens under the lake, forcing PCs to swim a 60-foot-waterfilled tunnel to surface in the center of the room. A pall of black smoke drifts over the water, the vapor wafting throughout this chamber. The stone ceiling is 15 feet overhead, and a rocky 5-foot-wide path runs around one side of the lake. The bottom of a brick-lined chimney cuts a square hole in the center of the ceiling. This chimney cuts through 400 feet of rock and dirt and opens in the middle of a surface lake. Iron rungs set into one side of the brick chimney go all the way to the surface. Purple mushrooms provide a soft phosphorescent light in the underground cavern. The room smells of sulfur and rotten eggs.

Two wings of 2d4+2 smoke dragons live in small caves just above the waterline of the underground lake. It's mating season for these dragons, and the males are fighting for the affection of the females (which are also vying to be with the top males). Half of the dragons encountered are male. The smoky blasts of the dragons' breath float about the room like small clouds, causing PCs to choke and cough. The dragons enter and leave the grotto through the chimney.

The purple mushrooms are a rare species that emit a flammable gas. This gas floats along the ceiling and fills the brick-lined chimney. The gas ignites in a fireball if a flame is lighted in the room. The flash fire does 5d6 points of damage (save for half). The smoke dragons dart into the caves to avoid the flames that roil along the upper part of the room. The fire erupts up the chimney as a column of fire that rises nearly 75 feet above the land above. There's a 2 in 6 chance that the column attracts the attention of nearby flying creatures, including griffons, sabrewings and dragons. It takes a full month for the gas to build up again. The smoke dragons pour out of their holes to finish off anyone who disturbed their courtship.

Dragon, Wrath (Draco Sanctus Benevolentia)

Hit Dice: 10-12
Armor Class: 2 [17]
Attacks: 2 claws (1d8), 1 bite (2d12)
Saving Throw: 5, 4, or 3
Special: Breathes holy fire, turn undead
Move: 9/24 (flying)
Alignment: Law
Challenge Level/XP: 10 HD (12/2,000), 11 HD (13/2,300), 12 HD (14/2,600)

A wrath dragon is 30 feet long and weighs about 30,000 pounds. It has a serpentine neck and glittering silver scales. They breathe holy fire in a cone-shape 90 feet long and roughly 30 feet wide at the base. Wrath dragons have 75% chance of being able to talk; talking wrath dragons have a 50% chance of being able to cast spells as a 6th-level Cleric. They can turn undead as an 8th-level Cleric.

Devotion

The forest long ago reclaimed a lost civilization that flourished hundreds of years ago in this area. Only the foundations and vague outlines of city streets remain. The one link to the past that has withstood the test of time and the harsh elements is a sprawling cemetery surrounded by a low stone wall topped with cast-iron fence. A marble entry arch enclosing an iron gate has the name of the cemetery written on it in an ancient common tongue: "Devotion." More a mystical garden than a cemetery, Devotion has working fountains, fantastic monuments and ornate mausoleums. Even to casual observers, the area seems too idyllic and serene. Visitors have a strong sense of being watched on the pristine grounds that have defied the ravages of time. Flocks of docile sheep and goats keep the grounds naturally maintained. Untold treasures of ancients lie undisturbed within the forgotten tombs.

A pact with a long-departed king keeps a wrath dragon within the compound as an eternal guuardian for the burial grounds. The dragon, who has adopted the name "Devotion," slumbers within a reflecting pool in the middle of the graveyard. It watches over the dead and dines on the protected flock when needed. Tomb raiders who try to steal from the dead invoke the dragon's wrath, and it fully lives up to its species odd name.

Recently, a coven of hags and their minions secretly burrowed into the cemetery and defiled a number of tombs and looted the dead. They stole jewels and magic trinkets, and even made off with the entombed bodies of the ancient dead. The dragon desperately needs the stolen items and mummies returned. It may reward righteous adventures with a choice of items from its private hoard.

Copyright Notice
Author Scott Greene.

Dragon Horse

Hit Dice: 8
Armor Class: -1 [20]
Attack: 2 hooves (1d8)
Saving Throw: 8
Special: Breath weapon, keen vision, limited empathy, magic resistance (30%), never surprised, sense alignment
Move: 30/60 (flying)
Alignment: Law
Challenge Level/XP: 12/2000

This creature resembles a horse with a smooth coat of scintillating blue hues that seem to flicker and wash over its body in waves as it gallops through the air. Its deep sky blue hooves do not touch the ground as it moves. The mane and tail of a dragon horse is of purest white and flows out behind it in an elegant cascade. The name "dragon horse" is something of a misnomer, as these creatures have no relation to true dragons. They are, in fact, more closely related to the noble ki-rin. Dragon horses are creatures originally from the Elemental Plane of Air that have decided, for reasons unknown to anyone but themselves, to reside more or less permanently in the Material Plane. Dragon horses visit the Elemental Plane of Air frequently, however.

Dragon horses are solitary creatures, but a mated pair will often remain together to raise their young. They have no need or desire for material possessions and so keep no treasure. Dragon horses are highly prized as steeds, but they are notoriously difficult to train. They have a very free spirit and do not tolerate captivity, thus only juvenile dragon horses have any chance of being tamed mounts. A captive foal can be raised only by a lawful being and doing so requires 10 years and a significant investment of time.

Three times per day, a dragon horse can create one of the following effects in a 30-foot cone: *cone of cold* (8 dice), *obscuring mist* or gust of wind capable of knocking weak or small creatures down if they fail a saving throw, a imposing a -5 penalty to ranged attacks while it continues.

A dragon horse can enter the Ethereal Plane, Astral Plane, Elemental Plane of Air, or the Material Plane. This ability transports the dragon horse and up to two other creatures, provided they are on its back.

Free Ride

The parlor of the silk merchant has long been renowned not for the rich curtains of damask or the thick crimson rugs across which the light feet of shaven slaves scurry back and forth with silver trays of exotic delicacies, but rather for the curious chandelier that hangs from the ceiling. Captured, the merchant claims, from a sacked mountain temple and given to him by the duke of a far away land with a nonsensical rhyming name, the chandelier consists of three bluish orbs hanging from golden chains attached to an ornately carved triangle of black wood connected to the ceiling by an iron chain. The orbs fill the room with a soft, silvery light that becomes noticeably stronger and more coppery whenever the merchant enters the room. Folk who are sensitive to such things may notice a disturbance in the aether whenever they are in the room, a disturbance that, they will discover with some concentration, has a voice - a weak voice, to be sure, but one that repeats the word "Freedom" over and over again with a desperation and longing that will melt hearts neutral and lawful alike (but not chaotics, the miserable bastards).

The presence of any elemental air magic in the room will focus itself upon the chandelier to the exclusion of all other targets, though such magic cannot harm the chandelier, which contains within the orbs three dragon horses. The horses can be freed by shattering the orbs, which have an AC of 4 [15] and can suffer 20 points of damage before they break. Once freed, the dragon horses will swiftly make their way from the home of the silk merchant, stopping only to dent his skull with their hooves and offer their rescuers a free ride.

Credit

The Dragon Horse originally appeared in the First Edition *Monster Manual II* (© TSR/Wizards of the Coast, 1983) and is used by permission.

Copyright Notice

Author Scott Greene, based on original material by Gary Gygax.

Dragonfly, Giant

Hit Dice: 7
Armor Class: 2 [17]
Attack: Bite (1d8)
Saving Throw: 9
Special: None
Move: 9/30 (flying)
Alignment: Neutrality
Challenge Level/XP: 8/800

Giant dragonflies appear as normal dragonflies about 5 feet long. Their skin glitters in the sunlight and, if it can be removed and preserved, brings a very good price on the market. Giant dragonflies are dangerous predators and hunt humans and other humanoids as prey. A giant dragonfly is very aggressive and hunts warm-blooded creatures fearlessly. It attacks until either it or its prey is dead.

Fly, My Pretties, Fly!

A battered stone tower rises from the midst of the swamp, its tumbling stones covered in swamp creepers and patches of green slime. The lower floor of the tower is empty save for a rusty iron ladder. The ladder leads to the lair of a hermit-like ogre mage. Despite the ramshackle appearance of the tower, the ogre mage live in luxury - thick, patterned rugs, tapestries containing gold and silver threads, beautiful (though slightly warped) furniture upholstered in velvet, etc. The walls of the ogre mage's chamber are lined with wooden cages containing 2d6 dazzlingly beautiful giant dragonflies. The ogre mage hunts with them as humans hunt with falcons. He carries a tin whistle covered in blue lacquer that allows him to control (to a very limited degree) the dragonflies. Should intruders enter his abode, the ogre mage will first attempt to release his pets.

Credit
The Giant Dragonfly originally appeared the First Edition module *EX2 The Land Beyond the Magic Mirror* (© TSR/Wizards of the Coast, 1983) and later in the First Edition *Monster Manual II* (© TSR/Wizards of the Coast, 1983) and is used by permission.

Copyright Notice
Author Scott Greene, based on original material by Gary Gygax.

Dragonnel

Hit Dice: 8
Armor Class: 2 [17]
Attack: 2 claws (1d8), bite (2d6)
Saving Throw: 8
Special: None
Move: 15/30 (flying)
Alignment: Neutrality (with chaotic tendencies)
Challenge Level/XP: 9/1100

Dragonnels are believed to be either related to dragons or an abominal crossbreed of dragon and pteranodon, as they share the physical characteristics of both those monsters. Dragonnels are semi-intelligent and use this ability to their advantage when hunting or stalking prey. Dragonnels are fierce hunters, though some have been trained by evil humanoids as mounts and guardians. A typical dragonnel is about 25 feet long. It is thought that dragonnels speak or at least understand Common. A solitary dragonnel is usually either hunting or returning to its lair from hunting, while more than one dragonnel usually indicates a mated pair or family. In such a case, all dragonnels attack in concert with one another and usually fight to the death.

A dragonnel requires training before it can bear a rider in combat. To be trained, a dragonnel must have a friendly attitude toward the trainer. Training a friendly dragonnel requires six weeks of work by an animal trainer. Riding a dragonnel requires an exotic saddle. A dragonnel can fight while carrying a rider, but the rider cannot also attack unless he or she succeeds on a saving throw. Dragonnels can carry up to 1,000 pounds without reducing their movement rate, up to 2,000 pounds at half their movement rate and 3,000 pounds at a third of their movement rate.

Dragonnel eggs are worth 4,500 gp apiece on the open market, while young are worth 9,000 gp each. Professional trainers charge 1,500 gp to rear or train a dragonnel.

The Maidens of Devi's Roost

The Devi's Roost is a tall mountain, its peak obscured by clouds and its lower slopes covered by a thick tangle of coffee bushes. The bushes are harvested by a timid population of halflings, fearful of the terrible beasts who live above the clouds and their fierce mistresses. The upper reaches of the Devi's Roost are inhabited by a small band of women, maidens all if the stories are true. The maidens ride dragonnels, using them to dive down and snatch up trespassers on the lower slopes of the mountain. Those so snatched are never heard from again.

The maidens dwell in a series of caverns, stacked one atop another, accessible from a large cave entrance high atop the mountain. The upper cave is a simple guard post. Below it is a much larger cavern that serves as a home to 1d4+4 dragonnels, usually tended by two or three halfling slaves. The deeper caverns hold living quarters for the maidens, tall women with ebon skin and golden hair, and deeper still the great vats from which they are born. In all, there are twenty of these vat-born beauties, who are completely devoid of emotion and seem to live solely to create sisters, the primary ingredients being the bodily humors of captured halflings not kept as servants.

Credit

The Dragonnel originally appeared in the First Edition *Monster Manual II* (© TSR/Wizards of the Coast, 1983) and is used by permission.

Copyright Notice

Author Scott Greene, based on original material by Gary Gygax.

Dragonship

Hit Dice: 20
Armor Class: 3 [16]
Attacks: 4 slams (2d6+2) and 1 bite (1d8+2)
Saving Throw: 3
Special: Breath weapon, vulnerable to fire, winds, immune to magic
Move: 18 (swim)
Alignment: Neutrality
Challenge Level/XP: 23/5300

A dragonship is an animated sailing vessel—essentially a massive wood golem in the form of a longship. It is identical to a longship in every way except that it is only 20 feet long. It has a standard square-rigged sail, and 10 oars (5 on each side). The front of the ship sports a great wooden dragon-like figurehead. It has a near perfect knowledge of local sea charts and navigation routes. It can be told a destination and it will sail there by the quickest route possible. As a sailing vessel a dragonship has a crew of 30 and can carry up to 35 tons of cargo. At will, a dragonship can cause winds to fill its sails to carry it along. Three times a day, a dragonship can breathe a line of fire up to 30 feet that does 8d6 points of damage (save for half). A dragonship is vulnerable to fire, and takes one-and-a-half times damage from fire-based spells. No other magic harms a dragonship.

Raiders in the Storm

A wide underground river flows through a broad natural cavern beneath the treacherous Sabergnaw Peaks. The water is clear and cold, filled with trout and catfish. The waterway runs for four miles underground. The roof looms 300 feet overhead, with jagged spikes of stone reaching downward.

A band of vicious raiders called the Devourers of the Dead live in a side branch of the massive tunnel. These burly warriors eat the dead, and steal women and children from the surrounding mountain villages to work in their underground camp. The marauders sail a dragonship along the river and use it on their scavenging raids. A particularly vile fighter named Kreskinarl leads the raucous band. He is a beefy man with a grimy red beard who takes what he wants. He carries a large double-bladed axe notched with numerous nicks. He wears a metal helm with two large horns that sweep down around his face.

The Devourers live in a group of dirty wood-and-stone buildings set into the cavernous tunnel. A rickety wooden dock extends over the black water, and the dragonship moors itself beside it, always ready to sail – sometimes on its own if it feels the need.

The marauders keep a druid named Jendle tied to the dragonship's mast. This poor man is barely fed and tortured daily by the vicious Devourers. The rest of his friends were eaten raw in front of the anguished man. The Devourers know the weak little man can create a fog cloud a few times a day. Kreskinarl sticks a knife into the druid when he desires this concealing vapor to hide the dragonship. The cloud rolls through the tunnel ahead of the marauders.

Copyright Notice
Author Erica Balsley.

Drake, Fire

Hit Dice: 4
Armor Class: 4 [15]
Attack: Bite (1d6)
Saving Throw: 13
Special: Breath weapon, pyrophoric blood, resistance to fire (50%)
Move: 9/30 (flying)
Alignment: Neutrality
Challenge Level/XP: 6/400

Fire drakes look like small dragons with translucent scales of mottled mauve and burgundy, black wings and crimson eyes. Heat and steam rises from the dragon's body. Fire drakes lair in caves and caverns deep within the hills and mountains. Fire drakes are carnivorous creatures and very territorial, fighting other drakes that move into their area. They are tolerant of other fire drakes, but view them with suspicion. On occasion, a mated pair is encountered, but only in the late summer months or early autumn.

A fire drake can spit a cone of fire to a range of 40 feet five times per day. Creatures in the cone suffer 2d8 points of damage (saving throw for half damage). A fire drake's blood is highly flammable and ignites in a burst of flame upon contact with the air. A creature that makes a successful attack with an edged or pointed weapon (including natural weapons like claws) against a fire drake must succeed on a saving throw or take 1d3 points of damage from the splashing blood.

Fire Drake Blood

The blood of a fire drake can be sealed in an airtight container and used as a firebomb, equivalent to a burning flask of oil. It can also be used to create temporary flaming weapons. A weapon coated with fire drake's blood inflicts an additional 1d6 points of damage with each hit for 1d4 rounds.

Flame on!

In the center of the maze-like city of basalt blocks and roofs of brilliant tin there rises the Grand Temple of Celestial Fire, home to the city's theocrat. The stifling city rests at the bottom of a deep crater, gouged from the earth by a meteor a thousand years ago and now surrounded by basalt fortifications flying red dragon-shaped pennons. The people of the city are miners and smiths, extracting from the ground all manner of metals and precious stones, and possessing the knowledge of building blast furnaces powerful enough to work the iron-nickel composites they extract from the reddish ore.

The Grand Temple is their pinnacle of their achievement - four stories tall and built in the style of a pagoda with golden roofs and walls clad in reddish marble veined with black. Storks of mechanical brass pose outside the temple in pools of crystal clear water (maybe the only clean water in the entire city) and brass hawks fly about the highest level of the temple day and night. The interior of the temple is one gargantuan space containing a 40-foot tall idol of the lord of celestial fire, posed with one leg raised, a massive glaive in his hands. The idol is constructed of wrought iron and decorated with crushed glass in shades of amber, ruby and maroon. A pool of fire surrounds the idol, the massive pedestal of which is home to a family of 1d3+5 fire drakes, the largest of the brood being the theocrat who "rules" via magical signs left in his steaming droppings and analyzed by the temple's priests, who dwell in small living cells the line the perimeter of the inner temple.

The fire drakes are pampered creatures, fat and lazy and no longer cut out for rugged combat (no more than 3 hit points per hit dice), but they are still dangerous enough. Their latest "communique" has set the people of the fire city to the task of constructing large aqueducts across the salt plains and into the snowclad mountains that surround them.

Credit

The Fire Drake originally appeared in the First Edition *Fiend Folio* (© TSR/Wizards of the Coast, 1981) and is used by permission.

Copyright Notice

Author Scott Greene, based on original material by Dave Waring.

Drake, Ice

Hit Dice: 3
Armor Class: 1 [18]
Attack: Bite (1d6), 2 claws (1d4)
Saving Throw: 14
Special: Breath weapon, spells, alternate form, immune to cold, double damage from fire, magic resistance (40%)
Move: 9/24 (flying)
Alignment: Chaos
Challenge Level/XP: 7/600

Ice drakes look like small, immature white dragons with icy white scales and sapphire eyes. Ice drakes are found in cold mountainous caves and caverns. Most encounters are with a solitary drake. Only in the winter months is it common to find a mated pair or family. An ice drake can spit a cone of freezing air to a range of 40 feet five times per day. Those in the cone suffer 2d8 points of cold damage (saving throw for half damage).

Ice drakes can cast the spells *fear* and *sleep*, each twice per day. Twice per day, an ice drake can assume the shape of a young white dragon as a standard action. It can remain in this shape for up to 2 hours at a time and while in this shape has the statistics of a 6 HD white dragon of age category 2. It retains its own ability to cast spells, loses its own breath weapon and does not gain the white dragon's breath weapon.

The Last Stand

The ice drakes of the high mountains and rugged plateaus once lived in relative peace until the bold legions of the fire city came, the swaggering rascals seemingly taking offense at being treated as an exotic and novel delicacy. Around the construction sites of their aqueducts the soldiers have constructed forts that are assaulted nightly by the ice drakes, who treat it as a dangerous game.

The elder drakes of the far patrols have recently caught wind of their children's sport, and are on their way to put an end to it by destroying the source of their amusement. One fort in particular is commanded by a rather surly dwarf - grumpy because he's an engineer and way in over his head when it comes to fighting dragons. He has but fifteen men-at-arms left under the command of a rather dashing sergeant-at-arms. A clutch of 1d4+1 ice drakes has surrounded the fort and awaits only the fall of dusk before they attack. Dozens of frozen corpses lie in various states of consumption around the makeshift wall of stone and timber.

Credit

The Ice Drake originally appeared in the First Edition *Fiend Folio* (© TSR/Wizards of the Coast, 1981) and is used by permission.

Copyright Notice

Author Scott Greene, based on original material by Mike Ferguson.

Drake, Salt

Hit Dice: 11
Armor Class: 1 [18]
Attack: 2 claws (1d8), bite (2d6)
Saving Throw: 4
Special: Spit salt, regenerate 2 hp/round
Move: 15/60 (flying)
Alignment: Neutrality
Challenge Level/XP: 13/2300

Salt drakes resemble blue dragons with mottled black wings and crimson eyes. They are found in warm, arid climates such as deserts or salt flats. Salt drakes are omnivorous creatures and very territorial, even fighting among themselves to protect their domains. Most encounters are with a solitary drake. Only in the midsummer months is it common to find a mated pair or family. A salt drake's scales range from dull blue to midnight blue, and it is often mistaken for a young blue dragon. Salt drakes range from 8 feet to 30 feet long. Though difficult to train, salt drakes are favored as mounts by goblins, gnolls, and hobgoblins. A salt drake's primary diet consists of large quantities of salt. This diet enables the drake to spew salt at its opponents five times per day. This blast of salt takes the form of a 60-foot cone that deals 3d6 points of damage (saving throw for half damage) from the grit and dessication.

Prince in Salt

The salt flats that surround the city of fire are home to a few roving bands of salt drakes. The drakes spend their days lazing in shallow burrows and their nights prowling about the flats hunting the stony, terrestrial crabs that also survived the destruction of their shallow sea by meteor storm. A clutch of 1d4+1 one of the beasts has been preying on the lines of bearers transporting stones across the flats to the mountains for the construction of aqueducts. The salt drakes recently hit the jackpot, seizing a prince of the blood royal who has crept away to adventure in the mountains, having heard stories of daring battles against dragons. The young moron has been tucked into a burrow and kept under guard by a sinuous female drake. His father has only recently gotten wind of his son's disappearance and has promised a rich reward for any who bring him back alive.

Copyright Notice
Author Scott Greene.

Drake, Splinter

Hit Dice: 8
Armor Class: 4 [15]
Attacks: 2 claws (1d8), 1 bite (1d8)
Saving Throw: 8
Special: Breathe thorns, thorn volley
Move: 12
Alignment: Neutrality
Challenge Level/XP: 9/1,100

A splinter drake is a wingless dragon made from wood. They are about 12 feet long and weigh around 800 pounds (24 points of damage). They breathe a blast of thorns in a cone-shape 40 feet long and 20 feet wide at the base. A splinter drake can also fire a volley of thorns in a 60-foot-line that deals 3d6 points of damage.

Hawthorn Hedges

A long brick-lined well connects the ceiling of this underground room with the surface above. The 10-foot-diameter tube is filled with thick vines and briars. Sunlight filters through the vegetation in beams of green light. The thorny vines spill into the chamber from above and dangle just inches from the floor. The vines look easy enough to climb, but are covered in sharp spines that make the task painful and difficult (1d3 points of damage every round climbing). The surface is approximately 80 feet above. The bones of hundreds of rodents and woodland creatures lie scattered on the floor of the room at the bottom of the well. A horrible smell of rotting meat is strong in the blocked well.

The shredded and entangled corpse of an elf hangs halfway up the passage. The well is the lair and ambush spot of a splinter drake. The drake is virtually invisible amid the dense vegetation. The drake hunts outdoors, but patiently waits for the opportune time to attack those climbing about in its lair.

Copyright Notice

Draug

Hit Dice: 6
Armor Class: 2 [17]
Attack: Cutlass (1d6) or 2 claws (1d4)
Saving Throw: 11
Special: Call storm, control ship, resistance to fire (50%)
Move: 12/12 (swimming)
Alignment: Chaos
Challenge Level/XP: 8/800

The draug is the vengeful spirit of a ship's captain who died at sea, thus being denied a proper burial. If an entire ship sinks at sea with the loss of all hands, the ship itself and its entire crew may return as ghostly wanderers. The captain usually rises as a draug and his crew rises as brine zombies (see that entry). A draug looks as it did in life, wearing the same clothes and bearing the same possessions it held at the moment of death. The arrival of a draug is often taken as a death portent, for even if it does not attack, some dire circumstance is likely to befall the witness. A draug often acts as a death token, rising out of the sea and staring at or pointing a bony finger at a sailor fated to drown. Once per day, a draug can summon inclement weather to harass its opponents. The effects are felt immediately (i.e., there is no gradual shift in the weather). Otherwise, this ability is identical to the *control weather* spell. A draug has full control over its vessel (wind notwithstanding) so long as it remains at the wheel or within 20 feet of the helmsman. Should it leave the area, its ship meanders in a random direction until the draug regains control.

When a ship sinks beneath the waves, it and its entire crew may return as ghostly wanderers, especially if the captain and crew had a less than scrupulous profession (as pirates, for example). A sunken ship of this nature may undergo a transformation from the evil surrounding it. When this happens, the ship rises from the deep, piloted by a draug and manned by skeletons, brine zombies, zombies, and lacedons. The ship appears as it did at the time of its demise. The sails are tattered and the decks covered with seaweed. When a draug is at the helm, the "ghost ship" gains several powers. Regardless of the condition of the hull, a draug-piloted ship remains afloat in any weather conditions. It is not affected by wind of any type (though the draug can still use the wind to maneuver and sail the ship) and can even sail against gale-force winds. Strong waves may toss the ship about, but will not capsize it as a result. A draug ship is so waterlogged that it is completely immune to all fire effects. A draug can maneuver his ship to leave the waves and take to the air as long as the draug remains on board. This functions as the *fly* spell cast by a magic-user with a caster level equal to the draug's HD.

Dead Men Tell No Tales, Or Do They?

For the past fifteen years, the ship of a terrible pirate has sat in the midst of a grand harbor, a prison hulk for members of its former crew. The ship was taken by a fleet of galleons after a storm had deprived it of masts and sent the ship's captain over the side, a dirk lodged in his spine. As members of his former crew died, they were tossed over the side, their ankle chains attached to an iron band around the remains of the main mast, their bloated bodies steeping in the brine. For all these fifteen years the captain, now a vengeful draug, has trod the sea floor on a direct course for his ship. He is now very close, and the bodies of his expired crewmen are responding to his presence, their waterlogged (1d6+5 brine zombies) or skeletal (2d4 skeletons) remains shifting gently. Soon, they will climb their chains and their old master will again command his ship and cut a crimson road of blood and plunder across the silvery waves.

Copyright Notice
Author Scott Greene.

Dream Spectre (Nightmare Creature)

Hit Dice: 8
Armor Class: 4 [15]
Attacks: 1 claw (1d4 + sleep)
Saving Throw: 8
Special: enchanted slumber, death gaze, +1 magic weapon to hit
Move: 14 (flying)
Alignment: Chaos
Challenge Level/XP: 10/1,400

Dream specters are incorporeal creatures that look like spectres. They are not undead, however. Their claw attack puts victims into an enchanted slumber (saving throw avoids). One creature per round seeing a dream specter must save or be reduced to 1 hit point. Unless healed, the victim dies in the next round. Dream specters can also enter the dreams of sleeping creatures within 100 feet. A dream is powerless in daylight.

Dreams of a Forgotten Shore

A dead tree dominates this bizarre room. Unusual mobiles and medallions made from twigs twirl from the tree's branching, each slowly spinning in an absent breeze. Tens of thousands of tiny carved faces cover the tree's bark-stripped trunk. The corpse of a man is impaled by iron spikes against the tree. The spikes pin him through his legs and left side, while his right hand still clutches a hammer strapped around his wrist with a leather strap. A bag of iron spikes hangs from his waist. It appears as if he crucified himself against the tree.

The tree sits in a concave depression of black dirt. A glass dome of white light is set in the ceiling above the tree, the glare illuminating the room. Ghostly humanoid figures swirl behind the dome, barely visible in the white glare.

A 10-foot-dimeter stained-glass wall sits directly opposite the room's entrance. The wall crudely resembles a scenic ocean landscape with a brilliant sun rising above the waves. After 2 rounds, the wall shimmers and transforms into a realistic nighttime view overlooking the same seashore. A full moon glows above the waves, and a ship's lights bob on the horizon. Vague silhouettes of gulls fly in and out of the picture. A reclining woman lies on the sand at the edge of the gentle surf. The woman seems to be focusing her attention on a sword protruding from the sandy beach where the waves crash against the beach. The image is a permanent illusion that changes multiple times each day.

A dream spectre hides in a narrow space behind the stained glass wall.

Copyright Notice

Drelb (Haunting Custodian)

Hit Dice: 5
Armor Class: 4 [15]
Attack: Incorporeal touch (1d4 plus nether chill)
Saving Throw: 12
Special: +1 or better weapon to hit, double damage from silver weapons, immune to mind-affecting spells and abilities
Move: 9/9 (flying)
Alignment: Neutrality (chaotic tendencies)
Challenge Level/XP: 7/600

Drelbs are energy creatures that make their home on the Negative Energy Plane. They appear as spectral figures of darkness with no discernable features save their eyes - two small pinpoints of light. They are summoned to the Material Plane by evil spellcasters who task them with the duty of guarding treasure or secret places to be left alone. Hence, they are sometimes referred to as haunting custodians. Drelbs are not undead and cannot be turned, though they sometimes feign being affected. A living creature touched by a drelb immediately drops anything it is holding and falls prone, shivering for 1 round. There is no save against this attack.

A drelb can rapidly diminish its form while it advances forward. To the onlooker, it appears as if the drelb is retreating. Creatures succeeding on a saving throw see through this illusion; otherwise, the drelb advances into melee range and its opponent is considered surprised for the first round of comnbat with the drelb.

A drelb can imitate any mind-affecting spell used within 30 feet of it as though a 5th level spellcaster. Further, any such spell that directly targets a drelb is reflected back on the attacker with full effect.

Watch Out!

At the pinnacle of the wizard's tower there is a tiny room accessible only via a trapdoor in the floor. The room is completely bare save for a tall, double-doored cabinet of cherrywood engraved with a scene of palms and playful apes. The cabinet has a seemingly simple lock that will defy all attempts to pick it without the use of a pair of lodestones, which must be run up either side of the lock while a stream of smoke is blown into the lock. The cabinet, once opened, will be found to be empty save for a scrap of parchment resting on the floor. The parchment has reversed writing on it, which can be easily viewed using on of the two mirrors on the interiors of the cabinet doors. The words on the parchment are written in elven and say, roughly translated, "Watch out!".

At about this point, a drelb will reach out from the mirror behind the reader of the parchment and snatch up the closest victim. The mirrors both lead into a strange dimension, a tunnel of swirly smoke and a throbbing amethyst light. Either end of the tunnel, which is about 50 feet long and 5 feet wide, connects to one of the doors, making the entire dimension something of a circuit. At the center of the tunnel there is a large casket of smoky glass with a silver frame. The casket holds the wizard's greatest treasure, a rickety old wooden sled he new well in his youth, a golden urn holding the dried eyeballs of a dozen of his rivals and three spell books, one a copy of the other and the third a tome of cursed reversed spells.

Credit

The Drelb originally appeared in the First Edition *Monster Manual II* (© TSR/Wizards of the Coast, 1983) and is used by permission.

Copyright Notice

Author Scott Greene, based on original material by Gary Gygax.

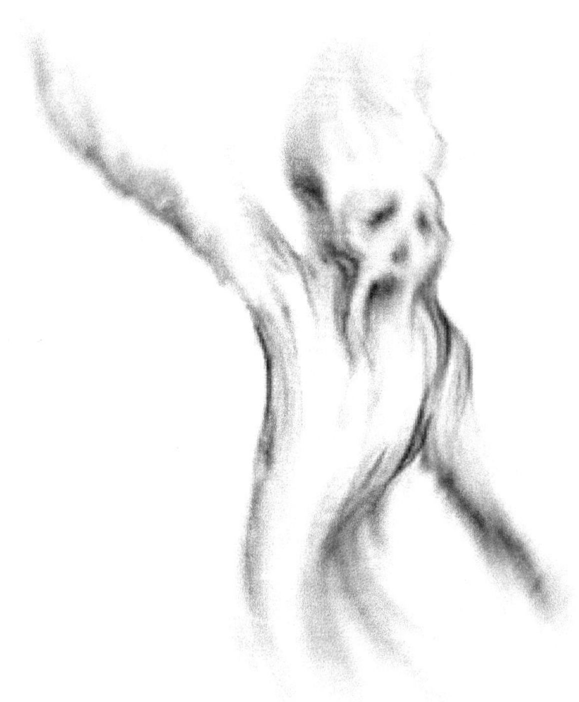

Dust Digger

Hit Dice: 4
Armor Class: 3 [16]
Attack: 5 tentacles (1d6)
Saving Throw: 13
Special: Sinkhole, swallow whole
Move: 6/6 (burrowing)
Alignment: Neutrality
Challenge Level/XP: 6/400

Dust diggers are nocturnal desert carnivores about 10 feet in diameter. They resemble brown starfish with five long tentacles ringing a central maw lined with sharpened teeth and fangs. The creature spends most of its life buried under sand and dirt, waiting for potential prey to wander too close or actually wander over the area where a dust digger is buried. A dust digger inflates its body with air, buries itself under a thin lair of sand or dirt, and waits for its prey to pass nearby. When a living creature walks over a dust digger, the creature deflates its body and folds its arms around the victim, attempting to shove the prey into its mouth.

A dust digger can try to swallow a grabbed opponent by making a successful attack. Once inside the dust digger's interior, the opponent takes 2d6 points of damage per round from the digestive fluids and the squeezing movement of the stomach. A swallowed creature can climb out of the dust digger with a successful saving throw made at a -3 penalty. This returns it to the creature's maw, where another successful saving throw is needed to get free.

A dust digger can glide through sand, loose soil, or almost any sort of loosely packed earth as easily as a fish swims through water. Its burrowing leaves behind no tunnel or hole, nor does it create any ripple or other signs of its presence. A *move earth* spell cast on an area containing a burrowing dust digger flings the dust digger back 30 feet, stunning the creature for 1 round unless it succeeds on a saving throw.

Sand Trap

Your subterranean travels have brought you to the silty remains of an ancient subterranean lake. The floor of the cavern is silt ranging from 2 to 12 feet deep and acting much as quicksand, as good a reason as any to have made a purchase from your friendly neighborhood pollier (for one must assume that any fantasy economy that keeps 10-foot poles in ready supply has a brotherhood of carpenters devoted to their manufacture).

The lake was drained when a crevasse opened up in the midst of it, now forming a long, submerged canyon, the upper reaches of which are pocked with small caves that support a population of aquatic troglodytes. Numerous insects and fungoid life forms dwell on this water course, preyed upon by bats (normal sized and giant) that make their home on the cave roof 300 feet above. The silt desert has its own inhabitants, a colony of 1d12+8 dust diggers, who lie patiently beneath the silt waiting for their next meal.

Credit

The Dust Digger originally appeared in the First Edition module *I3 Pharaoh* (© TSR/Wizards of the Coast, 1982) and later in the First Edition *Monster Manual II* (© TSR/Wizards of the Coast, 1983) and is used by permission.

Copyright Notice

Author Scott Greene, based on original material by Tracy and Laura Hickman.

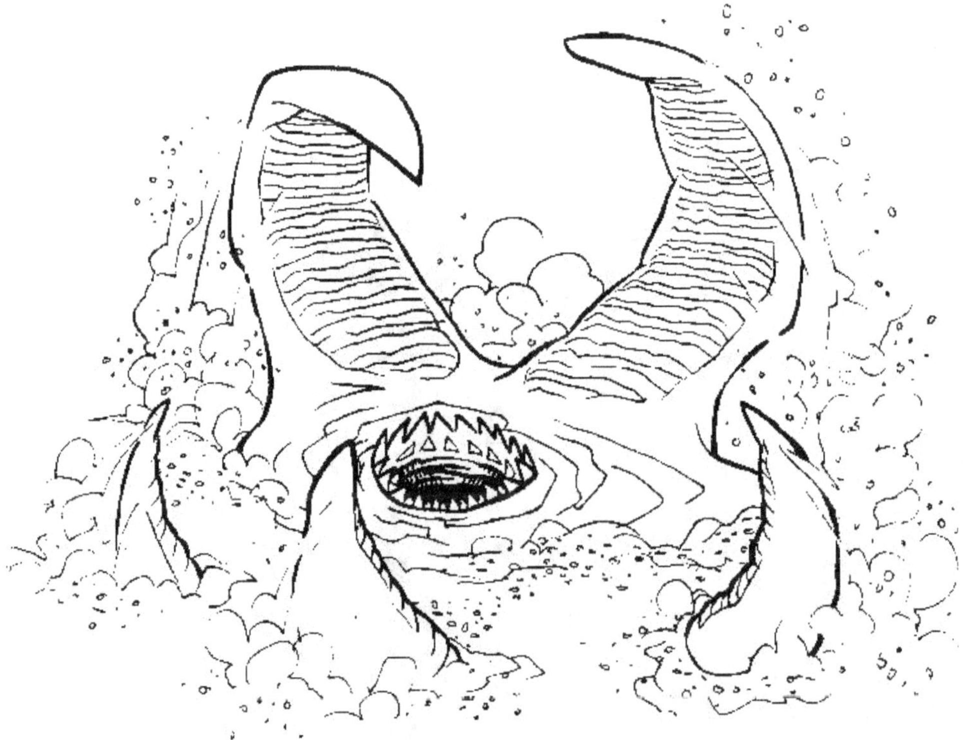

Ear Seeker

Ear seekers are small maggot-like creatures, white or brown in color. They are found lairing in rotting wood or similar organic materials. If the check fails, the ear seekers have contacted the creature and move toward any warm place on the creature (favoring places such as the ears) in which to lay their eggs. Once an ear seeker enters a warm place, it lays 2d8 eggs before dying. In 4d6 hours, the eggs hatch and the larvae devour the surrounding flesh, dealing 2d6 points of damage to the host each round thereafter. At 0 hit points, the host dies and the ear seekers crawl out to find a new host. A *cure disease* spell kills all ear seekers and any unhatched eggs.

Wood Parasites

The tunnel the party is moving through is shored up with thick, wooden beams. The wood creaks and groans. Gouts of steam explode periodically from the walls, making the tunnel quite hot and forcing adventurers to make a saving throw each round they spend in the tunnel or suffer 1d4 points of damage.

The damp wood is home to hundreds of ear seekers. The creatures sense movement below them and fall from the wooden beams onto the shoulders of victims. There is a 1 in 6 chance each round (per adventurer) than an ear seeker assaults them and makes a run for their ear.

Credit

The Ear Seeker originally appeared in the First Edition *Monster Manual* (© TSR/Wizards of the Coast, 1977) and is used by permission.

Copyright Notice

Authors Scott Greene and Erica Balsley, based on original material by Gary Gygax.

Eblis

Hit Dice: 4
Armor Class: 2 [17]
Attack: Beak (1d6)
Saving Throw: 13
Special: Spells, fire resistance (50%)
Move: 12/12 (flying)
Alignment: Chaos
Challenge Level/XP: 6/400

The eblis are a semi-civilized society of birdmen that make their homes in desolate swamps and marshes. They rarely have interactions with other races, preferring the company of their own kind and the serenity of their marshland homes. An eblis is a large bird that strongly resembles a stork — so much so that eblis are often called "stork men." An eblis stands about 8 feet tall, and the neck is extremely long and snake-like and is unnaturally flexible and capable of blindingly fast movements. An eblis' beak is long, sharp, and deadly. A male eblis has gray-brown feathers with reddish patches on its head, while a female lacks the red patch. Eblis speak their own language of clicks and chatters and some speak Common. Each eblis flock has one individual capable of using arcane magic. A spellcasting eblis has 1d6 spells, each spell usable once per day. Each spell is cast as though a 4th level magic-user.

1d6	Spell
1	ESP
2	Mirror image
3	Obscuring mist
4	Phantasmal force
5	Fear
6	Invisibility

At Home Among the Mangroves

In a swampy river delta thronged by thick woodland and itself lush with mangrove trees, there dwells a flock of 4d4 eblis led by a crested male, its thin neck adorned with a golden torque that allows it to become invisible once per day for 10 minutes. The eblis dwell on a large, royal pleasure barque that ran aground (or was forced aground) many years ago, its unhappy revelers forced into a march through the woods from which none emerged alive and intact.

The barque is partially submerged, its teak railings now warped, its canopy of silk and leather cracked and drapped with mossy vines. Here dwell the eblis, far away from humankind, plotting petty revenges upon one another. The hold of the ship is submerged and filled with all manner of once-expensive stocks, now mostly ruined save for a copper urn, sealed with wax, that contains brandy worth about 100 gp. In addition, a ragged tarp covers a pile of gold and silver bars, nearly 1 ton in all and worth 15,000 gold pieces should one manage to retrieve them.

The leader of the eblis can cast four spells: *ESP, obscuring mist, phantasmal force* and *fear*.

Credit

The Eblis originally appeared in the First Edition module *EX2 Land Beyond the Magic Mirror* (© TSR/Wizards of the Coast, 1983) and later in the First Edition *Monster Manual II* (© TSR/Wizards of the Coast, 1983) and is used by permission.

Copyright Notice

Author Scott Greene, based on original material by Gary Gygax.

Ectoplasm (Ghost Ooze)

Hit Dice: 7
Armor Class: 10 [9]
Attacks: 1 pseudopod (1d8 + weakness)
Special: +1 or better magic weapon required to hit
Move: 6 (flying)
Saving Throw: 9
Alignment: Chaos
Challenge Level/XP: 10/1,400

This incorporeal ooze resembles a faintly glowing, billowing cloud. Ectoplasms are not undead. The pseudopod attack of an ectoplasm imposes a -1 cumulative to-hit penalty to attack and damage with each strike. It does an additional 1 point of damage against undead.

Mystery Mist

Someone or something recently dug two rows of six graves in this chamber (or field). A shovel remains embedded in a mound of fresh grave dirt. A thick mist fills each of the graves, concealing their actual depths. A parchment listing 12 names (possibly including the name of a PC or a known NPC) is tacked to the shovel's wooden handle. Several of the names are crossed out. Someone has also drawn a crude smiley face next to one of the names.

A set of elegant garments lies across the dirt mound beside one of the open graves. The clothing looks carefully placed atop the dirt, as if someone who was wearing it lay down and then vanished. A mound of nearby dirt contains an abundant amount of burrowing grubs and worms. One (or more) of the graves contains an ectoplasm. The graves are empty aside from the ectoplasm and harmless mist. It is difficult to remove the mist, and it returns after 12 hours.

Copyright Notice

Elemental, Gravity

Hit Dice: 8, 12, or 16
Armor Class: 2 [17]
Attacks: Strike (2d8)
Saving Throw: 8, 3, or 3
Special: telekinesis
Move: 36 (flying)
Alignment: Neutrality
Challenge Level/XP: 8 HD (9/1,100), 12 HD (13/2,300), 16 HD (17/3,400)

Gravity elementals are circular regions of absolute blackness that attack by hurling objects using telekinesis. They warp and manipulate gravity within 20 feet of them, giving arrows and other missile attacks a -6 to-hit penalty. Spells such as magic missile ignore this warped gravity field and strike true.

Tetrominoes

A nondescript pedestal in the center of the room holds a large glass bowl. A 40-foot-diameter ring of bubbling water (actually caustic acid that deals 1d6 points of damage to anyone touching it) encircles the pedestal. The ring-shaped pool is five feet wide and appears to be about four feet deep. Spears, two-handed swords and one-foot-diameter metal globes circle the base of the pedestal in a symmetrical pattern. The room spans at least 50 feet on each side and a *darkness (15-ft. radius)* spell conceals the ceiling 40 feet above the pedestal.

A 5-foot-diameter black sphere of nothingness swirls 20 feet above the glass bowl. It absorbs light and random chaotic tendrils lash out of its depths. Silvery liquid fills the bowl just below the black mass. The liquid is platinum in a permanent fluid state. The platinum might fetch 5,000 gold pieces if a means of hauling it can be found. It slips and slides like mercury if picked up.

A gravity elemental guards the platinum pool. Over the years, it has amassed quite an arsenal that it keeps hidden in the darkness along the ceiling using its control gravity ability. Suspended against the chamber ceiling are 8 large stone blocks (2d6 points of damage), 3 bloated bugbear corpses soaked in acid (1d6 points of crushing damage and 1d6 points of acid damage) and a portable battering ram (2d8 points of damage). The gravity elemental can drop these at any time in any order within a 20-foot radius of itself. It can also cause the pool of acid to rise toward the ceiling or to hover in midair. Creatures bound by gravity (i.e. not flying or levitating) are at its mercy within 20 feet of the elemental.

Copyright Notice

Elemental, Negative Energy

Hit Dice: 8, 12, or 16
Armor Class: 2 [17]
Attacks: Strike (1d8 + energy drain)
Saving Throw: 8, 3, or 3
Special: Level drain (1 level with hit)
Move: 36 (flying)
Alignment: Neutrality
Challenge Level/XP: 8 HD (9/1,100), 12 HD (13/2,300), 16 HD (17/3,400)

A negative energy elemental appears as a sphere of translucent gray energy with small motes of light winking in and out of existence. The touch of a negative energy elemental drains 1 level with each hit. When slain, a negative energy elemental detonates in a 30-foot-radius blast that deals 1d6 points of damage per 2 HD.

Staff Infliction

The emaciated corpse of a man stands before you, leaning heavily on a staff carved of obsidian. His round hollow eye sockets and gaping mouth bear an expression of disbelief. His skin looks as if it was slowly baked into a fibrous shell with a skeletal framework. A magenta light pulses along the length of the staff. The man's garb hints that he once practiced the magical arts. The magic-user's equipment appears to be intact and untouched on his body. A belt pouch holds a pair of gloves.

The staff acts as a receptacle for a negative energy elemental that is attracted by living beings. Any living creature that touches the staff unprotected releases the elemental for 2d4 rounds. After the time lapses, the negative energy elemental is sucked back into the staff.

Handling the staff with gloves does not release the elemental. In fact, a person wearing gloves or gauntlets can effectively use the staff as a weapon. The staff deals 1d6 points of damage and drains one level with each strike (a successful save resists the level drain). The staff can be used to strike opponents a total of five times before the staff shatters and permanently releases the elemental to wreak havoc.

Elemental, Positive Energy

Hit Dice: 8, 12, or 16
Armor Class: 2 [17]
Attacks: Strike (1d6 healing)
Saving Throw: 8, 3, or 3
Special: Positive energy burst
Move: 36 (flying)
Alignment: Neutrality
Challenge Level/XP: 8 HD (9/1,100), 12 HD (13/2,300), 16 HD (17/3,400)

A positive energy elemental appears as a shimmering sphere of brilliant white energy with small motes of light winking in and out of existence. Its attacks imbue bonus hit points upon targets that last up to one hour. A creature reaching double its normal hit points explodes. When slain, a positive energy elemental detonates in a 30-foot-radius blast that heals 1d6 points of damage per 2 HD.

Solar Power

A 20-foot-diameter polished marble dais sits low to the floor. In its center stands a pure white statue of a glorious angel with its wings spread wide and its arms reaching toward the ceiling. A holy symbol made of platinum and encrusted with sapphires hangs from its neck, separate from the carved figure. Between its outspread fingers floats an orb of brilliant white light. Arcs of energy silently discharge from the sphere in chaotic, lightning-like rays. A scripture written around the base of the statues reads "Behold the power of the sun, blessed be the righteous in pain and cursed be the glutton and vain." A positive energy elemental hovers above the statue. It attacks undead outright and anyone who dares desecrate this small shrine. This encounter acts as a rejuvenation point for weary and wounded adventurers, but also poses a danger for those who stay too long.

Elemental, Psionic

Hit Dice: 8, 12 or 16
Armor Class: 1 [18]
Attack: Strike (2d6)
Saving Throw: 8, 3 or 3
Special: Psionic powers, +1 or better weapon to hit, magic resistance (30%), telepathy 100 ft., warp reality
Move: 24 (flying)
Alignment: Neutrality
Challenge Level/XP: 8 HD (12/2000), 12 HD (16/3200), 16 HD (20/4400)

Psionic elementals appear as a dark, semi-translucent clouds of swirling vapor. They have their origin on a plane composed entirely of psionic matter and seldom venture from their home except when summoned by a spellcaster. It is unknown whether psionic elementals can speak; all communication with these creatures thus far has been through telepathy. Looking closely at a psionic elemental's form reveals two small pinpoints and a mouth formed of solid bits of matter swirling in the elemental's form.

Psionic elementals can cast the following spells: *Dimension door*, *ESP*, *magic missile* (3/day) and *suggestion* (3/day). Large psionic elementals can also use *telekinesis* at will. They enjoy a +2 bonus to saving throws against mind-controlling or affecting spells or abilities.

By folding the dimensions around its body, a psionic elemental can automatically deflect one attack per round directed against it back upon the attacker. The attacker takes full damage just as if he had hit the psionic elemental (including any special effects of the attack). Spells can be reflected using this power, but only those that specifically target the elemental. Area of effect spells are not reflected and have full effect on the psionic elemental.

Essence of Desire

At the bottom of a dusty well (octagonal in shape, approximately 20 feet wide) in a forgotten dungeon there sits a sculpture in blue crystal. The sculpture depicts an elderly woman, beautiful and stately garbed in ornate platemail and holding before her a golden rod tipped with an amber sphere. The well is easily 60 feet deep and contains, at the bottom, four doors each carved from a single large crystal and apparently affixed to the wall with no opening behind it.

The crystal idol, for an idol it is, carved by a man who loved a woman from afar and imbued this magnificent scuplture with the fire of his passion and all the energy of his fevered, troubled mind. The golden rod if touched, gives off a powerful electrical shock that stuns for 1 full minute.

As the body lies seemingly dead on the ground, a dark vapor emerges from its mouth, forming into a 12 HD psionic elemental. The elemental offers passage through one of the crystal doors if those assembled can best it in combat. If reduced to fewer than half its starting hit points, the elemental inhabits the crystal statue, animating it. The combined creatures will fight as a stone golem with the mental powers of the elemental. If finally reduced to 0 hit points, the crystal doors become portals of light leading wherever the Referee has a mind to take his players.

Copyright Notice
Author Scott Greene.

Elemental, Time

Common

Hit Dice: 12
Armor Class: 0 [19]
Attack: 2 slams (2d6 plus cell death)
Saving Throw: 3
Special: Cell death, multi-manifestation, foresight, immunity to magic, magic resistance (40%), time jaunt, +1 or better weapon to hit
Move: 9 (flying)
Alignment: Neutrality
CL/XP: 20/4400

Noble

Hit Dice: 20
Armor Class: -3 [22]
Attack: 2 slams (2d8 plus cell death)
Saving Throw: 3
Special: Alter age, cell death, multi-manifestation, temporal displacement, time stop, foresight, immunity to magic, magic resistance (50%), time jaunt, +2 or better weapon to hit
Move: 9 (flying)
Alignment: Neutrality
CL/XP: 32/8600

Royal

Hit Dice: 24
Armor Class: -5 [24]
Attack: 2 slams (2d8 plus cell death)
Saving Throw: 3
Special: Alter age, cell death, multi-manifestation, summon time elementals, temporal displacement, time stop, foresight, immunity to magic, magic resistance (60%), time jaunt, +3 or better weapon to hit
Move: 9 (flying)
Alignment: Neutrality
CL/XP: 37/9500

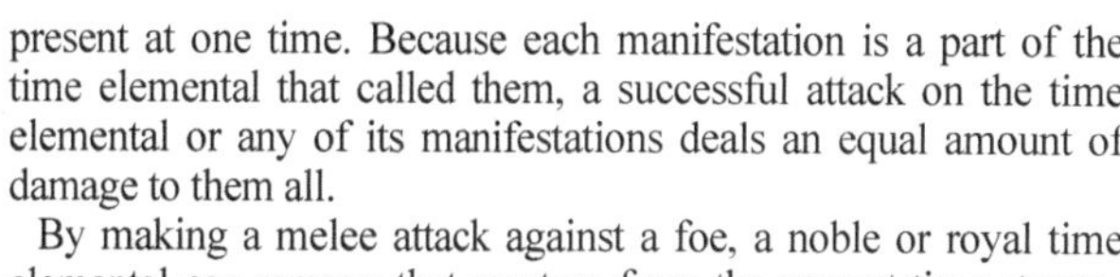

Time elementals are creatures from an elemental plane most sages are unaware even exists. A time elemental is a powerful creature formed of pure time and matter such as is unknown to even the most learned of sages. It is unknown how or why time elementals enter the Material Plane, as they cannot be summoned using the standard summoning spells. Time elementals appear as formless clouds of coppery vapor or sparkling dust about 5 feet in diameter. They attack by forming misty or smoky arms from their forms and lashing at opponents or by spraying a fine mist onto their opponents so as to induce aging. Damage dealt by a time elemental's slam attack does not heal naturally, but it can still be healed magically. A creature slain by a time elemental can only be raised through the successful casting of a *wish* spell.

Once per day, a noble time elemental can age a creature simply by touching it (this requires a melee attack that ignores one's armor bonus to AC). If successful, the target must succeed on a saving throw or advance forward one aging step (from adulthood to middle age, from middle age to old, from old to venerable, and so on). A venerable creature affected by this ability dies and cannot be restored to life by mortal magic. Alternately, a time elemental can use its alter age ability to reduce a character's age. A character that regresses in age does not revert to earlier mental states, retaining all memories and mental abilities. This ability does not affect a character that has died from old age. A time elemental can also use this ability to age vegetable matter 10-200 years (older or younger) or mineral matter 100-2,000 years (older or younger). Royal time elementals can use this ability twice per day.

A time elemental exists in several other dimensions at any given time. It can bring forth 1d4 of these manifestations to its current locale in order to gain multiple attacks that round. Treat each manifestation as a separate time elemental with hit points equal to the time elemental's current hit points. A manifestation cannot use any of the spell abilities of the time elemental except foresight. A time elemental cannot have more than four manifestations present at one time. Because each manifestation is a part of the time elemental that called them, a successful attack on the time elemental or any of its manifestations deals an equal amount of damage to them all.

By making a melee attack against a foe, a noble or royal time elemental can remove that creature from the current time stream. On a failed save, the creature disappears in a flash of white energy. For a number of minutes equal to the time elemental's Hit Dice, the displaced creature is effectively nonexistent. No form of magic, effect, or force can detect or aid such a creature. When the effect ends, the creature reappears in the same space it was in before being displaced. If the space is occupied when the creature returns, it is shunted aside to the first open space and takes no damage. A noble or royal time elemental can use this ability three times per day.

A time elemental can slip through the time stream and appear anywhere on the same plane of existence as if by teleporting. This ability transports the time elemental and up to four other creatures within a 30-foot radius. Unwilling creatures can attempt a saving throw to avoid being carried away.

Once per day, a royal time elemental can attempt to summon 1d4 common time elementals with a 70% chance of success or 1-2 noble time elementals with a 30% chance of success. Noble and royal time elementals can create an effect identical to a *time stop* spell once per day. All time elementals can see a few seconds into the future. This ability prevents it from being surprised. Time elementals are immune to all time-related spells and effects (though the *time stop* ability of the noble and royal time elementals can affect those time elementals of lesser power).

To Infinity and Beyond

The plane of time exist in between the ticks of a clock. It is limitless and vast, though mortals who enter it view everything as though with tunnel vision, perceiving only the merest shred of the place at any given moment (though the term moment ceases to have much meaning on the plane of time, it still governs the limited mortal mind and is a habit hard to give up).

The plane appears as just that, a vast plain of parched earth cut with a never ending array of parallel lines resembling the grooves on a vinyl record. These grooves appear no more than an inch deep, though a clumsy character may discover that each is really the width and depth of the grand canyon and holds representations of all the detritus of some moment in time. These representations are white and crude features, like copies of a real objects or persons carved from foam. Touching one of these objects allows one to understand everything about its double at the moment (a milisecond, perhaps) captured in this strange canyon.

On the plane above, one notices the completely black sky, and although there is no obvious source of light, the entire plane appears to be lit with a warm, reddish light. As one wanders this endless plane, they might come across one or another of the coppery mists that is a time elemental (roll 1d6: 1-3 = solitary common elemental; 4-5 = noble elemental plus 1d2 common elementals; 6 = royal elemental plus 1d2 noble elementals and 1d4 common elementals).

The goals of the time elementals are inscrutable, and they might just as likely ignore travelers as attack them or throw them into some far distant time from their own. The time elementals dwell in massive palaces formed of vaguely suggested geometries and filling the entire plane, though they are completely invisible to beings incapable of thinking fourth dimensionally. For those so attuned, they discover that the source of the plane's light, which to such enlightened individuals is be perceived as a rainbow-like aura rather than a reddish glow, is a giant symbol of infinity floating above the plane and corruscating in a neverending flux of colored light.

Credit

The Time Elemental originally appeared in the First Edition *Monster Manual II* (© TSR/Wizards of the Coast, 1983) and is used by permission.

Copyright Notice

Author Scott Greene, based on original material by Gary Gygax.

ELEMENTAL CONSTRUCTS

Elemental constructs are golems or automatons forged of one of the four basic elements—air, earth, fire, or water—bound to serve their creator. The creation of an elemental construct requires no less than five elemental spirits (of the same type) which are unwillingly bound into the form of the elemental construct.

Elemental constructs are used by powerful mages as servants, bodyguards, and assassins. An elemental construct, like any other automaton follows any order or command given to it to the best of its ability.

An elemental construct's creator can command it if the construct is within 60 feet and can see and hear its creator. If not commanded, an elemental construct usually follows its last instruction to the best of its ability, though if attacked it returns the attack. The creator can give the elemental construct a simple command to govern its actions in his or her absence. The elemental construct's creator can order the construct to obey the commands of another person (who might in turn place the elemental construct under someone else's control, and so on), but the elemental construct's creator can always resume control over his creation by commanding the elemental construct to obey him alone.

Each elemental construct appears as a humanoid creature about 9 feet tall and is composed entirely of its native element.

Elemental Construct, Air

Hit Dice: 90 hit points
Armor Class: 2 [17]
Attacks: Pummel (3d6) or wind blast 30 ft. radius (2d6)
Saving Throw: 3
Special: Immune to magic, +2 or better magic weapon required to hit
Move: 36 (flying)
Alignment: Neutrality
Challenge Level/XP: 17/3,500

An air elemental construct is a 9-foot-tall semi-vaporous humanoid composed of air and mist. An air elemental construct transforms the air in a 30-foot radius around it into a forceful blast of wind and debris that deals 2d6 points of damage. *Control winds* and *control weather* spells heal an air elemental construct (1d8 per spell level). Any cold-based attack slows an air elemental construct. No other type of spell affects an air elemental construct.

The Funeral Dahabeah

Ruins of looted tombs and shrines line the banks of the murky river. Tomb raiders centuries ago stole the tombs' treasures and carried off the remains of mummies entombed within. Vandals defaced the hieroglyphs and chipped at the memorials to leave them unrecognizable. Embedded atop a small mastaba is a massive bronze chain that extends into the sky. The chain is connected to a bronze boat floating hundreds of feet above the riverbank. The chain and boat are the only artifacts that have not been defiled by robbers.

The bronze dahabeah serves as a ceremonial funeral barge for a high priest of the wind demon, Pazuzu. The priest lich Khuenaton lies in repose in the barge above the river. Four **air elemental constructs** hold the ship aloft indefinitely. They remain invisible while they lift the bronze barge. Only one lets go of the barge to defend against intruders at a time. The boat drops a quarter of the distance to the river each time one of the air elemental constructs leaves its post. The last air elemental construct sets the barge gently down in the river before it turns to defend Khuenaton's resting place. Although the bronze barge floats, it was not intended for water travel and is sluggish difficult to navigate.

In addition to the lich Khuenaton, the boat holds the 6 mummies of his former wives, viziers and a vast amount of treasure.

Elemental Construct, Earth

Hit Dice: 90 hit points
Armor Class: 2 [17]
Attacks: Pound (4d6) or trample (2d6)
Saving Throw: 3
Special: Immune to magic, +2 or better magic weapon required to hit
Move: 8
Alignment: Neutrality
Challenge Level/XP: 17/3,500

An earth elemental construct is a 12-foot-tall humanoid composed of dirt and rock. An earth elemental charges opponents, dealing 2d6 points of damage with a hit. An *earthquake* spell immediately destroys an earth elemental construct. *Transmute rock to mud* and *move earth* heals an earth elemental construct (1d8 per spell level). No other type of spell affects an earth elemental construct.

Farmers in the Dell

The bustling farming village of Roudell thrives with hard workers and bountiful crops. In fact, the indentured servants and farmhands work with dedication and determination unlike any other village in the area. The town is pristine and perfectly manicured. Everyone seems ecstatically cheerful no matter what chore they do. The reason for the insane happiness? The landowners and town elders formed a cult to an earth elemental lord and regularly sacrifice farmhands and servants who do not meet their stringent expectations.

The townsfolk of Roudell built a crude shrine at the far end of the dell for when a worker needs to be "disciplined." Eight stone obelisks stand upright in a circle, and mounds of dirt encrusted with blood lie between them. Piles of skulls, some with dried flesh still attached, surround the dirt mounds. One or more of these mounds of dirt are earth elemental constructs left here to guard the shrine and the town's appalling secret. Within the confines of the obelisks are many small depressions, each filled with unrefined salt. In the midst of the enclosure is a servant buried up to his neck in the earth. His mouth and eyes are encrusted in salt in a horrific ceremony of sacrifice to the elemental lord. The headless bodies of other servants lie buried in the depressions.

Copyright Notice
Author Scott Greene.

Elemental Construct, Fire

Hit Dice: 90 hit points
Armor Class: 2 [17]
Attacks: Strike (3d6) or fire bolt (2d6)
Saving Throw: 3
Special: Immune to magic, immune to fire, +2 or better magic weapon required to hit, ignite materials
Move: 12
Alignment: Neutrality
Challenge Level/XP: 17/3,500

A fire elemental construct is a 9-foot-tall humanoid composed of flame. Their attacks cause flammable materials (including wood) to ignite. A fire elemental construct launches a bolt of fire 90 feet that does 2d6 points of damage. Fire-based spells heal a fire elemental construct (1d8 per spell level). Cold-based spells do double damage to the creature. No other spells affect a fire elemental construct.

Fire Chaser

Four shallow troughs create an intricate maze on the floor of this large room. The troughs are six inches deep and about a foot wide and create a five-foot-wide twisting path to the opposite side of the room to a landing. A clear oily substance fills the channels. A brass brazier on the landing contains a blazing fire in which floats a ring of cold resistance (as a ring of fire resistance, but the wearer is immune to cold). The ring is hot, but undamaged by the blaze. The fire in the brazier is actually a **fire elemental construct** holding the ring inside itself.

Four paths lead through the trough maze from the entry to the other side of the room. A route through the maze can easily be discovered by studying the grooves for just a few minutes. Once a path is stepped upon, however, four geysers of flame appear in the troughs on the entry side of the room. All four of the spouts extend from floor to ceiling. The flame spouts race along the trough maze, instantly creating a wall of fire as they move. Most creatures can outrun the flames, but it should be a close race. While the walls are hot and burn anyone passing through them, creatures remaining in the centers of the paths are safe. The walls remains for 1d4 hours until the flames consume the oily substance filling the troughs. The troughs refill in 1d4+3 hours and the flame geysers reset. The fire elemental construct attacks anyone attempting to remove the ring. If commanded to do so, it hands the ring over willingly.

Copyright Notice
Author Scott Greene.

Elemental Construct, Water

Hit Dice: 90 hit points
Armor Class: 2 [17]
Attacks: Slam (3d6)
Saving Throw: 3
Special: Immune to magic, +2 or better magic weapon required to hit, engulf, drown
Move: 12
Alignment: Neutrality
Challenge Level/XP: 17/3,500

A water elemental construct is a 10-foot-tall humanoid composed entirely of water. The elemental's slam attack engulfs opponents, and they drown in 2d4 rounds if they can't escape the creature's liquid form. *Create water* heals a water elemental construct (1d8 per spell level). *Lower water* instantly destroys a water elemental construct, while *part water* divides the creature into 2 equal halves. Fire-based spells do double damage. No other spell affects a water elemental construct.

When It Rains, It Pours

The damp door to this room is swollen with moisture and sticks in its frame. A trove of books, scrolls and gazettes fill shelves built along the wall in this chamber. The air is humid and laden with moisture. Black mold grows on nearly every inch of the room. Beads of water cover the ceiling and drop throughout the room like rain. Hundreds of glass containers, ceramic jars and metallic urns sit on the floor catching the falling water. Several large ceramic urns are large enough for a human-sized creature to climb into. A rocky mineral crust coats the containers and floor. Water overflows from many of the containers and eventually drains through cracks in the flagstone floor.

A water elemental construct guards this room. It hides in a shallow pool just above the ceiling and flows down through the holes to form its body in the library before attacking.

The library contains books related to water and the sea. The large majority are ruined beyond repair. A set of metallic plates written in the language of merfolk details the steps and materials need to create a helm that allows a surface-dwelling wearer to survive indefinitely underwater. The library's creator made a poor decision in creating a water elemental construct to serve as the room's guardian. The construct attracts water to keep itself sustained in the dungeon environment.

Copyright Notice
Author Scott Greene.

Elemental Dragon, Air

Hit Dice: 24
Armor Class: -2 [21]
Attack: Bite (2d10), 2 claws (2d8)
Saving Throw: 3
Special: Breath weapon, cyclone, spells, +2 or better weapon to hit
Move: 9/48 (flying)
Alignment: Chaos
Challenge Level/XP: 33/8300

The Elemental Plane of Air is home to many creatures: elementals, belkers, and the great djinni. Yet none are as feared as the elemental air dragons. Their great form and majestic aura strike fear into the bravest of souls. Elemental air dragons are as chaotic as their brethren (the other elemental dragons) and take joy and pride in swooping over a settlement or village and destroying it with their cyclonic powers. Watching the frightened creatures flee in terror provokes some sort of perverse excitement in these dragons. Luckily, elemental air dragons rarely enter the Material Plane. Elemental air dragons dislike cloud dragons and mist dragons and seek to slay them whenever they are encountered. The average air elemental dragon is 30 feet long and appears to be a huge dragon composed of vapor and smoke. Three times per day, an elemental air dragons can breath a cone of superheated air. The cone measures 50 feet long and 30 feet at the base and inflicts 10d8 points of damage (save for half).

By beating its wings rapidly back and forth, a hovering elemental air dragon can create a cyclone-like force of wind in a 30-foot radius around its body. This cyclone has the following effects: movement through the cyclone is one-third normal, ranged attacks suffer a -6 penalty in the area, and all non-magical unprotected flames are extinguished. Creatures in the area must succeed on a saving throw or take 3d6 points of damage each round they remain in the area. Human sized or smaller creatures in the area must succeed on a second saving throw or be knocked prone and back 1d4 x 10 feet, taking 1d6 points of nonlethal (i.e. cannot reduce hit points lower than 1) damage per 10 feet. Flying creatures are automatically grounded in this area.

Elemental air dragons can cast *control weather* once per day.

Wind Power

The pinnacle of the tallest mountain in the universe is ever buffeted by howling winds that create a deafening roar as they brush rapidly across a great cave entrance. The entrance is perfectly round, as though carved by intelligent hands and completely unadorned (nor will a dwarf be able to find any mark of tools). This round cave gives entrance to a round tunnel that worms its way into the heart of the mountain (and providing no hand holds to allow one to climb down it).

At the bottom of the tunnel is the lair of a great elemental air dragon, exiled from its home plane by a cabal of its brethren. Once a mighty king among its kind, the dragon's cruel whims drove its ambitious and jealous rivals into a shaky alliance that lasted as long as it took to shunt the beast into the mortal world. It now dwells in its hidey hole, brooding and bitter and unable to force its way back to its home plane.

When ejected into the Material Plane, the great king's soul was shattered and thrown to the four winds, where it now takes the form of ornaments worn by 12 queens of sylph-kind. Should the ornaments be gathered and swallowed by the beast, it can leave its exile and take its revenge on its surviving rivals. The beast charges those who enter its lair with this task, or promise them a most unpleasant death.

Copyright Notice
Author Scott Greene.

Elemental Dragon, Earth

Hit Dice: 24
Armor Class: -3 [22]
Attack: Bite (2d12), 2 claws (2d8)
Saving Throw: 3
Special: Assimilation, breath weapon, only harmed by +2 or better weapons, freeze, meld into stone
Move: 9/30/9 (flying/burrowing)
Alignment: Chaos
Challenge Level/XP: 33/8300

Elemental earth dragons are the strongest of the elemental dragons. Using their great stone tail or earthen claws, they can destroy almost anything in short order. The majority of their time is spent burrowing through the Elemental Plane of Earth devouring gems, minerals, and silicate life forms. On occasion, they are summoned to the Material Plane by evil (and foolish) spellcasters who usually live just long enough to regret their mistake. Elemental earth dragons are chaotic (perhaps the most chaotic of the elemental dragons in addition to being the strongest) and despise most other forms of life. They rarely associate with other creatures, though a few have been known to have dealings with the occasional earth elemental. Elemental earth dragons cannot enter water; they must burrow under it or walk around it. The average elemental earth dragon is 30 feet long and resembles a massive wyrm composed of polished stone. Its roar can be heard up to 5 miles away.

Three times per day an elemental earth dragon can breath a cone of scorched earth, 50 feet long and 30 feet wide at the base. Creatures inside this cone suffer 14d8 points of damage (save for half).

When an elemental earth dragon slays an opponent, it dehydrates the flesh with its breath weapon and pulverizes the bones. The residue is then absorbed into the dragon's body. An assimilated creature can only be restored to life using *wish*, but even then, there is a 50% chance that such powerful magic fails.

An elemental earth dragon can hold itself so still it appears to be a statue. An observer has a 1 in 10 chance (1 in 6 for dwarves) to notice that the elemental earth dragon is really alive. In addition, an elemental earth dragon can meld its body with any stone surface large enough to accommodate its entire body.

Metal Information Broker

There is a place amidst the sun-baked hills along a violent coast where the earth eternally churns, pebbles and stones of every size and worn perfectly smooth circle a dimensional vortex that leads into the Elemental Plane of Earth.

Should one take this passage, they find themselves in a cubical vault that measures 50 feet long, wide and high, entering through the ceiling and suffering falling damage as appropriate. Once the travelers, those who survive the fall, have dusted themselves off and splinted their broken bones, they discover that the entirety of the cavern is bathed in a rich, caramel light, thick with dust. Standing in the cavern, one almost feels the crush of many trillions of tons of stone and soil pressing in on them.

The cavern has a single exit flanked by two massive leonine dragons carved from polished stone, each with one mighty paw poised over the exit. As a group of adventurer's walk through this exit, the last finds themselves plucked up by one of those paws, its owner being an elemental earth dragon. The creature studies its captive, maybe jostle and toss it around a bit just to make sure it knows its place, and then quiz it about where it came from, what passes in the mortal realms and other bits of gossip.

Attempts at rescuing the victim are met with deadly force. When the dragon has heard enough (assume three hours of questioning, during which random encounters occur and encountered monsters neither bother nor perturb the earth dragon), he sends his captive on their way.

Copyright Notice
Author Scott Greene.

Elemental Dragon, Fire

Hit Dice: 24
Armor Class: -5 [24]
Attack: Bite (2d8 plus 2d8 fire), 2 claws (2d6 plus 2d6 fire)
Saving Throw: 3
Special: Breath weapon, fiery aura, rain of fire, only harmed by +3 or better weapons, immune to fire, double damage from cold
Move: 15/36 (flying)
Alignment: Chaos
Challenge Level/XP: 33/8300

This creature appears as a 30-foot long dragon composed of fire. Its eyes burn with a white-hot flame and flames lick the dragon's great mouth as it roars. As it flies overhead, its wings send sheets of flame roaring into the sky and crashing into the ground.

One of the most feared creatures from the Elemental Plane of Fire is the dreaded elemental fire dragon. Composed entirely of flames, these magnificent creatures fear little and are respected and feared by those that have encountered them. Elemental fire dragons are malign and vicious. They delight in killing and torturing others, especially magmin (whom they relish as a delicacy). They employ salamanders to aid them in their ventures, but once they have accomplished their goals, any survivors are devoured. Elemental fire dragons cannot enter water or any other nonflammable liquid. The typical elemental fire dragon is at least 30 feet long and looks like a sinuous dragon composed entirely of fire, with white hot eyes and gouts of smoke leaking from between its teeth.

Anyone within 60 feet of an elemental fire dragon must succeed on a saving throw or take 1d6 points of fire damage from the intense heat. Creatures attacking an elemental fire dragon unarmed or with natural weapons take 1d6 points of damage each time one of their attacks hits. Combustibles automatically catch fire if they contact an elemental fire dragon.

Three times per day an elemental fire dragon can breath a cone of elemental fire, 50 feet long and 30 feet wide at the base. This fire inflicts 16d10 points of damage (save for half).

An elemental fire dragon can hover and rapidly beat its wings causing fire to rain down on an area in a 100-foot radius. Creatures within the area must succeed on saving throw or take 2d8 points of fire damage as clothes catch fire or armor and weapons become searing hot. The damage continues for another 1d8 rounds after the attack or until the flames are extinguished. Combustibles in the area automatically catch on fire.

Lisping Conflagrant Grandiosity

On a basalt island in a sea of fire under a sky that seems filled by the raging fires of the sun broods an elemental fire dragon, unlucky rival of the emir of the efreeti. The fire dragon dwells within an active volcano, a basalt outcropping in the midst of an active lava flow its couch, a harem of fire nymphs (see entry) tending to its every need and a gaggle of 4d4 lava children (see entry) with maximum hit points and clad in tungsten harnesses and serving as the dragon's honor guard.

His *conflagrant grandiosity* (one must use this title when addressing it if they wish to have any chance of emerging from the encounter alive) looks like a great burning serpent with four wide splayed legs tipped in claws. It coils itself on its couch, head tucked under a roll of its body and seemingly drowsing, though really just conserving its energy. The beast speaks with a notable lisp, its head weaving back and forth while it speaks. It first wishes to know what visitors know of the efreeti and their master and then either consumes them or charges them with spying on the genies on its behalf, knowing full well the mission will probably kill the travelers.

While the fire dragon seems rather urbane and measured, its loses its temper quickly and violently, its court usually diving into the lava flow to escape their master's wrath.

Copyright Notice
Author Scott Greene.

Elemental Dragon, Water

Hit Dice: 24
Armor Class: -2 [21]
Attack: Bite (2d8), 2 claws (2d6)
Saving Throw: 3
Special: Breath weapon, capsize, drench, spells, only harmed by +2 or better weapons, transparency
Move: 15/36 (flying and swimming)
Alignment: Chaos
Challenge Level/XP: 33/8300

From the Elemental Plane of Water comes the elemental water dragon. They make their homes in the deep oceans of the Material Plane and are rarely found far away from large expanses of water. An elemental water dragon is composed entirely of water and commands respect from the more intelligent sea creatures as well as those humanoids that ply their trade upon the waters. Elemental water dragons are chaotic and take great pleasure in demanding sacrifice from those that dare enter their realm. If the sacrifice placates the dragon, it lets the creature pass unabated; otherwise, it attacks with all of its might and most often destroys those that offend it or fail to appease its desires. Water dragons take great pleasure in capsizing and sinking ships. On occasion, a group of sahuagin or locathah can be found allied with an elemental water dragon, but this alliance is usually short-lived and often shaky and ends with the death of the fish men.

When submerged, an elemental water dragon is effectively invisible (1 in 12 chance to spot, 1 in 10 chance for elves) until it attacks. A submerged elemental water dragon that surfaces under a boat or ship of less than 20 feet long capsizes the vessel 95% of the time. It has a 50% chance to capsize a vessel from 20 to 60 feet long and a 20% chance to capsize one over 60 feet long.

Three times per day an elemental water dragon can breath a cone of superheated water, 50 feet long and 30 feet wide at the base. The breath weapon inflicts 14d8 points of damage (save for half).

The elemental water dragon's touch puts out torches, campfires, exposed lanterns, and other open flames of nonmagical origin as long as they are no larger than a house fire. The creature can dispel magical fire it touches as the *dispel magic* spell. It can *part water* and *lower water* each once per day.

All Wet

The storm that capsized your vessel and lifted it bodily onto a desert island came out of nowhere; of the few survivors, none of the old tars will have ever seen its like. The island you find yourself on is about 100 feet wide and 200 feet long and composed entirely of white sand, with no life existing beyond the surf.

As the survivors collect themselves, they are set upon day and night by 1d4+2 giant crabs, who attempt to carry survivors one by one into the sea. When only three survivors remain, they are visited by a great elemental water dragon, looking like the sea itself has taken draconic form. The dragon is in constant motion, forward then back, rising then falling into the waters and rising again behind the survivors and speaking the entire time is a deep, resonant voice that is first a whisper and then a roar.

Should the three survivors fight and entertain him, the dragon promises riches to the sole survivor. Otherwise, it simply destroys them all and throws their boiled bodies to the fish.

Copyright Notice
Author Scott Greene.

Elusa Hound

Hit Dice: 3
Armor Class: 7 [12]
Attacks: 1 bite (1d6+1)
Saving Throw: 14
Special: Detect magic
Move: 15
Alignment: Neutrality
Challenge Level/XP: 3/60

The elusa hound appears as a powerful wolf-like dog with pale white, coarse fur (though some recent breeds have whitish-gray fur) and a short, bushy tail. Its eyes burn with a ghostly yellow glow and its teeth are ivory white. The dog is attuned to Magic-Users and can track them unerringly using its ability to detect magic at will.

Dogs and Bounty Hunter

The bounty hunter Koll Mange was recently hired by the magic-user-hating Insydions, a group of barbarians intent on ridding the world of the taint of spellcasters. The group pays Mange a bounty for every magic-user he slays.

Mange is a brute of a man, standing a seven feet tall with broad shoulders and gargantuan hands. His brow is a heavy furrow that hides his deep-set eyes, and his square jaw is framed by a dark red beard. Mange carries a huge axe with scratches carved in the ashen handle for every magic-user he has killed. Mange travels with Cur and Larz, 2 elusa hounds he uses to track magic-users for the bounty offered for their heads.

Cur unfortunately has focused his tracking skills on one of the PC magic-users, and is now following the PC through hell and high water, leading him to a date with the business end of Mange's axe.

Copyright Notice
Author Scott Greene.

Encephalon Gorger

Hit Dice: 8
Armor Class: 6 [13]
Attacks: 2 claws (1d6+1)
Saving Throw: 8
Special: mindfeed, resists cold, haste, regenerate 3 hp/round
Move: 6
Alignment: Chaos
Challenge Level/XP: 9/1,100

An encephalon gorger is a sleek, pale-skinned humanoid standing about 7 feet tall, with long, thin arms and legs. Its hands and feet end in four digits; the two middle digits being slightly longer than the outer two. Its mouth is lined with short, needle-like teeth, with the canines being most pronounced. An encephalon gorger's tongue is sleek and black. An encephalon gorger strikes and tears at its victims with its sharp claws. If it hits with two claws, it grabs the victim and automatic starts to mindfeed in the next round. To mindfeed, the gorger sinks its teeth into the prey's head to drain cerebral fluid (1d6 points of damage per round). Twice per day, a gorger can give itself an adrenal boost of speed (similar to a *haste* spell). An encephalon gorger heals 3 hit points per round.

The Vampire Wannabe

Castle Volkav sits high on the crags above the forlorn village that shares its name. People speak in whispers of the place, casting a wary eye toward the castle's turrets. Cloves of garlic hang doors and windows, and old-timers whisper of the return of the days when people went missing. Getting to the castle is easy, though no one willing goes there anymore.

All signs point to Castle Volkav being empty, but vile equipment and glass containers containing dried flecks of blood still stand in the laboratory. A surface of a wooden in the center of the stone room is marred by deep gouges. Thick chains run through rust-coated pulleys to the table's four corners and a single metal chandelier hangs from a rusted iron chain. Three sputtering candles give off a dismal yellow light. Thick mist rolls in the castle's high windows, and a trapdoor set in the ceiling opens to the outside air.

An encephalon gorger moved into the empty lab a few weeks ago and has been terrorizing the village ever since. The creature shares the lab with an invisible flesh golem created by the lab's original owner. The golem is enchanted to automatically turn invisible after it goes dormant for 1 hour. The golem stands in the corner, but follows the last command it was given and hold slams victims onto the table and holds them down. The gorger takes advantage of this and sucks victim's brains out of their skulls as the golem goes about its "job."

Flesh Golem (Invisible): HD 10 (45 hp); AC 9[10]; Atk 2 fists (2d8); Move 8; Alignment Neutrality; Save 5; CL/XP 12/2000; Special: Healed by lightning, hit only by magic weapons, slowed by fire and cold, immune to most spells.

Copyright Notice
Author Scott Greene.

Executioner's Hood

Hit Dice: 2
Armor Class: 4 [15]
Attack: Choke (1d4)
Saving Throw: 16
Special: Engulf, immune to sleep, vulnerable to alcohol
Move: 6/3 (climbing)
Alignment: Neutrality
Challenge Level/XP: 3/60

The executioner's hood is a deadly monster, black in color and 1 inch thick, that resembles an actual executioner's hood or a small black bag. It has two eyeholes that can be used to see into or out of the monster (if some unfortunate soul happens actually to pick it up — or worse, put it on). The executioner's hood is sometimes used to guard valuable belongings. It does so unerringly as long as a constant supply of food is available. The executioner's hood clings to the ceiling, waiting for prey to pass under it. When prey passes by, the hood drops and attempts to engulf the victim's head. Slain victims are slowly devoured by the hood.

An executioner's hood can try to wrap the head of a victim by making a normal melee attack against a surprised opponent. If successful, it establishes a hold and deals 1d4 points of damage each round it remains on the victim's head. Opponents can tear it off by making a successful open doors roll as though their strength was 3 points lower. A creature whose head is engulfed cannot breathe, but can hold her breath for 2 rounds per point of constitution. After this period of time, the character must make a saving throw each round in order to continue holding her breath, with each successive roll made at a cumulative -1 penalty. When the character fails one of these saving throws, she suffocates and dies. Attacks that hit an engulfing executioner's hood deal half their damage to the monster and half to the trapped victim. An creature whose head is engulfed cannot cast spells.

An executioner's hood is vulnerable to wine, ale, brandy, or any other strong alcoholic drink. Each quart poured on the hood deals 1 point of damage to the creature. After the hood has taken 4 points of damage, it releases its hold on its opponent and drops to the ground. The next morning it suffers from a terrible headache unless properly hydrated.

Bat Hoody

You disover a terrible scene of ancient battle, a lone warrior encased in ancient plane and mail with dozens of broken goblin skeletons littered around it. The skeletal warrior leans against a wall, three crossbow bolts hanging from its rib cage and at least twenty others broken on the floor around it or lodged in the wall.

Tangled vines of tiny, blood red roses grow from the cracks in the glazed, terracotta floor tiles despite the lack of natural light. Cutting through the roses to the other side of the room (and an iron door) takes about 10 minutes, while cutting a path to the skeleton takes half as much time.

The skeleton wears a large iron helm surmounted by leather horns and lined on the inside with what first appears to be black velvet. If placed upon one's head, the executioner's hood inside will wait a few minutes before fitting itself over the victim's head and choking it.

Credit

The Executioner's Hood originally appeared in the First Edition module *EX1 Dungeonland* (© TSR/Wizards of the Coast, 1983) and later in the First Edition *Monster Manual II* (© TSR/Wizards of the Coast, 1983) and is used by permission.

Copyright Notice
Author Scott Greene, based on original material by Gary Gygax.

Eye Killer

Hit Dice: 6
Armor Class: 2 [17]
Attack: Tail (1d6)
Saving Throw: 11
Special: Constrict, death gaze, light vulnerability
Move: 12
Alignment: Chaos
Challenge Level/XP: 8/800

Eye killers are subterranean dwellers that hate daylight. They dwell underground in dark places, where very little light can touch their sensitive eyes. They are evil, malicious creatures that delight in killing others, particularly those that wander to close to their lair. Eye killers are limbless spherical things at birth, but take a form that resembles a cross between a bat and a snake as they mature. The adult creature's upper torso is that of a large bat while its lower torso is that of a snake. Dark green fur covers its upper body, while yellow-green scales cover its lower body. Its eyes are large, lidless, white circles without pupils. The average adult eye killer reaches a length of 7 feet. Its bat wings are useless. Eye killers seem to communicate with each other through a series of low rumbles and growls. They do not speak any known language.

The victim of an eye killer's tail attack must pass a saving throw or be wrapped and constricted for 1d6 points of automatic damage each round until freed with a successful open doors check.

By using natural or magical light that illuminates it (i.e. it cannot be in the dark), an eye killer can amplify the light and refocus it in a line that functions as a death ray to a range of 50 feet. The eye killer must make a ranged attack against its target. If successful, the creature struck must make succeed on a saving throw or die instantly. Even if the save succeeds, the victim takes 3d6 points of damage. An eye killer can use this gaze once per day. Eye killers are immune to their own gaze attack and to the gaze attack of other eye killers. If the eye killer's gaze attack is reflected back upon it, it amplifies the intensity and projects it at a new target as a free action. The saving throw against this amplified gaze attack is made at a -2 penalty.

If natural sunlight is brought within 5 feet of an eye killer, it immediately releases a constricted foe and attempts to move as far away from the source of light as possible. On subsequent rounds, an eye killer is dazzled as long as it remains within 5 feet of the light source.

Umbral Eye Killer

The umbral or shadow eye killer is a variant of the standard eye killer. It uses the statistics above for the standard eye killer but can see perfectly even in magic darkness and can cast *darkness 20' radius* three times per day.

Evil Eye

In a 20-ft wide tunnel, the ceiling arched and the walls run through with veins of reflective quartz. Everburning torches, fastened tight to the walls, run the length of the corridor, dazzling the eyes with the flickering flames that reflect from the walls.

In the center of the corridor there is a 15-foot deep pit, 10 feet square, lined with mirrors and inhabited by an eye killer, bound here by cunning and ancient magics. Two other covered pits are located before and behind this central pit. Each of these is in all respect like the first save for the covering. The presence of torches and lanterns in the mirrors pits offers the beast fuel for its death rays.

The pits are connected by secret passages, the interiors of which are painted in scenes that forewarn one of deeper dangers of the dungeon. In the northernmost corridor, one will also find a key of some sort to an important door.

The pits contain 1d6 x 1,000 sp, 1d4 x 100 gp and a wooden idol of a pit fiend (worth 85 gp) wrapped in a sack made of shark skin (worth 30 gp).

Credit

The Eye Killer originally appeared in the First Edition *Fiend Folio* (© TSR/Wizards of the Coast, 1981) and is used by permission.

Copyright Notice

Author Scott Greene, based on original material by Ian Livingstone. Umbral eye killer, author Scott Greene.

Eye of the Deep

Hit Dice: 10
Armor Class: 4 [15]
Attack: Eye rays (see below), 2 pincers (2d4), bite (1d6)
Saving Throw: 5
Special: Constrict, eye rays, stun cone
Move: 3/9 (swimming)
Alignment: Chaos
Challenge Level/XP: 13/2300

The eye of the deep is a 5-foot wide orb dominated by a central eye and large serrated mouth. Hundreds of small seaweed-like bristles hang from the bottom of its body. Two large crab-like pincers protrude from its body, and two long, thin eyestalks sprout from the top of its orb. Eyes of the deep are found only in the deepest parts of the ocean, though on occasion one moves too close to the shoreline and ends up beaching on the sands. An eye of the deep stranded in this manner dies in 2d4 minutes unless placed back into the water. Eyes of the deep speak their own language and the common tongue of seafaring humans. Creatures struck by the eye of the deep's pincers must pass a saving throw or be caught and crushed for 2d4 points of automatic damage each round until they can pry open those pincers with an open doors check.

Each of the creature's eyes stalks can produce a magical ray once per round. The creature can aim both of its eye rays in any direction. Each of its eye rays resembles a spell cast by a 12th-level caster and requires a ranged attack (ignores armor) to hit. Each eye ray has a range of 150 feet. The left eye emits a *hold person* ray, while the right eye emits a *hold monster* ray. By combining both eye rays, the eye of the deep can replicate the *phantasmal force* spell.

An eye of the deep's central eye can, once per round, produce a cone extending straight ahead from its front to a range of 30 feet. Creatures in the area must succeed on a saving throw or be stunned for 2d4 rounds.

Lord of the Depths

A tremendous bubble of silvery glass floats in the sea. The sphere measures 1 mile in diameter, and though the surface appears perfectly smooth from a distance, a closer inspection reveals entrances on the top and bottom of the sphere and four spaced around the middle. Each of these entrances is circular and is opened by pushing (strength of 16 required).

These tunnels are immersed in water and form ten levels and run right, left, forward, backward, sideways, up and down, seemingly without rhyme or reason, many passages blocked by iron doors that variously slide, roll or pivot open. A great array of sea creatures lurk in these tunnels, all of which wind eventually toward the spherical (25-feet in diameter) center, the lair of an eye of the deep. Here, the lord of the aqueous orb directs its movements through the seven seas by the force of its mind, unleashing its denizens on aquatic strongholds and villages and gathering into its vaults all the wealth of the oceans.

Credit

The Eye of the Deep originally appeared in the First Edition *Monster Manual* (© TSR/Wizards of the Coast, 1977) and is used by permission.

Copyright Notice

Author Scott Greene, based on original material by Gary Gygax.

GIANT FALSE SPIDERS

False spiders are spiderlike creatures that are very aggressive and highly predatory in nature, often hunting at night when the element of surprise is theirs to be had. False spiders dwell in shallow burrows which the dig with their massive pincers. There are two kinds of false spiders: pedipalps and solifugids. False spiders are highly territorial and are likely to attack any living creature that enters their area.

False Spider, Giant

	Pedipalp	Solifugid
Hit Dice:	2	5
Armor Class:	3 [16]	4 [15]
Attack:	2 claws (1d4), bite (1d6)	2 claws (1d6), bite (1d6)
Saving Throw:	16	12
Special:	None	None
Move:	12	12
Alignment:	Neutrality	Neutrality
Challenge Level/XP:	2/30	5/240

Pedipalp

Pedipalps are called whip scorpions and look like a cross between a spider and a scorpion. They have eight legs and two thin antennae. Its front sports two spider-like eyes and a set of large mandibles. Two large scorpion-like pincers protrude from just in front of its foremost legs. The average pedipalp is 5 feet long but can grow to a length of 10 feet.

Solifugid

Solifugids are at least 6 feet long but can grow to a length of 12 feet. They have eight legs, two spider-like eyes and a set of large, clicking, hooked mandibles. Two large scorpion-like pincers protrude from just in front of its foremost legs.

Poisonous Pedipalp

The poisonous pedipalp is a rare variety of the species. Rarely encountered, the poisonous pedipalp is a solitary creature; no more than one has ever been encountered at a given time. They do not associate with others of their kind or with normal pedipalps. The poisonous pedipalp uses the same statistics as the normal pedipalp with save it has a challenge level of 3. When threatened, a poisonous pedipalp releases a cloud of noxious fumes in a 20-foot radius around its body. Living creatures within the cloud must succeed on a saving throw or be nauseated for 1d6 rounds. The poisonous pedipalp can use this cloud three times per day.

Hair Today

In a dry savannah there rise the towering nests of a large brood of giant termites. The termites, about the size of wolves, are now in hiding, their halls stalked by a giant solifugid. The solifugid has made a burrow in a deep pit within the termite halls, coming out occasionally to hunt down a termite.

The pit once belonged to the termite queen. Approximately 1d10+10 termites still lurk in the nest, scattered and confused. The solifugid has started making forays into the savannah to hunt mammals, needing their hair to line its new nest, which now holds a clutch of the beast's eggs.

Credit

The Pedipalp and Solifugid originally appeared in module *Q1 Queen of the Demonweb Pits* and later in the First Edition *Monster Manual II* (© TSR/Wizards of the Coast, 1983) and are used by permission.

Copyright Notice

Author Scott Greene, based on original material by Gary Gygax.

Fear Guard

Hit Dice: 4
Armor Class: 5 [14]
Attacks: Incorporeal touch (1d6)
Saving Throw: 13
Special: Fear aura, spell-like abilities, create spawn
Move: 12 (flying)
Alignment: Chaos
Challenge Level/XP: 6/400

Fear guards appear as translucent hooded figures wearing flowing robes of gray or black over a suit of incorporeal armor. Their hands end in terrible claws. Their faces are a swirl of maddening images, fluctuating between a serene and calm countenance to a face twisted in horror and fear. Fear guards strike from the shadows, using their incorporeal touch. Any creature slain by the creature becomes a fear guard within 1d6 rounds. A fear guard radiates *fear* (as per the spell) in a 10-foot radius. Twice a day, a fear guard can cast *darkness, 15 ft. radius*.

Fear and Loathing

A black slab of hardened shale juts out from the cliff face, forming a ledge above a 150 foot drop in the Porshire Peaks. Vines dangle from the cliff above to the slab. A gold sigil of intertwined snakes is etched into the shale and burns with a sickly green flame. A carved basalt doorway sits about 10 feet into a stone recess and has a similar glowing sigil carved into its otherwise featureless surface.

The door is the entrance to the tomb of Marlena Eboncore, the wife of a particularly jealous magic-user named Hagstrom. Marlena was a loyal wife (most of the time), but her eye was sometimes inclined to wander – a fault that Hagstrom put up with until he caught her with a visiting jester. In a blind rage, he slew the jester with a burst of magical fire, then locked Marlena in her chambers. He didn't know about the poison she'd hidden in the room.

Hagstrom buried Marlena on the cliff overlooking the sea where they met, but was left uneasy. He feared one of her many lovers – some powerful magic-users and clerics – might raise her from the dead, something he couldn't bring himself to do despite his undying love for her. Hagstrom loathed himself for what he drove his beloved to, and eventually drank the same poisonous concoction that killed her.

If the tomb door is opened by anyone other than Hagstom, it causes the sigil on the shale platform to explode (6d6 points of damage). The explosion shatters the shale and causes the entire platform outside the recess to drop into the ocean below. The mountain stone is enchanted and the platform regrows in three days.

Inside the tomb, a bier of black stone holds a burial vault engraved with Marlena Eboncore's likeness. A fear guard stands silently beside the tomb, protecting the woman's corpse. As soon as someone enters the tomb, a magic mouth on the effigy shouts "You'll never have her." The fear guard unleashes its horrid moan as it advances. It won't leave the tomb.

Fen Witch

Hit Dice: 6
Armor Class: 5 [14]
Attack: 2 claws (1d4)
Saving Throw: 11
Special: Death speak, horrific appearance, mind probe, magic resistance (25%)
Move: 12
Alignment: Chaos
Challenge Level/XP: 11/1700

The fen witch is a creature of legend, found only in the most remote of places. It is a female humanoid with one nostril, webbed feet and hands, fiery red eyes and long, unkempt hair. It is a solitary creature and disdains all that invade its realm. The sight of a fen witch is so revolting that anyone who sets eyes upon one must succeed on a saving throw or instantly be weakened, taking 1d8 points of strength damage. This ability loss cannot reduce a victim's Strength score to 0.

The fen witch can communicate telepathically with any creature within 100 feet that has a language. A fen witch can peer into the mind of a living creature within 60 feet in an attempt to extract the creature's true name. The target can resist the mental trespassing by succeeding on a saving throw that requires all of their concentration. If the save fails, the fen witch has learned the creature's true name and can use her death speak ability. Creatures with an intelligence score of 2 or less and non-sentient creatures are immune to this ability.

If the fen witch speaks the true name of an individual and the individual hears it, that creature must make a successful saving throw or die. If the save succeeds, that creature cannot be affected again by the same fen witch's death speak for one day. Whether the fen witch's death speak ability is successful or not, the target's name remains fresh in her mind for one day. After that, she must use her mind probe ability again to retrieve a creature's true name.

Defenseless Old Women In the Swamp Never Are

While tromping through a swamp, the ooze gathered about your ankles, you come across an old woman heading on a perpendicular course to your own. The woman is hunched and wears a deep, green hooded cloak over her head, a large bundle of sticks tied to her back. Noticing the strangers in her swamp, the old woman will turn to face them, making sure her cargo of human bones remain obscured behind her husky form and her face hidden in the shadows of her hood.

The old crone engages the adventurer's in conversation, introducing herself as Old Meg-o-the-Green and proclaiming herself either a canny sorceress, a spirit of the swamp or the humble widow of a woodcutter. She has a voice like two great stones sliding against one another, and a piercing, unnerving laugh. Although she asks many questions, she never seems to hear the answers, often repeating herself or asking new questions that have already been answered.

This is, of course, because she is busy probing minds for true names. When the adventurers tire of her, she will bid them farewell, speaking the true names she has already learned and then striking at the others with her claws after first hurling her bundle at the face of a spellcaster. If she manages to win her fight, she'll throw a body over her shoulder and leave the others to rot in the muck.

Copyright Notice

Fetch

Hit Dice: 3+2
Armor Class: 6 [13]
Attacks: 2 claws (1d4)
Saving Throw: 14
Special: Freezing touch, immune to cold, vulnerable to fire
Move: 6
Alignment: Chaos
Challenge Level/XP: 3/60

A ragged-looking and rotting humanoid leaps from the snow, its filthy nails slashing through the frosty air. Its eyes are stark blue and its skin is pale white. Ice hangs from its scraggly hair. A fetch stands anywhere from 5 to 7 feet tall and weighs between 100 and 250 pounds. Its rotting flesh is drawn tight around its bones and flushed grayish-white. Its hair is scraggly and frozen and ice crystals cover its skin. A fetch's eyes are stark blue. Fetches strike with their claws, which are supernaturally cold and deal 1d4 points of cold damage. A fetch is vulnerable to fire (taking an extra 50% damage).

Cold War

A frozen field stretches out between the snow-covered evergreen trees. Thousands of freeze-dried hands, arms and heads lie partially buried in the tundra. Gauntlets, golden rings and even weapons are still grasped in the icy dead hands. One skeletal hand holds a broken hand-and-a-half sword. Its pommel glows a cold blue aura. The elven name "Tazeen" is skillfully etched into the hilt.

The area looks as if the ground has slowly swallowed the remains of a large battle. Six goblins carefully pick through the remnants on the opposite end of the field. Holding broken and rusted weapons, they quickly flee with their plunder at first sight of any intimidating threats. In the midst of the field, 2d4 fetch hide just under the permafrost awaiting fresh victims to walk above them. The battle took place between humans and elves nearly a century ago. Other than the name Tazeen, no identifying clues have survived.

Copyright Notice
Author Scott Greene.

Fire Crab

Hit Dice: 1 or 4
Armor Class: 1 HD: 7 [12]; 4 HD: 5 [14]
Attacks: 1 HD: 2 claws (1d3 + 1d4 fire); 4 HD: 2 claws (1d6 + 1d6 fire)
Saving Throw: 17 or 13
Special: Heat, immune to fire
Move: 1 HD: 6/9 (swim); 4 HD: 9/12 (swim)
Alignment: Neutrality
Challenge Level/XP: 1 HD (1/15); 4 HD (4/120)

A fire crab resembles a large crab in most respects. Its carapace is reddish-brown with dark red or yellow markings and its body is slightly square-shaped. Tiny flames lick its body, erupting at irregular intervals from its underbelly. Its eyes are perched on the end of two large eyestalks that protrude from the center of the carapace. Fire crabs have large claws and in males, one claw is always larger (at least three times larger) than the other. Fire crabs have six segmented and spindly legs, blackish-red in color. Fire crabs generate intense heat, dealing heat damage with their claw attacks.

Playing With Fire

The Kulspout Volcano is alive with spurting flames and clouds of poisonous gases that roll down its jagged slopes. Burning boulders thrown into the air land with resounding crashes before the bounding rocks tear pine trees out by their roots. The air is thick with clouds of choking ash that turn the day into night.

A narrow fissure in the side of the volcano opens into a steamy cavern containing a 30-foot-wide pool of lava. Molten rock flows over a series of boulders in a hissing lava-fall that feeds the lake. Hollowed-out rocks sit on the edge of the lava. A 10-foot-wide flat slate platform sits in the center of the lava pool. A 10-foot-tall conch shell sits in the middle of the rock. Scattered gold coins lie on the slat platform. The coins are hot to the touch, and deal 1d6 points of damage to unprotected flesh.

A fire crab lives in the shell, and scuttles out to attack if anyone steps onto the platform. It is the largest and claimed the shell as its own. In the lava pool and hollow rocks are 5 more fire crabs.

Copyright Notice

Fire Nymph

Hit Dice: 2
Armor Class: 5 [14]
Attack: Dagger (1d4 plus 1d4 fire) or slam (1d2 plus 1d4 fire)
Saving Throw: 16
Special: Heat, spells, immunity to fire, magic resistance (5%), double damage from cold
Move: 12
Alignment: Chaos or Neutrality
Challenge Level/XP: 6/400

Fire nymphs are beautiful females with long, flowing, fiery-red hair, pale blue eyes and skin with the color and scent of cinnamon. Fire nymphs dwell on the Elemental Plane of Fire. Fire nymphs rarely visit the Material Plane, though mages are known to request their company on occasion. A fire nymph usually wears translucent robes of white or ash. Fire nymphs can all spells involving fire as 7th-level spell casters. A fire nymph's body generates intense heat, causing opponents to take an extra 1d4 points of damage every time the creature touches the fire nymph. A fire nymph's metallic weapons also conduct this heat.

Too Hot to Touch

For days you see a thick plume of smoke, often punctuated by momentary images of horrified spirits ascending into the heavens. Following it brings you to the smoldering remains of a palace. All that remains of the place are crumbling white walls, marble floors marred with soot and bare stone pillars once coated with precious metals that have pooled on the ground.

In the center of the palace there is a sunken chamber which has been turned into a fire pit fed by once expensive furniture and silks. The architect of the pit and the fire that destroyed the palace is a fire nymph, summoned by a sorcerous sheik who offered her an impertenance when his charm against fire proved inadequate to the touch of the nymph. In no time the great sheik found himself ablaze, his servants running about in a panic and the nymph luxuriating in the chaos.

The fire nymph is now building a shrine to her master that she might contact him and find deliverance from the frigid Material Plane.

Copyright Notice
Author Scott Greene.

Fire Phantom

This humanoid has raging fire for hair and flame-encased fists. Elemental fire plays across its body exposing patches of charred flesh. Its eyes and tongue look like tiny balls of molten fire. Blackened teeth fill its mouth and flames dance in the back of its throat.

Hit Dice: 6
Armor Class: 6 [13]
Attacks: 1 slam (1d4 + 1d6 fire)
Saving Throw: 11
Special: Fire blast, immune to fire, immolation
Move: 6
Alignment: Chaos
Challenge Level/XP: 7/600

Fire phantoms appear as humanoids with raging fire for hair, flame-encased fists, and elemental fire playing across their bodies. A fire phantom's eyes are tiny balls of molten fire, as is its tongue. Fire phantoms attack with fiery fists that deal an extra 1d6 fire damage. Once every 1d4 rounds, they can hurl a globe of concentrated flame up to 30 feet (2d6 damage, save avoids). As a last resort, a fire phantom can detonate itself in an inferno that does 6d6 points of damage to all creatures within a 10-foot radius (save for half). The explosion kills the fire phantom if it fails a save, and causes its flames to extinguish for 1 round if it succeeds.

Fire Lake

The volcano's caldera bubbles and seethes with noxious gases, the lava held in check – for the moment – inside the mountain. A narrow crevice leads into the peak, the steam and fire making the journey a torturous ordeal. The rocks glow red, and metal soon becomes too hot to touch. The path winds through the igneous rock until it opens onto a lake of lava. The rim of the volcano rises above the open lake.

The Buntau tribesmen in the jungle village below sacrifice their warrior dead by placing their bodies on shale biers that float on the lake of fire. The bodies ride the lava currents until the rocks break apart and sink.

Currently, five bodies float on the lava, the corpses blackened and hard, like charred cinders left too long in a fire. Each bier carries the person's favored weapons. One of the bodies clutches a *+1 flaming mace*. Another corpse wears a *necklace of firebaubles*, although it is blackened and charred and appears to be nothing more than rocks placed around the corpse's neck.

Five fire phantoms stand on the shale platforms to protect the dead. The creatures attack anyone disturbing the bodies.

Copyright Notice
Author Scott Greene.

Fire Snake

Hit Dice: 2
Armor Class: 2 [17]
Attack: Bite (1d4 plus paralysis)
Saving Throw: 16
Special: Paralysis, immune to fire, double damage from cold, surprise on a roll of 1-4 on 1d6
Move: 9/12 (climbing)
Alignment: Neutrality
Challenge Level/XP: 4/60

A fire snake resembles a normal snake with reddish-orange scales and stark white eyes. They range in size from 2 feet to 6 feet in length. Fire snakes make their homes in fires and rarely journey more than 30 feet from such an open flame. A fire snake's preferred method of attack is to hide in a nearby fire and then surprise its foes as they come nearby. A fire snake attacks by biting its opponents with its sharp fangs. A creature hit by a fire snake's bite must succeed on a saving throw or be paralyzed for 1d6 rounds.

Ayesha of the Flames

In the black mountains that serve as the border of Jinnistan, there is a miles long tunnel. The entrance to the tunnel is faced with blue jade carved in the shape of a mass of dancing apsaras, the eyes of several of them hiding poisoned darts that are triggered when one places a foot upon various of the 101 marble steps that lead up to the portal.

The tunnel is fairly straight and level, and appears to have been melted through the mountains rather than excavated. Every 100 feet, the tunnel is blocked by a coruscating curtain of flame. Lining the tunnel are hundreds of red marble statues of dancing fire nymphs surrounded by roaring pits of flame.

About 1 in 6 of these pits contains a pack of 1d4+1 fire snakes.

In roughly the midpoint of the tunnel there is an especially tall statue, the base engraved with the name Ayesha. This statue is surrounded by a shallow pit of white flames 30 feet in diameter containing three especially nasty fire snakes (maximum hit points) that will strike any creature entering the flames with a charisma score below 16.

Any who dare to throw a piece of gold into the pit may attempt to walk across the flames to the statue of Ayesha to retrieve a small sphere of rose quartz from those resting on the pedestal. The individual attempting the walk must possess supreme concentration (i.e. roll wisdom score or less on a 1d20). Every traveler to Jinnistan knows anyone exiting these tunnels without a quartz sphere will discover themselves violently unwelcome.

Credit

The Fire Snake originally appeared in the First Edition *Fiend Folio* (© TSR/Wizards of the Coast, 1981) and is used by permission.

Copyright Notice

Author Scott Greene, based on original material by Michael McDonagh.

Fire Whale (Burning Leviathan)

Hit Dice: 12
Armor Class: 3 [16]
Attacks: 1 bite (3d6), tail slap (1d8)
Saving Throw: 3
Special: Scalding blast, immune to fire
Move: 18 (swim)
Alignment: Neutrality
Challenge Level/XP: 13/2,300

A fire whale is about 30 feet long, though specimens as long as 60 feet have been seen swimming the fiery seas. The fire whale's body is crimson red mottled with yellow and orange spots, particularly along the back and shoulder area. The fire whale has a wide angular mouth. A fire whale attacks with its bite and tail slap. Surface creatures that threaten a fire whale are subjected to its scalding blast attack. The blast of superheated air from the whale's blowhole to burn opponents (4d6 damage, save for half).

The Great Red Whale

Captain Melvilic needs a crew to sail the whaler Acushnet. His last crew – may the briny deep give them peace – didn't survive the last voyage. Just one hardened sailor came back from that fateful trip when the good captain encountered the great red whale. It's been a month since the Acushnet last sailed. She's been in dry dock since the battering she took when the massive red whale charged the ship. Melvilic is determined to sell the whale's blubber to the candlemakers, and its meat to the fish markets. The captain will pay 200 gp per sailor who signs on to track the demon fish. No one in the port town of Queen's Run will sign, and one old sailor named Elijah warns PCs to be wary of Melvilic's destructive desire.

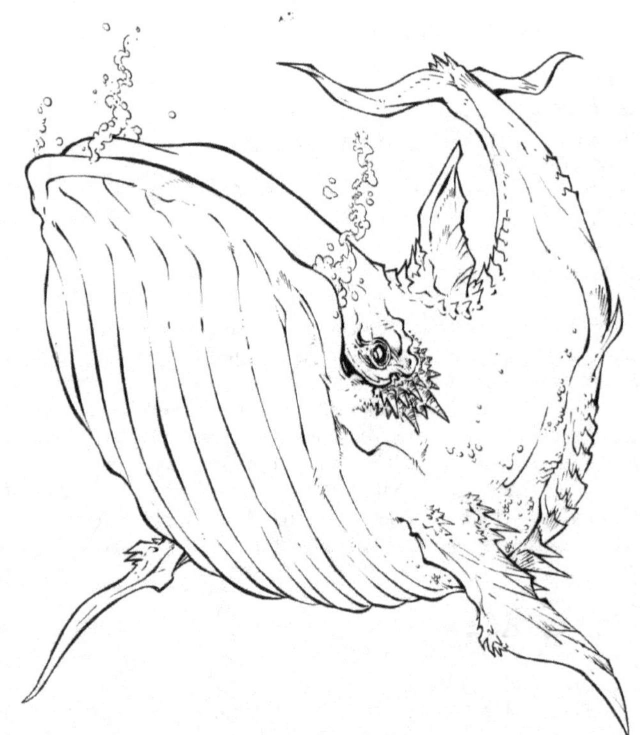

Copyright Notice

Author Scott Greene.

Firefiend

Hit Dice: 8
Armor Class: 3 [16]
Attack: 3 longswords (1d8 plus 1d6 fire)
Saving Throw: 8
Special: Spit, immunity to fire, double damage from cold
Move: 12
Alignment: Chaos
Challenge Level/XP: 9/1100

A firefiend is a rare creature from the Elemental Plane of Fire that takes the form of a three-sided column of fire, each side sporting a single arm, leg and face. In each arm the creature carries a flaming longsword. Upon first glance, a firefiend strongly resembles a fire elemental of the same size, but beyond that the resemblance ends. Its three faces constantly scowl and scream at opponents, cursing them in the flowery language of the efreet. If an opponent understands this language, he will comprehend only incoherent babbling and cursing. Once every other round, each of the firefiend's faces can spit a fiery cinder to a range of 10 feet at one opponent. A target takes 1 point of fire damage and must succeed on a saving throw or catch on fire. Because of their three faces, firefiends are very difficult to surprise.

Out of the Frying Pan . . .

You enter a completely black cavern, as hot as an oven and of indeterminate size, but at least 500 feet in diameter. The ceiling is rather low (8 feet), and in the center of the chamber there is a white pillar of light 10 feet in diameter. As someone in the party walks toward the pillar, it dims while the rest of the cavern becomes bathed in a rising light. When that person reaches the perimeter of the central "pillar", it will have become as black as night and the rest of the cavern almost blindingly brilliant and revealing no discernable exit in the smooth, gray walls of the round cavern.

Stepping into the blackness, elves and dwarves will find the ability of their eyes to pierce the darkness reduced, everything appearing hazy and indistinct. Light spells give off a wan, wavering light in the darkness. In the blink of an eyes, a firefiend will appear in the center of the pillar of blackness, brandishing its swords and babbling its curses. Any attempt to leave the blackness proves that it is now endless. The only way to escape is to destroy the fire fiend, at which point the blackness will contract into a pillar 3 feet in diameter. Stepping into the pillar will either lift one slowly through a hole in the ceiling or drop them slowly through a hole in the floor, depending on whether they wish to escape the dungeon or delve more deeply into it.

Copyright Notice
Author Erica Balsley.

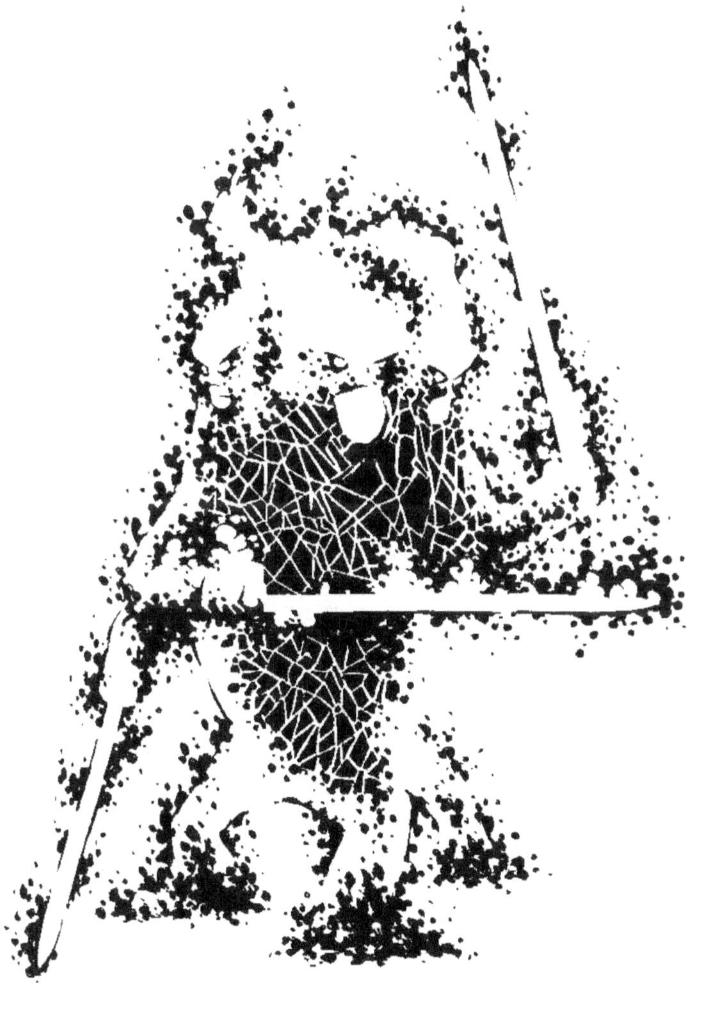

Flail Snail

Hit Dice: 4
Armor Class: 1 [18]
Attack: 4 slams (1d8)
Saving Throw: 13
Special: Immunity to fire and poison, light blindness, warp magic
Move: 6
Alignment: Neutrality
Challenge Level/XP: 6/400

Flail snails are solitary omnivores found in the deepest recesses of caverns, caves, and dungeons. There they sustain themselves on a diet of fungus, mold, and rodents. Flail snails are massive snails, the size of warhorses. Their heads are masses of four thick tentacles, each tipped with a mace-like ball. The snail's shell is striped in bright colors of red, blue, yellow and green, while its flesh is gray-blue. The shell of a dead flail snail can be sold on the open market for 3,000–5,000 gp. Abrupt exposure to bright light blinds flail snails for 1 round. Any time a spell targets a flail snail, there is a chance it produces a random effect rather than affecting the creature. Only spells that directly affect a flail snail are warped. Area spells are not affected by this ability. Roll 1d10 and consult the table below to determine random effects.

1d10	Result
1-2	Spell misfires; caster disoriented for 1d4 rounds and must make a saving throw to cast any spell while disoriented.
3-4	Spell misfires; creature nearest the flail snail is affected as if the spell had been cast on him.
5-7	Spell functions normally
7-9	Spell fails; nothing happens
10	Spell rebounds on caster

Greater Flail Snail

For a greater challenge, you can inflict a "greater flail snail" on your players by increasing the monster's Hit Dice. For every Hit Dice above 4, a flail snail has one additional mace-like tentacle with which it can attack. Thus, a 6 HD flail snail has 6 tentacles; an 8 HD flail snail has 8 tentacles; and a 12 HD flail snail has 12 tentacles.

It Rhymes, Too

As you traverse a narrow ribbon of a tunnel deep beneath the earth, you come upon a massive flail snail coming the other way, plodding slowly along. Beyond the snail the tunnel slant sharply upwards and is coated with the creature's slime. The way back should be long enough to force players into making a difficult choice.

Should one check the walls, they discover a secret door that gives access to a chute to a deeper level of the dungeon. The shell of the flail snail has been drilled through, an adamantine chain and manacles attached. These manacles are currently secured around the wrists of a slime-covered, beaten and bloody hobgoblin king, overthrown by his nephew and sent into the dungeon to meet his doom.

Credit

The Flail Snail originally appeared in the First Edition *Fiend Folio* (© TSR/Wizards of the Coast, 1981) and is used by permission.

Copyright Notice

Author Scott Greene, based on original material by Simon Tilbrook.

Flea, Giant

Hit Dice: 5 hp
Armor Class: 4 [15]
Attacks: 1 bite (1d2 + blood drain)
Saving Throw: 18
Special: Blood drain, disease, leap
Move: 6
Alignment: Neutrality
Challenge Level/XP: B/10

Giant fleas are blood-sucking parasites that prey on warm-blooded animals. They have strong hind legs with powerful tendons that allow them to leap up to three times their Move rate. A giant flea is about a foot long, with an oval, flattened body. If a giant flea hits with a bite attack, it latches on to automatically drain the creature's blood (1d4 points of damage) in the next round. After it drains 4 total hit points, it leaps away to digest its meal. There is a 5% chance that a giant flea carries a disease.

Dead Elephants

Several lumps of brown fur lie in heaps in a weed-covered field. Buzzards glide in lazy circles, their spirals descending toward the dead animals on the plains below.

The furry lumps are mammoths that collapsed after drinking from a watering hole poisoned by mineral runoffs. The giant animals only recently died.

But they haven't stopped moving. The furry hides of the mammoths part and shift, the hair moving in odd lines along the dead mammoths' backs and sides. A colony of 28 giant fleas burrows through the thick pelts. Four fleas hide on each of the seven mammoth carcasses. The fleas burst from the mammoths' fur and leap onto opponents who get too close to the dead mammoths.

Copyright Notice
Author Erica Balsley.

Flind

Hit Dice: 2+2
Armor Class: 1 [18]
Attack: Flindbar (1d6+1)
Saving Throw: 16
Special: None
Move: 12
Alignment: Chaos
Challenge Level/XP: 2/30

Flinds are a race closely related to gnolls. The two races share some strong similarities, and at first sight inexperienced adventurers could easily confuse the two. Flinds are much stockier than their lanky kin, much stronger and hardier, and are certainly more dangerous. It is unknown if flinds are a subspecies of the gnoll or a genetic anomaly produced among large gnoll packs. Flinds are often found among gnoll bands acting as leaders; their strength and relatively superior intelligence puts them above their lesser brethren. Flinds speak Gnoll and about 15% of them also speak the common tongue.

A flindbar is a weapon that consists of two iron bars, approximately 18 inches in length, connected by a length of chain. With a flindbar, the wielder gains a +2 bonus on attack rolls made to disarm an enemy. Flindbars inflict 1d6 points of damage. They weigh 2 pounds and cost 4 gp.

Gnoll Lords

The broad veldt that separates the jungle from the sea is the domain of the flinds, rapacious nomads who make temporary camps on rocky outcroppings, covering them with their graffiti and using their heights to spy potential victims on the plains. The Jagged Finger tribe, denoted by their copper-colored muzzles and back-turned pinkies (a rite of passage, and a painful one at that), are one such tribe of 1d10x20 flinds and their 1d10+10 gnoll servants.

The flinds are primarily scavengers, the sea coast abutting their native grassland littered with treacherous reefs and harried by a tribe of sahuagin. While the flind are happy to pick up odds and ends of cargo, they primarily prey on the crew of these ships, enslaving them and selling them to the ape men of the jungle.

The flind are led by a silver-haired male with 7 HD and a quick temper. He is assisted by 1d2 sub-chiefs with 4 HD and one 3 HD sergeant per 20 flind. The sergeants of the tribe are all females wed to the chief and acting as his executioners and advisors. The sergeants are adorned with copper jewelry (bandles, neck bands, nose rings) and carry two-handed bronze executioner's swords. Each female sergeant rules over a matriarchal clan and competes for the favor of the chief, hoping one of their cubs will one day replace him when he grows to old to defend his throne.

The flind's complete treasure consists of 1d8 x 1,000 sp, 1d10 x 100 gp and 20 square yards of lace (weighs 60 pounds, worth 100 gp) salvaged from a shipwreck.

Credit
The Flind originally appeared in the First Edition *Fiend Folio* (© TSR/ Wizards of the Coast, 1981) and is used by permission.

Copyright Notice
Author Scott Greene, based on original material by J. D. Morris.

Floating Eye

Hit Dice: 1d6
Armor Class: 3 [16]
Attack: Bite (1d2)
Saving Throw: 18
Special: Hypnotic gaze, surprise on a roll of 1-5 on 1d6
Move: 24 (swimming)
Alignment: Neutrality
Challenge Level/XP: 1/15

Floating eyes look like 6-inch long, semi-transparent fish with a single large eye located in the center of its body along its dorsal region. They are most often found underground in forgotten dungeon waterways and underground lakes and seas. The creature's eye is capable of bioluminescence, and it has such minute control over the intensity and patterns of the light that it can mesmerize other creatures that see it. Floating eyes are part of an unusual symbiotic relationship with a variety of predatory fish, including sharks. Once the floating eye has mesmerized its prey, predatory fish move in and consume it. After they have eaten, the floating eye moves in and gorges itself on the scraps. Floating eyes are small saltwater fish that have transparent bodies and a single large eye about the size of a walnut located in the center of their body. Creatures meeting the gaze of a floating eye must succeed on a saving throw or stare blankly at the floating eye for 1d6+1 rounds. A swimming creature that fails its save does not sink, but floats on the surface of the water.

From the Abyssal Depths To Your Local Aquarium

In the home of the cunning master of thieves there is a grandiose central chamber furnished with plush couches and low, mahogany tables set with decanters of potent spirits and boxes of snuff. It is here that the master thief entertains allies, clients and enemies. One wall of the chamber is shrouded in a heavy curtain of damask silk in an acanthus pattern.

A thick cord of golden silk hangs from the ceiling and parts the curtains, but only if one pulls it at an angle - pulling straight down releases a heavy stone block from the ceiling (4d6 damage, save for half damage). Behind the curtain is what appears to be a large, thick pane of glass - actually steel turned glassy via powerful magic.

The glass wall is part of an aquarium holding a variety of long, serpentine amethyst-colored fish. It also contains a school of 3d4 floating eyes. The master thief often introduces his guests to the wonders of the aquarium that the floating eyes might put them into a deep hypnosis, allowing the master thief to do as he will with them. Particularly hated or annoying visitors might be chained and dropped into the aquarium from above.

Credit

The Floating Eye originally appeared in the First Edition *Monster Manual* (© TSR/Wizards of the Coast, 1977) and is used by permission.

Copyright Notice

Author Scott Greene, based on original material by Gary Gygax.

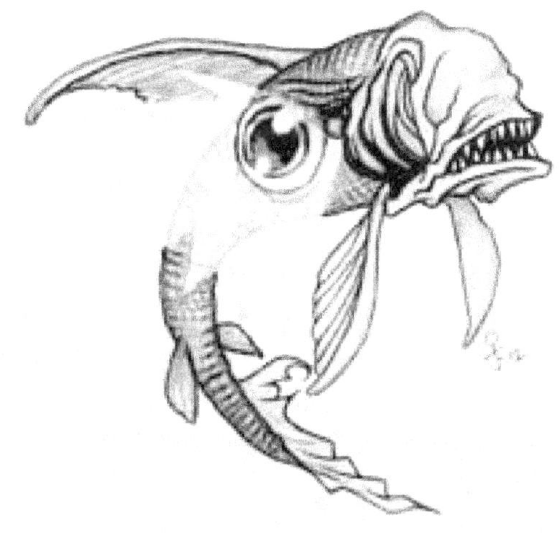

Flumph

Hit Dice: 2
Armor Class: -1 [20]
Attack: Nauseating spray (sickened) or spikes (1d6 plus 1d4 acid)
Saving Throw: 16
Special: Acid, nauseating spray
Move: 9 (flying)
Alignment: Law
Challenge Level/XP: 5/240

This small (2 feet in diameter) strange creature looks like a saucer-shaped jellyfish with many small spike-like tentacles dangling from its underbelly. Its body is milky-white in color. Two short eyestalks protrude from the top of its body. Its eyestalks are gray as are its tentacles. Its eyes are jet black. Flumphs are strange beings that spend their days floating along looking for food and water. They are non-offensive and only attack when actively hunting for food. Flumphs prefer the darkness of the underground and are rarely, if ever, encountered above ground.

A flumph that hits an opponent with its spikes injects acid into the wound, dealing 1d4 points of damage. The acid damage continues for the next 2d4 rounds. Immersion in running water or a *cure light wounds* spell stops the acid damage. A flumph's nauseating spray is a 20-foot line that it can fire twice per day. A creature hit by this poison must make a saving throw or be sickened for 5 rounds. The odor from this spray lingers in the area (and on any creature hit) for 1d4 hours and can be detected to a range of 100 feet. Creatures that come within 100 feet of an affected area or creature during this time must succeed on a saving throw themselves or become sickened for 5 rounds.

A flumph is helpless if turned over (requires a successful grapple attack).

Get Flumphed

The Temple of Transcendentant Wisdom occupies a great square clad in white stone in the middle of a great capital city. The temple is inhabited by 4d4 flumphs, the keepers of the pit of wisdom. The flumphs are lawful and very wise, but can only communicate with those who can contact their minds telepathically.

The pit is rumored to hold all sort of great treasures and secrets, but in truth is nothing more than a 200 foot deep well that, in its lower portions, connects with several tunnels into the underworld. One who is wise enough to communicate with the flumphs, who spend their days floating about the temple eating delicate viands from silver platters held by temple maidens, they will happily tell them everything they wish to know, provided they are polite and behave themselves.

Credit
The Flumph originally appeared in the First Edition *Fiend Folio* (© TSR/Wizards of the Coast, 1981) and is used by permission.

Copyright Notice
Author Scott Greene, based on original material by Ian McDowell and Douglas Naismith.

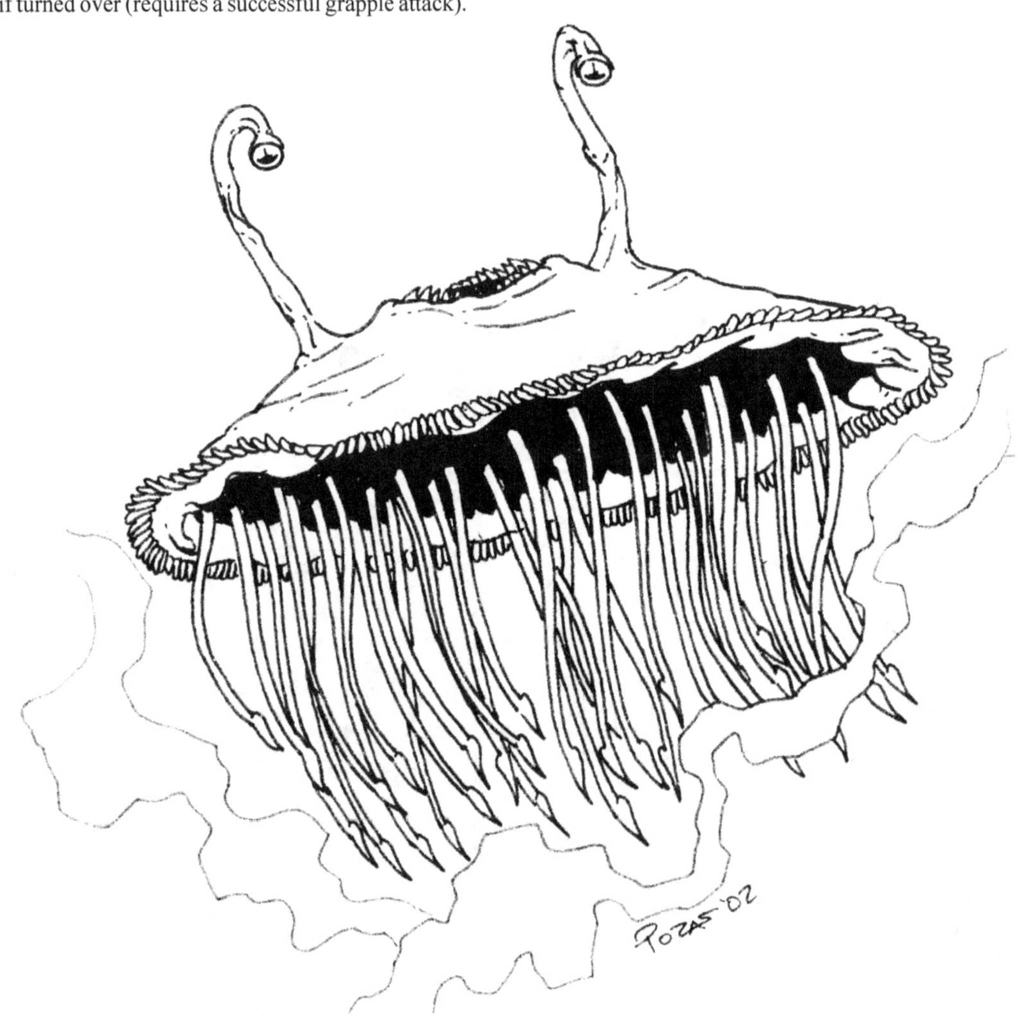

Fly, Giant

Hit Dice: 3
Armor Class: 5 [14]
Attack: Bite (1d6)
Saving Throw: 14
Special: None
Move: 12/24 (flying)
Alignment: Neutrality
Challenge Level/XP: 4/120

Giant flies are larger relatives of normal flies. Like their lesser cousins, they are most often found in areas of garbage, litter, and refuse. A giant fly resembles a normal fly and can grow to a length of 12 feet, though most average about 6 feet long.

You Are What You Eat

A swarm of 1d6+5 giant flies buzzes over the decapitated head of a titan. The head appears to have rolled into its present position in a gully from atop a craggy hillock, though what did the deed is unknown. The flies have planted their eggs in the head and are now digesting it bit by bit. The titan's ichor has made the flies especially aggressive, cunning and strong

(max hit points), and it has spread the titan's magical abilities among the giant flies.

Credit

The Giant Fly originally appeared in the First Edition *Monster Manual II* (© TSR/Wizards of the Coast, 1983) and is used by permission.

Copyright Notice

Author Scott Greene, based on original material by Gary Gygax.

Fogwarden

Hit Dice: 4
Armor Class: 4 [15]
Attack: Lightning bolt (3d6)
Saving Throw: 13
Special: Fear aura, lightning, animate dead, +1 or better weapon to hit, gaseous form, immunities (cold, electricity, poison), vulnerable to sunlight, surprise on 1-2 on 1d6
Move: 15 (flying)
Alignment: Chaos
Challenge Level/XP: 8/800

This creature resembles a humanoid formed of fog and mist. The only discernible facial feature is its icy blue eyes. It is sometimes called an ice apparition, for much like the standard apparition, the fogwarden feeds on the fear of its victims. The fogwarden, however, is not undead. A fogwarden is usually found inhabiting the coldest and most desolate areas of the world. The fog surrounding it flashes with its life force. These flashes are often mistaken for the will-o'-wisp. The fogwarden's natural is similar to the *gaseous form* spell, except that a fogwarden does not lose any abilities, can attack its foes, and has a fly speed of 15. A fogwarden radiates a 30-foot-radius fear aura. A creature in the area must succeed on a saving throw or be affected as though by a *fear* spell.

Electricity constantly plays across a fogwarden's form. A creature holding a metal object that contacts the fogwarden takes 3d6 points of electricity damage (save for half damage). Once every other round, a fogwarden can loose this electricity as a stroke of lightning in a 30-foot line (save for half damage). This electrical aura of the fogwarden can animate dead creatures within 20 feet as the *animate dead* spell. The animated creatures resemble zombies (and use their stats) and are under the control of the fogwarden that animated them. They are not truly undead however and cannot be turned. If the fogwarden is slain or moves more than 20 feet from a zombie, the animated creature collapses dead and cannot be animated again.

Fogwardens shun sunlight. A fogwarden exposed to sunlight can take only move or attack each round, and is destroyed utterly after 1 hour of exposure if it cannot escape.

Hard Water Vapor

In the still of a foggy night, a strange figure alights on a quay of a great mercantile city. The being looks like an amazonian woman formed of swirling mists and fog. As it makes its way into the city, people and animals flee and lightning flashes overhead. In a voice that howls like a hurricane, the creature will say repeatedly "I seek the cup of my lord, bring it to me."

The fog warden is heading for the home of a wealthy merchant prince, and as it draws closer it will become more destructive. Any men-at-arms who cross swords with the entity will likely die and be raised as a foot soldier in a growing army of the dead that attacks anything in reach, smashing weapons, cracking skulls, etc. The fog warden seeks a *bowl of water elemental command* taken from an island shrine by the aforementioned merchant prince, and it will not leave without the item.

If the item has passed into other hands, the fog warden does whatever it must to discover its new location and then proceed on its hunt, hiding in the daylight hours.

Credit

The Fogwarden originally appeared in the Second Edition *Monstrous Compendium Annual 4* (© TSR/Wizards of the Coast, 1997) and is used by permission.

Copyright Notice

Author Scott Greene, based on original material by Wizards of the Coast.

Foo Dog

Hit Dice: 7
Armor Class: 0 [19]
Attack: Bite (1d6)
Saving Throw: 9
Special: Strike chaotics, summon foo creatures, aura, etherealness, invisibility, plane shift, magic resistance (35%)
Move: 15
Alignment: Lawful
Challenge Level/XP: 9/1100

Foo dogs are extraplanar creatures that serve as guardians to those of the lawful alignment. They are rarely encountered on the Material Plane, but when they are, they are always in the employ of a lawful-aligned creature, acting as either a companion or guardian. A foo creature never associates with creatures of chaotic alignment. It tolerates those of neutral alignments.

This large dog has a slightly oversized head and large, bulbous eyes. Its paws end in sharp claws. Its fur is golden fading to crimson on the underside.

Foo dogs have a +2 bonus on to hit and damage rolls when fighting chaos-aligned creatures.

Once per day, by barking, a foo dog can summon 1d4 additional foo dogs with a 25% chance of success.

A foo dog is protected by an aura of goodness. A chaos-aligned creature that attacks a foo dog takes a –1 penalty on to hit and damage rolls.

A foo dog can become *invisible* and/or *ethereal* at will. A foo dog can enter the Astral Plane with up to six other creatures, provided they are all within 5 feet of the foo dog.

Tomb Guard Dogs

When the emperor died, his burial chambers had long ago been completed. The imperial corpse was placed in the center of many rings of chambers and tunnels dug into the bowels of a sacred mountain. There are five rings, to be precise, each more deadly than the last. The tunnels of these rings are studded with traps such as pits of mercury, barbed crossbows, pivoting stones, hollow stairs filled with green slime.

The inner chamber of the tomb is protected by two foo dogs, frozen into the form of fierce-looking statues, but released from this condition by the presence of intruders.

Within the tomb the body of the emperor lies encased in a jade coffin held aloft by four clay golems in the form of half-ogres in scale armor and holding halberds. The imperial treasury is kept in a lead chest sunk in a pool of mercury beneath the funeral slab. The chest holds a 1d4 x 1,000 sp, 1d12 x 1,000 gp, a terracotta lamp in the shape of a qilin (worth 1d3 x 100 gp), a lapis lazuli charm (worth 1d8 x 10 gp) and a belt of golden chains (worth 1d8 x 1,000 gp).

Credit

The Foo Creature originally appeared in the First Edition *Monster Manual II* (© TSR/Wizards of the Coast, 1983) and is used by permission.

15. Copyright Notice

Author Scott Greene, based on original material by Gary Gygax.

Forester's Bane (Snapper Saw)

Hit Dice: 5
Armor Class: 2 [17]
Attack: 6 stalks (1d6)
Saving Throw: 12
Special: Engulf
Move: 0
Alignment: Neutrality
Challenge Level/XP: 6/400

The forester's bane is a huge, immobile, and carnivorous shrub. Closer inspection reveals large, tough leaves radiating from its central stalk. These dark green leaves hide six purple serrated stalks inside its body. At the center of this low-growing shrub is a 3-foot diameter yellowish orb from which sprout many small green branches. Each branch has small, sweet smelling (and tasting) berries of various colors growing from it.

When a living creature moves near a forester's bane's leaves, it attempts to grab the creature. Trapped creatures are subjected to attacks by 1-6 serrated stalks that slash and cut until the opponent escapes. Trapped victims are attacked at a +2 bonus. The forester's bane releases a trapped victim when either it or the victim is dead, or the leaf holding the victim is destroyed. Because of its four leaves, it can grapple up to four different opponents at one time. Both leaves and stalks each have 10 hit points and can be attacked. Severing a leaf or stalk deals no damage to a forester's bane. Attacks that hit a leaf deal half their damage to the monster and half to the trapped victim. Destroyed leaves and stalks grow back in 2d4 weeks if the forester's bane is not killed.

Feed the Plants

In a narrow, wooded defile cut by a swiftly flowing brook, you see a struggling figure. The person wears a heavy, green cloak and appears to have its foot stuck in a trap of some sort that was hidden beneath a large shrub. The shrub is actually a forester's bane, and the struggling figure is an illusion created by the orc shaman that calls this place home.

The orc's burrow is located a few yards away from the illusion, the entrance flanked by a second forester's bane. Inside the burrow, the shaman has made a small, private lair for herself, hidden from the others of her tribe. She is a hideous creature with stringy white hair plastered on her flat head, only the suggestion of a nose and fierce, red eyes. She wears a cloak adorned by eagle feathers and bone ornaments pierce the loose folds of skin on her face and back.

The shaman can cast spells as a 3rd level cleric and 2nd level magic-user, and keeps a variety of odd ingredients, powders and tinctures in clay jars in her cave. Victims of the forester's banes are collected and stripped for parts - their flesh is eaten, their fat is boiled down to make ritual candles, their bones used to make tools and ornaments, etc. The berries from the plants are collected (carefully) and turned into a delicious jelly.

Credit

The Forester's Bane originally appeared in the First Edition module *S3 Expedition to the Barrier Peaks* (© TSR/Wizards of the Coast, 1980) and later in the First Edition *Monster Manual II* (© TSR/Wizards of the Coast, 1983) and is used by permission.

Copyright Notice

Author Scott Greene, based on original material by Gary Gygax.

Forgotten One

Hit Dice: 3
Armor Class: 3 [16]
Attacks: 1 weapon (1d3)
Saving Throw: 14
Special: Forgetful presence
Move: 3
Alignment: Neutrality
Challenge Level/XP: 3/60

A forgotten one is a foot-tall fey with pointed ears, slanted eyes, and long, nimble limbs. Most forgotten ones weave twigs and leaves into their hair for decoration and to help conceal themselves in the treetops. Three time per day, a forgotten one can cause any creature within 20 feet to forget meeting the fey (save resists).

The Brewer's Life

The mountain town of Alemint is renowned for its superb ales and frequent festivals. The Oberlyn family has a long history and a solid reputation as the town's premier brewer. An ill omen has recently settled over the town, causing the residences to contract a persistent stomach virus. Greed has overtaken Asleson Oberlyn, the eldest son and heir to the family business. Asleson has made a pact with a particularly mischievous forgotten one named Wizil Wixo. In exchange for all ale he and his companions can drink, Wizil Wixo uses his unique powers over memory to aid Asleson in his plan to rule the town. Under the forgotten one's ministrations, the senior Oberlyn and the town elders appear absentminded and make poor choices while Asleson always manages to say exactly the right thing. Asleson and Wizil Wixo bend the minds of others to achieve their goals. Wizil Wixo has a *ring of invisibility* and usually follows Asleson closely. Wizil Wixo has no allegiance to Asleson and departs if bored, discovered or at an opportune time in order to cause the most chaos.

Asleson has recently sublet a huge portion of farmland to a mysterious "druid" who promises to increase the quality and quantity of the family's barley crop.

*(See the **gargoyle, fungus** entry for more on this encounter.)*

Copyright Notice
Author Erica Balsley.

Forlarren

Hit Dice: 3
Armor Class: 2 [17]
Attack: 2 strikes (1d4)
Saving Throw: 14
Special: Heat metal
Move: 12
Alignment: Chaos
Challenge Level/XP: 4/120

The powers of a nymph are such that she can enchant and seduce nearly any creature that has the capacity to know beauty. Some say that even the great and terrible daemons are not immune to a nypmh's charms. The forlarren, they say, is the proof. The forlarren is a lonely creature that feels cursed by its own existence. They look like hairless satyrs, a small ruff of dark hair covering the back of its head, small horns protruding above its eyes and a twisted, leering visage upon its face. They detest themselves and everything they see, consumed by hatred of life itself. Such is their rage that they seek to vent their ire on law and chaos alike. Forlarrens speak their own language and some actually speak the common tongue or the language of nymphs and dryads.

The forlarren attacks with its fists, using them to pummel an opponent. It focuses on a single opponent in combat and attacks until it or its opponent is slain. If a forlarren succeeds in killing an opponent, the kindly traits of its fey mother surface and it shows profound remorse. It ceases combat, if possible, or flees if other opponents insist on continuing the fight. Should its opponents allow combat to end, the forlarren may offer its solace to the surviving companions amid wails and sobs. After a few days, however, the dominant evil nature of its fiendish father resurfaces and the forlarren once more attacks all creatures on sight—including those it had previously befriended.

Once per day, by making a melee touch attack, a forlarren can heat metal (as the druid spell). Once the affected metal reaches the searing stage, it remains at that stage until the forlarren breaks contact with the affected metal. Once contact is broken, the metal slowly returns to its normal temperature (reducing the effects each round just as the *heat metal* spell).

The Ugly Forlarren

Traveling through the woodlands you come across a massive limestone sarcophagus partially buried in the soil and overgrown with shrubs and shadowed by two large oak trees. A hideous little forlarren is sitting on the sarcophagus, a scowl on his face.

As soon as adventurers come into sight, the unpleasant little man will leap up and charge at the most heavily armored person in the group. Should the forlarren succeed in killing its victim, it flees into the woodlands weeping. Some time after, it finds the adventurers again and throws itself at their mercy for its dark deed. The forlarren tells them of the wonders hidden beneath the sarcophagus, a great, abandoned fortress of the ancient wood giants, littered with their relics and now inhabited by the terrible beasts that bubbled up from the depths and destroyed them. The halls are still haunted by the unquiet spirits of some of those giants, and it is said that their thane still sits on his ornate wooden throne, his magic axe clutched in his cold, dead hands.

Of course, once the forlarren has the party in the depths of the dungeon, his chaotic personality again takes over and sends him creeping away in the night to shut them in the lightless confines of the dungeon.

Credit

The Forlarren originally appeared in the First Edition *Fiend Folio* (© TSR/Wizards of the Coast, 1981) and is used by permission.

Copyright Notice

Author Scott Greene, based on original material by Ian Livingstone.

Frog, Giant Abyssal Dire

Hit Dice: 6
Armor Class: 2 [17]
Attack: Tongue (grapple), bite (2d6)
Saving Throw: 11
Special: Leap, smite law, swallow whole, +1 or better weapon to hit, magic resistance (10%) resistance to cold and fire (50%)
Move: 12/15 (swimming)
Alignment: Chaos
Challenge Level/XP: 9/1100

Abyssal dire frogs come from the Plane of Slime and are wholly chaotic. They have a demonic aspect to them, with a spiny and usually poisonous hide of blackish-green. Their red eyes flicker with demonic intelligence. They speak the language of demons. Abyssal dire frogs are about 12 feet long. Once per day, an abyssal dire frog can make a normal attack against a lawful foe to deal additional damage equal to the frog's total Hit Dice.

An Abyssal Dire Frog's tongue can be attacked. Damage dealt to the tongue is not dealt to the frog itself. If successful, the frog does not attempt a tongue attack against that opponent for the remaindof the combat. An Abyssal Dire frog's tongue has an AC of 4[15]

(See the Frog entry in the Animals Appendix for example encounter.)

Credit

The Giant Abyssal Dire Frog made its d20 debut in the Necromancer Games module *D1 Tomb of Abysthor*.

Copyright Notice

Authors Scott Greene and Clark Peterson, based on original material by Gary Gygax.

Froghemoth

Hit Dice: 16
Armor Class: 3 [16]
Attack: 4 tentacles (1d6), tongue (1d6), bite (4d6)
Saving Throw: 3
Special: Swallow, resistance to fire (50%), slowed by electricity, surprise on roll of 1-2 on 1d6
Move: 9/12 (swimming)
Alignment: Neutrality
Challenge Level/XP: 18/3800

This gigantic creature resembles a giant frog with 4 large tentacles in place of its front legs. A single eyestalk juts from the top of its head. Its underbelly is yellow, its body is green, and its tentacles and legs are mottled green. The froghemoth is a weird aberration that swells in marshes and swamps. Its tongue is 10 feet long and it uses it to capture its prey. The froghemoth is a carnivore and feeds on various swamp-dwellers.

The victim of a froghemoth's tentacle attacks must pass a saving throw or be held fast and pulled to the mouth for a bite attack. Victims of a bite attack must likewise pass a saving throw or be swallowed whole. Once inside the beast's belly, a creature suffers 3d8 points of damage per round. A swallowed creature can attempt climb to climb into the beast's mouth, where it must make a successful open doors roll to escape. A swallowed creature can also cut its way out using a dagger to deal 20 points of damage to the froghemoth's stomach (AC 6 [13]). A froghemoth's stomach can hold 1 human or elf or 2 dwarves or halflings.

The froghemoth takes no damage from electricity, but is instead *slowed* for one round (per the reverse of the *haste* spell).

Paladins are Tasty

In a dank bayou, a froghemoth guards a holy sword. The sword lies at the bottom of a pool of cloudy water, obscured further by thick vines and muck. The pool is the lair of the froghemoth. Large, black willows overhang the pool, their branches home to venomous serpents and a species of black squirrels with skull faces and eyes that emit a yellow, sulferous gas that causes those who breath it in to (if they fail a saving throw) fall into a fitful sleep beset by nightmares. About two dozen bodies, all belonging to paladins who sought the holy sword, are scattered about the shallows surrounding the pool.

Credit

The Froghemoth originally appeared in the First Edition module *S3 Expedition to the Barrier Peaks* (© TSR/Wizards of the Coast, 1980) and later in the First Edition *Monster Manual II* (© TSR/Wizards of the Coast, 1983) and is used by permission.

Copyright Notice

Author Scott Greene, based on original material by Gary Gygax.

Frost Man

Hit Dice: 4
Armor Class: 4 [15]
Attack: Weapon (1d8)
Saving Throw: 13
Special: Ice blast, immunity to cold, double damage from fire
Move: 12
Alignment: Chaos
Challenge Level/XP: 6/400

Frost men are hunters that make their home in the cold regions of the world. They appear to be brutish humans dressed in animal skins and furs and wearing a patch over one eye. Each carries his personal belongings in small sacks and takes them wherever he goes. A frost man's body radiates cold out to 30 feet, though not enough to deal damage. Frost men are only ever encountered as lone males. Perhaps there are villages somewhere with women and children, perhaps frost men are spawned from the freezing waste itself. Tribes that are aware of frost men fear them greatly for their deadly talent and refer to them as "ice demons. Frost men speak their own language and the common tongue. Three times per day, a frost man can release a blast of freezing mist in a 30-foot cone from the eye underneath its eye patch. A creature in the area takes 3d6 points of cold damage (saving throw for half).

The Ice Man Falleth

While traveling across the frozen landscape, you hear a terrible crack, as though the very earth was split asunder. Later that day, you come across a crevasse in the ice, about 5 feet wide and many miles long. The crevasse is about 20 feet deep, and one might come across a human figure at the bottom of the crevasse, chipping away at ice with an obsidian bladed knife. Apparently, the man's foot became stuck in the ice when he fell (he suffered normal falling damage). The man is dressed in furs and looks something like a neanderthal, only a bit taller and with a less pronounced jaw and forehead.

Should the party stop to rescue him, they will find him difficult to communicate with - he apparently does not speak common. The man has ruddy skin and a thick, curly black beard. Although one eye is covered by a leather patch, the other is sapphire blue. A leather bag seems to hold his possessions. Once out of the crevasse, the man might be persuaded to guide the party elsewhere if offered something he desires. More likely, he will guide them into a trap, use his frost power against them or in some other way seek to profit from their demise.

There is also the possibility that he guides them back to his village - a treacherous hike of seven miles into a maze of ice tunnels guarded by polar bears that hiding dozens of small burrows inhabited by the statuesque frost men and their families.

Credit

The Frost Man originally appeared in the First Edition *Fiend Folio* (© TSR/Wizards of the Coast, 1981) and is used by permission.

Copyright Notice

Author Scott Greene, based on original material by Julian Lawrence.

Fulgurate Mushrooms

Hit Dice: 1
Armor Class: 9 [10]
Attacks: lightning blast (2d6)
Saving Throw: 17
Special: lightning blast
Move: 0
Alignment: Neutrality
Challenge Level/XP: 2/30

Fulgurate mushrooms appear as normal mushrooms with faint blue stems and either bluish-white caps or sapphire blue caps. A typical patch covers a 10-foot area. When touched, the mushrooms send out a burst of lightning that deals 2d6 points of damage (save for half) to any creature within 10 feet of the patch. Fulgurate mushrooms are instantly destroyed when they release their lightning blast.

Lair of the Fungus Druid

The Fungus Druid Angus Sallow, or at least what's left of him, lives in an underground greenhouse called the Mushroom Grotto. The complex has a central circular chamber and six 50-foot-long spokes radiating outward into the damp earth. A central pool of clear water is filled with clinging vines of ivy and wet, spongy plants. Moss and mushrooms grow in solitude in the side halls. Each hall is lit by the soft blue glow of

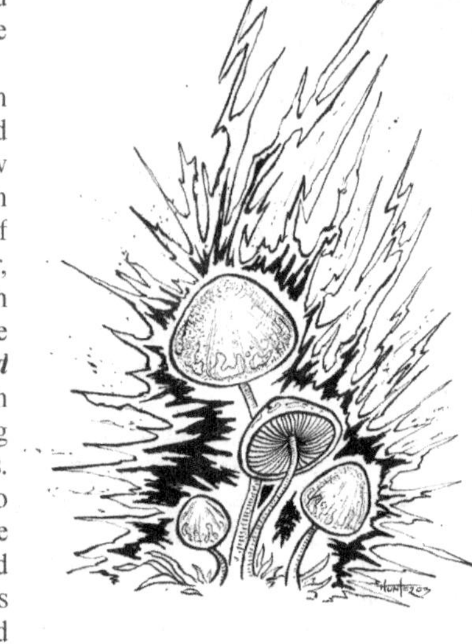

phosphorescent lichens that grow along the walls and across the ceiling in a cascade of color.

Planting boxes contain draping streamers of wild azalea dappled with yellow moss. At the entry of each dead-end tunnel is a row of small planters set on the floor, each containing a small patch of fulgurate mushrooms. The Fungus Druid (*see the **Fungoid** entry*) can safely walk through these boxes without triggering their explosive properties. Anyone else won't be so lucky. The repercussion of the blasts alerts the Fungus Druid to intruders, and summons his companion, a moss-covered shambling mound that rises out of the central pool.

Copyright Notice

Fungoid

Hit Dice: 5
Armor Class: 5 [14]
Attacks: 2 slams (1d8)
Saving Throw: 12
Special: Resists electricity, immune to charm
Move: 6
Alignment: Neutrality
Challenge Level/XP: 5/240

A fungoid resembles a 6-foot-tall, stocky and powerful humanoid formed of mushroom flesh. Coloration varies from brownish-green or brown to dark green mottled with brown splotches. It weighs about 300 pounds. A fungoid's facial features are discernible, but rough. Its arms end in powerful hands. Fungoids rush into combat swinging their powerful fists. They take half damage from electricity and are immune to charms.

A Fungi to Be With

In a nook just off his garden greenhouse (*see the **Fulgurate Mushroom** entry*), the Fungus Druid Angus Sallow rests in a bower of damp earth. After years of growing exotic plants, Angus' body is covered by the fungi he prefers. More mushroom now than man, Angus is now a fungoid, a mushroom behemoth with a limited intelligence whose sole intent is to protect his garden and the species of plants it contains.

The Fungus Druid sleeps in a three-foot-tall mound of wet earth and fertilizer bounded by oaken sideboards. Mushrooms poke through this dirt layer, their caps tilted to the blue phosphorescent light of glowing lichens lining the walls. Angus rises out of the dirt pile if anyone bothers his plants or mushrooms. Fulgurate mushrooms grow on the Fungus Druid's broad back, so that any PC striking Angus has a 2 in 6 chance of setting off a concussive blast of lightning. Angus' companion, a shambling mound, rests in a pool of clear water nearby. Angus calls on the shambling mound once he rises out of his earthen bower.

Buried in the rich loam is a *+1 mace* carved like a blooming rose, a sealed tube containing a scroll with *plant growth* written on it, and six flower-shaped garnets (50 gp each).

Copyright Notice

Fye

Hit Dice: 5
Armor Class: 4 [15]
Attacks: Incorporeal touch (1d6 + possession)
Saving Throw: 12
Special: Aura of despair, possession, magical abilities
Move: 24 (flying)
Alignment: Neutrality
Challenge Level/XP: 7/600

A fye resembles a translucent humanoid whose face is contorted and twisted as if frozen in an eternal scream. The fye is about 6 feet tall, and its lower torso tapers off around the knees into vaporous nothingness. Its face always has the appearance that the creature is screaming or howling though it never utters any sound. A fye continually emanates an aura of despair in a 10-foot radius that causes creatures to suffer a -2 penalty on attacks and saves (save resists). Once per round, a fye can attempt to possess an opponent with a successful touch attack (as per the *magic jar* spell, except it doesn't require a receptacle). At will, a fye can cast *ESP*; three times per day it can cast *cause fear*; and once per day it can cast *feeblemind*.

Cold at Heart

A granite statue of a nondescript woman stands among a dozen corpses. A glimmering heart-shaped amethyst adorns her bare chest, the gem bathing the room in soft purplish light. The dead in the room appear to have died from self-inflicted wounds. Most tore out their eyes while others carved into their chests with their own daggers. The corpses are a mixture of humans and goblin-kind. All of the deceased face the statue, kneeling in a semicircle in front of it.

An epitaph is inscribed in the stone floor at the statue's base. It reads: "Faen Tiensa: Heart weeps, age befall old, Tears become red. Life with no reason grows cold. Love gone, dead." This is the tomb of Faen Tiensa, the beloved wife of Glaeran the Faithful. Glaeran was a high priest who had more devotion to his spouse than his own deity. The deity cursed Glaeran to an existence as a fye tied to this monument to his wife. The heart-shaped amethyst serves as an anchor for the fye's eternal existence. Once destroyed, the fye's spirit is set free.

Copyright Notice
Author Scott Greene.

Fyr

Hit Dice: 2
Armor Class: 7 [12]
Attacks: head butt (1d4+1) or 1 weapon (1d6+1)
Saving Throw: 16
Special: Spell-like abilities
Move: 6
Alignment: Neutrality
Challenge Level/XP: 3/60

A fyr is a 3-foot tall, goat-headed humanoid with large slightly-backward-curved horns, goat-like legs, a small bushy tail, and a human torso. Its entire body, except its arms and hands, is covered in thick brown fur. Fyrs often adorn their body with rings, necklaces, bracelets, earrings, and other such trinkets. A fyr attacks by butting with its horns, but some use weapons. A fyr can use various spell-like abilities: at will—*speak with animals*; 4/day—*charm monster*; 3/day—*warp wood*; 1/day—*plant doorway*.

Nothing to Fear

The delicate chimes of elaborate spiraling wind chimes fill the air with a trilling melody. Nearly 30 fantastic creations hang from the limbs of a willow tree near the dirt path. Sitting in the middle of a blanket spread under the tree is a fierce-looking fyr. Anghus has large horns wrapped in spiraling bands of silver and platinum. Spread on the carpet are dozens of finely crafted rings, jewelry boxes, pendants, broaches, scroll tubes and necklaces. A small sign supported by a stick in the ground says "For Sale."

Anghus sells hand-crafted jewelry. Every piece sparkles a dazzling hue of colors when held up to the light. The jewels are incredibly cheap, despite their incredible beauty.

The fyr was cursed nearly a year ago by Egrella Grul, a vile annis, so that every piece of jewelry he sells brings bad luck to the buyer. The rings draw all spells cast (by friend or foe) toward the wearer. The broaches choke the life from the wearer while he sleeps. The scroll tubes fill with blood every morning, ruining anything kept within. The Game Referee is free to make up any other curses to inflict on PCs buying the fyr's wares.

The only way to stop the curse is to drop the cursed items into the muddy waters of the Sin Mire Swamp. The fyr knows of the bad luck following his items, but hopes to one day find someone to face the wicked hag, who makes her home in a gigantic rotten tree.

Copyright Notice

Gallows Tree

Hit Dice: 12
Armor Class: 0 [19]
Attacks: 6 slams (2d6)
Saving Throw: 3
Special: Create gallows tree zombies, grab, +1 magic weapons to hit, resists fire
Move: 6
Alignment: Neutrality
Challenge Level/XP: 15/2,900

A gallows tree is a 20-foot-tall tree with 6 or more humanoids hanging from its branches, each tightly secured by their necks with greenish-brown ropes. The gallows tree's canopy is thick and bushy, and its trunk is formed of leathery bark, mottled brown. Gallows trees sustain themselves on the internal organs and body fluids of living creatures. Gallows trees lower zombies to the ground when prey comes within 100 feet of the tree. Foes that get within 15 feet are struck by the tree's sharp branches. If two or more branches hit the same opponent, he is held and takes 2d6 points of damage automatically each round as the tree pummels him. The tree slices open victims for their organs, then fills them with a greenish sap that turns them into gallows tree zombies. The newly created undead rises in 1d4 days. A typical gallows tree has 6-11 gallows tree zombies hanging from it at any given time.

Gallows Tree Zombie

Hit Dice: 4
Armor Class: 5 [14]
Attacks: 2 slams (1d6)
Saving Throw: 13
Special: Spore cloud, tether-vine, regenerate 2 hp/round
Move: 9
Alignment: Neutrality
Challenge Level/XP: 5/240

Gallows tree zombies are humanoid creatures with deathly gray-green skin that feels coarse and rough to the touch. Their clothes are tattered and torn, and some still wear the armor they wore in life (though it is now rusted, dented, or damaged). Many have small plants, weeds, or fungi growing on or from their bodies. A long, sinewy cord of greenish-brown wraps around the zombie's throat and connects it to a gallows tree. Gallows tree zombies hang motionless from the tree that created them, being lowered to the ground only when a living creature comes within 100 feet of the gallows tree they are connected to. Once every 1d4 rounds but no more than 3 times per day, a gallows tree zombie can breathe a cloud of poisonous spores. Anyone caught in the spore cloud must make a save or be slowed (as per the *slow* spell). Gallows trees zombies regenerate 2 hit points per round as long as they remain connected to their tree by their tether-vine. The vine allows the zombie to move up to 100 feet away from the tree.

The Tree Cult

A thick fog rolls through the dense forest, obscuring the vines and thorny underbrush. The thick canopy overhead blocks the morning sun, the interlocking branches forming a natural ceiling.

A massive tree stands in the middle of a small clearing, its heavy branches arching outward to intermingle with the elms and oaks surrounding it. The thick foliage weeps with dripping condensation. Thick strands of green vines hang from the branches, each nearly touching the ground.

Swaying rhythmically beneath the gnarled and twisted tree are five robed human figures standing in a circle around a goat-like being perched atop a wood-and-bark altar. A curtain of vines surrounds the worshippers. The five humans bow deeply to the goat-like being, then raise their hands high above their heads. The satyr capers on the altar. The scene is eerily silent.

The massive tree is a gallows tree, while the five figures and the satyr are gallows tree zombies suspended by vines and manipulated like puppets to lure strangers closer to the tree's base. The altar is a natural formation of roots and rocks.

The gallows tree attacks with vines as it unleashes the robed zombies. It also holds two more zombies in the branches overhead and drops them down among opponents once it attacks.

Copyright Notice
Author Scott Greene.

Gambado

Hit Dice: 4
Armor Class: 5 [14]
Attack: Bite (1d8), 2 claws (1d4)
Saving Throw: 13
Special: Surprise on roll of 1-3 on 1d6
Move: 15
Alignment: Neutrality (chaotic tendencies)
Challenge Level/XP: 4/120

A gambado makes its lair in a 6-foot deep pit. It hides its body with rocks, leaves and anything else in the surrounding area, allowing only its head to be seen. Beneath the leaves, the gambado is a human-sized creature with a cylindrical torso. Two long arms ending in razor-sharp claws protrude from the body. Its torso ends in three long, single-toed feet. Its body is gray in color and leathery and can be compressed like a spring. This is its primary means of locomotion. By compressing its body, the gambado can spring up or forward.

Gambado are solitary creatures by nature, and on the rare occasion that more than one is encountered, each will have its own lair and pit from which it attacks. The pits are usually close together to maximize their attacks on creatures within the area. Any treasure collected by a gambado is stored on its pit floor or in a small and well-hidden hole in the side of its pit. It is unknown whether gambados can communicate or speak any languages.

Halfling Mysticism

You come across a plain of heliotropes studded with dozens of large stone heads, representation of obscure gods and goddesses. Atop each head there is a halfling mystic in a state of deep meditation, naked save for a loinclout. The area is inhabited by 1d4+1 gambado dwelling in their pits, the pits covered by woven grasses and flowers. The gambado prey on visitors to the halfling mystics, who pay no attention to the plight of the pilgrims.

Each halfling owns a single jewel worth 500 gp that it hides beneath its sculpted seat. With these jewels, each halfling can grant a single wish made on behalf of another. Upon granting such a wish, the jewel disappears in a great flash of light and the halfling is reduced to a pile of ashes, a ravenous gambado left in its place. Violence directed against a halfling results in its stone head rising from the ground to attack as a stone guardian (q.v.). These stone guardians are finely sculpted, but are far more powerful than they initially appear.

Credit

The Gambado originally appeared in the First Edition *Fiend Folio* (© TSR/Wizards of the Coast, 1981) and is used by permission.

Copyright Notice

Author Scott Greene, based on original material by Simon Shaw.

GARGOYLES

Several different varieties of gargoyles exist, and each is detailed below. For all their differences, they do share some common traits. They prefer to remain still and then suddenly attack or dive into their prey. Green guardians attempt to hold their victims and then fly off with them. A group of margoyles and/or gargoyles works in unison to bring down their opponents.

Gargoyle, Four-Armed

Hit Dice: 4+1
Armor Class: 3 [16]
Attack: 4 claws (1d4), bite (1d6), gore (1d6)
Saving Throw: 13
Special: +1 or better weapon to hit, freeze
Move: 15/24 (flying)
Alignment: Chaos
CL/XP: 6/400

Four-armed gargoyles have a great fondness for inflicting pain on their foes. When a four-armed gargoyle has the upper hand in battle, it often draws out the conflict as long as it can in order to deal as much pain and suffering as it can on its foes.

Forewarned is Fore-Armed

To the sound of a beating drum, a pleasure galley traverses a narrow straight, the walls of which are covered in friezes of elegant gentlemen and ladies dancing a minuet. The galley is defended by 10 archers (chainmail, longbow, short sword) and 20 ballestieri (leather armor, sling, short sword) and carries a noble wedding party. The party consists of a baronet and his fiance, the daughter

of a duke, as well as eight knights and dames and a multitude of servants.

Lurking atop the cliff is a wicked count who desires the lady for himself. To obtain her, he has summoned forth a wing of 1d12+4 four-armed gargoyles using a magical gong. The gong is made of a strange black metal that absorbs light and sound, but when struck sends vibrations through the aether and summons forth all monsters within 1 mile. The four-armed gargoyles usually dwell on the ledges of the massive frieze, appearing to be grotesque demons flitting over the heads of the dancers.

The gargoyles are to slay the baronet, seize the lady and bring her to the count, who has a fast horse tied to a scraggly apple tree. Unfortunately, the gargoyles are not under the command of the count and are apt to do as they will.

Gargoyle, Fungus

Hit Dice: 5
Armor Class: 4 [15]
Attacks: 2 claws (1d6)
Special: fungus breath, stench
Move: 14/18 (flying)
Saving Throw: 12
Alignment: Neutrality
Challenge Level/XP: 3/60

A fungus gargoyle stands about 6 feet tall and weighs up to 200 pounds and looks like it is carved from molds, fungi and mushrooms. Every 1d4 rounds, a fungus gargoyles can breathe a 30-foot cone of fungus particles that causes 1d6 points of damage to any opponent who inhales the substance (a successful saving throw keeps the fungi particles from taking root in the windpipe). A fungus gargoyle also exudes a horrible stench in a 10-foot-wide cloud around it that causes those who get too near it to spend the next round retching if they fail a saving throw.

Ergot Egotism

On the outskirts of the town of Alemint lies a prosperous barley farm with an exceedingly tall and abundant crop. The giant fields of barley stand taller than a man and conceal the farm. A narrow road leads through the fields to the farmhouse and barns. A druid has sublet the farm from the Oberlyn family. The "druid" Rhawtin Omphalotus is actually a cleric (8th level) of the Cult of Rachiss (a demigod of parasites). Rhawtin seeks to bring about the downfall of civilization through the spread of parasites, leeching fungi and virulent plagues. Rhawtin (following the teachings of Rachiss) wants nature to reclaim modern cultures through malicious activities and biological acts of terrorism.

Rhawtin and his gang of 6 infected gargoyles spread a fungal pestilence throughout the barley crops that makes the ale and other brews mildly toxic. In addition to fungus gargoyles, Rhawtin has planted several guards such as gas spores, shriekers and violet fungi around the barley field. He carries a magical egg that creates swarms of giant mosquitoes when it is broken.

Gargoyle, Green Guardian

Hit Dice: 4+1
Armor Class: 3 [16]
Attack: 2 claws (1d4), bite (1d6), gore (1d6)
Saving Throw: 13
Special: +1 or better weapon to hit, freeze, hold, reanimation
Move: 15/24 (flying)
Alignment: Chaos
CL/XP: 8/800

Green guardian gargoyles are carved of a strange green stone and have two eyes of jet (500 gp each). The eyes radiate magic and evil if detected. If a green guardian gargoyle hits an opponent with both claw attacks, that opponent must succeed on a saving throw or be *held* for 4 rounds as if by a *hold person* spell. Unlike the *hold person* spell, a held creature does not receive a new save each round to break the effects. A green guardian gargoyle that has been killed reanimates in 1d8+2 days at full strength unless its eye gems are crushed and disenchanted with both *dispel magic* and *remove curse*.

Gargoyle, Margoyle

Hit Dice: 6+1
Armor Class: 1 [18]
Attack: 2 claws (1d6), bite (1d6), gore (1d6)
Saving Throw: 11
Special: +1 or better weapon to hit, freeze
Move: 15/24 (flying)
Alignment: Chaos
CL/XP: 8/800

A margoyle is a slightly larger version of the standard gargoyle. It is meaner, more wicked, and deadlier than its smaller kin. Margoyles are most often encountered in subterranean regions and often have a pack of gargoyles with them. In such cases, the margoyle is looked upon as the master or leader of the group.

The Wizard of Babble's Safe Haven

You come across a strange, subterranean vault entered via one of three barred doors. In the middle of the room, which is furnished with Persian-style rugs, pillows of damask silk stuffed with goose down and a small, ebony table upon which rests an ornate hookah worth 1,200 gp.

Sitting before the hookah is a grinning skeleton, smoke curling up through its eye sockets. The skeleton is wearing silk robes and a tall turban of amethyst satin adorned with peacock feathers. On the skeleton's finger is a copper ring engraved with the word "Srijkaunsh", which magic-users might recognize as the name of a celebrated wizard famous for a lost spell that caused people to speak gibberish (actually the reverse of a *tongues* spell).

Gods of the Pillars

The main square of the little village by the oasis is dominated by a tall pillar topped by a sculpture of a ram-headed man. The pillar is composed of granite and clad in brass, and bathes the square in golden light while the sun shines. The sculpture is composed of malachite and has two eyes of jet worth 500 gp each. The pillar rises 20 feet above ground level, but is actually set in a 20-foot deep well filled with cool water. The well is 7 feet in diameter, the pillar 3 feet in diameter.

A trio of priests, their heads shaved, their faces painted black, armed with scourges and wicker urns, harrangue the crowds that move through the square, demanding offerings of food for themselves and riches for the god of the pillar, lest he descend and destroy them. Adventurers might be tempted to ignore the obnoxious priests, who apparently have no magical powers and are too cowardly to put up any kind of fight. If they do, they are visited that night by the green guardian gargoyle who stands atop the pillar. Should it succeed in gaining its revenge, their heads decorate the edge of the well the next day.

The walls of the vault are sculpted in the form of eight ugly, horned, winged demons standing on the backs of elephants and apparently holding up the ceiling. The sculptures are gargoyles - specifically, two margoyles and six gargoyles. The skeleton is animated, but only to draw people into the chamber, not to fight. Should people sit down next to the skeleton, it holds out a copper bowl. An offering of a gemstone is taken in the skeleton's fingers and held aloft, at which point a monkey wriggles through the bars of one of the exits, takes the stone, and capers away.

The offering placates the gargoyles and make the room a safe haven for the adventurers for the remainder of the day. At midnight, however, they are ushered out of the room by a stinging wind (save or suffer 1d4 points of damage per round).

Credit

The Four-Armed Gargoyle first appeared in the First Edition module *S1 Tomb of Horrors* (© TSR/Wizards of the Coast, 1978) and is used by permission.
The Fungus Gargoyle originally appeared in the First Edition *Fiend Folio* (© TSR/Wizards of the Coast, 1981) and is used by permission.
Green Guardian Gargoyles can be found in the Necromancer Games module *Rappan Athuk 1: The Upper Levels* (©2000 Bill Webb and Clark Peterson, Necromancer Games, Inc.).
The Margoyle originally appeared in the First Edition module *S4 Lost Caverns of Tsojcanth* (© TSR/Wizards of the Coast, 1982) and later in the First Edition *Monster Manual II* (© TSR/Wizards of the Coast, 1983) and is used by permission. It was called the "Marlgoyle" in S4 (note the extra "l").

Copyright Notice

Authors Scott Greene and Clark Peterson, based on original material by Gary Gygax.

Gas Spore

From a distance greater than 10 feet, the gas spore is likely to be mistaken for a beholder (1 in 6 chance to notice the difference). T The gas spore has a fly speed of 10 feet with average maneuverability.

When a gas spore contacts a living creature (or a living creature touches a gas spore unarmed or with natural attacks), it injects poisonous rhizomes into the foe if that opponent fails a saving throw. Each day thereafter, an infected creature must succeed on a saving throw (-1 cumulative penalty per day) or take 1d6 points of damage. Damage continues until the victim dies or the rhizomes are destroyed. At 0 hit points, a victim dies and 2d4 gas spores emerge from its body. A *cure disease* spell cast on an affected creature before it dies destroys the rhizomes and prevents any further damage.

If a gas spore is struck for a single point of damage (by a weapon, natural attack, spell, or effect), it explodes in a violent blast of gas that dcals 6d6 points of damage to all creatures within a 30-foot radius. A successful saving throw reduces the damage by half.

Credit

The Gas Spore originally appeared in the First Edition *Monster Manual* (© TSR/Wizards of the Coast, 1977) and is used by permission.

Copyright Notice

Authors Scott Greene and Clark Peterson, based on original material by Gary Gygax.

Gas Attack

A large, circular cavern (100 feet in diameter) with a funnel-shaped floor serves as the breeding ground for almost 100 gas spores. The spores float through the room aimlessly, sewing their spores in the bodies of the dead creatures that are thrown into the cavern by the denizens of the dungeon.

Gelid Beetle, Greater

Hit Dice: 12
Armor Class: 2 [17]
Attacks: 1 bite (1d6 + 1d8 cold)
Saving Throw: 3
Special: Cold, cold cloud, immune to cold
Move: 12
Alignment: Neutrality
Challenge Level/XP: 13/2,300

Greater gelid beetles are larger, meaner versions of the standard gelid beetle. They are almost always hungry and are usually encountered while hunting. Gelid beetles bite opponents, delivering cold damage with each hit. Once per minute, a gelid beetle can emit a cloud of ice cold vapors in a 20-foot radius around its body that deals 2d6 cold damage (save for half) to creatures caught within it. The cloud lasts for 1d4+3 rounds.

Lesser Gelid Beetle

Hit Dice: 4
Armor Class: 5 [14]
Attacks: 1 bite (1d4 + 1d4 cold)
Saving Throw: 13
Special: Cold, cold spray, immune to cold
Move: 15
Alignment: Neutrality
Challenge Level/XP: 5/240

Gelid beetles appear as stark white beetles with silvery-black legs and dull silver mandibles. Some specimens have a mottled silver or black carapace and an even rarer species has dull crimson wing covers. Gelid beetles have two sets of eyes equally spaced on their heads dull silvery-black in color. Gelid beetles bite opponents, delivering cold damage with each hit. Once per day, a gelid beetle can release a spray in a 10-foot cone that deals 2d4 cold damage (save for half).

Icy Death

A large cave opens into the edge of the Wailing Glacier, the opening a dark hole that slopes down from the frozen landscape. The cave is the lair of Belthorin the Ice Bellower, a monstrous white dragon that has terrorized the land for nearly three decades. Giant icicles hang from the rocky opening, and the cave beyond descends at a steep 60-degree angle. The 100-foot-long slope is coated with a thick sheet of ice, so any PC climbing down may instead go rocketing into a large circular chamber filled with frozen stalactites. Belthorin lies coiled in the center of the chamber, the white dragon's body resting on a low ice ledge. The dragon's head faces the tunnel entry. Its eyes are closed.

Belthorin has been dead for six weeks now, hollowed out from the inside by a colony of gelid beetles that ate into the soft belly of the infirm dragon while it slept. Two greater gelid beetles guard a clutch of eggs inside the white dragon's innards, while 12 recently hatched lesser beetles climb about the dragon's ice lair. The young beetles attack with their cold spray, while the larger beetles use their cold cloud to freeze attackers.

Copyright Notice

Author Scott Greene.

Genie, Abasheen

Hit Dice: 8
Armor Class: 4 [15]
Attacks: 2 slams (1d10+1)
Saving Throw: 8
Special: Spell-like abilities, whirlwind
Move: 9/24 (flying)
Alignment: Neutrality
Challenge Level/XP: 10/1,400

An abasheen stands about 8 feet tall and is always dressed in flowing robes colored to denote their current station. Their skin is dark and their build powerful. All have dark hair, either black or brown, and most wear their hair braided or pulled into a ponytail, tied with ribbons of gold or silver. They are akin to genie nobility and act the part. Abasheens slam opponents with their powerful fists and employ their spell-like abilities in combat: at will—*charm person*; 1/day—*quest*. An abasheen can turn itself into a whirlwind much like an air elemental, sweeping away creatures with one or fewer hit dice (the diameter of the whirlwind is 20 ft.)

Sultan's Pleasure Palace

Sitting quietly on the grassy plain is a grand nomadic tent. The flamboyant yak-wool tent looks like it belongs to royalty. Two muscular eunuch guards (5th-level Fighters) stand beside an open door flap that leads into the massive tent. They wield large curved scimitars (same damage as two-handed swords) and wear polished plate armor. Their tongues have been cut out, so they communicate with stern gestures and guttural grunts. They allow visitors to enter the tent if shown proper respect and permission is asked. The pavilion belongs to an abasheen genie named Khilafah al Abbasid. The tent itself is a magical creation that has many more rooms inside than possible. In fact, the open flap leads into an extra-dimensional space. The interior is a maze of veils, tent walls, corridors and extravagant rooms. The tent walls are immovable and unforgiving.

The woolen tent's sides have the consistency of iron, although it feels soft and cloth-like. If torn or destroyed, the tent evaporates, leaving all occupants sitting on the desert sand. The tent's center pole is a plain ash pole that holds the tent together. Once destroyed, the tent dissipates and all occupants and prisoners are set free. While in the pocket dimension tent, time ceases. Inhabitants do not need to eat or sleep, although they can do so if they desire. They do not age or contract disease, although poisons still work. Khilafah al Abbasid, an abasheen genie, controls the tent and can gate it to other places and planes by grasping the main pole and stating his destination.

The great Khilafah al Abbasid has wandered the planes for millennia. Khilafah al Abbasid has a unique passion among djinn-kind: He collects living creatures, in particular only the most desirable females of various intelligent species. He considers his harem a collection only, and allows nothing to disgrace or harm his beloved possessions. While Khilafah al Abbasid has fed his obsession for ages, his extreme prejudice and stringent standards severely limit who he accepts into his harem. Currently, there are fewer than 30 harem girls within the tent prison. The harem slaves are well-read, literate in many languages and have fantastic artistic talents (such as dancing, painting and musical abilities). Prisoners for centuries, there is little else for them to do except learn new skills. They are bored and show great fascination with males of any species.

Many eunuch guards protect the tent the palace pavilion. These guards are replaced often as the temptations within the tent are great and punishment by Khilafah al Abbasid is severe. Khilafah al Abbasid slays any guard who displeases him or soiled members of his harem. Khilafah always needs quality guards, but the job has horrific requirements, the first requiring the men be – or become -- eunuchs. In addition to the harem and guards, Khilafah particularly enjoys the company of noblemen, scholars and others of the genie races. He takes great pride in his harem and enjoys showing the women off to well-mannered visitors.

Copyright Notice

Genie, Hawanar

Hit Dice: 11
Armor Class: 4 [17]
Attacks: 2 fists (1d8 + fire)
Special: Magical abilities, immune to fire, fiery cyclone
Move: 10/16 (flying)
Saving Throw: 3
Alignment: Neutrality
Challenge Level/XP: 15/2,900

Hawanar are 12-feet-tall genies whose lower torsos are shrouded in a cyclone of flame. A hawanar can create food and water as well as wooden and cloth objects. They can create metal objects (including coins), but all such magically created metals disappear in time. Hawanar can become *invisible* at will and can create realistic illusions that disappear when touched. Finally, a hawanar can turn into a flaming whirlwind that sweeps away creatures with one or fewer hit dice and deals 1d6 points of fire damage. (The diameter of the whirlwind is 10 feet.) Some hawanars can grant true wishes. A hawanar's attacks cause flammable materials to burst into flame.

The Torchbearer of Bad News

Merdle Grunny has been a lackey and torchbearer for nearly 60 years. Mistreated and underpaid by countless adventurers, he dislikes their kind and talks bitterly of being exploited. Forever down on his luck thanks to cheap alcohol and friendly companions, he was forced to take on ever more dangerous jobs in the hope of cashing in on the goodwill of generous treasure-seeking adventurers. Grunny carried torches and equipment into forgotten tombs, into catacombs filled with foul goblins and through primeval forests laden with fiends. He always ended up lugging out heavy burdens of plunder.

And what did he get for his efforts? A few meager coins that quickly vanished. Grunny always tells his drinking buddies how he's the only reason many expeditions came back at all. In truth, Grunny survived through dumb luck and by cowering behind adventurers. He didn't escape unscathed, though. Disfiguring scars mar his face and hands, and he has developed twitchy mannerisms that make him jump at the slightest noise.

His last haul was different, though: With his employers (mostly) dead in a sandy tomb, Grunny happened upon a jewel-encrusted brass torch. Looking to be the envy of his torchbearer colleagues, he pocketed the torch and fled the tomb, leaving his employers to their doom.

It was only after lighting the torch that he discovered its terrible power. The torch is the prison of a powerful hawanar genie named Anta' Falegha. Hateful and cruel, she serves the person holding the torch resentfully. Once lit, Anta' Falegha erupts from the torch in a swirling column of flame and destruction. Cunning and wise, Merdle Grunny has yet to request any wishes from the genie. After discovering the limited duration of the hawanar genie's created coin, he devised a scheme to obtain a more permanent source of wealth. Using his skills as a torchbearer and hired laborer, he accompanies adventurers and releases Anta' Falegha when they are fighting for their lives. He steals their treasures and leaves them to their fate.

Copyright Notice
Author Scott Greene.

Genie, Marid

Hit Dice: 11
Armor Class: 5 [14]
Attacks: 2 fists (1d8)
Special: Magical abilities, whirlpool
Move: 10/16 (swim)
Saving Throw: 3
Alignment: Neutrality
Challenge Level/XP: 13/2,300

A marid is a blue genie standing about 16 feet tall and weighing nearly 2,500 pounds. These powerful beings can transform into a maelstrom in water to carry creatures and objects away. This watery cyclone overturns small boats and sinks larger vessels in 1d4+4 rounds. Marids also can rise out of the ocean to attack ships, and will batter vessels to pieces within 1 hour if not prevented or distracted. A marid can turn invisible, *polymorph self*, *create water* and *control water* at will. Some marids can grant limited wishes.

Tides of war

Defying gravity, a castle made of water steadily floats atop the sea. The castle's surfaces remain stationary, but the sea that makes up the walls flows in abnormal patterns. The seawater flows up from the base of the outer wall to the very peaks and then turns inward to form the interior surfaces while dropping back into the depths. The walls act just like water, but characters attempting to pass through the liquid curtain find themselves violently tossed around and unable to control their direction or destination. Unfortunate marine life crowds the 10-foot-thick walls as the castle sucks them up through the outer walls, hurls them throughout the inner walls and violently plunges them back into the sea at the castle's center. Even more mysterious, the floor and stairs of the watery citadel remain eternally frozen and support weight. There are no doors or windows into the citadel. The castle is filled with plunder from the sea protected by guards such as sea giants and giant squids that reach through the walls, and sharks that leap from one wall to another through the middle of rooms.

This is the sea fortress of Majnoon al Kali, a powerful marid genie who has ambitions of ruling the oceans. Only Majnoon can control the slow and unstoppable movement of the castle (which can also submerge after trapping air in its internal rooms). The sea citadel collapses upon his death, sending all its continents into the ocean. Majnoon currently has his sights set on a merman city that lies off the coast near the city of Bargarsport.

Credit

The Marid originally appeared in the First Edition module *S4 Lost Caverns of Tsojcanth* (© TSR/Wizards of the Coast, 1982) and later in the First Edition *Monster Manual II* (© TSR/Wizards of the Coast, 1983) and is used by permission.

Copyright Notice

Author Scott Greene, based on original material by Gary Gygax.

Geon

Hit Dice: 8
Armor Class: 3 [16]
Attacks: 2 slams (2d8+2)
Saving Throw: 8
Special: Animate boulders, spell-like abilities, vulnerable to cold, immune to fire and electricity
Move: 6
Alignment: Neutrality
Challenge Level/XP: 9/1,100

A geon appears as a large, boulder-like creature, though similar in a way to xorn. They have two large legs and feet, which also act as hands, allowing the geon to manipulate items with them. Two large recesses on its surface function as eyes. A geon has a large, wide mouth. Geons animate boulders to attack its foes and create walls of stone to contain them. The geon can animate any rocks within 180 feet at will, and can control up to two rocks at a time. Boulders (Move 6) fight as geons in all respects. Geons can: 1/day--*move earth, passwall, transmute rock to mud, wall of stone*. Geons are vulnerable to cold and take one-and-a-half damage. They take half damage (or none if they save) from fire and electricity.

A Rolling Stone Gathers Moss

An extremely pungent moss called Sylvan's Beard grows near the top of the steep slopes of the Enta Hillside, just outside a low stone cave of battered rocks set into the dirt. The entire hillock is covered in fragrant wildflowers and tall weeds. Thirty-foot-long muddy strips are torn through the flora. Ten 10-foot-tall boulders walk up the hillside in shambling gaits on short, stubby legs, all slipping and sliding on the steep hillside.

A geon tasked with protecting the moss was thrown out of its home (literally) by a drunken cave giant. The geon cared little about the cave, but animated the many boulders in the area to follow it up the hill to help guard the moss. But every morning, the giant stumbles out of the cave and tosses the rocks back down the hill where they bounce and spin, taking out trees and tearing up the dirt.

The geon needs help running the giant out of its cave. The animated boulders aren't doing any good (and just provide the giant with ammunition to throw). The geon is extremely thankful if PCs help return it to its post, but not so happy if they try to take any of the moss it protects. *(See the* **Giant, Cave** *entry to continue this encounter.)*

Copyright Notice
Authors Scott Greene and Clark Peterson.

Ghoul, Cinder

Hit Dice: 6
Armor Class: 4 [15]
Attacks: 1 slam (1d8 + 1d6 fire + level drain)
Saving Throw: 11
Special: Drains 1 level with hit, fire
Move: 12 (flying)
Alignment: Chaos
Challenge Level/XP: 8/800

A cinder ghoul is ghost-like spirit in the form of a swirling humanoid cloud of burning ash and charred body parts. Its dark, smoky shape is lit here and there with the red glow of perpetually burning embers, and the grisly remains of scorched body parts can occasionally be glimpsed floating within the mass. These baleful undead creatures reek of smoke and burnt flesh. A cinder ghoul's touch drains 1 level. Any creature struck by the ghoul's vicious touch also suffers 1d6 fire damage and must save or catch on fire.

Ashes of Vengeance

A blackened 5-foot-wide dais sits outside a cave constructed of perfectly fitted blocks of black glass. A 10-foot-diameter sheet of charred glass encircles the dais. Gold-colored sigils are carved into the stone dais and flame-like petroglyphs are etched into the glass sheet. The head of a fire giant sits on the altar. The top of the giant's head has been removed and filled with burning oil. A garish blue flame leaps upward from the severed head. The area around the altar smells of burning hair and flesh. Two small brass bowls filled with ash and bone fragments sit alongside the burning head.

The priests of the fire maiden Incindreia routinely sacrifice victims by setting them on fire. The bowls of ash contain the collected remains of a married pair of clerics caught by the wicked priests while on their honeymoon. The spirits of the clerics now rise as cinder ghouls from the brass bowls in a swirl of ash and bone fragments to attack anyone approaching the altar.

Copyright Notice

Ghoul, Dust

Hit Dice: 4
Armor Class: 7 [12]
Attacks: 2 claws (1d4), 1 bite (1d4)
Special: Animate dust, paralyzing shriek
Move: 10/6/4 (flying/burrow)
Saving Throw: 12
Alignment: Chaos
Challenge Level/XP: 5/240

Dust ghouls are dust-covered creatures with decaying flesh pulled tightly over their humanoid frames. Their teeth are pointed fangs and their hands end in wicked, dirt-covered and blood-soaked claws. Once per round, a dust ghoul can emit a hellish shriek that paralyzes any creature within 60 feet for 2d4 rounds if they fail a save. Once per day, a dust ghoul can animate 11d4 dust zombies. These zombies cannot be harmed by spells or weapons, but a gallon of water destroys them. The dust zombies attack with the ghouls to-hit bonus, but do no damage. If two hit the same opponent, they hold the creature immobile. Dust ghouls are immune to charms and sleep spells.

Paupers' Grave

A large stone-lined pit stretches across this room (or field), with corpses in various states of decay strewn across a rusted iron mesh grate. The pit drops 20 feet to the grate and 30 more to the floor of the pit below that. A fine coating of lye covers the corpses, and half a barrel of lye and a shovel sit next to the pit. An empty vial (that used to contain unholy water) can be found buried in the barrel of lye. The lye causes chemical burns to any exposed skin (1d4 points of damage per round until washed off).

The dust from centuries of corpses fills the floor of the pit beneath the mesh grate. Only coins, rings and other small valuables belonging to the dead filter through the grate. The grate sits on a rock ledge running around the interior of the pit. Lifting the grate is difficult due to its weight and precise fit. A dust ghoul rests below in the mound of ash at the bottom of the hole. It animates the remains into zombies before attacking.

Copyright Notice
Authors Scott Greene and Casey Christofferson.

Ghoul-Stirge

Hit Dice: 4+1
Armor Class: 4 [15]
Attack: Bite (1d6 plus parlaysis)
Saving Throw: 13
Special: Blood drain, paralysis
Move: 9/18 (flying)
Alignment: Chaos
Challenge Level/XP: 7/600

A ghoul-stirge resembles a large stirge with rotting flesh and broken wings. The origin of the ghoul-stirge has been lost, but it is believed to be the result of a failed magical experiment conducted in ages past by a group of evil and insane necromancers. Though they can generally be encountered anywhere, ghoul-stirges seem to favor desolate places such as ruins and caverns or dungeons deep underground. Being undead they do not have to eat, but seem to draw sustenance from the blood of enemies, much like a vampire.

Those hit by a ghoul-stirge's bite attack must succeed on a saving throw or be paralyzed for 1d6+2 rounds. A ghoul-stirge can drain blood from a paralyzed or pinned opponent. Each round it deals 2d4 points of damage each round. Once the ghoul-stirge has dealt 8 points of damage, it flies off to digest its meal. If its victim dies before the ghoul-stirge's appetite has been sated, the creature detaches and seeks a new target.

Comfortless Inn

A crumbling two-story coaching inn on the road between two rival city-states is called home by a gang of 1d3+1 ghoul-stirges. The ghoul-stirges dwell in the attic, the scene of a terrible fire that claimed the life of two smugglers who now haunt the grounds as poltergeists. One poltergeist dwells in the stable, throwing about horse shoes, whips, harnesses, brushes and other tools. The other dwells in the taproom, where he has pewter mugs and cuttlery to play with.

A monstrous large cask is embedded in one wall, the tap being the handle to a secret door if turned counter-clockwise three times. The cask holds smuggler's loot, mostly furs, pelts and horns taken from wisent that dwelled in the king's forest. The ghoul-stirges are only active at night or on cloudy days. They prefer to attack people in the open, where their flight ability can be used to its full effect.

Credit

The Ghoulstirge originally appeared in the First Edition module *L1 The Secret of Bone Hill* (© TSR/Wizards of the Coast, 1981) and is used by permission.

Copyright Notice

Authors Scott Greene and Clark Peterson, based on original material by Lenard Lakofka.

Giant, Bronze

Hit Dice: 12+1d6 points
Armor Class: 1 [18]
Attacks: Sword (6d6)
Special: hurl boulders, sardonic laugh
Move: 15
Saving Throw: 3
Alignment: Neutrality
Challenge Level/XP: 13/2,300

A bronze giant is huge muscular being often mistaken for a statue of the gods. It is well proportioned and has flesh that gleams like polished bronze and hair the color of copper wire. Bronze giants stand about 25 feet tall and weigh about 14,000 pounds. A bronze giant can unleash a bellowing laugh that strikes fear (save negates) into the hearts of any creature within 100 feet that hears it. They throw rocks for 6d6 points of damage.

Garden of the Gods

Deep within the Hollow Spire Mountains stands Mount Alluvial, a mountain encircled by fantastic rock formations. Phosphorescent evergreens, enormous ferns, blooming vines and gigantic flowers are dwarfed by colossal rock formations. Paved paths meander though the otherworldly garden. Titanic bronze and rock statues decorate the garden. These unique statues resemble the gods of the lands. These statues are the works of Alaxias, a bronze giant, who is said to wield a bronze shield with the image of the three Gorgons emblazoned on its face. The shield reportedly has the power to turn opponents to bronze or stone. Alaxias has served the will of the gods and man for centuries. Wealthy high priests seek out his skill and knowledge to sculpt statues of their deities to decorate their temples. Mages travel great distances to commission golems and other animated beings. The garden also contains golems, clockwork creations and other constructed creatures that wander freely or stand like magnificent statues until disturbed.

Alaxias does not welcome uninvited guests or treasure-seekers. The grounds are protected by a pack of chaotic, intelligent wolves. The large wolves have coats of silvery metallic fur that are reputed to reverse flesh to stone once skinned and tanned.

Copyright Notice

Authors Scott Greene and Casey Christofferson.

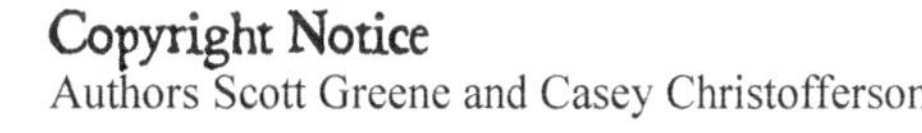

Giant, Cave

Hit Dice: 9+1d6
Armor Class: 4 [15]
Attacks: weapon (2d8) or slam (1d8)
Saving Throw: 6
Special: None
Move: 12
Alignment: Chaos
Challenge Level/XP: 9/1,100

Cave giants are the dumber, stronger cousins of hill giants. A cave giant is a massive creature, stocky and pot-bellied, with black scraggly hair streaming down over its shoulders. The skin of a cave giant is gray, mottled here and there with blotches of brown and black. The face of a cave giant has a bulbous nose between glaring eyes with thick, bushy eyebrows. A cave giant has two tusk-like teeth that extend down over its lower lip, causing it to drool almost constantly. Cave giants don't throw rocks, but instead try to grab victims and pound them into the ground, ceiling or any nearby objects.

Return Deposit

The cave giant Creel Rockcrusher has found the perfect cave. It sits high on a hill, a perfect vantage point to see his enemies (he's sure they're out there), and is surrounded by a red-colored moss that smells like rotting goat, Creel's favorite. Creel just had to clear out a few boulders in and around the cavern.

But the rocks came back the next morning, sitting right outside the entry to the cave. The rocks are animated boulders led by a geon. Creel unceremoniously tossed the geon out of the cave. The geon sits at the base of the hill, directing the boulders up the hill each day.

Creel's limited intellect is further hindered by the moss growing all around him. The moss, called Sylvan's Beard, gives off a highly intoxicating spores that can cause euphoria. Creel is in a drunk-like stupor most days, and the moving rocks are a nightmare taking root in his delusional and paranoid mind. He sees them as trying to get into his cave (they are, by the way) and kill him in his sleep (they're not).

The cave giant charges out of its cave and grabs any boulders in reach to smash into PCs who might side with the geon. *(See the **Geon** entry for more from this encounter.)*

Copyright Notice
Authors Scott Greene and Erica Balsley.

Giant, Ferrous

Hit Dice: 12+1d6
Armor Class: 3 [16]
Attacks: 1 weapon (4d6)
Saving Throw: 3
Special: Spell-like abilities, immune to fire
Move: 12
Alignment: Neutrality
Challenge Level/XP: 13/2,300

Ferrous giant stand 20 feet tall and have dark ruddy skin. They wear their hair long and most males are bearded. Hair color ranges from brown to black. Their eyes are typically brown, hazel, or green. Common dress consists of furs, skins, or armor. Ferrous giants grab opponents and pound them into the ground, ceiling or any nearby objects. Ferrous giants can employ various spell-like abilities: at will—*heat metal*, *levitate*; 1/day— *wall of iron*. Ferrous giants are immune to fire.

The Iron Giant

A small two-story wooden house sits inside a picket fence where chickens roam freely. A large barn sits on the edge of the clearing within sight of the farmhouse. A wooden porch wraps around the front of the home, and is painted a mix of colors, reds, blues, greens and yellows. Dirty clothes lie in piles in the weed-filled yard.

A 10-year-old boy sits in a creaking porch swing, carving an apple with a large dagger. The dagger has a gold hilt and the blade gleams brightly. The boy's hair is long, and the clothes he wears look a few sizes too large for him.

Cadmon Niddle is an orphan who was adopted by a rather unusual parent. The boy was snatched out of the orphanage he was sent to after his parents died, but was "found" while running away by Marsivin, a ferrous giant who had recently lost his own son to a thundershrike.

Cadmon lives alone in the now-vacant log-cabin (Marsivin ate the former residents a few weeks ago). The giant provides for the boy's needs by raiding nearby farms and villages. Cadmon already considers the giant his "dad," simply because the giant treats him better than any adult he's ever met. Marsivin is just as protective of his newfound son.

The ferrous giant sleeps in a pile of hay in the barn – well within shouting distance if Cadmon needs him.

Copyright Notice

Giant, Jack-In-Irons

Hit Dice: 16+1d6 points
Armor Class: 0 [19]
Attacks: Club (7d6)
Special: hurl boulders, shake earth, stun
Move: 15
Saving Throw: 3
Alignment: Neutrality
Challenge Level/XP: 17/2,300

A jack-in-irons looks like a huge orc adorned in chains. It stands 20 to 25 feet tall and weighs 13,000 to 15,000 pounds. Any creature struck by its weapon must save or be stunned for 1 turn. A jack-in-irons can stomp its foot on the ground to cause powerful vibrations that radiate around the giant and cause opponents to fall down. The giant can throw rocks for 7d6 points of damage.

Slave Caravan

The ground trembles at the approach of the jack-in-irons and its troupe. Two hill giants roll a 10-foot-diameter iron ball. The iron ball is covered in ancient runes and glyphs of an unknown origin. The giants use the ball for to destroy things by battering walls and buildings with it, and by rolling it into opponents from atop hills. The ball has one cavity that bears a stout iron loop. The jack-in-irons can attach a chain to the loop and use it as wrecking ball or massive flail to smash multiple opponents.

Behind the lead hill giants, two teams of tethered ogres pull two iron-and-wood prisoner wagons that hold captured slaves. A platoon of black orcs holding readied crossbows ride atop each wagon behind iron battlements. The black orcs serve as shock troops and raiding parties. The barbed wagons have wheels of iron with spiked treads. The wagons are cumbersome and slow to move. The monstrous wagons contain only the choice slaves, as the rest are eaten or slain for entertainment. The dreadful Rhobrus Krupp, a jack-in-irons giant, commands the motley band of slavers.

Rhobrus Krupp and his band travel down from the Hollow Spire Mountains yearly to raid and destroy. They leave nothing but destruction in their wake. None of the captives taken into the mountains has ever escaped to tell of their plight.

Copyright Notice
Author Scott Greene.

Giant, Sand

Hit Dice: 17
Armor Class: 2 [17]
Attack: Two-handed sword (4d6) or 2 strikes (1d10)
Saving Throw: 3
Special: Shape earth, spells, rock catching
Move: 15
Alignment: Chaos
Challenge Level/XP: 19/4100

Sand giants are brutal, somewhat barbaric giants that prey on those weaker than themselves. They have dark tan skin, brown hair, and dark brown or dark green eyes. An adult male stands approximately 20 feet tall. Males tend to wear their hair and beards braided. Sand giants wear light clothes and light armor (if any). In times of battle or war, males may don chainmail. A typical sand giant's bag contains food, 3d4 mundane items and no more than 12d10 coins. Sand Giants speak their own harsh tongue and the common tongue. They can live to be 500 years old.

Sand giants make their homes in warm desert lands away from human civilization. They live in tribes consisting of 8-9 families of 2-4 members each. On occasion, a tribe forms a raiding party that sets off to the nearest civilized place, returning at a later time with food, treasure and captives. For each adult in a sand giant's lair, there is a 40% chance that the lair has 1d3 captives of a random humanoid race.

Once per day, a sand giant can form a volume of sand within 40 feet into the shape of a 20-foot long arm that ends in a clenched fist. The arm has a reach of 20 feet, AC 0 [19] and 30 hp. It can attack once per round as a 12 HD monster and deals 1d10 points of damage on each attack and any creature struck must succeed on a saving throw or be stunned for 1 round. The arm remains for 17 rounds. A sand giant does not need to concentrate to maintain the arm and can direct it to attack a new target without sacrificing its own attack. The arm loses shape if it is reduced to 0 or less hit points, the duration expires, or the sand giant dies.

Sand giant scan also cast the following spells: *Transmute rock to mud* (2/day), *move earth* (2/day) and *earthquake* (1/day).

Simoom of the Sands

While traversing a blazing desert, the adventurers might come upon a little man in white robes and a crooked turban. The man has a thin, heavily wrinkled face reminiscent of a monkey, while creamy white skin and wisps of silver hair escaping from his turban. He carries a blue parasol and is well adorned in silver chains and bits of amber (worth about 60 gp). As they approach, he hails them and, standing as straight as his old spine will allow, pronounces that he is the herald of a great chieftain of the desert sands and seeks ladies or gentlemen of unrivaled puissance who would prove their mettle in the arena of his master for ten times their weight in gold.

If the adventurers are so uncouth as to attack the old man, he will call out for his master and a simoom will sweep over the scene, blinding the adventurers and forcing them to pass saving throws or be knocked over, tumbled and possibly buried in sand. When the wind dies down, the old man will have disappeared.

If they accept, the old man will lead them about a mile away and, reaching a large, white stone in the midst of the desert will call upon the adventurers to surround it. Tapping his parasol on the white stone, the sand surrounding them will begin to roll away in waves, eventually leaving the travelers and the old man standing upon an ancient, weathered courtyard of limestone paving stones, about 500 feet square with a round, iron trapdoor about 12 feet in diameter in its center. The white stone stands about six feet tall uncovered and just a few feet from the trapdoor.

A few minutes after the courtyard and trapdoor are revealed, the door is opened by the hand of a sand giant, a massive man swathed in thick robes with a saffron scarf wrapped about his head. He ushers the visitors through the trapdoor, a narrow, spiral staircase being provided for little folk. This entrance leads down about 150 feet. At the bottom are two doors, 30 feet tall, that lead into a massive hall. Within the hall are 1d20+7 sand giants and a third as many females and young. A tall chair at one end of the hall bears a sand giant chieftain in robes of pure, white cotton and holding a shepherd's crook of gold and lapis lazuli (worth 3,000 gp). He wears a tall, pointed helmet of brass wrapped with a crimson scarf of silk. Besides his normal abilities, the chieftain can also cast spells as a 9th level cleric.

The chieftain invites his visitors in, feeds them savories and sweet tea, entertains them with dancers and acrobats (it's hard to believe beings so large can be so graceful) and then calls on them to prove their prowess against his warriors. Each warrior will be asked to fight single-handed against a single giant. They may use weapons like clubs or staves (which will be provided) or their fists, but no bladed weapons are permitted. Should the warrior win, he is showered with gold coins equal to ten times his own weight. Should he lose, he will be clasped in irons and made a cupbearer to the chieftain and his warriors.

Copyright Notice

Author Scott Greene.

Giant, Sea

Hit Dice: 14+1d6 points
Armor Class: 2 [17]
Attacks: Trident (6d6)
Special: hurl boulders, magical abilities
Move: 15
Saving Throw: 3
Alignment: Neutrality
Challenge Level/XP: 15/2,300

Sea giants are bluish-green amphibious giants standing 10 feet tall and weighing about 6,000 pounds. Sea giants adorn themselves in loose flowing robes of white, blue, or green. Many wear wreathes of coral in their hair. Sea giants are the living embodiment of the sea's bounty and destructive wrath. They can *control water* as per the spell five times per day. They can also increase the pressure of the water in a 10-foot radius around them for 5 rounds. Any creature in this denser water must save or take 1d8 points of damage from the crushing water. Sea giants can move freely in water without hindrances.

Rock the Boat

The harbor in the seaport city of Bargarsport appears more like a battlefield than a bustling marina, with flaring tempers between sea captains and sailors reaching war-like levels. Ships have collided; anchor chains are entwined, and the disappearance of precious cargo has led the sailors to blame one another. Several cargo ships are openly hostile toward one another. The true culprits behind the tension lie below the surface of the bay. A group of sea giants wreak havoc on the ships while searching for a sacred giant conch shell. The powers or importance of the shell are a mystery that only the giants know.

The sea giants force ships to collide, pull on anchor chains, search the boat decks (eating any supplies they find) and move unattended ships. The sailors blame one another for these incidents. The smuggler's ship, The Miscreant Treant, is a rum smuggler who is hiding a shipment in hopes of avoiding the city's hefty harbor tax. While hiding another plunder of rum on a sandy island for their return, the sailors discovered the jeweled conch shell.

The leader of the sea giants carries a glass bubble helm that magically fills with seawater and allows him to move about on dry land indefinitely. The sea giants have not resorted to violence yet but have already sunk several ships by prying open hulls in search of their revered shell. If angered, the giants yank the anchor chains to sink the ships or rock the boats violently to send sailors overboard.

Copyright Notice
Author Scott Greene.

Giant, Smoke

Hit Dice: 8+1d6 points
Armor Class: 5 [14]
Attacks: weapon (2d6)
Special: hurl boulders, immune to fire, smoke form, smoke cloud
Move: 15
Saving Throw: 8
Alignment: Chaos
Challenge Level/XP: 9/1,100

This filthy giant resembles a 9-foot-tall humanoid with soot-colored skin. A smoke giant's form is solid, but it can turn into a smoky form similar to *gaseous form*. The giant can cause a billowing smoke cloud to surround it at will. The giant can throw rocks for 2d6 points of damage.

Smoke on the Water

A 50-foot-tall brick smokestack rises out of the center of a wide shallow lake. Billowing plumes of smoke drift out of the chimney and dissipate high in the clouds overhead. A thick mixture of mist and smoke settles back over the surface of the lake, obscuring its surface. Six large rowboats sit tethered to posts along the shore. The lake itself is no more than five to six feet deep, and the water is very warm but not hot enough to cause harm. The water becomes warmer closer to the chimney, and has a thin coat of oily ash floating on the surface. The lake bottom is a mire of sunken soot.

A group of smoke giants guards this chimney against intruders. They remain in smoke form hidden around the lake and use massive cinders buried within the sooty lake bottom as boulders. The chimney possibly leads into a great underground forge used by friendly dwarves or raging fire giants. An iron rung ladder set into the exterior and interior of the chimney appears to be the only entrance into the forge below. The size of the ladder and width of the chimney should meet the size requirements of the smiths below. *(See the **Dragon, Smoke** entry for a variant of what may be at the bottom of the chimney.)*

Copyright Notice
Author Scott Greene.

Giant, Volcano

Hit Dice: 14+1d6
Armor Class: 2 [17]
Attacks: 1 weapon (4d6)
Saving Throw: 3
Special: Throw boulders, breath weapon, immune to fire
Move: 12
Alignment: Neutrality
Challenge Level/XP: 16/3,200

A volcano giant is an 18-foot tall barrel-chested giant with black or brown hair and brown, black, or dark amber eyes. Its skin is leathery and tanned reddish-brown. The hair of a volcano giant is tough and wiry, with the strength and texture of copper. Three times per day, a volcano giant can exhale a cloud of sulfuric gas in a 30-foot cone. This gas causes creatures who fail a save to succumb to fits of coughing and choking. Volcano giants can throw rocks for 2d8 points of damage. Volcano giants are immune to fire.

The Soul of Truth

A giant-size basalt throne sits on the side of the Candledusk Volcano. Images of fire ravaging the countryside decorate its sides. Sitting in the throne is an 18-foot-tall volcano giant. He wears a dirty toga smeared with ash, and has a long beard flowing down to his lap. A 40-foot-long black chain shackles the giant's ankle to one leg of the throne. Far above, the volcano spits and hisses.

Yak Splitear sits quietly in the throne, his palms facing upward on the arms of the chair. His eyes are closed in contemplation. His face is serene, as if he is meditating. The giant's shadow appears nearly 40 feet away from him, a dark blot on the mountain plateau disconnected from Yak.

Stacks of food, coins and even old weapons and shields sit around the base of the throne. Three goats are tethered to a nearby rock. The townsfolk of Morlayne bring these offerings to the giant each month to gain his advice and to hear his predictions. Years ago, Yak offended a deity walking the land. This all-powerful being stole Yak's soul but made the giant an offer: If he would sit in this throne and answer questions truthfully, his soul would gradually return to him. The giant has been in the seat for 20 years, and his soul – the shadow rippling on the ground – is getting closer with every piece of advice he offers. The advice doesn't have to be true or even good, just so long as Yak speaks truthfully.

Anyone nearing the shadow draws Yak's immediate glare, and the short-tempered volcano giant attacks anyone daring to touch it.

Copyright Notice

Giant, Wood

Hit Dice: 7
Armor Class: 1 [18]
Attack: Two-handed sword (2d8) or longbow (2d6)
Saving Throw: 9 (7 vs. charm)
Special: Change self, surprise on roll of 1-3 on 1d6
Move: 15
Alignment: Law
Challenge Level/XP: 8/800

This giant resembles a wood elf of about 10 feet tall. It has brownish-green skin, a bald head, and bright green eyes.

Wood giants are peaceful, good-natured giants found in the forested areas of the world. The average wood giant stands 9 feet tall, weighs 900 pounds, and resembles a large wood elf. Wood giants have brownish-green skin, bright green eyes, large heads and prominent jaws; their elf-like ears sit high on their long, oval heads. Most wood giants (particularly males) are bald. Wood giants dress in greens or browns and prefer neutral colors to the bright or dull colors of other races. Wood giants speak their own language and the language of elfs, and may also speak common. Wood giants can live to be 400 years old. Three times per day, a wood giant can alter its form so as to appear as any humanoid creature between 3 feet and 15 feet tall.

Wood giants are on friendly terms with most benign creatures of the forest, particularly wood elves. Though contact outside their immediate clan is rare, they do occasionally have dealings with nearby tribes of wood elves. Wood giant villages are large and open expanses of land with few if any buildings or shelters. Wood giants prefer to spend their time under the warmth of the day and the serenity of the night. They do not associate with—and usually attack on sight—evil forest creatures. The leaders of wood giant clans might have the abilities of 1st to 3rd level rangers.

The Trees Are Still Taller

The tall, straight trees of the woodland are lit with a ghostly, white light at night. In the center of the forest there is a large oak tree - 150 feet tall - hung with long, glowing crystals. The oak serves as the centerpoint of a permanent camp of 1d4+1 wood giants and the 1d4 dire wolves they use as hounds. The wood giants dwell in tall patchwork tents of red deer pelts around a smoldering fire pit. They are currently entertaining a party of 1d3+1 wood elf traders who have brought gifts of tobacco and bricks of tea to win the alliance of these great hunters.

The tree is home to a dryad as tall as the wood giants, with auburn skin, flowing hair of pale green and bright, white eyes that have a gaze attack that *holds monster* (as the spell). The dryad is the tutelary spirit of the woodlands, and the wood giants are her devoted servants. They will be aghast at the arrival of outsiders in this holy place, and quickly attempt to seize them with the help of the wood elves.

Once bound, the intruders are hung by their feet from low branches and not permitted to sleep for 3 days and nights, while being whipped with switches cut from the surrounding underbrush. At the end of this purification ritual, they are cut down and given a brisk massage and medicinal soup of mushrooms and nettles. A dab of woad is applied to their foreheads and are pronounced the sons and daughters of the dryad and accepted into the society of the wood elves and giants. Resistance to this ritual is met with deadly force.

Credit

The Wood Giant originally appeared in the Second Edition *Monstrous Compendium 5* (© TSR/Wizards of the Coast, 1990) and is used by permission.

Copyright Notice

Author Scott Greene, based on original material by Wizards of the Coast.

Glass Wyrm

Hit Dice: 5-7
Armor Class: 1 [18]
Attacks: 2 claws (1d6), 1 bite (3d6)
Saving Throw: 12, 11, or 9
Special: Breathes shards of glass
Move: 9/24 (flying)
Alignment: Neutrality
Challenge Level/XP: 5 HD (8/800), 6 HD (9/1,100), 7 HD (10/1,400)

This semi-transparent dragon appears to be formed of crystal or glass. Its large wings are translucent and the sound of grating glass can be heard when it moves. It breathes razor-sharp shards of glass in a 60-foot-long cone that is roughly 30 feet wide at the base. Any light source brought within 30 feet of a glass dragon's reflective surface causes the light to reflect as a burst that blinds all creatures within 30 feet for 1d6 rounds unless a save is made. Spells that target a glass dragon have a 50% chance of reflecting in a random direction.

Misguided Intentions

Nestled among fields of barley and clear mountain streams sits the large town of Alemint. The town is renowned for its high-quality brew and spirits, and many breweries operate there. Large barley farms surround the settlement and the smell of grain and yeast fills the air. The town is serious about the brewing profession, but Alemint likes to let its hair down every 30 days during an alcohol-fueled celebration called the Straubinfest. During Straubinfest , beer flows freely and the town fills with loud music and wild dancing until the wee hours of the morning. The rest of the week is dedicated to cleaning up after the celebration and preparing for the next.

Recently though, things have gone sour in Alemint. The townsfolk are weak and ill, and the normally festive Straubinfest is a pale shadow of its former self, with the beloved smell of beer now invoking nausea for many of the townsfolk. Townsfolk wander the streets, holding their heads and stomachs as if they'd just woken up with a terrible hangover.

The elders blame the sickness on a glass dragon named Chalcedon that resides farther up the mountain in an abandoned quartz mine. Ten days before each new Straubinfest, the citizens of Alemint offer a maiden to the dragon in hopes of lifting the curse. The dragon has nothing to do with the sickness befalling the townsfolk; the actual curse is caused by a microscopic mold blight that infects the barley fields and spoils the brew. The bound maidens left outside the dragon's quartz mine lair die from exposure to the elements and are carried off by scavengers as the innocent glass dragon slumbers deep within the mines.

A 15-foot pillar made from a single quartz crystal sits outside the mine's entrance. Chains and shackles are embedded into its surface. Bones and garments litter the ground around the crystal pillar. The large mine adit is cut into the white quartz wall, and light gleams and reflects within the crystal mine shafts. Chalcedon lives a peaceful life and rarely leaves the comforts of his lair. Other monstrosities (such as crystal ooze, gelatinous cubes of enormous size and a colony of geons) live in the mines and serve as guardians to the glass dragon and its crystalline treasures. Adventurers may reason with the dragon, but persuading the town's folk of the true nature of their curse is another matter.

Gloom Crawler

Hit Dice: 10
Armor Class: 3 [16]
Attacks: 10 tentacles (1d6 plus constrict), bite (2d8)
Saving Throw: 5
Special: Constrict, all-around senses, vulnerable to sunlight
Move: 9
Alignment: Chaos
Challenge Level/XP: 11/1,700

Gloom crawlers resemble giant squid with many, 5-foot-long tentacles that end in a small, round, lidless eye with a stark blue pupil. These many eyes let it see in all directions at once, and let it sense the location of anything within 60 feet that is touching the ground. If a gloom crawler hits with a tentacle, it grabs the victim and constricts for automatic damage in the rounds thereafter until the creature is freed. Gloom crawlers take 1d4 points of damage from natural sunlight.

The Monkey House

Wooden bars fill this underground 50-by-50-foot square room, the horizontal poles rising to the ceiling 30 feet overhead. Taut ropes hang between the bars. Shredded netting dangles throughout the chamber and shrouds the doorways. Jungle plants grow throughout the chamber, and leafy green vines hang down from the ceiling. Monkey feces covers the floor, and a couple of dead chimps lie facedown in the dirt, their bodies twisted and crushed. A circus wagon with a crude monkey painted on its wooden side sits in the corner, one of its wagon wheels broken.

A pair of gloom crawlers took over the monkey house, and the primates inside were no match for the creatures. One gloom crawler lives in the broken wagon, while the other sleeps on a small dark ledge near the ceiling. The gloom crawlers can each get around quite well using all the odd protrusions, ledges and ropes filling the room. They often attack from above by swinging down to snatch victims into the air with their tentacles.

On the ledge near the ceiling is the remains of a dwarf. On his body remain a *+1 warhammer* (1d6) and a *potion of levitation*.

Copyright Notice
Author Scott Greene.

Gloomwing

Hit Dice: 5
Armor Class: 0 [19]
Attack: 2 claws (1d4), bite (1d8)
Saving Throw: 12
Special: Confusion, implant, weakness pheromone, summon gloomwings
Move: 3/15 (flying)
Alignment: Neutrality
Challenge Level/XP: 9/1100

Gloomwings look like a giant moths with black wings covered in spiraled patterns of silver. Eight legs run the length of the their bodies, each ending in a pearly-white claw. Their mouths have two large pearly-white mandibles. The gloomwing is native to the Plane of Shadow and is summoned to the Material Plane by spellcasters to act as a guardian. On occasion, a gloomwing slips through a tear in the fabric of the planes and enters the Material Plane on its own. The ivory mandibles of a gloomwing can be pried or broken from its carcass and sold for 100 gp each.

The coloration on the gloomwing's back and wings provide it with protection against some predators. Any creature viewing the gloomwing from above must succeed on a saving throw or be affected as if by a *confusion* spell for 6 rounds.

After the first round of combat, a gloomwing can emit a scent in a 30-foot radius that weakens living creatures in the area. An affected creature can make a saving throw each round it remains in the area to negate the effects. Otherwise, they suffer a -1 penalty on melee attacks and melee damage. The pheromone ceases when the gloomwing dies. Strength damage dealt by a gloomwing's pheromone heals at a rate of 1 point per hour. Each round a gloomwing emits its weakness pheromone there is a 20% chance that 1d4 additional gloomwings arrive in the area and join the battle.

Female gloomwings lay their eggs in the bodies of slain victims. In 12 days, these eggs hatch, releasing 1d6+3 tenebrous worms. The young emerge about 2 weeks later as a tenebrous worms (see that entry), literally devouring the host from inside. While implanted, a body cannot be brought back to life except by the casting of a *wish*. If *cure disease* is cast on the body, the eggs are destroyed and the body can be raised normally.

Cube in a Bubble

In the middle of a geest (a sandy heath) surrounded by flat marshlands and grazed upon by bison, there rises a crystalline dome of smoky glass. The glass cannot be scratched or damaged, not even by diamonds. When the dome is touched, there is a 1 in 6 chance it draws the toucher inside, which it turns out is actually a sphere.

The person drawn into the sphere slides to the bottom (save or suffer 1d4 points of falling damage). The sphere has a diameter of 50 feet. A number of adamantine cords extend from the walls of the sphere to a silvery cube suspended in the center. The cube gives off an intermitant, flickering glow, sending arcs of electricity across the cords and along the sphere walls as it does. These blasts of electricity occur on a roll of 1 on 1d8 (roll each round) and inflict 1d4 points of damage to people inside the sphere.

Separating the cube from the cords can be accomplished by depressing a button on each side of the cube that is not connected to a cord. The cords all release at the same moment, sending anyone who has climbed up the cords to the bottom of the sphere (a 50-foot fall). The cube remains floating in the center of the sphere and continues to electrify anyone touching it.

At this point, the remainder of the sphere becomes as black as night and people in the sphere might see flickers of movment in the blackness out of the corner of their eye. This is the movement of the sphere's guardian, a gloomwing. The gloomwing does its best to destroy intruders. If it fails, a second gloomwing is called forth in 1d4+2 rounds and then a third, etc.

The cube, having been rid of the adamantine cords, has four additional buttons on its surface. If pressed in the proper combination, they cause the cube to spin and give off a blinding light. When the light fades, the sphere will have disappeared (a crater is left behind) and the cube shrunk to the size of a human fist. The cube now grants its holder immunity to electricity and control over creatures infused with electricity, such as blue dragons.

Credit

The Gloomwing originally appeared in the First Edition *Monster Manual II* (© TSR/Wizards of the Coast, 1983) and is used by permission.

Copyright Notice

Author Scott Greene, based on original material by Gary Gygax.

Gnarlwood

Hit Dice: 11
Armor Class: 2 [17]
Attacks: 4 branches (2d6)
Special: magical abilities, animate dead, rend, protection aura
Move: 12
Saving Throw: 4
Alignment: Chaos
Challenge Level/XP: 10/1,400

A gnarlwood resembles a treant but instead of the kindly, gentle face of the tree-folk its face is twisted into a grim scowl. Its deep-set eyes and jagged mouth give it an almost skull-like grimace and its four twisted arms are tipped in sharp woody claws. Its leaves are deep green, almost black, and have ghostly white markings on them. Behind it, the skeletal remains of unfortunate animals shamble through the undergrowth. A gnarlwood exudes a 20-foot radius *protection from good* around it, and can *animate dead* within 60 feet at will. If a gnarlwood hits a single opponent with two branches, it grabs the creature and does an additional 1d6 points of damage as it rends the victim's flesh.

Save the Kitty

An abandoned and dilapidated cemetery sits atop a small knoll with a dead and twisted tree at its peak. The pleading bellows of a golden-furred cat emanates for high up in the tree. Ten undead zombies claw at the trunk in vain attempts to reach the stranded feline. Many of the graves have hollow depressions where the dead dug their way out of the earth. Many more skeletons and zombies remain buried in their rotting coffins. Some of the dead were buried with semi-valuable possessions, most of which remain in the grave or lie fallen on the ground. This gnarlwood purposely uses cats (in this case a golden cat) to attract would-be do-gooders. It remains inanimate until victims are close enough. The remains of dozens of cats, opossums and raccoons lie scattered around its trunk.

Gohl (Hydra Cloud)

Hit Dice: 12
Armor Class: -1 [20]
Attacks: 6 tentacles (1d6+3) and 3 acidic bites (1d8+3)
Saving Throw: 3
Special: Acid, constrict, +1 magic weapons to hit
Move: 15 (flying)
Alignment: Chaos
Challenge Level/XP: 13/2,300

A gohl is a 10-foot-wide, 10-foot-high, blob of mottled black and gray flesh, slimy and rubbery to the touch. From its central form sprout six long tentacles of brownish flesh and three snake-like heads, each head perched atop a long, thin neck. Each head is gold with red eyes and has a wide mouth lined with double rows of needle-sharp teeth. Many small tendrils appear from the gohl's central form at random intervals only to disappear back into its massive trunk. A gohl tries to grab victim in its tentacles. If an opponent is struck by two or more tentacles in the same round, he is constricted and takes 1d6+3 damage each round thereafter. Creatures held by a tentacle are pulled toward the creature's mouth. The toxic bite of a gohl deals 1d8 points of acid damage.

The Serpent Demon

Vine-covered stone steps head down into darkness from the step-pyramid's steep outer slope. The corridor is narrow, and colorful snakes and twisting jungle plants twine along the block walls. Every 10 feet, a leering face with a forked tongue sticking between fanged teeth is carved into the stone. Flickering torches are mounted in soot-covered sconces at head height. The air is stale and oppressive and smells of dried meat.

The corridor opens onto a 30-foot-tall chamber in the pyramid's heart. A 25-foot-tall towering statue of a snake-faced demon with a human body stands in the center of the room, his arms stretched out before him. The statue's fingers are splayed wide, and thick tendrils of vines hang down. Two struggling humans are held in the vines like puppets. The statue's demonic face peers down at the captives, and its forked tongue juts from its fanged maw. The statue's eyes are cinders that burn a hellish red.

Beneath the statue is a 15-foot-wide pit filled with the undulating bodies of thousands of serpents. The snakes – of all sizes – twist and squirm in a ball of serpentine flesh. Around the pit stand seven robed figures and 5 women cavorting in a rhythmic dance around the snakes. The struggling humans are held just on the edge of the pit. The dancers wind in and around the helpless victims. The women are naked, but their deformities are obvious: Each has a serpent growing at the end of her arms where her hands should be.

The women are inphidian dancer/charmers lost in the throes of ecstasy to their god and creator. The robed figures are four common inphidians, two cobra-back protectors and the "high priest," an inphidian night adder. The inphidians are intent on sacrificing the humans – two wandering fighters named Toral and Bethane – to the living embodiment of their god: a gohl in the serpent pit. The inphidians are from the serpent city of Uroborus in the Seething Jungle sent to protect the gohl.

The gohl rises out of the pit if the inphidians are attacked. Snakes drop off its slimy flesh as it flies toward PCs and lashes out with its tentacles. The inphidians join the fight, but flee if the gohl is slain.

Golden Cat

Hit Dice: 1
Armor Class: 9 [10]
Attacks: 1 bite (1d2)
Special: lucky/unlucky
Move: 10
Saving Throw: 17
Alignment: Neutrality
Challenge Level/XP: 1/15

A golden cat is a normal cat with rich golden fur and green eyes. When a golden cat selects an "owner," it grants that creature good fortune. Three times per day, so long as the golden cat is within 40 feet, the owner can reroll one die roll and take the most favorable result. Only one die can be rerolled each round. Each time the golden cat activates this ability and the owner rerolls a die, all other creatures (including the owner's allies) within 40 feet of the golden cat must reroll one die roll and take the least favorable result each time.

The Cat in the Bag

A large bag moves down the passage. A single cat's leg grasps the floor as it reaches out of the nearly closed sack. The leg strains as it pulls the bag blindly down the passage. The bag is a bag of devouring that has tightened around a golden cat. The golden cat managed to free one leg to prevent the bag from swallowing it whole. The bag has magical strength and does not give up its newest victim easily. Cutting the bag frees the cat but also opens a brief portal to another dimension and releases a trapped demonic marsh jelly.

Copyright Notice
Author Scott Greene.

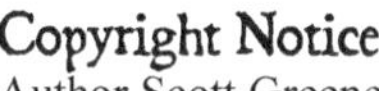

Golem, Blood

Hit Dice: 6 (25 hp)
Armor Class: 3 [16]
Attack: 2 strikes (1d8 plus blood consumption)
Saving Throw: 11
Special: Blood consumption, cell division, +1 or better weapon to hit, regenerate (2 hp/rd), immune to mind-affecting abilities, resistance to fire (50%)
Move: 12
Alignment: Neutrality
Challenge Level/XP: 9/1100

This creature looks like a hideous, bloated slug, blood red in color. Two long spindly arms protrude from its upper body. It has no other discernible features. Contrary to their name, blood golems are not constructs, but rather slug-shaped clots of living blood animated by a dark and ancient ritual. A typical blood golem is 10 feet long and weighs 700 pounds.

Each time a blood golem hits a living opponent with an attack, it gains a number of hit points equal to the damage dealt. These bonus hit points are added to the blood golem's total. When a blood golem absorbs enough blood to raise its hit points to the maximum for its HD, it splits into two identical blood golems, each with half the original's hit points. For example, a 6 HD blood golem that reaches 48 hit points splits into two 6 HD blood golems with 24 hit points each.

If a blood golem successfully hits an opponent with both of its slam attacks in a single round, that opponent suffers catastrophic blood expulsion, taking 2d4 points of constitution damage (saving throw for half). A blood golem gains 3 hit points per point of constitution damage it deals.

A blood golem is *slowed* (as the spell) for 1d4 rounds by any cold-based attacks or effects. A *purify food and water* spell deals 1d6 points of damage per caster level to a blood golem. A blood golem can attempt a saving throw to reduce the damage by half.

Blood Tribute

A procession of blue robed men and women, the monks and nuns of a large abbey dedicated to a deity of death is making its way through a crowded town on their way to pay a hated tribute to the town's Lord Mayor. Four of the monks are bearing a cassone of iron covered in shallow reliefs of dancing skeletons. The cassone is born on two thick poles of oak. At the head of the procession is the abbot, a gangly man with a scarred face and voluminous robe of blue velvet lined with sable.

Inside the cassone there is a blood golem, animated from the blood of numerous victims culled from the town and sacrificed on a hidden altar. The monks plan to carry the cassone into the city council's chambers and present it to the Lord Mayor in a bid to seize power.

Copyright Notice
Author Scott Greene.

Golem, Flagstone

Hit Dice: 9 (50 hit points)
Armor Class: 5 [14]
Attacks: 2 fists (2d8)
Saving Throw: 6
Special: Hit only by magic weapons, immune to most spells
Move: 8
Alignment: Neutrality
Challenge Level/XP: 12/2,000

A flagstone golem is composed of large flat stones and bricks jointed and fitted together so as to allow the creature to fold itself flat. A flagstone golem stands 10 feet tall and weighs 1,200 pounds. Spells that affect rock are the only ones that affect flagstone golems. Any energy-based (acid, fire, cold, electricity) attack that directly effects a flagstone golem is absorbed into its body dealing no damage. A flagstone golem can use the absorbed energy to repair itself, healing 1 hit point for every 3 points of damage the attack would have otherwise dealt. Or it can release the energy in a 30-foot cone that deals 3d8 points of damage to all within the area. An opponent can save to reduce the damage by half.

Mom

Brilliant and multicolored light fills this large domed room. A massive stain glass dome serves as the ceiling. Radiant lights shine through the dome, projecting vibrant images onto the floor. The lights behind the dome rotate, giving the projected image a sense of animation. Highly polished mirrors cover the curved walls and create a sense of endless space and light.

The images on the dome tell the life story of a wizard in 12 panels as she rose to power. Her deeds include slaying dragons, creating golems, protecting towns from encroaching armies of gnolls, building a floating tower, and finally a funeral panel where mortals and angels mourn her death. In each of the panels, the mage carries a ruby tipped staff. The light that passes through the rubies casts red ray onto the floor. Each ray deals 1d6 points of fire damage to anything that touches or passes through it. This beam heals the flagstone golem.

The stone and mosaic glass floor displays a family tree of sorts, with 10-foot-tall mosaic representations of the magic-user's female ancestors forming a circle on the floor. A flagstone golem protects the room. The animated creature lies in the spot on the floor where the magic-user's mother is represented.

Copyright Notice
Author Scott Greene.

Golem, Furnace

Hit Dice: 18 (75 hp)
Armor Class: 3 [16]
Attacks: 2 slams (4d8 + fire)
Saving Throw: 3
Special: Breath weapon, fire heals, cold slows, +2 weapons to hit, immune to most spells
Move: 6
Alignment: Neutrality
Challenge Level/XP: 20/4,400

Furnace golems are 20-foot-tall suits of black iron armor with a large grate opening in their abdomen covering roaring flames. The fires are magical and cannot be extinguished. Once every 1d4 rounds, the golem belches forth a 50-foot line of fire that does 10d6 points of damage (save for half). If a furnace golem hits a single opponent with 2 slams, it grabs the opponent (save avoids) and shoves the victim into its furnace interior (2d6 damage per round while trapped). Cold-based spells slow the golem (as per the *slow* spell), while fire spells restore hit points. No other type of spell affects a furnace golem.

Can't Stand the Heat

A pitiful halfling scavenges in the deep forest, filling a rusty wheelbarrow with branches and kindling. His fingers are blackened and covered by thick burns and scars. He wears soot-covered rags. His eyes are red and his hair is burnt to his scalp. His eyebrows are gone. Droog is a miserable being forced to care for the Unseen Tower of Archipor by a missing magic-user.

The tower is built of tightly packed gray stone rising four stories into the sky. The top is crenellated and topped by a metal fence. A single red oak door stands in the side of the tower.

A furnace golem sits like a pot-bellied stove in the middle of the tower's open first-floor room, connected to a network of pipes that snake throughout the tower. Hot water flows through the metal pipes, and steam hisses out of loose fittings. The golem doesn't bother anyone who enters the tower – unless they try to leave the entryway. A circular staircase rises through the ceiling to the second floor. Droog sleeps in a small bed under the staircase. Even he is not allowed above this floor. The golem belches fire and steam.

Droog thanks PCs profusely if they kill the golem and set him free.

Copyright Notice
Author Scott Greene.

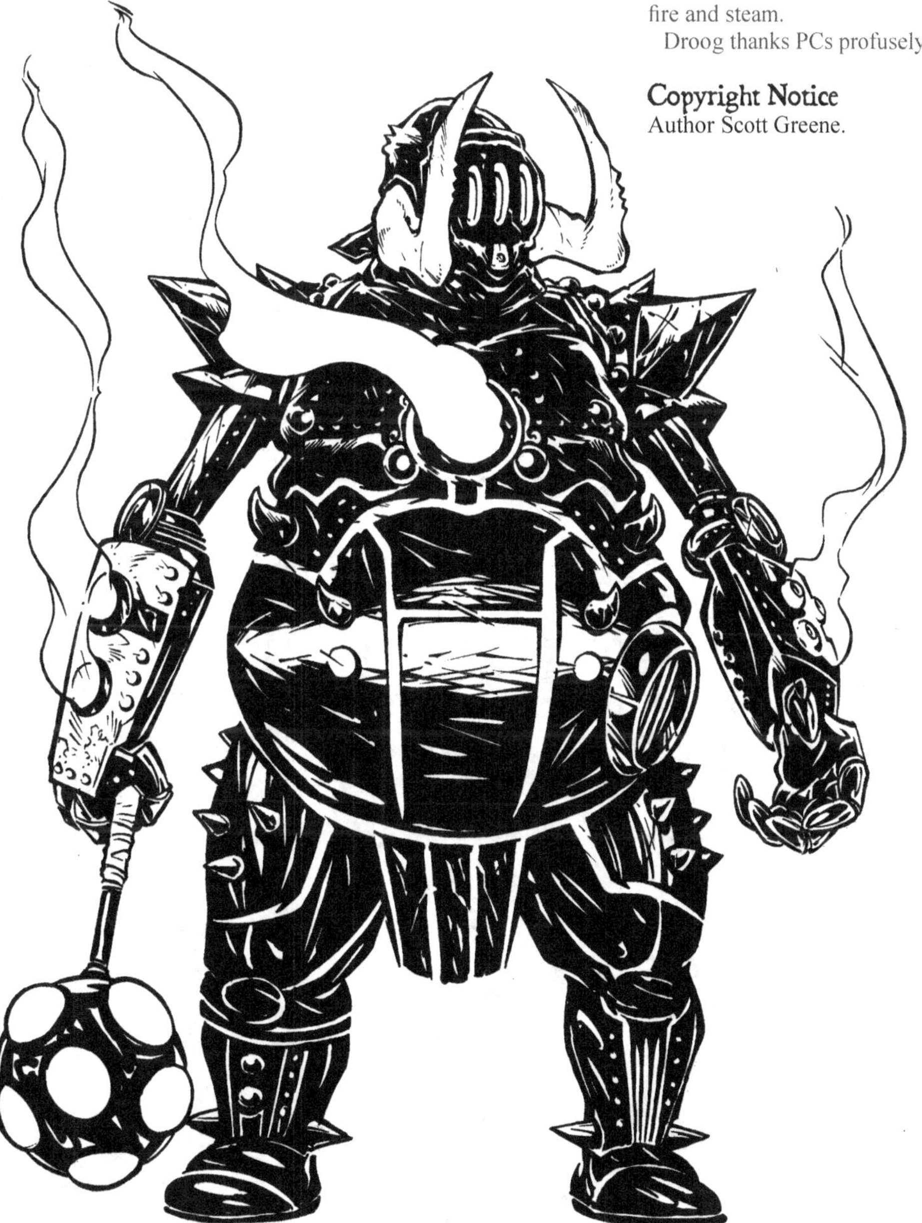

Golem, Gelatinous

Hit Dice: 10 (65 hit points)
Armor Class: 9 [10]
Attacks: 2 fists (2d6 + paralysis)
Saving Throw: 5
Special: Hit only by magic weapons, immune to most spells
Move: 8
Alignment: Neutrality
Challenge Level/XP: 11/1,700

A gelatinous golem is a humanoid-shaped, semi-transparent amoeba that stands 8 feet tall and weighs 600 pounds. It has rudimentary intelligence. A gelatinous golem secretes an anesthetizing slime that paralyzes opponents for 2d4 rounds who fail a save. If a gelatinous golem hits an opponent with both fists, it can decide to engulf the opponent automatically on the next round. An engulfed opponent takes 1d6 points of damage each round from the the gelatinous golem's acid each round it remains trapped. Attacks on a gelatinous golem deal half their damage to anyone engulfed by the creature. Cold slows a gelatinous golem. It is immune to all other spells.

Belly of the Beast

An idol of indescribable repugnance adorns this putrid shrine. The floors, walls and ceiling are coated in a thin layer of fatty gelatin and hardened stalactites of slime drip harmless sludge to the floor. A 15-foot-diameter bowl-shaped depression in the floor serves as an unholy altar of sorts. Fetid slime fills the pool and a dozen skeletal hands made of iron reach out from its depths.

The inanimate hands are merely decorative although the pool contains a dreaded green slime. Adjacent to the pool sits an idol of a demonic slime lord. The 15-foot-tall patchwork idol appears fashioned from the sewn skins of several humanoids and animals. Crudely made, the thing resembles a giant slug with the head and arms of an ogre. The distended belly of the decaying sculpture is like an overfilled wineskin. Beads of ooze and puss flow out of the seams and onto the floor. The stomach contents are actually a gelatinous golem that is the protector of the shrine. It bursts out of the distended stomach in a spray of gore and animal parts.

This recently abandoned shrine to the demon lord of ooze remains empty. The cultists took all valuables with them as they fled, but left the golem protector.

Copyright Notice
Author Scott Greene.

Golem, Ice

Hit Dice: 7 (30 hp)
Armor Class: 5 [14]
Attack: 2 slams (2d6 plus 1d6 cold)
Saving Throw: 9
Special: Breath weapon, cold, immunity to cold, immunity to magic, double damage from fire
Move: 9
Alignment: Neutrality
Challenge Level/XP: 10/1400

The ice golem is a humanoid formed of roughly chiseled ice, standing 10 feet tall and weighing around 800 pounds. Ice golems at rest appear to be normal ice sculptures and are often mistaken as such. An ice golem usually opens combat with its breath weapon, a blast of cold air in the shape of a cone 20-feet long with a 10-foot wide base. The breath weapon inflicts 3d6 points of cold damage (save for half damage) and can be used 3 times per day. An ice golem's body generates intense cold, dealing 1d6 points of damage with its touch.

An ice golem is immune to all spells except as follows: Lightning-based effects *slow* an ice golem (as the spell) for 2d6 rounds. Cold-based effects heal all of its lost hit points.

An ice golem's body must be constructed from a single block of ice weighing at least 1,000 pounds. The ice is treated with magical powders and unguents worth at least 500 gp.

Pantry of Souls

You come across an iron door in a corridor. The door cannot be pulled open and in fact can only be pushed open from the top, as its hinges are on the bottom of the door and parallel to the floor. The door forms a ramp into a room 20 feet wide, 30 feet long and with a 12-ft high ceiling. The room is quite frigid, owing to the presence of the room's guardian, an ice golem.

The walls of the room are lined with small niches, each holding a single bottle. The bottles contain all manner of liquids - water, poison, holy water, wine, bitters, spirits, etc. In addition, each bottle is inhabited by a disembodied soul with a connection to the liquid. If consumed, the soul possesses the drinker unless the drinker passes a saving throw. The bottles are sealed in silver and are worth about 20 gp each. A person who examines a bottle closely might see a ghostly image staring back at them.

Copyright Notice

Author Scott Greene.

Golem, Iron Maiden

Hit Dice: 12 (50 hp)
Armor Class: 3 [16]
Attacks: 2 slams (2d10)
Saving Throw: 3
Special: Animate host, +2 magic weapons to hit, slowed by lightning, healed by fire, immune to most spells
Move: 6
Alignment: Neutrality
Challenge Level/XP: 14/2,600

An iron maiden golem is a hollow torture device. The golem appears as a tall, well-muscled male or female warrior. An iron maiden golem has articulated arms and legs. If an iron maiden golem hits a victim with two slams, it must save or become trapped inside the golem. Trapped creatures take 20 points of damage each round from the dagger-like blades inside the lid. A creature slain inside the golem transforms into a zombie. Only +2 or better magic weapons can harm an iron maiden golem, and it is slowed by lightning spells. Fire-based spells heal the golem. No other type of spell affects an iron maiden golem.

Ungal's Angel

This 30-foot-by-30-foot torture chamber has thick chains hanging from the ceiling. Man-size iron cages swing at the ends of the chain. Pokers, serrated blades, whips and manacles hang from bones driven into the wall. Five wooden tables are scarred with slashes. Brass urns sit around the floor, each filled with congealed blood.

In the center of the east wall is a 10-foot-tall metal angel with wings spreading above it. The creature's face is serene, but its blank iron eyes seem to follow creatures in the room. The angel's arms are folded peacefully across its broad chest.

Ungal, the castle's ogre torturer, wears a blood-stained leather apron. Hanging from his belt are mallets, iron spikes and small saws. Ungal talks to the metal cages, blades and torture tables as if they were close friends. But Ungal saves his love for his pride and joy: an angel-shaped iron maiden golem named "Charlotte." Ungal rescued the golem from the smelting pit and relocated the creature to his lair.

The iron maiden golem reaches out and pulls PCs into a tight embrace as the razor-sharp wingtips fold inward and slam shut with a metallic clang over the entrapped creature. The golem releases the victim only when its soul is drained. Ungal can command the golem to release victims sooner, but he enjoys seeing others suffer too much to even think of doing so.

Ungal, Ogre Torturer: HD 7+1; AC 5[14]; Atk 1 weapon (1d10+1); Move 9; Save 9; CL/XP 7/600; Special: None.

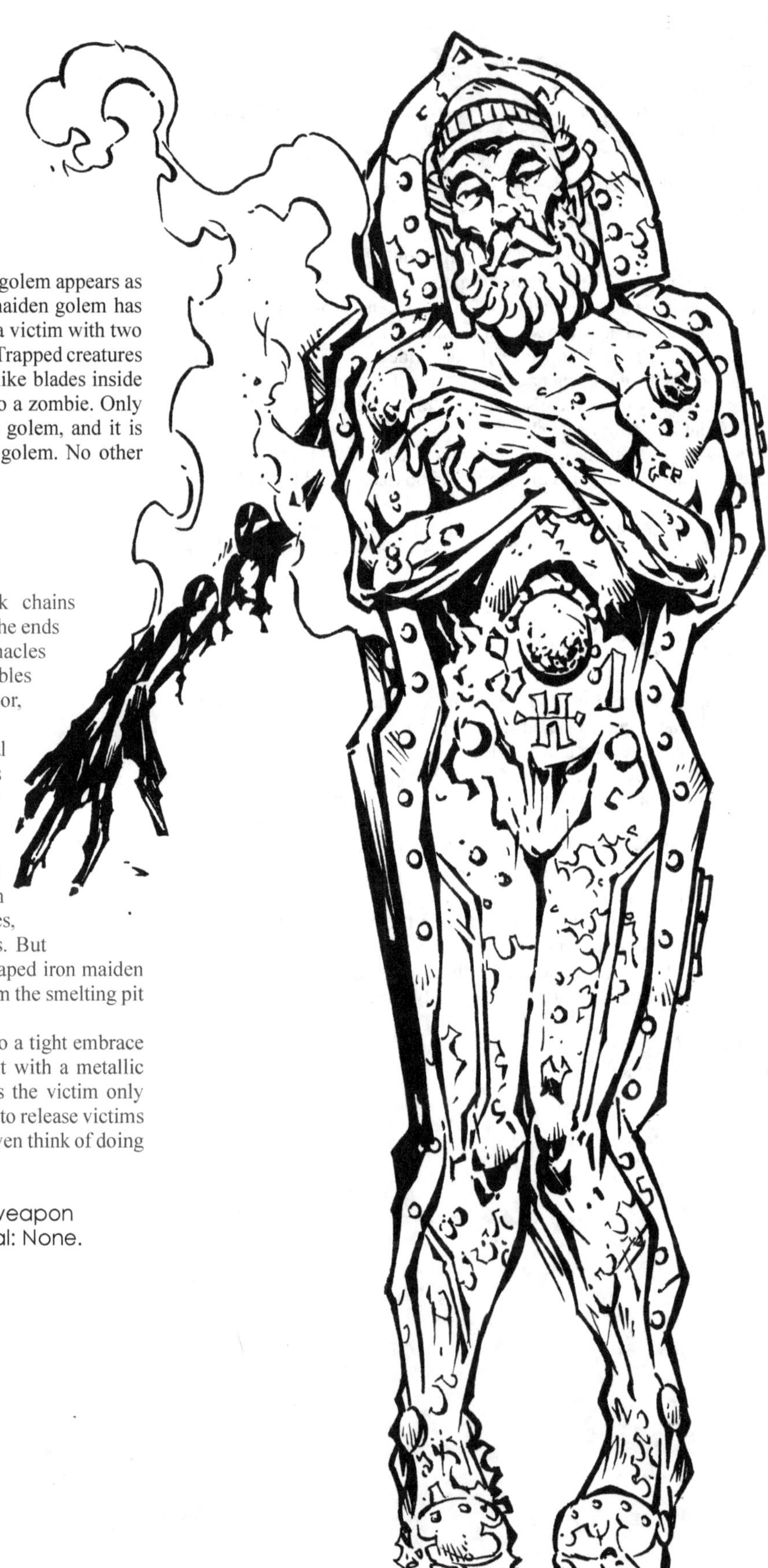

Golem, Magnesium

Hit Dice: 7
Armor Class: 5 [14]
Attacks: 2 slams (2d6+1)
Saving Throw: 9
Special: Sickness, +1 weapons to hit, immune to most spells
Move: 6
Alignment: Neutrality
Challenge Level/XP: 9/1,100

A magnesium golem is a silvery-white humanoid formed of magnesium standing 6-7 feet tall and weighing 600 pounds. The magnesium golem's features are smooth and perfect, though it has no discernable ears, nose, or mouth. Its eyes are indentations in its face. A 10-foot aura of sickness radiates around the magnesium golem that sickens any creature it hits or that gets near it (save avoids). This sickness lasts for 1d4 turns. Water-based spells slow a magnesium golem (as per the slow spell), while fire-based spells heal the golem. They are immune to all other spells, and +1 weapons are required to hit them.

Beneath the Surface

The air in the 10-foot-high tunnel is thick and oppressive and smells heavily of brine. Water seeps through the roof to splash against the paving-stone floor. Glowing lichens cover the walls, casting a wan light throughout the tunnel. An arching doorway opens into a much larger room.

The 80-foot-diameter circular room is topped by a massive glass ceiling keeping the ocean at bay. Glowing deepwater fish shoot past the window in bright arcs, their luminescence lighting the chamber with a pale blue hue. Heavy shadows fill the room. A thin layer of frost covers the floor from the bone-numbing chill radiating through the glass ceiling.

The room is decorated with dried fish, dolphins and squid attached to a pulley system that winds them throughout the room. Each creature flops, moves and twists along its track as if alive. A palanquin bed covered in silk sheets and piled with pillows sits in the center of the room, supported by two giant figures, each with their flesh sewn and stitched into place. Around the bed, propped up by metal posts, are the bodies of seven mermaids posed like revelers at a party. The room was the underwater home of the vampire Dicostia Green, who was slain as she sought out a giant clam to complete the décor.

The room is unoccupied, but not undefended. One of the giants holding the bed is covered in stitches and staples that hold its flesh together. In all ways, it resembles a flesh golem. It wears a dirty tunic fastened with two golden clam shells over its shoulders.

The creature is actually a magnesium golem with a hill giant's flesh sewn about its true form. The creature attacks, not caring if its "flesh" body is torn or burned away during the fight.

Hidden in a panel in the bed are potions of levitation, undead control and human control, plus a diamond ring (worth 1,000 gp) and a bag of gold coins (500 gp).

Copyright Notice

Golem, Mummy

Hit Dice: 9 (55 hit points)
Armor Class: 3 [16]
Attacks: 2 fists (1d8)
Saving Throw: 6
Special: Hit only by +1 magic weapons, immune to most spells, constriction
Move: 10
Alignment: Neutrality
Challenge Level/XP: 10/1,400

A mummy golem stands 6 feet tall and weighs 300 pounds. Its body is composed of tightly knotted and rolled bandages held together by magic (and more bandages). A mummy golem can wrap bandages from its body around a grappled foe's throat. The bandages can come from anywhere on its body, not just its arm or hand, so the mummy golem can continue using its fist. A strangled creature takes 1d6 points of damage each round. A mummy golem can strangle a maximum of 4 opponents. Fire and fire-based spells affect mummy golems normally. They are immune to all other spells.

Tomb of the Bull King

A sealed iron door blocks entry into this chamber. The sculpted metal head of a bull adorns the door, with a ring piercing its nose serving as a door knocker. The door opens if the ring is used to knock; otherwise, the door remains magically locked.

Hieroglyphs of bull-headed giants decorate the walls of the musty tomb behind the door. Three upright stone sarcophagi line the walls, two of which contain minotaur zombies that appear as minotaur mummies. The third sarcophagus contains a mummy golem created in the image of a mummified minotaur. In the center of the chamber's floor sits the crypt lid to a buried vault. A small golden bull figurine adorns the lid (500 gp). The crypt contains the dead king of a small clan of minotaurs that banded together to wreak havoc on the lands. The king wears a golden bull funeral mask (750 gp) and other finery fit for a king.

Minotaur Zombie (2): HD 7; AC 8 [11]; Atk 1 strike (2d6); Move 6; CL/XP 5/400; Save 11; Special: Immune to sleep and charm spells.

Copyright Notice

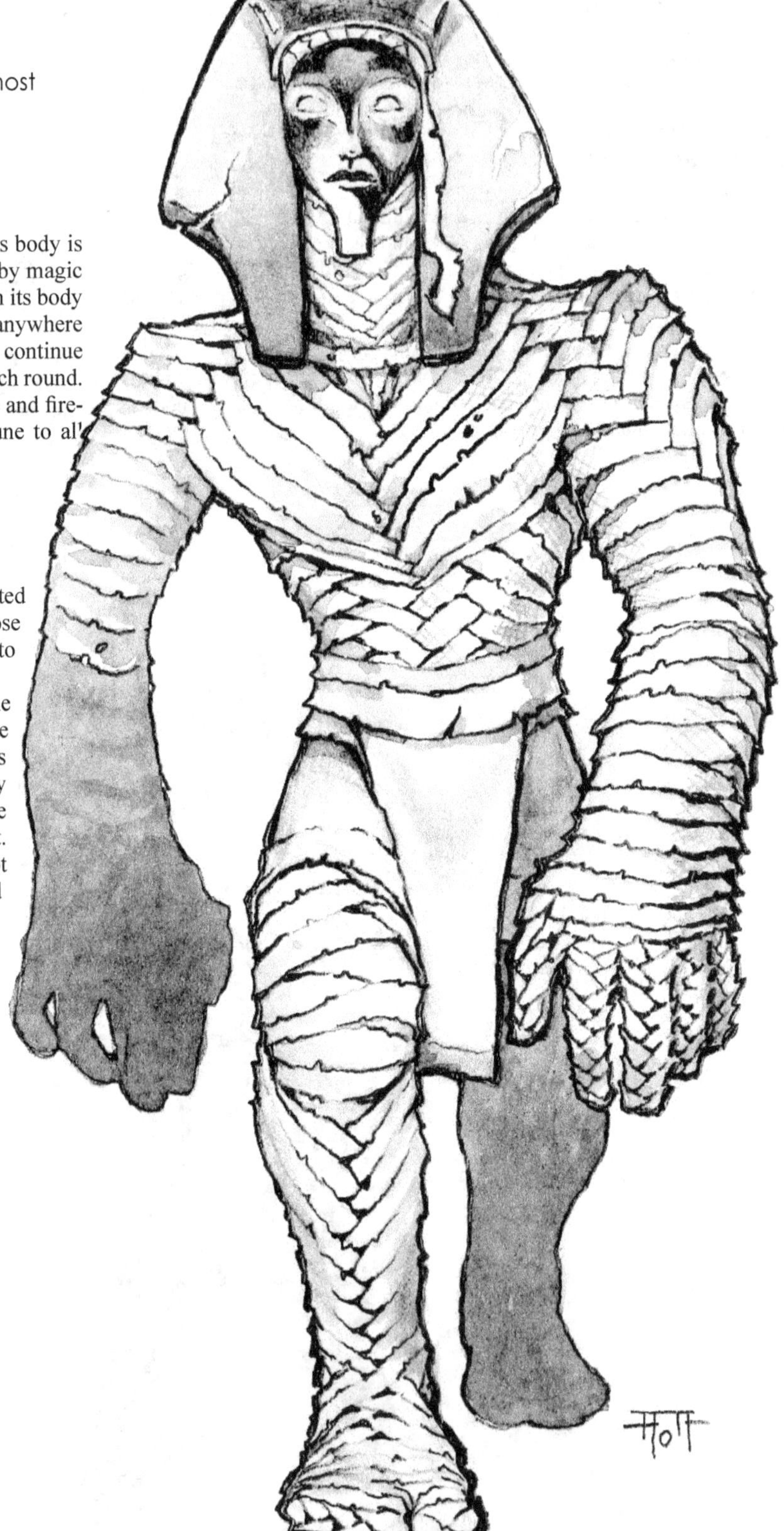

Golem, Ooze

Hit Dice: 10
Armor Class: 6 [13]
Attacks: 2 slams (2d8 + 1d6 acid)
Saving Throw: 5
Special: Acid, death throes, immune to blunt weapons, immune to most spells, regenerate 2 hp/round
Move: 6
Alignment: Neutrality
Challenge Level/XP: 12/2,000

Ooze golems are 10-foot-tall amorphous creatures of swirling colors that can alter their shape to appear roughly humanoid. Their natural form resembles a column or pillar with two large pseudopods extending from its central trunk that function as arms. In humanoid form, an ooze golem's lower torso ends in two powerful legs, and the creature can flatten its body to squeeze through cracks up to 2 inches in size. An ooze golem secretes a deadly acid that deals an extra 1d6 points of damage with each hit. Spells don't affect ooze golems. When killed, an ooze golem explodes in a burst of acid that does 2d6 points of damage to all within 10 feet (save for half).

Ol' Black Water

A burbling fountain sits flush against the wall, a semicircle of stones jutting 10 feet out into the room. A giant stone goldfish sits on the edge of the fountain, black oily sludge spurting from its open mouth into a stone catch basin. Another giant face carved into the wall vomits an incredible amount of the same dark ichor. The basin bubbles and boils with the churning fluid, the surface swirling with reds, greens, browns and grays.

Attached to the wall above the fountain is a golden replica of a long sword. The weapon is marked with a detailed scene of a god climbing down from the heavens to slay a massive dragon.

The gelatin-like water is an ooze golem that flows on its own through the fountain. It is harmless unless someone disturbs the sword.

The blade is useless as a weapon, but can be sold for 200 gp as a decorative item.

Copyright Notice

Golem, Rope

Hit Dice: 5
Armor Class: 7 [12]
Attacks: 2 slams (2d6)
Saving Throw: 12
Special: Strangulation, vulnerable to fire, immune to magic
Move: 6
Alignment: Neutrality
Challenge Level/XP: 6/400

A rope golem is a tangled mess of knotted and bundled ropes in roughly humanoid form. The typical rope golem stands 7 feet tall but weighs only about 100 pounds. Its long, gangly arms end in noose-like hands. Until it is activated, a rope golem appears to be nothing more than a pile of normal ropes. If a rope golem hits the same opponent with 2 slams, it twists the foe into its ropy clutches to strangle him for 1d8 damage for each round thereafter. A rope golem takes one and a half damage from all fire-based spells. *Rope trick* deals 1d6 points of damage. They are immune to all other spells.

Scuttle and Run

A galley under full sail appears on the horizon, its prow leaping from the water as the ship plows through the waves. Skeletons line the black freighter's rails and stand on the ship's masts. Each waves a short sword as the ship closes.

The Fortune Seeker and its skeletal crew are the scourge of the eastern seaboard. The galley rides low in the water, but seems to fly across the waves. The skeletons never take prisoners and sink vessels without plundering treasure.

Riding on the ship are 20 skeletons, but the ship is without a leader since a sea serpent plucked the captain off the deck. The ship gets through the waters via a massive rope golem that is the ship's rigging. The golem can sail the ship by itself, raising and lowering the sails at will. A rope wrapped around the helm lets the golem steer the ship.

When the Fortune Seeker slams into a ship, the rope golem reaches out and begins strangling victims on the opposite deck. The skeletons jump across to attack with their short swords. The rope golem also can grasp a ship to lash the vessel to the Fortune Seeker's side.

The forgotten treasures remaining on the ship include 2,000 gp in coins of different nations, a room full of diamonds (all worthless glass fakes), 10 bolts of expensive cloth (500 gp total), and a hidden compartment in the captain's empty quarters containing various spell components and a *ring of shooting stars.*

SKELETONS (10): HD 1; AC 8 [11]; Atk Short sword (1d6); Move 12; Save 17; Alignment Neutrality; CL/XP 1/15; Special: None

ROPE GOLEM (1): HD 12; AC 7 [12]; Atk 2 slams (2d6); Move 6; Save 3; Alignment Neutrality; CL/XP 13/2,300; Special: Strangulation, vulnerable to fire, immune to magic

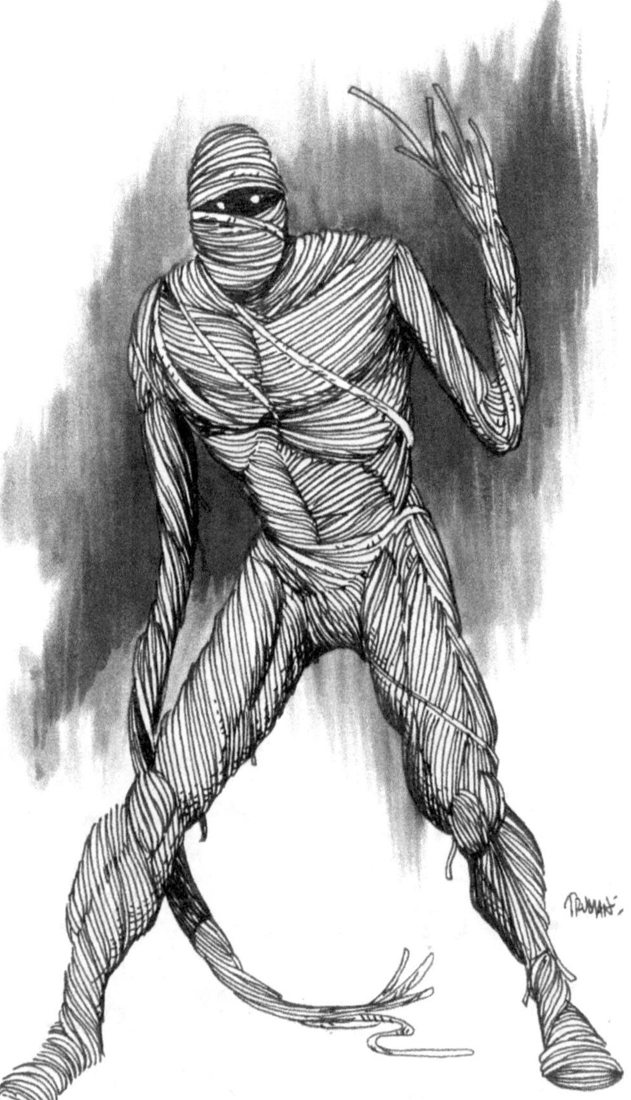

Golem, Stone Guardian

Hit Dice: 4 (20 hp)
Armor Class: 1 [18]
Attack: 2 slams (2d6)
Saving Throw: 13
Special: Resistance to cold, electricity and fire (50%), ring link, see invisibility
Move: 9
Alignment: Neutrality
Challenge Level/XP: 5/240

Stone guardians are sometimes referred to as lesser stone golems. It resembles a stocky humanoid formed of mud and stone. Stone guardians are often used as guardians by their creators. When the stone guardian is first constructed, the creator crafts a magical ring that offers himself (or anyone to whom he gives the ring) protection from that stone guardian. A stone guardian can see invisible creatures.

A stone guardian's body is constructed from mud mixed with rare herbs and powders worth at least 500 gp. A large chunk of stone inserted into the chest cavity functions as its "heart." The magical ring that links a stone guardian is constructed at the same time and costs 300 gp to create.

You Sink It or You Die

This large chamber is designed as a ball court for a hobgoblin game very similar to tlachtli, the Inca ball game. The room is 50 feet wide and 100 feet long, with a ceiling 30 feet high. The room is clad in gray stone tiles about 1 foot square. Squat, grimacing demons flank the "baskets" in the two short walls.

The room is a sacred place for the hobgoblins. Those who enter the room must propitiate the hobgoblin god of physical education by picking up the rubber balls in the center of the room and throwing them into the baskets. This requires a ranged attack against an AC of 5 [14].

Each time a basket is missed, one of the stone demons leave the wall to throttle the person who missed. The "demons" are stone guardians Successfully throwing the balls into the holes causes a large area in the center of the room to sink into the floor, revealing four hidden doors that go deeper into the dungeon.

Credit

The Stone Guardian originally appeared in the First Edition module *L1 Secret of Bone Hill* (© TSR/Wizards of the Coast, 1981) and later in the First Edition *Monster Manual II* (© TSR/Wizards of the Coast, 1983) and is used by permission.

Copyright Notice

Author Scott Greene, based on original material by Lenard Lakofka.

Golem, Tallow

Hit Dice: 10 (40 hp)
Armor Class: 6 [13]
Attack: 2 slams (1d8)
Saving Throw: 5
Special: Chemisorb, only harmed by sharp weapons, immunity to cold, double damage from fire
Move: 9
Alignment: Neutrality
Challenge Level/XP: 12/2000

The tallow golem is a humanoid construct composed entirely of wax. It bears no facial features unless the creator chooses to render a lifelike "wax dummy," in which case the golem can appear quite real indeed. Wizards who specialize in the creation of tallow golems refer to themselves as "chandlers." Unlike other golem-sculptors, chandlers consider their work a form of art. The golem wears whatever clothing (if any) that its creator desires, usually rags or trousers. It has no possessions and no weapons. The golem cannot speak or utter any sound. It moves slowly, but relentlessly.

A creature hit by both of a tallow golem's slam attacks in a single round must pass a saving throw or be pinned. A tallow golem can break down and absorb chemicals from a pinned victim, dealing 1d12 points of damage each round the pin is maintained. Additionally, this causes skin discoloration. The victim must make a successful saving throw or lose 1 point of charisma permanently.

The tallow golem is formed from a large block of candle wax mixed with special powders worth at least 500 gp.

As the Tallow Burns

In a deep gorge divided by a rusty river there is a divided town. The town is joined by a long, wooden bridge, but the bridge is now off limits, protected by a gang of four tallow golems. The town is in an uproar, divided by a religious conflict precipitated by a young girl who claims to have heard the voice of a goddess when she stood in the middle of the bridge under a full moon.

The priests of the village have rejected this, and about half of the population support them. The lord mayor of the town supports the girl (he wishes to break the monopoly the priests hold on minting coins), again, with the support of about half the population. There have been a few skirmishes in the village, and the priests and their faction are now occupying and looting the north side of the river and the lord mayor and his faction are on the south side of the river. Anyone attempting to cross the bridge will be accosted by the tallow golems and thrown into the river, which is home to aggressive and hideous river dolphins.

The girl, as it happens, is lying. She came up with the story to explain why she crept out of her house in the middle of the night. Her lover is now trapped on the other side of the river, his family supporting the priests.

Copyright Notice

Golem, Witch-Doll

Hit Dice: 10 (65 hit points)
Armor Class: 2 [17]
Attacks: 2 fists (2d8)
Saving Throw: 5
Special: Hit only by +1 magic weapons, immune to most spells, linked damage
Move: 10
Alignment: Neutrality
Challenge Level/XP: 10/1,400

A witch-doll golem appears to be crafted from stuffed human skin dressed in a patchwork of ill-fitting clothes. Large needles and pins pierce the creature's body where a humanoid's vital organs would be. A witch-doll golem stands twice the height of a human and weighs about 1,000 pounds. A witch-doll golem can be commanded to target a specific foe. Against that foe, the witch-doll golem deals an extra 1d8 points of damage with each fist. Once the golem hits its intended target, half of any further damage the witch-doll golem takes is transferred to the victim so long as they are within 60 feet of each other. Only the linked target can attack a witch-doll golem and not take "linked damage." Witch-doll golems take full damage from fire and do not pass this damage to their linked target. They are immune to all other spells.

Blood Donor

A massive fluid-filled cylinder dominates this ruined laboratory. A crudely assembled humanoid made from the parts of many creatures floats in the translucent greenish liquid. The burnt corpses of orcs lie clustered together where they died by some sort of fiery blast. The decaying body of a man wearing a leather apron lies sprawled out on the floor. A battle axe is still embedded in the man's head. Broken glass, burnt paper and wrecked equipment litter the floor and workbenches. Only the cylinder and an attached complex mechanism made of gold remain unscathed. The device has many tubes, hoses and a dial lined with small needles.

The witch-doll golem in the fluid only needs a small sample of blood to become active. Handling the machinery in any fashion has a 50% chance of a needle sticking the victim and siphoning a drop of blood. Once active, the witch-doll golem stops at nothing to slay the blood donor. The fragments of paper hint at a lab journal and research on golems. One sheet displays a diagram of the gold mechanism with the words "golem completion: blood" written on it. The mechanism has a delicate pinwheel dial lined with needles used to extract blood from flesh or a test tube. Regardless, the witch-doll golem animates and attacks if the glass is broken but only has quarry to chase if blood is siphoned into the gold apparatus.

Golem, Wood

Hit Dice: 9 (40 hp)
Armor Class: 2 [17]
Attack: 2 slams (2d6)
Saving Throw: 6
Special: Alarm, immunity to cold and electricity, double damage from fire
Move: 12
Alignment: Neutrality
Challenge Level/XP: 10/1400

Arcane spellcasters used several ancient texts to arrive at a process to create inexpensive yet still quite powerful golems. They had master craftsmen create wood statues with articulating limbs and then performed the proper spells to animate and control them. The statues vary in shape and form and usually have weapons of some sort held in each hand. The wood golems were designed to act both as an alarm and a protection against intruders. Wood golems let out a piercing howl that lasts for 6 rounds when anyone other than its creator enters the area it is guarding or comes within 50 feet of the golem. This howl can be heard to a range of 100 feet. The pieces of a wood golem are assembled from blocks of fine wood and sprinkled with rare powders and crushed herbs worth at least 300 gp.

Lich Puppets

At the edge of a great glacier there is a sturdy little cavern. A plume of smoke rolling from the chimney invites chilled travelers to knock on the door, which is answered by a stout man with cloudy spectacles wearing a woolen tunic, leather boots and a leather apron. The man is actually a lich, his soul hidden in a pulsing bloodstone hidden under the fire. An illusion gives him the appearance of a kindly woodcarver.

The interior of the cabin is copiously covered in carvings of faces and animals (they take on a sinister cast when one views them from the corner of their eye), with dozens of shelves covered in dozens of wooden puppets. Four of the puppets - a mountain goat, dairymaid, knight with a long mustache and old hag, are actually small wood golems (stats are the same).

The lich uses his golems to strangle people in the night, revealing himself and his powers only if he must. Those killed have their souls drained into glass marbles, which are then used as they eyes of puppets animated as wood golems.

Credit
Wood Golems originally appeared in the Necromancer Games adventure *Hall of the Rainbow Mage*.

Copyright Notice
Authors Scott Greene and Patrick Lawinger.

Gorbel

Hit Dice: 2
Armor Class: 2 [17]
Attack: 2 claws (1d4), bite (1d6)
Saving Throw: 16
Special: Explosion, cannot be surprised, only harmed by sharp weapons
Move: 3/24 (flying)
Alignment: Neutrality
Challenge Level/XP: 3/60

This bizarre creature is a small orb with reddish skin. Atop its round body are six eyestalks, each ending in a sapphire-colored eye. Dangling beneath its body are two stubby legs that end in claws. A gorbel is approximately 3 feet in diameter. Its reddish skin is a thin, tough and rubbery membrane. The spherical body of a gorbel is highly elastic and filled to near bursting with a lighter-than air flammable gas that smells of rotten eggs (sulfur). A gorbel eats, breathes, and excretes through an aperture best described as a mouth. This mouth is lined with a ring of sharp teeth that face inward to help it force food into its gullet.

A gorbel's body is naturally buoyant. This buoyancy allows it to fly at a speed of 60 feet and also grants it a permanent *feather fall* effect.

When a gorbel is hit with a weapon, spell, or effect that deals piercing or slashing damage it must succeed on a saving throw or explode, dealing 1d4 points of damage to all creatures within 5 feet. This instantly kills the gorbel.

Bouncing Ball in the Corner Pocket

A wide river that flows through a jungle is embanked with massive stone blocks. The river is spanned by an arched bridge that is entered by an ivory spirit gate set with a blue crystal. The first person through the spirit gate is struck by a beam of blue light partially on the ethereal plane. The light cannot be blocked by any substance due to its origin. In the middle of the bridge span there is a round tile of blue jade depicting a leering eyeball. The tile is about 3 feet in diameter and stuck fast to the ground. Attempts to pry it out with metal implements result in powerful shocks (2d6 points of electricity damage, saving throw for half damage). If a person struck by the blue light steps on the tile they will fall through it into a pocket dimension.

This pocket dimension is a single chamber, cubical and measuring 30 feet wide, tall and long (and thus the person who enters it falls 30 feet to the floor). The walls are composed of blue jade and are perfectly smooth. A scepter lies in the middle of the chamber, topped by a faceted crystal. Should one breath on the crystal it throws off a reddish light as of from a mirror ball. As the reddish spots trace their way across the walls, 2d6 gorbels emerge from the walls to attack the holder of the scepter, bouncing off the walls as they do so. The walls will begin to shrink, losing about 3 feet per round as the combat continues. If the crystal is broken on the floor, the cube disappears and the person drops 30 feet to land in the middle of the bridge span, still holding the remnants of the scepter (treat as a *+2 mace*). Otherwise, the cube will shrink to the point that it folds in one itself, leaving the holder of the scepter alone in the negative material universe and on a vast, steaming plain of red trees under a blue sun. This plain is rife with gorbels that serve a massive beholder, the ruler of this strange dimension.

Others may enter this dimension by the same means as the first person, though they will have to re-enter the spirit gate to do so. Presumably, the palace contains all manner of weird treasures and a means of returning to the Material Plane.

Credit

The Gorbel originally appeared in the First Edition *Fiend Folio* (© TSR/ Wizards of the Coast, 1981) and is used by permission.

Copyright Notice

Author Scott Greene, based on original material by Andrew Key.

Gorgimera

This hideous creature has leathery dragon wings and three heads; a lion, a dragon, and a gorgon. Its hindquarters are that of a gorgon and its forequarters are that of a great lion.

Hit Dice: 10
Armor Class: 2 [17]
Attack: 2 bites (1d10), butt (1d8), 2 claws (1d6)
Saving Throw: 5
Special: Breath weapon
Move: 15/18 (flying)
Alignment: Neutrality
Challenge Level/XP: 13/2300

A gorgimera is a chimerical creature akin to the standard chimera. A gorgimera has the heads of a lion, dragon, and gorgon. A gorgimera's dragon head can be that of any of the chaotic dragons (see below). It has the hindquarters of a gorgon and the forequarters of lion. It is a highly territorial predator whose hunting range often covers several square miles around its lair. The creature makes its home inside caves high atop mountains or deep inside caverns. A typical lair contains a mated pair and one or two young.

A gorgimera has two breath weapons, each of which can be used independently of the other (thus it can breathe twice in a given round as a standard action). A gorgimera's dragon head breath weapon depends on the color of its dragon head, as summarized on the table below. Regardless of its type, a gorgimera's breath weapon is usable once every 1d4 rounds, deals 3d8 points of damage and allows a saving throw for half damage. To determine a gorgimera's head color and breath weapon randomly, roll 1d10 and consult the table below.

1d10	Head Color	Breath Weapon
1–2	Black	40-foot line of acid
3–4	Blue	40-foot line of lightning
5–6	Green	20-foot cone of corrosive gas
7–8	Red	20-foot cone of fire
9–10	White	20-foot cone of cold

A gorgimera's gorgon head breath weapon is usable once every 1d4 rounds (no more than twice per day), turns a creature to stone permanently, and allows a saving throw to avoid. The breath weapon is a cone 30 feet long and 20 feet wide at the base.

They Picked the Wrong Beast to Poke

Crossing the snowcapped mountains you might (1 in 10 chance) come across a grievously wounded man crawling along the ground dragging a shattered leg. The man was part of an army that was set upon by a gorgimera with the heads of a lion, gorgon and white dragon. The gorgimera was defending the cavern in which reside its mate and three young. The icy scarp beneath the cave is now littered with the bodies of soldiers in banded armor and steel helms, as well as a splintered chariot. The horses escaped the slaughter and now graze in a meadow about a mile away. Slumped over the side of the chariot is the body of Lord Elphston.

Elphston wears a brilliant red cape over a gilded cuirasse (treat as chainmail, worth 250 gp) and has a *+1 long sword* clutched in his cold, dead hand. A scroll case on his hip shows the location of a fabulous treasure in a cliffside temple. Taking possession of Elphston's longsword means certain doom for those not of the Elphston family, in the form of a curse that imposes a cumulative -1 penalty each week to all saving throws made by the person. When one taps the hilt of the longsword against a structure, all doors and windows in the structure fly open violently.

Credit

The Gorgimera originally appeared in the First Edition module *S4 Lost Caverns of Tsojcanth* (© TSR/Wizards of the Coast, 1982) and later in the First Edition *Monster Manual II* (© TSR/Wizards of the Coast, 1983) and is used by permission.

Copyright Notice

Author Scott Greene, based on original material by Gary Gygax.

Gorgon, True

Sthenno

Hit Dice: 18 (75 hp)
Armor Class: -1 [20]
Attack: 2 claws (1d10), bite (1d8), snakes (1d6 plus poison)
Saving Throw: 3
Special: Petrifying gaze, poison, +2 or better weapon to hit, regenerate (2 hp/rd), immortal, immunities, magic resistance (60%)
Move: 12/21 (flying)
Alignment: Chaos
CL/XP: 26/6200

Euryale

Hit Dice: 20 (80 hp)
Armor Class: -2 [21]
Attack: 2 claws (1d10), bite (1d8), snakes (1d6 plus poison)
Saving Throw: 3
Special: Petrifying gaze, poison, +2 or better weapon to hit, regenerate (2 hp/rd), immortal, immunities, magic resistance (65%)
Move: 12/21 (flying)
Alignment: Chaos
CL/XP: 28/6800

Though the word gorgon is often associated with the deadly bull-like creature that turns a victim to stone with its breath weapon, the true gorgons are three sisters; Euryale, Sthenno, and Medusa. They are the daughters of the god Phorcys and the goddess Ceto. Euryale and Sthenno were born immortal and are hideous creatures with writing snakes for hair, brass claws, wings, and a gaze that can turn any living creature into stone. Phorcys tasked them with guarding the entrance to the Underworld.

Medusa was born mortal and was very beautiful. Phorcys sent her to the Material Plane so all could gaze upon the beauty of his daughter. Medusa's beauty rivaled that of some of the goddesses, and some of them grew jealous of Medusa, particularly the goddess Athena. Her beauty also turned the heads of some of the gods, and when Poseidon seduced her in a temple to Athena, the goddess became enraged and changed the beautiful Medusa into a creature as hideous as her sisters. Poseidon turned from his love, never to return again. Medusa, enraged, fled into the desert and never came back to civilization.

The hero Perseus was tasked with killing the gorgon known as Medusa and bringing her head to King Polydectes as a wedding present. Using a magic shield given to him by the gods, he avoided Medusa's deadly gaze and severed her head. From her serpentine body sprang the children of Poseidon, creatures similar in appearance to their mother. These creatures escaped into the world and are called medusa.

Sthenno and Euryale long for their sister's return or their meeting with her in the Underworld. Yet being immortal, they cannot enter the Realm of the Dead. Thus, both know they will never see their beloved sibling again. Their cries are said to be audible on the wind as a high-pitched shrill akin to a bird's cry.

The sisters' gaze turns people to stone permanently. The poisonous bites of their snakes are deadly (i.e. pass a saving throw or die).

Sthenno and Euryale are immune to polymorph, sleep, stunning and paralysis.

Forgotten Sisters

Far to the north there is a bare stone promontory that juts into a frozen sea. Over this a piercing wind howls as it carries poisonous words and fierce shrieks. The rocky coasts of the promontory are inhabited by especially large and powerful harpies. Atop the promontory dwell the two true gorgons, Sthenno and Euryale.

The great scaled queens of the damned, whispering foul curses and wicked temptations and launching them out on the winds to find the ears of gullible men and women. The gorgons guard a chest of lead, unlocked, that contains a wide-brimmed *hat of invisibility* and *sandals of flying*. The hat and sandals were owned by the hero Perseus, and if touched by creatures with fewer than nine levels cause them to burst into flame (6d6 damage, no save).

Copyright Notice

Gorilla Bear

Hit Dice: 4
Armor Class: 3 [16]
Attack: 2 claws (1d8), bite (1d6)
Saving Throw: 13
Special: Squeeze
Move: 12
Alignment: Neutrality
Challenge Level/XP: 4/120

Gorilla bears are the result of a magical crossbreeding and merging of two distinct species: a gorilla and a black bear. A gorilla bear's fur is always dark and ranges in color from jet black to brownish-black. Its paws and feet end in elongated nails, brown in color. A typical gorilla bear stands 8 feet tall and weighs almost 1,700 pounds. Its eyes are always one of two colors: crimson or emerald green. No other eye color has ever been seen on a gorilla bear (though legends speak of an immensely powerful white-furred gorilla bear with eyes the color of amethysts). Gorilla bears make their lairs in caves or caverns, often hidden among the twisted tangle of trees and shrubs of jungles. They are diurnal hunters and feast on a diet of meat, savoring the taste of goblins and elves. A typical lair contains a mated pair and 1d4 young. A gorilla bear that hits a victim with both claw attacks squeezes them for 1d8+1 points of damage.

Experiment Gone Wrong

The map discovered in the crypt leads to an enormous crater filled with a thick, tanged wood of bloated trees and pale, sickly plants. The crater's scalloped edges descend 90 feet to the floor of the crater, where their air is heavy and has an acrid, unpleasant smell. It was formed when the skull of a dead god of sorcery (or some other elder thing as dictated by one's campaign) emerged from the astral plane and streaked through the atmosphere, slamming into the ground.

The skull, eight feet in diameter, is now buried 10 feet under ground and formed of crystal adamantine - a tempting prize for any dwarf. The soil around ground zero of the crater is rich in pitchblende, a uranium ore often used in the creation of magic items. The air in the crater is tainted with a subtle poison that slowly turns those who breath it into monstrosities called gorilla bears. Hundreds of these misbegotten creatures lurk in the woods, with encounters with 1d4+2 of the monsters occuring on a roll of 1-2 on 1d6 made hourly.

Credit

The Gorilla Bear originally appeared in the First Edition *Fiend Folio* (© TSR/Wizards of the Coast, 1981) and is used by permission.

Copyright Notice

Author Scott Greene, based on original material by Cricky Hitchcock.

Grave Risen

Hit Dice: 4
Armor Class: 8 [11] or 7[12] with shield
Attacks: 2 claws (1d4+2 + blood poisoning)
Saving Throw: 13
Special: Animate dead, blood poisoning
Move: 6
Alignment: Chaos
Challenge Level/XP: 5/240

Grave risen are rotting, worm-ridden, walking corpses draped in tattered and loosely fitting rags or outfitted in dented and rusted armor. Blackened eye sockets grant it sight and its body still clings to the stench of death. The clawed hands of a grave risen are filthy; its nails long and caked with dirt and soil from its grave. Once per day, a grave risen can animate up to 10 HD of corpses within 100 feet as zombies. A grave risen's claws are coated with a deadly poison that infects the blood.

The Pampered Dead

A fire recently devastated the mill in Jodea, a careless flame igniting the sawdust into a blazing inferno that killed 12 men. A few climbed from the burning debris, only to collapse with their lungs on fire. The town mourned as the workers were buried them in the small cemetery. Three nights later, someone dug up the bodies.

The recent dead weren't stolen; they got up and walked out of the graveyard after a grave risen passed through. The creature animated the recent dead to join its growing retinue of zombies.

PCs who follow the many footsteps leading out of the small cemetery uncover a horrid band of 20 zombies lurching across the countryside. Six of the undead carry a wooden palanquin on their rotting shoulders, struggling to support its weight. The litter has four wooden poles on the side that support rotting funeral shroud curtains.

A bloated grave risen rests aboard a palanquin. The undead creature wears a dirt-soiled toga and has a silver crown perched on its withered head. The creature's massive bulk wobbles from side to side with each lurching step of its servants. The grave risen's sharp claws are black and twisted, with cemetery dirt falling in dark specks in the palanquin's wake. Despite its bulk, however, the grave risen is fast and vicious, and attacks by leaping from its palanquin directly toward PCs.

Copyright Notice

Gray Nisp

Hit Dice: 8
Armor Class: 4 [15]
Attacks: 2 claws (1d6), 1 bite (1d8)
Saving Throw: 8
Special: Rend
Move: 6/18 (swim)
Alignment: Neutrality
Challenge Level/XP: 8/800

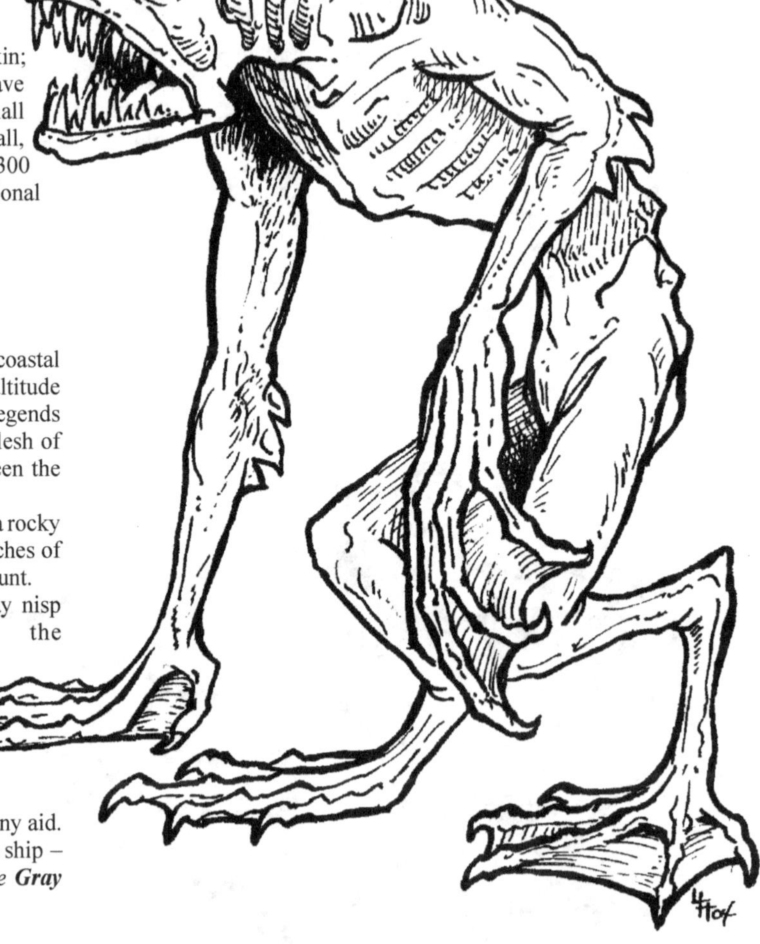

Gray nisps resemble hairless humanoids with smooth, slick skin; their hands and feet are webbed and end in claws, and their faces have large, dark pupilless eyes. They have no noses or ears, and its small fishlike mouth is filled with tiny, sharp teeth. Gray nisps are 9 feet tall, with light gray skin and a white underbelly, and weighs well over 300 pounds. If a gray nisp hits with both claws, it rends for an additional 2d6 points of damage. A gray nisp cannot survive on dry land.

Snatcher of Children

The town of Niborlyn has a reputation as a quaint and serene coastal village. The villager virtually shuts down at night (aside from a multitude of cats) as the doors and windows are boarded and locked. Legends say that a beast emerges from the sea each night to feast on the flesh of children who disobey their parents. Although no one has ever seen the monster from the ocean, all in town really believe it to be true.

The legend is partially accurate. A grey nisp lives just offshore in a rocky overhang. It mostly makes an easy living off of the refuse and catches of the fishing villages. Content with easy meals, it has no reason to hunt.

With the recent lack of discarded fish parts, however, the gray nisp began to snatch fishermen and locals who came too close to the water. Magdalena, a fishmonger's wife, lost her husband. While she cares little for the man, he had told her about a sunken ship he discovered before his disappearance. He claimed the ship carried chests of smuggled silver bound for Bargarsport. He carved a crude map of the wreckage on the mast of his skiff. The people of the village are too involved with their cats to offer any aid. She pleads with travelers to aid her in finding the location of his ship — and him if he's still alive. *(See more about life in Niborlyn in the **Gray Malkin** entry.)*

Copyright Notice

Author Scott Greene.

GRAYMALKINS

Graymalkins are magical creatures that resemble ordinary cats. To the casual observer, a graymalkin appear to be nothing more than a raggedy-looking cat with nothing unusual about it. This disguise aids the graymalkin in its travels, allowing it to move unmolested among living creatures.

Graymalkins always dwell near populated areas, preferring cities to towns, towns to villages, and so on. They often choose an owner (a living creature they deem gullible and easily manipulated) and convince that creature to take them home with them (by using their fascination ability). Once inside their owner's house, a graymalkin uses its special abilities to kill its owner and any other family members. Such attacks usually occur at night (in the case of the slinker) or over a period of time (in the case of the tether).

Graymalkins are often found serving as the familiar to an evil spellcaster or hag. They prefer females to males when serving as a familiar and very rarely do they ever use their special abilities against their true owner. (Some tales say that when a graymalkin is serving as a familiar, its master is actually immune to its special abilities.)

Graymalkins avoid direct confrontations with opponents, preferring to attack helpless or otherwise unobservant foes. If forced into battle, a graymalkin seeks escape as quick as possible.

Graymalkin, Common

Hit Dice: 1d4 hit points
Armor Class: 9 [10]
Attacks: 1 bite (1 point of damage)
Saving Throw: 18
Special: Charm
Move: 10
Alignment: Chaos
Challenge Level/XP: A/5

Graymalkins are magical creatures that resemble ordinary cats. A graymalkin can attempt to charm a single opponent. The target can make a successful save to resist the attempt. Graymalkins are magical creatures that resemble ordinary cats. They appear to be nothing more than a raggedy-looking cat with nothing unusual about it. This disguise aids the graymalkin in its travels, allowing it to move unmolested among living creatures. A graymalkin can fascinate a single opponent (save resists). A creature that fails its save "adopts" the graymalkin as a pet, clinging to the cat and always keeping it close by. The effect is similar to a *charm person* spell. Once inside their owner's house, a graymalkin kills its owner and any family members.

Graymalkin, Slinker

Hit Dice: 1
Armor Class: 9 [10]
Attacks: 2 claws, 1 bite (1 point of damage each)
Saving Throw: 17
Special: Breath stealing, fascination
Move: 10
Alignment: Chaos
Challenge Level/XP: 1/15

A slinker is referred to in legend as a witch cat, hell cat, or demonic cat that creeps into a family's house and steals the breath from their sleeping children. It appears as a large graymalkin. A slinker can fascinate a single opponent (save resists). A creature that fails its save "adopts" the slinker as a pet, clinging to the cat and always keeping it close by. The effect is similar to a *charm person* spell. Once inside their owner's house, a slinker kills its owner and any family members at night by sucking the air from their lungs as they sleep (save resists). If the save fails, the victim loses a quarter of its hit points. A successful save means the victim awakens, although it is still charmed.

Graymalkin, Tether

Hit Dice: 1
Armor Class: 9 [10]
Attacks: 2 claws, 1 bite (1 point of damage each)
Saving Throw: 17
Special: Level drain, fascination
Move: 10
Alignment: Chaos
Challenge Level/XP: 2/30

Tether are graymalkins with very long tails. A tether can fascinate a single opponent (save resists). A creature that fails its save "adopts" the tether as a pet, clinging to the cat and always keeping it close by. The effect is similar to a *charm person* spell. Once inside their owner's house, a tether kills its owner and any family members. A tether drains 1 level per hour from a charmed victim. A saving throw negates each level drain, but does not break the charm.

Cat's Meow

The fishing town of Niborlyn has always offered a peaceful and serene life for its citizens. The villagers live quietly, always looking down upon anything that forces them to deviate from the norm. Two years ago, the town elder Prelli Fishmeal adopted a slinker gray malkin found floating on wreckage from a lost ship. Prelli immediately fell in love with the animal and the creature has not left her side since that day. Over the years, the town has changed, and not for the better.

By charming Prelli, the gray malkin has methodically turned the town into a cat-worshipping cult. Thousands of cats fill the streets and homes of Niborlyn. Fields of catnip have replaced most crops, and massive sandboxes line the streets. Dogs are strictly forbidden anywhere near the village. Cat idols have replaced shrines to the sea gods. Fish and milk are standard rations for people and "pets" alike. Even the townspeople's clothing is made from spun cat hair. The townsfolk continually try to outdo one another by acquiring larger cats. Many of the more well-to-do keep large felines such as cougars, ocelots and tigers. The town has even attracted the attention of a weretiger.

The current state of Niborlyn does not please every citizen. Many of the older citizens hide their religious practices to the old gods. They may approach visitors to assist them in figuring out what has befallen their beloved town.

Copyright Notice
Author Scott Greene.

Gremlin

Hit Dice: 1d6 hit points
Armor Class: 9 [10]
Attacks: 2 claws (1d2), 1 bite (1d2) or 1 weapon (1d4)
Saving Throw: 18
Special: Magic resistance (15%), +1 magic weapon needed to hit, *invisible*
Move: 10
Alignment: Chaos
Challenge Level/XP: B/10

Gremlins are wicked faerie folk who revel in destruction and mayhem. They resemble a goblin with long floppy ears, pinched wrinkled faces, nasty claws, a mouth full of sharp teeth and a wicked glint to its eyes. A gremlin stands 3-1/2 feet tall and weighs about 40 pounds. Bright light blinds gremlins for 1 turn. They do an additional 1d6 points of damage to surprised opponents. Gremlins can turn *invisible* at will.

Misadventure

After a few very profitable years, Hooghly Slaw (Hoo Saw to his few friends) has quit adventuring. But his dream of owning a tavern didn't turn out so well. He now owns a defunct tavern named "The Vulgar Satyr".

Sixteen years ago, Hoo Saw found a locked chest while exploring ruins deep in the Hollow Spire Mountains. The locked chest contained a single wooden chess piece: a pawn. Intrigued by such a unique find, Hoo Saw kept the piece. Hoo Saw's misfortunes began that fateful day, and they've not let up.

Unbeknownst to the adventurer, the chest was a prison for a gremlin named Booglar who has followed and tormented poor Hoo Saw ever since he released the creature. Hoo Saw's attempts at adventuring, operating a successful business, finding a mate, even ending his life have all met with disastrous results because of the gremlin. The miserable Hoo Saw takes every misfortune in stride, however, which annoys Booglar to no end.

The Vulgar Satyr isn't a total money pit that Hoo Saw believes it to be, though. Over the years, Booglar has hidden nearly all of Hoo Saw's money within the tavern's stucco walls. Hoo Saw is in fact a very wealthy individual – if he could only discover the years of profit and treasure hidden in the walls around him. Booglar leaves just enough money for Hoo Saw to survive in misery. The Vulgar Satyr's only patrons are vagrants, drunkards, prostitutes and the deranged. Booglar takes great pleasure in tormenting anyone other than the dregs of society who visit the tavern.

The chess pawn sits on a table without chairs in the center of the room. Despite Hoo Saw's efforts to get rid of the game piece, it always returns. Hoo Saw has noticed that when he destroys the piece, it returns looking slightly different. He long ago accepted his bad luck and has given up on ever getting rid of the cursed chess piece.

None of the tables or chairs in the bar has level legs. Eating utensils are bent, and bowls and wooden tankards have small annoying leaks. Randomly loosened floorboards tilt to harmlessly hit clients in the face or back. Sand taints the salt and spice jars on the tables. Common pranks the gremlin plays are putting tadpoles in tankards, lighting of tinder twigs in boots, shaving a PC's horse, putting black powder in pipes, entwining boot laces, placing rotten potatoes in backpacks and pouches, loosening saddles on horses, greasing sword hilts and door knobs, placing bees in wineskins, removing arrowheads, spilling drinks on crotches and unloosening armor straps loosened. The Game Referee should feel free to make up more annoyances to torment the PCs with.

Hoo Saw feels indebted to anyone who aids him in getting his life back on track. If his treasure is found, he hands over the deed to The Vulgar Satyr (the chess piece comes with the tavern) and leaves on a permanent vacation.

Copyright Notice

Author Scott Greene.

Grimm

Hit Dice: 12
Armor Class: 0 [19]
Attacks: 2 claws (1d8), 1 bite (2d6)
Saving Throw: 3
Special: Magic resistance (35%), +1 magic weapons or better needed to hit, death aura
Move: 12
Alignment: Chaos
Challenge Level/XP: 13/2,300

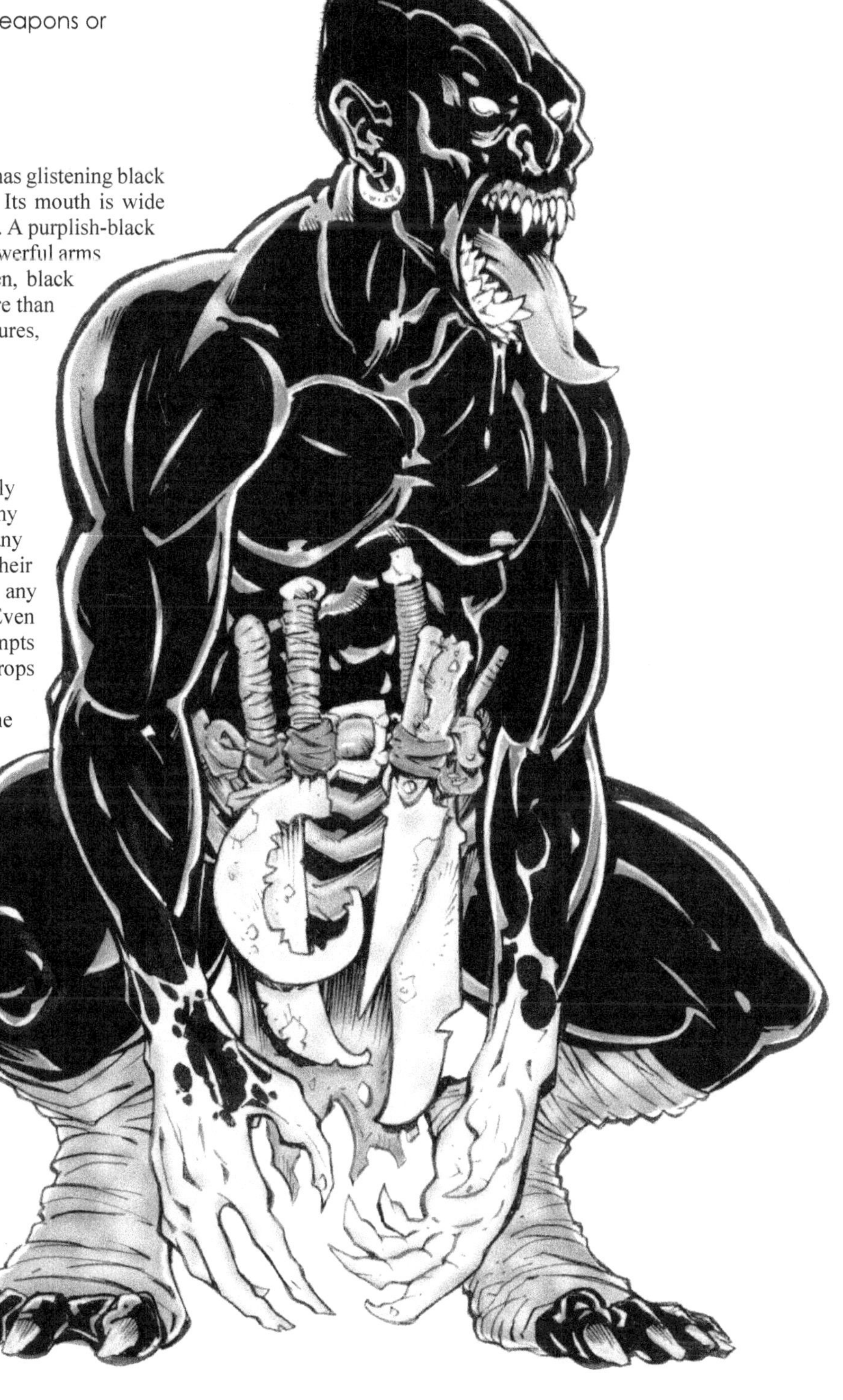

This monstrous beast stands well over 9 feet tall and has glistening black flesh. Its head is oval with deep sunken black eyes. Its mouth is wide and large and sports double rows of razor-sharp fangs. A purplish-black tongue flicks in and out of its mouth. The monster's powerful arms and legs end in filthy wicked claws that sport broken, black fingernails. A grimm stands 9 feet tall and weighs more than 1,200 pounds. A grimm drains life from Lawful creatures, dealing 1d6 points of damage each round.

Ebbing Acres

The extensive farmstead of the Ebbing family has remained profitable for generations. As wealthy landowners, the Ebbing family has made many enemies with their aggressive style of farming and their questionable ethics. None of the locals has seen any member of the Ebbing family for weeks, however. Even more mysteriously, no one has returned from attempts to contact them. Acres of neglected and wilting crops surround the homestead and barn.

The Ebbing family and their farmhands stand in the yard crucified in a circle upon wooden crossbeams. Their bodies bear no wounds and appear to be drained of blood. The corpses are surrounded by the carcasses of thousands of birds, rodents and vermin. Livestock and crops alike look as if all their fluids have been drained as well. Two grimms living under the family's home caused the deaths of the scavengers and livestock with their life-draining aura. The grimms slowly tortured the crucified people with their presence.

Copyright Notice
Author Scott Greene.

Grimstalker (Banaan)

Hit Dice: 6
Armor Class: 3 [16]
Attacks: 2 claws (1d4+1 + poison) or 1 weapon (1d6+1)
Saving Throw: 11
Special: Poison, spell-like abilities
Move: 6/3 (climb)
Alignment: Chaos
Challenge Level/XP: 7/600

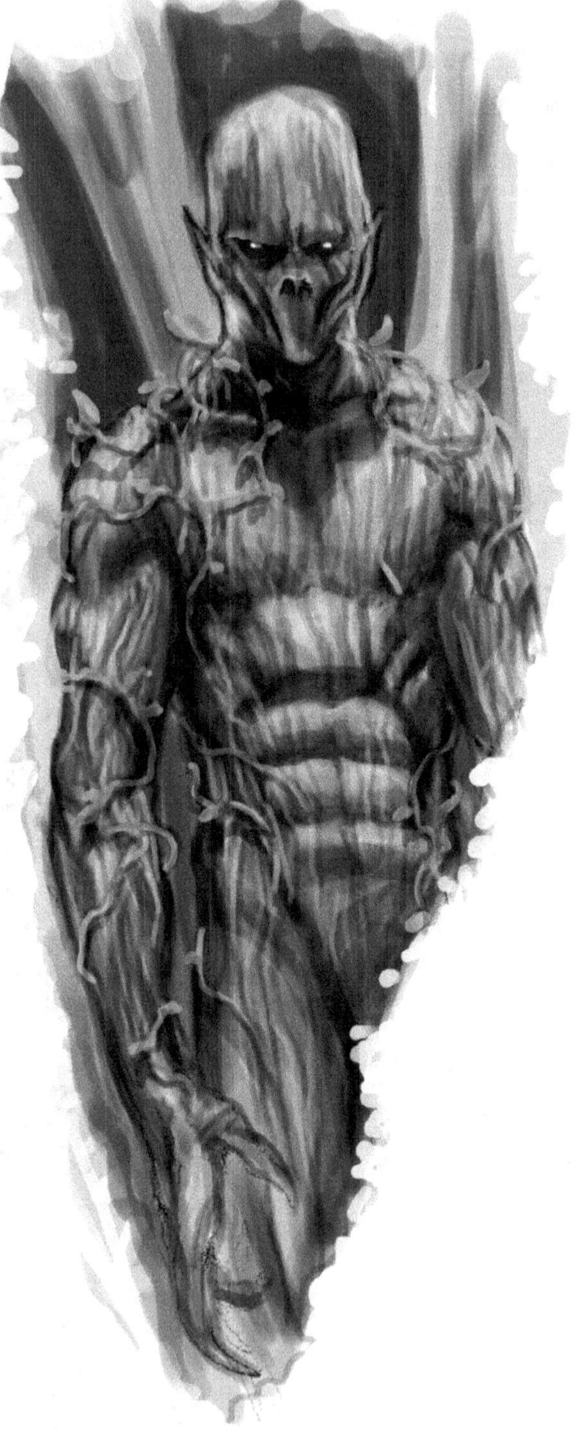

The grimstalker is a fey creature that does not share the beauty and goodness of its kin. They are hairless humanoid fey, slender and graceful, with long arms and legs. The grimstalker's skin is brown and woody, almost having the texture and hardness of tree bark, and their hands are tipped in sharp claws that drip toxic venom with the consistency of pinesap. They often decorate themselves with leaves and vines that actually take root in their skin and cover them with a protective layer as thick as leather armor. Grimstalkers deliver a paralytic poison with each claw attack that stuns victims for 1d4+1 rounds. Grimstalkers can cast *plant growth* and *warp wood* three times per day.

Hey Mr. Tally Man

Rows of banana trees stand on the grounds of the abandoned Horstman Plantation, ripening bunches of bananas hanging down from the serrated fronds. The ground is covered by patches of unruly grasses and piled high with rotting bananas. The grass causes flesh to itch and sting, and fire ants crawl in long lines over the ground. Other than the macaws calling through the trees, the banana farm is silent.

The pickers fled three days ago when a troupe of grimstalkers moved in and began terrorizing the farmhands. The miniature assassins drove poisoned splinters into the bananas, left snare traps in the thick grass, and even lured a corrupt banana tree treant onto the plantation. The grimstalkers consider the plantation their ancestral land and attack any trespassers. The grimstalkers ride in the banana tree treant, pelting enemies with poisoned arrows.

Banana Tree Treant (8HD): HD 8; AC 2[17]; Atk 2 strikes (2d6); Move 6; Save 8; CL/XP 8/800; Special: Control trees.

Copyright Notice
Author Erica Balsley.

Grippli

Hit Dice: 1
Armor Class: 6 [13]
Attack: Weapon (1d4)
Saving Throw: 17
Special: Marsh move
Move: 12/12 (climbing)
Alignment: Neutrality
Challenge Level/XP: 1/15

Gripplis are short, bipedal tree frogs that dwell in swamps and marshes. They can move upright or on all fours. A grippli stands 2 to 2-1/2 feet tall and weighs from 40 to 50 pounds. Its eyes are yellow with vertical-slit pupils of black. Gripplis often wear brightly colored or decorated clothes. They arc attractcd to and love brightly colored items. Gripplis speak their own language and some speak common or elven. Gripplis can move across marshlands, swamps, and mud without any penalty to their movement.

Grippli characters can take levels in fighter (up to 5th level) or thief (up to 7th level). They can see in the dark as well as elves and enjoy a +5% bonus to climb walls (maximum 99%).

Frog God House

Amidst the thick aerial prop roots of an ancient banyan, a tribe of 30 grippli adults and their 15 young. The grippli dwell in tiny huts of mud and grass, climbing into the tree to hunt lizards and gather figs. The grippli arm themselves with spears and slings and brew a powerful fig wine. The village is lead by a grippli who can cast spells as a 3rd level cleric or druid. A large hut in the middle of the village contains the tribe's nine eggs guarded by four large grippli with obsidian-bladed axes. In the upper branches of the banyan tree there is a thing the grippli refer to as the "god house".

The god house is the pinnacle of an ancient stone temple that was engulfed and mostly destroyed by the banyan in its youth. The peak of the temple, decorated with reliefs of dancing apsaras, now rests in the branches about 200 feet above the forest floor. One can enter the "god house" through a tiny hole. The interior is covered by a growth of orange crystals that the grippli believe allow communication with spirits, for they hum in the presence of light. The grippli's priestly leader carries a bronze lantern as part of her gear.

Credit

The Grippli originally appeared in the First Edition *Monster Manual II* (© TSR/Wizards of the Coast, 1983) and is used by permission.

Copyright Notice

Author Scott Greene, based on original material by Gary Gygax.

Groaning Spirit

Hit Dice: 7
Armor Class: 2 [17]
Attack: Incorporeal touch (1d8 + chill touch)
Saving Throw: 9
Special: Chill touch, fear aura, keening, immunity to cold and electricity, magic resistance (50%), unnatural aura, vulnerability
Move: 12
Alignment: Chaos
Challenge Level/XP: 12/2000

The groaning spirit is the malevolent spirit of a female elf that is found haunting swamps, fens, moors, and other desolate places. Groaning spirits hate the living and seek to destroy whomever they meet. A groaning spirit appears as a translucent image of her former self.

Anyone viewing a groaning spirit must succeed on a saving throw or flee in terror for 1d6+4 rounds. Damage caused by the groaning spirit's touch attack sends a chilling cold through an opponent's body. Any creature touched must succeed on a saving throw or suffer 1 point of Strength drain. Groaning spirits are the bane of other undead, and any undead they touch (except other groaning spirits) must succeed on a saving throw or flee in fear for 2d6 rounds.

Once per day, at night only, a groaning spirit can release a death wail audible to a range of 1 mile. All creatures within 30 feet of the groaning spirit must make a successful saving throw or die. Those that make their save still take 3d6 points of damage.

If a spellcaster uses *holy word* against a groaning spirit, the creature must succeed on a saving throw or die immediately.

Murder on High Street

A large city of granite walls tinted red from rust of the curved copper roofs on its tall, thin buildings has curved streets paved with chalk and lined with crowded, noisy shops. A single main street, the High Street, once thronged with people but has been abandoned due to the presence of a groaning spirit. The spirit once belonged to an elf, the victim of a murderous baker on the High Street.

The bakery is the tallest building in the area, with a mechanical clock tower on which a clockwork knight slays a clockwork dragon every hour on the hour. The bakery specializes in hot cross buns, tongue sandwiches (sheep tongues for a copper, beef tongues for a silver, peacock tongues for a platinum) and sticky pastries made with honey and almonds.

The baker concealed the body in a barrel of flour in his cellar, and until the body is found and properly buried, the spirit cannot rest. A number of brave knights have lost their lives to the groaning spirit, including the king's favorite nephew. Destroying the creature is probably a fine way to endear the king to a band of otherwise unwelcome adventurers.

Credit

The Groaning Spirit originally appeared in the First Edition *Monster Manual* (© TSR/Wizards of the Coast, 1977) and is used by permission.

Copyright Notice

Authors Scott Greene and Clark Peterson, based on original material by Gary Gygax.

Gronk

Hit Dice: 5
Armor Class: 8 [11]
Attacks: 2 slams (1d6) and horn (1d8), or 1 weapon (1d8) and horn (1d8)
Saving Throw: 12
Special: None
Move: 12
Alignment: Neutrality
Challenge Level/XP: 5/240

Gronks are the typical big, dumb brutes; a male gronk is on average approximately 9 feet tall, with females only slightly smaller. Gronks have mottled gray skin and shaggy brown hair that is thickest at its head and shoulders and gradually thins out around its waist. The arms and legs of a gronk are massive, like tree limbs attached to its thick barrel-like torso. The face of a gronk seems almost lost amid the long hair hanging from its head. The most notable feature of a gronk's face is the long, rhinoceros-like horn between its eyes.

Pitted Plains

A nomadic tribe of gronks has excavated huge pits throughout the rolling hills of a vast grassland. The gronks have worked long and hard through the years carefully digging the vast pits. The Horncrunk gronks, under the command of their tribal leader Uooteg, are fiercely territorial and secretive about their digging project.

The tribe has managed to domesticate rhinoceroses and yaks to aid in their quarrying activities and to serve as mounts and guards. Guard rhinos are leashed by heavy iron chains tethered to spiked collars. Occasionally, the gronks find something useful such as minor magical items left over from ancient wars. While unreceptive of intruders, diplomatic negotiations may avoid combat but won't divulge the reason for the dig. In fact, the gronks aren't sure either why they are digging the land. Some years ago, Uooteg had a dream of a buried weapon (a warhammer shaped like a boar) and convinced the tribe that this vision was a quest from the gods to find this weapon. Thus far, their work has yielded little.

Copyright Notice

Author Erica Balsley.

Gryph

Hit Dice: 2
Armor Class: 5 [14]
Attack: Touch (attach) or beak (1d8)
Saving Throw: 16
Special: Attach, implant eggs
Move: 3/21 (flying)
Alignment: Chaos
Challenge Level/XP: 5/240

Gryphs are small, jet-black birds about the size of eagles. They have four, six or eight legs and needle-like beaks. Gryphs are found in dungeons, ruins, and caverns. They are typically scavengers, feeding on dead rodents and other small animals, but in times when food is scarce they take on a more predatory role and become hunters, craving the flesh and blood of warm-blooded creatures. If a gryph hits with a touch attack, it uses its legs to latch onto the opponent's body. A female gryph that gets a hold injects 1d4 eggs into the host's bloodstream from a tiny thin tube projected from the creature's abdomen. Each day thereafter, the host takes 1d6 points of constitution damage and suffers a –2 penalty to hit and make saving throws until cured or until the eggs hatch. At the end of the third day, the eggs hatch and 1d4 young gryphs burst forth from the host's body. If the host is still alive when this happens, he immediately takes 2d6 points of Constitution damage. A *cure disease* spell rids a victim of the eggs.

Hell's Plumbers

This cavern is 40 feet high, with walls that slant down to the floor of the cavern, which is 60 feet long and about 12 feet wide. Twelve thick pipes span the cavern from wall to wall, about half of them warm and the other half cold. A bloated corpse is slung over one of the warm pipes incubating 7 gryph eggs.

A throng of 1d8+7 male gryphs (plus one female per 3 males) inhabit this cavern, roosting on the warm pipes. The pipes do not carry water, but rather move tortured souls between different planes of Hell. Rupturing a pipe releases the souls in the form of 2d6 screeching shadows. Such a rupture is likely if one is attacking the gryphs with sharp or piercing weapons. If such a rupture does occur, an imp is oily overalls will appear in 1d4+1 rounds to repair it. If the adventurers are not busy, it will make a clumsy attempt at trading its plumbing services for a soul.

Credit

The Gryph originally appeared in the First Edition *Fiend Folio* (© TSR/Wizards of the Coast, 1981) and is used by permission.

Copyright Notice

Author Scott Greene, based on original material by Peter Brown.

Gutslug

Hit Dice: 2
Armor Class: 8 [11]
Attacks: 1 bite (1d4 + blood drain)
Saving Throw: 16
Special: Blood drain
Move: 6/12 (flying)
Alignment: Neutrality
Challenge Level/XP: 2/30

A gutslug is a slimy, sticky worm that resembles entrails. The body is a lumpy, veined, gray tube approximately 10 feet long but usually no thicker than an inch in diameter. Gutslugs have no eyes, and their mouth is large, round, and resembles the suckered mouth of a leech. A gutslug latches onto a victim with a successful bite, automatically draining blood for 1d4 points of damage each round until it drains a total of 8 hit points or is removed.

A Slug in the Gut

The Capering Satyr is throwing a bash to beat all parties to celebrate the owner's recent good fortune. The party's been going for a week so far, with little signs of slowing down. Revelers come and go, and new kegs are brought up from the cellar every hour. The owner, Borum, won't talk about how he came into his wealth, but whispering bar patrons claim he found a gold vein in the Whispering Forest.

Borum did indeed find gold, but only after he tricked a leprechaun and stole its treasure. The leprechaun, an angry little fey named Marn McLir, searched high and low and just recently found the bar owner. Now that he's found the barkeep, his ire is about to be unleashed. Marn broke into the cellar and "improved" a keg by stuffing 50 gutslugs into the barrel. He rigged the keg to explode in a blast of splinters that launches the gutslugs over the entire bar crowd.

PCs partying in the bar find themselves covered in the slimy entrail-like worms.

All the while, Marn McLir dances in the rafters, laughing at the sport below.

Copyright Notice
Author Erica Balsley.

Half-Ogre

Hit Dice: 2
Armor Class: 4 [15]
Attack: Two-handed sword (2d6+1) or spear (1d6+1)
Saving Throw: 16
Special: None
Move: 12
Alignment: Chaos
Challenge Level/XP: 2/30

Half-ogres are rare crossbreeds of human and ogre. Standing a few feet shorter than their ogre kin and a few feet taller than their human kin, half-ogres have strength as well as speed and intelligence (relative to other ogres) in their favor. Their skin and hair color generally match that of their ogre parent, with dark tones such as gray, brown, or olive being the most prevalent. Half-ogres speak the common tongue, and those with an intelligence score of at least 10 also speak ogre.

Half-ogres, though generally outcasts among humans and feared for their ugliness and size, can find some acceptance among ogres. Half-ogres in an ogre band need to prove themselves constantly to their larger kin, however. For this reason, half-ogres found among an ogre band are cruel, violent, and strong; weaker half-ogres usually wind up in the stew pot. Most half-ogres found among full-blooded ogres are leaders of the ogre band or are at least well on their way to becoming leaders. Their long years suffering the harsh treatment of their kin help half-ogres develop a sense of cunning and a strong will to survive. Therefore, ogres under the leadership of a half-ogre fight more effectively, even engaging in planned ambushes and complicated tactics that are beyond most ogres.

On rare occasions, half-ogres collect into hybrid communities of other half-ogre races (such as orogs and ogrillons) or humanoids (such as orcs and half-orcs). These rogue bands of outcasts form bandit clans or marauding groups that are the bane of other humanoid communities in their area.

Half-Ogres as Characters

Half-ogre leaders tend to be barbaric fighters and can advance to the 6th level of ability (7th level if their strength score is 13 or higher). Half-ogre clerics worship "the Destroyer" and can advance to the 4th level of ability (5th level if their wisdom is 15 or higher). Half-ogres can also multi-class as fighter/clerics, reaching a maximum of 5th level as fighters and 3rd level as clerics.

Half-Ogre enjoy a +1 bonus to strength and constitution and a -1 penalty to intelligence and charisma at character creation. These modifications cannot take an ability score over 18 or below 3.

Half-ogres begin their careers with one additional hit dice (1d6).

Half-ogres can see in darkness as well as a dwarf.

Half Ogre, All Bandit

A gang of 1d3+1 half-ogre bandits has taken up residence in an abandoned watchtower that overlooks the moor road. The bandits wear hides and pelts (treat as leather armor) and carry a variety of hand weapons, including 4 javelins each. The leader of the band, a 3rd level fighter, recently lost a challenge he intitiated against the ogre chief of his former tribe. He now bears a nasty scar across his bald head for the effort.

The band has set up a rather ingenious (for ogres) device to attack passing caravans. The moor road runs directly past the watchtower. The half-ogres station themselves on the roof, where they have a thick rope tied between a crenelation and a large, loose piece of masonry. At the direction of a spotter, two ogres heave the heavy block off the roof in the opposite direction of the road. The rope then turns the heavy block into a powerful, pendulum like projectile that smashes into wagons and often kills or wounds horses or oxen. The half-ogres then, still on the roof, proceed to hurl smaller stones and javelins at the caravan until it gives up and flees the harassment.

So far, the half-ogres have managed to gather 20 head of goats (worth 1 gp each, penned behind the watchtower), 30 pounds of millet (worth 9 gp), five pounds of lentils (worth 1 gp), two square yards of lace (weighs 6 pounds, worth 10 gp), 20 pounds of red dye (worth 10 gp), 10 pounds of blue dye (worth 10 gp, in a barrel), 10 pounds of gum arabic (worth 10 gp), two barrels of ale (30 gallons, 250 pounds, worth 6 gp each), a granite holy icon (worth 65 gp to a dwarf), a bag of *dust of disappearance* (thrown to the side, deemed worthless), a soapstone bust of Millard Fillmore (worth 1d4 x 10 gp, once owned by a famous plane-hopping magic-user), 1d6 x 100 cp and 1d4 x 100 sp.

Credit
The Half-Ogre originally appeared in *Dragon #29* (© TSR/Wizards of the Coast, 1979) and is used by permission.

Copyright Notice
Authors Scott Greene and Erica Balsley, based on original material by Gary Gygax.

Hanged Man

Hit Dice: 3
Armor Class: 7 [12]
Attacks: 2 claws (1d4)
Saving Throw: 14
Special: Hangman's rope
Move: 6
Alignment: Chaos
Challenge Level/XP: 3/60

A hanged man appears much as it did in life, though its skin is pale and pulled tight over its bones. Its head hangs at an odd angle, unsupported by its shattered neck bones. A rotted noose and several feet of rope hang from its neck and trail off behind it as it walks. Its eyes have no pupils. A hanged man can only utter choked gurgles, gasps and strangled moans. It uses the rope that killed it to snare victims and drag them into the hanged man's waiting claws. The rope can be cast up to 20 feet away, and wraps around creatures with a successful hit.

The Well Hanged Man

The rotting corpses of 10 pirates and thieves hang from a scaffold outside of the village of Arndale. Crows sit haughtily on the corpses, cawing at anyone who approaches.

The village is empty, a ghost town sitting beside the sea. Buildings are vacant, with doors and windows wide open. Bloody scratches mar many wooden floors. People appear to have been dragged from their houses, clawing frantically for their lives.

A small 8-foot-diameter well sits in the center of town, a rope hanging over the stone ledge trailing down into the darkness. The rope twitches feebly.

A hanged man entered a cave network under Arndale a week ago. The creature discovered a dry well that let it move about the town without being noticed. The creature picked off victims every night, casting some down the well to savor later. The creature waits at the bottom of the hole. The noose tied around its neck hangs over the top of the well to snatch prey who might try to give it a good yank.

Copyright Notice
Author Erica Balsley.

Hangman Tree

Hit Dice: 8
Armor Class: 2 [17]
Attack: 4 vines (1d8)
Saving Throw: 8
Special: Hallucinatory spores, magic resistance (45%), strangle, swallow, surprise on 1-4 on 1d6
Move: 3
Alignment: Neutrality (chaotic tendencies)
Challenge Level/XP: 10/1400

Hangman trees look like nothing more than giant oak trees. Close inspection reveals a scar-like marking on the lower part of the trunk (this is where undigested creatures or gear is expelled after digestion). Hidden among the hangman tree's branches and leaves are its rope-like appendages that it uses to trap its prey. Hangman trees can speak broken Common. The hangman tree attacks by dropping its noose-like appendages around prey and yanking victims upwards. Trapped prey is held until it dies or is dropped into the hangman's trunk where it is digested. Hangman trees have no visual organs but can ascertain all foes within 60 feet using sound, scent, and vibration.

Opponents struck by a vine in combat must pass a saving throw or be strangled for 1d6+1 points of damage per round until the vine is cut (it has an AC of 4 [15] and can take 6 hp damage) or the strangled victim or a rescuer makes a successful open doors check. The hangman tree can attempt to swallow a strangling (or strangled) victim with a successful attack roll and a failed saving throw by the target. A swallowed victim suffers 2d6 points of crushing damage per round and can only escape with a successful open doors check. The tree's trunk can hold up to two human-sized victims.

Besides the danger of its vines and trunk, a hangman tree can also release a cloud of spores in a 50-foot radius spread. Creatures in the area must succeed on a saving throw or believe the tree to be of some ordinary sort or to be a treant or other such friendly tree creature. An affected creature becomes passive for 2d6 rounds and refuses to attack the hangman tree during this time.

A hangman tree takes half again as much (+50%) damage as normal from electricity, regardless of whether a saving throw is allowed, or if the save is a success or failure. Cold-based effects paralyze a hangman tree as if by a *hold monster* spell. Spells that generate darkness slow the hangman tree (as the *slow* spell) for 1 round per caster level.

Grim God of the Wood

A tunnel you have been traversing for the last hour ends in a flight of wide steps of black and white marble. They lead up maybe 60 feet to perpendicular tunnel. This new tunnel is arched and clad in checked black and white tiles. It is about 10 feet wide and 15 feet high and seems to run for at least one mile in either direction. Dried animal droppings in the tunnel suggest that it is an underground highway. Should one proceed east, they will eventually come to a point where the tunnel slants upward, disgorging travelers into a thick woodland of oaks. This woodland is inhabited by several tribes of goblins, discernable by the different colors of their ears and memorable for the violent hatred they feel towards one another. One tribe is particularly hated, for it dwells on the fringes of a meadow of sweet grasses and forget-me-nots in which dwells the "Grim God of the Wood". The god is a large, ancient hangman tree and the tribe that dwells closest to him holds the position of the "high holy tribe" and lords this rank over the others.

As one approaches the meadow of the Grim God, they will almost certainly encounter members of the high holy tribe, goblins with gray-fringed ears in leather armor and carrying shields, spears and daggers. Encounters with 1d4+4 goblins should be diced for once every hour, occuring on a roll of 1 in 4. The goblins will make an attempt to capture characters, using lassos that they throw from the branches. Captives are brought to the edge of the meadow and driven into it by the massed goblins of the high holy tribe, their hands unbound but weaponless (this strikes the goblins as a "fair fight").

A possible treasure for the high holy tribe consists of 1d4 x 1,000 gp, 1d4 x 1,000 sp, an obsidian mask worth 135 gp, a terracotta oil lamp decorated with black and white porpoises worth 135 gp and a wooden figuring of a child worth 45 gp.

Credit
The Hangman Tree originally appeared in *EX1 Dungeonland* (© TSR/Wizards of the Coast, 1983) and is used by permission.

Copyright Notice
Author Scott Greene, based on original material by Gary Gygax.

Haunt

Hit Dice: 5
Armor Class: 5 [14]
Attack: Ghostly touch (1d4 plus 1d3 dexterity)
Saving Throw: 12
Special: Alternate form, dexterity damage, immune to turning, malevolence, rejuvenation, strangle, vulnerabilities
Move: 9/12 (flying)
Alignment: Any (usually chaotic)
Challenge Level/XP: 8/800

The haunt is the spirit of a person who died before completing some vital task. A haunt inhabits an area within 60 feet of where its body died and never leaves this area. (Note—a haunt in possession of a material body can in fact leave its area and must do so in order to finish its task.) It desires but one thing: its final rest. To accomplish this, it must possess a living creature and finish the task that prevents it from achieving everlasting slumber. A haunt only attacks humanoid creatures.

A haunt's natural form is that of a translucent image appearing much as the person did in life, but it can alter its form so as to appear as a floating, luminescent ball of light. In this form, it cannot use its dexterity damage attack or its possession ability. It retains its ghostly form and can make an ghostly touch attack that deals normal damage, but not dexterity damage.

A haunt remains in one form or the other until it chooses to assume a new one (as a standard action). A change in form cannot be dispelled. A haunt cannot change forms while using its malevolence attack (that is, while possessing a host).

The touch of a haunt deals 1d3 points of dexterity damage to a living foe. A creature reduced to 0 dexterity by a haunt is subjected to possession by the spirit (similar to *magic jar* spell; saving throw permitted to negate the possession). Dexterity returns to normal while the haunt is in possession of a body, but drops back to 0 when the haunt leaves. Thereafter, dexterity returns at the rate of one point per hour.

If the haunt possesses a victim, it attempts to complete its unfinished task. If the haunt completes its task, it leaves the host and fades away forever. If the host body is slain while the haunt is in possession of it, the haunt becomes tied to that new area and can never leave. Its unfinished task remains the same.

If a creature possessed by a haunt has an alignment opposite to that of the haunt, it attempts to strangle the host using its own hands (i.e., the hands of the host body). Unless precautions are taken to restrain the possessed victim's hands, they immediately reach for the throat and begin strangling the haunt-possessed body. An opponent takes 1d4 points of damage each round until its hands are forcibly restrained (opposed strength checks to pry the host's hands loose), the haunt is ejected from the body, or the victim dies.

In most cases, it's difficult to destroy a haunt through simple combat, as the "destroyed" restores itself in 1d4 days. A haunt that would otherwise be destroyed returns to its area with a successful saving throw. The only way to get rid of a haunt for sure is to use *dispel evil* or allow it to finish the task that holds it to the material world.

A haunt can be forcibly ejected from a host if *hold person* is cast on the victim and the haunt fails its saving throw. A *dispel evil* spell instantly ejects the creature from the host and deals 1d6 points of damage per caster level to the haunt. A haunt slain in such a manner cannot rejuvenate and is permanently destroyed.

As a ghostly, incorporeal creature, a haunt can only be hit by magic weapons. A haunt's attacks ignore armor bonuses to Armor Class.

Possession Is 9/10ths of the Law

You emerge from the rain forest onto a sodden plateau inhabited by giant lizards (dull, grazing herbivores). In the middle of the pleateau there is a spear stuck in the ground, a brace of blue-gray feathers hanging from the end. The plateau runs for another 300 feet before it ends in the black, jagged cliffs of a chasm. The chasm is 100 feet across and spanned by a rope bridge. The bridge leads into a cave in the higher cliff on the other side of the chasm.

Approaching the spear will draw out a lawful haunt, the spirit of an ancient chief who died while trying to rescue his kidnapped son from a rival tribe. The chief's crushed bones are sunk into the plain beneath the spear. The chief will appear out of nowhere, running towards the adventurers, his incorporeal face tattooed in an awful grimace, intent upon possessing one of the travelers to complete his mission.

Rescuing the child will be nearly impossible. The chief died 20 years earlier, and his son is now a sub-chief in the tribe that kidnapped him and unlikely to allow himself to be rescued by a complete stranger.

The chief's spear is a *+1 magic weapon* that, when cast through the air, gives off a terrific war scream that forces those with 1 HD or less to make a saving throw or flee in terror for 5 minutes.

Credit

The Haunt originally appeared in the First Edition module *A2 Secret of the Slavers Stockade* (© TSR/Wizards of the Coast, 1981) and later in the First Edition *Monster Manual II* (© TSR/Wizards of the Coast, 1983) and is used by permission.

Copyright Notice

Author Scott Greene, based on original material by Harold Johnson and Tom Moldvay.

Helix Moth

Hit Dice: 12
Armor Class: 5 [14]
Attacks: 1 bite (2d4), sting (2d6 + poison)
Saving Throw: 3
Special: Immune to charm, drone, poison
Move: 12/30 (flying)
Alignment: Neutrality
Challenge Level/XP: 13/2,300

Helix moths are 20-foot-long black insects with spiraling bands of red, green, yellow, blue, purple, and white on their abdomens. Their underbelly is white. Their large mandibles are gray, as are their legs. Three sets of translucent wings protrude from the insect's body. A small black sword-like stinger protrudes from the end of the moth's abdomen, capable of delivering a highly toxic poison. If the moth beats its wings, the droning sound is audible up to 60 feet away and causes *confusion* (as per the spell) in all who fail a save.

Helix Moth (Larva)

Hit Dice: 5
Armor Class: 7 [12]
Attacks: 1 bite (1d8 + acid)
Saving Throw: 12
Special: Grab, acid
Move: 6
Alignment: Neutrality
Challenge Level/XP: 7/600

Helix moth larvae are 10-foot-long maggot-like creatures with rubbery gray flesh. Their cylindrical body is about 4 feet in diameter. Their entire body is coated in a thick, slimy mucous. Larvae have no eyes but use their other senses to detect prey. The mouth has two ridges along it that are formed of a hard, shell-like substance that function as teeth. Larvae lack most of the full-grown moth's abilities, but their bite is still deadly and delivers a powerful regurgitated acid (1d6 damage). Once the larva bites, it grips the creature with its mouth, dealing automatic bite and acid damage until removed.

Crystal Moth

Thin purple spindles of sharp glass tower in the air in the Amethyst Jungle. Spindly branches sprout from the glass trees. The wind warbles through the crystal trees with a delicate sound of clinking glass. The amethyst trees grow naturally and are incredibly sharp, dealing 1d4 points of damage to anyone touching the trunks. A 100-foot-wide cavern splits the forest into two sides. One side's glass is a deep violet, while across the canyon the glass is a lighter mauve. The chasm drops nearly 150 feet to another glass forest at the bottom of the canyon. A 30-foot-radius glass column stretches across the canyon. The giant trunk is shaved flat across its upper surface to form a bridge across the chasm.

A helix moth lives in a cave mouth 50 feet down the cliff wall. The female moth laid her eggs in the cavern a week ago. The moth is very territorial, and rises to investigate any noise. Anyone cross the bridge is immediately attacked. The drone caused by the moth's gigantic flapping wings sets up vibrations in the crystals that have a 1 in 6 chance each round of shattering the crystal trees – including the glass bridge.

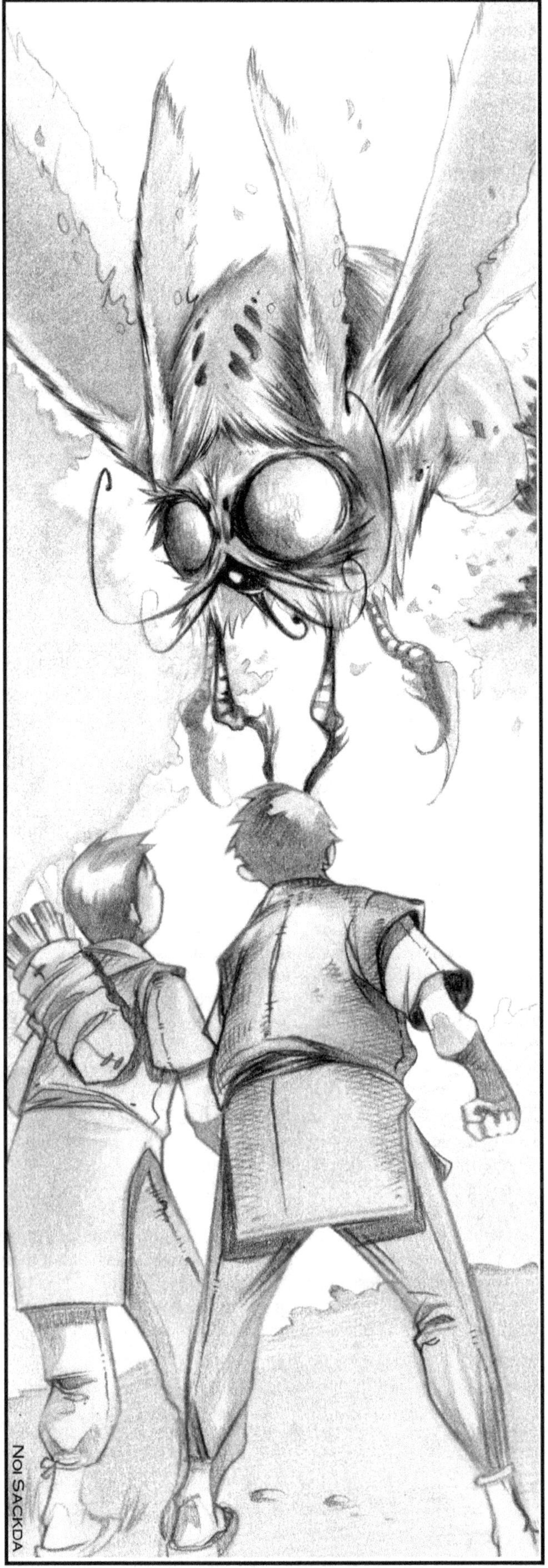

Hell Moth

Hit Dice: 9
Armor Class: 0 [19]
Attack: Bite (1d8)
Saving Throw: 6
Special: Engulf, immolation, resistance to fire (90%)
Move: 6/15 (flying)
Alignment: Neutrality (chaotic tendencies)
Challenge Level/XP: 11/1700

The hell moth looks like a giant gray moth with spiraling bands of red and black on its body. It has large, thin, reddish-hued wings. The hell moth is thought to have come from another plane, though sages are not quite sure of its exact origin. The hell moth attacks living creatures that wander too close to its lair. It otherwise resembles a large moth with an 8-foot wingspan.

A hell moth can try to wrap a human-sized or smaller creature in its body as a standard attack. If successful, it establishes a hold and bites the engulfed victim with a +2 bonus on its attack roll. Attacks that hit an engulfing hell moth deal half their damage to the monster and half to the trapped victim. A hell moth that has engulfed an opponent can detonate its body in a blast of hellish fire that deals 6d10 points of fire damage to itself and to the engulfed opponent (no save). Remember to reduce the damage dealt to the hell moth due to its fire resistance. A hell moth can immolate itself once every 3 hours, providing it survives the immolation. Creatures within 10 feet of the hell moth when it uses this ability must succeed on a saving throw or take 1d8 points of fire damage as clothes and combustibles ignite. The damage continues for another 1d4+4 rounds after the hell moth uses this ability or until the fire is extinguished.

Hell Gate Pearl

On a low, green island located about 100 yards off the coast of a pleasant harbor there is a large manor house that once belonged to the court physician of the local king. The wooden bridge to the island has been burned and three stone towers and a wall erected opposite the island on the shore. These towers and wall are patrolled day and night by a company of crossbowmen, each armed with three magical arrows.

The island measures about 1,200 feet in diameter. The shores are thick with willows, their branches trailing in the waters of the bay. Beyond the wall of willows there are pleasant gardens and goldfish ponds and the blackened husk of a stone manor house. The central stone tower of the manor still stands and is inhabited by a flock of 1d4+2 hell moths. The tower once had three floors and an observatory on the roof, but the roof and floors have been burned away.

At the center of the tower's floor there is a black pearl clutched in the hand of a charred skeleton. The black pearl bathes the tower's interior in darkness and attracts the hell moths the way a normal light attracts normal moths. The pearl was a gift to the physician from a rival, a wise woman of the hills who once enjoyed the patronage of the king. It has the ability to cause darkness in a 60 foot radius but allows its holder to see in that or any darkness. The holder of the pearl gains the ability to communicate telepathically with the creatures of the night, though he is unable to block their thoughts and might, if not possessed of a powerful will, succumb to their predatory instincts. The pearl, if touched by a lawful person, opens a swirling gate of black and red mists 30 feet overhead that draws in a flock of hell moths, who continue to lurk around the pearl until it is returned to its container, a black, metallic box stamped with the grimacing face of Yama, the death god.

Herald of Tsathogga

Hit Dice: 14
Armor Class: 1 [18]
Attacks: 10 tentacles (1d8) and 1 bite (2d6)
Saving Throw: 3
Special: Bellow, paralysis, swallow whole, regenerate, half damage from blunt weapons
Move: 6/9 (swim)
Alignment: Chaos
Challenge Level/XP: 17/3,500

A herald of Tsathogga is a gigantic pale yellow-green frog with oversized monstrous eyes. In place of its legs and forelimbs are many long, writhing tentacles it uses to pull itself along the ground. The body of the thing resembles that of a massive toad. These tentacles are covered in tiny lancets that inject paralytic venom. A herald can bellow once ever 1d4 rounds in one of two ways: one sound is a trilling croak that deafens all opponents within 30 feet (save avoids), while the other is a directed sound that targets one foe within 100 feet for 4d6 points of damage (save for half). If a herald of Tsathogga rolls a natural 20 on its bite attack, it swallows its opponent whole for 3d6 points of damage per round. A herald regenerates 5 hit points per round.

Creeping Swamp

A small dense swamp, roughly two miles in diameter, slowly moves across the ground. The Creeping Swamp moves at walking pace and moves like a plodding wave. The swamp bowls over stationary objects such as trees, rocks and buildings. Larger structures are destroyed and eventually pushed aside while things that stand in the swamp's way are crushed beneath its weight. Simply walking onto the swamp is sufficient to enter its perimeter. The swamp carries creatures or objects as if they were standing in a motionless swamp. Trees and animals alike live perfectly natural lives within the roving swamp as if it were normal wetlands. The swamp remains is constantly humid no matter whatever environment the swamp moves through. The Creeping Swamp contains common swamp life such as giant mosquitoes, prehistoric alligators, gnarlwood, undead treants and an occasional demon. Frogs and frog-like monsters overpopulate the swamp. A clan of powerful tsar has even established a temple to Tsathogga near the back edge of the Creeping Swamp.

The water gradually increases to a depth of four feet near the center. The swampy ground extends into the earth about 10 feet deep at its heart and tapers at the sides as it slides across the land. The swamp leaves a wide swath of flattened and drenched lands as it passes. The swamp moves with an uncanny intelligence and avoids rocky terrain, deserts, canyons and large bodies of water. The Creeping Swamp remains stationary for years at a time before beginning another journey to an unknown destination.

The Herald of Tsathogga controls the Creeping Swamp from a mud pit at the heart of the swamp. Four clay golems resembling giant toads surround the pit. A high priest of Tsathogga also attends to the sanctuary and speaks for the demon lord. The pit contains plunder collected from the swamp's victims and the settlements consumed by the swamp.

Copyright Notice
Authors Scott Greene and Erica Balsley.

Hippocampus

Hit Dice: 4
Armor Class: 4 [15]
Attack: Bite (1d4) or tail slap (1d6) or butt (1d4)
Saving Throw: 13
Special: None
Move: 0/24 (swimming)
Alignment: Law
Challenge Level/XP: 4/120

A hippocampus is often called a merhorse or sea horse, for it is indeed a half-horse/half-fish creature of the sea. The hindquarters of the animal are that of a great fish. Its body is covered in fine scales in the fore parts and large scales elsewhere. The hippocampus' scales vary in color from ivory to deep green, with shades of blue and silver. Aquatic races often tame these animals, and they make fine steeds, for they are strong, swift, and very intelligent. A hippocampus is about 8 feet long and weighs about 600 pounds. Hippocampuses speak the language of merfolk and tritons, and about 10% speak common. Though they are unable to move on land, a hippocampus can breathe air and survive out of the water for 15 minutes.

Training a Hippocampus

A hippocampus requires training before it can bear a rider in combat. To be trained, a hippocampus must have a friendly attitude toward the trainer. Training a friendly hippocampus requires six weeks of work and the assistance of an animal trainer. Riding a hippocampus requires an exotic saddle. A hippocampus can fight while carrying a rider, but the rider cannot also attack unless he or she succeeds on rolling 1d20 under their dexterity score, with fighters subtracting their level from the roll.

Hippocampus eggs are worth 1,500 gp apiece on the open market, while young are worth 2,500 gp each. Professional trainers (usually tritons) charge 1,000 gp to rear or train a hippocampus.

A light load for a hippocampus is up to 300 pounds; a medium load, 301-600 pounds; and a heavy load, 601-900 pounds.

Noble Steeds

On a mountainous island of tiny villages and terraced rice fields, there rules a powerful daimyo, the son of a nobleman and a mermaid. The daimyo rules not only the surface of the island, but also the seafloor around the island to an extent of 5 miles. A tribe of 300 merfolk dwell around the island, spending their time sunning themselves, singing and playing pranks on fishermen.

Among them is a retinue of seven merfolk samurai in shimmering scale coats and wielding barbed spears. On a green meadow in the midst of the undersea mountains, a trio of samurai and their servants look after their herd of nine hippocampuses. The hippocampuses are more loyal to their daimyo than the merfolk (who are always slightly chaotic, despite their best intentions), and the largest and most intelligent of the beasts belongs to the daimyo himself.

In the midst of that meadow of seaweed there is a tall, stone idol in the image of Kannon. The idol has a calming influence on the horses, and in fact acts of violence within 100 feet of the idol are impossible without making a saving throw. Should one perform a courtly dance for the idol, it may (10% chance + 1% per point of dexterity) a single golden teardrop might emerge from its right eye. This teardrop, collected and turned into an amulet, allows one to turn/command sea creatures as a 1st level cleric (+1 level if lawful, +1 level if their wisdom is 13+).

Credit

The Hippocampus originally appeared in the First Edition *Monster Manual* (© TSR/Wizards of the Coast, 1977) and is used by permission.

Copyright Notice

Authors Scott Greene and Erica Balsley, based on original material by Gary Gygax.

Hoar Fox

Hit Dice: 2
Armor Class: 3 [16]
Attack: Bite (1d6)
Saving Throw: 16
Special: Breath weapon, immunity to cold, double damage from fire, surprise on roll of 1-3 on 1d6
Move: 15
Alignment: Neutrality
Challenge Level/XP: 3/60

Hoar foxes are silvery-gray foxes with sapphire colored eyes. They hunt in packs and can often be found lairing near settled areas. Hoar foxes are often hunted for their fur as it brings a handsome sum on the open market. While attacking a hoar fox with fire seems like a sensible solution (given their vulnerability to it), such an attack destroys its pelt and renders it worthless. Three times per day, a hoar fox can expel a blast of frigid ice in a 30-foot cone. A creature in the area takes 2d6 points of cold damage (saving throw for half damage).

Trapped in the Trapper's Cabin

Traveling across the frigid taiga, the trees sparkling from the frost that covers their branches and the snow clinging to your ankles, you come across a cabin. The cabin appears to be in good repair, but it is covered in frost and no smoke curls up from its chimney. Four days ago, a lone trapper carried home a number of fur bearing critters, including a hoar fox that, he later discovered, was not yet dead. When the creature awoke in the cabin, it unleashed multiple cones of frost, icing the door shut and covering much of the interior with frost. The trapper was killed, and for the last three days has served as the hoar fox's only sustenance. It has tried in vain to escape the cabin, but the sub-zero temperatures outside have kept the ice from its own breath from melting.

Should adventurers enter the place, the will find the hoar fox hiding in a corner behind a wooden chair. It is as likely to attack as it is to flee. The floor in the cabin is covered in many patches of ice, making combat tricky. Those who miss on an attack or attempt to move more than 3 feet during a round must pass a saving throw or fall prone, suffering 1 point of damage in the process. Besides the half-eaten body of the trapper (could it rise as an undead due to its shocking death?) the cabin contains a store of foodstuffs (5 weeks of normal rations, 2 weeks of iron rations), fresh water in a large jug, the tools of the trapper's trade and animal pelts worth 1d6 x 20 gp.

Credit
The Hoar Fox originally appeared in the First Edition *Fiend Folio* (© TSR/Wizards of the Coast, 1981) and is used by permission.

Copyright Notice
Author Scott Greene, based on original material by Graeme Morris.

Hoar Spirit

Hit Dice: 4
Armor Class: 5 [14]
Attacks: 2 claws (1d4 + cold) or 1 weapon (1d8 + cold)
Saving Throw: 13
Special: cone of cold (1/day), immune to cold, paralyze
Move: 6
Alignment: Chaos
Challenge Level/XP: 5/240

Hoar spirits are believed to be humanoids that freeze to death and are doomed to haunt the icy wastes. A hoar spirit appears much as it did in life, though its body is gaunt and rotting, and its clothes are tattered. Its skin is pale gray with ice crystals randomly located on its form. Its hands end in wicked claws with pale blue, nearly translucent nails. Its eyes are frozen solid and show no signs of life. Any strike with by the creature's claws deals an extra 1d4 points of damage from the intense cold radiating off its body, and a victim must save or be paralyzed for 1d4+1 rounds. A hoar spirit can unleash a *cone of cold* once per day.

The Ice Maidens

The temperature in the Wailing Glacier's cavern is below freezing. The floor, walls and ceiling of the 30-foot-long by 40-foot-wide chamber are covered in a foot-thick layer of ice. A cold wind blows through the chamber.

Frozen in place are 16 humanoids of various sizes, shapes and races. PCs examining the figures find:

• Five elves wearing heavy furs and seal-skins. The furs are brittle to the touch. The elves hunch forward as if pulling a heavy weight.

• An ogre wearing animal pelts. The creature appears to have sat down next to a fire – and never gotten up again. It still holds a carved branch with a spitted rainbow trout on it.

• Six humans wearing furs, with frost-bitten features. Four appear rotted, with bloody ice crystals caking their torsos. The two "intact" humans embrace, their bodies frozen so completely to one another that no amount of pulling separates them.

• Two dwarves engaged in a tug-of-war with one another's beards. The dwarves each have a handful of beard in their hands. The beards are as frozen as their bodies. Their eyes are glassy and marble-like.

• An orc frozen while drawing his short sword. His feet are encased in heavy blocks of ice that keep him upright. Icicles hang from his protruding tusks.

• A seated satyr playing a small golden harp. The harp's strings are broken and twisted, but also frozen.

Two of the female

frozen undead humans are hoar spirits posing among their victims. The pair hunt together, and bring their victims' bodies back to this ice cave to devour at their leisure. The frozen glacier keeps the victims preserved and frozen.

One of the hoar spirits wears an iron crown set with six rubies (500 gp).

Copyright Notice
Author Scott Greene.

Hornet, Giant

Hit Dice: 7
Armor Class: 4 [15]
Attacks: bite (1d3) or sting (1d4 + poison)
Saving Throw: 9
Special: Poison, pheromone
Move: 1/24 (flying)
Alignment: Neutrality
Challenge Level/XP: 8/800

Giant hornets are 9-foot- long insects with black bodies and white markings on their thorax and abdomen. Giant hornets attack by biting their foes, only relying on their stingers when threatened. During combat, they release a pheromone that agitates all other giant hornets in the area, making them more aggressive (+1 attack, damage).

Riders in the Sky

The Hornet Riders of Olathe raise giant insects to carry them into battle. The kobolds fly in raiding groups of six. Each hornet wears a small saddle. The kobolds carry small crossbows and short swords. The kobolds demand tribute (all the gold PCs carry is a good start) and use hand signals to direct the giant hornets to back up their demands. The kobolds wear leather armor decorated with yellow-and-black stripes.

The Hornet Riders live in Olathe, a mountain village overrun by the foul creatures. A cave on the edge of town is the giant hornets' hive. The entire nest contains more than 60 hornets, although not all are capable yet of carrying riders. A small shack outside the cave entrance contains tack and weapons for the 25 kobold riders who live in the village.

Thirty humans walk with their heads down through the dirty streets. They are the only villagers still alive. They serve the kobolds to keep from being killed.

Copyright Notice
Author Scott Greene.

Horsefly, Giant

Hit Dice: 4
Armor Class: 7 [12]
Attacks: 1 bite (1d6)
Saving Throw: 13
Special: Blood drain
Move: 3/15 (flying)
Alignment: Neutrality
Challenge Level/XP: 4/120

Giant horseflies are 8-foot-long, black hairy flies. Their bodies are thick and their multifaceted eyes are black and dark gold. Their wings are translucent and their legs are long, bristly and jet black. Females have a slightly longer mouth tube than males. A giant horsefly that successfully bites an opponent latches on to drain the creature's blood for 1d4 points of damage per round until dislodged.'

A Wing and a Prayer

Screams and pleas for help bellow from overhead. The shrieks come from Ollie Nematoad, a halfling inventor. Ollie wove a large enclosed basket and tethered it to a giant horsefly in the hopes of harnessing overland flight without the use of magic. Unfortunately, Ollie forgot to figure out a way to guide the horsefly once it was airborne. The panic-stricken horsefly chaotically flees the shrieking Halfling, dragging Ollie along behind it. The giant horsefly is starving and greedily attacks anyone on the ground. After touching down, Ollie cannot stand and retches for several minutes due to hours spinning in the basket beneath the buzzing insect. Once slain, the giant horsefly releases pheromones that attract more giant horseflies.

Copyright Notice
Author Scott Greene.

Hound of Ill Omen

The hound of ill omen (only one is thought to exist) is a legendary monster that appears when a living creature offends his/her deity. The hound appears as a shadowy, translucent wolf about 5 feet tall at the shoulder. Only the creature that offended his deity can see the hound, and only he is affected by the hound's attack. The hound cannot be attacked or driven away by any known means.

The hound of ill omen unleashes a booming howl (audible only to its intended target) that curses the target. This curse causes the next 1d10 wounds the target takes to automatically deal double damage.

Until the target suffers the requisite number of wounds, no form of natural healing cures any damage the target takes. Likewise, any caster attempting to cast a healing spell on cursed target must succeed on a saving throw or the spell has no effect on the cursed creature.

The victim receives no save to avoid the howl's effects and it cannot be removed by any means short of a god's magic, but if *remove curse* is cast on the target within 10 minutes after the howl, the effects of the curse are halved (i.e., only 1d5 wounds automatically confirm as critical hits).

Howls of the Bloody Beast

While trouping across the moors, through the sodden ground and the purple lichens that grow on the white, spiky stones that give the Fangmoor its name, a band of adventurers might hear a mournful howl weaving its way through the stones and across the moor. As the howl reverberates, mists begin to gather on the ground. In the village or carriage inn on the edge of the moor, the adventurers will probably have been warned about the Bloody Beast, a ghostly hound that haunts the moor and presages the death of any who look upon it. If they turn back now, they will be safe, but if they press on there is a cumulative 1 in 6 chance per hour (i.e. 1 in 6 during the first hour, 2 in 6 the next, etc) that a hound of ill omen appears on a rise, looking down on the unfortunate adventurers.

Credit

The Hound of Ill Omen originally appeared in the First Edition *Fiend Folio* (© TSR/Wizards of the Coast, 1981) and is used by permission.

Copyright Notice

Author Scott Greene, based on original material by Mike Roberts.

Huecuva

Hit Dice: 2
Armor Class: 2 [17]
Attack: Claws (1d4+1 plus disease)
Saving Throw: 16
Special: Change self, disease, silver or +1 weapons to hit
Move: 12
Alignment: Chaos
Challenge Level/XP: 5/240

Huecuva are the undead spirits of good clerics who were unfaithful to their god and turned to the path of evil before death. As punishment for their transgression, their god condemned them to roam the earth as the one creature all good-aligned clerics despise — undead. Huecuva resemble robed, worm ridden skeletons and are often mistaken for such creatures. Three times per day, a huecuva can disguise their appearance with an illusion that makes them appear to be a normal cleric.

A huecuva attacks relentlessly until either it or its opponent is dead. During combat, if a lawful cleric attempts to turn a huecuva and fails, the huecuva concentrates all attacks on that cleric, ignoring all other opponents until the cleric or the huecuva is dead.

People struck in combat by the huecuva's claws must pass a saving throw or come down with a fever. The fever incubates for 1d3 days before its symptoms appear. Once the incubation period is over, the disease inflicts 1d3 points of constitution and dexterity damage each day until the diseased victim passes a saving throw at a -3 penalty.

Innocent Until Proven Guilty

The church of the village you just entered in search of healing has been bricked up. The work is fairly fresh and crudely done, as though finished in a hurry. Three days prior, the chief inquisitor of the church rode into town on a palfrey and ordered the parish priestess and her acolytes taken into custody. After a hasty trial in which evidence of involvement in the slave trade was presented, the priestesses were cast into the great hearth of the temple (the temple being dedicated to the hearth goddess). It was a terrible shock for the people to see their beloved priestesses accused, convicted and summarily slain (especially in so terrible a manner), but it was an even more terrible shock to see them emerge from the flames as smoldering skeletons and strangle the inquisitor.

The people fled and did their best to trap the huecuvas in the temple, but they were unaware of the tunnels dug beneath the temple and accessibly via a secret door. The huecuvas are now loose, and will begin to strike at night through numerous secret passages, dragging their victims into the tunnels and casting them into the slave pits to die of starvation or fever.

Hidden in the tunnels there are three treasure chests, each locked and guarded by a poisoned needle. The chests are hidden in different places - one buried in a slave pit, one behind a false wall next to the secret door from the temple into the tunnels, and one buried near one of the exits. In total, the chests hold 1d6 x 200 gp, 1d8 x 200 sp, a brass toe ring etched with the name "Melinda" worth 25 gp, a tiny hematite idol of the Mouse Lord worth 4 gp and a pearl worth 175 gp.

Credit

The Huecuva originally appeared in the First Edition *Fiend Folio* (© TSR/Wizards of the Coast, 1981) and is used by permission.

Copyright Notice

Author Scott Greene, based on original material by Underworld Oracle.

Huggermugger

Hit Dice: 2
Armor Class: 6 [13]
Attacks: 1 weapon (1d4)
Saving Throw: 16
Special: Confusion
Move: 6
Alignment: Chaos
Challenge Level/XP: 2/30

A huggermugger appears as a 3- to 4-foot-tall humanoid with short, cropped, black hair, hidden beneath a black hat, pulled low so as to hide its facial features. Its skin is pale and cold to the touch, regardless of the actual temperature in the surrounding area. A huggermugger's normal attire, in addition to its hat, is a robe of black or dark gray. Huggermuggers do not speak, other than the incessant chattering and mumbling they seem to constantly indulge in. If three or more huggermuggers surround an opponent and begin chattering, it causes *confusion* in the creature (as per the spell).

Capers at the Carnivale

The Carnivale of Plenty is a nonstop celebration lasting from early morning to late night in the city of Listor. Revelers stagger from one party to the next. Wine flows in abundance, and colorful outfits are expected. Horse carts stand outside taverns where their drivers abandoned them. Rose petals litter the roads.

A band of huggermuggers is living in the city and plans to abduct, rob, ransom and kill (in no particular order) as many people as possible. They use the carnival to hide their many schemes to get people alone. The Game Referee could use any or all of the following encounters– or craft your own – to build tension in the group before the huggermuggers make their move and finally abduct someone:

• A huggermugger stands at the end of a dark alley, barely visible in the darkness. It looks like a child torturing a cat and giggling crazily. If a PC approaches, a group of six huggermuggers surround and charm the victim before bustling him into an abandoned warehouse to disarm and rob. If a group enters the alley, the huggermugger "child" runs off and vanishes.

• PCs see a dark shape shadowing them across the rooftops. If anyone climbs or flies, they find a red velvet scarf tied around the neck of a child's doll waiting for them.

• A sewer grate gives way beneath a PC, dropping him 15 feet into the muck if he fails a save. A group of huggermuggers tries to surround and charm the victim.

• An wooden outhouse sits behind a tavern. Any PC who steps inside hears a strange "murmuring" as four huggermuggers surround the shack and try to charm the person inside. If they fail, they lock the door and stab through each wall.

Copyright Notice
Author Scott Greene.

INPHIDIANS

Somewhere in humanities lost aeons a race of malformed serpentine humanoids rose, now known as inphidians. While the truth of their origins has been long forgotten, most sages subscribe to one of two theories. The first states the creatures are the failed results of horrific experiments performed by the dark and nameless sorcerers of an ancient snake-cult in their attempts to ensorcel their followers. The second theory contends the inphidians were once a cult of snake-worshippers cursed by an ancient snake-god for some transgression against the ethos. Whatever the truth, it appears as of late that the inphidians have evolved into true race, beyond the machinations of arcane experiments or curses. While there exist several known species, recent reports describe encounters with yet unidentified inphidians and others are sure to surface as encounters with the race grow more frequent.

Inphidians, regardless of their subspecies, have viper heads in place of their hands. The creatures use these in combat to deliver a powerful bite that injects the victim with poison. Some inphidians, particularly the craftsmen, wear special gloves called *inphidian gauntlets* that let them use their hands like any other humanoid with five digits.

New Item: Inphidian Gauntlets

Inphidian gauntlets are nonmagical leather or metal gauntlets that provide a creature (normally an inphidian) without humanoid hands a set of fully functional hands. When wearing these gauntlets, the creature can manipulate items normally considered unusable (because the creature lacks hands).

Inphidian, Cobra-Back

Hit Dice: 5
Armor Class: 5 [14]
Attacks: 2 snake hand bites (1d4 + poison)
Saving Throw: 12
Special: Poison, spit poison
Move: 9
Alignment: Chaos
Challenge Level/XP: 6/400

Cobra-backs appear as roughly humanoid creatures just over 6 feet tall with a large flap of skin (known as the hood) that runs the length of their neck/spine. Cobra-backs are blue-green scaled like other inphidians, their eyes are crimson, and their forked tongue is gray. Like their brethren, their hands are actually viper heads complete with sharpened fangs that secrete a virulent poison (3d4 points of damage, save for half). When threatened or enraged, the hood of the cobra-back fans open just like that of a true cobra. A cobra-back can spit a line of poison 20 feet from its mouth every 1d4 rounds (2d6 points of damage, save for half).

The Slave Masters

Inside the city of Uroborus, a city being built in the Seething Jungle by the inphidians to honor their snake god Lachesiss, slaves are little more than cattle to be whipped and killed at the whim of the snake men.

A group of 15 captives toil in the jungle humidity, working on their bare and bleeding knees to place sparkling quartz and mica into a 300-foot-wide brick plaza. They are halfway done, but already the rearing head of a cobra can be discerned in the stonework.

A pair of female cobra-back inphidian taskmasters named Naja and Mia stand over the slaves, whipping them with cat-o-nine-tails made from the leathery bodies of dead serpents. The fangs remaining in the snake heads make the slaves jump and scream each time the whips strike flesh.

Copyright Notice

Author Scott Greene.

Inphidian, Common

Hit Dice: 4
Armor Class: 3 [16]
Attack: 2 snake-hand bites (1d4 plus poison)
Saving Throw: 13
Special: Blinding spray, poison
Move: 12
Alignment: Chaos
Challenge Level/XP: 5/240

A common inphidian appears as a humanoid standing about 6 feet tall. Its skin is covered with blue-green scales and its head is almost snake-like in appearance. It has no hair on its head or body. The most unusual feature of an inphidian is its hands; for where they should be, they are not. Each hand has been replaced with the head of a viper with scales of the same blue-green color as the other parts of the inphidian. Common inphidians make up the bulk of the population in inphidian communities. They are the laborers, craftsmen, workers, citizens, guards, and militia.

Once every 1d4 rounds, a common inphidian can spew forth a line of milky-white liquid that causes blindness (as the *blindness* spell) for 6 rounds to any creature struck. A successful saving throw avoids the spray. The spray has a range of 20 feet. The snake hands of the common inphidian deliver a debilitating poison with a successful bite from its snake-hands. The poison weakens the bitten victim, imposing a -2 penalty to hit and damage in melee combat.

Snakes in the Savanna

On a humid savanna you see a large outcropping of stone. The outcropping is composed of several large, flat stones set at different angles to one another and propped up on rounded stones that are carved to look like the top of human heads, their eyes peeking over the grasses of the savanna. A number of holes riddle the outcropping and are home to a tribe of 1d5 x10 degenerate serpent people called inphidians. The inphidians are led by a malevolent trio of females, all born from the same clutch and having golden markings on their skin and the ability to cast spells as 5th level clerics. The will of the clerics is carried out by a sisterhood of five warriors.

During the day, the inphidians can be seen sunning themselves on the rocks or encountered within 3 miles of their home hunting for small mammals. The burrow of the priestesses contains a number of terracotta jars - bulbous and etched with diamond patterns - containing pickled roots and animal organs. Feathered cloaks hang on hooks embedded in the walls but are only worn on ceremonial occaisions. The sisters also have an ivory scroll case in their possession. The case contains a parchment scroll depicting the savanna (one can make out the outcropping and a few other landmarks). A dotted line shows the path of a treasure caravan that a wicked mage has hired the inphidians to attack, for it is carrying a princess royal accompanied only by a bodyguard on her way to wed a bandit king of the plains.

The inphidian's treasure might consist of 4,500 gp (ancient, triangular coinage, with about one of every 100 coins coated with a deadly contact poison), 3,400 sp and a leather sack containing a tourmaline worth 100 gp, a banded agate worth 175 gp and a tiger's eye worth 100 gp.

Copyright Notice
Author Scott Greene.

Inphidian, Dancer

Hit Dice: 3
Armor Class: 7 [12]
Attacks: 2 snake hand bites (1d4 + poison)
Saving Throw: 14
Special: Poison, entrancing dance
Move: 9
Alignment: Chaos
Challenge Level/XP: 4/120

Most dancer/charmer inphidians appear as shapely female humanoids; lithe and elegant in their movements. A charmer's forked tongue is gray and their eyes are crimson. Like other inphidians their body is covered in blue-green scales and where their hands should be, a viper head sprouts from each of its arms. Each viper head is of the same blue-green color and scaled like the rest of the charmer's body. The snake head hands strike with a weak poison (1d4 points of damage), so the inphidian usually relies on its entrancing dance to charm those seeing it (as per a *charm person* spell).

Snake Charmers

A series of 10-foot-deep pits is dug into the earth inside the walls of Uroborus, and each is filled with 30 or so slaves. The pits are 60 feet across, and smell of sweat and feces. Ten-foot-tall metal poles are spaced every 15 feet around the edges of the pits. Slinking around the poles are 10 dancer/charmer inphidians who keep the slaves in line and charmed until they are needed to hoist the blocks and lay the bricks in the city's construction.

The female snake dancers move alluringly between the poles, twisting their bodies around the metal as they dance. Their bodies are covered in silky veils that leave little to the imagination, and charm the minds of all who see them. Rope ladders are lowered into the pit to let the charmed slaves out to work in the city. The inphidians attempt to charm PCs who get too close to the pit, and push them over the edge into the slave mob. The dancer/charmer inphidians shriek and flee if attacked.

Copyright Notice

Author Scott Greene.

Inphidian, Night Adder

Hit Dice: 6
Armor Class: 4 [15]
Attacks: 2 snake hand bites (1d6 + poison)
Saving Throw: 11
Special: Poison, spells
Move: 9
Alignment: Chaos
Challenge Level/XP: 8/800

Usually dressed in black robes, an inphidian night adder has black scales covering its entire body. Its head is serpentine and its arms end in snake-like hands resembling a black mamba. A night adder stands 6-1/2 feet tall and weighs 190 pounds. The snake hands of a night adder deliver a deadly poison. About 40% of night adder inphidians can cast spells as a 7th-level Cleric.

The Serpent Rises

In the sandy ruins of a forgotten temple dwells the clandestine cult of Lachesiss. Only curling columns and sand-covered foundations remain of this ancient space. The crypts below now serve as a vile temple. Poisonous snakes and scorpions coalesce into a moving carpet within the ruins. The desecrated remains of the mummies of Osiris' faithful lie scattered throughout the sand.

The inphidian cult has far-reaching tendrils that invade settlements throughout the lands. The cult mostly consists of human assassins and priests. Guarding the entrance to the temple's depths at all times are 1d4+1 inphidian rattlers from the snake city of Uroborus. This sect is led by a night adder inphidian who can cast an additional four spells: *sticks to snakes*, *charm monster*, *polymorph self* and *monster summoning II*. The cultists melted all the gold looted from the crypts into a huge jewel-encrusted cobra. The statue weighs 300 pounds. The inphidians hope to create a portal from this desolate spot to Uroborus – in the hope of constructing a second snake city here.

Copyright Notice
Author Scott Greene.

Eric Lofgren

Inphidian, Rattler

Hit Dice: 6
Armor Class: 5 [14]
Attacks: 2 snake hand bites (1d6 + poison)
Saving Throw: 11
Special: Death rattle, paralytic poison
Move: 9/6/6 (climb/swim)
Alignment: Chaos
Challenge Level/XP: 7/600

A rattler inphidian is 6 feet tall and about 8 feet long, with a viper head and the lower torso of a giant rattlesnake. Colors vary, but most are brown, black, or dark gray with bands and diamond-shaped patterns. Like all inphidians, its hands are viper heads. Once every 1d4 rounds, a rattler inphidian can unleash a death rattle that does 2d6 points of damage to all creatures in a 40-foot-radius (save for half). The snake hand bite of a rattler inphidian delivers a paralytic poison (2d8 points of damage, paralysis, save resists).

Serpentine Pillar

Beneath the Temple of Entwined Serpents within the inphidian city of Uroborus lie the crypts of a desecrated temple. Standing within this unhallowed space is the Serpentine Pillar. Inphidian cultists invaded and defiled the temple, subverting it to their wicked campaign before they began building their glorious city overtop it. The Serpentine Pillar represents the centerpiece of the new snake temple. This 20-foot-tall column of living, entwined snakes harnesses the dark powers of Lachesiss, the dark god of snakes. Its baleful aura slowly turns living beings into snake-like abominations.

Creatures within 10 feet of the pillar must make a successful save each round or gain serpentine characteristic such as a forked tongue, scaled skin, slit eyes or venomous fangs. The Game Referee can further expand the inflictions, if needed. After an hour of exposure, most creatures painfully transform into an inphidian. Currently, the room holds four inphidian rattlers that slither from the pillar. Only strong magic can remove the permanent transformations caused by the Serpentine Pillar.

Copyright Notice
Author Scott Greene.

Iron Cobra

Hit Dice: 1+1
Armor Class: 1 [18]
Attack: Bite (1d4 plus poison)
Saving Throw: 17
Special: Find target, poison, magic resistance 10%
Move: 15
Alignment: Neutrality
Challenge Level/XP: 3/60

The iron cobra is a construct that resembles a small, 3-foot long cobra. Its eyes give it an evil, determined and almost intelligent look. The iron cobra is most often used to guard a treasure or to act as a bodyguard to its creator, though on some occasions it can be ordered to track down and slay any creature who is within 1 mile and whose name is known by the creator.

When ordered to find a creature within 1 mile, an iron cobra does so unerringly, as though guided by magic. The being giving the order must have seen (or must have an item belonging to) the creature to be found.

The bite of an iron cobra is poisonous, but being a construct, it does not produce its poison. The creator must fill the iron cobra's poison sacs. The sacs can be filled with any poison type of poison, but the poison is usually fatal. The iron cobra can inject its poison three times before its sacs are emptied. It takes 5 rounds to refill the poison sacs.

Construction

An iron cobra's body is constructed from 100 pounds of iron costing at least 1,000 gp. Assembling the body requires the help of an armorer and a 10th level cleric.

Apples and Serpents

In a cavernous vault of mottled limestone there is a small shrine dedicated to a forgotten goddess. The ceiling of the cavern drips with a mild acid from the stalagtites on the ceiling. The shrine is carved into the floor of the cavern. It consists of a cubical chamber (20 feet x 20 feet x 20 feet) with 5-ft walls surrounded by a 5-foot wide trench. The shrine has a stone door that swings easily, as though its hinges are kept oiled. Three walls of the shrine are covered in the preserved skins of reptilian humanoids, their eyes replaced with spherical tiger eye gemstones (worth 10 gp each, 12 in all). The fourth wall is taken up by an idol depicting a white skinned woman, plump and attractive, entwined with four large, green-skinned serpents with garnets for eyes (eight garnets worth 50 gp each). Wooden bowls filled with mealy apples are placed in front of the idol and a chandelier of tallow candles hangs from the ceiling, casting long, leering shadows in the otherwise lightless shrine.

Attempts to steal the gemstones draw out the shrine guardians, four iron cobras. The cobras will emerge from the mouths of the serpents in the idol, surprising anyone involved in prying out the garnet eyes. The iron cobras will not leave the shrine, nor will they allow the bodies of tomb robbers to be retrieved. Once every three days 1d3+3 inphidian shrine keepers visit the shrine to replace the apples, refill the iron cobras with poison (they summon them with bull roarers) and take away dead tomb robbers.

Credit

The Iron Cobra originally appeared in the First Edition *Fiend Folio* (© TSR/Wizards of the Coast, 1981) and is used by permission.

Copyright Notice

Author Scott Greene, based on original material by Philip Masters.

Jack-O-Lantern

Hit Dice: 6
Armor Class: 5 [14]
Attack: 3 strikes (1d4) or *fire seed* (see below) or pitchfork (1d6)
Saving Throw: 11
Special: Fire seeds
Move: 12
Alignment: Neutrality
Challenge Level/XP: 7/600

A jack-o-lantern is an animated plant creature brought to life by a combination of druidic magic and fey sprits. It looks like a roughly humanoid shaped tangle of vines and leaves with a large pumpkin for its head. The pumpkin-head bears a leering face that appears to have been carved there, and glows from within with an eldritch fire. The nature of the face generally reflects the alignment of the animating spirit. Once per day, the monster can spit from its mouth up to four exploding pumpkin seeds. It can spit the seeds up to 100 feet and deals a total of 8d8 points of damage divided up between the seeds. The seeds explode in a 10 foot radius and those in the area may attempt a saving throw to halve the damage.

Creating a Jack-O-Lantern

To create a jack-o-lantern, the caster must be a druid of at least 11th level. Creating a jack-o-lantern involves placing a single pumpkin seed into the mouth of a corpse and burying it in an open field. The body must be that of a human or demi-human of at least 6th level or Hit Dice; the jack-o-lantern has the same HD and alignment as the humanoid did in life. Once the body is buried, the creator must cast *plant growth* and *produce fire*, in that order.

The pumpkin plant that grows from it must be carefully nurtured and tended. Several pumpkins will grow on the vine, one of which will contain the essence of the nature spirit that will eventually animate the plant. The creator must *commune with nature* to determine which pumpkin holds the essence-all others must be picked off the vine and discarded. By harvest time, if the creator chose the right pumpkin, the jack-o-lantern will animate and seek out is creator for instructions.

Melon Terraces

In the rocky highlands inland from the warm jungle coast the farms consist of narrow, rocky terraces planted with rice, melons and gourds. Above these garden terraces are small hovels made from volcanic rocks and palm fronds. Each of these villages has a wise woman or wise man who oversees what administrative needs the village has and coordinates the paying of tribute to the satrap on the coast. Most of these wise people are druids of 1st to 3rd level. All of the wise men pay homage to an 11th level archdruid who visits these villages on a set circuit. The archdruid travels on a friendly elephant and has in his train a court of lesser druids, ritual dancers and drummers, sacred smiths and brewers and an honor guard of spearmen. In each village, the archdruid has stationed a jack-o-lantern to defend the fields, forming them from the bodies of wise people who have died.

The villages possess no treasure beyond their wooden idols, instruments and farming tools.

Copyright Notice

Author Erica Balsley.

Jaculi

Hit Dice: 1
Armor Class: 4 [15]
Attack: Bite (1d6)
Saving Throw: 17
Special: Surprise on roll of 1-5 on 1d6
Move: 12
Alignment: Neutrality
Challenge Level/XP: 1/15

Jaculi are serpents with long, muscular bodies and a squat, flat heads. A mane-like ridge of sharpened bones surrounds its head. Jaculi average 8 feet long, but can grow to a length of 12 feet. Their natural coloration is a deep green fading to a dark brown near the tail and light gray on their underbellies.. Jaculi lie in wait for opponents, preferring places high above the ground where they can leap on their prey and gain surprise.

Ring Toss

Along the jungle coast there is a long stretch of chalk cliffs. Upon these cliffs one can find hundreds of white-naped parrots. The parrots are favored for their relative intelligence as pets and familiars and for their livers, the bile of which is useful in a number of alchemical operations. Embedded in the cliffs is a bronze sculpture 15 feet tall that depicts a winged goddess with four heads on long, serpentine necks. The locals believe they can summon good fortune for themselves by tossing garlands of flowers on those heads from the top of the cliffs. This operation, of dubious value anyways, is made more difficult by the swarm of 1d8+5 jaculi that occupy the fig trees that line the top of the cliffs. The bronze statue is actually a touchstone that transports people into the Elemental Plane of Air when touched under a full moon. This is a possible explanation for why those bits of earth that float in that plane are often colonized by jungle flowers.

Credit
The Jaculi originally appeared in the First Edition *Fiend Folio* (© TSR/ Wizards of the Coast, 1981) and is used by permission.

Copyright Notice
Author Scott Greene, based on original material by Philip Masters.

Jelly, Marsh

Hit Dice: 5
Armor Class: 4 [15]
Attacks: 4 tentacles (1d6 + poison)
Special: Death throws, disorienting glow, poison
Move: 4/18 (flying)
Saving Throw: 12
Alignment: Neutrality
Challenge Level/XP: 10/1,400

A marsh jelly looks like a hovering, flying jellyfish with a translucent sickly green body and four long dangling grayish-pink tentacles. When slain, a marsh jelly explodes in a blast of acid that deals 2d4 points of acid damage to anything within 10 feet. A successful save reduces the damage by half. When a marsh jelly first takes damage, its body begins pulsating and flashing rapidly, emitting an eerie greenish glow. Creatures viewing a pulsating marsh jelly are disoriented (–1 to-hit penalty) for 1d4 rounds. Opponents hit by a marsh jelly's poison tentacles must make a saving throw or be paralyzed for 1d4 round.

Up Through the Ground Came a Bubblin' Ooze

The swamp in this area is stagnant and lifeless. Once-luscious green moss draped from the trees hangs in brittle clumps. An oily skin covers the water's surface. Methane bubbles assault the senses as they release their putrid treasures. The bark at the base of the trees is dissolved from the swamp gases. The water erupts in great bursting boils that splash everything with rotten muck. A glowing bubble rises out of the brackish water, with long tendrils writhing below the radiance. A marsh jelly waits in this area for prey. The jelly eats everything in the area before moving on to more abundant hunting grounds. More jellies can be adding to increase the Challenge Level. The jellies could also hide in the trees and drop down on PCs or appear as a peculiar green glow in the thick mists that occasionally blanket the swamp.

Marsh Jelly, Demonic (Progeny of Jubilex)

Hit Dice: 15
Armor Class: 3 [16]
Attacks: 4 tentacles (1d8 + acid plus poison)
Special: 20% spell resistance, immune to poison and acid, death throws, disorienting glow, telepathy 120 ft., poison
Move: 4/18 (flying)
Saving Throw: 3
Alignment: Chaos
Challenge Level/XP: 15/2,900

A demonic marsh jelly looks like a larger, more sinister marsh jelly. These intelligent minions carry out the will of their slime lord. When slain, a demonic marsh jelly explodes in a blast of acid that deals 3d6 points of acid damage to anything within 10 feet. A successful save reduces the damage by half. When a demonic marsh jelly first takes damage, its body pulsates and flashes rapidly, emitting an eerie greenish glow. Creatures viewing this pulsating glow are disoriented (–2 on attack rolls) for 2d4 rounds. Opponents hit by a demonic marsh jelly's poison tentacles must save or be paralyzed for 1d4 round.

Thus the Lord of Slime Smites Thee

A babbling vagrant makes his way through the crowded street. His skin oozes with oil and filth. Snot streams from his nose and mucus collects in his dirty beard. Commoners hold their noses in disgust and cover their mouths as he passes. As the crowd disperses from the beggar, he raises his arms to the sky and proclaims "Juhl-da-poo! For thee has transgressed against the gory god of goo and gunk. Jook-a-spulck! Prepare to meet thy doom of dung and drudge thee infidels of glop! Haaack-sploomp-plaaa! Behold the strife of sludge!"

As the vagrant speaks the last words, sewage pours forth from all nearby culverts, drains and manholes. The ground beneath him bubbles in a disgusting morass. The vagrant falls to his knees, weeping with delight as the sludge engulfs him. A massive glowing dome emerges from the mire around the man, and long tendrils thrash about looking for victims.

Peligos was sent by the demon lord of slime to enact revenge upon PCs for the extinction of his beloved ooze followers. Whether the PCs are guilty or not makes little difference to Peligos.

Jelly, Mustard

Hit Dice: 7
Armor Class: 2 [17]
Attack: Slam (2d4 plus 1d4 acid)
Saving Throw: 9
Special: Acid, constriction, poison aura, +1 or better weapon to hit, divide, energy absorption, resistance to cold (50%), magic resistance (15%)
Move: 12
Alignment: Neutrality
Challenge Level/XP: 12/2000

Mustard jelly appears to be a yellowish-brown form of the ochre jelly and is thought to be a distant relative of said creature. However, the mustard jelly is far more dangerous than its supposed relative because it is intelligent. The mustard jelly gives off a faint odor of mustard plants to a range of 20 feet. The mustard jelly exudes an aura in a 10-foot radius centered on it that *slows* (as the *slow* spell) any creature in the area as long as it remains in the area and for 1d4 rounds afterward. A new save must be made each round a creature is within 10 feet of the mustard jelly.

A mustard jelly attacks by forming a pseudopod from its body and either slashing or enveloping its foes. A creature hit by a pseudopod must pass a saving throw or be constricted for automatic pseudopod damage each round.

A mustard jelly can split itself into two identical jellies, each with half of the original's current hit points (round down). A jelly with 10 hit points or less cannot divide itself. When divided, each jelly moves faster than the original (base speed 15 feet per round).

A mustard jelly is immune to electrical effects and *magic missiles*. If targeted by an electricity effect (including area effects) or a *magic missile* spell, the mustard jelly gains temporary hit points equal to the amount of damage it would have otherwise sustained. These temporary hit points last for 1 hour.

Mustard Apocalypse

Environment: Temperate marshes
Organization: Solitary

Walking across the marshlands, you come across the remains of a vast canal city. All that remains, unfortunately, are the canals - not a single building or foundation yet remains of the city, nor a brick of fallen masonry or a scrap of wood. It is as if the entire city was swept away into the ether in a single, terrible moment.

What does remain are the subterranean, flooded tunnels that once acted as a sewage system for the city and permitted the movement of goods into cellars. These tunnels harbor a number of alcoves and secret rooms and are inhabited by a race of troglodytic humans - scrawny and small of stature, with coarse black hair, jaundiced skin and pink eyes. These people hide in their secret chambers, hoarding what treasures remained from the ancient city and stockpiling what food they can glean from the marsh - edible fungi, fish, crawdads, beetles, etc.

All of these folk live in terrible fear of the "devil", a large mustard jelly that dwells in the abandoned canals, hunting the remnants of the ancient city. The jelly primarily dwells in a flooded wine cellar. What casks remain intact are now filled with vinegar, though a secret panel in one wall contains 1d4 x 1,000 sp, 1d6 x 1,000 gp, 1d6 x 100 pp and a malachite dagger used in dark rituals (it is stained with blood) worth 100 gp.

Credit

The Mustard Jelly originally appeared in the First Edition *Monster Manual II* (© TSR/Wizards of the Coast, 1983) and is used by permission.

Copyright Notice

Author Scott Greene, based on original material by Gary Gygax.

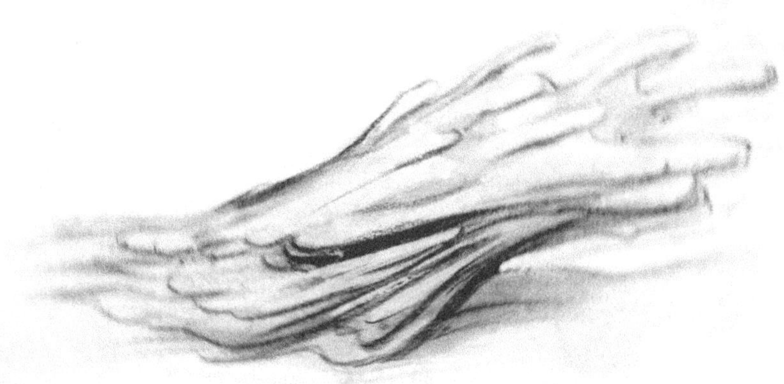

Jelly, Stun-

Hit Dice: 4
Armor Class: 5 [14]
Attack: Slam (1d6 plus 1d6 acid plus paralysis)
Saving Throw: 13
Special: Acid, engulf, paralysis, camouflage, immunity to electricity, surprise on a roll of 1-3 on 1d6
Move: 6
Alignment: Neutrality
Challenge Level/XP: 6/400

Stunjellies are distant relatives of the dungeon-dwelling gelatinous cube. It appears as a section of ordinary wall and covers an area of at least 10 square feet. A stunjelly is 2-1/2 to 5 feet thick. A stunjelly is gray in color and slightly translucent. It gives off a mild vinegar odor that can be detected at a range of 5 feet.

When a target moves within 5 feet of a stunjelly, it attacks with its slam attack. A stunjelly's acid does not harm metal or stone. Creatures hit by a stunjelly must pass a saving throw or be paralyzed for 3d6 rounds. Stunjellies automatically engulf paralyzed creatures, who then suffer automatic acid damage and paralysis each round. Attacks that hit an engulfing stunjelly deal half their damage to the monster and half to the trapped victim.

Stunjellies only surprise dwarves on a roll of 1-2 on 1d6.

Well Guard

A set of spiral stairs leads down into the center of a well-crafted stone vault. The stairs are encased in steel bars with a narrow gate at the bottom. The vault is 30 feet long and wide and 20 feet tall.

The vault is a trophy room (perhaps the owner is alive, perhaps not - Referee's choice) holding such treasures as a stuffed great white shark hanging from the ceiling by chains (a skeletal fighting man in *+1 plate mail* is still encased in its stomach), a wax figure of a damsel in silk robes with a tall, pointed hat and veil combination (the hat and veil act as a *ring of protection +1* when worn by a male, but gives off no magical aura), a sphere of thick glass filled with the stuff of the Abyss, including a school of transparent demonic fish and a night-black staff. The sphere will transport the viewers to a beautiful garden glade of fragrant roses, pear trees and two salt statues of young lovers locked in a kiss if the viewers hold their breath, close their eyes and ease into the sphere fingers first.

The trophy room would be a mere gallery of the bizarre if not for the stunjelly lurking within the vault. The stunjelly lurks on the wall near the wax dummy.

Credit

The Stunjelly originally appeared in the First Edition *Fiend Folio* (© TSR/Wizards of the Coast, 1981) and is used by permission.

Copyright Notice

Author Scott Greene, based on original material by Neville White.

Jelly, Whip

Hit Dice: 3
Armor Class: 8 [11]
Attacks: 4 whip tendrils (1d4 + 1d4 acid)
Saving Throw: 14
Special: Acid
Move: 8
Alignment: Neutrality
Challenge Level/XP: 3/60

A whip jelly looks like a bluish-gray quivering pile of goo with four long slimy tendrils jutting from its form. A whip jelly, like most oozes, is a mindless hunter that spends its time prowling the subterranean world for food. A whip jelly secretes a deadly acid that quickly dissolves organic matter but does not harm metal or stone. Any melee hit deals acid damage. Non-metal armor or clothing dissolves and becomes useless immediately unless.

Whipped

A knight in weathered plate mail armor stands where the hall widens to a 15-foot circular. The knight's visor is down, and he stands unmoving, bent slightly forward at the waist. His chest plate hangs loose and his entire body is covered in dust and translucent goo. He holds a rusted long sword in his gauntlet, but the tip of the blade is dug into the dirt of the cavern's floor. At the knight's feet lie various metal helms, weapons and bits of armor. A grime-coated *+1 ring of protection* can be found among the various cast-off items. A deep voice speaks from the knight if PCs approach within 15 feet: "Halt and identify yourselves!" The same voice speaks again if PCs defy the warning and come within five feet: "Drop your weapons or face my wrath."

The knight is a clockwork automaton a magic-user crafted from gears and pulleys, a poor-man's iron golem that barely functioned. The metal man marched with a stiff gait, swung its blade indiscriminately at anyone it encountered, and in general posed little threat to man or beast. The metal knight moved with a constant clicking and whirring of gears, and rubber and cloth bands inside the construct gave it life. Right now, the only thing still working on the knight is a *magic mouth* cast into the knight's helm to issue warnings to intruders.

The knight halted in place forever years ago when a whip jelly wormed its way into the knight's dented chest cavity. The jelly dissolved the bands that propelled the metal knight, causing the automaton to slump but not fall. The jelly lives inside the knight's hollow chest cavity, venturing out occasionally to find food. The metal objects at the knight's feet are the remains of past meals. The goo covering the knight is an acid secreted by the whip jelly that dissolves flesh and other organic matter, but leaves metal unscathed.

Copyright Notice

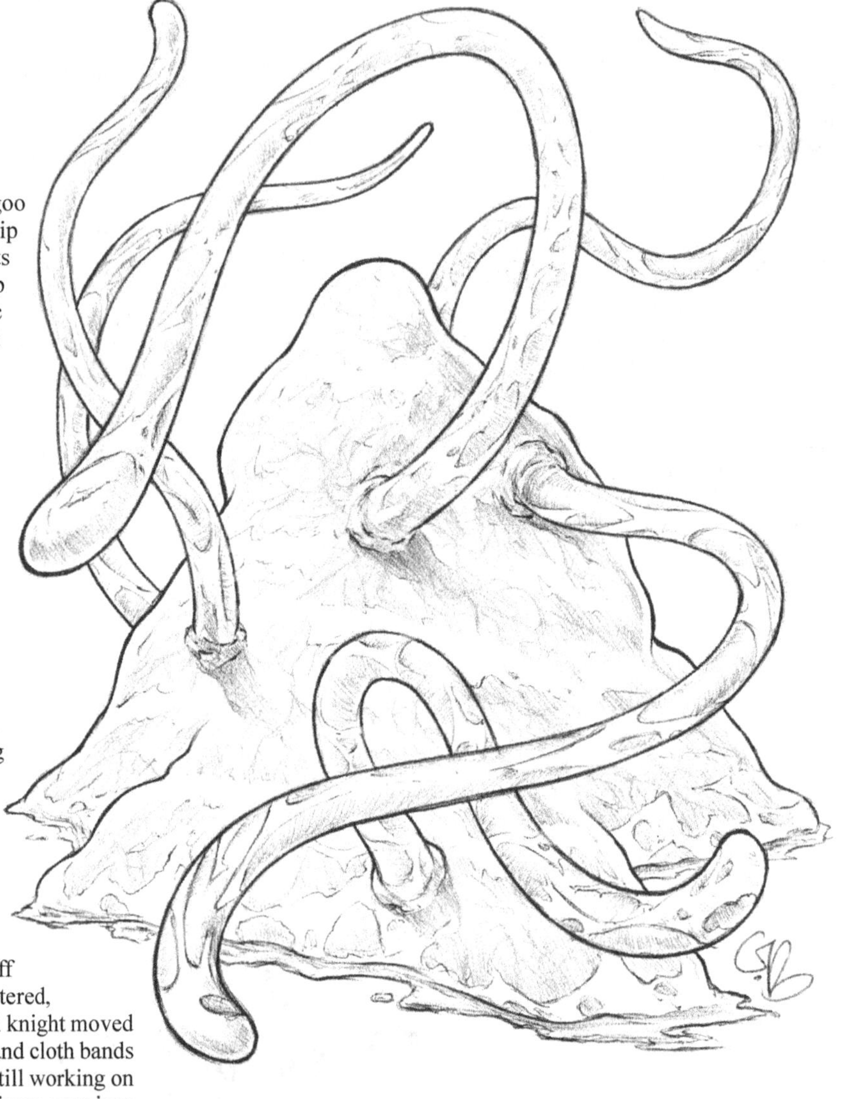

Jellyfish, Monstrous

Hit Dice: 3
Armor Class: 7 [12]
Attack: Tentacles (1d6 plus poison)
Saving Throw: 14
Special: Poison, transparent (surprise on roll of 1-2 on 1d6)
Move: 0/6 (swimming)
Alignment: Neutrality
Challenge Level/XP: 4/120

The monstrous jellyfish's body is a translucent pink, blue, or purple hollow form resembling an inverted umbrella of sorts. A giant jellyfish's body averages 8 feet or more in diameter, while its tentacles (trailing beneath it underwater) can reach lengths of around 50 feet or greater. Special muscles on the underside of the jellyfish's body push water out of it, allowing the creature to swim through propulsion. Jellyfish eat anything that contacts their tentacles — usually crustaceans, fish, algae, plankton and the occaissional *water breathing* adventurer.

A monstrous jellyfish's tentacles are highly poisonous, delivering a paralyzing poison when contacted or contacting a foe. The victim of the poison suffers 1d4 points of stinging damage and must pass a saving throw or be paralyzed for 1d6 rounds.

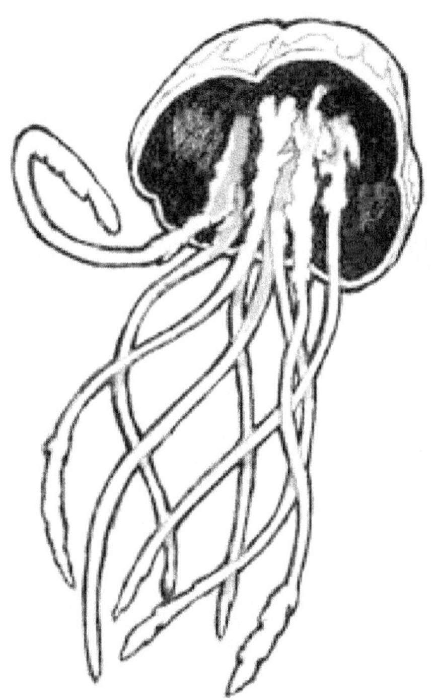

Blue Lagoon Resort

A fortified palace of white stone and elegant onion domes stands near a jungle lagoon. The palace is owned by the satrap of the jungle coast, a comely, artistic man more concerned with his poetry than the governance of his realm. Discipline and administraiton is handled by his wife, a tall, stately woman with deep, bronze skin, glossy black hair and a blood-red temper.

The palace is surrounded by gardens of orchids, ferns and fruit trees and a series of deep, salt water ponds connected to the lagoon and inhabited by a swarm of 1d12+10 monstrous jellyfish, their translucent pink and purple bodies beautiful in the crystal clear waters of the ponds. Entrance to the ponds via the lagoon is blocked by a bronze grate that can be lifted with a winch in a small, marble cupola nearby.

The palace grounds are guarded by a hobgoblin slave soldiers, klibanophoroi wearing heavy scale armor and carrying shields, long spears and curved short swords. Those who patrol the grounds do so mounted on striped jungle horses.

The satrap is a most generous and pleasant man, sitting on his portico in his wicker throne upon the kamadan rugs, dining on peacock eggs and jellied cobra while dwarven eunuchs in bulbous turbans and red loincloths fan him with palm fronds. His wife will be found roaming the palace, barking orders at her clarks and servants, raising a furor wherever she goes. Guests who have made themselves a bother might be tossed in the pools with the jellyfish.

The palace treasury contains 2d12 x 100 sp and 1d6 x 1,000 gp. The satrap wears a large moonstone worth 200 gp on his turban.

Copyright Notice

Jupiter Bloodsucker (Vampire Plant)

Hit Dice: 3
Armor Class: 4 [15]
Attack: 6 vine-leaves (1d6 plus blood drain)
Saving Throw: 14
Special: Blood drain, smother, double damage from fire
Move: 3
Alignment: Neutrality
Challenge Level/XP: 4/120

The jupiter bloodsucker, or vampire plant, is a man-sized, seemingly ordinary plant that looks like a tangle of leaves and roots topped by four large, dark green, serrated leaves with red veins. A creature looking closely at the roots may notice that the stems are transparent and that blood seems to course through them. On the bottom of each leaf are many small, sharp thorns. These are used to attach to a victim and drain its blood.

A jupiter bloodsucker deals 1 point of constitution damage per round per vine-leaf attached to a foe. If reduced to zero points of constitution, the victim has been completely drained of blood and dies. Constitution points lost to a jupiter bloodsucker heal at the rate of 1 per hour. Prying a leaf loose requires a successful open doors check.

A victim struck by more than one vine-leaf in a round must make a saving throw to avoid being smothered by them. For every vine-leaf beyond the first, the victim suffers a -1 penalty to its saving throw. An opponent so smothered must hold his breath or die. Again, one can pry leaves loose by making a successful open doors check.

Accident on the Trail

Tromping up a jungle trail, you come to the side of a small ravine where it appears a coach has gone over the side. Indeed, in the bottom of the ravine you see the coach, damaged but still whole, and the remains of the drivers and horses, their flesh pale and bloodless and their bodies bloated in the powerful sun. The ravine is covered with thick, green vegetation, including a bed of 1d6+4 jupiter bloodsuckers.

The passengers in the coach are alive, but injured and dying of thirst. If they hear travelers (2 in 6 chance) they will signal to let them know they are there. The passengers were on their way to a jungle stronghold, and include an armorer, a minstrel, the lord of the stronghold's tax collector (an attractive woman) and an animal trainer who specializes in horses.

The coach also holds a locked iron box containing the collected taxes: 2d10 x 100 sp, 1d20 x 20 gp and 1d6 turquoise buttons worth 65 gp each.

Credit

The Jupiter Bloodsucker originally appeared in the Basic module *B3 Palace of the Silver Princess* (© TSR/Wizards of the Coast, 1981) and is used by permission. It appears in the orange-covered version (the original), not the revised green-covered module.

Copyright Notice

Author Scott Greene, based on original material by Jean Wells.

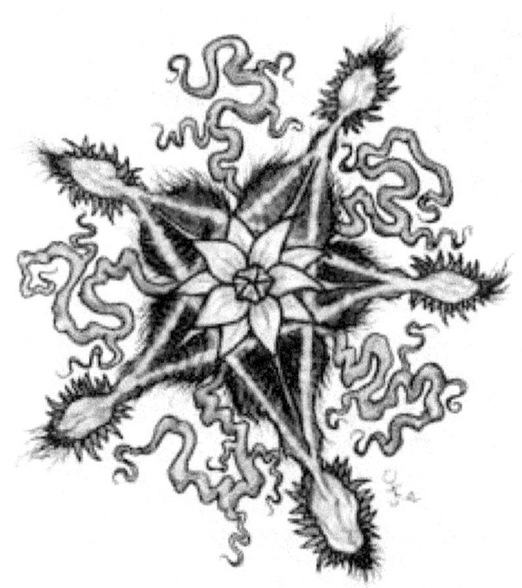

Kamadan

Hit Dice: 4
Armor Class: 3 [16]
Attack: 2 claws (1d6) or snakes (1d4) and bite (1d8)
Saving Throw: 13
Special: Sleep breath
Move: 15
Alignment: Neutrality (chaotic tendencies)
Challenge Level/XP: 6/400

The kamadan is a feline-like predator that may somehow be related to the displacer beast. The kamadan has coarse, yellowish brown fur and a leopard-like body and head with emerald green eyes. From its shoulders sprout six long serpents, blackish-green in color, each about twice the length of a normal human. The serpents' eyes are reddish-yellow. It is about 9 feet long and weighs about 600 pounds.

The kamadan is a fierce predator and highly territorial, hunting just about anything that spends too much time in its territory. The kamadan has a hunting range of about 5 or more square miles. It makes its lair under rocky outcroppings or within caves.

Kamadans are intelligent creatures and are capable of speaking the local common tongue with a thick accent, owing to their felinoid mouths.

Once every 1d4 rounds and no more than 5 times per day, a kamadan can exhale a cone of sleep 30 feet long and 20 feet wide at the base. Creatures with 4 HD or less are automatically cast into a deep slumber; creatures with 5 HD or more are permitted a saving throw to avoid drowsing.

Poisonous Kamadan

A variant kamadan, one with poisonous snakes, is rumored to exist. Encounters with such creatures are rare, for which most adventurers are thankful. The poisonous kamadan uses the same statistics as the normal kamadan, but each snake head delivers a deadly poisonous bite. The poisonous kamadan has a CL/XP of 7/600.

Nighttime Mine Supervisor

A balmy savanna of bushwillows, elephant grass, gum acacias and eucalyptus trees is home to an active population of bulettes and dwarven miners. On a large outcropping of bluish, mithral-rich stone, a dwarven armorer has established a forge fueled by the potent droppings of bulette. The forge produces some of the finest arms and armor in the world - ornate suits of platemail, round, mirror-like shields, axe-swords and flanged maces - often incorporating bulette scales. About 40 dwarves live in the adobe complex atop the outcropping, somewhat in fear of their master. Iron mines are tunneled into the outcropping and patrolled at night by the master's pet, an especially fierce kamadan. The kamadan is kept in a mithral cage in the mines and released each night using a winch located in the master's quarters. The adobe walls are patrolled by ten dwarves armed with platemail, crossbows and axes.

The master's treasure consists of 1d20 x 100 sp, 1d20 x 100 gp, 1d20 pounds of mercury used for etching armor, a granite icon of the forge god (worth 125 gp) and a jasper whistle worth 1 gp that the master uses to control the kamadan.

Credit

The Kamadan originally appeared in the First Edition *Fiend Folio* (© TSR/Wizards of the Coast, 1981) and is used by permission.

Copyright Notice

Author Scott Greene, based on original material by Nick Louth.

Kampfult (Sinewy Mugger)

Hit Dice: 2
Armor Class: 3 [16]
Attack: 6 tendrils (1d4)
Saving Throw: 16
Special: Strangle
Move: 6
Alignment: Neutrality (chaotic tendencies)
Challenge Level/XP: 2/30

This creature is a man-sized monster resembling a tree trunk with six long sinewy tendrils spaced evenly around the upper portion of its body. Six smaller tendrils located at the base of its trunk seem to aid it in locomotion. Its body is dark grayish-green and its tendrils are dark gray changing to dark green at the tips. The kampfult haunts subterranean realms in search of prey, grabbing any living creature that passes by. Creatures slain by a kampfult are slowly absorbed into the base of the trunk and digested. Kampfults do not speak, but it is thought that they can understand the language of the drow.

A kampfult attacks from surprise, waiting until its prey moves within reach and then lashing out with its tendrils, attempting to grab and entangle its prey. A kampfult rarely attacks creatures larger than itself unless it is extremely hungry. It fights until either it or its opponent is dead. Those struck by a tendril must pass a saving throw to avoid it wrapping around their neck and inflicting 1d4 points of damage automatically each round. Tendrils can be removed with a successful open doors check or severed with an edged weapon. The tendrils have an AC of 3 [16] and are severed with 4 points of damage.

Pool of the Lost

You enter a natural cavern about 40 feet in diameter and 25 feet high that has been carved to make the floor and walls smooth. Three holes near the west wall and two holes near the east wall allow steam to rise into the chamber. A chimney in the ceiling permits the steam to exit again, but the air in the room is always warm and moist.

The floor of the cavern is concave and filled with a few feet of water, with a 10 foot diameter island in the middle of the room. Besides the entrance and the holes (not even large enough for a halfling), the only obvious exit is a shaft located on the island. The shaft is covered by an iron grate that, though heavy, is easily moved.

The pool is inhabited by a species of prehistoric, bony fish that are only mildly dangerous (1 in 6 chance of 1d4 fish attacking, treat as 2 HD creatures with an AC of 6 [13] and a bite attack that deals 1d4 damage).

The island is inhabited by a kampfult that is very good at playing the part of a weird, but harmless, tree. It will not move a tendril until all but one person has descended down the shaft, attacking the straggler and closing the iron grate.

About 1d10x100 gold pieces lie at the bottom of the pool.

Credit

The Kampfult originally appeared in the First Edition *Monster Manual II* (© TSR/Wizards of the Coast, 1983) and is used by permission.

Copyright Notice

Author Scott Greene, based on original material by Gary Gygax.

Kathlin

Hit Dice: 4
Armor Class: 7 [12]
Attacks: 2 hooves (1d6), bite (1d4)
Saving Throw: 13
Special: Endurance
Move: 24
Alignment: Neutrality
Challenge Level/XP: 4/120

A kathlin resembles a heavy warhorse with six legs. Black or brown coats are the horse's most common coloring, although white-coated kathlins are sometimes found. Eye color varies as much as fur color, but again brown or black seems to be most common. Kathlins can be trained to serve as mounts, and their ability to run for days without rest makes them highly prized.

Steeple Chase

This encounter takes place when PCs are encamped in the forest some distance from the nearest town. The moon is new, leaving very little light in the sky. The land is alive with the sounds of burrowing animals and owls taking flight. In the middle of the night, a giant riderless black horse wanders into camp, its flanks heaving as if from a long run. A fine sheen of sweat drips off the animal's broad sides. The horse has six muscular legs. Leaves and pine needles stick to the animal's flanks.

A group of 15 goblins captured the kathlin and trained the horse to lead raids on unsuspecting campers. They call it Steeple, which in their coarse language means "far runner." The horse's body is coated in a very sticky pine resin that looks like sweat. Any PC running his hand down the animal's coat must save or become stuck to the mount. If someone gets stuck, the horse charges into the forest – dragging the unfortunate victim with it. Any PC stuck to the kathlin takes 2d4 points of damage each round as he hits small trees and gets hit by the animal's powerful legs.

The goblins wait until the horse charges into the forest before moving in to scavenge whatever they can carry from the PCs' camp. The resin wears off in an hour, when PCs – or their lifeless bodies – fall away from the horse. If rescued from the vicious goblins, the kathlin can easily be retrained to serve as a mount.

Copyright Notice
Author Scott Greene

Kech

Hit Dice: 5
Armor Class: 3 [16]
Attack: 2 claws (1d4) and bite (1d6)
Saving Throw: 12
Special: Rending claws, pass without trace, surprise on roll of 1-3 on 1d6
Move: 15/9 (climbing)
Alignment: Chaos
Challenge Level/XP: 5/240

Kechs are monkey-like humanoids standing about 6 feet tall and weighing about 150 pounds. They have azure eyes and their bodies are covered in leathery scales that resemble greenish-brown leaves. Kech make their homes in trees and prefer to move through the trees rather than on the ground. They have an almost human organization and society among the various tribes and clans. Family units dwell in a single lair (usually a hollowed tree or small hut built among the branches of a leafy tree). Kechs speak their own language and have a 15% chance of speaking the common tongue.

Kechs attack from ambush, preferring to ensnare their prey in pits, traps, or the like. If faced with a weak adversary, they attack with a frontal assault, seeking to kill as quickly as possible. Slain prey is dragged into the kech's lair and devoured at the creatures' leisure. If a kech hits with both claw attacks, it latches onto the opponent's body and tears the flesh for an extra 2d4 points of damage.

A kech can move across any ground— ice, snow, mud—without leaving any footprints. Tracking a kech by nonmagical means is impossible.

Kech Me if You Can

In a large, temperate woodland nestled between two granite ridges, several bands of 2d4 kech make sport of travelers who dare to pass through the woodland. Each band will attempt to steal something from the adventurers - a helmet, wine skin, jewel, etc - and carry it to a particularly tall, ancient oak near the center of the woodland overlooking a shallow, murky lake. The other bands will do their best to steal the object and get to the tree first. Although this might appear to be little more than a silly annoyance, for the kech it is how they assign rank, and thus territory, in the valley. The kech mean no harm (though they also aren't worried about returning the stolen item, which resides in the hollow trunk of the great tree with other stolen articles), and will react violently and in concert if the adventurers use violence to retrieve their article.

The kech do not value the items they have stolen, and will do nothing to stop adventurers from climbing the great tree to retrieve them. The tree holds a brass candlestick (650 gp), a brass bust of a bearded, toothless man (100 gp), a *+2 heavy mace*, a terracotta flask containing brandy (6 gp) and a moonstone worth 500 gp.

Credit

The Kech originally appeared in the First Edition *Monster Manual II* (© TSR/Wizards of the Coast, 1983) and is used by permission.

Copyright Notice

Author Scott Greene, based on original material by Gary Gygax.

Kelp Devil

Hit Dice: 8
Armor Class: 2 [17]
Attack: 6 fronds (1d6)
Saving Throw: 8
Special: Charm, immunity to electricity, resistance to fire (50%), resistance to blunt weapons (50%), underwater concealment
Move: 12/18 (swimming)
Alignment: Chaos
Challenge Level/XP: 10/1400

Kelp devils are relatives of kelpies. To the casual observer, the kelp devil resembles a large colony of slow moving seaweed about 20 feet in diameter. A closer look reveals six 10-foot long pseudopods extending from its body. Kelp devils speak the common tongue.

Kelp devils are patient creatures. They lie perfectly motionless until potential prey moves within 10 feet. Once their prey is within range, they strike quickly with their pseudopods, attempting to grab an opponent. Grappled creatures are dragged underwater and drowned. Slain creatures are devoured by the kelp devil.

Twice per day, on a successful hit with a frond, a kelp devil can affect the opponent as by *charm monster*. The creature can make a saving throw to resist the effects.

Creatures hit by a kelp devil's fronds must make a saving throw or be entwined and dragged under water to drown. Kelp devils are expert at squeezing the air from a creature's lungs, so their victims can only hold their breath for 1 round per 2 points of constitution before they drown.

Admiral's Rock

On a lonely sea mount in the middle of a green sea the ex-admiral of the Blue Brotherhood, a fleet of pirates, has constructed an impregnable keep. The keep is designed not only to contain the admiral's treasures but also to act as a bank for pirates. The walls of the keep are 8 feet thick near the base and 6 feet thick at the top, which rises 5 stories above the island and surrounding sea, with windows of leaded glass and thick, wooden doors at the back of tunnels barred with bronze portcullises.

The keep has the latest in war engines trained on the surrounding seas, and allows only men in small launches to approach the keep. The keep's battlements are patrolled by a dozen swaggering pirates (2nd to 4th level fighters), but they are not the primary defenders of Admiral's Rock. A large kelp devil patrols the waters around the rock, attacking any person not cleared by the admiral. This is done by blowing a trumpet in a particular tune. Without this sounding, the kelp devil shows no mercy in sending people to a watery grave.

Among the treasures held in the keep's vaults are 4d20 x 100 sp, 1d30 x 100 gp and a large turquoise scepter worth 650 gp.

Credit

The Kelp Devil originally appeared in the Second Edition module *Return to White Plume Mountain* (© Wizards of the Coast, 1999) and is used by permission.

Copyright Notice

Author Scott Greene, based on original material by Bruce Cordell.

Kelpie

Hit Dice: 5
Armor Class: 2 [17]
Attack: Slam (see below)
Saving Throw: 12
Special: Charm, amphibious, reshape form, resistance to fire (50%), telepathy 1 mile
Move: 9/12 (swimming)
Alignment: Chaos
Challenge Level/XP: 7/600

In their true form, kelpies are indistinguishable from normal seaweed. They are found in saltwater and freshwater, swamps, fens, and stagnated underground pools and lakes. In her human guise, a kelpie appears as a beautiful female with long flowing dark hair, emerald eyes, and soft, pale skin. She is cloaked in robes of seaweed or wears nothing at all. A kelpie often assumes a semi-human form in which her lower torso is composed entirely of seaweed. Kelpies speak the common tongue and possibly the language of merfolk and tritons.

Kelpies lie in wait for their foes, most often males, and when a target moves within range, they reshape their form to appear human. In most cases, they take the form of a drowning woman to lure the target closer. If the ruse is not detected and the opponent moves within reach of the kelpie, she attacks, attempting to drown her victim. Drowned foes are taken back to the kelpie's lair and devoured.

Once per day, a kelpie can produce an effect identical to the *charm monster* spell. The target can make a saving throw to avoid the effects. If the save fails, the victim believes the kelpie to be a very beautiful and attractive creature, and attempts to move as quickly as possible toward the kelpie. The kelpie can automatically grapple a charmed foe, for they do not resist the kelpie's embrace. A *charmed* foe can only hold his breath for a number of rounds equal to his Constitution. After that, he drowns.

Female creatures are immune to the kelpie's *charm* ability; only males can be affected. The *charm* is negated if the victim dies, the kelpie dies, or *dispel magic* is cast on the victim.

Kelpies can survive out of the water for 6 hours.

Leap of Faith

Saint's College is housed in an old, fortified manor built on a rocky peninsula that overlooks the ocean. The college trains men and women for the priesthood or lives as sages or major domos, and usually houses about thirty students drawn from pedigreed families. The college employs five sages as lecturers, one of them serving as the dean. Armed guards patrol the college grounds and the walls.

Recently, the school has run into a spot of trouble. Three young men, all from powerful families, have gone missing. One body has been found floating washed ashore about a mile up the coast. The guards have seen nothing, and the dean is not prepared to deal with a matter like this. His superiors in the church hierarchy are intent on calming matters down, and their inquisitors have questioned all involved and discovered nothing.

The kingdom is now in an uproar, with different political factions exchanging accusations and challenges. Two men of high birth have died in duels and civil war appears to be on the horizon. The real culprits of the crime are a bed of 1d4 kelpies that have taken up residence in the waters beneath the college's dormitory windows. They arise at night, when mists cloak the coast, and send their voices into the heads of the students, rousing them from their slumber, bringing them to the shuttered windows and commanding them to leap into the sea.

Credit

The Kelpie originally appeared in the First Edition module *S2 White Plume Mountain* (© TSR/Wizards of the Coast, 1979) and later in the First Edition *Fiend Folio* (© TSR/Wizards of the Coast, 1981) and is used by permission.

Copyright Notice

Author Scott Greene, based on original material by Lawrence Schick.

Khargra

Hit Dice: 6
Armor Class: 0 [19]
Attack: 3 claws (1d3) and bite (2d8)
Saving Throw: 11
Special: Ruin armor and weapons, earth glide, immunity to cold and fire
Move: 6/12 (burrowing)
Alignment: Neutrality
Challenge Level/XP: 9/1100

Khargra resembles a human-sized cylinder covered in metallic scales. It sports three large "fins" spaced even around its circumference. Between each fin is a metal sheath from which slide long claw-like arms. A large hole in the front of its cylindrical body is lined with many small curved metallic teeth and seems to function as its mouth. A khargra is a 5-foot long cylinder and weighs about 300 pounds.

Khargras are native to the Elemental Plane of Earth and are only encountered on the Material Plane when summoned. On occasion, a khargra slips through a tear in the planar fabric and enters the Material Plane to digest ores and metals not normally found on its native plane.

Khargras attack from ambush, preferring to wait just inside the wall of a dungeon or corridor and springing out when prey passes nearby. The khargra attempts to grab and devour any metal objects within the area. Nonmetallic objects may be bitten, but not devoured.

A khargra's bite can tear right through armor and weapons. Khargra can bite weapons by making a successful melee attack at a -5 penalty. If a khargra misses an attack due to armor or a shield, their attack instead affects the armor. In either event, the owner of the object must roll a saving throw, rolling 1d20 and adding either the armor bonus or weapon's damage dice and equalling or exceeding a roll of 15. If unsuccessful, the obect is ruined.

A khargra can glide through stone, dirt, or almost any other sort of earth, including metal, as easily as a fish swims through water. Its burrowing leaves behind no tunnel or hole, nor does it create any ripple or other signs of its presence. A *move earth* spell cast on an area containing a burrowing khargra flings the khargra back 30 feet, stunning the creature for 1 round unless it succeeds at a saving throw. Khargra can automatically sense the location of anything within 60 feet that is in contact with the ground.

Up From the Depths

A narrow defile in the far northern lands is the last resting place of a company of imperial surveyors. The surveyors, lead by a merchant venturer and consisting of twelve men-at-arms, two sergeants and three cartographers, were killed while moving through the defile on their way to the coast, where the empress believes there is an ancient diamond mine. The empress is quite correct; the rocky hills along the coast are very rich in precious stones and metals, but are also home to a pack of 2d6 khargra, summoned in depths of the mine by a wizard locked in battle with a pit fiend and now persisting in the material plane. The khargra often leap between the sides of the defile, and it was during one of these migrations that they encountered the armored men of the surveying team.

The armor and weapons of the surveying team were destroyed or consumed by the khargra, and even the sack of gems and gold coins hidden on the venturer's body were removed. The dead surveyors do still have a very accurate set of maps of the coast and highlands inside an ivory mapcase. On the back of one of the maps the venture scribed notes and sketched illustrations of a strange cavern that seemed to "breathe." The author believed this cavern granted access to a subterranean kingdom his people tell stories about.

Credit

The Khargra originally appeared in the First Edition *Fiend Folio* (© TSR/Wizards of the Coast, 1981) and is used by permission.

Copyright Notice

Author Scott Greene, based on original material by Lawrence Schick.

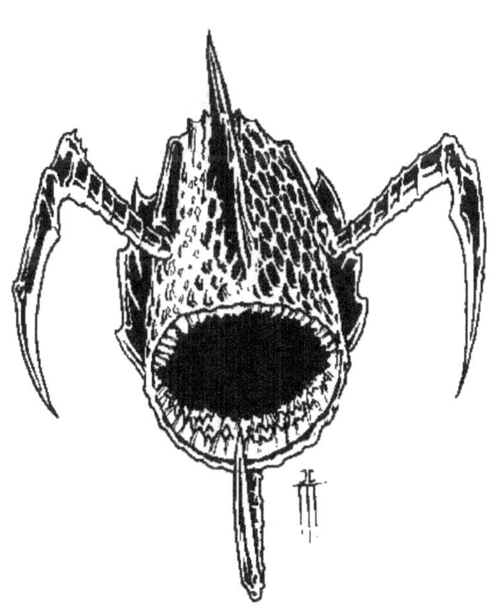

Killmoulis

Hit Dice: 1d4
Armor Class: 4 [15]
Attack: Needle (1)
Saving Throw: 18
Special: Magic resistance 25%, surprise on a roll of 1-3 on 1d6, telepathy 100 ft.
Move: 15
Alignment: Neutrality
Challenge Level/XP: B/10

A killmoulis is thought to be distantly related to brownies and other small, helpful fey, though it bears little physical likeness to its kin. Standing about 1 foot tall, they do not speak except through a limited form of telepathy. The race appears to be sexless. They are unnaturally thin and a bulbous head with no chin, seemingly no mouth and an immense, trunk-like nose. A kilmoulis has pale white skin and deep blue eyes.

A killmoulis gang always tries to take up residence in places of human habitation where foodstuffs are prepared or handled, dwelling beneath floorboards or in garrets or behind pantry shelves. The killmoulis has the same loyalty to its host family and eagerness to perform chores as the brownie, but unlike the brownie they are more prone to pointless but harmless mischief.

Killmoulises are inoffensive creatures, lacking any real combat capability. They do carry dagger-like needles, however, and use these to stab and pierce their opponents. Occasionally, these needles are poisoned with whatever poison is readily available.

Fey Hide-Away

A modest castle of gray bricks sits on a rocky mount overlooking an icy stream. The keep of the tower has a copper roof that rises to a peak and is topped by a brass statue of an archer. The archer in question is the mistress of the castle, a 12th level fighting-woman who won fame and glory competing in tournaments and wealth plundering the underworld. The castle has a population split between humans and dwarves, the dwarves being five religious scholars of their people who were persecuted and exiled from a neighboring kingdom. The humans are mostly shepherds, the scraggly hills around the castle supporting hundreds of the fluggy, white creatures. The mistress of the castle is a devout worshipper of the fey court, and all fey creatures, including the dwarfs, are given freedom on her lands provided they do not harm her people or their animals. A gang of 1d3+1 killmoulis dwell in the castle as its stewards, feasting on aromatic resins and nosegays hung from the rafters by the mistress to thank them for their work.

Credit
The Killmoulis originally appeared in the First Edition *Fiend Folio* (© TSR/Wizards of the Coast, 1981) and is used by permission.

Copyright Notice
Author Scott Greene, based on original material by Gary Gygax.

Korred

Hit Dice: 6
Armor Class: 4 [15]
Attack: Slam (1d4) or shears (1d6) or club (1d6)
Saving Throw: 11
Special: Animate hair, laugh, magic resistance (30%)
Move: 12
Alignment: Neutrality (chaotic tendencies)
Challenge Level/XP: 8/800

A korred has the upper torso of a small humanoid and the lower torso of a goat, thus giving it a satyr-like appearance. It has a long, flowing beard, and like its hair, is tangled and matted into frightful knots. It wears a simple leather covering on which hangs a large leather pouch. Its hair is dark and its wild, brown eyes have an almost feral-like gleam in them. Korreds speak their own language.

Three times per day, a korred can unleash a laugh that stuns all creatures within 60 feet that hear it for 1d2 rounds. A saving throw negates the effects.

A korred can weave its hair (contained in its pouch) into animated ropes that can entangle foes. The time it takes to weave enough hair to entangle one foe is dependent on the size of the creature as follows:

Size	Time
Dwarves, Halflings	1 round
Elves, Humans	2 rounds
Ogres	3 rounds

A korred cannot entangle an opponent larger than an ogre.

Whose Side Are You On?

While resting and recuperating in a roadhouse outside an apparently quiet village of tall, stone houses and alleys of black dirt, the adventurers will find themselves in the midst of a revolution. Recently, imperial convoys have been attacked by "bandits" that they know were really revolutionaries from the White Jasmine Society, a secret organization funded by local merchants who are angry about taxation they believe is excessive.

The leaders of the revolution, all mid- to high-level fighters, are hiding in the village. An imperial army of 60 soldiers under the command of a war hero have arrived to suss them out. The leader is a calm, honorable man, but he is also determined to put down the threat to his feudal lord. He will find the presence of the adventurers very provocative, questioning them often and keeping them under guard 24 hours a day.

A serving woman in the inn associated with the society will, at some point, pass a note on to the adventurers hidden beneath a loaf of bread. The note will explain that the society has a powerful ally in the greenwood who might be able to break the occupying army if he can be found. The ally is a korred (or perhaps a gang of korreds), who are difficult to negotiate with but will respond to a silk scarf embroidered with a white lotus.

Credit

The Korred originally appeared in the First Edition *Monster Manual II* (© TSR/Wizards of the Coast, 1983) and is used by permission.

Copyright Notice

Author Scott Greene, based on original material by Gary Gygax.

Kuah-Lij

Hit Dice: 4 hp
Armor Class: 8 [11]
Attacks: weapon (1d4)
Saving Throw: 18
Special: None
Move: 6
Alignment: Neutrality
Challenge Level/XP: A/5

A kuah-lij resembles a halfling who has been stretched vertically to the height of a human. Its features are knobby and elongated. Its hair is light and downy, more akin to a soft fur than anything else, and its skin is white with pale blue undertones. They are natural tinkerers and enjoy creating bizarre contraptions.

Aboleth, Aboleth, Where Do You Roam?

Ten people top the next rise, each walking stiffly through the prairie grasses. Their clothes and skin are coated with dripping slime. Dragging itself behind the walkers is a monstrous aboleth. The grotesque creature pulls itself along with its tentacles. Riding atop the aboleth in a small metal enclosure are five tall halflings. They caper and laugh uproariously when one of the walkers trips and falls. Each humanoid carries a slingshot he uses to hit the walkers in the backs of their heads with water-filled balloons. A trail of slime marks the aboleth's progress through the grasslands.

The five halfling-like creatures are actually kuah-lij. The walkers are villagers from Shum who offended the kuah-lij. The odd-looking humanoids returned with their enslaved aboleth and charmed and slimed the villagers. The metal box on the aboleth's head is a control station linked into the creature's brain that allows the kuah-lij to control its movements and attacks. The kuah-lij don't mean to kill the villagers, just humiliate them. They pelt the slimed villagers with water balloons to keep them damp to protect them from the adverse effects of the aboleth slime.

If the control platform is knocked loose from the aboleth's head, it frees the beast to attack on its own. It is fully aware of what has been done to it and lashes out at everyone nearby.

Credit

The Kuah-Lij can be found in the Necromancer Games module *Dead Man's Chest* (©2005 Bill Webb and Clark Peterson, Necromancer Games, Inc.).

Copyright Notice

Author Lance Hawvermale.

Land Lamprey

Hit Dice: 1
Armor Class: 3 [16]
Attack: Bite (1d3)
Saving Throw: 17
Special: Attach, blood drain
Move: 15
Alignment: Neutrality
Challenge Level/XP: 2/30

Land lampreys are 3-foot long, blackish-green eels with large, downward facing mouths lined with sharpened teeth. They can be found in all but the hottest and the coldest environments and prefer the dark and dampness of the subterranean world and so are most often encountered there.

If a land lamprey hits with a bite attack, it latches onto the opponent's body and drains 1d4 hit points per round by draining the victim's blood. An application of fire causes the land lamprey to releases its hold and move away from the source of the flame. The lamprey can also be pulled off with a successful open doors check, though doing so inflicts 1d4 points of damage. Once a land lamprey has dealt 8 points of damage, it detaches and slithers off to digest the meal. If its victim dies before the land lamprey's appetite has been sated, the land lamprey detaches and seeks a new target.

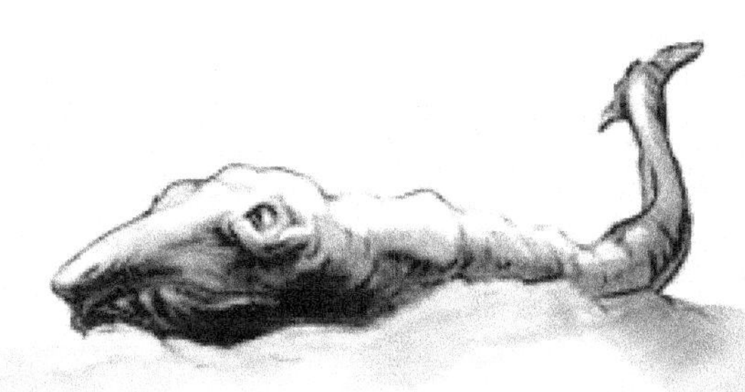

Fetid Sewers

Beneath a brick townhouse occupied by the owner of a scriptorium there runs a dank, cramped sewer tunnel - a remnant of the foundations of the ancient city but still in use for drainage from the driving rains that plague the city-state. Though most folk know nothing of these tunnels, the local thieves' guild long ago learned of their existance from an ancient map stolen from the city hall.

An iron grate in the arched ceiling of the brick tunnel allows access to the crawl space beneath the townhouse - perhaps adventurers will learn of its existance while in the townhouse as customers or thieves, or perhaps they will come to this spot via the drainage tunnels while hunting thieves or doing some thieveing themselves.

The tunnel is six feet high, the floor angled to create a stream of water during a rain, and a chain of brackish pools in between rains. The thieves always enter the tunnels with flaming oil and torches, for they know that encounters with swarms of 1d6+5 land lampreys occur often (3 in 6 chance per hour), not to mention giant rats and lesser slimes. Besides the iron grates that give access to crawlspaces, alleys and abandoned tunnels and buildings, there are a number of secret doors in the tunnels that lead to chambers that the thieves use as safe houses and places to store their loot. A typical hiding place might contain 1d6 x 100 gp worth of treasure.

The air in the tunnels is dank and foul and travelers in these tunnels must cover their mouths or save (-1 penalty per hour in the tunnels) or come down with a hacking cough.

Credit
The Land Lamprey originally appeared in the First Edition *Monster Manual II* (© TSR/Wizards of the Coast, 1983) and is used by permission.

Copyright Notice
Author Scott Greene, based on original material by Gary Gygax.

Lantern Goat

Hit Dice: 7 or 14
Armor Class: 3 [16]
Attacks: 7 HD: butt (1d8) and 2 hooves (1d6); 14 HD: butt (2d6) and 2 hooves (1d8)
Saving Throw: 9 or 3
Special: Fear light, soul capture
Move: 6
Alignment: Chaos
Challenge Level/XP: 7 HD (10/1,400); 14 HD (17/3,500)

A lantern goat has tangled and patchy gray-and-white hair, and horns and hooves that appear to be made of stone. Its eyes are stark white. Around its neck hangs a dented and ugly iron lantern that glows with a foul amber light. The scarred and battered lantern serves to channel souls into the undead creature. It emits an ugly yellow light that causes all creatures within 60 feet who see it to flee in fear (as per the spell of the same name) if they fail a save. Any creature slain while within 60 feet of a lantern goat must save or have its soul drawn into the goat's lantern to be digested. Only a wish can return creatures to life after they have been consumed by the lantern goat.

Chariot of Dire

Rumbling through the night barrels the chariot of death. Four lantern goats pull a black chariot resembling a horned grinning skull. The Harvester, a mercenary with the Dogs of Orcus, drives the goat team in a never-ending quest to collect mortal souls. He carries a lance, spear and a whip, and wears red plate armor made from the shell of a stygian turtle-shark. The Harvester is blind and his plated helm has no visor. The Harvester has a unique connection with the lantern goats where as he can "see" and detect life through their eyes. If the goats are slain, The Harvester is effectively blinded until he can enlist more goats. By day, the chariot, driver and goats are swallowed safely by the earth and only rerun when the moon once again shines. Once The Harvester is slain, the chariot sinks into the earth but resumes its quest for souls when a suitable cleric of Orcus is found to replace the slain Harvester.

The Harvester: HD 12 (cleric of Orcus); HP 64; AC 3[16]; Atk 1 lance (2d4+1), 1 spear (1d6+2) or 1 whip (1d2 + trip); Move 12; Save 4; CL/XP 12/2,000; Special: Spells. 4/4/4/4/4/1; Spells: **1**—*cure light wounds, detest evil, detect magic, protection from evil*; **2**—*bless, hold person (x2), silence (15-foot radius)*; **3**—*locate object, prayer, remove curse, speak with dead*; **4**—*cure serious wounds neutralize poison, protection from evil (10-foot radius), sticks to snakes*; **5**—*commune, finger of death, quest, raise dead*; **6**—*word of recall*; Equipment: +3 Red Stygian Turtle-Shark Plate Mail, +2 Dragon Bone Spear

Copyright Notice
Authors Scott Greene and Lance Hawvermale.

Lava Child

Hit Dice: 4
Armor Class: 3 [16]
Attack: 2 claws (1d4) and bite (1d6)
Saving Throw: 13
Special: Immunity to earth magic, fire and metal, double damage from cold
Move: 12
Alignment: Neutrality
Challenge Level/XP: 5/240

This creature is a stocky humanoid standing about 5 or 6 feet tall with sooty-black hair and green eyes. It wears crudely constructed hides of fur and leather. Its face has a curious, almost child-like appearance and seems to be imprinted with a permanent, non-changing smile. Its skin is pinkish-white. Lava children make their lairs deep underground and usually in warmer climates. Some lava children build their communities in dying or burned out volcanoes as well. Their society as a whole is reclusive, and rarely do lava children have dealings with outside races (magmin and fire elementals being the exception). Lava children speak their own gibberish-like tongue.

Lava children take one extra point of damage per caster level from water spells and suffer double damage from cold spells and effects. Lava children are immune to all earth spells and to any metal object or weapon and its effects (swords, armor, doors, walls, for example). Metal simply passes through the lava child as though it did not exist. Metal items are not destroyed, just ignored. Any metal weapon (including magic weapons) that strikes a lava child deals no damage and simply passes through its body. Likewise a lava child can simply walk through metal doors or walls as though they did not exist and ignore bonuses to an opponent's Armor Class due to metal armor.

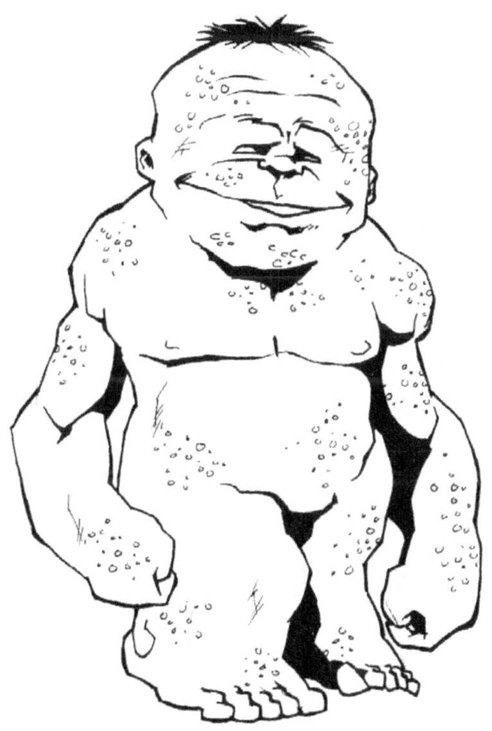

All Shall Burn

In lava tubes beneath a dormant volcano there dwells a band of 1d10+6 lava children. The lava children have constructed a number of chambers in the lava tubes, mostly through the use of slave labor taken from the tribes who dwell in the jungles surrounding the volcano. The lava children know secret tunnels beneath the forest and hidden paths. The jungle tribes carve images of the lava children - the mountain spirits - on wooden masks and basalt statues - images of smiling demons with empty eyes.

The chambers of the lava children appear have no real purpose. They are all octagonal, with precious stones set into the walls. A magic-user or cleric might be able to identify the gem patterns as constellations. The lava children are following the instructions of their master, a flame entity imprisoned on the Astral Plane that seeks escape. Each chamber is attuned to a collection of eight constellations, and when those constellations are in the correct positions in space a chamber is filled with a portion of the flame entity's spirit. Currently, six such chambers are filled with a roiling pillar of flame that deals damage as a *wall of fire* if touched.

There are still 12 empty chambers. When those chambers are filled, the entity will have returned to the Material Plane and woe betide the people of the jungle. Deeper than the fire chambers there are several more chambers, including a prison for the slaves (3d4 slaves at any one time), a living chamber for the lava children and a temple to the flame entity, complete with a basalt altar stone studded with tiny garnets (worth a total of 50 gp if collected) and a marble altar depicting an abstract column of flames - far too complex for it to have been the work of the lava children.

The living chamber of the lava children contains 2d20 x 100 gp, a brass trencher worth 750 gp, a copper brooch depicting a smiling lava child (worth 75 gp), a brass scepter inlaid with red marble (worth 145 gp), a tiger's eye gem worth 165 gp and a piece of jet worth 400 gp.

Credit
The Lava Children originally appeared in the First Edition *Fiend Folio* (© TSR/Wizards of the Coast, 1981) and is used by permission.

Copyright Notice
Author Scott Greene, based on original material by Jim Donohoe.

Leech, Giant

Hit Dice: 2
Armor Class: 8 [11]
Attack: Bite (1d6)
Saving Throw: 16
Special: Attach, blood drain, disease, salt vulnerability
Move: 3/9 (swimming)
Alignment: Neutrality
Challenge Level/XP: 3/60

Giant leeches appear as larger versions of the common leech. There is a 50% chance that any leech encountered carries disease. A giant leech attacks any living creature that comes within 30 feet of it.

If a giant leech hits with a bite attack, it latches onto the opponent's body. An attached giant leech drains blood, dealing 1d6 points of damage per round. Once it has dealt 12 points of damage, it detaches and slithers off to digest the meal. If its victim dies before the giant leech's appetite has been sated, the giant leech detaches and seeks a new target. A giant leech can be pulled off with a successful open doors check, but doing so inflicts 1d6 points of damage.

A giant leech takes 1d4 points of damage per pound of salt poured on its body.

Leeches Get Their Just Due

The swampy lowlands that the upland villages from the market town on the coast are dotted with a number of tall, bronze beacons. Each pillar is hollow and filled with several gallons of lamp oil, allowing them to burn for several days. The pillars are connected by thick ropes, allowing traders to traverse the swamp in their flat-bottom boats, pulling themselves along from one beacon to the next and finding their way to the coast without getting lost.

The swamp traders are a hardy breed, usually fighting-men of 2nd to 5th level, and they are assisted by groups of 4 to 9 men-at-arms in leather armor and carrying crossbows and spears. The boats carry all sorts of cargo, from foodstuffs to hides and pelts to rare herbs.

Among the dangers of the swamp, the most pernicious are the giant leeches. The leeches usually appear in swarms of 1d10+5, and the traders keep sacks of salt on board to drive them away.

Just three days earlier, a heist of the lord mayor's jewels took place, pulled off by a visiting band of thieves. The thieves sought to hide the jewels in the swamp, dropping a locked chest into the swamp at the base of a beacon that they marked with a glyph (those who know the cant will be able to identify it). Unfortunately, the thieves were ill-prepared for the giant leeches, and their bodies now lie at the bottom of the swamp with the jewels.

The locked chest contains two electrum hair pins tipped with rose quartz (worth 50 gp each), a steel tiara inlaid with the chitin of a giant crab and set with a moss agate (worth 150 gp), a gold signet ring bearing the lord mayor's arm (worth 200 gp) and a brass hookah with platinum filagree (worth 150 gp).

Credit
The Giant Leech originally appeared in the First Edition *Monster Manual* (© TSR/Wizards of the Coast, 1977) and is used by permission.

Copyright Notice
Author Scott Greene, based on original material by Gary Gygax.

Leprechaun

Hit Dice: 1d6
Armor Class: 5 [14]
Attack: Dagger (1d3)
Saving Throw: 18 (16 vs. magic)
Special: Spells, magic resistance 60%
Move: 15
Alignment: Neutrality
Challenge Level/XP: 3/60

Leprechauns are short fey creatures, about 2 feet tall. They favor brightly colored clothes, particularly greens and reds. Leprechauns are a jovial people, enjoying fine food and drink; some leprechauns also enjoy a good smoke from a long-stemmed pipe. They are a tricky folk and enjoy jokes and pranks, although they usually do not appreciate being the victims of such acts.

Most leprechauns are skilled pickpockets (as 8th level thieves), and it is a favored prank of these wee folk to filch items from unsuspecting travelers in their domain and then taunt the intruders into pursuit. The leprechaun so involved in the prank often alternates between being visible and invisible as he teases and pesters his pursuers in a merry chase. Leprechauns tire of pranks quickly, however, and will give up the stolen item and sneak away. Some say leprechauns are descendants of halflings and pixies. Leprechauns summarily dismiss this rumor, however, scoffing at those who repeat it.

Leprechauns can cast *invisibility* (self only), *phantasmal force*, *polymorph* (objects only) and *ventriloquism* at will.

Practical Joke

As you move through a shady wood, you come across a clearing. The clearing is marked by five pillars of chalk and in the middle there is a large, bronze cauldron. Three maidens, with long, braided hair and in diaphenous gowns sit around the cauldron, plucking at mandolins and singing drowsy love ballads. The cauldron is heaped with gold coins and jewels and covered by the pelt of an aurumvorax (q.v.).

This entire scene is, alas, a prank concocted by a terribly wicked gang of leprechauns. Perhaps the leprechauns have something against the adventurers or perhaps they're just world class jerks - it's hard to say with the fey.

The maidens are actually a trio of orc bandits (3 HD each) arguing over their empty cauldron. The chalk stones are their warriors, five orc warriors in leather armor with white shields, short swords and pole arms.

The orcs will not immediately understand why their visitors are so bold or refering to them as maidens and what not, but they're crafty enough to play along if it seems they can bag dinner. The 1d3+1 leprechauns will remain out of sight, though when the illusion is dispelled one will certainly hear their peels of laughter echoing from the woods.

The orcs have a treasure buried nearby in leather sacks. It consists of 2d12 x 10 cp, 1d10 x 10 sp, 2d12 x 10 gp and a small wooden box containing a pound of saffron (worth 15 gp).

Credit

The Leprechaun originally appeared in the First Edition *Monster Manual* (© TSR/Wizards of the Coast, 1977) and is used by permission.

Copyright Notice

Author Scott Greene, based on original material by Gary Gygax

Lich Shade

Hit Dice: 11
Armor Class: 6 [13]
Attacks: 2 claws (1d6 + chill)
Saving Throw: 4
Special: Chill, death throes, spell leech, resists cold and electricity, spell resistance (22%)
Move: 9
Alignment: Chaos
Challenge Level/XP: 14/2,600

A lich shade is a rotting and skeletal humanoid dressed in tattered and worn robes with ancient runes etched on their surface. Its eye blaze with a crimson fire. Lich shades are evil creatures who attempted to achieve lichdom but failed. A lich shade stands about 6 to 6-1/2 feet tall and weighs about 160 pounds. The robes and gowns it wears often denote its previous life's profession. A lich shade's touch is supernaturally cold, so any creature struck by one of its claws must save or be dazed for 1 round. When reduced to 0 hit points, a lich shade crumbles into a pile of dust equivalent to *dust of sneezing and choking*. When a spellcaster within 50 feet of a lich shade attempts to cast a spell, he must save or lose the spell as it is absorbed by the creature. The lich shade can cast the spell on its next turn, turn the spell into a bolt of magic energy (similar to a magic missile) that does 1d6 points of damage per two levels of the original spell cast, or gain a number of hit points equal to the spell level x 4.

Images of Ages Past

Only the top two levels of this crumbled tower remains. The upper portion floats 60 feet above the lower ruins of the foundation. A partial stone staircase that once followed the interior wall hangs down from the floating partial tower. The tower's foundation looks as if it exploded from the inside in a massive blast that scattered the black bricks outward across the land. Someone built a 40-foot-tall scaffold of bound wooden poles beneath the floating tower in a vain effort to reach the suspended stairs. Stout vines growing from the sides of the floating tower drape down until they are almost within arms reach of the top of the scaffold. The tower belonged to Ashten Un Shorn, a magic-user who died during an attempt to transition to lichdom. A single mistake in the ritual resulted in the blast that destroyed her tower. Ashten now haunts the upper floors as a lich shade, and slays all who seek her treasure. Stories tell of her wondrous lantern that lantern reveals past events in any area where its light shines.

Copyright Notice

Livestone

Hit Dice: 5
Armor Class: 10 [9]
Attack: Slam (1d8)
Saving Throw: 12
Special: Engulf, solidify, immunity to petrification, surprise on 1-4 on 1d6
Move: 9
Alignment: Neutrality
Challenge Level/XP: 7/600

Livestone is a strange species of ooze that can solidify itself into a consistency that very closely resembles that of stone. In its solidified form, a livestone is indistinguishable from a normal boulder or slab of rock. No one is quite sure from where livestones originated, but ancient legends say that the dwarves accidentally unleashed these horrors on the surface world by digging into their subterranean lairs. Eventually, some livestones found their way to the surface.

Livestones are incredibly long-lived, solidifying and entering a form of hibernation and remaining that way indefinitely until a food source wanders too near. Livestones have a simple chameleon-like ability to mimic local stone by ingesting a small sample and adjusting its own color and texture to match. A hibernating livestone can become covered in moss and lichens to further the deception.

Livestones generally attack from ambush, waiting for a potential meal to pass before flowing into their ooze form and rushing up to engulf the prey. If the surprise attack fails, a livestone resorts to hammering with pseudopods. When attacking in this manner, a livestone will solidify the tip of the pseudopod and strike with a hammer-like blow. A livestone's usual tactic is to solidify the half of its body facing the prey and then send hard-tipped pseudopods out from behind this shield.

A livestone can simply mow down human-sized or smaller creatures by moving over them. It cannot make a slam attack during a round in which it engulfs. The livestone affects as many creatures as it can cover. Opponents can attempt a saving throw to avoid being engulfed; on a success, they are pushed back or aside (opponent's choice) as the livestone moves forward. An engulfed opponent takes 1 point of damage per round as the livestone consumes it (unless the livestone solidifies itself).

A livestone that has engulfed an opponent can instantly solidify its form, dealing 8d6 points of crushing damage per round to the trapped victim (saving throw for half damage).

An engulfed creature can be freed by killing the livestone or by casting *stone to flesh* on the livestone. This deals 1d6 points of damage per caster level to the livestone and automatically ejects an engulfed victim.

An opponent attacking a livestone must succeed on a saving throw each time his attack hits. If the save is failed, the livestone actually solidifies the portion of its body at the instant it was hit, cutting damage in half. A livestone cannot attack if its entire form is solidified.

Livestones surprise on a roll of 1-4 on 1d6 in stony areas.

Dangerous Crossing

You come across a swift subterranean river, about 40 feet wide. Two large boulders rest in the middle of the river, which is about 5 to 7 feet deep. The stones rise about 3 feet above the surface and one has a rope tied to it and extending to rocks on each shore. A small boat on the shore (the side the adventurers are on) provides a way across, for swimming would be exceptionally difficult in the current and even pulling one's way across on the boat requires a combined strength of 20 to keep it from being pulled down the river.

The second stone in the river is topped by a livestone in its solidified state. When a band of adventurers reach the midpoint of the river, it will take ooze form, make a leap at the nearest adventurer and then attempt to drag them overboard while taking its solidified form. The ooze is a pure predator, uninterested in destroying the others or taking their loot.

Copyright Notice
Author Erica Balsley.

Living Lake (Agrath-Ogh)

Hit Dice: 16
Armor Class: 2 [17]
Attacks: 4 slams (3d8)
Saving Throw: 3
Special: Engulf, spellsww
Move: 6
Alignment: Neutrality
Challenge Level/XP: 17/3,500

Hundreds of feet across, a living lake is an ooze of truly colossal proportions. The protoplasmic body of a living lake is fluid in nature and transparent in water. A living lake attacks by forming pseudopods from its oozy form and pummeling its opponents. The ooze can raise a portion of itself off the ground and come crashing down on opponents who must save or be engulfed into the ooze and "drown" in the living lake. A living lake casts spells as a 9th-level druid.

Peace Among Evil

Hordes of orcs inhabit the badlands below the receding Wailing Glacier. The land is a jumble of rotting refuse and vast marshes left behind as the glacier melts. Many treasures have been revealed as the ice melts. One such treasure is the astonishing Parish of Iseleine, an exotic community built around a perfectly round lake of crystal clear water that remains pristine under an ice dome within the glacier. The lake has a ceramic tiled bottom and contains swarms of golden trout and edible freshwater anemones. The pool is also home to a living lake that has absorbed the pacifist ideas of the followers of Iseleine. The Wailing Glacier has thawed enough for explorers to navigate the ice caves to visit the parish.

The citizens of the city strictly follow the passive teachings of the dreaming goddess, Iseleine. They speak ancient common and have whimsical customs and mannerisms. The followers of Iseleine are passive to the extreme. The dreamy followers practice freedom and love in every sense of the words. They value art and harmony above all; values of the outside world are merely trappings of the flesh to them.

The living lake protects the Parish of Iseleine against all transgressors. The living lake is not above violence when defending the followers. The citizens still weep in anguish over the death of hundreds of orcs who attempted to destroy the Parish. The followers pray for Iseleine's forgiveness at the death of the orcs and are preparing the corpses for ceremonial burial.

Copyright Notice
Author Erica Balsley.

Lizard, Cavern

Hit Dice: 4
Armor Class: 5 [14]
Attacks: 1 bite (2d4)
Saving Throw: 13
Special: Grab
Move: 9/6 (climb)
Alignment: Neutrality
Challenge Level/XP: 4/120

Cavern lizard are 8-foot-long gray lizards with wide feet and sapphire-gold bulging eyes. Their legs are thick and muscled and their large feet have small suction cup-like pads on the bottoms that aid in climbing. Its head is angular and somewhat flat. Its mouth sports a row of long, serrated teeth. These very aggressive hunters latch onto prey with their bite, automatically dealing damage each round thereafter.

Leaping Lizards

The Noblett family has farmed the land for years, taking advantage of a water-filled cave entrance that provides water for their cattle year round. Just weeks ago the water began to slowly recede into the cave. Each day the farmers and cattle must travel farther back into the bore hole to get to the water. Once the water lowered, a pair of mated cavern lizards escaped into the surface world to hunt larger prey. Soon, the cavern lizards devoured the cattle and most of the Noblett family, leaving only Granny Noblett and her young niece and nephew. She pleads for any travelers to search the cave for her family or the lost cattle. She claims to have seen horned, cloven-footed demons wandering at night around the family's fields. Due to her failing eyesight, she actually mistook roaming goats standing to feed on low branches as the horned humanoid. Only Granny Noblett's son-in-law remains alive, trapped in the cave under a low rock shelf. The lizards scale the walls, waiting to leap down on anyone entering the cave.

Copyright Notice
Author Scott Greene.

Lizard, Fire

Hit Dice: 10+1
Armor Class: 2 [17]
Attack: 2 claws (1d8), bite (2d6)
Saving Throw: 5
Special: Breathe fire, immunity to fire, double damage from cold
Move: 12
Alignment: Neutrality
Challenge Level/XP: 11/1700

Fire lizards are often called "false dragons." Despite their general resemblance to dragons, sages have as yet found no evidence of these creatures being in any way related to them. Fire lizards look like wingless dragons with gray scales dappled in red and brown. Its underbelly is bright red and its yes are black with yellow pupils. A fire lizard is averages 30 feet long but can grow to almost twice that size. Fire lizards do not associate with or keep company with dragons. Once every 1d4 rounds, a fire lizard can breathe fire in a 20-foot cone. Creatures in the area take 2d6 points of fire damage (saving throw for half).

Shooting the Pipeline

A large fire lizard with a crooked leg and a crest like a rooster has taken up residence in an old lava tube that leads well into the depths of a dormant, though still quite warm, volcano. The slopes around the tube are quite verdant and support an especially rare orchid fed upon by a species of wasp.

Before the coming of the fire lizard, the tube was inhabited by a band of cast-off grimlocks who were driven into the jungle by the beast. They left behind an ivory sculpture of a portly man in a flowing robe that covers him from nose to feet and a conical hat that contains a secret poison needle that can be operated by pressing the small of its back. In addition, there are a number of leather sacks containing coins and a few arrows fletched with dire corby feathers in a quiver made from a fire beetle carapace.

The tube is about 10 feet in diameter for most of its length, with the outer tube (i.e. before it enters the volcano proper) often opened to the skies. Once one has entered the volcano things become notably warmer and the tube is intersected by several smaller tubes, home to a breed of especially nasty black rats and (if you're feeling particularly saucy) a pack of 1d6+2 wererats.

Credit
The Fire Lizard originally appeared in the First Edition *Monster Manual* (© TSR/Wizards of the Coast, 1977) and is used by permission.

Copyright Notice
Author Scott Greene, based on original material by Gary Gygax.

Lizard, Gnasher

Hit Dice: 8
Armor Class: 6 [13]
Attacks: 1 bite (1d8)
Special: swallow whole, severing bite
Move: 10
Saving Throw: 8
Alignment: Neutrality
Challenge Level/XP: 7/600

A gnasher lizard is typically 10 feet to 20 feet long and weighs about 1,000 pounds. Gnasher lizards have a wide gaping maw filled with double rows of dagger-like teeth. Its head is large and flat and sports a ridge of hardened bone that runs the length of its head before tapering off near the middle of its back. Its four legs end in large, flat clawed feet. A gnasher lizard that rolls 4 or higher than needed to hit a creature swallows the victim whole. If the lizard rolls a natural 20, it severs an opponent's limb.

Party Wagon

A large sled pulled by two gnasher lizards crashes through the countryside. A party of drunken goblins sits atop a dead bowhead whale strapped to the sled, some of the loathsome creatures missing arms and legs. The goblins sing and revel with vigor, many too inebriated to fight let alone stand. The goblins discovered the dead whale washed ashore a couple of days ago and decided to bring it home. The whale will feed their clan for many weeks and its bones will make excellent weapons. The goblins celebrate their prize as they drive the 50 miles inland to their camp. The whale has already begun to rot, a fact that doesn't seem to bother the goblins. It leaves a trail of blood and congealed blubber in its wake. The driver immediately releases the gnasher lizards at the first sign of trouble. The semi-trained gnasher lizards normally do not attack the goblins. Aside from the decaying whale, the goblins have little treasure.

Copyright Notice
Author Scott Greene.

Lurker Above

Hit Dice: 10
Armor Class: 4 [15]
Attack: Buffet (1d8)
Saving Throw: 5
Special: Amorphous, smother, half damage from blunt weapons
Move: 6/15 (flying)
Alignment: Neutrality
Challenge Level/XP: 12/2000

The lurker above is a subterranean carnivore that preys on any living creatures that enter its territory. It looks something like a massive manta ray. Its body is black on the top and gray on the underbelly. A lurker's underbelly tends to blend in with stone, allowing a lurker pressed against a ceiling a 4 in 6 chance to surprise opponents below.

Lurkers above are extremely territorial and are never encountered with others of their kind. Mating habits among lurkers is unknown to sages as no two of these creatures have ever been encountered together. A typical lurker above has a hunting territory of several square miles.

A lurker above can try to wrap a creature in its body as an attack that ignores armor bonuses to Armor Class. If successful, it establishes a hold and deals buffet damage each round the hold is maintained. A wrapped opponent must hold its breath or suffocate. A grabbed opponent can hold her breath for 2 rounds per point of constitution. Attacks that hit an engulfing lurker above deal half their damage to the monster and half to the trapped victim.

Lurker Below

The lurker below is an aquatic variety of lurker above that makes its lair in any body of water and in any climate (though it rarely lairs in extremely cold climates). Lurkers below are pale blue or black in color and are often mistaken for giant manta rays. Lurkers below cannot fly, but have a swim speed of 15. They are otherwise identical to their land-based counterparts detailed above, except they lie in wait on the sea floor and attack from below.

Gray Pavilion Oasis

While traversing the empty, blazing expanse of the desert, you come across what can only be a mirage. Rising above the cracked, red soil is a pavilion of gray stone with a rounded top held up by twelve pillars. Between the pillars, gauzy purple curtains billow in the wind. The pavilion is about 30 feet in diameter and contains a small pool of clear water. The ceiling of the pavilion is the lair of a lurker above, one of several that dwell in the caves that dot the sandstone hills around the desert. This one was driven out into the desert by competition with larger lurkers and now subsists on foolish travelers.

Credit

The Lurker Above originally appeared in the *Strategic Review #3* (© TSR/Wizards of the Coast, 1975) and later in the First Edition *Monster Manual* (© TSR/Wizards of the Coast, 1977) and is used by permission.

Copyright Notice

Author Scott Greene, based on original material by Gary Gygax.

Lythic

Hit Dice: 3
Armor Class: 4 [15]
Attacks: 2 slams (1d4+2)
Saving Throw: 14
Special: Earth glide, blend with stone
Move: 12/18 (burrow)
Alignment: Neutrality
Challenge Level/XP: 3/60

Lythics are 5- or 6-foot-tall humanoids composed of smoothly-carved rock. Their features are human-like but emotionless. Related to earth elementals, lythics are shy creatures that tend to flee rather than confront people. They are experts at blending into stone, and use this camouflage technique to seemingly vanish if threatened. Lythics can glide effortlessly stone and dirt like a fish through water.

The Sentinel of Ice and Stone

Jutting like serrated teeth from the icy waves leading into the Ebon Straits are the 10 Sentinels of Ice and Stone that presage the way to the icy northern seas. Each granite pillar is barely 80 feet in diameter, but rises more than 100 feet off the turbulent ocean. Ice winds in thick bands around the stone, creating slick cliff ledges that can nevertheless be carefully climbed like a winding ramp around the rock. The 10 pillars are all located within sight of one another in a quarter-mile ocean area.

Rumors says that atop one of the pillar stands a being of living stone – although which pillar is a matter of debate among seafarers. The creature is said to answers questions for sailors, but just as often predicts hideous fates.

The sentinel is actually a lythic cursed to live atop the stone pillars and await sailors seeking their fate. The lythic moves randomly between the pillars each day, vanishing from one perch to appear atop another stone column. Getting to the top of a pillar is difficult, as the ice ramps are treacherous and slick, and the waves and wind are always present to toss climbers into the brine. The lythic won't move or answer questions until at least 1,000 gp in coins are placed at its feet, and the truthfulness of its answer often depends on how it is treated by the questioners. The gold sinks into the pillar, never to be seen again, once the question is answered. If attacked, the lythic melts into the stone and reappears on another pillar.

Copyright Notice
Author Scott Greene.

Magmoid

Hit Dice: 8
Armor Class: 2 [17]
Attacks: 1 flaming slam (2d6)
Saving Throw: 8
Special: Melt normal weapons, magma blast, immune to fire, *sleep* and poison
Move: 9
Alignment: Neutrality
Challenge Level/XP: 9/1,100

Magmoids are large, sentient, spherical balls of liquid fire and rock about 10 feet across. Small bubbling pockets on the magmoid's form serve as sensory organs. A giant magmoid, measuring 30 feet across is thought to exist, though none have ever seen it. A magmoid attacks by spraying a blast of superheated magma at opponents or by slamming into and rolling over them. The magmoid's body is composed of molten rock that melts any nonmagical weapon that hits it. Once every 1d4 rounds, a magmoid can release a line of magma up to 40 feet (2d6 damage, save for half).

Great Ball of Fire

This encounter takes place in an extremely long 10-foot-wide corridor with a 10-foot high ceiling. The corridor rises at a 20-degree angle. The marble floor is scorched and burnt, with a trench coated in ash and soot cut through the center of the tiles. The walls and ceiling have similar grooves cut through them. Each trench is concave, with rounded edges. A flickering, fiery glow illuminates the end of the tunnel.

A magmoid lives in a chamber, and uses the corridor as a "track" to roll down on intruders into its underground lair. The fiery creature waits for PCs to get about three-quarters of the way up the corridor, then rolls at top speed toward them. Since the magmoid is rolling downhill, it gains +6 to its movement. The 10-foot-diameter ball of fire completely fills the tunnel as it rushes forward. Its edges fit perfectly into the grooves on the walls, floor and ceiling.

A burnt skeleton lies in a charred heap in the magmoid's chamber. The thief wears *boots of speed*, although they are dingy with gray ash. The thief ran down the hall before the magmoid entered the corridor, but collapsed, utterly exhausted. The angry magmoid rolled over him again and again.

Copyright Notice
Author Scott Greene.

Magnesium Spirit

Hit Dice: 6
Armor Class: 5 [14]
Attack: Touch (2 strength)
Saving Throw: 11
Special: Blinding flash, level drain, strength damage, possession, magic resistance (40%), vulnerability to holy water
Move: 18
Alignment: Chaos
Challenge Level/XP: 11/1700

A magnesium spirit is a human-sized column of heatless white fire with a wispy tail protruding from the bottom of it. The magnesium spirit is an chaotic creature from an unknown plane, though it is agreed among sages that its origin definitely does not lie on the Material Plane. Believed to have been summoned by magic-users to do their bidding, the magnesium spirit desires nothing more than to return to its home plane. Its incorporeal form prevents this, however, and it requires a physical body to complete the spell ritual needed to return it home.

Three times per day, a magnesium spirit can flare up its body in a blinding flash. All creatures within 20 feet viewing the flash must succeed on a saving throw or be blinded (as the *blindness* spell) for 1d2 hours.

A magnesium spirit's incorporeal touch ignores armor bonuses to AC. If the magnesium spirit touches a creature, it deals 2 points of strength damage and the victim must pass a saving throw or be drained of one level. This begins the process of possession (per a *magic jar* spell). A magnesium spirit that is possessing a victim automatically deals 2 points of strength damage and drains one level each round. After two rounds, the possessing magnesium spirit can only be harmed by holy water, which inflicts 2d4 points of damage. After three rounds, the possession is complete. If the victim still has at least 5 levels, the magnesium spirit completes the spell ritual and both body and spirit disappear. If the victim does not have at least 5 levels, the magnesium spirit abandons it and searches for another.

As an incorporeal creature, a magnesium spirit can only be harmed by magic weapons or spells.

Don't Go Into the Light

The mountain guides all know about the sarcophagus in the middle of the volcano, and everybody has a story, all a bit different, about how it got there and when. The volcano in question is a dead stratovolcano, the caldera filled with a pristine lake that freezes over in the winter. In the center of the lake there is a small, perfectly round island that the guides will assure visitors is not natural. They are correct on his fact. The island is a pillar of pumice, 10-ft in diameter and about 20 feet long. The pillar floats, with about 2 feet of it clearing the surface of the water. A thick chain keeps it anchored to the bottom of the lake.

Standing on the pillar is a sarcophagus of blue steel. The sarcophagus is 5 feet tall and cast in the shape of a hauntingly beautiful woman, eyes closed, hands clasped as in prayer. Thick chains are wrapped around the sarcophagus and secured by heavy locks of the same material, which, although not as strong as adamantite is stronger than steel.

A magnesium spirit has been sealed in the sarcophagus, although it is unknown by whom. The spirit is nearly crazed with its desire to return to its home dimension (or planet, depending on your campaign world).

Resting in the bottom of the sarcophagus there is a golden ring set with a large piece of smoky, gray glass that allows a person wearing it to transform their body into any material the glass touches, at will, for 1d6+1 rounds.

Credit

The Magnesium Spirit originally appeared in the First Edition *Fiend Folio* (© TSR/Wizards of the Coast, 1981) and is used by permission.

Copyright Notice

Author Scott Greene, based on original material by Nick Louth.

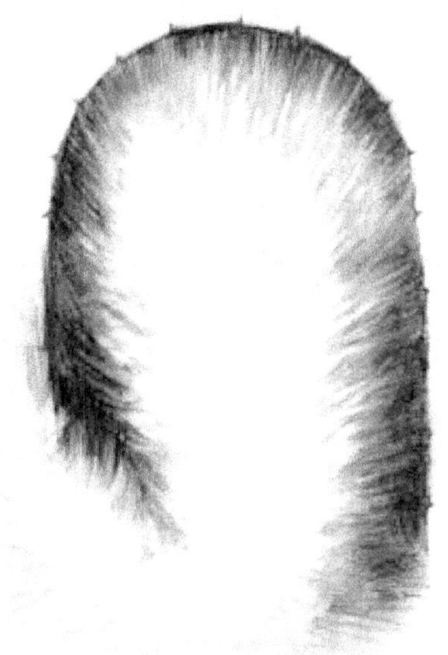

Mandragora

Hit Dice: 1
Armor Class: 3 [16]
Attack: 2 tentacle slaps (1d4)
Saving Throw: 17
Special: Constrict, light blindness, resistance to fire (50%), magic resistance (10%)
Move: 12/9 (burrowing)
Alignment: Chaos
Challenge Level/XP: 3/60

The mandragora is a vaguely humanoid looking plant creature with mottled green and brown flesh. Its lower roots are splayed and resemble legs and feet. Its upper roots are long and resemble humanoid arms. Its head, if it could be called that, is a mass of solid vegetable matter covered in lumps. The mandragora stands about 5 feet tall and weighs about 120 pounds.

The mandragora is carnivorous and relishes the taste of human flesh. If it goes more than three days without devouring flesh, it burrows into the ground and attaches to local tree roots, from which it draws its sustenance until living prey can be found.

A mandragora attempts to grab its prey and strangle it, inflicting 1d4 points of damage per round. Slain creatures are covered in a thick layer of mucus and slime and devoured at the mandragora's leisure.

Abrupt exposure to bright light stuns the mandragora for 1 round. On subsequent rounds, they are dazzled and suffer a -1 penalty to hit as long as they remain in the affected area.

Over the Woods and Through the Hills

Amala, daughter of King Theod was stolen away in the night by a band of crafty wererats who entered the stronghold of her father in the guise of animals and, with the help of the native rats (who despise the king and his Lord Keeper of the Royal Pantries), made their way to her room. The touch of a slim, crystal wand stole her soul away, leaving her body in a state between life and death.

The king is frantic with worry and has ordered all brave men of his kingdom to find his daughter, offering rich rewards and a potential royal wedding if they do (he has little intention of keeping all of these promises).

The rats escaped the stronghold and made their swiftly to the south, through the thick woodlands of the moss dwarves, over the craggy hills of the huldra-folk and finally into the infamous green chasm, a rent across the barren landscape populated by a thick, primordial wood and all manner of strange, reptilian beasts.

Hidden beneath the overarching boughs there is a small building of gray-green brick shaped like a rounded cylinder. The building has no entrance, per se, though a number of small cracks and gaps allowed the wererats to enter and place their precious burden atop a cruel, iron-toothed trap, itself hidden beneath a black bearskin. A grab for the crystal will trip the trap, which deals 1d8 points of damage unless a saving throw is passed. If the damage is "8", the trap has shattered the victim's arm.

The ground around the little building are infested with a colony of 3d6 mandragoras, all trained to ignore the wererats. The wererats use this building, and others like it spread around the kingdom, as hiding places to stash their loot.

The wererats were hired by a baronet, a gangly, awkward gentleman with high ambitions, to steal away the princess' soul and keep it well hidden for two weeks. At that point, they are to carry it to his manor that he might return it to the king and claim the princess' hand in marriage. A magic-user and hated rival of the king (old adventurers on opposite sides of the law vs. chaos debate) provided the baronet with the crystal and, unbeknownst to him, will provide the corpse of the supposed culprit.

Credit
The Mandragora originally appeared in the First Edition *Monster Manual II* (© TSR/Wizards of the Coast, 1983) and is used by permission.

Copyright Notice
Author Scott Greene, based on original material by Gary Gygax.

Mantari

Hit Dice: 1
Armor Class: 5 [14]
Attack: Tail sting (1d6)
Saving Throw: 17
Special: None
Move: 3/24 (flying)
Alignment: Chaos
Challenge Level/XP: 2/30

Mantari sustain themselves on a diet of rats, carrion, and subterranean plants, but prefer the taste of fresh meat, particularly humans and gnomes. Mantari appear as large manta rays, gray in color, with a long smooth tail that ends in a sharpened barb. The mantari flies silently through its underground world in search of prey, and when encountered, it is often hungry and immediately attacks.

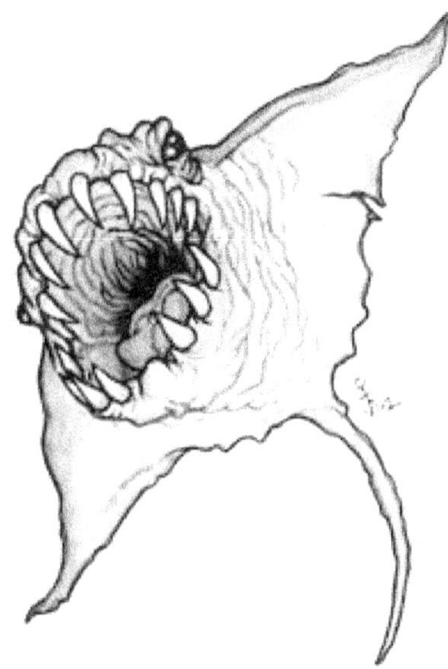

Pilgrims for Winter Solstice Feast

Not all underworlds are hidden from the view of men. In the far western portions of a great kingdom there is a great underworld complex of limestone caves often visited by pilgrims. The pilgrims seek out a stone formation called the Throne of Judgment, where they believe their cthonic deity once sat while he held court over the fey and spirits of the departed. Small bands of pilgrims might visit the Throne at any time, but on the shortest day of the year larger pilgrimages, including villagers from as far away as 20 miles, descend on the caverns wearing skull masks and swinging ritual flails made of ox bones and horse hair to celebrate the cthonic god's birth.

Recently, small bands of visiting pilgrims have fallen victim to a pack of 1d3+1 mantari who have come up from lower portions of the underworld and made the Throne's cavern their hunting ground. They lurk in the upper shelves of the cavern, descending while pilgrims are prostrate in front of the throne. Their shelf is littered with bones and the belongings of the pilgrims - a three pound ingot of silver (worth 30 sp), a 5 lb ingot of zinc (worth 4 sp), a large rock crystal worth 90 gp, a bronze goblet in the shape of a ram's head (worth 2 gp), a brass waist chain (worth 115 gp), 210 sp and 11 gp as well as shredded clothing and five staves.

Credit
The Mantari originally appeared in the First Edition *Fiend Folio* (© TSR/Wizards of the Coast, 1981) and is used by permission.

Copyright Notice
Author Scott Greene, based on original material by David Wormell.

M

Mantidrake

Hit Dice: 9+2
Armor Class: 3 [16]
Attacks: 2 claws (1d3), 1 bite (1d8), 6 tail spikes (1d6)
Special: breath weapon, spikes
Move: 12/18 (flying)
Saving Throw: 6
Alignment: Chaos
Challenge Level/XP: 10/1,400

A mantidrake is a cross between a dragon and a manticore. A typical mantidrake is about 10 to 12 feet long and weighs about 1,100 to 1,300 pounds. Its draconic head is scaled and is the same color as its dragon parent. A mantidrake's breath weapon depends on its dragon heritage. Regardless of its type, a mantidrake's breath weapon is usable once every 1d4 rounds, deals 5d8 points of damage, and allows a save for half damage: black, 60-foot line of acid; blue, 60-foot line of lightning; green, 30-foot cone of gas; red, 30-foot cone of fire; and white, 30-foot cone of cold). A mantidrake has 24 iron spikes on its tail. It can hurl up to 6 of the spikes per round, to a maximum range of 180 feet.

The Petrified Forest of Drevjen

Many scholars speculate about the origin of the Petrified Forest of Drevjen, but none has found the reason for the ancient cursed forest. Animal life is scarce at best in the forest, but all plant life has been turned to stone. No new living plants grow normally within its boundaries. Plants and plant-like creatures brought into the woods turn to stone within 24 hours. The crunch of brittle stone leaves and grass sounds with every step. The trees and brush in outlying areas of the forest have few remaining leaves, but deeper into the forest the stone trees remain pristine with their canopies filtering out almost all sunlight. The result is a vast cave-like room with only occasional pinpoints of light gleaming through. Damage done to the petrified forest seems to regenerate over time, as if the plants continue to thrive despite their current state. What horrors lie deep within the forest are unknown to all but the bravest adventurers.

A pair of mated mantidrakes nests high in the massive petrified tress on the outside edge of the Dravjen woods. The nest is built high in a stone snag made from rock branches and leaves. The mantidrakes guard a clutch of their eggs and fiercely protect their territory. The nest holds a mythical *horn of blasting* rumored to have incredibly destructive sonic powers.

Copyright Notice

Marble Snake

Hit Dice: 3
Armor Class: 7 [12]
Attack: Bite (1d6)
Saving Throw: 14
Special: Whistle
Move: 9/9 (climbing)
Alignment: Neutrality
Challenge Level/XP: 4/120

The marble snake has whitish-gray scales, translucent in places where its underlying veins can be seen. The snake's head is long and has a large lion-like mane of golden fur. Two long sharp fangs protrude from its mouth. Its multi-faceted eyes are red. A typical marble snake is 10 feet long and can grow to a length of 20 feet.

Unlike normal snakes, it adapts very well to its environment, hence it can be found just about anywhere, though underground encounters are rare. The marble snake prefers sunlight and warmth to the cold and darkness of dungeons and caverns and most often makes its lair in high, sunny altitudes.

Typically an encounter is with a single marble snake. In instances where more than one is encountered, they will a mated pair and young. A female marble snake is usually only encountered during mating season (when she lays 1d10 eggs). Marble snake eggs are milky-white with gray-brown flecks. An egg can fetch up to 5 gp on the open market.

A marble snake can whistle, gaining the attention of any creature within 50 feet that hears it. All creatures (other than marble snakes) with the area must succeed on a saving throw or become entranced. An entranced victim walks toward the marble snake, taking the most direct route available. If the path leads into a dangerous area, that creature gets a second saving throw. The effect continues for as long as the marble snake whistles and for 1 round thereafter. An entranced victim is effectively dazed, and cannot attack, but can defend itself. If an entranced opponent is attacked, the effect is immediately broken.

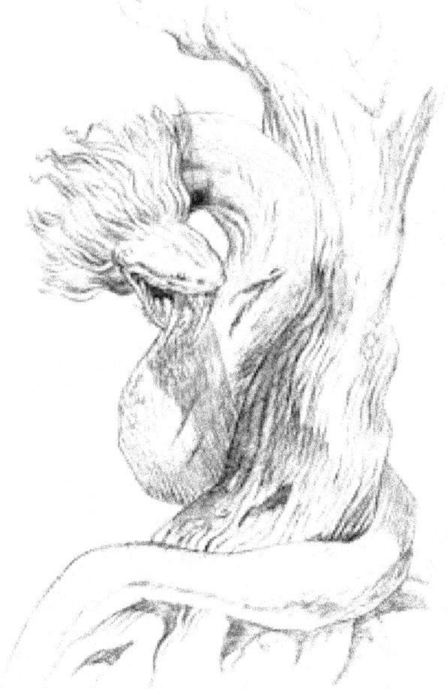

Aulos Snake Trial

A winding lane that descends from the south gate of a small town has been nicknamed Fear Street by the citizens, for it leads past an old colonial cemetery on its way to the lake. The cemetery is about a 500 feet long and 100 feet wide and runs along the lane. A low wall of white stones surrounds the cemetary, with two bronze gates allowing entrance - one on the north end of the cemetary, the other on the south end.

The stones in the cemetary date from the early days of settlement in the region, and many names are recognizable as belonging to the leading citizens of the town. On a few occaisions people have claimed to see a thin man sitting atop a marble slab playing an aulos (a double piped wind instrument) in the middle of the night.

The man, his face hidden by a black cloak, is the court jester of the town's duke, a cruel, paranoid man who has established a secret court in his family crypt. Enemies (or perceived enemies) are tried here and sentenced to death. The bodies are fed to a pack of 1d3+1 marble snakes that reside in the deep recesses of the crypt and sometimes wander the cemetary, hunting rats and other small game. The snakes are lulled into a dreamless sleep by the music of the aulos (and perhaps by other deep, wind instruments).

There is a 1 in 20 chance that court will be in session, and the court jester present, when adventurers pass by the cemetary one night. If they investigate, the jester will skulk away (4 in 6 chance of slipping away unseen in the darkness if adventurers do not declare themselves to be watching him intently) and head to the crypt, for which he has a key. The crypt is a small building of marble blocks barred by brass gates. Within, there are two sarcophagi, one of which opens to reveal a narrow staircase down to a larger crypt stacked with wrapped corpses on shelves. The floor of this area is cleared save for an iron chair equipped with manacles. The duke and his fellow hooded judges stand about the accused, hurling accusations and torturing confessions out of them with burning brands. They won't be happy to see intruders. If the jester is present, he can summon the marble snakes to attack.

Credit

The Marble Snake originally appeared in the First Edition module *B3 Palace of the Silver Princess* (© TSR/Wizards of the Coast, 1981) and is used by permission.

Copyright Notice

Mawler

Hit Dice: 4
Armor Class: 7 [12]
Attacks: 1 bite (1d4)
Saving Throw: 13
Special: Constrict, mimic shape, radiate magic, vorpal bite
Move: 6
Alignment: Chaos
Challenge Level/XP: 5/240

A mawler's natural form is that of a small blob of fleshy stuff approximately 2 feet across. Mawlers are rarely ever seen in their natural form, however, as they almost always take the shape of an article of clothing. A mawler can alter its texture, color and shape to match such substances as leather and metal. A single mawler usually takes on the form of a single article of clothing, such as a hat, helmet, scarf, codpiece or belt. A pair of these creatures encountered together can take the shape of a pair of boots or a pair of gloves. A mawler radiates as magic, which often lures victims to it who detect magic on the item the mawler is mimicking. When an unsuspecting person dons the mawler, it attacks with its bite. If a mawler hits, it automatically constricts for 1d4 points of damage in the next round. If a mawler rolls a natural 20 on its bite attack, it severs whatever appendage is within it at the time (a leg or hand, for example).

The Clothes Take the Man

A broken wall is all that remains of the Castrano Shrine. Wooden dowel rods are pushed in to the granite blocks, and each holds a piece of perfectly preserved clothing. The pegs are enchanted to keep cloth from disintegrating. Flowering plants climb the wall, but leave the clothes untouched. Ants and other insects never go near the cloth. Hanging from the pegs are a clean forest-green cloak, two loincloths, a pair of gloves and a toga. The pegs lose their magic if pulled from the wall.

The cloak and gloves belonged to a magic-user chased from the ruins by wild boars. One plain loincloth and the toga were left by a monk killed when the bath house collapsed during the massive quake that destroyed the shrine. The second loincloth is a mawler clinging to the wall peg. It appears to be woven from an expensive, shimmering gold weave.

Copyright Notice
Author Erica Balsley.

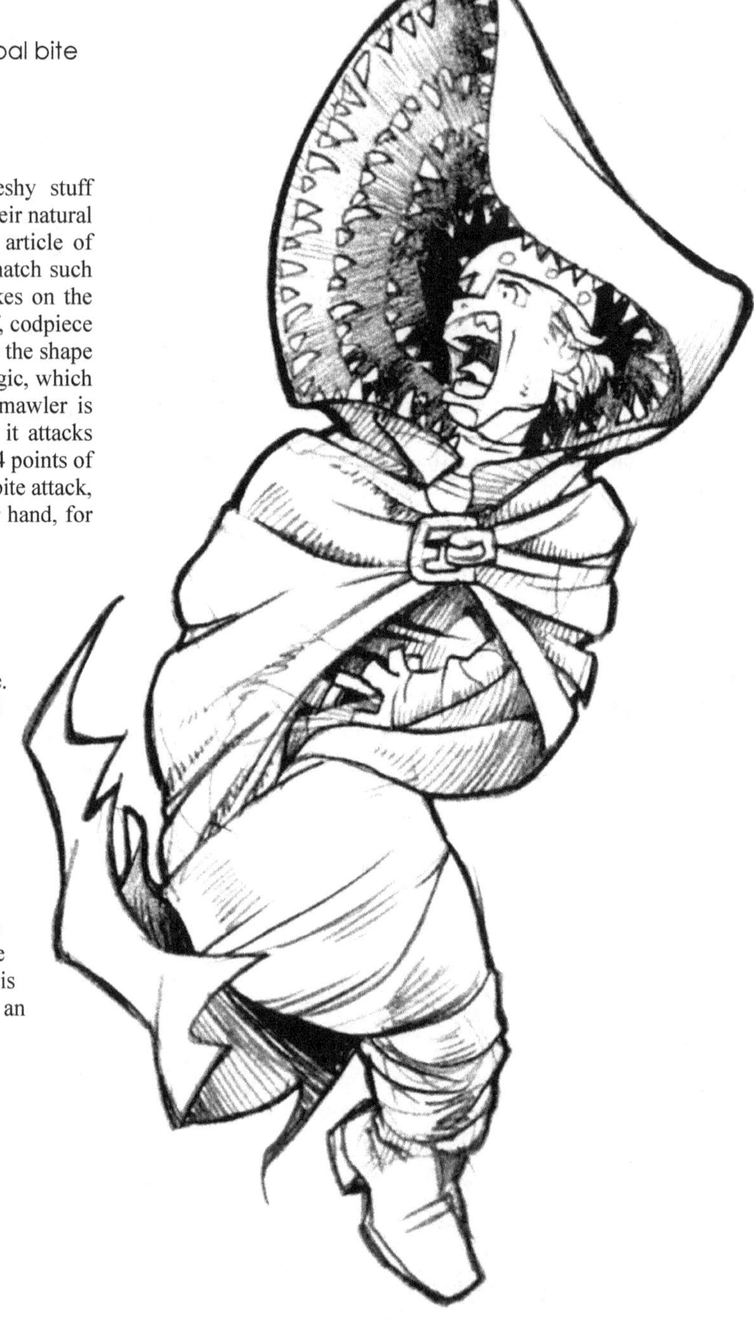

Medusa, Greater

Hit Dice: 8
Armor Class: 3 [16]
Attack: Shortbow (1d6) or dagger (1d4) and snakes (1d4 plus poison)
Saving Throw: 8
Special: Petrifying gaze, poisonous blood
Move: 12
Alignment: Chaos
Challenge Level/XP: 10/1400

A greater medusa looks like its lesser kin except that it has the lower torso of a giant snake. The greater medusa is a rare form of the normal medusa. They are very solitary creatures and dwell far from civilization, rarely leaving their lairs. In all other respects, they behave as the normal medusa.

A greater medusa's gaze turns people to stone and their snakes' fangs are poisonous. The blood of a greater medusa is highly poisonous even to the touch. A creature contacting the blood must succeed on a saving throw or take 2d6 points of damage. The blood loses its potency one hour after being exposed to air.

Art Objects

The finest sculptor in the kingdom works in a large, brick building, exceptionally grand. The building has a large, heavy iron door that is usually kepy locked, for the sculptor does not care to be interupted while at work. The sculptor is an old, blind man whose work decorates the temples and palaces of the kingdom. He does not take commissions of living people, but claims the images he sculpts are delivered to him in his dreams by his muse.

The workshop is visited daily by a serving wench from the largest inn in the city. She is the only person the genius will allow in his workshop, and she only visits for a few moments to bring him his daily repast (he eats but once per day, though the meal is quite large). The woman is often quizzed as to what wonders the sculptor is currently creating, but she always reports the same thing - everything hidden beneath large tarps. Once a month, a gang of laborers delivers several large slabs of stone, setting them up around the shop and then leaving.

A loose floor tile in the workshop gives one access to a subterranean river located about 30 feet below the workshop. The river runs from the mountain kingdom of a greater medusa. The sculptor once performed a great service for the medusa, ridding her of a terrible melancholy with a clever riddle. He alone of his party of adventurers survived this encounter, due to his lack of sight and his quick wit.

In exchange for his service, the greater medusa sends one of her two daughters (normal medusas) down the river once per month along with a bodyguard of goblins and several men and women taken by the medusa as tribute from the barbarian tribes of the mountains. No more than four or five captives make their way to the sculptor's workshop, where they are drugged, posed and then turned to stone by the medusas. Monies paid to the sculptor are sent back to the greater medusa with the sculptor's compliments, he only retaining what he needs to pay for his meals and his "raw materials". These raw materials are chipped away into gravel and tossed into the subterranean river.

Credit
The Greater Medusa originally appeared in the Second Edition *Monstrous Compendium I* (© TSR/Wizards of the Coast, 1989) and is used by permission.

Copyright Notice
Author Scott Greene, based on original material by Wizards of the Coast.

Memory Child

Hit Dice: 8
Armor Class: 5 [14]
Attacks: Mind drain (1d6)
Special: Mind flood
Move: 12
Saving Throw: 8
Alignment: Neutrality
Challenge Level/XP: 8/800

A memory child is an otherworldly being whose sole purpose is the collecting of memories. A memory child looks exactly like an ordinary child (male or female) about 7 or 8 years old. Regardless of its actual age, a memory child never seems to grow up or grow old. A memory child can absorb an opponent's thoughts and memories by touch. Draining memories is painful and does 1d6 points of damage to the victim. Alternatively the touch of a memory child can flood the opponent's mind with every single thought the child has ever collected from those that have come into contact with it. This effect overloads the opponent's brain, dazing it for 1d6+2 rounds and confusing it for 1 hour (treat as a *confusion* spell). A successful save negates the stunning effect and reduces the confusion effect to 1 minute. A memory child can use *ESP* at will.

The Daedalean Labyrinth

A fierce lightning storm envelops the top of a cragged stone mountain. The terrifying Daedalean Labyrinth is carved into its granite face. Arcs of lightning flash across the sky from billowing cloud to billowing cloud. The lightning is drawn to flying creatures but does not seem to strike within the maze.

The maze winds its way around the foundation of the mountain and eventually up the side before disappearing into the dark clouds. There are four entrances into the maze, one from each cardinal direction. The maze walls are 15 feet high and have no ceiling. Any flight above the walls draws the lightning bolts.

Memory children watch over the first section of the labyrinth. These beings steal the memories of anyone in the maze so they forget their current location and the direction to the entrances. No living creatures have ever exited the maze the same way they entered.

The memory children frolic and play in the entrances, but take the hands of anyone entering the maze as if to guide them through the twists and turns. They always appear friendly and helpful but do their best to mislead wanderers until they can steal their memories. The Daedalean Labyrinth holds many secrets and monsters. It is told that those lost within the maze over the centuries have formed a nomadic community wandering through the walls seeking a way out. Even the wisest of sages can only guess what lies at the end of the maze or why it was created.

Copyright Notice

Memory Moss

Memory moss appears as a 1-foot square patch of black moss. It grows in temperate or warm climates and is sometimes encountered in subterranean realms (though not often). Memory moss cannot abide the cold or the arid clime of the desert and is never encountered in such environments.

When a living creature moves within 60 feet of a patch of memory moss, it attacks by attempting to steal that creature's memories. It can target a single creature each round. A targeted creature must succeed on a saving throw or lose all memories from the last 24 hours. This is particularly nasty to spellcasters, who lose all spells prepared within the last 24 hours.

Once a memory moss steals a creature's memories, it sinks back down and does not attack again for one day. Any creature who loses its memories to the memory moss acts as if affected by a *confusion* spell for the next 1d4 hours. Lost memories can be regained by eating the memory moss that absorbed them. Doing so requires a saving throw, with failure resulting in the creature being nauseated for 1d6 minutes and suffering 2d4 points of damage.

A creature that eats the memory moss temporarily gains the memories currently stored therein (even if they are not the creature's own memories). Such creatures can even cast spells if the memory moss has stolen these from a spellcasting creature. Creatures eating the memory moss to regain their own lost memories do not lose them after 24 hours. Fire and cold kills a single patch of memory moss.

When first encountered, there is a 25% chance that the memory moss has eaten within the last day and does not attack by stealing memories. In such a case, the moss contains 2d4 spells determined randomly. When a living creature moves within 60 feet of a sated memory moss, it assumes a vaguely humanoid form and casts the stolen spells at its targets.

I Forgot, What?

An old oak forest, thick with moss and riddled with fungus, slopes every downward toward a gravel-filled gully. The gully shows signs of both infrequent campfires and flooding. Growing near the site of the campfires, there is a thick patch of black moss. The patch of memory moss grows in and around a number of skull-sized stones and does not give itself away during the day, waiting for a band of adventurers to settle in to camp. Once people have fallen into a slumber, the memory moss strikes at anyone left awake, stealing away their memories and sending them wandering aimlessly into he woods, where the local wolves finish them off.

Credit

The Memory Moss originally appeared in the First Edition *Monster Manual II* (© TSR/Wizards of the Coast, 1983) and is used by permission.

Copyright Notice

Author Scott Greene and Erica Balsley, based on original material by Gary Gygax.

M

Mephit, Lightning

Hit Dice: 2
Armor Class: 4 [15]
Attacks: 2 claws (1d2 + 1d4 electricity)
Special: breath weapon, immune to electricity, summon mephit
Move: 12/18 (flying)
Saving Throw: 16
Alignment: Neutrality
Challenge Level/XP: 2/30

A lightning mephit is a winged imp about 4 feet tall and weighs about 1 pound. It breathes a 15-foot cone of lightning (1d8 electricity, save for half). Once per day it can call down a bolt of lightning for 2d6 points of damage. A successful save halves the damage. Once per day, a lightning mephit can attempt to summon another lightning mephit with a 25% chance of success.

The Unnatural

A lightning-blasted tree is split in two, revealing a two-handed sword embedded in the burnt stump. It appears as if the tree grew around the sword until a lightning bolt freed it from its living prison. A web of camouflaged metal cords lies buried under the leaves and grass around the shattered stump. Two lightning mephitis hide within the split halves of the tree. Anyone standing on the metal cords when the lightning mephits strike takes an extra 1d6 points of damage as the metal conducts electricity around them.

Summoned by a magic-user, they have guarded the tree for centuries, never knowing that the tree contained a sword. The sword may have any number of abilities as decided by the Game Referee, but some ideas include absorbing electrical damage and turning it into healing magic for the wielder or improving the wielder's armor class by −1[+1] as it turns the bearer's skin as hard as bark.

Copyright Notice

Mephit, Smoke

Hit Dice: 2
Armor Class: 4 [15]
Attacks: 2 claws (1d2)
Special: breath weapon, immune to fire, summon mephit
Move: 12/18 (flying)
Saving Throw: 16
Alignment: Neutrality
Challenge Level/XP: 2/30

A smoke mephit is a winged imp about 4 feet tall and weighs about 1 pound. It breathes a 15-foot cone of hot soot (1d4 points of fire damage, save for half). Living creatures that fail their saves are tormented by burning eyes that impose a –2 to-hit penalty for 3 rounds. Once per day, the mephit can create a downpour of white-hot embers in a 20-foot radius that causes 2d6 points of fire damage to creature in the area. A successful save halves the damage. Once per day, a smoke mephit can attempt to summon another smoke mephit with a 25% chance of success.

Churning Oil

A large metal and canvas wind fan turns atop a narrow 60-foot tower. An iron ladder attached to the side of the tower leads to the only entrance at the top. Metal pipes protrude from the tower walls and pump crude oil into a series of iron barrel-like contraptions. Metal smokestacks emit plumes of thick smog into the air, the black clouds dumping an oily ash over the land.

Four smoke mephits burn off waste sludge inside the contraption to produce functional oil. The ground around the tower is a mess of mud, oil and unidentifiable sludge. Two ogres and six orcs fill barrels of oil from the machine and load the containers onto wagons. Twelve wagons sit nearby, each filled with barrels of oil. Six more wagons hold empty barrels. A herd of mistreated oxen suffer in a corral near the loaded wagons.

Any flame or flame-based spell near the tower ignite the land around the structure in a furious blaze as the oil-soaked ground ignites (6d6 points of damage, save for half). An enterprising magic-user named Oggsdul completes paperwork and tends to the pump controls in the top of the tower. He doesn't care for the safety of his minions; he can always hire more.

OGGSDUL (9th-level magic-user): HD 9; HP 19; AC 9[10]; Atk 1 dagger (1d4); Move 12; Save 7; CL/XP 9/1,100; Special: Spells: **1**—*charm person, light, magic missile, shield*; **2**—*invisibility, levitate, web*; **3**—*fireball, haste, hold person*; **4**—*confusion, wall of fire*; **5**—*transmute mud to rock*; Equipment: wand of pyrotechnics (8 charges)

Copyright Notice
Author Scott Greene.

Midnight Peddler

Hit Dice: 7
Armor Class: 3 [16]
Attack: Touch (death chill)
Saving Throw: 9
Special: Death chill, divination, plane shift
Move: 9
Alignment: Neutrality
Challenge Level/XP: 10/1400

The midnight peddler appears as a normal human, cloaked in a long gray hooded robe. A long protruding, sharp jaw can be seen under the hood. He wanders city streets and is normally only encountered on fog-covered nights. He is first detected by the audible squeaking of the cart he pushes, the sound growing louder as he draws closer. The midnight peddler moves with a slow gait as he pushes his wooden cart. The contents of his cart vary each time he visits the Material Plane, but at any given time, he has available any item listed in the equipment section with a value of 50 gp or less. The midnight peddler speaks the common tongue.

The touch of the midnight peddler drains 1d4 levels to a living creature.

The peddler provides advice and answers correctly any one question asked of him by any creature who buys something from his cart.

The midnight peddler can plane shift to any inner or outer plane as a move action. His cart (and any non-living matter contained therein) shifts with him. This ability otherwise functions as the spell of the same name.

Travelling Peddlers Are Always Sinister

The Worshipful Company of Augurs, Prophets and Prognosticators has run into a problem. Each night, at midnight precisely, a strange cart pulled by a man in a hooded cloak appears beneath the covered lane that runs between the home of the master armorer and the School for Impressionable Maidens. The peddler proceeds down the lane, past the old fountain and into a deadend alley, where he disappears in the shadows. The origins of the peddler are unknown, but what the fortune tellers of the city know is that he's cutting seriously into their business. Where people once visited their salons and parlors and paid well to learn of their future, they now creep out of their homes at midnight to buy a bauble from the peddler and have a single question answered.

In response to this crisis, the assembled diviners are seeking the services of foreign ne'er-do-wells to put a bloody end to the midnight peddler's poaching of their suckers. They are offering a 2,000 gp reward for any who can bring them proof of his end. The local assassins have turned down their contract, for reasons they will not share, and this alone has caused the soothsayers to wonder if they aren't making a miscalculation.

Copyright Notice
Author Scott Greene.

Mihstu

Hit Dice: 8
Armor Class: -3 [22]
Attack: 4 tentacles (1d6)
Saving Throw: 8
Special: Constitution damage, engulf, +1 or better weapon to hit, immunity to electricity, resistance to missile attacks, magic resistance (15%), susceptible to cold
Move: 9/9 (flying)
Alignment: Chaos
Challenge Level/XP: 13/2300

Mihstus are semi-solid creatures from the Elemental Plane of Air. They are found in cool, damp, dark areas such as ruins, dungeons, and underground caves and caverns. The mihstu can shape its body at will and almost always appears on the Material Plane as a cloud of swirling vapor. It can seep through small cracks and openings.

When threatened, a mihstu forms four tentacles from its body. Each tentacle ends in a razor-sharp, barb-like talon. A mihstu can try to wrap a creature in its body as an attack that ignores the victim's armor bonus to Armor Class. Even while engulfing a victim a mihstu can still use its tentacles to strike at other targets. A mihstu deals 1d2 points of constitution damage to an engulfed opponent each round the hold is maintained.

Ranged attacks (including *magic missile*) used against a mihstu have a 50% miss chance. Cold-based attacks and effects deal no damage to a mihstu, but stun it. If the cold-based effect allows a saving throw and the mihstu succeeds on its save, it ignores the stun effect. If it fails its save, or if the effect doesn't allow a save, the mihstu is stunned for 1d4+2 rounds.

Clinging to a Cloud

In a landscape of green, rolling hills and pleasant, balmy breezes, there is an ancient stone wall. The wall is all that remains of an ancient temple. It stands about 20 feet tall and is 45 feet long. Three large, arched windows pierce the wall, spaced about 10 feet apart from one another. Each of the windows is 6 feet tall and 4-1/2 feet wide.

The center window in the wall is a portal into the Elemental Plane of Air. A strong wind blows through the window at all times, and observers might (1 in 20 chance per day) see elemental air creatures pass through it into the mortal realms.

The window is easy enough to enter - one need only climb up to it and step inside. Once they do, they will find themselves in a 100-foot long tunnel of dark gray stone. The walls of the tunnel are slick and periodic bursts of lightning arc across them.

The guardian of the tunnel, a bound mihstu, can be found at its midpoint. The guardian permits no non-native of the Elemental Plane of Air to pass through the tunnel alive. Those who reach the other side find themselves looking out at an endless sky of rose and amber hues.

Credit

The Mihstu originally appeared in the First Edition *Monster Manual II* (© TSR/Wizards of the Coast, 1983) and is used by permission.

Copyright Notice

Author Scott Greene, based on original material by Gary Gygax.

Mimi

Hit Dice: 2 hp
Armor Class: 5 [14]
Attacks: 1 dagger (1d4)
Saving Throw: 16
Special: Spell-like abilities
Move: 3/18 (flying)
Alignment: Neutrality
Challenge Level/XP: 1/15

A mimi resembles a 1-foot-tall elf with small, bee-like wings, silver hair, milk white skin, and icy blue eyes. A mimi dresses in brightly colored clothing, preferring garments of blue, silver, or green. Mimis avoid combat, but blast foes with a *cone of cold* (once per day) if disturbed. They turn *invisible* (at will) and flee if threatened.

Snow Going

The mountain passes are snowbound, with man-sized drifts covering the ground and ice coating the rocky surfaces. Heavy flakes of snow continue to fall. Tree limbs sag under a thick blanket of ice. In the middle of the path leading up the next hill, a snowman stands facing downhill. It has two coal eyes, a carrot nose and what appear to be five small rubies forming a mouth. Two long branches are its arms. The cliffs rise slightly around the pass, leaving the snowman standing in shadows. When PCs get close enough, the snowman's head turns and it says, "10 gold to pass."

Six mimis live in the mountains and delight in tormenting travelers. The snowman is made of real snow, with a mimi crouched in the head to turn it and speak.

If PCs don't pay the toll, the hidden mimis pelt PCs with snowballs from the high ridges and roll a 10-foot-diameter snowball down the hill toward them. The snowball picks up more snow on its descent, so it is 15 feet wide by the time it smashes into the snowman and the PCs. It does no damage, but PCs who fail a save are smashed into the snowball as it continues to roll down the hillside. They are nauseated by the sickening ride (save avoids).

The mimis continue with their fun for as long as possible, not harming PCs as long as they are good sports and play along. If the snowball fight turns serious, the mimis use their *cone of cold* ability and escape.

Copyright Notice
Author Scott Greene.

Mire Brute

Hit Dice: 15
Armor Class: 3 [16]
Attacks: 2 fists (3d6)
Special: Disgorge vermin, disease, impale, magic weapon required to hit, immune to fire
Move: 9/20 (swim)
Saving Throw: 3
Alignment: Neutrality
Challenge Level/XP: 15/2,900

Mire brutes, when dormant, appear as large stretches of mud bristling with wooden stakes. Once per day a mire brute can vomit forth a spray of fetid water to a range of 30 feet. The spray contains small biting insects and worms. Treat these vermin as a *creeping doom* spell. A mire brute can try to impale smaller opponents. An impaled opponent immediately takes 4d6 points of damage and is stuck on the stakes jutting from the mire brute's body. The stakes protruding from a mire brute's body are filthy and diseased. A saving throw is allowed (versus poison). The effects of the disease are decided by the Game Referee.

The Tree People of Eanca

High in the mountains lies a fen nestled among giant redwoods. The redwoods thrive in the geothermal warmth in an unusual mountain swamp. The barbaric people of the mountains built their settlement high up in the redwoods above the swamp. The Tree People use the swamp, the trees and the swamp's creatures as natural defenses against their enemies. They are a simple, yet fierce and territorial people.

The Tree People worship a mire brute that resides in the swamp below their temple in the trees. The temple consists of a hole in a wooden platform through which they drop sacrifices to the mire brute "god." Their sacrifices consist of slaves and captives taken from neighboring tribes. The bodies (adorned with the best fineries available to the Tree People) lie impaled upon the submerged mire brute's back.

Copyright Notice
Author Scott Greene.

Mite

Common

Hit Dice: 1
Armor Class: 7 [12]
Attack: Club (1d4) and bite (1d3)
Save: 17
Special: None
Move: 9
Alignment: Chaos
CL/XP: 1/15

Pestie

Hit Dice: 1
Armor Class: 5 [14]
Attack: Dagger (1d3)
Save: 17
Special: Surprise on 1-2 on 1d6
Move: 15
Alignment: Neutrality
CL/XP: 1/15

Mites are thought to be distant relatives of the goblins. Mites live their lives deep under the surface of the earth and are never encountered on the surface world. While sunlight does not harm a mite, it prefers the darkness and dampness of its underground realm.

Common mites speak their own language of garbled twittering, though some can speak the language of goblins. Pesties generally prefer not to communicate with others (even those of their own race) except through body language and hand signals. It is unknown whether pesties simply cannot or choose not to speak.

Trickery and surprise are the forte of the mite. They avoid direct melee with opponents, preferring to attack from ambush. Often, the first tell-tale signs that mites may be nearby is the plethora of traps, snares, and tripwires encountered. Mites prefer to attack those they feel they can overpower or dispose of quickly. Extremely tough or powerful opponents are ignored and left to pass through unabated or swarmed by a massive number of mites. Though considered unintelligent and stupid by other races, there is a sort of weird cooperation and strategy to mite tactics (that only mites can understand).

A typical mite ambush has the creatures digging narrow tunnels that parallel a dungeon's corridors. When a foe traverses these corridors, the mites burst from the walls and tunnels and strike quickly with their daggers. Opponents are rarely killed, but any knocked unconscious are relieved of coins, weapons, or any other item of value. If forced into melee, mites seek escape at the first possible opportunity. Mites attack with clubs and a bite in combat, while pesties prefer to utilize hit-and-run tactics to keep opponents off-balance.

Mites make their homes underground in deep, dark dungeons and caverns where they survive by stealing from those unfortunate enough to wander near their lair. A mite lair is often a large central room or cavern from which many small and winding tunnels lead. A mite lair is a filthy place littered with garbage and refuse. Cleanliness and sanitation are virtually unknown in a mite community. Pesties often are found working with or lairing with goblins or (more usually) common mites. The trapmaking skills of the mite complement the pestie's adeptness at speed and hit-and-run tactics. Mite young are almost never encountered, but a typical lair contains a number of noncombatant young equal to the number of adult mites.t

Mitey Rift to Hell

A mob of 6d4 common mites is making its way through a triangular tunnel clad in porphyry, carrying their loot in leather sacks. If confronted, they will seemingly disappear into the walls. The mites actually use doors set sideways to reality, doors one can only find if they have fey blood or a wisdom score of 18. Two or three of the mites will make a show of fleeing down the tunnel and into a large chamber.

As one exits the tunnel, they will feel themselves hurled against the far wall of the chamber, suffering 2d6 points of falling damage. After they recover their senses, they will realize they are on the floor of the chamber, the tunnel through which they entered now being a seemingly solid, black triangle on the ceiling. Four other triangles around it form a pentagram lined in gold.

The chamber is about 50 feet in diameter and 20 feet tall. The walls are swathed in curtains of red velvet. The curtains hide thirteen barred circular caches, each about 3 feet in diameter and 2 feet deep. A polished stone is set in the back of each cache. The stones are of various types, but each is a sphere 4 inches in diameter, highly polished and worth about 500 gp. The mites the adventurers chased into the room are nowhere to be seen.

If a gem is pried from the wall, one will discover a powerful void behind it. This void will begin sucking the air and any small object not secured into it. The person who pried the gem must pass a saving throw or have their hand and arm sucked into the hole and suffer 1d6 points of damage from the pressure and cold. When a person has lost 25% of their total normal hit points from this damage, their arm will be left withered and useless.

The sucking of the void will begin to open a rift in the center of the chamber. The rift will appear as a black, crackling energy that gradually expands to fill an area roughly the same shape as the pentagram on the ceiling and extending from floor to ceiling. This process should take 15 rounds, but multiple void holes will quicken the rate of growth (i.e. 2 holes will cause the rift to grow in 8 rounds, 3 holes in 5 rounds, and so on). Once the rift is complete, a random demon or devil will emerge from it into the room and attend its petitioners as it sees fit. The void holes can be plugged with the gems or with a large enough object at least as strong as steel.

Credit

The Mite and Pestie originally appeared in the First Edition *Fiend Folio* (© TSR/Wizards of the Coast, 1981) and are used by permission.

Copyright Notice

Authors Scott Greene and Skeeter Green, based on original material by Ian Livingstone and Mark Barnes.

Mongrelman

Hit Dice: 2
Armor Class: 4 [15]
Attack: Fists (1d4) or club (1d6)
Saving Throw: 16
Special: Sound imitation, surprise on 1-2 on 1d6
Move: 12
Alignment: Neutrality
Challenge Level/XP: 2/30

Mongrelmen are hideous creatures seemingly pieced together from parts of other monsters as some sort of vile joke or blight on humanity. Though not inherently evil, mongrelmen are shunned from society because of their appearance. They make their homes far from civilization, and those few encountered in settled areas are usually slaves or servants of the local humanoid races. Mongrelmen that must travel among other races take precautions so as not to reveal their true identities, using cloaks, capes, and the like to hide their forms. Mongrelman society is a collection of close-knit tribes, each with its own leader. Mongrelmen never fight against other mongrelmen, preferring to live peaceably with others of their kind, for all mongrelmen know they are shunned by outsiders and must stick together if their race is to survive. Mongrelmen stand about 6 feet tall. The average lifespan of a mongrelman is 35 years. Mongrelmen speak their own guttural language.

Mongrelmen can imitate sounds made by any creature they have previously encountered, including monsters with special vocal attacks. They cannot, however, mimic the special vocal attack powers or damage dealt by such attacks. A successful listen check made by a listener detects the falsehood.

Mongrelmen as Characters

Mongrelman characters enjoy a +1 bonus to strength and constitution scores at character creation, but suffer a -3 penalty to their charisma score. These adjustments cannot increase a starting ability score above 18 or lower a starting ability score below 3. Mongrelmen can see in the dark as well as elves and retain their ability to imitate sounds. Mongrelmen can advance in levels as fighters (up to 6th level, or 7th level with a strength score of 13+) or thieves (up to 8th level, or 9th level with a dexterity of 13+).

Mongrelman Melancholy

You come upon a conclave of 1d10 x 10 mongrelmen living in a series of sea caves. The mongrelmen are preparing a feast (rather meager, if truth be told), though the celebration seems rather somber. The mongrelmen are quiet, simpering creatures, melancholic and not eager to entertain visitors, though they will not resist the intrusion of others into their home. The leader of the mongrelmen will explain that they have little to offer visitors, and that it is probably safer if they leave, for in the morning they expect the arrival of the red raiders.

The red raiders are pirates who sail in a red galley with black sails. At each full moon they sail the coast, visiting the mongrelmen and taking a tribute of seven slaves. The mongrelman slaves are put to work as rowers and treated no better than machines. The red raiders make no attempt to keep them alive any longer than they must.

The leader of the mongrelmen is Tovos, a 6th level thief. Tovos is, like all mongrelmen, a weird amalgam of creatures. The left side of its head looks like that of a flind, while the right is that of a sahuagin. Tovos' left arm is that of a crabman, the right is that of a goblin. He has the torso of a halfling, the right leg of a kobold and the left leg of a bugbear.

The leader of the red raiders, berserkers all of them, is called Yazima. Yazima is a tall, copper-skinned woman with orange-red hair and crystal blue eyes. She is an 8th level fighter who wears leather armor adorned with burnished bronze rings and carries a red shield and a heavy scimitar.

Credit

The Mongrelman originally appeared in the First Edition *Monster Manual II* (© TSR/Wizards of the Coast, 1983) and is used by permission.

Copyright Notice

Author Scott Greene, based on original material by Gary Gygax.

Randomly Generating a Mongrelman

Mongrelmen are a mixture of many different creatures, and no two mongrelmen ever look alike. The table below can be used to generate the appearance of any given mongrelman.

Roll one time for each of the following areas of a mongrelman: left side of head (includes ear and eye); right side of head (includes ear and eye); torso; right arm; left arm; right leg and left leg.

Random Mongrelman Generation

1d20	Type
1	Gnoll
2	Goblin
3	Hobgoblin
4	Human
5	Kobold
6	Merfolk
7	Locathah
8	Sahuagin
9	Dwarf
10	Elf
11	Gnome
12	Halfling
13	Orc or ogre
14	Troglodyte
15	Crabman
16	Bugbear
17	Minotaur
18	Flind
19	Lizardfolk
20	Missing body part (Use common sense on this one. Obviously, a mongrelman cannot be missing part of its torso.)

Description of Body Parts

A mongrelman gains abilities in addition to the ones noted in the stat block above based on the actual body parts that make up that mongrelman. Below are descriptions of the body parts and additional abilities gained.

Gnoll: *Eye:* See in darkness and spot concealed doors on roll of 1-2 on 1d6. *Ear:* Listen at doors on 1-2 on 1d6. *Arm:* +1 melee damage using that arm.

Goblin: *Eye:* See in darkness and spot concealed doors on roll of 1-2 on 1d6. *Ear:* Listen at doors on 1-2 on 1d6. *Arm:* -1 melee damage using that arm.

Hobgoblin: *Eye:* See in darkness and spot concealed doors on roll of 1-2 on 1d6. *Ear:* Listen at doors on 1-2 on 1d6.

Human: No additional abilities.

Kobold: *Eye:* See in darkness, spot concealed doors on 1-2 on 1d6, sensitive to light. *Ear:* Listen at doors on 1-2 on 1d6. *Arm:* -1 melee damage using that arm.

Merfolk: *Eye:* See in darkness and spot concealed doors on roll of 1-2 on 1d6. *Ear:* Listen at doors on 1-2 on 1d6. *Head:* If entire head is merfolk, the mongrelman can breathe water and air equally. *Leg:* Leg is actually a fin or flipper and the mongrelman moves at one-half speed while on land. *Torso:* Mongrelman has a land movement rate of 3, but can swim at a movement rate of 18.

Locathah: *Eye:* See in darkness and spot concealed doors on roll of 1-2 on 1d6. *Ear:* Listen at doors on 1-2 on 1d6. *Head:* If entire head is locathah, the mongrelman can breathe water and air equally.

Sahuagin: *Eye:* See in darkness and spot concealed doors on roll of 1-2 on 1d6 and light blindness. *Ear:* Listen at doors on 1-2 on 1d6. *Arm:* +1 melee damage using that arm. *Head:* If entire head is sahuagin, the mongrelman can breathe water and air equally.

Dwarf: *Eye:* See in darkness. *Head:* If entire head is dwarven, the mongrelman gains the dwarf's ability to notice unusual stonework. *Torso:* +1 to saves against poison.

Elf: *Eye:* See in darkness and spot concealed doors on roll of 1-2 on 1d6 and light blindness. *Ear:* Listen at doors on 1-2 on 1d6. *Head:* If entire head is elven, the mongrelman gains a +1 bonus to saves against charm and sleep.

Gnome: *Eye:* See in darkness. *Ear:* Listen at doors on 1-2 on 1d6. *Head:* If entire head is gnome, the mongrelman gains a +1 bonus to saves against illusions.

Halfling: *Ear:* Listen at doors on 1-2 on 1d6. *Arm:* -1 melee damage using that arm. *Torso:* Mongrelman is small.

Orc or ogre: *Eye:* See in darkness and light sensitivity. *Arm:* +1 melee damage using that arm (orc) or +2 melee damage using that arm (ogre).

Troglodyte: *Eye:* See in darkness. *Torso:* Gains the stench ability and surprises on 1-2 on 1d6 by changing its skin color.

Crabman: *Eye:* See in darkness. *Arm:* +2 melee damage using that arm. *Hand:* hand is actually a large pincer like that of the crabman; gains claw attack that deals 1d6 damage.

Bugbear: *Eye:* See in darkness. *Arm:* +1 melee damage using that arm.

Minotaur: *Eye:* See in darkness and spot concealed door on 1-2 on 1d6. *Ear:* Listen at door on 1-2 on 1d6. *Arm:* +2 melee damage using that arm. *Head:* Gore attack for 1d4 damage; if both sides of a mongrelman's head are minotaur, the gore damage increases to 1d6.

Flind: *Eye:* See in darkness and spot concealed door on 1-2 on 1d6. *Ear:* Listen at door on 1-2 on 1d6. *Arm:* +1 melee damage using that arm.

Lizardfolk: *Arm:* +1 melee damage using that arm. *Hand:* Gains claw attack that deals 1d3 damage. *Head:* Gains bite attack that deals 1d3 damage. *Torso:* Gains a lizardfolk's tail and swim speed.

Moon Dog

Hit Dice: 9
Armor Class: -3 [22]
Attack: Bite (1d8)
Saving Throw: 7
Special: Bay, shadow weave, spells, +1 or better weapon to hit, immunity to fear, lick, plane shift, magic resistance (30%)
Move: 18/12 (bipedal)
Alignment: Law
Challenge Level/XP: 15/2900

The moon dog is a large wolfhound from the outer planes (believed to have its origins on the plane of Elysium). Moon dogs often enter the Material Plane when chaos has grown to an immeasurable level in an area. Otherwise, they are found in the employ of deities, solars, planetars, and the most powerful devas.

Moondogs forepaws are prehensile and resemble human hands. Though moon dogs can move on two legs in a bipedal fashion, most do not do so, preferring the speed and grace they gain by moving on all fours. They have grayish-black fur and golden eyes.

A moon dog can produce one of the following effects when it howls or barks.

Fear: All evil creatures within 80 feet must make a successful saving throw or be affected as by a *fear* spell.

Dispel Evil: This effect works like the spell, and affects one evil creature within 80 feet.

Dismissal: This effect forces an extraplanar creature to pass a saving throw or be sent back to its home plane.

The following abilities are always active on the moon dog: *Detect evil, detect magic,* and *detect invisibility.* They can cast mirror image three times per day and *darkness, invisibility, light* and *obscuring mist* once per day. A moon dog can also *dispel magic* once per day, but doing so forces it back to its plane of origin.

When in shadows, a moon dog can move in such a way as to affect evil creatures within 60 feet as though by a hypnotic pattern. Any lawful creature in the area of the shadow weave will be affected as though by *protection from evil.* The moon dog cannot use its shadow weave and attack, and the moon dog must concentrate to maintain it.

By licking a person's wounds, a moon dog may use one of the following abilities: *cure disease, cure light wounds* or *remove disease.* Each is usable at will by the moon dog, but only once per day per recipient.

A moon dog can enter the Ethereal Plane, Astral Plane, or Material Plane.

Guardian Angel Hound

Stories abound in the farm village about the wolfhound who watches over the people. For several moons, the strange dog has been seen in glimpses moving through the woods around the old reservoir or in silhouette at night, baying at the moon. On at least three occaisions it has been credited with saving a person's life. The first time was when it rescued a child from drowning in the reservoir. It also chased away two brigands who threatened old Jed on the imperial road as he took his turnips to market and then again when he pulled three maidens out of a burning barn.

In all three cases, the moon dog, for a moon dog it is, was countering the actions of a band of 3d6 x 10 aquatic hobgoblins that has taken up residence in the murky waters of the old reservoir. The hobgoblins were chased from their old lair by a gang of fresh water trolls, and were fortunate to discover the reservoir a few miles up stream.

The leader of the hobgoblins has the abilities of a 2nd level magic-user and 3rd level cleric of the "Creeping Crud", an ooze god favored by the wicked water fey of the region. The moon dog was dispatched by the deva Soniznt, patron of the village's church, to protect the village until adventurers could be "led" to the village.

Encounters with the hobgoblins occur on a roll of 1-4 on 1d6. An encounter will usually be with 1d6+6 hobgoblins, for the creatures are beginning to patrol in force. In the event of an attack, the moon dog will make itself known and explain why the adventurers have come to the village (even if they think they arrived on their own volition).

Credit

The Moon Dog originally appeared in the First Edition *Monster Manual II* (© TSR/Wizards of the Coast, 1983) and is used by permission.

Copyright Notice

Author Scott Greene, based on original material by Gary Gygax.

M

Mortuary Cyclone

Hit Dice: 17
Armor Class: 0 [19]
Attacks: 1 fist (3d6 + level drain)
Special: 50% spell resistance, +2 magic weapons required to hit, create spawn, desecrating aura, whirlwind
Move: 16
Saving Throw: 3
Alignment: Chaos
Challenge Level/XP: 20/5,900

A mortuary cyclone is 5 feet wide at the base, 30 feet wide at the top and about 40 feet tall tornado composed of grave dirt, bone fragments, and body parts all swirling around in its whirlwind form. A mortuary cyclone emanates an aura of desecration within a 50-foot radius centered on its body. Undead within the area gain a +2 bonus on attack rolls, damage rolls, and saves. Once every 1d4 rounds, a mortuary cyclone can blast forth a mass of bone fragments, debris and negative energy in a 30-foot cone. Creatures caught in the cone take 6d6 points of damage. Creatures that save reduce the damage by half.

Opponents touching or entering the mortuary cyclone (if the cyclone moves into another creature) might be lifted into the air if they are smaller than the mortuary cyclone. A creature that comes into contact with the whirlwind takes 3d6 points of damage. It must also succeed on a save or be picked up bodily and held suspended in the powerful winds, automatically taking 3d6 points of damage each round thereafter. Creatures trapped in the whirlwind cannot move except to go where the mortuary cyclone carries them or to try to escape the whirlwind. Any living creature slain by a mortuary cyclone's whirlwind attack or energy drain attack becomes an undead creature in 1d4 rounds. Creatures with less than 3 HD return as a ghoul or ghast; 4-7 HD, a wraith; 8-11 HD, a spectre; and 12+ HD return as a ghost.

Negative Vortex

The sides of this small mountain have disintegrated, leaving a sheer cliff wall surrounding the peak. The top of the mountain levels off to form a quarter-mile-diameter plateau. Identical featureless obelisks symmetrically surround a solid octagonal tower of black granite. The outer wall of the tower is covered in petroglyphs and star charts. Sections of the tower rotate horizontally to align with the constellations. With careful study, a scholar may determine that the rotating sections seem to count down to a specific date when the stars will align. The only physical entrance into the tower's interior lies buried under 10 feet of earth on the north side of the building. The tower hosts a multitude of undead in the service of a lich king who rests within. A mortuary cyclone guards against interlopers to this sacred monument to undeath. The cyclone issues forth from the top of the tower if a living being touches the tower.

Copyright Notice
Author Scott Greene.

Mosquito, Giant

Hit Dice: 4 hp
Armor Class: 6 [13]
Attacks: 1 bite (1 point + blood drain)
Saving Throw: 13
Special: blood drain
Move: 6/15 (flying)
Alignment: Neutrality
Challenge Level/XP: B/10

Giant mosquitoes are 3 feet long and slender, with dark black bodies. Silver scales line their thorax, and like other insects, the giant mosquito is segmented. It has six legs of the same dark color as its body and its single pair of wings is translucent. The giant mosquito possesses a long, slender proboscis, the end of which contains its mouth. Females use this to pierce a living creature's flesh and drink their blood (1d4 hit points per round for 1d6 rounds).

Deadliest Catch

The annual fishing derby of Juloos Loch draws competitors from many leagues – all hoping to claim the 50 silver scales (normal silver pieces crafted to be more "fish-like") for catching the biggest fish. More than 100 fishermen are already on the lake by the time the morning fog parts and the sun begins to rise.

But it isn't long before screams drown out the celebration. A fisherman's boat drifts in, the angler sitting upright but completely drained of blood. His ashen face is pale and his cheeks and eyes sunken. He holds his homemade fishing rod in his desiccated hands. Even the fish lying in the boat are drained of blood.

Last year's tournament angered a druid living on the far side of the lake. A worshipper of the loathsome insect god Rachiss, the druid vowed to get his revenge on the fishermen invading his privacy with their annual contest. The druid raises giant mosquitos in a barn on his property, and nourishes them with the blood of cattle. He released them just before dawn to scour the lake in search of "fresh blood." Ten of the mosquitos buzz the lake, terrorizing fishermen and draining the blood of those who can't get away.

Copyright Notice
Author Erica Balsley.

M

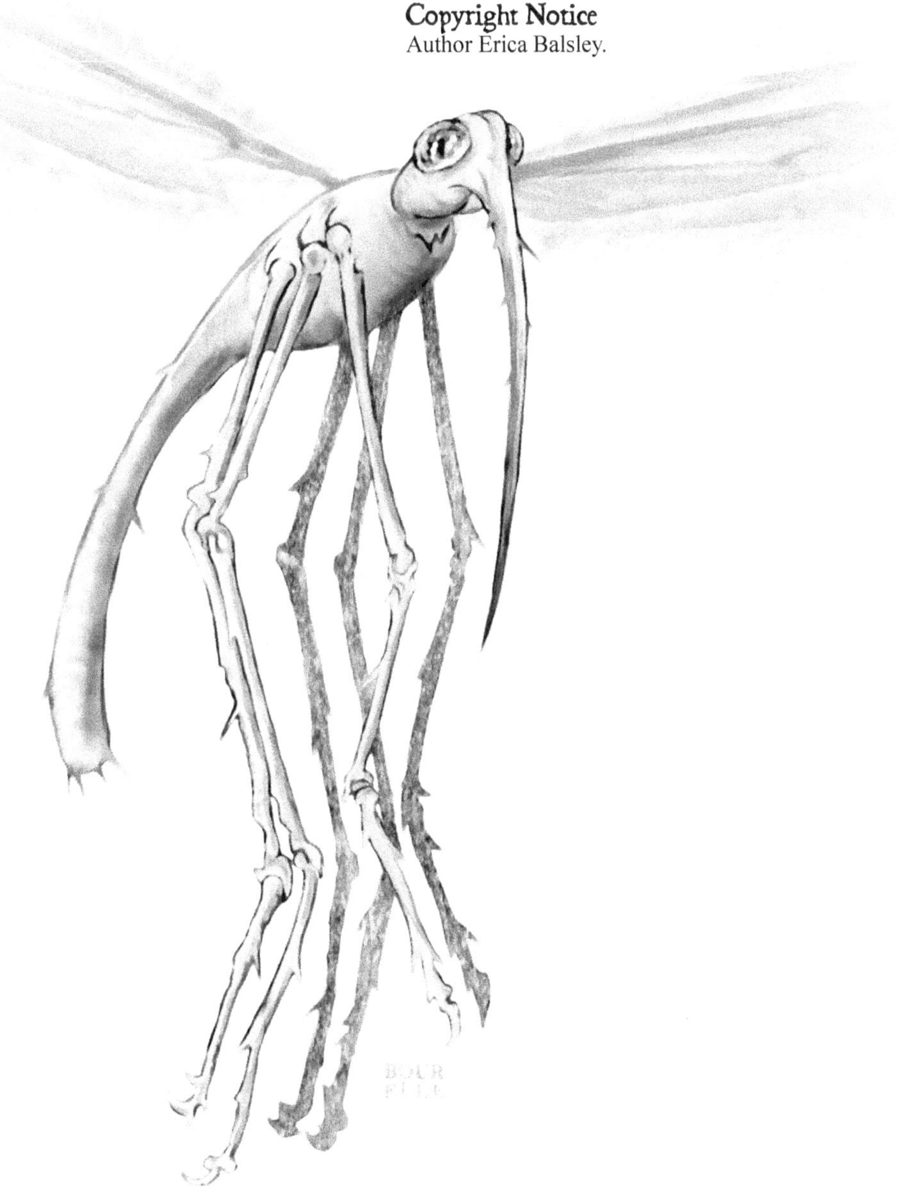

Muckdweller

Hit Dice: 1d6
Armor Class: 5 [14]
Attack: Bite (1d3)
Saving Throw: 18
Special: Blinding spray
Move: 6/12 (swimming)
Alignment: Neutrality
Challenge Level/XP: 1/15

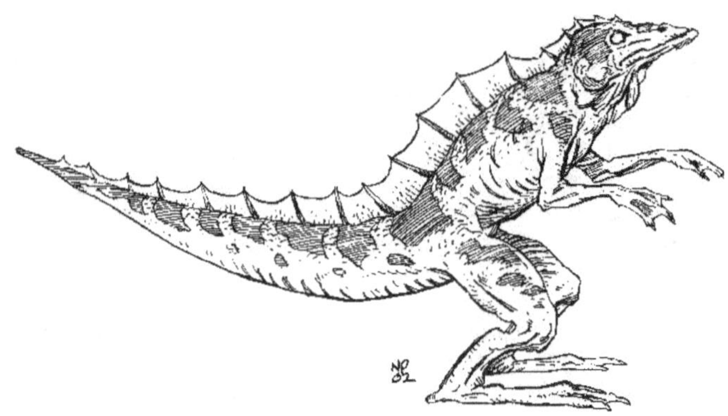

The muckdweller is a small, swamp-dwelling bipedal lizard that lives on a diet of carrion, fresh meat, plants, and insects. It has a long tail that allows it to swim rapidly through the water or maintain its balance when standing upright. Muckdwellers sometimes associate with lizardfolk. Muckdwellers stand about 4 feet tall. They speak their own language of croaks and hisses, and a rare few speak the language of black dragons.

By filling its mouth with muddy water, a muckdweller can fire a stream of muddy water in a 10-foot line. A creature hit must succeed on a saving throw or be blinded for 1d2 rounds. A muckdweller can take a move action to refill its mouth with muddy water so it can use its spray again.

Last Man Standing Wins

There is an old castle on the moor, ancient and moss covered and seemingly always surrounded by a gray miasma. The castle is divided between two rivals, 9th level clerics in service to the temple of the death god. The high priest of that god has recently passed on, and the cardinals both expect to be declared the new high priest in a conclave of high priests of the other deities of the pantheon.

Each of the bitter men has invited his supporters and hangers-on to a great party to celebrate his expected ascension. The revelers are sequestered in their own sides of the castle, but several raucous clashes have happened in the great hall, a sort of no-man's-land.

Over the past three nights, several followers of each claimant have been killed by some manner of wild animal. This has thrown each side into a fury of accusations, challenges and bloody (though nonlethal) duels.

The murderers in question are a pack of 1d4+3 muchdwellers that have been let into the castle from the murky moors by a third party, an 8th level cleric who serves as an abbot of the death god's monastery. The monk holds a scroll of protection from reptilians. He plans to provoke the two cardinals into open war, leaving himself clear to claim the position of high priest.

Credit

The Muckdweller originally appeared in the First Edition *Monster Manual II* (© TSR/Wizards of the Coast, 1983) and is used by permission.

Copyright Notice

Mudbog

Hit Dice: 3
Armor Class: 5 [14]
Attacks: Engulf
Saving Throw: 14
Special: Immune to blunt weapons, engulf, acid
Move: 3
Alignment: Neutrality
Challenge Level/XP: 3/60

Mudbogs are slow-moving, pudding-like creatures that are brownish in color, resembling nothing more than brackish mud. The average mudbog is roughly 10 feet across and 3 feet deep. Mudbogs dig holes in the swamp and wait for creatures to blunder into their bodies. A mudbog secretes a digestive acid that dissolves organic material (leather armor, wooden clubs, etc.) and deals 1d6 points of damage. Any being that stumbles into a mudbog is considered engulfed and takes 1d6 points of damage from the creature's acidic nature automatically in the rounds thereafter.

Pig Pen

Small sulfur springs continually feed into a muddy field. The area reeks of rotten eggs. A sod hut sits on a small island amid the soupy pasture. A hollow tree stands next to the hut and serves as a chimney. Sounders of wild hogs populate the fields, the animals wallowing in the mud, basking in the sun and licking the salty sulfur.

The abrasive druid Tungo Bramlett lives in the mud hut among the swine. The burly Tungo contracted Devil Swine disease that turns him into a wereboar. Easily angered, Tungo quickly transforms into a boar hybrid capable of uncontrollable violence. From his food to clothing, nearly everything in Tungo's daily life deals with swine. The field contains several mudbogs. The wild swine have learned to sense and avoid the deadly oozes, but Tungo regularly feeds the things pork scraps to ensure their survival. Tungo has adopted a primordial boar that shares his abode and rarely leaves his side.

Although normally offensive (both in hygiene and personality), Tungo has learned of an oakman who makes wondrous cakes from pork fat, asparagus and moss. He desperately wants to try these cakes but does not want to leave his beloved mud pits.

Copyright Notice

Mudman

Hit Dice: 2
Armor Class: 7 [12]
Attack: 2 slams (1d4) or mud bomb (see text)
Saving Throw: 16
Special: Engulf, mud bomb, +1 or better weapon to hit, mindless, mud pool
Move: 6
Alignment: Neutrality
Challenge Level/XP: 5/240

A mudman's natural form is that of a pool of mud about 5 feet in diameter. In this form, they cannot be discerned from normal mud. Mud pools are formed where the run-off from alchemical laboratories mixes with soil. Though not evil, mudmen look with disdain on any who trespass in their mud pools.

When a living creature enters a mud pool, the mudman forms its humanoid shape and attacks until the opponent is slain or leaves the mud pool. A mudman attacks by pummeling a foe with its fists or by hurling globs of mud. Mudmen are bound to the pool where they are formed.

A mudman attacks by hurling globs of mud at its opponent. These globs deal no damage and have a range of 30 feet. A successful ranged touch attack means the mud glob hits the target and solidifies in the same round. A creature hit by a mud bomb has its movement rate reduced by 3. A creature whose movement is reduced to 0 is stuck on the ground. A stuck creature cannot move without making a successful open doors check. A creature can scrape the mud off, taking one round to scrape it off for every mud bomb that hit them.

A mudman can hurl itself at any creature within 10 feet. If it succeeds on a ranged attack, the mudman engulfs the victim's head and upper body in mud that instantly solidifies and cuts off the victim's air. This attack destroys the mudman if its hits; otherwise it reverts to its natural form and must spend one full round reforming. A character that has no air to breathe can hold her breath for 2 rounds per point of Constitution. After this period of time, the character suffocates. The mud can be hit automatically and is destroyed when it takes 6 hit points of damage from a blunt weapon. Each successful attack deals half its damage to the mud and the other half to the engulfed victim. The mud can be pried off by a creature with a successful open doors check.

Mudmen are mindless, and thus immune to mind-influencing effects like charms, suggestions, fear and illusions. *Dispel magic* acts as a *fireball* spell against a mudman, dealing 1d6 points of damage per caster level to all mudmen in a 30-foot radius (no save). *Transmute mud to rock* deals 1d8 points of damage per caster level to all mudmen in the area of effect (save for half).

Mud Pies, Anyone?

What began as a simple magical experiment involving the Elemental Plane of Water has turned into a nightmare for the grand duke. His court magician was conjuring over a cauldron when a comet made an unexpected transit across Aquarius. Water in its pure, elemental form poured from the cauldron, flooding the tower occupied by the magician and creating a great, swampy mess around the castle. Worse yet, a pack of 1d6+6 mudmen now has the castle surrounded, essentially under siege. The grand duke has lost no fewer than 20 men-at-arms and 5 knights to the mudmen, his wine cellar is flooded and ruined and the food supply is running low. He should pay handsomely for assistance, though the crafty old miser probably will find a way out of showing his gratitude.

Credit

The Mudman originally appeared in the First Edition module *UK1 Beyond the Crystal Cave* (© TSR/Wizards of the Coast, 1983) and later in the First Edition *Monster Manual II* (© TSR/Wizards of the Coast, 1983) and is used by permission. It was called the "Mud-man" in UK1 (note the hyphen).

Copyright Notice

Author Scott Greene, based on original material by David J. Browne, Tom Kirby, and Graeme Morris.

Mummy of the Deep

Hit Dice: 6+2
Armor Class: -1 [20]
Attack: Slam (1d6 plus curse of the deep)
Saving Throw: 11
Special: Curse of the deep, despair, control water, resistance to fire (50%)
Move: 9/9 (swimming)
Alignment: Chaos
Challenge Level/XP: 9/1100

A mummy of the deep is an undead creature that lairs in the depths of the sea. It is the result of an evil creature that was buried at sea for its sins in life. The wickedness permeating the former life has managed to cling even into unlife and revive the soul as a mummy of the deep. It appears as a rotting humanoid wrapped in seaweed.

On a slam attack, a victim must pass a saving throw or be embraced by the mummy. The mummy presses its lips against an opponent's and regurgitates sea water into the opponent's lungs. Each round thereafter, for the next 10 rounds, the victim must make a saving throw or take 1d4 points of damage that round. Three consecutive successful saves means the character has coughed up enough water to shake the effects of this attack and takes no further damage. An affected creature can take no actions other than to defend itself in any round it takes damage from this ability. At 0 or less hit points, the victim falls unconscious. In the next round, he drowns. Holding one's breath does not prevent drowning because water is already in the lungs. A *remove curse* halts the damage if applied before the creature reaches 0 or less hit points.

At the mere sight of a mummy of the deep, the viewer must succeed on a saving throw or be paralyzed with fear for 1d4 rounds.

Once per day, a mummy of the deep can *part water* or *lower water*.

Beauty is Only Skin Deep

Beneath the waters of the frothy strait that now bears her name lies the body of the most beautiful woman ever born, now animated as a mummy of the deep. The creatures of the strait and some beyond fear her power and obey her commands, bringing beautiful young men beneath the waves to her. Alas, the young men do not survive the journey, and the mummy's desire for companionship is never satisfied.

The mummy of the deep dwells in a castle of white stones, constructed by her merrow and lacedon servants (she commands 2d4 of the former and 2d6+6 of the latter) and set in a "garden" of 1d3+1 kelpies. From atop the central tower the mummy looks up toward the surface and her former life. The mummy has the form of a shapely woman, tall and stately. Her body is wrapped in kelp. She has silvery hair that falls to her hips, hollow eyes that peek from behind the kelp.

When ships pass over the white castle, they traditionally drop a leather sack of coins and a garland of flowers into the water. The mummy's treasure might consist of 1d12 x 100 gp and a marble statue of herself in life worth 5,000 gp and weighing nearly 1 ton.

Copyright Notice
Author Scott Greene

Murder Crow

Hit Dice: 8
Armor Class: 4 [15]
Attacks: 2 claws (1d4), bite (1d6)
Saving Throw: 8
Special: Eye-rake, death throes
Move: 6/30 (flying)
Alignment: Neutrality
Challenge Level/XP: 9/1,100

Murder crows resemble standard crows except that they stand nearly 4 feet tall with a wingspan of 9 feet. Their tattered feathers are black and carry the stench of death. The eyes of a murder crow are bleak and hollow, showing no signs of emotion or life. Murder crows attack with their jagged beaks and sinister talons. If a murder crow hits an opponent with both claw attacks in the same round, the victim must save or be blinded for 1d4 days or until healed. When killed, a murder crow explodes into a murder of undead ravens.

Undead Raven Swarm: HD 7; AC 6[13]; Atk Swarm (3d6); Move 18 (flying); Save 9; CL/XP 8/800; Special: Disease, distraction, eye-rake

The Pealing Bell

A small stone bell tower rises in the Boneshay Cemetery. Toppled, broken stones surround the crumbling structure in a ragged circle. The ground is pawed and churned, with numerous decayed bodies clawed from their graves. Many corpses are missing arms and legs. The weathered headstones are heavily scratched.

A wooden ladder is propped against the squat tower and reaches to a landing where a 15-foot-tall iron bell lies on its side in the shattered cupola. The bell's iron shell is rusted through in ragged spots. The fetid smell of decay hangs heavy in the air. The bell rings out randomly, the lonely sound echoing across the graveyard. The sound is sharp and distinct, like a hammer strike on metal.

A murder crow makes its gory nest inside the toppled bell. The undead bird yanked off the arms and legs of many of the dead to layer its nest. The nest is six feet across with four foot high sides. The undead bird spies on PCs through the rust spots. It pecks at the iron shell with its ragged beak to draw prey closer.

The bird launches out of the bell's opening if the limbs are moved. It spreads its wings immediately and flaps viciously toward the nearest PC with a shriek. The crow aims for an eye-rake on its first pass, then sails into the sky to circle around to come in behind intruders. It caws just before it strikes, hoping to get them to look up just as its claws slice into their face.

Copyright Notice

M

Murder-Born

Hit Dice: 6
Armor Class: 4 [15]
Attacks: 1 incorporeal touch (1d6)
Saving Throw: 11
Special: Despondent wail, +1 magic weapons to hit
Move: 15 (flying)
Alignment: Chaos
Challenge Level/XP: 7/600

A murder-born appears as a ghostly image with translucent, yet delicate features. Its unholy eyes rage with absolute and thorough evil that reflects its hatred for the living. Spawned of hatred when both mother and child are murdered, the rapacious soul of the unborn sometimes rises as a foul and corrupt spirit. A murder-born's incorporeal touch does 1d6 points of damage. Twice per day, a murder-born can unleash a child-like wail that causes creatures to be overcome with despair (save resists) and results in a -1 penalty to saving throws for 24 hours. Magic weapons are required to hit the incorporeal murder-born.

The Sounds in the Walls

The Whaling Inn sits on the edge of a promontory overlooking the Scourging Sea. The inn is a two-story structure that has seen finer days; broken windows are boarded up, while the white banister leading to the front door is split and peeling. Boards creak underfoot in a well-worn path to the faded doorway. The old innkeeper Arl Nethup welcomes visitors, although he's as deaf as a post and as difficult to understand because of his thick accent.

The interior of the inn is pleasant, a far cry from the harsh surroundings of the fishing town. The inn was an orphanage before tragedy befell nearly 75 years ago. At the time, a young woman who worked with the orphans found herself pregnant by a fisherman who never returned from the harsh waters. She hid her shame, but the townsfolk soon knew of her condition. The fisherman's parents blamed her for leading their boy to distraction – and ending with his death on the open waters.

Their hatred bubbled over in their second son, who took a ragtag bunch of hooligans to help convince the girl to leave the village. One thing led to another, and the girl was murdered and her body boarded up within the walls. No one looked too hard for the missing woman.

It was a year after her murder that the screams began in the orphanage's walls. The wails were loud and unnerving, driving the owners to sell the building to an entrepreneur who reopened it as a tourist spot called the Wailing Inn. A spate of suicides by guests led to his downfall, and the inn fell into disrepair. Finally, Arj bought and reopened the inn, but misunderstood the name. When he repainted the signs, he unintentionally renamed it the Whaling Inn, a name that has stuck for the past 30 years. The inn is currently the only place to stay within the small village, and prices are reasonable.

At midnight, wails begin in the building, the sounds emanating from within the walls. Arj sleeps peacefully through it all; PCs staying the night won't be so lucky.

The inn is the home of murder-born twins that hide in the walls where they and their mother were killed and their bodies still rest. The twin spirits look identical, and flit through the hollow space between the walls, reaching through broken gaps in the bricks and floorboards to touch PCs.

Only one room is silent – the chamber where the murder-borns' mother is entombed. PCs can put an end to the murder-borns' rampage by removing the woman's bones and burying them in the nearby churchyard.

Copyright Notice
Author Scott Greene.

Nazalor

Hit Dice: 8
Armor Class: 4 [15]
Attacks: 2 claws (1d8) and bite (1d8)
Saving Throw: 8
Special: Stun
Move: 6
Alignment: Neutrality
Challenge Level/XP: 8/800

A nazalor is 7-foot-tall bipedal, stocky, bronze furred hyena with slightly oversized claws and fangs. Its fur is bronze in color with varying shades depending on the creature's age (young nazalors are brighter in color while an aged nazalor's coat is dull). Its eyes are usually green or brown. If a nazalor hits an opponent with both claws and its bite in the same round, the opponent must save or be stunned for 1d2 rounds from the ferociousness of the attack.

Night Hunter

A moonless sky leaves the scrublands draped in deep darkness. Fireflies flit in swirling paths, their glowing trails standing out against the night. The sounds of animals – the roars of lions, the huffs of wild boars, and the silent thumps of hooves in the dirt – fill the nighttime air. Stunted trees stand silent in the gloom.

A nazalor huntress named Fisi stalks the wildlands, her eyes glowing a faint green. Fisi is a vicious predator, and her scent drives even the great jungle cats to abandon the plains. Fisi bears the wounds of her run-ins with the lions, as the great claw marks across her face attest, but she also wears those same claws woven into the fur of her body after she ripped them from the dead cat's paws. The bipedal hyena lives in a stone cave where she raises three nazalor pups. The pups are a couple of months from setting out on their own to find their own hunting grounds to terrorize.

Copyright Notice
Author Scott Greene.

Necrophidius

Hit Dice: 3+3
Armor Class: 1 [18]
Attack: Bite (1d8 plus paralysis)
Saving Throw: 14
Special: Dance of death, paralysis
Move: 12
Alignment: Neutrality
Challenge Level/XP: 5/240

The necrophidius appears to be a great skeletal snake topped with a human skull. To the dismay of some, it is not undead and therefore cannot be turned or rebuked. The necrophidius is a construct created by a magic-user to serve as a guardian or assassin. A typical necrophidius is 10 feet long.

A necrophidius can entrance opponents by swaying back and forth. Those within 30 feet viewing the dancing snake must succeed on a saving throw (adding a +1 bonus for high wisdom) or be unable to act for 2d4 rounds. Victims are dazed for the duration of the effect and cannot take any action other than defending themselves.

A living creature bitten by a necrophidius must succeed on a saving throw or be paralyzed for 1d6 minutes.

Rattler

A variation of the necrophidius, the rattler is constructed from the skeletal remains of a giant rattlesnake. During the creation process, the tail rattle is left intact and magicked to create a *confusion* effect on those that hear it rattle. The rattler uses the same statistics as the standard necrophidius except it does not have the necrophidius's dance of death special attack. Instead it gains the special attack detailed below.

By shaking its tail rattle, the creature emits a rattling noise to a range of 30 feet. Those within the area that hear this rattle must succeed on a saving throw or be affected as by a *confusion* spell for 2d4 rounds.

Construction

A necrophidius' body consists of a human skull and the skeletal remains of a constrictor snake treated with rare oils and powders worth at least 1,000 gp. Creating the body requires the cooperation of a master sculptor and a 10th level magic-user that can cast *charm person* (or *confusion*) and *polymorph*.

Cone Experimentation

In the hills overlooking a lazy river there is a picturesque chateau, home to a miserly baroness. The baroness is not popular among her people, not so much because of cruelty, but rather because of her somber mood and the shabby state of the manorial village. The peasants of the manor graze sheep and keep swine and grow crops of wheat, barley and grapes. The vineyards belong exclusively to the baroness. The baroness grows tiny, sweet grapes and turns them into a light, sweet white wine, much favored by the swaggering young merchant class in the nearby market town.

Beneath the baroness' chateau there is a large cellar complex in which one can find pantries, an armory, two secret rooms (one containing an iron maiden) and a wine cellar. The wine cellar has a locked iron door - the stoutest door in the entire complex, even stronger than the door of the armory. Inside there are two wooden racks holding irregularly shaped bottles of wine. The racks reach from floor to ceiling and contain a total of 40 bottles of wine, worth about 10 gp per bottle. Five casks, each holding about 20 gallons, are set at the back of the room and sealed in parafin wax. Each cask holds a tincture of vinegar, blood and pitchblende, as well as a growing a homonculus.

The homonculi are in various states of completion. When finished, they will be almost perfect duplicates of powerful nobles in the region. The baroness is an alchemist and believes she has perfected the formula for creating these clones. At her next gala party, she will replace her rivals and become the power behind the palatine duchy in which she dwells. This operation has cost her most of her fortune (hence the shabbiness in her manorial village).

Another of her creations, a necrophidius, guards the chamber.

Credit

The Necrophidius originally appeared in the First Edition *Fiend Folio* (© TSR/Wizards of the Coast, 1981) and is used by permission.

Copyright Notice

Author Scott Greene, based on original material by Simon Tilbrook.

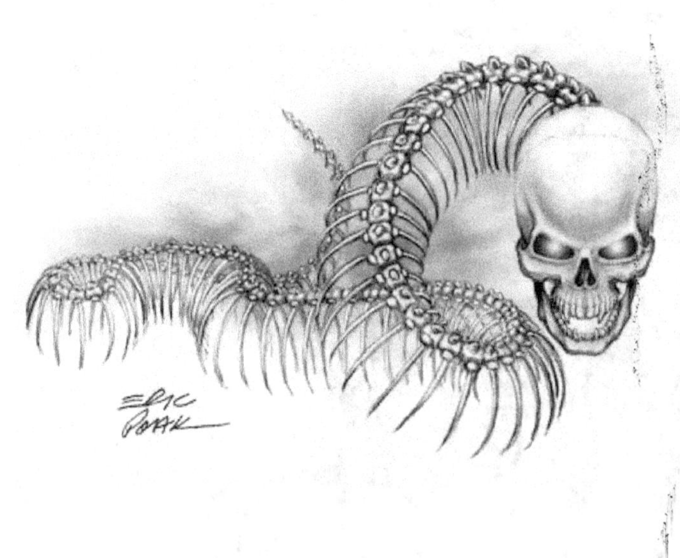

Nereid

Hit Dice: 4
Armor Class: 3 [16]
Attack: Poison spittle (ranged attack, poison)
Saving Throw: 13
Special: Beguilement, kiss, poison spittle, spells, change shape, magic resistance (40%), transparency, vulnerability
Move: 12/15 (swimming)
Alignment: Neutrality (chaotic tendencies)
Challenge Level/XP: 8/800

Nereids are elemental fey that spend most of their time swimming through the Elemental Plane of Water. Occasionally one finds her way into the Material Plane and takes up temporary residence in lakes, rivers, springs, pools, or inland seas. Many sailors, seafarers, pirates, and other sea-goers have met their ends at the hands of a nereid. Their natural beauty lures men to their doom, for behind the beauty of the honeyed ones lies certain death for any creature that tries to steal a glance or kiss from a nereid.

A nereid can assume the shape of either a male or female humanoid, and almost always assumes a female form unless encountering an all-female party of adventurers. In humanoid form, she can use any of her special attacks and special qualities and can wield weapons and wear armor (though a nereid rarely does so). In her water form, she cannot use any of her special attacks or special qualities, except as noted below. A nereid in water form moves at her swim speed and can flow through cracks, under doors, and through small openings. In this form she retains her damage reduction and AC and gains immunity to poison. A nereid is effectively invisible in water until she assumes humanoid form.

A nereid's natural form is that of a small pool of water. She can assume a humanoid form at will and usually employs this form when on the Material Plane. Some are arrayed in robes of white or gold, but most appear unclothed. All nereid in humanoid form wear a shawl of white or gold draped over their shoulders.

Nereids shy away from combat and flee at the first sign of conflict if possible. If a nereid encounters only female opponents, she assumes the shape of a handsomely striking male humanoid. A nereid that is attacked can attempt a saving throw. If successful, she takes no damage and assumes her natural watery form and flows away.

A creature of the opposite sex viewing a nereid must make succeed on a saving throw or be instantly smitten and beguiled. This effect is similar to an *charm monster* spell and lasts as long as the nereid is in view. Females viewing a nereid in male form gain a +2 bonus on their saving throw.

Any creature meeting the lips of a nereid must succeed on a saving throw or take 1d4 points of damage as the nereid floods the creature's lungs with sea water. Each round thereafter, for the next 10 rounds, the victim must make a saving throw or take 1d4 points of damage. Three consecutive successful saves means the character has coughed up enough water to shake the effects of this attack and takes no further damage. An affected creature can take no actions other than to defend itself in any round it takes damage from this ability. At 0 or less hit points, the victim falls unconscious. In the next round, he drowns. Holding one's breath does not prevent drowning (water is already in the lungs). A *dispel magic, break enchantment, remove curse, heal* spell, or successful DC 20 Heal check halts the damage if applied before the creature reaches 0 or less hit points. Nereids are not prone to giving kisses. An opponent that attempts to force a kiss must succeed on a successful grapple check against the nereid.

Once per round, a nereid can spit a stream of watery poison at an opponent within 20 feet. A successful ranged attack that ignores armor is required to hit. A target hit must succeed on a saving throw or be blinded (as the spell) for 2d6 rounds. A character can take a full round to wash away the poison using water or similar liquid.

A nereid can form a volume of water within 30 feet into the shape of a serpent formed of water. A watery serpent is about 6 feet long. It has the same number of hit points as the nereid who created it, and its AC is 4 [15]. Its attacks as the nereid and deals 1d6 points of damage on each successful attack against an opponent.

A nereid need not concentrate to maintain the watery serpent. She can direct it to a new target as a move action if she wishes. At hit points 0, the serpent collapses into normal water. A nereid can only have one such watery serpent in existence at a given time. The watery serpent lasts until destroyed or until the nereid dismisses it or dies.

At will, nereids can *lower water* and *part water*.

The nereid's shawl contains a portion of her life force. If it is ever destroyed, the nereid to which it belongs immediately and forever dissolves into formless water.

Sea God's Shrine

In a wild, mountainous district of the kingdom there is a magnificent shrine the sea god. The shrine is notable not only for its distance (40 miles) from the sea, but also for its inhabitant, a nereid.

The nereid most often takes the form of a beautiful woman, a woman who bears a striking resemblance to the grandmother of the present king. Her shrine consists of eleven thick, marble pillars surrounding a pool of crystal clear water so deep one cannot perceive the bottom. In fact, this pool is connected to the Elemental Plane of Water. A person swimming more than 100 feet into the pool will find themselves in the elemental plane. A statue in limestone of the sea god stands astride the pool.

The nereid shares her shrine with a giant, venomous serpent (3 HD, 15 hp). One of the pillars is hollow and can be accessed from beneath the surface of the pool via a narrow tunnel. The tunnel is located 12 feet below the surface and is small enough that only a halfling would be able to swim into it and have a hope of getting back out. Inside this hollow pool the nereid stores offerings to the temple. These offerings might include 3d10 x 100 sp, 2d8 x 100 gp and a silver ewer worth 1d4 x 50 gp.

Copyright Notice
Author Scott Greene, based on original material by Gary Gygax.

Netherspark

Hit Dice: 10
Armor Class: 3 [16]
Attacks: 2 slams (1d6)
Saving Throw: 5
Special: Negative energy ray, negative energy burst
Move: 6
Alignment: Neutrality
Challenge Level/XP: 13/2,300

A netherspark is a 6-foot-tall humanoid whose form is composed of dark matter. Its head is featureless and sports no eyes, ears, nose, or mouth. It wears no clothes, and bands of silver and white crackle and dance in its form. A netherspark radiates an aura of negative energy that does 1 point of damage to any creature in a 10-foot radius. Undead heal 1 point each round. Once every 1d4 rounds, a netherspark can release a burst of negative energy in a 20-foot radius that does 1d8 points of damage (undead heal 1d8 points). A netherspark can release a ray of energy in a 40-foot line that drains 1 level (save resists).

The Good, the Bad And the Netherspark

The iron door to this chamber is bolted and locked from the outside. Beyond the door lies a half-dome room with a flat stone floor. Two spheres the size of wagon wheels hover 10 feet above the ground. The spheres rotate around one another, seeming to attract and repel each other's presence. Silent white and black lightning fills the room originating from the spheres. The beams of energy leave short-lived trails of white and black marks on the room's surfaces. Below the spheres are two kneeling angel statues and two kneeling demonic statues with their arms raised as if reaching for the gyrating energy balls. The statues alternate between angel and demon.

Regardless of PCs' actions, a black energy beam flashes across any living creature viewing the room through the opened door. The beam appears harmless, but the spheres immediately begin rotating at incredible speeds. Within moments, the black sphere overtakes the white in a sudden burst of absolute darkness. The ebon burst extinguishes all light sources immediately, although they maybe relit or cast. Permanent magical light sources relight after 1d4 hours. The spheres disappear and the statues turn into oozing mud leaving a netherspark in their wake.

Copyright Notice
Author Scott Greene.

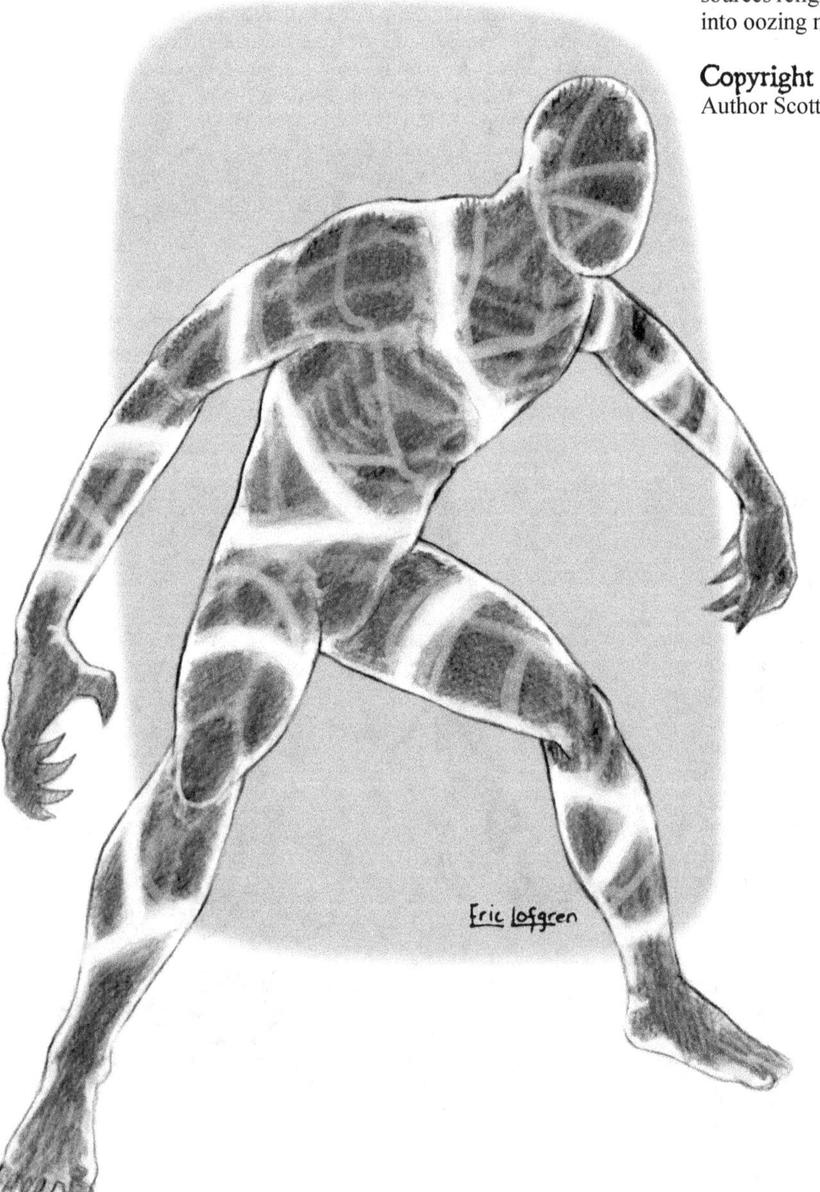

Nilbog

Hit Dice: 1d6
Armor Class: 4 [15]
Attack: 1 mace (1d6) or javelin (1d4)
Saving Throw: 18
Special: Spatio-temporal reversal, damage reversal
Move: 9
Alignment: Chaos
Challenge Level/XP: 1/15

The nilbog is a goblin afflicted with a strange space-time reversal disease known as nilbogism. The disease appears to occur when overly heavy use of magic strains the fabric of the space-time continuum and leads to some very strange localized events. The disease only affects goblins and is not transmitted by them. In appearance, nilbogs are indistinguishable from goblins.

A nilbog constantly emanates an aura of *confusion* in a 20-foot-radius. A creature in the area must succeed on a saving throw or be affected.

When struck by any attack that would normally damage it, the nilbog actually gains hit points equal to the damage the attack would have otherwise dealt. A nilbog gains any extra hit points above its normal total as temporary hit points, though it can never have more than twice its normal hit points.

The nilbog can only be damaged through the use of curative magic and effects (*cure light wounds* and healing potions, for instance). Curative magic deals damage equal to the amount it would normally heal.

Slavers of the Underworld

While circumnavigating a large lake set in the midst of low, tropical hills populated by several herds of elephants you come across a guest house. The guest house is built of white stone and set on a gentle rise overlooking the lake in a place where the elephants seem to enjoy congregating. On the other side of the rise there are terraced fields of tea and pepper and at the bottom of the hill, in a swampy area, rice fields. A wooden hand bridge spans the swampy area, allowing a number of free villagers who dwell on a hill in sight of the guest house to access their fields. The owner of the guest house, a pleasant but rather dull-witted fellow who claims to be an exiled duke, does not own the village, but he does purchase their goods.

If one can overcome the xenophobia of the villagers, they will learn that the duke is quite mad and that those of his guests that do not disappear end up leaving after no more than 24 hours, some a bit touched in the head themselves.

The duke will assure people that this is not the case. He sets a fine table, with heaping trenchers of fish on rice with slices of citrons, spicy curries of okra, peanuts and carrots and generous goblets of sura (a rice wine) and much smaller glasses of brandy wine. The quarters in the guest house are open to the night air, with only wooden latices and sheer cotton curtains protecting one from the large mosquitos that prowl the night. The guest house usually has four rooms available, each able to comfortably house two people and each set in the corners of the guest house's ground floor. A dining room, kitchen and entry make up the remainder of the ground floor while the upper floor contains a large, open patio/sitting area, a library of scrolls and books and the large bedchamber of the duke. A staircase separates the floors, with a door at the bottom and a second door at the top. Both doors are thick oak and locked at night.

There is a 1 in 6 chance each night that a band of nilbogs who dwell in caverns deep beneath the guest house will conduct a raid. The bizarre creatures are primarily slave traders of the underworld, taking captives down the weird, winding stair in the guest house's wine cellar to their own lair, which connects via tunnels to many other lairs of subterranean folk. Large captives are sold to the duergar to haul rock from their mines, attractive folk to the drow to be turned into house servants (they prefer eunuchs, so watch out fellas) and just about everyone else to the hobgoblins, grimlocks or bugbears to be used as slave labor and cannon fodder.

The nilbog band is composed of 1d10 x 100 nilbogs plus as many noncombatants. The nilbogs are led by one 3 HD sub-chief per 20 warriors and one 5 HD chief. Their lair consists of a large central chamber wherein is kept the sacred fire beneath an obsidian slab (used for cooking and the occaisional slow, painful sacrifice) and many smaller living chambers connected to the central chamber. The warriors wear leather armor and carry shields made from the hardened caparaces of purple-black beetles. They carry long, barbed whips and maces with large metal disc heads on flexible lengths of thick leather.

The nilbog's treasure might consist of 1d20 x 10 cp, 1d20 x 100 sp, 1d4 x 100 gp, and a brass buckle set with a moonstone worth 1d8 x 100 gp. The buckle is worn by the chief.

Credit

The Nilbog originally appeared in the First Edition *Fiend Folio* (© TSR/ Wizards of the Coast, 1981) and is used by permission.

Copyright Notice

Author Scott Greene, based on original material by Roger Musson.

Niln (Vapor Horror)

Hit Dice: 5
Armor Class: 3 [16]
Attacks: 1 slam (1d6)
Saving Throw: 12
Special: Drench, drowning fog
Move: 24 (flying)
Alignment: Neutrality
Challenge Level/XP: 5/240

Nilns are large, amorphous clouds of nearly transparent vapor. Small water droplets dance and play around their form and occasionally drop to the ground. Three large sapphire droplets function as eyes. When manipulating objects or attacking, nilns form wispy and vaporous tendrils that coat everything in water and put out open flames. Once per day, the niln can create a muggy cloud around it that spreads to fill a 20-foot radius. This moving fog fills a victim's lungs with water as if he is drowning (2d6 damage, save resists).

Steam Heat

The Haunted Bathhouse of Hylat is a three-room stone building on the grounds of the old Koilton Estate. Steam from a gurgling mineral hot spring fills the bathhouse with steamy vapors. The steam vents upward through a small circular opening cut into the floor in the center of the middle room. The temperature in the two outer rooms hovers at 90 degrees, while the center room is an uncomfortable 110 degrees. Enchanted gold rocks spit and hiss in the water, creating the thick clouds of steam. The water smells heavily of sulfur, and is supposed to healing properties. There are 6 gold rocks, each worth 50 gp.

A niln lives inside the watery hole, and rises out with the steam clouds if anyone disturbs the enchanted gold. The niln revels in the intense heat and drowns anyone who tries to take that away from it.

Copyright Notice

Nuckalavee

Hit Dice: 8
Armor Class: 2 [17]
Attacks: 2 hooves (1d6), bite (1d6) and 1 weapon (2d8)
Saving Throw: 8
Special: Breath weapon, fearful presence
Move: 18
Alignment: Chaos
Challenge Level/XP: 9/1,100

A nuckalavee is a large skinless warhorse with a rider of similar make-up, though closer inspection reveals the rider is actually part of the monster itself, growing straight out of the horse's back. The monster's internal organs, veins that carry its blackened blood, and corded muscles are all visible. Its body is covered with a thin layer of putrid reddish mucus. The sight of a nuckalavee incites fear in creatures within 30 feet that see it (as per the spell, save resists). Nuckalavee relish combat and attack with a combination of weapon, bite and hoof. Once every four rounds, the nuckalavee can breathe a cloud of noxious gas from its horse head that liquefies organs of those around it (6d6 damage, save for half).

The Warhorse Warlord

A partially skinned warhorse stampedes through the PCs' camp, the animal's hide ripped in wide flapping strips down its sides. Blood sprays in thick droplets behind it as it runs. The animal screams in terror and pain.

Chasing it is Death-Bringer, a self-named nuckalavee killer who refuses to allow any stallions into his Wyndes Forest home. The massive warhorse warlord arrives in a flash of blade, stamping hooves, skinned flesh and taut muscle. The Death-Bringer takes mares for his harem, and kills stallions – and their owners – for food. The nuckalavee gives up his pursuit of the fleeing horse (it'll be dead in a day if not healed) if PCs have mounts with them.

The Death-Bringer keeps a herd of 30 mares that graze around a mud-and-dirt lean-to in the center of the forest. The mares remain close to the nuckalavee's lair out of fear more than anything else. A saddle from a past meal contains 100 gp and a horse bowl that fills with clear water on command.

Copyright Notice
Author Scott Greene.

Oakman

Hit Dice: 3
Armor Class: 8 [11]
Attacks: +1 staff (1d6+1)
Saving Throw: 14
Special: Magic weapon, tree stride
Move: 6/9 (climb)
Alignment: Chaos
Challenge Level/XP: 3/60

An oakman stands just less than 4 feet tall. Its skin is brownish-green and as tough as tree bark, and he has unkempt green hair. Its eyes are either green or brown and its nose is slightly large and bulbous. Any oaken staff or club wielded by an oakman is considered a +1 weapon. An oakman is usually bound to a single enormous oak that he can never stray more than 1 mile from. He uses his tree stride ability to travel between trees to roam his territory. An oakman likes to sit in his tree and insult passers-by.

Mossy Oak

Along the path stands a mighty oak. Its limbs sag with an abundance of acorns. Hundreds of names and limericks have been carved into its monstrous trunk. A thin wisp of smoke drifts upward to where a small weathered man lounges on a limb just out of reach. Dressed in a muted green suit, he gnaws on a long pipe with knotty teeth. This wisecracking oakman goes by the name Dimbort Oakjob. He enjoys badgering travelers and smoking his pipe weed. He never gives a straight answer and is often cruel and rude in his taunts, puns and insults. Example of his jabs include:

• Your mother's armpits are so hairy, it looks like she has a bugbear in a headlock.

• You'll never be the man your mother is …

• Talking to you is as appealing as playing leapfrog with unicorns.

• I've met ghouls with less offensive breath than yours.

• You're as welcome as fleas in a gnolls' den.

• Now go away or I shall taunt you a second time.

• Someone said you are not fit to sleep with orcs. I stuck up for the orcs.

• The orc-breeding is certainly obvious in your family.

• He's so short, his hair smells like feet.

• He'd steal the straw from his mother's kennel.

• I certainly hope you're sterile.

• You're as strong as an ogre and almost as intelligent.

After a bit of fun, Dimbort requests an errand. In turn, he promises to make a special magical moss cake that will grant the consumer wondrous powers. Oakmen are known for their extraordinary culinary skills and magical talents. While he has plenty of moss locally to create moss cakes, it takes a rare exotic moss named Sylvan's Beard to make something truly great. Since he cannot venture far from his tree, he needs someone to harvest the rare moss. Just down the road a piece is a small rocky knob. A cave at the top of the hill has a mystical spring, around which grows the pink moss. Dimbort needs enough to fill a basket, of which he just happens to have a few lying around. He promises the rewards are well worth the stroll through the woods. The moss cakes he bakes have the ability to cure disease and rid the body of poisons. *(See the **Geon** and **Giant, Cave** for more on this encounter.)*

Copyright Notice
Author Erica Balsley.

Obsidian Minotaur

Hit Dice: 12
Armor Class: -2 [21]
Attack: 2 claws (2d8 plus 1d6 fire), breath weapon
Saving Throw: 3
Special: Breath weapon, burn, immune to magic
Move: 9
Alignment: Neutrality
Challenge Level/XP: 16/3200

An obsidian minotaur stands 12 feet tall and weighs roughly 2,000 pounds. It appears to be a minotaur carved from a single block of obsidian and then animated via some eldritch ritual. Small pinpoints of blue light can be seen in its eyes.

The obsidian minotaur is often employed by spellcasters as a guardian or assassin. As a guardian, the obsidian minotaur activates when trespassers enter an area it is programmed to protect. As an assassin, it actively hunts down the targeted victim.

Once every 1d4+1 rounds, an obsidian minotaur can expel a cloud of gas directly in front of it. The cloud fills a 10-foot cube and lasts for 1 round before dispersing. Any creature in the area must succeed on a saving throw or be slowed (as the *slow* spell).

The claws of an obsidian minotaur deal 1d6 points of burning damage each time they hit. A creature hit must succeed on a saving throw or take an additional 1d6 points of fire damage for 1d4+1 rounds as clothes ignite and armor becomes searing hot.

An obsidian minotaur is immune to most spells. Certain spells and effects function differently against the creature as noted below.

A *transmute rock to mud* spell slows it (as the *slow* spell) for 2d6 rounds, with no saving throw, while *transmute mud to rock* heals all of its hit points.

A *stone to flesh* spell does not actually change the obsidian minotaur's structure but negates its immunity to magic for 1 full round.

Construction

An obsidian minotaur is sculpted from 2,500 pounds of black obsidian worth at least 3,000 gp. Assembling the body requires a 17th level magic-user and a master sculptor. The magic-user must be able to cast fireball and wish.

Ceaseless Diligence

The story of the obsidian minotaur is well known in the low country. It seems that 200 years ago a thief by the name of Billy Mire stole something of value from a powerful magic-user (her daughter, to be precise). Billy Mire and his lady love escaped clean away, and the canny thief had the werewithal to keep their location hidden from the sorcerous powers of the magic-user.

Possessed with a powerful thirst for vengeance, the magic-user never forgave the thief and eventually put her fortune and her knowledge to the task of constructing an obsidian minotaur. Merchant vessels plying the waves between the new and old worlds brought her a massive slab of obsidian cut from the hills around a sacred volcano. Rare, expensive unguents were purchased from traders to the east. A master sculptor from the house of the golden patriarch of the south was hired to create the beast. With the magic-user's final breath, she charged her new creation with the task of killing Billy Mire. Unfortunately, she did this without passing on the knowledge of his appearance.

For 200 years, the obsidian minotaur has wandered the lowlands, stopping any it sees and bellowing out the same question, "Be you Billy Mire the Thief?". Of course, nobody, even a person unfortunate enough to share that legendary thief's name, is stupid enough to answer in the affirmative, and the beast plods on, unable to magically discern the thief's location and not bright enough to search outside the lowlands.

Copyright Notice

Author Scott Greene.

Ogren

Hit Dice: 2
Armor Class: 7 [12]
Attacks: 1 weapon (1d8)
Saving Throw: 16
Special: None
Move: 9
Alignment: Chaos
Challenge Level/XP: 2/30

Ogrens are 6- to 8-foot-tall stocky humanoids with hairy hides of dark brown, yellowish-brown, or gray. Their eyes are generally gray or black, though some do have green or blue eyes. Hair color ranges from brown or black to dark red or gray. Most ogren have long hair and rarely if ever sport facial hair. The typical ogren lives to 100 years of age. Ogrens are a mix of a male ogre and a female hobgoblin.

Stop the Wedding!

Occral Tusk-breaker of the Rockbasher Tribe has to find a bride before the new moon. He's already past the age when his warrior brethren took wives, and the daily taunts and beatings he endures are driving him over the edge.

Quarn Morningfever, the Rockbasher's shaman, told the young ogren he'd "find his mate in the vale." Quarn meant the Mastadon Vale, but Occral misheard "pale" and decided he was chosen to find a human or elf wife. He packed his weapons, put on his cleanest loincloth, and left the tribe that night.

He's been watching the entrance to the farming village of Horcross for three days, but no one so far has struck his fancy. The problem is further compounded by the fact that the ogren is fasting to purify himself for his marriage, leaving him starving, slightly dehydrated, and a little delirious.

He's beyond caring about what his "mate" looks like, and is ready to find any PC camping out in the open forest. He storms into camp, snatches up a sleeping "mate," and dashes into the forest. He heads immediately back to his tribe to "prove himself" by marrying his chosen during the next full moon.

Copyright Notice
Author Scott Greene.

Ogrillon

Hit Dice: 2
Armor Class: 5 [14]
Attack: 2 strikes (1d4+1)
Saving Throw: 16
Special: Reinforced fists
Move: 12
Alignment: Chaos
Challenge Level/XP: 2/30

Ogrillons are a fierce half-ogre race born of a union between a female orc and a male ogre. They tend to act like ogres, but they are far more violent and aggressive than their larger kin. Ogrillons are usually only slightly taller than orcs, with features that strongly favor their orc parent, so much so that most ogrillons are indiscernible from normal orcs. About 10% of ogrillons resemble their ogre parent. Ogrillon's skin is covered in closely fitting bony plates and nodes akin to an alligator.

Ogrillons love nothing more than combat. They are a race so inborn to be warriors that they seem almost depressed and dejected when they are not involved in melee. They only time an ogrillon laughs is when it is the center of a whirlwind of melee and covered in its opponent's blood. Ogrillons do not care for armor or weapons and in fact carry very little gear at all. They do, however, like gold pieces and usually keep a few in a filthy pouch with other shiny trinkets as lucky charms.

Ogrillons speak orc and ogre, and about 10% are intelligent enough to have learned the common tongue.

Ogrillons disdain the use of armor, relying solely on their natural armor to protect them. They also disdain the use of weapons, preferring to leap headlong into a fray with fists swinging madly. Ogrillons are considered to be armed even when unarmed (i.e., they do not provoke attacks of opportunity from armed opponents when attacking them and can themselves still make an attack of opportunity against an opponent that attacks unarmed). Additionally, they always deal lethal damage rather than nonlethal damage when fighting unarmed.

A Tale of Two Tribes

Between two sister cities (daughters of Marduk and thoroughly sentient) there is a thick range of mountains. The only pass through the mountains winds up on a rugged volcanic field of flat-topped volcanoes and domes of brownish-green volcanic glass and slowflake obsidian. The land is fairly barren save for some stubby, cantankerous stands of grass and woody fluorescing golden shrubs.

The volcanic field is inhabited by two tribes of ogrillons, the Eaters of Hearts and the Drinkers of Blood, both consisting of 5d6 ogrillons. The names of the tribes are quite accurate and do a fine job of summing up their key cultural traits. The Eaters dwell in the northern portion of the field in tents of animal hide set up at the obsidian base of a flat-topped volcano, while the Drinkers roam the southern portions in a number of small warbands that dwell in old volcanic tubes. Each tribe is ruled by a chief (5 to 7 HD) and has as its primary form of entertainment the capture of the royal post that runs between the sister cities.

The royal post consists of teams of adventurers and explorers hired to move correspondence and cargo between the cities. Few other outsiders venture onto the volcanic field. Post expeditions are sporadic, to keep the ogrillons from preparing elaborate attacks. Encounters occur on a roll of 1-3 on 1d6. A roll of one indicates a warband of 1d6+2 ogrillons from the Eaters of Hearts, a roll of two a similar warband of ogrillon from the Drinkers of Blood and a roll of three indicates a warband from each tribe. When a warband of both tribes is present, there is a fair chance they will attack one another instead of the intruders.

A typical tribal treasure consists of 1d12 x 10 cp, 2d12 x 100 sp and 2d12 x 10 gp.

Credit

The Ogrillon originally appeared in the First Edition *Fiend Folio* (© TSR/Wizards of the Coast, 1981) and is used by permission.

Copyright Notice

Authors Scott Greene and Erica Balsley, based on original material by R. K. R. Chilman.

Oil Shark

Hit Dice: 9
Armor Class: 6 [13]
Attacks: 1 bite (1d8+4)
Saving Throw: 6
Special: immune to fire
Move: 24 (swim)
Alignment: Neutrality
Challenge Level/XP: 9/1,100

Oil sharks are, on average, about 20 feet long, though they can reach lengths of 40 feet or more. Oil sharks resembles standard sharks with blackish-blue, metallic scales and dull gray eyes. They are blind and rely completely upon their "sonar" to hunt their prey. They are immune to fire.

Oil and Water

The sea blazes with burning oil, the air above the water thick with black smoke that is visible from miles away. Fire leaps from wave to wave, and burning dolphins and other sea creatures surface briefly before bursting into flame. Drifts of seaweed burn on the surface, a floating bonfire tossed by the currents. A dying mermaid lies across a chunk of drifting wood, her tail severed cleanly. Three other mermaids swim around their injured sister, slapping at the water as large fins split the sea.

A natural crevice on the ocean floor split apart during a recent undersea quake and released a natural reservoir of oil into the water. The oil burst upward in a billowing cloud, forming a patch of oil miles wide across the surface. A spark of lightning ignited the patch into this current inferno. Left alone, the oil burns for another week before the reservoir empties.

A dozen oil sharks swim around the conflagration in wide circles around and through the burning pitch. A colony of mermaids was the first victims of the voracious monsters, with a mere handful escaping the gnashing jaws. They plead with passing sailors for aid in getting rid of the foul creatures polluting their ocean. They offer 10 giant pearls (600 gp each) for helping them.

Copyright Notice

Olive Slime

Olive slime is a plantlike growth found in dark, damp underground areas. It is sticky, wet, and olive drab in color. It clings to walls, ceilings, and floors and consumes any organic matter it contacts. Olive slime can detect prey by vibration to a range of 30 feet and drops from ceilings and walls when it detects movement underneath it.

When a patch of olive slime drops and attaches to a foe (the host), it secretes a numbing poison that makes its presence go unnoticed. A creature viewing the host can successfully notice the olive slime on a roll of 1 on 1d6. Within 5 feet of the host, the olive slime is easily noticed.

An olive slime that has attached itself affects the thinking pattern of its host so the host's main concern becomes how to feed and protect the olive slime (including keeping the creature hidden from any adventuring companions). This effect is similar to a *charm monster* spell. If a creature attempts to remove the olive slime from the host, the host either attacks that creature or attempts to flee the area. The only way to successfully break the brain link is to destroy the olive slime, destroy the host, or remove the olive slime from the host.

A single patch of olive slime deals 1d6 points of constitution damage each day as it devours flesh, replacing skin and muscle tissue. Additionally, the host must double its normal food intake each day or sustain an additional 1 point of constitution damage each day. On days the host does not eat twice its normal food intake it does not naturally heal any damage (including ability damage). At constitution 0, the host dies and its body transforms into a slime zombie. (See the slime zombie below.)

Olive slime can be burned, frozen, or cut away (dealing an equal amount of damage to the host as well). Anything that deals acid, cold or fire damage, or a *cure disease* spell destroys a patch of olive slime.

Slime Zombie

Hit Dice: 3
Armor Class: 3 [16]
Attack: Slam (1d6 plus infestation)
Saving Throw: 14
Special: Infestation, death throes, mind link, telepathic bond, immunity to electricity
Move: 9
Alignment: Neutrality
Challenge Level/XP: 6/400

Slime zombies (or olive slime creatures) are created when a living creature is slain by a patch of olive slime (see that entry). The slime zombie's sole purpose for existence is to capture or kill new prey for its master (i.e., the olive slime that created it).

A slime zombie resembles a humanoid blob, olive drab in color. The creature bears no distinguishing marks or facial features. It can speak to others of its kind through telepathy, but otherwise makes no sound or noise.

Any creature hit by the slime zombie's attack must succeed on a saving throw or be infested with olive slime. This infestation works as described in the olive slime entry.

When a slime zombie is brought to 0 hit points, its structure collapses and it transforms in a single round as a pool of olive slime (see that entry in this book).

A slime zombie is linked symbiotically with the patch of olive slime that created it. This link has a maximum range of 200 miles. Both the slime zombie and olive slime must be on the same plane of existence.

Olive slime zombies have a telepathic bond with each other to a range of 100 feet if they were created by the same olive slime. This bond allows them rudimentary communication with one another.

Credit

The Olive Slime Creature originally appeared in the First Edition module *S4 Lost Caverns of Tsojcanth* (© TSR/Wizards of the Coast, 1982) and later in the First Edition *Monster Manual II* (© TSR/Wizards of the Coast, 1983) and is used by permission.

Copyright Notice

Author Scott Greene, based on original material by Gary Gygax.

Sweaty Palms

While traversing the deeper portions of the underworld, the adventurers come across a peculiar sound - a tinny clink-clank that echoes through the tunnels in a strange, lazy rhythm. The sound comes from a gray-headed tinker and trader. The trader walks next to a half-starved and frightened mule, his pots and pans clanging as he walks. His eyes are vacant, his skin clammy and pale. The man is under the control of an olive slime, the slime having attached itself to his back and now working its way down his arms. Being polite (and devious), he will offer his hand to visitors, allowing a portion of the slime to attack them.

Credit

The Olive Slime originally appeared in the First Edition module *S4 Lost Caverns of Tsojcanth* (© TSR/Wizards of the Coast, 1982) and later in the First Edition *Monster Manual II* (© TSR/Wizards of the Coast, 1983) and is used by permission.

Copyright Notice

Author Scott Greene, based on original material by Gary Gygax.

Onyx Deer

Hit Dice: 5
Armor Class: 5 [14]
Attacks: 2 hooves (1d4), 1 gore (1d8) and bite (1d6)
Saving Throw: 9
Special: Bellow, petrification
Move: 18
Alignment: Neutrality
Challenge Level/XP: 7/600

These intelligent herd animals resemble large deer, with dark brown heads and chests changing to light brown along the rest of its body. Most have a large white patch on their back and rump. An onyx deer has huge antlers, at least as wide as a human is tall. Twice per day, an onyx deer can unleash a bellow that instills fear (as per the spell) in any creature within 100 feet that hears it and fails a save to resist. There is a 10% cumulative chance each time an opponent is bitten by an onyx deer that he turns to stone (onyx).

Deerly Departed

Stone animals litter a mile-square area of the Hargstolt Woods. Petrified rabbits munch on leaves, deer stand unblinking in the treeline, and a lone stone wolf crouches in mid-growl. The animals are solid granite, and pitted and discolored from the elements.

Animals aren't the only things in the odd landscape. Lying on his back in a clump of thick weeds is Ernst Doxil. The naked woodsman's body is curled up asleep, although a large bite is visible on his bare thigh. A stone to flesh spell cures the sleeping woodsman, who doesn't realize he's been missing for nearly three years. He wakes up thinking it's the next morning and is surprised to find himself naked (his nightclothes disintegrated around him while his stone body slept).

An onyx deer chanced upon Ernst while he slept, and delivered the bite that turned the woodsman to stone. The same deer is responsible for the animals throughout the Hargstolt Woods. The territorial deer bellows at intruders, hoping to stun them long enough to deliver its bite.

Copyright Notice

Ooze, Amber

Hit Dice: 1
Armor Class: 6 [13]
Attacks: —
Saving Throw: 17
Special: Poison
Move: 4
Alignment: Neutrality
Challenge Level/XP: 1/15

An amber ooze is approximately 1 foot in diameter, and is a dark amber color and smells of ale. Attracted to liquor, the ooze hides in kegs and wineskins. If ingested, amber ooze secretes a poison that does 1d6 points of damage each day the ooze remains in a victim. The host is allowed a save each day to expel the ooze.

Drink and Be Merry

Five drunken men stagger into the Last Drop Tavern, each carrying a small keg of ale. The men are celebrating the groom's wedding in the morning and are making the most of his last day of bachelorhood with an all-night bender that has already made its way through three taverns. The group props the small ale kegs on the bar, pays the bartender a hefty sum to tap and serve them, and promises free ale for everyone.

Unfortunately, the groomsmen were too cheap to spring for the "good stuff" and bought the ale from a side alley dealer. Unbeknownst to them, three of the five kegs contain a mix of alcohol and amber oozes. There's a 3 in 6 chance that any PC who partakes of the free drinks gets an amber ooze in his frothy glass.

Copyright Notice
Author Erica Balsley.

Ooze, Crystal

Hit Dice: 4
Armor Class: 7 [12]
Attack: Strike (2d6 plus paralysis)
Saving Throw: 13
Special: Acid, paralysis, immune to acid, cold and fire, transparent, water dependent
Move: 3/6 (swimming)
Alignment: Neutrality
Challenge Level/XP: 6/400

The crystal ooze is an aquatic variety of the gray ooze. It is semitransparent and clear, almost impossible to see in the water and looks like nothing more than a puddle of water. The crystal ooze can grow to a length of up to 8 feet and a thickness of about 6 inches.

A crystal ooze secretes a digestive acid that quickly dissolves organic material, but not metal. Half of the damage from a melee hit is from this acid. Non-metal armor or clothing dissolves and becomes useless immediately unless its wearer succeeds on a saving throw. A wooden weapon that strikes a crystal ooze also dissolves immediately unless the wielder succeeds on a saving throw.

In addition to its digestive acid, a crystal ooze secretes a paralytic slime. A target hit by a crystal ooze's strike must succeed on a saving throw or be paralyzed for 3d6 rounds.

Crystal oozes can survive out of the water for 5 hours.

Drink to Health and Long Life

A company of yeoman archers is camped on the banks of a jungle river. Explorers from the north, they are clothed in tattered crimson tunics and wear chainmail hauberks and wide, flat helms of steel. The archers carry longbows and battle axes. The leader of the expedition is a smarmy merchant-prince who wears a long wig of flaxen curls and keeps a generous amount of wax on his long mustache. The merchant-prince and his men seek a *fountain of longevity*.

A stone's throw from the camp, but hidden by the thick foliage, is an ancient stone city. Little remains of it now but a few toppled pillars and overgrown piazzas. The largest pillar contains three ornate cisterns, each holding a shallow pool of water. Two of the three cisterns are home to crystal oozes, who use their resemblance to water to capture small birds and insects. The third cistern is actually fed by a underground spring via a number of thin tubes cut through the stone.

If more than 100 pounds is placed in the circular cistern the bottom corkscrews downward, finally coming to rest 30 feet under the surface in the bed of a swift, shallow stream if icy water. As soon as less than 100 pounds is resting on the descending stone pillar, it will corkscrew back up to its original position in the cistern. The stream originates as the run-off from a subterranean glacier that abuts a cavern warmed by volcanic action occuring beneath it.

The stream flows into a golden basin located in an alabaster cavern. The basin puts off a low, softly waxing and waning light. The water that fills the basin has the properties of a potion of longevity, though this magical effect only persists for 1 hour after the water is removed from the basin. A large (8 HD) crystal ooze dwells at the bottom of the basin, preserved by its magic but still devilishly hungry.

Credit

The Crystal Ooze originally appeared in the First Edition module *S4 The Lost Caverns of Tsojcanth* (© TSR/Wizards of the Coast, 1982) and later in the First Edition *Monster Manual II* (© TSR/Wizards of the Coast, 1983) and is used by permission.

Copyright Notice

Author Scott Greene, based on original material by Gary Gygax.

Ooze, Entropic

Hit Dice: 10
Armor Class: 8 [11]
Attacks: 1 pseudopod (2d6 + level drain)
Saving Throw: 5
Special: 25% magic resistant, devour soul
Move: 6
Alignment: Neutrality
Challenge Level/XP: 11/1,700

An entropic ooze is an amorphous mass of black protoplasm that covers an arca of 15 feet or more. It resembles a black pudding, for which it is often mistaken. Entropic oozes devour the souls of creatures they slay. Creatures that lose their souls in such a way cannot be returned to life until the entropic ooze containing the soul is slain. Living creatures hit by an entropic ooze lose two levels unless they save to resist the level drain.

Ooze, Entropic (Dark Matter)

Hit Dice: 20
Armor Class: 8 [11]
Attacks: 1 pseudopod (2d8 + level drain)
Saving Throw: 3
Special: 25% magic resistant, devour soul
Move: 6
Alignment: Neutrality
Challenge Level/XP: 23/1,700

Dark matter entropic oozes are amorphous masses of black protoplasm that cover areas of 25 feet or more. They are the larger cousins of regular entropic oozes. Dark matter entropic oozes devour the souls of creatures they slay. Creatures that lose their souls in such a way cannot be returned to life until the entropic ooze containing the soul is slain. Living creatures hit by an entropic ooze lose three levels unless they save to resist the level drain.

In His Hands

The 20-foot-tall corridor is topped by golden arches that raise the ceiling to a curving point. Columns line the white marble walls, and the floor is decorated with a checkerboard pattern of black-and-white tiles. The corridor is 30 feet from wall to wall and runs nearly 150 feet to a pale altar carved of feldspar.

Standing on each side of the corridor are 15-foot-tall stone statues carved into the image of a muscular man holding a black glass globe above his head. There are 16 of the statues, eight on each side of the hallway. One of the statues halfway down the corridor is actually a stone golem holding an entropic ooze trapped in a glass sphere. The golem slams the ooze to the tiled floor, splashing the creature across PCs in the area. The golem then defends the altar as the ooze devours PCs.

Copyright Notice
Author Scott Greene.

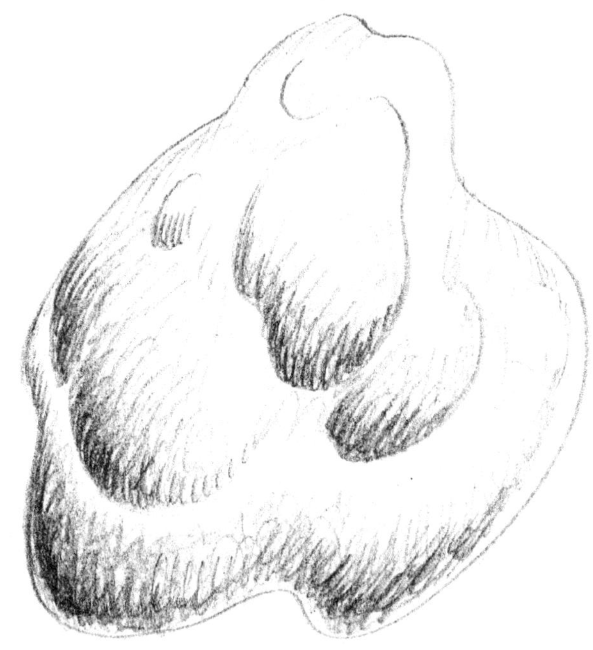

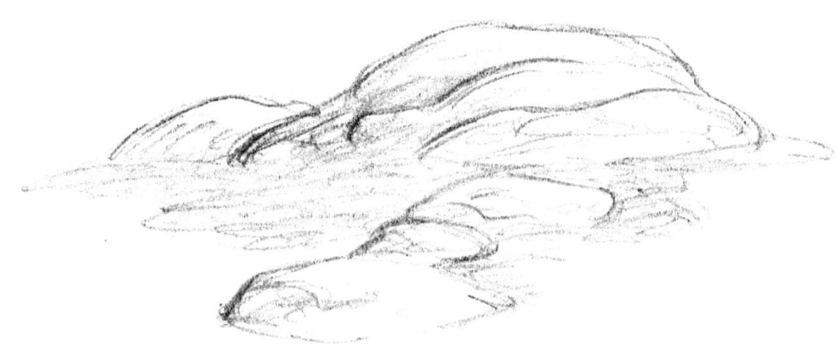

Ooze, Glacial

Hit Dice: 5
Armor Class: 8 [11]
Attacks: 1 slam (2d6)
Saving Throw: 12
Special: cold, engulf, transparent, immune to cold and blunt weapons
Move: 4/12 (swim)
Alignment: Neutrality
Challenge Level/XP: 6/400

A glacial ooze is an enormous jelly found in arctic climates. This creature appears as translucent bluish-white icy sludge about 10 feet on each side (though larger specimens have been encountered). This ooze is conjectured to be a relative of the gelatinous cube. Glacial oozes absorb all bodily fluids and liquids from a corpse, leaving behind a frozen and rotting husk. They can form a pseudopod to pummel foes, and their freezing touch deals 1d6 damage. If a glacial ooze strikes a foe, it can decide on its next attack to instead engulf that opponent (save avoids). Engulfed enemies take 1d6 points of cold damage until freed.

Icy Clutches

A moose skeleton juts from an icy wall in the frozen corridors of the Wailing Glacier. The skeletons gleams a bleached white. The tunnel is coated in a thick layer of ice that halves movement to avoid slipping on the treacherous ice (1d3 points of damage). The moose is caught in a glacial ooze controlled by the magic-user Paavo Janvarias, and is slowly being dissolved of flesh so the wizard can eventually animate its bones as one of his skeletal minions.

The ooze appears to be a portion of the wall, and lashes out to grab PCs who approach it. Riding alongside the moose skeleton are three animated skeletons ordered to defend the ooze. These skeletons step out of the glacial ooze's mass and attack if the ooze is struck.

Copyright Notice

Ooze, Magma

Hit Dice: 7
Armor Class: 8 [11]
Attack: Strike (2d6 plus 2d6 fire)
Saving Throw: 9
Special: Lava, immune to fire, double damage from cold, split
Move: 6
Alignment: Neutrality
Challenge Level/XP: 8/800

A magma ooze appears to be a pool of bubbling and churning molten rock. They are almost always found in or near volcanoes and other warm or hot places. Magma oozes do not approach water and are never found near such sources. Magma oozes can grow to a length of 10 feet, with a thickness of about 6 inches. A magma ooze can climbs walls and move across ceilings.

The magma ooze is formed of molten rock. Any melee hit deals 2d6 points of burning damage. The damage continues for 1d3 rounds, but deals only 1d6 points of damage per round during this time.

Slashing and piercing weapons deal no damage to a magma ooze. Instead, they split the creature into two identical oozes, each with half of the original's current hit points (round down). A magma ooze with 10 hit points or less cannot be further split.

Hot Bath!

In a pleasant valley of plum trees and tall, sweet grasses grazed upon by small, swift antelopes there is a chain of three small villages. Each village is built around an ancient, medicinal bath. These baths are small buildings of four chambers - an entry chamber clad in aged marble where people can disrobe, a side chamber where clothing is stored, a secondary chamber holding an idol that resembles a pot-bellied old man with large ears, squinty eyes, six arms (each holding a golden pear) and two long tusks jutting from his bottom jaw.

From the idol chamber one can climb down a narrow shaft into a grotto. The grotto holds a steaming medicinal spring with a few marble benches placed in it for bathers to sit on. The water is warm but not scalding and a long soak doubles a person's natural rate of healing and grants them a +1 bonus to save vs. disease and poison for 1d6 days.

The largest of the villages is dominated by a small castello, a stone keep ruled by the valley's prencipicu, a boy prince with golden ringlets and olive skin. His castello is surrounded by tall Italian cypresses and dozens of tall homes in orderly rows. In the prencipicu's cellars there is a deep grotto with a private bath, this one clad in marble with copper fixtures and attending servants. This bath is warmer than the others, for about 15 feet beneath it there is an active flow of magma. A magma ooze has recently flowed down to the cavern located directly beneath the bath. It has discovered a small crack through which it is working its way into the bath.

Copyright Notice

Author Scott Greene.

Ooze, Mercury

Hit Dice: 5
Armor Class: 7 [12]
Attack: Strike (2d4 plus mercury poisoning)
Saving Throw: 12
Special: Mercury poisoning
Move: 12/9 (climbing)
Alignment: Neutrality
Challenge Level/XP: 6/400

A mercury ooze resembles a swirling thick pool of silvery-white mercury about 8 feet long and 6 inches thick. It can compress its body to a thickness of 1 inch to slip into cracks and crevices.

A creature hit by a mercury ooze has 1 point of constitution and 1 point of dexterity permanently drained from them unless they pass a saving throw. One week after suffering the drain, the opponent must succeed on a saving throw or be affected as if by an *insanity* spell. The effects can be removed by the successful casting of a *wish* spell.

In Case of Emergency, Do Not Break Glass

A dusty, forgotten chamber in a dungeon is empty save for a crystal tube that runs from the ceiling to the floor. The tube is filled with a silvery gray fluid that seems to move at irregular speeds through the tube, sometimes from floor to ceiling, sometimes from ceiling to floor. The crystal tube is quite difficult to break. It will take 48 points of damage from metal weapons to finally shatter it and release the three mercury oozes that dwell within. Each time a weapon strikes the tube, a metallic keening fills the chamber, causing dust to fall from the ceiling and forcing all within the chamber to pass a saving throw or suffer 1d3 points of wisdom damage and become slightly disoriented. The tube connects two glass spheres, one embedded in the ceiling, the other the floor. The sphere in the floor contains a single diamond worth 2,500 gp.

Copyright Notice
Author Scott Greene.

Ooze, Metallic (Hoard Ooze)

Hit Dice: 7
Armor Class: 7 [12]
Attacks: 1 slam (1d8)
Saving Throw: 9
Special: Acid, irritating fumes, immune to blunt weapons
Move: 6/3 (climb)
Alignment: Neutrality
Challenge Level/XP: 8/800

A metallic ooze appears as a 9-foot blob of protoplasm of varying hue and color. Its form is coarse and rough giving it the appearance of piles of coins. A metallic ooze can flatten its body in order to squeeze through spaces and cracks. Metallic oozes come in a variety of sizes and colors: gold, silver, platinum, copper, brass, or bronze. They form pseudopods to attack foes. If a hoard ooze hits a creature, it can decide to engulf that opponent in the next round. Engulfed creatures are trapped inside its body, where the ooze's acid desolves organic matter (1d6 points of damage each round). If burned, the ooze emits a cloud of vapor that burns the eyes and lungs of creatures within 10 feet (2d6 damage, save for half).

Coin Collector

The underground passage opens into a 30-foot-square room lit by glowing globes that bob about the ceiling. Shadows dance around the chamber. In the center of the room, a 15-foot-long red dragon lies curled on the floor, a mound of coins scattered around its sides and snout. Steam rises in breathlike wisps from its nostrils, and the sound of its breathing fills the chamber.

The "dragon" is a life-like (but much smaller) ceramic idol to Horvorrance, a wyrm the underground Cult of Kalast worshipped before the creature was slain by a traveling knight. The dragon is incredibly detailed, and appears alive thanks to natural heating vents beneath it that create the wisps of steam and simulate its breathing.

The coins around the statue's base are a metallic ooze that presses against the false dragon's sides to draw heat from the underground vents. The ooze appears to be a mass of coins left to honor the dragon, but lashes out at anyone coming within range.

Copyright Notice
Author Scott Greene.

Ooze, Undead

Hit Dice: 6
Armor Class: 9 [10]
Attack: Strike (2d4 plus 1d6 cold)
Saving Throw: 11
Special: Engulf, skeletons
Move: 9/9 (climbing)
Alignment: Chaos
Challenge Level/XP: 8/800

This creature appears as a large, undulating mass of black goo from which rotted and broken bones protrude.

When an ooze moves across the grave of a restless and evil soul, a transformation takes place. The malevolent spirit, still tied to the rotting flesh consumed by the ooze, melds with the ooze. The result is a creature filled with hatred of the living and an intelligence and cunningness not normally known among its kind. The resulting undead ooze appears as a large, undulating mass of black goo from which rotted and broken bones protrude.

The undead ooze has an advantage over any other ooze: intelligence. It uses this new gift to its fullest in combat by attacking from surprise or by stalking its prey and attacking when the opportunity presents itself. The undead ooze attacks by slamming its body into its prey. It usually engulfs its foes or expels its skeleton allies to contend with its enemies. Undead oozes are undead and can be turned by clerics.

Although it moves slowly, an undead ooze can mow down creatures by moving over them. It cannot make a strike during a round in which it engulfs a creature. Targets who do not attempt to attack the ooze can attempt a saving throw to avoid being engulfed. An engulfed creature automatically takes strike damage each round.

Each round, in place of moving or striking, an undead ooze can expel 1d6 skeletons from its mass. Skeletons can act in the round they are expelled. Slain skeletons are engulfed by the undead ooze and can be reanimated and expelled again in 1 hour.

Just a Direction

You enter a chamber in the dungeon that is quite nondescript save for a large clockwork mechanism that takes up the center of the room. The mechanism consists of a number of gears and shafts connected to a spherical clock - that is to say, a sphere, half black, half white, with each side marked with twelve Roman numerals in brass. A stationary pointer indicates the time, the black and white sides of the rotating sphere indicate whether the time is A.M. or P.M. Atop the sphere there is the form of a squatting demon, also in brass.

The demon is animated, sentient and quick to strike up a conversation with visitors. It will claim that it can answer any question posed to it, but only at the appointed time (which will always be midnight). Any attempt to force information from the demon will end in a mild scolding, a wide, toothy grin and an admonition to return at midnight.

The demon is capable of answering most questions via a *legend lore* effect that it can evoke once per day. In truth, it can do this at any time, but prefers midnight, for that is when an undead ooze seeps slowly from the walls of the clock chamber. While adventurers' attentions are on the demon, the ooze can strike, entertaining the demon to no end.

Credit

The Undead Ooze originally appeared in Sword & Sorcery Studios' *Creature Collection* (© Sword & Sorcery Studios, 2000) and is used by permission. It has been modified from the original.

Copyright Notice

Author Scott Greene, based on original material by Sword & Sorcery Studios.

Ooze, Vampiric

Hit Dice: 8
Armor Class: 8 [11]
Attack: Strike (2d4 plus level drain)
Saving Throw: 8
Special: Level drain, create spawn, split, sunlight vulnerability
Move: 6/6 (climbing)
Alignment: Chaos
Challenge Level/XP: 10/1400

Some think the vampiric ooze was created by a lich using ancient and forbidden magic. Others believe the vampiric ooze was formed when an ochre jelly slew a vampire and absorbed it. Whatever the monster's origins, it looks like a thick, bubbling pool of mustard yellow muck. It can alter its shape so as to appear up to 12 feet long and 6 inches thick; it can also compress its body to slip through cracks as small as 1 inch wide. It spends its time slithering along floors, walls, and ceilings, or if above ground, hunting its prey at night.

The ooze's attacks drain one level unless the victim of the attack passes a saving throw. Any humanoid slain by a vampiric ooze becomes a zombie in 1d4 rounds. Spawn are under the command of the vampiric ooze that created them and remain enslaved until its death. They do not possess any of the abilities they had in life. For each such level drained, the vampiric ooze gains 1 Hit Dice.

Cold and electricity deal no damage to a vampiric ooze. Instead they cause the monster to split into two identical oozes, each with half of the original's current hit points (round down). A vampiric ooze with 10 hit points or less cannot be further split. Exposing a vampiric ooze to direct sunlight destroys it utterly if it cannot escape in one round.

Life Sucker

Your travels through the crooked woods bring you to the foot of a steep hill. Atop the hill there is the remains of a fortified temple that shows signs of a terrible and very hot fire. The ceiling of the temple has collapsed, taking much of the walls with it and leaving little more than a pile of rubble and melted metal.

Beneath the temple there is a crypt, once home to the vampire that seized the temple from an overconfident high priest (her husband) who sought to found a community of believers to extend the sway of Law into the chaotic wilderness.

After the fall of the bishop, his followers fled. In due time, a force of religious knights found their way to the temple and entered it intent on stamping out the curse of vampirism. As a result of their fight, the temple was burned and collapsed. The knights never left the temple, of course. Expecting a vampire, they were not prepared for the vampiric ooze that fell upon them as they threw open the vampire's casket and found it empty.

The vampiric ooze still dwells beneath the temple, oozing out of the rubble every so often to hunt. Beneath the rubble, in the crypt, one might find all that remains of the nine knights - their scorched platemail, melted holy symbols pressed to the cuirasses. In a secret cache beneath the casket there is 1d4 x 10,000 sp, 1d3 x 1,000 gp and a slender terracotta flask of sandalwood oil worth 200 gp.

Copyright Notice
Author Scott Greene.

ORCS

Orc tribes are feared and reviled throughout the planes for their depravities and their penchant for destruction and mindless violence. The vast majority of orcs are easy enough to identify by their jutting jaw, yellowed tusks, squinting eyes and hairy, brutally muscular frames. Their skin color tends to run the gamut from blue-black to grey, with putrid slime green being the most common. Many tribes of orcs however have adopted traits unique to their own species through interbreeding with other races, adaptation to climate and terrain, and the intervention of evil magicians or other-planar powers.

Orc, Black (Black Orc of Orcus)

Hit Dice: 2
Armor Class: 5 [14]
Attacks: Weapon, usually flail (two-handed) (1d8) or two-handed sword (1d10)
Saving Throw: 16
Special: None
Move: 12
Alignment: Chaos
Challenge Level/XP: 2/30

A head taller and slightly more intelligent than an ordinary orc, these foul brutes move in daylight as well as they do the darkness of their subterranean lairs. (They do not have the light sensitivity penalty normal orcs suffer).

Orc, Black (High Priest of Orcus)

Hit Dice: 7
Armor Class: 4 [15]
Attacks: Weapon, usually flail (two-handed) (1d8) or two-handed sword (1d10)
Saving Throw: 9
Special: Spells
Move: 9
Alignment: Chaos
Challenge Level/XP: 9/1,100

These black orcs are the undisputed leaders of massive orc tribes. Black orc high priests cast spells as 10th-level clerics.

The Siege Machine

A black iron juggernaut rolls through the forest just seven leagues outside the city walls. Its three-story walls are broken only by arrow slits near the crenellated roof. Bleached white skulls linked by iron chains decorate the sides. Two massive iron plated doors remain closed on the face of the iron behemoth, presumably concealing a battering ram. Two great smoke stacks bellow oily soot from its top. Two huge ballistae on swivel mounts are loaded with barbed spears. Long chains with hooks drag corpses from a recent siege.

The juggernaut is powered by the steam created by two enslaved fire elementals trapped within the boiler. Two dozen black orcs operate the machine, decimating all in its path. They use the juggernaut to attack defenseless villages and settlements.

Cyrene, a human high priestess of Orcus, holds an uncanny influence over the orcs as she commands the troops and controls the juggernaut. As a young lithe human with delicate features, she makes a stark contrast with her brutish crew.

Orc, Blood

Hit Dice: 2
Armor Class: 5 [14]
Attacks: Weapon, usually large two-handed axe (1d10)
Saving Throw: 16
Special: Frenzy
Move: 12
Alignment: Chaos
Challenge Level/XP: 2/30

A typical male blood orc stands over 6 feet tall and weighs around 200 pounds. Blood orcs' skin is dark reddish-black and their hair is black, dark brown, or crimson. A blood orc who smells or tastes blood (even his own) during combat flies into a frenzy and adds +2 to his attack rolls. Like normal orcs, they fight with a -1 to-hit penalty in sunlight.

To the Victors

In a remote corner of the known lands, smoke rises in large columns into the cloudless sky. A gnoll village once stood along a rocky creek bank. Piles of burning gnoll corpses surround the smoldering village. Severed gnoll heads are impaled on long spears embedded into the sward.

Most of the huts are burnt ruins, and gore and blood coat the ground. Two dozen blood orcs stand as victors amid the carnage. The orcs rummage through the spoils and ravage the gnoll survivors and slaves. The blood orcs are led by Two-Stump, a plump biclops. He carries a two-handed sword in each hand and a loaded ballista on his back.

Orc, Ghost-Faced

Hit Dice: 2
Armor Class: 5 [14]
Attacks: Weapon, usually large axe or two-handed sword (1d10)
Saving Throw: 16
Special: Invisible in shadows
Move: 12
Alignment: Chaos
Challenge Level/XP: 2/30

Ghost-faced orc are normal orcs that paint their faces with grotesque skull-like patterns. Whenever a ghost-faced orc stands still or moves slowly in shadows or darkness, it is essentially invisible. Their face paint makes them appear to be floating disembodied skulls. Like normal orcs, they fight with a -1 to-hit penalty in sunlight.

The Graves of Stone

Two rows of graves set into solid stone encircle a grotesque and bloated statue. Four graves sit in the inner row and sixteen in the outer. The graves are six feet by four feet wide holes cut three feet deep into solid rock. Each has a heavy stone lid lying atop it. The aged statue depicts Orcus grinning down upon the graves. Eight ghost-faced orcs guard the statue and the interred. Occasionally, a ranking priest of Orcus communes here to bask in the statue's presence. Panicked screams, pounding and scratching come from five graves. Fingers jut through small air holes in the stone lids.

Faithful of Orcus travel from afar to worship at this shrine. For many, it is the next and last step in their testament of devotion to the undead lord. The faithful sacrifice themselves by twos. Two unclothed and weaponless individuals lie down in the stone grave as the ghost-faced orcs seal them in with the stone lid. The sacrifices fight to the death inside the grave. The victor remains in the grave until death, surviving until his last moments on by consuming the flesh and drinking blood of his victim. Once the victor perishes, he returns as a ghoul, which the ghost-face orcs release into the world.

Orc, Greenskin

Hit Dice: 2
Armor Class: 5 [14]
Attacks: Weapon, usually spear (1d6) or scimitar (1d8) or short bow (1d6)
Saving Throw: 16
Special: Thieving abilities
Move: 12
Alignment: Chaos
Challenge Level/XP: 2/30

Wiry and quick, these slime-green orcs have long ears, smallish tusks, and coyote-like eyes. They shoot first and eat later. Greenskins are arboreal hunters with limited thieving abilities. They can use Climb Walls (86%); Hear Sounds (3 in 6); Hide in Shadows (15%); and Move Silently (25%). Greenskin orcs do not suffer any ill effects in sunlight like normal orcs.

Salt Mines

A young forest grows in the rich soil of a former lake. A massive sinkhole swallowed the water in the lake years ago, leaving a massive rocky gash in the ground. The trees reach a height of only 50 feet and the ground is soft and spongy. Methane seeping from the hole fills the forest with a horrible stench. The canyon-like sinkhole drops 150 feet into a seemingly endless natural borehole. The lakebed is filled with a bounty of quality salt crystals.

A tribe of greenskin orcs lays claim to the salt. Slaves mine the salt and the orcs then trade with local merchants to distribute the valued commodity. A 20-foot-tall wooden palisade built by the greenskin orcs surrounds the 300-foot-wide canyon. Six 30-foot-tall wooden towers overlook the saltpit and the surrounding woods. The canyon immediately drops away behind the wall. Wood, thatch and mud dwellings line the walls of the pit and provide shelter for the orcs and slaves. Wooden ramps, ladders and scaffolding line the cliff walls, providing access to the levels of the mine.

Bubbling pools of mud surround the wooden wall. These mud bubbles grow in massive mounds of hardened suds as the mud dries and traps the methane gas. The greenskin orcs discovered that flaming arrows ignite these mounds into fireball-like explosions. The damage dealt is relative to the size of the frothy mounds.

Orog

Hit Dice: 3
Armor Class: 2 [17]
Attack: Battleaxe (1d8+1) or javelin (1d4+1)
Saving Throw: 14
Special: None
Move: 12
Alignment: Chaos
Challenge Level/XP: 3/60

Orogs, also called elite orcs or greater orcs, are the much larger kin of normal orcs. They usually reach well over 6 feet tall but closely resemble normal orcs in all ways except build: orogs are much stronger and stockier. It is believed that orogs are the result of the union of a male orc and female ogre.

In contrast to lesser orcs, orogs are highly disciplined and straightforward. Orogs within an orc community quickly rise to leadership positions within their clan, although in orc armies the orogs will segregate themselves into all-orog military units. Orog military units are highly organized, tactically superior, and far more dangerous than those of normal orcs. Such orog units form the vanguard of the army to which they belong. Orogs do not separate themselves into their own clans, despite their tendency to self-segregate while in an orc army. Orogs wear platemail and carry large axes or swords.

Orogs speak orc, and about 25% master the common tongue, although their inflection often makes it appear every statement they make is posed as a question.

Lost Morale

The mountainous district you have wandered into is crawling with squads of orogs (1d10+10 in each, plus two 3 HD sergeants and one 5 HD lieutenant). There are a total of four roaming squads; encounters with them occur on a roll of 1-2 on 1d6 made each day and each night. The squads are attached to a besieging army that has cut off a stronghold built to hold a high mountain pass. The main army is encamped around the stronghold on the edges of a rocky meadow. The camp consists of leather tents and a number of timber and stone buildings hastily constructed to house supplies and officers. The main force consists of 2d4 x 10 warriors. There is one 3 HD sergeant per 10 warriors, five 5 HD lieutenants and three 7 HD captains. The orog warriors wear blackened chainmail and are armed with a variety of weapons. About 25% of the force is made up of crossbowmen (heavy crossbow, hand axe), 50% are heavy infantry (shield, pole arm, dagger) and the remainder sappers (pick and battle axe).

As is typical with the orcish races, the orogs are easily focused on killing, but tend to fall to infighting when forced to wait. Hurling stones from onagers and the odd raid into the countryside has not been enough to satisfy their lust for battle, and the camp is now divided into three camps, each based around its captain and existing in a tenuous peace with its rivals. The folk inside the stronghold are on the brink of surrender, with only their fear of the what the orogs will do to them keeping them throwing open their gates.

Credit

The Orog originally appeared in the Second Edition *Monstrous Compendium I* (© TSR/Wizards of the Coast, 1989) and is used by permission.

Copyright Notice

Authors Scott Greene and Erica Balsley, based on original material by Wizards of the Coast.

Paleoskeleton, Triceratops

Hit Dice: 15
Armor Class: 0 [19] front, 5[14] back
Attacks: 1 gore (4d8)
Saving Throw: 3
Special: Fossilize, charge, roar
Move: 12
Alignment: Neutrality
Challenge Level/XP: 17/3,500

A paleoskeleton triceratops is the fossilized remains of a long-dead dinosaur. The triceratops uses its horns to attack, and does double damage while charging. Once every 1d4 rounds, a paleoskeleton can turn any creature to stone with a successful strike (save resists). Once every other round, a paleoskeleton triceratops can unleash an eerie roar that causes creatures with fewer Hit Dice than the triceratops to flee in terror (as per a fear spell). Other types of prehistoric paleoskeleton dinosaurs are believed to exist.

No Bones About It

Deep in the southern jungles lies the fabled Bone Fortress of Danok Toh. The warlike indigenous tribes of the deep jungle unite against common foes behind the petrified bone walls of the massive stronghold. The ancient shaman Iztalkus rules the tribes with necromantic power, plant-imbued apes and hordes of juju zombies.

The petrified bones of thousands of dinosaurs line the stone walls of the fortress, some of the skeletons' bones jutting from the stone. One half of a triceratops skull adorns each of the front gates. The skull becomes complete when the doors are shut. At Iztalkus' command, the skull and some of the bones forming the gate step forth as paleoskeleton triceratops.

Copyright Notice

Author Erica Balsley.

Pech

Hit Dice: 4
Armor Class: 2 [17]
Attack: Heavy pick (1d4+1)
Saving Throw: 13
Special: Spells, stone knowledge, immunity to petrification, magic resistance (30%), light blindness
Move: 6
Alignment: Neutrality (lawful tendencies)
Challenge Level/XP: 6/400

A pech is a fey creature believed to have its origins on the Elemental Plane of Earth. On the Material Plane, pechs dwell deep underground in places rarely even seen by dwarves, drow, or other subterranean races. They are excellent stonemasons and are sometimes employed by other subterranean races for their skill at stoneworking (if such subterranean races can actually find the pech's lair). They are generally an isolated race and rarely venture far from their lairs.

Pechs never wear armor and most are arrayed in nothing more than a simple loincloth of brown or black fur. They stand as tall as a dwarf and have gangly arms and legs, broad hands and ochre-colored skin. Pech are universally bald and their large, bulbous eyes are stark white without any discernable pupils.

Pechs speak their own language, and some speak the languages of dwarves, gnomes, goblins and kobolds as well.

Pech are immune to all petrifying effects, such as a gorgon's breath, medusa's gaze or a flesh to stone spell. They are mastr masons and miners, and their extensive knowledge of stone gives them a +1 bonus to hit and damage against creatures made of stone or earth. Four times per day, a pech can cast *stone shape* and *stone tell*. Once per day, four pechs working together can cast *wall of stone*. Eight pechs working together can cast *conjuration of earth elemental* once per day.

Abrupt exposure to bright light blinds a pech for 1 round.

Antigravity Ore

In the deeper portions of a dungeon a band of delvers might come across what looks like a subterranean canal. The canal is about three feet wide and five feet high and runs at a slope of 20-degrees.

The "canal" is actually an aquifer constructed by a tribe of 1d20+20 pech miners and 1d10+10 pech females. The pech live about 2 miles away, the aquifer flowing into their stronghold from above. The aquifer runs through a stone lattice and down a 40-foot channel into a shallow pool that is also fed by three other aquifers. The pool is used by the pech for fishing, the gathering of molds and fungi and bathing.

The pool chamber is about forty feet in diameter. Two bridges arch over the pool, leading into long, low-ceilinged chambers used as living quarters, dining halls and kitchen facilities by the females of the tribe. The females live with their sisters and mother in these chambers, meeting their husbands only rarely in one of a dozen pleasant, secret grottos beneath the earth.

A number of ladders in the pool chamber lead up to the mine shafts where the males reside. The shafts are closed by heavy stone doors. The males live with their brothers and father in the shafts where they mine the deep earth for kavorite. The unrefined kavorite is unusually light; the metal's anti-gravity properties do not surface until it is refined by a skilled alchemist. The pech trade their kavorite with gnomes for foodstuffs and gems.

The total treasure of the pech consists of 1d10 pounds of hickory nuts (worth 200 gp per pound), 1d20 pounds of fagara (worth 100 gp per pound, 3d6 pounds of pistachios (worth 15 gp per pound), 1d10 sides of beef crusted with salt (worth 15 gp each), 1d6 terracotta icons depicting Ptah (worth 75 gp each), a silver and brass waist (worth 190 gp), a silver tiara worth 600 gp and a turquoise turtle (worth 20 gp).

Credit
The Pech originally appeared in *S4 Lost Caverns of Tsojcanth* (© TSR/Wizards of the Coast, 1982) and is used by permission.

Copyright Notice
Author Scott Greene, based on original material by Gary Gygax.

Phantasm

Hit Dice: 8
Armor Class: 3 [16]
Attacks: Incorporeal touch (1d6 + level drain)
Saving Throw: 8
Special: Level drain (1 level) with hit
Move: 9/15 (flying)
Alignment: Chaos
Challenge Level/XP: 9/1,100

Phantasms appear as translucent humanoid-shaped creatures with faintly discernable facial features resembling a human face twisted and corrupted by evil. Hair, if present, is formed of the immaterial stuff the phantasm is composed of. Their arms are long and thin and end in wisps of the very stuff they are made of. Likewise, their lower torso trails off into the same misty substance. The touch of a phantasm drains one level from living creatures.

Giving up the Ghost

A leprous stranger moves jerkily out of the Tallowstack Graveyard, his eyes wide and his mouth opening and closing silently. His clothes are torn and dirty, and his skin is sallow and sunken, his flesh hanging off his bones. Clumps of his hair are yanked out by the roots. Just three days ago the man weighed more than 300 pounds; he's now under 100. PCs looking in the direction he points see a yellowish glow rising from a crypt within the graveyard. The yellow light is a magical field that traps victims who enter it in a short stasis unless they save to avoid the effect. Dust and insects fly slowly through the wavering light, as if underwater.

Takaal Reel is a shell of his former self since he cut through the graveyard late one night and was possessed by a phantasm. The creature rides in the poor man now, draining his life. The phantasm knows poor Takaal won't last much longer, and is eager to find a new host. It has just a few hours remaining before Takaal dies. The phantasm is eager to find a new host before that time, and hopes to lure a PC into the ancient graveyard to switch bodies.

Copyright Notice

Phantom

Phantoms are translucent spirits of creatures that died a particularly violent death. A phantom appears much as it did in life, though its form is clearly translucent and incorporeal. Phantoms have no attack form other than causing fear. A phantom causes fear (by gaze) to any living creature within 30 feet of it (saving throw negates). Affected creatures flee in terror for 1d6 rounds. If the save is successful, that creature cannot be affected again by that phantom's fear for one day. A phantom is immune to all attack forms but can be destroyed through the casting of a *dispel evil* spell.

Phantom Treasure

In a crossroads of the dungeon you discover an iron chest, the surface of which it pitted and marred. About 30 feet away from the chest there is a skeleton that looks as though its clothing and leather armor was dissolved by acid. The acid is actually a trap activated by opening the chest, which is locked. The acid pours from the joints between the stones that make up the arched ceiling. If a person fails their saving throw, the acid pours on him and causes 1d6 points of damage per round until washed away with at least 1 gallon of water. To make matters worse, the skeleton's spirit now occupies the area as a phantom, making it difficult for adventurers to get through the intersection. The chest is, unfortunately, empty save for a gold filling from a tooth (worth 5 gp).

Credit

The Phantom originally appeared in the First Edition module *A2 Secret of the Slavers Stockade* (© TSR/Wizards of the Coast, 1981) and later in the First Edition *Monster Manual II* (© TSR/Wizards of the Coast, 1983) and is used by permission.

Copyright Notice

Author Scott Greene, based on original material by Harold Johnson and Tom Moldvay.

Phantom Stalker

Hit Dice: 6
Armor Class: 2 [17]
Attack: 2 burning claws (1d4 plus burn)
Saving Throw: 11
Special: Burn, death throes, find target, flames of healing, immunity to fire, polymorph, double damage from cold
Move: 12/24 (flying)
Alignment: Neutrality
Challenge Level/XP: 10/1400

Phantom stalkers live in the Elemental Plane of Fire. In its true form, a phantom stalker appears as a column of fire. It can take a human-shaped form, appearing as a muscular, fiery red humanoid about 8 feet tall. A phantom stalker rarely enters the Material Plane on its own. If encountered, it is usually in the employ of a spellcaster that has summoned it there to do his bidding. A phantom stalker can be summoned using a *summon monster IV* spell.

Anyone touching (or touched by) a phantom stalker must succeed on a saving throw or take an extra 1d6 points of damage as clothes ignite or armor becomes searing hot. The damage continues for another 1d4+4 rounds after the phantom stalker's last successful attack. Phantom stalkers can also ignite flammable materials with a touch. Once per day, a phantom stalker can alter its form per the *polymorph self* spell.

Any magical attack against a phantom stalker that deals fire damage heals 1 point of damage for every 3 points of damage it would otherwise deal. If the amount of healing would cause the phantom stalker to exceed its full normal hit points, it gains any excess as temporary hit points that last the remainder of the battle.

A phantom stalker reduced to 0 hit points or less expels a fiery blast equivalent to a six dice *fireball* to all creatures within 20 feet. A saving throw reduces the damage by half. A phantom stalker never uses this ability if it would harm the one that summoned it, unless the summoner itself is to blame for the phantom stalker's destruction (i.e., if the summoner attacks the stalker or orders it into battle against opponents that clearly outmatch it).

If the one who summoned the phantom stalker is slain while the stalker is on the Material Plane, the stalker can unerringly find the slayer. Once the slayer has been tracked and dealt with, the phantom stalker returns to its home plane.

Biding Time

It is a little known fact that many of the stars in the night sky are actually portals into the Elemental Plane of Fire. Around one such star in the sky there orbit dozens of large chunks of basalt. The largest of these was recently the scene of a terrible fight between rival wizards. In the course of their invocations and conjurations, one summoned into existence a phantom stalker. The other froze that stalker in place, giving her time to kill her rival and escape into the Astral Plane. The phantom stalker now sits and broods, calculating whether or not a leap into the star will bring him home.

This whole situation would mean next to nothing to your adventurers, save for the fact that the wizard in question holds an object of great value to the adventurers, and any attempt to locate that object by magical means will lead them to the chunk of basalt and the phantom stalker.

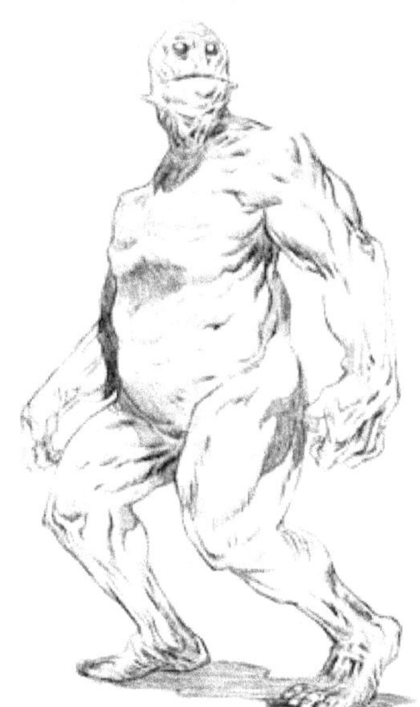

Credit

The Phantom Stalker originally appeared in the First Edition *Fiend Folio* (© TSR/Wizards of the Coast, 1981) and is used by permission.

Copyright Notice

Author Scott Greene, based on original material by Ian Livingstone.

Phase Flea, Giant

Hit Dice: 5 hp
Armor Class: 4 [15]
Attacks: 1 bite (1d3 + blood drain)
Saving Throw: 18
Special: Blood drain, disease, leap, phase shifting
Move: 6
Alignment: Neutrality
Challenge Level/XP: 1/15

A giant phase flea is about 1 foot long, with an oval flattened body. The insects live on the blood of warm-blooded animals. Up to three times per day, a phase flea can leap up to three times its Move rate. Phase fleas can shift out of phase with their surroundings (so they can be attacked only be ethereal creatures), only to come back into phase later for an attack. If a giant phase flea hits with a bite attack, it latches on to automatically drain the victim's blood (1d4 points of damage) in the next round. After it drains 4 total hit points, it leaps away to digest its meal. There is a 5% chance that a giant phase flea carries a disease.

Caught in the Mists

A swirling mist of ghostly vapors spins in the center of this small stone chamber. The vapors appear about a foot above the stone floor and end just short of the 10-foot-high ceiling. The mist is about three foot wide in the middle, and tapers at either end. Colors flash throughout the mist, and anyone staring into the vapors starts seeing scenes of his life playing out. The PC must save or become entranced by these images.

The mists are a shimmering portal to another plane that never fully closed. PCs can't travel to this empty void, but creatures on the other side don't have any trouble getting through. Four rounds after PCs enter the room, 10 phase fleas leap from the mists to attack.

Copyright Notice

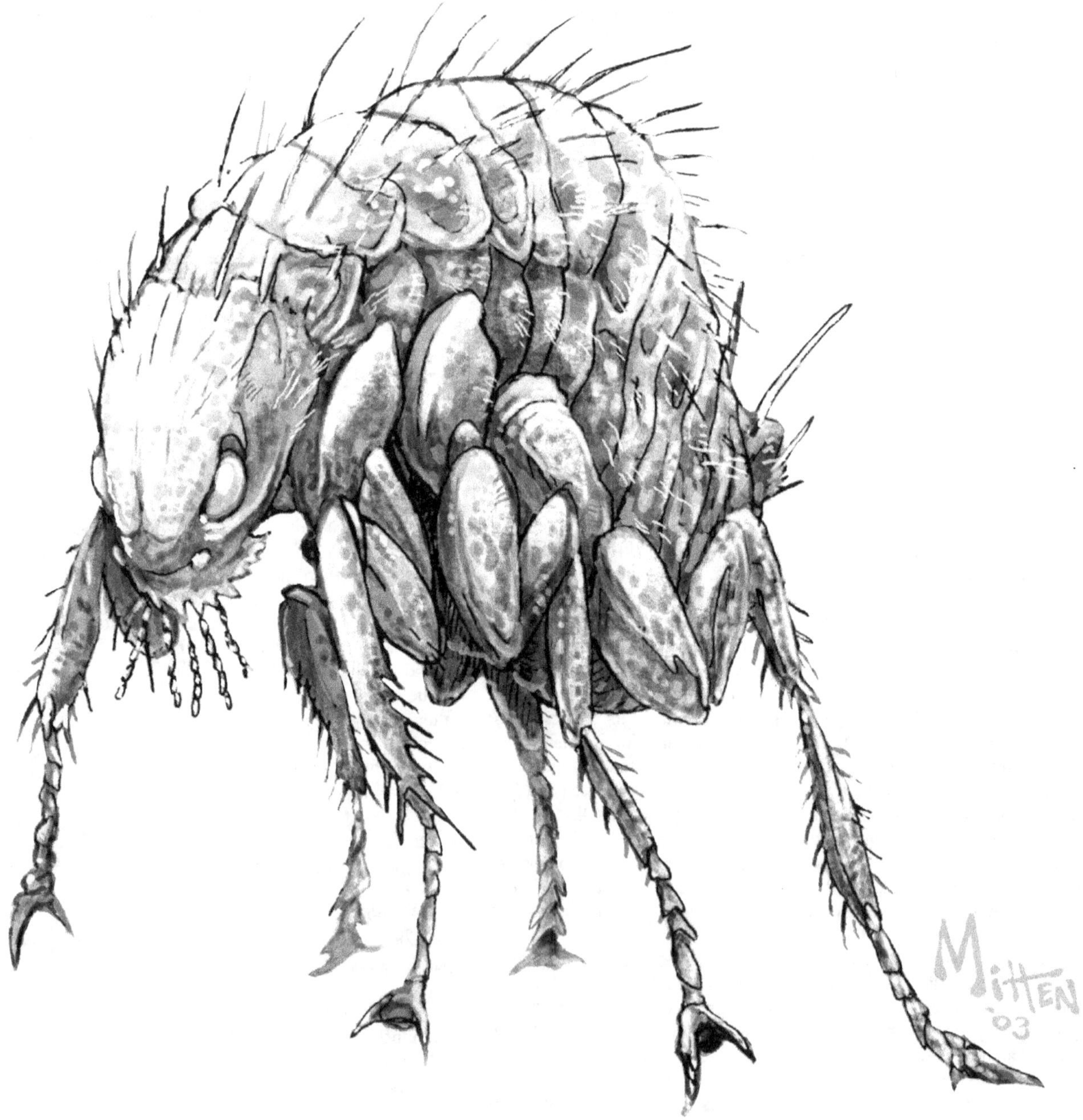

Phasma

Hit Dice: 7
Armor Class: 3 [16]
Attacks: Incorporeal touch (1d6)
Saving Throw: 9
Special: magical powers, create images
Move: 6/9 (flying)
Alignment: Chaos
Challenge Level/XP: 8/800

A phasma is a floating semi-transparent humanoid dressed in grayish robes. Its face is either nonexistent or concealed behind a translucent gray mask. A faint pulsating white light surrounds its form. Twice per day, a phasma can create a *phantasmal force* of the most fearsome creature imaginable to each subject within 30 feet. At will, a phasma can *detect good*. Three times per day, it can *dispel magic*.

All In Your Mind

The downward sloping tunnel empties into a nightmare of a chamber that is 30 feet wide by 70 feet long. The stone room's gray walls are covered in white scratches, as if someone dragged long fingernails down the rough bricks. The ceiling 10 feet overhead is covered in jagged mirror shards that reflect the floor one moment, then change to show a hellish chamber of fire pits where dead figures walk unheeded. Figures reach out of the floor, their faces pressed against the stones, and their arms reaching upward and clutching at freedom from the rock.

In the middle of the room, a pair of arms drops from the ceiling. Tied to the fingers of this set of hands are black threads supporting a twisted marionette dressed in an orange-and-yellow diamond-pattern outfit. The puppet's head is downcast, and the thing hangs five feet above the floor. The face is white and the eyes are sunken red orbs. Its lips are painted a midnight black.

At the far end of the room, a chair is turned away from PCs, although the top of the head of an old man with long wisps of gray hair can be seen. If PCs approach the chair, the hands reaching from the stone floor grasp at their legs to hold them in place. Shards of mirror fall from the ceiling to slice at their flesh. And the marionette dances and sways as if alive, then laughs at struggling PCs. The chair slowly rotates to face PCs, as a sibilant voice whispers their names. The old man in the chair is a corpse, his eyes gone and his mouth hanging open.

The entire chamber is a phantasmal force cast by a phasma residing in the corpse. The phasma waits for PCs to approach before it leaps from the old man to attack.

Copyright Notice
Author Scott Greene.

Phlogiston

Hit Dice: 4
Armor Class: 7 [12]
Attacks: 4 tendrils (1d6)
Saving Throw: 13
Special: Fire bolt, grab, death throes, resist fire
Move: 0 (immobile)
Alignment: Neutrality
Challenge Level/XP: 5/240

The phlogiston bush (known as a fire shrub by some sages) is an immobile plant found only in temperate regions. It resembles an ordinary shrub or bush with long leaves of silvery-green scattered sparsely across several small and twisted branches of brownish-green. Phlogiston bushes gain nourishment from the body fluids and organs of living creatures. The plant sends out tendrils to grab prey, then holds on while it digests the victim. If two tendrils hit the same victim, the plant grabs the creature and holds it, automatically inflicting 1d6 points of damage. Once every 1d4 rounds, the phlogiston bush can release a tiny bolt of fire in a 40-foot line that deals 2d4 points of fire damage (save for half). When reduced to 0 hit points, a phlogiston bush explodes in a concussive blast that deals 4d6 damage in a 10-foot radius (save for half).

Ignominious Assault

The Muricee Forest is thick with old timber and clinging vines. Animals scamper through the dense underbrush, and birds build large nests in the upper branches of the pines and termite-eaten elms. About an hour into the forest, the ground is scorched, and the remains of a small shack sit in an overgrown clearing. All that remains of the building are the burned stones forming its foundation, and heaps of charred wood collapsed on itself. A skeleton lies amid the clumps of burnt wood, its blackened bones broken and scattered. A rickety outhouse stands off to the edge of the clearing, its wooden door hanging slightly ajar. Inside the outhouse is a single hole cut through a wooden plank. Living in the smelly hole beneath the outhouse is a phlogiston bush that is barely getting by. The plant grew in the richly fertilized soil, but barely gets any light because of the outhouse above and the trees growing thickly around the clearing. The plant subsists on mice and other small animals that wander into the hole. The hungry plant shoots a fire bolt up through at anyone relieving themselves before sending its tendrils up to drag them down into the muck.

Copyright Notice
Author Scott Greene.

Phooka

Hit Dice: 4
Armor Class: 5 [14]
Attacks: 1 weapon (1d3)
Saving Throw: 13
Special: Alterate form, magical powers, tree stride, spell resistance (16%)
Move: 6
Alignment: Neutrality
Challenge Level/XP: 5/240

A phooka is a small hairy creature resembling a cross between a goblin and a child's fuzzy play bear. Phookas have wide-set, glowing, golden eyes and long, pointed ears like those of a donkey. They have a mouth to match their ears, complete with buck teeth. Phookas are tricksters and jokesters that revel in playing tricks on unwary travelers. A phooka's trickery may include turning itself into an enchanted pony and offer a stranger a ride, only to lead it through brambles and thorns at top speed, or to lead travelers to enchanted springs that cause them to fall into deep slumber and strip them of all their belongings and clothes, then leave behind clues as to where their possessions are hidden. A phooka can assume the shape of a mountain lion or wolf. They can create dancing lights three times per day. A phooka can enter a tree and move from it to another tree within 50 feet.

A Life of Jest

Ten-year-old Myrtie Mae is missing, and the only clue is a note in her room reading "I have the girl."

At first, her parents thought it was another of the endless pranks she and her "invisible friend" like to pull. They both remembered the time little Myrtie found a pony and took it to a friend's birthday party – and the horse charged across the field with the screaming boy clinging to its back. Or the time Myrtie said wanted to live in a pink house – and someone painted the house a phosphorescent salmon overnight.

But things became more serious when the girl didn't return last night. Neighbors are confused and scared. PCs who help search find odd clues about town: Giant footprints lead from the girl's window into trees, but vanish in the fresh loam between the oaks. A yellow sign on a small pole asks "Which way now?" Other signs say "That way" while more read "No, that way" with an arrow pointing in the opposite direction. One yellow sign simply points up … straight at a hornet's nest. Another points down, into waist-deep mud. A statue in town holds one of the girl's blonde pigtails.

Myrtie Mae is indeed with her mischievous invisible friend, a phooka named Jest. She's safe and sound in his burrow as the townspeople traipse through the forest looking for her. Jest pulls tricks on the searchers, then comes back to tell Myrtie about all the fun he's having. Myrtie plans to return home soon and slip into bed, although Jest puts a bucket of glue and feathers on top of the door to her room as one last joke.

Copyright Notice
Author Scott Greene.

Phycomid

Hit Dice: 4
Armor Class: 4 [15]
Attack: Fluid globule (1d6 acid plus spore infection)
Saving Throw: 13
Special: Acid, spore infection
Move: 3
Alignment: Neutrality
Challenge Level/XP: 5/240

A patch of phycomids is often found growing in garbage heaps, refuse, and other such places. A typical patch of phycomid covers an area of 2 feet. The actual number of mushroom-growths varies with the actual size of the patch. The mushroom caps are usually white, red, purple, or yellow in color, and the phycomid's body is milky white.

The phycomid attacks by extruding a small tube from its body and firing a glob of acid at a foe. The phycomid has a range increment of 5 feet and can fire a globule to a maximum range of 20 feet.

A creature hit by a phycomid's fluid globule attack must succeed on a saving throw or lose 1d2 points of constitution as tiny mushroom-like growths sprout from its body. Each turn (10 minutes) thereafter, until the victim receives a *cure disease* spell, he loses 1 point of constitution. At constitution 0, the victim dies and his body collapses to the ground, sprouting a new phycomid. Lost points of constitution return at the rate of 1 per day of rest.

Dungeoneer's Foot

The passage you are traversing runs into a large, hollow cavern, the walls of which appear to be cast from copper. The cavern is filled with brackish water and four "islands" of reddish stone allow one to pass from one side of the cavern to the exit on the other side without getting their feet wet, assuming they can leap about five feet from island to island.

The copper cavern is, in fact, an artificial construct. The walls are about one foot thick. It is located a larger cavern, such that knocking on a wall will produce a loud sound that echoes and reverberates for at least an hour.

The middle island in the cavern is inhabited by a patch of 1d3+1 phycomids growing on the remains of a dwarf. The dwarf still wears an amulet of protection from evil with a very basic map scratched into its reverse.

Credit

The Phycomid originally appeared in *Dragon #68* (© TSR/Wizards of the Coast, 1982) and later in the First Edition *Monster Manual II* (© TSR/Wizards of the Coast, 1983) and is used by permission.

Copyright Notice

Author Scott Greene, based on original material by Gary Gygax.

Piercer

Piercers resemble 1-foot long stalactites and are found underground in caves and caverns hanging from the ceiling waiting for living creatures to pass underneath. Those viewing a piercer have a 1 in 8 chance to discern its true nature (1 in 6 for dwarves); else it is overlooked and mistaken for a normal stalactite. Piercers gather in clusters of up to 20 creatures.

When a living creature stands in a square directly below a piercer, it drops and attempts to impale the unsuspecting foe. The creature can make a saving throw to avoid the piercer's attack. If the save fails, the target sustains 1d6 points of damage. If the save succeeds, the piercer misses its target and may not attack again until it climbs back into position. (Piercers have a move of 3). A piercer on the ground is easily dispatched, though touching or attacking it unarmed or with natural weapons causes it to secrete an acid that deals 1d4 points of acid damage to the opponent each time one of its attacks hits.

Piercers can grow to a length of 6 feet. Those of 2 to 4 feet in length deal 2d6 points of damage (plus 1d6 acid damage). Those of 5 to 6 feet deal 3d6 points of damage (plus 1d6 acid damage) if they hit.

That's Gotta Hurt

An underground chasm in a limestone cavern is spanned by a natural bridge of pinkish stone. The stone is damp from water dripping from stalactites overhead. The chasm is filled with a torrent of icy water that flows from higher caverns. Among the stalactites hanging over the bridge, which is about 6 feet wide and 36 feet long, there are 1d10+8 piercers. If one looks over the bridge into the torrent of water, they might notice the shells of a few pierces washed up on the sides, but otherwise must rely on their dungeoncraft to warn them of the danger of crossing the bridge.

Credit

The Piercer originally appeared in the *Strategic Review #3* (© TSR/Wizards of the Coast, 1975) and later in the First Edition *Monster Manual* (© TSR/Wizards of the Coast, 1977) and is used by permission.

Copyright Notice

Authors Scott Greene and Clark Peterson, based on original material by Gary Gygax.

Pit Hag

Hit Dice: 14
Armor Class: 3 [16]
Attacks: 2 claws (2d8) and bite (1d8), or pitchfork (1d8)
Saving Throw: 3
Special: Rend, spells, +1 magic weapons to hit, poison, immune to fire
Move: 12
Alignment: Chaos
Challenge Level/XP: 17/3,500

A pit hag is a 6-foot-tall female humanoid with crimson red skin, small upward pointing horns of golden-red and eyes the color of the fires of Hell. Its hands and feet end in wickedly sharp curved claws and its mouth is filled with razor-sharp fangs that they constantly lick with their forked black tongues. A pit hag has a small barbed tail. Pit hags attack with their claws or a wicked curved pitchfork. If she hits with both claws, the victim is held and the pit hag inflicts automatic damage with its claws and bites thereafter. Pit hags cast spells as an 11th-level Magic-User.

Dipped in Pain

The locked iron door to this chamber radiates unnatural warmth. The 120-foot-diameter room beyond resembles an image from hell. Five-foot-square marble flagstones encircle a 20-foot-diameter dais. The flagstones are composed of alternating bands of red and black tiles. The floor looks like a round chess board with the dais in the center. Evenly dispersed within each ring are five-foot-square pits set in the floor. There are seven bands of alternating red-and-black flagstones with four pits in all but the outer ring for a total of 24 pits. The pits contain:

Ring 1 (innermost): Fire, 1d6 points of damage.
Ring 2: Acid, 2d4 points of damage.
Ring 3: Oscillating spikes, 2d6 points of damage.
Ring 4: Grinding iron gears, 4d4 points of damage.
Ring 5: Whirling razor blades, 4d6 points of damage.
Ring 6: Green slime
Ring 7 (outermost): No pits.

Attached to a chain above each pit hangs a barely living human, elf or dwarf secured in locked manacles. The chains extend into holes in the ceiling. Once a ring on the floor (starting with the outer perimeter ring) is breached, the chains in the next inner ring begin dropping victims sequentially into the pit below them, one each round (determined randomly). Waving a hand, shooting an arrow or casting a spell over the floor ring releases a victim into the pit below and starts the process in motion. Any movement over the ring releases the chain so flying, jumping or climbing sets off the trap. Mostly commoners, the hanging victims instantly die horrible deaths once dropped into the pits. Helping the victims in any ring immediately starts the process in the next ring moving toward the dais.

In addition to torture devices, the dais holds an iron mechanism with levers and chains that extend into the ceiling above. This machine controls the chains to the hanging prisoners. Two obese black orc torturers carrying hooked halberds attend a pit hag who lounges on the dais. She cackles gleefully whenever anyone drops into a pit.

Only one of the prisoners has any experience as an adventurer. A bewildered dwarf located in the innermost ring is known as "The Baker of Molnar." He can survive a few rounds in the fire pit. He has neither baking skills nor any emotions to speak of. He simply follows orders and replies in vague disconnected thoughts.

Plant-Imbued Ape

Plant-Imbued Ape

Hit Dice: 7
Armor Class: 7 [12]
Attacks: 2 claws (1d6), 1 bite (1d6)
Saving Throw: 13
Special: +1 magic weapon needed to hit, magic resistance (10%), regenerate, vulnerable to acid and fire
Move: 12
Alignment: Neutrality
Challenge Level/XP: 8/800

A plant-imbued ape is a plant-like creature that assumes an animal shape. They act like standard apes. While in contact with the earth, they can regenerate 3 hit points per round as they draw new plants into their body to repair damage. The plant creatures can even regrow lopped-off heads and limbs. The only way to utterly kill a plant-imbued ape is to submerse it in acid or burn it. Through ancient rituals, elder druids can create diverse plant-imbued creatures.

The Entwining Temple

Legends from prehistoric times tell of the sacrifice of the virgin princess at the Hot Gates of Bythunova to appease the gods. But the gods, angered by the sacrifice of such beauty, turned the princess's corpse to jade as the plants of the wild consumed the temple. The city and its people have vanished with time, leaving only the remains of the temple.

A ring of vine-covered pillars topped by a roof of vegetation surrounds a pit in the temple's center. At the bottom of the pit lies a jade statue of the forgotten princess. A gold ceremonial dagger is imbedded in her chest.

The sentient vines grow on unhallowed ground, the tendrils slowly growing over and consuming living creatures. The vines spawn horrific replicas of those they consume. Currently, a band of plant-imbued gorillas thrives in the ruins.

Copyright Notice
Author Patrick Lawinger.

Poltergeist

Hit Dice: 2
Armor Class: 7 [12]
Attack: See text
Saving Throw: 16
Special: Fear, telekinesis, natural invisibility
Move: 3/6 (flying)
Alignment: Chaos
Challenge Level/XP: 5/240

Poltergeists are undead spirits that haunt the area where they died. A poltergeist has no material form and cannot manifest on the Material Plane. Most poltergeists are evil, as they are "trapped" in the area where they were killed and can never leave this area unless they are destroyed. This "prison" drives them mad and they come to hate all living creatures. Poltergeists are naturally invisible except when attacking. Their invisibility is inherent and cannot be dispelled or negated.

A poltergeist can create a telekinetic effect to hurl one object or creature within 10 feet to a distance of 60 feet. A creature hit by a thrown object must succeed on a saving throw or flee in terror for 2d6 rounds. A creature that successfully saves is immune to the fear effect of the same poltergeist for the remainder of the encounter.

Both wild and domesticated animals can sense the unnatural presence of a poltergeist at a distance of 30 feet. They will not willingly approach nearer than that and panic if forced to do so; they remain panicked as long as they are within that range.

Busted

A long gallery (20 feet wide, 40 feet long) in a dungeon has walls lined with thick shelves of oak. The shelves hang from iron chains. The shelves hold dozens of busts carved from soapstone, all of the same person, a man with an aquiline nose, high forehead, hair pulled back into a tail and thin, unforgiving lips. The sculptures are worth maybe 1 sp each and weight about 5 pounds a piece.

In the center of the gallery there is a low dais, atop of which there is an old wooden chair, battered and broken, the skeletal remains of a man (a close inspection might convince one that it is the man in the sculptures due to the size and shape of the forehead. Lying in front of this dais is the skeleton of another man, pierced in the back by an arrow, a rusty chisel covered in dried blood lying beneath one hand, a hammer beneath the other. Pieces of an shattered busts cover the floor, from the beginning of the gallery to the end.

The gallery was once owned by a subterranean warlord, a master of many orc tribes who was inordinately fond of his own face. A sculptor and amateur magic-user had the misfortune to have fallen into his hands on his first delve and was pressed into service as his "court sculptor". In time, he lost his mind and killed the warlord, dying seconds afterward by the hand of an orc archer. The orcs plundered their former master's underground lair and left, and so were not present for his rise as a poltergeist. The poltergeist will manifest in the center of the gallery, above its former skeleton. Once very fond of the busts, it now finds them excellent ammunition. A hit from a soapstone bust inflicts 1d6 points of damage.

Credit

The Poltergeist originally appeared in the First Edition *Fiend Folio* (© TSR/Wizards of the Coast, 1981) and is used by permission.

Copyright Notice

Author Scott Greene, based on original material by Lewis Pulsipher.

Proscriber

Hit Dice: 12
Armor Class: 1 [18]
Attacks: 1 weapon (1d8+2)
Saving Throw: 3
Special: Condemn, spell-like abilities, immune to poison, resists cold, fire and electricity
Move: 6
Alignment: Any
Challenge Level/XP: 15/2,900

A proscriber appears as an 8-foot tall warrior dressed in full plate armor, wielding a weapon (usually a sword or mace), and carrying a shield. Proscribers are the "messengers" of the gods and are sent to punish a cleric who has offended his deity. Proscribers vary in how they carry out this sentence, but it usually involves cursing the offending cleric (with blindness, a quest, or some other curse the Referee can devise). If particularly vile, the proscriber may cast *finger of death* or attack the cleric directly. Once per day, the proscriber can use its condemn ability to sever a cleric's connection to his god. If the cleric fails a save, he immediately loses the ability to cast spells and turn undead, and cannot be healed by any cure spells. Proscribers have various spell-like abilities – at will—*continual light*; 3/day—*power word stun*; 1/day—*blade barrier, quest, polymorph self, power word blind* – and cast spells as a 12th-level cleric.

Little Priest, Little Priest, Let Me In

A temple sits against the hillside. The building houses a worship room, and has a small parsonage attached to the side. Red shingles cover the roof, and the grey stone façade is decorated with carvings of angels in flight.

Standing on the parsonage's stone porch is a 7-foot-tall figure wearing blood-red plate mail armor. The towering figure holds a long sword in its gloved hand. The blade glows a sickening green. A shield that looks like a screaming skull is strapped to the man's forearm. His face is hidden beneath a visor of yellowed ivory fangs. Two long horns on his helm curve from his temples and nearly touch at the nape of his neck. The figure slams its heavy hand into the temple's oak door so hard that the frame shakes with each resounding thump. A scared priest inside the church screams with each pounding knock.

Anton Penn freely admits that he was an evil man in his past life. But he's turned things around for the better after nearly being killed. He rejected the death goddess he formerly served, and is trying to make a new way in a life of goodness. He thought he'd gotten out of the death cult cleanly.

But Hel had other ideas, and sent the proscriber to teach the wayward priest a lesson for turning his back on her. Wards on the temple keep the proscriber from simply breaking down the door, but it won't be denied punishing the priest – or anyone who tries to help the man.

Copyright Notice
Author Scott Greene.

Protector

Hit Dice: 7
Armor Class: 1 [18]
Attack: Longsword (1d8+1)
Saving Throw: 9
Special: Air walk, spells, know alignment, telepathy 50 ft.
Move: 18
Alignment: Law
Challenge Level/XP: 10/1400

Protectors resemble tall, powerful humans with green eyes and bald heads. They dress in long, flowing green robes that billow as though blown by an invisible and unfelt breeze. They are guardians of law that are sent to the Material Plane when the forces of chaos swing the cosmic balance in their favor.

Protectors move by means of their air walk ability; their feet never touch the ground, and they always float 6 to 10 inches above the ground.

All protectors can cast divine spells as a 7th level cleric. A protector automatically knows the alignment of any creature within 50 feet that it looks upon.

Penance

A troupe of 1d6+5 protectors has been assigned to serve a 13th level high priest of Law who has undertaken to circumnavigate the outer planes in an effort to categorize the flora and fauna and construct a magnificent botanical garden on the grounds of his fortress monastery. His travels are, in part, a pennance for indiscretions that occurred in the presence of his subordinates.

The high priest is a balding gentleman, elderly but vigorous and handsome, with a well worn face, strong jaw and keen, golden eyes. He wears a creaky suit of platemail and carries a leather sack and silver knife for collecting specimens and a *heavy mace +1, +3 vs. demons* and *+1 golden shield* (capable of emiting a burst of golden light 3/day that stuns chaotic creatures who fail a saving throw).

The high priest and his protectors travel in a curious cog of greenish metal (kavorite) that floats about five to six feet above the ground. Much of the deck is taken up by panes of glass, allowing light to pour into the hold for the living specimens kept within. The high priest is especially proud of the bright purple choke cherries he discovered on Elysium and the flowering spurge that emits a choral hymn in the moonlight that grew on the slopes of the Second Heaven.

Credit

The Protector originally appeared in the First Edition module *B3 Palace of the Silver Princess* (© TSR/Wizards of the Coast, 1981) and is used by permission.

Copyright Notice

Authors Scott Greene and Erica Balsley, based on original material by Jean Wells.

Psiwyrm (Draco Presentia Facultas)

Hit Dice: 7-9
Armor Class: 3 [16]
Attacks: 2 claws (1d8), 1 bite (2d6)
Saving Throw: 9, 8 or 6
Special: Breath weapon, spell-like abilities
Move: 9/24 (flying)
Alignment: Chaos
Challenge Level/XP: 7 HD (7/600), 8 HD (8/800) or 9 HD (9/1,100)

Psiwyrms are 15 feet long with sleek, muscular bodies. Their scales are a rich purple color, growing darker on the dragon's underside and its clawed feet. Its mouth is filled with sharpened fangs and two large downward curving horns protrude from its angular head. The psiwyrm's eyes are glossy black. They breathe a cone of force, with a length of 70 feet and a base of 30 feet. Psiwyrms have a 100% chance of being able to talk and a 50% chance of being able to cast Magic-User spells: 1d4 first-level, 1d3 second-level, 1d2 third-level, and 1 fourth-level spell.

Halcyon Canyons

The Halcyon Canyons serve as a pass into the heights of the Hollow Spires Mountains. Massive quartz crystals make up the 50-foot-high canyon walls. During the light of the midday sun, the Halcyon Canyons fill with brilliant, scintillating colors. The prismatic colors don't blind creatures, but they make seeing beyond ten feet difficult without proper eye protection. During daylight or in lighted areas, the canyon walls reflect and refract images. Creatures passing along the canyon floor have multiple reflections. Standing against a crystal wall acts as a *mirror image* spell except the images do not go away if attacked.

The psiwyrm Cheldelic roams the canyons. It has a lair hidden behind a heavy but movable sheet of white quartz. Cheldelic has accumulated a large hoard of treasure from travelers as well as a hefty number of uncut gemstones. Halcyon Canyons are also home to geons, cragmen, caterprisms and crystallis.

Copyright Notice

Pudding, Blood

Hit Dice: 5
Armor Class: 9 [10]
Attacks: 1 slam (2d4)
Saving Throw: 12
Special: Disgorge blood, grab, immune to blunt weapons
Move: 6
Alignment: Neutrality
Challenge Level/XP: 6/400

A blood pudding is a spheroid blob of protoplasm about 3 feet high; they are rounded at the top, but flatten out somewhat at the bottom as their own weight spreads out their form. The puddings are blood-red in color, and constantly seep a foul smelling and sticky slime. In bright enough light, blood puddings are translucent. A blood pudding strikes with a thick pseudopod. If it strikes a victim, the blood pudding grabs the opponent and attempts to infuse itself with the prey (save resists). If it infuses, it attempts to disgorge the victim's blood through its pores, eyes, ears and mouth on the next round (3d6 points of damage). Blunt weapons just bounce off a blood pudding, doing no damage.

The Black Skull of Kalitos

A yawning cavern of black stalactites lies in the deep tunnels beneath the Mines of Yurith. A stream of black water flows through the cavern, the undulating water rolling around a 20-foot-wide rock platform. Two small wooden bridges cross the stream to the platform. Atop the platform sits a 10-foot-tall black skull carved from basalt. The skull is wide and squat, but otherwise complete, with the jawbone resting on the rock platform. The giant skull has two long incisors that overlap the lower teeth.

Standing around the skull are 6 black-robed figures, each bearing a staff formed from fused leg bones. Each figure is a 6th-level cleric of Kalitos.

A bound and gagged body lies on the platform in front of the skull, held in a small stone trough. The Cult of Kalitos routinely sacrifices captured travelers at this profane altar to evil. An unconscious elf lies bound with barbed wire in the trough, ready to be offered to the dark deity.

The massive skull is hollow and contains the instrument of the god's wrath: a blood pudding. The pudding pours out of the eyes, nostrils and from between the teeth of the black skull to devour victims in the trough.

Copyright Notice

P

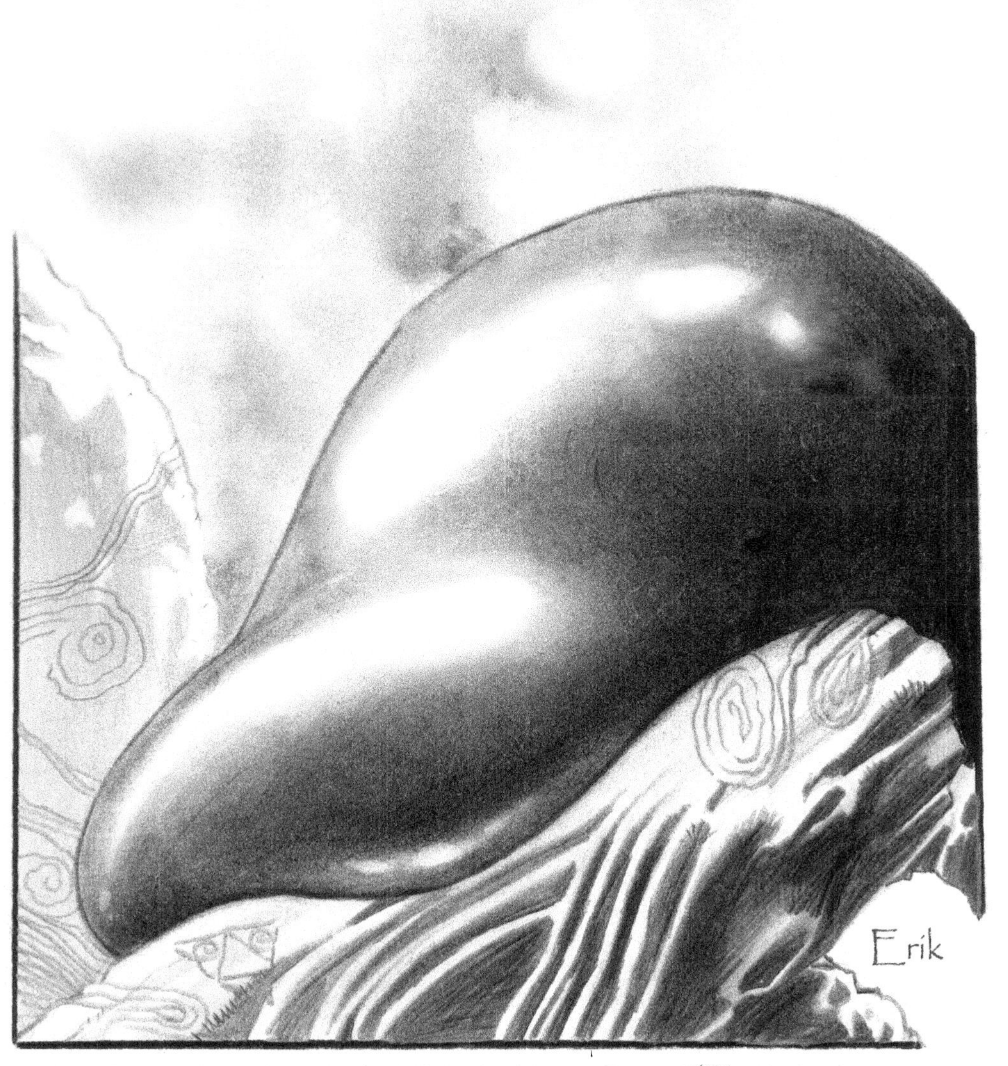

Pudding, Brown

Hit Dice: 11
Armor Class: 9 [10]
Attack: Strike (2d6 plus 2d6 acid)
Saving Throw: 4
Special: Acid, split
Move: 6/6 (climbing)
Alignment: Neutrality
Challenge Level/XP: 12/2000

A variety of the black pudding, the brown pudding is found only in temperate and subtropical swamps. It is dark brown in color. The creature secretes a digestive acid that dissolves organic material quickly, but does not affect metal. Any melee hit or constrict attack deals acid damage, and the opponent's clothing and armor (non-metal only) dissolve and become useless immediately unless they succeed on saving throw. A wooden weapon that strikes a brown pudding also dissolves immediately unless it succeeds on a saving throw.

Slashing and piercing weapons deal no damage to a brown pudding. Instead the creature splits into two identical puddings, each with half of the original's current hit points (round down). A pudding with 10 hit points or less cannot be further split and dies if reduced to 0 hit points.

Black Blot on an Exemplary Quest

In the humid grasslands of the southern continent, there is a lonely, snowcapped mountain surrounded by miles of wetlands. The wetlands are home to tall, blue cranes, a ragged wanderer and a cunning brown pudding.

The ragged wanderer is an archbishop of Law that hails from the colder northern lands. He came to the grasslands in response to a prophecy in search of a black blot that was supposed to have fallen from the sky and landed in these swamps. Try as he might, he has found nothing, and as a result is going through a severe crisis of faith. The archbishop wears rusty platemail and tattered, soiled priestly vestments, and looks more like a wild man than a member of the lawful clergy. Encounters with the man occur on a roll of 1 on 1d6, made each day and each night spent traveling through the swamps. He is mildly friendly to strangers, but maintains a healthy suspicion as well. While not averse to banding together with others, he will almost certainly attempt to take the lead, using the adventurers to accomplish his own ends.

The archbishop has become something of an expert at avoiding and fighting the other main inhabitant of the marsh, the brown pudding. The pudding appears on a roll of 6 on 1d6 when a wandering monster roll is made. It is clever enough to use the environment to its advantage, slinking up beneath the murky waters and engulfing a victim from below. If challenged, the beast will attempt to flee under cover of the water, stalking the party and sniping at them as long as they remain in the marsh.

The legendary black blot did fall in the swamp. The blot is a nexus of anti-matter contained in a sphere of pure force. The force sphere can be dispelled by playing a trilling rune on a flute. Should the sphere of force disappear, the blot will begin destroying everything in its path, growing as it does so. It grows at the rate of 1 foot per minute. It will take the blot about 3-1/2 days to destroy an area one mile in radius.

Credit

The Brown Pudding originally appeared in the First Edition module *S4 Lost Caverns of Tsojcanth* (© TSR/Wizards of the Coast, 1982) and later in the First Edition *Monster Manual II* (© TSR/Wizards of the Coast, 1983) and is used by permission.

Copyright Notice

Author Scott Greene, based on original material by Gary Gygax.

Pudding, Dun

Hit Dice: 8
Armor Class: 9 [10]
Attack: Strike (2d6 plus 2d6 acid)
Saving Throw: 8
Special: Acid, split
Move: 6/6 (climbing)
Alignment: Neutrality
Challenge Level/XP: 9/1100

A variety of the black pudding, the dun pudding is found only in warm, dry, arid regions. It is light tan or brown in color. The creature secretes a digestive acid that dissolves organic material and metal quickly, but does not affect stone. Any melee hit or constrict attack deals acid damage, and the opponent's armor and clothing dissolve and become useless immediately unless they succeed on a saving throw. A metal or wooden weapon that strikes a dun pudding also dissolves immediately unless it succeeds on a saving throw.

Slashing and piercing weapons deal no damage to a dun pudding. Instead the creature splits into two identical puddings, each with half of the original's current hit points (round down). A pudding with 10 hit points or less cannot be further spit and dies if reduced to 0 hit points.

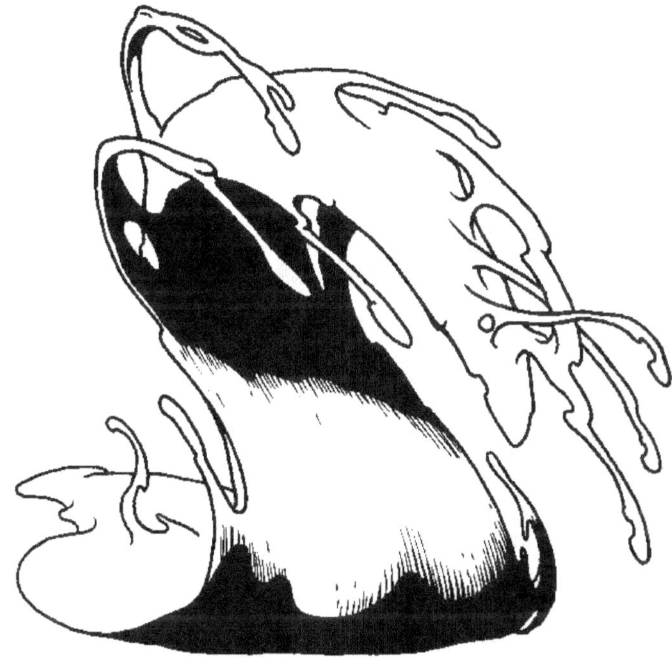

Can't Get Good Help These Days

A silk caravan making its way through the desert has fallen under attack from two separate bands of nomads. Each nomadic band is made up of 1d20+20 nomadic warriors mounted on camels. The nomads wear leather armor and carry short bows, spears and long, slim daggers. They dress in hooded white robes decorated with gaudy glass beads and mark their faces with chalk. One tribe uses triangle shapes on their faces while the other uses lines and circles. Each tribe is led by a chieftain (a fighter of level 1d6+2) and his harem of 1d3+3 wives. The wives are all magic-users and sages of mathematics, the youngest wife being 1st level and each additional wife being one level higher in turn. In other words, a group of six wives will be magic-users of level 1 through 6.

In both cases, the magical wives of the tribe discovered, via their auguries, that the caravan moving through their desert was carrying more than silk and foodstuffs. A bronze calculation device that looks like a series of gears within a circular case has been entrusted to the caravan master to be transported to a center of learning on the coast.

The caravan is now hunkered down atop a large, long sand dune. Most of its animals have been killed, and a mere ten guardsmen are still alive. The nomads harry the guards through the day, and then press their attack at night. By and large, the most intense night fighting is between the nomads as they struggle for the right to steal the device.

All of this fighting and motion has now attracted a dun pudding. The pudding slinks beneath the sands like a sidewinder, spreading itself out just beneath the surface of the sand and wait for a victim to walk over him. Two guardsmen have already been engulfed and digested by the creature, and the others are arguing over whether they should kill the caravan master, take whatever food and water they can carry, and abandon the caravan to the nomads.

Credit

The Dun Pudding originally appeared in the First Edition module *S4 Lost Caverns of Tsjocanth* (© TSR/ Wizards of the Coast, 1982) and later in the First Edition *Monster Manual II* (© TSR/Wizards of the Coast, 1983) and is used by permission.

Copyright Notice

Author Scott Greene, based on original material by Gary Gygax.

Pudding, Stone

Hit Dice: 10
Armor Class: 5 [14]
Attacks: 1 slam (2d6 + acid + petrification)
Saving Throw: 5
Special: Acid, petrification, immune to blunt weapons
Move: 3/3 (climb)
Alignment: Neutrality
Challenge Level/XP: 12/2,000

A stone pudding is a large, oozing gray blob about 16 feet across and from 2 to 4 feet thick, and weighing in excess of 20,000 pounds. A stone pudding secretes a digestive acid that dissolves organic material and stone, but not steel. They attack with a massive pseudopod. Anyone hit by a stone pudding must save or be held and take automatic slam (2d6) and acid (1d6) damage each round. The stone pudding's touch also can turn an opponent to stone (save avoids). Fire causes a stone pudding to split into two identical puddings with half the original's hit points.

Sewer Crawl

An abandoned tunnel in the sewers beneath Bargarsport is filled with accumulated trash and detritus washed in from the Reaping Sea. A thin stream of dirty water runs down the center of the stone floor. Brown moss and dirty seaweed are wedged into the stone block walls. Water rises and falls through the tunnel with the rising and ebbing tides. The stone ceiling along a 20-foot-long section sags noticeably.

A stone pudding clings to the ceiling during the day and drops to the sopping floor at night. The creature hunts in the narrow tunnels, slowly flowing through the corridors after mice and other helpless sea creatures left behind when the waters rush out of the sewers with the ebbing tides. The creature is an opportunistic hunter and greedily drops on any creature wandering beneath it when the tide is out.

Copyright Notice
Author Scott Greene.

Pudding, White

Hit Dice: 9
Armor Class: 9 [10]
Attack: Strike (2d6 plus 2d6 acid)
Saving Throw: 6
Special: Acid, split
Move: 6/6 (climbing)
Alignment: Neutrality
Challenge Level/XP: 10/1400

A variety of the black pudding, the white pudding is found only in cold, frigid lands. It is white in color and uses this to its advantage by ambushing its prey. Since a white pudding looks like normal ice and snow when at rest, it surprises prey on a roll of 1-4 on 1d6.

The creature secretes a digestive acid that dissolves organic material quickly, but does not affect metal. Any melee hit or constrict attack deals acid damage, and the opponent's armor (non-metal armor only) and clothing dissolve and become useless immediately unless they succeed on a saving throw. A wooden weapon that strikes a white pudding also dissolves immediately unless it succeeds on a saving throw.

Slashing and piercing weapons deal no damage to a white pudding. Instead the creature splits into two identical puddings, each with half of the original's current hit points (round down). A pudding with 10 hit points or less cannot be further split and dies if reduced to 0 hit points.

Frozen Dinner

In a far northern trading center there is a small but respected university. While its chancellor, the archbishop, has taken a leave of absence, leaving it in the charge of the vice chancellor, an ambitious man descended from minor (and cash strapped) nobility.

The university consists of three long, two-story buildings of whitish stone with slate roofs. The largest of these three buildings was once the property of a master thief, serving as the headquarters for his gang of cutthroats and smugglers. Concealed passages, mostly bricked up, lead into dank catacombs beneath the building. These catacombs were used to store stolen loot, make quick escapes and to each a sea cave that permitted them to smuggle goods and people out of and into the town under the nose of the authorities.

When the vice-chancellor discovered one such passage behind a wooden panel in the chancellor's office, he decided to set up a smuggling ring of his own. The deeper catacombs are now home to his "enforcer", a white pudding that came into the possession of the vice-chancellor via an adventuring party that captured it on the northern tundra while sacking the frozen fortress of a frost giant jarl. The beast roams the catacombs at will, and though the smugglers are aware of its existance and are forewarned to avoid it, they still hate being in the catacombs. Recently, two students of the university have disappeared. They came to suspect the activities of their vice-chancellor and were locked in the catacombs to be killed by the beast. One of the students has been so consumed, but the other has managed to avoid the beast for three days.

The smuggling ring keeps their treasure hidden behind a false stone in the catacombs. It currently numbers 1d4 x 1,000 gp and 3d6 pounds of calamus (worth 8 gp per pound).

Credit

The White Pudding originally appeared in the First Edition module *S4 Lost Caverns of Tsojcanth* (© TSR/Wizards of the Coast, 1982) and later in the First Edition *Monster Manual II* (© TSR/Wizards of the Coast, 1983) and is used by permission.

Copyright Notice

Author Scott Greene, based on original material by Gary Gygax.

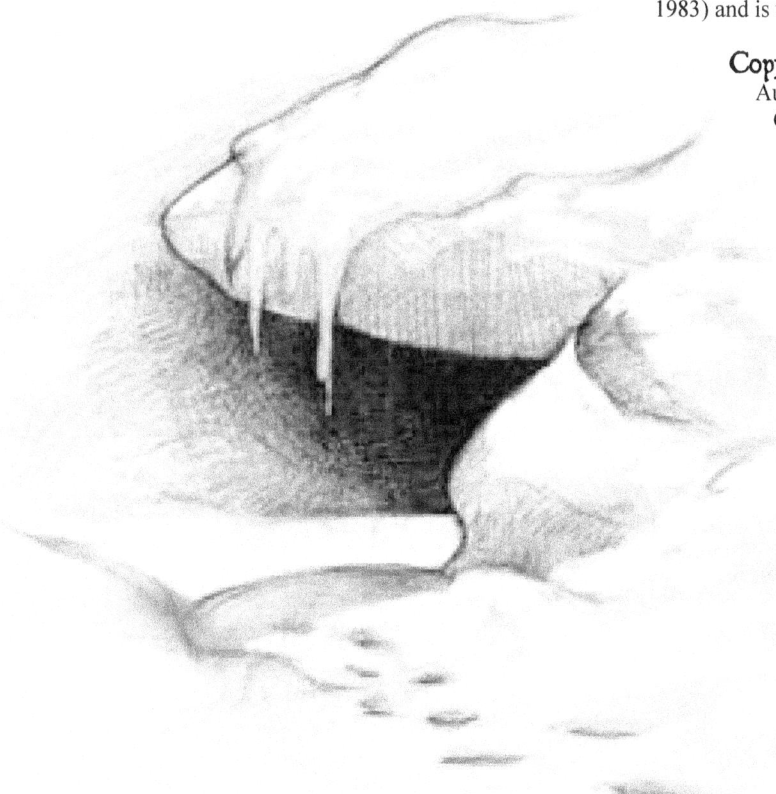

Purple Moss

This plant is a distant cousin of yellow mold. It feeds on moisture, so any area in which it grows is always extremely dry. Purple moss emits a sweet smell to a range of 10 feet that has the same effect as a *sleep* spell. A victim that falls asleep is quickly covered by the moss. It takes 1 round to cover a small creature and 2 rounds to cover a human-sized creature. A creature so covered suffocates in 1d4 rounds. Slain victims are digested in 1d2 hours by acidic secretions from the moss. Purple moss can be destroyed by fire.

Sleepiness Is Weakness of Character

In a finely crafted portion of a dungeon clad in black stone lovingly carved by dwarven hands. The dungeon was once the home of a flamboyant magician who wished to dwell away from other human beings. Taking residence in the upper levels of a dungeon, his power was enough to keep the local humanoids at bay.

Besides the requisite study (with its displacer skin rugs, preserved albino ape heads hanging on the wall, brontotherium foot umbrella holder and scrolls in leather cases) and the laboratory (overrun with pink giant rats and what looks like a giant, pulsating lung that they protect with their lives), there is a fine wine cellar. The cellar contains a number of bottles of exotic beverages, including a bamboo pipe containing mbege, three reddish gourds containing chicha, a crock of blaand and dozens of bottles of sweet and spiced wine. The cellar also contains the desiccated body of the magician, still clad in his velvet robes and floppy hat. The magician wears a conical mask over his face filled with bitter herbs. On the walls grows a sweet-smelling purple moss. The mask was intended to counter the scent of the purple moss, which he grew purposely in the cellar to keep it dry and cool. In the dry air the bitter herbs lost their effectiveness and the magician succumbed to the moss.

Credit

The Purple Moss originally appeared in the First Edition module *B3 Palace of the Silver Princess* (© TSR/Wizards of the Coast, 1981) and is used by permission.

Copyright Notice

Author Scott Greene, based on original material by Jean Wells.

Pyrolisk

Hit Dice: 4
Armor Class: 5 [14]
Attack: Bite (1d4)
Saving Throw: 13
Special: Conflagration gaze, pyrotechnics, immunity to fire
Move: 6/24 (flying)
Alignment: Chaos
Challenge Level/XP: 6/400

The pyrolisk resembles a cockatrice and is often mistaken for it. The difference lies in the coloration of its tail feathers and wings: the pyrolisk has a single red feather in its tail and a reddish tinge to its wings. Otherwise, it is identical to the cockatrice in appearance.

A creature within 30 feet that meets a pyrolisk's gaze bursts into flames, taking 4d8 points of damage (saving throw for half). The flames immediately burn out so there is no continuing damage or effect.

Once per round, a pyrolisk can use *pyrotechnics* as the spell. The pyrolisk can only use the fireworks version of the spell.

Furnace Punishment

On the banks of a subterranean river (reachable via a grotto, the entrance marked with a statue of the goddess of animals) a druidic hermit has constructed a strange parliament of awakened animals. The banks of the slow river are lined with stone couches upon which sit the assembled beasts of the surrounding jungle. The tiger has been elected the parliament's speaker, both for his deep, resounding voice and his threats to consume at least half of the parliament if he was not given the position. The beasts rule over the jungle, keeping it safe from the depredations of humanoids. The bats serve as the parliament's spies, hanging from the limbs of tall trees and always listening. The parliament's executioner dwells in dry, hot cave located beneath the parliament chamber. A person thrown into the opening will fall 20 feet to the floor of the cavern, where a flight of 1d3+1 pyrolisks dwells. The pyrolisks have not been awakened, but they really don't need to be to do their job.

The cavern lair of the pyrolisks connects to other subterranean passages and chambers, most of them volcanic vents and lava tubes that eventually wind up in a veritable sea of magma located 3 miles beneath the surface. The lair is littered with no fewer than thirty charred corpses, most of them goblins, but a few humans, elves and dwarves as well. All of the bodies were stripped of their valuables before being dropped into the "furnace".

Credit

The Pyrolisk originally appeared in the First Edition *Monster Manual II* (© TSR/Wizards of the Coast, 1983) and is used by permission.

Copyright Notice

Author Scott Greene, based on original material by Gary Gygax.

Quantum

Hit Dice: 11
Armor Class: 1 [18]
Attacks: 4 quantum tentacles (2d6+3)
Saving Throw: 4
Special: Dimension door, disintegrate, +2 magic weapons to hit, mirror image
Move: 12 (flying)
Alignment: Neutrality
Challenge Level/XP: 13/2,300

A quantum's outline flickers and changes randomly, at first appearing to have four tentacles, then eight more appear and waver menacingly before vanishing. Its general shape is serpentine, with an uncertain number of tentacles dangling beneath it. The only constant is its six glowing eyes, three on each side of what must be its head. Quantums lash opponents with their tentacles. Three times per day, it can attack with a single tentacle and set up a vibration in an opponent that causes the creature's molecular structure to shake apart (similar to a *disintegrate* spell, save resists). A quantum can appear to be in two places at once (as per a *mirror image* spell) and can create a *dimension door* each round.

Ring My Bell

The underground chamber is massive, a quarter mile from rock wall to rock wall, with a ceiling rising 80 feet overhead. Long tapering stalactites hang from the roof, some reaching the ground in slender columns of stone. Several of the stone pillars are shattered and broken. Rubble litters the cavern floor.

Splitting the room is a 200-foot-wide underground river that steams and bubbles. The water is 15 feet deep and burns at nearly 100 degrees. Clouds of steam rise from the stream, making the air thick with a white sulfurous mist.

A dented iron bell sits on a small island in the center of the river. The bell is nearly 5 feet tall, and hangs from a frame of water-slickened wood. The bell weighs nearly 1,000 pounds. A wooden striker sits near the bell. A small bridge of wooden planks held together by fraying ropes crosses from the shore to the island.

If struck, the bell sounds a loud peal that sets up a vibration on the water that soon sets the stone columns to quaking. The vibration attracts a quantum's attention within 1d6 rounds. The quantum flickers into the room over the bell. The thick clouds of steam hide its form as it drifts moves to investigate.

Copyright Notice
Author Erica Balsley.

Quasi-Elemental, Acid

Hit Dice: 2
Armor Class: 6 [13]
Attacks: 1 slam (1d4 + 1d4 acid)
Saving Throw: 16
Special: Acid, fumes
Move: 6/30 (swim)
Alignment: Neutrality
Challenge Level/XP: 3/60

Hit Dice: 4
Armor Class: 5 [14]
Attacks: 1 slam (1d6 + 1d6 acid)
Saving Throw: 13
Special: Acid, fumes
Move: 6/30 (swim)
Alignment: Neutrality
Challenge Level/XP: 5/240

Hit Dice: 6
Armor Class: 4 [15]
Attacks: 1 slam (1d8 + 1d8 acid)
Saving Throw: 11
Special: Acid, fumes
Move: 6/30 (swim)
Alignment: Neutrality
Challenge Level/XP: 7/600

Hit Dice: 8
Armor Class: 3 [16]
Attacks: 2 slams (2d4 + 2d4 acid)
Saving Throw: 8
Special: Acid, fumes
Move: 6/30 (swim)
Alignment: Neutrality
Challenge Level/XP: 9/1,100

Hit Dice: 10
Armor Class: 2 [17]
Attacks: 2 slams (2d6 + 2d6 acid)
Saving Throw: 5
Special: Acid, fumes
Move: 6/30 (swim)
Alignment: Neutrality
Challenge Level/XP: 11/1,700

Hit Dice: 12
Armor Class: 1 [18]
Attacks: 2 slams (2d8 + 2d8 acid)
Saving Throw: 3
Special: Acid, fumes
Move: 6/30 (swim)
Alignment: Neutrality
Challenge Level/XP: 13/2,300

At rest, an acid quasi-elemental is a clear puddle of liquid with a slightly green hue. It can rise up like a wave in a manner similar to a water elemental, or ooze along solid surfaces by sending out tendrils and pulling itself along. Wherever it travels, it leaves behind a shallow trough that emits wisps of smoke. In the midst of the acid quasi-elemental one can barely make out regions of darker green that form a vaguely human face. Acid quasi-elementals slam opponents with an acid attack. The bigger elementals have stronger acid attacks. Anyone within 5 feet of an acid quasi-elemental must make a save or be overcome by the acidic vapors rising off the creature (1d6 points of damage per round).

Acid Washed

New Spells

Transmute Water to Acid
Spell Level: Druid 5, Magic-User 5
Range: Close (Referee's discretion)
Duration: Instantaneous

This spell transforms a volume of normal or magically created water into an equal volume of highly corrosive acid. Any creature touching this acid takes 1d6 damage per round of exposure.

Transmute Acid to Water
Spell Level: Druid 5, Magic-User 5
Range: Close (Referee's discretion)
Duration: Instantaneous

This spell is identical to *transmute water to acid* but it changes an equal volume of corrosive acid into plain, clear (and safe) water.

A creature constructed of acid takes 1d4 points of damage per level of the caster (save for half).

This 40-foot-by-40-foot room is closed off by a set of steel doors set tightly into the stone on opposite walls. A stone sluice runs at a 45-degree angle down from a small glowing trapdoor in the 20-foot-high ceiling. The stone channel ends 4 feet above the floor, where a 10-foot-by-10-foot square frame of pitted metal stands. A 5-inch plate of copper is held horizontally off the floor in an iron frame. A brass plate in the frame is pocked and eaten through, and covered in green and brown swirls of color. A ring of powdered diamond grit fills a circle that runs completely around the metal frame. A partially dissolved skeleton lies on the stone floor beneath the sluice. A small handle on a silver chain hangs down from the underside of the ramp.

If the chain is pulled, an acid quasi-elemental pours down the ramp. Originally, the quasi-elemental poured over the copper plate to etch it so it could be sold as "acid-burned art." Now, a chink in the stone ramp allows the creature to escape and drop onto the person pulling the chain. Ten rounds after the chain is pulled, the quasi-elemental is automatically returned to an enchanted dimensional space in the ceiling.

Copyright Notice
Author Scott Greene.

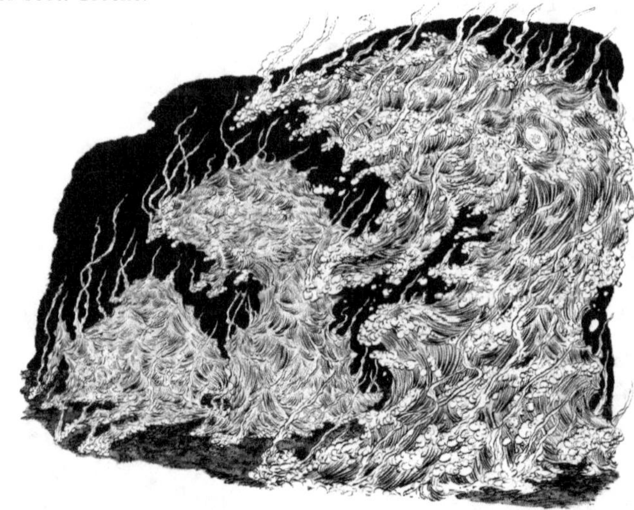

Quasi-Elemental, Lightning

This creature appears as a bluish globe of electrical energy. Lightning plays off and around its body.

	Small	Medium	Large
Hit Dice:	6	9	12
Armor Class:	1 [18]	0 [19]	-1 [21]
Attack:	Slam (1d6 electricity)	Slam (1d8 electricity)	Slam (2d6 electricity)
Saving Throw:	11	5	3
Special:	Electricity, globe weapon resistance (50%), immunity to electricity resistance to fire and (50%), vulnerability to water	Electricity, globe weapon resistance (50%), immunity to electricity resistance to fire and acid (50%), vulnerability to water	Electricity, globe weapon resistance (50%), immunity to electricity resistance to fire and acid (50%), vulnerability to water
Move:	24 (flying)	24 (flying)	24 (flying)
Alignment:	Neutrality	Neutrality	Neutrality
CL/XP:	9/1100	13/2300	16/3200

Lightning quasi-elementals are native to the Plane of Elemental Air, the Positive Energy Plane, and a rumored elemental plane situated in between (the Quasi-Elemental Plane of Lightning). They are sometimes summoned to the Material Plane by magic-users, but more often than not slip through a rift between the Material Plane and elemental plane during a lightning storm. They appear as bluish globes of electricity, arcs of lightning playing off and around its body.

A lightning quasi-elemental is composed entirely of electricity and deals electricity damage each time it hits. A creature striking the lightning quasi-elemental unarmed, or a creature striking the lightning quasi-elemental with a weapon take this same electricity damage each time one of their attacks hits. Metallic creatures or creatures using metal weapons take an extra 1d6 points of electricity damage each time one of their attacks hits.

A lightning quasi-elemental can discharge one globe of electricity per HD it possesses once per round. Globes hover 1 foot from the quasi-elemental and move with the creature. An opponent that moves within 5 feet of a globe discharges it and takes the electricity damage shown on the table below. An affected creature can make a saving throw to reduce the damage by half. Once a globe discharges, it is destroyed and a lightning quasi-elemental cannot recreate it for 4 hours.

A lightning quasi-elemental takes 1d8 points of damage per gallon of water it contacts.

Size	Electricity Damage
Small	1d6
Medium	1d8
Large	2d6

and thus require one to be swallowed to venture into the plane of question. Of course, most adventurers misunderstand the intentions of the golems and fight them. In the intervening decades, two of the golems - those of air (in the shape of a coiled serpent) and fire (in the shape of a lion) have been destroyed, throwing open their belly portals. The stone golems of earth (shaped like a lizard) and water (shaped like a hippopotamus) are intact.

The mixture of the hot, dry air of the fire plane and the cool, moist air of the air plane is responsible for the never-ending storm that now tops the mountain. Because of the elemental origins of the storm, it is inhabited by a large lightning quasi-elemental. Because of its presence, the malachite walls of the maze are charged with static electricity, causing the hair of adventurers who enter it to stand on end.

The Keeper's Tower in the center of the maze might offer clues as to the nature of the maze and its remaining golems, perhaps in tapestries hanging in the lower floor. The upper floor contains the Keeper's chamber, where his skeletal body still lies where he died in his bed. A large chest in the room (locked, poison needle trap) contains a smaller chest (also locked, poisoned) that contains 1,900 gp, 2,400 pp. The skeletal remains grasp a brass statuette of a sylph (worth 600 gp).

Credit

The Lightning Quasi-elemental originally appeared in the First Edition module *EX2 The Land Beyond the Magic Mirror* (© TSR/Wizards of the Coast, 1983) and later in the First Edition *Monster Manual II* (© TSR/Wizards of the Coast, 1983) and is used by permission.

Copyright Notice

Author Scott Greene, based on original material by Gary Gygax.

Tower of Elemental Portals

The top of the tallest mountain in the neighborhood is always shrouded in storm clouds, with terrific peals of thunder echoing through the surrounding valleys and fast, thuggish rivers pouring into the countryside beyond where they water some of the finest, sweetest grasses in the kingdom.

The cattlemen of the lowlands tell many tales about Thunder Mountain. Some say it is the home of a mighty storm giant, others that the gods have hidden a powerful magic item and posted the storm clouds as its guardians. The truth of the matter is nearly as fantastic.

The top of the mountain in question is flat and topped by a large maze of 20-foot tall malachite halls. In the center of the maze there is a stout, green tower once occupied by a wizard called the "Portal Keeper". The Keeper died long ago without an heir or apprentice to take over his job and in the ensuing decades the portals hidden within the maze have not been maintained.

The portals in question lead to the four elemental planes. They are located in the four corners of the maze and take the form of four stone golems in the shape of giant animals. The portals are located in the bellies of the golems,

Quasi-Elemental, Obsidian

This creature is a powerfully built, roughly humanoid-shaped monolith of black stone. Its hands end in wicked, serrated and jagged claws. No facial features can be discerned.

Hit Dice: 2
Armor Class: 6 [13]
Attacks: 1 claw (1d4)
Saving Throw: 16
Special: Death throes (1d6, 5 ft. radius), molten glass (1d4), resists fire
Move: 6
Alignment: Neutrality
Challenge Level/XP: 3/60

Hit Dice: 4
Armor Class: 5 [14]
Attacks: 1 claw (1d6)
Saving Throw: 13
Special: Death throes (2d6, 10 ft. radius), molten glass (1d6), resists fire
Move: 6
Alignment: Neutrality
Challenge Level/XP: 5/240

Hit Dice: 6
Armor Class: 4 [15]
Attacks: 1 claw (1d8)
Saving Throw: 11
Special: Death throes (3d6, 10 ft. radius), molten glass (1d8), resists fire and cold
Move: 6
Alignment: Neutrality
Challenge Level/XP: 7/600

Hit Dice: 8
Armor Class: 3 [16]
Attacks: 2 claws (2d4)
Saving Throw: 8
Special: Death throes (4d6, 30 ft. radius), molten glass (1d8), resists fire and cold
Move: 6
Alignment: Neutrality
Challenge Level/XP: 9/1,100

Hit Dice: 10
Armor Class: 2 [17]
Attacks: 2 claws (2d6)
Saving Throw: 5
Special: Death throes (5d6, 30 ft. radius), molten glass (1d8), resists fire and cold
Move: 6
Alignment: Neutrality
Challenge Level/XP: 11/1,700

Hit Dice: 12
Armor Class: 1 [18]
Attacks: 2 claws (2d8)
Saving Throw: 3
Special: Death throes (6d6, 30 ft. radius), molten glass eruption (1d8), resists fire and cold
Move: 6
Alignment: Neutrality
Challenge Level/XP: 13/2,300

Obsidian quasi-elementals appear as powerfully built, roughly humanoid-shaped creatures of blackened stone. Their hands end in wicked, serrated and jagged claws. No facial features can be discerned. Some obsidian quasi-elementals have flecks of dark green or white markings on their form. Obsidian quasi-elementals attack with their claws. If slain, the creature explodes in a cloud of razor-sharp bits of obsidian. Any hit on the elemental with a piercing or slashing weapon causes an eruption of molten glass that burns the attacker (save avoids).

A World of Hurt

Columns of jagged obsidian rise along the horizon, sharp pillars punching through the forest. Trees lie in splintered pieces, and boulders are split in half by the serrated towers rising 20 feet into the air. Towering buttes of blackened rock sparkle like dark glass in the middle of this encroaching forest. The obsidian is sharp and slices anyone moving through it for 1d6 points of damage.

The village of Keer-Toth is cut in half by shards of glass. Bodies lie in pieces amid the densely packed columns, and blood runs around the base of the shafts. The remaining villagers are fleeing the columns overrunning their homes. It appears the columns rose in the middle of the night to skewer half the stone houses.

A magic-user named Yurt McCallot is to blame. The lonely wizard tried to open a portal to a plane of lovelorn women – but instead unleashed an expanding rift to the Quasi-Plane of Obsidian. The tear is slowly switching the two planes, taking villages from this world into the barren bleakness of the Obsidian Plane. So far, 10 obsidian quasi-elementals are wandering free, with more arriving each day. The only way to stop the spread of the Obsidian Plane is to find McCallot's body in the middle of the forest and smash a small obsidian locket he holds. His body is currently held 10 feet off the ground, impaled on a serrated spike tree.

Copyright Notice
Author Scott Greene.

Quickling

Hit Dice: 2d6
Armor Class: 0 [19]
Attack: Dagger (1d3)
Saving Throw: 16
Special: Poison, spells, blur, natural invisibility
Move: 48
Alignment: Chaos
Challenge Level/XP: 5/240

Believed to be the offspring of an elf and a brownie (see that entry), the quickling is a chaotic faerie creature that hates all other races, especially the other fey races. How they came to be evil and malign is still a mystery, but legend speaks of the first quicklings as being great sorcerers. Elven scholars believe these quickling sorcerers unleashed some extradimensional force that was never meant for mortal creatures.

Quicklings resemble small elves with large ears that rise to points above their heads. Their skin is pale blue to blue-white and hair is either silver or white. They prefer clothes of bright and boisterous colors; reds, yellows, silvers, blacks, and blues are among their favorites. Quicklings never wear armor. They speak the common tongue and the language of pixies and brownies. Both are spoken so quickly that even those able to speak one of the languages may still find it difficult to converse with a quickling.

Because of their rapid metabolism, quicklings reach adulthood by the age of 2, middle age at 5, old age at 12, and venerable at age 15.

Quicklings employ daggers lined with poison extracted from kava plants. This poison induces sleep in its victims. When a quickling coats a weapon with this poison, the poison lasts for 1 turn or until it is touched or scores a successful hit.

A quickling that moves in a round appears as a blur. This gives all attacks against the quickling a 20% chance to miss their attack (roll the miss chance before an attack roll is made).

A quickling is effectively invisible (as the spell) when standing motionless. It loses this invisibility and remains visible (though blurred) in any round in which it moves.

Quicklings can cast the following spells, each once per day: *Dancing lights*, *flare*, *levitate*, *shatter* and *ventriloquism*.

Slicker Than Snot

You come across a forest clearing occupied by a highly agitated brown bear. The beast has been wounded, its flesh rended and torn and there are several trickles of blood matting its fur. It is circling in the center of the clearing, swaying its massive head back and forth as though looking for something. The bear is actually a werebear, and it has a mere 10 hit points between it and death.

The werebear's assailants are a gang of 1d3+1 quicklings. The quicklings are currently standing still and are thus naturally invisible. As much fun as they've had tormenting the werebear, they will not pass up the chance to kill adventurers (better treasure, you know).

If the adventurers and werebear come out of the encounter alive, the wearbear will gladly lead them back (or give directions if it must be carried) to its lodge. The werebear's lodge is a cabin built against a cave, thus making half of the lair subterranean. The lodge has a large fire pit and woven mats of fragrant grasses for sitting/sleeping. The subterranan portion of the lodge contains casks of mead, pots of honey, jars of berry preserves, two venison and a wild pig hanging from hooks in the ceiling and other foodstuffs.

The wearbear will take two or three weeks to completely heal from its wounds, and will invite his rescuers to spend that time enjoying his hospitality. If they consent, they will meet the other werebears of the district and might learn a great deal about the surrounding woodlands.

Credit
The Quickling originally appeared in the First Edition *Monster Manual II* (© TSR/Wizards of the Coast, 1983) and is used by permission.

Copyright Notice
Author Scott Greene, based on original material by Gary Gygax.

Quickwood

Hit Dice: 7 (or more)
Armor Class: 2 [17]
Attack: Root (entangle) or bite (2d6)
Saving Throw: 9
Special: Fear aura, grasping roots, immunity to electricity, immunity to fire (see below), remote sensing, surprise on roll of 1-4 on 1d6
Move: 6
Alignment: Neutrality
Challenge Level/XP: 9/1100

Quickwoods appear as nothing more than common oak trees and are indistinguishable from them at distances greater than 30 feet. Closer inspection (at a distance of 10 feet or less) reveals a human-like visage embedded in the trunk. They are carnivores and prefer the taste of human or elven flesh above all others.

A quickwood's body is brown and textured like bark, and many strong, rigid branches protrude from its trunk. Each branch has many smaller branches that sport leaves of a deep, rich green color. Quickwoods usually root themselves to a particular location and rarely move. When they do move, they pull themselves slowly along with their roots. A typical quickwood stands 16 feet tall.

Quickwoods speak the language of the nymphs and satyrs, and might speak the common tongue of men if it makes enough meals of them.

A typical quickwood (7 HD) has 7 roots it uses to grab foes. For every 2 HD above 7, a quickwood has one additional root it can use in combat (thus, a 9 HD quickwood has 8 roots and a 15 HD quickwood has 11 roots).

A quickwood can use a normal oak tree within 360 feet as a magical sensor to view its surroundings. This ability is similar to a *clairaudience/clairvoyance* spell and allows a quickwood to see (including with darkvision) and hear through a sensor. A quickwood does not need line of sight to establish a sensor. A quickwood can establish a new magical sensor in another tree within range within seconds, though it can never have more sensors at one time than its Hit Dice. A quickwood with multiple sensors can switch between them freely.

An oak tree utilized as a magical sensor takes on a human-like visage (similar to a quickwood). Ad adventurer has a 1 in 6 (2 in 6 for elves and halflings) of noticing the tree's visage.

If a quickwood is targeted by a spell (excluding area spells) and it makes its saving throw against the spell's effects, it takes no damage and absorbs some of the spell's energy and releases it as a fear effect in a 10-foot radius per level of the spell. Affected creatures must succeed on a saving throw or be affected as by a *fear* spell.

If a quickwood hits with a root attack, it entangles its victim unless the victim passes a saving throw. If it entangles a victim, it drags the foe 30 feet closer each subsequent round. A quickwood can draw in a creature within 3 feet of itself and bite with a +2 bonus in the same round. A root has 10 hit points. If the root is currently entangling a target, the root suffers a 2 point penalty to its Armor Class. Severing a root deals no damage to a quickwood.

A quickwood can perspire, granting it immunity to fire for one hour. Afterwards, it must wait one turn before using this ability again.

Rotten Wood

After a long journey in search of the secret druid's grove of the old forest, the adventurers will take great comfort in seeing a stone marker decorated by chalk and ochre drawings of hunters and deer. The marker is one of several dozen that form a circular boundary of the holy druidic precinct. Beyond this point, chaotics and lawfuls must not journey unless they are willing to have a curse (a cumulative -1 penalty to saving throws with each lawful or chaotic act they commit until the moon has passed through its phases) - or at least, they would be cursed if the grove was still sanctified.

Stepping into the holy precinct, they will find its outer portions thick with large oak trees covered in moss. The air is thick and seems to be charged with power and one will hear no animal noises - not even the buzzing of insects - in the area. Knowing they are entering a druidic holy place, the adventurers might not be alarmed by the presence of grave, staring faces on some of the oaks.

The staring oaks serve the new master of the grove, a massive (15 HD) quickwood. The quickwood dwells at the center of the grove, dipping its branches and roots in a fountain of longevity (per *potion of longevity*, only one dip per person). The quickwood destroyed the local druids (who happened to be neanderthals) and its chaotic presence has made the grove unholy. A druid that destroys the quickwood and re-sanctifies the grove should be awarded with 2,000 XP. Other neutrals that participate should be awarded 500 XP.

Credit
The Quickwood originally appeared in the First Edition *Monster Manual II* (© TSR/Wizards of the Coast, 1983) and is used by permission.

Copyright Notice
Author Scott Greene, based on original material by Gary Gygax.

Raggoth

Hit Dice: 10
Armor Class: 2 [17]
Attacks: 4 claws (1d6+2) and 1 bite (1d8+2)
Saving Throw: 5
Special: Grab, pounce, rake, tormenting howl,
Move: 9
Alignment: Neutrality
Challenge Level/XP: 12/2,000

A raggoth is a sleek black-furred creature with a gaping mouth full of sharpened fangs. Its head is wolf-like, and the creature has six muscular legs. Its body is about 8 feet long long and ends in a thick furred tail. A raggoth attacks with its claws and bite. If it hits one opponent with two claw attacks, it can rake the victim for an additional 2d6+4 points of damage with its middle claws. Once every 1d4 rounds, a raggoth can let loose a piercing howl that demoralizes any creature within 60 feet. Creatures hearing the howl that fail a save suffer a -2 penalty on attacks and saves.

Cats and Dogs

A cat's deep-throated growl sounds from the Kajaani Forest. The noise is punctuated by a cat's loud hiss. A horde of 8 scratched and bloodied tangtals rushes out of the woods and cowers behind the PCs. Only one of the giant cats is real; the rest are merely mirror images of the frightened and exhausted original. Just after the cat bursts out of the forest, its pursuers arrive: 3 mangy raggoths. The dogs paw the ground with their six legs and bare rows of sharp teeth. A guttural growl starts in its chest and vibrates along the slick fur of its throat. The raggoth is intent on catching the cat and ignores PCs unless they get in its way. If PCs help the battered cat, they may make a new friend who'll tag along with them as long as they feed it.

Copyright Notice
Author Scott Greene.

Rakklethorn Toad

Hit Dice: 2
Armor Class: 8 [11]
Attacks: Thorn volley (1d6 + poison), bite (1d4)
Saving Throw: 16
Special: Poison, thorns
Move: 4
Alignment: Neutrality
Challenge Level/XP: 3/60

A rakklethorn toad is a small 3-foot-long toad with dozens of small needle-like thorns protruding from its back. Its skin is mottled brown and green and glistens with a dull sheen, while its eyes are gray and its underbelly is pale white. The thorns are brownish-black. A rakklethorn toad attacks by arching its back and firing a volley of thorns up to 50 feet at an opponent. The thorns are coated with a debilitating poison that does 1d3 points of damage.

The Mating Game

The Sin Mire Swamp is alive with sounds and movement, birds flapping out of the moss-covered trees, fish splashing in the three-feet-deep water. Cattails sway in bunches, and marsh grasses buzz with swarming mosquitoes. The murky swamp is thick with viscous jelly-like balls that cling to anything dipped into the water.

Three colonies of rakkletorn toads – a total of 30 toads – have come together for their annual mating frenzy. The water is thick with the jelly-like eggs released by the females, and the males are hyper-aggressive toward anyone entering the area.

Copyright Notice
Author Scott Greene.

Rat, Barrow

Hit Dice: 1d4 hp
Armor Class: 7 [12]
Attacks: 2 claws (1d3), 1 bite (1d2)
Saving Throw: 18
Special: Toughen hide
Move: 12/6/6 (climb/burrow)
Alignment: Neutrality
Challenge Level/XP: A/5

Barrow rats are 15-inch-long brownish-gray rats with long gray or brown, hairless tails. Their underbellies are lighter in color than their fur often appearing white in some rare species, but usually appearing light brown or slate. Some barrow rats have a dark brown or black stripe on their dorsal side that runs the length of their body. Once per day, a barrow rat can toughen its hide to be as tough as stone (AC 3 [16]).

Trapped Like . . . You Know

The 10-foot-wide corridor continues in a straight line for 50 feet before turning to the right at a 90-degree bend. The walls are heavy rust-colored stones set flush atop one another. Copper lanterns hang every 15 feet, each casting a feeble greenish light down the hall. The center 15 feet of the corridor is a pit trap that drops into a 20-foot-deep hole beneath the passageway. The walls of the pit are pocked by hundreds of small holes. Rat droppings fill the floor of the hole.

The pit is home to a warren of barrow rats that swarm out to attack anyone falling into the hole. The aggressive rats consider the pit their territory and defend it against invaders.

Copyright Notice
Author Scott Greene.

Rat, Brain

Hit Dice: 1
Armor Class: 5 [14]
Attack: Bite (1d2)
Saving Throw: 17
Special: Psionic abilities, surprise on roll of 1-3 on 1d6
Move: 9/9 (climbing)
Alignment: Neutrality
Challenge Level/XP: 3/60

Brain rats resemble their normal cousins and are indistinguishable from normal rats. Brain rats (also called psionic rats) are intelligent relatives of normal rats. Brain rats cluster in large groups and wait for prey to pass by. Brain rats flee if combat goes against them. Brain rats can use *ESP* (as the spell) at will. Three times per day they can unleash a mind thrust that deals 1d6 points of damage per point of intelligence difference between the rat (has a 14 intelligence) and its victim. Brain rats can also use the spells *confusion* and *feeblemind* once per day.

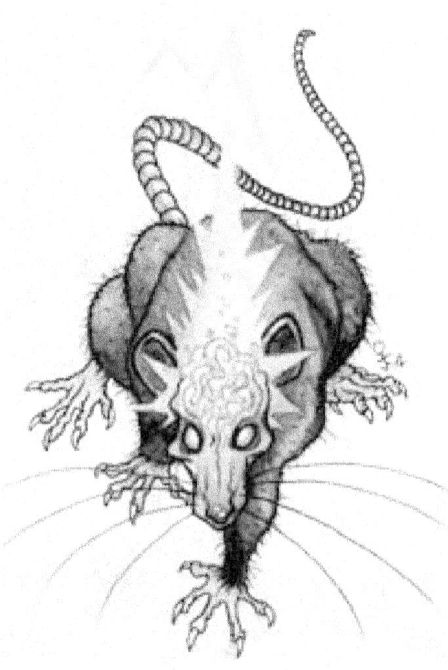

The Secret of Yimm

The weird house on the hill (built in the Jacobethan style of bluish bricks), the locals will tell visitors, belongs to the reclusive wizard Yimm. Though rarely seen, the wizard's presence was often felt by the locals, whether from the mysterious gifts that would appear on doorsteps when people were in need or from the stream of adventurers into the town to visit the wizard and beg for favors.

The interior of Yimm's home wasn't terribly strange - a foyer, study, sitting room, dining room (rarely used), kitchen, rooms upstairs and a lead-lined laboratory in the cellar. The rooms are packed with the mementos of a well-traveled wizard, most of them being interesting but not terribly valuable (after all, a wizard's experiments eat up most of their wealth).

Two rooms of the house are worthy of mention. The kitchen was no longer used for its intended purpose for two reasons. Firstly, Yimm practiced a strict dietary regemin, eating nothing but pottage and drinking nothing but claret. A cauldron of pottage was kept always over the fire in the study, while the casks of claret were kept in the downstairs broom closet. The kitchen, made of stone and containing a large fireplace, was now the home of a fire drake called Rix. Each morning after waking, Yimm would make his way into Rix's chamber, set some animated tools to cleaning up after the creature and teleport himself and his pet into the far mountains so that he could take his morning constitutional and the fire drake could romp and hunt. That being accomplished, Yimm and Rix would return home, Rix to take a nap next to the fireplace and Yimm to eat a bowl of pottage, drink a flute of claret and then head into his laboratory.

The laboratory is the other interesting room in the house, for it now holds the gibbering remains of Yimm, his mind completely broken. The night before, he discovered in the worst way possible that the two laboratory rats that escaped many months ago had been quite active, populating the walls of the wizard's house with 1d6+5 brain rats.

Entry into the house is not difficult, for the wizard never locks his front door. Rix will be found to be quite restless, missing his master and his customary romp in the mountains. The brain rats will be in the walls, watching all and preparing an ambush for the visitors.

The wizard keeps a treasure of 1d6 x 100 gp and a coral sculpture of a dolphin worth 450 gp hidden in an extradimensional place that one enters by staring for 3 solid minutes into the eyes of a painting of a hideous duchess hung on the wall.

Copyright Notice

Author Scott Greene.

Rat, Ethereal

Hit Dice: 2
Armor Class: 6 [13]
Attack: Bite (1d3 plus ethereal poisoning)
Saving Throw: 16
Special: Ethereal poisoning, etherealness, surprise on roll of 1-4 on 1d6
Move: 9/9 (climbing)
Alignment: Neutrality
Challenge Level/XP: 4/120

Ethereal rats, like normal rats, they can be found just about anywhere. They look like grayish-black rats about 2 feet long. Ethereal rats attack by biting a foe and then jumping to the Ethereal Plane. If badly wounded in battle an ethereal rat uses its ethereal jaunt ability to escape to the Ethereal Plane.

The bite of an ethereal rat deals 1d4 points of strength damage to a victim. At strength 0, the victim becomes ethereal (as if affected by the *etherealness* spell). The victim remains in this state until at least half of the victim's normal strength score is recovered. Strength returns at the rate of 1 point per day.

An ethereal rat can shift from the Ethereal to the Material Plane per *oil of etherealness*.

Into the Ether

The village of Thorper has been overrun by a pack of 1d6+5 ethereal rats, called into the Material Plane by a soothesayer attempting to manifest the spirit of the recently departed (and beloved) duchess of Thorper by her husband. The rats have made their way through the village, attacking people seemingly at random and sending them into an ethereal state. The arrival of so many people into the borderlands between the deep Ethereal and the Material Plane has created something of a feeding frenzy for the natural predators of the Ethereal Plane, their loved one's having to watch helplessly while many were savaged by seemingly invisible horrors, their dead, ethereal bodies dragged away into the deep Ethereal to be devoured.

The living ethereals have banded together, gathering in the space roughly analagous to the duke's great hall to wait for their strength to slowly return and send them back into the Material Plane. They would be very thankful (to the tune of 1,000 gp) for a party of seasoned adventurers to trap and destroy the ethereal rats.

Copyright Notice

Author Scott Greene.

Rat, Shadow

Hit Dice: 1
Armor Class: 3 [16]
Attack: Bite (1d4 plus 1d3 strength)
Saving Throw: 17
Special: Disease, strength damage, incorporeal, shadow blend, surprise on a roll of 1-3 on 1d6
Move: 15/9 (climbing)
Alignment: Neutrality
Challenge Level/XP: 4/120

Shadow rats are essentially undead rats that can assume an incorporeal form. Other than their semi-translucent form (which they maintain regardless of their incorporeality or not), they resemble their earthly counterparts in all respects save for their rotting flesh, torn and matted fur and blazing, red eyes. They are relentless when they attack. The bite of the shadow rat drains one level unless the victim passes a saving throw. Levels drained by a shadow rat return at the rate of 1 per day on a successful saving throw.

A shadow rat can assume an incorporeal form for up to 1 hour per day. In this form the shadow rat can only be hit by magic weapons and spells.

In any condition of illumination other than full daylight, a shadow rat can disappear into the shadows, giving it total concealment. Artificial illumination, even a *light* or *continual flame* spell, does not negate this ability.

Infinite Shadows

When adventurers enter this circuitous tunnel, a wall will quietly slide in place behind them after they walk about 20 paces. Once shut, only dwarves have a hope of finding the wall again (1 in 6 chance if not looking, 2 in 6 chance if actively looking), but they will find it impossible to shift (although it could conceivably be battered down with several hours of hard labor).

The tunnel takes the shape of a rough figure "eight". The walls of the tunnel are rough and black and seem to absorb the light of torches. Every few feet, these black walls are interrupted by a round plaque of golden-brown stone. Each of these stones measure about 3 feet in diameter and is carved to resemble a gorgon. These stones are used to seal tombs. Behind each seal is a small space carved into the stone wall - about 2-1/2 feet in diameter and six feet long wherein a skeletal body wrapped in brilliantly patterned silks is interred.

None of these bodies are undead, but they have been feasted on by undead shadow rats. As travelers move through the hallway, there is a 2 in 6 chance per turn that they are attacked by a pack of 1d6+1 shadow rats. The rats always come from behind one of the seals, using their incorporeality to phase through the material. They are clever enough to attack light bearers first.

At the intersection of the figure "eight", there is a slim pillar that extends from floor to ceiling. On this pillar are carved four thin faces, each looking in a different direction. When one stands before this pillar, the faces spring to life and proclaim themselves the Keepers of the Royal Tombs. They inform the adventurers that should they wish to pass from the tombs, they must first pay a toll of 30 dead shadow rats. Should this toll be brought before the pillar, it sinks into the ground, revealing a hole in the ceiling through which one can clamber (with the help of a boost) into an upper level of the dungeon. One turn after this exit is revealed, the sliding wall through which the adventurers originally entered the royal tombs resets itself in the open position.

The small tomb spaces contain about 1d4 x 1,000 gp worth of treasure and a pack of 1d6+6 shadow rats.

Copyright Notice
Authors Clark Peterson and Scott Greene.

Rat, Spore

Hit Dice: 3
Armor Class: 7 [12]
Attacks: 1 bite (1d2 + spores)
Saving Throw: 14
Special: poison, spore cloud
Move: 12
Alignment: Neutrality
Challenge Level/XP: 3/60

Spore rats are dog-sized rats with matted brownish fur and ruby red eyes. Its mouth is lined with sharpened teeth and its claws appear to be razor-sharp. A spore rat is typically up to 3 feet long and weighs about 30 pounds. Its fur is greenish-brown and is not actually fur at all, but tightly packed funguses and mushrooms. Its cycs arc ruby rcd or palc ycllow. Its claws and teeth are always filthy and are brownish-white in color. The bite of a spore rat injects spores that cause nausea for 1 round unless a save is made. Twice a day, a spore rat can release a cloud of spores in a 5-foot cloud that causes 1d4 points of damage to any creatures in the cloud.

You Dirty Rat

A 12-foot skiff floats toward the PCs, hovering three feet off the ground at all times. The boat is filled with mounds of mud and loose tree branches. Thorny vines drape over the edges of the floating vessel and drag along the ground. Miniature trees grow out of the dirt, and flowers and mushrooms grow across the bow. A skeleton stands in the stern of the skiff, using a 10-foot-long pole to push the hovering boat forward. The boat moves at walking speed. The words Bone Barge are engraved along its prow.

The boat is home to an infestation of 1d10+8 spore rats that burrow into the muck. The mud clings to their fungus hides, making them appear to be just large rats. The spore rats swarm over the sides of the vessel to bite anyone attacking their floating home. They climb the dragging vines to return to the lair once the threat is dealt with.

The floating skiff belonged to Daznashal the Vicious, who lost the boat during a storm when it burrowed into the Sin Mire and filled with swampy sludge.

Copyright Notice

Rawbones

Hit Dice: 8
Armor Class: 4 [15]
Attacks: 2 slams (1d8) or entrail lash (1d4)
Saving Throw: 8
Special: Nauseating aura, strangulation, vomit gore, +1 magic weapons to hit, immune to cold
Move: 6
Alignment: Chaos
Challenge Level/XP: 10/1,400

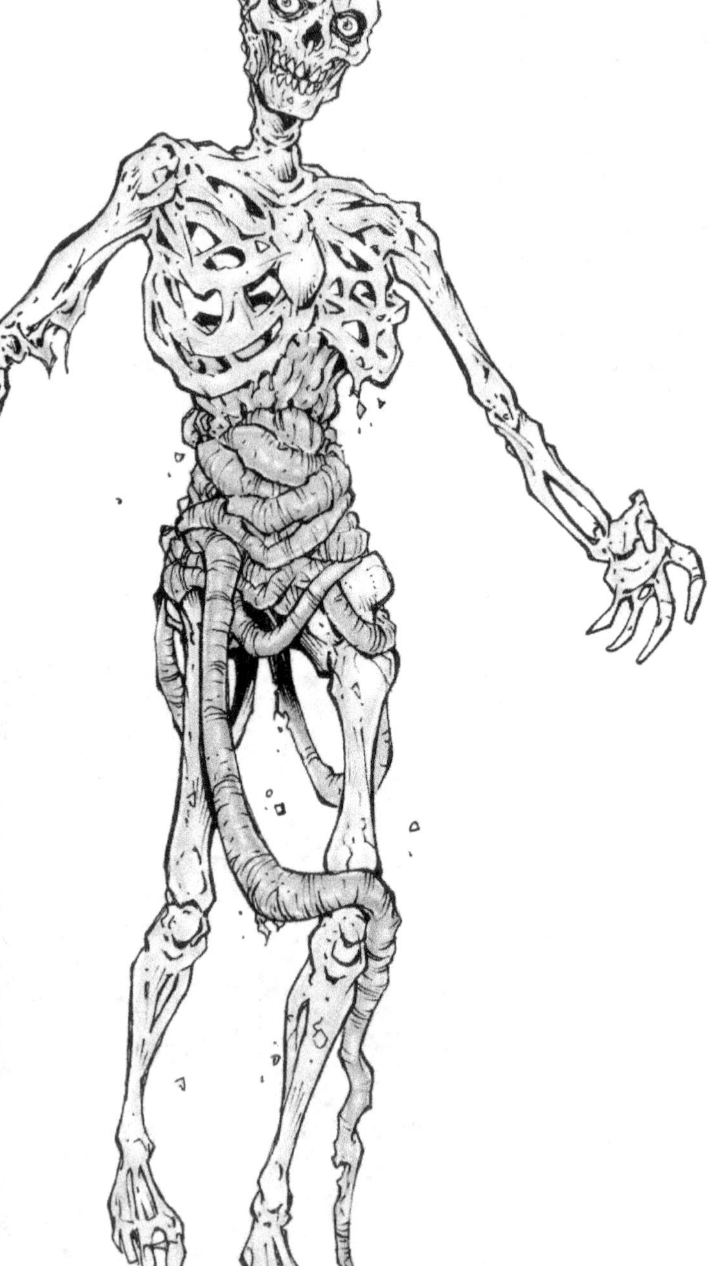

A rawbones appears to be a freshly skinned and cleaned corpse standing 6 to 6-1/2 feet tall and weighing roughly 140 pounds. Its bones are stained red with fresh blood which seems to continually weep from the creature's body. Bits of flesh and muscle fall away from it as it moves about and its entrails often drag the ground behind it or are wrapped around the creature's forearms. Rawbones reek of death in a 20-foot radius, requiring all creatures approaching them to save or become nauseated. If a rawbones hits an opponent with an entrail lash, the victim must save or become entangled and strangled for 1d4 points of damage each round thereafter until freed. Three times per day, a rawbones can spit a blast of blood and gore in a 20-foot cone that does 6d6 points of damage (save for half).

Collateral Damage

The ruins of Castle Caern are silent and foreboding, the collapsed ebon walls nothing more than jagged heaps of shifting stone in the desolate landscape above the town of Drulk. Markers stolen from the nearby graveyard to decorate the castle's outer walls poke through the rubble, each bearing the names of the dead. The gravestones still burn with an inner warmth.

Standing in the middle of the collapsed castle is a 20-foot-tall metal spike radiating cool silver light. The spike looks like it was cast down from the heavens to strike the center of the castle and punched all the way through to its stone foundation. Symbols of the god of justice are branded into the sliver. The silver needle is clawed and slashed, and dark blots are burned across its surface.

Three innocents held in shackles in the dungeon didn't survive the explosion that leveled the castle. They died underground, choking on the rock debris filling the tunnels around them. The three are now rawbones who clawed their way through the rocks. They slashed at the silver lance to exact their revenge, but went unsatisfied. They lie in wait among the rocks for anyone approaching the silver weapon of the gods.

Red Jester

Hit Dice: 12
Armor Class: 2 [17]
Attacks: +2 heavy mace of merriment (1d6+1) or jester's deck
Saving Throw: 3
Special: Fear cackle, jester's deck, merriment
Move: 9
Alignment: Chaos
Challenge Level/XP: 14/2,600

A red jester is a rotting humanoid wearing brightly colored clothes, floppy shoes, and a bright red jester's hat complete with jingling bells sewn to the ends. The creature has a permanent smirk or smile on its face, even during combat. Some red jesters, to disguise their undead nature, don masks or wear makeup. A red jester can unleash a fear-inducing cackle that causes *fear* (as per the spell) in all creatures that fail a save. A red jester uses a +2 heavy mace of merriment that causes any creature struck to save or fall to the ground laughing for 1d3 rounds. The jester also can draw a card from a deck of many things it carries and throw it at an opponent. If the opponent is struck by the thrown card, the card's effect takes place as if the person had drawn the card himself. The jester can draw and throw a card once per round, and can choose which card is drawn, even drawing the same card multiple times.

Dead Man's Hand

Fifty years ago, King Jepson IV demanded a joke, one so funny it would leave him laughing for days. But when his court jester couldn't deliver the perfect punchline, the king had him executed and his body tossed in the rubbish pile as a warning to future funnymen. But the jester took his job seriously and rose from the dead a night later. His corpse staggered from the kingdom, asking everyone he met for a joke that would allow him to return and please his king. He's still looking. The red jester now wanders into towns and asks everyone he meets for a joke, any joke. If one is offered to the undead creature, it weighs the riddle's merits and offers a reward – or punishment – for the effort. The jester purposefully picks a card from his *deck of many things* as a sign of thanks – or a way to get even for someone belittling his quest. Game Referees may ask players for their best joke: those who participate and try to come up with something funny may be rewarded. Those who dismiss the whole thing as childish – or worse, insult the jester – won't like the consequences.

Copyright Notice
Author Scott Greene.

Redcap

Hit Dice: 1d4 hp
Armor Class: 7 [12]
Attacks: 1 weapon (1d4 + poison) or claws (1d2)
Saving Throw: 18
Special: Poison, spell-like abilities
Move: 4
Alignment: Chaos
Challenge Level/XP: B/10

Redcaps stand just about 20 inches tall with wrinkled gray skin, gray or white hair, and gray or blue eyes. Their mouths sport small upward curving fangs, and their hands end in eagle-like talons. Redcaps prefer to dress in greens, browns, or other drab colors, except their hats. Their hats are always red, having been soaked in the blood of those they have slain. They coat their weapons with a toxic poison. Redcaps can turn *invisible* at will, cast *dancing lights*, *detect good* and *mirror image* once per day.

Hate Mill

An abandoned mill sits along a dry riverbed. A giant waterwheel is still, the boards broken and dry. Birds make nests in the water troughs. The three-story mill is built of gray bricks and sits dark and silent. Weeds and flowering plants grow through the wood-slat floor. Piles of rotting grain lies in heaps on the mill floor.

Hanging from the dusty rafters inside the mill are the bodies of nixies, grigs, squirrels, mice, owls and moles. Each body hangs from taut nooses, the bodies black and blue and beaten. Many are dried and rotted. The odor of decay fills the large room. Scattered on the wood floor are hundreds of insect bodies, some sliced in half. Limbs, thoraxes and wings lie in heaps.

A group of redcaps lives in an overturned grain bin inside the mill, while their pet and protector – a giant chameleon – lives in a 12-foot-tall pile of moldy corn. The redcaps collect insects at night for the chameleon. They kill any other small animals or fey they encounter and hang their bodies from the mill's rafters. The mill is built on an ancient redcap village, and the redcaps fight to protect their land.

Copyright Notice

Reigon

Hit Dice: 5
Armor Class: 6 [13]
Attacks: 2 claws (1d6) and 1 bite (1d8) or weapon (1d6) and 1 bite (1d8)
Saving Throw: 12
Special: Camouflage, spell-like abilities
Move: 6/6 (climb)
Alignment: Chaos
Challenge Level/XP: 6/400

A reigon is a gorilla with thick, brownish-black fur. Its face is white and its eyes are brown. Its mouth is lined with rows of sharp teeth with the canines being slightly longer than the rest. Its hands end in wickedly sharp black nails. Reigons stand about 8 feet tall and weigh around 600 pounds. Reigons are masters of blending into their surroundings. They can release a concussive force blast once per day that deals 2d8 points of damage to an opponent (save for half).

Ape God

Lush trees and thick vegetation form a natural dome 50 feet overhead. Only the midday light manages to break through the green ceiling. A flagstone terrace sits under the dome. A 15-foot-tall pillar carved with ancient runes erupts from the patio's center. A one-foot-tall diamond-shaped purple amethyst defies gravity as it spins atop the pillar. Daylight shining through the amethyst sends flashing violet rays to the ground around the pillar. The amethyst is a relic from a forgotten religion. Under certain conditions and prayers, the amethyst grants ordinary animals the gift of sentience and some minor magical powers. The runes on the pillar describe these details, if deciphered.

Currently a troop of relgons adopts the area as a shrine to an obscure deity. The reigons live in nearby cliffs. The reigons learned the secrets of the amethyst's power and brought chimpanzees and orangutans to the crystal to gain sentience. They use the lesser apes as servants. Many have greater intelligence and compassion than the reigons, but are too weak to fight against the more-powerful apes.

Copyright Notice
Author Scott Greene.

Reliquary Guardian

Hit Dice: 60 hit points
Armor Class: 5 [14]
Attacks: +1 long sword (3d6) or slam (3d8)
Saving Throw: 3
Special: +2 or greater weapons to hit, immune to most spells, pronouncement, magical powers
Move: 6
Alignment: Neutrality
Challenge Level/XP: 16/3,200

A reliquary guardian is a 12-foot-tall exquisitely carved statue weighing 5,000 pounds. Reliquary guardians are constructs found guarding the bones of saints or protecting religious icons and relics against would- be thieves or plunderers. They stand unmoving unless activated by intrusion into their protected sanctuary by unbelievers. Once per day, a reliquary guardian can make a pronouncement that affects all creatures within 60 feet that hear it as if by a *fear* spell. Once per day, reliquary guardians can also cast *detect magic*, *detect invisibility*, *dispel magic*, *confusion* and *feeblemind*.

The Bones of the Martyr

A ruined cemetery of unknown age lies in shambles amid the violently turned ground. Stone sarcophagi, obelisks and monuments lean at random angles across the tortured landscape. The land still shivers with temblors that cause monuments to topple and ancient caskets to rise out of the soil.

A reliquary golem stands amid the chaos, guarding an iron urn. The urn contains the bones and ashes of Invadak, the Sage of the Ancients. It is rumored that worthy petitioners can request answers from Invadak's remains. The remains swirl up from within the urn to form a dusty apparition of Invadak. The golem smites those unworthy to seek an audience or at the request of Invadak's shade.

Copyright Notice

Renzer (Devilfin)

Hit Dice: 8
Armor Class: 5 [14]
Attacks: 2 claws (1d6+1), 1 bite (1d8+1)
Saving Throw: 8
Special: Spell-like abilities
Move: 24 (swim)
Alignment: Chaos
Challenge Level/XP: 9/1,100

The renzer is a large predatory creature about 12 feet long that resembles a grayish-white shark with the head of a humanoid. The human head is hairless, having neither hair nor eyelashes or even eyebrows. Its teeth are long and pointed and the renzer's tongue is forked and brown in color. Its shark-like pectoral fins end in three-fingered claws and it has two dorsal fins, side-by-side. Its tail fins are sharply curved and are a bit lighter in color than the rest of its body. Twice per day, a renzer can cast *cone of cold* and *charm monster* (fish only).

Net Loss

A hemp net spreads on the water among the ships anchored in Rout's Harbor. A sailor floats face down in the center of the net, his arms splayed wide and his hands wrapped tightly in the strands. The sailor's face is bitten away, leaving a gaping hole into the man's skull.

The 20-foot-wide net is enchanted to wrap itself around anyone who comes within 5 feet of it and fails a saving throw. The net sinks like a stone when it entwines a victim, taking the PC into the depths. Lurking on the bottom of the harbor are 6 sahuagins and their leader, a renzer named Raxoc who dreams of conquering the port city.

Sahuagin: HD 2+1; AC 5[14]; Atk 1 weapon (1d8); Move 12 (Swim 18); Save 16; CL/XP 2/30; Special: None.

Copyright Notice
Author Scott Greene.

Retch Hound

Hit Dice: 3+2
Armor Class: 5 [14]
Attacks: 1 bite (1d8)
Saving Throw: 14
Special: Breath weapon, stench
Move: 18
Alignment: Neutrality
Challenge Level/XP: 4/120

Retch hounds are large, muscular dogs with sickly brownish-yellow fur, matted or torn in places. Small sores cover its body, each oozing a thick, yellowish-green liquid. Its mouth is filled with long pointed yellow teeth, some broken off on the ends. A retch hound has four large yellow eyes evenly aligned across its canine head. A typical retch hound stands 4 to 4 1/2 feet tall at the shoulder and weighs about 150 pounds. A sickening stench surrounds a retch hound, nauseating opponents who approach within 30 feet unless they make a save. Once per round, a retch hound can belch forth a blast of digestive acid in a 10-foot cone (2d6 damage, save for half).

Walking the Dogs

Corpuzon the Putrescent is a haughty lich who enjoyed a hedonistic life when he was alive. A beefy man, Corpuzon lost much of his fat in death, and his skin sags in loose flappy layers off his five-foot frame. His eyes are gone, leaving ragged holes that burn with an inner green fire. A three-pronged platinum crown (worth 600 gp) sits on his desiccated skull with the words "Feast of Life" engraved into its surface. He wears dirty green-and-yellow robes, and the stench of death wafts off his body in nauseating waves.

Corpuzon always travels with his companions, Feast and Famine, two retch hounds he fawns incessantly over. The sickening smell of the retch hounds doesn't affect the lich, and he's powerful enough to stop them when the aggressive animals occasionally turn on him. Each wears a diamond-studded collar (1,000 gp each) around its neck, to which Corpuzon attaches a 10-foot-long leather leash.

The lich recently decided to treat the hounds to a "night on the town" for their birthday, and strides into the nearest city with Feast and Famine leading the way. The hounds strain at their leashes, waiting to pounce on anyone they encounter. Corpuzon lets the dogs have their fun, but defends himself if necessary. The 12-HD lich uses his spells to protect his pets if they get into trouble.

Copyright Notice
Author Scott Greene.

Riptide Horror

Hit Dice: 6
Armor Class: 3 [16]
Attacks: 6 tentacles (1d4 + poison) and 6 bites (1d6)
Saving Throw: 11
Special: Grab, poison, half damage piercing and slashing weapons
Move: Chaos
Alignment: 6/15/9 (swim/climb)
Challenge Level/XP: 7/600

Riptide horrors are grayish-tan tubeworms about 7 feet in length with six eyeless heads. Each mouth is lined with inward curving, serrated teeth. The underside of the riptide horror is white and six long grayish-tan tentacles protrude from the middle of its body. If a riptide horror hits with two tentacles on the same opponent, it grabs the victim and pulls it to its mouths for automatic bite damage.

Belly of the Whale

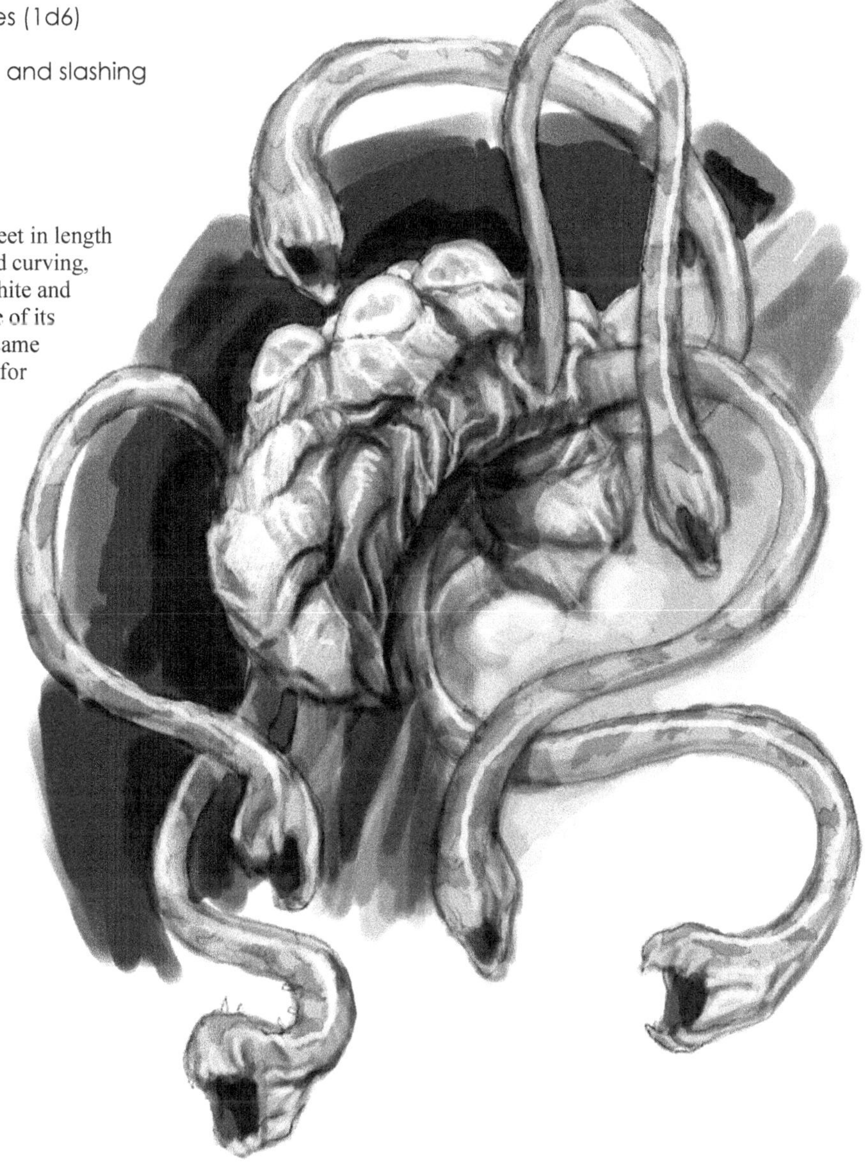

A dead whale lies on the sandy strip of shore near the wharfs of Squall Harbor, the giant creature bloating in the midday sun. Its skin is rubbery and soft, and the smell of dead fish wafts off the carcass. The sea creature's eyes are rolled up and its mouth hangs open. Seaweed hangs in verdant strands inside the gaping maw. The whale's tongue lolls from the side of its mouth, and is coated with a sticky, greenish-tan mass of eggs. A bony chittering sound rises out of the mouth.

Two riptide horrors found the dying whale shortly after it beached itself, and crawled into its open mouth to mate. The creatures move freely inside the whale's body as they await high tide to slip out and back into the sea. They lash out with their tentacles to pull PCs into the whale's mouth.

Copyright Notice
Author Erica Balsley.

Rock Reptile

Hit Dice: 5
Armor Class: 2 [17]
Attack: Bite (1d6)
Saving Throw: 12
Special: Surprise on roll of 1-3 on 1d6
Move: 9
Alignment: Neutrality
Challenge Level/XP: 5/240

A rock reptile is a 5-foot long chameleon-like lizard that lairs in rocky areas such as caves and outcroppings. It is fond of darkness and only leaves its seclusion when it is ravaged by hunger. Its chameleon-like ability allows it to blend with its surroundings where it is often mistaken for a pile of rocks.

Rock reptiles are ambush hunters and lie quietly in wait for prey to come within range. Once prey is within range, the creature springs from its hiding place with blinding speed and bites at its prey. On the first round after it emerges, it gains a +2 bonus on its attack roll.

Three Hermits

Beyond the green and pleasant mountains there is a vast expanse of badlands. The badlands are composed of acre after acre of ochre-colored stones, rounded and haphazardly stacked, some appearing as though they could topple at any moment. There is only minor vegetation in the badlands - some scrub, a few cacti and stiff grasses fit only for the iron stomaches of goats.

The dominant predator in the badlands is the rock reptile. The creatures' rocky hides blend perfectly with the landscape, making travelers easy prey. Encounters with rock reptiles occur on a roll of 1 on 1d6 made each hour one travels through the badlands.

It is in this wilderness that the three holy hermits of Azucar chose to make their homes. The hermits dwell in small, shallow caves at the foot of stone pinnacles. The least of the hermits has the power to cure all diseases, while the greatest can return the dead to life.

Seekers of the hermits have a 1 in 6 chance per day of coming upon one. The hermits are called Azka, Eris and Ullo. Azka can cure all diseases, but cannot speak the truth. Eris can restore lost levels, but is cursed to do the opposite of what is requested of her. Ullo can bring the dead back to life, but is blind, deaf and mute, making communication with him very difficult. When found, a hermit will be sitting in the lotus position in front of a fire fed by creosote bushes. The hermits have the stats of normal humans and they possess no treasure.

Credit
The Rock Reptile originally appeared in the First Edition *Monster Manual II* (© TSR/Wizards of the Coast, 1983) and is used by permission.

Copyright Notice
Author Scott Greene, based on original material by Gary Gygax.

Ronus

Hit Dice: 3
Armor Class: 4 [15]
Attacks: 1 bite (1d6+2)
Saving Throw: 14
Special: None
Move: 24
Alignment: Neutrality
Challenge Level/XP: 3/60

A ronus is a brownish-gray wolf with the head of a falcon. Its falcon-head is covered with light brown or tan-colored feathers that slowly fade in color near the neck and blend with the fur on its canine torso. Its eyes are a rich brown color and its beak, razor-sharp, is dark grayish-black. The neck is lighter, almost white, and slowly blends with the lighter brownish-gray fur on the ronus's chest.

Death Race

This encounter takes place as PCs are camping in the forest. At some point during the night, the sound of twigs snapping is heard as something moves toward the campfire. Four ronus step out of the trees. Each wears a black leather collar around its neck with a gem hanging on a silver chain. Each animal has a different color gem hanging below its beak. The gems glow with a soft inner radiance.

The ronus are owned by a cruel magic-user named Holis Wastburn. The gems are enchanted to permanently give off a *fear* effect (as per the spell of the same name) in creatures within 20 feet. The gems cease to function if removed from the collars. The gems are worth 150 gp if sold as a set.

The ronus immediately chase any PC who runs in fear from them. If PCs don't run, the ronus flee back into the trees.

Copyright Notice
Author Scott Greene.

Roper, Stone

Hit Dice: 6
Armor Class: 0 [19]
Attack: Strand (drag) or bite (1d8)
Saving Throw: 11
Special: Drag, freeze, stony hide, strands, venom, resistance to normal arrows and bolts (50%), surprise on 1-3 on 1d6
Move: 6
Alignment: Chaos
Challenge Level/XP: 8/800

Stone ropers are distant relatives of the common roper though the two species do not associate with one another. Stone ropers are always found underground and never venture forth to the surface world. They have a dislike for sunlight, though it doesn't harm them in any way.

Stone ropers are primarily predators, dining on a diet of fresh meat taken from whatever they can find and kill. When food is scarce, stone ropers become scavengers and dine on carrion.

Stone ropers are mottled gray and brown like stone and have a rock-like body. Cutting a stone roper open reveals its treasure hiddin inside its gizzard. A typical stone roper stands 5 feet tall and weighs about 1,000 pounds. Stone ropers speak their own dialect of the roper language.

Most encounters with a stone roper begin when it fires its strong, sticky strands. A stone roper attacks anything that comes within 50 feet by suddenly shooting out its tentacle strands. It prefers to attack two victims at once, each with three strands. If a stone roper hits with a strand attack, the strand latches onto the opponent's body. This deals no damage but drags the stuck opponent 10 feet closer each subsequent round unless that creature breaks free, which requires a successful open doors roll. A stone roper can draw in a creature within 10 feet of itself and bite with a +2 attack bonus in the same round. A strand has 10 hit points. Severing a strand deals no damage to a stone roper. If a strand is severed, the stone roper can extrude a new one on its next turn.

The first two victims successfully attacked are injected with the stone roper's venom. Twice per day, a stone roper can secrete venom from each of its strands. A creature hit by a strand must succeed on a saving throw or be paralyzed. A paralyzed creature appears to have been turned to stone (close inspection reveals that this is in fact not the case). One round after being paralyzed, the victim recovers and must succeed on a saving throw or act as if under the effects of a *charm person* spell for 2d4 rounds. A charmed creature fights for and defends the stone roper. If the stone roper is killed, a charmed victim acts as if under the effects of a *confusion* spell for 1d6+2 rounds.

If the venom fails, the stone roper continues to hold the creatures. A stone roper's strands sap an opponent's strength. Anyone grabbed by a strand must succeed on a saving throw or take 2d4 points of strength damage.

A stone roper can hold itself so still it appears to be a statue. An observer must succeed on a roll of 1 on 1d6 to notice the stone roper is really alive. A stone roper can automatically detect the location of anything within 200 feet that is in contact with the ground.

Obstacle

While exploring the underworld, a band of adventurers will experience a truly frightening thing - an earthquake. The quake is not terribly damaging - folks might be knocked prone, dust will fall, but nobody is hurt or put through a major inconvenience.

As they delve deeper, they come across a newly created crevasse. About 20 feet below the upper edge of the crevasse there is a rend in the granite forming a small cave. A band of 1d3+2 gnomes are in this cave trying to avoid the tendrils of a stone roper at the top of a crevasse.

The crevasse is about 30 feet wide, the near side about 6 feet below the far side. The crevasse is 300 feet deep, with a number of dead gnomes at the bottom. The gnomes were transporting expensive spices worth 1,300 gp when the event happened, and though some of the casks they were transporting are now broken at the bottom of the crevasse, about 400 gp worth are still intact.

Credit
The Stone Roper (Storoper) originally appeared in the First Edition module *A3 Assault on the Aerie of the Slave Lords* (© TSR/Wizards of the Coast, 1980) and later in the First Edition *Monster Manual II* (© TSR/Wizards of the Coast, 1983) and is used by permission.

Copyright Notice
Author Scott Greene, based on original material by Allen Hammack and Gary Gygax.

Ryven

Hit Dice: 3
Armor Class: 7 [12]
Attacks: 2 claws (1d4) and bite (1d6), or 1 weapon (1d6)
Saving Throw: 14
Special: Rage
Move: 6
Alignment: Neutrality
Challenge Level/XP: 3/60

Ryven are known as badger-folk by those of other races. In appearance, they resemble man-sized, bipedal badgers. Ryvens are 5 or 6 feet tall and weigh about 450 pounds. Their arms are broad and well-muscled as are their legs. Their hands and feet end in sharpened claws with elongated nails. Ryvens have short, bushy, brown tails. Their bodies are covered in brown or gray fur with lighter coloration on the abdomen and chest; facial fur is brown or gray with black patches or rings. A long stripe of white fur runs from its nose, across its head, and down its back, terminating near its tail. A ryven that is injured in combat can fly into a berserk rage three times per day, clawing and biting with a +2 bonus to its attacks and damage.

The Animal King

A group of monk's sits in a circle in a small marble and glass atrium to the side of the road. Columns holding up the atrium's roof depict a wild hunt, with rabbits and foxes outrunning hounds. They wear long red robes and hoods that cover them from head to foot. Their hands are folded into the elaborate robes. Mesh screens sewn into the hoods conceal their features. Their whispered chant is a soft hum radiating out of the quiet atrium.

The six monks surround a glass spindle rising four feet high in the middle of the atrium. A delicate crystal decanter filled with a golden liquid sits in a niche carved into the glass. The liquid gleams in a shaft of sunlight filtering through stained-glass panels set in the roof.

The monks are 6 ryven awaiting the resurrection of their true leader. They don't speak and don't make a move to stop anyone approaching the decanter. They stop chanting in anticipation should a PC prepare to drink the draught. The golden liquid tastes like elderberries. It refills automatically once set back into the glass pillar.

PCs who drink from the decanter have a 1 in 6 chance of gaining an animal trait: whiskers, a bushy fox tail, pointed ears, fur, etc. Those who gain an animal characteristic further have another 1 in 6 chance of turning fully into a ryven. If this happens, the ryven monks bow to their newly risen leader. Those who don't gain an animal trait are healed for 1d6 points of damage. This healing occurs only if the liquid is sipped from the crystal decanter within the confines of the atrium. It loses all potency if removed.

Copyright Notice
Author Scott Greene.

Sabrewing

Hit Dice: 5
Armor Class: 5 [14]
Attacks: 2 wing slashes (1d6+2)
Saving Throw: 12
Special: +1 weapons to hit
Move: 6/12 (flying)
Alignment: Neutrality
Challenge Level/XP: 5/240

A sabrewing is a 6-foot tall, muscular humanoid with two large, leathery wings in place of its arms. Each wing has a plate of razor-sharp and rigid bone on its outer side. Its flesh is rubbery and black in color while the bony edges of its wings are slate gray or dull silver. A sabrewing's head is hairless and humanoid in appearance. Its eyes are small and slitted with golden pupils. A sabrewing's long, muscular legs end in three-toed clawed feet and its mouth is wide and filled with rows of sharp teeth.

The King and Eye

King Narsh II is uneasy. A mysterious box arrived for him three days ago, with no note or any information about who sent it. The courier vanished before he could be detained and questioned. Inside the felt-lined container was the plucked-out eye of a storm giant staring up at him.

As King Narsh stared into the bloody depths of the eye, he realized he was seeing through the pupil into another plane of existence. He spied on jagged citadels of stone and iron that rose into the dull sky. He saw a forest of moving steel blades slicing all life to ribbons. The king recoiled at the visions, but the damage was done as a hairless head appeared in the vision and two golden eyes stared malevolently at the king.

Two sabrewings are zeroing in on the royal court, and await the chance to strike and slay the king spying on their home world. The king requires protection, and offers PCs a hefty fortune (and the storm giant's eye, which serves as a *crystal ball*) if they'll protect him.

Copyright Notice
Author Scott Greene.

Sand Kraken

Hit Dice: 8
Armor Class: 6 [13]
Attacks: 10 tentacles (1d6) and bite (2d6)
Saving Throw: 8
Special: Constrict, camouflage
Move: 0 (immobile)
Alignment: Neutrality
Challenge Level/XP: 9/1,100

Sand kraken are bloated, eyeless, formless octopi ranging 15 feet across. The coloration of a sand kraken is a revolting pale yellow. From its shapeless body sprouts ten long tentacles tipped with cruel barbed pads. A sand kraken lies hidden under the desert sands, waiting to use its tentacles to grab prey passing above it. If a sand kraken hits a single opponent with two or more tentacles, it constricts the victim for 1d6 damage and drags him into the sand to the kraken's mouth for automatic bite damage.

House of Sand

The desert village of Rankaap was abandoned 100 years ago during the War of the Winds when scouring blasts of desert air lifted the sand in a scouring wall. A dozen or so stone buildings sit abandoned, the doors and windows open to the surrounding desert. Heat rises past 130 degrees during the day, and plummets to 30 degrees at night. Most of the buildings are dilapidated, but a two-story building still appears habitable.

The outer stone walls of the manor house are sandblasted smooth from the driving winds, but the interior remains relatively intact. Tables and chairs, paintings, and other fixtures can be found in almost every room, although up to six feet of drifting sand covers the floors and objects. The drifts are less on the second floor, but the wooden floors still creak ominously because of the weight of the sand.

A gold chandelier with crystal glass globes hangs from the 15-foot-high ceiling of the 20-foot wide family room on the first floor. The room is bare of furniture. A smooth layer of sand three feet deep appears to fill the room. In fact, the sand is closer to 12 feet deep after the wooden floor collapsed into a wine cellar. The splintered furniture rests amid the wreckage of the wine racks below tons of sand.

A sand kraken lairs in the basement, waiting for creatures to enter the family room above.

Copyright Notice
Author Erica Balsley.

Sand Stalker

Hit Dice: 7
Armor Class: 4 [15]
Attacks: 1 bite (1d6+2 + poison)
Saving Throw: 9
Special: Paralytic poison, sound lure
Move: 15/12 (burrow)
Alignment: Neutrality
Challenge Level/XP: 9/1,100

Sand stalkers are aggressive 12-foot-long hunting spiders with light gray underbellies. Desert dwellers, sand stalkers burrow just beneath the sand, leaving only their front forelegs exposed. The wind plays over their forelegs, producing an eerie flute-like sound that attracts and hypnotizes prey into approaching the creature (save to resist). A sand stalker's bite delivers a poison that paralyzes its prey (save avoids) so they can be consumed at the creature's leisure.

Wind in the Willows

A small oasis sits among the desert dunes, the 30-foot-wide pool of clear water surrounded by swaying reeds. Stunted palm trees stand about the lake, their roots draped into the placid water. A light breeze plays a trilling melody of notes as it flits through the reeds.

No animal tracks approach the oasis, despite the harsh desert stretching for miles around the tiny patch of serenity. The water is clear and refreshing, although it has a slight mineral taste.

The real danger is a sand stalker that lives under the sand among the reeds growing wild around the small pond. The creature has its hollow forelegs sticking up among the reeds to create the music drifting around the area.

Copyright Notice

Sandling

This creature appears to be a large snake formed of earth and sand. A slit seems to function as the creature's mouth.

Hit Dice: 4
Armor Class: 3 [16]
Attack: Bite (1d8)
Saving Throw: 13
Special: Resistance to edged weapons (50%), vulnerability to water
Move: 12/9 (burrowing)
Alignment: Neutrality
Challenge Level/XP: 4/120

Sandlings are creatures from the Elemental Plane of Earth. A sandling in its natural form resembles a mound of sand that covers a 10-foot area. They are most often summoned to the Material Plane by clerics and wizards, though on occasion a sandling slips through a vortex connecting the Elemental Plane of Earth to the Material Plane.

Sandlings live on a diet of minerals and cannot digest plants, herbs, meat, or other substances. Opponents killed by a sandling are left for scavengers.

Sandlings have no real society and are highly solitary in nature. Though they harbor no ill-will towards others of their kind, it is very rare to find more than one sandling operating near another. Reproduction methods among sandlings is unknown to sages but it is believed they create others of their kind by division (that is, an adult sandling splits into two or more smaller creatures).

A typical sandling is 10 feet long but can grow to a length of 20 to 25 feet.

For every 2 gallons of water that hit a sandling, it is slowed (as the *slow* spell) for 1 round (no save).

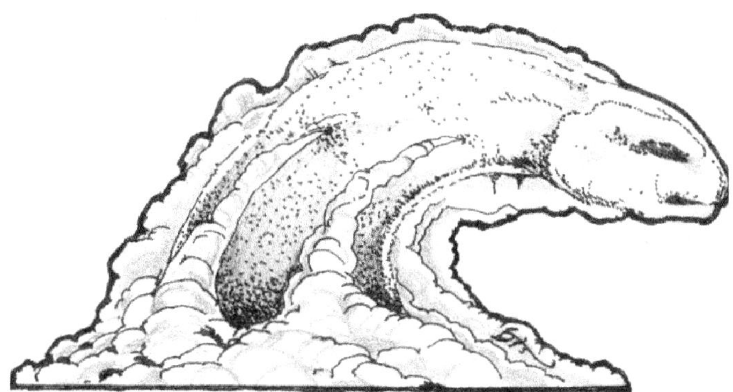

Little Maker of Death

A band of evil masterminds erected a stone pagoda in the middle of a woodland of towering teaks. The pavilion is constructed for pearly white stones quarried on the Elemental Plane of Earth and then expertly cut in the workshop of an ancient house of svirfneblins, impressing within each stone a three-dimensional rune of mithral. These runes, properly assembled as they now are, turn the pavilion into a terrible engine of destruction. All the pavilion lacks is a final trigger, a six-pointed star carved from an immense opal.

The star trigger was lost, and the mad elementalists thwarted, by a band of paladins from a nearby city-state. The star opal is now inlaid into the large, round teak table that dominates the great hall of their chapter house. The paladins and their soldiers wear a multi-colored patchwork six-pointed star on their mantles, for it has become the symbol of their order.

Should the star opal be brought into the pavilion and placed in the space awaiting it in the ceiling, the pavilion will become the single safe haven in a hemisphere of destruction that grows outward from the pavilion at the rate of 1 mile per day, until it finally extends to a radius of 500 miles. Within this hemisphere the earth is wracked by quakes, landslides and tornadoes. Lakes and rivers are swallowed by the earth, leaving behind a parched, broken landscape fit only for monsters and the tougher humanoids.

Within the pavilion, there is a pit of sand that is warm to the touch. A large sandling dwells in this pit, emerging only to attack those who do not identify themselves as friends by pricking their fingers with copper needles and dropping those needles into the sand pit. All others are marked for destruction.

Credit

The Sandling originally appeared in the First Edition module *A4 In the Dungeons of the Slave Lords* (© TSR/Wizards of the Coast, 1981) and later in the First Edition *Monster Manual II* (© TSR/Wizards of the Coast, 1983) and is used by permission.

Copyright Notice

Author Scott Greene, based on original material by Lawrence Schick.

Sandman

Hit Dice: 4
Armor Class: 3 [16]
Attack: Strike (1d4 plus sleep)
Saving Throw: 13
Special: Sleep aura, resistance to non-magical ranged weapons (50%), magic resistance (25%)
Move: 12
Alignment: Neutrality (chaotic tendencies)
Challenge Level/XP: 6/400

Sandmen are silicate creatures from the Elemental Plane of Earth. They appear as slender humans constructed of sand. They have delicate facial features and long, slender fingers. Their purpose on the Material Plane is unknown, but spellcasters often summon them when they want to protect someone or something. Though sandmen have chaotic tendencies many willingly serve summoners of other alignments.

Sandmen have an immense dislike for humans (reasons unknown) and attack them on sight—human spellcasters take heed when employing their services!

A sandman can radiate a 20-foot-radius sleep aura as it pleases. A creature in the area must succeed on a saving throw or be affected as though by a *sleep* spell cast by an 8th level magic-user. There is no limit to the number of Hit Dice a sandman can affect with this aura. A creature that successfully saves cannot be affected again by the same sandman's sleep aura for one day.

A creature struck by or touching a sandman must also succeed on a saving throw or be affected as though by a *sleep* spell cast by an 8th level magic-user. Again, there is no limit to the number of Hit Dice a sandman can affect with this ability.

Bring Me a Dream

In the stony desert that covers a great peninsula you might come across the palace of a great conqueror. The palace is constructed of sandstone and boasts 1,000 grand pillars, some rising as high as 50 feet, over one hundred chambers and a network of troughs fed by a spring. The troughs allow the palace servants to cultivate a massive garden in the center of the palace that features fruit trees, vines, vegetables, song birds and a variety of small game. Most of the palace's needs are fulfilled by tribute from more fertile lands conquered by the sultan with the help of a slim whistle.

The whistle is carved from the finger bones of an elemental earth dragon. It looks like ivory but has the strength of steel. The whistle always hangs around the sultan's neck. By blowing into the whistle and concentrating on an object made of stone, the sultan can turn that stone into sand. Obviously, this has been most helpful in toppling the walls of many towns and strongholds. The whistle can also be used to summon a gang of 1d8+1 sandmen, who serve the sultan loyally for a period of one week before seemingly blowing away on an etheric wind back to their home on the Elemental Plane of Earth. A gang of these sandmen dwell in the sandpits that surround the palace, where glassblowers do a steady trade in art glass.

The sultan can usually be found in his gallery, admiring glass statues of lovely jinni swathed in veils and striking fetching poses. These twelve statues are actually sandmen that have been trapped in glass. With a blow of his whistle, they return to their normal form and become fierce guardians. Hidden behind a wall in the gallery is the sultan's treasure: 17,540 sp, 3,820 gp and a brass idol of a terrifying efreet with carnelian eyes (worth 6,000 gp, weighs 1,000 pounds).

Credit

The Sandman originally appeared in the First Edition *Fiend Folio* (© TSR/Wizards of the Coast, 1981) and is used by permission.

Copyright Notice

Author Scott Greene, based on original material by Roger Musson.

Scarecrow

Hit Dice: 5
Armor Class: 5 [14]
Attack: Strike (1d6 plus fascination)
Saving Throw: 12
Special: Fascination, immunity to cold, double damage from fire
Move: 9
Alignment: Neutrality
Challenge Level/XP: 6/400

The animated scarecrow is nearly indistinguishable from a normal scarecrow. Close examination, however, reveals a tiny spark of red light in its eyes (1 in 6 chance to notice). Each scarecrow is unique in construction and design, but most are about 6 feet tall, constructed of wood and ropes, and stuffed with straw or grass. Scarecrows are most often used as guardians to keep out would-be treasure hunters or trespassers.

Any living creature within 30 feet meeting the gaze of a scarecrow must succeed on a saving throw or be fascinated for as long as the scarecrow is "alive" or remains within 300 feet of the fascinated person. A fascinated creature can take no actions but can defend themselves. A fascinated creature can attempt a new saving throw any time it is attacked. The touch of a scarecrow fascinates a foe in the same way its gaze does.

Construction

Each scarecrow varies in appearance: one may have a stuffed straw head, for example, while another may have a pumpkin for its head. Whatever the differences, scarecrows do have some elements in common: their bodies and all limbs are constructed of wood and bound by ropes; their clothes are almost always dirty and ragged; and most scarecrows are stuffed with straw or grass. Regardless of the materials used, unguents and special powders totaling 500 gp are also required.

Assembling the body requires a skilled woodworker and a magic-user of at least 12th level that can cast *charm person, hold person* and *geas*.

Not For Scaring Crows

A solitary scarecrow leans against a bower of roses that marks the gateway to a crumbling stone farmhouse. The scarecrow has a burlap face painted with the face of a fierce warrior. On its frame of sticks is draped an ancient, tattered robe. For hands it has bamboo rakes.

The scarecrow was constructed by a magic-user called Kimbuk, a leader of rebellious peasants, to guard their hideout in the ruined farmhouse. The farmhouse belonged to a popular yeoman farmer who made the mistake of standing up to the fell lord that has seized power in this land. The rebel band is made up of 1d30+20 peasants (1d6 HD) who arm themselves with little or no armor, bamboo shields and a collection of farm implements, spears and short bows.

The fell lord in question is a rakshasa lich called the Venerable Claw. He is served by a band of 1d20+20 scythe wielding berserkers. Prophecies state that the Venerable Claw can only be destroyed with his own two-handed sword, a handsome weapon edged in silver runes with a deep azure sapphire in the hilt. The sapphire is the lich's phylactery, and an ancient curse by a vanquished wise woman ensures that if the sword strikes the Venerable Claw, his phylactery will shatter. The peasants seek the sword, but it has been well hidden in a misty swamp guarded by a nine bog mummies.

The Venerable Claw dwells in a fine manor of white stones and gracefully arched roofs of blue-green slates. He walks by day swathed in silk robes and wearing a porcelain demon mask, and is always accompanied by ten of his toughest warriors. The Claw's treasure consists of 21,500 sp in the form of 10 pound trade bars (there are 215 in all), 2,060 gp and a moss agate imbroglio depicting the goddess of mercy (worth 165 gp).

Credit

The Scarecrow originally appeared in the First Edition *Fiend Folio* (© TSR/Wizards of the Coast, 1981) and is used by permission.

Copyright Notice

Author Scott Greene, based on original material by Roger Musson.

Screaming Devilkin

Hit Dice: 3
Armor Class: 1 [18]
Attack: Tail-barb (1d4)
Saving Throw: 14
Special: Scream
Move: 3/12 (flying)
Alignment: Chaos
Challenge Level/XP: 4/120

Shrill wails echoing through the night signal the arrival of a screaming devilkin. Screaming devilkins are smallish beasts, humanoid in appearance but with frail and spindly arms and legs. These weak limbs are nearly useless for combat and locomotion, but the screaming devilkin makes up for this disability with its bat-like wings. Although screaming devilkins are fast fliers, they are not particularly agile on the wing. Screaming devilkins also have a long, muscular, barbed tail that is their primary means of physical attack. It should be noted that despite its appearance and name, the screaming devilkin has no connection with outsiders of any type.

A typical screaming devilkin is 3 feet tall and has a wingspan of about 5 feet. Its skin is reddish-brown in color and its eyes are black. Its tail is about 2-1/2 feet long.

A screaming devilkin howls continuously. This painful howling affects all creatures within 60 feet that hear it. Affected creatures must succeed on a saving throw or can take no actions other than defending themselves for as long as the screaming devilkin continues to scream. A dazed creature can attempt a new save each round to break the effect. A creature that successfully saves cannot be affected again by same screaming devilkin's scream for one day.

Conversation, even shouting, is impossible within 60 feet of a screaming devilkin using this ability. Spellcasters in the area must succeed on a saving throw each time they try to cast a spell. *Silence* negates the devilkin's scream for the duration of the spell.

Invasion of the Baby Snatchers

In the boughs of a gigantic banyan tree in a steamy rain forest, there dwells a pack of 1d4+1 screaming devilkins. The devilkins have made a home for themselves in what was originally a giant wasp nest. The nest looks like a great globule of dried mud, twigs and leaves, and measures approximately 15 feet in diameter and 25 feet tall. The presence of the devilkins has driven the other inhabitants of the banyan far away, and the wicked creatures are now occupying themselves by attacking the scattered villages of the area, including a sprawling fishing village and a tribe of hunters that dwell within in a palisade of polished iron trees in mud brick houses decorated with bits of jagged crystal mined in the hills. The hunters are known for their pet worgs, and are willing to trade a trained worg for the services of a band of adventurers. The devilkins have proven too powerful for the hunters, and they have lost several children to the beasts already.

The devilkin's lair contains about 80 gp worth of the copper trade bracelets used by the people of the rain forest (the equivalent of 8,000 cp) as well as a lapis lazuli brooch that, when placed upon one's forehead, leads them to pure water and a small jasper worth 3 gp.

Credit

The Screaming Devilkin originally appeared in the First Edition *Fiend Folio* (© TSR/Wizards of the Coast, 1981) and is used by permission.

Copyright Notice

Author Scott Greene, based on original material by Philip Masters.

Screaming Skull (Cacophony Golem)

Hit Dice: 6
Armor Class: 9 [10]
Attacks: None
Saving Throw: 11
Special: Cacophony, insanity, *magic missile*, +1 weapons to hit, immune to magic
Move: 0 (immobile)
Alignment: Neutral
Challenge Level/XP: 8/800

A screaming skull is the skull of a humanoid or other creature, bleached white, and with a single gemstone of varying size and type embedded into each eye socket. Whenever a being approaches within 30 feet, a screaming skull emits an ear-shattering roar that does 1d6 damage to creatures within 60 feet. The screaming lasts for 1d4 rounds. Anyone touching the golem must save or be driven insane for 1d6 hours. Once per round, a screaming skull can shoot up to 3 *magic missiles* from its eyes (1d4+1 points of damage each). *Disintegrate* slows a screaming skull. Cold-based spells heal a screaming skull. They are immune to all other magic.

Swinging Skulls

This 20-foot-by-20-foot room is filled with random clutter. A small cauldron sits on the stone floor, surrounded by animal totems decorated with colorful feathers. A fireplace in the east wall is filled with embers, and the wall is covered in a thick layer of creosote. Hanging from the 10-foot-high ceiling on knotted twine are various bits of bone, including femurs, a crooked spine and numerous skulls of various animals and humanoids. Each of these skeletal remains is decorated with odd trinkets, feathers or swirls of color. The bones dance, sway and swing on their strings as if alive. Deer antlers are fixed to the walls.

The room belongs to a temperamental witch named Gurthred the Shriveled who collects remains of her kills. She hangs the assorted bones as good-luck charms to protect herself. Gurthred casts a simple spell on the strings to make them move on their own to give the bones "life" as they swing wildly

To protect her trinkets, Gurthred hung a screaming skull amid her treasures. The cacophony golem swings on a length of twine, waiting for someone to bump into it before it begins to wail. The golem is tasked with protecting the room from anyone trying to make off with the random bones.

Gurthred keeps a metal lockbox in the embers of the fire that contains 100 gp, a small ruby (50 gp) and a *potion of levitation* that's been spoiled by the heat. Anyone drinking it must save or float helplessly into the sky without control for 4d6 rounds before the potion wears off and they fall back to earth.

Copyright Notice

S

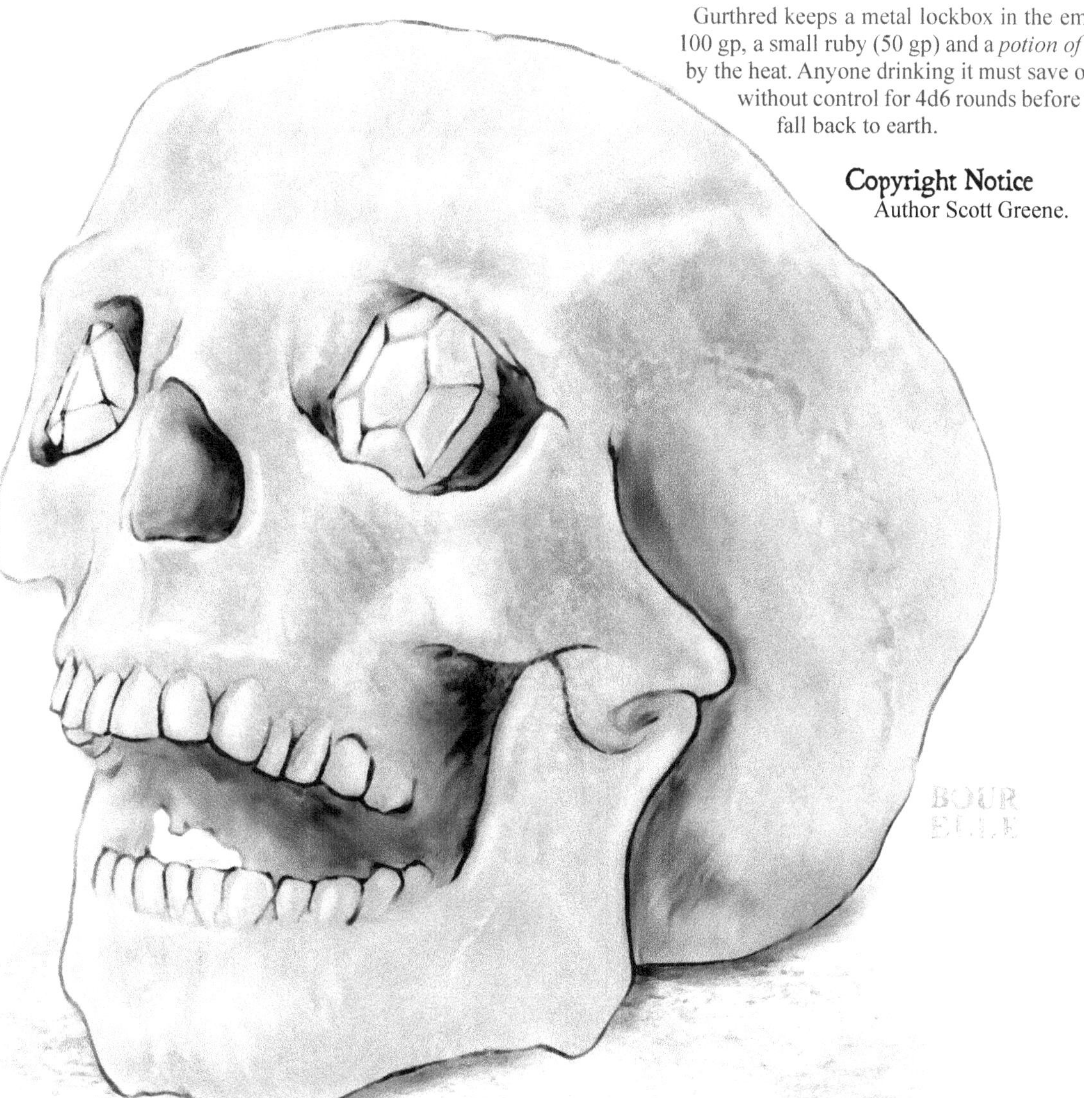

Scylla

Hit Dice: 12
Armor Class: 2 [17]
Attacks: 6 bites (1d10+3)
Saving Throw: 3
Special: Boil water, scalding blast
Move: 6/18 (swim)
Alignment: Neutrality
Challenge Level/XP: 13/2,300

Scyllas are great sea-monsters about 20 feet long with a rounded lower body, four large fins, a short tail, and six heads, each perched on top of a long snake-like neck. A scylla is gray-blue to dark gray in color with a lighter shaded underbelly. Its fins are gray-blue to dark gray. Its eyes are golden or gray and each mouth is lined with triple rows of whitish-gray teeth. Scyllas can grow to a length of 50 feet. The body of a scylla is extremely hot, and causes the waters around them to boil. The heated water does 3d6 points of damage. A scylla can gulp the boiling water and blast it in a line of scalding steam. Each blast does 3d6 points of damage (save for half).

Back to the Surface

A plume of smoke and ash rises above the ocean above the Vestus Maw volcano. The violent eruptions are slowly pushing the ancient city of Pompellos to the surface again, nearly 300 years after it sank beneath the ocean waves. A scylla, the city's original defender, slithers through the still-partially submerged streets, awakening to once again protect the city's treasures. The scylla swims through the wide columns lining the streets, and circles the island, creating crashing waves. It blows spouts of superheated water high into the air to warn off ships.

The scylla originally protected the city from ships seeking to reach the city's shores without flying the proper flag. That flag design was forgotten long ago, so any ship approaching now is considered an enemy by the deadly sea serpent.

Copyright Notice

Scythe Tree

Hit Dice: 6
Armor Class: 1 [18]
Attack: 4 scythe-branches (2d4)
Saving Throw: 11
Special: Resistance to slashing weapons (50%), double damage from fire, surprise in woodlands on a roll of 1-3 on 1d6
Move: 6
Alignment: Chaos
Challenge Level/XP: 6/400

Scythe trees are malevolent plant creatures found in heavily forested areas where they naturally blend in with normal trees. Scythe trees are carnivorous by nature and draw very little sustenance from sun, air, or water, preferring a diet of dryad or elf flesh.

A scythe tree, on average, is 20 feet tall, but may reach or exceed heights of 30 feet. It weighs about 3,500 pounds and has a trunk diameter of 3 feet. Its bark is dark brown, shading darker as it nears the roots. What few leaves a scythe tree has are reddish-brown (and do not change color or fall out as the seasons change).

The branches of a scythe tree resemble wicked-curving scythes (this is where the tree gets its name). The scar that appears on the trunk is the tree's mouth (it appears as a scar when closed). Scythe trees hate treants and dryads and attack both on sight (though a scythe tree usually only confronts a treant when it outnumbers it).

A scythe tree speaks its own language and the language of treants. Some (15%) can also speak the language of dryads and wood elves.

Little Mother's Judgment

Just beyond the crowded streets of a great city there is a network of alleys that rarely see the light of day, for they are hemmed in by tall buildings. In the center of this maze of passages there is an exceptionally lovely old building that was once a monastery but is now used as the headquarters of a brotherhood of seven butchers. The butchers are the adopted sons of a wicked fox maiden who has become the de facto (and secret) ruler of the old city through the use of guile and fear. The Little Mother's sons are all assassins. The gang primarily run a protection racket. A number of her rivals and hold-outs have disappeared under mysterious circumstances, keeping everybody else in line.

The ground floor of the monastery is run as a tea house that serves a heady oolong and a spicy soup infused with jasmine. Little Mother has a small table in the rear of the teahouse. The table is obscured by a lovely frame depicting crane maidens bathing in a waterfall. She sits behind the table, her eldest son by her side, sipping oolong and seeing one petitioner after another. Some petitioners come asking favors and others are summoned to make an account for themselves.

Those who are brought before the Little Mother because they have displeased her might be forgiven if they have enough gold, or instead lead into the old monastery's courtyard and told to make their way to a stone bench adorned with lion heads sitting beneath a strange tree and await the Little Mother's judgment. The tree is, of course, a scythe tree, and there mere fact that the person has been lead into the courtyard is proof that Little Mother has made her judgment. At the sound of a brass bell, the scythe tree strikes and Little Mother's reign of fear continues.

Copyright Notice
Author Scott Greene.

SEA SERPENTS

Nearly as old as the dragons that roam the sky are the sea serpents, great snakelike creatures that have roamed the oceans for ages. Unlike the classical dragon, these great, scaly, serpentine beasts are generally agreed to be a product of evolution, though many suspect magical influence, either deliberate or natural, somewhere in their evolution.

Whatever their origins, sea serpents are a highly varied species, with a great variation in size, coloration, intellect, and temperament. However, all sea serpents bear certain similarities. They are long, serpentine, warm-blooded creatures that closely resemble snakes in appearance, though they all have two sets of flippers, which may be large or so small and atrophied as to be nearly unnoticeable. Sea serpents are aquatic creatures, though some can make their way about on land. All sea serpents can breathe both water and air with equal efficiency, another fact that distinguishes them from marine mammals and reptiles. Further, all sea serpents are sentient, with an intellect ranging from little greater than moronic to supra-genius level.

One trait that sea serpents share in common with their draconic brethren is a sense of innate superiority, a feeling that they are masters of the sea, at least in whatever manner they choose to pursue their expertise.

Unlike dragons, however, sea serpents are not distinguished by color or age category. And while some species are as acquisitive as dragons, others have no interest in hoarding wealth, and live lives little better than beasts.

All sea serpents can speak and understand Aquatic, and many know Draconic as well. The more intelligent species may also learn the languages of marine civilizations, or the languages of sea-traveling surface dwellers.

Due to their physical similarities, sea serpents use fairly consistent tactics in combat situations. All sea serpents have venomous bites, and they use this to their advantage to slow or immobilize multiple attackers so they can concentrate on one foe. In addition to their lethal bite, all sea serpents have the ability to ensnare prey in their coils as a giant constrictor does and crush the life out of them. The larger sea serpents may even use this constriction attack against sea vessels, and mariners in their smoky dens delight in recounting tales of horror and woe of great serpents that splinter hulls and then devour the helpless sailors in the water.

Because they are sentient beings, sea serpents can often be reasoned with, even if the reasoning is no more complex than simple intimidation. They are adaptable to circumstances, and none throw themselves into battle rashly.

Sea Serpent, Brine

Hit Dice: 16
Armor Class: 4 [15]
Attacks: bite (4d6)
Saving Throw: 3
Special: Breath weapon, constriction, swallow whole
Move: 20 (swim)
Alignment: Chaos
Challenge Level/XP: 18/3,800

This 60-foot serpentine creature has two sets of large flippers and a wide body. A finned crest runs the length of its back, head to tail. A brine sea serpent can release a blast of acid and salt water in a 50-foot cone dealing 6d6 points of damage (save for half). These beasts swallow their prey whole on a roll 4 higher than the needed number, and always on a natural 20. Swallowed victims take 8d6 points of damage each round. After a successful bite, a brine sea serpent can constrict automatically to deal 4d6 points of damage.

The Icebound Terror

A small galleon sits atop an iceberg floating in the otherwise calm sea. The ship looks battered but possibly still seaworthy. The iceberg extends 20 foot above sea level and has a rough diameter of about 80 feet. The top of the ice appears to have supported life for a while. The remains of a small campfire, utensils, sleeping mats and skeletal fish waste all show signs of recent survivors from the ship. None of them remain on the berg. A brine sea serpent has hallowed out the core of the chunk of ice. It uses the galleon as bait to draw in potential prey. It exits the cavity in the iceberg through a tube below the iceberg or through a hole in the top covered by the ship. The brine sea serpent has accumulated some treasure it keeps in the interior of the iceberg. Among the loot of sunken ships are a rusted iron statue of a triton king, a bag of pearls (8d12, 25gp each), 23 anchors, a bronze church bell, a giant-sized scepter topped with a garnet the size of a man's head and a frozen satyr.

Sea Serpent, Deep Hunter

Hit Dice: 18
Armor Class: 2 [17]
Attacks: bite (4d10)
Saving Throw: 3
Special: Constrict, poison, swallow whole
Move: 0/24 (swim)
Alignment: Neutrality
Challenge Level/XP: 20/4,400

Deep hunters are smooth sea serpents with scales the size of a large shield. These beasts swallow their prey whole on a roll 4 higher than the needed number, or if the serpent rolls a natural 20 to hit. After a successful bite, a deep hunter sea serpent can constrict and deal 4d10 points of damage. Their bite inflicts a lethal poison (save resists).

Flounder

A small galleon thrashes in the sea. Sailors scream in terror as the ship is tossed about the waves and sometimes goes underwater completely. A huge winch on the galleon secures a chain and leathery tube that extend into the water. The chain and tube connect to an iron sphere with glass windows.

Ollie Nematoad, a halfling inventor, explores the sea's depths inside the rudimentary diving bell. A deep sea hunter snatched Ollie and his diving bell, but the contraption is now lodged in the serpent's jaws. The sea serpent thrashes about trying to dislodge the sphere. It is angry and aggressive. If the PCs rescue him, Ollie would gladly reveal the locations of the sunken treasure he has found, absentmindedly neglecting to mention the various dangers.

Copyright Notice
Authors Scott Greene and Patrick Lawinger.

Sea Serpent, Fanged

Hit Dice: 8
Armor Class: 3 [16]
Attacks: bite (1d8)
Saving Throw: 8
Special: Constrict, poison
Move: 0/18 (swim)
Alignment: Neutrality
Challenge Level/XP: 9/1,100

A fanged sea serpent is 12 to 15 feet long and 5 feet thick. Its scales are thick and hard, which slows it somewhat in water but provides good protection. Fanged sea serpents tend to travel in packs. On a successful bite, a fanged sea serpent deals 1d8 points of automatic constriction damage. Their bite inflicts a lethal poison (save resists).

Serpent Surprise

Recent storms caused a backwash of seawater into the neighboring rivers and sewers of the Eminence. The water backs up into wells and basements of the lower city. The city has incurred many problems as result. The arrival of fanged sea serpent has led to perhaps the worst of the troubles. The serpent seeks easy prey through the sewers. It surprises pedestrians by popping out of sewer grates or bursting through the floorboards of buildings after coming up through the flooded cellars.

Copyright Notice
Authors Scott Greene and Patrick Lawinger.

Sea Serpent, Gilded

Hit Dice: 5
Armor Class: 3 [16]
Attacks: bite (1d8)
Saving Throw: 12
Special: Constrict, magic or gold weapons needed to hit, poison
Move: 0/18 (swim)
Alignment: Neutrality
Challenge Level/XP: 6/400

A gilded sea serpent is about 8 feet long and 2 feet thick. Its body scales shine with the brilliant luster of gold. It has a long, narrow crocodilian snout and a cluster of antenna-like whiskers sweeping back from just above its jaws. Their skins can be crafted into exceptional armor. On a successful bite, a gilded sea serpent deals 1d8 points of automatic constriction damage. Their bite also inflicts poison (save resists) that numbs the flesh and induces a catatonic stupor.

The Chariot of the Triton King

In a serene lagoon filled with silver sand sits an enormous chariot made of golden shells. The Chariot of the Triton King rests here in this secluded lagoon. The boat-like chariot does not have any wheels and sits atop a column of white coral. A bridle made of gold chains droops into the water. Sea elves stole the chariot long ago and hid it above the water to prevent the tritons from finding it. A cluster of 1d6+2 gilded sea serpents guards the chariot. The tritons desperately want the chariot returned, although they may not have a friendly disposition to those having it in their possession.

The chariot can comfortably hold five man-sized beings. Once grasped, the reins summon eight gilded sea serpents to pull and protect the chariot's occupants. While the gilded sea serpents draw the chariot, it moves with the speed and grace of a dolphin. The chariot can move atop the water or submerged. Once activated, a bubble of infinite air surrounds the chariot while underwater. Occupants are free to move on or off the chariot, but suffer normal water consequences once they leave the conveyance's safety.

Golden Bliss

Golden bliss is a drug made from the venom of a gilded sea serpent. A serpent that is milked of its venom produces enough poison to make 2d4 doses of golden bliss. When inhaled, the drug produces a euphoric catatonia that lasts 10-30 minutes, with a secondary effect being a –4 drain to Wisdom that lasts 1 week. Golden bliss also temporarily increases Charisma by +4 and provides complete protection against mind-influencing magic lasting 1 week. Golden bliss is highly addictive. Each time an addict goes without golden bliss long enough to experience withdrawal, there is a 25% chance that the first point of Wisdom loss suffered is permanent.

Copyright Notice
Authors Scott Greene and Patrick Lawinger.

Sea Serpent, Shipbreaker

Hit Dice: 24
Armor Class: 0 [19]
Attacks: bite (5d10)
Saving Throw: 3
Special: Constrict, poison, swallow whole
Move: 2/24 (swim)
Alignment: Neutrality
Challenge Level/XP: 26/6,200

The devastating shipbreaker sea serpent is more than 120 feet long and 15 feet thick. Its body scales are dark gray-brown, festooned with barnacles, seaweed, and other sea life. Its maw is the size of a large wagon, with teeth the size of great swords. The legendary shipbreaker is thought to be the largest of the sea serpents, a true behemoth that rules the seas. These beasts swallow their prey whole on a roll 4 higher than the number needed to hit, or on a roll of natural 20. A shipbreaker can crush even the mightiest seagoing vessels in its great coils. With a successful bite, a shipbreaker sea serpent does 5d10 points of automatic constriction damage. Their bite also inflicts a lethal poison (save resists).

Poseidon's Horn

Drudgery's Cove has been a safe haven for ships for as long as anyone can remember. This city-state within a 6-mile-wide volcanic crater serves as a protected port along the busy coast. The city is cut off from easy land access by the immense cliff wall that rises around and above the city. Drudgery's Cove sits on a sandy expanse at the base of the crater. The other half of the six-mile-wide crater is filled with natural breakers and a geothermal lagoon.

Since it has few laws and no naval force, Drudgery's Cove is a safe haven for pirates, slave traders and smugglers. The city honors Poseidon (or some other sea-related deity that fits the Game Referee's campaign). No other shrines or temples exist in Drudgery's Cove.

A retired pirate named Captain Ikas Storn oversees the city. For reasons long-forgotten, a shipbreaker sea serpent guards the city. A 60-foot-long curving horn carved from fossilized coral sits embedded in volcanic slag at the city's center. Stairs cut into the volcanic rock wind up the rock to the human-sized mouthpiece. The horn summons the shipbreaker to defend Drudgery's Cove.

When the Bubble Bursts

A giant bubble pops out of the Reaping Sea in an explosion of water and flies nearly 100 feet into the sky. Inside the bubble are the splintered remains of the Lusty Sail, a merchant vessel attacked three days ago by a shipbreaker sea serpent. A wily magic-user on board the vessel cast a spell that engulfed the Lusty Sail in a solid air-filled bubble just before the serpent bit down on the ship's hull. The bubble expanded to fill the creature's mouth and became stuck in the serpent's open jaw. The monstrosity dove into the black, icy depths. The crew died and the ship was reduced to kindling within the first day as the sea serpent violently shook its head back and forth trying to dislodge the bubble.

The serpent finally shook the bubble free, and the air-filled orb rocketed to the surface near the PCs' ship. The bubble pops when it smacks heavily into the water in a violent splash that sends plumes of water soaring into the air.

The serpent is angry and aggressive and chases the bubble to the surface. It leaps from the water, looking for the ship that caused it so much pain. It attacks any ship on the surface.

Copyright Notice

Authors Scott Greene and Patrick Lawinger.

Sea Serpent, Spitting

Hit Dice: 12
Armor Class: 4 [15]
Attacks: bite (1d8)
Saving Throw: 3
Special: Acid spit, constrict, poison
Move: 4/18 (swim)
Alignment: Chaos
Challenge Level/XP: 13/2,300

A spitting sea serpent is roughly 15 to 18 feet long, with a girth of up to 3 feet. They are covered with rough-edged scales of brown, green, or blue, giving their hides a mottled appearance. With a successful bite, a spitting sea serpent deals 1d8 points of automatic constriction damage. A spitting sea serpent can eject a sticky glob of concentrated acidic mucous (2d6 points of damage) up to twice a round, with a range of 60 feet. Their bite inflicts a numbing poison (save resists). The poison does 2d6 points of damage.

Maiden on the Rocks

A mermaid reclines atop an outcropping of rocks, singing a beautiful melody across the ocean waves. The mermaid holds a coral-encrusted harp while singing the sorrowful tune. Bones and scales cover the small rock jutting out of the sea, as well as jewelry and other valuables. The mermaid is dehydrated and weak, but still sings her song without missing a beat. A spitting sea serpent lies in a hollow cavity in the rock outcropping below the surface. For its own nefarious reasons, it regularly snatches up mermaids and other aquatic folk and forces them to sing and play for it. The victims die of exposure or become a meal for the serpent when they can't sing anymore.

Copyright Notice
Authors Scott Greene and Patrick Lawinger.

Sea Slug, Giant

Hit Dice: 15
Armor Class: 6 [13]
Attacks: 1 bite (2d8+2)
Saving Throw: 3
Special: Capsize, paralysis, swallow whole
Move: 18 (swim)
Alignment: Neutrality
Challenge Level/XP: 17/3,500

A giant sea slug is about 30 feet long and has nine sets of gills along its body. It is variable in color: some are gray or greenish-blue; others are white mottled with yellow or brown; and still others are gray mottled red or yellow. It has a large set of antennae that it uses for sight and navigation and its mouth is lined with serrated teeth used to grind its food. Tiny threads cover the slug's body. These cilia cause paralysis for 1d6 rounds. Giant sea slugs bite if provoked, but also can rise beneath ships to capsize them. If a sea slug rolls a natural 20 on a bite attack, it swallows the opponent whole. A swallowed creature takes 3d8+2 points of damage from the slug's digestive acids.

The Prince's Party Barge

Prince Lander's birthday party is already the talk of the city. Queen Mashay is sparing no expense, bringing in mastodon steaks from the frozen northlands, jellied giant octopus tentacles cooked on barracuda flanks, and the fabled exploding yellow custards of the barony of Anatary. The wittiest jesters and the finest musicians are already staying in the city's inns, awaiting their chance to honor the young prince. And the queen has found the perfect spot for the massive party: a series of floating barges floating on the calm waters of Loch Kinrain.

But the overprotective queen is concerned someone might attempt to kidnap her darling boy on the night he becomes king. She's offering 1,000 gp per person (provided they can prove themselves honorable folk with references) to help guard the party and protect her son from the threats (mostly imagined) she's sure will surface. And she's right about a threat, but it won't come from outside the party but from below.

Queen Mashay disregarded the fishermen's warnings of avoiding the lake at this time of the year, and has floated the barges across a giant sea slug migration route. The noise, scraps of food and wine tossed into the loch attract two of the 30-foot-long slugs, which surface beneath the barges during the party. The barges tip, dumping partygoers and prince alike into the chill waters.

Copyright Notice

Sea Spider

This creature resembles similar arachnids found on land. Its color ranges through various shades of blue and green with distinct black markings. Its legs and bodies are covered with thousands of fine, sticky hairs.

Sea Spider (Common)

Hit Dice: 16
Armor Class: 6 [13]
Attacks: 3 pinchers (1d6) and 1 bite (2d6)
Saving Throw: 3
Special: Swallow whole
Move: 4/20 (swim)
Alignment: Chaos
Challenge Level/XP: 16/3,200

A sea spider resembles similar arachnids found on land. Its color ranges through various shades of blue and green with distinct black markings. Its legs and bodies are covered with thousands of fine, sticky hairs that trap air bubbles, which aid in floatation and mobility. With its long, strong legs a sea spider can propel itself underwater as easily as it can glide upon the surface. A sea spider is about 16 feet long and resembles a monstrous spider with fur of varying hues of blues and greens. If a sea spider hits with its bite attack, it can swallow its opponent whole in the next round.

Sea Spider (Pelagos)

Hit Dice: 18
Armor Class: 3 [16]
Attacks: 1 bite (2d8)
Saving Throw: 3
Special: Poison, spells, resists acid, fire and cold
Move: 4/20 (swimming)
Alignment: Neutrality
Challenge Level/XP: 20/4,400

This great sea spider makes its home in the deep ocean never venturing close to the coast or shorelines. Its lair is often made in sunken ships or underwater caverns and caves. Its legs and bodies are covered with thousands of fine, sticky hairs that trap air bubbles, which aid in floatation and mobility. With its long, strong legs a sea spider can propel itself underwater as easily as it can glide upon the surface. A sea spider is about 16 feet long and resembles a monstrous spider with fur of varying hues of blues and greens. If a sea spider hits with its bite attack, it can swallow its opponent whole in the next round. The bite injects a deadly poison (save resists). Any creature that dies from the poison turns into water and flows away. Three times per day, pelagos giant sea spiders can *cast cone of cold* and *lightning bolt*. Once per day, they can cast *stinking cloud*.

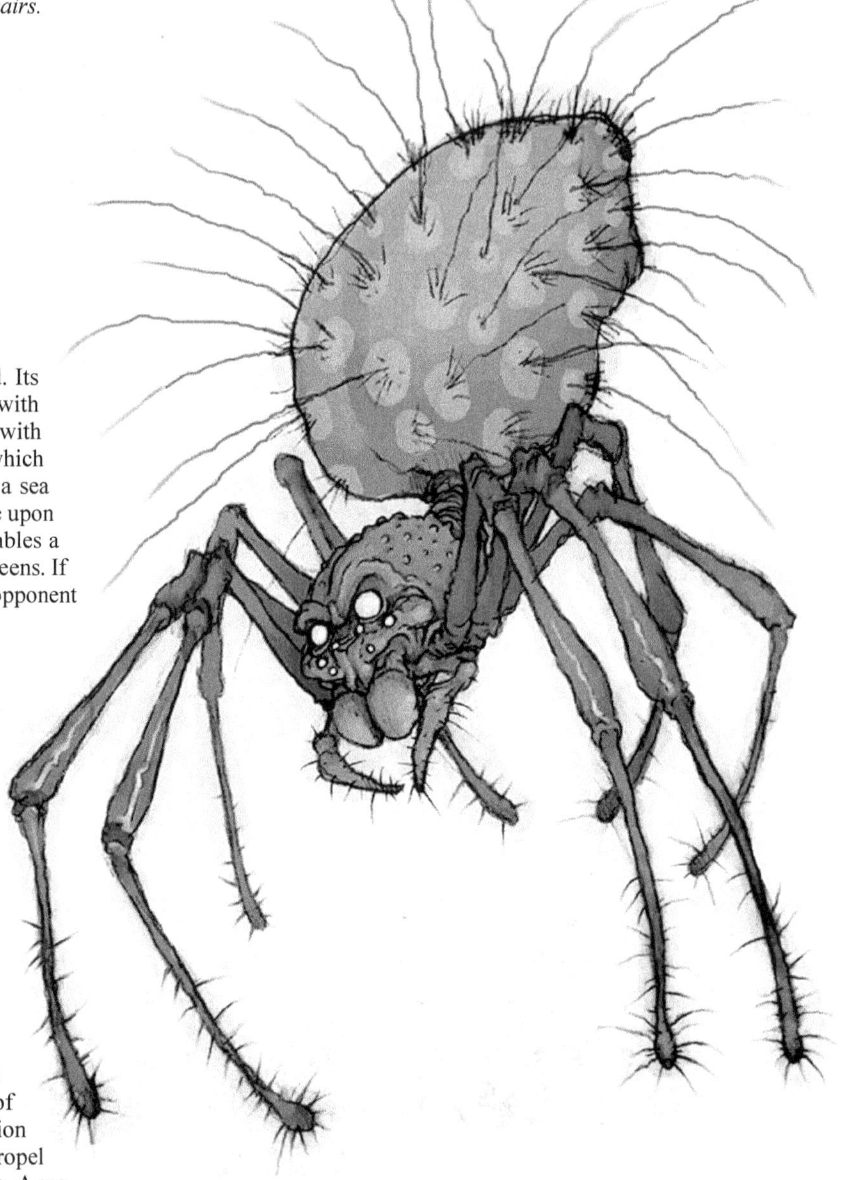

Island of Junk

A wide island of plankton and seaweed floats in the sea. The island seems to be a collective mass of sea junk floating atop the waves. Small wrecked boats, driftwood, dead sea life and other detritus float amid the green mash. A floating bridge of solid and stable junk traverses the jumble to the center where half of a large galleon bobs in the water. The flag of the infamous pirate the Gray Otter flies above the bent mast. Moving corpses peer over the edge of the ship remains. The corpses are puppets attached to thin spider silk from a giant sea spider that stands on the underside of the algae island. The spider uses the lures to attract would be treasure-seekers.

Copyright Notice
Authors Scott Greene.

Sea Wasp, Monstrous

Hit Dice: 2
Armor Class: 7 [12]
Attacks: tentacles (1d4 + poison)
Saving Throw: 16
Special: Poison, entangle, transparent, jet
Move: 9 (swim)
Alignment: Neutrality
Challenge Level/XP: 3/60

Hit Dice: 4
Armor Class: 7 [12]
Attacks: tentacles (1d8 + poison)
Saving Throw: 13
Special: Poison, entangle, transparent, jet
Move: 15 (swim)
Alignment: Neutrality
Challenge Level/XP: 5/240

Hit Dice: 8
Armor Class: 6 [13]
Attacks: tentacles (2d6 + poison)
Saving Throw: 8
Special: Poison, entangle, transparent, jet
Move: 15 (swim)
Alignment: Neutrality
Challenge Level/XP: 9/1,100

Hit Dice: 16
Armor Class: 5 [14]
Attacks: tentacles (2d8 + poison)
Saving Throw: 3
Special: Poison, entangle, transparent, jet
Move: 18 (swim)
Alignment: Neutrality
Challenge Level/XP: 17/3,500

Monstrous sea wasps are deadly aquatic creatures with long, writhing and highly poisonous tentacles. Sea wasps are translucent blue in color rendering them nearly invisible in water. Its main body, or bell, is cube-shaped, having four distinct sides. A bundle of 60 tentacles, which reach lengths of 50 feet in the largest sea wasps hang from its bell. Sea wasps have four eyes, one on each side of the bell, connected to a nerve ring inside the main body. They have no brain, but are able to process visual information. Sea wasps float in the water waiting for creatures to swim into their mass of tentacles. When it detects prey in its tentacles, it folds them around the prey, and stings it. A monstrous sea wasp's poison (particularly the larger ones) is meant to instantly kill its prey so it does not struggle and damage the sea wasp's delicate form. A monstrous sea wasp can jet backward in a straight line once per round at a speed equal to four times its swim speed.

The Seaweed Island

A three-mile-wide woven net of seaweed supports the Denrot Tower as it floats atop the Sargot Sea. The tower is made of coral and white stone encrusted with thousands of colorful shells. The tower sits atop a chunk of thick seaweed nearly a mile deep. Tunnels descend below the tower into the hardened mass.

The seaweed plain surrounding the tower is less dense, and filled with plant-based creatures such as shambling mounds, sea crocodiles and seaweed-wrapped mummies of sailors who died on the island. Thin stretches of seaweed across the island collapse beneath weight, dropping travelers into the sea below the island.

A monstrous sea wasp floats beneath the island, its long tentacles spread to catch anything falling into its clutches. The sea creature jets away from danger if attacked.

Copyright Notice
Authors Scott Greene.

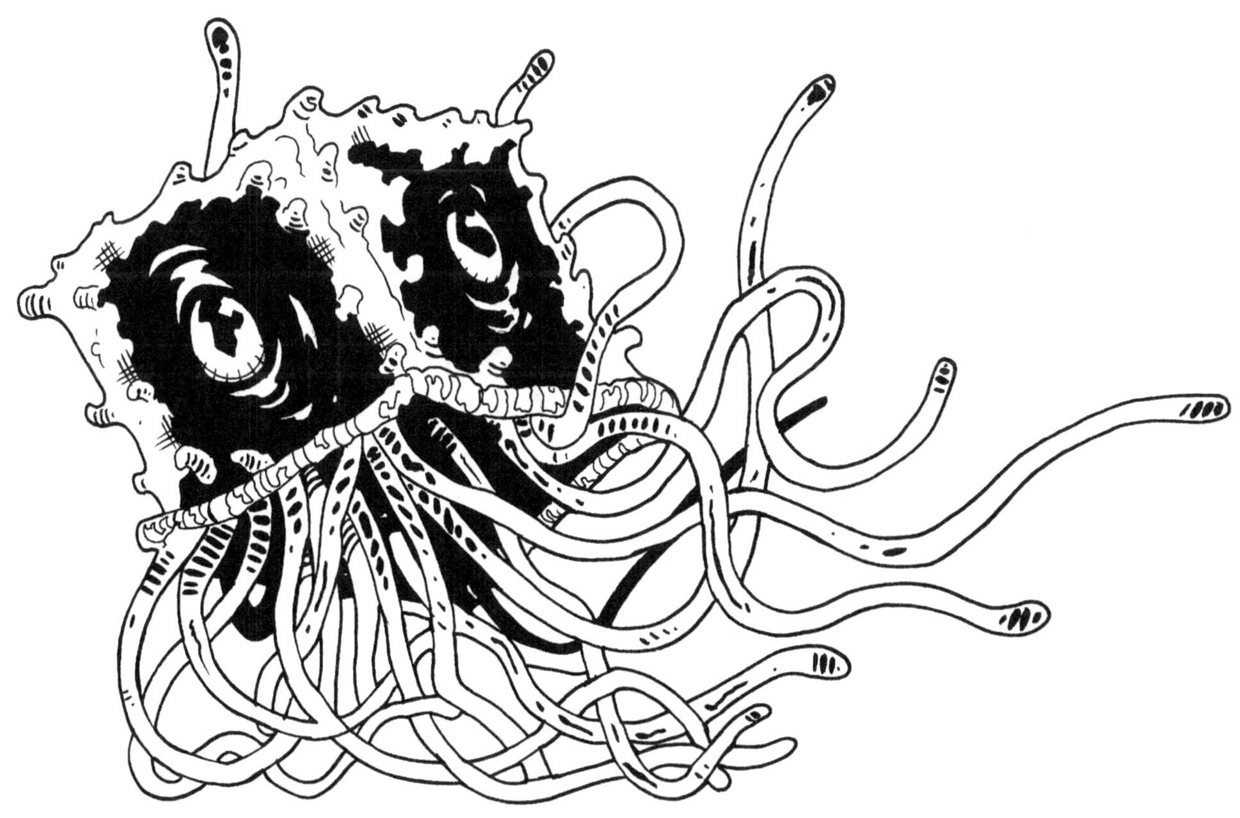

Sepia Snake

Hit Dice: 12
Armor Class: 3 [16]
Attacks: 1 bite (1d8) and tail sting (1d8 + poison)
Saving Throw: 3
Special: Cocoon, poison
Move: 9/12 (flying)
Alignment: Neutrality
Challenge Level/XP: 13/2,300

A sepia snake is an anaconda-like creature that grows to be up to 30 feet long and nearly two feet thick. Although this strange snake can fly, it has no wings and no apparent means of airborne travel. Its scales are muddy brown in color, with strange patterns and symbols on its dorsal side. The tail of a sepia snake ends in a vicious-looking barbed sting that injects a poison into victims. The eyes of a sepia snake are two large glowing yellow orbs set in its wide, triangular head. Three times a day, a sepia snake can fire a line of webbing up to 20 feet to cocoon a victim (save to avoid).

Snake Charmer

Four 5-foot-diameter columns of carved marble stand at the corners of a raised dais. Veins of purple bands swirl within the white marble. A wicker basket sits in an oval depression carved into center of the dais. A hollow gourd with a flute-like instrument attached to one end sits on a wooden table beside the basket. The instrument is bright red and decorated with small gems near a mouthpiece at the tip of the gourd.

Six web cocoons are stuck to the columns. Five of the sticky masses contain bones, while the last holds a dehydrated, nearly comatose woman. Slicing through the webs yields a total of 200 gp, three small garnets (30 gp each) and a *ring of invisibility* around a mummified finger.

If the flute-like pungi is played, the purple veins on the columns writhe and twist into strange designs. Two rounds after the instrument's first notes are sounded, patterns form a different *symbol* (as per the spell) on each of the columns. The four symbols displayed are *symbols of sleep*, *fear*, *discord* and *stunning*.

When the symbols appear, a sepia snake is summoned into the wicker basket. The snake rises out of the container and floats in the center of the room. It tries to cocoon anyone not stunned or put to sleep by the columns.

The trapped woman is a thief named Quay who stumbled into the room and played the instrument. She was cocooned three days ago and is barely alive. She cannot speak or move until healed. She screams and tries to get away from the basket if awakened.

Copyright Notice
Authors Erica Balsley.

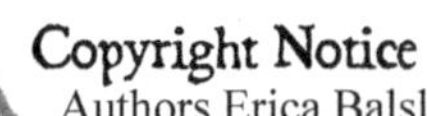

Sepulchral Guardian

Hit Dice: 10
Armor Class: 3 [16]
Attacks: 1 sword (1d8)
Saving Throw: 5
Special: Disease, dread, +1 magic weapons to hit, spell resistance (15%), immune to cold and fire
Move: 12
Alignment: Neutrality
Challenge Level/XP: 11/1,700

Sepulchral guardians are humanoids standing just over 6 feet tall. Their entire body, save their face, is encased in a suit of iron. Its face, while humanoid, shows no signs of life, and its eyes are filled with the emptiness of an automaton. Most sepulchral guardians wield long swords, battleaxes, or other such weapons. A sepulchral guardian weighs about 900 pounds. Sepulchral guardians are created to guard the final resting place of a now dead creature. Once activated, a sepulchral guardian performs its task until it is destroyed. Any creature struck by a sepulchral guardian's slam must make a save or contract a rotting poison that does 2d6 points of damage per hour. Creatures seeing a sepulchral guardian must save or flee in fear (as per the spell of the same name).

The Warden's Tomb

A 10-foot-tall iron fence cuts through the forest, vines and weeds growing up around it. Beyond the fence is a weed-covered clearing. One-foot-square grave markers set into the ground are aligned in perfect rows. Each bears a single, unknown number.

Dunkire Prison is lost to memory, but its cemetery remains. The graveyard is nearly a mile square, but overrun by the forest it was hidden within. Hundreds of bodies are buried here, each nothing more than a prisoner number. These were the worst of the worst who died within the prison's walls.

A stone mausoleum in the center of the graveyard is the only structure within the clearing. Cherry trees surround the stone building. Four carved caryatids hold the roof. A weathered name on a marker over the door is illegible, but the words "beloved warden" can be made out.

Inside the structure is a sarcophagus set into the tiled floor. It is carved to resemble the man buried within. Standing before the grave is the warden's guardian, a sepulchral guardian assigned to protect the body from grave robbers.

Copyright Notice

Authors Scott Greene.

Shadow, Lesser

Hit Dice: 1
Armor Class: 6 [13]
Attack: Incorporeal touch (1 Str)
Saving Throw: 17
Special: Strength damage, blend with shadows
Move: 15 (flying)
Alignment: Chaos
Challenge Level/XP: 2/30

Lesser shadows appear to be humanoids constructed of living darkness. Though not as powerful as their stronger relatives, lesser shadows are every bit as wicked. A lesser shadow is completely indistinguishable from a standard shadow. A lesser shadow is 5 or 6 feet tall and weightless. Lesser shadows do not speak.

Lesser shadows hide in darkness, springing to attack when living opponents wander too close. Unlike normal shadows, lesser shadows do not create spawn.

The touch of a lesser shadow deals 1 point of Strength damage to a living foe. A creature drained to Strength 0 by a lesser shadow dies.

In any condition of illumination other than full daylight, a lesser shadow can disappear into the shadows. Artificial illumination, even a *light* spell, does not negate this ability. In shadowy areas, a lesser shadow surprises opponents on a roll of 1-3 on 1d6.

Only the Shadows Know

While wandering through a dungeon, you come upon a door painted bright red. Opening the red door reveals a circular room 30 feet in diameter and shrouded in magical darkness. The walls of the room are lined with seven doors of multiple colors - red, blue, green, yellow, purple, orange and white - though this is not apparent in the darkness. A lantern hanging from the ceiling. The only light that can cut through the darkness is from the lantern, and even then the light is quite dim. Once the lantern is lit, the darkness slowly slinks away and seven shadows are formed on the walls.

The shadows mimic the adventurers in the room, but a careful observer can tell they are not natural. As one approaches a door, a shadow stands in their way, tight against the door. As the person reaches for the handle of the door, the shadow attempts to touch their hand. If the adventurers show a capability of destroying the shadows they slink away, avoiding them or disappearing into the actual shadows cast by the adventurers.

Copyright Notice
Authors Scott Greene and Clark Peterson.

Shark, Giant Landwalker

Hit Dice: 13
Armor Class: 5 [14]
Attacks: 1 bite (1d10+8)
Saving Throw: 3
Special: Amphibious, feeding frenzy
Move: 9/18 (swim)
Alignment: Neutrality
Challenge Level/XP: 13/2,300

A landwalker giant shark is a great white that has evolved the ability to walk on its fins to leave the water and breathe air. The shark attacks with its giant tooth-filled mouth, and the smell of blood sends the beast into a feeding frenzy where it attacks mindlessly and deals an additional 1d4 points of damage per bite.

Blood in the Water

Sides of cow hang from the slaughterhouse ceiling, blood dripping onto the stained wooden floor. Gore sits in fatty blobs on the slatted floor. Blood drips through the open slats into the Krell River that runs beneath the building. Reddish-tinged water flecked with bits of castoff flesh flows out of the port city of Lem. This bloody slurry mixes with the tide at the breakwater.

The bloody trail has lured a giant landwalker shark into the river from its ocean home. The monster bursts through the slat floor in a leap that sends splinters exploding into the room. The shark lands in the slaughterhouse in a blood frenzy, rending cow and PC flesh with every shake of its tooth-filled maw. The landwalker shark focuses PCs before sating itself with the hanging cow sides.

Shedu

Common Shedu

Hit Dice: 9
Armor Class: 3 [16]
Attack: 2 hooves (1d6
Saving Throw: 7
Special: Spells, etherealness, telepathy, magic resistance (30%)
Move: 12/24 (flying)
Alignment: Lawful
CL/XP: 13/2300

Greater Shedu

Hit Dice: 14
Armor Class: 1 [18]
Attack: 2 hooves (1d8)
Saving Throw: 3
Special: Spells, etherealness, telepathy, +1 or better weapon to harm, protection from evil 10' radius, magic resistance (40%)
Move: 15/30 (flying)
Alignment: Lawful
CL/XP: 21/4700

Shedus have the body of a chestnut-colored horse, large brown-feathered wings and the head and face of a bearded human. They are lawful creatures found roaming the Material Plane seeking out evil and destroying it wherever and whenever they encounter it. Shedu aid lawful creatures in need and never knowingly associate with chaotic creatures. They are on good terms with lammasu and ki-rin.

Priests and holy men sometimes seek the advice and wisdom of a shedu and will journey great distances to find the knowledge they seek. Some ancient cults even worship and pray to the shedu holding them up as deities in their culture.

Shedu found on the Material Plane make their homes in abandoned and ruined temples and shrines dedicated to gods of law.

Both shedu and greater shedu can shift from the Ethereal Plane to the Material Plane at will. Both forms of shedu can communicate telepathically with any creature within 100 feet that has a language.

Shedu can use the following spells at will: *Astral spell* (self only), *charm monster* (3/day), *detect evil* and *ESP*.

Greater shedu can use the following spells at will: *Astral spell* (self only), *clairaudience, clairvoyance, detect evil, detect magic, invisibility* (self only), *suggestion* (2/day), *telekinesis* (2/day). They can also cast spells as a 10th level cleric.

A greater shedu radiates a continuous *protection from evil, 10' radius*.

Repent Ye Sinners

The party's travels bring it into a region of tall, sandstone pillars and orange sands. For miles, they will see no sign of animals, plants or water until they reach the base of a tall butte, the top of which is covered in a thick woodland of knotty, white pines. This butte is the home of a greater shedu called Nabirsu. A few hours of searching will eventually uncover a cave in the base of the butte. The cave has smooth walls and extends about 300 yards into the butte before branching into two separate sets of stairs leading up. The first set is wide and grandiose and set with alcoves containing brass censers set with mother of pearl and burning cones of fragrant incense. The other set of stairs is narrow and plain, with a low ceiling that forces one to stoop as they climb. The fragrant stairs are guarded by a number of large panthers chained to the walls. There are twelve panthers in all, and they are quite unfriendly. The rough stairs are unguarded.

The fragrant stairs lead to a cave in the northern half of the butte that opens onto a stone shelf overlooking a gorge filled with bubbling, acidic water (1d4 damage per round). A 30-foot long rope bridge spans the gorge, and though it is sturdy the fumes from the acid force people crossing it to make a saving throw or become dizzy and fall into the acid.

Beyond the gorge are the woods, inhabited by a ivory-colored lions, golden owls, serpents, squirrels, insects and other animals common to a woodland. Encounters with 1d4 hunting lions occur on a roll of 1 on 1d6.

The rough staircase exits into a palace of golden brown marble. This palace is the home of a greater shedu, the tutelary spirit of the wasteland. The shedu is fierce and unyielding. Lawful characters are warmly welcomed and shown to comfortable chambers by the shedu's brownie servants. Neutrals are shown to a grotto temple that holds an idol of Marduk and told to reflect on their lives and priorities. After a few hours they are welcomed back into the presence of the shedu and either welcomed into the lawful fold or given supplies of fresh water and crusty bread and sent on their way.

While the others are led away, chaotic individuals are left before the shedu. Then they are dropped into a pit. Moments later, the shedu will enter the pit (it is quite large) in ethereal form, and in this form they are given a chance to beg forgiveness and leave behind their wicked ways. Should they accept, they are helped from the pit, their equipment is taken and they are given clothes of sackcloth, wooden staffs and supplies to see them through the waste. Should they make it through the desert alive, the shedu will return their goods to them and wish them well. Chaotics who refuse are attacked by the shedu, who will flee in ethereal form if losing only to drink a healing draught and then return again and again until the chaotics have repented or are dead.

Credit

The Shedu originally appeared in the pre-First Edition book *Eldritch Wizardry* (© TSR/Wizards of the Coast, 1976) and later in the First Edition *Monster Manual* (© TSR/Wizards of the Coast, 1977) and is used by permission.

The Greater Shedu originally appeared in the First Edition *Monster Manual II* (© TSR/Wizards of the Coast, 1983) and is used by permission.

Copyright Notice

Author Scott Greene, based on original material by Gary Gygax.

Sheet Fungus

Hit Dice: 3
Armor Class: 4 [15]
Attacks: 1 pseudopod (1d6)
Saving Throw: 14
Special: Camouflage, engulf
Move: 15 (flying)
Alignment: Neutrality
Challenge Level/XP: 3/60

Sheet funguses are flat, sheet-like plant creatures about 6 feet long and 2-1/2 or 3 feet wide. It weighs about 3 pounds. Two small dark circles "sewn" into its design function as eyes. They resemble tapestries or rugs and use this to their advantage when hunting for food. Sheet funguses are fond of blood and flesh, especially that of humans. If a sheet fungus hits an opponent with its pseudopod, it can decide to engulf a victim automatically on its next round. An engulfed opponent is held until it dies or until the sheet fungus takes three-quarters of its hit points at which time it releases its prey and flees.

Holy Sheet

A canopy bed stands in a corner bedroom of the abandoned castle, its yellow bedspread covered in a fine layer of dust. The poles supporting the draping veil canopy are ringed with green mold. A holy symbol depicting a raptor with its wings spread rising toward a burning sun is embroidered into the top of the comforter, and the blanket radiates a pleasant heat on its own. A mural of the forgotten deity graces the wall at the foot of the bed, the image showing a radiant bird-like being striding through a crowd of people reaching upward. The people all have vaguely birdlike features, including beaks and feathers. The raptor design is etched into the ceiling above the bed, the image appearing ghostly through the veiled canopy hanging from the four pillars supporting the bed.

A pile of wet plush pillows rots in the corner beneath a steady leak dripping through the brick ceiling. The entire chamber smells of mildew and rot. The bed is comfortable and soft, and the magical blanket adjusts its temperatures to keep the sleeper warm. A sheet fungus replaced the canopy that once hung over the bed. The fungus waits for PCs to lie down before dropping onto them, preferably as they sleep alone.

Copyright Notice
Author Scott Greene.

Silid

Hit Dice: 1
Armor Class: 7 [12]
Attacks: 1 weapon (1d6)
Saving Throw: 17
Special: Blur, -1 to hit in sunlight
Move: 9
Alignment: Chaos
Challenge Level/XP: 2/30

A silid is a small, 3- to 4-foot tall humanoid with pale gray, leathery skin. Though slightly thick in stature, a silid is quick on its feet and extremely graceful. Its hair is always unkempt, short, and jagged, and its ears are slightly pointed. Its eyes are slightly bulbous with red pupils. A silid's arms are long and slender and end in four-fingered hands. They attack at -1 in full sunlight. Once per day, a silid can create an effect that blurs their image, causing opponents to miss 20% of the time.

Sounds in the Dark

A baby's cry shatters the stillness of the underground. The wailing echoes off the rock walls. The Dark Crawlers, a tribe of 20 vicious silids, slink through the Maspar Caverns in search of prey. The creatures avoid fair fights, preferring to set up ambushes. One of the silids is adept at imitating creatures it hears. His favorites are a mewling cat, a whistling songbird, a whinnying horse and the baby crying.

The silids hide in the darkness under black-cloth lean-tos near a 30-foot-deep pit covered by the black tarps. The silid sound mimic sits on a ledge halfway down the pit, hidden under the black cloth.

Anyone falling into the pit is attacked with spears and arrows. The silids are cowards at heart and run from PCs who gain the upperhand.

Copyright Notice

Skeleton, Black

Hit Dice: 6
Armor Class: 4 [15]
Attacks: 1 weapon (1d6) or 2 claws (1d4)
Saving Throw: 11
Special: Shriek
Move: 12
Alignment: Neutrality
Challenge Level/XP: 6/400

A black skeleton is a 6-foot-tall skeleton with glistening, black bones, seemingly constructed of blackened steel. Small red pinpoints of light burn in its hollowed eye sockets. Black skeletons wear any clothes or armor they had in life, and some still carry their gear and weapons. A black skeleton can shriek a hellish sound that causes fear (save avoids).

Back in Black

This dungeon chamber is 100 feet long by 40 feet wide, with a 10-foot-wide stone pathway running around a three-foot-deep tar pool that dominates the room. A row of white marble blocks form a lip around the bubbling tar. The ceiling 30 feet overhead is crisscrossed by a giant white pentagram carved from the same white stone. Three arching bridges cross the pool, each rising 10 feet above the sticky surface.

A skeleton holding a burning torch aloft in its bony hands stands in the center of each bridge. The flickering flames cause shadows to dance around the chamber. A dais sits in a recess carved into the room's far wall. A black stone altar sits in the center of the dais. Atop it, a dagger carved of sharpened onyx sits beside a black human skull.

The skeletons drop the torches into the tar pit if PCs enter the chamber. The torches instantly ignite the tar into an inferno that raises the temperature in the room to an uncomfortable level. Anyone within 5 feet of the tar pit must save or take 1d6 points of damage each round from the blistering heat. When the blaze ignites, 6 black skeletons submerged in the tar rise from the sticky, burning pitch. The black skeletons each carry short swords. Their bodies burn for an hour (dealing 1d6 extra points of damage to anyone they attack) before the pitch coating their bones is burned away.

Copyright Notice
Authors Scott Greene and Bill Webb.

Skeleton, Lead

Hit Dice: 10
Armor Class: -1 [20]
Attack: 2 strikes (1d8)
Saving Throw: 5
Special: Resistance to normal weapons (50%), immunity to acid, cold, electricity and fire, immunity to magic
Move: 12
Alignment: Neutrality
Challenge Level/XP: 13/2300

Lead skeletons appear simply to be skeletons coated with metal. Despite their outward appearance, they are actually golem-like constructs and not undead. Therefore, they cannot be turned.

Lead skeletons appear as 6-foot tall skeletons constructed of metal. Some have gemstones encrusted in the body and eye sockets. A lead skeleton is expensive to create. Those who choose to create such creatures prefer the added fear and awe the skeletons tend to receive, and have a great deal of additional wealth and time.

Lead skeletons can be programmed to attack only certain creatures or be programmed to accept certain passwords or types of clothing. More complex programming tends to fail. In combat, they attack a single target until it is dead.

Lead skeletons have no eyes. They "see" their opponents by emitting high-frequency sounds, inaudible to all other creatures, that allow them to ascertain objects and creatures within 90 feet. A *silence* spell negates this ability and effectively blinds the lead skeleton.

A lead skeleton is immune to most spells, except magical attacks that deal sonic damage which slow a lead skeleton (as the *slow* spell) for 1d4 rounds, with no saving throw.

Construction

Bones from a full humanoid skeleton are carefully sheathed in an alloy of lead and iron and rejoined with iron or steel hinges. The total cost of the body must be at least 2,000 gp. An elemental spirit is summoned during the creation and bound to the body. To bind the elemental spirit, the creator must summon and confine an elemental using a *wish* spell. Assembling the body requires a master armorer and a magic-user of at least 17th level that can cast *conjuration of elementals, geas, polymorph* and *wish*.

Not-So-Mini Lead

Dropping through a trapdoor you enter a long chamber decorated as though it were a drawing room in a baronial manor. The floor is polished blond wood and the walls are carved ebony panels depicting mermaids and sea lions. On one wall there hangs a painting of a warlord wearing a powdered wig and bright cuirass and holding a sword, the point resting on the floor. The warlord wears a large, gold ring on his right pinky.

In the middle of the room there a large slab of lead, about seven feet long and three feet wide and bearing the image of a skeleton in deep relief. Any attempt to touch the slab of lead causes the skeleton to rise up from it, grabbing at the person's arm and leaving a skeleton-shaped hole in the lead. This hole reveals a lit chamber below. This lit chamber can only be reached via a secret door in one of the wood panels. The secret door can only be opened by sliding a sword point into a small, narrow slit in the floor in front of it - a slit that looks like nothing more than a deep gouge in the wood floor. Behind the secret door there is a spiral set of stone stairs, damp with moisture.

At the bottom of the stairs there is a locked iron gate. The room beyond is littered with bones. A stone slab against one wall contains what appears to be a second lead skeleton (unfinished), along with a leather tome containing instructions for building one of the constructs.

Copyright Notice

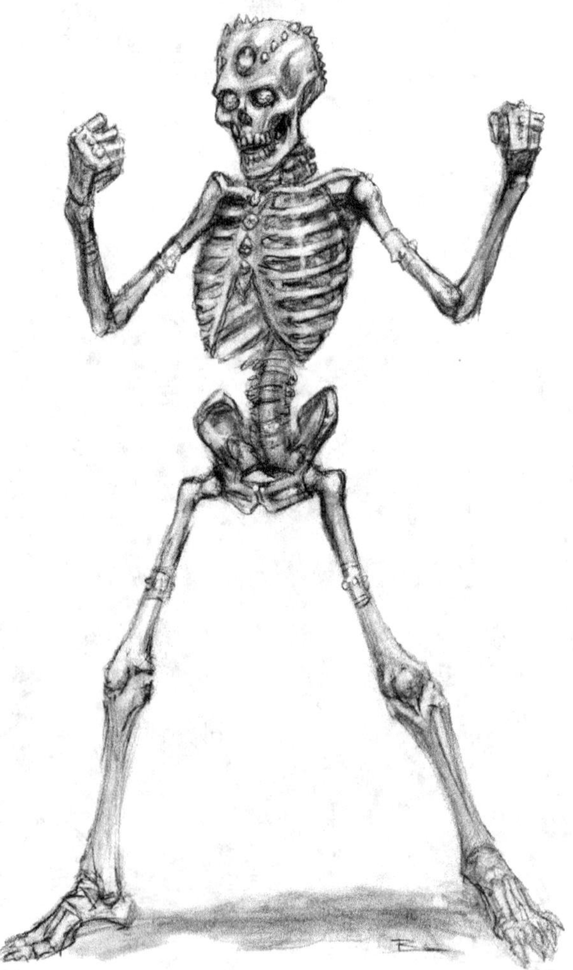

Skeleton Warrior

Hit Dice: 12
Armor Class: -1 [20]
Attack: *+1 long sword* (1d10+2)
Saving Throw: 3
Special: Fear aura, find target, +1 or better weapon to hit, immune to clerical turning, magic resistance (60%)
Move: 12
Alignment: Chaos
Challenge Level/XP: 12/2000

The skeleton warrior is a lich-like undead that was once a powerful fighter of at least 8th level. Legend says that the skeleton warriors were forced into their undead state by a powerful demon prince who trapped each of their souls in a golden circlet. A skeleton warrior's only purpose is to search for and regain the circlet containing its soul.

A skeleton warrior appears as a lich-like creature dressed in the same type of armor and clothes worn during life. Its clothes and armor usually show signs of wear and age.

Skeleton warriors are shrouded in an aura of fear. Creatures with less than 5 HD and in a 30-foot radius must succeed on a saving throw or be affected as though by *fear*.

A skeleton warrior can track and find the possessor of its circlet unerringly. Using this ability, it can also find the last person to possess its circlet.

Unrelenting

A skeleton warrior has been tracking its circlet for the better part of a century. Originally stolen by a thief that delved deep into a dungeon, it passed from his hands to a hoary sage in a sylvan kingdom. The sage lived peacefully for many years, and was a mere week away from meeting the skeleton warrior when an army from the steppe invaded the pleasant kingdom in the woods and rode off with the circlet, many tons of gold and silver and three princesses of the royal blood.

For a dozen years the circlet passed between the chieftains of the steppe in the form of tribute, wedding gifts and loot, forcing the skeleton warrior to zigzag its way across the rolling grasslands. Finally, it ended up in the possession of the duke of a seafaring people. The duke had it added to his crown and suffered from many years of strange visions and waking nightmares before going mad and burning down his own palace, ending his line.

The crown ended up in the dank dungeons beneath the haunted palace, and would have remained there had a band of enterprising kobolds not tunneled into the dungeons in search of loot. The crown now rests on the head of the kobold chieftain, where it might be found by a band of adventurers, who might discover they are a mere 1d6 days ahead of that skeleton warrior, still seeking its circlet.

Credit

The Skeleton Warrior originally appeared in the First Edition *Fiend Folio* (© TSR/Wizards of the Coast, 1981) and is used by permission.

Copyright Notice

Author Scott Greene, based on original material by Nigel Morgan.

Skeleton Warrior's Circlet

The transformation into a skeleton warrior traps the character's soul in a golden circlet. Anyone possessing one of these circlets may exude control over the skeleton warrior (whose soul is trapped therein).

In order to establish or maintain control, the controller must be within 300 feet of the skeleton warrior and must wear the circlet on his head and spend one full round concentrating on the skeleton warrior. If the controller is interrupted during this time, he must succeed on a saving throw to establish control. If the check fails, the controller can try again. While wearing the circlet, the controller cannot wear any other item on his head. Doing so causes the circlet to cease functioning until the other headgear is removed. (A skeleton warrior can still detect the location of its circlet even if the controller wears something on his head to nullify the circlet's powers.)

While wearing the circlet and within 300 feet of the skeleton warrior, the controller can see through the skeleton warrior's eyes and force it to act (attack, search, and so forth). This is called "active" mode. While the skeleton warrior is in active mode, the controller himself cannot take any action other than minimal movement.

Alternately, the controller can place the skeleton warrior in "passive" mode. In this mode, the skeleton warrior stands motionless and inert. The controller cannot see through the skeleton warrior's eyes but he himself is free to act. If the controller moves more than 300 feet away from the skeleton warrior or if the circlet is removed from the controller's head, the skeleton warrior automatically enters passive mode.

The controller can switch the skeleton warrior between active and passive mode as a free action. Should the controller ever lose the circlet (through accident, theft, or simply by discarding it), the skeleton warrior instantly stops what it is doing and moves as quickly as possible toward the former controller and attempts to destroy him (or her). If a skeleton warrior ever gains control of the circlet that contains its soul, it places the circlet on its head and "dies", vanishing in a flash of light. The circlet falls to the ground and crumbles to dust.

Skin Stitcher

Hit Dice: 7
Armor Class: 4 [15]
Attacks: 2 claws (1d4) or 2 barbed chains (2d4)
Saving Throw: 9
Special: chain rake
Move: 12
Alignment: Chaos
Challenge Level/XP: 7/600

This gaunt skeletal humanoid has heavily scarred flesh randomly stitched together. Its eyes are sunken and burn with hatred. A skin stitcher is a malevolent and violent creature that kills for food, pleasure, and the skin of humanoids (which it keeps and collects). The skin stitcher stands about 6 feet tall and appears as a skinless humanoid. Its natural body appears to be bone wrapped tightly with corded muscle and covered with a dark red-purplish slime. The skin stitcher's long, lanky arms end in claws as do its thick, muscled legs. It carries two large chains covered with many sharpened barbs. If a skin stitcher rolls a natural 20 with its chain rake, it does triple damage to its opponent.

The Skin Clan

A small knoll covered in the skeletal remains of countless creatures sits at the edge of a rocky wasteland. The natural rock formation has smooth sides. Crows and vultures fight over meaty rotting morsels. The birds caw warning as they flee approaching wanderers. The bone field conceals large anchor-like barbed hooks. Groups of these multi-pronged hooks lie under the bones with only their barbed tips protruding above the cast off bone. The hooks are painted white and difficult to detect. Ropes and chains attached to the hooks lead up the slope to an encampment above and are attached to large round boulders. A small clan of 12 skin stitchers (3 noncombatants) has claimed this knoll as their permanent settlement. Once enemies are detected among the bone field below, the skin stitchers roll the boulders off the opposite side of the knoll. The boulders rapidly drag the chains and ropes through the bones and over the other side. Creatures within the bone field must save or be snagged by the grappling hooks (2d6 points of damage).

Large tents of leather and chain make up the skin stitcher compound. These skin stitchers use the hides of humanoids and other intelligent races to sew tents and armor. They are hostile to most races but do trade with orcs and goblins for metal goods and supplies.

Copyright Notice

Skulk

Hit Dice: 2
Armor Class: 6 [13]
Attack: Short sword (1d6)
Saving Throw: 17
Special: Surprise on roll of 1-4 on 1d6
Move: 12
Alignment: Chaos
Challenge Level/XP: 2/30

Skulks are a race of humanoids that dwell on the fringe of other societies. They are a parasitic race—the humanoid equivalent of rats that survive by theft, subterfuge, and at times outright murder. Skulks are consummate cowards, sneaking into humanoid communities under cover of darkness and taking what they desire. They freeze to immobility and blend in with the background if they are detected and flee at the first opportunity.

Skulks are human-sized, but are very lightly built. They have slender, graceful arms and legs. Skulks have no hair, and their eyes are usually pale blue or pink. The grayish skin of a skulk is leathery to the touch, but the skulk has the natural ability to vary its skin tone to match nearly any environment. A typical skulk stands 6 feet tall and weighs 140 pounds. They speak their own whispered language and the common tongue.

Skulks can pass through forest and subterranean settings almost without a trace (-20% chance for rangers to track).

Skulk Society

Skulks dwell in small bands or family groups, living a nomadic existence as they travel from place to place. They move constantly so as not to attract undue attention from local militias. A skulk lair will usually be located in an area that is easily concealed, such as a cave or forest. Occasionally, skulks will sneak into a large city's sewer system and set up a more or less permanent presence there, moving their lair from place to place under the city.

Skulks remain hidden during daylight hours, leaving the safety of their lair to conduct forays into the humanoid community under cover of darkness. A favored tactic of a skulk band is to sneak into a residence under cover of darkness and slaughter the entire family. Once that grisly task is complete, the skulks remain to take what they will from the home and leave the following dawn.

Skulk leaders might have the abilities of thieves or assassins of 3rd to 5th level.

Pleasant Valley Vampire

A band of 1d6+2 skulks has recently taken to terrorizing an otherwise pleasant valley. The men of the valley raise tall, red cattle with massive black horns as much as 4 feet wide. The skulks have convinced the farmers that a vampire has come to the valley by attacking the cattle in broad daylight and stabbing at their necks with double-bladed stilettos, filling glass bottles with the blood.

The skulks have found a hiding place in a copse of twisted pines that grace the top of a rocky butte. The locals have always believed the butte to be haunted, but overcoming their fear have searched it and found nothing. They have recently begun demonstrating outside their baron's manor, demanding something be done. The baron has sent his men out several times in search of the beast and called on the assistance of clerics from the next valley, but with no success.

As the peasant's grow more restless and frightened, one young man, an errant knight, is fast becoming their spokesman and leader. Perhaps he and the skulks are working together, or perhaps the knight is just taking advantage of a bad situation. In either event, the tension in the local inn is terrible and the baron is not inclined to welcome outsiders into his valley.

Credit

The Skulk originally appeared in the First Edition *Fiend Folio* (© TSR/ Wizards of the Coast, 1981) and is used by permission.

Copyright Notice

Author Scott Greene, based on original material by Simon Muth.

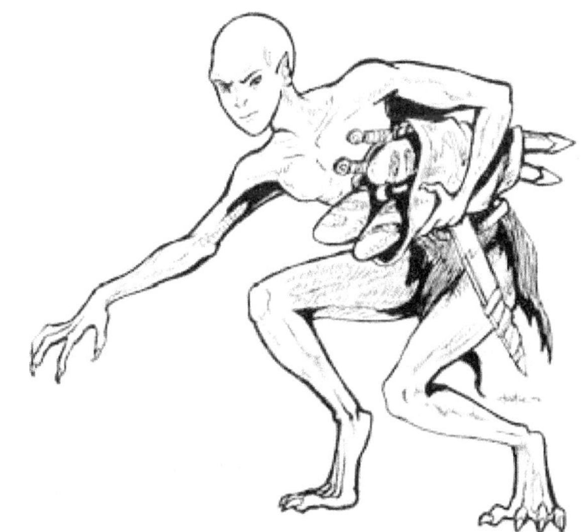

Skulleton

Hit Dice: 4
Armor Class: 5 [14]
Attack: Bite (1d3 plus disease)
Saving Throw: 13
Special: Disease, dust
Move: 6 (flying)
Alignment: Chaos
Challenge Level/XP: 6/400

Skulletons are undead creatures believed to have been created by a lich or demilich, for the creature greatly resembles the latter in that it is nothing more than a pile of dust, a skull, and a collection of bones. The gemstones inset in its eye sockets and in place of its teeth are not gemstones at all, but painted glass (worthless).

The skulleton is thought to have been created to detour would-be tomb plunders in to thinking they had desecrated the lair of a demilich.

The bite of a skulleton infects its victim with a fever unless they pass a saving throw. The fever has an incubation period of 1d3 days and inflicts 1d6 points of damage and imposes a -1 penalty to all missile attacks and armor class due to swelling of the joints.

The skulleton can use its crumbled remains to attack any creature that comes within 10 feet. As a standard action, it can billow forth a cloud of dust that covers a 10-foot area in front of it. Creatures caught within the area must succeed on a saving throw or be affected as if by a *stinking cloud* for 6 rounds. The dust cloud remains for 2 rounds and can be affected by wind. A skulleton can use this ability twice per day.

Creating a Skulleton

To create a skulleton, the creator must be at least 9th level. The following ingredients are required.

— The skull of a humanoid or monstrous humanoid.
— A few bones from a humanoid or monstrous humanoid.
— A small quantity (at least 1 pint) of earth (dirt).

Powder the bones (but not the skull) and mix with the earth or dirt in an iron bowl. Pour the powdered mixture over the skull. Cast the following spells in this order: *cause disease, fly, stinking cloud,* and *animate dead.* Within 1 hour, the skulleton animates.

Like a Skeleton, But Not

In a rather dusty, apparently long unused passage in a dungeon there is an oval door of brass inlaid with hundreds of skulls & crossbones. The door is unlocked, but appears to be stuck. It takes a total strength of 18 to pry the door open. This is because the door does not open into a chamber, but rather tears open a dimensional rift. The rift opens onto a dimension that seems to consist of an endless, black crystalline plane and a white sky with wispy ivory clouds. The air of the dimension is breathable, but smells of a coppery, electric tang. As people step out onto the glassy ground of the plane, they might notice that their reflections appear to be x-ray versions of themselves.

This dimension has but a single inhabitant, a skulleton placed here by the archimage that wove the dimension. The strange creature sits about 1 mile away from the door in any direction atop a pile of dust. The creature's reflection looks much the same, save for the piles of coins and jewels that surround it. The skulleton does not initiate combat with the adventurers, but fights to win if attacked.

The only way to reach the reflected "other side" of the plane (and the treasure) is to die. In truth, one cannot truly die on this plane. Once dead, a person finds themselves on a white, glassy plane with a black sky painted with wispy gray clouds. In this flip-side to the dimension, the adventurers appear as skeletons, their reflections as their normal selves. Here, the skulleton is surrounded by a large horde of treasure and, unfortunately, this skulleton is actually a demi-lich.

The treasure, should one manage to claim it, consists of 7,300 gp, potions of healing, dragon control and clairaudience, a *cursed shield -1*

(attracts missiles) and the following gems: a hematite worth 300 gp, jade carved to look like a pudgy infant, worth 400 gp, smoky quartz worth 200 gp, jasper worth 400 gp, a gold armband worth 315 gp, a brass and turquoise buckle worth 300 gp, a wooden bust of a hideous hag worth 75 gp and a silver locket worth 90 gp.

Demilich: HD 21; AC -2 [21]; Atk 1 touch (10d6 plus paralysis); Move Fly 60; Save 3; CL/XP 28/6800; Special: *Magic jar,* fear aura, cast spells as 21st level magic-user, +2 or better weapon to hit, resistance to fire (50%), immunity to cold and electricity, immunity to *polymorph* and mind-affecting effects.

Copyright Notice

Author Scott Greene.

SLAAD LORDS

Also known as Chaos Lords, the Slaad Lords exist in the maelstrom of Limbo and serve as agents of Chaos and rulers of a primordial race called the slaadi.

Slaad Lord of Entropy (Chaos Lord of Entropy)

Hit Dice: 16 (211 hp)
Armor Class: -8 [27]
Attack: 2 scythe attacks (6d6 or death)
Saving Throw: 3
Special: Control undead, dragon mount, plane shift, spells, +2 or better weapon to hit, magic resistance (85%), resistance to cold and fire (50%), summon slaad, telepathy 100 ft.
Move: 15
Alignment: Chaos
Challenge Level/XP: 25/5900

The Slaad Lord of Entropy is believed by some to be the supreme ruler of the slaadi race. He is a true agent of Chaos as can be seen in his actions and mood. Few have witnessed his true power, and those who have never speak of such experiences.

Although he usually appears as a black, bat-winged skeletal figure, hushed whispers among the slaadi say this is in fact not his true form. It is believed that his true form is that of a 15-foot tall black salad.

On the Material Plane the Lord of Entropy always rides an ancient red dragon. He can command undead as a 16th level cleric. The Slaad Lord of Entropy wields a *+3 scythe* that deals 6d6 damage unless a saving throw is failed, in which case it causes instantaneous death. Unique extra-planar creatures are immune to this effect. The Lord of Entropy strikes twice per round with his scythe. His true form is of a black slaad.

The Lord of Entropy can use the following spells: *Astral spell, darkness 15-ft radius, detect invisibility, detect magic, dispel magic, ESP, invisibility, produce flame, phantasmal force, power word - blind* (1/day), *power word - kill* (1/day), *sleep* and *symbol* (1/day) and *unholy word* (1/day).

The Slaad Lord of Entropy can enter any of the outer planes, the inner planes, or the Material Plane. This ability transports the Slaad Lord of Entropy and up to six other creatures, provided they all link hands.

Three times per day, the Slaad Lord of Entropy can summon three red, blue, or green slaadi or two gray or death slaadi.

The Slaad Lord's Mount

When visiting the Material Plane, the slaad lord rides an ancient red dragon named Ryssk.

Ryssk, Ancient Red Dragon: HD 11 (88 hp); AC 2 [17]; Atk 2 claws (1d8) and bite (3d10); Move 9 (Fly 24); Save 4; CL/XP 13/2300; Special: Breathes fire, speaks, can cast magic-user spells - four 1st level spells, three 2nd level spells and two 3rd level spells.

The Heart of Darkness

At the heart of Limbo there is a place of complete and awful darkness. Spells and magical effects of light create only a dim globe, illuminating an area 10 feet in diameter at a maximum and the light seemingly spiraling off at a curve into what must be the center of the globe of darkness. In the dim light, one can see thousands of bubbles that are also traveling in a spiral toward the center of the darkness. One can reach out and touch these bubbles, grab them even, and should they peer into the bubble they will see what appears to be visions of an alien world (or maybe even their own world).

At the center of the globe of darkness there sits the form of the Lord of Entropy (who some call Azathoth) atop a rough sphere of the world-bubbles. He casually reaches into the mass of bubbles, pulls one out, and pierces it with his finger, creating a terrible chorus of screams as a world pops out of existance. Surrounding the Lord of Entropy are a dozen lesser slaadi, swimming about in the darkness as though to some unheard, alien rhythm and croaking their approval as each world is destroyed.

Should visitors prove troublesome, and his slaadi unequal to the task of destroying them, the Lord of Entropy calls Ryssk to his side and destroys them himself.

Credit

Ygorl, the Slaad Lord of Entropy originally appeared in the First Edition *Fiend Folio* (© TSR/Wizards of the Coast, 1981) and is used by permission.

Copyright Notice

Author Scott Greene, based on original material by Charles Stross.

Slaad Lord of the Insane (Chaos Lord of the Insane)

Hit Dice: 16 (198 hp)
Armor Class: -7 [26]
Attack: 3 pseudopods (2d8 plus 1 level)
Saving Throw: 3
Special: Change shape, level drain, spells, regenerate 3 hp/round, +2 or better weapon to hit, magic resistance (85%), plane shift, resistance to cold and fire (50%), summon slaad, telepathy 100 ft.
Move: 15/18 (swimming)
Alignment: Chaos
Challenge Level/XP: 26/5900

The Lord of Insanity looks like a dark gold amoeba with an oversized humanoid brain floating in its center. Three long, black tentacles extend from its body, writhing constantly. It is one of the most powerful slaad lords in existence, and no slaadi questions his authority or rulership, even the other slaad lords.

The Slaad Lord of the Insane is one of the few slaad lords that enjoys traveling the planes and often enters the Material Plane disguised as a tall, mystical warrior adorned in black plate armor. In the outer planes, he is often encountered in his amoeba form or that of a great golden slaad. In any form, it has the strength of a storm giant.

The Slaad Lord of the Insane generally covers an area about 5 feet wide and feet tall, but being similar in makeup to an ooze, can flatten his form and cover a greater area or squeeze through openings much smaller than would normally be allowed. His tentacles are 10 feet long.

The Lord of Insanity can use the following spells: *Astral spell, charm monster, darkness 15-ft radius, detect evil, detect magic, detect invisibility, dispel magic, ESP, fear, fireball, invisibility, locate object, power word - any* (1/day), *shape change, symbol of insanity, unholy word* (1/day), *wish* (not self) (1/day).

The Slaad Lord of the Insane can assume the shape of a humanoid. In humanoid form, the slaad lord cannot use its natural weapons and does not deal level drain. He usually assumes the form of as a human male fighter in black plate armor wielding an iron black longsword (purportedly the legendary *black sword*: a *+3 longsword* that stuns any creature struck, as if by the *power word stun spell*, for 1d10 minutes if the victim fails a saving throw).

The Slaad Lord of the Insane can enter any of the outer planes, the inner planes, or the Material Plane. This ability transports the slaad lord and up to six other creatures, provided they are all touching the slaad lord.

Three times per day, the Slaad Lord of the Insane can automatically summon three red, blue, or green slaadi or two gray or death slaadi.

Cult of Insanity

In the depths of a dungeon or the bad part of a city there is a temple. The temple is built of reddish-gold stone. The temple is only one story high on the exterior, but the interior has a sub-level and a deep pit. From the outside, the temple is an exceedingly simple square building, about 40 feet wide and long and 12 feet tall. The temple has a single entrance, a thick wooden door painted black.

The cultists of the temple worship an entity they call Istnynia. The cult is not recognized by the authorities, but to date it has only been a minor annoyance. The cultists wander the streets of the city-state at dusk, blowing on ram's horns and loudly accosting pedestrians with the phrase "Wake up, gentle dreamer and embrace insanity!"

The cultists wear yellow dhotis and black leather sandals and loincloths. They shave their heads and carry black staves topped by a cluster of jingling bells on leather cords. They have recently taken their cult to a new level by kidnapping sacrificial victims to throw their incarnate god, who has taken up residence in their pit.

Through the temple's single door, one enters a hallway that runs around the perimeter of the building. At several points in the hallway there are iron grates that allow folks in the crawlspace above to fire arrows or pour acid on intruders. The crawlspace is usually empty, but there is a 1 in 6 chance of someone being up there and on guard. The crawlspace looks over the inner sanctum of the temple. A second door on the other side of the hallway and *wizard locked* by a 5th level magic-user leads into the inner sanctum of the temple via a set of rough-cut stone steps.

The inner sanctum is about 24 feet from side to side and set 10 feet below the floor of the hallway. In the middle of the inner sanctum there is a pit that appears to bottomless and as black as pitch. Most of the temples 14 cultists (10 normal humans, three men-at-arms and a dual-classed 9th level cleric/5th level magic-user called Aspeth) are usually to be found here. In the daytime, the cultists are usually lounging about. At dusk, only the high priest and the men-at-arms are present. At night, the men-at-arms are either out searching for a sacrificial victim or returning with one.

The pit is inhabited by the slaad Lord of Insanity, who has chosen to grace the Material Plane with its presence in this temple of chaos. It will enjoy tussling with adventurers only until they appear to threaten it, at which point it will return to Limbo and dispatch various lesser slaad to torment and harass the adventurers until they are dead.

Credit

Ssendam, the Slaad Lord of the Insane originally appeared in the First Edition *Fiend Folio* (© TSR/Wizards of the Coast, 1981) and is used by permission.

Copyright Notice

Author Scott Greene, based on original material by Charles Stross.

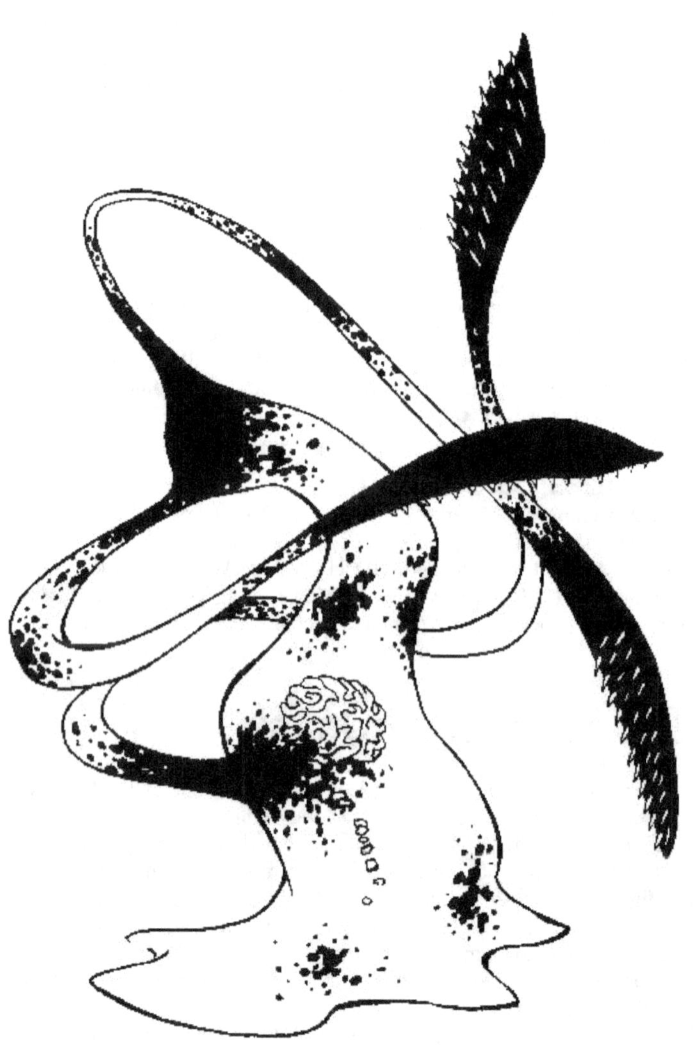

Slag Worm

Hit Dice: 24
Armor Class: 3 [16]
Attacks: 1 bite (4d6)
Saving Throw: 3
Special: Deafening roar, immunity to fire, heat, swallows whole
Move: 3
Alignment: Neutrality
Challenge Level/XP: 26/6,200

This massive wormlike creature of burnt iron and glistening hematite grinds with the roar of the forge. A slag worm's fanged lamprey-like mouth opens to reveal the molten fires burning in its gut. Slag worms average about 40 feet long and weigh about 60,000 pounds, though specimens as large as 100 feet or more have been rumored to exist. Its massive form radiates abysmal heat and when the worm opens its maw, fires can be seen burning and raging in its interior. A slag worm causes a deafening roar as it moves that deafens creatures within 50 feet for 2d4 rounds. Any non-magical weapon that strikes a slag worm melts into slag. A creature striking a slag worm with a natural attack takes the same 4d6 points of damage. If a slag hits with its bite attack, it automatically swallows its opponent on its next turn. The worm's body generates incredible heat, so that anyone within 10 feet takes 2d6 points of damage each round (save for half). A swallowed creature takes 4d6 points of damage each round. Fire heals a slag worm, and cold does one and a half damage to them.

The Worm Crawls In

The Villogas Clan, a ruthless fire giant tribe from the Hollow Spire Mountains, suffered a crushing defeat against the high walls of Holslot. The fire giants tried to assault the structure head-on, but the catapults, archers and heavy ballistae on the crenellated walls forced them to retreat. They want desperately to get into the city, as the High Crown of the Flame Giver is reportedly hidden in the city's temple. The fire giants think the crown will lead them to great victories – if they can recover it.

The giants recruited a slag worm to their cause, and convinced the worm to circle under the city's outer wall. The worm does as instructed, which causes the entire wall to drop straight down in one fell swoop around the city. The giants rush out of underground tunnels while the slag worm rises out of the center of the city like a demonic force as the giants rush the temple. The crown exists, but it's not the mythical relic the giants hope it to be.

Copyright Notice

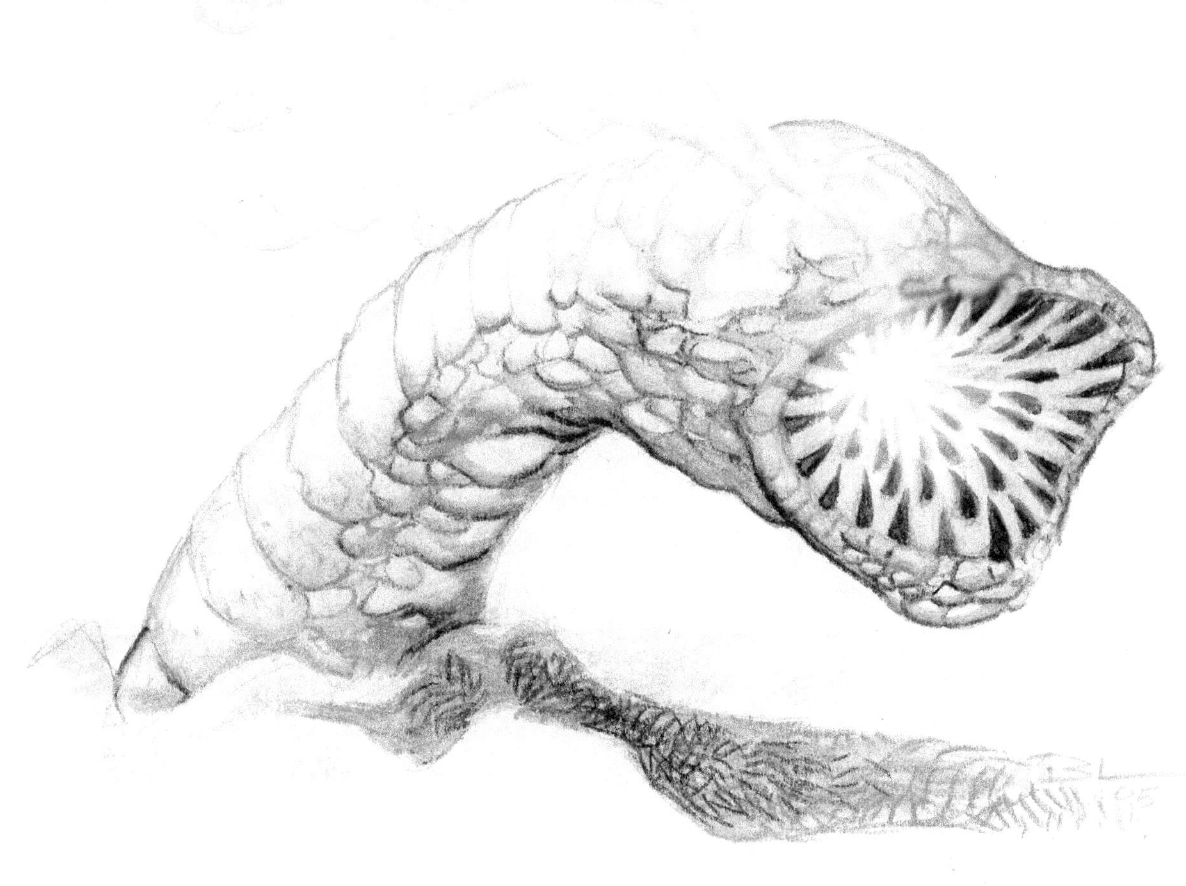

Slaughterford (Reaperborn)

Hit Dice: 10
Armor Class: 3 [16]
Attacks: 2 arm blades (1d8+2)
Saving Throw: 5
Special: Rend armor, magic resistance 20%
Move: 9
Alignment: Neutrality
Challenge Level/XP: 12/2,000

A slaughterford is a strong, wiry creature that looks almost inhumanly slender and weak, with long bony arms and legs. Slaughterfords have four arms. Its primary arms are very strong and, rather than hands, the forearms end in long sharp blades made of an extremely hard and sharp bony material. Their secondary arms, immediately below the first, are much weaker and used for simple manipulation. If a slaughterford rolls a natural 20 with its arm blade strike, it deals 3d8 points of damage. If a slaughterford hits a single opponent with both arm blades, the victim must save or his armor is ripped apart around him, dealing 2d8 points of damage.

Lever Age

The underground caverns beneath the dwarven collieries of Anvil Plunge are filled with the past greatness of the dwarves before the Ashenchisel clan moved their extended families aboveground. Flying buttresses of stone soar over the grand halls and delicate spindles carved from rock columns support cavern roofs. Inlaid blocks of stone on the floor bear the merged forge and chisel Ashenchisel clan symbol.

But deeper still in the silent earth, deeper even than some of the hardiest dwarves dare to delve, lie long-forgotten chambers carved by an unknown hand. These precise, geometric rooms are sterile and empty, and a harsh white glare glows from trapezoidal lanterns sunk into the walls. In one room, three dozen red-handled metal levers rise out of a block of white stone similar to marble sitting in the center of the chamber. Sitting cross-legged atop the block is a wizened man holding a fist-sized diamond (worth 2,000 gp). The gem pulses with strobes of blinding white light. The man is nearly mummified and ancient, his wispy white hair hanging over his skeletal features. His dried fingers are locked around the gem.

Two slaughterfords walk in unison around the block, each pulling levers at random, intent on their duties. The creatures won't let anyone approach the marble block or the diamond. If the creatures are slain, the figure seated on the block begins aging in reverse, growing younger by the second. The figure is Sutur Anrovat, a 12 HD lich trapped in the chamber for nearly 300 years. He rises at full power within 2d4 rounds.

Sleeping Willow

Hit Dice: 11
Armor Class: 1 [18]
Attacks: 4 slams (2d6)
Saving Throw: 4
Special: Sleep, spores, vulnerable to fire
Move: 6
Alignment: Neutrality
Challenge Level/XP: 13/2,300

A sleeping willow appears as a normal willow tree (and is often mistaken for such) standing 15 or more feet tall. Its trunk is 2 feet or more in diameter and dark brown in color. From the trunk sprout branches that end in long drooping and graceful twigs. The sleeping willow is crowned with leaves of green or brownish-green. A sleeping willow can grab an opponent in its branches if it hits with two or more branches (save avoids). A creature held in the branches is drawn closer to the trunk and drained of its body fluids (1d4 hit points of blood loss per round). A sleeping willow can eject a cloud of yellowish pollen in a 30-foot radius that causes creatures to fall asleep for 10 rounds (save resists). Sleeping willows are vulnerable to fire-based spells and take one-and-a-half times damage (no save).

The Kite-Eating Tree

A thick-trunked willow tree stands among a dreary line of termite-eaten trees. Its branches rustle and shake. Grass grows in thick, verdant clumps around the lone healthy trunk and yellow wildflowers bloom in abundance. A shimmering stream of azure blue water flows over slick red rocks near the tree's roots. A bright red kite hangs from the willow's branches, the tail of the child's toy entwined in the leaves. The canvas rustles and shakes.

The tree is a sleeping willow growing in the willow orchard. The kite is left from its last meal. Hidden in the tree's upper branches are three skeletons. The victims were strangled and absorbed by the deadly tree. One wears yellowed plate mail armor with a jagged slash cut across the chest. The knight's *+1 long sword* is wedged into a branch in the treetop.

Copyright Notice
Author Scott Greene.

Slime Crawler

Hit Dice: 1
Armor Class: 4 [15]
Attack: Tentacles (1d3) and bite (1d4)
Saving Throw: 17
Special: Constrict, slippery
Move: 9/6 (climbing)
Alignment: Neutrality
Challenge Level/XP: 1/15

Slime crawlers are the immature version of the carrion moth (see entry in this book). The process of maturity usually takes two to three weeks, at which time the slime crawler feeds on any living organisms encountered. More slug-like at this larval stage, the slime crawler's legs appear as small buds or stumps. These legs allow the slime crawler to climb walls and other surfaces, albeit slower than an adult carrion crawler. Four tentacles sprout below its throat, eventually splitting (losing their grappling ability) and growing into the pseudopod-like tentacles of the carrion crawler. A typical slime crawler is about 6 feet long and weighs about 300 pounds.

A slime crawler attacks with its tentacles, attempting to grab an opponent and squeeze it for 1d3 damage per round. Slime crawlers have a nasty bite, but prefer to use their tentacles in battle.

A slime crawler exudes a thin, oily film from its mouth that leaves a slug-like trail behind it as its moves. A creature stepping in a space covered with this slime must succeed on a saving throw or slip and fall prone. The slime remains in the area for 1d2 hours before losing its slipperiness.

Because of its slippery secretions, a slime crawler is very difficult to grab or hold. Attacks intended to grab or hold a slime crawler are made at a -4 penalty.

Slime Pit

You enter a level of the dungeon with broad (10-foot wide) passages and generously proportioned chambers. All have peaked ceilings that are 12 feet tall at the highest point. Set into the ceilings of the passages are glowing green orbs that cast a bright, verdant light on the passages and allow a variety of exotic plants to grow. Set in the center of each passage there is a bronze statue of a fertility goddess covered in verdigris. These statues are actually automatons programmed to care for the plants. The automatons hold objects akin to holy water sprinklers (they are actually part of the automaton). Once per day, an enchanted pebble inside the hollow automatons casts a *create water* spell.

The chambers one can access from the passages are decorated with mosaics depicting lush gardens inhabited by sprites, satyrs, nymphs and dryads. Lurking in one of these chambers in what appears to be a gladiatorial pit is a brood of 1d6+5 slime crawlers, recently hatched from large, russet eggs that were stuck to one of the walls of the pit. The slime crawlers have begun to make forays out of the pit to search for food, bringing it back to the pit to be devoured. The pit currently contains a lantern (there is a treasure map in the base, which is empty) and a backpack holding 56 gp, a smoky quartz worth 55 gp and three pounds of chickpeas in a sealed jar (worth 9 gp).

Copyright Notice

Authors Casey Christofferson, Scott Greene, and Greg A. Vaughan.

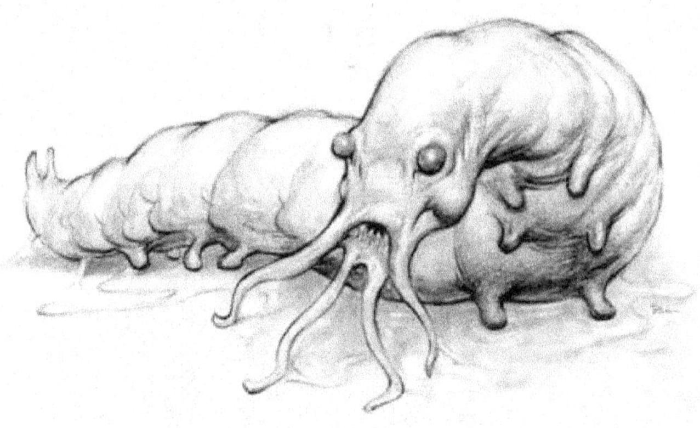

Slime Mold

Hit Dice: 4
Armor Class: 9 [10]
Attacks: slam (1d8+1 + disease)
Saving Throw: 13
Special: Fungal rot, immune to fire
Move: 3
Alignment: Neutrality
Challenge Level/XP: 4/120

Slime molds appear to be an undulating mass of plant matter when in actuality they are a rare form of non-acidic ooze. Something in the creature's protoplasmic substance causes mushrooms, molds, mosses, and other fungal plants to take root and grow on its surface in a symbiotic relationship. A slime mold attacks with a pseudopod slam that causes a creature's skin to darken as small patches of fungi and mold sprout in random locations. Each day, the victim loses 1d6 hit points until it dies and becomes a patch of slime mold. Slime molds are immune to fire.

Home Sweet Home

A bamboo and reed hut sits amid jungle vines. The walls are slanting outward and propped up by the trees growing around it. Mushrooms grow along the flat roof. The interior of the shack is covered in fungi that grow abundantly in the wet jungle. Crude furniture is nothing more than clumps of moss and mushroom. A carpet of grasses grows across the floor of the single-room shack. The air smells of rot.

A slime mold crawls through the grass, its body spread across the floor. The creature is the remains of a hermit who used to live in the shack away from civilization. Over the years, he moved less and less and eventually became the slime that still lingers in his home.

Copyright Notice
Author Scott Greene.

Slithering Tracker

Hit Dice: 5
Armor Class: 4 [15]
Attack: Strike (1d4 plus paralysis)
Saving Throw: 12
Special: Engulf, paralysis, plasma drain, sealed mind, transparent, surprise on 1-2 on 1d6
Move: 6/6 (climbing)
Alignment: Neutrality
Challenge Level/XP: 8/800

The slithering tracker is an amorphous and transparent creature that inhabits dark underground areas of the world. It looks like a long, thin, transparent protoplasm, almost snake-like in form. Unlike other oozes, the slithering tracker does not feed on organic matter. It survives by devouring living creatures. A typical slithering tracker is 3 feet long and has a thickness of about 6 inches. It can grow to a length of about 8 feet.

A slithering tracker secretes an anesthetizing slime. A target hit by its attack or that touches it with its exposed flesh must succeed on a saving throw or be paralyzed for 1d4 hours.

A slithering tracker can engulf a paralyzed foe up to twice its own size in place of making an attack. The slithering tracker merely has to move over a paralyzed creature to engulf it. An engulfed opponent is subjected to the slithering tracker's paralysis and plasma drain. A slithering tracker only uses this ability against a paralyzed, sleeping, or otherwise helpless opponent.

A slithering tracker drains the body fluids from an engulfed opponent. Each 5 rounds an opponent is engulfed, it loses 1 point of constitution. A freed victim regains points of constitution at the rate of 1 per day.

Even though a slithering tracker is intelligent, it is immune to all mind-affecting effects (charms, compulsions, illusions, and fear).

It Came From the Sewers

In the deeper portions of a dungeon, the adventurers come upon a sewer system. The system consists of two levels of clay pipes built between square chambers of cut stone with channels for the liquid waste that filters into the system from the upper portions of the dungeon. The channels and pipes are filled about two feet deep with the run-off. Lurking about this sewer is a single slithering tracker that preys on the rats and insects of the dewer and larger, more intelligent inhabitants.

The middle level of the sewers is inhabited by a small clan of sewer dwarves, rat faced dwarves in dirty smocks and high leather boots covered with tar to make them somewhat water-tight. The dwarves live in chambers reachable via secret doors in the square chambers that connect the pipes. Despite the rather horrid conditions of the sewers, the dwarves live in relative comfort. Their natural resistance to disease helps them survive on a diet of giant rats and other denizens of the sewer. Within their living quarters, which all link into a central common chamber, the dwarves are scupulously neat, burning incense to clear the air and making as warm and comfortable an environment as they can by scavenging and trading.

The common chamber of the dwarves is taken up by a tangle of glass tubes, copper pipes and oddly shaped decanters. The dwarves use this still to distill the raw sewage into pure water and a variety of other alchemical compounds (some of the run-off comes from ancient laboratories). The dwarves power their still with methane gas piped in from the lowest level of sewers. They trade some of the compounds for goods they cannot scavenge or make themselves.

Credit

The Slithering Tracker originally appeared in the *Strategic Review #5* (© TSR/Wizards of the Coast, 1975) and later in the First Edition *Monster Manual* (© TSR/Wizards of the Coast, 1977) and is used by permission.

Copyright Notice

Author Scott Greene, based on original material by Gary Gygax.

Slorath

Hit Dice: 17
Armor Class: 0 [19]
Attacks: 1 bite (2d8)
Saving Throw: 3
Special: Paralyzing gaze, spell-like abilities, magic resistance 30%, immune to cold
Move: 9/6 (burrow)
Alignment: Chaos
Challenge Level/XP: 20/4,400

A slorath is a 40-foot-long viper with glossy-white scales and a bluish-white underbelly. The mouth lacks the fangs of a viper and is lined with sharpened teeth and a long, slender, icy blue flickering tongue. The eyes are greenish-blue with vertical-slit pupils. The gaze of a slorath can paralyze opponents (save avoids). Sloraths live in freezing climates and are immune to cold. Three times per day, they can create a *cone of cold* and *ice storm*. One per day it can unleash a glacial storm (similar to a *meteor swarm*, but the swarm inflicts cold damage).

The Winter Carnival

Kruest, a village of barbegazi in the icy north, has a terrible secret. The homes, inns and taverns in the village are carved from sparkling ice – some standing nearly three stories tall. Ice sculptures sit on every ice road through the city. The Harbin House, an inn complete with ice fireplaces has 30 rooms and an underground hot spring spa. Carved satyrs, curling dragons, giant grinning faces and delicate carriages stand outside the building in an ice garden. The barbegazi are expert ice sculptors.

The barbegazi struck a terrible bargain five years ago with a slorath that threatened the town. The villagers at first sacrificed their kin – until they realized no one would miss a few visitors who came to see the ice sculptures. The entire village speaks of a "white dragon" outside town that won't leave them alone. Gullible PCs who fall for the trick are shown a path to the slorath's lair. If adventurers don't fall for the kill-the-dragon-save-the-town scenario, the barbegazi drug them and cart them to the slorath's cave.

The slorath is a massive creature that has grown fat off its "deal" with the barbegazi. It keeps its treasure frozen in the walls of its lair.

Copyright Notice
Author Scott Greene.

Sloth Viper

Hit Dice: 5
Armor Class: 6 [13]
Attacks: 1 bite (1d4 + poison)
Saving Throw: 12
Special: Poison
Move: 9/6/6 (climb/swim)
Alignment: Neutrality
Challenge Level/XP: 6/400

Sloth vipers are emerald colored snakes with bands of gold and black ringing their body. Their tails are tipped with black and their eyes are amber or brown in color. The typical sloth viper is 9-10 feet long, though they can grow to a length of 20 or more feet. A sloth viper's bite delivers a deadly poison.

Pit Vipers

The thick jungle canopy is alive with colorful birds that squawk and flap off into the sky, noisy tree frogs that croak a discordant melody, and all manner of snakes wrapping around the gnarled branches. Vines hang in bundled clumps, and the trees present an almost impenetrable barrier. The path through the trees is nothing more than a narrow game trail, but is still the fastest way through the nearly impenetrable jungle.

In a wide clearing, the ground is a churned mess of swampy, thick sand covered in a thin layer of decaying fronds and wild clumps of tangled weeds. The jungle canopy is just 10 feet above the marshy ground, with leafy vines dipping into the muck. The clearing is a shallow pit of quicksand that won't kill PCs who blunder into it (it's only three feet deep), but does slow movement to a quarter normal.

A sloth viper lives in the tree branches over the quicksand. It uncoils to deliver a quick venomous strike to anyone floundering in the quicksand pit beneath it. The viper waits for creatures to die in the muck or on its outer banks before descending to enjoy a meal.

Copyright Notice

Slug, Giant

Hit Dice: 12
Armor Class: 3 [16]
Attack: Bite (2d6 plus 1d8 acid) or acid spit (4d8)
Saving Throw: 3
Special: Spit acid, resistance to sharp weapons (50%), malleable, vulnerable to salt
Move: 9/3 (burrowing)
Alignment: Neutrality
Challenge Level/XP: 13/2300

Giant slugs are found in moist or wet environments such as swamps, marshes, rain forests, and dungeons. They are both scavengers and predators feeding on both plants and animals. Giant slugs are nocturnal creatures and spend the daylight hours away from the heat of the sun. On extremely hot days, giant slugs bury themselves in debris where they secrete a thick coating of mucus that covers their entire body and protects them from the heat.

Giant slugs are larger versions of normal slugs. They are pale gray in color with a dull white underbelly. They have a single pair of long, thin tentacles or antennae. The giant slug uses them to sense brightness, heat, and to smell. A typical giant slug is 20 feet long but can grow to twice that length.

A giant slug begins combat by spitting a line of corrosive saliva at an opponent. Every 1d4 rounds, a giant slug can spit a line of acid at an opponent within 60 feet. A successful ranged attack that ignores armor bonuses to AC is required to hit. If struck, a target takes 4d8 points of acid damage. Each piece of equipment carried by the struck creature must also pass a saving throw or be ruined.

A giant slug can squeeze its body through openings 4 feet wide or larger.

A giant slug is highly susceptible to salt and takes 1d6 points of damage per pound of salt it contacts.

Slow Moving Vengeance

Seeking passage to an out of way corner of the globe, the adventurers are fortunate to find a large junk heading their way. The junk is captained by a jovial looking giant of a man with a long, white mustache and a shaved head that seems always to beaded with sweat. Two capuchin monkeys decorate the man's arms and shoulders most of the time, the man absentmindedly feeding them bits of sweet potato and spicy pickles while he barks out orders. The crew looks particularly seedy on this vessel, probably because they are pirates. They have been hired by a magic-user to transport a very dangerous cargo to his tower (which is conveniently located wherever the party is heading, or close to it). The magic-user apprentice, a comely lass with sparkling eyes and a wry wit, is aboard to make sure everything goes as planned.

The dangerous cargo is kept in the forward hold. Naturally, approaching the forward hold is forbidden. It is guarded by three of the pirates (one tall, one short, one fat), who seem terribly annoyed by their duty below decks and just itching for something to punch. Inside the hold there is a massive construction of force that can only be the creation of a powerful wizard. Inside the "aquarium" there is a giant slug, apparently frozen in time.

While the captain is under the impression that he has been hired to transport the beast to the magic-user, he is sadly mistaken. The magic-user's wife was, many years ago, lost to the depredations of the pirates. A few days into the voyage, the aquarium simply disappears and the slug is released from its spell to wreak havoc on the ship. The magic-user regrets losing his apprentice this way, but there is always a price to pay for revenge.

Credit
The Giant Slug originally appeared in the First Edition *Monster Manual* (© TSR/Wizards of the Coast, 1977) and is used by permission.

Copyright Notice
Author Scott Greene, based on original material by Gary Gygax.

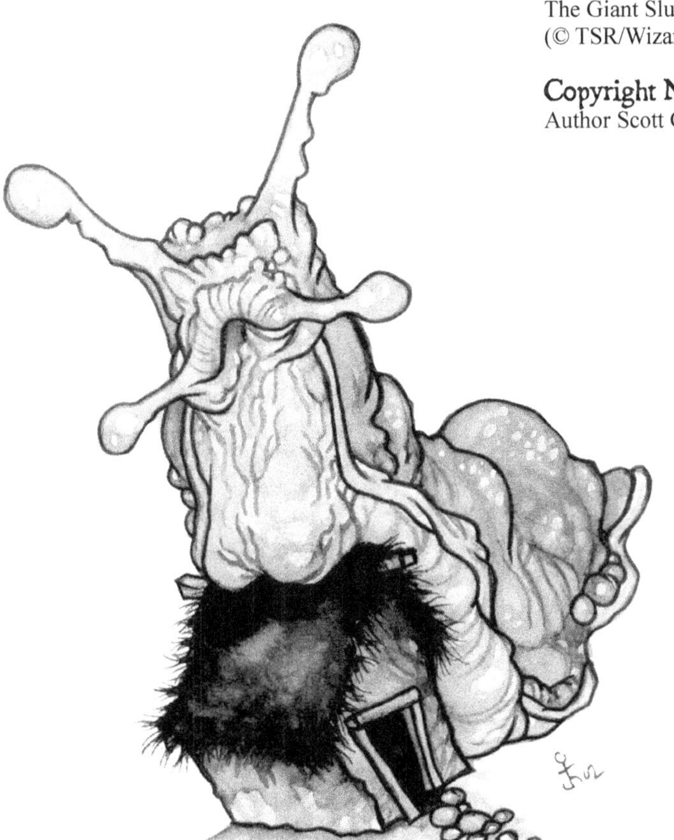

Soul Eater

Hit Dice: 10
Armor Class: -1 [20]
Attack: 2 claws (1d6 plus 1d6 wisdom)
Saving Throw: 5
Special: Level drain, soul drain, only harmed by +1 or better weapons, find target, immunities, surprise on 1-3 on 1d6 in darkness or smoke
Move: 36 (flying)
Alignment: Neutrality
Challenge Level/XP: 14/2600

A soul eater is an extraplanar creature of great power. Its plane of origin is unknown but is thought to be some sort of void plane. Soul eaters are summoned to the Material Plane for one purpose—to slay living creatures. When given a target, a soul eater can track it unerringly.

Soul eaters look like billowing clouds of inky darkness. Two long, pale arms protrude from the darkness, each ending in a clawed hand. Soul eaters sustain themselves on the life energies of living creatures and derive this sustenance by draining the souls of living targets.

A creature hit by a soul eater's claw attack must succeed on a saving throw or lose one level. When a soul eater slays a foe, it devours the victim's soul. Such a creature cannot be returned to life by any means save a deity's intervention.

When a soul eater is summoned to the Material Plane, it creates a mental link between itself and the caster who summoned it. If a soul eater's victim (i.e., the creature it is summoned to slay) is killed before the creature can devour its soul, the soul eater returns to the caster and attacks him. Likewise, if a soul eater is defeated in battle (but not slain) by its target, the creature returns to the caster and attacks him. So long as both the caster and soul eater are on the same plane of existence, the soul eater can successfully locate the caster. If the caster leaves the plane, the link is temporarily broken. Once the caster returns, or the soul eater enters a plane the caster is on, the link is immediately restored.

When ordered to find a creature, a soul eater does so unerringly. The being giving the order must have seen the creature to be found and must know the target's name.

Soul eaters are immune to poison, sleep, paralysis, and stunning. Since they have no clear front or back they cannot be back-stabbed.

The Harpist of Souls

In a large city square a bedraggled harpist moves into the center of the square and sits on the ground, disrupting traffic and drawing the attention of the guards. The man has glassy eyes and a tangled mustache and beard. His clothes are soiled and tattered. Sitting on the ground, ignoring the shouts of townsmen and the guards, he begins to pluck his harp.

As the music winds its way through the market, people begin to listen, intently. The crowd quiets, those few people still talking finding themselves elbowed in the ribs or otherwise quieted. The song slowly grows louder and the crowd begins to sway back and forth. As they do so, a gray haze forms over the harpist. The haze spreads out over the heads of the crowd and grows blacker and blacker until it fills the sky over the marketplace. As the people turn their faces to the blackness, two long, pale arms appear above the harpist's head. They appear to be very far away, but quickly move nearer, until they reach out of the cloud and grab one of the crowd. The person wriggles for a moment and then drops lifeless to the ground.

As this, the harpist finishes his song and slumps over, chin on chest. The crowd awakens from their fascination and begins to scream and flee from the square as the arms pursue them. After thirteen people have been killed, the blackness and the soul eater suddenly disappear. The harpist awakes, gets to his feet groggily, and then moves on. Those attacking the harpist discover that he is incorporeal. Should one have weapons or spells that affect incorporeal creatures, the harpist is merely a normal human, a minstrel who had the misfortune of trading a few gold pieces to a cloaked stranger for the harp.

Credit

The Soul Eater originally appeared in the First Edition module *X4 Master of the Desert Nomads* (© TSR/Wizards of the Coast, 1983) and is used by permission.

Copyright Notice

Author Scott Greene, based on original material by David Cook.

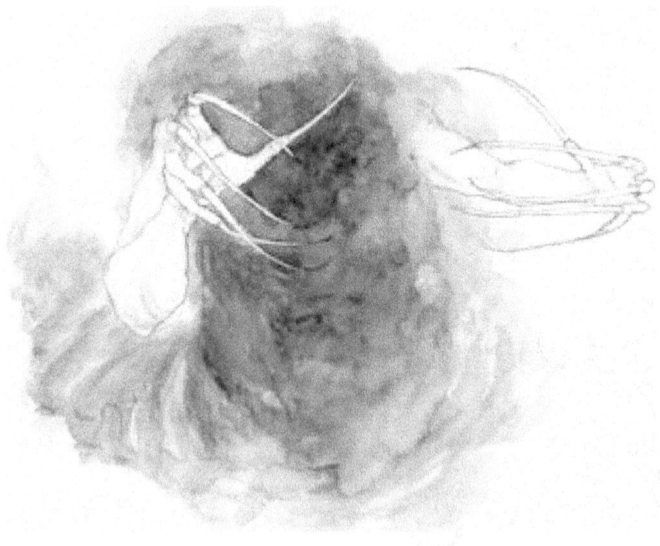

Soul Nibbler

Hit Dice: 1d6
Armor Class: 4 [15]
Attack: Bite (1d3)
Saving Throw: 18
Special: Level drain, immune to necromancy, surprise on roll of 1-2 on 1d6
Move: 6/6 (climbing)
Alignment: Neutrality
Challenge Level/XP: 2/30

Soul nibblers are rats that have undergone genetic mutation due to continued feeding on essence ingots (see sidebar). The biological effects of a prolonged consumption of soul stuff are minimal. Soul nibblers are always black in color, and their eyes sometime glow with a sickly light. The magical changes wrought by their unholy diet, however, are more profound, granting the soul nibblers unique necromantic abilities.

Having begun life as normal rats, soul nibblers behave in combat much like their mundane cousins. The primary difference between soul nibblers and standard rats is their bond to dark magic, which grants them the powers of level drain and necromantic immunity.

Living creatures hit by a soul nibbler's bite attack lose one level unless they pass a saving throw.

Soul nibblers are immune to a cleric's *cause wounds* spells (i.e. reverse of *cure wounds*) as well as spells that cause death or energy drain.

Eternal Scholars of Darkness and Deceit

In a dingy flat overlooking a narrow alley three young scholars have gathered to perform a magic ritual - a real one. One of three, who have dubbed themselves the Eternal Scholars of Darkness and Deceit, procured a scroll from his master at the university while said master was in his cups. The scroll contains the true name of a devil (an erinyes, it turns out) and the summoning ritual to bring it into the Material Plane and bind it. The scroll case that contained the scroll also contains a number of small, black metallic pellets.

As adventurers walk through the alley, perhaps on their way to the Carmine Unicorn to buy a few pints, they see crimson smoke, pungent and choking, pouring from the windows and filling the alley. Following closely behind the crimson smoke is a swarm of 1d10+10 soul nibblers, rats fed the pellets as proscribed by the ritual.

Once the soul nibblers appear, the erinyes is only 6 rounds behind. The ritual has a 50% chance of success. If successful, the erinyes is bound to serve the ambitious young scholars. If not, it kills them and then turns its attention to conquering its new home.

Erinyes: HD 9; AC -2 [21]; Atk Longsword (1d8+1) or longbow (1d8 + 1d6 fire) or rope (entanglement); Move 12 (Fly 24); Save 7; CL/XP 17/3500; Special: +1 or better weapon to hit, immunity to fire and poison, resistance to acid and cold (50%), magic resistance (50%), telepathy 100 ft., see invisibility, immune to illusions. Erinyes can cast the following spells: Charm monster, teleport, phantasmal force.

Credit

The soul nibbler first appeared in module *G3 What Evil Lurks* by Lance Hawvermale (© Necromancer Games, Inc., 2002).

Copyright Notice

Authors Travis Hawvermale and Scott Greene.

Essence Ingots

Essence ingots are small rectangular bricks of blackened stone that contain the soul of a living creature. Creatures are trapped in *essence ingots* through the use of a great smelter, the location of which has been lost.

A trapped spirit can be released by casting *remove curse* (or similar and more powerful magic). A released soul reforms its material body in 1d4 rounds. If an *essence ingot* is broken, the trapped soul is not released but is lost forever.

Soul Reaper

Hit Dice: 18
Armor Class: -3 [22]
Attacks: 1 scythe (2d4 + soul slash)
Saving Throw: 3
Special: +2 or better magic weapons to hit, magic resistance (60%), soul slash
Move: 12
Alignment: Chaos
Challenge Level/XP: 20/4,400

Soul reapers are 12-foot-tall undead creatures shrouded in long, black hooded cloaks. No discernible facial features are visible under the hood. The creature's hands end in wicked claws of inky blackness that are always clutched tightly around its gleaming, sharp scythe. If a soul reaper hits with its scythe, an opponent must save or have its soul torn from its body and pulled into the reaper's scythe. The victim's soulless body collapses into a desiccated husk and crumbles to dust within 24 hours. To reclaim a soul, the reaper must be destroyed and its scythe shattered on holy ground. All souls trapped within are released and seek their original body (if it's been less than 24 hours since it was killed). Creatures without a body are left to wander in spirit form, although a *wish* or *resurrection* can restore them. Soul reapers can see invisible creatures, and can cast *confusion* and *symbol of pain* once per day.

Fear the Reaper

An ornate metal stand of dark wrought iron stands at the dusty crossroads. A voluminous tome with a mahogany leather cover lies open atop the stand. Names are scrawled across the open page, but plenty of space remains to add more. A quill taken from the corpse of a roc slain under a full moon sits in a vial of squid ink in a metal recess.

The Book of Possibilities is a magical volume that appears randomly and offers potential signers a blind choice: Sign their name and receive powerful rewards or face the consequences of their decision. Each time someone signs his name to the book, the pages randomly flip for the next signer. There is an even chance this new page brings wealth and power for the PC (although it is up to the Game Referee to decide how this occurs and when, although the wish could be twisted as per an infernal pact). There is the same chance the PC finds himself facing a soul reaper that forms out of the sepia ink on the stand. If a soul reaper is summoned, the creature targets the signer until his death, then fades away until summoned again (at full strength). The book and stand evaporate with the coming dawn.

Copyright Notice
Author Scott Greene.

Spectral Troll

Hit Dice: 6
Armor Class: 7 [12]
Attack: Incorporeal bite (1d8) and 2 claws (1d6)
Saving Throw: 11
Special: Corrupting touch, create spawn, manifestation, rend, regeneration 2 hp/round
Move: 12/12 (flying)
Alignment: Chaos
Challenge Level/XP: 9/1100

A spectral troll stands nearly twice as tall as a human. Its arms are long and gangly and its nose is droopy and slightly oversized. Its arms end in powerful claws. Filthy black, matted hair streams down from its head.

A spectral troll that hits a living target with its incorporeal bite or an incorporeal claw attack deals 1d6 points of damage. Any humanoid killed by a spectral troll rises 1d3 days later as a free-willed spectre unless a cleric of the victim's religion blesses the corpse before such time.

A spectral troll dwells on the Ethereal Plane and, as an ethereal creature, it cannot affect or be affected by anything in the material world. When a spectral troll manifests, it partly enters the Material Plane and becomes visible but incorporeal on the Material Plane. It can be harmed only by other incorporeal creatures, magic weapons, or spells, with a 50% chance to ignore any damage from a corporeal source. A manifested spectral troll can pass through solid objects at will, and its own attacks pass through armor. It always moves silently and its incorporeality helps protect it from foes on the Material Plane, but not from foes on the Ethereal Plane.

In most cases, it's difficult to destroy a spectral troll through simple combat: The "destroyed" spirit will often restore itself in 2d4 days. Even the most powerful spells are usually only temporary solutions. A spectral troll that would otherwise be destroyed returns to its old haunts with a successful saving throw. As a rule, the only way to get rid of a spectral troll for sure is to determine the reason for its existence and set right whatever prevents it from resting in peace. The exact means varies with each spirit and may require a good deal of research.

Spectral trolls vanish in direct sunlight. They are not harmed by it, nor does it cause them any discomfort: they simply do not appear in sunlight. Spectral trolls that are *held*, restrained, confined, or imprisoned vanish in direct sunlight. Once night has fallen, a spectral troll reappears. If the spectral troll was magically held or restrained, the magic does not resume when it reappears.

Hunter or Hunted?

The adventurers, wherever they might be, have wandered into the territory of a spectral troll. The troll dwells on the ethereal plane in a twilight cave on a bleak moor of reeking spirits and ghostly white willows. The troll is always on the hunt for prey, and there is a 3 in 6 chance it will catch the scent of the material creatures walking through its territory.

The troll is canny and cunning, and waits for one person to become separated or for the group to slumber before striking. If the group has men-at-arms or animals that are easier targets than the adventurers, the troll takes them first. If the group proves clueless as to what is attacking them in the night, it will follow them for many days, killing victims, dragging them away and gorging itself on them before the dawn arrives and it must return to its home plane.

On the Ethereal Plane, the troll keeps 1d6 x 100 sp and 1d4 x 1,000 gp in its cave, along with a massive collection of knuckle bones.

Credit
The Spectral Troll originally appeared in the Second Edition *Monstrous Manual* (© TSR/Wizards of the Coast, 1993) and is used by permission.

Copyright Notice
Author Scott Greene, based on original material by Wizards of the Coast.

Spider, Skull

Hit Dice: 1
Armor Class: 0 [19]
Attack: Sting (1d8 from poison)
Saving Throw: 17
Special: Poison
Move: 9/6 (climbing)
Alignment: Neutrality
Challenge Level/XP: 2/30

Skull spiders are tarantula-like creatures that reside in the skulls of their victims. The two front legs of a skull spider contain poisoned barbs that they use to sting their victims. The weak and fleshy body of a skull spider is about the size of a grapefruit and is easily damaged. Its eyes grow on the end of long, slender stalks. Skull spiders take up residence within skulls as a means of protecting themselves in a manner similar to hermit crabs.

Their eyestalks protrude through the empty eye sockets of their skull, and their legs have a backwards curve in the first joint that enables them to extend out of the bottom of the skull to allow rapid locomotion. Skull spiders can also fold their legs under their skull so they cannot be seen. Many an adventurer has been unnerved by the sight of dozens of skulls seemingly sprouting long, spidery legs and skittering toward them.

A colony of skull spiders is led by a king and queen, which are the only two members of the colony that are capable of reproducing. After a victim is subdued, the queen deposits an egg in the skull. Queen skull spiders are always 3 HD. The larva hatches, consumes the brain over a period of weeks, and then enters a pupae stage. After several months, when the corpse is sufficiently deteriorated, the new skull spider hatches, uses its strong legs to detach the skull, and goes to join its colony.

A skull spider delivers a virulent poison with a successful bite attack. A successful saving throw cuts the poison damage in half. Every 10 rounds after suffering poison damage, a victim takes an additional 1d4 points of damage until they pass a saving throw by 3 points or receive a *neutralize poison* spell.

Chamber of Skulls

The catacombs (beneath the city streets or on some level of a dungeon) are lined with hundreds of grinning skulls. The skulls are set in long compartments set in the glistening walls (they contain copious amounts of iron pyrite) at eye level. Hidden among these skulls is a swarm of 1d10+10 skull spiders. As people enter the catacombs, the spiders begin tracking them, waiting until they reach an octagon shrine in the middle of the catacombs. The shrine is set a few feet below the level of the catacombs and is 10 feet wide in each direction and 10 feet tall from floor to ceiling. Four of the walls of the shrine open into other corridors, while the other four contain totem-like statues of stacked, toad-faced demons. The top of the totem has a wide, gaping mouth that begins releasing a cloud of sleeping gas as soon as a pressure plate in the center of the chamber is activated. The sleeping gas fills the top foot of the chamber in the first round, and another foot with each additional round until the upper six feet of the chamber is fairly inundated with the gas. Anyone in the gas cloud must pass a saving throw each round (at a cumulative -1 penalty per round) to avoid falling asleep (per the *sleep* spell).

Copyright Notice
Author Erica Balsley.

Spider Collective

Hit Dice: 6
Armor Class: 6 [13]
Attacks: 1 bite (1d6)
Saving Throw: 11
Special: Engulf, swarming body, poison
Move: 6/12 (climb)
Alignment: Neutrality
Challenge Level/XP: 6/400

A spider collective is a human-size spider composed of thousands of smaller spider swarming into the familiar shape. A spider collective can sling individuals spiders from its body at a single target within 10 feet to deal 1d6 points of damage. Any creature attacking a collective creature unarmed or with natural attacks automatically takes 1d4 points of damage as the smaller spiders swarm over the attacker. At will, a collective spider can break into smaller swarms or even into individual creatures and disperse. Other collective creatures such as collective fire ants, wasps and leeches are rumored to exist. A spider collective's poison is derived from the thousands of spiders in the group, and deals 3d6 points of damage (save for half).

Cluster Yuck

Plaques and display cases holding the pinned remains of thousands of insect specimens line the wall of this chamber. Short bookshelves contain volumes on arthropods and insect diagrams. Dissection drawings and notes relating to spiders lie on a podium. Strapped to a wide metal table is the body of a large spider-human hybrid. Its split abdomen contains rotting internal organs. A mechanical device incorporating vials of green liquid sits partially sewn into the chest cavity. Oozing bile and pus drip from the table to the floor. The creature – whatever it was – is dead and poses no threat.

The shadowy ceiling is covered in a thick layer of normal black spiders. The height of the room and light sources make the spiders difficult to discern. The spiders drop from the ceiling in a huge teardrop shape and form a collective spider to defend their master's laboratory.

Copyright Notice

Spinal Leech

These vermin appear as 3-inch long transparent leeches. A typical encounter is with a swarm of 10-20 leeches. They are found in swamps, marshes, and stagnant underground pools. They attach to their prey and drain spinal fluid, thereby inducing paralysis in the victim. When encountered, the spinal leeches crawl onto their victim (1 in 6 chance of noticing), moving quickly to its spine. A spinal leech needs only a single round to reach its destination. If the target is wearing chainmail armor, an additional round is added to the time as the leech finds a way underneath its host's armor; 2 rounds are added if the victim is wearing platemail.

When a leech attaches itself, the victim has a 1 in 6 chance of feeling a strange sensation run down his spine; otherwise, the spinal leech's bite goes unnoticed. Each round thereafter, a saving throw must be made or the victim takes 1d6 points of dexterity damage. At dexterity 0, the victim is paralyzed until his dexterity score is brought to 1.

An application of fire or salt instantly kills all leeches. They can also be pulled from a host with no ill effects.

Who's Watching Your Back?

You enter a long tunnel that curves downward. The tunnel was dug by a purple worm. Where the tunnel dips, there are pools of stagnant water inhabited by swarms of 1d10+10 spinal leeches and the remains of some of their victims - mostly giant rats, but also a bugbear and two dwarves. The bugbear is dressed in piecemeal armor and carries a spear, while the dwarves are dressed in dark gray buckskin and carry backpacks, daggers and 1d6+10 gold pieces and a few other adventuring supplies. The tunnel runs about two miles, and intersects with other similar tunnels cut by purple worms, as well as natural caverns. The tunnels would make a fine underground highway were it not for the spinal leeches.

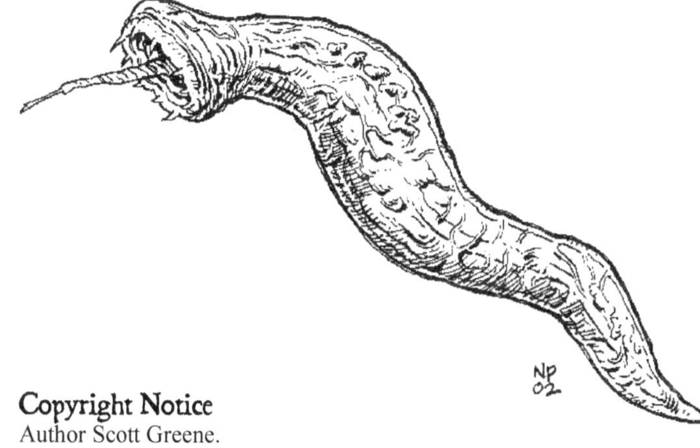

Copyright Notice

Spriggan

Hit Dice: 4
Armor Class: 3 [16]
Attack: Short sword (1d6) or pole arm (1d8)
Saving Throw: 13
Special: Spells, size alteration
Move: 9
Alignment: Chaos
Challenge Level/XP: 6/400

Spriggans are among the ugliest and certainly the most foul tempered of all gnomes. At one moment a normal-sized gnome, a spriggan can grow to giant-sized in an instant, gaining immense strength and taking unsuspecting opponents by surprise.

Spriggans are, by human standards, quite homely. They have stocky bodies and sickly ochre-colored skin and dark hair of brown of black. Male spriggans favor facial hair such as shaggy mustaches and ratty beards, but any head or facial hair they have is unkempt and filthy. Female spriggans do not have facial hair. Being unhygienic creatures, spriggans never bathe or clean their clothing or equipment. Thanks to their filthy lifestyle, spriggans reek with the foulness of dirt, body odor, and other unpleasantness. Despite being gnomes themselves, spriggans despise all of their gnomish kinfolk.

A typical spriggan stands 3-1/2 feet tall and weighs 50 to 55 pounds. An enlarged spriggan stands about 8-1/2 feet tall and weighs 500 to 550 pounds. Spriggans speak the language of gnomes with a thick accent and they trill their "r"'s. Some speak the common tongue as well.

Spriggans can cast fear, pyrotechnics and strength at will. They cannot use these abilities when they are enlarged.

At will, a spriggan can enlarge to triple its normal size and ten times its normal weight. Weapons, armor, and other inanimate objects on its person grow proportionately with it when it changes size. The spriggan can changes sizes at will in place of making a move in comat. An enlarged spriggan doubles its Hit Dice and doubles its damage. While enlarged, a spriggan cannot use its spells.

Spriggan Society

Spriggan mobs are almost always comprised of males; female spriggans rarely venture out of their dismal lairs other than to gather food. Mobs of spriggan males are nomadic in nature, roving from place to place and never settling down for more than a few days unless there is promising a opportunity for rewarding raids on local communities. Female spriggan mobs are unusually stable for such chaotic creatures, often lairing in the same place for years before moving on. Spriggan leaders are 7 to 9 hit dice.

Down and Out Gnomes

A mob of 1d10+2 spriggans has established a lair in the broken remains of a caravan. The caravan, or what remains of it, consists of three wagons, human-sized, in terrible shape. The wagons have been overturned, some of the wood splintered, the wheels missing, etc.

The destroyers of the caravan are the same spriggan who now inhabit it. The broken and bloodied bodies of the guards and drivers have been stripped of their valuables and thrown into a gully about 1 mile away. The bullocks were eaten, their charred bones cast into the surrounding woods.

The spriggans welcome outsiders, posing as down and out gnome cobblers, the survivors of an attack who are without rations (they bury their food) and have had little luck hunting. The spriggans allow travelers to do a few things for them before enlarging themselves and attacking.

The gnomes have a treasure of 3,840 sp, 1,310 gp, a brass bracelet set with an obsidian shark (worth 210 gp) and a scroll of protection from magic wrapped in a wolf skin (worth 8 gp) and buried in the ground twenty paces away from their camp.

Credit

The Spriggan originally appeared in *Dragon #59* (© TSR/Wizards of the Coast, 1982) and later in the First Edition *Monster Manual II* (© TSR/Wizards of the Coast, 1981) and is used by permission.

Copyright Notice

Authors Scott Greene and Erica Balsley, based on original material by Roger Moore and Gary Gygax.

Sprite

Hit Dice: 1d6
Armor Class: 4 [15]
Attack: Short sword (1d3) or shortbow (1d4)
Saving Throw: 18 (16 vs. magic)
Special: Sleep arrows, speak with animals, spells, magic resistance 25%
Move: 12/24 (flying)
Alignment: Neutrality (lawful tendencies)
Challenge Level/XP: 2/30

A reclusive folk, sprites live in meadows and woodland glens, where they have appointed themselves the monitors of their lands. They stand about 2 feet tall and fly by means of their tiny diaphanous wings. Sprites have very delicate features with tiny, upturned noses and large pointed ears. Their eyes sparkle like moonlight on a forest lake, and their tiny, high-pitched voices sound almost like music.

Sprites are very capricious creatures, even finding elves a bit stodgy and serious; only druids have regular contact with sprites, and indeed many druids get their training from sprites.

Sprites speak the common tongue and the language of elves, gnomes, pixies, dryads and satyrs. They can also communicate with woodland animals.

Sprites detest evil and attack it on sight. Opponents are knocked unconscious with sleep arrows and then spirited away to some reclusive locale where they are placed, without weapons or gear and left to their own accord. Extremely evil creatures are usually slain outright by the usually fun-loving and good-natured sprite.

Sprites coat the tips of their arrows with an ointment that causes any creature struck (regardless of HD) to fall asleep (as the *sleep* spell) for 1d6 hours unless they succeed on a saving throw.

Sprites can cast *detect evil* (range 150 ft.), and *invisibility* (self only) at will.

Sprites are one of the few races that are truly immortal, never aging. They cannot die from natural causes. They still need to eat, sleep, and breathe, and can be killed normally.

Sea Sprite

Sea sprites are the aquatic version of normal sprites. As their name implies, they are joyful fey who dwell in the sea. Their hair resembles strands of seaweed and they have large, fish-like eyes. The skin of a sea sprite is pale blue. Lacking wings, sea sprites cannot fly, but thanks to fine webbing in their fingers and toes they can swim at a speed of 24. The weapons and abilities of the sea sprites are identical to those of their land-dwelling cousins, except they employ crossbows rather than shortbows. Sea sprites can breathe both air and water without difficulty. Like normal sprites, sea sprites make use of special ammunition that put their opponents to sleep.

Faerie Fair

A tribe of 1d10 x 10 sprites is hosting a pleasant fair in the woods about 5 miles away from a large human village. Under the light of the full moon, the market is set up between several large liveoaks with gray trunks and broad, dark green leaves. The sprites are hawking plump golden grapes, full pomegranates, dates, sharp bullaces, damsons, bilberries, rare pears and greengages.

A number of strange folk are wandering through the fair, pinching grapes, tasting sparkling wines poured from silver decanters. The fairgoers include a band of lusty satyrs, a few quiet hamadryads poking their green faces from the oaks, several elven merchants, abacuses in hand, clerks scrawling notes on parchment scrolls with silver-tipped quills, a number of young maids from the nearby village and even a few warty hobgoblins holding baskets bulging with fairy fruit.

Credit

The Sprite originally appeared in the First Edition *Monster Manual* (© TSR/Wizards of the Coast, 1977) and is used by permission.

Copyright Notice

Sprite: Author Scott Greene, based on original material by Gary Gygax.
Sea Sprite: Author Scott Greene.

Squealer

Hit Dice: 12
Armor Class: 2 [17]
Attack: Bite (1d8) and 2 claws (1d6)
Saving Throw: 3
Special: Rend with claws, sound imitation, surprise on 1-2 on 1d6 in woodland environments
Move: 15/12 (climbing)
Alignment: Neutrality
Challenge Level/XP: 12/2000

A squealer is about the size of a large gorilla. Its fur is long and yellowish-green in alternating splotches. Its shoulders are hunched and it has a forward-thrusting, pig-like head. Razor-sharp teeth line its mouth. Its four forelimbs sprout from its body—two from the hunched back and the other two from high on the hindquarters. A fifth limb grows from the middle of its back.

Squealers are carnivorous predators found in dense forests. They are voracious creatures and spend a good part of their day hunting food.

A typical squealer stands 9 feet tall and weighs about 400 pounds. Squealers communicate with others of their kind using a series of grunts, growls, and squeals. They cannot speak any known language.

A creature hit by a squealer's bite attack must pass a saving throw or be grabbed and held tight. A held creature is rended by the squealer's claws, suffering an automatic 2d6 points of damage.

A squealer can mimic any animal or magical beast sound it has previously heard. Listeners who succeed on a saving throw detect the ruse.

Lipstick Goblins and Pigs

While traveling through a forest of tremendous blue gums that rise 200 to 300 feet in height one might have the misfortune of running into a gang of 1d3+1 squealers. The curious beasts dwell in the upper branches of the trees, listening for out of place sounds on the ground below and then crashing down through the foliage to subdue their prey.

Once killed or knocked senseless, a body is dragged up into the tree and eaten. Belongings are tossed onto the floor below or become lodged in the trees. The local goblins scavenge for these treasures in the hours just before dawn, when the squealers are usually asleep. They stow them in their burrow, located in a copse of lipstick trees. The goblins use the paste made from the seeds in their cuisine (they mix them with mangoes and onions and use it to flavor their stews) and use it as a dye to color the left half of their faces.

Credit

The Squealer originally appeared in the First Edition module *S3 Expedition to the Barrier Peaks* (© TSR/Wizards of the Coast, 1980) and later in the First Edition *Monster Manual II* (© TSR/Wizards of the Coast, 1983) and is used by permission.

Copyright Notice

Author Scott Greene, based on original material by Gary Gygax.

Stegocentipede

Hit Dice: 9
Armor Class: 2 [17]
Attack: Bite (2d6 plus poison) and tail (2d6 plus poison)
Saving Throw: 7
Special: Poison, spines
Move: 15
Alignment: Neutrality
Challenge Level/XP: 10/1400

A stegocentipede resembles a gigantic centipede covered with chitinous plates of hardened bone that run along its back in double rows. Its rear portion ends in a long, scorpion-like stinger. They are greatly feared by adventurers and other dungeon dwelling denizens for their poisonous bite and sting. A typical stegocentipede is 18 feet long. A stegocentipede ranges in color from brown to green.

A stegocentipede delivers a debilitating poison with its bite and tail attacks. The poison causes the victim's joints to swell and causes numbness in the extremities. The victim must pass a saving throw or suffer 1d6 points of damage to their dexterity score. A dexterity 0 means total paralysis. Lost points of dexterity return at the rate of 1 per hour.

A stegocentipede raises its spine-plates during combat, and moves rapidly back and forth while attacking. Creatures in a space directly in front of a stegocentipede must succeed on a saving throw or take 2d8 points of damage from the spine-plates each time they attack (whether successful or not).

Mage Duel Gone Awry

While delving in a deep dungeon or visiting an important market town, the adventurers are unlucky enough to happen upon a very unhappy stegocentipede. If in a dungeon, the beast is in the middle of trampling a bugbear camp in a large, smoky cavern. In a town, it will have flattened the better part of the town center, sending hundreds of people screaming for the town gates in a panic.

The beast was summoned by a rat-faced (literally, lab accident) magic-user to destroy his rival, a marble-skinned elf who drapes herself in silks and satins. The two wizards have made a game out of trying to kill one another, usually through the summoning of wondrous creatures. All the other folk of the dungeon or area have grown unfortunately used to these attacks, but unfortunately lack the ability to put an end to it.

Credit

The Stegocentipede originally appeared in the First Edition *Monster Manual II* (© TSR/Wizards of the Coast, 1983) and is used by permission.

Copyright Notice

Author Scott Greene, based on original material by Gary Gygax.

Stench Kow

Hit Dice: 3
Armor Class: 3 [16]
Attack: Gore (1d8)
Saving Throw: 14
Special: Charge, trample, stench, immunity to cold, fire and poison
Move: 15
Alignment: Neutrality
Challenge Level/XP: 5/240

The stench kow is the cattle of the lower planes. It resembles a large bison with a hunched back, long, downward-curving horns and grotesque facial features. They are used as food by the denizens of the lower planes and are often found in large herds wandering the wastelands of the nether regions. A typical stench kow is 8 feet long and weighs about 3,000 pounds. Its fur is orange or brown in color and mottled green throughout.

A charging stench kow deals double damage with a successful gore attack. It can move over opponents, inflicting 1d8 points of trampling damage unless the person passes a saving throw and leaps out of the way.

A stench kow exudes a foul body odor. All living creatures (except stench kine) within 5 feet of a stench kow must succeed on a saving throw or be nauseated for as long as they stay in the area and for 1d4+1 rounds after they leave.

Hell's Stampede

A vast herd of 1d4 x 15 stench kows (plus 50% as many stench kalves and one 6 HD strench bull per 5 females) is mulling about a copper spiral sculpture. The sculpture puts an electric tang into the air and one will discover a static electric aura around the device, which stands about 15 feet tall and is 5 feet in diameter. The sculpture, if that is what it really is, is smooth to the touch and gives one an electric shock for 1d4 points of damage.

There is a 1 in 20 chance when touched that a charge of elecricity will surge across the landscape and into the sculpture. Besides this charge causing a stampede of the stench kine, anyone touching the sculpture suffers 3d6 points of damage and is vaulted across dimensions from the Nine Hells to the Material Plane.

Credit
The Stench Kow originally appeared in the First Edition *Monster Manual II* (© TSR/Wizards of the Coast, 1983) and is used by permission.

Copyright Notice
Author Scott Greene, based on original material by Gary Gygax.

Stone Maiden

Hit Dice: 10
Armor Class: 0 [19]
Attacks: 1 long sword (1d8) or 2 fists (1d6)
Saving Throw: 5
Special: Animate rocks, +1 magic weapon needed to hit, magical abilities
Move: 12/12 (burrow)
Alignment: Neutrality
Challenge Level/XP: 10/1,400

Stone maidens are exquisitely carved statues, female and shapely in design. Loose-fitting robes clothe her form and a veil hangs across her shoulders and wraps around her head, though her face is not obscured. Her skin is the color of shale. A typical stone maiden stands about 6 feet tall. A stone maiden can animate rock and control up to two rocks at a time. Animated rocks are vaguely humanoid-shaped (most often resembling a stone maiden) and use the same statistics as stone maidens. Once per day, a stone maiden can create a *wall of stone*.

Made in Stone

Wide flagstone steps encircle a round altar. Four 20-foot-tall pillars surround the steps, each connected to the adjacent pillar by thick iron chains suspended 10 feet above the floor. Four bull heads made of stone crown each pillar. Closer examination reveals that the bull heads are those of gorgons. Between the pillars are eight kneeling stone maidens. They have knelt in prayer for over a year and appear to be nothing more than stone statues. Vines grow over their bodies but do not hinder their movements. A toothed stone chisel made of adamantine rests on the altar. The stone maidens are the guardians of the Chisel of Zemlya. Legends state that this chisel and Zemlya's Hammer have the power to slay any mortal by engraving their true name into stone.

Copyright Notice
Author Scott Greene.

Stormwarden

Hit Dice: 3
Armor Class: 6 [13]
Attack: Longsword (1d8) or longbow (1d8)
Saving Throw: 14
Special: Conjure storm
Move: 12
Alignment: Chaos
Challenge Level/XP: 4/120

Stormwardens dwell high in the mountains and hills away from civilization. They are hunters by nature and spend their time hunting and trapping game. They are isolationists and solitary, rarely found in groups of more than 6 individuals. Their hair color and eye color range across the spectrum just as a normal human, though most tend to have dark hair and eyes.

Quite intelligent, stormwardens speak their own tongue and at least two other languages.

Once per day, a stormwarden can create an effect similar to a *control weather* spell as cast by a 10th level magic-user, except that it affects an area in a 1,000-foot-radius circle and the weather effects are immediate rather than gradual. The effects last for 1 turn before the weather in the area returns to normal.

Stormwardens as Characters

Stormwarden characters retain the ability to control weather once per day. Stormwardens can take levels as fighters (up to 6th level, or 7th level with strength of 13+), druids (up to 7th level, or 8th level with wisdom of 13+) or magic-users (up to 5th level, or 6th level with intelligence of 13+). They can also multi-class as fighter/druids (maximum 5th level/6th level) or druid/magic-user (maximum 6th level/4th level).

Children of the Swarm

A gang of 1d4+2 stormwardens dwells in the narrow valleys of a range of tall mountains. Storm clouds often blanket the mountain tops and swift floods pour down the mountains into the valleys below, carrying with them gold and silver dust. The mountains are composed largely of granite with large veins of quartz running through them.

The stormwardens live off the land, trapping animals and collecting juniper berries and a variety of spicy wild radish that grows in the valleys. The stormwardens are brothers, sons of the local storm god and a daughter of a storm giant that dwells much deeper in the range of mountains. These grandsons of the storm giant form the first line of defense of his mountain top kingdom.

Despite their rugged ways, the brothers live in a subterranean hall with walls of quartz and thick bearskin rugs on the floor. Their treasure consists of 120 cp, 2,110 sp, 355 gp, a scroll with three low level spells and a rock crystal worth 115 gp.

Copyright Notice

Strangle Weed

Hit Dice: 4
Armor Class: 5 [14]
Attack: Slam (1d6)
Saving Throw: 13
Special: Constriction, camouflage, resistance to fire (50%), surprise on roll of 1-4 on 1d6
Move: 3
Alignment: Neutrality
Challenge Level/XP: 5/240

The strangle weed is a large, 12-foot wide plant that resembles a patch of seaweed. It attacks by grappling its foe and then squeezing it or drowning it (in the case of air-breathing creatures). Slain creatures are digested by the strangle weed. The strangle weed is dark green and slightly slimy. Three to ten fronds, each about 10 feet long, protrude from its main body, though the strangle weed can easily hide them from potential prey.

A subterranean version of the strangle weed is believed to exist, though encounters with it are very rare. It is dark blackish-green and is found in underground pools, stagnant water, and the like.

Creatures struck by a strangle weed must pass a saving throw or be grappled in its long fronds. Grappled creatures suffer 1d6 points of damage automatically each round. Escape is possible with a successful open doors check.

Druids, rangers and elves are only surprised by strangle weeds on a roll of 1-3 on 1d6.

Bad Weed

Just off a stormy coast there is a small, rocky promontory. The promontory rises about five feet above the surface of the surging surf. A group of 1d3+1 fronds of strangle weed are rooted just beneath the waves here, and they wait eagerly for people to be blown or knocked off the stone and into the water.

Embedded in the rocky pillar there is a golden goblet. The rim of the goblet sticks about three inches above the rock and cannot easily be chipped out (most folks have a 1 in 12 chance of chipping away enough rock to loosen the goblet without destroying it, dwarves and gnomes a 1 in 6 chance).

If the goblet is filled with wine, no matter how cheap or fortified, the stone of the pillar begins to slough away as sea sand. After about 5 minutes, a woman with sapphire skin, long black hair and garbed in a panther pelt is revealed. This woman is a sorceress of elder days, trapped in the stone for millennia by a rival. The woman is an 11th level magic-user who still has most of her daily spells memorized. She is dazed when first released, but when she regains her senses is smart enough to turn the situation to her advantage.

Credit

The Strangle Weed originally appeared in the First Edition *Monster Manual* (© TSR/Wizards of the Coast, 1977) and is used by permission.

Copyright Notice

Author Scott Greene, based on original material by Gary Gygax.

S

Stroke Lad

Hit Dice: 7
Armor Class: 4 [15]
Attacks: 1 slap (1d6 + Dexterity drain)
Saving Throw: 9
Special: Magic resistance (15%), +1 magic weapon needed to hit, spells
Move: 12
Alignment: Chaos
Challenge Level/XP: 7/600

Stroke lads are handsome and wicked looking young men of sleight build with sharply pointed ears, with small goat-like horns jutting from their broad temples. They dress in fine silk robes and ermine lined cloaks and often bear a scepter or some other symbol of nobility. Stroke lads exact their punishments on servants and enemies who displease them with a touch of their long fingers, withering arms and legs to make one lame, and permanently disfiguring faces of those deemed more handsome than themselves. They can use *ESP* at will. Once per day, stroke lads can cast *confusion*, *dancing lights*, *detect evil* and *dispel magic*.

William the Squire

Sir Garin's manor has sat empty ever since his tragic jousting accident. A young man has laid claim to the manor, declaring himself to be William, the squire of Sir Garin. William the Squire, a stroke lad, does not have a legitimate claim to the manor. He does have forged deeds and a falsified title to back up his legitimacy. William the Squire hosts lavish parties and has two satyrs as manservants who tend to his needs.

The manor looks nothing like the esteemed mansion of Sir Garin. Coats of lavender and chartreuse paint cover the white marble walls. Wine flows through majestic fountains. Strange and obscene statues have replaced refined artwork. Household servants employed for generations were fired with no warning. Strapping young men and fickle girls now frolic within the manor. Neighbors constantly complain to the city guards about outlandish parties lasting well into the night. The helpless guards simply do not have the authority to challenge William the Squire's inheritance.

Seliana Von Truqué, an actress paid by the neighbors, pleads with travelers to throw William the Squire out of her uncle's manor, which she claims should rightfully belong to her. If confronted, William the Squire delicately removes his white gloves before slapping the offender. The flamboyant stroke lad does not stoop to combat with barbaric adventurers, and prefers to let his servants do his dirty work. He does not give up his newfound home or wealth easily.

Copyright Notice

Stygian Leviathan

Hit Dice: 25
Armor Class: -6 [25]
Attacks: 1 bite (4d6)
Saving Throw: 3
Special: Capsize, digestive acid, swallow whole, immune to fire
Move: 24 (swim)
Alignment: Neutrality
Challenge Level/XP: 28/6,800

The stygian leviathan is a gigantic whale, about 70 feet long. Its flesh is dark gray or blackish-blue turning yellowish-white on its underbelly. Its dorsal fin is sharply curved and short, mottled white or pale silver on the edges. Its enormous mouth is lined with nearly 600 teeth of white or pale ivory color. A stygian leviathan can use its massive bulk to capsize ships, with ships less than 20 feet capsizing 100% of the time; 20 to 60 feet long, 75% of the time; and vessels over 60 feet 50% of the time. If a stygian whale rolls a natural 20 on its bite attack, it swallows an opponent whole. Inside the whale, an opponent will be drenched in acid from the whale's stomach and the infernal seas it normally swims within. The victim takes 4d6 points of damage each round. A stygian leviathan is immune to fire.

Purgatory Falls

A horrible wound in the earth sits at the edge of the known lands. A bottomless chasm splits the land. The chasm is a half mile long but is only 500 foot wide. Great plumes of steam rise from the depths. Visitors claim to hear the agony of tortured souls echoing out of the depths of despair. Nine of the world's largest rivers converge and fall into the chasm's depths. The area is known as Purgatory Falls, where converging rivers feed the River Styx that winds through the realms of the underworld.

A barge of iron and bone powered by two stygian leviathans floats tethered to a rusted wharf. Great iron hooks pierce the leviathans' skin, permanently attaching them to the barge with massive chains. The boatman Haros waits patiently for his next fare. Haros is the brother of Charon. He is identical to the daemon Charon (*see* **daemon, Charon** *elsewhere in this book*), except that Haros appears to be a living, compassionless man. Haros requests only two things for safe passage to the underworld.

Haros requests the true name of each passenger and requires a small personal token or possession (such as a locket of hair, piece of clothing, or other personal affects) from that named being. If paid, the boatman carries his fares safely over the edge of Purgatory Falls to their desired destination. Those giving their true names and possessions remain on the barge as if it were level ground, despite the trip over the falls. Travelers giving false names or objects that don't truly belong to them fall from the barge as it tips over Purgatory Falls. Those falling are transported to a random layer of Hell, possibly lost forever. The gaping rift prevents travel out of the pit unless someone is traveling on Haros' hellish barge.

Copyright Notice
Author Scott Greene.

Stymphalian Bird (Bronze Beak)

Hit Dice: 4
Armor Class: 3 [16]
Attack: 2 claws (1d6), bite (1d8) and 2 wing slashes (1d6) or 4 feathers (1d4)
Saving Throw: 13
Special: Throw feathers
Move: 15/30 (flying)
Alignment: Neutrality
Challenge Level/XP: 5/240

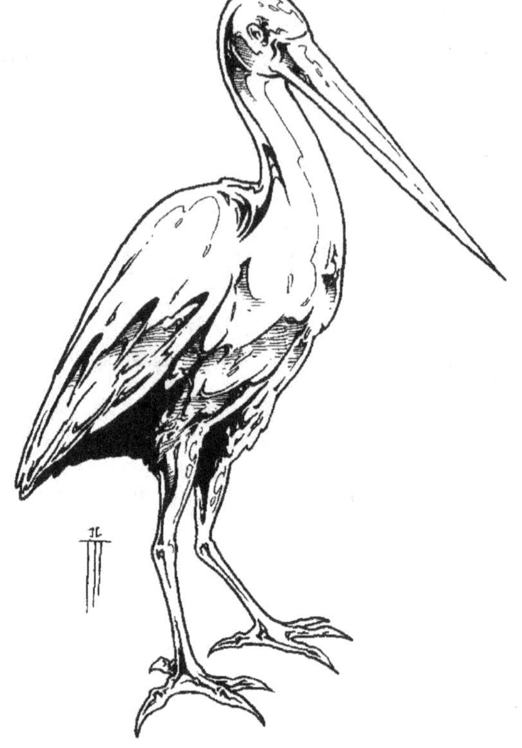

Stymphalian birds are crane-like predators found in dense forests and lowland hills. They are voracious predators that sustain themselves on a diet of livestock, cattle, and the like. They are particularly fond of the flesh of humans and elves, so always attack them on sight.

A stymphalian bird stands 7 feet tall and has an ibis-like body. Unlike an ibis, however, the stymphalian bird's beak is long and straight rather than curved. Its feathers, talons, and beak are made of bronze.

A stymphalian bird attacks from the air by loosing a volley of bronze feathers at its opponents. This ranged attack has a range of 60 feet and all targets must be within 30 feet of each other. The creature can launch only twelve feathers (3 volleys) in a single day.

A stymphalian bird that rolls a natural '20' on an attack with its feathers, bite, wing-slash, or claws deals double damage.

Stork Pond

A pond of warm, but not hot, water lies in the middle of a region of red hills covered with patches of tall, deep green grass. The pond is surrounded by a copse of white elms with golden leaves. The elms are inhabited by hundreds of jet black lorises (a small mammal with a sweet face, large eyes, long fingers and a poisonous bite).

The pond is notable for two reasons. First, it is inhabited by a flock of 1d4+1 stymphalian birds. The birds feed on the lorises, silvery goldfish that dwell in the pond and any travelers unfortunate enough to stumble upon the pond.

The other point of interest in the pond is a crystal statue of a magic-user, cobalt in color and pointing to the sky. At dusk, the light of the setting sun strikes the crystal statue in such a way to cause a beam of azure light to spring from the pointing finger of the statue at a strange angle. The light falls on a portion of the shore that hides stone doors that lead into a dungeon.

Copyright Notice

Sudoth

Hit Dice: 4
Armor Class: 6[13]
Attacks: 2 fist (1d6) and tail tentacles (1d8 + paralysis) or 1 weapon (1d8) and tail tentacles (1d8 + paralysis)
Saving Throw: 13
Special: Paralytic enzyme
Move: 5/12 (swimming)
Alignment: Neutrality
Challenge Level/XP: 4/120

Sudoth are vaguely humanoid creatures with a head that resembles a large jellyfish. Extending down from its large head is a manlike torso and arms that again change into a long knot of feathery writhing tentacles which it uses as a means of propulsion beneath the waves. A small almost unnoticeable band of eyes ring the circumference of its head. A sudoth can survive out of the water for 7 hours outside of water. Its lower torso is a mass of writhing and twitching tentacles. A sudoth's tail tentacles excrete a powerful enzyme that paralyzes any creature coming into contact with them (save resists) for 1d6 rounds. A sudoth can survive out of the water for just a few hours. They often carry wicked tridents or long spears.

Captain Fleck

PCs spy the salvage vessel Black Trollop adrift in calm seas, her rigging snapped, her sails in tatters and her crew absent. The Trollop sits low in the water, her belly obviously full of cargo. Sitting on deck is a 15-foot-tall glass bowl with an open top. The bowl is filled with sea water, and a strange man-jellyfish creature floats inside. The creature is a sudoth named Fleck who captains the Trollop. At least the creature did until the ship's most recent salvage expedition cost the creature its crew and nearly its life.

The sudoth leads all salvage operations by being lowered into the water and searching sunken ships at its leisure. When he finds something, he pulls the item to a net lowered from the Trollop and the sailors pull it aboard. On his last dive, Fleck found a blood-red coral skull with a fist-sized crystal skull fastened to the headband. The sudoth didn't realize the crown was a relic of Orcus that drained the Trollop's crew of life as soon as it was brought aboard.

Fleck made it back aboard and into his command jar on deck just before the curse turned his men into zombies. The Black Trollop is now out of control, with Captain Fleck unable to do anything. The 15 zombie sailors are in the Trollop's hold. Fleck promises PCs their choice of items from his last salvage operation if they help him right his ship – and rid it of his zombie crew. He also requires that they cast the coral skull of Orcus back into the briny depths where it belongs.

Swarm, Adamantine Wasp

Hit Dice: 15
Armor Class: 0[19]
Attacks: stings (3d6 + poison)
Saving Throw: 3
Special: poison, magic resistance (12%)
Move: 5/14 (flying)
Alignment: Neutrality
Challenge Level/XP: 16/3,200

An adamantine wasp is 1 foot long and looks like its namesake only made out of metal. Its body is segmented like a normal wasp (head, thorax, and abdomen) and has carefully and delicately been fitted together to form the wasp. A wicked-looking adamantine stinger protrudes from its abdomen. Its wings are formed of paper-thin adamantine, specially treated during the construction process. An adamantine wasp swarm delivers a debilitating poison that causes a victim to harden into ice (save resists), causing 1d6 points of damage each round until the creature dies and shatters.

Behind the Red Door

A stone clock tower more than 100 feet tall stands majestically in of the Tangletorn Thicket. A low rock wall with a decorative gate surrounds the single tower. A tidy flower garden lies in the courtyard. Riveted metallic statues of satyr, centaurs and giant insects adorn the garden. The statues appear mechanical but are not animated.

The windowless tower has one entrance: a pair of red steel doors. Anyone inspecting the doors sees a complex jigsaw pattern on the red doors. The doors are actually a swarm of adamantine wasps intricately locked together to fill the doorway. The doors appear solid but quickly disengage to attack uninvited guest. Behind the adamantine wasp swarm stands an iron portcullis barring entrance into the tower.

Sceliphron, a reclusive magic-user who specializes in clockwork creatures, resides in the tower. He disdains intrusions and travels often on mechanical giant dragon fly. A clockwork dryad who serves acts as a servant and trusted companion always remains in the tower. The elderly Sceliphron currently is seeking to transfer his soul into a mechanical body in a bid for immortality.

Copyright Notice

Author Scott Greene.

Swarm, Grig

Hit Dice: 7
Armor Class: 6 [13]
Attacks: Swarm (2d6)
Saving Throw: 9
Special: Spell-like abilities, fiddle
Move: 6/9 (flying)
Alignment: Neutrality
Challenge Level/XP: 8/800

A grig swarm is a large mass of flying grigs. The individual grigs that make up the swarm have light blue skin, forest-green hair, and brown hairy legs, and usually wear tunics or brightly colored vests with buttons made from tiny gems. A grig stands 1-1/2 feet tall and weighs about 1 pound. They attack with weapons, or use their fiddles or to cause a victim to dance uncontrollably (save avoids). Once per day, a grig can cast *polymorph self*, *plant growth*, *invisibility* and *pyrotechnics*.

The Minstrel's Minions

A creaking covered wagon painted in bright colors and veiled in layers of silk curtains sits at the side of the road. A dappled mare grazes freely on the roadside.

Sitting cross-legged atop the wagon is a diminutive man, his head covered in a wide-brimmed green hat. His whiskers are long and his crinkled skin is covered in thick age lines. His eyes are alive, though, and his mouth tilts up in a sly grin. He holds a well-maintained violin in his long fingers.

Tomasi Vitali tips his hat and stands when PCs approach. The minstrel smiles disarmingly and begins playing a light, cheery jig on his violin. When he stops, he throws his hat to the ground and demands payment for his music. Tomasi is a brigand, although he doesn't consider it theft since he entertains his victims first with his delightful music.

If threatened, Tomasi plays a discordant jangle of notes on his violin and a grig swarm rises out of the covered wagon. Tomasi charmed a get-together of grig tribes with his music, and the miniature musicians claimed his wagon to remain near the musician. Tomasi makes the best of it, and uses the grig in his schemes to steal from travelers.

Swarm, Heat

Hit Dice: 12
Armor Class: 2[17]
Attacks: engulf (3d6)
Saving Throw: 3
Special: heat, immunity to fire
Move: 12/14 (flying)
Alignment: Chaos
Challenge Level/XP: 13/2,00

A heat swarm is a mass of flying, aggressive, foul-tempered elementals that resemble a thumb-sized ball of fire with vaguely discernable facial features. A heat swarm engulfs its foe, dealing 3d6 points of damage. Those hit by a heat swarm must save or catch on fire. Anyone within 20 feet of a heat swarm must save or take 1d6 points of damage from the extreme heat radiating off the elemental.

Point and Shoot

A 15-foot-long brass instrument similar to a baritone horn lies on its side in this chamber. The horn is mounted on a wooden trolley with fixed steel wheels. Ropes beneath the massive golden bell allow the trolley to be pulled. An assortment of pipes and fluttering billows are mounted to the trolley near the middle of the horn. There is no mouthpiece to blow, as the stem is twisted into the odd machine. A red lever on the control panel is in the up position.

Near the lever is a crude note with words written in block letters that read: "Aim. Pull. Stand back." Following the instructions causes the bellows to pump and inflate, and 1d4 rounds later a mournful blat sounds. Gouts of fire erupt from the horn's bell, and a reddish mist filled with tiny skull-like faces floats out to engulf the horn and control panel. The heat swarm rapidly spreads to attack creatures within 50 feet. The lever cannot be raised, and automatically rises to the up position in 10 rounds. The heat swarm is sucked back into the bell as the instrument of death resets itself.

Copyright Notice
Author Scott Greene.

Swarm, Piranha

Beneath your dangling feet swarms a roiling school of fish. Their tiny mouths flash with the glint of sharp, razor-like teeth.

Hit Dice: 4
Armor Class: 7 [12]
Attacks: swarm (1d6)
Saving Throw: 13
Special: None
Move: 24 (swim)
Alignment: Neutrality
Challenge Level/XP: 4/120

Piranhas are small, 8- to 12-inch-long black or silvery-black fish with large bulging eyes and a tiny mouth lined with razor-sharp teeth. They are generally black or silver with a red underbelly or mottled red spots on their scales. Eye color is usually gray or silver. Piranhas attack using their razor sharp teeth, biting and gnashing their prey. Once blood is spilt, the piranha swarm enters a killing frenzy.

Wrong Step

The warm river steams in the Seething Jungle's humidity. Heavy vines hang from branching rubber trees, and thick foliage traps the heat. The river is a narrow ribbon as it races through the jungle in a turbulent rush. The far bank is a mere 20 feet away.

Looks are deceiving, however, as the river actually undercuts the land by about 10 feet on either side. A swarm of piranha lives in the shadows beneath the carved-out bank, where the rushing waters can't push them madly downriver.

Anyone venturing within 10 feet of the water's edge has a 2 in 6 chance of stepping through the thin soil and into the water below. The piranhas mercilessly strip to the bone any creature that falls through the dirt bank into their midst.

Swarm, Landwalker Piranha Angry, Gnashing Teeth

A dilapidated shack stands in a clearing in the middle of the Seething Jungle, its windows boarded up against the elements. The flat roof is covered in layers of giant palm fronds to keep the water out, and the entire building is raised four feet off the ground to keep the river from flooding in when it overflows its nearby banks. The slat door of the shack stands slightly open, pulled off its hinges.

Banyan trees grow in thick, twisted groves to the north of the shack, while the southern edge of the clearing ends in the river flowing through the dense foliage. A covered still sits in the middle of the clearing, a firepit beneath it containing week-old ash. The clearing is sliced by hundreds of shallow grooves in the dirt that lead from the river to the shack.

The interior of the shack is covered in streaks of dried blood that paint long smears on the walls and floor. Two skeletons wearing torn and ragged clothing lie curled on the floor, their bones nipped and gnawed. The bones gleam whitely. The sound of clacking bones can be heard clearly within the shack.

Hidden under the raised floor is a swarm of landwalker piranhas taking refuge in the cool, dank environment. The swarm hunts at night, but won't pass up a free meal walking into its nest. The swarm boils out of rat holes and openings in the floor in 1d4 rounds. The piranhas gnash their sharp teeth constantly, creating a buzzing drone.

Landwalker Piranha Swarm: HD 4; AC 7[12]; Atk swarm (1d6); Move 12/24 (swim); Save 13; CL/XP 4/120; Special: Amphibious.

Copyright Notice
Author Scott Greene.

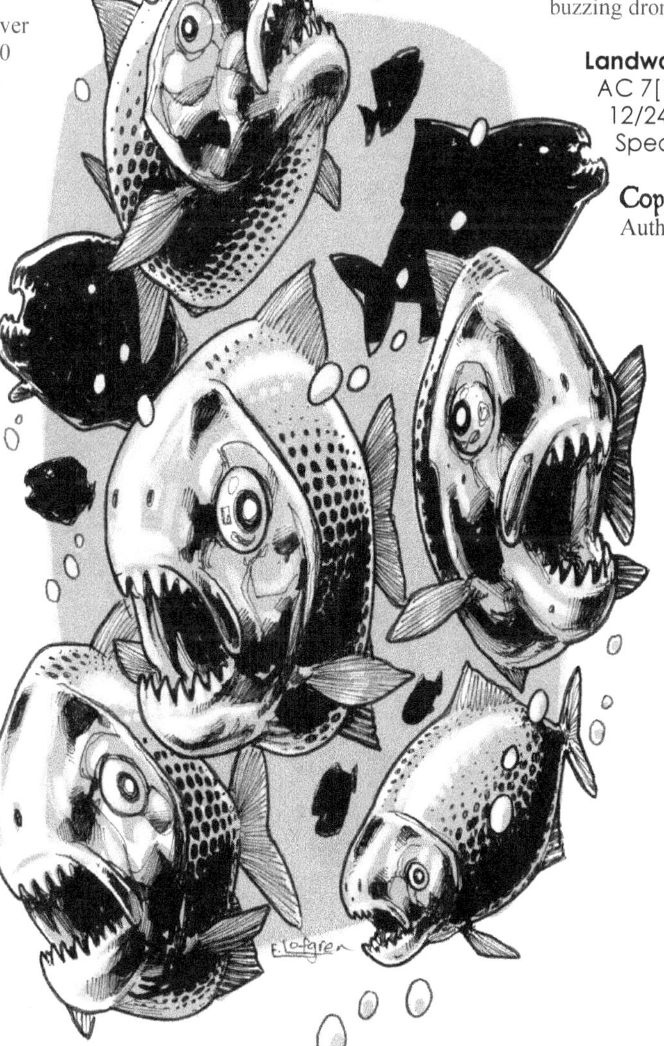

Swarm, Poisonous Frog

Hit Dice: 4
Armor Class: 8 [11]
Attacks: Swarm (1d6 + poison)
Saving Throw: 13
Special: Poison
Move: 9
Alignment: Neutrality
Challenge Level/XP: 4/120

Poisonous frog swarms are composed of small, fierce, poisonous frogs. A single poisonous frog is a small dark green frog with black bands or stripes on its hind legs. These stripes function as a warning to predators that the frog is poisonous. The skin of a poisonous frog is very smooth to the touch. The middle digit on each of its extremities is slightly shorter than the others. A poisonous frog swarm delivers its poison with a successful swarm attack.

Raining Frogs

The fronds of the banyan trees dip low with water as the jungle downpour continues. The nearby river swells over its banks as the torrential rainfall pounds the earth. Rivulets flow along the ground, and water drops heavily out of the trees. Storm clouds on the horizon promise the rain may continue for days.

A colony of poisonous tree frogs nest in the upper branches of the banyans. The rain washes out the colony's home, dropping the frogs through the branches to the river and ground. The frogs – already angered by the heavy rains – swarm anything they land on.

Swarm, Raven

Hit Dice: 3
Armor Class: 8 [11]
Attacks: Swarm (1d6)
Saving Throw: 14
Special: Eye-rake
Move: 3/18 (flying)
Alignment: Neutrality
Challenge Level/XP: 3/60

A raven swarm is a disorienting mass of angry birds that pecks, scratches and claws an opponent. They specifically target the heads and eyes of victims.

Come for the Wedding, Stay for the Food.

This encounter takes place as a wedding is letting out of a city temple. PCs may be in the crowd, members of the bridal party or simply passing by. As the bride and groom descend wide stone steps outside the church, the guests toss handfuls of rice, birdseed and small grains over the happy couple to wish them a fertile life together. The crowd is festive and raucous, celebrating the happy couple.

A passing swarm of starving ravens sweep down in a flock of black feathers and cawing voices to peck and claw at the bride and groom and any guests covered in the birdseed. The ravens don't hesitate to go for the "fleshy bits" of the people in the crowd, starting with the eyes, lips and ears. PCs may have their hands full trying to save people and shoo the birds away.

Raven Swarm, Undead

Hit Dice: 7
Armor Class: 6 [13]
Attacks: Swarm (3d6)
Saving Throw: 9
Special: Disease, eye-rake
Move: 3/18 (flying)
Alignment: Neutrality
Challenge Level/XP: 8/800

An undead raven swarm is a teeming mass of sinister, rotting, disease-ridden birds that seek to destroy any living creature encountered. A single undead raven appears as a rotting and diseased black bird whose feathers are torn, matted and dirty. Its eyes are inky black. The beaks and claws of an undead raven can spread disease.

The Blood Mashes

The ground seems to bleed in the marsh fields. The ground seeps blood from a cursed war that took place eons ago. Ghosts and spirits haunt the bloody fields, each forever seeking an end to their cursed existence. Fresh corpses and ancient relics of battle churn up through the soft earth, only to be slowly swallowed again.

Ravens that drink from the bloody marsh die and sink into its depths. By midnight, these unfortunate birds rise again as an undead raven swarm that flies off into the night to wreak havoc. An undead raven swarm always circles above the bloody field, sometimes landing in the nearby dead trees.

An executioner's axe juts from a snag rising from the field. The axe was used to slay the survivors of the battle. The snag bleeds into the marsh field. If the axe is reached and buried within the Blood Marsh, the curse breaks and the land no longer bleeds. Once broken, all undead within the area are freed of their bindings.

Copyright Notice
Author Scott Greene.

Swarm, Scarlet Spider

Hit Dice: 3
Armor Class: 1 [18]
Attack: Swarm (1d6 plus disease plus painful bite)
Saving Throw: 14
Special: Swarm, distraction, painful bite, surprise on roll of 1-3 on 1d6
Move: 6/6 (climbing)
Alignment: Neutrality
Challenge Level/XP: 4/120

Scarlet spiders dwell in temperate forests and make their homes in the hollows of trees, under fall trees, and in dense foliage. They are deadly, aggressive black spiders about 3 inches long. Their legs are long, thin, and covered in a thin layer of dark hair. Their bodies are solid black with horizontal bands of scarlet ringing them. Scarlet spiders are not web-spinning spiders; therefore, they do not possess the standard web ability of other spiders.

Scarlet spiders swarm over their prey, literally moving over them. Any creature caught in a swarm suffers numerous bites. Swarms can only be harmed with bludgeoning or area attacks.

The bite of a scarlet spider is extremely painful. A creature bitten takes a -1 penalty on attack rolls, weapon damage rolls and saving throws until cured by a *neutralize poison* or *cure disease* spell.

A scarlet spider carries disease and attempts to infect any creature it bites. The disease is called the red ache. It has an incubation period of 1d3 days. Each day after the incubation period, the victim must pass a saving throw or lose 1d6 points of strength, dying if their strength score reaches 0. If a victim passes a saving throw two days in a row, they throw off the disease.

Scarlet Scourge

In the middle of a tangled jungle there is a stone shaft descending into the earth. The shaft is about 8 feet wide and high and descends at a 45-degree slant. Hundreds of stone hands reach out from the floor and ceilings; the hands are not animated, nor will they attempt to grab people as they walk through.

The shaft runs for 100 feet and then ends in a pool of brackish water that gives off a sickening sweet odor. about the time the adventurers reach the bottom of the shaft, a colony of 1d6+4 scarlet spider swarms begins creeping down the shaft.

There is no apparent exit from the shaft, but should one grasp the stone hand nearest the water, a stone face emerges from the wall and says, in a gravely voice, "Your salvation lies in the water". At this, a secret passage will open beneath the water, dropping the water and anyone standing in it down a 10 foot deep shaft. The secret door remains open for 3 rounds and then closes. What lies beyond the shaft is up to you!

Copyright Notice

Swarm, Shadow Rat

Hit Dice: 6
Armor Class: 6[13]
Attacks: bite (2d6)
Saving Throw: 11
Special: envelop, immunity to fire
Move: 12
Alignment: Chaos
Challenge Level/XP: 7/600

Shadow rats are undead rats that can assume an incorporeal form. Other than their semi-translucent form, they resemble their earthly counterparts in all respects. A shadow rat swarm is simply a massive number of shadow rats that have cluttered or banded together for survival or food. A shadow rat swarm attempts to surround and envelop its opponent in its form. A shadow rat swarm deals 2d6 points of damage.

The Died Piper

The faint fluttering trill of a flute rises in the dungeon hallway, the sound coming from everywhere – and nowhere – at once. Moments later, a ghostly figure steps through the wall. He is gaunt and pale, and black hair hangs limply down around his narrow face. His legs are long and he wears high black boots. His ghostly torso is covered by a blood-stained shirt, and his cloak is ripped and flutters around his body. The Died Piper does a capering jig and blows a sorrowful tune on his flute. He then vanishes through the wall, the flute music trailing off until it stops.

Within 1d4 rounds, a shadow rat swarm answers the summons, boiling out of the walls to find the piper. They attack any creatures they see for 1d6+1 rounds before moving on in their never-ending quest.

Copyright Notice
Author Scott Greene.

Swarm, Velvet Ant

Hit Dice: 5
Armor Class: 7 [12]
Attacks: swarm (1d6 + poison)
Saving Throw: 12
Special: Poison
Move: 6/4 (climb)
Alignment: Neutrality
Challenge Level/XP: 5/240

Velvet ants are not really ants at all but a form of wasp. Velvet ants have a bright red abdomen and thorax and a black head and black legs. Its thorax and abdomen are covered with short, coarse, red hairs. Typical adults reach a length of 1 inch. A swarm of velvet ants delivers a large amount of toxic venom to a victim.

The Hornet Swarmed

A giant hornet – 9 feet from head to stinger – flies through the fir trees at head height. The insect's flight is erratic, zigging left to right and rising and falling in the air, as if the creature were in a drunken stupor. It slams heavily tree branches, recovers before it slaps the ground, then resumes its dodgy flight. The giant insect finally crashes down in front of PCs, its wings twitching feebly. The giant hornet flew through a velvet ant swarm and the smaller insects are eating the hornet from the inside out. Anyone approaching the dying hornet stirs up a cloud of velvet ants, which viciously attack everything around their new "nest." If left alone, the velvet ants form a new colony nest in the ground around the dead hornet's husk.

Copyright Notice
Author Scott Greene.

Swarm, Warden Jack

Hit Dice: 5
Armor Class: 3 [16]
Attacks: swarm (1d6 + trip)
Saving Throw: 12
Special: Trip
Move: 4
Alignment: Neutrality
Challenge Level/XP: 5/240

Warden jacks are miniscule metal objects in the shape of a ball covered in sharp spikes. These things are able to move on their own by retracting their spikes, and rolling along the ground. Warden jacks typically range from 1-3 inches in diameter. Warden jack swarms have two modes of attack: as moving caltrops, or as rolling marbles. If an opponent tries to walk through a field of warden jacks, he must make a save or trip on the moving spheres and fall for 1d6 points of damage.

Toy Story

The castle playroom sits empty, dust covering toys sitting on shelves and in toy boxes. Dolls sit on shelves, their hollow glass eyes following PCs entering the room. Stuffed wooden horses stand beside carved knights. A toy drum is propped against the wall. A plush 6-foot-long green and purple stuffed snake doll sits on the floor facing the door. A long-faced marionette dangles from a hook in the wall.

The toys begin moving if PCs enter the playroom. The drum begins thumping a random beat, the snake twists on the wood floor. The stuffed horses fall over and the dolls vibrate on their wooden shelves. Within 1d4 rounds, a swarm of warden jacks erupt from the playthings, bursting through the toys to roll around the room after PCs. The warden jacks were sewn into the toys to protect the royal children.

Copyright Notice

Author Scott Greene.

Symbiotic Jelly

The symbiotic jelly is a small, sickly yellow blob of slimy ooze about 3 inches in diameter. It is found in subterranean realms, caverns, and damp, dark caves. The symbiotic jelly possesses several mental abilities that it uses to assail its foes.

When a living creature moves within 30 feet, the jelly attempts to charm it (as if by the *charm monster* spell). The victim must succeed on a saving throw to resist the effects. If successful, the victim feels a tingling sensation but nothing more. The jelly then lets the creature pass unharmed, as it can only attempt its charm ability on the same creature once per day. If the save fails, however, the creature has fallen under the symbiotic jelly's sway.

The jelly telepathically orders the victim to remain in its lair and attack the next living creature that ventures into the area. The jelly uses its innate illusion powers to make the host appear to be a much weaker monster or an entirely different monster all together. It also generates an illusionary treasure horde in which to draw potential prey into its lair. A creature can see through either illusion by succeeding on a saving throw.

When the jelly's symbiotic link kills a trespasser, the jelly draws sustenance as the charmed monster feeds. If the symbiotic jelly's host is slain, it attempts to charm the creature that killed it and use it to replace its former host. The symbiotic jelly, if it can be found, is easily killed by an application of fire, cold, or acid.

Big Dumb Guard

You enter a stony cavern about 15 feet in diameter with a ceiling 13 feet high. Two large boulders rest in this cavern and there is a smallish natural alcove in one wall. Perched on a ledge above the alcove there is a symbiotic jelly. It has recently charmed a minotaur, which now guards the ooze's lair. Piled in the alcove is a horde of (illusory) treasure.

Minotaur: HD 6+4; AC 6 [13]; Atk 1 butt (2d4), bite (1d3), weapon (1d8); Move 12; Save 11; CL/XP 6/400; Special: Never gets lost.

Credit

The Symbiotic Jelly originally appeared in the First Edition *Fiend Folio* (© TSR/Wizards of the Coast, 1981) and is used by permission.

Copyright Notice

Author Scott Greene, based on original material by Roger Musson.

T'shann

Hit Dice: 4
Armor Class: 10 [9]
Attacks: 1 strike (1d4)
Saving Throw: 13
Special: Alien thoughts, spew
Move: 5/5 (burrow)
Alignment: Neutrality
Challenge Level/XP: 4/120

The slug-like t'shann has a cylindrical body and a mass of dripping, writhing tentacles at its head. It is brownish gray, with patches of green and black blotches scattered unevenly over its body. Its underside is pasty off-white in color and ripples with the muscular contractions that move the creature along. T'shanns burrow through earth and stone to consume the minerals trapped in the rock. They range anywhere from 2 to 4 feet long. The alien brainwaves of a t'shann have a bizarre effect on intelligent creatures. Within 30 feet of a t'shann, all opponents with an Intelligence score greater than 5 must save or be affected as if by a confusion spell. If the opponent approaches to within 10 feet, he must succeed on another save or suffer 1d4 points of damage for as long as he remains within 10 feet of the t'shann. A t'shann can emit a spray of powerful acids from nearly every pore on its body, affecting any creature within 10 feet of it. This acidic spray does 1d4 points of acid damage (save for half damage).

Matter Over Minds

The dwarves of the underground halls of the Granite Holdfast are losing their minds. Every day, the best and brightest – and everyone else – forget where they are, what they are doing and even who they are. Groups roam like zombies through the claustrophobic stone halls, their eyes and minds clouded and confused. A few simply stop in their tracks, their minds gone and their life soon to follow. The mineral-rich halls of the Holdfast are rapidly emptying as dwarves wander into the deep tunnels never to return.

Sitting in the center of the dwarven stronghold is a large anvil composed of mineral-rich rock. This 20-foot-tall stone block was said to have been used by the dwarven gods to forge the dwarves. The dwarves found the block during a delve and hauled it back to their throne room. The block is infested with 6 t'shann that are slowly eating away at the stone's innards as they eat away the minds of the dwarves.

Copyright Notice
Author Erica Balsley.

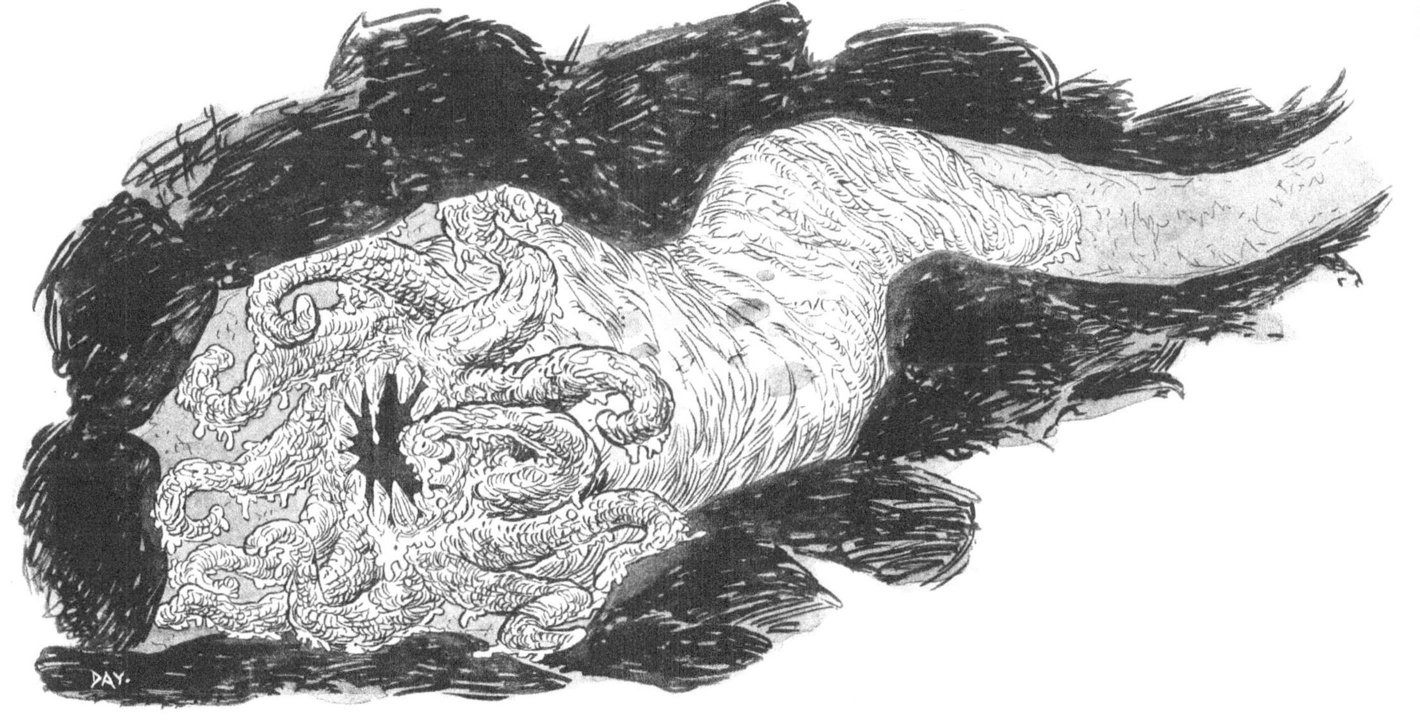

Tabaxi

Hit Dice: 2
Armor Class: 6 [13]
Attack: 2 claws (1d4) and bite (1d3) or weapon (1d6)
Saving Throw: 16
Special: Pounce, track by scent, surprise on 1-3 on 1d6
Move: 15/9 (climbing)
Alignment: Neutrality (proclivity for chaos)
Challenge Level/XP: 2/30

The tabaxi (called cat-people or tigerfolk by some) are a reclusive race of feline humanoids that dwell away from settled areas, making their home deep in the forests and jungles. They rarely engage in trade or dealings with other races, preferring to keep to themselves most of the time.

Tabaxis are very graceful and catlike in their movements. They resemble humanoids with feline-like characteristics most akin to a tiger. A typical tabaxi stands 6 feet tall and weighs about 150 pounds. They speak their own language, and a few tabaxi understand and speak the common tongue.

Tabaxis rely on their claws and bite in combat, though they have been known to employ weapons (usually javelins and short swords). They prefer to attack from ambush, using their natural coloration to their advantage. A tabaxi that successfully strikes an opponent with both claw attacks can make an additional rake attack that deals 1d4 points of damage.

Tabaxis as Characters

Tabaxi characters possess greater than normal speed (+3) and when with others of their own kind or away from non-tabaxi surprise on a roll of 1-2 on 1d6. They retain their specie's claw and bite attacks, but lose the ability to rake with their claws. Tabaxi has darkvision to a range of 60 feet. Tabaxi can advance as fighters to 5th level (6th level with a strength of 13 or higher) and as thieves to 7th level (8th level with a dexterity of 13 or higher).

Can You Run?

While chopping their way through a dense rainforest of durians, tualangs, bamboo and strangler figs, adventurers might (1 in 6 chance) come across a field of wreckage. The wreckage is composed of twisted steel and looks something like a long tube with metal wings - it's quite unlike anything they have ever seen (well, depending on what kind of campaign you run).

Tracks lead from the wreckage that rangers might be able to identify as both human and feline. The tracks lead deeper into the rainforest, finally leaving the ground entirely and making their way into the leafy canopy. A very skilled ranger might track the party to a tall tualang surrounded by dozens of bunches of bamboo.

Keen eyes might see four figures suspended from a thick limb overhead by ropes. These figures are the survivors of the wreck, three men and one woman. All four are dressed in strange clothing and look badly beaten up. Three tabaxi sit on the branch, guarding the prisoners while their high priestess consults with the Great Tiger God over the correct way to sacrifice these intruders to his divine glory.

The tabaxi dwell on several small bamboo platforms in the branches of the tualang. There are 1d3+5 in all, including the aforementioned guards and the high priestess. On their platforms they have tents formed from animal skins as well as bamboo lockers to hold their kills. The high priestess' tent, which also serves as a shrine of the tiger god, holds the pride's treasure, 1,750 sp and a wooden tiger figurine carved from teak and worth 75 gp.

Credit

The Tabaxi originally appeared in the First Edition *Fiend Folio* (© TSR/Wizards of the Coast, 1981) and is used by permission.

Copyright Notice

Author Scott Greene, based on original material by Lawrence Schick.

Taer

Hit Dice: 3
Armor Class: 2 [17]
Attack: 2 slams (1d4+1) or weapon (1d6+1)
Saving Throw: 14
Special: Stench, immunity to cold
Move: 18
Alignment: Neutrality
Challenge Level/XP: 4/120

Taer are shaggy, primitive, naked humanoids that may be related to the yeti. They resemble prehistoric humans but are more bestial and apelike. Their fur is coated with an oily, fatty substance excreted through the pores, which protects them from cold. Taer can see clearly even in heavy snowstorms due to a second transparent eyelid that protects the eye from blowing winds and heavy snow. Taer never wear clothing, although they do sometimes wear necklaces and bracelets of tooth and horn. Taer communicate through grunts, hooting, and yelling, as well as a body language similar to that of apes.

Taer attack with their claws and bite, but occasionally use stone spears in combat. They are fierce creatures and very territorial, attacking any living creature that wanders into the area. Taer use their knowledge of the land to their advantage during combat by creating avalanches, burrowing under snow and attacking from surprise, and using snow-covered pits to trap their prey. They prefer to drive intruders off rather than kill them.

A taer's body secretes a foul-smelling oil that nearly every form of animal life finds offensive (even troglodytes). All living creatures (except taers) within 10 feet of a taer must succeed on a saving throw or suffer a -1 penalty to hit and damage.

Taer Society

Taers are nomadic creatures that band together in clans for protection, hunting, and social reasons. During the day, adults hunt for food, which consists of fruits, berries, nuts, insects, and game (goat, sheep, rodents, and the like). Though they do eat meat, taer do not hunt or eat humans or humanoids. Taer are extremely superstitious and fear metal and clothing and those that use and wear them. No taer ever wields or wears items of cloth or metal. Taer clans worship a snow-god to whom they offer sacrifices for protection and guidance. Each clan has a large stone idol of this snow god that is often located in the very heart of the clan or near the clan leader's cave.

Cut 'Em Off at the Pass

A small silver mining operation depends on a high mountain pass to get its silver to the great city beyond the mountains. Unfortunately, severe snowstorms and the presence of a clan of 1d4 x 10 taer has closed the pass.

The taer dwell in a high cave complex and haunt the ledges and chasms surrounding the pass hunting for food. They have raided one caravan (for food), and the rather cowardly merchant that owns and operates the mine is hesitant to send more people through. The hooting and hollering of the taer can be heard echoing through the mine's valley at night, and people are terribly unnerved.

The taer's cave complex consists of a large common room containing sleeping pallets (or nests) for the common taer. A lower cavern has become the clan garbage pit and now contains hundreds of splintered bones and other refuse. A higher cavern is clad in ice (from water seeping from the mountains above) and is now used as a sort of temple by the taer. Animal skins and teeth have been placed next to the ice pillars as offering for the gods. This cavern leads to an icy chute that heads deeper into the mountain and a higher cavern, mostly free of ice, being used as the living quarters of the clan's leader, a large 6 HD male with a black patch of hair on the top of its head. The taer have no real treasure - perhaps 1d4 x 100 gp worth of animal skins and teeth.

Credit

The Taer originally appeared in the First Edition *Monster Manual II* (© TSR/Wizards of the Coast, 1983) and is used by permission.

Copyright Notice

Author Scott Greene, based on original material by Gary Gygax.

Tangtal (Dupli-Cat)

Hit Dice: 3
Armor Class: 6 [13]
Attacks: 2 claws (1d4+1), 1 bite (1d6)
Saving Throw: 14
Special: Duplicate
Move: 15/6 (swim)
Alignment: Neutrality
Challenge Level/XP: 4/120

A tangtal is about 7 feet long from nose to tail and weighs about 350 to 400 pounds. It has short, stiff fur, dark brown in color. Small white flecks cover its head, throat and neck, and shoulders. Its legs are long and powerful and end in sharpened claws. It has a long, upward curving tail with a white tip. Once per day, a tangtal can create up to 8 duplicates of itself (otherwise similar to *mirror image* spell).

Mirror Image

The Terashee Carnival pitched its multicolored tents on land outside Landrey. A midway attracts people with games of chance and separates them from their hard-earned coin. Magister Anxes' Mirror Maze is especially popular, drawing people in droves to negotiate the twists and turns of the mirrored passages, the thrill of seeing so many versions of themselves walking along with them in the silver-backed glass something they'd talk about for days and days on end. What the visitors see as a nice diversion from their humdrum lives, a tangtal that lairs in the nearby forest sees as a fantastic hunting ground. The big cat dug an entry tunnel beneath one of the outer walls and quietly slipped inside to stalk prey. The carnival trapped the cat inside the maze once the screaming began, but no one is willing to go in after the beast or to help the people trapped inside.

Copyright Notice

Tazelwurm

Hit Dice: 7
Armor Class: 3 [16]
Attacks: 2 claws (1d6), 1 bite (2d6)
Saving Throw: 9
Special: Camouflage, frightening exuviation, resists fire
Move: 12
Alignment: Neutrality
Challenge Level/XP: 8/800

Tazelwurms appear as 9-foot long serpents with gray-colored scales. Their head is leonine and resembles a maneless lion with brownish-tan or gray fur. Two long, powerful humanoid arms of the same gray color as its body protrude from its serpentine body. Each arm ends in a slender, four-taloned hand. Its talons average 9 inches in length and fade to black near the tips. Very old tazelwurms may even have lichens and mosses growing on them, enhancing their rocky appearances. If a tazelwurm is hit by a fire attack or effect that deals at least 10 points of damage, it takes no damage, but instead allows its scales, flesh, and fur to be consumed and burned away in a single round, exposing its skeletal structure. A creature viewing this must make a save or be paralyzed with fear for 1d3 rounds.

The Snake Warrens

The Kylar Pass is a narrow route through the high peaks of the Khandibat Mountains, but anyone daring the treacherous switchback trail risks life and limb doing so. Fierce storms roll through the peaks, with driving rains and gusting winds.

The high peaks contain a maze of round tunnels about 4 feet in diameter. These winding tunnels twist and turn throughout the granite peaks. Two tazelwurms live in the warrens. The male is a 10-foot-long creature, while the female is a true beast: 25 feet from lion's head to the tip of her snake tail. The pair target travelers.

Inside the warren are the bones of past meals, as well as 600 gp, a *ring of human control*, and a battered suit of *+1 plate mail armor*.

Copyright Notice
Author Scott Greene.

Temporal Crawler

Hit Dice: 6
Armor Class: 5 [14]
Attacks: 1 bite (1d6 + paralysis)
Saving Throw: 11
Special: Paralysis, slowing webs
Move: 12/6 (climb)
Alignment: Neutrality
Challenge Level/XP: 8/800

A temporal crawler is a 6-foot-long hairy, gray spider with a large hourglass-shaped patch of silver fur dominating its back. Upon closer inspection, it appears that the hourglass is animated and that sand runs from one chamber to the other. The temporal crawler's mandibles seem to be constructed of silver and bounce light off of them. The creature's many eyes are bright red. Temporal crawlers spin webs to catch creatures. Once a victim enters the web, it must save or be affected by a *slow* spell. The spider paralyzes its prey with its bite for 1 round.

A Place Where Time Stands Still

An underground cavern is filled wall to wall with sticky webs. Hundreds of bodies are ensnared in the spider silk, hanging from the ceiling walls and even cocooned as lumps on the rocky ground. Most of the bodies are desiccated and brittle. A few are nothing more than bones stuck in the webs. Two human travelers and an elf magic-user struggle in the webs.

A large crystal globe hangs down from the 40-foot-high ceiling. The eight-sided globe is suspended by a number of thick spider webs. The glass sides of the globe are opaque. A temporal crawler sleeps inside the glass globe.

All movement in the cavern is slowed to half speed by the giant spider. It is a vicious hunter that crawls to the surface every night to snatch travelers to cocoon in its web.

Copyright Notice

Tendrul

Hit Dice: 9
Armor Class: 2 [17]
Attacks: 1 bite (1d8) and 1 tail (1d6)
Saving Throw: 6
Special: gnashing teeth
Move: 9/30 (swim)
Alignment: Neutrality
Challenge Level/XP: 9/1,100

The amphibious tendrul is *the size of a small whale and has a pair of powerful flippers with which it pulls itself from the waters to sun itself on the stones. It has a head reminiscent of a piranha, the body of a giant grayish-black seal, and a bony razor-sharp scythe-like tail.* An average tendrul reaches 12 feet long and weighs several hundred pounds. If a tendrul scores a natural 20 on its attack roll with its gnashing-teeth bite, it deals triple normal damage. A tendrul notices creatures by scent in a 90-foot radius and detects blood in the water at ranges of up to 500 feet.

Don't Go In the Water

The white sandy beach near the northern merchant city of Ivor is covered in blood and blubber. The tail of a half-eaten sperm whale lies near the waterline. The tide is frothy and pink with rivers of blood, and chunks of the whale float atop the waves. The whale's tail section is torn and jagged, the blubbery flesh bitten clean through by sharp, serrated teeth.

A tendrul caught the poor whale in the open water, and dragged it to shore to devour. The huge beast is submerged in the silt offshore, but bursts out of the sand once it realizes PCs are disturbing the rest of its meal. The giant carnivorous beast flops onto the beach, chasing PCs and slashing with its scythe-like tail. Anyone caught in its mouth is instantly ground between its sharp teeth.

Copyright Notice
Author Scott Greene.

Tenebrous Worm

Hit Dice: 10
Armor Class: 1 [18]
Attack: Bite (2d6 plus 1d6 acid)
Saving Throw: 5
Special: Acid, bristles
Move: 9
Alignment: Neutrality
Challenge Level/XP: 11/1700

A tenebrous worm resembles a 6-foot long, sleek, gray caterpillar. The front half of its body, including its head, is covered in long, dull, black coarse bristles. Two large, multi-faceted eyes dot its head and two large, pearl white mandibles flank its mouth.

The tenebrous worm is native to the Plane of Shadow and is rarely encountered elsewhere. On occasion, a tear in the fabric of the planes allows the worm to slip through to other planes of existence. Tenebrous worms enjoy attacking and devouring living creatures, though they do not normally attack anything larger than themselves.

Its mandibles can be broken off or pried from a dead tenebrous worm and sold for 1d3 x 1,000 gp each. The tenebrous worm is the larvae stage of the gloomwing (see that entry).

A tenebrous worm's head and upper body is covered in many small bristles. When biting, the creature thrashes about striking with them. An opponent hit by a tenebrous worm's bristles must succeed on a saving throw or be paralyzed for 1d4 rounds. When the paralysis wears off, the opponent takes 3d6 points of damage from the poison. A creature attacking a tenebrous worm unarmed or with natural weapons must succeed on a saving throw each time one of their attacks hits or be subjected to the same paralysis and subsequent damage as above.

Water Rights in the Desert

In a blasted wasteland of reddish-gray sand, creosote bushes and bear-paw poppies, a devilish shaman has brought forth a portion of the plane of shadow into a complex of sandstone caverns that overlooks a lonely river. The shadowy caverns are inhabited by a tenebrous worm that is only held at bay by the unforgiving desert sun. At night, it stalks forth in search of prey (its first meal being the foolish shaman that summoned it).

Worse yet, the shadowstuff has begun to spread out of the cavern. It now covers an area 1 mile in diameter and has caused the river that emerges from it to freeze for 2 miles beyond the shadow. The human fishing village built on the shores of a lake fed by the river have seen the river run almost dry and the lake become freezing, killing off their fish. The villagers suspect it was their old shaman, recently exiled for "inhuman acts", but do not know of his whereabouts.

Credit

The Tenebrous Worm originally appeared in the First Edition *Monster Manual II* (© TSR/Wizards of the Coast, 1983) and is used by permission.

Copyright Notice

Author Scott Greene, based on original material by Gary Gygax.

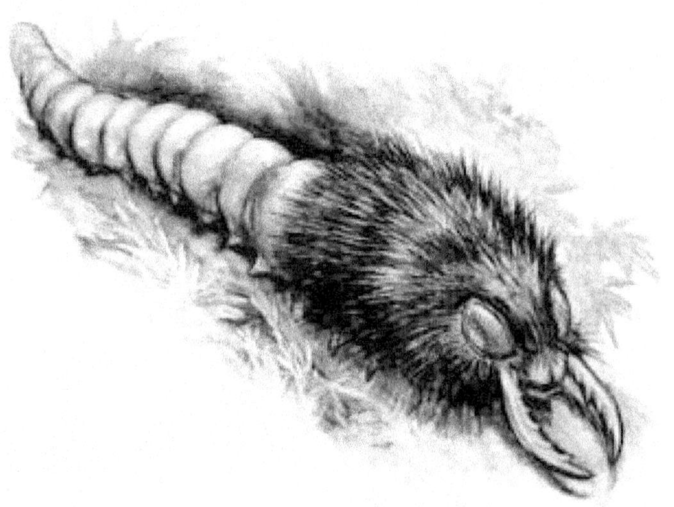

Tentacled Horror

Hit Dice: 12
Armor Class: 1 [18]
Attacks: 4 tentacles (1d8), 1 bite (3d6)
Saving Throw: 3
Special: Constrict, regenerates 5 hp/round, aura of insanity
Move: 6
Alignment: Chaos
Challenge Level/XP: 14/2,600

Exuding a foul oily slime wherever it goes, a tentacled horror has a powerful humanoid torso that ends in a thick slug-like foot. Sprouting from the torso are four whip-like tentacles tipped in cruel barbs. A tentacled horror has a shapeless head with a single, huge, unblinking eye. The mouth is a yawning chasm of sharp teeth. Above the eye is a glistening black 2-foot-long horn. Tentacled horrors attack with their tentacles to rip and tear at opponents. If two tentacles hit the same opponent, the foe is held and constricted for automatic 2d8 damage and pulled toward the creature's mouth for automatic bite damage (3d6) on the next round. Creatures with fewer than 6 HD who view a tentacle horror must save or be affected as if by a *fear* spell. Tentacled horrors regenerate 5 hit points per round.

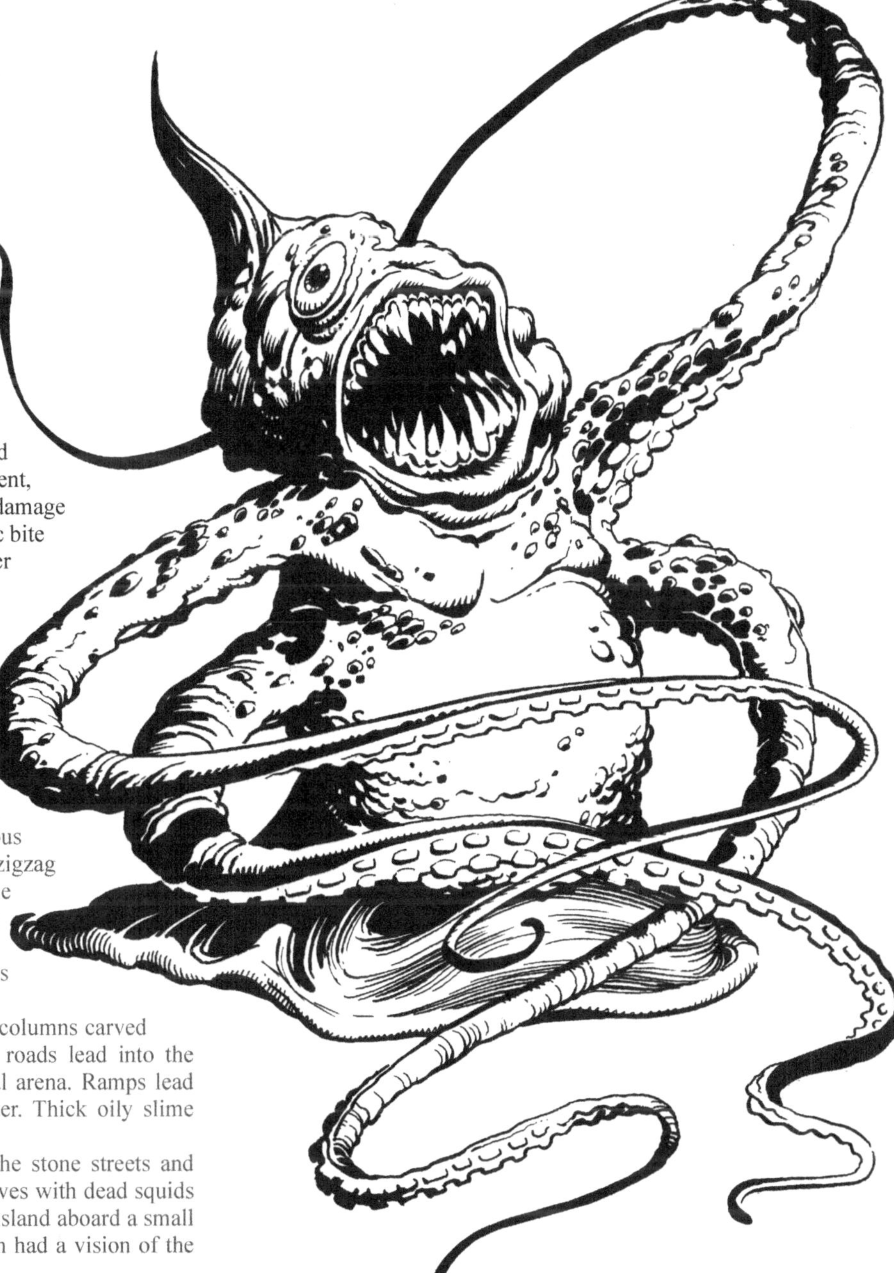

The Island Rises

Moss-covered ruins rise in ocean. The island is nearly 2 miles across, and every inch is covered in stone ruins that nearly merge into one continuous structure. Twisting alleys of claustrophobic tunnels zigzag through the buildings. Red brick and slick pale marble fit together in a patterned mosaic on the streets. The buildings are filled with hanging strands of seaweed, scuttling crabs and dead fish. Indecipherable sigils are carved into the stone walls.

A stone arena in the center of the island has high columns carved to resemble tentacled sea creatures. Three paved roads lead into the amphitheater, and stone benches surround a central arena. Ramps lead into water-filled dungeons beneath the amphitheater. Thick oily slime leads down the ramps.

A tribe of 40 goblins make their way through the stone streets and abandoned buildings. The goblins decorate themselves with dead squids left on the brick streets. The creatures sailed to the island aboard a small ship that broke up on the rocks. The tribe's shaman had a vision of the island and led his minions here.

A tentacled horror rose from the sea with the island and lives in the pools beneath the arena. It slides up the ramps to face creatures entering its arena. The island is tied to the creature's life force. If it is slain, the island crumbles quickly and sinks back into the sea. Creatures in the center of the island face a gauntlet of breaking stone and waterspouts as they race for the shoreline.

Copyright Notice

Tentamort

Hit Dice: 4
Armor Class: 0 [19]
Attack: 2 tentacles (1d4)
Saving Throw: 13
Special: Grab, liquefy organs
Move: 3/3 (climbing)
Alignment: Neutrality
Challenge Level/XP: 6/600

A tentamort has a small spherical body of gray flesh. Two long tentacles protrude from the upper half of the sphere while eight smaller tentacles hang from the bottom of its spherical body. One tentacle ends in a squid-like appendage while the other ends in a needle-like barb.

Tentamorts are rarely encountered above ground, preferring the darkness of underground caverns and dungeons. The tentamort resembles a squid. Its body is a small, 3-foot diameter sphere of gray, hard flesh. Two 10-foot long tentacles protrude from the upper half of its body while eight 2-foot long tentacles hang from the bottom of its spherical body (it uses these for movement only). Of the two large tentacles, the left ends in a squid-like appendage and the right in a long, needle-sharp barb. A tentamort uses its small tentacles to hold itself to ceilings and walls. When prey passes underneath, it drops on its opponent, grabbing it with its tentacles and injecting it with its deadly acid.

Creatures struck by the tentamort's tentacles must pass a saving throw or be held fast and squeezed for an automatic 1d4 points of damage each round. They can escape by chopping off a tentacle (12 hit points each) or making a successful roll to open doors. A tentamort always attempts to grab a foe with its rightmost tentacle so it can stab the opponent with the needle-like barb on its left tentacle.

After grabbing a foe with its rightmost tentacle, a tentamort can insert the needle-like projection from its leftmost tentacle into the foe's body (requires a successful melee attack). Once inserted, the tentamort injects its acidic saliva through the hollow barb and liquefies the victim's internal organs, which the creature then draws through the tube and into its own body. This attack deals 1d4 points of constitution damage each round the tube remains inserted in a foe and 1 point of constitution damage for 1d2 rounds after the needle is removed.

A *cure disease, restoration* or *wish* spell halts the constitution damage after the needle has been removed. A creature slain by this attack can only be raised by the casting of a *wish*.

Liquefaction or Liquification?

At the confluence of three rivers there is a vast moorland of twisted trees and tall grasses. In the lagoons of the moorland there dwell pelicans, swans, ermines, wolves and wild boars (2 in 6 chance of a significant encounter each day). On the edges of the moorland there are signs of former human habitation in the form of old mills and abandoned, toppled cottages.

The moorland once supported a large population, as population pressures in nearby city-states drove farmers into the moors. One of the ex-residents was an alchemist, who chemical infusions into the swampland gave rise to a number of strange creatures (owlbears, for example), including a brood of 1d4+1 tentamorts that hatched from befouled swan eggs. The tentamorts eventually ran people out of the area, and even claimed the life of the alchemist. His ruined tower still stands in the middle of a pond inhabited by the descendants of the original tentamorts.

Rumors in the nearest city-state claim that the alchemist was working on coating seven magic swords with an alchemical essence of silver when he was killed.

Credit

The Tentamort originally appeared in the First Edition *Fiend Folio* (© TSR/Wizards of the Coast, 1981) and is used by permission.

Copyright Notice

Author Scott Greene, based on original material by Mike Roberts.

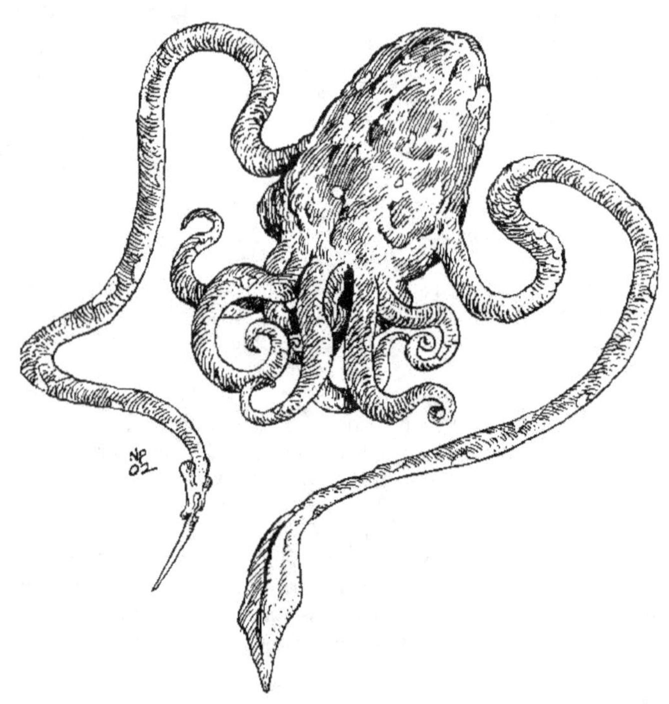

Thermite

Thermite, Worker

Hit Dice: 3
Armor Class: 3 [16]
Attacks: Bite (1d4 + 1d4 fire)
Saving Throw: 16
Special: Burn, heat (1d4), immune to fire
Move: 18
Alignment: Neutrality
Challenge Level/XP: 4/120

Thermites are reddish-hued giant termites. Immense heat radiates from their bodies. They are 5 or 6 feet long with large biting mandibles and segmented antennae. A hive can hold as many as 100 thermites, in a worker-to-warrior ratio of 1:5. A hive also contains one giant queen thermite. When a thermite hits with its bite attack, the opponent must save or catch on fire. Touching or being touched by a thermite automatically deals 1d4 points of fire damage. There are tales of winged thermites.

Thermite, Warrior

Hit Dice: 5
Armor Class: 3 [16]
Attacks: Bite (1d6 + 1d6 fire)
Saving Throw: 12
Special: Burn, death throes, heat 1d6, immune to fire
Move: 18
Alignment: Neutrality
Challenge Level/XP: 6/400

Thermite warriors are reddish-hued giant termites. Immense heat radiates from their bodies. They are 5 or 6 feet long with large biting mandibles and segmented antennae. When a thermite warrior hits with its bite attack, the opponent must save or catch on fire. Touching or being touched by a thermite automatically deals 1d6 points of fire damage. A warrior thermite explodes in a ball of fire dealing 3d6 points of fire damage to all within a 10-foot radius when slain. A successful save reduces the damage by half.

Thermite, Queen

Hit Dice: 8
Armor Class: 2 [17]
Attacks: Bite (1d8 + 1d8 fire)
Saving Throw: 8
Special: Burn, death throes, heat 2d6, immune to fire
Move: 12
Alignment: Neutrality
Challenge Level/XP: 9/1,100

Thermite queens are reddish-hued giant termites. Immense heat radiates from their bodies. A thermite hive contains one queen. When a thermite queen hits with its bite attack, the opponent must save or catch on fire. Touching or being touched by a thermite queen automatically deals 2d6 points of fire damage. A thermite queen explodes in a ball of fire dealing 8d6 points of fire damage to all within a 10-foot radius when slain. A successful save reduces the damage by half.

The Glass Desert

The blistering heat of the desert blasts PCs, with winds whipping sands into their faces and the sun baking their flesh. Shifting dunes make travel difficult. One large section of the desert is covered by a foot-thick field of clear glass that stretches for nearly a mile. The glass is incredibly hot as it reflects the sun, but safe to walk on. Skeletons sunk to the waist – or deeper – stick out of the glass plain. Those above the glass are bleached white by the sun and stinging grit, while below the glass their bodies are sun-burned, mummified flesh. Wagon wheels jut from the glass, although the wagons are missing. Weapons can be found completely, each completely encased in the clear surface.

Broken holes descend into man-size tunnels. These tunnels are slick glass tubes cut into the sand with sharp ridges slicing upward. Any PC sliding down a tube takes 3d6 points of damage from the sharp edges.

The glass plain is the creation of a colony of thermites. Their bodies generate the heat that turns the sand into glass around them as they burrow. The tubes lead into the colony's home, where hundreds of worker and soldier thermites can be found. A queen is protected in a glass chamber deep inside the colony. The thermites react to anyone making too much noise on the upper glass and defend their tunnels from invaders.

Copyright Notice

T

THERIANTHROPES

Therianthropes (sometimes called anthromorphs or weretherions) are animals that can assume a human or hybrid form (the latter combining traits of both their human and animal forms). They are akin to lycanthropes (in that they are shapechangers), but therianthropes are not lycanthropes and do not carry or induce lycanthropy. All therianthropes in human form have slightly feral characteristics.

Asswere

Hit Dice: 3
Armor Class: 4 [15]
Attack: Bite (1d4) or weapon (1d8)
Saving Throw: 14
Special: Bray, only harmed by silver weapons
Move: 12
Alignment: Chaos
Challenge Level/XP: 5/240

Assweres in humanoid form are indistinguishable from other humanoids. In hybrid form they look like donkey-headed humanoids covered in blackish-gray fur and standing 6 feet tall.

An asswere can loose a loud bray as a standard action. All creatures within 30 feet that hear it must succeed on a saving throw or be affected as by a *confusion* spell for 1d4+3 rounds.

Copyright Notice
Author Scott Greene.

Foxwere

Hit Dice: 3
Armor Class: 3 [16]
Attack: Bite (1d4) or weapon (1d6)
Saving Throw: 14
Special: Charm gaze, only harmed by silver weapons, surprise on roll of 1-2 on 1d6
Move: 15
Alignment: Chaos
Challenge Level/XP: 5/240

Foxweres in humanoid form are indistinguishable from normal humanoids, though most have reddish-colored hair. In hybrid form, they look like fox-headed humanoids standing 5 feet tall and covered in reddish fur. A sleek, white stripe runs the length of its back.

Any creature within 30 feet that meets the creature's gaze must succeed on a saving throw or be affected as by a *charm monster* spell.

Copyright Notice
Author Scott Greene.

Jackalwere

Hit Dice: 3
Armor Class: 3 [16]
Attack: Bite (1d6) or weapon (1d8)
Saving Throw: 14
Special: Sleep gaze, only harmed by silver weapons
Move: 15
Alignment: Chaos
Challenge Level/XP: 5/240

Jackalweres in humanoid form usually have dark eyes and dark skin, but are otherwise indistinguishable from other humanoids. In hybrid form they look like jackal-headed humanoid with dark fur and dark eyes.

Any creature within 30 feet that meets the creature's gaze falls asleep for 3 minutes if it fails a saving throw. This ability functions as the *sleep* spell, but there is no HD limit to the number of creatures it can affect.

Credit
The Jackalwere originally appeared in the First Edition *Monster Manual* (© TSR/Wizards of the Coast, 1977) and is used by permission.

Copyright Notice
Author Scott Greene, based on original material by Gary Gygax.

Lionwere

Hit Dice: 6
Armor Class: 2 [17]
Attack: 2 claws (1d4) and bite (1d8) or weapon (1d8) and bite (1d8)
Saving Throw: 11
Special: Weakness gaze, only harmed by silver weapons, surprise on roll of 1-2 on 1d6
Move: 15
Alignment: Chaos
Challenge Level/XP: 8/800

Lionweres appear as normal humanoids when in humanoid form, though most are stocky and muscular. In hybrid form the appear as lion-headed humanoids with large golden mane. Its body is covered in golden brown fur and its eyes are greenish-gray.

Any creature within 30 feet that meets the creature's gaze takes 1d4+1 points of strength damage. A successful saving throw negates the damage. A lionwere can use this ability twice per day.

Copyright Notice
Author Scott Greene.

Mulewere

Hit Dice: 3
Armor Class: 4 [15]
Attack: 2 hooves (1d4) or weapon (1d8)
Saving Throw: 14
Special: Bray, only harmed by silver weapons
Move: 12
Alignment: Chaos
Challenge Level/XP: 5/240

Muleweres in humanoid form are indistinguishable from other humanoids. In hybrid form it appears as a mule-headed humanoid with grayish-black fur and brown eyes.

All creatures within 30 feet that hear the mulewere must succeed on a saving throw or become panicked for 2d4 rounds. Creatures further away but within 200 feet must succeed on a saving throw or become frightened for 2d4 rounds.

Copyright Notice
Author Scott Greene.

Owlwere

Hit Dice: 3
Armor Class: 3 [16]
Attack: 2 talons (1d4 plus disease) or weapon (1d6)
Saving Throw: 14
Special: Disease, only harmed by silver weapons, surprise on roll of 1-2 on 1d6
Move: 12/15 (flying)
Alignment: Chaos
Challenge Level/XP: 5/240

Owlweres appear as normal humanoids in humanoid form, often timid and shy. In hybrid form it appears as a lithe and small owl-headed humanoid with brownish-yellow feathers and white eyes. An owlwere's talons can infect people who fail a saving throw with an aching disease that imposes a -2 penalty to hit and damage until two daily saving throws are made back-to-back.

Copyright Notice
Author Scott Greene.

Wolfwere

Hit Dice: 3
Armor Class: 3 [16]
Attack: Bite (1d6) or weapon (1d8)
Saving Throw: 14
Special: Song of lethargy, only harmed by silver weapon
Move: 15
Alignment: Chaos
Challenge Level/XP: 5/240

In humanoid form, a wolfwere appears as a normal humanoid, often with grayish hair. In hybrid form it has a wolf's head and its body is covered in short gray fur. Its hands end in sharpened claws.

By speaking or singing, a wolfwere can *slow* all creatures within 60 feet that hear it if they fail a saving throw. The *slow* effects last 1d4+3 rounds.

Council Rock

Overlooking the savannah, near the forested gorge and a many miles south of the blazing desert is the outcropping called Council Rock. Here, the eldest of the therianthropes, the animal men that dominate the surrounding lands, meet to plan their campaigns against the humans that press them from every direction.

On the nights of the full moon they gather atop the old outcropping of granite, its slopes decorated with trailing vines bearing fragrant blossoms.

There is the seductive foxwere, whose people govern the underbrush and collect tribute from the rodents and birds; the asswere, whose people run the desert sands, preying on superstitious caravaneers; the lionwere, who considers his people the kings of all beasts - whether two or four-legged; the owlwere, whose people haunt the night and carry their terror into human lands; the jackalwere, always listening, rarely speaking and the wolfwere, whose people rule the forested gorge and who council most vehemently for the destruction of man.

Dug into the granite outcropping are three pits covered by wooden grates held down with large stones. Here, the beast lords place their prisoners, questioning and torturing them at their leisure.

Dire Wolfwere

Hit Dice: 6+6
Armor Class: 4 [15]
Attacks: 1 bite (2d4), 1 weapon (1d8)
Saving Throw: 11
Special: hit only by magical weapons, weakness gaze
Move: 12
Alignment: Chaos
Challenge Level/XP: 20/3,400

Primeval wolfweres in human form stand around 6 to 6-1/2 feet tall and have grayish-brown or grayish-black hair. Their features are sharp and well-formed, but otherwise unremarkable. A primeval wolfwere in hybrid form looks like a bipedal wolf with dark gray fur and yellow eyes. It stands about 9 feet tall and weighs about 800 pounds. The gaze of a primeval wolfwere makes opponents physically weak, imposing a -1 to-hit penalty. Therianthropes are animals that can assume human and hybrid form (the latter being bipedal and combining traits of its human and animal form. Unlike lycanthropes, therianthropy is not contagious and is an inherent ability of the creature. Therianthropes cannot be hit by normal means, only magical weapons can affect them. They do not have a weakness for silver weapons.

River Pirates

A sizable flatboat named the the Wastrel cruises up and down the Krell River looking for passengers. The boat is powered by two enchanted paddlewheels on each side that propel it through the water. The ship has three decks, with curving railings carved by a master carver. The bridge sits at the front of the top deck, affording the pilot a full view of the river ahead. The ship's figurehead is a snarling wolf of gleaming silver.

During the day and most nights, the Wastrel and its crew pose as wealthy revelers out enjoying the river. The flatboat has a reputation for outlandish revelry and all-day parties where expensive wines flow freely. On nights of the full moon, however, their true nature is revealed: The Wastrel's crew and passengers are river pirates infected with lycanthropy. Stella, a primeval wolfwere, leads the vicious werewolves.

A bronze nozzle attached to a large bellows below deck lets the flatboat spew burning oil on the wealthy merchant vessels with devastating effects. Treasure from the pirates' victims fills the belly of the ship. No one who encounters the Wastrel during nights of the full moon is left alive to spread the crews' secret.

Credit

The Wolfwere originally appeared in the First Edition *Monster Manual II* (© TSR/Wizards of the Coast, 1983) and is used by permission.

Copyright Notice

Author Scott Greene, based on original material by Gary Gygax.

THESSALMONSTERS

Thessalmonsters are nocturnal predators that resemble a cross between an eight-headed hydra and another monster. The true origin of the thessalmonster lies shrouded in mystery, but many sages speculate the creature is the result of an arcane experiment gone awry involving an ancient thessalhydra and other monsters.

Thessalmonsters are a combination of a thessalhydra and another creature. Thessalmonsters resemble hydras, complete with reptilian torso and eight serpentine heads around its central front. Some thessalmonsters retain the base creature's head while others lose it and have it replaced with a central maw filled with serrated teeth.

Thessalhydra

Hit Dice: 12
Armor Class: 2 [17]
Attack: 8 serpentine bites (2d6 plus 1d6 acid) and tail slash (2d6)
Saving Throw: 3
Special: Spit acid, heal 2 hp/round, immunity to acid
Move: 15/9 (swimming)
Alignment: Chaos
Challenge Level/XP: 13/2000

This creature is a massive reptilian beast with four stump-like legs and a multitude of heads surrounding a central maw filled with oversized teeth. Its body is reddish-gold and scaled. A long serpentine tail extends from its body and ends in a pincer-like claw. A typical thessalhydra stands almost 20 feet tall and measures 30 feet from front to tail. It weighs about 15,000 pounds.

A thessalhydra deals 1d6 points of acid damage with a serpentine bite. Once per day, a thessalhydra can spit acid in a 40-ft. line that deals 4d6 points of acid damage (save for half damage).

Credit

The Thessalhydra originally appeared in the First Edition *Monster Manual II* (© TSR/Wizards of the Coast, 1983).

Copyright Notice

Author Scott Greene, based on original material by Gary Gygax and Wizards of the Coast.

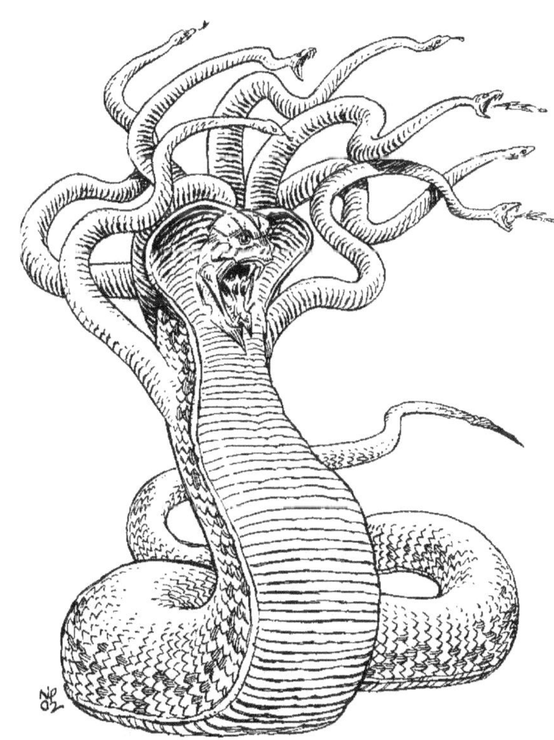

Thessalgorgon

Hit Dice: 8
Armor Class: 0 [19]
Attack: 8 serpentine bites (2d6 plus 1d6 acid) and gore (2d6)
Saving Throw: 8
Special: Breath weapon, immunity to acid, heal 2 hp/round
Move: 15
Alignment: Chaos
Challenge Level/XP: 12/2000

Thessalgorgons are a cross between a gorgon and a thessalhydra. They attack intruders on sight, attempting to trample, gore, or petrify them. There is no way to calm these furious creatures, and they are impossible to domesticate.

A thessalgorgon has a large central bull-like head is ringed by eight snake-like heads, each spitting and hissing. Its entire body is covered in thick, metallic scales of coppery-green. A typical thessalgorgon stands over 12 feet tall at the shoulder and measures 24 feet from snout to tail. It weighs about 8,000 pounds.

A thessalgorgon deals 1d6 points of acid damage with a serpentine bite. Once every 1d4 rounds and no more than five times per day, a thessalgorgon can exhale a 60-ft long and 40-ft wide cone of gas that turns people to stone (saving throw to negate).

Credit

The Thessalgorgon originally appeared in the *Monstrous Compendium (MC 3)* (© TSR/Wizards of the Coast, 1989). All are used by permission.

Copyright Notice

Author Scott Greene, based on original material by Gary Gygax and Wizards of the Coast.

Thessalisk

Hit Dice: 6
Armor Class: 2 [17]
Attack: 8 serpentine bites (1d8 plus 1d6 acid) and tail slash (1d8)
Saving Throw: 11
Special: Acid, petrifying gaze, spit acid, immunity to acid, heal 2 hp/round
Move: 15
Alignment: Chaos
Challenge Level/XP: 10/1400

A thessalisk is a cross between a basilisk and a thessalhydra. Its body grows to about 12 feet long, not including its tail, which can reach an additional length of 10 to 20 feet. The creature weighs about 800 pounds. It has eight, short legs, a short, powerful tail that ends in a pincer-like claw and a thick, barrel-like body. A large reptilian head with emerald green eyes is encircled by eight serpentine heads.

A thessalisk deals 1d6 points of acid damage with a serpentine bite. Once per day it can spit a 40-ft line of acid that deals 4d6 points of damage (save for half damage).

The creature's gaze turn to stone permanently people within 30 feet who look into its eyes. A saving throw negates the effect.

Unstable Bridges

The tunnel the adventurers have been following finally ends in a sheer drop. The cavern beyond is massive. The floor is 40 feet below and covered in slimy, brackish water, which is itself 5 to 8 feet deep. The ceiling is 30 feet above and covered in dripping stalactites. The cavern is at least 300 feet in diameter, the walls sheer and slick. Phosphorescent swamp gasses illuminate the cavern with the equivalent of twilight, and gouts of flame often erupt from the floor. Acrid fumes and the scent of rotting vegetation assault the nose.

Rising from the subterranean swamp there is what appears to be a mountain in miniature, only 40 feet tall, with sloping sides that must have been carved by humanoid hands. The top of this mound is flat and can be reached by a long bridge of rope and metallic discs. Two other bridges extend from the mound to other walls of the cave that are pierced with caves.

The bridges are sturdy enough to hold up to eight encumbered individuals at a time, though they sway uncomfortably as one walks and running or fighting on a bridge carries a 1 in 10 chance each round of causing the bridge to flip and deposit people into the waters below.

When one reaches the mound they will likely step on a pressure plate adjacent to the bridge they have just crossed. This pressure plate triggers a slim, brass pole that rises from the center of the mound and causes every third metallic disk of each bridge to become ethereal (1 in 6 chance to notice this intangibility, 2 in 6 for elves). This bar hums with energy and gives off minor shocks if touched. The top of the bar is a loop of metal, into which one can shove a wooden or metal pole (or staff, club, haft, etc). Turning the loop to face a bridge causes its discs to become material again.

Stepping on an ethereal disc forces one to pass a saving throw or fall into the swamp, which is inhabited by three thessalhydras. The thessalhydras live in submerged lairs in the base of the mound. Each lair holds 1d4 x 1,000 sp and 1d4 x 1,000 gp contained in cylinders of the same metal as the discs. The cylinders have no obvious way of opening them, but can be turned intangible with the application of electricity.

Copyright Notice

Thorny

Hit Dice: 4
Armor Class: 3 [16]
Attack: Bite (1d6)
Saving Throw: 13
Special: Thorns, surprise on 1-2 on 1d6
Move: 18
Alignment: Neutrality
Challenge Level/XP: 4/120

Thornies are the pets and companions of the vegepygmies. They are rarely encountered outside of a vegepygmy tribe or hunting party. Vegepygmies often use them to hunt prey. They look like hunting dogs formed of tangled briars, vines, leaves and sticks.

Thornies reproduce by planting egg-like seeds (that the female lays) in the ground. Three to six months later, a small tree sprouts, buds, and from these buds are born the thornies. An average thorny tree is capable of producing 1d6+4 thornies. The tree dies once it buds and the thornies "hatch."

A thorny's body is covered with sharp wooden thorns. Any creature attacking a thorny unarmed, with a handheld weapon, or with natural attacks takes 1d4 points of damage from the thorny's sharpened thorns. A creature that grapples with a thorny takes this same damage each round.

Midriff Protection is Necessary

A pack of 1d6+2 wild thornies has made a lair for itself in a patch of brambles. In the middle of the patch there are three thorny trees growing, each supporting 1d6+4 wriggling buds. The thornies patrol the surrounding landscape of tall pines and golden river gorges. Half the pack is always lurking around the clearing where they have planted their trees, and defend the area ferociously.

Just beyond the thorny trees there is an old cave with a low ceiling and significant piles of rubble. From the appearance of the rubble, the cave was a gold mine. Under one pile of rubble there is a partially buried skeleton wearing a dried out shirt of ringed armor with a rusty dirk (a *+1 dagger*) lodged in its ribs. Behind this pile of rubble there is a small tunnel entrance to a lower set of limestone caverns filled with spectacular formations and a veritable sea of slime.

A second skeleton, this one wearing what is best described as a mail halter and loinclout, is draped over one of the stalagmites that rise from the slime. The skeleton still has long, golden hair and wears a silver ring (*protection from undead*) one one bony finger. The cave is also inhabited by three ochre jellies.

A high stone shelf in the slime cavern gives access to a dry, dusty cavern. One must scoot on their belly through a 3-foot high and 10-foot wide passage to access this cavern. Here, there is a large idol carved from the native limestone and stained in purples and rust-reds with two large eyes of mirror-like platinum (worth 100 gp each). This demonic idol is surrounded by bowls containing long dried grapes and plums, apparent offerings. One every three months, the idol gives out a long, low groan that causes the ground to rumble and attracts the vegepygmy tribes in the area to come and worship. All those in the presence of the idol when it groans find themselves covered in a silvery dust that falls from the ceiling. The dust makes their skin sparkle (until washed) and grants them a +2 reaction bonus from all plant creatures.

In addition to the silvery dust, the idol becomes ethereal for a few minutes after groaning, revealing a round shaft located beneath it. This shaft leads to whatever adventures the Referee has a mind to run.

Credit

The Thorny originally appeared in the First Edition module *S3 Expedition to the Barrier Peaks* (© TSR/Wizards of the Coast, 1980) and later in the First Edition *Monster Manual II* (© TSR/Wizards of the Coast, 1983) and is used by permission.

Copyright Notice

Author Scott Greene, based on original material by Gary Gygax.

Thorny Tyrannosaurus

Hit Dice: 19
Armor Class: 4 [15]
Attacks: Bite (4d8)
Saving Throw: 3
Special: Thrash, thorns
Move: 18
Alignment: Neutrality
Challenge Level/XP: 20/2,700

A thorny tyrannosaurus is a dinosaur constructed entirely of thorns, tangled brush, and leaves. If the creature bites a victim, it draws the victim into its jaws and inflicts automatic bite damage each round thereafter as it thrashes and chews the creature. Any creature attacking a thorny tyrannosaurus unarmed or with weapons automatically takes 1d6 points of damage from the large thorns that make up its body.

The Island City of Verdurn

Austallos Lake formed in the high peaks of a massive volcanic crater within the remote mountain frontier. The warm lake is shallow, making travel by large ships hazardous. The algae-filled lake spans nearly 10 miles and is 5 miles across at its widest point. The lake reaches a depth of 10 feet but averages around 4 foot. Large natural rock formations and boulders lie strewn in the lake, creating a natural maze. Lost in time there existed an island city in the midst of the mountain lake. The vanished inhabitants left all possessions and structures.

A band of vegepygmies claimed the island as their domain. A thorny tyrannosaurus guards the island, roaming through the vegetation on the edges of the beach. In addition, the vegepygmies have planted patches of russet mold and shriekers and have plant-imbued apes guarding their lair inside one of the empty buildings in the heart of the island.

Throat Leech

The throat leech is a 1-inch long grey leech that lairs in fresh streams, pools, underground springs, and the like. When a living creature consumes liquid containing a throat leech, the leech attaches itself to the back of the victim's throat and begins draining blood. This deals 1d6 points of damage each round. Once the leech has inflicted 12 points of damage, it ceases draining (but does not detach). When a throat leech has sated itself, its body swells thereby suffocating the host.

A *cure disease* spell kills a throat leech as does an application of fire that deals at least one point of fire damage.

Clear Your Throat

As you approach this next chamber, the sound of running, splashing water is clearly heard. The room appears to have once been a bath of some sort. The center of the chamber (22 feet by 22 feet, 16 foot high ceiling) is sunken about 4 feet to form a 14-foot y 14-foot pool. The pool is clad in dingy marble and the walls are covered in sparkling blue tiles. Water pours into the pool from a tarnished brass pipe in the ceiling crafted in the shape of a curvaceous mermaid. Water also spills into the pool from two places in the ceiling where the plumbing has apparently burst. A drain in the bottom of the pool allows water to escape. The water pouring from the ceiling is warm, but the water in the pool is tepid. The pool is inhabited by a number of throat leeches that blend in with the dingy marble and are usually hidden by the froth kicked up in the pool by the water pouring into it. A large copper medallion (worth 3 cp) has fallen into the pool, and bears the image of an ancient king on one side and the goddess of victory on the other.

Credit
The Throat Leech originally appeared in the First Edition *Fiend Folio* (© TSR/Wizards of the Coast, 1981) and is used by permission.

Copyright Notice
Author Scott Greene, based on original material by Ian Livingstone.

Thunder Beast

Hit Dice: 6
Armor Class: 5 [14]
Attack: Bite (2d6)
Saving Throw: 11
Special: Breath weapon, trample
Move: 12
Alignment: Neutrality
Challenge Level/XP: 8/800

A thunder beast is huge animal with a hippo-like head with pointed pig-like ears. It has a large, wide mouth with small upright tusks jutting from its lower jaw. Its long body is thick and hunched. Six powerful legs aid the creature in locomotion. A typical thunder beast is about 20 feet long. It is yellow-brown, ochre, or olive in color, mottled dark brown or black.

Thunder beasts are herd animals that spend their time roaming the uncountable layers of the Abyss sustaining themselves on a diet of rotted plants, manes demons, and other inconsequential life forms.

Every 1d4 rounds, a thunder beast can exhale a semi-noxious cloud of gas that spreads to fill an area 20 feet high in a 20-foot radius. Living creatures in the area must succeed on a saving throw or suffer a -1 penalty to hit, damage and make saving throws as long as they remain in the area and for one round after leaving the area. The cloud lasts 1d4 rounds before dispersing. A strong wind (21+ mph) disperses the cloud in 1 round.

The thunder beast can trample creatures by simply moving over the top of them. Thunder beasts cause 2d6 points of damage when they trample. Trampled folk who attempt to dodge receive a saving throw to negate half of the damage. Those who stand their ground can make an attack at +2 to hit and damage.

Arena of the Damned

One of the myriad planes of the Abyss is home to a reeking jungle of eternally rotting vegetation, roaming herds of 5d4 thunder beasts (+50% as many noncombatant calves) and bands of manes set loose in the jungle by more powerful demons as a punishment for displeasing them. Rising above the jungles is a basalt spire. The spire does not appear to be a construction, rather rising from the plane fully formed. The spire is slightly crooked. At the top of the spire, which is about a 1/2 mile in diameter and 7 miles tall, there is a prison holding a movanic deva. The light of the movanic deva once shone across the twilight jungle, but has dimmed considerably over the centuries. The angel was imprisoned here by mighty Orcus, who is waiting for the creature to slowly lose its faith and become a demon.

The prison chamber looks like a vast arena with a diameter of 500 feet and a vaulted, rust red ceiling. The angel is chained in the center and tormented day and night by succubi, vrock and marilith demons, who emerge via passages that lead to the lower levels of the spire. The spire is a prison and dungeon for powerful prisoners of the various demon princes. It is guarded by retrievers and inhabited by a myraid of oozes and puddings furnished by the Faceless Lord.

Each day spent in the jungle carries with it a 1 in 6 chance of encountering a band of 1d4+5 mane demons and a 2 in 6 chance of encountering a herd of thunder beasts. The thunder beasts are sometimes trapped by the more powerful demons, who use them like war elephants in their struggles against rivals.

Retriever: HD 10; AC -2 [21]; Atk 4 claws (2d6) and bite (1d8) and eye ray; Move 18; Save 5; AL Chaos; CL/XP 13/2300; Special: Eye rays (10d6 fire ray, 10d6 cold ray, 10d6 bolt of lightning, or petrification), infallibly track targets, regenerate 2 hp/round.

Credit
The Thunder Beast originally appeared in the First Edition *Monster Manual II* (© TSR/Wizards of the Coast, 1983) and is used by permission.

Copyright Notice
Author Scott Greene, based on original material by Gary Gygax.

Thundershrike

Hit Dice: 13
Armor Class: 4 [15]
Attacks: 2 claws (3d6), 1 bite (3d12)
Saving Throw: 3
Special: Spell-like abilities
Move: 3/30 (flying)
Alignment: Neutrality
Challenge Level/XP: 15/2,900

Thundershrikes are majestic birds, 20 feet tall with a wingspan that reaches about 40 feet. Coloration varies from black to brown to gray with beak color ranging from gold to white (though white-beaked thundershrikes are extremely rare). The bird can cast *control winds* at will. Twice per day, the eagle-like raptor can create a *lightning bolt*. Once per day, it can cast *control weather*.

Sturm and Drang

Black clouds roll across the land, the storm dropping low tendrils toward the earth. Thick columns of twisting winds bob and weave through the gray sky, none quite reaching the ground – yet. A gray mist of rain pummels the muddy earth, the sheets of rain so thick they obscure the trees whipping in the gale.

Striding through the destruction is a giant, the horns on his helmet nearly touching the low-hanging clouds. His beard crackles with a rime of sparking energy from the storm, and the massive battle axe thrown over his shoulder draws the lightning in arcing, popping strikes. From the delight on his face, he's reveling in the fierce storm.

Sturm the Lightning Bringer walks in the magnificent chaos, taking it all in. Anyone attacking the giant, however, soon finds he's not alone. His pet thundershrike Drang is also enjoying the deadly winds and savage lightning, but inside the thunderhead. She sweeps down out of the blackness at Sturm's call to defend her master.

Sturm, Storm Giant: HD 15+5; AC 1[18]; Atk 1 weapon (6d6); Move 15; Save 3; CL/XP 16/3200; Special: Throw boulders, control weather.

Copyright Notice
Author Scott Greene.

Tick, Giant

Hit Dice: 2
Armor Class: 2 [17]
Attack: Bite (1d4)
Saving Throw: 16
Special: Blood drain, disease
Move: 6
Alignment: Neutrality
Challenge Level/XP: 3/60

Giant ticks appear as 3-foot long ticks. They are otherwise similar to normal ticks. They attack by dropping on their prey from above and stabbing with a hollow mouth tube. If subjected to fire or immersed in water, a giant tick detaches from its victim.

If a giant tick hits with a bite attack, it latches onto the opponent's body. The giant tick holds on with great tenacity. An attached giant tick can be struck with a weapon or pulled away with a grapple attack.

A giant tick drains blood, dealing 1d8 points of damage in any round when it begins its turn attached to a victim. Once it has dealt 12 points of damage, it detaches and crawls off to digest the meal. If its victim dies before the giant tick's appetite has been sated, the giant tick detaches and seeks a new target.

Fifty percent of all giant ticks carry and deliver a fever with a bite attack. Roll individually for each giant tick in the cluster or nest. The fever takes 1d3 days to incubate and 1d6 points of strength damage each day that a saving throw is failed. If a victim's strength is reduced to 0, they die. If they succeed at two daily saving throws in a row, they shake off the fever.

Ticklish

In the midst of an cork oak forest there is a massive cave mouth, 25 feet tall and 30 feet wide. The cave is carved into the side of a low, weathered mountain covered with thick grasses and blackberry bushes. The cave is inhabited by a giant bear that stands 15 feet tall at shoulder. The bear, called King of the Forest by the local druids, spends most of its time hibernating. Every 30 years the great beast awakens, devours the blackberries on the mountain, tops them off with a few dozen woodland creatures (and any hunters unlucky enough to be nearby) and then retires to its cave.

The chances of it being awake when adventurers come to call is minor. The great beast is fairly helpless while asleep, but the surrounding woods are home to a cluster of 1d4+2 giant ticks that are happy to attack anything that might threaten their regular meal. Attacks on the bear awaken it, but it remains groggy for 2 rounds. The giant bear has 12 Hit Dice and its attack deal triple normal damage for a brown bear.

Credit
The Giant Tick originally appeared in the First Edition *Monster Manual* (© TSR/Wizards of the Coast, 1977) and is used by permission.

Copyright Notice
Author Scott Greene, based on original material by Gary Gygax.

Time Flayer

Hit Dice: 13
Armor Class: 0 [19]
Attacks: 1 weapon (1d8+3)
Saving Throw: 3
Special: Temporal displacement, +1 magic weapons to hit, bend reality, time jaunt
Move: 9
Alignment: Neutrality
Challenge Level/XP: 16/3,200

Time flayers appear as shimmering white humanoids with eyes of sparkling fire. Their long, thin arms end in relatively humanoid hands and their legs end in humanoid feet. They move with an elegant grace, almost as though they were floating inches above the ground. With a touch, a time flayer can send an opponent a few seconds into the future. If the opponent fails a save, he vanishes for 1d4 rounds. The time flayer can use its temporal displacement ability three times per day. A time flayer can also fold the dimensional space around itself to hide its true location from attackers (50% chance of missing). A time flayer can slip through the time stream and appear somewhere else (as per the *teleport* spell).

The Party Never Ends

Tarkin Tower is crumbling into ruin, the top half of the tower open to the elements. Weeds grow rampant around the stone base, and animals disappear into the piles of fallen stone. A rotting drawbridge crosses a dry moat. The portcullis is down, but gaping holes have rusted through it. Just inside the stone entry, a line of checkerboard tiles runs from wall to wall.

Anyone crossing the tiles vanishes to those standing outside the castle. The person stepping across the checkboard pattern steps from ruin into opulence. The interior of the tower is grand and complete, and a magnificent party is still going on. Women sway across the floor, their gowns lavish and decorated with jewels. Men stand in groups, talking quietly. A banquet table is filled with a large ice sculpture of a swan sitting among roast pig, crepes, bowls of fruit and pitchers of sweet wine. There are about 50 people in the room.

If a PC crosses the tiles and appears, the party stops, and the revelers rush to introduce themselves. They are from all over, although a few claim to be from kingdoms that fell into ruin years ago. Many ask for the latest news, while others bring food for the hungry guest. Succulent grapes are offered to the PC as well as suckled ham and peach cobbler. Others push the PC toward a throne set on a low dais at the front of the room. It is covered in plush velvet pillows. Red curtains rise 30 feet to the ceiling behind the throne.

A time flayer appeared in the tower nearly 100 years ago during a grand celebration. Its unexpected arrival set off a host of protection spells that warped time inside the ballroom. The time flayer and the revelers are stuck in a time loop that keeps them from aging, but won't let any escape the ballroom. PCs who stay realize that the food is never replaced, the ice sculpture never melts, and the sun never rises through the windows. The open doors and windows are like solid walls to anyone trying to leave the ballroom.

The revelers and the time flayer have an understanding of sorts. It won't kill all of them if they sacrifice one person every year to the creature. The guests draw straws every year, and the loser is forced into the throne for the time flayer to claim. The time flayer lairs in the curtained off area behind the throne.

The revelers eagerly try to get the PC into the chair to put off their lottery another year. If the time flayer is slain, the time loop rights itself and releases everyone in the ballroom.

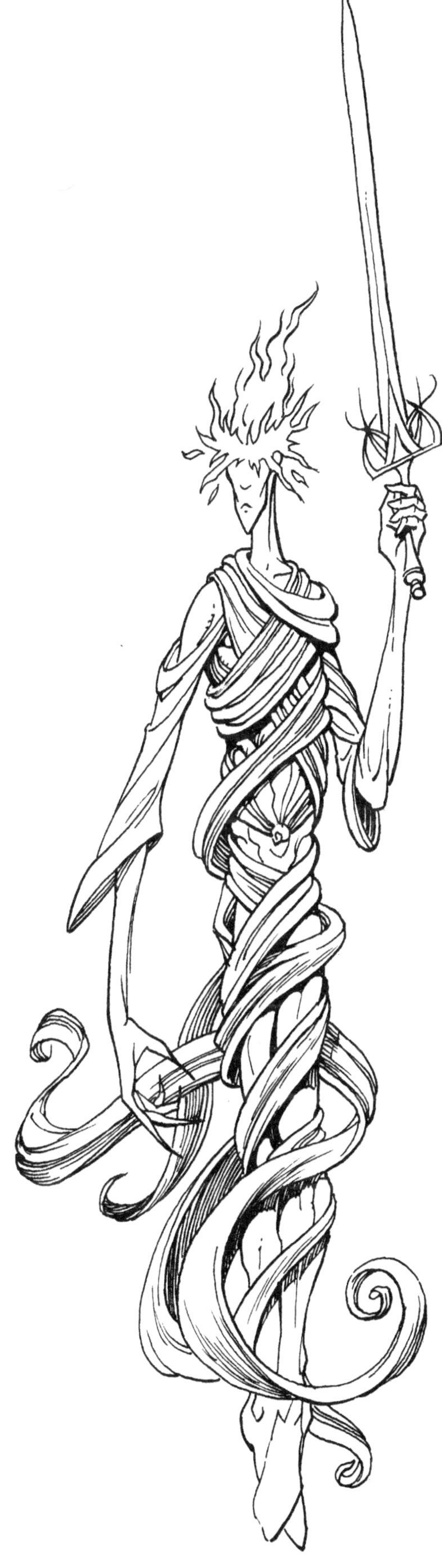

Tombstone Fairy

Hit Dice: 9
Armor Class: 3 [16]
Attacks: 1 weapon (1d2)
Saving Throw: 6
Special: Spell resistance 20%, danse macabre, spells
Move: 6
Alignment: Chaos
Challenge Level/XP: 9/1,100

Tombstone fairies are wicked little creatures dressed in the garb of an undertaker and resembling tiny gargoyles. *They have tiny black close-set eyes, and their skin is slate gray.* Tombstone fairies are wicked beings that dwell within graveyards, raising murderers and evil heroes from the dead to go out and continue their deadly work. They often demand some form of repayment for the raising of such beings, keeping the creature's funeral shroud as a bargaining chip. This payment could range from magical or monetary treasures, the murder of a specific enemy and so on. Failure to make payment within 30 days usually results in the raised individual dying again. Upon payment, the formerly dead is given their shroud and is free to go about committing whatever foul deeds they wish. A tombstone fairy stands about 3 feet tall and weighs around 35 pounds. Its skin is always slate gray and its hair is either dark brown or black. Its eyes are always black. Once per night, a tombstone fairy can invoke a ritual (danse macabre) to raise any evil creature from the dead. The ritual takes 10 minutes to perform and the target cannot have been dead longer than one day per HD of the tombstone fairy. During the ritual, a portion of the target's soul transfers to its funeral shroud or cloth. The tombstone fairy often retains this shroud so as to force compliance from the returned target. A tombstone fairy can have only one funeral shroud (containing a target's soul) in its possession at one time. A tombstone fairy can cast *detect evil*, *dispel magic*, *protection from evil* thrice per day and can use *ESP* at will. Once per day it can cast *suggestion*.

Hang Him High . . . Again

A weather-beaten gallows sits in the small town of Sod, with nearly seven severed ropes dangling from the center beam. A pile of seven bodies lie beneath the scaffold. Each has been hanged and the body cut down to rot beneath the gallows.

Sitting on the gallows is a gaunt man wearing a dusty black cloak wrapped around his body. A cut noose hangs loose around his neck. A black blade with a wickedly serrated edge is stuck into the wood in front of him. A young woman stands behind the man, her hands bound in front of her and a noose resting around her neck. She begs for her life.

Garn the Grievous killed all people who condemned him and dumped their bodies beneath the instrument of his death. The remaining townsfolk now cater to the evil man's whims. To disobey him is to join the rotting bodies under the gallows. Garn was hanged three days ago, but returned that night to seek his revenge. Every day, he randomly selects and hangs one townsperson. No one knows how the killer returned from the dead.

Near the unmarked grave where the killer's body was dumped lives a miserable tombstone fairy named Grim. The fey took a liking to Garn immediately, and raised the killer from the dead. If PCs slay Garn again, Grim seeks out the body and resurrects him that same night. The only way to stop Hanley returning to claim more townsfolk is to destroy Hanley's cloak, which the fairy possesses in a tiny grotto near the cemetery. The cloak is imbued with a portion of the killer's soul. Garn dies forever if the cloak is destroyed.

Copyright Notice

Author Scott Greene.

Transposer

Hit Dice: 6
Armor Class: 6 [13]
Attack: 2 slams (1d6 plus transposition)
Saving Throw: 11
Special: Transposition, change self
Move: 12
Alignment: Neutrality
Challenge Level/XP: 8/800

A transposer looks like a featureless humanoid whose arms end in large sucker-like membranes. Transposers are thought to be of an alien culture; how they came to the Material Plane remains a mystery to sages. Most transposers avoid contact with sentient races, preferring to live in seclusion among their own kind. Transposers speak their own alien tongue and a few that have spent time on the Material Plane speak the common tongue as well.

When it first encounters potential prey, a transposer takes the shape of a creature of the same race as its potential prey. Once its prey is in range, the transposer lashes out with its arms. Once it transposes a target, it pummels it relentlessly with its arms.

An opponent hit by a transposer's slam attack becomes linked (i.e. transposed) to it by an invisible and undetectable field of energy for 1 hour if it fails a saving throw. A transposer can have a number of opponents equal to its HD linked to it at one time. An opponent can be linked to more than one transposer (if it fails its save against each transposer's attack).

When a linked opponent attacks a transposer it is linked to, the creature gains hit points equal to the damage the attack would normally deal, and the attacker takes the damage. Other opponents linked to that transposer are unharmed. A transposer can gain up to the maximum hit points allowed by its Hit Dice (i.e. HD x 8). It cannot gain bonus or temporary hit points from this ability.

Curative magic cast on a transposer by a transposed opponent damages the creature by the amount it would normally heal, and heals a like amount of damage on the one who cast the spell. (Other linked creatures are unaffected.) Curative magic cast on a transposed opponent works normally but does not heal or harm a linked transposer. Curative magic cast on a transposer by a non-linked opponent functions normally.

Opponents not linked to the transposer can attack and affect the creature normally.

Someone Call the Men in Black

Three days after a clutch of asteroids struck the fields of a backwater village, a transposer stalks the area. The transposer seeks a strange, metallic helm that was found by a peasant in the smoldering woods near the site of the strike. The helm is precious to the creature, but its ultimate workings are unknown (i.e. it'll do whatever the Referee needs or wants it to do).

The peasant traded it to a traveling merchant for a few sacks of corn. The merchant is on his way to give it as a gift to the ruler of neighboring kingdom. The transposer has already tracked the peasant down and killed him in his lonely cottage. It has taken the peasant's form and is now looking for information on the man who received the helm.

Credit
The Transposer originally appeared in the First Edition *Monster Manual II* (© TSR/Wizards of the Coast, 1983) and is used by permission.

Copyright Notice
Author Scott Greene, based on original material by Gary Gygax.

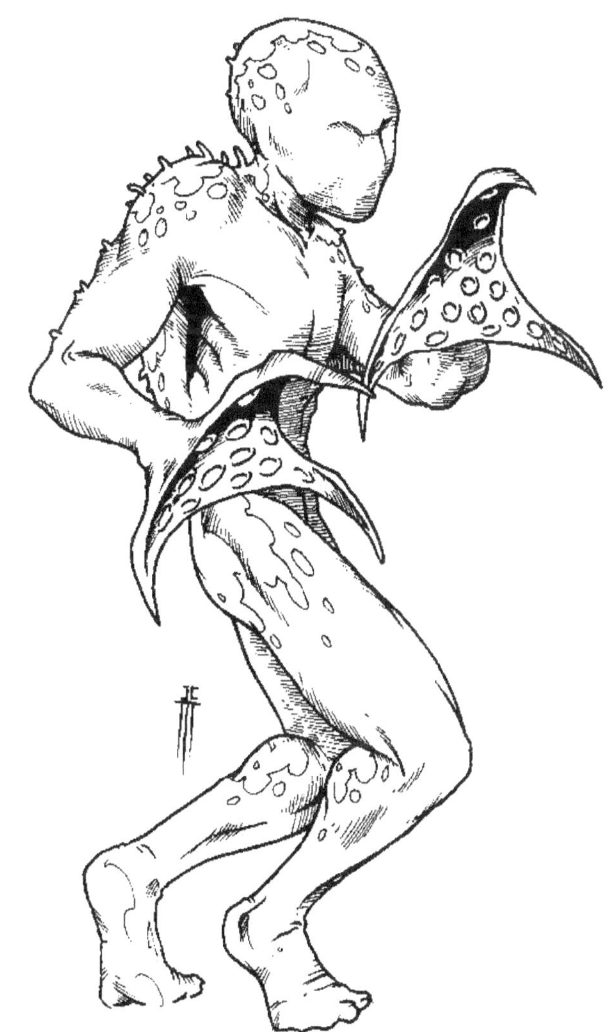

Trapper

Hit Dice: 12
Armor Class: 0 [19]
Attack: Buffet (1d8+1)
Saving Throw: 3
Special: Smother, resistance to edged or piercing weapons (50%), resistance to cold and fire (50%), surprise on 1-3 on 1d6
Move: 6
Alignment: Neutrality
Challenge Level/XP: 14/2600

A trapper resembles a manta ray with brownish-gray flesh turning lighter on its underside. No discernible eyes or appendages can be seen. Trappers are thought to be distant relatives of the lurker above (see that entry). Unlike their relatives, however, trappers mimic the floor of a building, dungeon, or other structure. By manipulating their body structure while covering the floor, trappers can form a box that resembles a small trunk or chest. This is usually enough to lure would-be-adventurers to their doom.

A trapper waits until its prey is almost centered on its body near the "trunk" or "chest" before it strikes. It then quickly folds and wraps its body around its unsuspecting prey attempting to smother and squeeze it until it is dead.

A trapper can try to wrap a creature in its body as an attack. If successful, it establishes a hold and deals buffet damage each round the hold is maintained. Further, a grappled opponent must hold its breath (2 rounds per point of constitution) or suffocate. After this period of time, the character must make a saving throw in order to continue holding her breath. When the character fails one of these saving throws, she suffocates.

Attacks that hit an engulfing trapper deal half their damage to the monster and half to the trapped victim.

Answer Me These

Questions Three

You come to a crossroads in a dungeon. The crossroads is composed of a chamber of red stone. The chamber measures 15 feet wide and long with an 8-foot ceiling. The center of the chamber (10 feet x 10 feet) is sunken about five feet below the rest of the chamber. On each wall of the upper chamber there is a straight passage leading away to other adventures. Each of these passages is closed by a door that looks like a stained glass window. Each window appears to show events in the romance of a learned duchess and a scribe.

In the sunken portion of the chamber there is a small platform holding an amethyst-colored lyre. In skilled hands, the *amethyst lyre* produces lovely music that has as a side effect the ability to animate images (on tapestries, stained glass windows, bas-relief, etc), allowing the musician to ask these objects (i.e. if only these walls could speak) three questions. Once an object has been asked these three questions, it can never be questioned again.

This treasure is guarded by a trapper mimicing the form of the sunken floor.

Credit

The Trapper originally appeared in the *Strategic Review #5* (© TSR/Wizards of the Coast, 1975) and later in the First Edition *Monster Manual* (© TSR/Wizards of the Coast, 1977) and is used by permission.

Copyright Notice

Author Scott Greene, based on original material by Gary Gygax.

Treant, Lightning

Hit Dice: 8
Armor Class: 2 [17]
Attacks: 2 strikes (2d8)
Saving Throw: 8
Special: magical powers, electric healing, immune to electricity, resists fire
Move: 12
Alignment: Neutrality
Challenge Level/XP: 10/1,400

A lightning treant is an animated, yet dead, moss-covered tree. Its bark is darkened with age and no leaves appear on its branches. At will, a lightning treant can create *faerie fire*, and three times per day, it can cast *lightning bolt*. Any attack that deals electrical damage heals 3 hit points per spell level. The hardened bark of a lightning treant resists fire, so that the creature takes half damage from flames.

The Tree House

The arch-druid Gorebourne lives in the Tanglethorn Thicket. Gorebourne (who is chaotic toward civilization and also happens to be infected with lycanthropy) has enslaved a lightning treant to entertain his youngsters. He attached a stout tree house high in the lightning treant's upper branches. He young sons ride the treant through the woods, wreaking havoc on all who cross their path. His sons respect nature, but have inherited their father's disdain for civilization. They attack and destroy any settlements that arise too close to the Tanglethorn Thicket. If given warning, the treant poses as a tree while the two boys taunt travelers. They have amassed a stockpile of rotten fruit, bags of feces, chestnut burs and bladders of putrid fish oil to throw at passers-by. Other than taunting PCs, the boys are too young to have any combat experience.

Copyright Notice
Author Casey Christofferson.

Tri-Flower Frond

Hit Dice: 2
Armor Class: 6 [13]
Attack: 4 tendrils (1d3 plus sleep)
Saving Throw: 16
Special: Acid, fluid drain, sleep, camouflage, surprise on a roll of 1-3 on 1d6
Move: 0
Alignment: Neutrality
Challenge Level/XP: 4/120

A tri-flower frond has stalks 5 to 8 feet tall. It is deep green with trumpet-shaped flowers of red, yellow, and orange topping its stalks. Tri-flower fronds are carnivorous plants found in warm (and occasionally temperate) forests. They are immobile creatures that reproduce by releasing seeds into the air and allowing either the wind (or creatures who happen to come into contact with them) to carry them wherever they go. Seeds take root once they touch the ground, and within a few months, a new tri-flower frond appears. These creatures are generally most active during the day and dine on fresh meat, having no preference as to the source.

A tri-flower frond attacks by firing a number of tendrils from its orange flower. The creature has 4 tendrils, plus 1 per Hit Dice above 3. A fired tendril causes an opponent struck to fall into a deep, coma-like sleep if it fails a saving throw. This effect is similar to a *sleep* spell, except it can affect a creature of any Hit Dice and slapping or attacking an affected creature does not wake it. A slept creature awakens on its own after 1d4 hours. A *dispel magic* spell ends the sleep effect.

If a tri-flower frond sleeps a victim, it pulls the opponent close and droops over it, allowing its yellow bloom to drip a shower of caustic acid (1d6 damage) on the sleeping victim while it inserts a needle-like tendril from its red bloom into the victim's body and drains fluids.

Against a sleeping or helpless foe, a tri-flower frond releases a needle-sharp tendril from its red bloom that pierces the opponent and drains its body fluids. This deals 1d4 points of constitution damage each round. At 0 constitution, a victim dies.

Flowers of the Triskelion

In the midst of a steamy rain forest there is a sort of labyrinth constructed of white stone and surrounded by a small lake of still water. The labyrinth is actually in the form of a triskelion. It has three entrances, tall, narrow doors of polished white wood at each foot of the triskelion. The walls, inside and outside, are scupulously clean.

At the center of the triskelion, where the three passages meet, there is a shrine built to honor Tricrucia, the goddess of forked passages. Tricrucia appears as a woman with three arms and three legs. In one of her hands she holds a military fork. This particular state, carved from the same white stone as the labyrinth, stands in the middle of a patch of three tri-flower fronds. Although obscured by the dangerous foliage, one of the idol's feet rests upon a golden sphere. The sphere cannot be removed without damaging it, leaving it worth about 50 gp. Those who do not molest the sphere, and instead place their foreheads against it while whispering a prayer to the strange goddess receive the equivalent of a *find the path* spell the next three times they come to an underground crossroads.

The pixies and sprites of the forest come to the shrine each day at midnight to clean the labyrinth, collect corpses (they are thrown into the lake for the fish) and their equipment (it is retained by the fairies as treasure) and tend the tri-flower fronds. The carnivorous plants regard the fairies as friends and do not harm them. If they discover the plants dead and the idol molested, they will hunt down the profaners and exact revenge.

Credit

The Tri-Flower Frond originally appeared in the First Edition module *S3 Expedition to the Barrier Peaks* (© TSR/Wizards of the Coast, 1980) and later in the First Edition *Monster Manual II* (© TSR/Wizards of the Coast, 1983) and is used by permission.

Copyright Notice

Author Scott Greene, based on original material by Gary Gygax.

Troblin

This hideous humanoid creature is a twisted amalgamation of extra limbs, thickened hide, and protruding growths.

Hit Dice: 3
Armor Class: 8 [11]
Attacks: 2 claws (1d4) and bite (1d6), or weapon (1d6) and bite (1d6)
Saving Throw: 14
Special: Regenerates 2 hp/round, mutation
Move: 9
Alignment: Chaos
Challenge Level/XP: 4/120

A troblin is a twisted creature, born of the union of a troll and a goblin. In general, troblins stand 5 feet tall, with crooked noses, long arms and legs, and large flapping feet. A troblin shares in the characteristics of both its parents, resembling a very tall goblin with troll-like facial features. Its skin is blotched in shades of green, grey, and dull yellow. Its eyes range from pale red to an ochre color. Troblins dress in drab-colored clothing and furs made from the hides of animals. Troblins often suffer hideous mutations after they regenerate as their body warps into inexplicable shapes.

Troblin Mutations

Each troblin has the potential to possess 1d2 random mutations brought about by its bizarre regeneration. Roll on the table below for each mutation.

1d20	Mutation
1-2	Dual forearm; claw damage increased (1d6)
3-4	Dual foreleg; move increases by 3
5-6	Massive scarring; armor increases -1[+1]
7	Multiple muscles; damage bonus to claw attack (1d8)
8	Shortened tendons; move increases by 9
9	Redundant vital organs; +2 hit points per HD
10	Third leg; move increases by 6
11	Two arms on one side; gains an additional claw attack
12	Two heads; never surprised
13-20	No mutation

Eye of the Beholder

A small figure moves among the trees, being careful to stay just outside the flickering light of campfires. The creature barely four feet tall and wears a dark wool robe cloak that covers it from head to foot. The creature hides its face behind a delicate porcelain mask. The mask is expressionless, just a painted-on mouth set beneath two small holes for the creature's eyes. Fine curls of dark paint wend down the mask's cheeks like tears. The creature shuffles through the underbrush, dragging one leg miserably. One misshapen hand stretches forth, holding a bright red apple in a gloved hand. The other hand is palm up, expecting payment.

Errax Boneshiver, a misshapen troblin, is a lonely creature who just wants to make friends. Unfortunately, his deformities – the left side of his face is a mass of scar tissue, and he drags a useless third leg that extends backward from behind his right knee – mark him as an outcast. Errax lives in a small lean-to in the forest, where he tends a small apple orchard. The trees are hearty and produce bright red, delicious apples. Errax's secret? He mixes a little of his sweat and blood into a smelly fertilizer he sprays on the trees and their fruit each morning.

Unknown to Errax, the apples are mutating under his ministrations. Any PC eating one of the fruit must save or suffer a troblin mutation from the "special brew" used to fertilize the apples. A PC might grow a third arm over the next week, or suffer intense scarring after his next fight. Roll on the troblin mutation chart or create your own deformity to inflict on the unlucky PC.

Copyright Notice
Author Erica Balsley.

Troll, Cave

Hit Dice: 4
Armor Class: 0 [19]
Attack: 2 claws (1d4) and bite (1d4)
Saving Throw: 13
Special: Rend, regenerate 2 hp/round, *haste, spider climb*
Move: 24
Alignment: Chaos
Challenge Level/XP: 7/600

This ugly humanoid appears to be about 6 feet tall. Its leathery skin is blackish-gray and its eyes are yellow. It has long, upright ears, almost elven in nature. Its arms and legs are long and slender and end in wicked-looking claws.

Cave trolls are smaller cousins of the normal troll and are found in all types of subterranean realms. They are as deadly, or more so, than their larger brethren. Cave trolls have the same voracious appetite of the normal troll and sustain themselves on whatever they can find in their underground realms. Cave trolls have blackish-gray hides and yellow eyes.

Cave trolls stand 6 feet tall and weigh 300 pounds. They do not walk with the same hunched gait of their larger relatives. They stand upright and move with blinding speed. They speak the language of trolls.

Cave trolls rarely venture to the surface world, preferring the security and tranquility of the darkness they inhabit. If extremely hungry or if food is scarce, however, a cave troll ventures to the surface and attacks whatever it finds near its lair.

Cave trolls often use deception when they first encounter prey, especially intelligent prey. Their troll heritage often leads to the misconception that they are slow in combat, which they gladly allow their opponents to believe — until the cave troll strikes or moves. Only then is the ruse negated and the true nature of the troll revealed. Cave trolls attack by grabbing and rending an opponent. If a cave troll hits with both claw attacks, it latches onto the opponent's body and tears the flesh. This attack automatically deals an additional 2d4 points of damage.

A cave troll is affected by permanent *haste* and *spider climb* effects. The haste ability can be dispelled, but the spider climb cannot.

Fire and acid deal normal damage to a cave troll. If a cave troll loses a limb or body part, the lost portion grows back in 3d6 minutes. The creature can reattach the severed member instantly by holding it to the stump.

Gold Was the Worst of It

You enter a chamber that measures 30 feet long and 15 feet wide, with a 10-foot high ceiling. The chamber is lined with reddish-brown bricks in a fishbone pattern. Every three feet, running down the length of the walls at chest height to a human are black ceramic disks. There are 12 disks in all, 6 on each wall, they are always set facing one another. The disks are flat and unadorned and measure about 2 feet in diameter. Set in the floor there is an iron hatch, the only exit from the room besides the entrance.

Coursing between each set of disks is what looks like a swarm of shadowy particles. Touching this stream of particles causes 1d4 points of damage and causes the body part to throb - throbbing hands cannot hold anything for 1 hour, while a throbbing foot reduces a person's movement rate by half for one hour. Mirrors do not reflect the particles and nothing short of lead blocks them at all. If damaged (AC 1 [18], 45 hp) or blocked by lead (see below), the particle stream ceases and a cave troll appears in its place. The trolls fight until killed, disappearing into the flow of particles if it flow is returned to normal.

If the iron hatch is opened, the shadow particles immediately change direction, running from the disks (on both sides) and into the revealed shaft. Each stream that hits a person causes damage as described above. The shaft leads into a small chamber (10 feet wide and long, 7 feet tall) that contains another black disk, this one floating in mid-air and spinning like a coin. If touched and any particle flows are still active above, the person immediately disappears and replaces one of the cave trolls in the particle flow, the troll appearing in the chamber with the floating disk. If no flows continue, the disk throbs with shadowy energy, causing the damage described above each round one is in the room with it. If destroyed, the release of energy causes 4d4 points of damage to all in the room and causes all metal in the room to change to gold.

Copyright Notice

Troll, Flame-Spawned

Hit Dice: 6+3
Armor Class: 4 [15]
Attacks: 2 claws (1d4 +1d6 fire), 1 bite (1d8 + 1d6 fire)
Saving Throw: 11
Special: Fiery, regenerates, immune to fire, vulnerable to acid and cold
Move: 12
Alignment: Chaos
Challenge Level/XP: 10/1,400

Flame-spawned trolls look like normal trolls, but with fire dancing around their reddish-tinged skin. Flame-spawned trolls regenerate 3 hit points per round. The only way to utterly kill a troll is to submerse it in acid or freeze it. Flame-spawned trolls can even regrow lopped-off heads and limbs. Flame-spawned trolls take double damage from acid and cold, and do not regenerate such damage.

Troll God

A 15-foot-diameter ball of fire dominates this area. It appears as if a fireball spell failed to detonate and remains in a permanent suspended state. The fireball produces heat and damage if touched but does not explode. It remains in the room and never burns out.

A group of trolls have adopted this as a holy site and worship at the fire. The trolls bring regular sacrifices to the fireball and have even made up an elaborate (for a troll) religion based on the fireball. They have built a "safety wall" of bones to signify the danger area. The ball of fire conceals Gulumpus, a flame-spawned troll who is the self-proclaimed troll god.

Long ago, the misfired spell transformed Gulumpus into his current state. Since then, Gulumpus rules this small clan with fear and brute force. Normally, 2d4 trolls tend to Gulumpuses' needs. The center of the fireball holds a molten pool of miscellaneous coins given to the troll god. The mound of slag is worth 7,000 gp if cooled and the metals separated. It weighs 300 pounds and has a mixture of iron and other metals infused within the mass.

Copyright Notice
Author Scott Greene.

Troll, Ice

Hit Dice: 2
Armor Class: 7 [12]
Attack: 2 claws (1d6)
Saving Throw: 16
Special: +1 or better weapon to hit, immunity to cold, double damage from fire, regenerate 2 hp/round, vulnerability to slashing weapons
Move: 12
Alignment: Chaos
Challenge Level/XP: 4/120

Ice trolls are relatives of normal trolls, but are decidedly more cunning, ruthless, evil, and despicable. They make their homes in very cold climates, always near a pool of water (either natural or troll-made). The strongest (and sometimes most intelligent) member of a band is usually the leader. They have semitransparent flesh of light blue and cold, stark white eyes.

Ice trolls savor the taste of human flesh and construct their lairs near civilized areas where humans are plentiful. Ice trolls often set traps for humans and either devours them immediately or captures them and carries them back to their lair. Captured humans are caged and fattened up before they are eaten.

An ice troll stands about 8 feet tall and weighs 450 pounds. Ice trolls do not possess any body hair. They speak the language of trolls.

If an ice troll hits with both claw attacks, it latches onto the opponent's body and tears the flesh for an additional 2d6 points of damage.

If an opponent rolls a natural 20 with a slashing weapon against an ice troll, the ice troll must succeed on a saving throw or lose a limb (roll 1d6: 1-3 arm, 4-6 leg; 50% chance of either right or left). An ice troll that loses a leg falls to the ground, but can continue moving at one-half speed. Severed limbs cannot attack but move at a speed of 30 feet toward the nearest source of water or ice.

Fire and acid deal normal damage to an ice troll. If an ice troll loses a limb or body part, the lost portion grows back in 2d6 minutes so long as both the ice troll and lost body part are within 30 feet of each other and are both in contact with ice or water. The creature can reattach the severed member instantly by holding it to the stump, but only if the severed member has been in contact with ice or water for at least 1 round.

Sorceress on Ice

Your adventures take you into a cave of ice. The cave measures 30 feet wide and 40 feet long with a ceiling 20 feet high in the center. The walls and ice pillars in the room are faceted and are as reflective as mirrors. The cave is inhabited by a band of 1d4+2 ice trolls. The cave is very unstable, and loud noises or shocks (such as from fireballs or lightning bolts) have a 1 in 6 chance of causing giant icicles to fall from the ceiling. Each round the icecicles fall, roll an attack against each creature in the cavern as though from a 3 HD monster. A successful hit indicated 1d6 points of damage.

A small tunnel, for all intents and purposes a secret passage due to the reflective nature of its surroundings, leads to a deeper ice cave. This ice cave holds the frozen corpse of a sorceress wrapped in an ermine cloak and wearing a crimson dress and fur-lined boots. The corpse's face is twisted in a look of hopelessness. There is a 1 in 6 chance the corpse's spirit still haunts the chamber as a spectre. In her frozen hand there is a silver flute. When blown, the flute summons a murder of ravens from mid-air. The ravens remain for 10 rounds before disappearing.

Credit

The Ice Troll originally appeared in the First Edition *Fiend Folio* (© TSR/Wizards of the Coast, 1981) and is used by permission.

Copyright Notice

Author Scott Greene, based on original material by Russell Cole.

Troll, Rock

Hit Dice: 8
Armor Class: 0 [19]
Attack: 2 claws (1d6), bite (1d6)
Saving Throw: 8
Special: Rend, regenerate 3 hp/round, vulnerability to sunlight
Move: 12/9 (burrowing)
Alignment: Chaos
Challenge Level/XP: 9/1100

A rock troll stands nearly twice as tall as a normal man. Its hide is earth-colored and its hair is dark. Its eyes are deep brown. The creature's arms and legs are long and thin and end in sharpened talons. Its feet end in three-toed feet.

Rock trolls are relatives of the normal troll and make their lairs deep within the subterranean realms of the earth. Most underground creatures avoid rock trolls, as they are completely malign and evil, attacking any living creature, especially when hungry. They are quite fond of human and halfling flesh. Unlike common trolls, rock trolls cannot regenerate lost limbs, though they do possess the ability to quickly heal damage. A rock troll regenerates damage only if it is underground and touching dirt or earth.

Rock trolls are 10 feet tall and weigh about 600 pounds. They resemble their smaller relatives in most respects. The rock troll's hide is stone gray or brown, its hair is black or brown, and its eyes are dull brown. Rock trolls peak the language of trolls.

If a rock troll hits with both claw attacks, it latches onto the opponent's body and tears the flesh. This attack automatically deals an additional 2d6 points of damage.

A rock troll exposed to sunlight (not merely a *light* spell) is instantly turned to stone (as if by a *flesh to stone* spell) in the next round if its fails a saving throw. This effect is permanent, but can be dispelled if the rock troll is removed from the source of the sunlight and *stone to flesh* is cast on it. A rock troll must make a new saving throw each round it remains in sunlight.

Tuscadero Hideaway

A gang of 1d3+1 rock trolls has made a camp for itself in a large cavern with walls that appear to drip with fresh blood. The "blood" is actually a harmless organism related to green slime. Although slightly acidic, the slime feeds only on bacteria plucked from the air or from the surface of the damp stone.

The trolls have a few palettes of soiled furs and pelts and a treasure of 3,400 sp and 700 gp tucked underneath them. Although most of the beasts fight with sticks and stones, the largest owns a *+1 halberd* taken from an errant knight.

On the far eastern end of the cavern, there is a steep slope that leads to a sandy cavern filled with cracked and splintered bones. This cavern is inhabited by an undead ooze. Beyond this cavern there is an old hiding place once used by a notorious band of halfling highwaymen called the Tuscaderos. The halflings constructed a secret entrance that leads into a small, tunnel-like passage. They once hung their equipment and bags of treasure from hooks on the walls of the tunnel, which is about 30 feet long and runs at a slight curve. The only treasure yet remaining in the tunnel is a silver hip flask holding a very potent sleeping potion (imbiber sleeps a minimum of 24 hours and has strange nightmares the entire time, nightmares he believes are prophetic).

Copyright Notice
Author Scott Greene.

Troll, Swamp

Hit Dice: 3
Armor Class: 3 [16]
Attack: 2 claws (1d6), bite (1d8)
Saving Throw: 14
Special: Swamp dependent, surprise on 1-2 on 1d6
Move: 12
Alignment: Chaos
Challenge Level/XP: 3/60

Swamp trolls are large, stocky, dark gray or brown hunched humanoids with large, upward-curving fangs jutting from their lower jaws. Their flesh is slick and slimy like moss. Swamp trolls make their lairs deep in swampland and marshes away from more settled areas, but not far enough away where they cannot hunt humans if game and other food runs scarce in the swamps.

Swamp trolls are 7-foot tall hunched humanoids and weigh about 400 pounds. Swamp trolls speak the language of trolls.

Swamp trolls keep their bodies covered in a thick coating of mud and swamp water. Without such a coating, they eventually suffocate. They can survive away from their murky home for 10 hours. After that, they suffocate.

Troblin Feast

In the midst of a deep marsh of cool, black water, white and yellow water lillies and cattails there is a ruin of narrow raised walks constructed of black, porous stone. These stone walkways are crumbling in spots and seem to lead to a central platform marked by a dozen basalt pillars in various states of decay. On the night of each new moon, a gang of 1d4+4 swamp trolls gathers at this place for a gruesome feast.

The central platform is actually a pit carved from a single piece of basalt, and thus fairly water tight (though it is covered with a sheen of water, various mosses and lichens and the odd jelly or ooze. The pit is about 10 feet deep and 40 feet in diameter, with gently sloping walls.

At each new moon, the trolls of the swamp gather here with dozens of troblin captives taken in the surrounding marshes and hills. The troblins are kept in crude wooden cages, which are piled in the middle of the pit. At the proper moment, one swamp troll releases the troblins, who quickly try to scurry away. The gathered swamp trolls waste no time in falling upon the creatures, tearing away their limbs and wolfing them down. The horribly injured creatures are allowed to writhe about in pain, still desperately trying to escape. Those that escape into the swamp are granted their freedom. Those that do not, but still live, are re-caged and kept for the next midnight feast.

Troll, Two-Headed

Hit Dice: 10
Armor Class: 3 [16]
Attack: 2 weapons (1d10) or 2 claws (1d6)
Saving Throw: 5
Special: Rend, regenerate 1 hp/round, only surprised on roll of 1 on 1d8
Move: 12
Alignment: Chaos
Challenge Level/XP: 11/1700

The two-headed troll is thought to be the hideous offspring of an ettin and female troll. Sages contend that no other explanation is possible concerning this monster. Two-headed trolls prefer to make their lairs underground and away from civilization. Although believed to be the offspring of an ettin and troll, they do not associate with the former, but are often found leading the latter during raids or wars.

A two-headed troll stands about 10 feet tall and weighs about 2,000 pounds. Its hide is mottled green or gray, and its facial features resemble that of a standard troll. Two-headed trolls typically dress in rags or tattered clothes or even battered and rusted armor on occasion. Their legs end in three-toed feet, and their powerful arms end in sharpened claws. The two-headed troll has the slow moving gait of the normal troll, but does not walk hunched over.

Two-headed trolls speak the language of trolls and the language of ettins.

If a two-headed troll hits with both of its claw attacks, it latches onto the opponent's body and tears the flesh for an additional 2d6 points of damage.

A two-headed troll heals 1 point of damage each round so long as it has at least 1 hit point. It cannot regenerate limbs.

Troll Blood Soup

A deep pit in a dungeon is occupied by a two-headed troll. The pit is 20 feet in diameter and the ceiling is 30 feet high. The pit is entered via two tunnels set about 10 feet above the floor of the pit. The troll's leg is chained to the floor by a thick, iron chain. Four shadowy alcoves are set into the walls about 15 feet above the floor of the pit, two on either side of the entrance/exit tunnels.

The troll is in bad shape, currently possessing about 15 hit points. Creatures hidden in the alcoves are casting iron darts at the two-headed troll, making sure they do not kill the beast. The troll's ichor runs onto the floor and into little channels, then drains and then into a cauldron a level below. This blood is collected by four shamans and used in their magic.

In each alcove there is a shaman of the underworld tribes - an orc, a hobgoblin, a bugbear and a goblin. Each alcove holds a secret door to a spiral stair that leads into the cauldron chamber about 10 feet below. Each shaman is accompanied by a single bodyguard with +2 HD and five normal members of their tribes in the cauldron chamber. From the cauldron chamber there are passages that lead into the remainder of the dungeon.

Credit

The Two-Headed Troll originally appeared in the First Edition *Fiend Folio* (© TSR/Wizards of the Coast, 1981) and is used by permission.

Copyright Notice

Author Scott Greene, based on original material by Oliver Charles MacDonald.

Tsathar

Tsathar, Common

Hit Dice: 2
Armor Class: 3 [16]
Attack: Weapon (1d8) and bite (1d4); or 2 claws (1d6) and bite (1d4)
Saving Throw: 16
Special: Leap, *summon hydrodaemon* amphibious, implant, slimy
Move: 12/12 (swimming)
Alignment: Chaos
CL/XP: 3/60

Tsathar Scourge

Hit Dice: 4
Armor Class: 3 [16]
Attack: Weapon (1d8) and bite (1d4); or 2 claws (1d6) and bite (1d4)
Saving Throw: 13
Special: Leap, amphibious, implant slimy
Move: 12/12 (swimming)
Alignment: Chaos
CL/XP: 5/240

A tsathar (pronounced "suh-Thar") resembles an upright, humanoid frog with gray flesh and reddish-gold eyes. Its humanoid arms end in wicked claws.

Tsathar have little contact with surface-dwelling races, preferring to make their lairs deep underground or in dark swamps. When they lair above ground, they are nocturnal. Some few surface-dwelling tsathar have joined cults of assassins. Though cults and gods vary in makeup and worship, nearly all tsathar worship the foul, slime-covered demon-god Tsathogga.

Tsathar scourges are special tsathar in charge of breeding the dangerous "killer" frogs. They wear a badge of station that indicates their control over the various beasts. All frogs bred by the tsathar obey scourges. Tsathar scourges never become priests and thus do not have the *summoning* ability of common tsathars.

Tsathar are sexless and reproduce by implanting an egg into a host, which can be any form of living creature. Normally, creatures are captured or bred to serve as hosts—dire rats and giant frogs being common hosts. It is said that priests must be born of an egg implanted into a humanoid or other creature of great intelligence.

A typical tsathar stands 6 feet tall and weighs about 300 pounds. Tsathar speak their own strange, guttural language and the eldritch speech of demons.

Tsathar prefer to use short, barbed spears and curved daggers in combat. They sometimes employ nets as well. They charge into combat with maniacal fury, and rarely use elaborate tactics, unless a scourge or priest is present to control them. They favor leather armor crafted from the hides of the frogs they breed. Priests favor the curved dagger in battle.

Scourges prefer to loose their servant frogs on opponents, allowing common tsathar soldiers to engage opponents hand-to-hand. This is not to say that they are not able fighters, for they certainly are. They favor barbed spears, curved daggers, and light armor such as leather or ring armor. They also often carry nets to snare their charges or foes. If their frogs are in danger, they leap in with their spears and attack.

Tsathar can leap up to 30 feet horizontally (10 feet vertically) and make an attack in the same round. Tsathar wearing armor heavier than ring armor cannot use this ability.

A tsathar with at least five levels of cleric can, once per day, attempt to summon a hydrodaemon with a 40% chance of success. Tsathar scourges do not possess this ability.

Tsathar are sexless, reproducing by injecting eggs into living hosts. An egg can be implanted only into an unconscious or restrained host. Giant frogs, bred for this very purpose, are the most common host. Accompanying the egg is an anaesthetizing poison that causes the host to fall unconscious for the two-week gestation period of the egg unless the host succeeds on a saving throw. If the save succeeds, the host remains conscious, but is violently ill (-10 penalty to hit and save) 24 hours before the eggs hatch. When the eggs mature, the young tsathar emerge from the host, killing it in the process. A *cure disease* spell rids the victim of the eggs.

Abrupt exposure to bright light (such as sunlight or a *light* spell) blinds tsathars for 1 round.

Because tsathar continuously cover themselves with muck and slime, they are difficult to grapple. Webs, magic or otherwise, do not affect tsathar, and they usually can wriggle free from most other forms of confinement.

Tsathars as Characters

A tsathar can advance as a fighter (3rd level maximum, 4th level with a strength of 13+) or cleric (5th level maximum, 6th level with a wisdom of 13+) or as multi-classed cleric/fighters if they have both a strength and wisdom score of 13+.

The Tsathar first appeared in the **Necromancer Games** adventure *Tomb of Abysthor* (©2001, Clark Peterson, Necromancer Games, Inc.) as servants of the demonic frog god Tsathogga.

It's Not Easy Being Green

A pack of 1d6+4 tsathar is holed up in a tower of white chalk set in the middle of a noisy swamp. The tower is 15 feet in diameter and 20 feet tall. The chaotic frog men are accompanied by 1d4+1 tsathar scourges and a clutch of 1d4+1 giant frogs. The frog men were dispatched from their clanhold to see to this building, a shrine to their demon god Tsathogga. The shrine has three round doors set about 10 feet above the surface of the mucky swamp and are barred with bronze bars.

The tower is currently under siege by a swarm of 1d10+10 giant wasps. The wasps were spurred into action by a quasit in service to another demon prince. The frog men are running out of food and are getting nervous about the scourges' ability to control their giant frogs.

The idol in the shrine is a copper idol covered in verdigris and set with dozens of moss agates (worth about 500 gp in total). The idol is surrounded by four stone pots filled with everlasting fires under piles of red hot river stones. These pots are used to create a ritual steam bath, a recreation not currently being enjoyed by the beleaguered tsathar.

Credit

The Tsathar first appeared in the Necromancer Games adventure *D1 Tomb of Abysthor* (©2001, Clark Peterson and Bill Webb, Necromancer Games, Inc.) as servants of the demonic frog god Tsathogga.

Copyright Notice

Authors Clark Peterson, Bill Webb, and Scott Greene.

Tumblespark

Hit Dice: 5
Armor Class: 4 [15]
Attacks: Roll-over (1d6 + 1d6 electricity)
Saving Throw: 12
Special: electrical arc, immune to electricity, insubstantial form
Move: 12
Alignment: Neutrality
Challenge Level/XP: 5/240

A tumblespark looks like a giant tumbleweed whose form crackles and sparks with electricity. A tumblespark can grow to a diameter of 10 feet or more. A tumblespark is not solid, nor is it incorporeal. It attacks by rolling over all in its path dealing 1d6 points of damage plus 1d6 points of electricity damage. Once every 1d4 rounds, a tumblespark can release an arc of electricity against a single opponent within 10 feet that deals 4d6 points of damage. A successful save reduces the damage by half.

Spark of Attraction

This 50-foot-diameter circular chamber is built from black stone blocks fitted perfectly atop one another to create smooth outer walls. Set flush into the walls are 16 portals. Two opposite one another lead out of the room. The rest are filled with smooth black stone that glistens like a starless night sky.

In the center of the room is a burnished copper column rising from floor to ceiling. Elaborate sigils are carved down the column. At waist height, sixteen graphite buttons inlaid with silver patterns ring the metal. Each button corresponds to the door it faces.

When a button is pressed, the copper hums and a noticeable vibration fills the room. Sparks of lightning dance over the metal surface. The selected door opens two rounds later, the black stone sluicing away into nothingness to leave a black spongy void. The doors lead wherever the Game Referee wishes.

Pushing a button has a 1 in 6 chance of releasing a tumblespark into the chamber. The tumbling ball of energy is drawn by the energy created in the copper column and arrives fully charged and agitated. Each successive button raises the chance of an encounter by 1, so pressing three buttons in a row means a 3 in 6 chance of a tumblespark arriving.

Copyright Notice
Author Scott Greene.

Tunnel Worm

Hit Dice: 9
Armor Class: 3 [16]
Attack: Bite (2d6)
Saving Throw: 7
Special: Rend armor
Move: 9/9 (burrowing)
Alignment: Neutrality
Challenge Level/XP: 10/1400

A tunnel worm appears to be a 30-foot long sleek, black centipede with a long segmented body and many slender legs. Its huge mandibles are serrated and razor-sharp, and its eyes are multi-faceted. A ring of chitinous bone rings its oversized head.

The tunnel worm is a burrowing creature related to the monstrous centipede. It is a very aggressive predator and hunter, though it can sustain itself by scavenging. Its preferred food is fresh, raw meat.

A typical tunnel worm is 30 feet long, but can grow to a length of 60 feet.

Tunnel worms are very aggressive and attack anything that enters their territory. They usually wait beneath the surface of the ground and then burrow out to surprise and attack their opponents (treat this attack as a charge attack). A tunnel worm that has taken more than half its hit points in damage retreats to its lair unless it is cornered, in which case it fights to the death.

If a tunnel worm hits with its bite attack, it pulls apart any armor worn by its foe. This attack reduces the armor bonus of the armor by 1d4. Armor with an armor bonus reduced to 0 or lower is destroyed. Creatures not wearing armor are unaffected by this special attack.

Prime or Tunnel

In a secret glade in a trackless forest there are two golden pillars standing about 7 feet tall and 3 feet apart. The top of each pillar is concave. Scattered around the shady clearing are nine stones, each bearing a number from one to nine.

The golden pillars are a planar portal that is activated by placing stones atop both pillars. If the double digit number is prime, the portal is activated, with each prime number keyed to a different plane (Referees should tie the numbers to the planes he or she is using in their campaign). If a non-prime number is placed on the pillars, the portal activates and 1d4+1 tunnel worms pour into the glade.

Scratched into the ground before the pillars is "135", a clue to the mathematical logic involved in the portal.

Credit

The Tunnel Worm originally appeared in the First Edition *Monster Manual II* (© TSR/Wizards of the Coast, 1983) and is used by permission.

Copyright Notice

Author Scott Greene, based on original material by Gary Gygax.

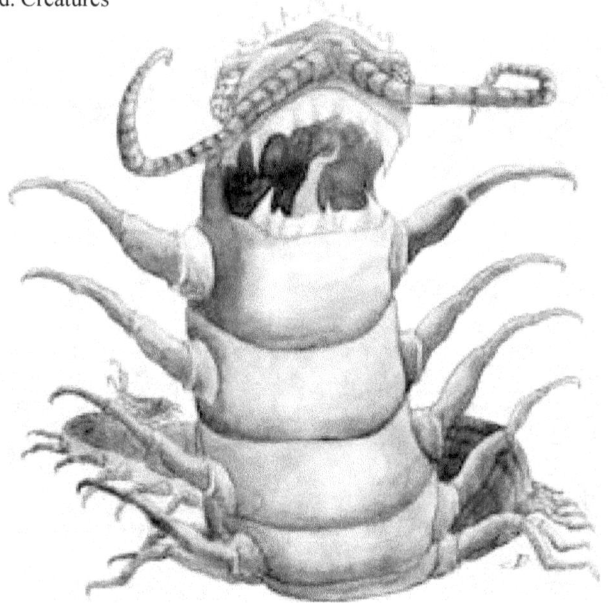

Turtle, Giant Bog

Hit Dice: 16
Armor Class: 3 [16], 5 [14] head, flippers
Attacks: 1 bite (4d6)
Saving Throw: 3
Special: swallow whole
Move: 3/12 (swim)
Alignment: Neutrality
Challenge Level/XP: 16/3,200

A giant bog turtle is about 20 feet long. Its carapace is brown or dark green and mottled with darker spots. Younger bog turtles have light stripes ringing their shell. As they age, the stripes slowly fade. A giant bog turtle's head, neck, and limbs are dark green or brown and leathery to the touch. Its undcrbclly is always lighter and is colored light green, gray, or pale yellow. If a bog turtle rolls a natural 20 on a bite attack, it swallows the victim whole (6d6 damage).

Slow Chase

The raft-city of Twain's Landing lives an idyllic existence on a redwood raft that supports wood-and-stone buildings housing nearly 300 people. Many of the residents are born and die on the raft without ever setting foot on dry land. The city floats around the Sin Mire's swampy waters. A giant movable series of paddlewheels in the center of the raft-city let it when it needs to, and giant rudders mounted on each edge of the massive square platform direct the raft's path. A line of giant turtle shells tethered to the city bob along in its wake.

The villagers trap the 20-foot giant turtles for food, and set the shells out as bait to attract more of the creatures. The plan worked a little too perfectly; a monstrous 50-foot snapping turtle now follows the village, forcing the city to keep moving to stay ahead of the beast. The lovelorn creature is big enough to capsize the floating city if it gets close enough.

Copyright Notice

Turtle-Shark

Hit Dice: 6
Armor Class: 3 [16]
Attacks: 1 bite (2d6)
Saving Throw: 11
Special: Capsize boat, shell, swallow whole
Move: 8/14 (swim)
Alignment: Neutrality
Challenge Level/XP: 6/400

A turtle-shark is a cross between a giant snapping turtle and a shark. Turtle sharks average 20 feet in length and weigh about 10,000 pounds. A submerged turtle-shark that surfaces under a boat or ship less than 20 feet long capsizes the vessel 95% of the time. It has a 50% chance to capsize a vessel that is 20 to 60 feet long, and a 20% chance to capsize one over 60 feet long at the Game Referee's discretion. Turtle-sharks swallow their prey whole on a roll 4 higher than the number needed to hit. If threatened, a turtle-shark can withdraw into its shell, leaving it almost completely impervious to attack.

Turtle-Shark, Stygian

Hit Dice: 18
Armor Class: 0 [19]
Attacks: 1 bite (4d8)
Saving Throw: 3
Special: +1 or better weapons needed to hit, capsize boat, spell resistance 35%, shell, swallow whole
Move: 8/14 (swim)
Alignment: Chaos
Challenge Level/XP: 20/4,400

The stygian turtle-shark averages 40 feet in length and weighs about 30,000 pounds. A submerged stygian turtle-shark that surfaces under a boat or ship less than 20 feet long capsizes the vessel 100% of the time. It has a 75% chance to capsize a vessel from 20 to 60 feet long, and a 50% chance to capsize one over 60 feet long. Stygian turtle-sharks swallow their prey whole on a roll 4 higher than the number needed to hit.

What Evil Beast Slouches Forth?

The rainy season has struck, six days and nights of water pouring out of the skies in buckets to drench the earth and anyone caught out in it. The trees and grasses are thriving, but the ground is a muddy mess that sinks beneath the boots of anyone slogging through it. Movement is halved in the sticking morass, and it's hard to see more than a few feet through the driving rain. Villagers are hunkering down indoors, only going out when they have to.

They may have to move soon, as a large turtle-shark is using the rain to move overland. It is wreaking havoc on everything in its cross-country trek, seeking food wherever it goes. A herd of cattle weathering under a grove of mangroves was the first victims, and most were sliced in half and eaten before they could shamble away. The turtle-shark decided to follow the mooing meat and its path is leading it directly into the small village of Fen-Krall.

Copyright Notice

Author Erica Balsley.

Twilight Mushrooms

Twilight mushrooms are purplish-black mushrooms about 4 to 6 inches in height. They grow in patches of 5-10 mushrooms and are only found in damp, dark underground areas. Twilight mushrooms sense vibrations and burst forth a cloud of noxious and choking dust when a living creature comes within 10 feet of a patch. Creatures within the area must succeed on a saving throw or take 2d6 points of damage. One minute later another saving throw must be made—even by those who succeeded on the first one—to avoid another 1d6 points of damage. Whether or not the saves are successful, a creature is disabled for 2d4 rounds from fits of choking and coughing. Such a creature can take no action other than to defend itself.

Sunlight renders twilight mushrooms dormant, and cold instantly destroys them.

Shortcut to the End of the Line

A slope of nearly bare stone sits in the midst of an otherwise verdant wood. Water seeps from cracks in the slope's face, indicating that a natural spring is located beneath it. This has made the slope slick with greenish slime (but not "green slime") and has furthermore covered it with 1d4 patches of 1d4+6 twilight mushrooms. The bloated remains of two young halflings lie at the bottom of the slope. The pair apparently stopped to investigate the mushrooms and were overcome by their noxious spores. The halfling bodies have not been touched, for the woodland is rife with game and the predators have learned to avoid the twilight mushrooms. Each halfling is dressed in green suits and leather cloaks. They both carry slings and daggers, and one has a leather sack filled with cuttings and safe mushrooms.

Copyright Notice
Author Scott Greene.

Ubue

Hit Dice: 3
Armor Class: 2 [17]
Attack: 3 clubs (1d8) or 3 strikes (1d6)
Saving Throw: 14
Special: Multiple personalities
Move: 9
Alignment: Chaos
Challenge Level/XP: 3/60

Ubues are a bizarre race that is among the rarest of intelligent races. They are so rare, in fact, that most people believe their existence to be only legend. At first sight, many adventurers assume that ubues are a race of three-headed ettins or trolls. Adventurers who have actually seen these strange creatures claim that the middle head of an ubue is a different sex from the other two. This is not true, however, and is in fact merely a side effect of the bizarre biology of these creatures. Ubues are ashen-skinned giants dressed in ragged animal hides. They have three heads, three arms and three legs. Ubue speak their own language.

The three heads of an ubue rarely get along with each other. Due to this division of personalities, there is a 15% chance in any given situation (usually once per encounter) that the heads get into an argument. An ubue engaged in an argument with itself takes a –2 circumstance penalty on attack rolls, saving throws and AC.

Ubues have a very primitive social system. The strongest male of any ubue tribe is the leader. Any adult male ubue has the right to challenge the tribal leader in ritual combat. The loser is banished from the tribe for a period of one full year, along with his family; ubues cannot tolerate weakness.

Female ubues usually give birth to only a single child. The birth of twins is seen as an ill omen, so one child is slain by the tribal shaman as a sacrifice to their god. The shaman casts bones or sticks to determine which child is to be the sacrifice. Because ubue society is strongly male-dominated, if one twin is male and the other female, it will always be the female child that is sacrificed.

Down by the Sea

Down by the shores of a frothy, beryl sea there is a village of squat, brick houses that look like bulging pumpkins. The village is inhabited by about 50 whalers and their families and would be unremarkable save for the tower that casts its shadow over the village. The tower is a temple dedicated to the sea god Proteus.

The tower is constructed of highly polished sea green stone and rises to a point. The tower stands 90 feet tall and is 30 feet in diameter. The walls are (apparently) 10 feet thick, leaving a 10-ft wide space in between them that is taken up by a long, spiral staircase. The stairs lead to a chamber in the conical top of the tower. This chamber holds several spiral horns taken from narwhals and lashed together into a roughly humanoid shape. When whalers are about to go out to sea, their captains climb these stairs, lighting candles at various alcoves set into the walls and making sure to bow at several extra-wide steps to avoid the hook-like blades that spring out from the ceiling.

The walls of the tower are not, in fact, solid. They contain a second set of spiral stairs that allow a clan of 3d10 ubue to follow the progress of people climbing the stairs. A number of secret doors that can only be opened from the secret stairs allow them to enter the main stairs and take away intruders that have been felled by the traps or who threaten the idol at the top of the tower.

The ubue dwell in a secret grotto beneath the tower. The grotto consists of a main living chamber and three smaller chambers. One of the smaller chambers is inhabited by the ubue chief, his rather ferocious wife and three noisy children. Another chamber is used as a dungeon/storage chamber. The ubue block it with a crude wooden gate fastened with a lock and chain. The final chamber is home to a phasm, a creature the ubues believe is the god Proteus himself. The phasm's chamber contains the

ubue's chamber, 1d3 x 1,000 sp, 1d6 x 1,000 gp and a piece of skrimshaw worth 10 gp.

Phasm: HD 15; AC 2 [17]; Atk 1 strike (1d3); Move 12; Save 3; CL/XP 17/3500; Special: Immune to poison, *sleep*, paralysis and *polymorph*, can assume any form up to 12 feet tall.

Credit
The Ubue originally appeared in the First Edition module *B3 Palace of the Silver Princess* (© TSR/Wizards of the Coast, 1981) and is used by permission.

Copyright Notice
Authors Scott Greene and Erica Balsley, based on original material by Jean Wells.

Vampire Rose

Hit Dice: 4
Armor Class: 4 [15]
Attack: Stalk (1d4)
Saving Throw: 13
Special: Camouflage
Move: 3
Alignment: Neutrality
Challenge Level/XP: 4/120

Vampire roses look like normal white rose bushes and are often mistaken for such. A vampire rose stands motionless until its prey moves within range, when it strikes with a thorny stalk. Opponents are grabbed and drained of blood. When fully sated with blood, a vampire rose's petals flush red.

A vampire rose can suck blood from a living victim with its thorns by making a successful attack with its stalk. If it gets a hold, it deals 1d6 points of damage each round until the victim breaks the hold with a successful open doors check.

Since a vampire rose looks like a normal white rose bush when at rest, it surprises on a roll of 1-3 on 1d6 (or 1-3 on 1d8 against druids and rangers).

Would Still Prick You With Its Thorns

The wealthy coastal kingdom you have entered is in a terrible state. The princess has been cast into a eternal, deathless sleep by pricking her finger on a deep crimson rose, the origin of which is unknown. A number of scholars and alchemists have been consulted, but none can find a cure. Archmages, enchantresses and wizards have been sent for, but none have yet arrived.

Adventurers who wish to try their hand at solving the problem will find a clue when they first step out of the city walls. An old woman carying a basket approaches them on the road. The basket is full of bouquets of deep crimson roses with thorny stems. If questioned about them, she reveals that they are to be found deep in the forest.

The old woman is an annis hag who disappears as soon as she answers the question. Naturally, the entire set up is a trap to lure worthies into the woods to be killed, their souls harvested for her demonic master. The black annis lives in a crumbling cottage surrounded by a patch of 1d3+1 vampiric roses. The annis hag keeps a treasure of 2d8 x 100 gp and a jargoon worth 15 gp in the cottage under the floorboards.

Annis: HD 7; AC -1 [20]; Atk 2 claws (1d6+1), bite (1d6); Move 15; Save 9; CL/XP 9/1100; Special: Magic resistance (50%), cast *obscuring mist* 3/day.

Credit

The Vampire Rose originally appeared in the First Edition module (revised edition) *B3 Palace of the Silver Princess* (© TSR/Wizards of the Coast, 1981) and is used by permission.

Copyright Notice

Author Scott Greene, based on original material by Tom Moldvay and Jean Wells.

Vapor Rat

Hit Dice: 1d4 hp
Armor Class: 7 [12]
Attacks: 1 bite (1d3)
Saving Throw: 18
Special: death throes, gaseous form, slowed by cold, heal 2 points/round, 5% are diseased
Move: 12
Alignment: Neutrality
Challenge Level/XP: 1/15

Vapor rats resemble normal rats in all respects. Though more intelligent, they possess a lot of the same traits and conduct themselves in much the same way as normal rats. When slain, their bodies burst in a cloud of grayish green vapors that fill a 10-foot radius and acts as a stinking cloud. Vapor rats can assume gaseous form once per day, and they heal 2 points per round. They are slowed by cold.

Rats on a Sinking Ship

A three-masted galleon sits broken across the Slister Reef, its central mast splintered at the deck and canted against the forward sail. A ragged hole at the waterline shows where sharp coral sliced open the wood. The ship sits atop the coral reef, but won't sail until repairs are made.

The hold is filled with the galleon's last cargo: a few tons of grain molded beyond use. Bits of string, a silver serving dish, a gold-braided sash and a handful of various coins (worth 120 gp total) sit atop the moldy grain. A colony of 3d6 vapor rats lives in the rotting grain.

Copyright Notice
Author Scott Greene.

Vapor Wasp

Hit Dice: 4
Armor Class: 7 [12]
Attacks: 1 sting (1d4 + poison)
Saving Throw: 13
Special: death throes, gaseous form, slowed by cold, heal 2 points/round, poison
Move: 1/18 (flying)
Alignment: Neutrality
Challenge Level/XP: 5/240

Vapor wasps resemble giant wasps in all respects. In some rare species their coloration seems to vary slightly (a blue stripe on the abdomen is the giveaway). When slain, their bodies burst in a cloud of grayish green vapors that fill a 10-foot radius and acts as a stinking cloud. Vapor wasps can assume gaseous form once per day, and they heal 2 points per round. They are slowed by cold.

Smoke and Stings

A bloated body lies on the ground beside a fallen tree in the Kajaani Forest, the man's features and hands puffed up beyond recognition. His skin is beet red and his clothes stretched so tightly on his body that his corpse looks like an overstuffed sausage. A canister emitting a stream of smoke sits beside the man, gray wisps rising into the still air. Hanging from his belt are a small axe, a wedge and a length of coiled rope.

A nest of vapor wasps lives in an underground nest nearby, and the man had the foolhardy idea of smoking the creatures out so he could chop down timber to repair his home. He had no idea the creatures were anything other than normal wasps, and assumed his "smoke 'em out" strategy would work this time as well. The man merely angered the vaporous creatures, which swarmed out and stung him to death. The insects are still extremely riled up, and anyone approaching the body is bombarded by 3d8 vapor wasps.

Copyright Notice
Author Scott Greene.

Vegepygmy

Hit Dice: 1
Armor Class: 3 [16]
Attack: 1 strike (1d4) or weapon (1d6)
Saving Throw: 17
Special: Immunity to electricity, resistance to piercing weapons (50%)
Move: 12
Alignment: Neutrality
Challenge Level/XP: 2/30

A vegepygmy resembles a humanoid with green vegetable-like skin and razor-sharp claws. Its head sports two large yellow eyes, a wide mouth, inset nose, and a topknot of dark brown leaves. Leafy tendrils protrude from its shoulders, midsection, arms, and legs.

When a living creature is slain by russet mold (see that entry), it rises as a 1 HD vegepygmy. Vegepygmies are plants possessed of a primitive intelligence. They make their home deep in the forests or underground away from most settled areas. They are hunters and scavengers, and carnivorous, preying on living creatures weaker than themselves. A 1 HD vegepygmy stands 2 feet tall, gaining 6" to its height with each additional HD. The largest vegepygmies, called chiefs, have 6 HD and stand 4-1/2 feet tall. Though they do not seem to have ears, it is well known that vegepygmies can hear.

Vegepygmies do not speak, but communicate with others of their kind by thumping their chest or rapping their spears on rocks, earth, or some other solid surface. It is not known if or how they communicate with other creatures.

The chiefs are the only vegepygmies with a spore attack. A chief vegepygmy can release a cloud of spores in a 40-foot spread. A living creature caught within the cloud must succeed on a saving throw or be paralyzed for 2d6 rounds. After the paralysis wears off, the character must succeed on another saving throw or take 3d6 points of constitution damage.

At constitution 0 a creature dies, and rises as a 4 HD vegepygmy in one day. If a *cure disease* spell is cast on a paralyzed victim before the paralysis wears off, he does not have to attempt the second saving throw and takes no constitution damage.

Vegepygmies often share their lairs with shriekers and russet molds.

Brass Tubes and Glass Prisms

Via a secret passage in a dungeon one might come upon an underground vault inhabited by a tribe of vegepygmies. The tribe consists of 3d10 x 10 vegepygmies (1 HD), 2d4 guards (2 HD), 2d4 bodyguards (3 HD), one subchief (4 HD) per fifty vegepygmies and a single 6 HD chief. The vegepygmies also keep 1d4 patches of russet mold, 1d3 shriekers and 1d20+4 thornies as guard animals.

The vault of the vegpygmies is about 1 mile wide and 2 miles long, with a ceiling that rises as high as 300 feet. The vault has numerous ledges and side caverns, all lit with a greenish light that emanates from a deep pit in the center of the vault. The pit is 30 feet deep and contains a glowing orb of glassy metal. The tribe's patches of russet mold grow on the sides of this pit. Captives of the vegepygmies are thrown into this pit.

Although the vegepygmies live as primitives, making weapons from flint deposits in their vault, they possess a wondrous library that was clearly handed down from a more advanced people. The library is located in a long tunnel that spurs from the main vault. The library consists of a number of brass tubes. Inside each tube there is a glass prism. When a prism is held up to the light and one looks in the end, a stream of strange glyphs seems to rush at the eye. Those who understand these glyphs can read these prisms as though they were books. Several of the prisms are alchemical reference tomes, and one is the spellbook of a 6th level alien magic-user.

Vilstrak (Tunnel Thug)

Hit Dice: 1
Armor Class: 1 [18]
Attack: 2 thumps (1d4)
Saving Throw: 17
Special: Merge with earth, surprise on roll of 1-3 on 1d6 in rocky areas
Move: 12
Alignment: Neutrality (chaotic tendencies)
Challenge Level/XP: 2/30

Vilstraks (or tunnel thugs) dwell underground, away from the surface world. A vilstak is a bipedal, man-sized semi-humanoid seemingly carved of stone. It has an insect-like head, long, large arms and thick, trunk-like legs that end in hoof-like feet. Though they have no allergy or reaction to sunlight, they disdain its existence, preferring the cold, damp blackness of their underground world. A vilstrak's lair is a "pocket" formed deep inside the earth. These pockets have no exits or entrances and are only reachable by those who can pass through stone or earth.

A typical vilstrak stands 6 feet tall and weighs about 200 pounds. Its arms have an extra joint between the elbow and wrist, and its arms end in large, powerful fists of stone. Vilstraks are gray or brown. They speak their own grating language.

A vilstrak can merge with earth or stone at will. A vilstrak can see what goes on outside the stone and it can remain merged as long as it desires.

Angry Spirits of the Mountains

A band of 2d8+4 vilstraks has taken up residence in a mountain pass. The resident barbarians of the mountains call them the spirits of the mountains and consider the pass to be taboo, attacking any who would venture into the pass and "anger the spirits". Adventurers have a 5 in 6 chance of encountering a band of resident barbarians including 1d10+10 berserkers, accompanied by a shaman (cleric or druid of 3rd to 7th level) wearing dozens of strings of cave bear fangs around their necks, ankles and wrists.

Three winters ago, a caravan carrying various parts needed to construct an iron golem was sacked by the vilstraks, who scattered the parts around their pass. The bodies of the victims were left to rot, and successive snows and icy winds have preserved the corpses in a macabre rictus. One of the corpses wears chainmail and carries a *+1 shield* emblazoned with the image of a white lily.

The vilstraks dwell in caverns beneath the pass, caverns that can be reached via a small cavern, big enough for a halfling, located about 300 feet up the side of one of the mountains that flanks the pass. The actual lair of the vilstraks measures about 20 feet in diameter, with a 10-foot high ceiling. It contains a treasure of 1d6 x 100 cp, 2d8 x 100 sp, 2d12 x 10 gp an orichalcum necklace (worth 2d8 x 10 gp) and an obsidian sphere worth 1d12 x 10 gp.

Credit

The Vilstrak originally appeared in the First Edition *Monster Manual II* (© TSR/Wizards of the Coast, 1983) and is used by permission.

Copyright Notice

Author Scott Greene, based on original material by Gary Gygax.

V

Volt (Bolt Wurm)

Hit Dice: 2
Armor Class: 3 [16]
Attack: Bite (1d4 plus blood drain) and tail slap (2d4)
Saving Throw: 16
Special: Blood drain, shock, immunity to electricity
Move: 0/12 (Flying)
Alignment: Neutrality
Challenge Level/XP: 4/120

A volt is a small, spherical beast with a long, sinewy tail trailing it. Its body is covered with thick gray bristles. Two large eyes resembling those of a fly dominate its head. Small horns protrude above these from its head.

Volts inhabit underground caverns and caves, preferring to lair in areas dampened by water. A typical grouping consists of up to 20 creatures, though it's anyone's guess which are male and which are female (if such a thing among volts actually exists).

A volt's spheroid body is about 3 feet across. Its tail is nearly 3 feet long and formed of semi-hardened tissue. Its mouth, unseen at first by those viewing it, is located near the underside of its body and is filled with rows of needle-like teeth.

If a volt hits with a bite attack, it latches onto the opponent's body. An attached volt has an AC of 6 [13], and holds on with great tenacity. An attached volt can be attacked or removed with an open doors check.

An attached volt drains blood, dealing 1d6 points of damage in any round when it begins its turn attached to a victim. Once it has dealt 12 points of damage, it detaches and flies off to digest the meal. If its victim dies before the volt's appetite has been sated, the volt detaches and seeks a new target.

A volt delivers an electrical charge with its tail slap that deals 2d4 points of damage. This damage cannot reduce a person's hit points below 0. An attached volt can attack its victim with its tail slap with a +2 bonus to hit in the same round.

Take Their Joules

A long, seemingly endless tunnel underground is traversed by swarm after swarm of 1d10+10 volts riding fierce, electrically charged winds. The schools of volts originate from a sparkling portal located about 60 feet down the tunnel and then re-enter a second portal 60 feet further up the tunnel. These portals lead to the borderlands between the elemental planes of air and water, which manifests as an eternally stormy sky.

The volts are dangerous enough that adventurers might wish to avoid the tunnel, but the portals also block further progress into the dungeon. Each portal is ringed in a collar of silver measuring 10 feet in diameter and 6 inches wide. Each of these collars weighs about 1 ton, and is thus worth 2,000 gp if it could be removed from the stone and transported out of the dungeon. The only way to switch off the portals is to link them with a conductive metal. Just touching a portal delivers 3d6 electrical shock damage (save to avoid bursting into flame, suffering 1d6 points of damage per round and possibly losing flammable objects).

Credit

The Volt originally appeared in the First Edition *Fiend Folio* (© TSR/Wizards of the Coast, 1981) and is used by permission.

Copyright Notice

Author Scott Greene, based on original material by Jonathon Jones.

Vorin

Hit Dice: 8
Armor Class: 3 [16]
Attacks: Sting (2d6 + poison) and bite (2d6 + poison)
Saving Throw: 8
Special: Paralytic poison, spit, immune to acid, resists fire, breathes water
Move: 12
Alignment: Chaos
Challenge Level/XP: 9/1,100

A vorin is an immense greenish-black thing with intense yellow eyes. It is 30 feet long and a foot thick. The body of the thing is a worm-like mass of pulpy flesh with several gill-like apertures along its length with which it propels itself through the water. The front of the beast has a long trunk similar to that of an elephant. Its skin glistens as if coated with a fine sheen of oil. A vorin can deliver a paralytic poison through a barb in its bite or via its sting. Once per round, a vorin can spit a blob of this poison at a single opponent within 50 feet (save avoids).

The Cistern Dweller

The floor of this 20-foot-square dungeon room contains five 5-foot-diameter pits filled with stagnant water. Each pit is surrounded by a 1-foot-high raised lip of bricks. Water pools on the stone floor in wide puddles. Each water-filled pit goes straight down for 20 feet where it opens into an underground cistern. Sitting next to each pit are a number of buckets. The buckets are useless, the wooden slats burned and blackened.

A vorin lives inside the cistern, and rises out to attack anyone disturbing the water. The creature leaps from pit to pit around the room to target creatures trying to get away from it. The pits form an X on the floor and allow the vorin to reach every corner of the room.

The water is contaminated by the vorin's poisonous bile, and kills anything that drinks it (save avoids).

Copyright Notice
Author Scott Greene.

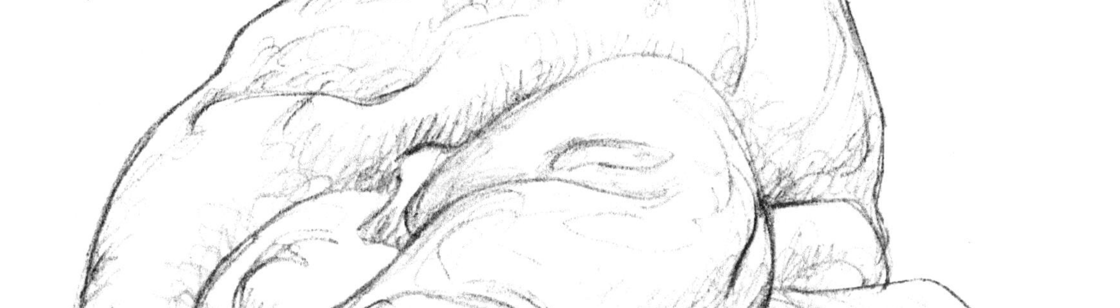

Vulchling

Hit Dice: 1+1
Armor Class: 6 [13]
Attack: Bite (1d6) and 2 claws (1d4)
Saving Throw: 17
Special: Track by scent
Move: 9/6 (Flying)
Alignment: Chaos
Challenge Level/XP: 2/30

Vulchlings are a malevolent race of avian creatures akin to the vulture. Their faces, though bird-like, seem to have an almost human quality to them. Vulchlings are not only scavengers but also predators, feeding on living prey as well as carrion. Vulchlings can occasionally be found in the company of harpies or vrocks, but most of their time is spent in their lairs—usually large nests found deep within the earth. Vulchlings speak their own language. Some (15%) speak the common tongue as well.

Vulchlings prefer to attack from secret or ambush by lying in wait for their prey and then swooping in to attack with their razor-sharp talons and beak. Slain opponents are carried back to the vulchlings' lair and fed to the young vulchlings.

Mad Scientists Associates

The craggy landscape the adventurers have wandered into is dominated by a stronghold of leaden gray bricks and latten doors. The stronghold is a tower keep, triangular in shape with three tall, slim towers with conical roofs missing some of their roof tiles. Perched on the battlements above is a flock of 1d8+8 vulchlings, the associates of the resident mad scientist (a magic-user of 9th level).

The stronghold has a few windows located about 20 feet above the ground. A wide staircase leads up to the front door, which in turn leads into a barren hall. Staircases from the hall lead to the towers (themselves leading to the upper floors of the keep) and doors lead into a kitchen and study. The study is equipped with a number of scholarly tomes (including a portion of a *manual of flesh golem creation*).

A secret passage in the study grants access to the laboratory in the cellar, a laboratory containing workbenches stained with acid, a stone slab embedded with manacles and a copper cabinet containing vials of bodily humors, jars containing preserved organs, etc.

The floor of the laboratory has several iron grates set into it, each leading to a small, 6-foot by 6-foot cell inhabited by 1d4+1 zombies.

The mad scientist's chambers contain a lead coffer (poison needle in the lock) of treasure: 1d4 x 100 sp, 1d4 x 10 gp, 1d6 x 100 pp, 1d12 pounds of frankincense (worth 150 gp per pound), a slab of malachite and white marble squares (a chess board) worth 1d6 x 10 gp and the magic-user's spellbooks.

Credit

The Vulchling originally appeared in the First Edition *Monster Manual II* (© TSR/Wizards of the Coast, 1983) and is used by permission.

Copyright Notice

Author Scott Greene, based on original material by Gary Gygax.

Wang Liang

Hit Dice: 3
Armor Class: 7 [12]
Attacks: 1 Bite (1d6 plus poison) and 2 claws (1d4 + poison)
Saving Throw: 14
Special: Magic or silver weapons needed to hit, immune to disease and poison, regeneration, spells
Move: 12
Alignment: Chaos
Challenge Level/XP: 4/120

Wang liangs are completely hairless feral humanoid creatures with gray skin and a mouth lined with rows of shark-like teeth. A wang liang delivers a virulent poison with its bite or claws. The poison imposes a -1 cumulative to-hit penalty to attack rolls unless a save is made. The poison effect lasts 1 hour. Wang liangs regenerate 3 hit points per round. They may cast *darkness 15-foot radius* at will.

The Wang Liang Clan

A mountain cave opens onto an infernal spectacle. Red rocks coated with oil burn brightly, filling the cave with a thick pall of smoke. Demonic faces painted in ash and soot decorate the walls, and bloody strips of flesh hang from twine strung across the room. A giant statue of a demonic figure reclines against the far wall, its razor-taloned hands holding a glowing black orb. Its eye glow with a furious red light.

Surrounding the statue are six humanoids wearing heavy woolen robes completely hiding their features. These same figures have been visiting towns and villages in the guise of traveling minstrels, and always leave shortly before tragedy strikes. A bounty of 200 gp has been placed on these traveling monks' heads for their capture, but no one has had any luck bringing them to justice. The "monks" are neither monks nor even human and have no intention of going quietly.

This group of 6 wang liangs wants to incite chaos in the Hollow Spire Mountains. The creatures hide their features unless confronted, at which time they whip off their robes and attack with their poisonous claws.

The black globe in the statue's hands is a gate to Hell that activates if touched. The ball of swirling darkness expands with a tortured shriek to swallow the person touching the orb. Screams fill the cave as the globe shrinks back to its normal size. The wang liangs try to force PCs near the orb.

WEIRDS

Weirds are creatures from the various inner and outer planes (including the demi-, para-, and quasi-elemental planes as well as the elemental planes).

They are sometimes encountered on the Material Plane, often in the employ of a powerful spellcaster. Bribery is the usual means of gaining the services of a weird, though some spellcasters resort to even more deceitful practices or trickery to gain the services of these creatures. Spellcaster beware! Weirds are intelligent creatures and do not take kindly to deception (unless they are the ones engaging in such trickery).

All weirds, regardless of their makeup, are serpent-like creatures about 10 feet long, and being of an evil and malign nature. Weirds speak the common language of weirds and the language native to their home plane. Some speak more languages, and still some can speak Common.

Weird, Blood

Hit Dice: 8
Armor Class: 5 [14]
Attacks: 1 bite (1d8)
Saving Throw: 8
Special: Grab, drown, transparent, reform
Move: 12 (swim)
Alignment: Chaos
Challenge Level/XP: 8/800

Blood weirds resemble 10-foot long, crimson serpents with glistening dark red scales. Some have bands of black that spiral the length of their body. Their eyes are a deep reddish-brown in color. Blood weirds are virtually invisible in their pools until they attack with a vicious bite. If a blood weird bites an opponent, it attempts to pull the victim into its pool to drown (save resists). When a weird is slain, it collapses back into its pool and reforms in 1d4 rounds.

In Cold Blood

This icy chamber sits deep within the twisting ice caverns of the Wailing Glacier. The room is roughly 100 feet wide and long, and the jagged ice ceiling soars 60 feet overhead. Water droplets fall in a steady beat from the melting roof, the drops plunking into the frozen surface of a 60-foot-wide circular pool contained by a three-foot-tall shimmering wall of clear, diamond-hard ice. An inch-thick ice layer on the surface of the pool covers three feet of blood swirling within the basin. The air smells of copper.

Three skeletons waving short swords are frozen in place from their waists down in the bloody basin. Icy fingers of frost climb among their bones and hold them fast in the pool. They wave their weapons menacingly, but cannot escape the ice.

The true threat is a pack of 4 blood weirds that live in the frigid pool of blood. The creatures punch through the ice easily to get at creatures outside the basin.

Copyright Notice
Author Scott Greene.

Weird, Fungus

Hit Dice: 5
Armor Class: 8 [11]
Attacks: 1 bite (1d8)
Saving Throw: 12
Special: Camouflage, fungus pool, sleep spores, reform, vulnerable to fire
Move: 0
Alignment: Neutrality
Challenge Level/XP: 6/400

A fungus weird is a 10-foot long serpent formed of fungus, plants, and tangled vines that resides in a 20-foot "pool" of brambles, mosses, leaves, fungi and plants. A fungus weird can never leave its pool, and is effectively invisible until it attacks. Once every 1d4 rounds, a fungus weird can release a puff of spores in a 10-foot cone. These spores induce sleep (as per the *sleep* spell) if the opponent fails a save. Unlike the *sleep* spell, there is no HD limit or maximum HD affected. When reduced to 0 hit points or less, a fungus weird collapses back into its pool. Four rounds later, it reforms at full strength minus any damage taken from fire.

The Forest Altar

A hill rises in the middle of the deep woods. Vines of yellow ivy and brilliant red dahlias prosper on the rise as it climbs nearly 30 feet above the forest floor. A 20-foot-wide dirt swath surrounds the hill, cutting it off from the rest of the forest. Plants grow thick on the hill, rising to about waist height. Atop the hill, a small golden altar gleams in the sunlight.

The altar is all that remains of a forest cult that met under the full moon each month. It is carved from stone and covered in flaking gold leaf. PCs searching the hillside find broken and bent bones scattered throughout the undergrowth. The bleached skeletal remains include human skulls, crushed femurs and splintered thigh bones.

A fungus weird is trapped on the hill and survives on the travelers who unwittingly stumble into its lair. The fungus weird was summoned by the cultists who barely managed to trap the creature from getting loose into the rest of the forest. Enchantments cast on the bare strip of earth around the hill stops the weird from escaping into the forest.

Copyright Notice

Weird, Lava

Hit Dice: 8
Armor Class: 5 [14]
Attacks: 1 bite (1d8 + 1d8 fire)
Saving Throw: 8
Special: Grab, drown, fire, transparent, reform, control elemental, immune to fire
Move: 12 (swim)
Alignment: Chaos
Challenge Level/XP: 9/1,100

A lava weird appears as a 10-foot-long serpent formed of elemental fire. Closer examination reveals liquid rock in scale-like patterns across its body, growing darker across its back. Two small flickers of white fire located on its head serve as eyes. The bite of a lava weird deals bite damage plus 1d8 points fire damage. Lava weirds can command any fire or earth elemental within 50 feet. The elemental gets a save to resist this command. Lava weirds are virtually invisible in their lava pools until they lash out at victims with a vicious bite. If a weird bites an opponent, it attempts to pull the victim into its pool to drown (save resists). When a lava weird is slain, it collapses back into its pool and reforms in 1d4 rounds.

To the Hilt

The corridor opens into a smithy's dream, with a river of lava flowing through a channel in the stone-cut floor. The air is thick with soot and noxious gases, and smoke hangs like dark clouds against the 30-foot-high ceiling. A stone bridge crosses the lava flow where a basalt anvil sits on a 20-foot-tall platform. Ash-covered steps rise around the platform, although no railing protects climbers from falling into the lava flow. A set of glowing metal tongs and a sword hilt sit on the anvil.

A lava weird lives in the lava flow, and is tasked with keeping intruders from reaching the anvil. The weird is nearly 30 feet long and rises out of the magma if PCs climb the stairs. The lava weird can reach anyone on the platform or stairs.

The hilt sitting on the anvil is white-hot, although it appears normal. Anyone touching it takes 2d6 points of damage (save for half) from the burning metal. The tongs are cool to the touch, but are coated with a gluey substance that sticks to flesh (1d6 points of damage to pull the tongs free). The hilt can be dipped into any normal fire to create a flaming blade for 2d4 rounds that does 2d6 points of damage.

Copyright Notice

Weird, Lightning

Hit Dice: 8
Armor Class: 5 [14]
Attacks: 1 bite (1d8 + 1d8 electricity)
Saving Throw: 8
Special: Control elemental, electricity, immune to electricity, transparent, reform
Move: 12
Alignment: Chaos
Challenge Level/XP: 9/1,100

Lightning weirds resemble 10-foot-long serpents composed of yellow or white crackling lightning. Brilliant flares of electricity function as the creature's eyes and small bolts of electricity leap and dance from its form. The bite of a lightning weird deals bite damage plus 1d8 points of electrical damage. Lightning weirds can command any air elemental within 50 feet. The elemental gets a save to resist this command. When a lightning weird is slain, it collapses into a sparking pool and reforms in 1d4 rounds.

Its Alive!

Miredown Keep sits on a lonely promontory jutting out over the Sagarran Sea. Lightning dances in the dark clouds roiling around the peaks, and ball lightning dances along the rooflines of the once-proud structure. The majority of the castle's floors are just shadows of the place's former glory, but the dungeon laboratory is still alarmingly clean and well-maintained.

A slab of metal swings in the center of the room from long gleaming metal chains that run to a door set in the ceiling. Winches and pulleys line the room's walls, and four 10-foot-tall metal spikes ringed by ceramic plates stand in the chamber. The ceramic plates are decorated with indecipherable sigils. Lightning sparks and cracks along the tips of each metal spike. Standing in the corners of the room are two 9-foot-tall flesh golems, each fitted with a metal-studded collar. Two-foot-long metal spikes jut from their sewn flesh.

The flesh golems defend the apparatuses scattered around the room, while the metal spikes hum with electricity. In 1d4 rounds, the spikes harness enough electrical energy from the outside air to create a ring of electricity 10 feet off the floor. The lightning arcs and cracks, and jumps from the metal posts to the spikes sticking out of the flesh golems. The golems heal 2d8 points of damage each round from the electrical bursts. Any PC caught in a lightning stream takes 4d6 points of damage.

Four rounds after the lightning ring ignites, a rift opens above the metal slab and draws a lightning weird into the room. The lightning weird's arrival instantly short-circuits the current, shutting down the lightning show in the room (and removing the healing current arcing to the flesh golems). The lightning weird leaps from metal spike to metal spike as it arcs about the room in a burst of radiant blue fire. It can also jump to a flesh golem to heal it for 1d6 points of damage each round it maintains contact.

Flesh Golem (2): HD 10 (45hp); AC 9[10]; Atk 2 fists (2d8); Move 8; Save 5; CL/XP 12/2000; Special: Healed by lightning, hit only by magic weapons, slowed by fire and cold, immune to most spells.

Copyright Notice
Author Scott Greene.

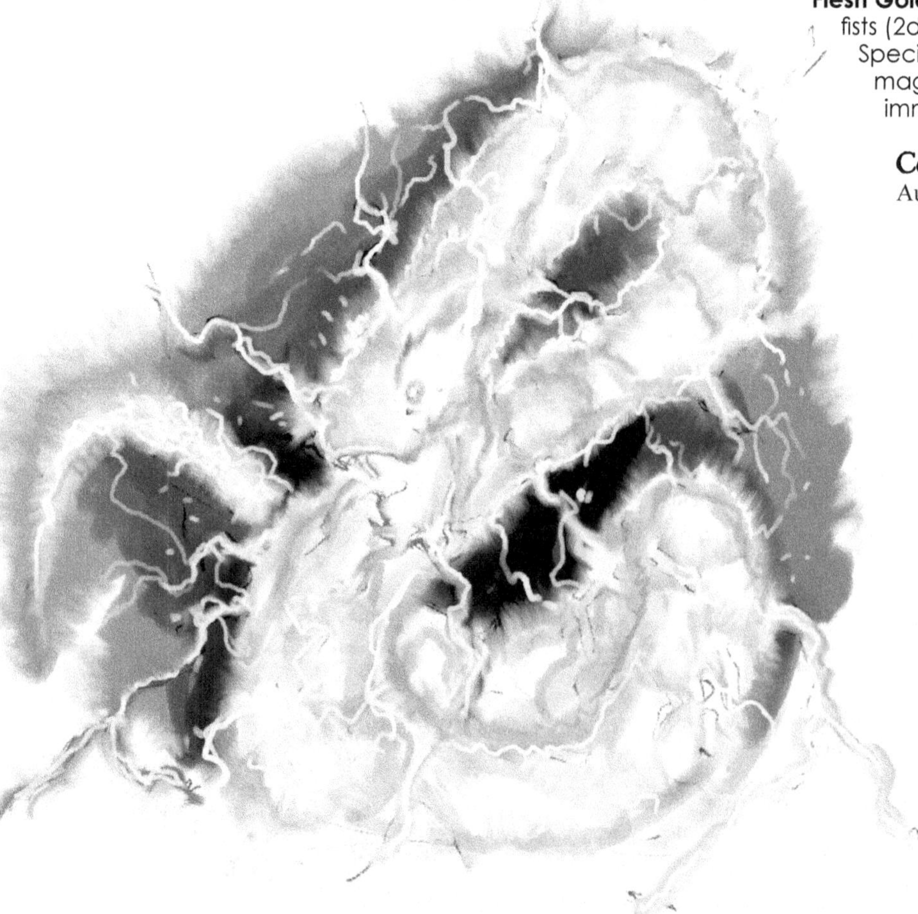

Well Lurker

Hit Dice: 8
Armor Class: 5 [14]
Attacks: 6 tentacles (1d8)
Saving Throw: 8
Special: Swallow whole
Move: 6
Alignment: Neutrality
Challenge Level/XP: 10/1,400

A well lurker looks like a freshwater well, with the beast's 10-foot-long tentacles and devouring mouth hidden behind a rock-like collar sticking out of the ground. A typical well lurker covers a 10-foot area, though specimens can cover a 30-foot area. If a well lurker's tentacle hits, it wraps around the target and pulls the creature toward the lurker's mouth to be swallowed automatically on the next round. It can swallow a man-sized creature or smaller (a save resists). Animals can detect the unnatural presence of a well lurker and are generally nervous in its presence.

All's Well

The grounds of Brull Keep are littered with the broken stones of four collapsed towers. The central complex is nothing but broken walls. The dungeons beneath the once-grand keep are inaccessible unless tons of stone blocks are carefully removed.

Sitting in the middle of the destruction, like an oasis in the middle of the deadliest desert, is a small green rectangle of verdant grasses and daisies. Miniature apple trees grow in small copses, and a small stone well sits nearby. A garden of vegetables grows naturally in the middle of the rubble.

This small paradise used to be the keep's central courtyard and was used to grow fruits and vegetables. When the building fell during a requiem beetle's assault, the central courtyard survived. Now, it serves as a resting spot for travelers and others looking for riches in the keep's abandoned dungeons. A well lurker also uses the spot as its hunting grounds, hiding in plain sight in the middle of the high grasses as it waits for prey. The lurker assumes the shape of the small stone well nestled among the apple trees.

Copyright Notice
Author Scott Greene.

Widow Creeper

Hit Dice: 9
Armor Class: 5 [14]
Attacks: 2 tentacles (1d8) or entangle
Saving Throw: 6
Special: Control plants, drain fluid
Move: 12
Alignment: Neutrality
Challenge Level/XP: 11/1,700

A widow creeper is an 8-foot-tall giant black widow formed from leaves, weeds, and tangled brush. Two long, sinewy vine-like tentacles protrude from its body and aid the creature in capturing and securing its prey. A widow creeper fires a mass of sticky, clinging vines and weeds up to 60 feet at a target to entangle a victim (save avoids). If a widow creeper hits with a tentacle, it grabs and automatically maintains a hold. The next round it sucks bodily fluids from its captive, dealing 1d6 points of damage. A widow creeper can animate plants (as *animate objects*) 3 times per day.

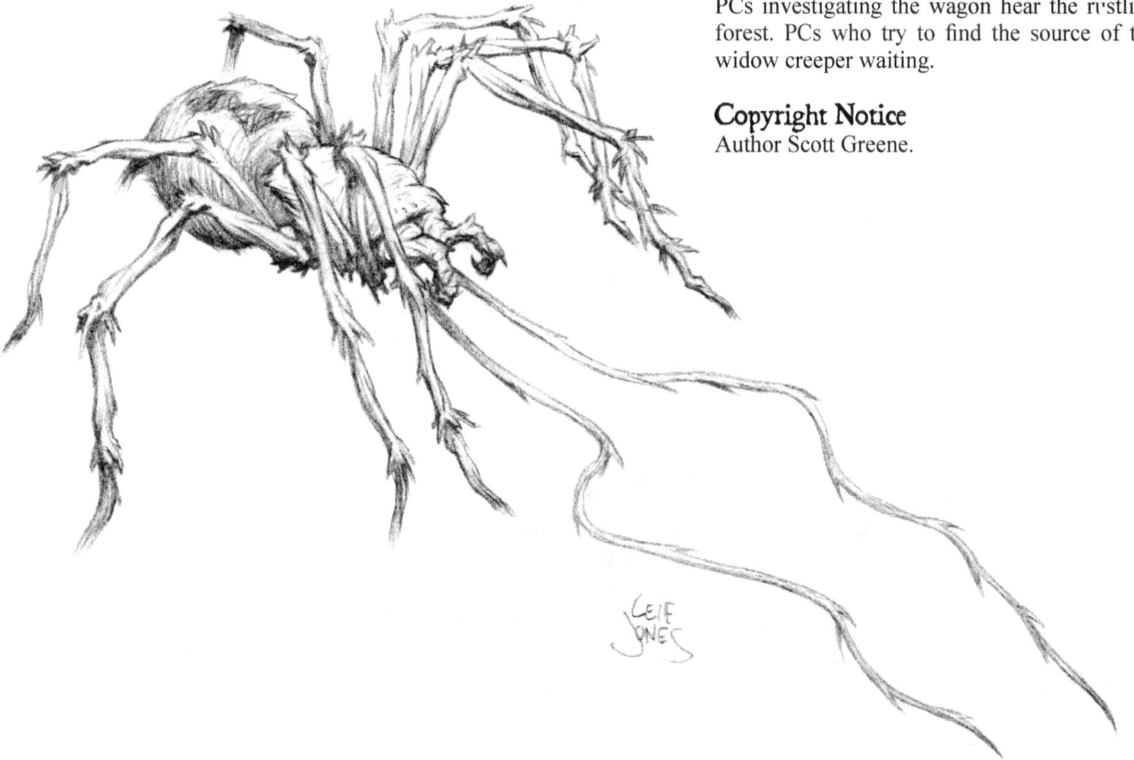

The Patient Widow

Bodies litter the Tanglethorn Thicket. Two satyrs lie in a clump of thick grass, their flesh ashen and cheeks sunken. A human traveler slumps against a fir tree, his lifeless body wan and pale. His green cloak is slashed and torn. His horse lies dead on its side, still tied to a tree. A covered wagon is overturned nearby, its large wheels broken and yanked off the axle. Gouges mar the wooden transport's sides, undercarriage and roof.

Inside the wagon is a wizened old woman named Hertha Oxley and her granddaughter, Beatrice. The pair were sleeping when the wagon was roughly overturned as Beatrice's father screamed from outside where he stood watch. They've been trapped for three days, although an abundance of baked goods and rainwater has sustained them. They didn't see what overturned the wagon, but the old woman proclaims it to be "vampire from the old country" chasing her family. The lack of blood in and around the bodies seems to bear this out.

The family made the mistake of camping near a widow creeper's web. The giant spider-like creature overturned the wagon but couldn't get at the people inside. The creature now waits patiently for them to come out. The spider leaves its victims where they fall, each body drained of blood. PCs investigating the wagon hear the rustling of leaves in the tangled forest. PCs who try to find the source of the noise find the immense widow creeper waiting.

Copyright Notice
Author Scott Greene.

Wight, Barrow

Hit Dice: 6
Armor Class: 3 [16]
Attack: Slam (1d4 + energy drain)
Saving Throw: 11
Special: Level drain, insanity gaze
Move: 12
Alignment: Chaos
Challenge Level/XP: 10/1400

Barrow wights are undead creatures akin to normal wights, but they are always found in or near barrows, usually guarding the treasure contained therein. Creatures hit by a barrow wight's slam attack are drained of one level. Creatures killed by this level drain rise as barrow wights in 1d4 rounds and remain under their creator's control until it is destroyed. Anyone with 30 feet that meets a barrow wight's gaze is affected as if by a *symbol of insanity* spell unless they make a successful saving throw.

Cold Heart

As one travels across the steppe, they may come across a strange embankment. Circular and 100 feet in diameter, the embankment rises about 4 feet. Just within the embankment there is a small ditch about 3 feet deep. The area inside the embankment is otherwise flat, save for a 9 foot high man-made hill in the center. The hill is 30 feet in diameter. It contains a barrow tomb holding the cremated remains of a neolithic king and his four wives, who were buried alive. Unlike the happily cremated king, the four wives have not rested peacefully. Their horrified spirits reanimated their corpses, turning them into barrow wights.

The queen's were tied with leather thongs (long since rotted away) and placed into small, stone coffins measuring about 3-ft x 3-ft and covered with stone lids. It is in these coffins that they await the arrival of tomb robbers, being fully capable of casting the lids from their resting places to surprise (on a 1-2 on 1d6) their prey. The king's ashes and bones are stored in a stone urn, along with his valuable burial objects. More mundane objects - stone knives, arrowheads, ancient pelts - litter the floor of the tomb. The entrance to the tomb points west and is completely obscured by earth. If the earth is cleared away (takes about 1 hour), one sees a short corridor lined with megaliths that have been painted with hunting scenes and depictions of the spirit world. At the end of this passageway is the tomb proper, sealed by another megalith weighing 3 tons.

The sealed tomb contains a sapphire worth 800 gp, two lapis lazuli worth 135 gp each, a terracotta cup worth 45 gp, 1d4 x 100 gp and 1d12 x 100 sp in the form of ring coinage.

Copyright Notice
Authors Clark Peterson and Scott Greene.

Wight, Blood

Hit Dice: 10
Armor Class: 2 [17]
Attacks: 2 claws (1d6)
Saving Throw: 5
Special: Engulf, wounding, magic weapons to hit
Move: 12
Alignment: Chaos
Challenge Level/XP: 12/2,000

Blood wights are powerful undead standing 8 to 10 feet tall and weighing 400 to 550 pounds. The wight's body constantly oozes blood. It is immune to nonmagical weapons. If a blood wight hits an opponent with two claws, it engulfs the victim in the next round and holds them inside its body until the person drowns. The blood wight's claws cause a persistent wound that bleeds for 1 hit point per round until healed.

Blood Drive

The rumble of a fast-moving wagon and galloping horses can be heard. From down the road comes a large stagecoach-type carriage that bounces out of control as a team of 6 horses flees in fear. Thin wisps of smoke trail from the carriage's closed windows. Blood drips from the doors and the undercarriage as the coach races past. The driver lies tangled in the ribbons as she dangles over the side of the driver's box. Garments stream from partially opened baggage compartments strapped to the back of the carriage.

The stagecoach continues on unless stopped. Within the coach is a blood wight. How or why it came to be in a stagecoach is up to the Game Referee. The bloody creatures may attempt to drag PCs into the coach or burst from the door once someone is close enough.

The driver clings to life after hours of being battered along the side of the coach. Within the coach are three passengers who drowned in blood from the monstrosity in their midst. PCs may feel the need to contact the next of kin. This information and more may be obtained from the remaining personal effects of the deceased. One possibility is that one of the passengers was a frail magic-user carrying vital information or a dangerous artifact to be delivered to a noble.

Copyright Notice

Willow Dusk

Hit Dice: 8
Armor Class: 5 [14]
Attacks: 2 branches (2d8)
Saving Throw: 8
Special: Droning, magic weapons needed to hit, misery, regeneration, swallow whole
Move: 8
Alignment: Chaos
Challenge Level/XP: 10/1,400

A willow dusk is a willow tree that grows to a height of 40 feet or more. Once every 1d4+1 rounds, a willow dusk can emit a wave of negative energy that affects all living creatures within 10 feet. Creatures hearing the sound become sad and disheartened, with a 10% cumulative chance per wave of lying down in despair. Once per round, a willow dusk can emit a droning audible sound up to 100 feet away that causes creatures to become lethargic (save resists). Affected creatures cannot move (as if held by a *hold person* spell) for 1d6 rounds. If 2 branches hit the same target, the willow dusk grabs the opponent and swallows him on the next round (save resists). While touching the ground, willow dusks regenerate 3 hit points every round. It does not regenerate fire or acid damage and dies if it reaches 0 hit points.

The Captive Willow

A magical doorway opens in the Cold Laurel Forest when the full moon rises above the trees. The shimmering portal flows like a watery curtain between two ancient pine trees and opens into a dimensional pocket where a willow dusk is trapped. The magic is weak after centuries containing the creature. The pull of the full moon now warps the energies and allows the deadly tree to escape. The tree is starving and charges through gate and into the hills in search of food.

The portal slices violently shut after three days, sealing the forest world away for another month – along with anyone trapped inside it. Woodland creatures can pass easily through the open gate, and forest animals frequently wander into the extradimensional world. Their bones litter the one-square-mile forest. Most of the animals are hunted and killed by the vicious willow dusk when it returns. If the willow dusk fails to get back through the portal before it closes, it withers and dies in the real world.

Copyright Notice
Author Scott Greene.

Wind Walker

Hit Dice: 6
Armor Class: 2 [17]
Attack: Wind blast (2d6)
Saving Throw: 11
Special: +1 or better weapon to hit, detect thoughts, immunity to magic, telepathy 100 ft.
Move: 15/24 (flying)
Alignment: Neutrality
Challenge Level/XP: 9/1100

Wind walkers are creatures from the Elemental Plane of Air. They are often summoned to the Material Plane by magic-users or clerics who employ them as guards. On occasion, a wind walker is encountered in the service of a cloud giant, storm giant, efreet, djinn, or other such creature.

A wind walker's natural form is that of a roaring and whistling column of wind about 12 feet tall. No discernable features can be seen in the wind walker.

A wind walker attacks using the air surrounding it, transforming it into a forceful blast that deals 2d6 points of damage to all creatures within 10 feet. The wind walker makes a single attack roll against each opponent within reach.

A wind walker can continuously use *ESP* as the spell, except it has a range of 100 feet. If two wind walkers are present, they can link their minds together to increase the range to 200 feet. If three or more wind walkers are present, they can link their minds to increase the range to 300 feet. All wind walkers that are mind linked gain this range boost.

A wind walker is immune spells and spell-like abilities. In addition, certain spells and effects function differently against the creature as follows.

Mind-affecting spells and effects function normally against a wind walker.

A *control weather* spell instantly slays a wind walker if it fails a saving throw.

A *haste* spell deals 1d6 points of damage per two caster levels to a wind walker. A saving throw halves the damage. In addition, a *haste* spell increases the damage the wind walker deals with its wind blast attack by +1d6 for one round.

An *ice storm* spell deals no damage to a wind walker, but affects it as if by a *fear* spell.

A *slow* spell deals 1d6 points of damage per caster level to a wind walker. A saving throw halves the damage.

A summoned or called wind walker is affected normally by magical barriers that restrict or inhibit called or summoned creatures.

A wind walker can communicate telepathically with any creature within 100 feet that has a language.

An Ill Wind Blows

An otherwise unremarkable cave in a range of werewolf-haunted mountains leads to a storm giant's castle in the upper peaks. The cave is located on a rough slope blanketed by spruce. About a mile east of the cave there is a ruined castle of granite blocks and sweeping, gothic buttresses. The ruins are now the lair of a pack of 1d4+1 werewolves, the former lords of the area (and a persistent annoyance to the storm giants).

The cave itself has a wide mouth overgrown with lichens and liverworts, but with a well beaten path from the cave mouth to the valley below. Above the mouth of the cave a coat of arms has been carved into the stone and shows signs of once being painted. The arms depicted an eagle sable on a field gules flanked by a sun and moon proper.

The lower portions of the cave are inhabited by 1d3+2 cave bears. The cave bear lair is littered with cracked bones and a rusted shirt of mail. There are signs that the cave was once used as storage, perhaps by the lords of the ruined castle. A high gallery in the cave leads to tunnels that climb higher in the mountain. One of these tunnels leads into a subterranean fairyland of oreads lounging around a shrine of Elemental Earth consisting of a granite block bearing bas-reliefs of grotesque faces. Another tunnel leads up to a higher vault guarded by a gang of 1d3+1 wind walkers.

The wind walkers' vault contains a number of bronze poles that run from the ceiling to the floor, most of them placed at odd angles. The poles are places about 8 to 12 feet apart. The poles do not bother the wind walkers in the least, but they make fighting difficult for others (players can choose to accept a -2 penalty to their Armor Class or a -2 penalty "to hit"). The poles are not just an annoyance, but also a means of traveling to the upper plateau and the storm giants' castle. The poles are activated with electricity, with all those touching the pole while it is electrified being transported to the castle above.

Credit

The Wind Walker originally appeared in the First Edition *Monster Manual* (© TSR/Wizards of the Coast, 1977) and is used by permission.

Copyright Notice

Author Scott Greene, based on original material by Gary Gygax.

Winter Bloom

Hit Dice: 2
Armor Class: 9 [10]
Attacks: spore cloud (2d4)
Saving Throw: 16
Special: Spore cloud
Move: 0 (immobile)
Alignment: Neutrality
Challenge Level/XP: 2/30

Winterblooms are small flowers with bluish-white petals, dark sapphire-colored stems, and small white leaves growing near the base. Winterblooms can generally be found in temperate and cold climates during the winter months when it is in full bloom. It gives off a slightly sweet scent that can be detected to a range of 30 feet. If a patch of winterbloom is disturbed, the plant releases a burst of poisonous spores in the form of a bluish-white cloud of chilled vapor. Creatures within 10 feet of the winterbloom must save or take 2d4 points of damage as the inhaled spores form ice crystals on the victim's lungs. The cloud remains in the area for 1d3 rounds.

To Die For

Prince Inferian IV is furious. He recently requested a very special courtship bouquet from Emil Hattan, a flower grower who specializes in rare blooms. The flowers were to be delivered before the arrival of his bride-to-be, Princess Marinal of the Northlanders. The Hattans haven't arrived yet with the special arrangement, and the prince is sure their negligence is going to jeopardize the fragile peace this planned marriage would bring. The Hattans have a small growing operation on the outskirts of Hullmay Valley, but the winter has made travel near impossible. The Northlanders sled dogs could be slowed by the drifts, however, so the prince is desperate to get the flowers.

The Hattans' growing shacks are three wooden buildings connected by three covered trenches. A cloyingly sweet scent of blossoming flowers drifts over the ice-covered lands around the shacks. Temperatures are controlled inside each building, with one a hothouse for desert flowers, a second for temperate climes, and the third kept barely above freezing. Inside the frost-filled greenhouse are the six frozen members of the Hattan family, each body writhing in unimaginable pain on the carpeted floor. Prince Inferian's special rush request caused the Hattans to cut a few corners – and they paid for it with their lives. Growing in the cold greenhouse are 10 winterblooms. The flowers killed the flower sellers with their spores and the cold froze their bodies. Fortunately, the Hattans finished the bouquet before the rest of the plants killed them. The arrangement sits on a table in the center of the living winterblooms.

Copyright Notice
Author Scott Greene.

Witch Grass

Hit Dice: 2
Armor Class: 9 [10]
Attacks: None
Saving Throw: 16
Special: Seed spray, spell failure
Move: 0 (immobile)
Alignment: Neutrality
Challenge Level/XP: 2/30

Witch grass is a summer-blooming, broadleaved plant that stands 1 to 2 feet tall at maturity. It is very bushy and its leaves and branches have a purplish hue. Its base and roots are thick and have the same purplish hue. A typical patch of witch grass covers a 10-foot area, though it often covers an area as large as 50 feet or more. It is only found in temperate or warm climates and in areas of naturally occurring grass such as forests, plains, and hills. Witch grass causes Magic-User spells cast within 20 feet to fail (10% chance). Anyone approaching within 10 feet of a patch of witch grass causes the patch to release a cloud of seedlings that attach to the creature. These seedlings disrupt spells as per the normal host patch.

Bar Fight

Magic doesn't work right in Monk's Quarry. Spells cast go awry as the magical energies sputter and fail. Years ago a traveling gypsy cursed the village after an angry magic-user killed her son for messing around with the mage's trollop of a daughter. The mother's jinx didn't do much more than scare the locals. However, the seed pods and pollen on the gypsies' traveling wagons infested the village with a quick-growing, magic-consuming plant called witch grass.

The Magician's Wand is a two-story inn and tavern in the center of town that caters to the needs of dusty travelers and thirsty locals. The building is painted white and has a green sloping roof. The inn is run by a fussy old woman named Madame Pritta who has no magical abilities. Purple broad-leaf plants grow wildly about the building and throughout the rest of the town. The purple plants are witch grass and can be found all over town. The locals even pluck the strangely colored stems and roll them into cigars to smoke. The cigars give off a sweet-smelling, cloying smoke.

A gang of 12 greenskin orcs has been casing the tavern from the nearby Kriegh Forest for the past week. The orcs don't know about the town's curse, and believe powerful magical items must be stored within the Magician's Wand. The orcs are led by a brawny orc named Gredal who has jangling earrings in his floppy ears and wears an eye-patch made of cured dwarf skin. The orcs attack the inn head-on, charging through the tavern doors and leaping through the windows. The orcs don't rely on spells, but any cast by the PCs may go awry because of the abundant witch grass.

Copyright Notice
Author Scott Greene.

W

Witch Tree

Hit Dice: 8
Armor Class: 3 [16]
Attacks: 4 tendrils (1d6)
Saving Throw: 8
Special: Constrict, spell-like abilities, resists electricity and fire
Move: 0 (immobile)
Alignment: Chaos
Challenge Level/XP: 9/1,100

A witch tree combines the features of a tall, beautiful woman and a willow tree looking somewhat like a female willow treant. Her hair and fingers form the fronds of the willow, while her arms and parts of her hair form the branches. From a distance, the witch tree is almost indistinguishable from a normal willow tree. Its skin is thick and dark, resembling the bark of a tree. Its legs join together to form the roots. A witch tree attacks with its tendrils. If two tendrils strike the same opponent, the tree grabs the victim and constricts the creature for an automatic 2d6 damage each round thereafter. A witch tree can employ various spell-like abilities: 5/day—*charm monster*; 2/day—*charm person*. A witch tree takes half damage from fire and electrical attacks.

Bewitched

The villagers of Mydwich have vanished, all 40 people simply gone as if they never existed. Footprints lead into the forest, where the muddy ground still shows they docilely walked into the willow trees that border the town. Homes sit vacant, fires are nothing but embers in the hearths, and meals sit rotting on wooden tables. A few stray dogs roam in and out of the homes.

A lascivious woman sits dressed in sheer silks sits atop the peak of one of the houses. She holds a willow branch in her hands, caressing the fronds lovingly. She seems deep in thought, but aware of PCs entering the village. A bag of willow branches and logs sits beside her on the steep roof.

Aubrien is a dryad protector of the willow trees around the village. She is an evil creature who delights in the misfortune of others and took revenge on the townsfolk for chopping down one of the willows under her care. She has been going from empty house to empty house collecting the remains of the tree.

Aubrien lured a witch tree to her grove, and the deadly tree – assisted by the dryad – lured the people of Mydwich into the plant's grasping tendrils. Crushed bones litter the ground about the witch tree's roots. The soil is a nutrient-rich mixture of dirt and blood, which Aubrien scoops up and uses to lovingly fertilize the other willows in her grove.

Copyright Notice
Author Scott Greene.

Witherstench

Hit Dice: 2
Armor Class: 5 [14]
Attack: 2 claws (1d3)
Saving Throw: 16
Special: Stench
Move: 9
Alignment: Neutrality
Challenge Level/XP: 3/60

A witherstench (also called skunk beast) is a mutated relative of the common skunk. It resembles a putrid yellow skunk with very little fur and whose body is splotched with tiny, purple spots. It is about 4 feet long and weighs around 50 pounds. Its diet consists of carrion, and the creature is always found in areas where such "food" is plentiful.

Witherstenches shuns combat, but attacks if cornered, raking at their opponents with their filthy claws.

A witherstench constantly emits a putrid stench that nearly every form of animal life finds offensive. All living creatures (except witherstenches) within 30 feet of a witherstench must succeed on a saving throw or be nauseated (unable to attack, cast spells, concentrate on spells, or do anything else requiring attention) for as long as they remain within 30 feet of the creature. Moving out of the affected area leaves the character sickened (-2 to hit, weapon damage rolls and saving throws) for 1 round after which time he recovers immediately.

Creatures that successfully save cannot be affected by the same witherstench's stench for 24 hours. A *neutralize poison* spell removes the effect from the sickened creature. Creatures with immunity to poison are unaffected, and creatures resistant to poison receive their normal bonus on their saving throws.

Irradiated and Irritated

A sandstone outcropping on the savannah holds a fantastic secret. The sandstone sits atop a layer of uranium ore, and the entire outcropping sits on top of granite bedrock. When inundated with groundwater, the uranium begins a chain reaction that produces fission.

The waves of energy given off by the natural nuclear reactor have twisted the surrounding flora and fauna. The plantlife is noticeably twisted and stunted, and strange animals are common in the area - tigerillas in copses of trees, owlephants on the savannah, cockatrices in the brush and a pack of 3d4 witherstenches living in a cave near the outcropping.

The skunk beasts are left alone by the other mutants of the savannah. More than a few magic-users have led expeditions to find the outcropping and study it, with more than a few of their retainers and bearers falling prey to the witherstench. Though the creatures have no use for the treasure, the bodies are dragged to their caves, which now contain 1d12 x 100 sp, 1d4 x 100 gp, a broken terracotta vase and packs containing about 12 weeks of iron rations (poisonous to eat).

Credit

The Witherstench originally appeared in the First Edition *Fiend Folio* (© TSR/Wizards of the Coast, 1981) and is used by permission.

Copyright Notice

Author Scott Greene, based on original material by Jonathon Jones.

Witherweed

Hit Dice: 5
Armor Class: 6 [13]
Attack: 5 frond (1d4)
Saving Throw: 12
Special: Death smoke, dexterity damage, camouflage
Move: 0 (immobile)
Alignment: Neutrality
Challenge Level/XP: 7/600

Witherweeds resemble large patches of dry grass and weeds and are most often found in areas where their natural makeup allows them to blend in with their surroundings. A subterranean version of this monster exists and makes its lair in desolate caves and caverns.

Hidden among the creature's body are many long, sinewy strands that it uses to trap its prey. The average witherweed covers an area of 20-square feet, though specimens as large as 60-square feet have been encountered by a few dungeon delvers.

A witherweed attacks any living creature that comes within 10 feet of it, slashing and striking with its fronds. Slain creatures are devoured as the witherweed releases enzymes to break down its food and absorbs the nutrients.

A witherweed has one frond for each HD it possesses (thus, the typical 5 HD witherweed has 5 fronds while a 10 HD witherweed has 10 fronds).

A witherweed that takes at least 1 point of damage from a fire effect releases a cloud of deadly smoke that billows forth and quickly fills a 20-foot radius surrounding it. Creatures within the area must succeed on a saving throw vs. poison or take 2d6 points of damage. One minute later, another saving throw must be made to avoid another 3d6 points of damage.

The cloud remains for 1 round per HD of the witherweed but a strong wind (21+ mph) disperses the cloud in 1 round.

An opponent struck by a witherweed's frond takes 1d4 points of dexterity damage. A successful saving throw reduces the damage by half.

Since a witherweed looks like normal grass and weeds when at rest, it surprises on a roll of 1-5 on 1d6 against most folks, and on a roll of 1-3 on 1d6 against elves, druids and rangers and against dwarves against the subterranean version.

Overgrown Mine

Ages ago, a clan of dwarves tunneled through a range of mountains, linking a high lake around which they had constructed their mansions to the lowlands, making it easier for them to bring their products to the human markets beyond.

The tunnel is about 30 feet wide with an arched ceiling 30 feet tall. It extends about 5 miles long and climbs a total of 800 feet from the bottom to the top. Throughout the route are a number of drops of up to 30 feet with pulley systems to move cargo and wide, spiral stairs to allow humans leading animals to pass. There are also a number of side tunnels leading to subterranean inns, storage areas, guard posts and shrines.

Alas, the days of caravans of sturdy mountain ponies moving fine dwarven crafts through the tunnel are long since over. An over-ambitious miner managed to connect his shaft to the lake, draining most of it into the underworld, but a portion flowed through the caravan tunnel, drowning hundreds of dwarves and making the high plateau quite uninhabitable. Many dwarves hung on for a century or two tapping out their mines, but most took the grim journey through the ruined tunnel into the human lands beyond as refugees.

The dwarf tunnel is now mostly inhabited by bats, rats and the scourge of witherweed, its vines clogging up stairwells and climbing the walls. More than a few adventurers have killed themselves trying to burn the stuff out of tunnels or stairwells. Perhaps there is an inn holding some forgotten treasure left by a merchant or adventurer. Maybe something unwholesome dwells in a forgotten shrine or one of the abandoned manors overlooking the dry lake bed.

Credit
The Witherweed originally appeared in the First Edition *Fiend Folio* (© TSR/Wizards of the Coast, 1981) and is used by permission.

Copyright Notice
Author Scott Greene, based on original material by Simon Eaton.

W

Wizard's Shackle

Hit Dice: 1d4
Armor Class: 5 [14]
Attack: Bite (1 point plus spell drain)
Saving Throw: 18
Special: Attach, spell drain, sense magic-users, sealed mind
Move: 3
Alignment: Neutrality
Challenge Level/XP: B/10

The wizard's shackle is a 6-inch long, gray-green leech-like creature. Though it is small in size, it is greatly feared by spellcasters, for its bite drains arcane magic from a caster's mind. In some rare instances, evil spellcasters have harvested these monsters and set them loose in an enemy spellcaster's tower or laboratory.

A wizard's shackle attacks from ambush. It favors hiding on ledges, bookshelves, doors, and other such places where it can drop on spellcasters that pass underneath it. A wizard's shackle injects an anesthetic when it bites, so it is possible that its bite goes unnoticed (only 1 in 6 chance of noticing).

If a wizard's shackle hits with a bite attack, it latches onto the opponent's body. The wizard's shackle holds on with great tenacity. An attached wizard's shackle can be struck with a weapon or removed with a successful open doors check.

A wizard's shackle drains spells when attached to a magic-user. Each round the wizard's shackle remains attached, it drains 1d6 levels of prepared spells or unused spell slots, beginning with the highest level spell or slot available. For example, on a roll of 4 against a 5th-level magic-user, a wizard's shackle drains four levels of prepared spells. The magic-user currently has one 3rd-level spell, two 2nd-level spells, and three 1st-level spells prepared. The wizard's shackle drains the 3rd-level spell and one of the 1st-level spells (determined randomly).

A creature drained of spells or slots can attempt a saving throw with a +2 bonus to notice that something is wrong, though unless he searches his body, he might still overlook the wizard's shackle. Once a wizard's shackle has drained at least 4 spell levels, it detaches and crawls away to digest its meal. Lost spells or slots are regained the next day.

A wizard's shackle can automatically detect the location of any arcane spellcaster within 30 feet. This functions as a *detect evil* spell.

Wizard's shackles are immune to mind-influencing spells and effects.

Wait, What's on Your Neck?

The coasts of a lonely wilderness are home to a strange marsh, quite unlike any other. The coasts consist of a range of limestone mounts - terribly ancient and quite worn down. Weathering has left these hills looking worm eaten, with hundreds of caves joining the highlands to the shore. Over the centuries, these limestone caverns have really become more like a series of sodden shelves connected by natural arches and tunnels. The sodden, opened vaults are like tiny marshes connected via ground water and waterfalls, the fresh water eventually straining through the stone and reaching the sea.

All manner of fish, frogs, marsh birds and rodents live in these quiet, sheltered marshes. A tribe of 1d6 x 100 kobolds hunts the marshes, dwelling in small burrows and never appearing in groups larger than ten - the kobolds are all linked by blood, and females are swapped between family groups, but they otherwise distrust and despise one another.

The most interesting creature in these marshes is the wizard's shackle. Those traveling up or down the marshy shelves have a 1 in 6 chance of running into a swarm of 1d6+5 wizard's shackles each hour. The kobolds are canny enough to recognize when a magic-user has been drained of spells - they have a certain look in their eyes - and will wait for the feeding to be complete before they launch an ambush.

Copyright Notice

Author Scott Greene.

Wolf, Abyssal

Hit Dice: 7
Armor Class: 2 [17]
Attacks: 1 bite (1d8+1)
Saving Throw: 9
Special: Paralyzing gaze
Move: 18
Alignment: Chaos
Challenge Level/XP: 8/800

The abyssal wolf is a man-sized wolf that stands 5 feet tall at the shoulder. It has deep blackish-blue fur and eyes of fiery orange. Its coat is usually caked with blood, and bits of flesh hang from its toothy mouth. Anyone within 40 feet meeting the gaze of an abyssal wolf must save or be paralyzed for 2d4 rounds. The wolf's keen sense of smell lets it detect prey within 60 feet, or 120 feet if opponents are upwind.

Let Slip the Dogs

Partiers fill the Sable Manse for Midsummer's Feast, the women's flowing party gowns swirls of garish color on the marble dance floor beneath floating green paper globes burning with soft orange candlelight. The sultan Reysis II sits loftily on his pillowed throne, exhorting the dancers to grander sweeps and bows in his honor. For this night is all about him, a birthday party to end all parties, where the wine flows freely, the women are beautiful and the morning is a long ways off.

And it might just be the last party, as a stranger now walks through the lavish halls, his multicolored robe drinking in the revelry around him and reflecting it back a thousandfold. The tall stranger stands every inch of 7 feet tall and covers his features with a white porcelain mask decorated with sparkling gemstones. His eyes are afire with mirth at the pomp going on around him as he travels through each decorated hall, grabbing at the women and tasting every drop of fruity wine. Darnyl Bloog is a wanted man, and knows this could well be his last night to enjoy the pleasures of the land. So he's making the most of his last days by sneaking into Reysis' monthly celebration

Bloog isn't being sought by any law local enforcement. He's the half-son of a demonic matron of Hell, and he's heard the baying of the hounds of his mother's rival coming for him for the past week. But he's not going down without one last revel. It's just too bad that the Grand Hunting Hounds of Entrium have found him before the party's last dance. The 6 monstrous hounds, led by a reddish-colored abyssal wolf named Gnawbone, burst into the reception like the party crashers they are, intent on their prey … or anyone who gets in their way.

Copyright Notice
Author Scott Greene.

Wolf, Ghoul

Hit Dice: 4+1
Armor Class: 5 [14]
Attack: Bite (1d6 plus paralysis)
Saving Throw: 13
Special: Paralysis, undead, surprise on 1-2 on 1d6
Move: 18
Alignment: Chaos
CL/XP: 5/240

Ghoul wolves are carnivorous undead wolves that delight in hunting living creatures, catching them, and tearing them to shreds. These creatures are most often found haunting desolate moors and marshes. They hunt in packs, surrounding their prey and circling as they move in for the kill.

Those hit by a ghoul wolf's bite must succeed on a saving throw or be paralyzed for 1d4+2 rounds. Elves are immune to this paralysis.

Dire Ghoul Wolf

Hit Dice: 12+1
Armor Class: 2 [17]
Attack: Bite (2d6 plus paralysis)
Saving Throw: 3
Special: Paralysis, undead, surprise on 1-2 on 1d6
Move: 18
Alignment: Chaos
CL/XP: 13/2300

Dire ghoul wolves resemble their lesser kin, but are much larger. Those hit by a dire ghoul wolf's bite must succeed on a saving throw or be paralyzed for 1d4+2 rounds. Even elves can be affected by a dire ghoul wolf's paralysis.

Blight Below the Demon's Peak

In an alpine landscape there is a small village of herdsmen. Looking down on the village there is a crooked, snow-covered mountain called Demon's Peak. Located halfway between the mountain and the village there is a small shrine carved into the mountain and faced with red marble. The shrine was tended by a hermit and contained an ancient clay tablet inscribed with glyphs of power. These glyphs kept the terrible secrets of the mountain hidden until a band of raiders (or adventurers) forced their way into the shrine and absconded with the tablet.

One the tablet was removed, the foul energies inside the Demon's Peak let loose a contagion on the valley below. With the streams poisoned, the cattle died away and those people who did not flee the valley were struck with a debilitating disease approximating mummy rot. The people, now afraid to spread their contagion elsewhere, survive by gathering mushroom and roots from the meadows and woodlands in the valley. They all dwell in the parish house in the village, barring entry to others for fear of infecting them.

At night, a mob of 1d3+1 dire ghoul wolves and 2d4 ghoul wolves prowl the valley in search of victims.

Copyright Notice
Authors Clark Peterson and Scott Greene.

Wolf, Shadow

Hit Dice: 4
Armor Class: 6 [13]
Attack: Ghostly bite (1d4 strength)
Saving Throw: 13
Special: Incorporeal, strength damage, shadow blend
Move: 18
Alignment: Chaos
Challenge Level/XP: 6/400

Shadow wolves are large black hounds formed of darkness. Their eyes burn with a crimson fire. Shadow wolves are nocturnal hunters and hate all living creatures. Their eyes flash with a crimson fire when prey is sighted.

Shadow wolves prefer to attack from ambush, using the shadows and darkness to their advantage. When prey wanders nearby, a shadow wolf leaps to the attack. A shadow wolf pack leads its prey into an ambush and then strikes when opponents are completely unaware.

As incorporeal creatures, a shadow wolf can only be harmed by magic weapons and magic spells like *magic missile*. Likewise, their ghostly bites ignore bonuses to Armor Class due to armor.

The bite of a shadow wolf deals 1d4 points of strength damage to a living foe. A creature reduced to strength 0 dies.

In any condition of illumination other than full daylight, a shadow wolf can disappear into the shadows, making it impossible to see. Attacks against a shadow wolf hidden in shadow are made at a -10 penalty to hit. Artificial illumination, even a *light* spell, does not negate this ability.

Shadowy Red Herrings

A band of rat-faced assassins has taken up residence in the slimy, limestone catacombs beneath a tropical city-state. The assassins are led by an aggressive, cold-blooded magic-user with coffee-colored skin, green eyes and dark brown hair hidden beneath a white wig. Tall and pinched-faced, the man poses as a physician by day and runs his small guild at night.

The assassins have been hired by the local patriarch to bump off a rival theologian. They are currently exploring the catacombs for one that might allow them access to the theologian's townhouse. To cover their explorations, the magic-user has simmoned a pack of 1d8+4 shadow wolves. The wolves have been terrorizing the city-state at night and then hustling back into the catacombs by day to protect the assassins.

The physician/assassin works and lives in a gray, brick building with marble accents near the city hall. He keeps a coffer (locked, trapped with a poisoned needle) hidden in his wardrobe. The coffer contains 1d6 x 1,000 gp and a piece of rose quartz worth 1d10 x 100 gp.

Copyright Notice
Author Scott Greene.

Wolf-in-Sheep's-Clothing

Hit Dice: 9
Armor Class: 4 [15]
Attack: 7 tentacles (1d4), bite (2d4)
Saving Throw: 7
Special: Constriction, all-around vision, lure-growth
Move: 3
Alignment: Neutrality
Challenge Level/XP: 10/1400

The wolf-in-sheep's clothing is perhaps the single strangest monster adventurers have encountered to date. It appears as a gray-brown tree stump about 3-4 feet in diameter. Two 10-foot long eyestalks protrude from the creature's base. Each eyestalk is brownish-green in color and is topped by a violet flower-like eye. Seven to ten root tentacles, black-brown in color, give the monster its means of locomotion. Its mouth is located on its trunk-like body and appears to be nothing more than a deep scar, except when the creature opens it. The mouth is lined with razor-sharp and jagged greenish-white teeth. Its strangest and perhaps deadliest characteristic is its ability to "sprout" a growth on its top that resembles a small furry animal (such as a rabbit or squirrel). The wolf-in-sheep's clothing uses this ability to lure in its prey, when it strikes with deadly force and aim.

The wolf-in-sheep's-clothing uses its lure-growth ability to draw in prey. When a creature moves within 10 feet of the wolf-in-sheep's-clothing, it lashes out with a tentacle. If it hits, the victim must succeed at a saving throw or be grabbed and constricted for 1d4 points of damage per round. A grabbed victim is dragged to the monster's mouth and bitten until dead.

A tentacle has 10 hit points and can be attacked by making a successful attack against an Armor Class of 2 [17]. Severing a tentacle deals no damage to a wolf-in-sheep's-clothing. Severed tentacles grow back in 1d4 weeks.

The wolf-in-sheep's-clothing's 7-foot long eyestalks allow it to look in any direction, thereby making it nearly impossible to surprise or attack from behind.

Disturbing the Peace

On a long, forested island there are two villages. One belongs to a gangly race of men with reddish-brown skin and narrow, close-set eyes while the other belongs to a race of men with black skin, angular faces and cornflower blue eyes. The two peoples do not care for one another, and their respective rulers are convinced that the "others" wish to conquer the entire island.

The island is rich in tin, and a nearby kingdom, just across the straits, has an interest in keeping those mines open and productive. To this end, they have negotiated an unsteady peace and placed a small army on the island to maintain it.

The army consists of 20 crossbowmen, 50 pikemen and a squadron of 10 light horsemen. It is led by a stately old knight with dark brown skin, curly, reddish hair and walnut-colored eyes. The knight and his army occupy the heights at the center of the island. The heights are in a defensible position and nearby, in the middle of their camp, there is a fresh water spring. A single, well worn path connects the two villages and runs very near the camp. The knight has posted sentries on the road every night since the army took up residence, but in the past week they have been disappearing.

The villagers, of course, blame each other and tensions have grown particularly high. The actual culprit is a wolf-in-sheep's-clothing. It and its ancestors have dwelled on the forested island for centuries and, though they have taken a few villagers (probably the cause of the enmity between the villages) they mostly prey on the island's wolves, badgers and hawks.

Credit

The Wolf-In-Sheep's-Clothing originally appeared in the First Edition module *S3 Expedition to the Barrier Peaks* (© TSR/Wizards of the Coast, 1980) and later in the First Edition *Monster Manual II* (© TSR/Wizards of the Coast, 1983) and is used by permission.

Copyright Notice

Author Scott Greene, based on original material by Gary Gygax.

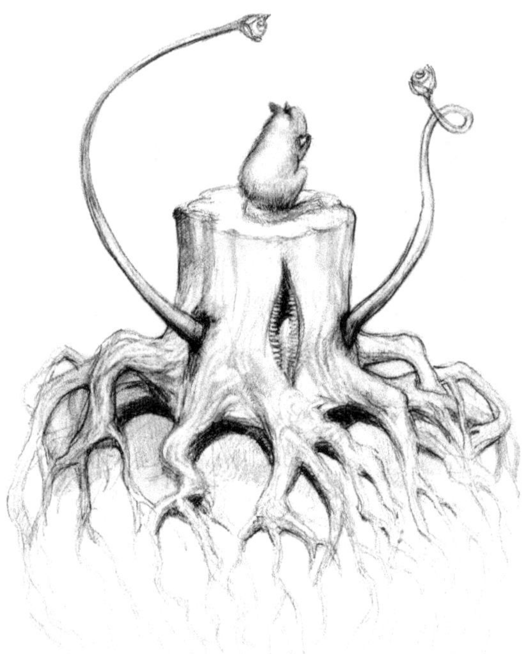

Wolf-Spider

Hit Dice: 6
Armor Class: 4 [15]
Attack: Bite (1d8 plus poison)
Saving Throw: 11
Special: Poison, web, surprise on roll of 1-3 on 1d6 when in their webs
Move: 15/9 (climbing)
Alignment: Chaos
Challenge Level/XP: 8/800

A wolf spider appears as a large monstrous spider with the head of a wolf. Its eyes are multifaceted like a spider's, and its fangs are complimented by a set of spider-like mandibles. Wolf-spiders are very territorial creatures and hunt their prey, kill it, and drag it back to their web lair. Wolf-spiders speak the language of goblins and might speak the common tongue.

A wolf-spider delivers a debilitating poison with a successful bite attack. Victims must pass a saving throw or suffer 1d6 points of strength damage.

Wolf-spiders can throw a web eight times per day. This is similar to an attack with a net but has a maximum range of 50 feet and is effective against targets up to hill giant size. An entangled creature can escape with a successful open doors check.

Wolf-spiders often create sheets of sticky webbing up to 30 feet square. They position these sheets to snare flying creatures but can also use them to trap prey on the ground. Approaching creatures have a 1 in 6 chance to notice a web (2 in 6 for elves). Otherwise they stumble into it and become trapped as though by a successful web attack. Each web has 12 hit points.

A wolf-spider can move across its own web at its climb speed and can pinpoint the location of any creature touching its web.

Rescue the Princess

There is a small native village over the next rise, beneath steep chalk cliffs pocked with small caves and home to a colony of brightly colored birds (or are they feathered reptiles) making a cacophony of shrieks and screeches. The villagers live on the shores of a placid lagoon of blue-green water so crystal clear it is like looking through a glass to the white sands below. Swimming in the lagoon are a shiver of five tiger sharks.

In the midst of the lagoon there is a weathered pillar of basalt - natural, and rising about seven feet above the surface of the lagoon. To long walkways lead out to the pillar from either shore. Standing on the pillar are two men, their ochre skin glistening in the noon sun. At a signal from a man in a feathered cloak and headdress on the shore, the men begin to wrestle. If the adventurers do not interfere, one of the men eventually is thrown into the water and torn limb from limb by the sharks. At this, a maiden on the shore gives out a terrible shriek. When the victor reaches the shore, he takes the woman by the wrist, gives the man in the feathered cloak a hard stare and heads for a cave in the cliffs.

The victor is under the control of a powerful witch doctor, and the witch doctor shall soon have his prize. Inside his subterranean lair he is preparing a ritual that will summon forth the demon queen of poisonous things from the Abyss, and all he lacked was a maiden of royal blood and a new moon. The maiden is now in his possession and the new moon comes tonight.

The witch doctor's lair is a collection of three caves, each larger than the first. The first cave is smallish and trapped with poisoned darts set off by a tripwire. The second has smooth walls painted with images of horror. This is an echo chamber that magnifies every sound twenty fold (and triples sonic damage of any kind). The final chamber is the witch doctor's lair, which he shares with two large wolf-spiders, envoys of the demon queen. One is usually stationed above the entrance, the other by the witch doctor, allowing the old man to stroke its bristles and ruffle the fur on its neck. During the ritual, the controlled warrior is present and the maiden will be suspended over a beating human heart on the ground, the heart surrounded by silver powder tracing out a magic circle. When the ritual is completed, the demon queen's essence will flow up from the heart and into the maiden. In four rounds, the transformation is complete.

The chieftain (the man in the feathered cloak) is distraught over losing his daughter and the finest warrior in his tribe. He cannot help but believe there was trickery involved, and should he catch sight of the outsiders, he will beg for their help. His people know that the witch dcotor's caves are taboo, and they will not enter. In return he offers his daughter's hand in marriage and half of his kingdom.

Copyright Notice

Woodwose

Hit Dice: 6
Armor Class: 6 [13]
Attacks: 1 weapon (1d8) or 2 fists (1d4)
Saving Throw: 10
Special: Spells, spines, immune to wooden weapons and plant-based spells
Move: 9
Alignment: Chaos
Challenge Level/XP: 7/600

Woodwose are green gnarled old men with skin-like tree bark and moss beards. A woodwose can cause sharpened wooden spines to protrude from its body that deal 1d6 points of damage to any creature in contact with or holding the woodwose. Woodwose cast spells as 5th-level clerics. They are immune to wooden weapons (such as clubs) and plant-based spells.

Wood Woes

Dark clouds the color of a bruise fester over the dead forest, spitting jagged streaks of lightning that burst the decaying tree trunks in explosive blasts of brittle bark. Trees crash and fall with booms that echo loudly through the leafless oaks and elms. In the middle of a clearing, a dryad is strapped with coarse vines to two stout broken branches crossed into an 'X'. The dryad Idylia struggles weakly against her bonds. A line of salt forms a perfect circle around the woman. On the far side of the clearing, a crude lean-to of split branches and dead leaves sits against the gnarled wood of a dead elm. Vines draped over the single entry form a makeshift curtain.

This dead area in the Kajaani Forest used to be alive and beautiful under the protection of a dryad, but a vengeful woodwose changed all that. The angry forest creature captured the dryad and tortures the beautiful creature as the forest decays around her. The crude crucifix holding her is all that remains of her tree.

The woodwose lives in the lean-to, but often can be found capering through the dead trees. His bark-like skin lets him hide in plain sight among the dying trees simply by standing still. Idylia will last just a few more hours under the woodwose's ministrations.

Copyright Notice
Author Scott Greene.

Yellow Musk Creeper

Hit Dice: 3
Armor Class: 4 [15]
Attack: Pollen spray (see below) or 2 tendrils (1d8)
Saving Throw: 14
Special: Create yellow musk zombie, intelligence damage, pollen spray, rejuvenation
Move: 3
Alignment: Neutrality
Challenge Level/XP: 5/240

The yellow musk creeper is a slow-moving plant that attacks living creatures and feeds on their intelligence, eventually turning such creatures into yellow musk zombies. Creepers can be found in moderate to warm climates or underground, and are rarely encountered elsewhere.

The plant is a large, green clinging vine with ivy-like leaves of dark green. Small, dark green bulbs and bright yellow flowers mottled with purple adorn the plant. The actual root of the plant is a large bulbous, brown sac that lies beneath the surface of the ground where the yellow musk creeper grows.

Yellow musk creepers lie silent until prey approaches within 10 feet. The small flowers of the creeper then puff a musky-smelling fine powder at a single target, attempting to entrance the target. If attacked, a yellow musk creeper lashes out with its tendrils.

Yellow musk creepers are never encountered alone. They always have a retinue of yellow musk zombies with them. These zombies will defend the creeper against all attacks.

A yellow musk creeper can spray a tiny cloud of hypnotic pollen at a single creature within 30 feet. An opponent hit by the cloud must succeed on a saving throw or be entranced for 1d4 minutes (as by a *charm monster* spell). Entranced creatures can take no action other than to move to the yellow musk creeper. An entranced creature resists any attempt to halt its progress. A victim within reach of the yellow musk creeper stands there and offers no resistance to the monster's attacks.

A yellow musk creeper can insert hundreds of tiny roots into the head of an entranced foe within any space occupied by the creeper. An entranced foe does not resist this attack and does not receive a saving throw to break free of its entranced state. This attack deals 1d4 points of intelligence damage each round. A victim reduced to intelligence 0 becomes a yellow musk zombie under the control of the creeper that created it in 1 hour (see that entry in this book). The transformation can be prevented by the casting of *neutralize poison* followed by a *restoration* spell.

A yellow musk creeper can be killed only if its root is dug up, then burned, hacked apart, or otherwise destroyed. Reducing the creeper to 0 or less hit points puts it out of commission, allowing excavation of its roots. The main root has an AC of 1 [18] and 10 hit points. As long as the root remains intact, a yellow musk creeper regrows in about 2 weeks.

Do Not Sniff the Yellow Flowers!

In the midst of a jungle there is a low depression with fairly steep, rocky sides covered with green vines of yellow and purple flowers. The vines extend into the depression and partially obscure a giant stone head with a demonic face. The stone head was carved for a stone golem that was never completed (or, for a more challenging encounter, a stone golem that was completed and activated and is now buried just under the surface of the depression.

The vines belong, of course, a yellow musk creeper. Its 1d6 yellow musk zombies are stationed in the jungle around the depression. It's not uncommon for a band of adventurers to be "herded" by the zombies into the depression and the waiting tendrils of their master.

The stone head contains a crystal matrix composed of a ruby, sapphire, emerald and diamond encased in a golden sphere. Each jewel is worth 1,000 gp and the gold sphere is worth 500 gp.

Credit

The Yellow Musk Creeper originally appeared in the First Edition *Fiend Folio* (© TSR/Wizards of the Coast, 1981) and is used by permission

Copyright Notice

Author Scott Greene, based on original material by Albie Fiore.

Yellowjacket, Giant

Hit Dice: 4
Armor Class: 4 [15]
Attacks: bite (1d3) or sting (1d4 + poison)
Saving Throw: 13
Special: Poison, pheromone
Move: 1/20 (flying)
Alignment: Neutrality
Challenge Level/XP: 6/400

Giant yellowjackets are 8 feet long with alternating bands of black and yellow on their thorax and abdomen. Workers generally have thicker black bands than the queen or soldiers. The yellowjacket's stinger is slightly curved and barbed and their mandibles are well-formed and developed, allowing them to chew their food. They attack by biting foes, saving its sting unless confronting a more powerful opponent. If attacked, a giant yellowjacket releases a pheromone that makes all yellowjackets in the area more aggressive (+1 to attack, damage).

The Apple Orchard

The branches of a dozen blossoming apple trees hang low with ripe fruit. On the ground around the trunks, daisies, peonies and lilies grow rampant. Bloody chunks of meat are scattered among the flowers, the barely identifiable flesh sliced and diced into gory pieces. A goblin lies in the bushes, its head severed at the neck, and one leg missing entirely. Blood pools in thick puddles under the grasses. A massive 15-foot-long snake skeleton is wrapped around the upper branches of one of the apple trees. The orchard is the home of a nest of giant yellowjackets that drove the giant snake from its underground burrow and moved in. The snake was slaughtered in the tree where it crawled to escape, and its flesh used to feed the young yellowjackets. The yellowjackets live in the underground warrens, and send 12 warriors out to attack anyone wandering around the insects' food sources.

Copyright Notice

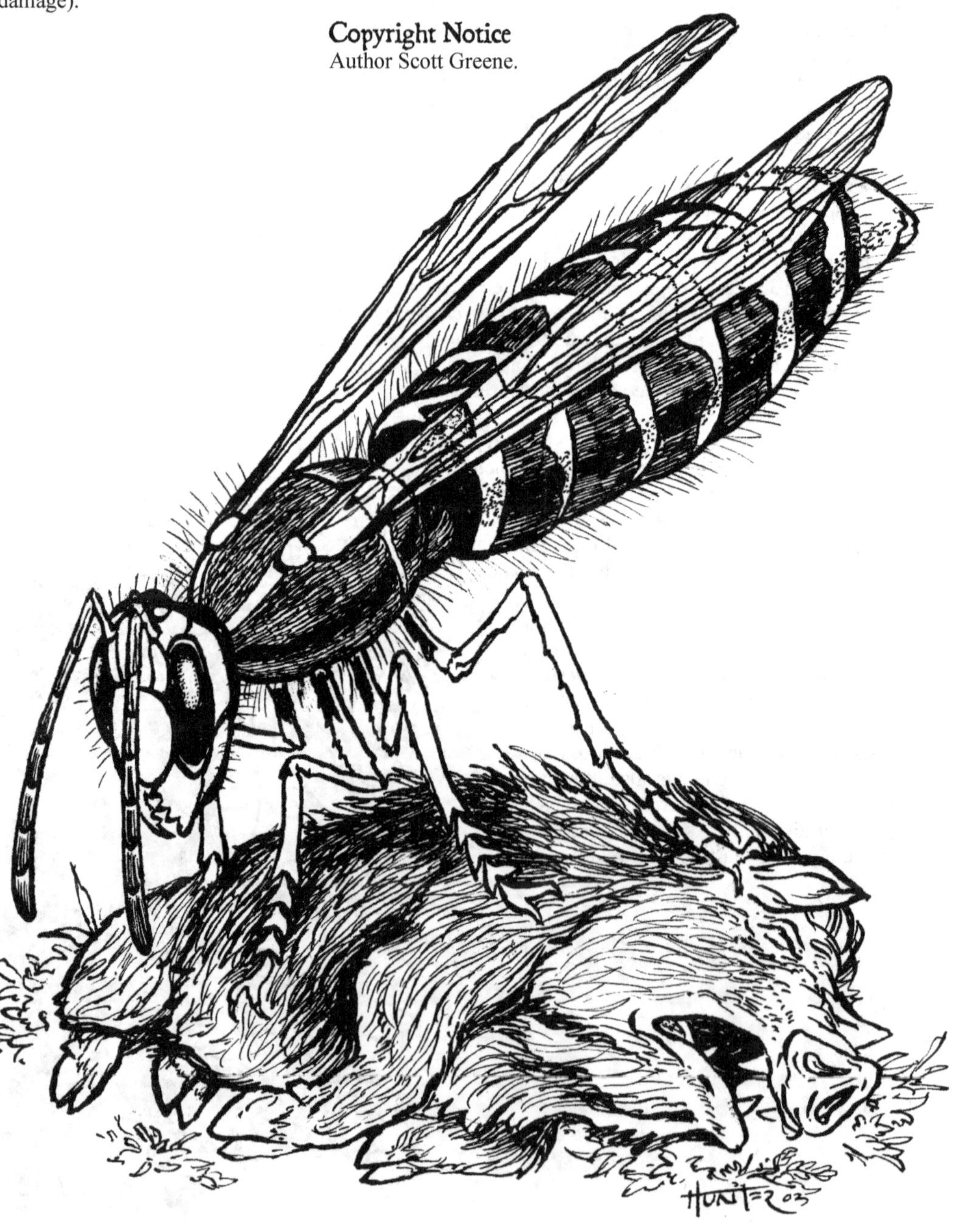

Yeti

Hit Dice: 4
Armor Class: 5 [14]
Attack: 2 claws (1d6)
Saving Throw: 13
Special: Cold, frightful gaze, squeeze, immunity to cold, double damage from fire, surprise on roll of 1-4 on 1d6 in snowy areas
Move: 15
Alignment: Neutrality
Challenge Level/XP: 7/600

A yeti is a large, hulking humanoid covered in white, shaggy fur. Its hands end in razor-sharp claws. The yeti's head is large and sports a large round mouth filled with fangs. The typical yeti stands 9 feet tall and weighs 600 or more pounds.

Yetis make their lairs in remote mountains and hills. They are fierce predators with ravenous appetites, dining on mountain goats, sheep and humanoids. They are particularly fond of human and elf flesh.

Creatures within 30 feet that meet the eyes of a yeti must succeed on a saving throw or stand paralyzed in fear (treat as a *hold person* spell) for 3 rounds. A creature that successfully saves cannot be affected again by the frightful gaze of that yeti for one day.

A yeti's body generates intense cold, dealing 1d6 points of damage to those that contact it for at least one round. An opponent hit by both of a yeti's claw attacks in the same round must pass a saving throw or be squeezed for 2d6 points of damage (plus 1d6 points of cold damage) each round the hold is maintained. The victim can escape with an open doors check.

Everyone Knows They Bounce

An ancient stone lamaserie is constructed on cliffs overlooking a sprawling village. The lamaserie and village are located on a high plateau inhabited by blue-furred tigers, takins, gazelles, cranes and snow chickens.

The villagers keep goats and yaks and grow fields of barley during their short growing season. The village is ruled by a brotherhood of 1d10+3 monks who dwell in a newer, smaller monastery within the village. The lama is a 6th level monk named Shamar, a stately, elderly gentleman with kind eyes and a sharp nose and chin.

The old lamaserie is a sprawling complex with tall walls that have, over hundreds of winters, developed deep cracks and partially tumbled to the bottom of the cliff. The lamaserie is two-stories tall and has an enclosed courtyard and a three-story stone watchtower. Stairs wind up the side of the cliffs connecting the lamaserie to the village. The stairs climb 60 feet and are often slick with ice or moisture.

The lamaserie is now inhabited by 1d6+3 yeti. They have made a few raids into the village and the monks are preparing a response, though they would much rather hire a band of adventurers to do it for them.

Credit

The Yeti originally appeared in the First Edition *Monster Manual* (© TSR/Wizards of the Coast, 1977) and is used by permission.

Copyright Notice

Author Scott Greene, based on original material by Gary Gygax.

Zombie, Brine

Hit Dice: 4
Armor Class: 6 [13]
Attack: Cutlass (1d6) or fists (1d4)
Saving Throw: 13
Special: Resistance to fire (50%)
Move: 12/12 (swimming)
Alignment: Chaos
Challenge Level/XP: 4/120

A brine zombie appears as a rotting humanoid dressed in tattered and ragged clothing. Its semi-bloated body glistens from the slimy mixture of water and seaweed that hangs from its form. The creature's rotting flesh is blue-green in color. No semblance of life burns in its eyes.

Brine zombies are the remnants of a ship's crew that has perished at sea. They are mindless creatures, not very pleasant to look at, and relentless in their attacks on the living. The spark of evil that brought them back from the ocean depths drives them to seek the living so they may join them in their watery graves. Brine zombies appear much as they did in life.

Revenge Is a Dish Best Served Briny

Every year, dozens of ships laden with spices enter the ports along the jungle coast, dropping their cargo and picking up timber and exotic birds for the desert kingdoms across the sea. The prince of the coast is a generous man with those who serve him loyally, but he is merciless toward those he suspects of betrayal.

So it was, a month ago, that the *Kingfish* left the port with a load of ironwood and a bit of sabotage. It went down about 10 miles off shore and its crew has been walking along the bottom ever since to enact their revenge on the prince and his precious city.

On the night of a visit by a band of adventurers (such bad luck), 40 brine zombies will rise from the waters and do their best to destroy the city. Their first target is the local temple and the clerics. After that, they'll cut a road of red ruin through the village on their way to the palace.

Copyright Notice
Author Scott Greene.

Zombie, Corpsespun

Hit Dice: 3
Armor Class: 6 [13]
Attacks: weapon or strike (1d8)
Saving Throw: 14
Special: Poisonous spider bites, immune to sleep and charm spells
Move: 6
Alignment: Neutrality
Challenge Level/XP: 3/60

Corpsespun zombies are the victims of a corpsespinner, whose poison animates the dead as an automaton sheathed in webs. The victim's insides are replaced by thousands of tiny spiders crawling over its body and into and out of its ears, eyes, and mouth. These spiders take over and devour the insides of the creature, but keep it moving with a semblance of its former self. Corpsespun zombies transfer 1d4 spiders with each attack to their foes. Each spider delivers a weak poison that does 1 point of damage.

The Spider Piñata

Four figures shamble through the thick webs filling this rocky cavern, their slow gait marking them as zombies even before the rotten meat stench of death betrays them. Thousands of spiders crawl across their bodies, and move in and out of their gaping wounds. Hanging in the center of the chamber is a giant spider, its body shriveled and its legs curling against its drooping abdomen. The spider is tangled in its webs and obviously dead. The corpsespun zombies have infested nearly every nook and cranny of the room with their spiders, and the dead spider is filled to bursting with the small arachnids. Anyone pushing the spider aside to get to the zombies causes the spider to burst like a piñata, showering the PCs with hundreds of venomous corpsepun spiders. Each PC within 10 feet is covered in 3d6 spiders that swarm over the victim as the zombies close in and attack.

Copyright Notice
Author Scott Greene.

Zombie, Juju

Hit Dice: 3
Armor Class: 2 [17]
Attack: Weapon or fists (1d6)
Saving Throw: 14
Special: +1 or better weapon to hit, immunity to electricity and cold, immunity to magic missile, resistance to fire (50%)
Move: 12
Alignment: Chaos
Challenge Level/XP: 5/240

A juju zombie looks like a desiccated humanoid with grayish, leathery flesh. It is dressed in filthy rags, and its eyes are small pinpoints of crimson light. An odor of death hangs in the air around the creature.

Juju zombies' hatred of living creatures and the magic that created them are what hold them to the world of the living. When a humanoid or monstrous humanoid is slain by an *energy drain* or a similar spell or spell-like ability, it may rise as a juju zombie.

All-Seeing Eye of Mojango

The swamp holds many terrors and strangenesses, none more terrible than the All-Seeing Eye of Mojango. The eye is actually a sphere of smooth, black stone (unidentifiable, even by dwarves). It is placed in a tree top and gives off arcs of purple and gold light that have the ability to hypnotize the weak-minded. If touched, the sphere drains 1d4 levels (a saving throw is permitted to reduce this to 1 level). Those that have had levels drained by the sphere have their eyes turn purple and gain the ability to see in darkness for one month.

Many adventurers have come across the Eye, and its location in the swamp seems to change from sighting to sighting. Wherever the Eye appears, its "handmaidens" appear as well, a troupe of 1d4+1 juju zombies, past victims of the object.

Credit

The Juju Zombie originally appeared in the First Edition *Monster Manual II* (© TSR/Wizards of the Coast, 1983) and is used by permission.

Copyright Notice

Author Scott Greene, based on original material by Gary Gygax.

Zombie, Spellgorged

Hit Dice: 2
Armor Class: 8 [11], or 7[12] with shield
Attacks: weapon or strike (1d8)
Saving Throw: 16
Special: Immune to sleep and charm spells, store spells, spell conflagration
Move: 6
Alignment: Neutrality
Challenge Level/XP: 4/120

A spellgorged zombie is a zombie crafted from the corpse of a Magic-User or Cleric to serve as a *ring of spell storing*. Spells can be cast directly into the zombie's mouth to store them until needed. A spellgorged zombie can store 1d6 spells (either Magic-User or Cleric). The zombie's creator can cause the zombie to explode by detonating the stored spells in a blast that does 4d6 points of damage to all within 20 feet (save for half).

Spell Bombs

A line of shambling 10 zombies wanders into Loodis, their shuffling gait slowed by a leather strap tied around their waists. The ropes link the undead to a skeletal kathlin walking behind them. A robed figure rides on the back of the six-legged horse.

Xun Marush is a 10th-level magic-user who controls the line of spellgorged zombies. He stores his spells in the undead. If outnumbered, Xun unhooks a zombie from the horse's saddle, and lets it shamble forward before he detonates it. Xun rides into towns and demands gold to leave. He detonates a number of the undead if he has to just to show his power.

Copyright Notice
Author Scott Greene.

Zombie, Yellow Musk

Hit Dice: 2
Armor Class: 3 [16]
Attack: Weapon (1d8) or fists (1d6)
Saving Throw: 16
Special: Link to creator, sprout new creeper
Move: 12
Alignment: Neutrality
Challenge Level/XP: 5/240

A yellow musk zombie has pale yellow skin and stark white eyes. Its clothes hang in tatters around its decaying form. Despite being called zombies, they are not undead and cannot be turned or controlled by clerics.

After about 2 months of service to a yellow musk creeper, the yellow musk zombie wanders up to 1 mile away from its creator (the link to creator is broken) and dies. Where it falls, new yellow musk seedlings sprout from its head and the corpse, take root, and within one hour, a new fully grown yellow musk creeper blossoms.

Credit

The Yellow Musk Zombie originally appeared in the First Edition *Fiend Folio* (© TSR/Wizards of the Coast, 1981) and is used by permission.

Copyright Notice

Author Scott Greene, based on original material by Albie Fiore.

Appendix A:
Animals

Archerfish, Giant

Hit Dice: 2
Armor Class: 7 [12]
Attacks: 1 bite (1d4)
Saving Throw: 16
Special: Water spray
Move: 15 (swim)
Alignment: Neutrality
Challenge Level/XP: 2/30

Giant archerfish are 3 feet long and have silver-colored bodies with vertical black stripes that begin just behind the head and fade as they near the tail. Their eyes are either cloudy blue or silver and its fins are slightly darker than its body. Some species of giant archer fish are yellowish-gray with dark-colored eyes, but all have the vertical black stripes. Giant archerfish can grow to be 5 feet long. The archerfish can shoot a jet of water up to 30 feet to knock prey into the water (save to avoid).

One Fish, Two Fish, Big Fish . . . Bigger Fish

The canal city of Venexia is a marvel of engineering, with buildings built on hundreds of small islands. Arching stone bridges cross the canals that wind through the city. Open boats poled through the canals allow residents to get from landing to landing. Low railings along the canals are designed more for show than to keep people from falling into the waters. Landings scattered throughout the city allow the shallow rafts to dock and take on passengers.

People are scared to go near the water, however, and those who must use the boats do so quickly. Residents speak of the "killer fish" in the canals that spit water and then swallow people whole. Signs posted about the city offer a 10 gp reward per "killer fish" caught, with a crude drawing of the archerfish.

Twenty giant archerfish did indeed recently swim into the canal system, and the aggressive fish attack anyone standing along the canals or poling the boats that ply the waters. But the archerfish so far haven't killed anything besides a few pets that got too close to the water's edge. The real culprits are six sharks that followed the tasty archerfish treats into the canals. People knocked off boats and bridges by the archerfish end up splashing in the water, which draws the hungry sharks.

Copyright Notice
Author Scott Greene.

Axe Beak

Hit Dice: 3
Armor Class: 5 [14]
Attack: 2 claws (1d6) and bite (2d6)
Saving Throw: 14
Special: None
Move: 18
Alignment: Neutrality
Challenge Level/XP: 3/60

The axe beak is a prehistoric flightless, carnivorous bird that resembles a 7-foot tall ostrich. It is an aggressive hunter and has a strong, thick neck and a sharp beak. The axe beak makes a honking noise that can be heard clearly up to one-half mile away. An axe beak lair contains 1d4 eggs worth 50-80 gp each. Hatchlings fetch the same value on the market. The creatures attack by kicking and biting. It is a very aggressive hunter and runs down its prey should an opponent flee. If extremely hungry, an axe beak attacks until it or its prey is dead.

Looking for a Nest Egg

Beneath an umbrella tree on a plain of yellowish grasses a female axe beak stands guard over her flock's egg pit. The dominant hen of the flock, she is highly aggressive in the defense of the 1d4+1 eggs buried in the pit, and enjoys a +1 bonus to hit and damage while fighting for them. Any aggressive action brings a chorus of honking that attracts the other 1d4+1 members of her flock. The local halflings have made the stealing of these eggs something of a cottage industry, and as a result the birds now attack small humanoids on sight and in preference to taller humanoids. One such halfling, a thief of little note, has been treed in the umbrella tree and is desperate for rescue. He claims he has a treasure map that he's quite willing to share if only the adventurers extract him from his predicament.

Credit

The Axe Beak originally appeared in the First Edition *Monster Manual* (© TSR/Wizards of the Coast, 1977) and is used by permission.

Copyright Notice

Author Scott Greene, based on original material by Gary Gygax.

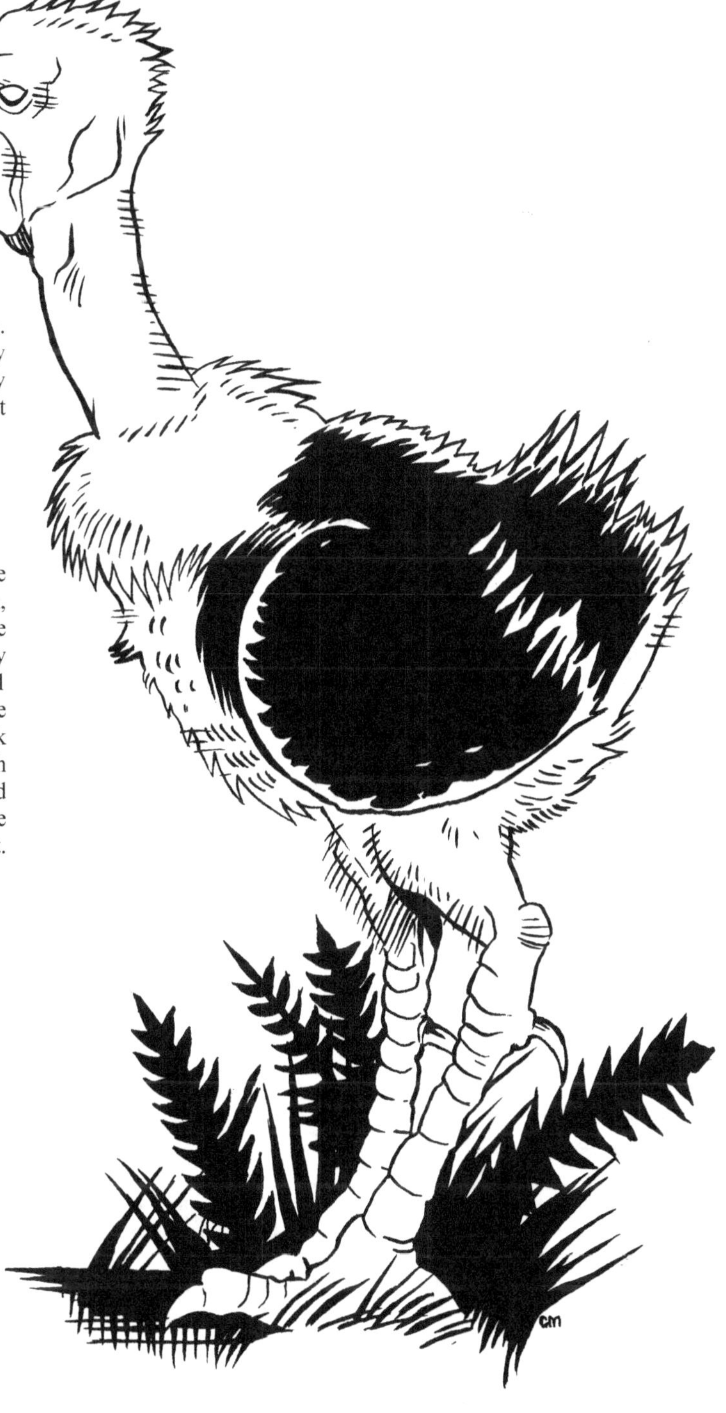

Barracuda

Small
Hit Dice: 1
Armor Class: 5 [14]
Attack: Bite (1d4)
Saving Throw: 17
Special: None
Move: 0/27 (swimming)
Alignment: Neutrality
CL/XP: 1/15

Medium
Hit Dice: 4
Armor Class: 5 [14]
Attack: Bite (1d6)
Saving Throw: 13
Special: None
Move: 0/27 (swimming)
Alignment: Neutrality
CL/XP: 4/120

Giant
Hit Dice: 7
Armor Class: 5 [14]
Attack: Bite (1d8)
Saving Throw: 9
Special: None
Move: 0/27 (swimming)
Alignment: Neutrality
CL/XP: 7/600

The barracuda is a predatory fish that averages about 2 feet long and weighs 10-15 pounds. Its body is bluish-gray near the front changing to silver mottled with black spots in the rear. Its mouth is filled with razor-sharp teeth. Medium barracudas are about 6 feet long and weigh 30-45 pounds. Large barracudas are about 10 feet long and weigh 50-80 pounds. The barracuda strikes quickly in combat. Slain prey is devoured immediately.

Battery or Barracuda

Just off the shore of a busy river port there is a popular tavern and inn called the *The Battery*. *The Battery* is composed of the remains of a small watch tower, with additions constructed of wood on a wooden platform held aloft by posts driven into the sea floor.

The Battery is run by a foul-mouthed old pirate the locals call Corvey (though few believe that he was ever a pirate). *The Battery* serves fortified wines, grog and dark, bitter ales, along with a wide variety of seafood. The cook (who people are positive has goblin blood flowing through her veins) makes a habit of tossing scraps out her window into the sea. This chum attracts schools of 1d6+5 barracudas (of whichever size you desire). Rumor has it that Corvey throws troublemakers to these barracuda, watching their struggles from a wicker chair set next to a bay window (and the rumors are true!)

Copyright Notice

Brontotherium

Hit Dice: 10
Armor Class: 4 [15]
Attacks: Gore (2d6+2)
Saving Throw: 5
Special: Trample
Move: 9
Alignment: Neutrality
Challenge Level/XP: 11/1,700

Brontotheriums weigh two tons, are about 14 feet long, and stand eight feet tall at the shoulder. They have dark brown or grayish-brown fur. Brontotheriums are herd animals and charge foes to gore them with their massive horn. If the herd is in danger, the animals charge, trampling opponents for 4d6 points of damage (save for half).

Crossing the Ice

Herds of wild brontotherium scatter before an ironbound warship being pulled slowly across the frozen tundra. The aged ship sits atop a crude wagon sled pulled by a team of domesticated brontotherium. Ogre handlers wrapped in furs walk alongside the massive beasts, leading them across the icy ground.

The Kintok ogre clan found the ship abandoned on a mountainside and is carting it toward the sea nearly 80 miles away. The centuries old warship remains stout and seaworthy. It is equipped with an operable catapult and several ballistae. Ogres walk the decks of the slow-moving vessel. A number of rocks sit on the deck, ready to be loaded into the catapults. Sharpened tree trunks serve as missiles for the ballistae.

Ogres riding brontotherium guard the warship on each side. Equipped with oversized lances, these ogres use the brontotherium's forked horns to guide the lances with uncanny precision.

Where the ogres found the ship and what they plan to do with it are unclear.

Copyright Notice

Caribe, Giant

Hit Dice: 3
Armor Class: 5 [14]
Attack: Bite (1d6)
Saving Throw: 14
Special: Frenzy
Move: 0/15 (swimming)
Alignment: Neutrality
Challenge Level/XP: 3/60

The giant caribe is a rare form of giant saltwater piranha. They are pale bluish-green in color and about 6 feet long, though larger specimens have been encountered.

Giant caribes attack by swarming an opponent and biting with their razor-sharp teeth. Once blood is drawn, the entire pack goes into a frenzy, attacking twice each round and gaining a 1 point bonus to Armor Class. Frenzied giant caribes attack until either they or their opponents are dead.

A giant caribe can notice creatures by scent in a 90-foot radius and detect blood in the water at ranges of up to 500 feet.

In the Shadow of Truth

The head waters of a tropical river are home not only to river dolphins, an aquatic form of pseudodragon and crocodiles, but also schools of 5d6 giant caribes, the apex predator of the river. A number of barges move up and down the river, carrying supplies to the villages and market towns along the river and bringing back timber and tropical fruits.

Aside from the giant caribes, the most famous thing about the river is a tall, bronze post that rises about 15 feet above the surface of the water. Suspended from the top of the post by a chain is a gleaming morningstar. Folk tales tell of the time that the pillar rose from the water amidst a shower of multi-colored sparks. The locals believe it was set there by a devil as a temptation, and many have succumbed to the caribes trying to claim the prize.

The morningstar is a +1 weapon. Creatures hit with the morningstar must pass a saving throw or be shrouded in shadow - essentially making them appear to be a shadow and completely blinding them. The bearer of the morningstar gains the ability to see in the dark, but loses the ability to tell truth from deception. Whether the morningstar is the product of deviltry is unknown, but likely considering its powers.

Catfish, Giant Electric

Hit Dice: 8
Armor Class: 3 [16]
Attacks: Bite (1d8)
Saving Throw: 8
Special: Electric discharge, swallow whole
Move: 9 (swim)
Alignment: Neutrality
Challenge Level/XP: 10/1,400

Giant electric catfish are about 8 feet long but can grow to lengths of 12 feet or more. Its bloated body is generally gray or grayish-brown in color fading to a dull white or cream color on its underbelly. Its eyes are small and its snout wide and round. Three sets of barbels (or feelers) are located around its mouth. Unlike many fish, a giant electric catfish has no dorsal fin. Once every 1d4 rounds, a giant electric catfish can produce an electrical charge that deals 2d6 points of damage (save for half) to everything within 10 feet of it. If a giant catfish rolls a natural 20 on its bite attack it swallows an opponent whole.

Old Sparky

Shouts for help shatter the still of the night. The screams lead PCs to the riverbank of the Quell River, where a glowing circle of light cast by a fisherman's lantern bobbles wildly as his small boat goes round and round in wide circles. The fisherman – an old salt named Grumby – holds on for dear life as the rowboat races through the water, pulled by something holding the rusty chain anchor.

A giant electric catfish is hooked on the other end of the anchor. It swallowed the spiked metal chain when Grumby tossed it overboard. The fish is swimming wildly in the 20-foot-deep river trying to dislodge the hook. Lightning flashes across the water as the angry fish sends jolts of electricity up the chain. Grumby pleads for help.

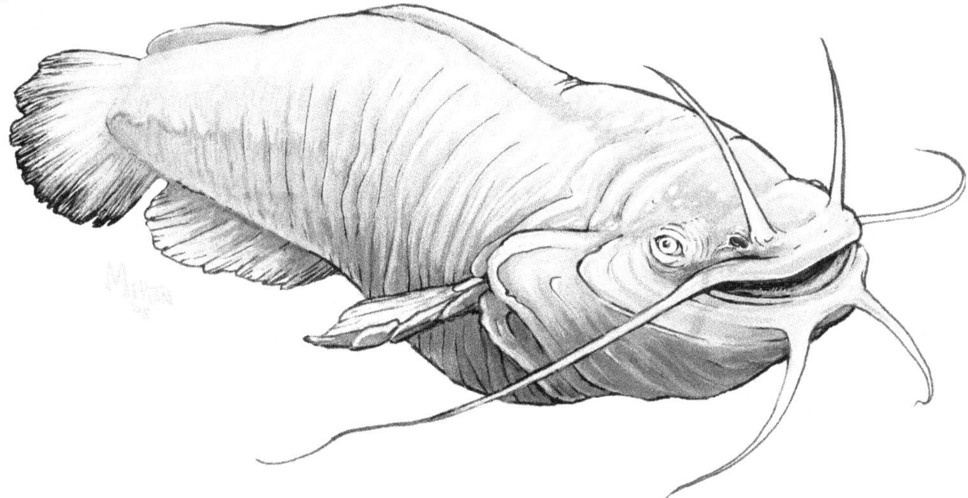

Chameleon, Giant

Hit Dice: 3
Armor Class: 7 [12]
Attacks: bite (1d8+1)
Saving Throw: 14
Special: tongue grab, swallow whole
Move: 6/6 (climb)
Alignment: Neutrality
Challenge Level/XP: 3/60

Giant chameleons are either green or brown in color with the females being slightly darker and heavier than the males. Males are distinguished by the white lateral line running the length of their bodies and the dark bands extending from head to tail. Females usually possess a dark yellow lateral stripe. Both species have striped throats and lips. Giant chameleons attack with their tongue. If the tongue hits, it wraps around the victim and pulls it to the creature's mouth for automatic bite damage in the next round. If the chameleon rolls a natural 20 for its bite attack, it swallows its prey whole. Anything swallowed whole suffers 1d8+1 points of damage plus 1d4 points of acid damage from the creature's digestive juices. Giant chameleons can rotate their eyes independently in a 180-degree radius, making it impossible to sneak up on them.

Chameleon, Giant Horned

Hit Dice: 4
Armor Class: 6 [13]
Attacks: bite (1d8+1)
Saving Throw: 13
Special: tongue grab, swallow whole, gore
Move: 6/6 (climb)
Alignment: Neutrality
Challenge Level/XP: 5/240

Giant horned chameleons are green or dark green. Males are distinguished by the three large horns protruding from their head. This grants them a gore attack (1d6 damage) that they can use in lieu of a bite or tongue attack. These chameleons have a crest on the back of their head, and bony ridges and spines running the length of their back. Giant horned chameleons can also attack with their tongue. If the tongue hits, it wraps around the victim and pulls it to the creature's mouth for automatic bite damage in the next round. If the chameleon rolls a natural 20 for its bite attack, it swallows its prey whole. Anything swallowed whole suffers 1d8+1 points of damage plus 1d4 points of acid damage from the creature's digestive juices. Giant horned chameleons can rotate their eyes independently in a 180-degree radius, making it impossible to sneak up on them.

Chameleon, Rock

Hit Dice: 3
Armor Class: 7 [12]
Attacks: bite (1d8+1)
Saving Throw: 14
Special: tongue grab, swallow whole
Move: 6/6 (climb)
Alignment: Neutrality
Challenge Level/XP: 4/120

Rock chameleons resemble common giant chameleons but their natural coloration is gray and they are only found in warm and temperate mountains where their coloration allows them to blend in with their surroundings. Rock chameleons attack with their tongue. If the tongue hits, it wraps around the victim and pulls it to the creature's mouth for automatic bite damage in the next round. If the chameleon rolls a natural 20 for its bite attack, it swallows its prey whole. Anything swallowed whole suffers 1d8+1 points of damage plus 1d4 points of acid damage from the creature's digestive juices. Rock chameleons can rotate their eyes independently in a 180-degree radius, making it impossible to sneak up on them.

Wildebeest Buffet

The stench of rotting meat flows down the corridors leading into this rocky underground chamber. A dim ghostly light rises off the caps of giant iridescent mushrooms, glowing beacons in the gloom. Ten-foot-wide stone ledges rise throughout the 50-foot-high room. The buzz of flies is a discordant drone echoing from rock to rock. Lying in a furry tangle of rot in the center of the chamber are the remains of four wildebeests that descended into the cave and couldn't escape. Feasting on the carcasses are 4 giant flies, which largely ignore PCs unless they try to hone in on the wildebeest buffet. The flies stay in the center of the room, avoiding the walls. Lounging on three of the stone ledges, waiting to pick off any stray flies or PCs, are 3 giant chameleons.

Copyright Notice
Authors Scott Greene and Meghan Greene.

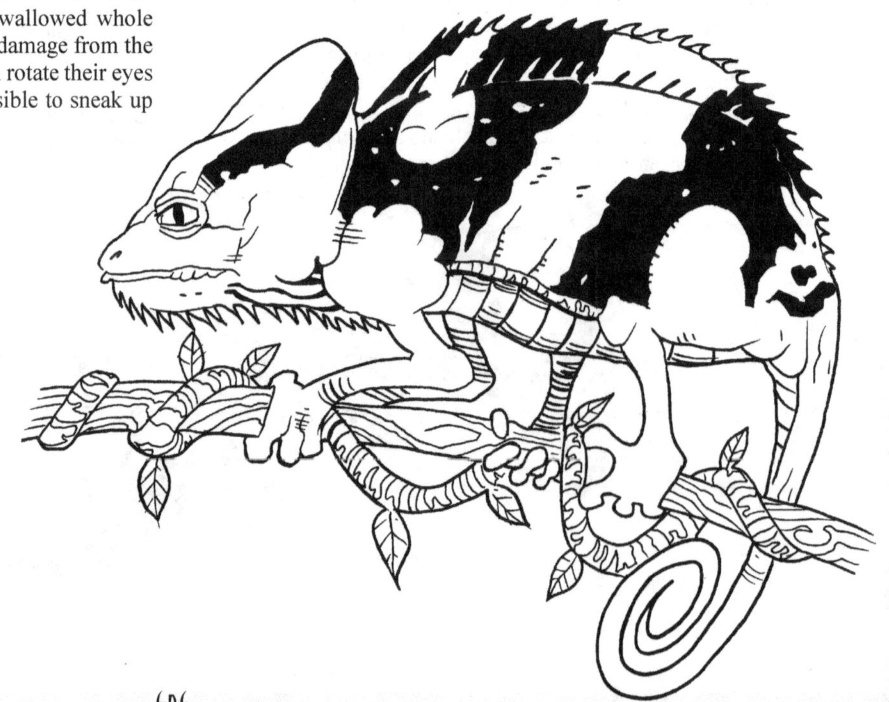

Deer

Hit Dice: 2
Armor Class: 6 [13]
Attack: 2 hooves (1d4) or gore (1d6)
Saving Throw: 16
Special: Surprise on roll of 1-2 on 1d6
Move: 15
Alignment: Neutrality
Challenge Level/XP: 2/30

Shy and wary, deer range from the arctic to the tropics. They are very flexible creatures, adapting easily to their climate and able to survive in all but the harshest of temperatures. Deer are very flexible in their diets as well, able to exist on plants, insects, fish, and even dead birds. Deer arc excellent swimmers and have been known to swim to a distance of five miles in the water. These statistics represent the typical white-tailed deer; they can also be used to represent other deer-like animals such as caribou and antelope.

Deer attack with their hooves or antlers. Antelopes, when defending their herd, attack by charging an opponent and butting with their horns (gore). The gore attack only applies to bucks with antlers.

Black-Tailed Deer

The statistics above can be used to represent the average black-tailed deer as well, with a few minor changes. The black-tailed deer prefers plains, hills, and other open ground as its habitat. In combat, a black-tailed deer jumps about in an effort to confuse its attackers before stotting (hopping) away.

Salt Lick Fool

A few miles away from a farming village there is a salt lick in the form of a cliff about 25 feet tall. The land slopes down gently from the salt lick and supports a number of pine trees and blueberries.

Herds of mule deer visit the rock regularly, and thus encounters with predators around the salt lick occur on a roll of 1-3 on 1d6. The villagers generally avoid the area, though they do stalk the trails that lead to it.

The prime attraction for humans is a strange statue nicknamed "the idiot". The statue sits atop the cliff, and looks like a rotund man with wild hair and a large smile on its face. It is said that one can climb to the top of the salt lick and whisper their plans into the statue's ear. If the plan is likely to fail, a small tear forms in the statue's eye and rolls down its cheek.

Copyright Notice

Dragonfish

Hit Dice: 2
Armor Class: 3 [16]
Attack: Bite (1d4)
Saving Throw: 16
Special: Poison spines, surprise on 1-4 on 1d6
Move: 9 (swimming)
Alignment: Neutrality
Challenge Level/XP: 3/60

This small flat fish has brown scales mottled with black. A series of needle-like spines runs the length of the fish on its dorsal side.

A dragonfish is a small, 2-foot long, flat fish that makes its home on the bottom of shallow lakes, rivers, or streams. They are non-aggressive and spend their days eating miniscule water creatures, insects, and aquatic plants. A dragonfish's back is covered with long, sharp spines. A creature stepping on a dragonfish or attacking it unarmed or with natural weapons must succeed on a saving throw or have a spine snap off in his or her flesh. Lodged spines impose a -1 penalty on attacks and saving throws per spine and inject the victim with poison, inflicting 1d6 points of damage. A spine can be removed safely by a barber, healer or surgeon; otherwise, removing a spine deals an extra 1d4 points of damage.

Tread Carefully

It is an age old tradition that those who would petition the pasha must first walk the 500 steps to his throne through the black pool. "Black pool" in this case is not just a clever name, but an accurate description, for the 2-foot deep pool, lined in azure tiles, is ensorcelled with an impenetrable darkness. Though filled with water, at might just as well be filled with shadow. The pool is about five feet wide, and runs down the center of the pasha's throne room, itself clad in tiles of white marble and no fewer than 500 columns of porphyry with brass capitals depicting in miniature the 3,000 year history of the pasha's kingdom, starting with its foundation by a man raised by giant cockroaches on the banks of a dismal swamp and including its recent foray into a campaign of genocide against the orcs of the western hills.

While the walk is most often taken by visiting diplomats and noblemen seeking redress for wrongs done by other noblemen (all 400 of the kingdom's noblemen are either sons, cousins or nephews of the pasha, who is married to 45 wives), it is also walked by those condemned to die for such crimes as plundering tombs and other subterranean venues without holding legal charter. The pool is home to a single dragonfish, and should one manage to walk the length of the pool without stepping on the beast, they will often find their wishes granted by the pasha.

Credit

The Dragonfish originally appeared in the First Edition *Fiend Folio* (© TSR/Wizards of the Coast, 1981) and is used by permission.

Copyright Notice

Eel, Electric

Hit Dice: 3
Armor Class: 5 [14]
Attack: Bite (1d6)
Saving Throw: 14
Special: Electricity, immunity to electricity
Move: 0/15 (swimming)
Alignment: Neutrality
Challenge Level/XP: 3/60

Electric eels resemble snakes ranging from 9 to 20 feet long and weighing 50 to 120 pounds. Its body is grayish-brown and lightens near the head. Small yellow splotches can be seen near the mouth. The electric eel is slimy to the touch and has no scales (the electric eel is not a true eel, but a fish).

An electric eel prefers to discharge its electricity when it first enters combat. Those slain or rendered unconscious by the shock are devoured. Should any opponents survive the attack, the eel either flees (if outnumbered) or attacks its remaining foes with its bite.

Once per hour, an electric eel can produce a jolt of electricity (about 800 volts at 1 ampere current) in a 10-foot radius centered on its body. Creatures within 5 feet take 3d8 points of electricity damage. Those further away than 5 feet but within 10 feet take 2d8 points of electricity damage. Affected creatures can make a saving throw to reduce the damage by half. Electric eels are immune to their own electrical attacks and that of other electric eels.

Eel Count

On the banks of a river that cuts through a rain forest, an unsuspecting band of adventurers might have the misfortune of running into a gang of trained red howler monkeys (see below). The monkeys have been trained by a man who calls himself the River Count to steal from the travelers and caravans that travel along the banks of the river.

The River Count dwells in a ramshackle castle that stands on a small, rocky island in the middle of the wide river. The banks of the island are clogged with dwarf banana plants and the castle is alive with the sights and sounds of monkeys. The count "owns" about 20 of the red devils, treating them as his court and stashing away their ill-gotten goods in a locked, bronze chest hidden in the half-submerged cellar of the castle.

The cellar consists of two small rooms connected by a short tunnel with a low, arched ceiling. The entry chamber is filled with water up to about 2 feet. Shelves above the water hold molding foodstuffs and a few bottles of fine, sweet wine.

The bronze chest is kept in the second chamber, which is lower than the first and filled up to chest height with river water. One wall of the cellar has partially collapsed, letting in the river water and a pair of large electric eels (maximum hit points). The chest is kept in a high alcove and is retrieved by gangs of monkeys.

Copyright Notice

Eel, Giant Moray

Hit Dice: 5
Armor Class: 3 [16]
Attack: Bite (1d8 plus disease) and tail lash (1d4)
Saving Throw: 12
Special: Disease, immune to disease and fear, surprise on roll of 1-3 on 1d6
Move: 3/9 (swimming)
Alignment: Neutrality
Challenge Level/XP: 6/400

Giant moray eels are greatly feared predators found in warm oceans and seas. They sustain themselves on a diet of crustaceans, fish, and unlucky swimmers who happen to swim too close to their lair. Giant moray eels make their lairs in underwater caves or hollows, a typical lair consisting of two adults and up to 6 young. The bite of the giant moray carries a disease that rots the flesh. The rotting sets in one minute after the bite is delivered and a saving throw is failed, robbing the victim of 1d6 points of constitution and 1d6 points of charisma each day unless a daily saving throw is passed. The disease persists until a saving throw is passed by 5 or more points, a *cure disease* spell is received or the victim's constitution is reduced to 0, at which point they die. Charisma cannot be reduced to below 1. When (or if) the disease is cured or overcome, constitution and charisma return at the rate of 1 point per day, though scarring from the disease permanently destroys one point of each score. Giant moray eels can survive out of the water for 12 rounds, after which they begin to drown.

Heart of Stone

On the banks of a tropical estuary a small tribe of hobgoblins, no more than 20 males and 30 to 40 females and children, works a network of salt pannes and pools, drying the salt into cubes and wrapping it in banana leaves for shipment to the larger tribes in the volcanic mountains located many miles inland.

While the hobgoblins do a bit of spear fishing, they never stray far into the estuary for fear of the school of 2d4 giant moray eels that dwell therein. The hobgoblins worship a granite idol, weathered and almost devoid of features, standing on a sandbar in the middle of the estuary - the distant god, they call him.

The hobgoblins make sacrifices to their god by directing strangers into the estuary or simply not warning them away. Any goods or survivors who come ashore are considered a blessing by the granite god and belong the hobgoblin's shaman (a large, warty male who cast spells as a 4th level cleric).

Credit
The Giant Moray Eel originally appeared in the First Edition *Monster Manual* (© TSR/Wizards of the Coast, 1977) and is used by permission.

Copyright Notice

Eel, Gulper

Hit Dice: 6
Armor Class: 7 [12]
Attacks: 1 bite (1d8)
Saving Throw: 11
Special: Swallow whole
Move: 9 (swim)
Alignment: Neutrality
Challenge Level/XP: 8/800

A gulper eel averages 10 feet in length but can grow to reach 30 feet or more. Its body is long, sleek, and black in color and its tail ends in a luminous organ. Its eyes are small for its body and close to its snout. It massive mouth is lined with rows of sharpened teeth. A gulper eel can unhinge its jaw and stretch its stomach to swallow opponents whole on a roll of 15 or greater on a bite attack.

From the Depths

A wide lake spreads out from the base of a slender stone tower rising into the sky. Lily pads drift lazily atop the azure water, blown about by a gentle breeze. Frogs croak a discordant tune along the edges of the nearly quarter-mile-wide lake. Bobbing lights flit beneath the surface like underwater fireflies.

The magic-user Isen Frong stocks his private lake with truly unique monstrosities. The lake is enchanted to duplicate pressures found nearly 3,000 feet underwater, to better accommodate deep-sea monsters rarely seen by those on land.

In the lake are a menagerie of humpback anglerfish, giant squid and Frong's prize possession: two gulper eels he personally traveled nearly 8,000 feet into the ocean depths to retrieve. The gulper eels are vicious monsters that leap from the water to snatch at creatures too near the shore. Anyone falling or jumping into the water feels the crushing weight of the deep ocean pressing in on them, like being hit by a mace on all sides at once, and suffers 2d6 points of damage per round while in the water.

Copyright Notice

Falcon, Giant

Hit Dice: 3
Armor Class: 5 [14]
Attacks: 2 talons (1d6+1), 1 bite (1d8)
Saving Throw: 14
Special: Rend (2d6)
Move: 3/30 (flying)
Alignment: Neutrality
Challenge Level/XP: 3/60

A typical giant falcon stands 9 feet tall and has a wingspan of up to 18 feet. Feather coloration varies, but typically ranges from brownish-red to brown. Its eyes are brown and its wings are tapered. The giant falcon has a short, slim tail consisting of brown, white, and black feathers. Most giant falcons have a light-colored chest with white predominant on the neck and throat and slowly fading as it reaches the abdomen. A giant falcon attacks by swooping down on its foe and raking with its talons and stabbing with its beak. If a giant falcon hits with both claws on a single opponent, it latches on and tears at the victim's flesh for 2d6 points of damage.

The River Wild

The Peregrin River is a deep, slow-moving waterway winding through the Granite Dive Cliffs. Tall cattails sway on the shallow banks leading to the brilliant blue waters, and salmon leap and splash. Tall pines overhang the water.

Stretching across the water is a thick hemp rope tied to one of the bigger pines. The rope sags across the 600-foot expanse of open water. A small ten-foot-wide square raft made of weathered logs sits in the water near the bank, with two ropes tied to its edges. The end of one is anchored to a nearby tree stump with a coil of rope lying on the ground. The second rope is tied to a tree stump on the other bank, the hemp strand floating on the surface of the river.

The raft is designed so one or two people at most can stand on it and pull themselves across the channel. The ropes attached to the raft allow it to be retrieved by others wanting to cross. Crossing is easy, as the river is slow-moving although it is nearly 60 feet deep at its center. The only real threat is a giant falcon that terrorizes travelers trying to cross. The bird of prey makes its aerie on one of the granite cliffs. It swoops down on PCs once they are halfway across the lake. It tries to pluck them off the raft and return to its mountain nest.

Copyright Notice
Author Scott Greene.

Fox

Hit Dice: 1
Armor Class: 4 [15]
Attack: Bite (1d4)
Saving Throw: 17
Special: Surprise on roll of 1-2 on 1d6
Move: 15
Alignment: Neutrality
Challenge Level/XP: 1/15

Foxes are opportunistic eaters with a diet that consists of mice and voles, rabbits, birds, eggs, amphibians and small reptiles, fish, mollusks, earthworms, carrion, and plants. Foxes are also known to scour garbage and refuse in settled areas. The statistics above describe the common red fox, but can be used for other foxes such as the grey fox or arctic fox.

The fox is a very territorial creature and spends about one-third of its day hunting for food (most hunting is performed at night). Foxes are excellent hunters and have even been known to bring down prey much larger than themselves. When prey is encountered, the fox leaps at it and dispatches it with a series of quick bites.

Arctic foxes surprise on a roll of 1-3 on 1d6 in snowy surroundings.

Fox Hunt

A party of 1d6+4 nobles in mail shirts and pointed helms is running down a fox. The nobles are being led by a huntsman, a wiry, olive-skinned man with strawberry blond hair and a cruel glint in his eye.

The nobles have been at it for some time. The woodlands they are coursing through belong to oldest of the noblemen, a terrifying man with a scarred face and raven hair that is turning white at the temples. His son looks like a younger, chubbier verson of him, with a kindly face and afable demeanor.

The son has paid a gang of 1d6+6 bandits to kill his father. The bandits are hiding in the woods and expect the son to lead his father into their ambush. It will only be too unfortunate if a band of adventurers were to stumble into the middle of the hunt or ambush.

Copyright Notice
Author Scott Greene.

Frog

Giant Frog

Hit Dice: 2
Hit Dice: 6 [13]
Attack: Tongue (grapple), bite (1d8)
Saving Throw: 16
Special: Leap, swallow whole
Move: 9/12 (swimming)
Alignment: Neutrality
Challenge Level/XP: 3/60

This creature is a larger version of a frog. It has razor-sharp teeth lining its mouth.

Giant Dire Frog

Hit Dice: 4
Armor Class: 2 [17]
Attack: Tongue (grapple), bite (2d6)
Saving Throw: 13
Special: Leap, swallow whole
Move: 12/15 (swimming)
Alignment: Neutrality
Challenge Level/XP: 5/240

This frog appears to be at least 10 feet long. It resembles a feral amphibian with dark mottled skin and black splotches on its body.

Killer Frog

Hit Dice: 1
Armor Class: 5 [14]
Attack: Bite (1d6), 2 claws (1d3)
Saving Throw: 17
Special: Rake with claws
Move: 6/12 (swimming)
Alignment: Neutrality
Challenge Level/XP: 2/30

Killer frogs are similar to their dire cousins, except that they stand partially erect and use their front claws as well as their bite. Killer frogs are created by an evil mutation of dire frogs through a practice thought to be known only to the worshipers of Tsathogga. Killer frogs, being more humanoid in appearance, do not have adhesive tongues.

Poisonous Frog

Hit Dice: 1
Armor Class: 4 [15]
Attack: Bite (1d2 plus poison)
Saving Throw: 17
Special: Poison
Move: 3
Alignment: Neutrality
Challenge Level/XP: 2/30

This small, greenish-brown frog with black striped legs is very poisonous and anyone contacting them risks being poisoned. Poisonous frogs secrete poison from their mouth and skin. A creature hit by or touching a poisonous frog must succeed on a saving throw or take 2d6 points of strength damage. Lost strength returns at the rate of 1 point per hour. A creature whose strength is reduced to 0 is paralyzed for 24 hours before lost strength begins to return.

When Frogs Attack

You find yourself in a large, bowl-shaped cavern lit by floating witch-lights. The cavern is about 60 feet in diameter and the ceiling is 40 feet overhead. The walls of the cavern are terraced and home to an astouding array of frogs. Their cacophony can be heard for miles underground, but as soon as people enter the cavern it ceases. The floor of the cavern is filled with a brownish-green ooze. A pedestal of rusting iron rises from the center of the ooze. Atop the pedestal there is an iron sculpture of a large frog, its eyes gleaming like rubies and its open mouth filled with a phosphorescent liquid. The terraces of the slime cavern are occupied by 3d6 poisonous giant frogs, a couple giant frogs, a single giant dire frog and 3d6 giant killer frogs. The frogs will not attack the adventurers - merely watch them in complete silence.

If one enters the slime, they find it initially ankle high and growing to knee high a few yards from the "shore". More importantly, as one enters the slime they will notice that the walls and seem to grow farther apart with each step the take toward the pedestal. Likewise, a yard of movement toward the pedestal seems to bring it no more than an inch closer.

When one finally reaches the iron pedestal, they will find the walls about 1,000 feet away and the pedestal now occupied by an abyssal dire frog sitting on an iron throne. If destroyed, the demonic frog will melt into a black slime and leave behind a ruby decanter filled with a glowing liquid that confers upon a person immunity to all energies, diseases and poisons for 24 hours. Upon reaching the shore of the slime lake, space will again bend back to normal, though the iron frog sculpture will not be there and the frogs on the terraces will be locked in combat with one another, the destruction of their liege apparently unleashing chaos in the cavern.

Credit

The Killer Frog originally appeared in the First Edition *Monster Manual* (© TSR/Wizards of the Coast, 1977) and is used by permission. The Giant Dire Frog made its d20 debut in the Necromancer Games module *D1 Tomb of Abysthor*.

Copyright Notice

Hamster, Giant

Hit Dice: 4
Armor Class: 6 [13]
Attack: Bite (1d8)
Saving Throw: 13
Special: Cheek pouch, grab, immunity to disease
Move: 9/6 (burrowing)
Alignment: Neutrality
Challenge Level/XP: 4/120

Giant hamsters are larger, more aggressive relatives of the normal hamster. Like their smaller cousins, they come in a variety of colors, shapes, and sizes. Giant hamsters are omnivorous, but prefer to feast on a diet of grains, berries, nuts, and water. On occasion, they indulge in and eat meat, usually insects and the like. Also like its smaller cousin, the giant hamster can store food in its cheek pouches. The average giant hamster can store about 200 pounds of food at any given time.

Giant hamsters normally shun combat, but if cornered or extremely hungry they may attack. Note that even domesticated giant hamsters attack if their young are threatened. The giant hamster attacks by biting with its long, sharp teeth.

A giant hamster can try to stuff a grabbed opponent of dwarf size or smaller into its cheek pouch by making a successful bite attack. The victim gets a saving throw to avoid being grabbed. A creature stuffed into the giant hamster's cheek pouch takes no damage, and can escape by making a successful open doors check or can cut its way out by using a light slashing or piercing weapon to deal 10 points of damage to the cheek (AC 8 [11]). A giant hamster's cheek can hold 1 dwarf or halfling.

Of Hamsters and Witches

In a land of dry, rocky hills, a cabal of witches tends a vast orchard of pistachios. The eldest of the witches has long, silky hair and warm, hazel eyes. She and her sisters worship the star goddess and maintain a small shrine in her honor, complete with a small silver idol (50 gp).

The orchard is beset by ankheg, which mostly dwell in the lowlands but make forays into the orchard to nibble on the bark of the pistachios, which ruins the trees. The sisters use their magic to protect the sacred trees, but also employ a pack of 1d4+2 giant golden hamsters, which prey on giant insects.

The giant hamsters prowl the orchard at night, and are as apt to attack humanoid intruders as they are to go after ankhegs. One of the witches (there are seven in all, the leader being a 5th level magic-user, the others ranging in level from 1st to 3rd) keeps vigil each night and will rouse the others if there is an attak.

Credit

The Giant Hamster originally appeared in the Second Edition *Monstrous Compendium (MC 7)* (© TSR/Wizards of the Coast, 1990) and is used by permission.

Copyright Notice

Hippopotamus

Hit Dice: 6
Armor Class: 5 [14]
Attack: Bite (1d8)
Saving Throw: 11
Special: Capsize, trample, hold breath
Move: 12/12 (swimming)
Alignment: Neutrality
Challenge Level/XP: 7/600

The hippo is a peaceful creature, but will defend its lair and young if provoked. They are found dwelling near rivers and lakes. Hippos in the water move by running along the bottom of lakes and rivers, surfacing occasionally to gulp air. A hippo can trample opponents by moving over them, inflicting 1d8 points of damage on each person who fails a saving throw. Those who succeed leap aside and suffer only 1d4 points of damage.

A submerged hippo that surfaces under a boat or ship less than 10 feet long capsizes the vessel 95% of the time. It has a 50% chance to capsize a vessel from 10-20 feet long. Huge hippos have a 20% chance to capsize a vessel over 30 feet long. Large hippos cannot capsize vessels over 20 feet long.

A hippo can hold its breath for an hour and a half before it risks drowning.

Temple of the River Horses

A bloat of 2d6 hippopotamuses luxuriates in the waters around a sandstone temple dedicated to the local river goddess. The temple is an ornate affair, decorated with blue tiles and onyx capitals on the supporting pillars. The temple consists of a central sanctum and a dozen side chambers used as living quarters and storage by the river priestesses. The sanctum holds a tall idol of sandstone and terracotta, glazed to appear as a luminous woman with blue hair and eyes and ochre colored skin.

The aforementioned idol is a mere illusion. The illusion hides a 10-foot wide hole in the floor of the sanctum. This hole leads to a half-submerged tunnel that connectes with the river. Despite the illusion, one can hear the water lapping at the sides of the tunnel, and sometimes hear a hippo inside, for they are used to traveling up the tunnel when they hear a bell rung to get treats from the high priestess.

The priestesses have a somewhat menacing look in their eyes today. They are wrapped in brown robes and have curved, poisoned daggers in sheaths hidden beneath their robes. The "priestesses" are actually assassins, hired by a rival wind temple to destroy the river priestesses. The remains of the six real priestesses are hidden in one of the storage chambers behind barrels of rose water.

Copyright Notice

Hyaenodon

Hit Dice: 5
Armor Class: 6 [13]
Attacks: 1 bite (2d6)
Saving Throw: 12
Special: None
Move: 18
Alignment: Neutrality
Challenge Level/XP: 5/240

Hyaenodons have large, upward pointing ears and dark spots along their bodies. As they age, these spots grow darker. They range in size from 5 to 8 feet long and weigh anywhere from 300 to 330 pounds. The largest hyaenodons reach lengths of 14 feet and weigh up to 600 pounds. Hyaenodons have massive jaws and large bone crushing teeth. They walk on their toes, and their claws are blunt and non-retractile.

Death on the Plains

A wildebeest lies in a clearing in the Burning Grasslands, the corpse ringed by a patch of dried blood splashed over the low scrub. The beast's stomach is ripped open, and its bowels lie in long strands across the grassy plain. The stench is overpowering. A small herd of exhausted wildebeests stands slightly away from the dead one. The living wildebeests are tired and thirsty, and have been hounded for days by a pack of 5 hyaenodons. The hyaenodons are accompanied by 12 normal hyenas. The bigger hyaenadons slink in the low scrub to get close to prey, then bite and disembowel opponents. The wildebeest herd is too tired to run at the sight of the creatures. The hyaenadons only take down a wildebeest to consume whenever they hunger – but they surround PCs they encounter, looking for fresh meat.

Copyright Notice
Author Scott Greene.

Jaguar

Hit Dice: 3+2
Armor Class: 6 [13]
Attacks: 2 claws (1d3), bite (1d6)
Saving Throw: 14
Special: None
Move: 24/12/12 (climb/swim)
Alignment: Neutrality
Challenge Level/XP: 3/60

Jaguars are sometimes confused with leopards. Both cats have a brownish-yellow base fur with dark spots or markings. The jaguar can be distinguished by the smaller markings inside the spots. A jaguar's forelimbs and head are slightly larger than the average leopard (another distinguishing characteristic). Black jaguars are often called black panthers (a misnomer applied to black leopards sometimes as well).

Death From Above

Twisted banyan trees form a wooden maze of trunks through the dense jungle. Bonobo monkeys bounce from limb to limb, chattering angrily and raining feces and rotten fruit down on PCs who venture too close. The monkeys shriek and scream at intruders, bouncing frantically on the limbs, before grabbing the thick vines and swinging away from danger.

As bad as the monkeys are, they aren't the true danger in the jungle. A jaguar slinks along the higher limbs, stealthily hunting the monkeys – and anyone else who gets in its way. The great cat pounces from above, a brown and yellow blur that leaps from the treetops with its sharp claws leading the way. The cat is an opportunistic hunter and retreats into the jungle to strike again at its prey when least expected.

Copyright Notice

Author Scott Greene.

Leopard, Snow

Hit Dice: 3+2
Armor Class: 6 [13]
Attacks: 2 claws (1d3), bite (1d6)
Saving Throw: 14
Special: None
Move: 18/12 (climb)
Alignment: Neutrality
Challenge Level/XP: 3/60

A snow leopard is about 5 feet long with light gray or smoke gray fur that turns white on its underbelly. Its fur is covered with large rings that contain smaller and darker spots of dark gray or black. Its fur is over 1-inch thick and provides it with warmth against the harshest of temperatures. Eyes are gray or dark blue. Its paws are large and thick-furred which enables it to maintain its footing on the most treacherous of snow-covered ground.

Night Hunter

Drifting piles of snow roll through the winter darkness, pushed by a screaming banshee-like wind that blows across the frozen tundra. The temperature is frigid, with metal sticking to unprotected skin, and movements slowed by the waist-high snow and ice.

Lurking in the darkness, unhindered by the deep snow, a snow leopard waits for lone creatures to leave the safety of their camps before it attacks in a bounding leap that carries it through the driving snow in a killing force of sinewy muscle and sleek fur.

The big cat has a small lair in a nearby rock wall where it retreats during the worst of the storms. It kills its prey on the open ice and drags the carcass back to its hole to consume at its leisure. Inside the den is the remains of its most recent meal, a thief caught out in the bitter storm. A *+1 dagger* is still strapped to his body.

Copyright Notice

Author Scott Greene.

Lion, Cave

Hit Dice: 7+2
Armor Class: 6 [13]
Attacks: 2 claws (1d4), 1 bite (1d8)
Saving Throw: 9
Special: None
Move: 12
Alignment: Neutrality
Challenge Level/XP: 7/600

Cave lions grow to a length of 14 feet and weigh in excess of 900 pounds, though the typical cave lion is about 10 feet long and weighs about 600 pounds. They have a broad face and rounded ears, and unlike common lions, neither males nor females possess a mane. They range in color from dark yellowish-brown to gold. Many have a mottled coat with darker spots of brown or gray. Their underbellies are lighter in color, even white on some species. Eyes vary from green to gold to brown. Their mouths are lined with rows of sharp teeth and oversized canines measuring about 5 inches in length.

The Lion Tamers

The Barnabas Circus has lost its lion. The great old cat that was the star of the show died three days ago during a center-ring performance. Overfeeding and a lack of exercise did the beast in. Now, Kyrin Barnabas desperately needs another lion, and he's willing to pay anyone who'll capture another big cat for him. He's even tracked down where a perfect specimen is hiding; he just needs someone to go and get the beast.

The cat Barnabas discovered is a monster that lives in a rocky mountain cave above the village of Thornwild. He'll pay 1,500 gp to a group that traps the cat, and may go up to 2,000 gp if they do so without injuring the beast too badly. The big cat's cave is in a barren stretch of rocky crags, with granite rock ledges and fallen oak trees surrounding it. A half-eaten zebra lies outside the dark cave, and bloody tracks lead into the dark recess. The pawprints are large and pressed deep into the dirt. What Barnabas doesn't know is that the cat is actually a cave lion, and the feral monster doesn't take kindly to people poking around its lair.

Lion, Mountain

Hit Dice: 3+2
Armor Class: 6 [13]
Attacks: 2 claws (1d4), 1 bite (1d8)
Saving Throw: 14
Special: None
Move: 18/12 (climb)
Alignment: Neutrality
Challenge Level/XP: 3/60

Mountain lions stand about 2 feet tall and are about 4 to 5 feet long with a 2 to 3 foot long tail. A typical mountain lion weighs around 125 pounds. It has short, coarse, fur with a white underbelly and a black-tipped tail. Its fur color (except its underbelly) is typically brown, black, rust, or gray. Its eyes are golden.

Claws of the Wild

The forested paths winds through tall strands of pines and aspens. The landscape is broken by huge boulders fallen from the mountainside, and thick green moss covers the fallen stones.

A pair of mountain lions makes their lair in a hollow beneath two fallen boulders. The den is accessed via a narrow hole between the rocks that opens into a 10-foot-wide hollow. Three cubs prowl the den's interior, rolling over one another in thick bundles of fur and claw.

The parents hunt the hillsides for rabbits and deer, but won't hesitate to attack anyone coming too near their cubs. The female is particularly cunning, launching herself from tree branches to hit and roll intruders. The male goes more for speed, driving himself from hiding to claw and bite before darting into the underbrush.

Lizard, Giant Rock-Horned (Blood Lizard)

Hit Dice: 4
Armor Class: 2 [17]
Attack: Bite (1d8)
Saving Throw: 13
Special: Spit blood, surprise on roll of 1-2 on 1d6
Move: 12/9 (swimming)
Alignment: Neutrality
Challenge Level/XP: 4/120

The rock-horned lizard is commonly referred to as the blood lizard because of its ability to shoot a stream of blood from its eyes when threatened. The rock-horned lizard grows to a length of 8 feet. Its head is wedge-shaped, and small horns protrude from the sides and top of its head. Its scales are dark reddish-brown or gold in color.

Once per hour, a rock-horned lizard can fire a stream of caustic blood from its eyes in a 20-foot line that deals 2d8 points of acid damage to a single target within range (saving throw for half damage).

Blood in My Eye

In a red desert with tall saguaros and barrel cactus and a variety of wildlife, there dwells a solitary giant rock-horned lizard. The lizard dwells in an abandoned mine dug into a slop that overlooks the sea. The mine was dug into the golden sandstone and runs about 30 feet back before ending in a cave-in. There doesn't appear to be any useful or precious material in the mine, making its reason for existance a mystery.

The giant rock-horned lizard dwells near the mouth of the cave, for the back parts of the cave give it the creeps. Should one travel to the back of the cave, they must pass a saving throw each turn or become drowsy and fall into a deep sleep. While sleeping, the astral form is carried away beyond the world one knows and to a place quite different and startling.

Copyright Notice

Lynx

Hit Dice: 2
Armor Class: 6 [13]
Attacks: 2 claws (1d3), bite (1d4)
Saving Throw: 16
Special: None
Move: 18/12 (climb)
Alignment: Neutrality
Challenge Level/XP: 2/30

A lynx has thick, gray fur that is spotted, striped, or plain. During the winter months through the summer months, its coat varies from spotted to plain. Its short tail is ringed and tipped with black fur. Its pointed ears are tipped with tufts of long black hairs and its eyes range from green to gray to brown. Its paws are large and covered with thick fur. This helps the lynx distribute its weight when moving across snowy terrain. The average lynx is 2 1/2 feet to 4 feet long and weighs 20-40 pounds.

Caracal

Hit Dice: 2
Armor Class: 6 [13]
Attacks: 2 claws (1d3), bite (1d4)
Saving Throw: 16
Special: None
Move: 24/12 (climb)
Alignment: Neutrality
Challenge Level/XP: 2/30

The caracal is a small cat, very similar to the lynx, and is commonly referred to as the desert lynx (even though it doesn't live in desert regions). The caracal is found in warm or temperate plains and hills.

Wolf Hunt

The snow drifts are high around the small village of Sil-Walden, the weather hovering just above freezing. The villagers walk about in thick layers of wolf-hide to keep the cold at bay.

Five men stand in the center of town, each armed with whatever weapons they could find. Some have bows, while some wave thick clubs. One carries a dagger. The leader is a man named Collins, a big burly hunter whose thick layers of fat provide more than enough protection on its own from the cold.

A pack of wolves has been sneaking into town and preying on the village's pack animals and sled dog pups. Tracks can be found throughout the village every morning. Collins has had enough. He's gathered these amateur hunters to track down and find the wolves. He's convinced the men that the wolves are more scared of them and won't be a match for their skills.

Unfortunately, Collins misread the tracks, which do indeed appear to be wolf prints. Instead, the men are facing a pride of 12 lynxes. The wild felines are hungry and feral, and attack from high and low, leaping from the rocks and trees to rake opponents with their claws. The lynxes have a small underground den in the middle of the snowy forest where they are raising a litter of six kittens.

Copyright Notice

Mammoth

Hit Dice: 12
Armor Class: 5 [14]
Attacks: 1 trunk slam (1d10), 2 gore (1d10+4), 2 trample (2d6)
Saving Throw: 3
Special: None
Move: 12
Alignment: Neutrality
Challenge Level/XP: 12/2,000

The mammoth is a relative of the elephant and the mastodon though its head is slightly taller than an elephant's and slightly wider than a mastodon's. Its upward curving tusks are longer than those of the mastodon, and its trunk ends in two, small finger-like projections used for grasping branches, fruits, and other such small items. The mammoth stands about 22 feet tall and is covered in a thick coat of gray, brown, reddish-brown, yellowish-brown, or black fur with a coarse "under-fur" beneath it to protect it in harsh climates.

In This Ring . . . Revenge

Barnabus Freep's Traveling Circus is in town, boys and girls, so get your parents and bring your gold, for the time of your lives! The nomadic circus performers have pitched their multi-hued tent on the outskirts of Fairhaven this fine day, and signs throughout town promise wonders and delights for all ages.

But a disgruntled dwarf clown known only as Quip is tired of the constant abuse he takes in every town the circus visits. He's decided to have his revenge for the years of insults, and Fairhaven is about to know dwarven clown wrath in the form of a herd of stampeding mammoths.

During the center ring spectacle as 6 mammoths perform various tricks, Quip gleefully lets loose a dozen white mice, then stands back laughing as the circus comes crashing down. The mammoths charge the crowd, looking to escape.

Copyright Notice
Author Scott Greene.

Mandrill

Hit Dice: 2
Armor Class: 8 [11]
Attacks: 1 bite (1d4)
Saving Throw: 16
Special: None
Move: 9/9 (climb)
Alignment: Neutrality
Challenge Level/XP: 2/30

This brightly-colored primate has a bushy mane, dense fur, and a long ridged snout. The average adult mandrill reaches a height of just under 3 feet tall and weighs around 35 pounds (though some males generally weigh around 50 pounds). A mandrill's fur is olive brown fading to a paler color on its underbelly. Adult males have a bright blue and red snout and a yellowish "beard." Females and young mandrills are likewise colored, but their colorations are duller.

Guerilla Warfare

The warrior-cultist Amad Thorct's life took an unexpected turn when he died. A roc falling from the sky smashed the evil man's life and halted his grand schemes of conquest before they even got started. His companions grudgingly brought him back to life, but the resurrection didn't go as planned. Instead of returning to his youthful, brawny body, Amad found himself in the form of a 5-foot-tall mandrill. He fled into the jungle to hide his shame.

Amad has adjusted to his new life in the trees, and now leads a colony of mandrills as the alpha male. Amad still dreams of conquest and organized the 20 mandrills into a scavenging force that attacks travelers near the Seething Jungle. He leads the colony to scatter pack animals and raid caravans. The monkeys carry crude spears and fight as a ragtag guerilla force.

Copyright Notice
Author Scott Greene.

Margay

Hit Dice: 2
Armor Class: 7 [12]
Attacks: 2 claws (1d2) and 1 bite (1d4+1)
Saving Throw: 16
Special: Rake
Move: 9/6 (climb)
Alignment: Neutrality
Challenge Level/XP: 2/30

Margays are jungle-dwelling cats similar to the ocelot. A margay is a small, slender, spotted cat with fur that ranges in color from tan to brown or cinnamon. Its spots are darker and run in longitudinal rows along its body. Margays generally average about 2 feet long and weigh about 8 pounds. If a margay hits a single opponent with its 2 claws, it rakes the victim with its back claws for an additional 1d4 points of damage.

Cat and Canary

A green-and-yellow parrot flutters down out of the trees and alights on a PCs shoulder. The bird can't be shooed away, and tells PCs that its master Lornil Zamph needs help and will pay handsomely if they come quickly. The magic-user is stuck in a portal to the netherworld, and needs someone to pull him out while dispelling the portal.

The PCs may not get a chance to find out more than this, however, as a margay is stalking the parrot. It leaps out of the woods to snatch at the colorful parrot. If allowed, it swipes the bird to the ground, pounces on it, and snatches it up in its mouth. It dashes back into the woods to feast on its catch. The parrot screams for help the entire time.

Marmoset, Giant

Hit Dice: 3
Armor Class: 4 [15]
Attack: 2 claws (1d6), bite (1d8) or 2 claws (1d6), tail (1d4)
Saving Throw: 14
Special: Only surprised on roll of 1 on 1d8
Move: 15/12 (climbing)
Alignment: Neutrality
Challenge Level/XP: 3/60

Giant marmosets are larger, more aggressive relatives of the smaller marmoset. Their fur is gray or black, with black fur predominant over the back and neck. Their tails reach a length of 5 feet and are colored in alternating bands of black and pale gray. They sustain themselves on a diet of tree saps and gums (using their sharp teeth to gnaw holes in the bark), small animals, and various fruits and nuts. Giant marmosets make their homes among the trees, rarely touching the ground unless hunting living prey. They are, on occasion, tamed by wild tribes of halflings and used as mounts in times of war.

Giant marmosets prefer to attack from surprise, tossing large stones from the sides of cliffs at their prey, hanging from branches by their tail and swinging down to surprise their prey, or dropping from the trees on their unaware foes. They attack using their claws and bite or claws and a tail slap.

Fountain of Tempest

A tropical island of lush, green hills and dense rain forest plays host to a number of giant marmosets. The marmosets grow thicker in number as one moves deeper into the rain forest, until finally they come to a stand of towering junipers crawling with no fewer than two dozen giant marmosets. In the midst of this stand of trees there is a small landing built of pure, white marble with broad steps into a shallow pool of water - apparently a hot spring judging by the steam that hangs over it.

The pool of water is the legendary *Fountain of Youth*. Bathing in the fountain acts as a *potion of longevity* (one dose per ten minutes spent in the bath), but bathers are always harried by the screaming marmosets before they can do so. The marmosets are quite aggressive until two or three have been killed, at which point they retire into the woods, content to harass adventurers as they leave the clearing.

There is a 1 in 12 chance that when one reaches the pool they find a hearty and hale man bathing there. The man has old, wise eyes and a noble bearing. His clothes, laying on the landing, are all velvet and silk and include a tall, pointed cap of blue velvet covered with stars and moons in silver thread. The man is a duke and a very powerful magic-user (9th level at least). He lives on the island in a cave complex he has turned into a palace with his command over the spirits of the island. He is always accompanied by his brutish guard, a 5th level fighting-man with half-orc blood.

Credit

The Giant Marmoset originally appeared in the Basic Edition module *B3 Palace of the Silver Princess* (© TSR/Wizards of the Coast, 1981) and is used by permission.

Mastodon

Hit Dice: 15
Armor Class: 4 [15]
Attacks: 1 trunk slam (2d6), 2 gore (1d12+2), 2 trample (2d8)
Saving Throw: 3
Special: None
Move: 12
Alignment: Neutrality
Challenge Level/XP: 15/2,900

The mastodon is a distant relative to the elephant though it is slightly longer and lower to the ground, with shorter and thicker legs than the common elephant. Its head is slightly longer and taller than an elephant's and the mastodon's entire body is covered in thick fur of brown, gray, reddish-brown, yellowish-brown, or black. Its long, upward curving tusks are formed of ivory and are white or yellowish-white in color. Its eyes range from gray to brown to green. An average mastodon stands 20 feet tall.

The Ichor Pit

Tall grains sway in a field of wildflowers, the gold wheat dancing in the light breezes playing over the rolling hills. Stunted trees – their bark rubbed away to reveal naked wood – stand in sad clumps along the hill. A loud trumpeting echoes through the valley, a horrible sound of distress. PCs who follow the sound find a large tar pit stretching between a series of cliff faces. The black tar bubbles and spits, and a noxious steam rises off in a miasmic cloud.

Struggling within the tar trap are six mastodons. The decayed bodies of other mastodons, a cave lion and other herd animals stick out of the ichor. The lead mastodons in the herd blundered into the tar. Two young bull elephants remain free and trumpet angrily as they walk the edges of the morass. One is coated in tar after barely escaping the muck. The pair are scared and angry, and the frantic bellows of the females is driving them crazy.

The mastodons charge PCs who advance on the trapped elephants. The bull elephants try to grab creatures and toss them into the tar.

Copyright Notice

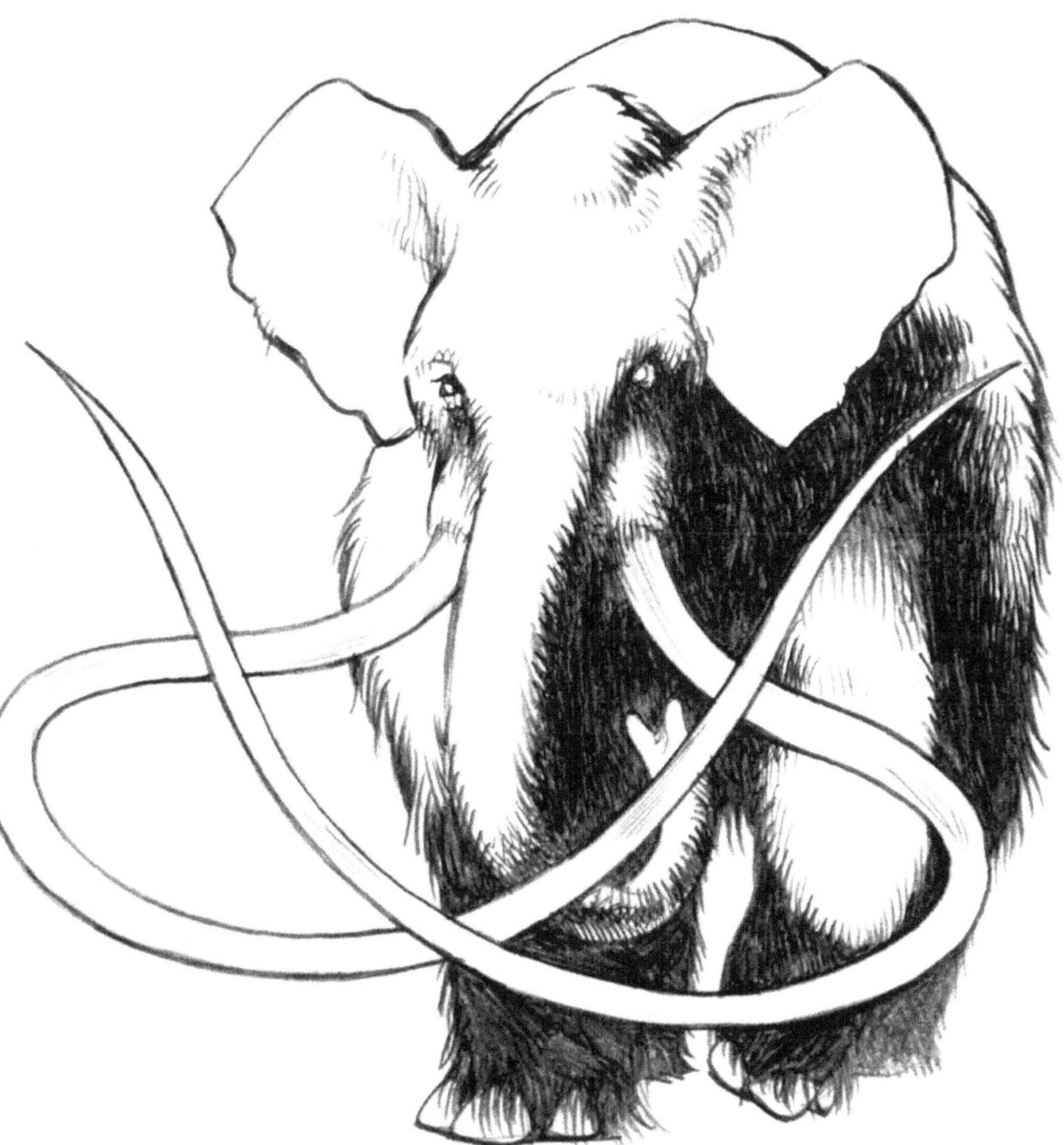

Moose

Hit Dice: 5
Armor Class: 5 [14]
Attack: Butt (1d8) or 2 hooves (1d6)
Saving Throw: 12
Special: None
Move: 12
Alignment: Neutrality
Challenge Level/XP: 5/240

Moose are the largest members of the elk family, ranging in size from 4 1/2 feet to over 8 feet tall at the shoulder and weighing from 440 to over 1,000 pounds. Males have broad, flat antlers that can reach a length of 5 feet or more. These antlers are shed each year after mating season. The moose's fur ranges from brown to black, changing to a dull gray in the winter months. They are excellent swimmers, often swimming into deep water to feed on aquatic plants.

Generally non-aggressive if left alone, moose can become quite aggressive if approached. They have poor eyesight, but excellent hearing, and tend to flee rather than fight as soon as would-be attackers are detected. If forced into combat, a moose attacks with its antlers or hooves

Just Don't Eat the Pie

In a boggy lowland of hawthorns, a dangerous bull moose has managed to tree a halfling princess. The princess and her handmaidens were bathing in a warm spring near a hook-shaped, buff-colored rock when the moose came upon them. The halflings scattered and the princess was unlucky enough to be chased. She just managed to make her way up the tree before the moose trampled her.

One of the handmaidens is heading towards her village to fetch a band of bravos. The village is set into a wooded hill and consists of a number of burrows braced by moose antlers and bones. The warriors of the tribe wear shirts of leather scales and carry shortbows and hand axes.

The other handmaiden headed for an old cleft in a nearby range of granite hills, seeking an ancient stone golem placed there many generations ago by a friendly human shaman. The stone golem exists under orders to protect the wee folk, and with some urging will scoop up the maiden and head for a confrontation with the aggressive moose.

Copyright Notice

Oliphant

Hit Dice: 8
Armor Class: 3 [16]
Attack: 2 stomps (2d8), gore (2d10)
Saving Throw: 8
Special: None
Move: 15
Alignment: Neutrality
Challenge Level/XP: 8/800

The oliphant is a 20-foot long creature resembling a mastodon. It is omnivorous and rarely makes its home near civilized or settled areas. Each of the creature's tusks brings 400 gp on the market. The oliphant's fur is thick, brown, and aids in protecting it from cooler climates and precipitation. Oliphants are sometimes trained as mounts or beasts of burden by various humanoid races. Oliphants seem to understand the common tongue, but they do not speak it.

Training an Oliphant

An oliphant requires training before it can bear a rider in combat. To be trained, an oliphant must have a friendly attitude toward the trainer. Training a friendly oliphant requires six weeks of work and an animal trainer. Riding an oliphant does not require an exotic saddle. Oliphant young are worth 2,000 gp each. Professional trainers charge 1,000 gp to rear or train n oliphant.

Carrying Capacity: A light load for an oliphant is up to 2,400 pounds; a medium load, 2,401-4,800 pounds; and a heavy load, 4,801-7,200 pounds. An oliphant can drag 36,000 pounds.

Crystal Cone Angel

The northern portion of a vast kingdom is noted for three lofty peaks that rise from an otherwise flat plain. The peaks are called the Tricruxia's Trident, after an obscure goddess once worshipped in the region. The lands around the mountains are inhabited by a number of oliphant families, each consisting of 2d4 animals (with a 25% chance that a calf is present).

The oliphants are the first line of defense for the temple hidden in the central mountain. The temple is actually the remnants of a volcanic cone that collapsed in on itself. The inner surface of this cone is covered by reddish-brown crystals, some growing as long as two feet. In the center of this crystal cavern there is statue of unbreakable metal that looks like gold. The statue looks like a solar encased in ruby red plate armor with only its outstretched wings and golden eyes visible underneath the armor.

The statue and temple are tended by a flock of 1d6+3 giant owls, celestial blue in color with intelligent, golden eyes. The statue they protect is an actual solar that has been frozen in time. The solar, Izbeniel by name, awaits the arrival of a pure human heart to awaken it from its slumber and set it on a quest to purify the petty kingdoms surrounding the plains.

Credit
The Oliphant originally appeared in the First Edition module *EX2 Land Beyond the Magic Mirror* (© TSR/Wizards of the Coast, 1983) and later in the First Edition *Monster Manual II* (© TSR/Wizards of the Coast, 1983) and is used by permission.

Copyright Notice

Pike, Giant

Hit Dice: 3
Armor Class: 7 [12]
Attacks: 1 bite (1d4)
Saving Throw: 14
Special: None
Move: 18 (swim)
Alignment: Neutrality
Challenge Level/XP: 3/60

The giant pike averages about 9 feet long and can grow to a length of 20 feet. Its coloration varies from dark green to brown and its body is covered in lighter colored spots. It has a single dorsal fin and a white or cream-colored underbelly.

The Flash of Scales

The Sin Mire Swamp is marked by varying depths of murky water, thick stands of trees, and the deep sounds of bullfrogs hidden in the reeds. PCs moving through the marsh must do so on a boat or by magic or risk getting sucked into the sticky muck for good.

A pair of giant pike hunts in the five-foot-deep water of the watery grassland. The large fish investigate disturbances caused by poles or oars slapping the water and savagely attack shiny or metallic objects. The fish leap from the water to attack reflective armor or flashing swords.

Copyright Notice
Author Scott Greene.

Quipper

Hit Dice: 1/4
Armor Class: 3 [16]
Attack: Bite (1d2)
Saving Throw: 18
Special: Frenzy
Move: 0/12 (swimming)
Alignment: Neutrality
Challenge Level/XP: B/10

The quipper is a rare form of cold-water piranha. They are dark green in color and are found in freshwater lakes and stream. Quippers attack by swarming an opponent and biting with their razor-sharp teeth.

A quipper that detects blood in the water goes into a killing frenzy, as do all other quippers within a 90-foot radius. Frenzied quippers attacks until either they or their opponents are dead.

A frenzied quipper can make two attacks each round. Additionally, it gains a +1 bonus on attack rolls and a 1 point bonus to AC. A frenzied quipper's swim speed increases by 3. This frenzy lasts for 1 minute (10 rounds) and can only be used once per encounter.

Frenzy of Greed

In mountains rich with quartz, gold and silver, a band of greedy dwarves has made a home for themselves in a mine dug into a rocky slope overlooking a cold, mountain lake. The lake is ringed by tall cliff walls that support a few evergreen shrubs large flocks of blackbirds.

The lake is populated by a school of 1d2 x 50 quipper, and the dwarves are quite aware of their presence in the lake, having set several traps that spill intruders into the lake from holes dug into the cliffs.

The leader of the dwarves is a scoundrel called Gwael, who wears a striped kilt and arms himself with a coat of mail, a buckler and a broadsword. He wears a long, golden earring in one ear and a conical helm set with tiny opals. His dwarves number 1d20+15. They have living quarters dug into the mine and do a fairly good business in gold and silver ore and bits of valuable rose quartz.

The lake connects to a trading post higher in the mountains (and located next to a mountain pass), and the traders there take turns coming down the river in keel boats to fetch loads of ore. The ore is lowered via barrels and ropes from the mine entrance above. The traders are very cognizant of the quippers, and take care not to fall into the water.

Credit
The quipper originally appeared in the First Edition *Fiend Folio* (© TSR/Wizards of the Coast, 1981) and is used by permission.

Copyright Notice
Author Scott Greene, based on original material by Albie Fiore.

Raccoon

Hit Dice: 2 hit point
Armor Class: 8 [11]
Attacks: 1 bite (1d2)
Saving Throw: 18
Special: None
Move: 4/4 (climb)
Alignment: Neutrality
Challenge Level/XP: A/5

Raccoons are about the size of a small dog with brownish-grey fur and a bushy tail ringed in black. Their paws and ears are black, and they have a black-and-white mask-like marking on their faces. Raccoons are small nocturnal omnivores that live in all but the warmest and coldest forests. They are curious animals and like to steal whatever they can carry off.

Thieves in the Night

Campers in the Kriegh Forest must keep track of their belongings as roving bands of feral raccoons plunder any item they can carry off. Travelers tell tales of waking with the sun to find everything but their bed missing. The raccoons are the furry eyes and stealthy hands of a group of primeval raccoons that live in the forest's depths. The raccoons take their stolen goods to these larger animals as tribute. PCs camping in the forest are targeted by the furry bandits, with anything left on the ground – including clothes, food, tent spikes, books and weapons – carried off by the opportunistic critters. By the time PCs awake, their items may be far into the depths of the forest. *(See the **Raccoon, Primeval** entry if PCs go searching for their missing gear.)*

Copyright Notice
Author Scott Greene.

Raccoon, Dire

Hit Dice: 4 hit points
Armor Class: 7 [12]
Attacks: 1 bite (1d4)
Saving Throw: 18
Special: Disease
Move: 6/6 (climb)
Alignment: Neutrality
Challenge Level/XP: 1/15

Dire raccoons are nocturnal animals about the size of a large dog. They have brownish-grey fur, and a bushy tail ringed in black. Its paws and ears are black as well, and it has a black and white mask-like marking on its face. The bite of a giant raccoon can spread disease.

King of Thieves

The abandoned ruins of Morgal-Uth sit silently in the heart of the Kriegh Forest, the once-proud stone village overgrown by towering elms and oaks. The village is the home of a family of 8 primeval raccoons. Most are the size of large dogs, but the matron is about the size of a small brown bear, standing nearly 6 feet tall when she rises onto her hind feet. The normal raccoons revere these larger cousins and instinctively bring "tribute" to these giant animals. The primeval raccoons now live a life of excess and don't have to hunt on their own. Mundane items are scattered within the stone ruins. Any equipment PCs might have lost to the thieving raccoon family may be scattered anywhere within the ruins. The family of primeval raccoons doesn't take kindly to anyone "stealing" from them, and ambush PCs at every opportunity. They are often accompanied by normal raccoons that leap from trees and ruins to bite and scratch intruders.

Copyright Notice
Author Scott Greene.

Rhinoceros, Woolly

Hit Dice: 10
Armor Class: 5 [14]
Attacks: 1 horn (2d6)
Saving Throw: 5
Special: Double damage on charge
Move: 12
Alignment: Neutrality
Challenge Level/XP: 10/1,400

The woolly rhino averages about 11 feet long and has two ivory horns, the longest averaging about 3 feet in length. Its body is covered in a thick layer of black, brown, ruddy, or yellowish-brown fur that enable it to withstand its harsh climate. The creature has poor eyesight, and relies on its senses of hearing and smell to locate sources of food and warn of impending danger. If a rhino charges, it tramples its opponent and does double damage with its horn attack.

Elasmotherium

Hit Dice: 15
Armor Class: 2 [17]
Attacks: 1 horn (4d6)
Saving Throw: 3
Special: Double damage on charge
Move: 12
Alignment: Neutrality
Challenge Level/XP: 16/3,200

The elasmotherium stands as tall and as long as an elephant, averaging almost 15 feet long and weighing around 4 tons. Its fur is thick, and its underlying body is tough and very resilient. Its single horn is thick, ivory colored, and almost 6 feet long. Its fur tends to be a bit darker than the common woolly rhino's. Like its brethren, its eyesight is poor, thus it, too, relies on its keen sense of hearing and smell. If an elasmotherium charges, it tramples its opponent and does double damage with its horn attack.

Bull (Rhino) in a China Shop

The sound of glass shattering and screams fill the street of the river community of Shalebend. People flee in panic down the dusty main street that splits the village. Mooing and squeaking noises can be heard in a large glass foundry called "Morto's Glassworks."

A female woolly rhinocerous and its mate, a prehistoric rhino called an elasmotherium, swam through the Shale River and charged into the rear of the buildings built along the edge of the water. The elephant-size elasmotherium knocked a hole in the back of the glass shop big enough for both animals to hide inside, although just barely. The elasmotherium's 15-foot-body is destroying the shop, and its 6-foot-long single horn is ripping holes in the roof. The smaller woolly rhinoceros is having an easier time, although her every movement is knocking over shelves and trampling delicate glass sculptures.

The rhinos are on the run from a female cave giant named Tolla Tarstump who raises the rhinos as pets. Each animal has giant glass beads woven into its furry hide and their long hair is dyed deep purple. The giant is trying to find her pets. The animals would rather take their chances in the wild. Both animals charge anyone trying to approach them. Tolla shows up in 2d4 rounds, angry that the town is hiding her rhinos.

Copyright Notice
Author Scott Greene.

Scythe Horn

Hit Dice: 5
Armor Class: 7 [12]
Attacks: butt (1d8) or horn-slash (2d6)
Saving Throw: 12
Special: Stampede
Move: 15
Alignment: Neutrality
Challenge Level/XP: 5/240

Scythe horns are 10 to 13 feet long and stand 5 to 6 feet tall at the shoulders. Scythe horns are covered in a thick brownish-black or brownish-gray fur. Its horns are black or gray and curve upward and inward in a scythe-like shape. Its legs are short and thick and its black hooves are circular in shape. An enraged scythe horn butts or slashes with its scythe-like horns. If startled, a herd generally flees, starting a stampede in the process. A frightened herd runs over anything in its path, dealing 1d12 points of damage per five scythe horns in the group.

Scimitar Horn

Hit Dice: 5
Armor Class: 7 [12]
Attacks: horn-slash (2d6)
Saving Throw: 12
Special: Stampede
Move: 15
Alignment: Neutrality
Challenge Level/XP: 5/240

A relative of the scythe horn, the scimitar horn is found only in cold plains and hills. They use the same statistics for the scythe horn, but have no butt attack, and attack by slashing with their scimitar-like horns.

Lost in the Fog

A thick fog blankets the hills, dropping visibility to barely 10 feet through the clinging burs and prickly thorns covering the land. The swampy ground squelches from recent rains, and slick mud makes each step tricky. A wolf howls in the distance, and is answered by another nearby predator. In the fog, sounds seem louder and directions are harder to pinpoint.

A raucous bleating and thrashing from a briar patch can't be missed. A herd of scythe horns got lost in the thick fog, and blundered into the briar patches. One of the young animal's horns is tangled in the thick vines. The rest of the 14 animals in the herd gather around the trapped animal. The males thrash at the thorny vines, tearing them out by the roots. The animals are frantic to free the young scythe horn and be on their way before a wolf pack trailing the herd catches them. The animals turn their anger on any PCs who come too near the herd.

Copyright Notice
Author Scott Greene.

Seahorse, Giant

Hit Dice: 4
Armor Class: 7 [12]
Attacks: butt (1d8)
Saving Throw: 13
Special: None
Move: Swim 15
Alignment: Neutrality
Challenge Level/XP: 4/120

A giant seahorse is about 8 feet long from the top of its head to the tip of its tail. Its body is covered in fine scales and its head is horse-like with a long snout. Its back is lined with small dorsal fins. Near the base of its head are pectoral fins that help the giant seahorse turn while swimming. A giant seahorse ranges in color from yellow to dull green or brown. Its eyes are almost always brown with the occasional giant seahorse having blue eyes.

The Seahorse King

Princess Polyena has lost her crown … but she knows exactly where to find it. She was swimming off her dad's barge, when it fell off her head and into the pearlescent waters of the stretch of ocean her father rules. She immediately ordered her servants to dive in to get it back, but not a single one of them did as she ordered and came back with the gold and diamond crown. She had to lock every single one of them in daddy's dungeons for disobeying her. Daddy promised to have another crown made, and she agreed to that idea wholeheartedly, but she's determined to get back the original as well (it is hers after all).

The crown has been spotted, although no one has figured out how to get it. When it fell off her golden tresses, it snagged around the curling tail of a giant seahorse that glides through the ocean near her father's compound with a herd of 25 other seahorses. The animal doesn't even realize the golden tiara is wedged on its body, and how rude is that? The princess has offered a 1,000 gp reward (which she'll expect Daddy to pay) for the return of the crown.

Copyright Notice

Sheep

Hit Dice: 2
Armor Class: 6 [13]
Attack: Bite (1d4)
Saving Throw: 16
Move: 12
Alignment: Neutrality
CL/XP: 2/30

Ram

Hit Dice: 3
Armor Class: 6 [13]
Attack: Gore (1d6)
Saving Throw: 14
Move: 15
Alignment: Neutrality
CL/XP: 3/60

The statistics here describe the common sheep and ram. Sheep generally flee from danger and avoid combat if possible. If cornered, they attack by biting. Rams are male sheep and are usually encountered leading a flock. Rams attack using their horns. They become aggressive if the flock is threatened.

Sheep Rustlers

Skunk

Hit Dice: 1d4
Armor Class: 6 [13]
Attack: Bite (1d4)
Saving Throw: 18
Special: Musk
Move: 12
Alignment: Neutrality
Challenge Level/XP: A/5

The stats here describe the common nonaggressive skunk. Skunks squirt their musk at potential predators in hopes of forcing the predator to flee. If this fails, the skunk looks for the quickest route possible for itself to escape. If cornered, a skunk bites its opponents.

Once per round, and no more than 5 times per day, a skunk can release a cloud of stinking musk that quickly fills a 5-foot area in front of it. A creature within or entering the area must succeed on a saving throw or be sickened for 1d4 rounds. One round later a second saving throw must be made (whether the first one succeeded or not) or the affected creature is blinded for 1d4 rounds.

A *neutralize poison* spell removes the effect from the sickened creature, but does not remove the blindness. Creatures with immunity to poison are unaffected by the sickened effect but can still be blinded if they fail their save, and creatures resistant to poison receive their normal bonus on both saving throws.

The stench is highly potent, and short of magical means of cleaning, all cloth and such material continue to reek for 1d6 months. The odor is so strong that it doubles all chances for wandering monster encounters and imposes a severe penalty on attempts to hide in shadows while wearing clothing contaminated with a skunk's musk. Flesh, leather goods, metal goods (weapons, armor, and the like) must be washed in a concentrated mixture of vinegar for a period of 1d3 days. Otherwise, the stench clings to them for at least 1 week, imposing the same modifiers to wandering monster encounters and hide in shadows checks.

In the rolling hill country, the main source of wealth (and conflict) is the keeping of sheep. A large flock of 1d10x10 sheep (plus one ram per 10 adults and 50% as many noncombatant lambs) roams one hill in particular. A village is located at the bottom of the hill and consists of a number of red brick cottages with thatched roofs running parallel to a rushing stream. A wooden bridge allows one to cross the bridge to the hills beyond. The village has no tavern or inn, and is populated by freemen who make a living selling wool to a canny old trader with a touch of orc blood who comes up in the fall with a caravan of wagons and guardsmen. The village has a few warriors equipped with longbows and short swords and wearing leather or ring armor, but it mostly relies on the patrols of the nearby baron.

There is a 1 in 10 chance, one evening, that a band of raiders attempts to rustle the sheep. The raiders wear bearskin cloaks and odd bits of armor and are armed with axes and darts. Their leader is a frightening old man with long, white hair and one blind eye that emits a silver radiance. The old man is a 6th level fighting-man. He wears a coat of mail and carries a spear and silver sword. He also owns a mithril harp set with a single sapphire that, when plucked, allows him to control animals. The raiders will attack any guards while their master plays his harp and leads the sheep into the deep hills.

Copyright Notice

Skunk Femerell

A slim, crooked tower of bleached limestone dominates an otherwise barren, rocky landscape. A bright, greenish light shines from the top of the tower, casting long, hideous shadows across the morose landscape. The source of the light is a simple lanthorn of emerald panels and wrought iron. While the lanthorn illuminates a dark environment with its green light, it casts twilight in a 1 mile radius when brought into bright light.

Two armies are encamped on the plain, surrounding the tower and locked in a stalemate over its possession. One army is composed of 300 goblins, the other of 360 kobolds. Both races are sensitive to light an contemptuous of the surface races, and thus would like to claim the magic lanthorn.

Currently, one force stops them - a family of 1d4+1 skunks. The skunks have taken up residence in the tower, feeding on rats and insects and defending their home with a tenacity matched only by the cowardice of the goblins and kobolds.

Credit
The Skunk originally appeared in the First Edition *Monster Manual II* (© TSR/Wizards of the Coast, 1983) and is used by permission.

Copyright Notice

Smilodon (Saber-Toothed Cat)

Hit Dice: 6
Armor Class: 6 [13]
Attacks: 2 claws (1d4+1), 1 bite (2d6)
Saving Throw: 11
Special: Rear claws
Move: 12/6 (swim)
Alignment: Neutrality
Challenge Level/XP: 6/400

Smilodons average about 5 feet long and weigh nearly 500 pounds, but can grow to a length of 8 feet and weigh up to 900 pounds. Their fur is golden or spotted (similar to a leopard). Their legs are short but powerful and their tail is short and bobbed. The smilodon has two 8-inch long, downward-curving canine teeth. These saber-like fangs are very sharp and are used for stabbing prey. This creature can open its jaws almost twice as far as other big cats. If a smilodon hits with its two front claws, it can pull itself up to rake with its rear claws (2 additional attacks).

Big, Sharp Teef

A 6-year-old approaches the PCs, her golden hair done up in bouncing polka-dot pigtails. Her frilly blue dress is wrapped in delicate white lace. But her expression is stern as she crosses her arms and demands in a babyish voice, "You better give me what I want, or you'll be sorry."

And Coralee means it, too. She is the only daughter of Corrigan Sheel, the only entrepreneur in Sheel (named after his grandfather, who founded the village). Coralee's mother died in childbirth, and her father feared the worst would befall his precious little girl. So he found his darling daughter a companion and protector, a trained smilodon named Teef.

Coralee learned over the years that shop owners give her whatever she wants when Teef is around. Despite her age, she's developed into quite the little bully. Even her father backs off punishing the girl when Teef gives him a look.

If Coralee gets whatever catches her fancy, she skips off with the treasure to a secret treehouse in the woods where she keeps her prizes. If she doesn't get what she wants, her expression darkens and she yells "Get'em, Teef." The smilodon lurks in the woods awaiting just such a command.

Copyright Notice
Author Scott Greene.

Smilodon (Giant and Homotherium)

Smilodon (Giant)

Hit Dice: 15
Armor Class: 6 [13]
Attacks: 2 claws (1d6+1) and 1 bite (3d6+1)
Saving Throw: 3
Special: Rear claws
Move: 12/6 (swim)
Alignment: Neutrality
Challenge Level/XP: 8/800

This massive golden-furred cat is about 10 feet long. It has short, powerful legs and a small, bobbed tail. Two 12-inch long, downward-curving canines protrude from its mouth. Giant smilodons are larger, much more aggressive versions of the standard smilodon. If a giant smilodon hits a single opponent with both claw attacks, it grabs the victim and rakes it with its rear claws for an extra 2d6+1 points of damage.

Homotherium

Hit Dice: 7
Armor Class: 6 [13]
Attacks: 2 claws (1d4+1), 1 bite (2d4)
Saving Throw: 12
Special: Rear claws
Move: 12/6 (swim)
Alignment: Neutrality
Challenge Level/XP: 8/800

This white-furred saber-toothed cat is a relative of the smilodon but makes its home in arctic regions. Its canines are much shorter than the smilodon (averaging only about 4-5 inches long) and its front legs are longer than its rear legs (similar to a hyena's leg structure).

The Clan of the Great Cat

On the mountainous edge of civilization lies the receding Wailing Glacier that is home to the reclusive primitive people called the Clan of the Great Cat. The Neanderthal clan seldom interacts with cultured races other than to wage war. These fierce legendary warriors are experts with primitive weaponry. Each member carries ingrained combat knowledge that increases with age. They pass these skills on to their children.

Clan members adorn themselves with mail made from bone. Each warrior wears a helm fashioned from the skull of a saber-toothed tiger. These helms are masterfully created and passed down through generations. They wear clawed bone gauntlets and wield saw-toothed swords. The clan has domesticated smilodons and even has trained a few giant smilodons as mounts.

Copyright Notice
Author Scott Greene.

Stingray

Stingray (Small)

Hit Dice: 1
Armor Class: 7 [12]
Attacks: tail sting (1d3 + poison)
Saving Throw: 17
Special: Poison
Move: 30 (swim)
Alignment: Neutrality
Challenge Level/XP: 2/30

Stingray (Medium)

Hit Dice: 4
Armor Class: 6 [13]
Attacks: tail sting (1d6 + poison)
Saving Throw: 13
Special: Poison
Move: swim 30
Alignment: Neutrality
Challenge Level/XP: 5/240

Stingray (Large)

Hit Dice: 8
Armor Class: 5 [14]
Attacks: tail sting (1d8 + poison)
Saving Throw: 8
Special: Poison
Move: swim 30
Alignment: Neutrality
Challenge Level/XP: 9/1,100

Stingrays are completely flat with no discernible head. At one end is a long, whip-like tail that ends in a razor-sharp and serrated barb. Their eyes appear as small bumps on the end opposite the tail and their mouth is located on the underside of their body. The sides of a stingray are composed of large, wide pectoral fins (mistakenly referred to as wings sometimes). Stingrays are brown, black, or slate gray and their underbelly is white. Small stingrays are about 3 feet across, while the largest ray measures 12 feet across. A stingray's tail sting causes paralysis. Small stingrays paralyze opponents for 1d3 rounds; Medium stingray for 1d4+1 rounds; and large stingray for 1d6+2 rounds.

Water Hazard

Ocean waves crash on the rocky beach in heavy riptides that pull sand and rock into the water. The land angles sharply down to the waterfront, where a small group of people stand on the beach. A small boy lies on his side on a sandbar rising slightly out of the water about 50 feet offshore. In the water between the boy and the shore, a man's body floats face down in the waves, bobbing in the surf.

Lying in the sand about 30 feet offshore is a large stingray. The creature is perfectly camouflaged in the dirt and tides, its coloration making it difficult to spot until it moves.

The boy waded into the surf on a dare, then became stuck when the stingray stung him just as he reached the sandbar. He collapsed in a paralyzed heap on the rise, safe but unable to move and warn rescuers. The first man into the water wasn't so lucky and was stung and fell facedown into the water. The man has just a few minutes until he drowns.

Copyright Notice
Author Scott Greene.

Tiger Barb, Giant

Hit Dice: 5
Armor Class: 6 [13]
Attack: Bite (1d6)
Saving Throw: 12
Special: None
Move: 0/15 (swimming)
Alignment: Neutrality
Challenge Level/XP: 5/240

The giant tiger barb is peach with black-striped gills that resemble the stripes of a tiger. It is 10 to 15 feet long and weighs about 50 pounds. Tiger barbs sustain themselves on a diet of plants, but eat any sort of food if hungry. They are very territorial and attack anything that enters their domain.

Fish Spy

Traversing a deep level of a dungeon, one comes upon a large chamber. The chamber measures 50 feet in length and 30 feet in width with a ceiling 30 feet high. The walls of the chamber are composed of orange stone carved to look as though they are covered by grape vines. The chamber is girded by a stone platform fifteen set feet above the floor. The chamber has four doors, all on the 30 foot walls and one at floor level and one at platform level. The chamber is filled with fifteen feet of water. Three pillars, each 20 feet tall and 6 feet in diameter, run down the middle of the chamber between the facing doors. The pillars are approximately 15 feet apart. Set in the bottom of the each pillar is a locked copper door. The water that fills the chamber is murky, hiding those doors from those above the surface of the water.

The chamber is inhabited by 1d6+5 giant tiger barbs. Where the fish get their food is unknown (perhaps one of the nearby dungeon denizens), but they are commonly kept hungry and thus more aggressive.

The doors in the pillars open inward and drain the chamber of water - it and the tiger barbs flowing into another chamber below. Once the water has flowed past (and the opener of the door has managed not to be swept away), one will see a ladder of copper rungs in each pillar leading up to a small trapdoor. The trapdoor in each pillar leads into a small chamber (4 feet in diameter and 8 feet tall) lined with a mosaic of mirrors. One pillar's mirrors are capable of showing things happening at that moment on the level above. Another is capable of showing things happening at that moment on the current level. The third shows events on the level below. The mirrors are activated by concentration alone.

Copyright Notice

Tuatara, Giant

Hit Dice: 5
Armor Class: 7 [12]
Attacks: 1 bite (1d8)
Saving Throw: 12
Special: None
Move: 6/3 (burrow)
Alignment: Neutrality
Challenge Level/XP: 5/240

A giant tuatara is a burrowing reptile with a sharp beak designed to crack and tear through the carapace or scaled hide of its prey. The creature is about 10 feet long and weighs close to 400 pounds. Its color ranges from gray or olive to dull red. It lacks ears but has two small openings on either side of its head that seem to function as such. On top of its head is a "third eye" (or parietal eye) that helps the tuatara to regulate its body temperature. Males have a noticeable crest down the center of its neck and back; females have the same crest, but it is much less pronounced. Tuataras stalk their prey at night, having excellent vision in low light and a keen sense of smell. When threatened, a tuatara inflates its body, raises and flares its crest, and darkens the scales between its shoulders and neck.

Gladiator Pit

A crude gladiator pit sits in an otherwise desolate land. The stone-lined pit sits 20 feet in the ground. Blood and bodily fluids stain the sandy dirt. A few body parts and pieces of armor dot the ground. Sturdy planks serving as bleachers surround the pit. Scavengers scratch through the mounds of trash looking for morsels. The spectators, gamblers and vendors have all gone until the next games, leaving smoldering fire pits, grooved wagon trails and waste of all kinds. Wooden cages to hold captives, animals and fighters sit empty behind the bleachers.

A giant tuatara remains in the pit. The lizard is slightly wounded but otherwise alert. A chain binds one its back legs to a post in the center of the pit. A young human man clings to life at the top of a 30 foot post in the pit. The man self-impaled his hands onto iron spikes near the top of the pit to prevent falling. He has been trapped here for four days and is on the brink of death. The chain does not allow the lizard to reach the man. The post is 25 feet from the edge of the pit.

The man is a local mercenary who failed to fulfill a contract and was sold into slavery. After he climbed to the top and impaled his hands, the crowd grew bored and left. The games are closed until the master of ceremonies arranges another night of fighting, gambling and carnage.

Copyright Notice

Turtle, Giant Snapping

Hit Dice: 12
Armor Class: 1 [18]
Attack: Bite (2d8)
Saving Throw: 3
Special: Swallow whole
Move: 6/9 (swimming)
Alignment: Neutrality
Challenge Level/XP: 13/2300

Giant snapping turtles are very large and very aggressive versions of their smaller cousins. They are found in large lakes, rivers, and inland seas. The average giant snapping turtle is 40 feet in diameter, but they can grow to a diameter of 75 feet.

A giant snapping turtle lurks near the shore or on the bottom of a body of water, where it remains motionless and hidden in its shell. When prey passes near, it shoots its neck out and bites.

The victim of a giant snapping turtle's bite must pass a saving throw to avoid being swallowed whole. Once inside, the opponent takes 2d8 points of crushing damage plus 1d8 points of acid damage per round from the turtle's stomach. A swallowed creature can cut its way out by using a light slashing or piercing weapon to deal 25 points of damage to the stomach (AC 3 [16]). A giant snapping turtle's interior can hold up to 8 human-sized victims.

Turtle Star

Any group of adventurers looking for (insert name of an artifact or powerful magic item from your campaign here) must eventually come to the vast Skeletal Sea. The "skeletal" in the sea's name refers not to human or animal remains, but to the remnants of buildings. Two or three hundred years ago, a vast, fruitful plain was flooded - perhaps a god or goddess took a disliking to the men of the plains or an earthquake drained a lake in the mountains.

Whatever the cause of the flooding, the people of the plain were forced to settle elsewhere, leaving their towns and villages behind. The stone ruins of those buildings remain, and one in particular holds interest for treasure seekers. The ruin in question is an ancient temple. All that remains of the temple are three walls, one with an arched opening into the flooded courtyard and a large, stained glass window on the opposite wall. The stained glass window depicts a warrior saint engaged in combat with a green wyrm. Above the saint's head is a constellation with one star larger than the others. Other clues in the window suggest that one must follow that large star in the dead of winter for 30 miles from this spot. At that point there is a dungeon in which the artifact in question resides.

Figuring out the clues in the window would be trying enough if one didn't have to tangle with the 1d3+1 giant snapping turtles that have made the ruined temple their home.

Credit
The Giant Snapping Turtle originally appeared in the First Edition *Monster Manual* (© TSR/Wizards of the Coast, 1977) and is used by permission.

Copyright Notice
Author Scott Greene, based on original material by Gary Gygax.

Appendix B: N'gathau

N'gathau

The n'gathau are a sadistic and cruel race of extraplanar creatures that journey the planes in search of living flesh to further their craft and trade. The n'gathau collect the flesh of their enemies, flay and destroy it, and reconstruct the tortured in blasphemous likenesses of their former selves. Additionally, they sometimes capture the essence of a slain outsider and bring it to their native plane where it remains in eternal torture.

Most horrifying of all, the n'gathau were once humanoids themselves: taken by beings known as the Twelve and transformed via disfiguring tortures. Living creatures are the n'gathau's desire, for the dead serve no purpose; the n'gathau cannot enjoy the suffering of one that cannot scream.

The average n'gathau is a walking collection of bizarre tortures, piercings, chains, flayed skin, and hooks. No two n'gathau are identical in their suffering; the pain endured by each is unique.

The Pain Trade

The n'gathau engage in a bizarre trade with other extraplanar races. In exchange for living creatures, the n'gathau offer reliquaries that contain the power that mortal pain and suffering offers. These reliquaries are most often used as spell components, used to craft constructs, or used in the creation of magic items.

When a living creature is tortured and mutilated, its screams and suffering are captured by machines of alien construction and fabricated into small reliquaries. These items are in turn traded to those who offer the n'gathau what they desire in return — flesh.

N'gathau Tortures

N'gathau are monstrously sadistic, and engage in the torture of captive beings for the simple pleasure of it. Any creature subjected to torture by a n'gathau loses 1d2 points of Constitution per day. A n'gathau will not let its plaything die as a result of the torture. When the captive's Constitution drops to 1 the n'gathau grants it a reprieve from the torture until it is back to full health.

Aagash "The Broken"

The Rulers of the Plane of Agony

The n'gathau are ruled by an enigmatic sect of frighteningly powerful beings called the Twelve. Very little is known about them except for their names and appearances; their history and true origins are locked away in the minds of the Twelve themselves and the catacomb of vaults lining the Plane of Agony. Though reclusive and secretive, it is known (supposedly by one who has seen the Plane of Agony and lived to tell about it) that the Twelve, as mighty as they are, are but servitors of a greater being called the Quorum.

Below is listed all known information about the beings known as the Twelve.

Aagash "The Broken"

Hit Dice: 13
Armor Class: 3 [16]
Attacks: 2 claws (2d8+3) and bite (1d6+3)
Saving Throw: 3
Special: Magical powers, spine break
Move: 9
Alignment: Chaos
Challenge Level/XP: 15/2,900

Aagash is called The Broken because he once greatly displeased the Quorum. He has been bent completely in half backwards, and his head now protrudes through a large opening in his back and out his belly. His neck is completely flayed, and steel rods screwed into his chin and braced against his hips support his head. Aagash is the personal servant of the Quorum. At will, Aagash can use *ESP*, *detect magic* and *hold person*. Once per day he can cast *massmorph*. If Aagash hits a single opponent with both claws, the foe must save or be grabbed by the n'gathau and bent backward for an additional 3d8 points of damage.

Asagin "The Assassin"

Hit Dice: 16
Armor Class: 1 [18]
Attacks: 2 slams (3d6)
Saving Throw: 3
Special: Hooks, fear gaze
Move: 9/15 (flying)
Alignment: Chaos
Challenge Level/XP: 17/3,500

Asagin is general to the armies of the Quorum and leads them in battle. He is known as "The Assassin" or "The Winged One." Some refer to him as the "Angel of Death." Nailed to his back by iron spikes are a pair of large membranous wings. Two large scars crisscross his face in an "X" pattern. His eyes are hollow sockets with small hooks piercing the skin of the upper and lower eyelids, and connecting to his shoulders by small lengths of chain. Small iron hooks are embedded the entire length of his arms, from shoulder to hand. A large hook protrudes from the palm of each hand. Any creature hit by both of Asagin's slam attacks is automatically drawn into his body and grabbed by the myriad hooks lining his torso for 1d8 points of damage each round until freed. By flexing his muscles, Asagin can open his eyes wide to cause anyone who meets his gaze to save or be overcome by *fear* (as per the spell). At will, Asagin can cast *feeblemind*, *confusion*, *mirror image* and *shield*.

Chaadon "The Slayer"

Hit Dice: 18
Armor Class: -1 [20]
Attacks: 4 slams (2d8+2)
Saving Throw: 3
Special: Crush, sever limbs, magical abilities
Move: 9/12 (flying)
Alignment: Chaos
Challenge Level/XP: 20/4,400

Chaadon is known as the Slayer and is the Quorum's bodyguard. He is a four-armed creature that serves unswervingly and never questions

Asagin "The Assassin"

By pulling one of the nails from his flesh and driving it into an opponent (1d8 damage), Chaas can enslave the being (as per a *charm person*) to do his bidding (save resists). At will, Chaas can cast a version of *rope trick* that affects any chains within 100 feet.

Ghehzi "The Mutilator"

Hit Dice: 17
Armor Class: 2 [17]
Attacks: 2 claws (2d8+3) or impale (2d8+3)
Saving Throw: 3
Special: Fire, impale, rend skin, immune to fire
Move: 15
Alignment: Chaos
Challenge Level/XP: 18/3,800

Ghehzi is Veruard's assistant and co-engineer. His entire body is a pallid, yellowish-gray color. Every visible portion of his skin has been flayed, charred, or mutilated. His ears have been crudely cut off and his nose flayed from his body. His mouth is hidden beneath a thick metal collar. Ghehzi's eyes are sewn shut with thick black cables. His hands sport small, razor-sharp curved blades in place of his fingernails. Two large metal spikes have been driven through his back, through each shoulder blade, and exit his upper chest. If Ghehzi hits a single opponent with both claws, he rips and tears at the opponent's skin with his sharpened razor blades for and extra 4d6 points of damage. Ghehzi can also lunge at a foe to impale him for 2d8 points of damage on the massive spikes sticking from his chest. The impaled victim is considered held, and takes automatic rend damage until freed. Four times per day, Ghehzi can pull his mouth free of the collar and utter a tortured scream that detonates a fireball on top of his form in a 40-foot-radius. The blast does 8d6 points of damage (save for half).

Greixas "The Destroyer"

Hit Dice: 21
Armor Class: 3 [16]
Attacks: 2 slam (3d6+2)
Saving Throw: 3
Special: Symbols, acid burst, siphon blood
Move: 12
Alignment: Chaos
Challenge Level/XP: 22/5,000

Greixas is a blood-thirsty warrior whose chest has been split open, the skin peeled back to expose his ribs and chest muscles. Long, thin feeding

his post. All of his arms are prosthetic and mechanical. It is believed he once possessed real arms and wings, but stories among the n'gathau say they were devoured by N'hror (see below) and he was reconfigured by Veruard the Creator. Large screws are driven into his eyes, and his lips are mutilated to leave his teeth exposed. His head is hairless, his flesh gray. Long, thin steel rods driven into his shoulders reside at an angle and attach to each side of his head. If Chaadon hits an opponent with two slam attacks, the being must save or be grabbed and crushed on the next round by Chaadon's powerful appendages for 4d6 points of damage. On a roll of natural 20, Chaadon rips the limb off an opponent. At will, chaadon can cast *silence (15-foot radius)* and *hold person*.

Chaas "The Flayed"

Hit Dice: 16
Armor Class: 3 [16]
Attacks: 2 slams (2d6+1) or 6 chain whips (2d8+1)
Saving Throw: 3
Special: Flense skin, chain whip, sever heads, enslaving nails
Move: 15
Alignment: Chaos
Challenge Level/XP: 18/3,800

Chaas stands over 6 feet tall and is a gray-skinned, hairless humanoid whose entire body upper torso, head, face, and arms have been made completely flayed of flesh. A double row of long, thin nails are driven into his back from shoulder to waist. A small chain hangs from each nail, almost dragging the floor, but each returns and disappears into his spine. His eyes are deep, sullen and gray. A row of nails driven into his throat and neck form a sort of collar. Chaas's true position in the Order of the Twelve is unknown, but it is assumed he serves the Quorum as Chancellor. Chaas can command the chains to swing in dangerous arcs around his body to grab and hold opponents. If two or more chains hit a single foe, the chains flense the skin from the opponent's body for 4d6 points of damage. On a natural roll of 20, the whipping chains sever an opponent's limb (chosen randomly, exluding the head; the N'gathau live for the pain, not instantaneous death).

Chaadon "The Slayer"

Chaas "The Flayed"

tubes run from his head and face to his internal organs beneath his ribcage. His head is devoid of hair and has intricate designs and patterns cut into it. His eyes are dark and gray. Greixas's hands are sewn and nailed shut in an "everlasting fist." Besides his fist slam, Greixas can cause his feeding tubes to back up and spew a thick sludge of digestive acid in a 20-foot radius that does 3d6 points of acid damage. The symbols on Greixas' head are various *symbol* spells that Greixas can cause to detonate by turning his head toward foes who face off against him. The symbol detonates if the opponent fails a saving throw to avoid seeing the spell sigil. If Greixas hits an opponent with both fists, he bear hugs the victim so his feeding tubes can attach and drain 2d6 points of blood from the victim automatically thereafter.

Modar "The Avenger"

Hit Dice: 21
Armor Class: 2 [17]
Attacks: 2 claws (2d8)
Saving Throw: 3
Special: See invisible, wirebind, kiss, magical powers
Move: 12
Alignment: Chaos
Challenge Level/XP: 22/5,000

The first of only two female members of the Twelve, Modar appears as a grotesquely mutilated woman whose mouth has been wired shut with thick black cables. Her breasts have been removed and her abdomen stitched in various patterns. Her lips are peeled away, revealing almost pearl-white teeth. Her eyes are pulled from their sockets on stretched out optic nerves and held away from her face by metal rods with small metal rings. Her disfigured hands end in wicked claws. On a successful hit, Modar transfers 2d6 coiled lengths of barbed wires from her body to an opponent. These wires wrap around appendages and bind arms to the torso or both legs together and do 1d8 points of damage (save resists binding). If Modar hits an opponent with both claws, she can choose on the next round to pull the victim close and kiss him (save avoids kiss). The kiss transfers tiny wires that burrow through the victims lips and seal his throat closed (2d6 points of damage each round as the victim suffocates). Three times per day, Modar can cast *ESP*, *charm person* and *suggestion*.

Greixas "The Destoyer"

N'hror "The Eater"

Hit Dice: 18
Armor Class: 1 [18]
Attacks: 2 claws (1d8), bite (3d6)
Saving Throw: 3
Special: Bite severs limbs, strangulation (2d6), immune to blunt weapons
Move: 6
Alignment: Chaos
Challenge Level/XP: 19/4,100

N'hror is a large, obese creature that has been cut open from navel to chest and whose intestines hang loosely from the wound. A thick, purplish liquid oozes from the gash. His chest, back, and arms are tattooed with intricate patterns and designs. His head is round and hairless, and his jaws have been stretched open to twice their normal capacity. His mouth sports a double row of sharpened fangs. His eyes are solid black. N'hror answers only to the Quorum. He is the Inquisitor of the n'gathau, and is the punisher of those who displease his triumvirate master. N'hror's hanging intestines can whip out of his body to grab an opponent. On a successful hit, the opponent must save or be wrapped in the purplish gore and dragged back to N'hror's body and strangled slowly for 1d8 points of damage each round thereafter. N'hror's bite on a roll of a natural 20 severs a victim's limb (chosen randomly, excluding the head). N'hror's corpulent body makes him immune to blunt weapons.

Raauka "The Ravager"

The Quorum

Raauka "The Ravager"

Hit Dice: 22
Armor Class: 3 [16]
Attacks: 2 claws (1d8 + poison) and bite (2d4)
Saving Throw: 3
Special: Flesh inversion injection, +1 weapons to hit, magical powers
Move: 12
Alignment: Chaos
Challenge Level/XP: 23/5,300

Standing about 6 feet tall, Raauka appears as a humanoid creature whose head and face has been severely mutilated. Small metal hooks embedded in his forehead attach to small links of chain that peel away the flesh around his eyes. His pupils and irises are blackened. Sharpened fangs protrude from his mutilated mouth. Several small, thin feeding tubes exit each forearm and enter his neck. His fingers have been amputated and replaced with long hollow needles that drip a sapphire blue liquid. Raauka is often sent to the Material Plane to retrieve powerful female mortals for transformation. Raauka's claw attack jabs opponents with a poison that turns their flesh inside out (save avoids). This does 6d6 points of damage as the character's internal organs push out through his skin and his flesh is replaced with muscle and sinew. A gel-like blue ooze coats the victim's new skin to hold the organs in place externally. Raauka can cast *charm person*, *suggestion* and *polymorph self* at will.

Ulaska't "The Twisted"

Ulaska't "The Twisted"

Hit Dice: 19
Armor Class: 3 [16]
Attacks: 1 slam (3d6)
Saving Throw: 3
Special: Twine skin, trample
Move: 9
Alignment: Chaos
Challenge Level/XP: 21/4,700

Ulaska't's entire lower body is missing, with his entrails draped and woven around a metal framework. Instead of legs, he has two rigid metal poles around which his leg muscles are stapled to allow movement. He is

N'hror "The Eater"

Veruard "The Razor and the Creator"

Hit Dice: 25
Armor Class: -3 [22]
Attacks: 2 slams (3d6 + wounds)
Saving Throw: 3
Special: Bind skin, create N'gathau
Move: 15
Alignment: Chaos
Challenge Level/XP: 28/6,800

Veruard is called the Creator for it is he who, at the Quorum's desire, reconfigures chosen subjects into their N'gathau form. He reworks, mutilates, destroys, tears, and reshapes creatures brought to him into a more "pleasing" form. He is a 7-foot-tall humanoid with pale gray flesh whose entire body is wrapped tightly and horizontally in razor-sharp filament wires that cut deep and tear into the flesh. His irises are gray and his pupils black. His fingernails are blackened. His body sports multiple piercings of various sizes and in various locations. His clothing and armor are sewn to his flesh. The artist of pain hits opponents with his massive slam attacks. Each hit slices away the flesh of his opponent, causing wounds that can't be healed by normal means. These wounds fester and expand for 2d6 points of damage per minute until a *remove curse* is cast on the victim. Veruard can pull free a piercing from his skin and smash it into an opponent. This attack causes minimal damage (1d6), but the piercing attaches to the victim. In 1d6 rounds, metal filaments erupt from the victim's hands and throat and wrap out his arms and neck (save resists). These razor-sharp wires deal 6d6 points of damage as they dig into the creature's body and immobilize him. These metal razor wires must be cut free of the victim's body for an additional 3d6 points of damage. If Veruard hits an opponent with both fists, he can grab an opponent and start crafting him into a N'gathau in the next round. At will, Veruard can cast *polymorph self, polymorph other, massmorph, charm* and *suggestion*. He can also cast spells as a 12th-level Magic-User.

The Quorum

Hit Dice: 32
Armor Class: -5 [24]
Attacks: 1 paralyizing touch (4d6)
Saving Throw: 3
Special: Gaze attacks, binding strands, magical abilities, +3 magic weapon to hit, confusion, paralyzing touch
Move: 6
Alignment: Chaos
Challenge Level/XP: 35/8,900

The Quorum consists of three creatures back to back, sewn together at the arms; one male, one female, and one that is a formed from a male and a female that have been bisected and crudely stitched together down the middle. The backs of their heads are sawn open and their brains are interconnected by a complicated tangle of wires and cables of various thickness. They move as one, and speak in three voices in perfect unison.

The Quorum is a tribunal of demigods acting in perfect harmony with one another, three gods in one, each chained, sewn, hooked, and pierced to the other. It is the Quorum that controls the Twelve and sends n'gathau on missions of flesh. It is the Quorum who sits in judgment over the n'gathau that have failed or disappointed it. And it is the Quorum who decides which mortals are worthy of joining the ranks of the N'gathau.

The multiple voices of the Quorum cause confusion (as per the spell) in creatures when it speaks. It can cast *charm person, suggestion* and *feeblemind* at will. The touch of the Quorum sends a jolt of electricity through an opponent that deadens the creature's nerves for 4d6 points of damage and causes paralysis (save for half damage and to resist being paralyzed for 2d4 rounds). Anyone attacking the Quorum must save or be infected by binding strands of wire that lash out from the creature's body to tie the foe to the Quorum's body for 1d8 points of damage each round until freed.

The Quorum's three separate gazes each have different gaze attacks. The male head can cause a victim who meets its gaze to burst into flame

---

the only one of the Twelve with hair, though it is matted and torn. His face is a masterpiece of scars and cuts. His eyelids have been removed and his nose cut off. Embedded in his arms and chest are small metal hooks and rings. Ulaska't is the sage and loremaster of the Quorum. There is little that transpires in any plane that Ulaska't is not aware of. Ulaska't uses his metal bulk to smash into opponents. If he hits with a slam, his myriad hooks snag the flesh of an opponent (save avoids). His upper body then spins on its platform to twist the skin off the foe's body for 3d8 points of damage. Ulaska't can also trample foes with his metal legs for 2d6 points of damage.

Veenes "The Blademistress"

Hit Dice: 21
Armor Class: -1 [20]
Attacks: 2 scythes (3d6+2)
Saving Throw: 3
Special: Seduction pheromones, sever spine, magical abilities
Move: 12
Alignment: Chaos
Challenge Level/XP: 23/5,300

The second of the female who comprise the Twelve, Veenes has a very beautiful and shapely torso. Her head is hairless with the skin removed; the top of her skull is sawn off, exposing her brain. Several small tubes pumping purplish liquid are inserted into her brain and run the length of her back where they enter her spine at waist level. Small, curved hooks protrude from her shoulders, forearms, and upper back across her shoulders. Embedded in each forearm and gripped with each hand is a razor-sharp scythe. An agent of Veruard, the strangely seductive Veenes is often used as a tool to capture powerful male mortals for transformation. Veruard is surrounded by a 10-foot cloud of pheromones that breaks down the will of any male who breathes in the potent scent. This ever-present cloud is similar to a *charm person* spell that affects only men. Veruard can cast *suggestion* and *polymorph self* at will. If Veruard rolls a natural 20 with her scythe attacks, she severs an opponent's spine.

for 4d6 points of damage (save for half). The female head causes the opponent to think it is the Quorum's ally and attack its former friends (save resists). The sewn-together head causes an opponent's skin to split asunder and peel apart from the top of its skull to its chest, causing 5d6 points of damage (save for half).

Creating a N'gathau

Any humanoid can be turned into a N'gathau. It is up to the Game Referee to decide what the creature looks like, and what extra attacks it gains after its conversion. The Random Mutilations table below is provided to help offer different possibilites.

N'gathau Random Mutilations

To randomly determine the mutilations of a particular n'gathau, first roll 1d3+3 to see how many mutilations the n'gathau has. Next roll 1d12 on the **Body Part Table** to determine the affected body part for each mutilation. Finally, determine the effects of each mutilation using the **Mutilation Table**. Some mutilations have side effects; any side effects are given with the description of the mutilation.

Body Part Table

Roll 1d12 for each mutilation on the table below to determine the body part affected.

1d12	Body Part
1	Head
2	Face
3	Neck
4-5	Chest or Back
6	Abdomen or Back
7	Upper Arm (roll 1d6; odd = left, even = right)
8	Lower Arm (roll 1d6; odd = left, even = right)
9	Hand (roll 1d6; odd = left, even = right)
10	Upper Leg (roll 1d6; odd = left, even = right)
11	Lower Leg (roll 1d6; odd = left, even = right)
12	Foot (roll 1d6; odd = left, even = right)

Sample N'gathau

The following example creatures use a 9th-level fighter as the base character.

Donlan, Male N'gathau Fighter 9: HD 9; AC 4[15]; Atk long sword (1d8); Move 9; Save 6; CL/XP: 9/1,100; Alignment: Chaos; Special: Chain mail, shield, long sword
Possessions: +3 studded leather armor, +2 razor-hook.
N'gathau Mutilations: Lower right arm encased in latticework of wires and cables charged with electricity (deals 1d2 points of electricity damage with slam attack or metal weapon), chest is pierced with rows of small upward curving hooks (grappled foe takes 1d2 points of piercing damage each round), head has been seared (ears are burned off, but organs still there, so he can hear), thick copper wires charged with electricity wrapped around head and hooked into shoulders, right leg has been fully scarified in intricate designs and patterns.

The Daedalean Cube

Only the base of the ruined Ziggurat of Mushussu remains in the dusty wasteland. A triad of reliquary golems (representing Good, Neutrality and Evil) stand atop the temple foundations, each facing outward as they forever guard the terror trapped inside. Horrific traps and eternal guardians are stationed in the depths beneath the ziggurat's remains. A lead-lined burial vault within the ziggurat contains a 15-foot-tall conic pillar of lead. The floor around the pillar is layered with barbed iron chains. The chains are animated guardians that rise up to stop thieves.

A fist-sized cube floats above the pillar's tip. The fabled Daedalean Cube is a cubic gate designed to unlock the mysteries of the planes. The enigmatic cube can open gates to six random planes, one assigned to each side of the cube. (The Game Referee could use a six-sided die to determine which plane the PCs end up on.)

Using the cube drains one level from the user and draws the attention of the N'gathau, who arrive via their own planar gates to torture and enslave the victim tampering with the energies of the universe.

Copyright Notice

Random Mutilation Table

Roll 1d20 for each mutilation determined above and apply the effects as detailed on the table below.

1d20	Mutilation
1	**Attachment:** The body part has some sort of gear attached to it via hooks, pins, or barbs. Examples include chains, pouches, jewelry, bones, or any other small object that can dangle from hooks. There is a 50% chance the attachment is actually a weapon either grafted to or embedded in the flesh. Weapons are always of the slashing or piercing type such as daggers, knives, scythes, etc.
2	**Degloving:** The body part has been completely skinned, revealing muscle, bone, and sinew. If the degloving is to the torso, the n'gathau's natural armor bonus is reduced by +1 [-1].
3	**Dislocation/Disjointed:** The body part is horribly dislocated and has been braced and bolted into an unusual configuration.
4	**Electrification:** The body part is encased in a latticework of metal bars and wires that constantly crackle with electricity, causing the entire body to twitch. The electrical charge deals an extra 1d2 points of electricity damage with slam attacks and attacks with metal melee weapons.
5	**Extension:** The body part has been fully disarticulated and artificially extended with metal plates and rods. The extension provides a +1 bonus to attacks using that limb (where applicable).
6	**Flaying, Major:** The body part has been flayed open down to the bone, and the incision is held open with hooks, metal staples, or brackets. If the affected body part is the head, roll 1d6; on a roll of 1, the top of the head has been removed and the brain is fully exposed. The exposure results in a +1 [-1] penalty to the creature's armor class.
7	**Flaying, Minor:** The body part has had several small square sections of flesh cut away or flayed open. A minor flaying to the head is a trepanation, which exposes a small portion of the brain.
8	**Metal Plate:** A metal plate has been crudely bolted, stapled, or in some way attached to the body part. The plates provide a -1 [+1] armor bonus.
9-10	**Piercing, Single:** The body part has a single metal spike, hook, ring, screw, or other object fully embedded in it or driven through it. A piercing to an arm, hand, foot, or leg provides a +1 bonus to damage using natural attacks with that limb (where applicable).
11-12	**Piercing, Multiple:** The body part is lined and pierced with several small metal spikes, hooks, rings, screws, or other objects. Hooks, spikes, nails, and other such devices can be used to deal 1d2 points of piercing or slashing damage.
13	**Prosthetic:** The body part has some sort of prosthetic or mechanical replacement. On a roll of 1-4 on 1d6, a prosthetic hand or arm is a bladed weapon of some kind that deals 1d6 damage (for just a hand) or 1d8 damage (for an entire arm). If the body part is a leg or foot, a metallic device that roughly duplicates the function of that limb has replaced it. A prosthetic on the chest, abdomen, head, or neck is a strange device of unknown function.
14–15	**Stitching:** The entire body part is covered in random surgical-looking stitches of either metal or cloth. If the stitching is on the face, roll 1d6; on a roll of 1 the eyes have been sewn shut, and on a roll of 2 the mouth has been sewn shut. Otherwise, the stitching is in a random pattern across the face. If the eyes have been sewn shut, the creature is effectively blind. If the mouth has been sewn shut, the n'gathau is effectively mute and cannot speak. If the stitching is to the torso, the n'gathau's natural armor bonus is increased by -1 [+1].
16	**Tubes:** The body part has 1d3 tubes embedded in it, each leading to another body part (determine randomly on the **Body Part Table**). Flowing through each tube is a sickeningly colored liquid of unknown origin.
17	**Utter Mutilation:** The body part has been totally mutilated and carved beyond recognition. It has been subjected to nearly every mutilation on this table, and some that aren't. If the mutilation is to the torso, the n'gathau's natural armor bonus is increased by -1 [+1] as well.
18	**Wire Wrapping:** The body part is wrapped tightly in a fine wire or wire mesh that digs into the flesh.
19	**Searing:** The body part is completely burned almost beyond the point of recognition. If the searing is to the torso, increase the n'gathau's natural armor bonus by -1 [+1] and takes half damage from fire-based attacks.
20	**Carving/Scarification/Branding:** The body part has a unique pattern of strange and elaborate symbols cut into the flesh or the flesh has been burned and branded. The base character's natural armor bonus increases by -2 [+2] if this mutilation is to the torso.

Appendix C: Monsters by CL

MONSTERS BY CL

Challenge Level (CL) A to 1

Barracuda, Small (1HD)
Bookworm
Brownie
Cave Cricket
Clockwork Drone
Clockwork Scout
Dire Skunk
Ear Seeker
Eye Leech Swarm
Fire Crab (1HD)
Flea, Giant
Floating Eye
Fox
Gas Spore
Golden Cat
Graymalkin, Common
Graymalkin, Slinker
Gremlin
Grippli
Hound of Ill Omen
Jaculi
Killmoulis
Kuah-Lij
Memory Moss
Mimi
Mite, Common Mite
Mite, Pestie
Mosquito, Giant
Muckdweller
Nilbog
Olive Slime
Ooze, Amber
Phantom
Phase Flea, Giant
Piercer
Purple Moss
Quipper
Raccoon
Raccoon, Giant
Rat, Barrow
Redcap
Skunk
Slime Crawler
Spinal Leech
Symbiotic Jelly
Throat Leech
Throat Spider
Twilight Mushrooms
Vapor Rat
Wizard's Shackle

Challenge Level (CL) 2

Archer Bush
Archerfish, Giant
Al-mi'raj
Atomie
Baric
Blood Hawk
Buckawn
Caracal
Carbuncle

Clockwork Overseer
Clubnek
Dakon
Dark Creeper
Deer
Dire Corby
Dire Dog
Dire Porcupine
Dire Skunk
False Spider, Giant (Pedipalp)
Flind
Frog, Killer
Frog, Poisonous
Fulgurate Mushrooms
Graymalkin, Tether
Gutslug
Half-Ogre
Huggermugger
Kampfult (Sinewy Mugger)
Land Lamprey
Lynx
Mandrill
Mantari
Margay
Mephit, Lightning
Mephit, Smoke
Mongrelman
Ogren
Ogrillon
Orc, Black
Orc, Blood
Orc, Ghost Faced
Orc, Greenskin
Shadow, Lesser
Sheep
Silid
Skulk
Soul Nibbler
Spider, Skull
Sprite
Stingray (Small) (1HD)
Tabaxi
Vegepygmy
Vilstrak (Tunnel Thug)
Vulchling
Winterbloom
Witch Grass

Challenge Level (CL) 3

Asrai
Axe Beak
Barbegazi (Ice Gnome)
Beetle, Giant Blister
Beetle, Giant Water
Boneneedle
Caribe, Giant
Chameleon, Giant
Clockwork Brain Gear
Crab, Monstrous
Crabman
Death Dog
Demon, Skitterdark
Devil, Amaimon
Dire Dog

Dire Goat
Dire Sloth
Dragon, Smoke (Draco Fumo) (3HD)
Dragonfish
Eel, Electric
Elusa Hound
Executioner's Hood
Falcon, Giant
Fetch
Forgotten One
Frog, Giant
Fyr
Gargoyle, Fungus
Gorbel
Hanged Man
Hoar Fox
Iron Cobra
Jaguar
Jelly, Whip
Leech, Giant
Leopard, Snow
Leprechaun
Lion, Mountain
Lythic
Mandragora
Marmoset, Giant
Mudbog
Oakman
Ogren
Orog
Pike, Giant
Quasi-Elemental, Acid (2HD)
Quasi-Elemental, Obsidian (2HD)
Rakklethorn, Toad
Ram
Rat, Brain
Rat, Spore
Ronus
Ryven
Sea Wasp, Monstrous (2HD)
Sheet Fungus
Silid
Swarm, Raven
Tick, Giant
Troll, Swamp
Tsathar, Common Tsathar
Ubue
Witherstench
Zombie, Corpsespun

Challenge Level (CL) 4

Abyssal Larva
Baccae
Banderlog
Barracuda, Medium (4HD)
Blood Bush
Bonesnapper
Cadaver
Cave Fisher
Cave Moray
Clam, Giant
Chameleon, Rock
Chupacabra
Clockwork Warrior
Cooshee
Crayfish, Monstrous
Dark Stalker
Devil, Nupperibo
Diger
Dire Deer

Dragon, Smoke (Draco Fumo) (4HD)
Fire Crab (4HD)
Fire Snake
Fly, Giant
Forlarren
Gambado
Gorilla Bear
Gronk
Hamster, Giant
Hippocampus
Horsefly, Giant
Inphidian, Dancer/Charmer
Jellyfish, Monstrous
Jupiter Bloodsucker (Vampire Plant)
Kathlin
Kul
Lizard, Cavern
Lizard, Giant Rock-Horned (Blood Lizard)
Marble Snake
Ongki
Rat, Etheral
Rat, Shadow
Retch Hound
Sandling
Seahorse, Giant
Screaming Devilkin
Slime Mold
Storm Warden
Sudoth
Swarm, Piranha
Swarm, Poisonous Frog
Swarm, Scarlet Spider
T'shann
Taer
Tangtal (Dupli-Cat)
Thermite, Worker
Thorny
Tri-Flower Frond
Troblin
Troll, Ice
Vampire Rose
Volt (Bolt Wurm)
Wang Liang
Zombie, Brine
Zombie, Spellgorged

Challenge Level (CL) 5

Abomination, Tigrilla
Adherer
Ahlinni (Cackle Bird)
Babbker
Beetle, Giant Boring
Beetle, Giant Saw-Toothed
Blindheim
Bumblebee, Giant (Worker)
Chameleon, Giant Horned
Clockwork Parasite
Coffer Corpse
Dire Ram
Dragon, Faerie (Draco Fraudatio Minimus)
Dragon, Smoke (Draco Fumo) (5HD)
False Spider, Giant (Solifugid)
Flumph
Frog, Giant Dire
Fungoid
Gallows Tree Zombie
Gelid Beetle, Lesser
Ghoul, Dust
Grave Risen
Golem, Stone Guardian

Gronk
Gryph
Hoar Spirit
Huecuva
Hyaenodon
Inphidian, Common
Kech
Lava Child
Lythic
Mawler
Moose
Mudman
Necrophidius
Nightshade Mastiff
Niln (Vapor Horror)
Phlogiston
Phooka
Phycomid
Poltergeist
Quasi-Elemental, Acid (4HD)
Quasi-Elemental, Obsidian (4HD)
Quickling
Rock Reptile
Sabrewing
Scythe Horn
Scimitar Horn
Sea Wasp, Monstrous (4HD)
Sirine Flower
Stench Kow
Strangleweed
Suchfed
Swarm, Velvet Ant
Swarm, Warden Jack
Stingray (Medium) (4HD)
Stymphalian Bird (Bronze Beak)
Therianthrope, Asswere
Therianthrope, Foxwere
Therianthrope, Jackalwere
Therianthrope, Mulewere
Therianthrope, Owlwere
Therianthrope, Wolfwere
Tiger Barb, Giant
Tsathar, Tsathar Scourge
Tuatara, Giant
Tumblespark
Vapor Wasp
Wolf, Ghoul
Yellow Musk Creeper
Zombie, Juju
Zombie, Yellow Musk

Challenge Level (CL) 6

Baobhan Sith
Bat, Mobat
Belabra (Tangler)
Boalisk
Bog Beast
Caterwaul
Cave Leech
Church Grim
Churr
Demon, Corruptor - Barizou (Assassin Demon)
Demon, Ooze (Lesser)
Drake, Fire
Dust Digger
Eblis
Eel, Giant Moray
Fear Guard
Fire Nymph
Flail Snail

Forester's Bane
Frost Man
Gargoyle, Four-Armed
Golem, Rope
Inphidian, Cobra-Back
Jelly, Stun-
Kamadan
Ooze, Crystal
Ooze, Glacial
Ooze, Mercury
Pech
Pudding, Blood
Pyrolisk
Reigon
Sandman
Scarecrow
Scythe Tree
Sea Serpent, Gilded
Skeleton, Black
Skulleton
Slime Zombie
Spider Collective
Sloth Viper
Smilodon (Saber-Toothed Cat)
Spriggan
Tentamort
Thermite, Giant (Warrior)
Turtle-Shark
Weird, Fungus
Wolf, Shadow
Yellowjacket, Giant

Challenge Level (CL) 7

Algoid
Amphisbaena
Barracuda, Giant (7HD)
Basilisk, Crimson
Bloody Bones
Bogeyman
Bone Cobbler
Brykolakas
Bunyip
Cadaver Lord
Caryatid Column
Clamor
Clockwork Swarm
Cobra Flower
Corpse Rook
Crag Man
Decapus
Demon, Corruptor - Azizou (Pain Demon)
Disenchanter
Drake, Ice
Drelb (Haunting Custodian)
Fire Phantom
Fye
Ghoul-Stirge
Gosa
Grimstalker (Banaan)
Helix Moth (Larva)
Hippopotamus
Inphidian, Rattler
Jack-O-Lantern
Kelpie
Lantern Goat (7HD)
Lion, Cave
Livestone
Lizard, Gnasher
Murder-Born
Onyx Deer

Psiwyrm (7HD)
Quasi-Elemental, Acid (6HD)
Quasi-Elemental, Obsidian (6HD)
Riptide Horror
Skin Stitcher
Swarm, Shadow Rat
Stroke Lad
Troll, Cave
Witherweed
Woodwose
Yeti

Smilodon (Homotherium)
Swarm, Grig
Swarm, Raven (Undead)
Tazelwurm
Temporal Crawler
Therianthrope, Lionwere
Thunderbeast
Transposer
Weird, Blood
Wolf, Abyssal
Wolf-Spider

Challenge Level (CL) 8

Ant Lion
Arcanoplasm
Ascomoid
Assassin Bug, Giant
Basidirond
Bat, Doombat
Beast of Chaos
Beetle, Giant Slicer
Bhuta
Bloodsuckle
Bog Creeper
Boggart
Brume
Carrion Moth
Caterprism
Chrystone
Clockwork Titan
Corpse Candle
Death Worm
Demon, Corruptor - Geruzou (Slime Demon)
Devil, Hellstoker (Marnasoth)
Devil, Lilin
Devil Dog
Dragongly, Giant
Draug
Eel, Gulper
Eye Killer
Fogwarden
Gargoyle, Green Guardian
Gargoyle, Margoyle
Genie, Abasheen
Ghoul, Cinder
Giant, Wood
Glass Wyrm (5HD)
Gnetch (Brain Stinger)
Gray Nisp
Gulper Eel
Haunt
Homotherium
Hornet, Giant
Inphidian, Night Adder
Korred
Memory Child
Nazalor
Nereid
Oliphant
Ooze, Magma
Ooze, Metallic (Hoard Ooze)
Ooze, Undead
Phasma
Plant-Imbued Ape
Psiwyrm (8HD)
Raven Swarm, Undead
Roper, Stone
Screaming Skull (Cacophony Golem)
Slithering Tracker
Smilodon, Giant (Saber-Toothed Cat)

Challenge Level (CL) 9

Aberrant
Apparition
Arach
Astral Shark
Burning Dervish
Crypt Thing
Demon, Gallu-Demon (Faceless Demon)
Demon, Mehrim (Goat Demon)
Dire Bison
Dire Moose
Dragonnel
Drake, Splinter
Elemental, Gravity (8HD)
Elemental, Negative Energy (8HD)
Elemental, Positive Energy (8HD)
Encephalon Gorger
Firefiend
Foo Dog
Frog, Giant Abyssal Dire
Geon
Giant, Cave
Giant, Smoke
Glass Wyrm (6HD)
Gloomwing
Golem, Blood
Golem, Magnesium
Khargra
Magmoid
Mummy of the Deep
Murder Crow
Nuckalavee
Oil Shark
Orc, Black (High Priest of Orcus)
Phantasm
Psiwyrm (9HD)
Pudding, Dun
Quasi-Elemental, Acid (8HD)
Quasi-Elemental, Lightning (6HD)
Quasi-Elemental, Obsidian (8HD)
Quickwood
Renzer (Devilfin)
Sand Kraken
Sand Stalker
Sea Wasp, Monstrous (8HD)
Sea Phantom
Sea Serpent, Fanged
Spectral Troll
Stingray (Large) (8HD)
Tendrul
Thermite, Giant (Queen)
Tombstone Fairy
Troll, Rock
Vorin
Weird, Lava
Weird, Lightning
Wind Walker
Witch Tree

Challenge Level (CL) 10

Abomination, Owlephant
Amphisbaena Basilisk
Basilisk, Greater
Bedlam
Bleeding Horror
Bog Mummy
Bonesucker
Catfish, Giant Electric
Crystalline Horror
Darnoc
Demon, Alu-
Demon, Balban (Brute Demon)
Devil, Tormentor (Tormentor of Souls)
Dragon, Dungeon (Draco Carcer Dominus) (8HD)
Dream Spectre (Nightmare Creature)
Ectoplasm (Ghost Ooze)
Genie, Abasheen
Glass Wyrm (7HD)
Gnarlwood
Golem, Ice
Golem, Mummy
Golem, Witch-Doll
Golem, Wood
Hangman Tree
Jelly, Marsh
Kelp Devil
Lantern Goat (7HD)
Mantidrake
Medusa, Greater
Midnight Peddler
Ooze, Vampiric
Phantom Stalker
Protector
Pudding, White
Rawbones
Rhinoceros, Woolly
Stegocentipede
Stone Maiden
Thessalmonster, Thessalisk
Treant, Lightning
Troll, Flame-Spawned
Tunnel Worm
Well Lurker
Wight, Barrow
Willow Dusk

Challenge Level (CL) 11

Angel, Chalkydri
Beetle, Giant Death Watch
Brontotherium
Cerebral Stalker
Daemon, Guardian
Dragon, Dungeon (Draco Carcer Dominus) (9HD)
Fen Witch
Gloom Crawler
Golem, Gelatinous
Hell Moth
Lizard, Fire
Magnesium Spirit
Ooze, Entropic
Quasi-Elemental, Acid (10HD)
Quasi-Elemental, Obsidian (10HD)
Tenebrous Worm
Troll, Two-Headed
Widow Creeper

Challenge Level (CL) 12

Beetle, Giant Rhinoceros
Brass Man
Bumblebee, Giant (Queen)
Chain Worm
Demon, Shadow
Dragon, Wrath (10HD)
Dragon Horse
Demon, Cambion
Demon, Nysrock (Cobra Demon)
Dragon, Dungeon (Draco Carcer Dominus) (10HD)
Elemental, Psionic (8HD)
Golem, Flagstone
Golem, Ooze
Golem, Tallow
Groaning Spirit
Jelly, Mustard
Lurker Above
Mammoth
Psiwyrm (Draco Presentia Facultas) (10HD)
Pudding, Brown
Pudding, Stone
Raggoth
Skeleton Warrior
Slaughterford (Reaperborn)
Squealer
Thessalmonster, Thessalgorgon
Thogg
Wight, Blood

Challenge Level (CL) 13

Anemone, Great (Giant) Sea
Aurumvorax (Golden Gorger)
Biclops
Corpsespinner
Daemon, Hyrdodaemon
Demi-Lich
Demon, Mezzalorn (Wasp Demon)
Demon, Ooze (Greater)
Devil, Blood Reaver (Garugin)
Dire Hippopotamus (Behemoth)
Dragon, Wrath (11HD)
Drake, Salt
Elemental, Gravity (12HD)
Elemental, Negative Energy (12HD)
Elemental, Positive Energy (12HD)
Eye of the Deep
Fire Whale (Burning Leviathan)
Gelid Beetle, Greater
Genie, Marid
Giant, Bronze
Giant, Ferrous
Gohl (Hydra Cloud)
Gorgimera
Grimm
Helix Moth (Adult)
Mihstu
Netherspark
Psiwyrm (Draco Presentia Facultas) (11HD)
Quantum
Quasi-Elemental, Acid (12HD)
Quasi-Elemental, Lightning (9HD)
Quasi-Elemental, Obsidian (12HD)
Scylla
Sea Serpent, Spitting
Sepia Snake

Shark, Giant Landwalker
Shedu, Common Shedu
Skeleton, Lead
Sleeping Willow
Slug, Giant
Swarm, Heat
Thessalmonster, Thessalhydra
Turtle, Giant Snapping

Challenge Level (CL) 14

Demiurge
Demon, Greruor (Frog Demon)
Demonic Knight
Dracolisk
Dragon, Cloud (12HD)
Dragon, Mist (9HD)
Dragon, Wrath (12HD)
Golem, Iron Maiden
Lantern Goat (14HD)
Lich Shade
Psiwyrm (Draco Presentia Facultas) (12HD)
Red Jester
Soul Eater
Tentacled Horror
Trapper

Challenge Level (CL) 15

Angel, Empyreal
Angel, Movanic Deva
Crucifixion Spirit
Daemon, Charonodaemon
Demon, Chaaor (Beast Demon)
Demon, Demonling Nabasu (Death Stealer Demon)
Demon, Shrroth (Squid Demon)
Dragon, Cloud (13HD)
Dragon, Mist (10HD)
Gallows Tree
Genie, Hawanar
Giant, Sea
Marsh Jelly, Demonic (Progeny of Jubilex)
Mastodon
Mire Brute
Moon Dog
N'gathau, Aagash "The Broken"
Prosciber
Shedu, Greater Shedu
Thundershrike

Challenge Level (CL) 16

Clockwork Bronze Giant
Corpse Orgy
Daemon, Derghodaemon
Demon, Stirge
Dragon, Cloud (14HD)
Dragon, Mist (11HD)
Elasmotherium
Elemental, Psionic (12HD)
Giant, Volcano
Obsidian Minotaur
Quasi-Elemental, Lightning (12HD)
Reliquary Guardian
Sea Spider (Common)
Swarm, Adamantine Wasp
Time Flayer
Turtle, Giant Bog

Challenge Level (CL) 17

Abyssal Harvester (Fourth-Category Demon)
Crystallis
Demon, Choronzon (Chaos Demon)
Demon, Nerizo (Hound Demon)
Draconid
Elemental, Gravity (16HD)
Elemental, Negative Energy (16HD)
Elemental, Positive Energy (16HD)
Elemental Construct, Air
Elemental Construct, Earth
Elemental Construct, Fire
Elemental Construct, Water
Giant, Jack-in-Irons
Herald of Tsathogga
Lantern Goat (17HD)
Living Lake (Agrath-Ogh)
N'Gathau, Asagin "The Assassin"
Paleoskeleton, Triceratops
Pit Hag
Sea Slug, Giant
Sea Wasp, Monstrous (16HD)

Challenge Level (CL) 18

Angel, Monadic Deva
Daemon, Cacodaemon
Demodand, Tarry
Devil, Flayer (Marzach)
Froghemoth
N'Gathau, Chaas "The Flayed"
N'Gathau, Ghehzi "The Mutilator"
Sea Serpent, Brine

Challenge Level (CL) 19

Demon, Aeshma (Rage Demon)
Demon, Daraka (Swarm Demon)
Giant, Sand
N'Gathau, N'hror "The Eater"

Challenge Level (CL) 20

Aerial Servant
Beetle, Requiem
Daemon, Piscodaemon
Demon, Mallor (Serpent Demon)
Devil, Lilith (Former Queen of Hell)
Elemental, Psionic (16HD)
Elemental, Time (Common)
Golem, Furnace
Mortuary Cyclone
N'Gathau, Chaadon "The Slayer"
Sea Serpent, Deep Hunter
Sea Spider (Pelagos)
Slorath
Soul Reaper
Therianthrope, Dire Wolfwere
Thorny Tyrannosaurus
Turtle-Shark, Stygian

Challenge Level (CL) 21

Animal Lord, Mouse Lord
N'Gathau, Ulaska't "The Twisted"

Challenge Level (CL) 22

Demodand, Shaggy
Demodand, Slime
Demon Lord, Caizel (Deposed Queen of the Succubi)
Demon, Gharros (Scorpion Demon)
N'Gathau, Greixas "The Destroyer"
N'Gathau, Modar "The Avenger"

Challenge Level (CL) 23

Afanc
Demon, Mature Nabasu (Death Stealer Demon)
Demon Lord, Kostchtchie (Demon Prince of Wrath)
Devil, Ghaddar
Dragonship
N'Gathau, Raauka "The Ravager"
N'Gathau, Veenes "The Blademistress"
Ooze, Entropic (Dark Matter)

Challenge Level (CL) 24

Devil, Titivilus (Duke of Hell)
Dire Elephant

Challenge Level (CL) 25

Demon Lord, Beluiri (The Temptress)
Slaad Lord of Entropy (Chaos Lord of Entropy)

Challenge Level (CL) 26

Animal Lord, Cat Lord
Demon, Vepar (Duke of Hell)
Demon Lord, Vepar (Duke of Dagon)
Devil, Baal (Duke of Hell)
Devil, Demoriel (Twice-Exiled Seductress)
Gorgon, True (Sthenno)
Sea Serpent, Shipbreaker
Slaad Lord of the Insane (Chaos Lord of the Insane)
Slag Worm

Challenge Level (CL) 27

Cherum
Demon Lord, Sonechard (General of Orcus)
Devil, Gorson (The Blood Duke)

Challenge Level (CL) 28

Devil, Alastor (Executioner of Hell)
Devil, Baaphel (Duke of Hell)
Devil, Hutijin (Duke of Hell)
Gorgon, True (Euryale)
N'Gathau, Veruard "The Razor and the Creator"
Stygian Leviathan

Challenge Level (CL) 29

Ceberus

Challenge Level (CL) 30

Demon Lord, Dagon (Demon Prince of the Sea)
Demon Lord, Jubilex (The Faceless Lord)
Demon Lord, Maphistal (Lieutenant of Orcus)
Devil, Amon (Duke of Hell)

Challenge Level (CL) 31

Devil, Geryon (Arch-Devil)
Devil, Moloch (Arch-Devil)

Challenge Level (CL) 32

Demon Lord, Pazuzu (Demon Prince of Air)
Devil, Caasimolar (Former President of Hell)
Elemental, Time (Noble)

Challenge Level (CL) 33

Elemental Dragon, Air
Elemental Dragon, Earth
Elemental Dragon, Fire
Elemental Dragon, Water

Challenge Level (CL) 34

Daemon, The Oinodaemon
Demon Lord, Baphomet (Demon Lord of Beasts)
Demon Lord, Tsathogga (The Frog God)

Challenge Level (CL) 35

Demon Lord, Fraz-Urb'luu (Demon Prince of Deception)
N'Gathau, The Quorum

Challenge Level (CL) 36

Colossus, Jade

Challenge Level (CL) 37

Elemental, Time (Royal)

Challenge Level (CL) 38

Devil, Xaphan (Duke of Infernus)

Challenge Level (CL) 40

Daemon, Charon (Boatman of the Lower Planes)
Demon Lord, Orcus (Demon Prince of the Undead)
Devil, Lucifer (Prince of Darkness)

Legal Appendix

Legal Appendix

This printing of *Tome of Horrors Complete* is done under version 1.0a of the of the Open Game License, below, and by license from Mythmere Games.

Notice of Open Game Content: This product contains Open Game Content, as defined in the Open Game License, below. Open Game Content may only be Used under and in terms of the Open Game License.

Designation of Open Game Content: All text contained within this product (including monster names, stats, and descriptions) is hereby designated as Open Game Content, with the following exceptions:

1. Any text on the inside or outside of the front or back cover or on the Credits or Preface pages is not Open Game Content;

2. Any advertising material — including the text of any advertising material — is not Open Game Content;

3. Any material contained in the "Credit" section of each monster is not Open Game Content. See the "Note on the 'Credit' Section," below;

Use of Content from *Tome of Horrors* Series: This product contains or references content from the *Tome of Horrors Revised, Tome of Horrors II* and *Tome of Horrors III* by Necromancer Games, Inc. Such content is used by permission. Further, some content reprinted here from the original *Tome of Horrors* and/or *Tome of Horrors Revised* contains content owned by Wizards of the Coast and is used under the Open Game License based on prior permission from Anthony Valterra of Wizards of the Coast.

Use of Other Content: The turtle shark (© 2002 Erica Balsley) originally appeared in *Asgard Magazine #1* and is used herein by prior permission. The Paleoskeleton template (© 2002, Erica Balsley) is from the *Book of Templates: Deluxe Edition*, © 2003, Silverthorne Games; Authors Ian Johnston and Chris S. Sims.

Note on the "Credit" Section: The Credit section for each creature contains information detailing the origin of the particular monster. This content is not Open Game Content, as explained above. Some material within the Credit section is copyright TSR/Wizards of the Coast and/or Necromancer Games, Inc., and is used within the Credit section by prior permission of Wizards of the Coast. You are not allowed to use any of the information in the Credit section under the Open Game License.

Designation of Product Identity: The following items are hereby designated as Product Identity as provided in section 1(e) of the Open Game License:

Any and all material or content that could be claimed as Product Identity pursuant to section 1(e), below, is hereby claimed as product identity, including but not limited to:

1. The name "Necromancer Games" and "Frog God Games" as well as all logos and identifying marks of Necromancer Games, Inc. and Frog God Games, including but not limited to the Orcus logo and the phrase "Third Edition Rules, First Edition Feel" as well as the trade dress of Necromancer Games products and similar logos, identifying phrases and trade dress of Frog God Games;

2. The product name *Tome of Horrors, Tome of Horrors Revised, Tome of Horrors II, Tome of Horrors III* and *Tome of Horrors Complete* by Necromancer Games, Inc. as well as any and all Necromancer Games Inc. and/or Frog God Games product names referenced in the work;

3. All artwork, illustration, graphic design, maps, and cartography, including any text contained within such artwork, illustration, maps or cartography;

4. The proper names, personality, descriptions and/or motivations of all artifacts, characters, races, countries, geographic locations, plane or planes of existence, gods, deities, events, magic items, organizations and/or groups unique to this book, but not their stat blocks or other game mechanic descriptions (if any), and also excluding any such names when they are included in monster, spell or feat names;

5. Any other content previously designated as Product Identity is hereby designated as Product Identity and is used with permission and/or pursuant to license.

6. All logos and identifying marks of Mythmere Games and Matthew J. Finch, including but not limited to the name "Swords & Wizardry" and the Swords & Wizardry logo, any trade dress, identifying words or phrases of Mythmere Games or Matthew J. Finch products and similar logos;

independent Agreement with the owner of such Trademark or Registered Trademark. The use of any Product Identity in Open Game Content does not constitute a challenge to the ownership of that Product Identity. The owner of any Product Identity used in Open Game Content shall retain all rights, title and interest in and to that Product Identity.

8. Identification: If you distribute Open Game Content You must clearly indicate which portions of the work that you are distributing are Open Game Content.

9. Updating the License: Wizards or its designated Agents may publish updated versions of this License. You may use any authorized version of this License to copy, modify and distribute any Open Game Content originally distributed under any version of this License.

10. Copy of this License: You MUST include a copy of this License with every copy of the Open Game Content You Distribute.

11. Use of Contributor Credits: You may not market or advertise the Open Game Content using the name of any Contributor unless You have written permission from the Contributor to do so.

12. Inability to Comply: If it is impossible for You to comply with any of the terms of this License with respect to some or all of the Open Game Content due to statute, judicial order, or governmental regulation then You may not Use any Open Game Material so affected.

13. Termination: This License will terminate automatically if You fail to comply with all terms herein and fail to cure such breach within 30 days of becoming aware of the breach. All sublicenses shall survive the termination of this License.

14. Reformation: If any provision of this License is held to be unenforceable, such provision shall be reformed only to the extent necessary to make it enforceable.

15. COPYRIGHT NOTICE

Open Game License v 1.0a Copyright 2000, Wizards of the Coast, Inc.

System Reference Document. Copyright 2000, Wizards of the Coast, Inc.; Authors Jonathan Tweet, Monte Cook, Skip Williams, based on material by E. Gary Gygax and Dave Arneson.

Swords & Wizardry Core Rules. Copyright 2008, Matthew J. Finch

Swords & Wizardry Complete Rulebook. Copyright 2010, Matthew J. Finch.

[Insert the name of monster used — incorporated here by this reference — in place of this bracketed text, with each monster used requiring a separate entry in Section 15] from the *Tome of Horrors Complete*, Copyright 2011, Necromancer Games, Inc., published and distributed by Frog God Games; [see the individual monster entry or entries for additional Section 15 information and insert that information here — incorporated here by this reference — in place of this bracketed text when reusing].

How To Do It

To use Open Game Content from this book, you must take *our* Section 15 Copyright Notice information and put it in the Section 15 Copyright Notice of *your* book. So now let's take a look at our Section 15 Copyright Notice for this book. It reads:

"[Insert the name of monster used — incorporated here by this reference — in place of this bracketed text, with each monster used requiring a separate entry in Section 15] from the *Tome of Horrors Complete*, Copyright 2011, Necromancer Games, Inc., published and distributed by Frog God Games; [see the individual monster entry or entries for additional Section 15 information and insert that information here — incorporated here by this reference — in place of this bracketed text when reusing]."

What does that mean? Simple. To construct the copyright notice for your product based on Open Game Content from this book, just follow the directions in the bracketed text. Doing so, you go to the specific monster page that you are using and get the monster name from the top of the page and the rest of the information there from the Copyright Notice section at the bottom of the page and put it in place of the bracketed text. It couldn't be easier. Just in case, let's do an example.

Example

Let's say you wanted to use the adherer in your new Swords & Wizardry product. Here is how you would cite it. You know its name, the adherer, so you plug that into the first part of bracketed text, so that it now reads:

"Adherer from the *Tome of Horrors Complete*, Copyright 2011, Necromancer Games, Inc., published and distributed by Frog God Games;"

Alright. To deal with replacing the next bracketed text, you to go to the Copyright Notice section of the adherer entry, and there you find:

"Authors Scott Greene and Clark Peterson, based on original material by Guy Shearer."

Now, all you need to do is replace the final bracketed text with that information and you are done. It should now look like this:

"Adherer from the *Tome of Horrors Complete*, Copyright 2011, Necromancer Games, Inc., published and distributed by Frog God Games; Authors Scott Greene and Clark Peterson, based on original material by Guy Shearer."

That is what you now must put in *your* Section 15 Copyright Notice since you used the Open Game Content that we distributed.

Reusing the Monsters in This Tome

This book contains tons of Open Game Content. We want other producers of open content products to use these great monsters in their products. To help make that happen, here are instructions on how to reuse the creatures contained in this book and comply with the Open Game License from our perspective.

Our Promise: If these instructions are followed properly, Necromancer Games, Inc., will not allege that you have failed to comply with the license from our standpoint.

Using Multiple Monsters

The monsters in this book are so cool that we are sure you will want to use several of them in your products. Does that mean you have to do a whole new entry in your Section 15 for *every* monster you use? Yes, yes it does. That is a side effect of our desire to credit each author and the original source material properly and accurately. We thought it was so important to give proper credit that we are sure subsequent publishers will not mind this slight inconvenience. We just couldn't find another way to do it.

So, for example, let's say you want to use the dark creeper, the pech, the mobat, and the shadow demon in your product. You have to go to the respective monster pages for each of those monsters and compile the names of the monsters and the respective Copyright Notice information for each of the monsters and create a separate Section 15 entry in your product for each of those monsters, just as we did in the adherer example, above.

• Dark Creeper, Author Scott Greene, based on original material by Rik Shepard.

• Pech, Author Scott Greene, based on original material by Gary Gygax.

• Mobat, Author Scott Greene and Clark Peterson, based on original material by Gary Gygax.

• Shadow Demon, Author Scott Greene, based on original material by Neville White.

You would need to make four entries in your Section 15 reflecting each monster you use. Taking the above four monsters, you would need to add the following entries to your Section 15:

"Dark Creeper from the *Tome of Horrors Complete*, Copyright 2011, Necromancer Games, Inc., published and distributed by Frog God Games; Author Scott Greene, based on original material by Rik Shepard.

Pech from the *Tome of Horrors Complete*, Copyright 2011, Necromancer Games, Inc., published and distributed by Frog God Games; Author Scott Greene, based on original material by Gary Gygax.

Mobat from the *Tome of Horrors Complete*, Copyright 2011, Necromancer Games, Inc., published and distributed by Frog God Games; Author Scott Greene and Clark Peterson, based on original material by Gary Gygax.

Shadow Demon from the *Tome of Horrors Complete*, Copyright 2011, Necromancer Games, Inc., published and distributed by Frog God Games; Author Scott Greene, based on original material by Neville White."

Important Reminder

Remember, at no time can you use or refer to any of the content in the "Credit" section of any monster. That content is provided to us by prior permission, and we do not have the right to contribute it as Open Game Content. If you use any content from the "Credit" section of any monster, you will be in violation of the license.

Conclusion

There you have it! Not only a ton of Open Game Content, but instructions on how to use it properly, too!

If you have any questions about how to use the Open Game Content contained in this book, please contact Bill Webb at Frog God Games at www.talesofthefroggod.com and he will forward your question to Clark Peterson.

Disclaimer

The above is not legal advice. It is a helpful summary to aid you in reusing the content contained in this book. Though the above language warrants that Necromancer Games, Inc. and Frog God Games will not allege you have failed to comply with the Open Game License if you follow the above instructions, this does not prevent third parties from possibly making such a claim. If you have concerns, please consult an attorney.

SWORDS & WIZARDRY

COMPLETE RULEBOOK

AVAILABLE NOW FROM FROG GOD GAMES
WWW.TALESOFTHEFROGGOD.COM

ULTIMATE BOOK OF ADVENTURE DESIGN

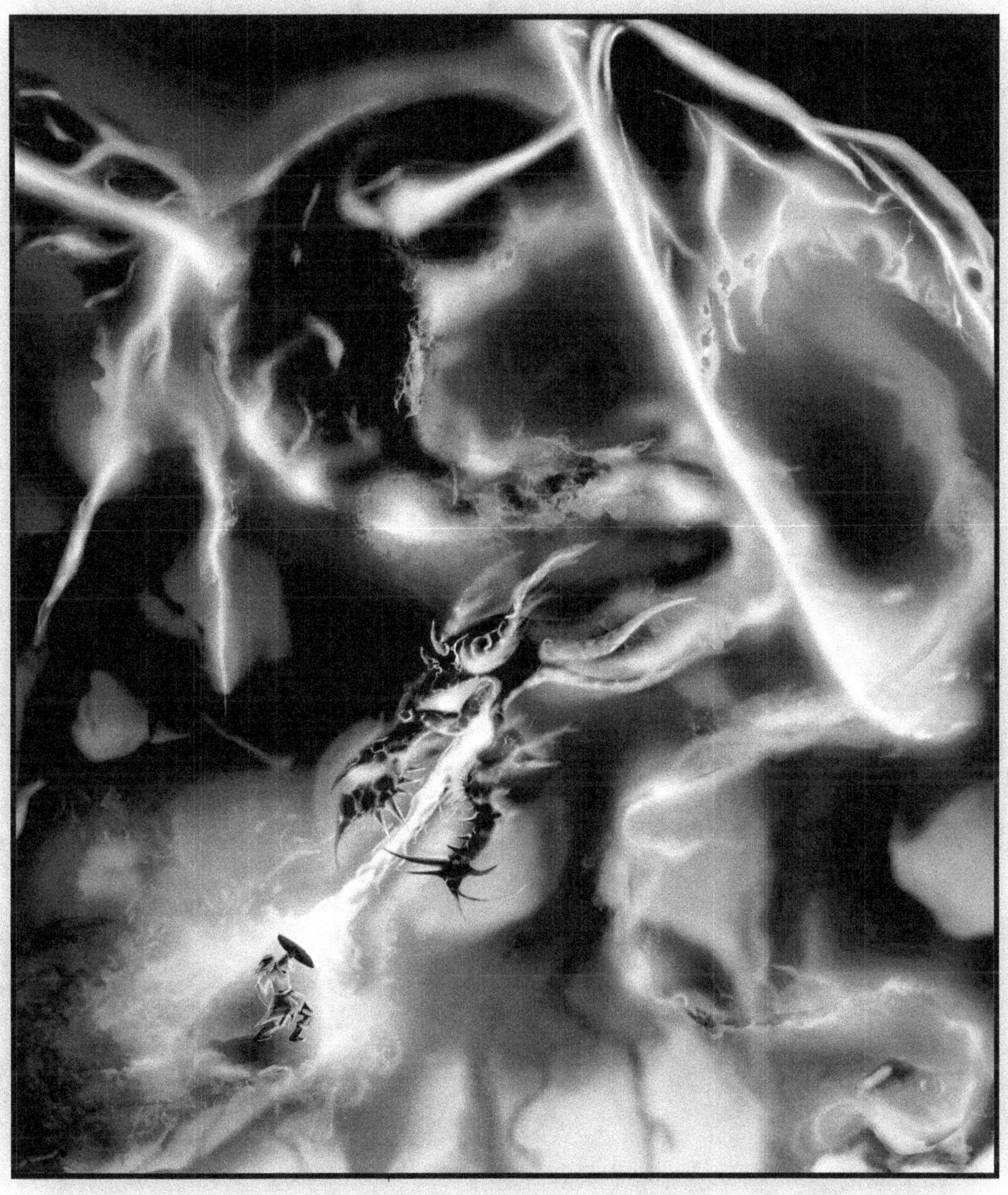

FROM THE MIND THAT BROUGHT YOU SWORDS & WIZARDRY
COMES A TOOL FOR ANY FANTASY CAMPAIGN

COMING SOON FROM FROG GOD GAMES
WWW.TALESOFTHEFROGGOD.COM

Also available for the Pathfinder Roleplaying Game

Purchase the PDF at www.talesofthefroggod.com

Fane of the FALLEN

By William Loran Christensen

All is not as it seems when a large scale orc raid preys upon the city of Brookmere. PCs are sent to parlay with the orcs believed to be responsible, and after many exciting battles and investigation, the characters learn of the masterminds behind the attack, a faction of murderous elves bent on the destruction of the kingdom. Can the characters penetrate the foreboding Harwood Forest and defeat the denizens of Castle Novgorod? Or will they succumb to the fallen elves and their depraved succubus goddess?

Fane of the Fallen™ is a d20 adventure of epic proportions, designed to take characters from 13th-level to 18th-level. Fane of the Fallen™ introduces the Kingdom of Myrridon, a mini-campaign of grand scale, and the fallen elves, a new race of murderous beings seduced by evil.

Available now for Pathfinder and Swords & Wizardry at
www.talesofthefroggod.com

Hex Crawl Chronicles

By John Stater

THE NORTHLANDS SAGA

By Kenneth Spencer

This series of adventures takes place in the frozen north, where men are men, beer is ale and monsters are, well, scary. Who has not loved the setting of the 13th Warrior or wished to relive the Frost Giant's Daughter by R.E. Howard? Heroes will fight evil in the cold lands, sail the treacherous ice filled seas where sea monsters swallow ships and crews and feast in fire-lit halls with Vikings! This series is sure to send shivers up even the bravest adventurer's spine!

Available now for Pathfinder and Swords & Wizardry at
www.talesofthefroggod.com

One Night Stands

Jungle Ruins of Madaro-Shanti - Available now!

Jungle Ruins of Madaro-Shanti is a Frog God Games adventure for a party of 4-8 characters of 4th through 7th level. Like other Frog God Games resources, it is compatible with the Pathfinder Roleplaying Games ruleset. Some of the monsters found in this module were previously published in Mythmere Games' Monster Book, converted for Pathfinder play.

Retail Price: $11.99 plus shipping.

Death in Painted Canyons- Available now!

A band of gnolls has been attacking caravans passing from the caravanserai at Salt Springs through the Painted Canyons and on towards the oasis town of Beni-Hadith. The Satrap of Salt Springs has offered a bounty on their heads.
Can the PCs stop the attacks once and for all?

Retail Price: $11.99 plus shipping.

Spire of Iron and Crystal - Available now!

Deep in the wilderness stands the legendary Spire of Iron and Crystal, a bizarre structure of twisting iron and four enormous crystals that seem to grow from the very ground itself. The fabled riches of the Spire have never been plundered, for no entrances have ever been found. . . . Until now.
Your party of adventurers has discovered the long-hidden secret of entering the Spire.

Retail Price: $11.99 plus shipping.

Many more titles coming soon!

One Night Stands are primarily non-dungeon adventures.

Remember when the world was a sandbox and you just inserted modules into your campaign whenever and wherever you wanted to? Remember when companies like Judges Guild and TSR produced short stand alone modules, not tied to any setting or campaign? Remember when the cost 5 bucks (ok we can't do print books for 5 bucks anymore , but we can do that for the pdfs)? Remember when you directed the action independent of what the "world" rules said was there? We do, and in response we decided to fill the gap with our One Night Stands and Saturday Night Specials series.

These modules are designed to be played over the course of 1-2 nights. Each is a sandbox style short adventure (One Night Stands) or a short dungeon crawl (Saturday Night Specials).

Frog God Games knows that in this day and age, sometimes a gamemaster just needs a short trek to take his players on, or to fill those regular gaps and interludes in his campaign. Sometimes its just fun to enter a dungeon and kill things for a night! Old school feel is the trademark of these product lines. Look for easy deaths and tough puzzles. Frog God Games is not made for rookie players.

These series are designed as stand alone modules and are typically between 24 and 32 pages. We have designed just one piece of cover art for each series in order to keep the price point low (though the cover art is rockin', and the interiors and maps are all of usual Frog God Games quality!). All of these books will be released in both Pathfinder and Swords and Wizardry format.

The nice part about these books is that some of the best authors in the industry, including Matthew J. Finch, Casey Christofferson, Patrick Lawinger, Anthony Pryor, Nate Paul, WDB Kenower, Scott Casper and James C. Boney have been enticed to write for us. You may even see some work from Old Tsathogga himself in these soon as well!

Saturday Night Special

Hollow Mountain - Available now!

When a peaceful tribe of nomadic wood elves suddenly become hostile and start raiding human settlements with murderous zeal, adventurers are hired by the local baron to investigate why.

They soon discover that the wood elves have left their nomadic lifestyle and have taken up residence inside a famous local landmark called the Hollow Mountain.

Castle Baldemar's Dungeon - Coming soon

An adventure for levels 5 to 7. The Town of Ravensrook was just a point between here and there, but the local wizard has plans for you before you leave – enter the dungeons below the dead baron's castle and retrieve his stolen staff from an evil dragon, or die trying!

Many more titles coming soon!

Saturday Night Specials are primarily dungeon-delving adventures.

The Sleeper Awakes!

At last, after languishing in its crypt for an age, the secrets of the slumbering city of Tsar burst forth in all their macabre glory. Poured forth from the eldritch furnaces and crucibles of the Necromancer and Orcus himself comes **Frog God Games** bringing you at long last **The Slumbering Tsar Saga™**.

Something Stirs in the City of Evil

Over the distant northern hills, beyond The Camp, and past the Desolation stand the pitted walls of Tsar. A hundred armies have crushed themselves against this bulwark in futile attempts to breach the city. Even the combined might of the Heavens and Earth were unable to break through in the final battle of Tsar. So why was the city suddenly abandoned on the verge of victory, and what waits for those foolish enough to enter the Temple-City of Orcus?

The Black Gates Await

Only the bravest and most powerful of heroes dare the depths of the Desolation and live to tell of it. But what happens when they penetrate that blasted landscape and look upon the gates of the very center of evil on the earth. Can even heroes of such renown breach the Walls of Death and live?

The Slumbering Tsar Saga™ began its journey years ago as a single mega-adventure for the masters of Third Edition rules and First Edition feel, then became a trilogy of adventures, then a trilogy of mega-adventures, and now finally comes to you as a monthly series culminating in a massive book with over a half million words of pure First Edition-style adventure. Updated to the Pathfinder Roleplaying Game to accommodate today's audience of the classic fantasy roleplaying game, **The Slumbering Tsar Saga™** brings you 14 chapters, released monthly in electronic format, each chapter the size of a full adventure in its own right (30-50 pages). Then when the final chapter has been released, the whole will be available in a classic edition, hardcover adventure book.

The Eamonvale Incursion

The Long-lost prequel and sequel to the infamous and best-selling Grey Citadel. This one never got published, and is available here for the first time. One of the long-lost Necromancer Games books for sale in all its original glory as a real book!

Adventures in the Valley of the River Eamon

Hard times have fallen on the frontier realm of Eamonvale. Economic hardship, inexplicable kidnappings, strange politics, raids by feral elves and rising brigand activity on the Trade Road combine to spell trouble for the people of the valley. Can the heroes sort fact from fiction and unearth the connections before uncertainty gives way to fear and panic?

Far worse things than dragons draw their shadows over Eamonvale.

The Eamonvale Incursion is a mini-campaign of urban investigation and wilderness exploration designed for 4 or more characters of at least 7th level. Finding the connections between recent disturbances takes the heroes from the bustling market town of Broadwater to the sleepy rural village of Fagan's Hollow, from the boggy wasteland of the Bleak to the shaded depths of the Elfwood, and into the hearts and minds of the people whose whole world is Eamonvale. Expanding on the setting of the author's first book The Grey Citadel (but fully useable without it), The Eamonvale Incursion features challenging parallel plot threads, a richly developed setting, vibrant NPCs and numerous secondary plot hooks to foster ongoing adventures in Eamonvale.

FORMATS V3.5

Page Count: 226 - Authors: Nate Paul - Retail: $29.99 for pdf or $34.99 for pdf and perfect bound softcover.

Demonheart

The Lost Necromancer Books...ready to print but never printed! This is one of the 3 books that never made the trip back from China...available for the first time as a print book.

Darkness in the Heart of the Forest

Generations ago, a fearful battle between raged in the depths of the Westwood. An entire tribe of forest elves gave up its very existence to turn back the rising tide of evil. Despite their noble sacrifice, a fragment of evil remained, and has now begun to awaken, drawing allies both old and new and transforming the Westwood into a place of fear and darkness.

Ancient Wrongs To be Righted

Today, the past lies forgotten and a settlement of innocent humans has sprung up near the old battleground. Little do the inhabitants of Tanner's Green suspect that a remnant of the old enemy has returned, and that its followers plot their downfall. Creatures of unspeakable evil lurk in the dark shadows of the forest, and only a small band of adventurers can find and stop them before the enemy rises once more.
Demonheart is mini-campaign for 3-5 player characters, beginning at levels 6-8 and rising to levels 10-12, with adventures that range from intrigue in the town of Tanner's Green to a life-or-death contest in the court of the king of the dark fey, all leading to a final confrontation with the ancient enemy.
Terror grows with each beat of the Demonheart. Can the adventurers stop it in time?

FORMATS V3.5

Page Count: 98 - Authors: Anthony Pryor - Retail: $14.99 for pdf or $21.99 for pdf and perfect bound softcover.

Splinters of Faith

Ancient Evil Awakens

In a long-buried tomb, a grave robber restores a death-cult leader to life, and his cloud of evil spreads across the land. Left behind are the broken Scepter of Faiths and a litany of shrines to restore the weapon. But the evil one and his minions wait to destroy any who try...

Temples of faith, bastions of evil

Splinters of Faith™ is a collection of 10 adventures for characters of levels 1 to 15 that can be played individually or as part of an epic campaign to restore the Scepter of Faiths. Adventure in 10 fully detailed temples such as the Shield Basilica of Muir or the dwarven city of Anvil Plunge, and conquer the nightmarish Nether Sepulcher to restore the balance of good.

Ten complete adventures for low- to high-level characters, usable separately or as a massive linked campaign.

• Eighteen unique temples (10 fully detailed) ready to drop into any campaign world.
• New monsters and magic items to discover, and ideas for further adventures.

Retail Price: $8.99 plus shipping and handling

Page Count: each module is 20-40 pages
Authors: Gary Schotter and Jeff Harkness

Splinters of Faith 1: It Started With A Chicken - Available now!
Splinters of Faith 2: Burning Desires - Available now!
Splinters of Faith 3: Culvert Operations - Available now!
Splinters of Faith 4: For Love of Chaos - Available now!
Splinters of Faith 5: Eclipse of the Hearth - Available now!
Splinters of Faith 6: Morning of Tears - Available now!
Splinters of Faith 7: The Heir of Sin - Available now!
Splinters of Faith 8: Pains of Scalded Glass - Available now!
Splinters of Faith 9: Duel of Magic - Available now!
Splinters of Faith 10: Remorse of Life - Available now!

Swords and Wizardry and Pathfinder versions are sold separately

strange bedfellows

By Carla Harker

A circus show erupts in mayhem when goblinoids crash the performance, slaughtering performers and audience members alike. PCs investigate the attack, leading them into an ancient dungeon and uncovering ancient secrets and harbored grudges. Their decisions affect the politics and economics of three unique towns.

Strange Bedfellows is a d20 adventure for 4-6 PCs of level 2 or higher and includes three fully-developed towns, numerous unique NPCs who offer an extensive assortment of side quests, and a wide range of challenging opponents.

Uncover ancient evils and secrets while discovering the reason for the attack at the circus. Fight unique monsters. Make decisions that affect the long-term politics and economics of three towns.

Available now for Pathfinder and Swords & Wizardry at
www.talesofthefroggod.com